Homeland

John Jakes

HOMELAND

D O U B L E D A Y
New York
London
Toronto
Sydney
Auckland

PUBLISHED BY DOUBLEDAY
a division of Bantam Doubleday Dell Publishing Group, Inc.
1540 Broadway, New York, New York 10036

DOUBLEDAY and the portrayal of an anchor with a dolphin are trademarks of
Doubleday, a division of Bantam Doubleday Dell Publishing Group, Inc.

With the exception of historical figures, all characters in this novel are fictitious.
Any resemblance to living persons, present or past, is coincidental.

Book design by Paul Randall Mize

Library of Congress Cataloging-in-Publication Data

Jakes, John, 1932–
Homeland/John Jakes.—1st ed.
    p.   cm.
1. German Americans—Illinois—Chicago—History—Fiction.
2. Chicago (Ill.)—History—Fiction.   I. Title.
PS3560.A37H66   1993
813′.54—dc20   92-43894
CIP

ISBN 0-385-41724-1
Printed in the United States of America
July 1993
First Edition

10   9   8   7   6   5   4   3   2   1

Dedicated to my grandfather
William Carl Retz
b. Neuenstadt-am-Kocher, 1849
d. Terre Haute, Indiana, 1936

There is a photo of him in old age,
handsome still with his white imperial,
seated in dappled sunlight
with a small boy on his knee.
I remember that day, or one like it;
the sunlight, and a copy of *Argosy*
with a bright yellow cover
lying nearby. My grandfather
loved good stories.

In loving memory.

Author's Note

THIS NOVEL is the first of a projected cycle about the members of an American family moving into and through the explosive events of the twentieth century.

It's impossible to understand this century without some knowledge of the last one. This story therefore attempts to present a tapestry of American life and history in the years between 1890 and 1900, the decade in which a naive young giant flexed its muscles and began to understand and use its enormous strength.

The Crowns live in Chicago because it is, and was, a quintessentially American place and, probably just as important, because I have always wanted to write about the rowdy prairie melting pot in which I was born and raised.

A second theme of the story, which I was also eager to write about, is the immigrant experience. My maternal grandfather, to whom this book is dedicated, was one of those immigrants; he arrived at Castle Garden about 1870. The young German woman he married in Cincinnati was an immigrant too. The roots of my mother's family stretch back to Germany, where cousins of mine still live in Aalen, the town from which my grandfather set out for America. Germany, the country that gave us the totalitarian horrors of the twentieth century, also gave us by far the largest immigrant group that came to these shores in the nineteenth. Strong people; good Americans, despite their occasionally strained loyalties.

My grandfather and his family prospered in Ohio and Indiana. Not all immigrant stories ended that way. The baker of Wuppertal, a minor but significant character in the book, was a not uncommon figure at the time.

J.J.

Contents

Part One   BERLIN   1

Part Two   STEERAGE   31

Part Three   CHICAGO   91

Part Four   JULIE   199

Part Five   PULLMAN   243

Part Six   LEVEE   355

Part Seven   FLICKERS   473

Part Eight   TAMPA   565

Part Nine   WAR   659

Part Ten   HOMECOMING   747

For he said, I have been a stranger in a strange land.

Exodus 2

And homeless near a thousand homes I stood.

WILLIAM WORDSWORTH

All happy families resemble one another; every unhappy family is unhappy in its own way.

LEO TOLSTOY

GERMAN 1: "I have a relative in America."
GERMAN 2: "Everybody has a relative in America."

Anonymous, circa 1900

Part One

BERLIN

1891–1892

Here at our sea-washed, sunset gates
    shall stand
A mighty woman with a torch,
    whose flame
Is the imprisoned lightning,
    and her name
Mother of exiles.

1883
The New Colossus by EMMA LAZARUS, written to raise
funds to complete the Statue of Liberty

1

Pauli

HE THOUGHT, *Where's my home? It isn't here.*

From a flimsy shelf beside his narrow bed he pulled a wrinkled paper.

It was a map of the world, torn from a book he'd bought at a secondhand shop with money he could ill afford to squander. He bought the whole book in order to have the map.

He scrutinized various locations as if he were some godlike being, able to choose any place on earth to live. But he was in Berlin, and that was that. Sometimes he loved the city but sometimes, as now, he felt trapped.

He'd come home at midnight, exhausted from work, and lay now under the old duvet, unable to sleep, studying the map. It was almost two in the morning, and Aunt Lotte hadn't yet returned. Out with one of her *Herren*, he presumed. He worried about her. Once the kindest of women, now she was short with him, as if she disliked him. Hated having him around. She was drinking more heavily than usual. That very morning, before he left, he'd seen her stumble into furniture twice.

His room felt tiny and cramped, like a cell. Barely enough space for his single bed, an old wardrobe with a missing leg replaced by a wood block, one shaky taboret with a kerosene lamp. A night jar was tucked into a corner, beside a wooden box containing some childhood toys. The room was part of a cellar flat; he had not even one window.

Often his room was cold; most of the time it was damp. Aunt Lotte complained that it was messy; very un-German. That could be said of him too. His clothes were almost always awry, his shirttail often hung out, his pockets were constantly stuffed with old pencils, chalk, scraps of paper on which he wrote down thoughts or things to do, rocks, crackers or sweets he forgot to eat, leaving them to crumble or melt.

He was no longer in school; he'd never liked it, and had left it a year ago. Though dropping out was against the law, no one came to find him. No one cared.

Pensive, he touched the map, putting his finger in the middle of America, where his uncle lived.

As they often did at night, painful questions arose. Questions usually buried so deep, he'd never uttered them aloud to another soul. Probably because he feared there were no answers. There were no answers tonight. Slowly he stretched out his hand and put the wrinkled map back on the shelf.

His name was Pauli Kroner.

He was thirteen years old.

Spring rain hammered the streaming glass. Lightning flashed and glared. Pauli peered in the window of Wertheim's on Leipzigerstrasse; window dressers had draped a variety of gentlemen's and ladies' coats around a marvelous globe, multicolored and exquisitely painted. The globe had brass fittings at its axis and rested in a heavy wooden stand, fancifully carved.

The globe's painted seas and continents seemed full of mysteries, possibilities, wondrous sights Pauli yearned to see. If only he had enough money to buy a globe like that . . .

Something hard whacked the back of his head. *"Lump."* Ragamuffin. "Get away from that glass, you're leaning too hard."

Pauli spun around to confront Wertheim's giant doorkeeper, sodden in his greatcoat with gold shoulder boards and ropes of braid. Rain dripped from the bill of his braided hat.

"I was only looking."

"Look somewhere else. We don't want trash like you loitering around, it scares off the customers."

"Es wird überall nur mit Wasser gekocht," Pauli exclaimed. It was an old proverb, meaning literally, They cook everywhere with water. Pauli meant it to say he was as good as the next man.

"Oh yes?" said the doorman. "You're a good customer? Big spender? Get away from here before I whistle for the police!"

Pauli gave the doorman a hot stare, but the defiance hid his real feelings about himself. The doorman knew him for what he was. Nothing.

He disappeared up the rainy boulevard, hands in his pockets, head down.

On a Sunday morning soon afterward, Pauli walked into the Tiergarten with a block of cheap paper under his arm. Returning from work the night before, he had found Aunt Lotte bemoaning the absence of gentlemen on a Saturday evening. Her speech was slow and slurred. She was drinking strong fermented *Apfelwein* from a goblet. She had still been asleep when he left this morning; he'd heard her snoring behind her closed door.

Pauli walked through the Tiergarten with a strong, fast stride. He looked older than his years. He would never be handsome, but he had friendly, lively blue eyes, and wide shoulders, and a sturdy build that enhanced his masculinity. The blood of southern Germany ran in him, and there was a red-haired strain in the family that sometimes gave his brown hair russet glints. Whenever he was feeling good about himself or his circumstances he exuded an air of strength and competence that people noticed.

The great park was green and misty this summer morning. Pauli hurried to a site, and a subject, that had caught his eye. On a grassy hillock, an old gentleman had laid aside his straw boater and his meerschaum pipe and gone to sleep with his belly jutting up like a mountain under his vest. At a discreet distance, Pauli dropped to his knees, smoothed the top sheet of the block and rummaged through his pockets for his charcoal stick. He licked a smear of chocolate off the end and poised the stick over the pad.

He was tight inside, with anticipation and anxiety. He wanted to do a good sketch of the sleeping gentleman, but he feared he'd fail.

He began with an outline of the sleeper, from the side. After four strokes, he rubbed out what he'd done; the proportions were all wrong. Somehow his hand couldn't understand or execute the signals from his eye and mind. Pauli tore the paper off the block and crushed it, cursing. The old gentleman started, sat up and looked at him. Pauli grew red. He jumped up and ran off with the paper block and charcoal, quite forgetting to pick up the discarded sheets he'd left on the grass.

Why did he keep it up? He wanted to draw the marvelous sights and subjects that abounded in the world. But his talent was poor. He struggled and struggled, and every time he came out with nothing. Sometimes it seemed he had no talent for anything.

Once again Pauli was on the pavement outside the great department store, Wertheim's, on Leipzigerstrasse. The doorkeeper was nowhere to be seen. It was late July; the long summer twilight was golden and warm.

Pauli saw an old lady in black emerge from the store with a string bag. Instantly, a bearded man sprang from the crowd and brutally shoved the old woman to the ground.

The old lady cried out as the man snatched her string bag, pulled out two tins of department store tea and swore furiously. He turned to flee through the crowd, in Pauli's direction.

Pauli didn't hesitate. He threw himself on the sidewalk. The thief couldn't stop in time, and tripped over the boy.

Pauli grabbed the frayed hem of the thief's long coat and brought him down. The man cracked his head badly.

The dreaded doorman appeared, but he ignored Pauli, fussing and clucking over the old woman while helping her to her feet and into the store.

The groggy thief tried to rise. Pauli sat on him. Two of Wertheim's store detectives came out to collar the man. Pauli stood up, brushed himself off. A few angry people gathered around, shaking fingers at the robber.

The police arrived. They insisted Pauli accompany them to the station.

"But I'm waiting here to meet my friend." The friend was Tonio Henkel, whose father owned a thriving sweet shop on Unter den Linden.

"No argument, you're coming along." One of the policeman seized his arm to settle the matter.

They took him to a room with dingy yellow walls and the inevitable large heroic lithograph of Kaiser Wilhelm II.

Two stern detectives shot off questions like bullets.

"Your name?"

"Pauli Kroner."

"Age?"

"Fourteen, last month, June 15."

"Address."

Reluctantly, he gave the number on Müllerstrasse. The detectives exchanged quick looks. They recognized a cheap street in one of the workers' districts. Almost a slum.

Pauli spent an anxious half hour repeating his story. All at once a distant bell rang. One detective was called out. When he came back in three minutes his whole demeanor had changed.

"I was speaking on the telephone," he said to Pauli. "You helped a very important lady. Frau Flüsser. The mother-in-law of the store's deputy director. She wants to see you at her flat tomorrow morning. Nine sharp. I think she wants to give you a reward. I'll write down the address."

The other detective patted his head. *"Ein scharfsinniger Junge."* A quick-witted youngster.

Dazed with delight, Pauli ran out of the building, then dashed toward Unter den Linden.

"And the policeman actually called you that, quick-witted?" Tonio Henkel said. He and Pauli were seated at a back table at Konditorei Henkel.

"Yes, he did," Pauli said with a shrug of false modesty. He stuffed another Othello into his mouth, disposing of it with a few bites.

Tonio smiled. His large, rounded forehead bobbed over the table. His head was too big for his frail body. Pauli and Anton Henkel had become fast friends in *Grundschule,* which Pauli had quit at Easter a year ago; the end of his seventh term. He had not been transferred to the *Oberschule* in his fifth year, as many bright pupils were. Remaining in the lower school marked him as one of those who would never receive a higher education at the *Gymnasium.* Aunt Lotte had made only minimal objections to his quitting; they needed whatever extra money he could earn.

Pauli's departure from school hadn't affected his friendship with Tonio. He liked Tonio's gentleness and good disposition. "I was scared when I got to Wertheim's and you were gone," Tonio said to him.

"Couldn't help it," Pauli said, taking another Othello and devouring it with his usual speedy efficiency. He glanced at the gilded wall clock. Almost ten. He had to get home, so he'd be sure to get up on time.

"When do you see the old lady who wants to reward you?" Tonio asked.

"Tomorrow morning, nine o'clock sharp."

"What do you think the old lady will give you? Anything you ask for?"

"Oh, I doubt that."

Tonio grinned. "Maybe she'll give you a ticket to America."

"Oh yes, I wish," Pauli said in a derisive way. Then: "I'd better leave. Aunt Lotte keeps track of my shifts. She'll be wondering why I'm late."

Tonio followed him to the front, his big head inclined forward like a heavy burden. "How's school?" Pauli asked.

Tonio seemed reluctant to answer. "School. Yes—well—I have bad news."

At the doorway to Unter den Linden, Pauli stopped. Lime trees along the curb swayed in the wind. Smart carriages rattled by. The evening was crisp and breezy; cool weather had rolled in from the North Sea. Pauli saw an uncharacteristic fear in his friend's eyes.

"You know how the doctor inspects us weekly for signs of infirmity or slowness?" Pauli nodded. "Today I was inspected and—uh—taken out. From now on I'm required to go to the special school. Actually they say it's more like a camp. I'll go there in the autumn. The doctor said he was sorry, but it's necessary."

"Tonio, that's awful." When a student was pulled from school because he was lame or feebleminded, there was no appeal. As the school doctor had once remarked when he was examining pupils, "It's the only way to keep up standards. It's the new German way."

If so, Pauli didn't like it much. Perhaps that was why he had such a strong interest in the country to which his uncle had emigrated years ago.

"Tonio, I'm really sorry."

"Yes, me too. But don't worry, I'll get along."

Pauli squeezed his friend's arm and left.

His heels clicked on the pavement as he walked along. Dark leaves rustled in the cool breeze. The streets resounded with the laughter and lively conversations of passersby, the raucous voices and thumped tankards of celebrants in beer halls, the tuneful grind of a street minstrel's *Leierkasten,* a barrel organ transported on a small two-wheeled wagon. With the appointment looming tomorrow, the night was full of anticipation and magic. Pauli loved Berlin again.

Well, why not? It was one of the world's great cities. A million and a half people crowded its old streets, creating constant noise and turmoil but at the same time a sense of energy, power, importance. The din of carriages and horse-cars wouldn't stop until early morning.

Athens on the Spree, the old residents called it. Because of the smoke, dirt, relentless industrial expansion, Rathenau, the electrics tycoon, called it Chicago on the Spree. Aunt Lotte had other, less flattering names. "This shithole of misery," for one.

On the streets you saw every sort of person. Elegant women and ragged gypsies. Travelers, officers, businessmen, Jews with their beards and hairlocks and long black gowns; Pauli had never spoken to a Jew, excepting those who were shopkeepers. You saw old Junkers in from their country estates, disdainful, and thin as their expensive cigars. Tonio's father said the Junkers ran the country, the new imperial Germany. He said the Iron Chancellor, Bismarck, had brought back something called the old steel and rye clique—the soldiers and the landowners. He said their influence was good for Germany, along with Bismarck's policy of promoting Germany through armed strength.

Yes, Berlin was a pageant, all right. But he was no longer sure that Berlin would be his permanent home. He'd begun to think often of America. Of a particular city, Chicago, and of the uncle he'd never met. The uncle who was a brewer, and rich.

Also, he disliked his job in the kitchen at the famous and elegant Hotel Kaiserhof. There Pauli swabbed the tiled kitchen floor, emptied trays of dirty dishes and smelly buckets of preparation scraps while avoiding the fists and kicks of the short-tempered chefs. Sometimes he worked days, and sometimes half the night, but the drudgery never varied. The single compensation was the opportunity to spend a few minutes with Herr Trautwein, the hall porter, a burly bachelor who crawled into the beds of female guests whenever possible. He was also an enthusiast about modern inventions of every kind, and talked endlessly but interestingly about the new age of mechanization that would enlighten the world in the next century.

In Müllerstrasse, the sanitary workers—women—clanked the lids of the sewer tanks as Pauli approached. Someone leaned out a window to complain about the noise. The reek of waste filled the drab street. Only the warm hearty smells that blew down from the Norddeutsche Brauerei several blocks away relieved the pervasive stench of dung and dirt.

The bell of the Catholic church on the next street sounded the quarter hour. Pauli hurried down the steps to the door of the cellar flat he occupied along with Aunt Lotte and her innumerable *Herren*. For a long time, before Aunt Lotte made a decision about entertaining *Herren*, a corner of the sitting room had been occupied by one or two *Schlafburschen*, renters who came and went by day and slept behind a temporary curtain at night. Now every guest wound up in Aunt Lotte's room.

Pauli let himself in. The flat was small, with a painted plaster ceiling that pressed down oppressively. The inevitable yellowing lace curtains masked what few windows there were. Dark furniture crowded the sitting room, where Pauli found his aunt in her best flowered wrapper, together with her visitor, an American who showed up about every six months.

"You're late, where have you been?" Aunt Lotte said. "You look even messier than usual." Lotte was forty-three, a handsome and full-bosomed woman with auburn hair like a tight cap of curls, pale blue eyes, and a deformed left foot. Her shoe had a sole several inches thick, and when she walked she exerted enormous effort to avoid listing from side to side. Pauli always thought it was the foot that had robbed her of a good life. Of course she was willful too; very independent and full of herself, which he found strange for someone in poor circumstances.

Intimidated by her question, Pauli didn't know where to start. Lotte waved her glass. "Well, come on, what's the explanation?"

"I was held awhile at the police station—"

"Police!" she cried. "My God, what have you done now?"

"Hey, let the kid explain," said the guest. He rose to pour himself another glass of the champagne he always brought. Phil Reynard traveled through Europe selling Globus sewing machines. He was a gangly, paunchy man who used dye to keep his hair a sleek glossy brown. His German was excellent.

"Explain, then, and be quick about it," Aunt Lotte said. Pauli told the story.

"Not bad, not bad. Got a reward out of it," Reynard said, chuckling.

Aunt Lotte poured herself more champagne. "All right, I guess you did the correct thing. It doesn't excuse the fact that you could have been injured. Don't make a habit of interfering with criminals, Pauli. One more thing. Tomorrow, if the nature of your reward is open for discussion, ask for money. Now go to bed and leave us alone."

Pauli walked down the long dark corridor to his room. There he lit the lamp—no electrification for this cellar yet. He shut the door and latched it with a hard push.

As he peeled off his jacket, he wondered unhappily, as he had so many times lately, what had come over his aunt. Until about a year ago they had enjoyed an affectionate, tolerant relationship. Then something began to change her. He couldn't guess what it was, but it was real, he could even see it in her face, once so ruddy, but now a spectral gray.

He stared around the pathetic room, and his eyes came to rest on the collection of souvenirs tacked to the old wallpaper with its pattern of weedy-looking flowers.

The largest part of the collection consisted of postal cards on which photographs were reproduced, mostly exotic foreign scenes. The Sphinx. A ricksha man at the Great Wall of China. The onion domes of Moscow. An American cowboy on his horse. A spectacular massive rock formation called El Capitan, in a far-off place in America called Yosemite Valley. Scenic and comic postcards were a craze in Germany. When the imprinted information was in English, Aunt Lotte translated it for him. Because of the international nature of her trade, she knew smatterings of several languages. Pauli never tired of studying the photographs.

Two tacks held the small black, red, and gold flag of the failed Revolution of '48. Hanging below it were streamers of red, white, and blue salvaged from a diplomatic party at the hotel. They symbolized and reminded him of his uncle in America.

He tried not to think too often about his longing to follow his uncle, because the dream was so impossible as to seem absurd. He had a symbol for it, however, tacked up somewhat apart from the other cards and souvenirs. It was a rectangle of cardboard for a parlor stereoscope, sepia-tinted, badly bent at two corners. Another of his aunt's *Herren* had presented it to him; a fat American trying to sell huge electrodynamos to compete with Siemens-Halske. On the card, in the dual images, the camera looked out across the bow of a great ship entering the harbor of New York. The huge city loomed in the background. In the foreground a magnificent statue rose from a rocky island. In her upraised right hand she held a torch of freedom. In the crook of her left arm rested a large tablet. Below the rays of her crown, her face was strong and beautiful. She was the first thing seen by new immigrants, the fat American said. Her name was "Liberty Enlightening the World." She welcomed millions of others; would she welcome him if he sailed there?

He laughed at himself for the ridiculous thought. How could he ever manage an ocean voyage? He was barely surviving day to day, handling backbreaking loads of *Ochsenfleisch* at the Kaiserhof just to stay alive.

Quickly he made ready for bed, put out the lamp and slipped under the skimpy comforter. The summer night had turned sharply colder. He couldn't relax, thinking of the morning. Dust from his pillow made him sneeze and bolt up wide-eyed. When he lay down again, noises from the other bedroom bothered him. First Aunt Lotte's faint cough, then familiar creakings and squeakings, followed by loud groans from the sewing machine salesman. Pauli had lived on the streets long enough to know what men and women did with, and to, each other, although he had no firsthand experience as yet. He'd heard that women enjoyed it, but were forbidden to admit it. Surely Aunt Lotte didn't enjoy it. She gave no sign of enjoying anything anymore.

2

Charlotte

LOTTE KRONER stared at the picture on the table next to the bed. The sewing machine salesman snored softly, one hand with a gaudy sapphire ring thrown over her heavy thigh.

The low-trimmed lamp flickered, making the faded metal plate in the gold frame shimmer. The adolescent girl in the picture had beautiful regular features and thick shining hair that Lotte knew to be red. The girl was her illegitimate daughter, whom she refused to discuss with Pauli no matter how much he questioned her.

She pulled up the down-filled comforter. Sewn and patched in many places, the comforter had come to her in her trousseau, along with all the other linens she still used. Then she hitched herself up so the triangular bolster gave her back more support. Reynard stirred and muttered a complaint. She didn't care. She had other, deeper concerns, chief among them her nephew. She had very little time to set his life on a better course. Very little time.

As if to remind her, raspy pain seared her throat. She put her fist to her lips to mute a cough, and the spasm passed.

Pauli's face haunted her, particularly his hurt eyes when she spoke to him sharply in the sitting room. She didn't really want to be unpleasant, ever. She loved him. Harsh words and angry looks were part of her deliberate campaign to set a distance between them, and thus make it easier to get him out of Berlin. He didn't understand. How could he?

Another familiar image pushed into her thoughts. Pieces of the lovely blue-gray pottery of south Germany, smashed at her doorstep by girlhood friends the night before her wedding. The breaking of crockery for *Polterabend* was supposed to keep the evil *Poltergeist* from bedeviling a marriage. A lot of good it had done for her. Ever afterward, the broken crockery was Lotte's symbol of her wretched life.

The market town of Aalen lies some forty kilometers east of Stuttgart, in the state of Württemberg in the pleasant green foothills of the Swabian Jura. At the midpoint of the nineteenth century little had changed in the town since the far-off time when a Roman cavalry detachment was garrisoned there to guard the imperial frontier.

The roots of the Kroner family went deep into the earth of that little sector of Germany. Swabians were and always had been a prickly, individualistic lot. Hard-working, and extremely protective of every mark they earned.

Württemberg and nearby Bavaria were tinder for the revolutionary fires that were ignited in Paris in 1848 and blazed across the frontier, sweeping all of Germany.

Lotte's father, Thomas Kroner, owned a small hotel and brewery on Radgasse —Wheel Street—in the town of Aalen. He was a revolutionary ringleader in his district. He rushed off at once to join the demonstrations centered in Baden.

Meantime, a National Assembly convened in Frankfurt. After enacting a few reforms, and struggling toward the unification of many small states, the delegates foundered. They couldn't agree on the boundaries of a new nation. Nor could they find a ruler for it. When offered the crown of a constitutional Germany, the King of Prussia declared he would not touch "a diadem molded out of the dirt and dregs of disloyalty and treason."

Thus encouraged, the landed class, the Junkers, stiffened their resistance, and the Assembly dissolved. The following spring, Württemberg erupted again. The grand duke asked Prussia for help, and two army corps under Crown Prince William advanced on Baden. July 23, 1849, saw the final capitulation of the revolutionaries; the end of the great hope for a new, democratically united nation symbolized by the tricolor. The aristocrats had won. Hundreds of "Men of '48" fled to America, embittered and fearing for their lives.

Thomas Kroner was identified as one of the leaders of the uprising. He had four children and a wife, the former Gertrud Retz. He also had his business to think about. So, despite danger, he refused to run or even hide. The authorities arrested him, tried him, and hanged him three days before Christmas.

Charlotte Kroner was the third child of Thomas and Gertrud. During her father's detention, her oldest brother, Alfred, was also seized and thrown into a cell. There he was held for forty-eight hours. He was nine years old.

Sadistic prison guards abused the boy with truncheons. The beating broke his left leg. Damage was permanent. Lamed, Alfred Kroner was unable to earn more than a minimal living thereafter. Perhaps out of fear, for the rest of his life he enthusiastically supported authority, and the monolithic German state gradually emerging.

Lotte herself had been born with her foot deformed. Sometimes, she reflected bitterly as she grew older, it seemed as if fate, history—or some malignant heavenly power—had crippled almost everyone in the Kroner family. Lotte was determined to see that a wretched life didn't cripple her nephew's mind and heart.

Lotte's mother had died in 1853. In 1861, her crippled brother Alfred married Karoline Wissen, a young woman from Aalen, who gave him no children.

In 1871, the new German Empire was proclaimed in the Hall of Mirrors at Versailles following the quick defeat of France in the Franco-Prussian War. It was the age of Bismarck, the Iron Chancellor, who threw violent baronies and city-states and robber fiefdoms into the furnace of nationalism, melted them in the heat of the Franco-Prussian victory, and on the anvil of his will hammered them into the shape of his personal vision—the First Reich.

Alfred's wife Karoline died in '73, as the new Germany was rising. Alfred soon married a woman named Pauline Marie Schönau, who bore one son, Lotte's nephew Pauli, and died not long thereafter.

Lotte had two other brothers. The second oldest, Josef, was the shining pride of her life. On his own initiative, Josef had left Aalen in 1857. He was fifteen. He made his way across the ocean to the American metropolis of Cincinnati, where many other Germans had already settled. In the state of Ohio, Josef developed great skill in the brewer's trade, of which he had learned something as a boy. He fought in America's bloody Civil War, striking a blow for the abolition of Negro slavery. After the war he married a good woman and moved to an even larger city, Chicago. From there he sent Christmas gifts to Lotte, along with greetings and news of his family penned on costly engraved stationery. He changed the spelling of his name, just as his German-born wife had; he took out citizenship, and became American in every respect. He was raising his three children under the name Crown.

Lotte's younger brother, Gerhard, was a baker by trade. After the family hotel and brewery were sold for debts, he chose to stay in Aalen. Pious, wildly unambitious, he baked his *Brot* and *Kuchen* in smug provincial isolation. Lotte knew that Gerhard thought her immoral, and considered Josef a dead man because he'd forsaken Germany. She hadn't seen Gerhard for over twenty years, and wanted nothing to do with him. To Lotte's way of thinking, she had no family left in Aalen at all.

Lotte's marriage to a cabinetmaker from a village near Aalen had broken almost as quickly as the blue-gray pottery of *Polterabend*. She converted to Catholicism to please her husband, a burly man who believed absolutely that a woman owed her whole life to the three *K*'s—*Kinder, Küche, Kirche*. Children, kitchen, church. When Lotte showed in various ways that she thought otherwise, her husband used his fist to enforce his viewpoint. One night after eleven months of marriage Lotte simply packed her things, put dressings on her bruises, boarded the local for Stuttgart, and never looked back.

Her ultimate destination was Berlin. Longing to experience the high life of the city, she had placed herself in the path of wealthy gentlemen who would take her to the opera or a fine restaurant in return for her carefully rationed favors. It was one of these who had fathered Christine out of wedlock.

Unfortunately Lotte didn't have either the perfect physique or the wits to be a highly successful courtesan. To care for herself and her infant daughter, she was reduced to factory jobs, which she hated, and with reason. A man slaved six days a week for a wage of eighteen or twenty marks—if he was lucky. Women usually received 40 to 50 percent less.

As Lotte grew older, it became apparent that she couldn't do an adequate job of raising her daughter. Christine was a ravishingly beautiful child. She was also headstrong. When she was ten, Lotte placed her in domestic service with a respectable and prosperous family in Ulm, south of Aalen. She prayed that Christine was not too beautiful and willful to stay in their employ, but she never knew, because, as she was doing with Pauli, she went out of her way to make the child believe she was unwanted, thus insuring greater contentment for Christine in her new home. It was after Christine's departure that Lotte began to drink more heavily.

Lotte's options steadily dwindled. She despised them all. She absolutely would not surrender herself to a *Stift*, a charity institution for females who had failed in achieving a woman's purpose—marriage, children, the maintenance of an orderly home. She refused to consider remarriage, because German men wanted nothing but a servant whom they could dignify with the name wife. A few months before his final condemnation of her, brother Gerhard had made overtures by letter, suggesting that she might come back to Aalen and live with him, his wife, and his growing brood of children. No thank you. Lotte had seen that arrangement in other families; the poor relation, the spinster, became a slave and gave up her independence in exchange for a tiny room, daily drudgery, and a role as an object of pity for the rest of her life.

So, between distasteful jobs, Lotte entered a number of unsatisfactory short liaisons. From these it had been but a short step to her current, one might call it professional, approach.

She wasn't a streetwalker. Nothing so degrading. By means of well-placed bribes and tips at the good hotels, she made contact with visiting foreigners of a certain class. She enjoyed theaters and cafés in their company, and later entertained them in her cellar flat. Thus she survived.

To shopkeepers and other acquaintances in the district round about Müller-strasse, she presented herself as Frau Kroner, a Swabian widow of private means. None of her neighbors threw the obvious lie back in her face. The greengrocer even played the game fully, asking solicitous questions about the security of her principal. In reply, she invented other elaborate lies.

Pauli's father Alfred had died in 1881, four years after his wife Pauline bore the boy, and Pauline herself succumbed in '85. Gerhard, perhaps irked by the various failures and deficiencies of family members, said that his household was too crowded for him to take Pauli in. At New Year's, 1886, Pauli Kroner, age eight and growing fast, arrived at the Berlin *Bahnhof* with his few clothes in a cheap valise.

He presented a brusquely worded note from Gerhard, saying he refused to go the trouble of contacting Josef in America. Pauli was transferred to Lotte's care. She detected a certain spiteful glee between the lines of Gerhard's note.

Never mind; she joyfully accepted responsibility for Pauli. She was happy for his company; for his energy and good cheer. Of course she soon realized it wasn't a pleasant existence for him. At *Grundschule* he was treated like one of the poorest charity cases. Given his books of Latin and German composition, rather than being required to pay for them. Given his breakfast of bread and milk in winter, and his free weekly ticket to a public bath. She saw how the stigma hurt him. She yearned for something better for him.

The trouble was, there was no longer much time. Her mirror told her so every day. She was growing gray and gaunt, and each month her little account book noted fewer *Herren*. She knew she would inevitably be driven to knock at the gates of the Charité Hospital.

She suppressed another cough, then leaned to the side and groped under the bed, where she had dropped the doily from the bedside table.

Her fingers closed on the stiff old lace. She drew it up into the light and gazed without flinching at the smear now dried to brown.

No, there was not much time left.

3

Pauli

THE OLD LADY lived in a one-family brick villa on a quiet street in *der alte Westen,* the Old West section, near the Tiergarten. Here you found the finest and wealthiest, who didn't care to exhibit themselves, or their riches, by living in some ostentatious, overdecorated flat in the New West, a rising district out along the Ku'damm.

Extremely nervous, Pauli presented himself at the front door at three minutes before nine. He'd put on his best jacket and knee breeches, and for once tried to clean his pockets of pencils and other objects. But there was still a large charcoal smudge on his left lapel that no amount of rubbing would remove.

A butler with a severe face answered his ring. He led Pauli through a succession of large rooms crowded with heavy dark furniture. So much furniture, he thought he was in some nobleman's palace.

The old lady awaited him in a wicker chair in a sunny room at the front. A shiny black cane with a large silver knob rested across her knees. Her dress looked hellishly hot; meters and meters of black silk. She had lively brown eyes set amid deep wrinkles.

"The young gentleman," the butler said, and retired.

"Good morning," the old lady said. "Take this seat next to me. We will have refreshments, I think."

A maid appeared almost by magic, bearing a silver tray with a plate of *Lebkuchen,* dark honey-sweetened cookies stamped out in the shape of stars, lions, hearts, elephants, even a soldier or two. There was a small pewter pot of dark beer for Pauli, and tea for the old lady, into which she poured rum from a decanter to make *Teepunsch.*

"Well, now," the old lady said after she'd sipped. "I am Frau Flüsser, and you are my benefactor. The police told me your name is Pauli."

"Pauli Kroner, yes," he said, clearing his throat in the middle. He held the pewter pot in his left hand, his plate on his right knee, and felt he was in danger of dropping one or both at any moment.

"You acted quickly and bravely when that rascal tried to rob me, so I feel you are entitled to a reward. You know my son-in-law, Otto, is deputy director of Wertheim's?" Pauli nodded. "I have spoken with him. Your reward will be your choice of anything reasonably priced from the store. Do you have any thoughts? Any wants?"

He thought for a moment.

"Do you have globes?"

"I beg your pardon? Speak up, please. I'm hard of hearing."

"Globes. A small globe. I like to look at other countries and imagine what they're like."

"A globe," she said. "That is an unusual request, but I believe it can be fulfilled. I will telephone Otto this morning. Where shall we send it?"

"Müllerstrasse." Reluctantly, he repeated the number.

"That is your home?"

"Right now, yes. I live there, with my Aunt Charlotte."

"Do you hope to have a home somewhere else someday?"

"Yes, that's what I hope most of all."

"Where will it be?"

"I don't know."

"Any ideas?"

"My uncle lives in Chicago, perhaps that's it. That's why I like a globe, it shows me all the possible places."

Frau Flüsser beamed. "America, that's a good place, I'd consider it seriously if I were you. My brother Felix lives in St. Louis. My niece Waltraud also. Many Germans live in St. Louis. I might go there myself if I weren't so old, and didn't know I belonged here."

She gave a glance at her gold watch, whose face was upside down, hanging on her large sagging bosom at the end of a gold pendant. "I will see that you get your globe promptly, so you can continue your search."

Kindness softened her wrinkled face. "I am very grateful for your courage and assistance. You may kiss me if you like."

He rose and kissed her cheek, wishing she were his own grandmother.

"Goodbye, Pauli Kroner."

"Goodbye, Frau Flüsser."

"If your true home isn't Berlin, I hope you find it, wherever it may be."

"Thank you, I also."

"Take my word, when you find it, you'll know. Something unexpected will tell you. When I was nine, my father was a choirmaster in the town of Luchow. He received an appointment as assistant in a church here. On the day we arrived in Berlin, there were beautiful cloud formations in the sky. I saw a cloud shaped like a harp. My father could play the harp exquisitely. I loved the music of the harp. When I saw the cloud I knew Berlin was where I belonged and would live the rest of my life. That was my sign. There will be one for you someday."

She blew him a kiss.

He smiled and squared his shoulders. He left the house and never saw her again.

After work that night, he couldn't wait to tell Aunt Lotte about his reward.

"A *globe?*" She squinted at him through smoke from one of her strong French cigarettes. "What a silly, stupid request. I told you to ask for money. You already have enough maps and cards to paper a palace. What are you planning to do, become a great *Herr Doktor Professor* of geography? Not likely." She lurched away, to the cabinet where she kept her schnapps bottle.

□ □ □ □

Frau Flüsser was true to her word. Wertheim's sent the globe by delivery van, in one of their own boxes, tied with silver ribbon. It was a splendid little wooden globe, painted with bright enamel colors. It sat freely in a four-legged stand of lacquered wood.

He threw away his paper map and cleared a special place on his shelf. At night he took the globe from the stand and held it close in front of him, where he could survey it in detail. Turn it and touch it at different places, wondering about each. More and more, he found his eye drawn to America, with its green plains, blue lakes, brown mountains. More and more, his finger was drawn to the bottom of one narrow blue lake, which was the location of Chicago; the home of his uncle.

Posters appeared, on kiosks and walls all over the city.

Beginn der 1. Vorstellung
am 24.August
—Dem Original und Einzigen—
Buffalo-Bill's
W I L D — W E S T

"Are you going?" Tonio asked Pauli. It was a welcome change of subject. Tonio had been chattering about the special school in which he would enroll in a few weeks. His poor head looked larger, more swollen, than Pauli remembered.

"No, I don't have the money," Pauli said. They were again seated at a rear table in Konditorei Henkel.

"Papa said he'd take me. Perhaps he'll pay for you, too."

"No, that's charity, I don't take charity. Don't worry about me, I'll see the cowboys and Indians some way or other, you can count on it."

On the morning of the arrival of the Wild West troupe, he was awake at five. He was dressed five minutes later. He stuffed a plaid cap in his pocket, picked up his drawing materials and tiptoed past Aunt Lotte's closed door. Reynard was back in town. It had been noisy in the flat until one in the morning.

He dashed up the steps into Müllerstrasse. A cool mist blurred the roof lines of the four- and five-story flats lining the street.

He raced into Wöhlertstrasse and went full speed, straight to the *Rangier- und Güterbahnhof*—the freight and marshaling yards that sprawled just to the east of Pflugstrasse. He heard the clanking of cars and the hooting of steam engines while he was still several blocks away.

He crossed a strip of weedy ground to the yards. On the first track in front of him, a devilishly long freight train was departing, effectively blocking his way. He spied an open car, stuffed his drawing paper into his belt and ran along beside the car until things felt just right. He jumped and flung one leg into the open doorway.

He caught hold of the door with both hands. He was aboard in a second. He rolled back the door on the other side and leaped out, sprawling on gravel. He bounded up and brushed himself off, undamaged save for a small tear in the knee of his pants. There was always a way around an obstacle if you looked for it.

He ran on across the next two tracks. To his dismay, he saw that the special train had already arrived. But it must have just pulled in, for the unloading hadn't yet started.

The train was long, eighteen cars plus the locomotive. Several of the cars were decorated with large gaudy paintings of frontiersmen firing pistols, Indians howling and flourishing tomahawks, a stagecoach racing away from red-skinned pursuers—and of course there was a portrait of the star, raising his white sombrero in salute as his splendid stallion reared. The image was magnificently heroic; horse, hat, and Cody's goatee and mustache shone pure white in the sunlight breaking over the yards.

Pauli waited until a little Borsig switch engine chugged by, then crossed the next track. He wasn't too late after all. Roustabouts in checked shirts were just starting to lay iron plates between the cars of the special train, while others dropped an iron ramp from the end of the last car. Pauli forgot Müllerstrasse, Aunt Lotte, poor Tonio—everything.

Activity around the train quickened rapidly. The roustabouts rolled back the doors of livestock cars and pulled canvas covers from vehicles tied and chocked in place on flatcars. The train was arranged in a precise order. At the rear, one livestock car held dray horses, first to be unloaded down the iron ramp.

Going forward, the flatcars carrying wagons were next in line, then the rest of the livestock cars whose occupants Pauli both saw and smelled. Saddle horses; mules; three shaggy bison; Colonel Cody's own milk-white horse, Isham. At the front of the train were passenger cars with doors in the ends, not the sides, and the unfamiliar word PULLMAN blazoned on them.

The roustabouts shouted and swore in English, a little of which Pauli understood because of his association with men such as Reynard. He took care to stay out of the way of the roustabouts as he gawked his way along the train. He almost collided with a brown-skinned man with long black braids. An Indian! Wearing a suit, stiff collar, tall silk hat.

Boldly, Pauli nodded a greeting. The Indian scowled and raised his hand, palm out. Pauli grinned and imitated the gesture. The Indian laughed and clapped him on the shoulder.

He stood for a while by a passenger car bearing the legend BUFFALO BILL'S WILD WEST & CONGRESS OF ROUGH RIDERS—GRAND EUROPEAN TOUR. A tall gentleman with mussed white hair staggered out of the car and down the steps. Colonel Cody! He was world famous; Pauli recognized him instantly.

Pauli stepped back. He needn't have bothered; the colonel ignored him. Cody wore old boots, stained pants, and a singlet. Braces hung down over his hips. He waved a whiskey bottle as he stomped to the rear of the train, swearing and shouting orders. Pauli was disappointed with the colonel's shabby appearance and rough behavior.

A somewhat more genteel personage appeared a moment later: a little lady, sleepily leading a poodle on a leash. It was Fräulein Annie Oakley, the celebrated sharpshooter. He recognized her from pictures on the posters.

Men uncoupled the last car, empty now, while others moved the ramp to the car in front of it. A switch engine backed up, coupled, and pulled the empty car away. It all seemed marvelously efficient to Pauli. But it didn't suit the colonel, who waved his whiskey bottle and screamed, "Get those damned pull-up horses hitched, we're behind schedule." Pauli caught his meaning, if not the exact words.

A team moved alongside the flatcar and was hitched to the first wagon. They pulled it from the ground, while roustabouts guided the wagon off the flatcar and down the ramp. The men led the team and wagon out of the way so a second team could unload the next vehicle, the gleaming lacquered Deadwood stagecoach. Pauli had found an advance flier at the hotel and read all about the various scenes of the show. The rescue of the Deadwood mail coach was the most famous. He still couldn't afford a ticket into the special show park newly fenced off at the corner of Augsburgerstrasse and the Ku'damm, but he'd imagined the action—the thrilling Indian attack, then the cavalry rescue—many times.

While the unloading went on, Pauli retired to some boxcars standing on the adjacent track. He rolled open the door of one and took a seat, determined to sketch something. His eye was drawn back to the gaudy painting of Buffalo Bill. He'd try that. He started his sketch with a dark blue pencil.

All at once a figure appeared from between his car and the next. A man, standing there, staring at him. The man had dark eyes that seemed to glare with an inner fire. For a terrible instant, Pauli thought he was looking into the eyes of Death.

The man was tall, and he looked underfed. He had a long, narrow face and large white teeth. His skin was the color of oat porridge; perhaps he hid from the sun. He was at least ten years older than Pauli, in his middle twenties.

He wore spectacles of cheap gold-plated wire, with round lenses no bigger than pfennigs. His clothes were dark and shabby—grimy collar and a cravat with a greasy sheen, a duster that reached below his knees, and a derby that had seen better days. He had a gray spat on his right shoe, a white one on his left. In his nicotine-stained right hand a stubby cigarette burned.

Poor as he was, the man affected a cocky air as he strolled toward Pauli, drawing on his cigarette with quick little puffs. His eyes were hot, and vaguely accusing—as if Pauli were some kind of lowlife.

With arrogant casualness, he leaned against the boxcar near Pauli. He glanced down at the sketch of Cody. Sneering, he said, "That's terrible."

Pauli stuck out his chin. "Oh, are you an art critic?"

"No, a journalist. But I know bad art when I see it, the same as I know sour cheese when I smell it." The man spoke German with a pronounced but unfamiliar accent.

Pauli thought the man was lying. "What newspaper do you work for?"

"Any one that will buy my paragraphs. I am independent. There is an interesting new term for that, I heard it in Zurich last week. Free lance. I travel, I write, I observe, I predict—" The young man shrugged. "Sometimes prophecy isn't popular, especially if the prophet dispenses anything other than candy and dreams. They killed some of the Old Testament prophets, you know. I'm often forced to leave a city on a moment's notice. I thought there might be a story possibility here."

"You're foreign—"

"According to you," said the man, with another sneer. But it was banter he seemed to enjoy. "My name is Mikhail Rhukov. At least in Russia. In this country you would say Michael, I suppose."

He lounged against the boxcar, pulling out a second cigarette which he lit from the stub of the first. "Amazing people, these Americans. They're going to own the earth, I think. I wish they'd export a little of their democracy to my country. It's an astounding time we live in, don't you think? Old governments, old ways, old orders going down in blood and fire. Anarchism on the rise. The red banners of socialism flying high. Tsars and kings trembling, proletarians marching—exciting."

"I don't know a thing about it," Pauli said, in what he hoped was a hostile tone.

Rhukov eyed him with that burning gaze. "Look, I'm only being friendly."

"Oh, is that what you call it?"

Rhukov laughed. "Cheeky little shit. I like you."

"Fine, leave me alone," Pauli said, no longer frightened, merely annoyed. Unfortunately, he seemed to have found a new friend, or at least a new companion, whether he wanted it or not.

Rhukov pulled a cheap notebook from his duster and wrote a few lines with a pencil.

Pauli jumped down from the freight car and walked toward the train. The Russian followed him. Pauli wished the obnoxious chap would find someone else to befriend.

Startled by the sound of men speaking German, Pauli turned to the right. He was surprised to see a group of six army officers standing near the iron ramp. Four were older, with the broad red stripe of the general staff on their trousers of *feldgrau,* the army's standard field gray. Their matching tunics had red epaulets and piping.

The two young lieutenants wore gray trousers and dark blue tunics, signifying that they belonged to a particular line regiment. Pauli couldn't immediately identify their collar insignia. He sidled closer, hands in pockets, trying to look casual. All but one of the officers were busily writing in small leather-bound notebooks or comparing the time on pocket watches.

Up close, Pauli recognized the metal insignia worn by the lieutenants. They belonged to the newest and most modern unit in the army, *Eisenbahn-regiment 1,* the railway regiment. Both lieutenants wore the *Pickelhaube,* the spiked helmet seen throughout the army.

"I have heard about these people," Rhukov remarked to Pauli. "They follow Herr Cody everywhere in Germany. They are studying his methods. A sneery lot, aren't they?" Pauli thought the Russian had a lot of nerve to criticize someone else's arrogance. Besides, German officers, especially the Prussians, were always haughty, because they were revered throughout the fatherland, and feared throughout Europe, for their steely professionalism.

The senior officer, a stout *Brigadegeneral,* studied the train through a monocle held in front of his eye. "I have read reports of this procedure but have not had a chance to observe it before. They move quickly."

"And as you notice, sir, everything comes off the train in correct order for their parade," said a stoop-shouldered major. "They have a written plan for loading and unloading. I have examined it. It covers the smallest items, down to the personal trunks of the performers, and describes where everything is hung or placed within each. It's a marvel of efficiency."

"I am surprised that Americans are capable of such clear thought. Very impressive."

"Perhaps Büffel Bill is German," the major said. The officers laughed, but not until the brigadier laughed first.

One of the young lieutenants from the railway regiment tapped his notebook. "They are twenty-eight minutes behind schedule." Leaning against a trackside signal, Pauli studied the man. He was of medium height, trim and erect, very fit-looking. No doubt he practiced his gymnastics and calisthenics daily. What struck Pauli most was a certain contrast. The lieutenant's features were not especially strong; his jawline formed a moderate V; his nose was ordinary; his cheeks strewn with light freckles. But his eyes commanded. Gray eyes, large and widely spaced, cool and hard. A smile seemed about to spring to the young officer's lips any moment, but that pleasant aspect of his face could never reach into his chill, darting eyes.

The young officer tucked his notebook into his belt, pulled out a flat gold case and offered it to his superiors. The brigadier and major took cigarettes. When the lieutenant turned to hold a match for the brigadier, Pauli saw a scar, hook shaped, on his left cheek. Probably he'd gotten it at Heidelberg, in one of the *Burschenschaften*, the elite student fraternities. They were notorious for demanding that members regularly engage in saber duels. A scar was a mark of prowess, a badge of honor.

"Twenty-eight minutes, hmm," the brigadier murmured, blowing smoke. "That is not impressive."

The major said, "We didn't see them arrive, perhaps the train was late."

"Arrival from Braunschweig was only six and one half minutes behind schedule," the lieutenant said. "I consulted several switchmen to confirm it."

"That would never do for artillery arriving in the field," said the brigadier. "Lieutenant von Rike, kindly ask a few more questions. Ascertain, if you can, the reason they have lost almost twenty-two minutes."

The lieutenant snapped his hand to his cap, then pivoted. Pauli stepped aside, but not in time. The officer had his eye on the train and didn't see Pauli until he blundered into him.

"I'm sorry, sir," Pauli began. Color rushed into the lieutenant's cheeks. His hands and clothing gave off a tobacco smell as strong as Rhukov's. He grabbed Pauli's collar and flung him down on the gravel. A sharp stone nicked Pauli's cheek, drawing blood.

"In the future be more observant, you little dumbhead."

Angry, Pauli started to jump up. Before he could, Rhukov stepped in.

"That was uncalled for. The young man bumped you by accident."

The lieutenant eyed Rhukov up and down. "We don't need advice from dirty foreigners."

For all his peculiarity, Rhukov was brave. He didn't move. "You need a lesson in deportment, I'm afraid. An apology to this boy would be in order."

"Fuck your apologies. When the day arrives, we'll deal with your kind. Now stand aside." He pushed Rhukov and stalked by.

The journalist stretched out one yellowed hand to help Pauli rise. The other officers were giving them threatening looks. Rhukov sneered and turned his back.

"Thank you," Pauli said, trying to smooth his unruly hair.

"Don't mention it."

"Do you know what he meant when he said 'the day'? He made it sound important."

"The day? It is important. I've seen it written with the *D* capitalized. It's the day some of your countrymen think about all the time. The Day is that day in the future when they fancy they'll get their own back. Punish all their enemies. Take all the territory they want and believe they deserve. Come on, move away."

Rhukov guided him a safe distance from the officers, talking the while. "What a bunch of strutting popinjays. Just imagine what dreams dance around in their heads. Invincible Teutonic knights in Prussian castles raising black falcons to hunt and kill. Emperor Barbarossa sleeping under his mountain, ready to waken and lead, the moment Germany needs a savior. What shit. The problem is, I think they believe it. I fear the Kaiser and the whole army believe it. You Germans are a people mired in myths. Myths of superiority. Myths of the grandeur of war, the nobility of death. Not to mention Herr Wagner's water nymphs, magic gold, and sublime heroes who fuck their sisters. I beg your pardon, I hope you're not too young for such language."

"I've heard it before." Pauli decided this fellow had some substance, seedy as he was. He certainly knew a lot about Germans and Germany. Or acted like he did. He also liked the sound of his own voice.

Rhukov lit his next cigarette. "Mark my word, German myths will destroy Germany one day—if they don't destroy the rest of the world first. Of course we can count on a slight reprieve, because they'll start with revenge against the French. I refer primarily to the German high command, you understand. The generals, plus their strongest allies, the nobility. You're exempted. You may be a rotten artist, but you seem a decent sort otherwise."

"Thank you very much." Pauli's sarcasm amused Rhukov. He gave a grudging smile.

"You're a tough little nut. Where's your home?"

"I don't know," Pauli snapped. "I don't want to talk about it." For the first time Rhukov was caught short. Pauli enjoyed it.

Lieutenant von Rike returned, marching by stiffly and glaring at them. "The delay was not their fault," he announced to his superiors. "It lay with the yard-master. He misinterpreted instructions and didn't have the switch engine here on schedule."

Rhukov put his notebook away. "I've seen enough. I can write a page or two. Goodbye, my friend." He extended his hand and they shook in a formal way.

"I will see you again," Rhukov said. He strolled away toward the head of the train, down the center of a wide gravel area. He tipped his derby when he passed Fräulein Oakley. Curious fellow. Some of his pronouncements about the future were alarming.

Activity at the train distracted Pauli for a few seconds. When he looked again,

Rhukov had vanished from the open area, as if he were no more than smoke in a windstorm. It was spooky.

What a strange man. Just a little while ago, when they first met, Pauli was repelled. Now he was sorry Rhukov was gone. He had the oddest feeling that they would indeed meet again somewhere.

Pauli went back to his perch in the open boxcar, but he gave up further sketching. The *Brigadegeneral* and his men returned to observing the Wild West train. All the show wagons had been unloaded and lined up, and now the horses, donkeys, bison, deer, and elk were being led from their cars, which had doors in each end.

The morning was well advanced. Pale yellow sunshine spilled over the fuming chimneys of the ugly cement barracks-apartments nearby. Colonel Cody had disappeared, but Fräulein Oakley continued to exercise her poodle, accompanied by a man in a fringed jacket. Pauli recognized him. Fräulein Oakley's husband, the marksman Butler. Several Indians stood chatting. All of them wore ordinary jeans pants. Two had suit vests. Very disappointing.

Now suddenly there came another diversion. A group of four well-dressed tourists, two men, two women, pointing and chattering. One man carried a small black box. Pauli jumped down from the boxcar in order to move closer again.

"*Engländer,*" said the brigadier.

"*Nein, mein General. Mit respekt—Amerikaner.*" The major said something else, and the men responded with smiles and chuckles.

The visitors were finely dressed. The gentleman with the black box wore a tall hat and velvet-collared chesterfield, the second man a sporty Norfolk jacket and knickerbockers with a strong brown plaid on a tan ground, and white linen spats. One of the ladies was drab, but the other won Pauli's admiration with her dress of Venetian red and matching toque decorated with a stuffed gray bird. She'd gotten gravel dust all over her hem; the sporty man went to his knees to brush it away. The tall-hatted man, meantime, leaned over his black box, which he aimed at the Indian in the silk hat. The Indian put his left hand under his lapel, Napoleon-style, and raised his right hand.

Fräulein Oakley's companion approached the photo maker. Butler asked a question; Pauli thought he heard Butler say the word *American*.

The tourist nodded vigorously; introduced himself. His name was something like Jasper or Jaster. The latter, Pauli decided. He heard a reference to a place called Syracuse, New York.

Colonel Butler and the tourist shook hands. The marksman was interested in the black box. Pauli heard the words *George Eastman Kamera*.

Jaster nodded to Butler. "A Kodak." Kodak was a strange word, but Pauli had heard it before, from Herr Trautwein at the hotel. Herr Trautwein bragged about his Kodak *Kamera* from America. The new word with its hard knife-blade sound was easy to remember.

Jaster's wife urged him to show Butler the camera. Somewhat reluctantly, Jaster handed it over. Butler examined it, then whistled. He bounced it on his palm to show its light weight.

Jaster snatched the camera back, on the pretext of showing Butler how simple it was to take a picture. Because Jaster was a man who spoke with broad gestures, Pauli thought he understood. You simply pressed a button on the box to magically produce a picture. It was an exciting thought.

Jaster indicated that he wanted to photograph Butler and his wife. The marksman was flattered. He waved to Fräulein Oakley. She joined them, dragging her leashed poodle. Jaster's wife posed with the performers, then the Butlers excused themselves. The tourists circulated up and down the length of the assembling procession of animals and wagons, yawning cowboys wearing sombreros and colorful neckerchiefs, twelve men in United States Army blue, four booted and fur-hatted Cossacks, or very good imitations thereof. The Indians reappeared in shirts and leggings of animal hide, their faces decorated with multicolored slashes of paint. Feathers on their enormous war bonnets fluttered in the light air.

Pauli followed the tourists, almost delirious from the thrill of seeing both the Buffalo Bill troupe and a genuine Kodak camera. He didn't know how a camera worked, but he understood what it did. It produced those breathtaking views of other people, other places, which decorated his bedroom wall. A camera brought the whole world into the parlor of ordinary persons like Aunt Lotte and himself.

Herr and Frau Jaster and their friends passed between Pauli and the shining Deadwood coach, now hitched to six snorting horses. Pauli reminded himself that he was due at the Kaiserhof at half past seven. How could he hope to keep his mind on slop buckets and swabbed floors, having witnessed so many exciting things?

Jaster's wife wanted a photograph of the German officers. Jaster stopped about ten feet from them, and they suddenly took notice. The brigadier waved sharply.

"You there," he called in German. "Stop that. No photographs of officers on duty."

"What's he saying?" asked the sporty man. Jaster lowered his camera but his wife jabbed him with a gloved finger. She didn't want him to back down so easily.

The officers looked annoyed. Pauli couldn't understand why they should object to being photographed, unless it was their usual arrogance coming into play. The scowls and dark glances didn't seem to deter Herr Jaster, who went on readying his shot.

"Someone stop him," the brigadier said. The lieutenant, von Rike, thrust his notebook in his pocket. "Teach him a lesson while you're at it."

The lieutenant rushed forward and violently tore the Kodak from Jaster's hands. Frau Jaster shrieked in alarm.

Her husband lunged for the camera. Von Rike feinted to the left gracefully, drew Jaster off guard, then jumped back while prying the box open. Agog, Pauli watched the lieutenant whip out a long paper streamer with a dark coating on one side. Von Rike dropped the camera and stamped on it. Frau Jaster wailed.

Jaster was in a fury. Although he was twenty years older than the lieutenant, he hoisted his fists and swung a right without hesitation. Von Rike drew approving exclamations from his colleagues by simply stepping out of the way. When Jaster swung a second time, von Rike knocked off his tall hat and smacked Jaster's forehead with his palm. It jolted the tourist and threw him off balance. He fell on his right knee.

The lieutenant walked back to his comrades and took his place, having done his duty. The brigadier offered no special compliments or approval. The major did, though; a terse "Neatly done."

"Thank you, sir. The best medicine for obstinacy is the one His Majesty prescribes. The mailed fist."

The brigadier chuckled approvingly, then gestured at the Americans, ordering them away. Herr Jaster was cursing and protesting as his friends helped him up. He wanted to resume the fight but they restrained him. A minute later the backs of the four tourists could be seen retreating around the corner of a switchman's shack.

Pauli perched in the boxcar doorway once more. The officers closed their notebooks and they too soon strolled out of sight behind the Wild West train, the junior officers trailing their superiors at a respectful distance. Pauli thanked heaven that he didn't have to be a soldier. He wouldn't want to take orders from some hothead who destroyed property and abused people without a qualm.

Colonel Cody came out of his car, resplendently dressed in knee-high boots, whipcord trousers, fringed buckskin coat enlivened by Indian beadwork and quills, flowing neckerchief and sombrero. Mounting Isham, he trotted up and down the line of the assembled parade, bellowing more instructions. He sounded cross.

Pauli's fascination with the Wild West show was waning, replaced by intense concentration on the object he feared to stare at because someone else might notice. The camera. Smashed; ruined. But a real camera. Abandoned there in the gravel . . .

With a popping of whips and a creaking of axles, the cavalcade began to move out of the yards, bound for the morning parade down Unter den Linden. Pauli's mouth was as dry as fireplace ash. Eyes darting, he eased down from the boxcar, then ran to the camera, snatched it up and sped away. He knew the camera was no longer any good, yet it was a rare treasure.

He sensed that he was late for work. He alternately ran and walked to the tram stop, eager to reach the Kaiserhof for once, and show his prize to Herr Trautwein.

It was four o'clock before he had a chance to sneak out of the kitchen to the cubicle behind the hall porter's desk. Herr Trautwein rhapsodized over the camera.

"Yes, this is a genuine Eastman snapshot camera, a Kodak Number One, like mine. Do you realize what a marvel it is? It weighs less than a kilogram, takes one hundred round photographs on a roll of paper film that's packed inside the camera before you buy it. When you finish the roll you send the camera to the factory in America—I have done that, twice!—they develop the pictures, pack in another roll and send back the whole affair. Eastman has a slogan. 'You push the button and we do the rest.' It's entirely true. Photography is the new art of the new age. It's too bad you couldn't have found a Kodak that works."

"I'd like one someday," Pauli said. He was fascinated by the slogan Trautwein had quoted. He had made a sudden and stunning leap in his head from "You push the button," to all the photographs on the cards on his wall, and from there to his constant and frustrating attempts to draw. To make photographs might be the answer. The way to capture a piece of the world when you had no talent, only one strong finger for the button.

He left the hotel at half past eight that night. Forgotten for the moment were Aunt Lotte's strange moods and deeds, the sense that she no longer wanted or cared for him. His enthusiasm possessed him, to the exclusion of everything else.

He found his aunt in her wrapper, seated like a lost child in the front room, an empty beer glass in hand. Her eyes were red raw from crying.

"Aunt Lotte, what's the matter?"

"Nothing, *Liebchen*. Everything's fine." She turned away from him.

"I can see things aren't fine at all." He pulled an old footstool near her and sat down. "You must tell me. What's wrong?"

She covered her eyes. "Herr Reynard."

"Did he hurt you?"

"No, he didn't touch me, he just—oh, Pauli." Weeping, she mussed his hair affectionately. "How can I explain? It's so sordid."

He rested his hands on her knees, and felt her trembling. "It's—all right."

Presently his aunt composed herself. "Pauli, do you know the meaning of the word 'consumption'?"

"I've read it in the newspapers. It's a kind of sickness."

"Yes, a terrible sickness that affects a person's lungs. It wastes you away. I have it. I've known for over a year. I've debated many a night about telling you, but now I must, because I don't want you to fall ill. You mustn't stay in this apartment until it becomes a pesthole. Also, because of my sickness, other things are going bad."

She walked to a Biedermeier cabinet gleaming with elaborate fruitwood veneer. It was her best piece, bought at an open-air furniture market. She found a packet of French cigarettes and lit one.

"This evening, after we had supper, Herr Reynard wanted to embrace me again, is that a decent way to say it? I had another spasm, the worst yet. I stained the bolster. Ruined it completely. Herr Reynard was disgusted. He cursed and walked out without leaving me so much as one mark."

She leaned close to him. "He said he was never coming back. He said that I belonged in a hospital. He said he'd blacken my name in the hotels and cafes where commercial travelers congregate. Soon no gentlemen will want to visit me. So you see—"

She puffed on the cigarette.

"We must make a different arrangement for you."

The room, the whole cellar, was absolutely still. Pauli felt something momentous was about to happen.

"It's out of the question for you to go back to Aalen, to your Uncle Gerhard. He's a narrow, stupid man. I'd sooner turn you out in the streets. What I think, Pauli—what I think is this."

She touched his cheek.

"You must go to America."

"America!"

"Yes, why not? It's a wonderful land of opportunity, hundreds of thousands of our people have gone there, and more are leaving every week. Don't forget we have a relative in the city of Chicago, my brother Josef, the brewer. He's rich and important. I'll write him this very night, and I'll pray he won't dismiss the letter. I haven't kept in good touch with my family, you see." He understood the reason. Perhaps the family members were glad. Perhaps they knew about her business with *Herren* . . .

He was excited. The house of his uncle might be the very home he longed for. On the other hand, his aunt's illness was something he couldn't overlook.

"I can't leave you when you're feeling so—"

"Of course you can. You're almost grown, you're quick and strong, furthermore, you can make the journey by yourself. Your uncle did. Is the idea of America so terrible?"

"Oh, no, I've longed to see it."

"I'm talking about living there, permanently. Could you do that?"

"I think so. I would try with all my might to be happy. To please my uncle—"

"You must go. There really isn't any choice. I'll write Josef, and we will begin immediately saving every pfennig to purchase your ticket. I've already investigated the price from Hamburg. Approximately a hundred five Deutschmarks for steerage passage on a decent ship. That's roughly—hmm—twenty-four dollars American."

"A hundred and five Deutschmarks! That's a fortune, Aunt Lotte."

"Yes, it is for poor people like us. It will take us a while to save what we need now. Months, perhaps a year."

"I'll work hard to help save the fare," Pauli promised. "I'll work extra whenever I can."

"Then perhaps we'll have the price sooner than we think. However long it takes, we'll use the time to good advantage. I'll teach you all the English that I can."

"What about American, can you teach me that?"

Lotte laughed heartily. "Oh, Pauli. American speech is English. Well, no, not quite, it's cheekier. More jokes. More slang. It's like English with pepper in it."

"Is it decided, then?"

"Yes, Pauli. It's decided. America will be fine, you'll see. It will be just fine."

He closed his eyes, shivering as a picture flashed into his head. New York Harbor; the lady of Liberty with her light upraised. She seemed to be signaling, beckoning, just to him.

The reply to her letter came late in the autumn. It was written in a fine neat hand, in proper German, on thick creamy paper with elegant engraved script across the top of the sheet. *JOS. CROWN, MICHIGAN AVENUE, CHICAGO USA*. Above this was an embossed crown of gold.

Dearest sister—

How splendid to hear from you once again. I hope your health is excellent. We are fine, and prospering. In response to your question, yes, I enthusiastically endorse the idea that Pauli come to us if it is no longer feasible for him to stay with you. Please do send him as soon as convenient.

You said you hoped it would be possible by the spring or summer of next year, and we will now share that hope. Whenever he arrives, Ilsa and I and our children will welcome him to America, and attend diligently to his needs, education, and settlement in a new country. I am confident he will not be disappointed with what he finds in America, and I also trust he will not be disappointed in his new home.

> Yours with affection,
> Joseph

On a spring day in the following year, 1892, Pauli took a horse tram out through the western suburb of Charlottenburg to the end of the line. From there he walked along the Spree, nearly all the way to Spandau.

He heard voices from the special camp before he saw it. Several plainly designed wooden cottages surrounded a large meadow where listless figures moved to and fro in the sun, or sat limply in white-painted wooden chairs. Pauli's mood turned dark at the sight of so many sad, helpless boys and girls, some of them hideous cases, with slack mouths, blank eyes, or enormous swollen heads.

In a swath of sunshine near a cottage, Pauli found Tonio. His friend was white as dough, and his poor distended forehead looked larger than Pauli remembered. Tonio sat tilted back in one of the heavy summer chairs. He didn't lift his head, just rolled it to one side when he heard the visitor. He smiled.

"Hello, Pauli."

"Hello, Tonio. How are you?"

"Oh, just fine. It's good of you to come all the way out here."

"I think it will be my last visit. I'm leaving soon. For America, to live with my Uncle Josef."

"Yes, I know. My father told me when he came on Sunday. It's a wonderful chance for you."

Pauli held out a paper bag. "I brought you something."

"What?" Tonio tried to sit up straighter but couldn't, and fell back. From the sack he took a twist of baked bread sparkling with salt crystals. "*Kringeln.* My favorite." He bit off the end and chewed. A shining line of drool ran from the corner of his mouth.

"Tonio, is this place—I mean—how do you feel about it? It seems cruel to weed out children and keep them hidden away."

"Oh, the sisters treat us very well. The doctors are kind. They tell us we're doing good for society—that it's important to keep everyone at his or her own level, so others aren't impeded. It's the new German way."

That might be, but Pauli didn't like it. If this was how Germans treated other Germans, it wasn't for him, and he was glad to be leaving. Tonio's mistreatment reminded him in a strange way of Rhukov's comments about the German army, its lust to make war.

Five minutes later he said his farewells and hugged Tonio, who wept. Pauli couldn't walk fast enough to get away from the sad camp in the middle of the sunny pine forest.

□ □ □ □

In his tiny room, he took down the cards, photographs, and mementos.

He piled them neatly inside the old wardrobe, which was empty now save for the box holding the toy village. He kept four items back. One was the paper flag of the revolution—red, gold, and black. The second was the globe from Wertheim's. The third was the ruined camera; though it was useless, he felt it was important that he take it.

The last item had become a very special talisman. It was the stereoscope card of the lady Liberty standing beyond the bow of the ship. Soon he'd see that same sight with his own eyes.

Carefully he put the card and the paper flag and the globe and the ruined Kodak into his traveling grip, which Aunt Lotte had bought secondhand. He laid them one by one on top of a few clothes wrapped around an English grammar and phrase book he'd been studying for months. It was called *Englisch für Reisenden.* English for travelers.

About to leave the tiny room for the last time, he turned back. He opened the wardrobe again. Took out the souvenir postcard picturing Kaiser Wilhelm II stiffly posed with Her Majesty and their children. He thought a moment, then made up his mind. He tore the card in half and tossed the pieces on the bed.

It seemed a very bold, courageous thing to do; the right thing for someone going to a new homeland, a real home, at last.

He spoke then, in clumsy halting English. It was practice, and perhaps even a bit of a prayer.

"America. Chicago. Hello, Uncle Josef. I am your nephew Pauli."

4

Charlotte

IN THE STEAM and bedlam of the Zoo Bahnhof, they said goodbye.

How young and strong he looked. How full of hope and purpose, standing there with clear eyes and his clothing in its customary disarray. His third-class rail ticket to Hamburg hung out of his breast pocket. Another pocket bulged with an apple she'd provided, and some hard candies. He'd combed his brown hair but it was all blown again. He looked so young; he had no idea of the snares of woe and mischance the world would set for him. Nor would she tell him.

Still, he might do better than she had, given the sponsorship of her rich brother in Chicago, and the promise of a young country unencumbered by musty old ideas. Now that Pauli was leaving she brimmed with love for him; fully as much love as she felt for her lost daughter, Christine. Somehow, in spite of her failings, she'd managed to care for the boy responsibly. It comforted her, and partially relieved the guilt she felt because she'd failed with her own child.

She'd hardly slept all night, worrying about Pauli. She'd heard of evil men who preyed on immigrants on both sides of the ocean. There were rumors of smallpox and cholera in Hamburg.

The spear of pain in her bosom was sharp this morning. It had taken all her will to rise up from bed, perform her meager toilet, wash her hair with a henna rinse she could ill afford, then dress herself in her best outfit, a cloth suit with silk braid and a bonnet of lace trimmed with artificial pink roses, very French in design, but ten years out of date. Some deep, nearly unfathomable impulse had driven her to search through bureau drawers until she found her rosary, from the days of her marriage. This she put into her reticule. Finally she donned her cape of dark green loden. There seemed a melancholy suitability to the heavy fabric that resisted water so well. Pauli asked her why she wore the cape when the weather was warm. She shushed him, rather sharply.

Speaking above the clangor of the station, she said, "I want you to do well in your new homeland, Pauli. You take with you all of the good characteristics of Germans. We Germans are a fine and ancient people, you know. Very diligent, smart, efficient. But we love life. We sing, we hike, we write great music and poetry." Despite her pain, her gray cheeks that no amount of rouging could hide, she felt uncharacteristically sentimental and forgiving.

"However, you're going to be an American, and you must be a good one, never forgetting you have changed your old country for a new one. It's an excellent time to leave Berlin. Frankly, I'm suspicious of the military clique. In my estimation, they harbor dangerous ideas. I don't believe America has that kind of warrior caste, but if she does, be wary. Above all, guard your money and don't lose the letter your Uncle Josef sent."

Trainmen blew their whistles and began shutting doors to the carriages. The actual farewell was hasty, a mere exchange of hugs and breathless goodbyes. She saw him into the third-class carriage, jammed there between a nun and a worn little man who might have been a junior clerk. With a ringing of the bell, a grind of great iron wheels, a hissing of jets of steam, the locomotive pulled the train and Pauli away from her forever.

When she left the huge station she discovered rain falling. Warm summer rain.

At a box marked with the horn of the postal service she dropped her letter into the slot. A letter for her daughter Christine, whom she'd abandoned. "For her own good"—that was the lie she'd told herself, so she could put the girl into service, go off and live her own life selfishly. She hadn't corresponded with Christine for years. It was time. The only address for her was the household in Ulm. She prayed that if her daughter had moved on, they would know where to send the letter.

She walked to Unter den Linden and took a turn along it, under the dripping trees. In a café she chose for its modestly priced *Speisekarte* posted at the door, she spent the very last of her money. Her light supper consisted of wursts, black rye bread, hard-boiled eggs, a glass of delicate Mosel wine followed by three glasses of *Weissbier*, the strong "white beer" millions of Germans still preferred over lager. She needed alcohol tonight, for courage.

As the light waned, she walked to the Schlossplatz and paused to admire the heroic statue of the Great Elector. She strolled on the bridge over the Spree.

Evening was settling on Berlin, muting some of the clangor, some of the ugliness. The rain had become an intermittent shower, hardly heavy enough to dampen her; quite pleasant actually.

Lotte leaned against the railing with her eyes fixed on the rain-dappled river. Reflections rippled and gleamed invitingly.

She slipped her hand into her reticule, found the rosary. The feel of the beads was comforting. She silently begged forgiveness for what she planned to do. Her faith in God had not suddenly been restored, but it was always well to play every card, in case one was a trump.

She thought of the train hurtling through the night toward Hamburg. Thank heaven her brother Josef in Chicago had responded favorably to the idea she proposed in her letter. Not that it was so surprising, really; Josef was always generous, besides being smart and rich. As for that shit Gerhard in Aalen, he could burn in hell, provided there really was such a place.

She took pleasure in having set Pauli's feet on a better road. He was young, clever, didn't give up easily; perhaps he would indeed find a better home than the mean and shabby one she'd provided, and from there would follow his new road to a happy end.

As for herself—well, she didn't feel so bad with wine and *Weissbier* in her. She felt composed, in fact, leaning against the wrought-iron rail and watching the lighted ripples on the Spree. She took out the rosary and held it.

She drew a deep breath, realizing like a delighted child that the Spree was her friend; the Spree was welcoming; the Spree held the answer to all of life's problems.

"Godspeed, Pauli," she whispered to the night.

Part Two

STEERAGE

1892

I marched away to the ocean's shore—
I trusted myself to the waves,
Not yet was my spirit broken,
Nor yet lay I in hateful chains,
Strength remained to save myself.
America welcomes me!
I shall stay in the faraway land.

1855
Poem by Jacob Gross, a German immigrant

5

Pauli

"CHANGE YOUR MARKS for dollars. Best rates. You need dollars on the ship, boy. How about it?"

Pauli looked up from his grammar and phrase book. He was tired and tense and uncomfortable. He'd been sitting on the packing box, amid six or seven hundred other travelers, since early morning. The angle of the light threw the steamship's great shadow on the pier, dark as a funeral drape. He hoped it wasn't an omen.

The wind blowing along the Elbe into the harbor basin was hot and damp. The day was more like August than late spring. The river smelled incredibly foul. Pauli had seen human waste floating in it. Like everyone else on the pier, he was fretful because boarding had been delayed. He was nervous about rumors of contagious disease in the city. For three days and two nights he'd been penned up in the shipping line's filthy emigrant barracks. It wasn't a rumor but a fact that there was cholera in Russia. Pauli had been one of the last Germans emigrants to arrive by regular train. Special sealed trains were bringing them into Hamburg. now.

All around him on the long pier, the steerage passengers sat or lay or wandered, crowded together just as they had been in the barracks and would be again on board ship. America was attracting not only Germans but Austrians and Romanians, Russians and Poles, and plenty of Jews from those countries. The hopeful travelers were a shabby lot. They spoke a variety of strange and incomprehensible languages, including one, vaguely like German, which Pauli guessed to be Yiddish. They had packed their worldly goods in knapsacks and old valises, wicker baskets and feather pillows tied with rope. Some of them looked pleasant, others disagreeable. The latter included a pair of young Germans, big and blond, who talked loudly, stared openly at women's bodies, and punched and roughhoused each other like playful dogs.

The man who'd spoken to Pauli leaned closer. "Come on, how much do you want to exchange?"

The man looked respectable until you noticed his soiled collar and worn coat cuffs. Pauli remembered the booths below a big sign in the company's drab and drafty ticket hall. BANK WECHSEL UND PASSAGE GESCHÄFT. This man was no banker.

"Nothing," Pauli said. "They only take marks on the ships. I asked."

"Smart boy," someone nearby called to him. "Give him your money, you can kiss it goodbye."

Someone laughed. The man spit on the pier and walked off quickly.

All at once Pauli felt utterly homesick. He had an impulse to jump up and race for the *Hauptbahnhof,* abandoning this foolish dream of America. Visions of his room in Müllerstrasse filled his head. In memory it didn't seem so bad. At least it was warm and cozy—

Stop, that's nonsense.

He wished he could rid himself of the bitter medicinal reek of his clothes. The shipping line was strictly enforcing its medical quarantine for steerage passengers. After a cursory examination on his day of arrival, he and everyone else had been fumigated with a noxious spray: hair, armpits, groin—everywhere. They were then reassembled and led to the company barracks, where they slept on the floor in similar, segregated rooms.

Besides smelling bad, he was famished. He'd had nothing but an apple since getting up; the core was in his pocket, forgotten. The food in the barracks consisted of tea and bread in the morning, tea and bread and bad-tasting sausage at noon, tea and bread at night. The emigrants had to pay for each serving; Pauli ate but once a day. He was eager for a regular meal on the ship. The food was advertised as excellent and plentiful.

He tried to resume his study. It wasn't easy. English was a damnably hard language. Although there were plenty of words similar to German—*Keller* and cellar, *Wein* and wine, *Lilie* and lily, among hundreds—English had too many words that sounded alike but were spelled differently. You *threw* a ball but passed *through* a doorway. After the number one came *two,* but you spoke *to* someone. *Too* was another word for also. Maddening.

There was no *du,* no familiar form of address for family and friends. Most confusing of all, English grammar shoved the verb somewhere in the middle of a sentence, not at the end, where a verb properly belonged. How would he ever learn it, let alone speak it?

With a sigh he closed the book. He wasn't learning fast enough. But he was learning other lessons; unpleasant ones.

When he'd stepped from the train, he expected the Hamburgers to be friendly and eager to help their countrymen who were setting out to create new lives for themselves. Altogether wrong. The Hamburgers pretended to friendliness, all the while looking for ways to deceive and take advantage of the travelers.

Pauli met one such fellow in the exercise yard—a greasy *Neulander,* a "New World man." These were fast talkers he'd been warned about by a passenger on his train. A *Neulander* acted as agent for a shipping line or an employer overseas. Most of the breed had never set foot in America.

The *Neulander* shoved a gaudy pamphlet in Pauli's hand. The cover featured a crude painting of the Statue of Liberty, made of gold and glowing with a golden halo. Behind it the artist had depicted tall buildings, each crowned with a giant diamond.

"Got your ticket, youngster?"

"Yes."

"Have a job waiting for you? If not, in Baltimore, I can offer—" The *Neulander* clenched his teeth when he saw Pauli's reaction. "What the hell's the joke?"

"This." Pauli waved the pamphlet. "Do you think I'm from the sticks? I'm from Berlin."

"So?"

"So the statue isn't gold. I'll show you, I have a picture of the real thing." He started to rummage for it, but the *Neulander* abruptly told him what he could do to himself. The man snatched the pamphlet and stalked off.

On the pier, remembering, Pauli sighed. So many thieves, Germans, preying on other Germans. He had expected better from his countrymen, and the world.

The *Auswanderung*, emigration, had been a fact of German life for more than forty years. It had sundered families, depressed the economy in certain parts of the country, and had even become a hot political issue several times. Aunt Lotte had told Pauli that hundreds of thousands had already gone, including his uncle, and the tide showed no sign of slowing. Gazing around the pier packed with the *Auswanderer,* he believed it.

The outcome of a journey to America wasn't always happy. He had learned that somewhat depressing lesson from a traveler who sat down on the same bench in the ticket hall. This was just a half hour after Pauli's train arrived; he'd gone directly to the hall to check in and have his ticket stamped. Then he'd sat down to examine it.

The man seated next to him uttered a weary sigh. Lonesome after the long rail journey among strangers, Pauli spoke to him. "Are you going to America, sir?"

"I'm going home to Wuppertal. My brother is supposed to meet me here with train fare. I've just come from America."

The traveler was an old man. Not old in years but old in the face, his skin seamed with worry lines, his eyes sad. "Are you going there?" he asked.

Pauli replied with a vigorous nod. "Definitely."

"Thousands go, but hundreds come back. They never tell you that, do they? I was in St. Louis for twelve years. I hated every moment. I'm a baker. There are a lot of bakers in America. Too many. I barely made enough to keep myself alive. One Easter my shop was completely looted at night. I almost came home then. I hated every moment."

"I'm very sorry you had bad experiences, sir, but they say in most respects it's a wonderful country."

"Oh, no. The people aren't your own kind, but all kinds. They throw out everyone's traditions as quickly as you or I would throw out slops. They tear everything down in America. They tear down buildings ten years old, they tear down whole neighborhoods for new boulevards, they tear down any person with a new or unpopular idea. For a while after you arrive you'll think everything's wonderful. But soon enough you'll see the dirt and despair—the truth behind the illusion you've created for yourself. You and all the rest of these cattle. If I were you I'd save myself grief and cash in my ticket, now."

"I can't do that. My relatives are expecting me in Chicago. That's my new home."

"Well, in a few years, you'll be back to stay. Count on it."

Pauli excused himself and moved away quickly. He wished he'd never met the baker of Wuppertal.

□ □ □ □

The day was waning. The sounds of the harbor—the mighty ship's horns, the screech of tug and barge whistles, the crisply rung bells—grew less exciting every moment.

On the vessel, amidships, a bell rang. People exclaimed and pointed. Pauli jumped on the packing box to see. Sure enough, back at the gangway for the cabin-class passengers, the velvet rope had been removed. Well-dressed ladies and gentlemen with their families were proceeding aboard with much waving and laughter.

The cabin-class gangway was covered with a peppermint-striped awning, and carpeted. The steerage gangway still lashed to the side of the ship at the bow was uncovered, narrow, rickety. The steerage entrance hatch in the hull was open, but no one could board until the gangway was swung out and dropped. Pauli sat down again.

Under his jacket and shirt, a canvas belt chafed his belly. Aunt Lotte had sewn the belt for him. It held his uncle's letter and his last eighteen marks. To buck himself up, he fished in the belt for his uncle's letter and was rereading the encouraging sentences, which he'd practically memorized, when a couple of sunburned seamen appeared at the hatch.

Responding to orders from a tall emaciated man in a braided cap and dark blue uniform, the seamen undid the lines and swung the gangway outward. One rode it down until it thumped the pier. People around Pauli jumped up, exclaiming or even shrieking in their eagerness to be first. Pauli was caught with the letter in hand. He barely had time to grab his grip before he was hurled forward by the crowd.

"Not so fast, not so fast, stand back." That was the skinny steward, shouting in German from behind a frayed rope tied across the gangway.

Angrily, someone cried, "Come on, when do we board?"

"When I say so." Non-Germans gestured and yelled at the steward, trying to tell him they didn't understand. Contemptuous, he turned his back and checked his manifest.

"Julius—Margaretta—I beg you for the last time, don't go." That was a man just behind Pauli. He turned around, saw the man imploring a younger couple. Hairlocks hung from under the older man's black hat. "Come back home with me, you won't survive if you go. You've heard the stories of these ships. Darkness, foul air, pestilence, unkosher food—there are very few for whom this journey isn't fatal."

Still holding the letter, Pauli stared into the Jew's blazing eyes over the shoulder of the younger man. The older man spoke to them, and to him, once more.

"*Fatal.*"

Shivering, Pauli was again jostled forward. When the steward finally untied the rope and stepped down to the pier, boarding went quickly. Pauli was still struggling to return the letter to his money belt when he was thrust to the foot of the gangway.

"Last name?"

"Kroner."

The steward checked it off. He noticed Pauli's hand fumbling at his waist. He saw the money belt.

"Move on, get aboard," he said with a jerk of his head. Pauli jumped forward, grip in one hand, the other hand frantically pulling his shirt down. A bad start. *Very few for whom the journey isn't fatal . . .*

Pauli climbed the swaying gangway to the hatch, a maw of darkness.

She was named MS *Rheinland.* Her capacity was three hundred and twenty-five passengers in two cabin classes, and a maximum of nine hundred in her steerage. She was owned by the Flying Stag Line. On flags, pennants, even the blouses of her crew, she carried the emblem of a winged stag in flight.

The steerage was located deep in the ship, forward, where both the anchor chain and the screws made noise. It was presided over by the steward and two boys who resembled street toughs more than crewmen on an international steamship line.

The emigrants were divided into two groups—married couples with children, and all others. Quarters for both were identical: large holds, each with only a few small portholes that resisted opening. The holds were equipped with iron-framed bunks stacked five high and three across. Each bunk had a thin straw-filled mattress and a flimsy blanket. Pauli rushed to claim what he thought would be a good bunk, on the end, in the lowest tier. It quickly proved no better than any other, because in all of them you couldn't sit up without striking your head.

The decks in steerage had been freshly whitewashed, and the spaces fumigated, but it didn't take long for the bewildered passengers to litter the former with paper trash and orange peelings, and foul the latter with strong odors of bodily dirt.

The line promoted its "excellent and nutritious" food, but there too, reality was somewhat different. Even before the ship was tugged out of port that night, gongs rang and the passengers practically ran to long trestle tables in the steerage saloon. Their "excellent" meal consisted of a lukewarm potato soup, platters of herring in a dubious vinegary sauce, and loaves of stale black bread. Pauli rushed through his meal with more than his usual speed and efficiency.

The steward circulated among the tables, unctuously dry-washing his hands and asking if all was well. He introduced himself as *Herr Steward* Blechman. One of the raucous blond brothers challenged him. "Where's the beer? You advertised beer, I damn well remember that."

"It's available," said the steward, rubbing his thumb against his other fingers. So were wine and potable water, for a price. Pauli decided he'd stay thirsty and snatch a mouthful from the men's washroom. When he went into that small facility later, he gagged at the smell of the iron troughs over which, so far as he could figure out, you crouched one way to piss and another to shit. Four iron basins with faucets lined the wall opposite the troughs. He turned a handle and filled his cupped hands. He spat out the first mouthful. The water was salty.

At the foot of a narrow iron stair, he found the steward. "Sir? Where is the drinking water?"

"It's available. See me any time you want it. You can afford it, can't you?" His thin hand dropped to Pauli's waist and pinched the hidden bulk of the money belt.

Pauli pulled away and fled. The steward's laugh drifted down the stinking hall behind him.

Rheinland sailed at midnight. Pauli was awakened by the hooting of the tugs, the thump and clank of hawsers and anchor chain, the terrified multilingual outcries of fellow passengers.

The man in the bunk next to him beat his fists against his chest and wailed in a language that might have been Russian. Directly above, a woman sobbed like a mourner at a funeral. These lamentations were duplicated by others, all the voices rising in a medley of fright that played at fortissimo when the vessel began to throb with movement. To compound it, steerage was dark. The few spots of light came from weak bulbs that shone like remote stars in a vast black space. A space that smelled bad again; someone had passed strong rancid wind.

Pauli dragged his grip up and covered his head and tried to sleep that way. He was awake for hours.

Daylight, and passage out of the Elbe, brought a respite, in the form of escape to the small steerage deck located at the bow. Trying to fit all the emigrants onto it was something like trying to assemble the entire population of Berlin in a village square.

Even with the crowd, Pauli, being quite agile, managed to wriggle into a spot at the rail. He leaned against it, feeling the wind, filling his lungs with clean air. Others on deck were playing cards, or reading, or gazing worriedly at the horizon. One family group was practicing the arrival in America. The father acted the part of an official who shouted questions at the children, poked and pinched them, then examined their eyes so roughly, the smallest girl cried. In Hamburg, Pauli had heard of the dreaded examiner, the "eye man," who turned back scores of newcomers. The American authorities were strict about matters of health.

Many of the steerage women wore bright head scarves or aprons, in a contrast to the fine but drab clothes of the cabin-class passengers, who gathered at the forward rail two decks above, just below the wheelhouse, to observe the emigrants, make remarks about them, and toss down half-eaten breakfast rolls and even some pfennigs. These treasures set off a great scramble. The two blond brothers shoved others aside to get what they wanted. They were Germans of a kind Pauli disliked. Further, he was unhappy to be looked down upon, literally and symbolically, by those above.

Presently another family attracted his attention. It consisted of a short, corpulent woman, the mother, two daughters nearly as heavy, and a boy one or two years younger than Pauli. The boy was frail, with pale skin, merry blue eyes, a quick smile, spiky black hair that seemed to stick up in many different directions. He had an old concertina on which he played lively airs with considerable skill. His animation and good humor set him apart from his mother and sisters, who looked miserable. Pauli edged closer to the boy, hoping to start a conversation. He heard the sisters speaking a foreign language and gave up.

□ □ □ □

That night, in the open Atlantic, a storm struck, and steerage turned into hell.

In one day's time, the dim hold had lost its faint scent of fumigation and begun to reek with the odors of bodily wastes. These spewed out the open doors of the washrooms but arose elsewhere too, because the sick and the careless were relieving themselves in corners, under the stairways, or right in their bunks.

Rheinland rolled and pitched violently. Pauli's stomach seemed to ride up and down, bringing sour fluid into his throat. Even flat on his back in his bunk he grew dizzy.

The man in the bunk across the aisle was crying. Others pleaded for help, or prayed aloud as the storm worsened. Thunderclaps rang the great hull like an iron bell.

"Help me, someone help me, I'm dying," a woman wailed in German in one of the bunks above Pauli. Pauli exclaimed, "Wait, I'll help you."

He grabbed the bunk overhead and started to pull himself out. His head was in the aisle when the woman retched. A torrent of puke drowned Pauli, causing him in turn to vomit uncontrollably.

By the time he was on his feet in the slippery aisle, the woman was gasping that she felt much better. Heaving and retching and wanting to die, Pauli ran to the washroom. Under a dim light he turned the tap and bathed away the worst in cold salt water.

"If you and your friends want a decent sleep, you should clean up the mess in there. Want a couple of rags? Plenty available." It was Herr Blechman, leaning in the doorway, wearing only his uniform trousers and a dingy singlet.

"Isn't it your job to clean up, *Herr Steward?*"

"Not until morning, *Neunmalkluger.*" Smart aleck.

"All right, how much?"

"Shall we say one mark?"

Pauli didn't want to do business with the man, didn't want to pay his thieving price. But he didn't want to sleep in vomit, either. He paid and was given two towels, small and ragged. With these he cleaned up the bunk and the floor around it.

Through the night of storm and sickness, he forced himself to picture the stereopticon card, or Buffalo Bill, or his uncle's letter with the small gold crown —all in a desperate effort to convince himself that what was waiting for him was worth this agony.

Fair weather returned next day, and a calm sea. Passengers tried to pry open the tiny portholes to air out the hold but found them sealed shut. "Policy of the line," the steward snapped when questioned.

Pauli discovered that he had good sea legs, which allowed him to spend every available moment on deck. He didn't fraternize, mostly out of shyness. About midmorning, a fat gentleman, Hungarian perhaps, sat down beside him. Speaking bad German, the man invited Pauli to play cards. He uttered the invitation softly, blowing garlic fumes in Pauli's face. The man's hand seemed to drop accidentally to Pauli's thigh. Pauli exclaimed, "No, I don't play," and bolted. Thereafter he brought the broken Kodak on deck with him and pretended to be busy photographing the anchor chains, lifeboats, the bridge—anything available. He had never been so lonely. He wished he could talk to someone, but it was dangerous.

One passenger who bunked in another aisle intrigued him. This was an old gentleman, emaciated but very correct in his posture. A mane of silvery hair and a luxurious mustache gave him a distinguished air. His clothes were peculiar: royal blue trousers with a white seam stripe, and a military-style overcoat, dusty rose, with royal blue braid and trim all over the sleeves, shoulders, and breast. The coat was threadbare and dirty, yet the old fellow wore it with style. Pauli couldn't imagine that any regiment, no matter how prideful, would choose such colors.

The old gentleman brought a small wooden box to the deck, always placing it carefully and then dusting it with a big kerchief before he sat. When he wasn't gazing at the sea he cleaned his cracked boots with spit and his thumb. Finally Pauli's loneliness overcame his fear.

"I don't mean to be forward, sir, but I've watched you dust that box every day. You're so neat, you could be German."

The old gentleman laughed. "On my mother's side. Where are you from?"

"Berlin. My name's Pauli Kroner."

"Berlin, you say. Fancy that. I worked nine years at the Kaiserhof. Out in front, on the curb—whistling up cabs, handling baggage, greeting dignitaries—"

"I can't believe this!" Pauli exclaimed. "I worked in the kitchen of the same hotel. We never met."

"Well, you shouldn't have stayed in back all the time. Besides, it was ten years ago." Both of them laughed.

Thus Pauli made the acquaintance of old Valter, a Silesian by birth and a hotel doorman by profession. Which explained the garish outfit. Valter had held doors at some of the finest: Paris, Brussels, Warsaw, Madrid. He proudly said he spoke nine languages. He was going to live with his second son in a small town in the American province of Pennsylvania.

Again the weather changed. A fog bank rose up out of the sea about four one afternoon, and by six it enveloped *Rheinland.* All night the monster horn gave its great bellow, a desolate and terrifying sound. Pauli prayed for the American shore to appear soon. But it wouldn't, not for another week at least.

In the forenoon the fog began to thin. Pauli went below to wash his face in the cold salt water. He noticed the gaunt Herr Blechman strolling through the sleeping area, eying various bundles and suitcases with his queer popeyes. Pauli darted back before Blechman saw him.

He climbed the iron stairs and noticed a hint of yellow sun behind the racing clouds. Old Valter was absent. Pauli recognized a few scattered groups, among them the blond brothers and the two young women of sixteen or eighteen traveling with the boy with the concertina; today he was not with them.

The sisters were stout as beer barrels. The elder was jowly and had a dark downy mustache. The other was almost pretty, with a well-shaped bosom and soulful eyes. They were playing a card game. It was the more attractive one who caught the attention of the brothers.

Pauli was alarmed when the blond louts exchanged nudges and smarmy grins. The fatter of the two pulled down his fisherman's cap and sauntered over. By pretending to aim the broken camera, Pauli could watch without attracting attention.

The blond youth leaned down to whisper something in the prettier sister's ear. She jumped up, spilling cards from her lap. The young man laughed and pushed the back of his hand against the girl's corseted bosom. Her sister was too frightened to move.

Pauli didn't want to interfere. Compared to the blond brothers, he was a runt. Yet others on deck—what few there were—deliberately looked away. Pauli found himself hurrying forward, his hands sweaty despite the cool sea air.

"—generally don't like kosher meat, but a starving man can't be choosy," Pauli heard the blond lout say. He sounded like a Bavarian. "Come on, *Jüdin*, don't be stuck up. I'm a good sort. Franz is the name. This is my brother Heinrich. The Messer boys."

The other sister, finally terrorized into action, began to wave her arms and jabber in her own language. The second brother was less jocular. "Shut up with that yid talk."

"It's Polish, Heine," Franz said. "At least I think so." Pauli danced around to the right of Franz, raising the Kodak while concealing most of it with his hands; he didn't want them to see it was broken.

"Here, what are you doing, you little shit?" Heinrich shouted.

"Taking your snapshot, for the captain."

The Messer brothers eyed the camera with surprise and even worry. "Is that one of those picture-boxes?"

"Yes, and it'll show the captain that you bothered these girls." The bluff was insane; steerage passengers never saw the captain. But these two Bavarians were stupid.

"Recognize his accent?" Heinrich asked his brother. "He's one of those snotty Berliners." Berliners looked down on most Bavarians, considering them peasants with lazy dispositions produced by the southern climate.

"He's an interfering little turd, too. Excuse us, girls, be right back." Franz Messer pivoted around and reached for Pauli with huge pink hands. Pauli saw dirt under every nail. He knew that the price of helping the sisters would be a beating, at best—

"That will be all, gentlemen." The stern voice sounded like a soldier's. Pauli sagged with relief as old Valter stepped from behind him.

Valter wagged his wooden box under Franz's nose. "If you can leave off bullying women and boys smaller than yourself, I'll accommodate your itch to fight. Then we'll get the steward to lock you up for the rest of the voyage."

With murderous eyes the Messers appraised the old man. They noticed a few other passengers watching, then spied Herr Blechman standing by a hatch with his arms folded. Franz yanked his brother's arm. "Come on, Heine, we'll square this later." He glowered at Pauli. "You especially, prick."

He stormed off, his brother following.

The two young women leaped on Pauli, hugging him and jabbering incomprehensibly in Polish.

Old Valter was able to translate. "These young ladies are the Wolinski sisters.

Here is Mira Wolinski—" The object of Messer's attention, the prettier one, curtsied nervously. "And here is Renata. They both want to thank you heartily."

Again he listened to the excited girls. "Their mother Slova Wolinski will want to thank you, but unfortunately she's ill and lying in her bunk. Also, their brother will want to tender his thanks. They are all on their way to America from the vicinity of Lodz, Poland."

"Well, I'm glad I could help," Pauli said.

But he knew that by interfering, he had guaranteed that he'd have to look over his shoulder for the rest of the voyage. The Messers were that kind, no doubt of it.

Still, the encounter had a happy side. Pauli escaped the bondage of loneliness and made the acquaintance of the boy with the concertina, Herschel Wolinski.

From the moment they met they were a triumvirate: Pauli, the Polish boy who was one year younger, and the former doorman who sat with them with an amused expression, translating their breathless exchanges.

"I love America. I've never seen it, but I love it," Herschel declared. It was two days after the incident with the Messers, a flawless sunny morning with a mild northerly breeze. "You don't know how long and hard we've planned and schemed to make this trip. It's hard for poor people in Poland, harder still for Jews."

"Are you persecuted?" Pauli asked.

Herschel's first answer was a casual shrug. "We're used to it. Ten thousand years or more, you get used to it, that's what the rabbi always says." Herschel seemed to have a sunny disposition, augmented by great energy. He was always pointing, darting his bright blue eyes here and there, jumping and fidgeting as if he couldn't contain all of life's joys and excitements. The mere sight of him brought a smile; his brushy black hair seemed to grow six different ways at once.

Pauli was fascinated with all the Wolinskis because he'd never known any Jews intimately. Of course he didn't see much of Slova, the mother, because she had been sick from the bad air and rotten food ever since leaving Hamburg. "She cries day and night." Herschel sighed. "She says we were the worst of fools to leave without papers, and walk to Hamburg."

"You walked all the way?"

"We walked with over a dozen others. There are thousands doing it, in Poland and in Russia. America's wonderful. They know."

Herschel picked up his concertina and began a lively march tune. Valter leaned against the rail, his silver mane tossing in the wind. He packed a curved pipe during his translations.

"This is an American song, from their great war," Herschel said. "I had a cousin in America for a while. A watchmaker in a village called Buffalo." He pronounced it *Boffla*. "He visited us in '87, the year before he died. He taught me the song. The soldiers sang it when they freed the colored slaves in the war; it's called 'Marching Through Georgia.'" He pronounced it *Marzhin Throw Zhor-zh-ia*. Pauli listened to the music, inhaled the salt air, savored the ship's rise and fall, soothing now. He liked all of it.

When Herschel finished the song, he asked, "Were you sorry to leave Germany?"

"Not very. I still love my fatherland, but I didn't have a real home. I'm eager to get to America."

Herschel eyed the cerulean sky. "Me too."

"Things will be better there."

"Definitely," Herschel said. He began to play a sad little theme, a lullaby perhaps. "I made this up."

"It's very pretty."

Another shrug. "I make up tunes all the time. Someday, when there's less to think about, I'd like to write them down." He played more softly. "You were talking about America. You'll have to work there, all of us will."

"Of course."

"Nothing wrong with a hotel career," old Valter said, pipe smoke streaming from between his lips as he spoke.

"On the curbstone, maybe, but not back where I was," Pauli responded. "I'll find something interesting—" On an impulse, he showed the broken camera. "Something new and scientific, perhaps. Like taking photographs."

"Can you earn any money doing that?" Herschel asked.

Pauli blinked. "I don't know."

"Well, I don't know what I'll do," Herschel said, "but whatever it is, it will be very exciting. I want to become American in every respect. That will include taking a new name."

"I've thought the same thing. My uncle did it; he was born Josef Kroner but now he's Joseph Crown. Here, I'll show you." He laid the camera aside, pulled up his shirt and unbuttoned the canvas money belt. He unfolded the letter with the embossed gold crown.

Herschel touched the embossing in way that was almost reverent. "Your uncle must be rich."

"Pretty rich, yes."

The fire in Herschel's eyes seemed to burn out suddenly. "So you've a sponsor in America."

"*Ein Bürge,* yes. Uncle Joseph. He soldiered in that war you talked about. He helped free the colored people. Maybe he even sang your marching song."

Herschel said, "We don't have a sponsor. They say it's helpful when the authorities question you. Mama said we should stay home because we didn't have one. I argued till she changed her mind. Now she's wishing she hadn't."

Over the soft crash of bow waves, old Valter sucked noisily on his pipe and touched Pauli's sleeve.

"I'd put that letter away. No, don't look around."

"What's wrong?" Pauli whispered.

"That damned steward's watching. I'm afraid he spied the money belt."

Pauli fastened the last button and yanked his shirt down. "Oh, he's known about it since Hamburg."

"Yes, but he's cozying up to someone else and I think they're chatting about it."

"Who is it?"

"Franz, isn't that his name?"

Pauli stiffened but didn't move. Herschel watched for nearly a minute, gazing into the sun directly behind Pauli's shoulder. Finally he relaxed. "All right, they've gone. Let's talk about America some more."

6

Herschel

THEY HAD BEEN AT SEA five days already. The crossing was scheduled for eight to ten, depending on conditions on the ocean. Herschel's new friend told him many things about America. Pauli seemed to know a lot about the country, including its cowboys and Indians. Talking of them, he liked to fire his finger like a pistol. "Bang, bang!" Soon he and Herschel were exchanging volleys and laughing uproariously, to the annoyance of some other passengers. A spate of fine weather set in. You could hardly move on the crowded steerage deck. Herschel took his concertina into the sunshine. He played tunes from home for Pauli. Soon old Valter laid aside his pipe, planted his fists on his hips, and began to dance. Quite agilely for a grandfather, in fact. Others joined him. Finely dressed men and women came to the railing above them to watch, comment, and clap.

Herschel played joyously. Music danced in his soul. Unfortunately so did a powerful dissatisfaction with things as they were. Which was why, young as he was, he'd been the one who pushed and wheedled and finally persuaded his confused mother and pliable older sisters that America was their best, most logical hope.

Back in the dim days of childhood (Herschel now considering himself at the age of fourteen almost grown up), he listened to his inner voice of discontent, which convinced him that to prosper—even to survive—he must escape the grimy confinement of the *shtetl*.

The *shtetl* was located not far to the southwest of the city of Lodz. Like similar settlements of the Jews, it was a poor, overcrowded place, the small wooden houses arranged in complete disorder along twisted muddy lanes.

In the market square, Herschel's late father had maintained his booth, one among many. He was a sad man with round shoulders, missing whatever elusive quality it took to conquer the world. But he knew carpets, which he obtained from Lodz. Since not that many carpets were sold in a year, he also hung cheap work shirts on a rope at the rear of the booth; they sold well. Some of Herschel's earliest memories were of his father haggling with a customer, amid stalls and booths selling everything from onions and potatoes to fish and raw meat dripping blood on smelly butcher blocks. Herschel had come to hate the squalor around him. He didn't want to spend his life hawking carpets or herring or boots or veal chops.

There were other forces working on him too. When Herschel was six, Papa wrapped him in a prayer shawl and led him to his first day of religious school. The *melamed* who would instruct him picked him up and set him on a bench like some statue on display. Then the teacher pronounced a formal blessing on the new student of Torah. He emphasized the wondrous benefits that would develop as the boy learned the *mitzvot*, the commandments, all six hundred thirteen of them, which a devout Jew had to observe. Herschel was appalled. Six hundred and thirteen *rules?* Never!

But he might have surrendered to that sort of future had it not been for his father's untimely death, and a visit to Warsaw made by the entire family in the winter six months before that happened.

They went to Warsaw against Slova's objections, to visit Uncle Moritz, the black sheep brother of Herschel's father. As a young man Uncle Moritz had run away from another *shtetl* to become, of all things, an actor. He had apprenticed with one of Europe's most famous troupes, the players of the Duke of Sachsen-Meiningen. Slova Wolinski cried that it was a godless occupation. Indeed, Uncle Moritz had converted to Christianity to increase his chances in the profession. Now a practicing Catholic with fourteen children, he was a tragedian of great repute. Herschel's mind was forever imprinted with the sight of Uncle Moritz, his face blacked, strutting and declaiming under old-fashioned calcium lights as Othello the Moor.

After the performance Uncle Moritz welcomed the Wolinskis backstage, a fascinating and exotic place of shadows and half-dressed women who smelled of powder and laughed a lot. Uncle Moritz took them all home to his stout *goyische* wife and rowdy children in their eleven-room flat, and it was there that Herschel had a chance to speak to his distinguished relative about going to America.

"I'd say it's a good idea, do it," Uncle Moritz advised, picking up the boy and setting him on his knee. "You won't fully understand why it's good until you're older, but I'll tell you this much now. There is a disease in Poland, and all of Europe. I might say an epidemic. 'The Jew is to blame.' Are shares on the bourse plunging? The Jews manipulated them. Is our army defeated? The Jews sold our secrets. The Jew did this, the Jew did that, the Jew did the other reprehensible thing. Why? I know a few reasons. The Jew is visible, the Jew is clever and resourceful, the Jew is often highly successful—even if he has to kiss the Pope's ring in the process," he added with a wink. "Therefore it's a convenient disease. If you intend to remain a Jew, flee from it. Surely they don't have the disease in America."

That was the moment Herschel made up his mind.

Easier said than done, though.

Herschel began his campaign with Slova right after Papa fell down dead in his booth, blood gushing from his mouth onto a stack of new carpets. Probably Herschel would have failed to persuade his mother, had he not enlisted Mira and Renata, and also written Uncle Moritz, who sent them just enough money to allow them to make the journey in order to escape Asiatic cholera. There had been outbreaks in Europe before, and Uncle Moritz warned that it had again invaded Russia from a mysterious place called Afghanistan. The epidemic had already swept from Kiev to Moscow, and when the summer came on—cholera being most prevalent in the hot months—Uncle Moritz predicted that it would march west. It killed swiftly. *You sit down to your soup a healthy person and you're dead by dessert,* Uncle Moritz wrote. *Go! Immediately! Only my career and numerous responsibilities prevent me from joining you.*

Herschel trudged to Lodz and there endured long waits in drafty hallways, harassment by bureaucratic clerks, and a night's sleep under sheets of newspaper in a rat-infested alley, all for the purpose of obtaining the necessary travel papers. Finally he got them. The family set out with eighteen other people from the district, all having agreed to band together for safety and companionship as *fusgeyer.* They trudged in sunshine or rain, along parched roads, or roads that had turned to mire, fighting fatigue, vermin, hunger, icy river crossings, clouds of blowing dust, even a hailstorm and a pack of wild dogs on separate occasions.

When they neared the frontier with East Prussia, a farmer warned them of military patrols, something entirely unexpected. Because of the epidemic, Prussia had sealed its borders.

For two days they debated the impasse among themselves, sinking deep into despondency. Herschel was one of only three who argued for hanging on—hoping for a miracle.

It came in the persons of two smugglers who turned up at their camp. For an outrageous fee per head, the smugglers offered to guide them over the border. They knew routes around the various guard stations on both sides. The shipping companies weren't too scrupulous about an immigrant's history so long as he got to Bremen or Hamburg and could pay the passage, they were assured.

That night, with a full moon in the sky, the smugglers led them to a ford in a fast-flowing stream, then warned them: "This is by far the easiest place, but there is a Polish guard post on the road just up there. The Polish army is cooperating with the Prussians because the disease endangers everyone. So be silent."

Moments later, just as the smugglers were hurrying them into the cold rushing water, they heard someone approaching on a fast horse from the direction of the Polish border post.

"Hurry, Mama," Herschel cried, knee deep in water and fully visible under the huge moon. He clasped Slova's elbow to assist her and urge her on. She staggered, lurched sideways, then fell into the water before Herschel could catch her.

"Halt there," came a cry from the unseen horseman. A loud crack followed; the bullet fractured the moonlit water into thousands of quicksilver droplets. Dripping and floundering, Slova Wolinski burst into tears. Others exclaimed or screamed for mercy. And Herschel, small and frail though he was, found that fear had pumped him full of unbelievable strength: he grasped his mother under the arms and pulled her up, then he pushed her to the far bank while bullets continued to bite the silver water. All of the emigrants crossed over without a single mishap.

Soaked and shaken, they huddled under the moon. There was no further pursuit by the horseman. With the aid of the smugglers they crept on through a deep wood, thus avoiding the first guard booth on the German side.

Soon the smugglers left them to make their own way. It was as hard as before; perhaps harder, because they were exhausted by fear and privation.

Reaching Hamburg days later didn't end the family's travail. You had to be on watch constantly in the company's quarantine barracks and on the piers. Herschel was warned of crooked ticket agents, baggage men, licentious doctors who attempted to force themselves on young girls they were examining. He stayed so close to Mira and Renata that it annoyed them, but he never saw anyone even remotely menacing, save for one burly baggage man who spoke Yiddish and threatened to punch Herschel when he refused the man's offer of help.

So now the ordeal of Europe was behind them, leaving only the ordeal of entrance to America. Herschel listened alertly in steerage and heard many conversations about the perils of the reception depot in New York Harbor. The authorities could be capricious, turning you back because they were tired or didn't like the tilt of your cap. Then there were the medical examiners, all reputed to have supernaturally keen eyes for spying out the slightest illness or deformity. The legendary "eye man" was dreaded most. The condition for which he inspected was something called trachoma, evidently common.

Herschel imagined various ways that he might deal with or outwit the authorities. He was confident that he could. His confidence completely drained away the moment Herr Blechman announced that they should be sighting "the Long Island" within forty-eight hours. Now they had to go through with it.

He noticed that his new friend looked worried too. Like Herschel, Pauli the German burned with a desire to live in America. Soon, very soon, it would be decided whether they would or not.

7

Pauli

AS *RHEINLAND* APPROACHED AMERICA, Pauli noticed the Messer brothers paying a lot of attention to him. He would look up in the dining saloon and see one or the other of them watching him. They idled near him on deck during the day. He knew the object of their interest was the money belt, which that damnable steward had surely mentioned to them. Pauli didn't know what to do, except to make sure he was always with other people.

At the same time, he was sleeping badly because he was getting sick. Fierce cramps stabbed his belly and there were wet rumblings in his bowels. He felt quarrelsome and glum. He noticed a similar mood in others. Passengers shouted at each other for no reason. They abandoned courtesy to push and shove to the dining tables or the washroom troughs. Several fist fights broke out among the men. To Pauli it was clear that they would all arrive on the threshold of America worn out and worn down, in no condition to face the ordeal that awaited.

On the night before the promised landfall, a night of rising wind and exceptionally heavy seas, he could eat nothing for supper. Instead, he went reluctantly to the steward's table near the dining saloon entrance and there bought a small tin can of warm beer. He was nauseated by the smells and the stifling, tobacco-choked air of the dining saloon. Did he dare go to the open deck?

Herr Blechman was again writing in an account book, paying no attention to him. From the corner of his eye Pauli searched for the Messers. They were at their regular place, talking in their usual loud and oafish way. They were just about the only cheerful passengers. Pauli decided to chance it. He slipped out.

He stopped at his bunk for the broken camera. He carried this and the can of beer up to the deck. To his relief, he found it totally deserted.

The wind cleared his head and relieved a spell of dizziness. The ship was heaving and crashing through high waves under a cloudless sky full of crystalline stars. Above him, like an illuminated castle, the decks belonging to the rich passengers mocked the dark steerage with the glow of their electric bulbs. Any emigrants traveling on a more expensive ticket didn't have to pass through the New York processing depot, Valter had explained. Only those arriving in steerage were screened there. "Because America wants no poor people who might become public charges."

Pauli sat with his back to the iron hull and his head well under the rail. There he sipped the warm beer. It calmed his stomach. He felt better almost at once.

He began to toy with the Kodak, imagining himself a photographer hired to picture the dazzling milky sweep of stars over the ship. He was clicking off imaginary shots when he heard a faint metallic ring, then a footstep. Instantly tense, he glanced up. Two burly figures blacked out sections of the sky.

"Here he is, Heine. Trying to hide from us."

"Just where Blechman said we might find him."

Heinrich Messer kicked Pauli's outstretched foot. "Hallo, you little shit. Did you think you could dodge us forever?"

Pauli scrambled to his feet but the brothers moved quickly to block an escape. Pauli backed against the rail. Franz said, "Blechman told us you bought beer from him."

"Right here it is," Heinrich said, picking up the can. He drank the remainder. "Good, I was still thirsty." He threw the can overside.

"He said you bought it with money from that belt you wear. Care to loan us a few marks? We could use extra in New York, they say it's an expensive town."

"I don't have any more money." Pauli's face was hot from the lie.

Franz grinned. "Is that right? You won't mind if we check."

"Franz, look, he's got that picture box, too."

"I've never seen one, give it here," Franz said. Pauli hid the camera under his right arm. Franz kicked his shin. Pauli gasped, staggered, and Franz snatched the camera. Pauli lunged at him. Franz laughed and danced back. "Here, Heine, catch."

The brothers tossed the Kodak back and forth, whooping and taunting Pauli while he strained on tiptoe on the tilting deck, reaching for the flying camera.

"We might let you have it if you hand over your money," Heinrich said, holding the camera over his head. Driven to the limit, Pauli shouted, *"Schmutziger Schweinehund,"* and hit Heinrich in the stomach.

Heinrich was unprepared for such a determined offense. The Kodak flew out of his hand and sailed overboard, lost the moment it struck the waves.

Pauli couldn't believe it. Open mouthed, he stared at the sea. Incredible rage exploded inside him. He clutched the rail, ready to push off and tear into them both, the hell with their size. A pounding blow from behind knocked his jaw against the teak rail. He bit his tongue and spat out blood.

"Call me a dirty bastard, will you?" Heinrich kicked him in the small of the back. "Come on, Franz, he's got it coming."

"Twice over, Heine, he's a Jew-lover, too."

"You are dirty bastards, both of you," Pauli shouted in German, staggering around and bringing his fists up. Franz kicked his shin again, then grabbed Pauli's crotch and twisted. Pauli let out a yell; Franz laughed.

Heinrich locked his fists together and swung them sideways, into Pauli's ribs. Pauli flew prone on the deck.

Franz knelt on Pauli's back and pulled his shirt out of his pants. "Here it is." He yanked, and the laces of the money belt broke. The belt scraped Pauli's skin as Franz dragged it from under him.

"Take the money," Pauli gasped. "Just give me the letter from my sponsor, I need it for—"

Franz Messer was on his feet, flourishing the belt. He kicked the side of Pauli's head. Hot tears filled Pauli's eyes. The Messers laughed and walked off.

In a moment, Pauli heard a hatch door clang. He lay on the cold iron deck while the great ship crashed and creaked on toward America.

At dusk next evening, *Rheinland* came within sight of a small vessel identified as the Ambrose lightship. *Rheinland* was a few hours ahead of schedule, hence the pilot wouldn't be put aboard until morning.

All of the steerage passengers who were up to it rushed to the deck, pointing and gesturing at scattered lights in the distance. In weary but excited voices they repeated one word: "America. America."

Pauli heard the cries while he was still down below. A man ran in to summon two friends from the miasma of the washroom. After days at sea, everything smelled of shit; every inch of floor, wall, mirror, basin was foul and sticky to the touch.

"It's America, hurry," the man shouted to the others. They all ran out, leaving one occupant—Pauli. In pain that defied belief, he sat with his rear in the trough.

He closed his eyes, cold but sweating. The spasms wouldn't stop. He had no money. The letter from Uncle Joseph was gone. He was sick. The Americans turned back sick immigrants at the place of arrival, which they would reach tomorrow.

Pauli dragged himself to the deck just at daybreak. Rain squalls blown by a north wind hid the horizon intermittently. There were rumbles of thunder.

Rheinland was steaming into a broad channel between an island on the port side and a larger, dimly seen land mass to starboard. Gulls were chasing garbage dumped from the stern.

Despite the thunderclaps and occasional gusts of rain, the deck was packed.

Almost everyone was gray-faced from exhaustion, if not illness. Still, they wanted an early glimpse of their destination, and they seemed to think it necessary to bring their worldly goods with them for this. It made the small slippery deck all the more congested.

Pauli managed to wedge in beside Valter on the port side. The old gentleman had brushed up his doorman's uniform and combed his hair, which now gleamed with rain. With an expression of excitement he was reading from a small German-language guidebook. "This is called the Narrows. There are almost as many ships as in Hamburg."

It was true. Freighters carrying the flags of England, the Netherlands, Scandinavian countries, Pauli's own homeland could be seen moving in and out of the harbor behind the low rain clouds.

Pauli dashed rain from his eyes and saw, directly ahead, a thicket of tall buildings spanning a quarter of the horizon. "New York," someone cried. There was handclapping. An elderly woman sat down on her roped suitcase and burst into tears.

Pauli still felt dizzy, drained, dangerously weak. He fought it. He had to stay alert; devise a plan. Worse than having no money was having no proof of sponsorship by his uncle in Chicago. What if the authorities denied him entrance? All this way for nothing . . .

He wouldn't let it happen. Weak and sick as he was, he would win through somehow.

Suddenly old Valter tugged his sleeve. "Look, Pauli, look! It's your picture card come to life."

And then Pauli forgot everything except the sight of the colossus rising ahead.

In all his dreams he had never imagined her so tall and mighty. She towered to the sky, seemed to float slowly and majestically toward him. The low-hanging clouds hid the island on which she stood, but he could see part of her base, a giant stepped pyramid of concrete, and above that, her pedestal of granite.

Valter too was transported, reading eagerly from his book.

"The island is called Bedloe's, an old army fort. She was placed there six years ago; she is the tallest statue in the world, three hundred five feet. That is ten times taller than Michelangelo's statue of David, almost three times taller than the Great Sphinx of Giza."

Pauli trembled as he gazed at her. Her robe and her face, her torch and her crown were a deep reddish brown, agleam with rain.

"She was created by the sculptor Bartholdi, but her inner skeleton was designed by the great engineer, Eiffel," Valter read breathlessly. "There are seven rays on her crown to represent the seven seas and seven continents. On the tablet, in Roman numerals, there is inscribed the date America won its independence. July 4, 1776."

She was almost opposite the prow, and Pauli wanted to sob and yell and somehow reach up to embrace the magnificent woman whose strong yet kindly face was already gazing past them, out beyond the stern of *Rheinland*, out to the vast ocean, searching for the next newcomers. Wind streamed the rain from her crown, blew it into her eyes. But she seemed stronger than all the forces battering her, strong enough to withstand any storm . . .

In the ecstasy of the moment, Pauli twisted completely around to watch the statue moving astern. Valter peered at the little book. "There are broken chains at her feet. She is striding ahead, free of the shackles of tyranny. We can't see that. We're on the wrong side, and too low."

The mighty statue floated away in scudding mist clouds. "Germania our mother—Columbia our bride," Valter said. "I heard that many times in Hamburg. Germania our mother—Columbia our bride. You grow up and you leave your family to take a wife. You'll always look back, but you can't go back."

Rain dripped from Pauli's eyebrows, nose, chin. He wiped his eyes. A lump filled his throat. *Germania our mother—Columbia our bride.* He wouldn't forget that, or anything else about this momentous experience. Here, in the new land, he would find a home, and a calling.

A sputtering engine attracted everyone's attention. A trim steam cutter bearing official insignia pulled alongside. *Rheinland* lowered a midships gangway to receive three men in uniform. Valter said, "Those are the immigration officials."

"For us?"

"No, the passengers upstairs. We're going there." He pointed off to port, where a gap in the low clouds revealed another small island dominated by a large buff-colored wooden structure. The building was two or three stories high, with a peaked roof of blue slate and four sharply pointed towers at the corners.

"It looks like a spa or hotel," Pauli said.

"On the outside maybe." Valter leafed through his little book. "It was built as a replacement for the older station, Castle Garden. It has only been open since January. It's called Ellis. Ellis Island."

As the morning advanced, *Rheinland* steamed up the Hudson River past the incredible sprawl of wooden and brick buildings that comprised the city of New York. The wind was finally blowing away all the rain clouds, bringing first occasional patches of blue sky and then cool dry air, and a brilliant sun.

With tugboats to assist, *Rheinland* tied up at one of the long wooden piers. A German band, men in Alpine hats, white blouses, lederhosen, played welcoming music. Herr Blechman appeared, nattily buttoned up in his uniform with the flying stag patch. He carried a megaphone.

"Travelers," he announced in German. "While the regular passengers disembark, you will be allowed onto the pier, but you must remain in that roped enclosure. No pushing, no shoving, be sure to remove all of your personal belongings because you will not be returning to the ship."

A woman called, "Is the pier America?"

"Yes, you'll be standing on the soil of a new country for the first time. And who knows? Perhaps the last."

"Nasty man," Valter said above the sudden hubbub: people snatching up their grips, their bundles, rushing and shoving toward the port and starboard stairs.

Valter and Pauli went down the steerage gangway together. The moment Valter stepped on the pier he stopped, braced his legs, pulled Pauli in front of him to protect him. People shoved by on either side. Valter's face was lifted to the sunshine.

"Feel it under your shoes, Pauli. Feel it and remember. Wednesday, the first of June, 1892. A most significant day, never forget it."

"I won't, how could I?"

Others were buffeting them and complaining from behind. They moved on.

The wooden pier was still wet from the rain. Burly policemen with clubs herded them into the large rope enclosure. Other policemen stood guard around the perimeter. Near Pauli, the Wolinski children huddled around their mother, who was sobbing and swaying as though on the point of collapse. Herschel flung his new friend a despairing look.

Pauli felt remote from all of it. Thrilled to stand on American territory, yes, but dreadfully afraid because he still had no plan for getting past the authorities.

Then, just when he felt most hopeless, he thought of something disarmingly simple. He dove into his grip and retrieved *Englisch für Reisenden.* He turned pages and with agonizing slowness picked out words, to construct phrases, which he began to repeat under his breath.

"What are you saying?" Valter asked while packing his pipe.

"Something to tell the authorities." Pauli repeated the phrases.

Valter waved his pipe toward the river. "Well, you'll soon see them. Here comes the vessel for Ellis Island."

A small harbor ferry and five open barges were required to carry all the steerage passengers. Another stampede occurred when the ferry tied up at the end of the pier. "Line up, get in line, don't run," the policemen yelled, with little effect.

Pauli and Valter were a good way back in line, near the Wolinskis. Soon the ferry was full; men closed her stern gates and cast off. As soon as the ferry chugged into the river, the first barge docked.

The sun grew hotter. The line moved slowly. The newcomers were sweaty and uncomfortable in their heavy clothes. There were complaints about hunger; only stale rolls had been served for breakfast. Pauli repeated his phrases silently at frantic speed.

At the front of the line, officials dealt with the immigrants one by one, using manifests provided by the ship. Each manifest had a number. Individual lines were likewise numbered. The officials checked off names and flung a paper tag at each new arrival, hectoring them in English until they got the idea that they must hang the tag somewhere on their person. Pauli's tag said 8–11. Manifest number eight, line eleven.

On Ellis Island, the barge tied up at an esplanade running along the front of the main building; the empty ferry was backing past them into the main channel. The moment a starboard plank was swung out from the barge, another mad exodus began. Pauli and Valter were buffeted toward the main doors, urged along by uniformed officials shouting, "Into the baggage hall, hurry up." Behind Pauli, a woman said, "They look like police." In Europe, *police* meant terror; the enemy; a knock on the door in the night.

Suddenly disoriented by darkness, Pauli found himself in a vast, gloomy hall with a wide staircase rising in the center. The hall smelled of fresh paint and new lumber. Other officials were waving numbered cards and screaming, "Manifest 2 this way, step lively," or "Manifest 11 here, you can leave your baggage."

Pauli heard a man say, "I'll not leave my valuables for thieves to pick over, I'm carrying them." But Pauli and Valter took a chance and piled their luggage in a roped enclosure over which hung a placard bearing a big black 8. The officials kept shouting. "Fall in at the foot of the stairs. Stay with your group!"

The baggage hall quickly filled with the odors of dirty bodies and clothing. Pauli kept repeating his phrases. The groups moved slowly up the stairs. Old Valter was on Pauli's left, the Wolinskis in the group ahead. Pauli heard a new sound from above. A buzzing and humming of hundreds of voices.

Shafts of sunlight from high arched windows reached into the top of the stairwell. Valter tugged Pauli's arm sharply, to show him a number of Americans wearing military-style caps and blue uniforms with epaulets. They stood along the railings beside the head of the stairs, observing the crowd.

"Inspectors," Valter whispered, as though he meant *the police*, or something even worse.

Pauli had never been in such a huge room, or one so noisy. By groups they were herded between waist-high iron railings which covered most of the floor, rather like animal runs. In each of several aisles, a uniformed inspector scrutinized the immigrants one at a time. Ahead of Pauli there was a mother with a small boy in her arms. The inspector spoke to her in a tired, harsh voice. "How old is your child?" She shook her head to show she didn't understand. A younger interpreter behind the inspector repeated the question.

In German she said, "He was just two last month, Your Excellency."

After the translation: "I'm not an excellency, I'm from the U.S. Public Health service. Put the boy down. Any child over two must walk without aid."

More translation. Trembling, the woman set her son on his feet. The boy stuck a finger in his mouth, hesitating. His mother gave him a hard shove. Tears filling his eyes, he toddled past the examiner, who immediately waved the next person forward.

Pauli kept watching. The inspector had a piece of chalk. When something didn't suit him he chalked a big letter on the immigrant's coat. *F, H, X*—Pauli had no idea what the letters meant. His heart was hammering when his turn came.

"Name?"

"Pauli Kroner. Number 8-11." Nervousness garbled the rehearsed phrases. "I work—yes, I—*ich bin*—I—good worker."

"What'd he say?"

Valter, a little more fluent in English, helped out. "He is good worker. He will work hard."

"Not so fast. He won't work or do anything else unless we pass him. You're pale, youngster—"

"*Blass,*" snapped the interpreter.

"Have you been sick?"

"*Krank?*"

"Sir, yes—here." He touched his stomach. "But—" Sweat broke out all over

Pauli's forehead. He struggled for the English; didn't dare reach for his book. "Only little. All right now."

The inspector seemed to study him forever. "You don't look all right. But you're young, I guess you'll live." Again a long scrutiny. Then he waved his piece of chalk. "Go on."

The words eluded Pauli, but not the meaning. He dashed past the inspector with a new and grim appreciation of the part that chance and whim played in these proceedings. All of the inspectors had a tired, irritated air, as if their hours were too long, their tasks too hard. They might turn anyone back on any pretext. It made the odds all the worse.

Bad as he felt, Pauli vowed he'd get through the ordeal. He started to move forward in the aisle. His hair nearly stood up when a familiar voice cried out. Horrified, he looked down the adjoining aisle and saw the widow Wolinski collapsed in her daughters' arms . . . wailing.

8

Herschel

THE WOLINSKIS had reached the station of the third inspector, the dreaded "eye man." He was standing with a helper at a table on which sat his cap, a basin of strong-smelling disinfectant and a pile of hand towels.

Herschel was relieved to see that the inspector was middle-aged, comfortably stout, with a face as rosy and kindly as that of a Christmas saint. His little blue eyes sparkled as he summoned Slova Wolinski to his side with a gesture. He took a moistened towel from his helper and gently cleansed her left eye, then her right. Next he picked up a small instrument which looked like a common buttonhook and with it lifted Slova's left eyelid for inspection. "Ah," he said, not happily.

By then fat tears were running down Slova's face. The inspector examined her right eye in similar fashion. "Here too." He removed the hook and clasped her hands in his.

"My dear woman"—the helper translated into Polish—"both of your eyes display the characteristic granulation of trachoma. It's a degenerative eye disease, very common in people who come through here. I'm afraid you must go to quarantine, and your relatives with you, unless you choose to separate."

Yes, yes, we will separate, Herschel thought as his ears rang and the floor seemed to ripple beneath him. He tried not to cry; Slova was crying loudly enough for both of them.

"No, sir," he said, "we agreed to stay together—" The helper translated; he had to raise his voice because Slova was wailing like a madwoman, overcome by her surroundings, so many strangers, the terrifying examination. "We would all land or we would all go back, that was our promise to each other."

Sadly, the inspector said, "That way, then," pointing.

9

Pauli

PAULI PASSED THE EYE MAN without incident. He advanced between the iron rails to the end of a line of people in single file. Similar lines flanked it. All led to the inspectors who conducted the final interviews at a row of trestle tables stretching across one entire side of the hall. The sight of the tables made Pauli's stomach tighten. As if sensing this anxiety, Valter laid his hand on Pauli's shoulder. Pauli shut his eyes and rehearsed his phrases yet again.

Person by person, the line ahead of him melted. And then it was his turn.

The inspector had sleek dark hair like wet otter fur, and a veined nose, and the ugliest, most villainous features Pauli had ever seen. The man motioned. "You, lad. Step up."

"Manifest 8, line 11," the translator said. The inspector grunted and ran an inky finger down the page of a thick ledger. "Name?"

"Kroner, sir. Pauli Kroner." With a scratchy pen the inspector wrote in the ledger.

"Age?"

The second man translated it into German. Pauli said, "Fourteen years. But I will be fifteen on the fifteenth of this month." The inspector wrote again.

"Traveling with anyone?" Pauli shook his head. "Can you read or write any English?"

Pauli burst out with his phrases. "Yes, thank you! America wonderful country!" The translator laughed, not unkindly. Then he asked a question:

"Where in the old country did you start from?"

"Berlin, sir. But my family is Swabian."

"I guessed it from the red in your hair. Fine people, Swabians. I'm from the region myself, came over eighteen years ago."

Despite the translator's friendliness, the inspector continued to regard Pauli with a blank expression. "Who paid your passage?" he said.

"My aunt back in Germany. But I worked to earn part of it." More English: "I will work hard here—good worker!"

Slitting his eyes, the inspector said, "Do you have a job waiting for you?"

Valter had coached him on that question. If you answered yes, you would be turned back, because you might be taking work from an American. Pauli said, "No, sir, although I hope to have one someday. My uncle will help me with that, I think."

"Is your uncle here?"

"No, he is in Chicago."

"But he's your sponsor?"

"Yes, sir."

"Show me something to prove it."

"I had a letter from him, in German, but two bullies on the ship stole it."

The inspector eyed Pauli for a long time. Then, without emotion, he said, "Lad, there's a problem here."

"Sir?" Pauli's ears rang again. Pains like knife blades tortured his vitals.

"United States immigration law prohibits entry of unaccompanied children under sixteen. Your uncle should have come for you personally. Then we wouldn't have a problem."

"I'm sure he thought—ah—" Pauli turned red, struggling. *"Der Brief—"*

"The letter," the translator said.

"Yes, thank you, I expect he thought the letter would be enough."

"So it would. If you had it."

"Sir, he couldn't come here, he is a very busy rich man, my uncle—"

"I appreciate that, but the law is the law. You will be detained and examined by the Board of Special Inquiry."

"What is that?" Pauli's courage was flagging with this bad news and the avalanche of strange words.

"Three officials who pass on all cases like yours. You'll be held here on the island until you have your hearing."

"Then they will let me go to Chicago?"

The translator looked away. The inspector said, "To be honest, probably not, unless you are a very persuasive speaker. You aren't allowed to have help in making your case. No lawyers, relatives, friends—no one."

Pauli's nerve almost crumbled then. But he held on; dug his nails into his palms. "Sir, I *did* have proof that my relatives are waiting for me. It was stolen." His mouth twisted. "I should have lied about my age."

After a moment his shoulders drooped. "No, I am not a good liar."

The ugly inspector pondered. Then he swung around to face his assistant. "Mr. Steiner, I would hate to make a mistake in this case. Don't you think this young man looks sixteen? He looks sixteen to me."

"Sir, I feel sorry for him too. But he's already stated—"

"Sixteen." The inspector scratched out the age previously written down in the ledger; wrote a new one. He took a square of colored pasteboard from a cigar box and handed it to Pauli, who turned it over, unable to decipher the English printing.

"Sirs—what is this?"

"Your landing card," the translator said, faintly smiling.

"Welcome to America," said the ugly inspector. "It's a long way to Chicago. Be careful."

He waited until he saw old Valter receive his card and then rushed to the holding area where the Wolinski children were trying to console their exhausted, defeated mother. Herschel tried to hide his sadness as he ran to the rail separating the rejected ones from all the others.

"Goodbye, goodbye," Pauli said, waving his card.

That English word Herschel understood. Tears appeared in his blue eyes as he shook Pauli's hand. Valter came up and stood silently by the boys.

Herschel spoke in Polish and Valter translated. "Goodbye, you've been a good friend. I'll go back with mama and my sisters now but I promise you I won't give up. They can ship me back to Poland a thousand times, I'll still try once more. We will meet in this country one day. I am going to be an American—you can be sure of that!"

He leaned over the rail and gave Pauli a strong hug. Then he shook Valter's hand. "Goodbye to you, sir."

"Please tell him to take care of himself," Pauli said to Valter in German.

Herschel replied, "Oh, definitely. You too." He managed to smile as he cocked his index finger. "Bang, bang."

Herschel rejoined his mother and sisters. Pauli and Valter walked away. After a few steps Pauli looked back, standing in a broad moted beam of sunshine falling through one of the arched windows. Somehow the babble of tongues, the occasional wails of rejection, the loud voices of the inspectors, no longer seemed threatening. Despite the hubbub, the great registry hall had a solemn beauty, churchlike and holy.

Pauli waved. Herschel waved back. Pauli took a breath and, with his landing card tight in his hand, went on with Valter toward double doors marked as the exit in half a dozen languages. One ordeal was over. Now the next began.

"Here's something interesting," Valter said to him just on the other side of the doors. "The inspector didn't like my name. Either that or he couldn't understand it when I said it. I am now Walters." He showed a paper with the name written in block letters. "See? Mr. Walters. He put it in his book that way."

"Do you like it?"

Valter was bemused. "Why, I don't know yet. I suppose I had better, it's official."

Along the upstairs corridor they came upon several offices. The largest displayed a big sign. CAMBIA VALUTA—WECHSELGESCHÄFT—BUREAU DE CHANGE. They passed it by; Pauli had nothing to take him in there.

They also bypassed the mail and telegraph rooms. But one smaller room attracted him. It advertised itself in two languages:

DEUTSCHE GESELLSCHAFT
German Aid Society
Jeder willkommen!

"I'd like to go in here for a minute," Pauli said.

"Fine," Valter said, "I'll see you downstairs in the baggage hall."

Inside, a woman wearing a billowy white long-sleeved blouse and spectacles greeted Pauli from behind a desk. Speaking German, she asked his name. He gave it. She asked his destination. He wanted to impress her with English.

"I am—uh—*zu* uh, to—Chicago going."

Still in German, she said, "Very good, but don't put the verb at the end. 'I am going to Chicago.'"

"Yes, I forgot, it's hard," he muttered, red with embarrassment.

"You will learn soon enough," she said in a kind way. She handed him a ticket. "This is good for passage on the scheduled barge service to the New Jersey Central railway terminal, just a short distance north of here. You must have seen it from the ferry." Pauli nodded. "It's the policy of the agency to give every new arrival from Germany a ticket plus one dollar."

She pressed the large heavy coin into his hand. He clasped it tightly, feeling a little more secure.

"It's a very long way to Chicago, Herr Kroner. Hundreds of miles. I want to advise you of possible dangers. First, avoid strangers. If one happens to accost you, leave immediately. Second, if you have valuables, keep them hidden. Under no circumstances deal with labor contractors who promise jobs in distant cities. Most of them are unscrupulous, and if they have any jobs at all, the jobs pay slave wages."

Pauli hated to hear such things. He was still glowing with the euphoria of his successful arrival.

"You'll find that Americans are wonderful folk, by and large," the woman continued. "But the nature of the American system permits a great deal of latitude when it comes to making money. Some therefore make it dishonestly."

"I will remember."

"Goodbye, then, Herr Kroner. All the best of luck to you."

Standing, she shook his hand with great gravity, as though he were undertaking a journey to China, or possibly the nether regions.

Pauli met old Valter in the baggage hall, near the railroad room where busy agents sold tickets to all parts of the country. Valter showed another scrap of paper. "My son Willi is traveling from Pennsylvania to meet me at a lodging house in New York. Here is the address. How-stone Street, I suppose that is the way it's pronounced. Come with me and meet my son and we can discuss how you'll travel from here."

Pauli thought this over and decided he didn't want to lose any time getting to Chicago. He had no plan for that yet, but he would formulate one very soon.

"No, sir, thank you, I'm going straight over to the place called New Jersey."

"But you haven't any money."

"I have this ticket for the ferry. I have one dollar from the German aid office. After I spend that, I'll work." He grinned and said in English, "I am good worker."

So they embraced, and parted.

The sun shone down on the open barge. The day had grown hot. The barge's little steam engine chugged roughly, noisily. Pauli sat apart from the other eight passengers, watching the railway sheds of the New Jersey Central terminal rising up ahead. The terminal stood on land that thrust into the river; behind it was an ugly panorama of decaying houses and ramshackle commercial buildings. The picture seemed to daunt the others; they said little. To Pauli, the vista was exciting, magical—flawless. He remembered the baker of Wuppertal, who had predicted just such a reaction—then warned that it would fade.

Ridiculous. It wouldn't happen to him.

He recalled something Herschel had said. *"I want to become American in every respect."* Yes, absolutely. That meant abandoning his German name; taking a new one. He relished the idea of examining choices, rejecting all until one stood out, shining and perfectly right. The search would make the long but informative journey to Chicago that much more enjoyable.

The barge nudged the terminal pier. Oily slick on the water reflected white clouds drifting overhead. Pauli was overwhelmed with happiness, and when he stepped on the pier he couldn't contain it. He dropped his grip and whirled around. Yes, he could still see her, rust-red and beautiful in the sunshine sparkling on the surface of the harbor. Standing so tall as she looked seaward for the next ship . . .

She had welcomed him without reservation.

He flung out his arms, and began to spin and hop in a storklike dance. The other immigrants stared at him.

"America," he cried. "America, America!"

"Fucking crazy greenhorn," said one of the two deckhands tying up the barge. "They're all alike."

The other deckhand said, "He'll learn."

For a while Pauli wandered the waterfront, just looking around. He tried to ignore his empty stomach, which was snarling at him. The day got hotter, and sticky. He sat on his grip in the shade of a warehouse wall. It was no cooler there. He needed to calm down, curb his excitement, organize his thoughts.

He must get to Chicago. He needed to do it before autumn brought bad weather, which would make traveling difficult. He ordered his problems, and their solutions, logically. First, how would he travel?

That was easy; surely freight trains ran back and forth across America. He knew how to catch rides on those, Berlin had taught him.

He didn't know the route, however. He needed to study maps. It occurred to him that, just as in Germany, there might be libraries he could consult.

Fine, now to the third problem. Even traveling free on freight trains, he would need money to eat, and he had only one United States dollar. That wouldn't go far. He needed to work a little, perhaps a few weeks, to put some cash in his pocket. Where could he find a job?

Again, a little concentration answered the question. There were many Germans in America, and there had to be some in this town. Germans could always be found where there was beer.

Pauli set out to find a beer garden in Jersey City.

In the late afternoon he located one, a small noisy establishment on a side street. In the soggy heat, more oppressive than any he remembered from his homeland, he crossed the outdoor garden in search of the proprietor. About a third of the tables were occupied, the patrons cheerfully red-faced and perspiring. The place had a familiar *Gemütlichkeit,* a friendly and cozy atmosphere; it could have been a beer garden in Berlin.

A waiter pointed out the proprietor seated on a stool behind a cash register. Pauli approached and addressed him haltingly, in English. "Sir? Any work?"

"No." The man scratched his formidable chin. "But Geizig over there, he's looking for a boy, his helper quit last Friday."

Pauli was baffled by the confusing flow of words. The proprietor saw it, and repeated it in German.

"Are you just off the boat?" he asked.

"I am."

The man gave him a paternal smile and patted his arm. "I'll bet you're hungry. You surely look hungry." He turned on his stool, beckoning. "Otto, this country-man of ours needs a plate of sauerkraut and a glass of beer. Take that table in the back, lad. Compliments of the house. You'll do better asking about a job with a little food to buoy you up. Oh, and before you ask, slip into the kitchen and wash your face. Geizig is a stickler for personal cleanliness. Don't worry, Geizig will be here for a while, he seldom goes back to his place before seven o'clock."

"Thank you, sir," Pauli said with enthusiasm. The smell of sausages and bread and beer floating in the steamy air made him feel faint. He was liking America better every hour.

Herr Geizig weighed about two hundred and fifty pounds. His head was large and shaped like a cabbage. His ears stuck out prominently. He affected great joviality, but Pauli saw no humor in the small, shrewd eyes of light blue. He approached Herr Geizig's table and respectfully asked in labored English about a position.

"Speak German, English is a language for barbarians," Geizig said with a sneer. Five empty beer steins sat in front of him, and a small ledger filled with figures, which he'd been studying between swallows.

"What's your name?" Pauli told him. Geizig asked some other particulars. "Well, I do need someone to clear and wash dirty dishes and glasses, sweep, mop —what do you know about my place?"

Pauli admitted he knew nothing.

"It's a social club for Germans. Newcomers, like you—though my clientele is older. It's small, cozy, not noisy like this. We serve light suppers in the evening, plenty of beer, wine, and coffee. I also help my guests with correspondence, railway tickets, that sort of thing. It's a nice arrangement. I can pay thirty—uh, twenty cents a day, plus your food, and you can sleep in a shed behind the club."

"It sounds fine, sir."

"Not so fast. Are you willing to wear an apron?" Pauli nodded. "You'll have to be neater, too. You're a mess."

He reached for a stein with fingers resembling white sausages. "Wait for me outside, I'll be along presently."

The name of the social club was *Die goldene Tür,* the Golden Door. Geizig told Pauli he'd taken the name from a poem written to commemorate the Statue of Liberty in the harbor. He said it with a snickering contempt in his voice.

Pauli was distressed when he actually saw the club. It was no more than two airless rooms with adjoining kitchen on the second floor of a tenement-like building which backed up to an alley, within sound of the hooting horns of the river. Only one room in the club had a window, the first room as you came in the door. The outside stair leading up to the club was shaky, with several rotting risers. The solid door, perhaps a bright yellow once, had weathered and faded to a dirty mustard hue.

A loft on the building's top floor served as a dormitory with flimsy cots where newcomers could stay, for a price, until they settled locally, or made plans to travel farther. The shed which was to be Pauli's domicile stood in a small, trash-strewn yard on the other side of the alley.

But Pauli couldn't be choosy. He would stay a month, no more, pocket his earnings and hop a train for Chicago. He would use his spare time to map his route.

Die goldene Tür did a small but steady business, Pauli was surprised to discover. Most of the guests were young German immigrants in their twenties or thirties, bachelors; there were no female customers. The club apparently offered something immigrants wanted. Everyone spoke German, guests and workers alike; Herr Geizig's rule.

The club employed two barmaids who served drinks and food, which was prepared by Geizig's gray and taciturn wife, in very indifferent fashion. Pauli quickly noticed that one or both of the barmaids usually disappeared with a customer at the end of an evening. The ritual of departure involved Herr Geizig handing a key to the woman, and the man handing some bills to Herr Geizig.

One of the barmaids, Magda, had a pocked and hardbitten face, but a good disposition; she was more friendly than the other woman, Liesl. Pauli worked up nerve to ask her a question.

"What's the key for, Magda?"

"A locked room upstairs. Don't get nosy."

Thus he learned that the Golden Door was not quite the innocent social club it pretended to be.

Pauli didn't start work until noon. His first job was to sweep up trash, mop the clubrooms and wipe down the tables. He was on duty until the club closed, sometimes as late as half past two in the morning. When she wasn't cooking and her husband nagged at her sufficiently, Frau Geizig hammered out German songs on a scarred piano in the room with no windows. The customers might sing with drunken abandon, but Frau Geizig's face remained strained and sour while her hands chopped up and down on the keys.

Other occurrences in the club disturbed Pauli. On four separate occasions he saw a patron overcome by an apparent fainting spell. These guests were helped down the stair by Herr Geizig personally. None of the four had been drinking very much, Pauli was aware of that. Why they fell ill was a mystery. He never saw any of them a second time. Whatever luggage they had disappeared.

The atmosphere of *Die goldene Tür* made him uneasy, eager to be away. And never more so than the night he heard a man shouting threats in the alley.

Herr Geizig jumped up to soothe the half dozen customers. "It's nothing, don't trouble yourselves, I'll take care of it." He rushed outside. Pauli peeked around the door jamb. In the dark at the foot of the stairs, Herr Geizig was brandishing something silvery at a bearded young man.

Someone pressed against Pauli's back, making him start. "Magda," he whispered, "Herr Geizig has a gun."

"Yes, come back in, it's none of your affair."

"But who's that man shouting and cursing?"

"A friend of mine. He's very jealous. He usually stays away when he's sober. He must have drunk too much tonight. Come back in," she repeated, with noticeable alarm.

After a few minutes the stranger's voice was suddenly stilled, and Herr Geizig lumbered back up the stairs. Of the silvery pistol there was no sign.

Herr Geizig went straight to Magda and grabbed her by the wrist. "Keep your crazy friend away from my club or it'll go hard with you."

Magda twisted free. "Yes, sir."

Geizig shot truculent looks around the room dimly lit by oil lamps—the tenement, empty on the first floor, didn't even enjoy the luxury of gas. No one dared ask a question or comment about the altercation, least of all Pauli.

His birthday passed. He didn't mention it to anyone. It was enough that he was filling out, growing taller. Hard work developed thick bunches of muscle on his upper arms.

When he wasn't on duty, he studied his grammar and phrase book furiously. Forced to deal with the new language every day, he learned faster than he had in Berlin or on the ship.

He and Magda talked whenever they had a chance. He told her about his uncle, and Chicago, and his need to get there before bad weather set in. She came around at ten one morning, wearing a poor threadbare cape and bonnet, and showed him the way to the Jersey City free library, a small one-story building of granite. There, she said, he could find the maps that he needed.

Hesitantly, he went inside. There was a rich, warm smell of paper and book bindings, then a rustle of skirts belonging to the librarian who came from behind her great mahogany desk.

"May I help you, young man?"

Phrase book in hand, he attempted to tell her what he needed. Maps of America. She seemed kindly, interested in helping. She was a stout young woman, ten or fifteen years older than Pauli.

She sat him at one of the tables, then disappeared down a shadowy aisle between tall shelves. She brought back two large atlases.

"I'll assist you with these. I am the librarian, Miss Lou Stillwell."

With Miss Stillwell seated next to him, he pored over colorful maps of the United States. Miss Stillwell took his hand and guided his index finger from Jersey City across a likely route to Chicago, a word printed large over the blue of a long slender lake. On the route there was at least one range of mountains, in a province named Pennsylvania. Then came another large province, Ohio, and another, Indiana—strange, musical names, but he was finding many of those in America. They were not provinces, Miss Stillwell told him, but *states*.

He came back several mornings in the following week, to study and dream over the maps. "It would be thoughtful of you to write your uncle," Miss Lou advised him during one visit. "To tell him you arrived safely. Do you have his address?"

"In his—uh—letter. I lost it. But he said Chicago. Mitch-i-gun Avenue."

"He said what?" She couldn't help giggling.

He tried to pronounce it more carefully. "Mich-i-gan. But I don't have no street number."

"Any street number."

"Yes, that is what I said."

"Not quite, but never mind, sweet boy. You'll be going to Chicago soon, won't you?"

"Soon, yes, I save money now." He had not, however, revealed that he planned to travel by stealing rides on freight trains.

He was going to Chicago sooner than Miss Lou Stillwell knew. He'd had his fill of the grim, vaguely sordid atmosphere of *Die goldene Tür,* and had made up his mind to leave at the end of the week. It would take a bit of nerve to inform Herr Geizig and ask for all the wages which the owner had credited to him, and retained for safekeeping. It was the first week of August; he'd been working for two months. Herr Geizig owed him something like twelve dollars.

"About your uncle," Miss Stillwell said. "I have an idea. We'll write him, care of Michigan Avenue, Chicago, and we'll just hope he is prominent enough to receive the letter without a street number."

It was a simple letter, three sentences, in English. The first said Pauli had landed on the first day of June. The second said he was well. The last was three words. *Expect me soon.* At Miss Stillwell's insistence, he closed by writing *Your affectionate nephew, P. Kroner.* The librarian promised to post the letter that afternoon.

"Thank you," Pauli said to her. Outside, another hot rain was pelting down, hiding Jersey City in a heavy murk. The library was stifling; overheated rooms seemed to be popular in America.

"Thank you," he said again. "I have learned from the maps. I may not be here again soon."

"I hope you'll come back," Miss Lou said with an odd catch in her throat.

"I will try." He would be gone by the following Monday, but he didn't want to tell her and possibly hurt her feelings.

"Yes, please do," she said. "Don't lose these." She handed him a packet of tracings from the atlases. She had traced the states that lay between New Jersey and his uncle's house. On these she had neatly printed the names of major cities, and drawn precise lines indicating railways.

Miss Lou Stillwell brushed her fingers against his cheek. "You're a fine person, Pauli. A lovely boy." She seized his head between her hands and kissed him, thrusting her tongue between his lips.

Then, with a little cry of shame, she ran back into the gloomy stacks.

Pauli didn't quite know what to make of the experience.

□   □   □   □

After a day of debating with himself, he decided to confide in Magda, and ask her to help him understand the incident.

"Why, Pauli, first, I expect the lady was lonely. But there's another reason, and you may not have guessed it yet. You're only fifteen, but even so, you're attractive. Strong shoulders, muscles in your arms—definitely an attractive young man. Women are drawn to you. Oh, you aren't the handsomest thing I've ever seen. But you're smart, you have a good nature—those qualities are in short supply in men. So women prize them. Also you have a wonderful smile. You'd turn my head if I weren't such an old lady." She said this teasingly, planting a kiss on his cheek.

"I'll tell you one more thing. You'll always have a lot of girls falling for you. Of course when you find one you want to keep, she'll probably be the one you can't get. Life has a funny way of pulling tricks like that, Pauli."

That Saturday night, his plans were abruptly changed.

Magda came in late, looking drawn. Herr Geizig shouted at her. She ran into the kitchen, weeping. As the door swung shut, Pauli saw a purpling bruise under her left eye. Her jealous friend again?

There were six men in the club. Four were drinking and playing cards. Herr Geizig was helping two with a railway itinerary; he often bought train tickets for newcomers who were baffled by English, or too intimidated to arrange transportation for themselves. Magda had told Pauli in confidence that Herr Geizig routinely cheated the men by charging fifty percent more than the actual price.

Just before nine o'clock the owner put on his hat and went out without an explanation. About half past nine, Pauli was wiping down a table when the other barmaid, Liesl, stopped near him. "What is that funny smell?"

"Coming from downstairs," one of the card players said.

Frau Geizig burst from the kitchen. "Something's burning, what is it?"

Magda dropped a full stein of beer that shattered and splattered. Deathly white, she clutched her bruised face. "Oh my God, he's done it." Pauli's eyes popped. Did she mean her jealous friend? Had he set the place on fire?

The frightened guests jumped up from their chairs. Pauli smelled smoke and saw a faint orange glow outside the single grimy window. He ran for the door, blindly, and bumped into a chair, hurting his leg. Full of rage and fear, he seized the nearest table and threw it over. He could feel heat in the floor; curls of smoke were seeping between the pegged boards. He could hear a roaring down below. The light outside the window glared. The whole rickety building was ablaze.

He yanked the door open. A blast of heat drove him back. He clung to the frame of the door while he looked down into an inferno of flame and sparks and disintegrating wood. "God in heaven. The stair's gone."

He slammed the door and leaned back against it to think. The wood was hot on his palms. He jumped away.

Frau Geizig wrung her hands. "We must escape."

"Did you hear me? The stairs are useless."

"We'll die, we'll all die," Liesl moaned.

"Isn't there another door?" one of the guests screamed at Frau Geizig. The rest knew the answer. Sobbing, Frau Geizig shook her head.

Everyone seemed stupefied with fear. Thick choking smoke was boiling from the kitchen, as if the fire had already eaten through the floor in there. Pauli shook himself out of his dazed state; he was cursed if he'd die in this mean, filthy place, accidentally, after struggling so hard to reach America. He shot across the room, yelling, "Out the window, that's the way."

"Oh, I can't jump, I can't," Frau Geizig wailed. One of the greenhorns, trying to find someone to blame for the sudden horror, slapped her across the face.

"Shut up, you old bitch."

The heat and smoke were intensifying. Pauli knew there wasn't much time. He ran to Magda. Ruddy light from the kitchen was reflecting off the tears on her bruised face. "Come on, we're not going to die here," he yelled, pulling her arm so hard she cried out.

He forced her to the window. Flames were licking up from the vacant floor below. In the darkness on the other side of the alley he glimpsed the faces of neighbors, round white blurs.

He shoved the window all the way up, struck in the face by a gust of scorching air. The flames were shooting up directly beneath the window; they'd have to leap wide. "Come on, the rest of you, it's the only way," he shouted.

"Right behind you," one of the greenhorns said, but Liesl was nowhere to be seen in the smoke, and Frau Geizig had collapsed on the floor.

"Hold on, Magda."

"I can't, I'm scared—"

"No you aren't, don't say that." Panting, he boosted her to the sill and worked his arm around her thick waist. For a moment he was truly terrified—the fire would consume his possessions: the stereopticon card, the globe, the map tracings—but then he remembered those things were stuffed in his grip in the shed, across the alley.

"Jump," he cried, and pulled Magda with him, out into the dark and the smoke and the billowing flames. As he plummeted, his left trouser leg caught fire. Then the ground rushed up to strike him.

10

Joe Crown

JOSEPH EMANUEL CROWN, owner of the Crown Brewery of Chicago, was a worried man. Worried on several counts, the most immediate being a civic responsibility he was scheduled to discuss at an emergency meeting this Friday, the fourteenth of October; a meeting he had requested.

Joe Crown seldom revealed inner anxieties, and that was the case as he worked in his office this morning. He was a picture of steadiness, rectitude, prosperity.

He wore a fine suit of medium gray enlivened by a dark red four-in-hand tied under a high collar. Since the day was not yet too warm, he kept his coat on.

Joe's hair was more silver than white. He washed it daily, kept it shining. His eyes behind spectacles with silver wire frames were dark brown, rather large, and alert. His mustache and imperial showed careful attention; he had an appointment at twelve for the weekly trim. His hands were small but strong. He wasn't handsome, but he was commanding.

Three principles ruled Joe Crown's business and personal life, of which the most important was order. In German, *Ordnung.* Without order, organization, some rational plan, you had chaos.

The second principle was accuracy. Accuracy was mandatory in brewing, where timing and temperatures were critical. But accuracy was also the keystone of any business that made money instead of losing it. The primary tool for achieving accuracy was mathematics. Joe Crown had a towering belief in the potency of correct information, and the absolute authority of numbers which provided it.

In Germany, he'd learned his numbers before he learned to read. Though a mediocre student in most school subjects, at ciphering he was a prodigy. He could add a column of figures, or do calculations in his head, with astonishing speed. In Cincinnati, his first stop in America, he'd begged the owner of a Chinese laundry to teach him to use an abacus. One of these ancient counting devices could be found in his office, sitting on a low cabinet, within reach. Money measured success; counting measured money.

Questions he asked of his employees often involved numbers. "What is the exact temperature?" "How large is the population in that market?" "How many barrels did we ship last week?" "What's the cost, per square foot, of this expansion?"

As for his third principle, modernity, he believed that, too, was crucial in business. Men who said the old ways were the best ways were fools, doomed to fall behind and fail. Joe was always searching for the newest methods to improve the brewery's product, output, efficiency, cleanliness. He hadn't hesitated to install expensive pasteurization equipment when he opened his first small brewery in Chicago. He'd been among the first to invest heavily in refrigerated freight cars. He insisted that modern machines be used in the office. From his desk he could hear the pleasing ratchet noise of a mechanical adding machine. This blended with the clicking keys and pinging bell on the black iron typewriter used for correspondence by his chief clerk, Stefan Zwick.

Originally Stefan had resisted Joe's suggestion that he learn to operate a typewriter. "Sir, I respectfully decline, a quill pen suits me perfectly."

"But Stefan," Joe said to him in a friendly but firm way, "I'm afraid it doesn't suit me, because it makes Crown's look old-fashioned. However, I'll respect your feelings. Please place a help wanted advertisement. We'll hire one of those young women who specialize in using the machines. I believe they too are called typewriters."

Zwick blanched. "A woman? In my office?"

"I'm sorry, Stefan, but you leave me no choice if you won't learn to typewrite."

Stefan Zwick learned to typewrite.

□ □ □ □

Every solid house or building was supported by a strong foundation; and so there was a foundation on which Joe Crown's three principles rested. It was not unusual, or peculiar to him. It was the cheerful acceptance, not to say worship, of hard work. Among other artifacts, advertising sheets, flags and fading brown photographs of annual brewery picnics decorating his office there was a small framed motto which his wife had done colorfully in cross-stitch and put into a frame of gilded wood. *Ohne Fleiss, kein Preis,* it said. In rough translation, this reminded you that without industry there was no reward. From his desk Joe Crown couldn't see the gold-framed motto; it hung on the wall behind him, slightly to his right. But he didn't need to see it. Its truth was in him deeper than the marrow of his bones. He was a German.

Joe Crown's brewery occupied the entire 1000 block on the west side of North Larrabee Street. All the brewery buildings were of fine red brick with granite trim. The office, which faced Larrabee, resembled a brick fortress, with a square tower at each of the two front corners. From the towers flew the brewery's flag with the gold crown emblem. On patriotic holidays the American flag was raised. Cut into the cornice were the words BRAUEREI CROWN. The German spelling of brewery was a token of pride and respect for the proprietor's homeland.

Joe Crown occupied a spacious corner office on the second floor of the main building. The front windows of the office overlooked Larrabee, the side ones Crown's outdoor *Biergarten.* The garden had an elaborate gate on the street, and a doorway, directly below Joe's office, leading inside to the *Bierstube,* which occupied most of the first floor. The taproom served beer and food from noon until late in the evening, as did the garden when the weather was fine. Large breweries commonly had such facilities.

In one corner of the paneled office, the black, white, and red tricolor of Germany jutted up from a heavy walnut base. In the corner opposite, similarly displayed, stood an American flag, twice as large. Stuffed heads of an elk and a black bear further ornamented the walls. Joe had bought these, deeming them masculine decorations; he wasn't a hunter.

The morning was dark, the sky threatening. Through the open office windows came a steady background noise—the voices of laborers, the clang of heavy pipe being moved and hammered. New pipes were being installed between the second floor of the brewhouse and the bottling house across the alley to the west. National tax laws had once dictated that no beer could be bottled in the same building in which it was brewed. Recently, as a result of pressure and lobbying by major brewers, the laws had been rewritten. Although still continuing to move tax-stamped barrels across the alley by hand, Crown's was racing to install connective piping to eliminate the practice. The numbers that would result from greater productivity were impressive.

This morning Joe faced an unwelcome task at his noon meeting, and although he was prepared—the folder sat ready on one corner of the desk—he didn't look forward to delivering bad news.

Questions involving his family were bothering him too. Where was his nephew Pauli who was coming from Germany? The boy should have arrived by now. And when he did arrive, what of Joe's own children? How would they treat the newcomer?

He strove to put the worries aside and deal with some of the ever-present, ever-increasing work connected with the presidency of a successful and expanding brewery. Deciding he was now too warm, he hung his coat on a wall hook and worked in shirt sleeves after fixing sleeve garters just below each elbow. Distant thunder rumbled.

He read and marked an article on advances in refrigeration equipment clipped from *Der Amerikanische Bierbrauer,* the paper of the U.S. Brewers' Association. He corrected a draft letter to a real estate agent down in Terre Haute. The agent was negotiating on property near the main railway depot. Joe had distribution agencies in carefully chosen cities around the country, and he wanted to open one for southern Indiana. Expansion was mandatory if you wanted to be more than a local brewer.

He approved a bill for next season's box at games of the Chicago White Stockings; baseball was one of his guilty pleasures. He declined an invitation to join a new German singing society. He had a fine baritone, and loved to sing, but he had no time.

Next he read a memorandum on yeast cultures from his brewmaster, Fred Schildkraut. He inked his pen and put a comment on the margin. He stepped to the door and asked Dolph Hix to come in.

Hix was Joe's senior sales agent, one of three men who roved Chicago and neighboring states to promote the consumption of the brewery's products. They did this in a variety of ways, perhaps the most important being use of a generous expense account to buy customers free samples of Crown beer in saloons.

Hix brought in a layout for a new advertisement to go in the city directory. He and Joe spent five minutes dissecting it. Joe's requests were simple and terse. He expressed them in excellent English, still with a fairly heavy German accent. "This barley stalk illustration is a waste. Get rid of it, or at least reduce the size. I want the name of the brewery much larger. Crown's is what we're selling, Dolph, not barley stalks."

As soon as Hix left, Joe turned to study of a catalog sheet for a device which very much interested him—the latest basket-style pasteurizer for bottled beer. Crown's produced both bottle and keg beer; several kinds of each. The best seller was Crown, a pale, light-bodied, effervescent Pilsen-style lager. Heimat Bier, old-fashioned, darker, with a heavier alcohol content, was a strong second in popularity. It was much favored among older Germans. Its slogan was *Qualität "Superior."*

For the last twenty years, Americans had preferred lager over porter, ale, or any other stronger brew, English or German. Joe Crown was part of a small circle of brewers who had sensed that preference, and built fortunes upon it. The group included the Schaefer brothers of New York; Joe Schlitz and Valentin Blatz and Fred Miller in Milwaukee; Theo Hamm up in St. Paul; Michael Diversey, the successful and esteemed German Catholic whose earlier Chicago Brewery had been a model for Joe's own; and perhaps the most audacious and formidable of them all, Adolphus Busch, who had taken over the struggling Bavarian Brewery in St. Louis in the 1850s, in partnership with his father-in-law, Eberhard

Anheuser. Of the lot, Joe liked Busch the least. He was a crude, ruthless man who served and drank expensive French wines at his own table and sneered at his brewery beer as "that slop." He had come to America enjoying a handsome stipend from his father in the city of Kastel on the Rhine. He had never starved, never really struggled; his history was hardly the typical immigrant story, though he liked to boast that it was.

Still, there was no avoiding a man such as Busch. In many cities and small towns he was a direct competitor. So were the other major brewers. And while they might hate one another as competitors, they also had a quiet pride in their membership in a small and elite fraternity. They were countrymen, they made beer—and they had one moral millstone around their collective necks. As Germans, they regarded beer as a food, a normal and healthy part of life. More puritanical Americans, people of other nationalities, thought differently. Beer wasn't food, but a tool of the Devil. It was sinful to drink it anytime, but blasphemous to drink it on Sunday. That fundamental cultural difference created a problem for brewers that never went away.

Eleven o'clock. Joe was marginally aware of a drop in the noise level outside. It was the hour of *zweites Frühstück*, the second breakfast. The brewery and construction workers were lounging about munching hard-boiled eggs, sandwiches of bacon or sliced wurst on black bread, cups of beer. Joe was studying the drawing of the pasteurizer when, jarring in the stillness, footsteps pounded on the stairs and along the outer hall. After a frantic knock the door burst open.

"Mr. Crown, help. Benno is killing Emil Tagg." The panting white-haired man was his chief clerk, Stefan Zwick.

Joe jumped up and ran after Zwick without asking questions. Benno Strauss had caused trouble before, and Benno's kind of trouble was always serious. Disputes between the men were handled by the front office, never the brewmaster.

Joe ran down the back stairs past an open window. The noise level had risen again; men were yelling and egging on the participants in a fight. Going out the door, Joe dashed past Zwick, and crossed the alley to the forecourt of the bottling house. A ring of about twenty men surrounded the combatants. As he pushed through, Joe quickly looked away from one of them who was watching him for a reaction.

Benno Strauss had both hands clamped on the throat of Emil Tagg, who was bent backward over a keg on a hand truck. The hand truck lay flat on the uneven bricks. Tagg was foreman of the bottling house. The machinery in his care clanked away beyond an open door.

Though Joe Crown was about Emil's size—much smaller than Benno—he rushed straight at the bigger man, hooking an arm around Benno's neck, which was only possible because Benno was leaning over. "Get off of him, Benno. Get off this instant." He tugged and yanked.

The red drained from Benno's face. Joe felt the tension leave Benno's body. He let go; stepped back. Benno released his stranglehold on Emil after giving him a final furious shake. Emil eyed Benno and rubbed his throat.

"The rest of you back to work," Joe said. His eyes raked the circle of men. Most of them left immediately, with only some muttered comments.

Joe dusted his shirt sleeves. "Now what's this all about?"

Emil and Benno continued to eye each other. Benno Strauss was huge. Because of his strangely oriental eyes, his shaved head and his bushy mustache, Benno always reminded Joe of some kind of genie. He was a "Man of '48"—one of the exiles who fled Germany after the failed revolution. Benno had the distinction of actually having taken part in fighting. At age ten he'd carried water for a band of rebel students, all of whom had been shot down or arrested. Or so he said.

Benno was chief of the Crown teamsters. A fifty-four-year-old bachelor, he was twice as strong as most men of twenty. He belonged to the National Union of Brewers, the organization of brewery engineers, firemen, maltsters, teamsters that was trying to strangle the industry with its exorbitant demands. In fact he was the only member on the premises. Joe Crown didn't recognize the union.

"Out with it, I want an explanation. It's up to you, Benno, you're the aggressor." He was testy; the disruption irked him. Especially since the culprit was an avowed radical.

Benno wiped his sweaty jaw with the sleeve of his smock. "This one called me a name." Benno's accent was heavy, his English poor.

"What name? Out with it."

"It was filthy. About my mother. I ain't going to repeat it. But I don't allow nobody to say such a thing."

"Is this true, Emil?"

"Yes, Mr. Crown. But, damn it, am I supposed to ignore it when he rags me? He never shuts up. He came at me preaching that same old stuff about an eight-hour day. The same stuff that got Spies and Parsons and the other Haymarket reds hung or jailed. You understand, don't you?"

Joe avoided the question. Tagg was a highly capable man, but Joe disliked his toadying. "Is that all?"

"No. He started in on the pardon."

Ah, the pardon. Perhaps the hottest public issue of this or any recent year. Governor John Peter Altgeld, a stalwart German but disgracefully liberal, wanted to commute the sentences of Fielden, Neebe and Schwab, the three Haymarket conspirators still living. The other five who had been arrested after a bomb went off during an 1886 labor demonstration at Haymarket Square were dead.

Governor Altgeld had always insisted that the trial of the eight accused conspirators, three of whom were German, had never proved their guilt. Indeed, it was conceded that the actual bomb thrower hadn't been caught or even identified. Sentences had been handed down on the grounds that the defendants had *caused* a bomb to be thrown, by staging the demonstration and working the crowd to a frenzy with radical rhetoric.

Benno wasn't even slightly upset by Tagg's accusation. "Sure, we want pardons for the Haymarket men. Want an eight-hour day here at Crown's, no more ten and a half. To keep silent about these things is yellow. I am for propaganda of—"

"Propaganda of the deed," Joe finished. "I told you before, Benno, don't spread your red doctrine on my time. And don't disrupt work. One more fight— one—and you'll be discharged."

"Okay, sir, I hear what you say." The words were surprisingly meek. Joe wasn't fooled.

He brushed his sleeves again, unconsciously, then did a quick about-face and marched back in the direction of the administration building.

What shall I do about him? Joe thought. Benno would continue to agitate, he was sure of that. In the wrong circumstances—any widespread labor dispute in the city, for instance—he would be a highly dangerous man to have around.

But he's a bull, he can do the work of three men when it's necessary.

He stopped abruptly. His way was blocked by a young man with arms folded. The young man was smiling. Joe reddened.

"Didn't you hear my instructions? Get back to work."

The young man let his arms drop. "Sure, Pop. You're the boss here."

Here.

Joe Crown pushed his son aside and walked on, grim-faced.

In his office he continued to think about Benno Strauss. Benno was one of the thousands who'd arrived in Chicago during the second great wave of German immigration in the 1880s. He claimed he'd lived in half a dozen European countries after the revolution. That he'd been jailed more than once, but had also outwitted and eluded the police many times. It was hard to tell which of his stories about past escapes and heroics in the socialist-anarchist cause were invention. Benno was *ein Schaumschläger;* a windbag; enthralled by the sound of his own voice, the expression of his own opinions. When he got going in German, he was a stirring speaker, Joe had to give him that.

Benno belonged to the *Lehr- und Wehr-Verein,* the league of armed workingmen. They preached self-defense against capitalist enemies. Benno had carried a pistol to work until Joe saw it and banned it. That was the first issue that had arisen between them.

Further, Benno refused to become a naturalized citizen, or even consider it. Joe held that against him, though he knew he shouldn't. He employed at least a dozen men who had the same resistance, from either an excess of pride in the fatherland, or some feeling that they might pack up and go home if they didn't do well in America.

Benno was a fine worker when he felt like it. So, for the present, Joe decided to put up with his agitation, hoping it would get no worse. If it did, Benno would go. Joe's tolerance was not infinite.

He pulled out his gold pocket watch and found his hand shaking slightly. The confrontation had upset him, especially that moment with his son.

With his nail he lifted the thin gold watch cover. The dial showed twenty-two minutes past eleven. His driver was due to arrive in precisely eight minutes, to take him first to the Palmer House, then to his club, the Union League, for the meeting with two other members. One was the traction magnate Charles Yerkes, a man of shady origins who had served time in Pennsylvania for stock fraud. The other was the former congressman from the Eighteenth District downstate, Joseph Gurney Cannon, commonly called Uncle Joe, or sometimes Foul Mouth Joe because of a tendency to lace his utterances with profanity; often when he rose to speak in Congress, women left the gallery. After long service, Cannon had been voted out in the Democratic sweep of 1890.

Joe put on his coat and white felt homburg with a fancy ribbon edging the brim. He took his gold-knobbed cane and the meeting folder and went downstairs to the *Stube*. On the front counter stood the newest token of modernity, a gleaming golden cash register. It was the latest model from the National Cash Register Company of Dayton, incorporating a cash drawer, bell, indicators that popped up in the window, and a daily detail strip that provided an exact record of individual sales in chronological order. Ah, numbers!

His headwaiter, Mickelmeyer, came out of the service pantry. Tapping the register, Joe asked, "How is this working?"

"She's a beauty, Joe, just wonderful," Mickelmeyer said. "I have something wonderful of my own to report. Peter is accepted for the fall."

"Oh, that's splendid. When did you learn?"

"Letter came yesterday." Mickelmeyer beamed. "I never thought the boy would finish *Gymnasium*, let alone enter a fine university." The University of Chicago was fine only in the eyes of Chicagoans; it had no record to speak of. It was new, built in large part with money donated by John D. Rockefeller.

"Maybe Peter will have time to play football for that new coach, Stagg."

"I'd like it," Mickelmeyer said. "His mama's against it."

"Women can sometimes be persuaded. I want Peter to have fifty dollars with my congratulations. Stop by the office later, I'll write you a draft."

"Typically generous of you, Joe. God bless you."

Joe waved and went out. Mickelmeyer had been grateful, but not particularly surprised. He probably expected some such gesture from the head of the firm. Like Joe, Mickelmeyer was an old-timer in the business. At Imbrey's in Cincinnati where Joe had apprenticed, the owner and his men had always eaten together at trestle tables, and shared each other's lives as fully as they shared the daily work. Mickelmeyer had had similar experiences. It was typical of the business years ago, and one aspect of the past that Joe tried to preserve. The socialists and anarchists made it hard, sowing suspicion and hostility.

In the *Biergarten*, the first noontime customers were beginning to fill the tables under the oak and elm trees. The air was heavy and damp, but full of the aroma he'd loved since boyhood: the smell of grain and water, yeast and hops mingling to create the sweet hearty odor of a brewery.

He counted the remaining empty tables, as was his habit. One table caught his eye. He studied it, then signaled a waiter, the newest, whose table it was. Joe showed him the cutlery laid out in a haphazard way.

"This piece goes here, so. The fork goes so." Joe demonstrated. "All neat and square, that's how it should be. See that you do it from now on."

"*Ja*, Herr Crown," said the sheepish waiter. He knew what would happen if he didn't heed the owner.

"We speak English here, unless the customer doesn't. Good morning."

He stepped through the gate to the splashing fountain dominated by a six-foot statue of Gambrinus, the legendary Flemish king and patron saint of brewers. King Gambrinus had supposedly gained his fame from his capacity to drink up to a hundred and fifty pints of beer on any occasion.

How satisfying to be Gambrinus, Joe thought. He looked calm and happy. Perhaps from all that good beer . . .

He heard wheels rattling and checked his watch as a team of handsome bays pulled the carriage to a stop. It was an English-quarter landau; a rich man's carriage. Black moldings, boot, and a horizontal accent stripe provided discreet decoration. The interior seats were leather dyed to match the outside finish. Even the driver's seat was fancy, dark red cloth with black leather welting. On each door, a small golden crown was displayed. The front and back top sections were raised because of the threatening weather.

"Five minutes late, Nick," Joe said, snapping shut the cover of his watch.

"Truly sorry, Mr. Crown," said Nicky Speers, the robust and ruddy driver-groom employed by the family. Nicky was a middle-aged Englishman; British drivers were highly prized among Chicago's gentry. "Big smash-up of drays on the Clark Street bridge. Couldn't turn around for near twenty minutes."

Joe Crown gave a quick nod to say the explanation was accepted, though not appreciated. He stepped into the carriage and it sped away under the ominous sky.

Joe settled against the cushion and thought about the luncheon meeting.

What lay behind it was the great fair scheduled to open, for one season only, on May 1 the following year. The World's Columbian Exposition would be a mammoth exhibition of arts and industry, commemorating the four hundredth anniversary of the discovery of America. International in nature, it would focus global attention on Chicago.

To house all the exhibits, enormous pavilions were being rushed to completion in Jackson Park on the South Side. Congress had chosen Chicago for the fair over competing cities, and mandated that the new buildings be dedicated "with appropriate ceremony." This led to immediate complications, because the obvious date, October 12, was ruled out when President Harrison insisted he must attend the parade honoring Columbus in New York.

The alternate day chosen was the following Friday, October 21. Dedication would be preceded by a full week of civic celebration, including a gala ball sponsored by Armour, Field, Pullman and General Nelson Miles, among others.

A great parade would take place on Thursday; President Harrison would review it. That evening, he and other dignitaries would be entertained at a dinner arranged and paid for by selected guests.

Friday would be the capstone. Every business proprietor save the most Scrooge-like would close his doors to celebrate the dedication. The morning would include a second parade to the Exposition grounds, then a dedication ceremony inside the cavernous Manufactures and Liberal Arts Building, already being promoted as "the largest building in the known world." All night long, Chicago's parks would be lit by fireworks.

The entire week had been planned by the Exposition Corporation's Committee on Ceremonies, which included every rich or important person in Chicago, and dozens who pretended to that status. Joe Crown's subcommittee was responsible for arrangements for the Thursday night presidential reception and dinner. On that subject, Joe was now bearing bad news.

He opened his folder, perused the menu written in a flowing hand. Thirty-five different items. *Oysters. Eggs "Florentine." Roast of Woodchuck. Veal Chops,*

Castilian Sauce. Strawberry Shortcake, Kirsch. Cognacs. Beers. Crown's would provide three kinds of beer, at no cost. Other suppliers weren't so generous; their avarice had necessitated the emergency meeting. Joe closed the folder. He didn't need to look at the dismal numbers again; he knew them by heart.

Despite the favorable attention the Exposition would generate, the millions of tourist dollars it would bring in, the fair was at the same time unleashing a floodtide of greed and venality. Even a quasi-respectable personage such as the mayor, Carter Harrison, Sr., had enthusiastically endorsed "progress and a wide open city" during the fair's run.

The mayor's cheerful callousness was typical of the town, but Joe thought it typical of the times as well. The tide of greed and venality had been rising in his adopted country for twenty-five years, ever since the administration of U. S. Grant, the war hero and avowed political innocent. Grant's advisers and cronies had used their positions to enrich themselves illegally, most notably in the Whiskey Ring that defrauded the government of millions in distillery taxes.

After that, Jay Gould and Jim Fisk had tried to corner the nation's gold supply and nearly wrecked the economy. The Tweed Ring in New York had looted millions from the city treasury before they were stopped. Four shareholders of the Union Pacific and the Central Pacific railroads had built personal fortunes by siphoning off government subsidies during construction of the transcontinental railroad. John D. Rockefeller of Cleveland had organized Standard Oil and ruthlessly used the corporation to drive competitors to the wall; now he went about wearing the purifying garments of a philanthropist.

For every one of these great scandals there were a thousand lesser ones. Stock manipulation, land fraud, stuffing of ballot boxes, fixing of prices, consolidation of industries in the hands of a few men who conspired together—all were commonplace. Children were hired illegally to work in factories that were dirty and unsafe, and some of those children became diseased or maimed for life. In Chicago, the votes of a majority of the aldermen—the notorious "gray wolves"—were openly for sale. Even today's meeting was the direct result of naked greed. There seemed to be very little idealism left in America, only a cynical belief in the almighty dollar. Get it honestly or dishonestly—by graft at city hall or sharp dealing in the boardroom—but get it.

The sensational press boosted circulation with stories about "robber barons" and "trusts," crooked bosses and slum landlords, and the stories were wearily shrugged off by a majority of decent folk who presumed themselves helpless. Obscure authors wrote books demanding reform but few read them save women, preachers, and impressionable young men such as Joe's older son.

A few public figures cried out against the worship of money and the attendant corruption. Joe's close friend Carl Schurz was one. Unfortunately such men were lonely prophets in a wilderness of apathy. The rich got richer by circumventing the law and the poor starved or died in submissive silence. The glory of the American business system—the freedom it allowed—was also its curse, for it virtually invited the wolves to enter the fold, to kill and plunder without hindrance. Reform was desperately needed. But where would it start? What man of good character would rise to lead it?

Joe still believed in the fundamental rightness of the American system. He believed in the opportunity it gave a man willing to work hard. He didn't fancy himself a saint or, praise God, a radical. But neither did he think himself as stupid as some of his peers. Businessmen with utter disregard for the human side of commerce. Gus Swift and Pork Vanderhoff, for example; two packing house tycoons who blandly said that if one of their workers hurt or crippled himself at one of their plants, it was not their fault or responsibility, but rather the injured man's—he knew and accepted the risks when he took the job. When such unfortunates fell on the human scrap heap, Swift and Vanderhoff looked the other way.

George Pullman was hardly any better. He'd built his model workers' town, Pullman, twelve miles south of the city. On the surface it seemed a wonderful and humane experiment. But he packed the town with company spies to prevent labor agitation, and he charged his tenants three times the normal rate for gas and light and water.

Sow the wind, reap the whirlwind, Joe thought. What the Pullmans, Swifts, Vanderhoffs ignored was a growing number of Bennos around the world. Men dedicated to "propaganda of the deed." Which could include arson, dynamiting, even murder.

He chastised himself for letting his thoughts flow into such morbid channels. It was probably the sum of many things, including the sinister dark sky. And a pervasive worry about his nephew from Germany.

In the basement of the Palmer House, Joe took the waiting chair in the barbershop. He greeted a couple of acquaintances—the shop was a haven for the city's business leaders—and apologized to the barber, Antonio, for being five minutes late. Antonio's smile and shrug said it didn't matter; Mr. Crown had his regular time each week, and he tipped generously.

The Palmer House barbershop was equipped with huge chrome-trimmed chairs and decorated with potted palms and dozens of silver dollars imbedded in precise rows in the floor. Important patrons had their own shaving mugs and brushes in racks on the wall. Joe Crown's mug was brightly enameled with a picture of a merry king wearing an enormous crown and lolling on a throne. Above the picture, in gold, was the word CROWN. Below, likewise gold, the word REX.

Antonio stropped his razor and lathered Joe's cheeks just above his beard. Joe usually enjoyed these tonsorial visits, but this morning his mood didn't allow it. The sight of the painted mug brought memories of the great war, his Union Army service that had exerted such a profound influence on the course of his life. In the war, a vague predisposition toward neatness and order had changed to a ruling passion, reaching deep into his German soul and enslaving him to *Ordnung* forever.

The mug. There had been another like it, on a tragic night when—

No, he didn't want to relive that now. Things were quite grim enough without it. He leaned back in the chair and closed his eyes while Antonio brushed sweet-smelling soap onto his cheeks.

The handsome red sandstone clubhouse of the Union League was at the corner of West Jackson and Custom House Streets. Formed in 1862 as a patriotic organization whose members swore an oath to preserve and defend the Union, the Union

League had spread through the North, and social clubs had sprung from it after the war.

Joe's subcommittee members were waiting for him in the spacious main lounge. The two men were a sharply contrasting pair. Both were in their middle fifties. Charles Yerkes, of German descent, was a pallid, dark-eyed man with a luxuriant handlebar mustache and leonine hair turning white. Someone who didn't know his reputation as a piratical businessman might have guessed he was a professor, with a professor's reserve and palpable aura of superiority—although no professor could have afforded his English suits and handmade shirts. Congressman Joe Cannon's appearance was also deceptive. He gave a first impression of rubelike sloppiness, with his crushed felt hat and sloppy clothes and a chin beard badly in need of trimming. Joe Crown had noticed, however, that Cannon's suits were not cheap, merely worn carelessly. Cannon often joked about it:

"My noble constituents down in Vermilion County, they're just a bunch of good old dirt farmers, how'd it look if I high-hatted them dressed up like a dude? Poor old Chester Arthur, he couldn't get renominated in '84 because he dressed fancy. I always say Chester was beat by his pants."

Cannon's hayseed act concealed a dictatorial nature, a shrewd mind and an awesome strength of will.

Chatting, the three repaired to the two-story main dining room, and the table Yerkes had reserved in a quiet corner. Behind an ornate screen in a small musicians' gallery, an unseen entertainer softly plucked a mandolin.

During the heavy meal, they discussed the uneasy state of the country. Yes, Americans considered the monopolistic trusts obscene, symbols of an evil and crushing influence on humble lives. By extension, all businessmen were suspect. There were political consequences. In the West and the South, farmers and workingmen were organizing a third party, called Populist. The gulf between rich and poor, capital and labor, was growing ever wider, ever more divisive. Witness Joe's problems with Benno Strauss, which he mentioned. Yerkes brought up the violence at the Carnegie Steel plant in Homestead, Pennsylvania, last July. State troops had been called in to quell a strike; men had died in a hail of gunfire.

If Joe's outlook on all this tended to be a little bleak, that of Yerkes was dismal:

"I have thousands of shares of Philadelphia & Reading in my portfolio, and they're practically worthless. All the railroads are teetering on the brink of bankruptcy. In New York last week I had dinner with Belmont and Morgan. They're both certain that we're headed for disaster. They've tried to warn Washington. No one there seems to give a damn," he said with a sidelong look at Cannon.

Uncle Joe scratched his nose. "Don't exactly know what we can do, Charlie. 'Tisn't up to the government to regulate a free market. You're right about the mess, though. I have some grain and cotton shares. Sky high one day, lower than a whore's reputation the next. You need a swami with a God damn crystal ball to predict what's going to happen." He signaled the waiter for more coffee. To Joe he said, "Your business all right?"

"Yes, always. Sales may dip a little in bad times, but they never dip too far. Beer is a cheap balm for the soul." He wasn't making a joke, but Yerkes snickered, as if he thought the statement contemptible.

When each man had more coffee, Joe opened his folder and showed them the final revised menu. "Charles, do you approve?"

Yerkes shrugged. "Why not? If we have a crash between now and next Thursday, we can serve the President stale rolls and water."

"Uncle Joe?"

"I'd say it's fine. I like you two fellas all right, but if you dragged me onto a C. & E. I. car from Danville, bumping my ass on a bad roadbed for a hundred miles just to okay a God damn menu—" With his foot he moved the spittoon closer under the table. He leaned over and expectorated noisily. "Then look out. You may think you've heard me cuss, but here comes a blue norther."

He pulled out one of his cheap cigars and lit up. Joe said, "No, there's something much more important to discuss. The two houses supplying our wild game and our liqueurs have arbitrarily increased their estimates. By very substantial amounts."

"Well, hell, just dump 'em and find new ones," Cannon said, waving.

"It can't be done, we're out of time. I'm damned angry but at this point anger is futile. Nor will it solve the problem. Even sold out—which we are—we will not take in enough money to cover our costs. Here, look."

He showed them his sheet with the numbers.

"Our subcommittee is responsible for keeping the menu within the budget. The Committee on Ceremonies will hang the three of us if we're in the red."

Cannon reared back in his high velvet chair. "Don't look at me, boys, my pockets got nothing in 'em but lint and small change. How much do you think a country lawyer makes when one shitkicker drags another into court over some pissant property dispute? I'll tell you what I make: chicken feed." He leaned over for another emphatic spit.

Looking put upon, Charles Yerkes sighed and said, "All right, I'll subscribe enough to make up the difference. I presume that's the reason I'm on the committee in the first place."

Greatly relieved, Joe said, "I was hoping you'd offer. If you'll be responsible for half of the deficit, I'll make up the other half."

"Done," Yerkes said, looking happier.

"Now that it's settled, suppose I can get another God damn drink?" Uncle Joe said, looking bored.

Joe left the Union League Club shortly after two. His carriage headed north for Larrabee Street. He knew he should be pleased that his subtle strategy had resolved a significant problem. Instead, his mind immediately fixed on another. Where *was* the boy?

There had been no word from him. He ought to write his sister Charlotte and inquire, just as a precaution. No doubt he had waited too long already. Then again, perhaps he was worrying needlessly. How was the boy supposed to communicate? He probably knew little or no English.

Assuming that he simply showed up one day, how would he get along? Would he be happy in America, or grow disillusioned and leave? Should he have more schooling, or a job? The most troubling concern was the first one. Would Joe and Ilsa's children fully accept a newcomer into the family?

There were three children in the Crown household; three problematic responses to the arrival of a stranger. The oldest, Joseph Junior, was seventeen. He was a small-boned boy with a triangular, almost elfin face, and a quick mind. Ilsa had trained him to read avidly. Very much like his father physically, temperamentally he seemed to reject everything Joe Crown stood for; to revel in rebellion. He had been dismissed from no fewer than three schools of high quality. In desperation, Joe had put him to work in the brewery. There he'd promptly fallen in with the worst element, the radical socialists whose ringleader was Benno Strauss.

Frederica, called Fritzi, was eleven. At the moment she said she hated boys. She was a skinny child, with a lot of wild blond hair that must have come from Ilsa's side of the family. Fritzi was lively, sometimes stridently so. She was always competing for attention. She lived under a double burden: being the second child, always compared to the firstborn, and being a female in a family, and a world, dominated by men. Joe adored her but she often taxed his patience. He feared he'd never understand her completely.

Carl was the youngest. He would be ten in November and he was already as tall as his sister. His face resembled Ilsa's, but his shoulders were so wide, his trunk and waist so thick, he looked like he'd come from a different set of parents. Carl appeared rather slow-witted until he talked or smiled; then his charm, and his smile, won every heart. He was sometimes clumsy around the house but never in games and sports, which he loved.

Carl was a complex little boy. Almost as strong as his passion for athletics was his love of things mechanical. At four, he had nearly driven Joe and Ilsa mad with a sudden interest in padlocks, safe dials, locks and keys of every shape and kind. Each year thereafter brought a new and different obsession.

Three children, all wary of the coming of a new and permanent member of the household. They were not eager to have their lives disrupted that way. They made no secret of it.

Joe tried to believe that the children would accommodate themselves to their cousin, but he wasn't sure.

11

Pauli

FOUR PEOPLE died in the blaze that consumed *Die goldene Tür*. Frau Geizig, Liesl, and two greenhorns sleeping in the loft on the third floor.

Herr Geizig had come back just as the blaze broke out, and didn't raise a hand to help those inside. The arsonist, Magda's jealous friend, was never caught.

Pauli's left leg had been wrenched so badly by the jump from the second floor that he couldn't take a step without excruciating pain. Magda suffered two broken ribs and many bruises.

The local police questioned Pauli but didn't hold him. He was, after all, something of a hero. He told the officers that Geizig owed him wages. They said the jailed owner claimed to have no money. A station house detective, a man with a German last name, heard about Pauli's situation and gave him five dollars from his own pocket.

Pauli's plan to ride freight cars to Chicago wouldn't work now. With his leg injured, he didn't dare try to jump aboard a moving train. He was worried about the lateness of the season. The weather was sharply cooler. Leaves were turning yellow and scarlet, and falling.

Magda went with him to the depot. She helped him buy a second-class ticket for four dollars; the rest he'd use for food, as long as it lasted. The ticket agent said four dollars would take him as far as Pittsburgh. Pauli marked one of his map tracings with a dot and the letter P.

"But what will you do after Pittsburgh?" Magda wanted to know, standing with him as bells rang, steam hissed, and the train prepared to depart.

"Walk," Pauli said, with far more assurance than he felt.

He didn't like the second-class car. It was dingy, the benches were hard, soot and cinders constantly flew in the open windows to sting his eyes and settle in his hair. Two ceiling lamps provided light, but of such dimness that he had to strain his eyes to read his phrase book. Second-class cars in Germany were much better.

Passengers got on and off at each station, most of them country people. A different person sat next to him every hour or so. No one bothered to make conversation, especially after they heard a few words of his broken English.

He bought a small bag of licorice twists from the news butcher who walked through the train. He ate candy and stared out the window, trying to lift his spirits by studying the changing landscape. The coastal plain gave way to hills, then to low mountains, their slopes aflame with the foliage of autumn. It turned cold that night, and the conductor lit a wood fire in the iron stove at the head of the car. Smoke billowed out, producing coughs and smarting eyes. But at least the car was warm. No, it was hot. It was an oven. How strange that Americans liked such heat in their rooms and public spaces. He wondered if he'd ever get used to it.

He was thankful when the smoky, dirty train lurched into a huge shed and the conductor shouted, "Pittsburgh!"

In Pittsburgh he spent the rest of his money on a sack of apples, crackers, and hard candies, which seemed the best foods to carry on the road. He set out westward on foot, asking directions of anyone who'd speak to him—schoolchildren, tramps, women hanging wash in their yards when breezes blew. The first few days he made very slow progress because of his leg. Each step was a struggle; often he had to clench his teeth against the pain. Several times he had to sit down by a roadside fence, gasping and sweating, till the pain passed. But he wouldn't be deterred.

The sky in the late afternoons was a dark blue. The light slanted; the sun hung a little lower every day. Fields were already harvested for winter. His wool coat was already too thin.

He slept in haymows, or burrowed into frost-withered weeds on the side of a hill. His sack was soon empty, and after that he ate when and where he could. Sometimes he begged water and food at a farmhouse, in exchange for work. He split logs at one place. At another he carried jars of preserved fruits and vegetables to an underground cellar for over two hours. At a third he was asked to feed pigs, an experience decidedly foreign to a boy raised on the streets of Berlin.

Now and again he rode a few miles with farmers driving wagons, or peddlers traveling between towns. One of these, an itinerant tinsmith, carried him for almost thirty miles in the state of West Virginia, then bought him a huge meal of beefsteak, onions, and beer, before sending him on his way.

Just over the border in the state of Ohio, in a cold twilight pricked with sparkling stars, he crept into an orchard where a few unpicked apples hung withering on the boughs. He plucked a gnarled brown apple and bit into it voraciously because he'd had nothing else for twenty-four hours.

"Hello, who's that yonder?" The gruff voice took him by surprise. A hound started to bark. He heard the farmer running toward him in the dusk. He snatched up his grip and ran in the other direction.

He stepped into some kind of animal burrow and was hurled down, smacking his forehead on the trunk of an apple tree. The farmer came up with a leveled shotgun. Pauli spent seven days and nights in the village jail for the crime of stealing one worthless apple.

At least the food in the jail was plentiful and good. Corn meal mush, homemade breads and preserves, tasty stews, thick strong coffee. The jailer's sister was married to the local physician. He came by with his leather bag. He looked like a consumptive but he had a gentle touch, and he examined Pauli's leg carefully. The skin was still purple and yellow in places, and Pauli had trouble putting his full weight on it.

"Nothing broken so far as I can tell," the doctor concluded. "I have some liniment you can rub on. You must be careful, though. Not strain it. How far are you going?"

"Chicago."

The physician shook his head. "That's a long way. How will you make it?"

"I don't know. But I will."

The doctor sniffed. "Before you travel, I want you to come by our house. My wife will heat some water. You need a bath. If you keep smelling the way you do, you'll be arrested as a public nuisance."

Pauli didn't understand the word "nuisance." But he enjoyed the bath, in a zinc tub, and a generous meal set out by the doctor's stern wife. ("I've never seen a human being eat so fast, is that a German trait?") After the meal came a blissful night's sleep in a real bed, under a thick comforter.

Under gray skies threatening winter, he set out west again, his clothes clean, his leg smelling of liniment, still limping.

□ □ □ □

On the journey he encountered many strange new names. Wheeling. Erie. Bucyrus. Toledo. He tried to learn and pronounce each one. It wasn't easy.

He saw advertising signs with strange pictures and legends on them. Voluptuous young women in diaphanous gowns held up bars of yellow soap. Fetching little girls in nightdresses bit into brown biscuits. Stalwart farmers in straw hats held out plugs of tobacco. APPLEBAUM'S DIGESTIVE ELIXIR. FENWICK & HERMAN, MORTICIANS. HOLY GHOST TENT REVIVAL. He understood most of the pictures but few of the messages. Still, he was fascinated by the zest and brashness of the signs; their bright colors. This, too, was something new; singularly American.

He traveled into the state of Indiana with an itinerant blacksmith. It was by now December, and the bleak weather had unexpectedly reversed itself in a spate of sunshine and warmth. The blacksmith said such weather was very unusual for the Middle West so late in the year.

The blacksmith let him off at a crossroad, waved and drove away on the road leading north. Pauli trudged on for about a mile, reaching another small farm town with a single unpaved main street. He stopped at an apothecary's, a crowded, fragrant shop which also sold harness, shirts, bonnets, work boots, ear trumpets, artificial limbs and glass eyes.

The apothecary was a craggy middle-aged man with a fan beard and a right leg that seemed stiff, as if he had an injury like Pauli's. Pauli got out his phrase book for help with his question. The apothecary listened gravely, then said Chicago was but a couple of hundred miles away.

"I advise you to conclude your trip speedily; this weather won't last. We could have a snowstorm any day." He cocked his head as he studied the visitor. "On the other hand, you look like you could use at least one night's rest in a real bed."

"I could, yes, very much."

"Splendid. I'll be glad to have the company."

He led Pauli to rooms above the shop, there opening the door to a large bedroom that smelled of dust and disuse. "My wife and I shared this room for years. A heat seizure took her a year ago August. I've slept in the small bedroom ever since. Can't bear this one. You make yourself comfortable. Here's one of my nightshirts. Put it on and I'll wash your clothes. My name is Llewellyn Rhodes."

"Pauli Kroner. Sir, very much I thank you."

Rhodes cooked Pauli a big supper. He ignored his shop and stayed in the upstairs kitchen with a mug of coffee, as if hungry to talk to someone, even someone much younger. He told Pauli that he served as unpaid choir director for the little church in town.

"Germans sing much," Pauli said. "Always they have singing clubs."

With melancholy eyes, Rhodes seemed to look at some place far away. "We sang a lot in the war. In the early days anyway. I served forty-six months with the 20th Indiana. Volunteers, all of us. Indiana farm boy volunteers, green as new corn. You've heard of our Civil War, have you?"

"The war to free the *Negerin?* Yes."

"The war to save the Union. A lot of us gave up parts of ourselves for that. Do you understand what I'm saying?" He stretched out his right leg and raised his pants. Pauli's eyes widened. Rhodes's leg was wood.

"It's wood clear up to the knee. How old are you?"

"Fifteen years."

"I wasn't but four years older when I lost it, at North Anna River, in Virginia. I've never felt bitter about it. The war was the greatest experience of my life. Most men my age who served feel that way. It was like marching in the Crusades. Everything else since has been pale and tame. We all had a purpose then. Now I just live to make a little money, take care of my business, get through the days." His haunted eyes held Pauli's.

"You need a purpose like that. Something you care about. Money is all right, money's necessary. But it isn't enough. Not nearly enough. Do you understand?"

Pauli nodded, though he wasn't absolutely sure.

In the morning, Pauli prepared to leave. Despite a good night's sleep, he felt strange. His teeth clicked and he was alternately sweaty and chilled. The apothecary noticed and put the back of his hand on Pauli's forehead.

"You're ill. You'd better stay another day or two."

"No, already I have taken too long. I must hurry to Chicago."

"Well, the Pittsburgh, Fort Wayne & Chicago runs through here. I'll buy you a ticket to take you the rest of the way. Don't say no, I've made up my mind."

So Llewellyn Rhodes took him to a depot, just as Magda had done.

The sky was dark. Wind blew. The air had grown bitterly cold overnight. Rhodes seemed broken by sadness as he waved goodbye from the platform. *America,* Pauli thought as he gazed out the window of the local to Chicago. *There are people here just as defeated as Aunt Lotte.* It was a disillusioning lesson.

The passenger car was little different from the one he'd ridden to Pittsburgh. Within an hour, Pauli's face was running with sweat. This time the cause was not the old stove heating the car. He was weak, intermittently dizzy; getting sicker. He huddled against the window and watched gray fields, wire fences, and bare trees through slanting snow that fell faster each minute.

Gale wind whined around the car, rattling the windows. Soon the train slowed to ten miles an hour. Then five. Everything outside disappeared in whiteness. The train was caught in a raging blizzard.

Drifts piled up. The train chugged, stopped, jerked forward, chugged again, then stopped a second time. This time it didn't move.

The conductor jumped off. Soon he was back, snow on his shoulders and cap visor. "The track's drifted this high. We're stuck till a work train with a plow gets here. Shouldn't be long."

Twelve hours later, in the midst of a long freezing night, they were still waiting.

Wood for the stoves ran out. There was no oil to refill the lamps. The snow stopped, the wind slackened, but the train remained trapped. The hardiest travelers began to gather their belongings and leave.

"You're damn fools," the conductor warned.

"I ain't goin' to freeze to death here," a man said. "How far's Chicago?"

"Seven or eight miles. There's a suburban station and switchyard about three miles up the line, but—"

"I'm goin'."

Pauli picked up his grip. He was going too.

□ □ □ □

The snow along the right-of-way reached up to his thigh in some places. Behind him, false dawn grayed the east, but day brought no warmth to the earth or sky.

His bare hands turned stiff as he struggled ahead. A good way up the track, he saw the half dozen hardy passengers whose example, and trail, he was following. But they weren't sick, and despite the drifts they outdistanced him easily. Soon they dwindled to specks against the snowscape.

The sunless day gripped him in its icy clutch. He staggered on, falling several times, plowing face first into drifts and pushing himself out again by the power of his tingling arms, and the power of his desire to reach his uncle's house. He'd come this far, he was damned if he'd be defeated by weather, sickness, or anything else.

About the middle of the morning, he came to the tiny suburban depot, lonely and isolated at one side of a switchyard. He saw no sign of a train with a snowplow. Nothing at all was moving. Two dozen boxcars were ranged along sidings, and in the extreme distance smoke curled from the tin chimney of a tall switch house.

He couldn't walk that far. He'd shelter in the depot.

On the snow-covered platform, he gasped with relief when he reached the door. Turned the handle—

Locked.

Desperate, he searched the silent yards. He couldn't stand out here, he'd die. But he was too sick to walk far. If he could get an hour's sleep, he could move again.

Bleary-eyed, he staggered across one track, then another, and down a line of boxcars. Every car bore the same big and gaudy lettering. BIG "V" PACKING. Like so many signs he'd seen, Pauli had no idea what it meant.

The first car was padlocked. The second also. His numb hands bled from scrapes and nicks as he fumbled with the iron padlocks. After trying six cars he was ready to give up but he tried one more.

The padlock was broken. He lifted it out of the hasp and rolled the door back. Straw littered the floor of the freight car. The inner walls had a crystalline white coating: refrigerator piping, covered with rime ice. Pauli had seen similar piping at the Kaiserhof in Berlin.

He pushed his grip inside, flung his right leg up, dragged himself into the car, gasping again. He rolled the door shut and sank down in the darkness. He piled straw on his legs and chest. He shoved his frozen hands between his legs to warm them if he could. Lying on his side, he fell into feverish sleep.

He heard wind blowing; a low-pitched sound, like someone moaning. Cold powder drifted down on him; he felt it on his face and lips. He licked it and groaned.

He rolled on his back and groggily opened his eyes. The snow was falling through a gap in the ceiling of the car. He was covered with snow. He heard men outside.

"Mikey, the lock's gone on this here one."

"Better have a look."

The door rolled back. Bitter wind streamed in. Shafts of lantern light cut back and forth above him like swords.

"All clear, Mikey."

"Okay, let's—no, hold it, there's somebody over there. You. Stand and come out, right now." The second man was gruffer than the first.

Shaking, Pauli lurched to the door. The two railroad policemen were standing on the ground outside. He could see little else because the day was so dark. The men had lanterns that illuminated the snow blowing around them, making it sparkle.

"Just a youngster, Mikey," the first man said.

"A little bit more than that. What's your name?"

"Kroner. Pauli Kroner."

"Listen to him," Mikey, the gruff one, said. "Greenhorn. Just off the boat, are you, boy?"

"Yes, the boat," Pauli nodded. "Please, can you tell me—this place is where?"

"This here's the south switchyard of the Pittsburgh & Fort Wayne."

"Chicago?"

"I'm the one to ask the questions," Mikey said. "Don't you know you ain't permitted to sleep in these cars? You can be arrested."

"The snow—" Pauli began.

"Don't matter, you're still not allowed."

"I don't expect he understands, Mikey."

"Trying to find my uncle," Pauli said, laboring every word. "In Chicago he waits for me—" *If I don't die first.* His teeth chattered furiously.

"That a fact?" The gruff one was unimpressed.

"Y-yes." Pauli grabbed the edge of the door to keep from pitching into the snow.

"Mikey, he's sick, look at the sweat on his brow."

"Who's your uncle?" the other demanded.

"Josef—uh, Joseph Crown."

"Not the brewer?" said the first, the more kindly one.

"Yes, sir, do you know him?"

"Sure, what beer drinker don't? Can you prove he's your uncle?"

"Ah, the hell with this," Mikey said. "Let the coppers sort it out while he's in the Bridewell."

"What is that, please?" Pauli had a premonition that it was a prison.

"You'll know soon enough."

Pauli swayed, dizzy again. But he couldn't quit, not this close to the home he'd dreamed of for so long. If necessary he'd try to fight these men. Anything but give up—

"Mikey, don't rag him so," the first one was saying. "He musta got caught in this storm. Let's leave him go. It's Christmas. Well, nearly. That counts for something, don't it?"

Christmas? *Weihnachten?* Was it that season already?

Mikey scratched his chin while he thought about his partner's remark. "Got any idea where your uncle lives?"

Pauli's lips felt numb as he said, "Michigan Avenue."

"That's right, I know the house, everybody knows it," the first man said. "Michigan Avenue, east side, corner of Twentieth Street. Big place. Takes up half the property. You'd recognize it right off, there's crowns all over the outside."

The gruff one made a small pleased sound. "Your uncle brews a fine lager, I'll say that."

"It's reason enough to let him go, Mikey."

"Can you—" Pauli coughed, long and painful. "The way tell me? I mean—tell me the—"

"I understand," the gruff one said. "I s'pose we could." He set his lantern in the car and laid his long polished stick beside it. He lifted a mittened hand. "Climb down. The trains aren't runnin' yet. You'll have to walk; it's a pretty good hike."

"I can walk," Pauli said, against all reason, only his determination whipping him on. He grasped the hand and jumped, but his weak leg buckled and he fell, crying out. They helped him up.

It was noon when Pauli left the Pittsburgh & Fort Wayne boxcar. All of Chicago was still paralyzed by the storm. By early evening the streets were still deserted save for an occasional police wagon or horsecar laboring through the drifts. It was snowing lightly again. Pauli followed the directions given him by the railroad men, putting one filthy aching foot ahead of the other, as he'd done for weeks.

They had spelled the name of the street for him, M-i-c-h-i-g-a-n, until he felt he'd be able to identify it on a sign. He had, and now he staggered along the boulevard flanked with rows of looming houses.

He peered at street signs in the gray dusk, working steadily northward on Michigan Avenue, reading the numbers of the cross streets until he found Twentieth. There was the house, a veritable castle on the corner. Electric light streamed from almost every window.

It was three stories, built of blocks of gray limestone. It had a mansard roof, a covered carriage entrance on the side, and an iron fence surrounding the whole. It occupied one half of the block on which it was situated. With his bare head white as a snowman's, Pauli stood gazing at it with amazement.

He knew it was the right house. On the wrought-iron gate on the Michigan Avenue side, forming part of the decorative pattern of the arch above, there was a crown. A crown exactly like the one embossed on his uncle's letter. Pauli noticed other crowns worked into the fence design. In several places on the house itself, crowns had been carved so as to stand out from the stonework.

The huge residence intimidated him. Should he look in back for the servants' entrance?

No, this was America. This house belonged to his own family.

He pushed the gate inward. Saw a spot of color on his fingers. The skin had cracked open. He was bleeding.

He dragged his grip up a flight of stone steps to the relative protection of the covered front porch. He took hold of a filigreed metal tab projecting from the carved door and twisted it.

Deep in the house, a bell rang.

□   □   □   □

Pauli's heart fell when he saw the severe expression of the man who answered. His uncle had a pale sickly horse face, suspicious eyes.

"If you will go to the rear door, Cook will find you some food."

"I am not *ein Bettler*—uh, beggar, I am your nephew from Germany."

"I beg your pardon?" The pale man scowled. Pauli realized his mistake. The man wore a pin-striped shirt with suspenders and a starched white apron with a high bib tied around his neck. On the bib was an embroidered crown.

"Wait just a moment." The door slammed, but not before Pauli was enfolded in a cloud of warmth, a sweet odor of pine, a sparkle of ornaments on a tall Christmas tree, a spectacular radiance from somewhere above.

The wind keened. Pauli's legs felt like broken twigs, too weak to support him. The door opened again. There stood a man even more severe than the servant Pauli had mistaken for his uncle.

This gentleman was rather short and wiry, with sleek silver hair, mustache and beard. His posture was correct, his brown eyes large and alert behind wire spectacles. He wore patent leather slippers, gray trousers, a dark blue smoking coat of some shiny material with a secondary brocade pattern discreetly visible in the fabric. He smelled pleasantly of shaving talc. He instantly inspired respect and a touch of fear in Pauli.

But the man's welcome was hearty. "Come in, come in, won't you? Close the door, it's bitter out there."

Pauli obeyed. "Uncle Josef? Here is your nephew Pauli," he exclaimed, instinctively thrust back into German by the excitement.

"In diesem Haus, sprechen wir gewöhnlich Englisch. I am saying we usually speak—"

"Yes, English. I understand. I understand a little."

From another room a young girl called out. "Who's there, Papa?"

Then a male voice; older. "Is it someone for us? Is it Julie with her skates?"

"Kindly be patient, I'll be there in a moment." The man spoke excellent English, though strongly accented. He leaned forward, his eyeglasses flashing back reflections of twinkling glass balls and tinfoil strips on the great Christmas tree. Dozens of white candles, unlit, decorated the limbs. The tree stood at the back of a vast foyer, by a broad staircase.

The man laid his right hand on Pauli's shoulder. A plain gold ring gleamed. The right hand was the traditional hand for wedding rings in Germany. Pauli was reassured.

"So. You are my nephew—at long last."

"Yes, sir. Your nephew. All the way from Berlin. I am calling myself—" He didn't know where it came from, but it was suddenly there, in his head, perfect; the name he needed and wanted.

"Paul Crown." He gulped. "Is it all right?"

Joseph Crown stared at the sick bedraggled boy. A smile crept out between his sleek mustache and his shining silver imperial. "Paul Crown. Yes, all right, why not? You've mixed some of the old with some of the new. That's what we do at the brewery, blend ingredients to make something fine and new." His eyeglasses glinted as he cocked his head. "I am your Uncle Joe. Come in, get warm, you don't look good."

"My letter. Did it here come?"

"Letter? No. This way, the family's gathered—"

Pauli put down his grip and moved toward an open double door flooded with light. Joe Crown stood aside to let him pass. He coughed and briefly covered his mouth when he caught a whiff of Pauli.

Pauli didn't notice. His head tilted back in awe. The foyer he was crossing rose up in marble splendor, two stories, like a cathedral. From the center of the ceiling hung a huge chandelier, hundreds of strands of cut glass beads or prisms shaped into a huge glittering bowl. In two concentric rings above the prisms, a dozen electric lamps made the chandelier wink and flash in a dazzling way.

Uncle Joseph prodded him forward with a touch. "Come, let's go in. Don't be shy. The family is eager to meet you. We've been quite worried about you."

Ears ringing, heart pounding, Pauli shuffled toward the tall doors from which the light streamed and the warmth rolled in waves. Doors to a new life . . .

Filled with sudden terror, he halted just inside the room. The blaze of electric fixtures beat against his eyes. From the ceiling hung a smaller twin of the foyer chandelier. People were gathered, blurry figures. It took him a moment to begin to sort them out.

He saw a woman. Little registered about her except her stoutness, and a great mass of dark reddish-brown hair piled up on her head, and a golden gleam on her right hand. A wedding ring that matched his uncle's.

He saw three young people. The smallest, a boy, was burly. The older boy was slightly built, with a russet beard and mustache, quite luxuriant. All that registered about the girl was a flat chest and frizzy hair. The three were staring at Pauli. So was the servant in the apron.

Logs blazed in the hearth of the *Wohnzimmer;* not the formal parlor, but the room in which the family gathered privately for talk and relaxation. Behind his aunt, Pauli saw the traditional large table decorated with red candles and green boughs and piled with packages of all sizes, in gold and silver and bright scarlet paper. On a smaller taboret there was a plate of *Pfefferkuchen,* traditional gingerbread Christmas cookies in the shape of stars and crescent moons, hearts and rings. Across the room he saw the *Adventshaus,* made of wood, brightly painted and lacquered; three of its four small stained glass windows were open. In each opening a candle shone to celebrate the passage of a week. Things were familiar. He wanted to weep for joy.

"Look here, everyone," his uncle said. "It's Pauli from Germany, at last. He has a new name, he will tell you about that. You know, Pauli, your Aunt Ilsa and I were expecting you long ago. We were concerned. Was the trip especially difficult?"

"Oh no," he said, perhaps foolishly, but he didn't want to spoil the moment. He stiffened his legs. Dizziness was assaulting him again.

"I am pleased to hear that. When did your ship dock in New York?"

"*Juni.* Ah—June. The first day."

"And you've been traveling ever since?" Pauli nodded. "How did you make the journey?"

Struggling again: "Some—uh—*mit dem Zug*—train—but more with walking."

"Amazing," his uncle said. "What a valiant effort. No wonder we didn't hear from you. We thought that something dire had happened, a terrible accident perhaps. You've certainly struggled, my boy. My journey from Castle Garden to Cincinnati in 1857 was easy by comparison. I remember—"

"Joseph," the stout woman interrupted, "can't we go into this later? The boy looks famished." She stepped forward, taking control gently, skillfully, without seeming to assert herself. Pauli took to her instantly.

Ilsa Crown slipped her arm in his. "We have Christmas *Stollen*, fresh and hot. You'd like a bath and a rest, I'm sure." She touched his brow. "Joseph, he has a fever!" With another gesture she turned Pauli's attention to a huge sofa with heavy dark claw feet and upholstery of some pale ivory stuff, delicate as a new snowfall. "Please, sit down, rest yourself."

Pauli couldn't believe this. The sofa. The family place of honor. No guest ever sat on a German sofa except by special invitation. He shuffled forward.

From a sideboard his aunt brought the delicious-looking *Stollen*, large and plump as a loaf of bread, with raisins peeping from the dough, and powdered sugar covering the top.

He started to say that he'd like nothing better than a piece of the Christmas cake; started to thank them all in a burst of gratitude. Words stuck in his throat. The ringing in his ears grew to a din. Everything tilted. The candles went out, and the fire in the hearth, and all the electric bulbs, at the same time.

12

Joe Crown

PAULI FAINTED onto the pale sofa. He slid off, leaving dirty streaks, and bloodstains where his hand touched the fabric. There were shrieks from Fritzi, exclamations from Joe Junior and Carl. Joe's wife covered her mouth.

Joe Crown stared at the filthy heap on the carpet. What appeared to be bread crumbs or bird seed leaked from the boy's coat pocket in a slow stream. Melted snow dripped from his heels, soiling Ilsa's fine carpet with gray spots. Through a hole in the sole of one shoe, the boy's naked foot was visible. The skin had a brown cast, as of dried blood. Fritzi said, "Papa, I've never seen anyone so dirty."

"Is he really going to live here?" Carl asked.

"If he is, we'd better dunk him in a wash tub," Joe Junior said, laughing.

"We could bathe him in some of Mama's toilet water," Fritzi said.

"Children," Ilsa Crown said, shaking a finger.

"Your mother is quite right, we need no unkind remarks," Joe Crown said. "The boy is exhausted and sick. A bath, a bed and plenty of rest will improve him. Also a doctor's care, if needed." The expressions of the children suggested those remedies wouldn't make the newcomer any more welcome. It seemed to Joe that his fears were realized.

From the fallen boy there came a strange sound, partially a whistle, partially a long unconscious sigh of contentment. The servant could hardly contain his ire. "Frau Crown, the sofa is badly damaged. I must say at once that I don't know whether we can clean it."

"Furniture is furniture, Manfred," Ilsa said.

"That's right, and the boy is family," said her husband. But even he was profoundly dismayed by the state of the newest member, the circumstances of his arrival, and the general reaction to it. As Joe Crown gazed at his nephew, he quite forgot his own admonition about language. "*Grosser Gott, was für ein Anfang!*"

Great God, what a start.

Part Three

CHICAGO

1892–1893

I will write you about Chicago next time. This young city is one of the most marvelous phenomena of America, or indeed of the world.

1854
CARL SCHURZ, a recent immigrant, to his wife

13

Paul

SPACE AND LIGHT. Light and space. He'd never known so much of either.

His room was beyond believing. It was fit for a palace. It was five times larger than the cellar in Berlin. Ten! Aunt Ilsa said it had been the *Kinderstube;* the nursery in which Carl, the last of the children, had been raised until he was old enough to move to a regular bedroom. It was located on the second of the three stories of the enormous house. It overlooked the yard and gardens which ran north all the way to Nineteenth Street.

Aunt Ilsa informed him of all this while seated on the edge of his large—immense!—four-poster bed. Aunt Ilsa's English was even more strongly accented than his uncle's. She was a stout, round-faced woman with blue eyes. She moved so purposefully, with such quiet authority, that he quickly decided she was not nearly as soft and meek as she pretended.

She made it clear by a word, a pat, a glance, that she liked him. He felt an immediate outpouring of love for her. He felt he'd known her forever.

Space and light symbolized the miracle that had taken place in his life. Space, light, and a real family.

When he awoke the first time in the four-poster bed, he was covered by a duvet of incredible softness. The clean starched sheet under him smelled strongly of laundry soap.

While he was still gazing at the room's profusion of furniture, the patterned wallpaper, the green plants, the two tall windows with expensive lace curtains, Uncle Joe brought in a rotund man with a goatee and a black satchel. Uncle Joe introduced him as the family's physician, Dr. Plattweiler.

"How do you feel, my boy? Your name is Paul, *nicht wahr?*"

"Yes, sir."

Paul. It sounded so odd. But it wasn't, it belonged to him completely now. He would be called Paul by everyone. From this moment, he would think of himself as Paul, never again Pauli.

Dr. Plattweiler asked Paul to remove the knee-length flannel nightshirt in which someone had dressed him after he collapsed. ("We burned all your clothes, it was the only thing to do," Aunt Ilsa said later.) Dr. Plattweiler poked and squeezed and peered into Paul's orifices for five minutes, then turned to Uncle Joe and Aunt Ilsa.

"I find nothing of a serious nature. He is suffering from exhaustion, malnutrition, and a bad case of the grippe. I prescribe, first, bed rest; second, plenty of nourishing food. I will have the apothecary deliver some medications to address his various symptoms." Dr. Plattweiler stuck a finger in the air. "Follow directions to the letter."

"What else?" Uncle Joe replied, with great gravity.

A few minutes after the doctor left, Paul made another wonderful discovery. In the corner immediately to his left, there was a three-cornered whatnot, perfect for his globe, the paper flag, and the stereopticon card.

But where were they?

Alarmed, he reared up on his elbows. Wildly gazed around the room. Then, with a gasp of relief, he fell back. His old grip was resting on the carpet, partially hidden by an expensive marble-topped washstand. He relaxed and lay marveling at the play of winter sunshine through the two tall windows.

He couldn't get over his good luck. On his third day, when he was allowed out of bed to visit the separate bathroom down the hall instead of using the enameled chamber pot, he was overwhelmed by the size and opulence of the house. There were twenty-four rooms on the three floors—Aunt Ilsa filled in this detail—and a large storage and work area in the cellar. The family quarters were on the second floor. A narrow back stair just beyond the large bathroom led up to rooms where some of the servants lived. Everything was modern, from the porcelain toilet with its pull chain to the brilliant electric lights. Ceiling and wall fixtures in the rooms and hallways, and huge chandeliers elsewhere, illuminated any area at the throw of a switch.

Because of the season, the house was full of lovely and tempting smells. The freshly cut greens hanging everywhere brought the sharp tang of the pine woods indoors. Even through his closed door, he could smell the smoky tallow odor of holiday candles and the yeasty aromas of baking bread and pastries. He was almost delirious with happiness.

He lay in bed for six days, fussed over constantly by his aunt and by a short, heavy woman with a pale freckled face and a cheerful disposition who introduced herself as Helga Blenkers. She was the housemaid. Her husband, Manfred, was the steward, in charge of the servants. Paul guessed that he was the unfriendly man who'd first opened the door to him. Based on that incident, he had already decided that he didn't like Manfred.

But Mrs. Blenkers was fine. She brought him trays laden with good German food. Thick slices of home-baked pumpernickel and its lighter cousin, *Schwarzbrot.* White bread sticks, warm and soft on the inside, the golden crust sprinkled with caraway seeds. There were roast pork and roast veal—always with dumplings—and to start every noon and evening meal, *Hühnersuppe,* hot chicken soup. For desserts he had either *Kompott,* stewed fruit, or one of Aunt Ilsa's delicious *Torten.*

Beginning on his second day in bed, he was visited by the different members of the family. He had seen them as little more than blurs when he staggered in from the storm. By means of the visits, he began to form impressions of each of them.

□ □ □ □

Uncle Joe's first visit occurred at nine in the evening, after *Abendessen,* the evening meal, which was seldom eaten in German households before 8 P.M. Paul's uncle appeared at the bedside in both coat and cravat. He smelled of talc and seemed to move in a very precise way. Paul noticed this when his uncle pulled a chair into the pool of light to the right of the bed. He considered the position of the chair for a few seconds, and adjusted it before he sat down.

"How are you feeling, Paul?"

"I am fine, Uncle," he answered, still laboring over every word of the English. "How are you?"

"Just splendid. Today we added up some figures, and we will have our best year yet. If nothing untoward occurs, by the thirty-first of this month *Brauerei* Crown will have manufactured and shipped the equivalent of six hundred thousand barrels of beer. That is a record for us. I am very proud."

"Yes, sir," Paul said, not knowing how else to reply. Despite his slight stature, Paul's uncle was a profoundly imposing man. Paul wanted his uncle to respect and like him.

"Are you getting enough to eat?"

"Oh, yes."

"We want you to be happy here. We want you to be happy in Chicago. I haven't much doubt on that score. You'll find many countrymen in this city. At the last census, there were one hundred sixty thousand persons in Chicago who were born in Germany. That represents almost 15 percent of our total population of one million ninety-nine thousand and some."

Paul murmured and strove to look impressed.

"Tell me something about my sister Lotte. How was she when you left her?"

A warning signal rang in his head. He mustn't say a word about the *Herren,* it would hurt his uncle. "She was hard-working—uh, working hard, but not feeling well."

"The tuberculosis," Uncle Joe said, sad for a moment. "I must write her. You were very lucky to get out of Germany when you did. There was a huge outbreak of cholera in Hamburg soon after you left. Thousands died."

Paul shivered. "How awful. I didn't know."

"Tell me a little about your journey, won't you? What kind of troubles did you encounter? Surely there were some, it took you so long—"

"There were." Paul nodded. He began with a description of *Die goldene Tür,* but minimized his heroic performance in saving Magda. He described some of the other incidents: his incarceration for stealing an apple; the kindness of Llewellyn Rhodes; the blizzard that stopped the train.

"And you walked all the way from there, as sick as you were?"

"I did, sir. I was—uh—*eifrig*—" In frustration, he stopped.

"Eager," said his uncle gently, with not the slightest hint of superiority or impatience.

"Yes. Eager. Thank you. I knew I had taken too long already."

His uncle stood up. "That is impressive, Paul. Very impressive. It testifies to your character."

Uncle Joe leaned over and patted his arm. "Rest now. I really hope you'll be on your feet soon. I want you to get acquainted with your cousins. I know you'll like them."

"Oh, certainly."

"I want them to get to know and like you."

"I too," Paul said, fervently hoping it would be so.

Fritzi paid a visit and then came back at least twice each day thereafter. She was rather long-nosed and plain, and flat-chested, and less than a month away from her twelfth birthday. She had dark brown eyes, like her father, and a lot of disorderly blond hair.

Fritzi was lively and friendly. As Aunt Ilsa had done, she sat on the edge of his bed, bouncing up and down while she shot questions at him. Questions about Germany, the ocean crossing, Chicago—which he hadn't even seen, except through dual curtains of snow and delirium. They were questions he had trouble understanding and answering in English. He knew he sounded like a clod, but she didn't seem to mind.

"I like to mimic people, I want to be an actress," she said to him on her fourth visit. "Can you guess who this is?" She jumped off the bed, planted her fists on her hips and pulled a long face. Deepening her voice, she said, "See here, my boy, don't you dare smile in this house."

Paul laughed. "It's the man who answered the door when I came."

"Yes," Fritzi cried, clapping her hands in delight. "It's Manfred, Helga's husband. How did you know? Have you seen him up here? Has he come to visit?"

"No, I only saw his face that first evening. Once was enough."

"My, you have sharp eyes. A good memory, too. My brother Joe calls him the Melancholy Dane. I don't know why Papa keeps him, he's such a grouch. Strict, too. Better watch out for him; if you make him mad he'll always get back at you somehow."

"I won't make him mad."

"I'd better go now. Please get well soon, it's almost Christmas, we want you to be downstairs with us for the holiday." She stood up, twisting her apron. "We're awfully glad you're here, Cousin Paul." She darted forward without warning, planting a kiss on his cheek. Red in the face, she ran out.

He fell back on the bolster with a frown. This was something unexpected. He wanted all the cousins to like him, but Fritzi was just a child, just a girl—and he'd developed no strong interest in any girl as yet. When had he had the chance?

What he really cared about was getting close to his male cousins, particularly Joseph Junior, who was two years older—a huge, significant difference to young boys in adolescence. In Paul's eyes Joe Junior was a grown-up, practically a man. He was old enough to let his beard grow out. He was abroad in the world; he worked six days a week at the brewery. He was the one whose friendship and respect Paul craved most.

He thought about Cousin Fritzi again. He hoped that the adoring light he'd seen in her eyes didn't represent a new problem.

Carl came in too, with wishes for Paul's good health, and a question.

"Do you want to see my baseball?"

"Yes, yes."

"Good," Carl said, showing the ball, which had heavy red stitching along its seams. "It's an official league ball, from Mr. Spalding's store downtown. Mr. Spalding, they call him A.G., he was one of the greatest pitchers ever. The ball cost a whole dollar. This is my fielder's glove, it's buckskin." Carl smacked the ball into the curious right-hand glove whose separate fingers were thick as sausages. He was a burly, dark-haired boy, with bright brown eyes like his sister's. His features and build favored his mother. "Will you play baseball with me?"

"You will have to teach me that game. I have heard of it, but I do not know the rules."

"I'll teach you," Carl said with an emphatic nod. "When spring comes, maybe Papa will take us to watch the Chicago White Stockings. We all love the White Stockings. Papa used to take Joe and me but Joe won't go anymore."

"I'll go."

"Good," Carl cried, leaping up from the bed so forcefully that his shoulder banged the whatnot and sent it over with a crash. "Oh-oh."

Hastily he righted the whatnot and collected Paul's scattered treasures. "I don't think it's hurt," he said as he handed the globe and stand to Paul for inspection. "I'm sorry."

"No, it's all right." Paul realized that Carl was a little boy blessed with a strong body and an excess of energy. It might not be a happy combination.

Finally, on his third day of confinement, Cousin Joe dropped in.

Joseph Crown, Jr., resembled his father, except in the color of his eyes. They were a blazing blue, lighter and more vivid than Aunt Ilsa's. He had slim hips, short legs, and a slender torso. He looked delicate, but not weak. His full beard and mustache made him appear older than seventeen.

He had just arrived home from his job. He wore heavy-soled shoes, dark corduroy trousers, a faded work shirt damp at the collar, as if he'd just washed his neck.

Joe Junior was cordial, yet reserved. When he asked about Paul's health, he called him "old man"—which Paul felt meant just the opposite. His cousin didn't sit on the bed, he sat in the chair, as Uncle Joe had.

"You work at the brewery," Paul began.

"Yep. Right on the front line, I guess you could say."

"I beg your pardon?"

"The front line of the class war. The war between capital and labor. It's just a war of words right now, but it's been bloody before, and it'll get bloody again. The exploiters never learn. They never reform."

How solemn and earnest he was. And Paul didn't have the slightest idea of what he was talking about. Joe Junior saw this and said, "It isn't so hard to understand, Cousin. My pop's a capitalist. Or couldn't you tell by looking around?" His wave embraced the furniture, the room, the house. "He isn't as bad as some, but he's still part of that class. He's always wanted me to sign up too. Work in the front office someday. But I'll be damned if I will." He showed his palms. "I work with my hands, and my back. I sweat just like all the fellows at the brewery. Just like 99 percent of the human race. We sweat and die, so the other one percent can get rich."

Still baffled, uncertain about what response to make, Paul decided to say nothing. Joe Junior watched him with those blazing blue eyes. "Well, now that you're here, what are you going to do?"

"I don't know, I suppose your father will tell me."

"He's good at that, ordering people around." There was a pause. "Should I call you kid? That means somebody younger. How old are you?"

"Fifteen."

"Just a baby." Crimson flowed into Paul's face. Joe Junior grinned. "Come on, I'm ragging you. Got a girl back in the old country?" Paul shook his head.

Cousin Joe hitched his chair closer. "Well, I've got a girl. Prettiest thing you ever saw. You wouldn't believe she's a Bohunk."

Confounded yet again, Paul mumbled, "What?"

"That's what they call Bohemians over here, Bohunks."

"Oh, Bohemians, yes." He was making a fool of himself. "What is her name?"

"Roza Jablonec. Roza, spelled with a *z*. She hates it, she's going to change it someday when she's a famous singer. I call her Rosie, she doesn't mind that too much. I met her at a Sunday labor picnic that Benno—well, skip that." He looked over his shoulder at the closed door; lowered his voice. "Rosie is hot stuff. *Titten* out to here." He cupped his hands six inches in front of his chest. Paul's eyes bugged.

"Is that so!"

"Maybe we can find that kind of girl for you," Cousin Joe said, getting up. "For your first time, know what I mean?"

"Oh, yes." Joe Junior gave him another of those long, appraising looks, then chuckled through his well-combed beard.

"See you soon, Cousin. Get well."

He went out, leaving Paul disturbed by the hint of animosity between Joe Junior and his father. He desperately wanted his cousin to like him and accept him as a friend. He wanted Uncle Joe to like him too. He didn't want to be caught in the middle of some family quarrel.

Two days later, Dr. Plattweiler pronounced him well. "Just in time, eh? Christmas is next Sunday. *Fröhliche Weihnachten!*"

Aunt Ilsa brought in clothes and underwear and a pair of shoes. The clothes still had creases from the store, the shoes were tight and stiff, but everything was clean and wonderfully new. After all of the sleep and gargantuan helpings of food, he felt strong again. He was eager to leave his room, join the others downstairs, begin to explore, to really live in the great house.

That evening, he put his hand on the newel post on the second-floor landing and stood gazing down into the foyer for a long moment. His uncle was home; he could hear the clatter and talk of *Abendessen* from the dining room. Trepidation seized him.

Go on, don't be scared, this is what you wanted. This is home.

But he wasn't sure he believed it yet.

Stepping very slowly from riser to riser, gripping the banister, he went down the great stair. He hesitated a second time near the enormous and fragrant tree, heavily decorated but still with its myriad of white candles unlit, as custom dictated. Ornamental sliding doors of a room on his left—the front of the house—were tightly closed. Locked too, he supposed; that was how Germans hid their family gifts until the important day.

Conversation and delicious odors drifted from the slightly parted doors of the dining room. He took another half-dozen steps and stopped a third time. Then, swallowing hard and taking a deep breath, he grasped both doors and pushed them back.

Aunt Ilsa jumped up from the long table. "Why, here's Pauli."

"Come in, we're eating," Carl cried, waving his fork. Fritzi fell back in her chair with a long sigh. He was put off by Cousin Joe's folded arms and quizzical half smile, but Uncle Joe pulled a chair up, then hurried around the table and flung an arm around him.

"Yes indeed, Paul, welcome. Sit. Have some food."

Paul's tension snapped, and with a dizzy delight close to swooning, he grinned and walked to the empty chair, knowing it would be all right.

In the week that followed he learned many things, including the reassuring fact that, although he was in America, Christmas in the house of his relatives still had strong German overtones.

Traditional mistletoe was hung up, even though Germans no longer believed it had a mystic power to ward off evil spirits, bad luck, and poor health.

Each night after dinner, the family gathered around the small pump organ in the music room. Aunt Ilsa played and Uncle Joe led the caroling. He had a truly fine voice and informed Paul that he would have joined one of the city's German singing societies had it not been for the time involved. Everyone sang "*O Tannenbaum*" and "*Stille Nacht, Heilige Nacht*" and other favorites. Everyone except Joe Junior, that is, who absented himself, visibly annoying his father.

Uncle Joe announced that the brewery would be closed on Monday, December 26. Aunt Ilsa was already doing some of the cooking for the huge Christmas Eve meal which traditionally featured fish as the main course. Joe Junior and Uncle Joe went off to work every day, and Carl and Fritzi would be in school until Friday, so Paul was left by himself. It gave him a chance to explore the house, meet the servants, familiarize himself with the daily routine.

The routine was not so different from that of a typical household in the fatherland. *Frühstück*, breakfast, was a large and important meal of hard rolls and unsalted butter, jam and marmalade, plates of cold sliced meats and cheeses, a selection of wursts. Pots of hot coffee, tea, and cocoa waited on the sideboard. A pitcher of cold milk, too. All this was set out at daybreak by Louise, the cook.

Family members came and went, ate quickly or slowly, as they pleased; there was no set time for *Frühstück*. What was customarily the largest meal of the day, *Mittagessen*, was not served unless Uncle Joe could arrange to get home from work. It happened only once during the first week Paul was up, and there were just three of them at the table, Paul and his aunt and uncle. Nevertheless, Louise served a complete meal—oxtail soup, followed by a bowl of dumplings as a filler before the main course, which this day featured roast pork, potatoes, and three kinds of vegetables, along with plenty of bread and butter. Uncle Joe also had his own special dish of herring rolled up around pickles. He was partial to herring, he told Paul, and also to mounds of whipped cream on his dessert *Torte*. He drank his coffee with a similar fluffy mound slowly dissolving on top.

The dining room was spacious; sunny and darkly paneled in the same walnut found throughout the house. The table was long, the furniture heavy and intricately carved. A large painting in a gold frame dominated the wall above the sideboard. It was a landscape, picturing a snowy mountain peak with a sunlit meadow below. Paul thought he'd seen it before.

"Yosemite Valley, California," Uncle Joe said in reply to his question. Paul then remembered a photo card of the same majestic peak. "I bought it because the artist, Bierstadt, is a German. I'm not sure he's a first-class talent."

"Oh, I think so," Aunt Ilsa said. "The man does exceptional work." Uncle Joe didn't seem annoyed about the disagreement, as many husbands in the old country would have been.

The meal was enjoyable until the moment Uncle Joe folded his napkin and said, "I've been meaning to speak to you about something important, Paul. After New Year's we'll make some plans for you. How much schooling have you had?"

Suddenly tense, Paul said, "I left school three years ago. I needed to work."

Uncle Joe's brown eyes bored into him. "Did the authorities permit that?"

"Sir, I did not ask. Aunt Lotte, she and I needed money. It was a very hard time just then." He would never say anything about Aunt Lotte's *Herren*. Never.

"All right, fair enough," Uncle Joe said after a moment. "We nevertheless must discuss the matter. We can't leave anything to chance—certainly not your future."

That week also, Paul was formally presented to the servants.

At the head of this small group was the dour steward Paul had mistaken for his uncle; the one Fritzi had mimicked, and Joe Junior called the Melancholy Dane. He said nothing after Aunt Ilsa's introduction, merely shook Paul's hand with a hand that was chilly and dry.

Manfred moved about the house in perpetual silence; he didn't so much inhabit the place as haunt it. When he did speak, it was usually to give an order. He was inclined to be bossy with the children. Paul soon observed that Fritzi was careful not to antagonize him, and that Carl was plainly scared of him.

Although Aunt Ilsa supervised the kitchen and did a great deal of the cooking, as wives always did, the Crowns employed a regular cook, a mite-sized widow whose full name was Louise Volzenheim. She lived on the third floor, along with Herr and Frau Blenkers. The gardener, Pietro de Julio—Pete—was Swiss-Italian. He lived somewhere in the city. Nicky Speers, the stableman-driver, was English. He lived above the stable located on the Nineteenth Street side of the property, at the alley which ran parallel to Michigan.

Paul felt swamped by all the new words, ideas, experiences pouring down on him. Sometimes, attempting to ask a question or make table conversation, he felt as though he was struggling with Chinese, not a language he'd studied. Carl made it worse by using slang that was incomprehensible. A baseball player was "swell." If you were excited, you cried "Gee!" But if you were disappointed, you slumped your shoulders and also said "Gee." This was the spicy language Aunt Lotte had referred to; Paul had to watch faces, and gestures, to catch on. He sometimes grew discouraged but he refused to give up. He would speak English as well as they did one day.

With so much to see and learn, the first week passed quickly. Saturday brought a special and palpable excitement to the household. Uncle Joe came home early, at half past three. So did Joe Junior, who seemed almost jocular for a change.

Around four o'clock, Carl begged Paul to come out and play. Paul bundled himself into a coat Aunt Ilsa had provided and followed his cousin to the side yard. Carl handed him the baseball.

"Throw it," he said, crouching and raising his fielder's glove. Paul threw the ball underhand, as hard as he could. It smacked into Carl's glove. He didn't even blink.

"Overhand," Carl said. "Like this." He demonstrated. Paul tried it and after a couple of pitches got the hang of it.

"Now throw it hard as you can."

Paul windmilled his arm, as Carl had done, and threw the ball with great speed. It smacked the glove louder than before, but Carl merely rocked back on his heels.

"Throw it harder."

Joe Junior strolled into sight on the path from the formal garden—an arrangement of shrubbery, gravel walks, stone benches, and a small reflecting pool, empty now that it was winter. Everything was laid out so as to direct the visitor's eye to the end of the garden nearest Michigan. There, framed by shrubbery planted in a half circle behind it, stood a large statue of a praying angel, head bowed, wings outstretched. Into its pedestal was chiseled the word FRIEDE. Peace.

Joe Junior's magnificent beard blew in the cold wind. "There isn't a ball my little brother can't catch. Here, I'll show you." He held out his hand.

Paul gave up the ball and stepped back. Joe Junior wound up with all of his strength and power. He hurled the ball with incredible force. This time Carl blinked but he didn't step back. Joe Junior kept pitching and Carl caught them all.

He ran up to his brother and hugged him around the waist. "All you've got to do is throw the ball and he loves you," Joe Junior said over Carl's head. He mussed Carl's hair affectionately. Carl leaned back to look his brother in the face.

"Joe, we'll go see the White Stockings in the spring, all right?"

Joe Junior's smile disappeared. "No, I don't think so, kid. It hasn't been the same team since Billy Sunday gave up the outfield for preaching. Things change."

With a look at the looming house, he walked off. "So long, Paul," he said over his shoulder.

"So long," Paul said, too eagerly.

Joe stuck his hands in his pockets and didn't deign to give him a second glance.

At six o'clock a light snow began to fall. With great ceremony, family and servants gathered at the tree. Aunt Ilsa brought a single candle in a brass holder. Manfred set up a stepladder. Uncle Joe, fully dressed in coat and cravat, touched a taper to the candle, climbed the ladder, and lit a white candle. He lit others. Soon the whole tree was aglow; the candles were held in special spring clips that kept them away from the branches, and there were sand and water buckets nearby in case of an emergency.

The candles, white for the purity of the Christ child, were never lit until this special and holy evening. It was a familiar ceremony, but Paul and Aunt Lotte had only been able to afford a small, scruffy tree, with a few candles; two years in a row they'd had no tree at all. Paul was filled with exaltation and joy; a sense of truly belonging here. The feeling was even stronger when Aunt Ilsa hugged him against her side.

They trooped to the dining room for the special meal of carp and a dozen appetizers and side dishes. Joe Junior and Paul were served Crown lager in gorgeously enameled steins with silver lids and handles. Even Carl and Fritzi were allowed a small glass. Aunt Ilsa drank punch. Uncle Joe floated a double-size helping of *Schlagsahne* on top of his coffee. Twice Paul caught Fritzi staring at him with misty eyes. Everyone was talkative and jolly, save for Joe Junior, who said little.

After supper they sang around the pump organ for half an hour. Then all the servants appeared again, and followed the family to the doors of the formal parlor. With great ceremony, Uncle Joe produced a brass key and unlocked the doors. He reached in and switched on the lights. Fritzi gasped and Carl jumped up and down at the sight of the presents heaped everywhere.

The servants received small gifts and cash from the Crowns. Paul was surprised and touched when Aunt Ilsa handed him several packages—Fritzi and Carl were busy tearing the shiny wrapping off their own. Paul's gifts consisted of three shirts, a school slate in a smooth wood frame, a straight razor with his name engraved on a small brass plate—"You're old enough for it," Uncle Joe said—and, finest of all, a gold pocket watch.

"Joey, what did you get?" Fritzi exclaimed from behind a brightly painted marionette theater.

"Clothes mostly. Do you s'pose I should give them to the poor people who are out there starving tonight?"

Uncle Joe threw a sharp look at his son. Joe Junior stared back, his bright blue eyes calmly defiant. Paul wound the pocket watch nervously.

The Saturday after Christmas brought the eve of *Sylvestertag*—the feast day of St. Sylvester, celebrating the new year of 1893. Like Christmas, *Sylvestertag* was partially a religious holiday and partially a secular one. The Crowns, Protestants, celebrated it enthusiastically. There was another huge evening meal, and special treats from the kitchen—marzipan in fanciful shapes, and good-luck pigs made of chocolate.

Carl arrived late from playing ball with Nicky Speers. "Carl," Uncle Joe said, "when you've been outside, I remind you to clean your shoes. Your mother doesn't want dirt and mud all over her good carpets."

Carl mumbled something. Firmly but gently, Uncle Joe added, "Take care of it in the kitchen, please." Carl left.

A moment later, Uncle Joe said, "While I'm speaking of matters of deportment, I have something to say to you, Fritzi. And you, Paul." Paul immediately lost his appetite.

Aunt Ilsa frowned at her husband but didn't interrupt. Uncle Joe continued, "Fritzi, I observed you doing one of your imitations for Cook last night. I was hunting something in the pantry. I don't believe you knew I was there. You have a marvelous talent for mimicry, I recognized Mr. Carney the postman right away."

Fritzi giggled and blushed.

"His shoulders were slumped, his eyes were crossed. You caught him exactly. However, I want to point out that he slumps because he walks five and one-half miles every day, and he's no longer a young man. As to his eyes—it's cruel to make fun of a person's infirmity. He can't help the condition, so please don't call attention to it, it doesn't become you."

Fritzi looked crestfallen. She obviously loved her father and hated to incur his disapproval. His sudden warm smile took some of the sting from his remarks.

He turned in his chair. "Now, Paul—"

"Sir," he exclaimed, like a recruit fervently answering a sergeant.

"Please tuck in your shirt and take a comb to your hair before you come to the table. Orderly habits promote an orderly mind."

"I will do it, Uncle Joseph," Paul said, practically doing contortions to get the errant shirttail hidden. Uncle Joe smiled at him too. Then he said to his older son:

"Joe, I compliment you on the neatness of your beard. You're rather young to wear one—most of them that you see belong to Union veterans, it's rather a badge of honor for old soldiers—"

Paul couldn't read Joe Junior's expression, or what was going on behind his eyes.

"You have kept your beard looking quite handsome, which I confess I didn't expect when it first emerged as stubble."

"I've tried, Pop," Joe Junior said. "I know what you like and don't like." Paul wondered why he didn't thank his father for the compliment. Uncle Joe nodded and resumed eating. Aunt Ilsa seemed to be examining the gold rim on her plate. Soon, enjoying his food, Paul forgot all about it.

At midnight everyone rushed down the tall stoop and out the gate to Michigan Avenue, bundled in coats and scarves and gloves, ringing bells brought from the house, shouting to neighbors, and—in Carl's case—gleefully setting off strings of firecrackers on the curb.

From all over the city came the sounds of revelry—church bells, firecrackers, gunshots. Carl gave Paul a lighted piece of punk which he applied to a fuse. He and Carl leaped back, fingers in their ears. The crackers went off like the rifles of an infantry regiment. Fritzi shrieked, ran to Paul, leaped up and kissed him on the cheek. She ran away just as fast. He saw Aunt Ilsa rubbing her sleeves and smiling. Everything was perfect.

Until the next morning, when Joe Junior appeared at *Frühstück*, so changed that Paul didn't recognize him for a second.

Paul and Uncle Joe were already eating. Uncle Joe was in shirtsleeves, finishing a cup of hot tea. "Happy New Year, son, I—"

He stopped. He stared.

Joe Junior had shaved off his beard. And his mustache.

"Why did you do that?"

"Because I woke up and decided I was tired of it."

"Is that the reason? Or is it because I complimented you? Get some food, sit down, we are going to have a talk about this."

"No, I don't think so, Papa, I don't have an appetite. I've got to go catch a car."

As he started out, Uncle Joe called, "Where are you going?"

"To Pullman, to see Rosie."

"When will you be back?"

"I don't know."

He disappeared. A moment later Paul heard the front door slam.

Uncle Joe looked at Paul suddenly. He was a different person. Livid. His hand was shaking noticeably. When he picked up his teacup he rattled it against the saucer, spilling a little.

Paul cast his eyes down. A family fight, just as he'd feared. A crack appearing in the smooth shining surface of life in the Crown house. How quickly he'd discovered it.

14

Ilsa

EARLY ON MONDAY, the second day of the new year of 1893, Ilsa was seated at one end of the long dining table, her usual collection of Chicago newspapers, both English- and German-language, spread in a fan in front of her. She was startled to hear her husband's tread in the hall. She had assumed he'd already left for the brewery. Joe Junior was gone, and so were the younger children; school had resumed after vacation.

Joe Crown came in briskly, kissed his wife on the cheek, then took his place at the far end of the table. He was fully dressed. His dark brown eyes seemed fatigued, circled by shadows.

He broke a roll and put marmalade on it with a small silver spoon. Ilsa said, "You're a bit late this morning, aren't you?"

"Yes, I wanted to have a little talk about our nephew. Where is he?"

"Outside, with Pete. The sun yesterday dried the lawns nicely. Pete and Pauli are raking out dead grass. Last night I had Pauli fetch in firewood. He works willingly. He's eager to please."

Joe Crown looked up from pouring tea. "I believe the boy wants to be called Paul."

With a smile, she said, "Well, I can't seem to use that name, he's been Pauli ever since he walked in covered with mud and fainted on my carpet. What did you want to discuss about him?"

"First, the matter of a tutor."

"We already agreed it's a good idea."

"All right, I'll have Zwick place an advertisement. Now as to the boy's general welfare—it seems to me that he has a rather low opinion of himself. I sense that, it isn't something he speaks about. He needs a trade. Respectable work, at some establishment where he can see his accomplishments, and have them recognized."

Ilsa sighed. "Not the brewery, Joe. Not yet. He needs schooling. Formal schooling, not merely a tutor."

He said nothing.

"Joe?"

"All right. Schooling. I wanted your opinion." He was looking at her, and not warmly. "You reject a job in the brewery very quickly, Ilsa."

"No, no, not at all. But first he needs—"

"After all these years," he interrupted, "my work is still an issue."

"You know the reason. Papa—"

"Spare me," he said, with an untypical curtness. It annoyed her.

"There's also the question of reputation, which we have discussed many times. You can't avoid it, Joe. Many, many people think of a brewer only one way. As a man who makes money promoting drunkenness."

Joe Crown began to tap and rub a large polished boar's tooth hanging from his watch chain.

"I do not promote drunkenness, Ilsa. I make and sell a wholesome, nourishing drink. A traditional drink. As good for you in its way as cheese or meat or milk. I was given my first sip when I was six or seven, I take it in moderation, and I've always been in excellent health. I'm sick of the way the industry is constantly accused of promoting idleness, crime, sexual license, the disintegration of families. We're charged with adulterating our product. Contaminating it with 'impurities and poisons'—never named, of course. We're always lumped in with the whiskey distillers—a further insult. Furthermore, I run an honest brewery. I don't allow my men the usual drinking privilege, and they accept that or they don't come to work for me. If someone sneaks a few swallows on the job, I can't help it."

"You employ three spending agents."

"Blast it, woman, Dolph Hix and his men are *sales* agents."

"Sales agent, it's a fine title. But Dolph and the others still carry rolls of cash, which you provide, and they spend the money in saloons, buying sample steins of Crown's for the house."

He pushed his teacup away. His face was red above his silver imperial. "This is a fruitless discussion. Each time we have it, we end up in the same deadlock."

"That's true, but I can't help my feelings about—"

"Excuse me, Ilsa, I'm already behind schedule. I won't be home for dinner today. Goodbye."

He didn't stop at her end of the table to give her a second kiss, as he usually did on his way out. He left the room with an aggrieved air. Ilsa heard the back door of the house close loudly.

She was both annoyed and sad. She really didn't like to make Joe angry, or hurt his pride. But she had her own opinions and convictions. At age twenty, a proper German girl in Cincinnati, she would have kept them deeply hidden. No longer.

Ilsa was almost sure that her husband was again descending into one of his dark phases. At least twice a year he went south by himself. He said it was to look over a particular town for a possible brewery agency, or to check on certain investments he had in the state of South Carolina. He usually took his trips after a period of mounting stress, or some setback in the business.

The trips seemed to calm him, help him reorder his thoughts. Sometimes when he came home he would talk for hours about where he'd been, what he'd done. After other trips, however, he said nothing, not even mentioning his destination. Ilsa didn't distrust her husband, or imagine he had a mistress somewhere. Yet the silences disturbed her, for she felt they were occasioned by some deep spiritual darkness that never entirely left him. Pessimism born in the dark and cold of northern Europe was expected, even joked about among Germans. Joe's malaise was more profound. It was a side of his nature that baffled her; a room in his soul from which he excluded her; a wall he built that she could never scale.

Ilsa Crown loved her husband unreservedly. She knew and accepted all of his characteristics, good and bad. His moods. His ferocious ambition. Joseph Crown was a man driven to succeed. He'd been that way since the day she met him, and it was this drive that had brought him success and riches. His drive enabled her to live and raise her children in fine surroundings. But there was a bad side to it. Joe was also driven to order the world as he wanted it. Which, given the haphazard and changing nature of life, and the contradictions in human beings, frequently led to conflict.

During the merriment of the holidays it was easy to forget or ignore conflicts within a family. But the season was over, there was only the celebration of the Epiphany remaining. Pauli had brought diversion, novelty, good cheer to the household, but that too would soon wear off. And she and Joe had argued over alcohol again, as they'd argued before, many times.

In the kitchen hung a plaque in German. It had belonged to her mother. It said *Des Hauses Glück Zufriedenheit*. "The house fortune is contentedness." Ilsa sat at the breakfast table an unusually long time that morning, wondering whether the contentedness of her house was about to be disturbed even more in the months to come.

Ilsa Crown was four years younger than her husband. She had been born Ilse Schlottendorf, in Bavaria, in 1846. Her parents were farm people who produced only one child.

She had grown up in surroundings she loved—a typical Bavarian *Bauernhaus*, a sturdy wooden structure which combined the family residence and the family barn under one steep red-tiled roof. Her bedroom was located directly above the barn, and her childhood lullaby was the restless lowing of the milk cows. One of her best memories was of the family gathering in the farmhouse kitchen on a winter night, eating their supper in the warmth from the great stone stove covered with geometric-patterned glazed tiles. From that room had come the kitchen plaque with its message about contentment.

In Bavaria, she had helped with chores, growing strong and tough from the work. She had displayed a keen intelligence, and something of an independent spirit. But she didn't rebel, she was a respectful and conventional girl. When her mother went out wearing a bonnet, the symbol of a *Hausfrau,* Ilsa dutifully slipped on a wreath, the mark of a young woman still unmarried.

Her favorite time of the year was *Ostern,* Easter. After the mountainous snowfalls of winter, and the somber penitence of Lent, *Ostern* brought the springtime, and the village bonfire in which the straw man representing Judas was burned. It brought the unforgettable sight of large wooden wagon wheels stuffed with straw, set alight in the dusk, and rolled down hillsides. To this day, she occasionally dreamed of the Easter wheels tumbling through the darkness, shooting off sparks and fire.

Several years of bad weather and poor crops, and her father's talent for failure, drove the family to the wall in Bavaria. The farm was sold for much less than its value. Just enough money for railway tickets to Bremen, and steerage tickets to New York. The Schlottendorf family made the journey in 1856, when Ilsa was ten.

They passed through Castle Garden and, on the advice of friends in the old country, traveled directly to Cincinnati. The city on the hills above the Ohio River was one of three in which Germans from the first great midcentury wave of immigration settled in large numbers, the others being Milwaukee and St. Louis. It was in Cincinnati that Ilse Americanized her name by changing the *e* to *a.* Someone suggested she consider the name Elsa, but she wrote it a few times and didn't like the look of it.

The Schlottendorfs rented a small house in the Fifth Ward, near the canal, in the large German section called Over-the-Rhine. When Josef Kroner arrived in Cincinnati a year later, he took a cheap room in another part of town.

Despite a new infusion of hope, and enthusiasm for visionary schemes, Ilsa's father failed once again. With two partners, he bought a hillside tract on the river near the city. The partners were convinced that, since this part of America resembled the wine regions of Germany, they could import cuttings from the Rhine and the Mosel, and after a few years have a profitable winery. But the climate was wrong, the growing season too short, the winters too severe. The fledgling industry quickly died, and with it her father's last hope. What happened in the months after the vineyard failed scarred her forever.

Ilsa didn't meet her future husband until the stormily eventful summer of 1861. The Union was at war with the rebel South, young men were enlisting, young girls like Ilsa were thrilled by the sight of so many uniforms, and Cincinnati itself, though officially in the Northern camp, seethed with divided loyalties. The city was a major depot for runaway blacks following the Underground Railroad north to Canada and freedom. It was also heavily infested with secesh sympathizers, many of them related to former slaveholders in the torn and bloody state of Kentucky across the river.

The "Men of '48" who settled in America were almost solid in their loyalty to the Union. They hated slavery and all those who practiced it. So did their wives. Ilsa's mother worked as a volunteer nurse for Quakers operating the local Underground Railroad. The Schlottendorf household contained a small library of abolitionist literature, including Mrs. Stowe's famous novel and the writings of Frederick Douglass and William Lloyd Garrison. Attendance at abolitionist rallies was another part of this discipleship of freedom.

Thus, on a muggy night in August of 1861, Ilsa Schlottendorf went with her twenty-year-old second cousin, Mary Schimmel, to an abolitionist gathering at the local hall of the Odd Fellows Lodge.

Several white orators addressed the crowd in turn, mixing their denunciations of slavery with emotional declarations that the war was necessary to destroy the system forever. The evening's final speaker was a black man with woolly gray hair, an Alabama-born Dahomian named Turk. He told of the sale of his wife and two tiny children by his financially pressed white owner. He then described what happened when he protested this enforced sundering of a family.

Turk slipped off his shirt and stepped forward to the row of smoking lamp chimneys at the front of the platform. When he turned around the audience cried out with one voice. Young Ilsa almost swooned at the sight of the crisscrossed scars on Turk's back.

By the end of Turk's presentation, the audience was howling for Rebel blood. Everyone left the hall with a renewed determination to support the war, even though it now seemed unlikely that a Union victory would come quickly, or at small cost.

Ilsa and Mary were buffeted by others as they passed through the doors. A steamy darkness awaited, thick with river vapors that blurred the stars. *Now where did we tie the buggy?* Ilsa asked herself. The vacant lot, nearly pitch-black, ran beside the wooden lodge hall from front to back, all the way to the next street. Because of the crowd they'd been forced to picket their horse and buggy at the extreme rear of the lot.

People from the meeting were hurrying to leave, pulling out in their wagons and shays. Ilsa fanned herself as they walked in clouds of dust churned up by the departing vehicles. Suddenly she gripped her cousin's arm.

"Mary, look, there's our buggy. What are those men doing to it?"

Two men, silhouetted against the lanterns of a grogshop on the next street, had apparently chosen a buggy at random and were slashing at the traces of the horse. The freed horse bolted into the street and galloped away.

"Here, what do you think you're doing?" Ilsa exclaimed, running. Her overweight cousin panted to keep up. Ilsa was too angry to be frightened. "Get away, that's our property," she cried, flinging herself on the nearest man.

"Ow, you Dutch bitch," the man yelled, ramming his elbow into her breast. Hurt, Ilsa reeled against Mary. "Let's take care of these two nigger lovers, Jud."

"Oh, my God, my God," Mary moaned in German. Terrified, Ilsa looked around the vacant lot. People were still leaving, the wheels of their vehicles raising huge dust clouds. The dust made vision poor. Ilsa and her cousin were completely alone, unnoticed . . .

"Grab her, Tom," Jud said. The other man leaped at Ilsa and held her from behind.

"You Reb monsters," Ilsa cried, wrenching and kicking. The man holding her spun her around.

"Quit that, God damn you." He hit her in the face with his open palm. Everything whirled: the dust, the dim lamps on the grogshop, the blurry summer stars. Ilsa staggered and fell on one knee in a clump of weeds. Suddenly she heard the man called Tom exclaim, *"Jesus, look out!"*

In heavily accented English, someone was shouting. "Leave those women alone, what kind of vermin are you?" Ilsa saw a small, spare figure snatch their buggy whip from its socket. He laid it across Tom's face.

Tom howled. The stranger kept whipping him. "Get out of here, you yellow dogs. Get out of here before I kill you both."

The Rebs wasted no time. They limped from the lot and disappeared down the rutted street. The stranger dusted off his heavy black coat and smoothed his hair. He was a young man, small and trim. He carried himself with authority.

He stepped over to the clump of weeds where Ilsa had fallen. He held out his hand. She clasped it, feeling the strength in it. With his help she stood up.

In German he asked, "Are you all right?"

"Yes. But my cousin—what about her?"

The stranger knelt over Mary, who lay near the buggy, eyes closed. "Only fainted, I think. This is terrible. Friends told me there might be Southern partisans outside the hall, but I had no idea they would get so ugly." He began to pat Mary's cheek with one hand and massage her wrist with the other. Suddenly his head lifted.

"Oh, forgive me, I'm being impolite. I failed to introduce myself."

Ilsa managed a shy laugh. "Well—under the circumstances—"

Mary Schimmel groaned and sat up. The stranger stepped away, and faced Ilsa. By the grogshop's light Ilsa clearly saw his strong young face for the first time.

"My name is Josef Kroner," he said, and bowed.

Ever afterward, Ilsa said that was the exact moment she fell in love with him. If it wasn't absolutely true, memory made it so, and it became part of the family history.

Josef Kroner, age nineteen, was employed at Imbrey's Brewery, one of several such firms, all German-owned, in Cincinnati. He had been at Imbrey's four months, having moved over from a lowly job at Rugeldorfer Ice, which furnished ice to many homes and business clients, including Imbrey's.

The moment the Ohio River froze, so Josef told Ilsa during the time they were getting acquainted, virtually the whole work force at Rugeldorfer's devoted itself to harvesting ice with crosscut saws. They worked sixteen and eighteen hours a day, in snow, sleet, or subzero temperatures; the season was short, and the demand was great. Lager beer was becoming popular, but before lager could be sold it had to be allowed to age, or rest, in cool cellars or caves. This required ice, tons of it. Most breweries didn't have ice plants. Imbrey's hired young Josef specifically to design, build, and run an ice plant on the premises.

While Imbrey's was a good old company, dependable if not spectacular, Josef's future there became uncertain the moment war broke out. The whole community of Over-the-Rhine was afire with patriotic zeal. After Josef and Ilsa met, one of the first things he told her was that he shared that zeal, and wanted to march off with thousands of other Germans, many of whom couldn't even speak English, to fight for his new country. He had in fact already signed enlistment papers with Colonel W. H. H. Taylor's 5th Ohio Volunteer Cavalry—"I handle horses at the icehouse, it's more experience than most cavalry recruits can offer." He would report to Camp Dick Corwin, near Cincinnati, in early September.

Hearing that, Ilsa was excited, yet strangely sad. The oddly mixed reaction was her first realization that she liked this brown-eyed, straight-backed young man very much.

Josef didn't propose to Ilsa until after the war. By that time he'd adopted the name Joe Crown. He was a toughened veteran, having ridden all the way to Savannah and through the Carolinas with the cavalry of Generals Sherman and Kilpatrick. He had been wounded twice, but he talked very little about his war experience and evaded Ilsa's direct questions about it. He seemed to brood whenever the subject came up. Ilsa decided it was a mystery she would never fully understand.

Joe made his proposal simply. "Will you do me the honor of becoming my wife, Ilsa?"

She answered from her heart. "I don't know."

He looked stunned, then wounded. "You say you love me. You've said it several times."

"I do love you. But I don't love your business."

There was the problem. He'd declared his ambition as soon as he came home to Cincinnati. He intended to leave Imbrey's as soon as he could. Launch out on his own, build his own brewery. His own fortune; his own life.

"You see, I want no part of anyone connected with brewing or distilling," she added.

"Wait," he exclaimed. "Those are two different trades. Beer's good, beer's German, brewers are fine upright people." He reminded her that it was the German brewers of America who had helped finance the war by encouraging and supporting the 1862 Internal Revenue Act that put a one dollar tax on every barrel of beer sold.

"I know that," she said. "But I have memories, Joe. Memories of my poor father."

"Your father's dead. You've never told me much about him, but you said he died while I was away."

"Papa is the reason Mama is an exhausted woman. For more than five years, she has worked six days a week at Kammel's Bakery. She had to support us because Papa couldn't. He was a drunkard. You met him only once or twice before you went to war, you probably never suspected."

Joe said nothing. Perhaps he had suspected. She didn't want to know.

"He always drank," she said. "Mama thought drink was the reason he couldn't do well managing the farm. Here in America it got worse. After his vineyard failed he drank almost constantly. He drank anything, wine, corn whiskey—even grain alcohol. For a while his men friends tried to help, find work for him, but he couldn't hold the most menial job. The night the town celebrated the defeat of the South at Gettysburg, he got drunk again, fell in the canal and drowned. So you see why I don't care very much for anyone who helps another human being to that kind of end."

Ilsa Schlottendorf married Joe Crown anyway, because her enormous love overcame her distinctly un-German feelings against beer. For many years, as a young wife, a young mother, she fitted into the expected pattern, and never criticized her husband's business, or spoke against it.

Of late that had changed.

Of late many things were changing for the Crowns.

When Ilsa composed herself and left the dining room, she went to the largest room on the first floor; her personal domain. The kitchen.

In many ways Ilsa Crown's character and interests were unusual for a person of her background and station. Her relationship to her kitchen, however, was distinctly conventional. Since long before her wedding to Joe, she had recognized that a *perfekte Küche* was the sign of a proper German home, and as a wife she devoted hours and years to achieving and maintaining it. The effort—the kitchen itself—comforted her spirit when things were unsettled.

Ilsa and Louise, a small and gray and mouselike woman, exchanged nods and murmured greetings. Louise was just finishing preparation of the light dough for *Nudeln*. Joe liked *Nudeln* sprinkled with vermicelli and fried in country butter. Ilsa would work the dough, and Louise wouldn't object; indeed, she expected it. A German-American wife cooked much of her family's food, even if she had a whole squad staffing her kitchen.

Ilsa's kitchen was equipped with a great old claw-footed monster of a wood stove, but otherwise it was airy and neat. Copper pans of all sizes hung from precise rows of ceiling hooks. Wooden and metal utensils—spoons, knives, cleavers, meat saws—were likewise racked on the walls so as to be easily seen and reached. In the arrangement and operation of her kitchen, the *Hausfrau* demonstrated her precious *Tüchtigkeit*. Her skill; her efficiency.

Louise laid a heavy pastry board on the work table, next to the butcher block. Then she turned the dough from a basin onto the board. Ilsa brought a flour canister to the board. After opening the eyelets on the lace cuffs of her dress, and pushing the cuffs up near her elbow, she sprinkled out a carefully considered handful of flour and began to knead it into the dough.

Louise lifted the lid from a pot on the stove. The smell of simmering chicken stock enriched the already flavorful aromas of the kitchen and the adjoining pantry, where Ilsa heard someone knocking about.

"Who is in there, Louise?"

"Delivery boy from Frankel's. He's new. I gave him coffee because he asked." Then Louise whispered behind her hand, "Asked in a very nervy way, too. I'll bet you Frankel won't keep him long."

Ilsa felt the dough stiffening slightly. But it had to be stiffer yet. She didn't work the dough by recipe, or by the clock, but by experience and instinct. She had first helped her mama prepare *Nudeln* when she was four. The rhythmic push and tug of the dough began to lift her spirits.

Whistling, the butcher's delivery boy sauntered out of the pantry. He was a tall gawky thing, perhaps nineteen or twenty. His skin was very white, his eyes dark brown and darting. He wore black trousers, a black vest, a white shirt with the sleeves pink-stained by the products of Frankel's meat market. He set his empty coffee mug on a chair and tipped his cloth cap. His black hair was combed and curled into an oiled lock on his high forehead.

To Louise he said, "Thanks for the coffee, it was swell. My mother always made wonderful coffee. The best."

Louise gave her mistress a look. To the delivery boy she said, "Did you put the chops where I asked?"

"Right in the ice chest. That's a big pantry. We had a huge one at home. Half again as big, I'd say. Morning, ma'am," he said to Ilsa, who gave him a smile and a nod although she was put off by his eyes. They roved the kitchen, jumping from copper pot to silver ladle as though appraising each for some unknown purpose.

"What is your name, young man?"

"Daws. Jimmy Daws."

"Louise tells me you are new with Abraham Frankel."

"Yeah, started two weeks ago."

"Mr. Frankel is a fine gentleman. Do you like the butcher trade?"

"I guess," the delivery boy said with a shrug whose lazy indifference annoyed her. "It's better than selling papers or blacking boots on the street. I've done that and a hell—uh, plenty more."

"Is it your intention to be a butcher?"

"I don't know about that, I'm afraid I'd die of boredom. But a guy's got to eat, don't he? Well, good morning, ladies, I'll be going now. Thanks again, cookie."

He left. Little Louise Volzenheim seethed. "Cookie, what kind of word is *cookie?* Impertinent young lout. I've met a few like him, always telling you they're better off in this or that respect. Usually they mean worse." She whispered again, although there was no one to overhear. "Frankel won't keep him. He said the boy's a malingerer."

Frowning, Ilsa stared at the heavy door to the back stair. "I don't like his looks either. I can't say why. Something about him . . . something suspicious."

Fritzi made her smile when she bounded breathlessly to her mother's side in the formal parlor, moments after she clattered in from school.

"Mama, I want to ask you a question. I must!" Ilsa smiled; Fritzi loved plays, actors, and actresses. Often she didn't speak, but declaimed.

"Ask, please," Ilsa said with a nod.

"I was talking with Gertrude Emmerling at school. We argued and I got mad because Gert said it's wrong for first cousins to get married."

"First . . . ?" Ilsa stopped, realizing the import of it. She immediately banished even a hint of a smile. "Is that a subject on your mind, Fritzi?"

"Well—" Fritzi squirmed. "Some. I'm just curious. It's just a *question,* Mama."

Ilsa clasped her daughter's hands in hers. "I'm sorry to tell you that Gertrude Emmerling is correct. Marriage between first cousins is generally frowned upon. In some places it's actually illegal. I'm not certain of the law in Illinois—" She hugged her daughter. "But don't worry, it will be quite a few years before you must think seriously about matters of marriage."

"I was just *asking*," Fritzi cried, and dashed out.

Ilsa leaned back and folded her arms. So Fritzi was smitten. Ilsa understood. She'd experienced several schoolgirl crushes herself. Fritzi would get over hers.

15

Joe Crown

JOE'S ARGUMENT with Ilsa upset him. It was well into the morning before he calmed down sufficiently to call Yerkes, something he didn't enjoy even under ideal circumstances. They needed to discuss another reception of dignitaries for which their committee was assigned responsibility. The reception would be held at the Union League Club on Monday, the first of May—the opening day of the Exposition. The President would again attend. The Infanta of Spain was coming, together with a lineal descendant of Christopher Columbus. If anything, the celebration would be bigger and more lavish than dedication day the preceding fall. Joe had already decided to close the brewery on opening day. Many Chicago businesses planned to do the same.

He and Yerkes talked for ten minutes. The connection was scratchy, and there was an intermittent whistling on the wire. These modern conveniences were far from perfect.

Joe liked Yerkes no better than before. The man was a bandit, preoccupied with his personal fortunes. His civic duties were performed in a calculated way, as he revealed when he asked, "Are any of the papers aware of the work we're putting into this?"

"You mean have our names been mentioned? Not that I've seen." Joe didn't add that he didn't habitually look for his name in the local columns. "Does it make a difference?"

"Certainly it does. If we're going to expend all this effort, we deserve recognition. Why don't you get in touch with someone? Perhaps that gossip hound Gene Field at the *Daily News.*"

"If it's important to you, Charles, why don't you? I have my hands full." He spoke more sharply than he intended.

"Very well, Joe, if that's how you feel, I will."

With a click and another eerie whistle, the connection was broken.

Joe hung up the earpiece and stepped away from the large wooden box mounted on his wall. He was profoundly annoyed for the second time that day. The annoyance brought him back to the argument with Ilsa.

He understood her dislike of the brewery, but he resented it. Her feeling was emotional—quite human—but he also considered it unwarranted. He meant what he'd said to her. He ran Crown's in an honorable and upright way. He had never engaged in some of the vicious practices common in the industry. Fixing of prices by a few men who met in secrecy. Selective price juggling in a chosen town or neighborhood, to hurt competitors. He didn't allow or condone the *Sternwirth*, the drinking privilege, for his employees—as he had reminded her. He withdrew or withheld his beer from any establishment found to engage in prostitution, or any that allowed streetwalkers to solicit openly on the premises. He didn't hire children.

Some of his colleagues said he'd lost a lot of business that way. "Fine," he would answer, "I don't want business at that price."

And still it wasn't enough for Ilsa—because of her father, and her radical female friends. Miss Frances Willard of the Women's Christian Temperance Union, Miss Jane Addams of the Hull House settlement, and that lot.

Joe Crown was proud of his wife's independence and intelligence. He only wished that independence, and all the churning forces of the new age—socialism and anarchism, free love, bimetallism, rights for women, to name a few of the worst—had not carried her so far.

Modernity was fine for a man. For a wife, no.

In the afternoon he shut his door in order to concentrate on a letter to Lotte. He wrote with black ink on a heavy sheet of paper with the gold crown embossed at the top. His handwriting was small, precise, and neat.

My dear sister—
  I am remiss in not writing to you sooner. I wish to report that our
nephew arrived safely. He is calling himself Paul Crown, which is flattering.
Be assured that we will look after his interests.

He thought a moment before writing the next lines, and he frowned unconsciously as he did so.

We shall see about some further schooling for him. I sincerely hope you are
in good health, that your Christmas was pleasant, and that the New Year
will be a happy one. I shall write in greater detail when time permits. The
family and I send you our love and thoughts.
                              Your affectionate brother—

He inked his pen again and, with a flourish, inscribed a large capital J at the bottom.

He stepped into the busy outer office and pulled a colored postal card from a rack holding two or three dozen. All the cards were the same; a rendering of the facade of *Brauerei* Crown with American flags flying from its towers. Joe had paid a lot for the work of the commercial illustrator, and for the printing. He was proud of the card, which he considered useful promotion, given the worldwide craze for collecting picture cards of all kinds. Paul had added one of the cards to the already cluttered display board in his room.

Joe enclosed the card with the letter, addressed the envelope and asked Zwick to post it by ocean mail.

As he traveled home that night, relaxing in his carriage, he reflected on Paul's presence in the family. Some of his worst fears had not been realized. The boy was accepted. Carl clearly admired him, no doubt because Paul was older. Joe had never imagined, however, that Fritzi would be romantically taken with her cousin. The only dark spot was Joe Junior's reaction to Paul. Not resentment, exactly, but indifference; a cool remoteness.

Paul was surely suffering over that. Joe Junior was closest to Paul's own age, and Paul probably looked up to him, as Carl looked up to Paul. Joe Crown didn't understand the reasons for his older son's behavior, unless it was another example of his rebellion against parental authority.

Ah, but who could analyze or explain the actions of a young man who was willful, and influenced by a man such as Benno Strauss? That Joe Crown himself had been willful at a similar age, and had set out for America against the objections of the timid and the envious, was no longer a consideration. He must speak to Joe Junior, he decided. He must do something about his son's quiet rejection of Paul.

That evening, after supper, he knocked on the door of Joe Junior's room. A brusque monosyllable bade him come in.

Joe Junior was sprawled on his bed in stocking feet, a book resting on his stomach. He closed it, keeping a finger at his place. To his disgust, Joe saw what it was. *Progress and Poverty* by Henry George. That scurrilous tract! Henry George was a radical who damned the concept of private ownership of land, as he damned those who profited from such ownership. He wanted them crushed under a burdensome tax. Henry George was poison.

"Hello, Pop," his son said.

"Joe, I have come to ask a favor of you."

"Yes?" The old respectful *sir*, drummed into his children since infancy, was no longer part of Joe Junior's vocabulary. Unconsciously, Joe's hand came up to his vest. His thumb and index finger closed on the boar's tooth hanging from the gold chain.

"I would like you to spend some time with your cousin. Be more friendly."

Joe Junior sighed. "Pop, I work six days a week, remember? I come home so tired I can't see. Just like everybody else who works at the brewery," he added in a pointed way. Joe Crown's thumb moved back and forth over the polished tooth.

"Not too tired to read radical trash, I notice. You could spend time with Paul on Sunday."

Joe Junior's eyes seemed to turn colder, a glacial blue. "Sunday's my only day to see Rosie."

"Nevertheless, I'd like you to be more cordial to Paul. He's a likable boy—"

"Yeah, he's all right," Joe Junior said with a dismissive shrug. "Young, though."

"When the weather warms up, I wish you would show him around the city. Be his guide to interesting places. I don't ask much of you, Joe, but I am making this a special request."

Their eyes locked in a test of wills. Joe Junior grew red-faced. He was the first to look away.

"All right, Pop. I'll do it if I can."

"Thank you, Joe. Good night." He wheeled quickly, anxious to leave while he had his victory. As he shut the door, his son's muffled voice startled him.

"You may not like the things I show him."

With a muttered curse, Joe Crown stalked away down the hall.

The breakfast table quarrel wasn't mentioned when he and Ilsa got into bed together. Joe reached under the covers to grasp her hand. She pressed against him in the darkness, smelling of one of the creams she dabbed on her skin at night. She kissed his chin and touched it affectionately.

"About Paul's enrollment in school—"

"At the end of the week I'll speak to him. I am already making inquiries."

"Thank you, Joe." She kissed him again, and in a few moments he heard the gentle susurrus of her breathing as she fell asleep.

He was wide awake. The house creaked and cracked in the grip of the iron cold of the January night. He thought about Paul. His troubles aboard ship; the tragic fire in New Jersey; his frequently hazardous trek to Chicago. He couldn't help contrasting that with his own emigration as Josef Kroner. He'd experienced hardship, hunger, and, on occasion, hostility. But his long journey from Aalen to Cincinnati in 1857 had never been violent. Certain parts of it had been thoroughly enjoyable.

He recalled the first stage of his trip, on a coal barge down the Rhine. He'd paid the captain a pittance, and worked for his keep. He traveled in the early summer. On several nights he lay on the deck watching a thousand stars sparkle overhead. Once he'd seen a star fall, trailing fire; a spectacular sight.

He left the port of Bremen on a vessel of the North German Lloyd Company. The steerage was spartan, but not unhealthy. The food was plain but plentiful, and the summer ocean was smooth all the way. In New York City, he landed at a place called Castle Garden, a vast, shedlike building with a conical roof, located in a pleasant park at the tip of Manhattan Island. Someone identified the park as the Battery.

It took young Josef only three and a half hours to be processed by the brusque, badgering officials, and to be cleared by their medical examiners.

He knew there were many Germans settled in and around a thoroughfare called the Bowery, which he found without too much difficulty before it grew dark. He drank beer and ate wursts and bread at a German saloon, then asked for work. He talked himself into a short-term job of helping the owner repair his roof. He needed money for passage to one of the heavily German cities inland.

Still calling himself Josef Kroner, he finished the roof repair in two months. He then sought work elsewhere. Communication wasn't hard; so many of the people in New York spoke his language. He had already purchased a little book of English grammar, and was studying.

He found a job as a general helper at the large and gloomy Bowery Theater. The plays he watched standing at the back of the house featured frequent fist fights, knifings, pistol shots, and attempted ravishments of a heroine. The audience chatted and laughed and loudly insulted one another from the hard backless benches on the main level, called the pit.

Those up in the cheap gallery seats were no better. Street urchins, prostitutes, and whole families tossed down coins and orange peels at actors who pleased or offended. Josef Kroner conceived a strong dislike of theater as he first saw it in America.

As soon as he'd saved enough money, he planned to buy a cheap train ticket to St. Louis, a mecca for newly arrived Germans. The theater's box office cashier happened to have a brother in Cincinnati who ran an ice company. The cashier liked Josef, and gave him a letter of introduction. "Forget St. Louis," he said. "Cincinnati's a whole lot prettier. Plenty of our people there, too."

How amazing, the small turns that sent a man down one road instead of another. But for the cashier of the Bowery Theater, he might have settled in St. Louis. Had he done that, he might not have apprenticed at a brewery, or envisioned his own brewery, or slaved to make it a success after he opened it in Chicago, with mostly borrowed money.

He would never have met Ilsa, or known the faces of his own dear children, or given shelter and opportunity to his nephew, or found himself a rich though often troubled man in a new homeland . . .

It was pleasant to contemplate all that in a warm bed on a cold winter night.

Joseph Crown the man had been shaped by Josef Kroner the boy. As Josef, his earliest memories of Aalen were good ones. The smell of yeast, beer, bread baking. The lively chatter of colorful and worldly guests who occupied the ten rooms of the Hotel Kroner—the small brewery being directly in back. Young Josef played in front of the hotel on cobbled Radgasse, or romped in the surrounding hills with other boys of the town. He was excellent at his studies but impatient with the rigid routine of school.

His father Thomas was a studious man with a perpetual frown. Thomas worried about politics, the ruthless nobility who controlled the land, the fate of Germany. His mother Gertrud was the practical one. She supervised the hotel and kept the books. She was exceptionally quick with figures, a trait Josef inherited.

He didn't understand the significance of the Revolution of 1848 until many years later. He only knew it was a terrifying time for the family, because his father rushed off to join the rebels, and then his older brother Alfred was seized by soldiers one night and thrown in jail. Alfred was nine years old; Josef was seven. Josef was lucky not to be snatched too. Gertrud hid him in a wardrobe. Alfred had been caught while dusting the tiny lobby.

Alfred came home profoundly changed. He had been beaten and abused. He never walked normally again.

Christmas, 1849, was one of the worst times of Josef's life. Thomas Kroner was hanged in Stuttgart and then brought home to Aalen for burial. The first night the closed coffin was in the house, resting on trestles in the black-draped lobby, Josef came into the room trembling. He realized his father was lying inside the cheap unpainted box. He threw himself on the coffin, pounding on it, screaming his hatred and grief until he was dragged away by the family's Lutheran pastor.

The pastor hauled Josef up to his bedroom on the third floor while Gertrud stood by, too drained by grief to interfere. The pastor flung Josef into his room, slammed the door and turned the key. Josef screamed and beat on the door.

A few minutes later he heard a scraping sound outside. Alfred, with his crippled bandaged foot.

Alfred whispered to him through the door, trying to soothe him. Josef screamed again, louder than ever. Finally the key was turned a second time and the Lutheran pastor came in with a pitcher of cold water, which he dumped on the ranting boy. Josef was jolted to sanity by the dousing.

He ran out of the room, and downstairs, and fell sobbing into his mother's arms. He had never acted so crazily before. He never acted that way again.

With Thomas Kroner in his grave, the little hotel and brewery fell on hard times. There was simply too much work. And Josef's mother was a broken woman. First, in 1851 the brewery closed. The hotel grew dirty, acquired a bad reputation. Regular guests stopped coming. When Gertrud died of a heart seizure in 1853, family friends helped arrange a sale of the property. It fetched a very low price, barely enough to cover debts.

Josef moved in with a family from their church, and so did his brother and his sister. They lived that way for several years, passed from family to long-suffering family like parcels no one claimed. In 1855, embittered about Germany, the cruelty of its rulers, the hopelessness of life there, Josef began to listen to stories about America, and to save his money. In 1857, at fifteen, he left Aalen forever. His sister Charlotte was only ten when he said goodbye. Gerhard was barely nine and already a disagreeable boy, perhaps because he'd never known a proper father. Later, a series of vituperative letters to Josef from Gerhard alleged that their sister had become someone's mistress in Berlin, if not an outright whore.

Josef, who by then called himself Joseph Crown, preferred not to believe that. He never made inquiries. He did, however, stop writing to Gerhard. He didn't even send Christmas greetings, which Ilsa said was un-Christian.

Fourteen inches of snow fell on Chicago at the end of the first week in January 1893. On Sunday, with the temperature low and the drifts still piled high, Joe organized everyone to go outside. Everyone except Joe Junior, who had already left for Lincoln Park, to ice-skate with friends. His girl was indisposed, he'd announced at *Frühstück*.

Ilsa and the children bundled up in their heaviest coats, with mufflers and mittens and boots. Joe settled for a long red woolen scarf wrapped round and round his throat over his coat and vest. He stuffed his leather gloves in a pocket because they made his hands too clumsy. He took his Kodak camera.

"Everyone stand in a line, please. I want to take your picture against the drifts."

"Joe, the sun is so bright," Ilsa said. "I can scarcely see. Will a picture be anything but a white blur?"

"I don't know, this is new to me, we'll find out."

Joe's fingers were numb on the pebbled black box. As he squinted, lining up his picture, he noticed Paul's face. The boy's eyes were fixed on the camera. The only word for his expression was enthralled.

Fritzi stuck her tongue out at Carl, then giggled and pulled Paul's sleeve to say something. He paid no attention.

After they went inside for hot cocoa in the kitchen, Joe said, "Paul, please come along to the study. I've been meaning to speak to you all week. This is a good time."

Joe Crown's study was a small room on the first floor of the mansion. Here he often sequestered himself in the evening or on Sunday after church and dinner, dealing with brewery work he'd brought home or with family matters—discipline, advice, whatever was called for.

"Close the door, please, Paul. Sit down." Paul drew a chair close to the desk. Joe laid the boxy black Kodak on some papers. Winter sunshine flooded the room. It seemed to cause Paul to blink nervously. Before Joe was quite ready to begin, Paul spoke.

"Uncle Joe, how much did that cost?" He pointed to the camera.

Surprised, Joe said, "Do you want one?"

"Very much, someday, yes." Paul's English was still awkward, heavily accented, broken by frequent pauses and hesitations.

Joe picked up the camera. "Eastman's company offers several models now. This one cost exactly eight dollars and twenty cents. Save your pennies. Now—"

"I have another question, Uncle. Does anyone earn money from photographs?"

Joe thought about that. "Perhaps the printers who produce postal cards, or pictures for parlor stereoscopes."

"I mean—does anyone make money—pushing the button?"

"Ah. Taking pictures. No, I think not. Not a decent living, anyway. I've seen a few portrait galleries around town. Pretty shabby places." Paul frowned. "Shabby. Poor." Paul smiled, nodded. "This is a remarkable invention, but I can't see that it will ever be much more than a novelty. After all, how many family portraits or views of the Great Wall in China does one person want?"

He laid the camera aside, noting his nephew's look of disappointment.

"Paul, I must speak to you about two things, both related to your education. I have interviewed one man who can tutor you in English, and I will be interviewing another on Tuesday. I will then make a choice. Lessons here at home will be helpful, I think."

"Thank you, Uncle."

"Your aunt and I have discussed the subject of your welfare at great length. We feel"—*she* feels—"that you should enroll in public school. While your English is far from perfect—please don't misunderstand me, you've learned marvelously in a short time—I believe you're well enough prepared to understand classroom teaching, though at a lower level than your age would otherwise dictate. The tutor will help, too. Accordingly, we will start you in school as soon as possible."

"The same school as Fritzi and Carl's?"

"No, a different one, across town. I consulted with a friend of mine, George Hesselmeyer, who is on the Chicago Board of Education. There are several Germans on the Board. Hesselmeyer recommended this school because of its superior faculty."

"What kind of school is it?"

"*Volksschule.* Elementary school. But you will be in the highest grade. There you will find other boys and girls who—what's wrong?"

Paul's palms were pressed down tightly on the knees of his knickerbockers.

Pressed down so hard his knuckles were white. "Sir, I am not good with studies. I don't know why, but it's true."

"You dislike schoolwork?"

"Truly, sir—yes. The books—they are so dull. The schoolmasters also. I like to learn things about America. But freely, in the city. Walking, looking—"

"As your whim dictates, is that it?" Sunlight was falling on the right side of Joe Crown's face, paling it till it resembled white marble. He was no longer smiling.

He strengthened his voice, asserting his control. "I'm afraid you'll get nowhere in this world living by whim and caprice, Paul. You must be educated."

"I will teach myself, sir. Study hard alone—"

Sharply, Joe said, "You've never heard the old proverb?" He spoke it in German first. "He that teaches himself has a fool for a master." He waited. "You have something more to say?"

"Yes, sir. My cousin, Joe, he works in your brewery. Couldn't I?" There was a clear desperation in Paul's voice now.

"In a year or two, when we see how you've gotten along, that may be possible. I don't want to seem harsh, Paul, but you are living in my house, you are my responsibility, therefore I will decide. You will be enrolled."

Softly, Paul said, "Yes, sir." He was clearly defeated. The look on his face was one of utter dread.

Joe Crown started to churn inside. *Ilsa was wrong, he's not suited for it.* But he couldn't undercut his own authority by reversing himself, or seeming to vacillate. Husband and wife had to present a united front.

"It will be all right," Joe said, more gently. "You'll soon feel at home in school." Paul nodded bleakly.

"Thank you, Paul, that will be all."

Paul rose, replaced the chair and went out without a sound. Joe Crown laid a hand on the Kodak and sat there, frowning.

The boy is smart. Hundreds of men educate themselves. I did it successfully. I should have resisted Ilsa. I have a definite feeling, no good will come of this.

16

Paul

HE HATED THE VERY THOUGHT of school. But he felt warmly toward his aunt and uncle for all the care and consideration they'd shown him, and he didn't want to appear an ingrate. So he had surrendered to Uncle Joe. He'd do his best but he had little hope of success. For example, unlike his uncle, who thought the study of mathematics noble and important, Paul was poor at numbers; they didn't interest him, never would. Yes, the prospect of school was terrible indeed.

□ □ □ □

Every day Paul learned more about his cousins.

Carl's favorite sports were baseball, wrestling, and another unfamiliar game called football. They were sports in which Carl could pit his strength against other boys. He loved that. He was always wanting Paul to engage in a wrestling match in some forbidden place like the formal parlor. Occasionally Paul obliged. He was bigger than Carl, and stronger, but it was never a one-sided contest. Carl had amazing power in his chunky body.

Joe Junior was less competitive, more solitary. He liked things you could do alone. He made reference to swimming in Lake Michigan in the summer. Swimming far out, against towering waves, dangerous tides. He liked ice-skating, and went often to Lincoln Park any winter Sunday when he couldn't see his girl in the town of Pullman south of the city. Skating was hugely popular in Germany, but Paul had never learned; Aunt Lotte said they couldn't afford to squander money on skates.

Paul wished Joe Junior would invite him along some Sunday afternoon but he didn't. Probably his older cousin regarded him as some stupid little boy.

Fritzi was more openly emotional, about everything, than either male cousin. She sighed constantly. Often fell onto the furniture in a mock swoon, her wrist against her brow, which amused Aunt Ilsa. Paul thought it was silly.

Fritzi devoured novels, and books on the meaning of dreams, but her great passion was the stage. Actors, actresses, their world of canvas and powder and illusion. Fritzi said she attended the theater with her mother and, sometimes, with her father. She said her father didn't care for the theater much.

Fritzi pursued Paul relentlessly. Did he want to see her collection of theater programs? Her latest imitation? Did he want a description of the divine Edwin Booth? The maddeningly handsome James O'Neill, star of *The Count of Monte Cristo?* What about the fiery Polish actress, Helena Modjeska, or the great Eleonora Duse? Paul had never heard of any of the actors; he said so, but it didn't deter Fritzi.

And she had a way of embarrassing him at the dinner table. If he chanced to make some quite ordinary remark, and accompany it with a smile, Fritzi would fling herself back and laugh as if he were the cleverest person alive. No, it was more than a laugh. It was a shriek; a bray. It caused Aunt Ilsa to sigh and Uncle Joe to raise his silver brows and Joe Junior to growl, "Oh, grow up."

While Paul was awaiting news of his tutor, Carl revealed another side of himself. He came up to Paul on an unseasonably warm afternoon, as Paul was washing and polishing windows on the lower floor of the stable.

"Hello, Paul."

"Hello." That English word now came to his lips with relative ease.

"How is your watch?"

"My watch? Fine. It keeps excellent time."

"Do you want to see my watch?"

"Yes, all right."

"Papa and Mama gave it to me for Christmas, a year ago." Carl pulled it from his pants pocket. The gold-plated case gleamed in the sunshine.

"I dropped it in Lake Michigan last summer. Papa doesn't know. It stopped running so I fixed it. I like to take things apart and fix them. Want to see?"

Paul nodded.

Carl took out a small clasp knife. He inserted the tip under the tight-fitting back of the watchcase. He pried but the watch wouldn't open. Biting his lips, he kept prying. The cover flew back. A spring flew out.

Without a thought, Paul lunged for it. He caught the spring but nearly stepped in his bucket of wash water. When he handed Carl the spring, Carl said, "You're quick, you ought to play baseball."

Carl poked the watch innards with his knife. A tiny brass-colored gear fell onto the sere grass. Both boys got down on their knees to search. After several minutes Carl found the gear. He forced it into the case and snapped the back shut with a sheepish look. "Guess it needs more fixing."

Paul said nothing. Carl put the watch and the knife in his pocket. From the rear porch, Aunt Ilsa called him to come in and do his studies. Carl started away, then broke stride and glanced back.

"I like you, Paul."

He ran to the house. *There,* Paul thought, overjoyed. *That's two. One to go.*

One afternoon at the end of January, Paul sat in the kitchen with a cup of hot cocoa Louise had fixed for him. Aunt Ilsa was busily mixing rye flour, a little water, and some old hard pieces of pumpernickel to make her starter dough for a new batch. She paused in her work to ask Paul whether he had any hobbies. He didn't understand the word.

"Anything you especially like to do for enjoyment."

He said he liked to collect cards with photos of distant places on them.

"Ah, picture postcards. You'll find plenty of those in America. I expect you need a way to display them in your room."

She assigned Carl to help him find a smooth board in the cellar. Nicky Speers located a can of paint, a neutral gray, and a brush. Helga Blenkers helped Paul hang the freshly painted board in his room with hooks and wire. It was crude, but Aunt Ilsa said it looked nice.

With some pins she supplied, he carefully mounted the stereopticon card on the board. From her apron Aunt Ilsa produced a mint-new picture card showing mighty waves breaking on the shore of Lake Michigan. Paul pinned that up too.

Aunt Ilsa examined the wood globe and stand. She turned the stand over and discovered the inscription of its German maker. "Pauli, I have another suggestion. You realize you are a traveled young person now. Perhaps you should keep a sort of record here. A small mark for every important place you've seen."

He was enthusiastic, so out of the cellar came a second paint can, smaller, and a delicate brush. With his aunt watching, he put a tiny dot of dark red enamel on Berlin, then a dot on Hamburg, a third on New York, a fourth on Chicago.

"Ah, it looks fine," she said. "It doesn't detract at all from the beauty of the globe. There will be many more places marked as you go through life, fascinating places. I am sure of it." She hugged him.

He was melted by this latest outpouring of caring. For Aunt Ilsa—Uncle Joe, too—he would endure the sentence of school, even though it was sure to be hellish.

▫ ▫ ▫ ▫

There came trudging through five inches of snow, wearing a long threadbare coat with a fur collar and a soft brown hat with a drooping brim, Mr. W. E. Mars. Winston Elphinstone Mars, native of Genesee Depot, Wisconsin, the tutor.

Mr. Mars was in his thirties, and pale as a new snowdrift. He parted his inky black hair in the center, and spruced up his shabby clothes with odd bits of ornamentation. A flowing pocket kerchief of flame-red silk; a large sunflower made of several colors of felt. In his pocket he carried a slim book by a Mr. Wilde, whom he apparently idolized. Paul had never heard of Mr. Wilde.

Mr. Mars had been engaged to work with Paul in his room every afternoon from three until six. The tutor was a gentle and patient man; Paul liked him. He taught reading by putting into Paul's hand a book called *McGuffey's Fifth Eclectic Reader*, and he taught the devilish intricacies of English grammar with a slate and chalk.

The reader contained selections from the speeches and writings of noted orators, politicians, philosophers, and poets. Mr. Mars's instruction consisted of hours of patiently listening to Paul read aloud, slowly and laboriously, and gently correcting each mispronunciation. The tutor explained complicated words, but he didn't insist that Paul memorize anything.

"When you start school—probably in the second term, February—you will read aloud this way—drill this way. But you will also be forced to commit long word lists to memory. I try to be more progressive."

On Wednesday in the last week of January, Paul felt comfortable enough to engage Mr. Mars in a personal conversation, to find out whether teaching was all that he did.

"Oh, no, I have had many positions, though I think I am best at pedagogy. Some time ago I decided that my purpose on this earth is to experience the beautiful in life. Employment, food, the necessity to wash and dress each morning—all else is but the means to a sublime end."

Baffled, Paul said, "I'll read some more."

That evening, as Mr. Mars was putting on his overcoat and hat in the lower hall, Paul listened from the upper landing while the tutor spoke with Joe Junior. He referred to a "new age of truth and beauty."

"Hell," Joe Junior said, daringly, "the only new age we'll see is a new age of revolution in the streets."

"That is an ugly thought, young man. Only beautiful thoughts make life itself beautiful."

Joe Junior contradicted him by uttering another word, even more daring. Mr. Mars left in a huff, slamming the door. Joe Junior slapped his knee and laughed. How worldly his cousin was, Paul thought, leaning his cheek against the hard polished banister.

That same night, Uncle Joe called Paul to the study again. He stood in front of his uncle's chair, nervous, as he always was in this room.

"I have made a further decision about your schooling, Paul. Let me explain. Long before your aunt and I came to Chicago, Germans were building excellent private schools to educate their children. Those schools are still thriving. They are unquestionably better than the public schools in most respects. Still, I consider them elitist—*elite*, it's the same word in either language."

Paul nodded.

"A public school is more democratic. This family is American by choice, therefore Fritzi attends public school. Carl also. Joseph Junior attended one until we were forced to put him into private schools. With equal lack of success."

He was quiet a moment, his lips pursed. His hand fell away from the boar's tooth, which he'd been rubbing.

"Public schools in Chicago—I might say the whole country—badly need an overhaul. They teach almost no science, which is criminal in this age of industry and invention. They don't have physical training or sports programs. Nevertheless—your aunt agrees with me—it will be a public school for you."

Paul waited.

"Today I spoke by telephone with the principal of the school you will attend. He understands your situation, that you are a newcomer. He will see to it that you receive special attention, and are placed in the right class. Next Monday morning I will accompany you to school in our carriage—don't worry, I'll go no further than the office, to sign any necessary papers. After that, you will ride the streetcar to and from school." Uncle Joe paused. "Do you have anything to say?"

Resentment bubbled up in Paul. He felt his uncle had been discussing a choice between a gallows and a firing squad. He drew himself up tall and straight. Looked his uncle in the eye.

"I would rather not go, sir. I would rather work."

"I know that. But it's settled. Good night, Paul."

He had turned back to his desk before Paul reached the door.

Saturday night another snowstorm struck Chicago. It passed through swiftly, leaving half a foot of new snow on the sidewalks surrounding the Crown mansion. After Sunday morning church—which Joe Junior seemed free to skip, perhaps with parental consent—Paul, Carl, and Joe Junior dressed warmly and started shoveling the walks.

After a few minutes, Joe Junior leaned on his shovel and said to Paul, "Tomorrow's the big day, huh?" Joe Junior's vivid blue eyes sparkled in the sunshine. His smile was sardonic. "Don't tell me you're eager."

"No, no, I hate it." Paul's breath formed a plume as he spoke.

"So did I. I got out of it. You can too."

"I don't know how."

"Refuse."

Paul gnawed on his lower lip; it was raw and cracked from the cold weather. "I can't, I said I'd go."

"Damn shame. It isn't the real world. The rough and tumble. Teachers have got nothing to say that's worth a nickel. But I've got some friends at the brewery who could teach you plenty." With a glance at the windows of the house, panes of glass flashing back the sunlight, he growled it again. "Plenty. Put your mind to getting out of school and you will. Don't study. Act like a dunce when you recite. Raise a little hell—play tricks. Make the teacher hate you. I got out of three schools that way. You can do it, you seem pretty smart to me."

Paul searched his cousin's face. So far as he could tell, Joe Junior meant the compliment sincerely. Paul was thrilled to realize that his cousin wanted him for an ally—perhaps a friend eventually. Nothing would have made him happier, except for the price Joe Junior wanted him to pay.

"Joe—your mother, your father—they have been so kind. If I did what you say, they'd be sad. They'd be angry. I could not do it to them."

"That's how it is, huh?" Joe Junior's face twisted with contempt. "They've got you hornswoggled."

"Horn—? I don't understand horn—"

"Forget about it," Joe Junior said, walking away. He bent over an uncleared section of walk and began to shovel with quick, angry motions.

At the conclusion of supper on Sunday night, Aunt Ilsa rose from the table, smiling. "We have a surprise for you, Pauli."

She came out of the kitchen bearing a large plate with a *Zuckertüte*. A large horn of plenty, made of flaky pastry and crammed full of hard candies, cookies, walnuts that threatened to roll off the plate.

Aunt Ilsa set the plate in front of him. "You might consider yourself much too old for this, but it's an important tradition, the *Zuckertüte* for the first day of school. When you come home tomorrow afternoon, having completed your first day successfully, you may have everything you see here."

Uncle Joe smiled. Fritzi cried, "Hurrah!" Carl shouted, "Can I have one of the jawbreakers?" Joe Junior folded his arms and leaned back, silent. Paul was almost moved to tears. How could he rebel against people who were so kind to him?

Monday morning, gray as death. A freezing damp day. A few snowflakes drifting down. The carriage pulled up before the two-story school. It seemed huge, forbidding, an ugly hulk of bricks and granite. A prison, save for the absence of bars on the lighted windows.

Moments later, Paul and his uncle were moving up the worn wooden steps. They had been asked to come to the office an hour after the regular schoolday began. At the top of the steps, Paul looked over his shoulder at the quarter landau, the steaming muzzles of the bay horses, the drab empty street beckoning with a thousand imagined allurements . . .

His uncle's face intruded, the dark eyes intimidating behind the silver-wire spectacles.

"Go in, please," Uncle Joe said impatiently.

The principal, Mr. Relph, shook Paul's hand and said to Uncle Joe that, because the new pupil was undoubtedly not acclimated to America as yet, he should have every advantage, and would therefore be placed in the class taught by one of the school's finest, Mrs. Petigru. Uncle Joe said that sounded excellent. He wished Paul well and bade him goodbye.

Paul followed the principal down a musty, gloomy hall to a wooden door with a small pane of glass set in. In horror, Paul saw the pupils in the room. Many looked at least a year younger, and many were smaller; mere children. The principal opened the door; led him in.

"Mrs. Petigru, this is your new student, Paul Crown."

The principal left. Paul waited beside the teacher's desk. A dozen heads were turned in his direction. A dozen pairs of eyes scrutinized him. The room was an oven. With frost patterns on the windows, how could that be?

"Take your seat in the second row. The last desk. There." Mrs. Petigru pointed. She was a plain, drab woman with a heavy bosom, graying hair in a severe bun, a slit for a mouth. And a tongue like a whip.

She pointed downward with one chalk-dusty hand. Mortified, Paul saw melting slush forming pools under his shoes. "When you report tomorrow, make sure your feet are wiped before you enter. And comb your hair, you're a sight."

"Please, I combed it before—"

"Don't answer back, young man. If you answer back, you and I will have trouble." Her smile was chilly. "That's rule number one. Rule number two, I demand neatness from my pupils. You don't appear to live up to that standard, but you'll live up to it in my class. Sit quietly today. Don't speak unless you're addressed. Come to my desk at the end of the day and we will draw your books. That's all."

"Yes, ma'am," he said, as he'd often heard Carl say to his mother.

The day passed in a haze of misery. In the lunchroom, a few of the pupils from his class spoke to him, but no one sat with him. He had a table and bench to himself, among hundreds of staring eyes.

He rapidly ate two sausages, then pulled a hard-boiled egg from the sack Aunt Ilsa had packed personally. She had included a small glass salt cellar; Paul liked salt on his hard-cooked eggs. He had the egg halfway to his mouth when something stung his left ear and made him yelp.

Nearby, he heard giggles. He could only see the thin face of Mrs. Petigru, who had stolen up behind him and thwacked his ear.

"Look at the mess. Salt all over the floor." She leaned down. She smelled of mothballs, like Aunt Ilsa's closets. She banged the glass salt cellar on the table. "Take this home tonight and never bring it back."

She folded her arms and glanced sharply at some of her pupils at the next table. They quickly bowed their heads over their lunch sacks and pails.

"I'll be frank with you, Paul," the teacher said. "I did not want you brought into my class. I protested, and I was overruled. I'll tell you why I didn't want you. First, you are too old. Second, your uncle is a brewer, and he's German. I consider that a Satanic combination. I am a religious God-fearing woman. My husband Samuel is a lay preacher. We don't like godless Germans who profane the Sabbath with revelry and strong drink."

Paul couldn't endure it. His chin lifted. Anger danced in his eyes. "Mrs. Petigru—Germans go to church on Sunday. Only after do they enjoy a little glass of—"

"I distinctly told you not to answer back." Again that cold smile. "I have had other pupils who tried to get the better of me. They always lose."

17

Joe Crown

JOE CROWN dutifully noted that, during his nephew's first weeks at school, the boy was withdrawn, and much less prone to smile. Paul excused himself after *Abendessen* every night and disappeared to his room, presumably to study.

Several times, Joe made a point of asking Paul how he was getting along. The answer was always the same.

"Fine, Uncle."

Joe was soon suspicious. And when he looked into Paul's eyes, he saw something that hadn't been there before. A look that reminded him of a whipped dog. Shaken, he thought, *I had a premonition about this. Has it come true already?*

April arrived, brushing the city with warmth and sunshine; a foretaste of summer. At Joe's request, Mr. Mars was now coming to the house two nights a week. The tutor's obvious intelligence and devotion to his task had quite overcome Joe's initial aversion to Mars's glaring effeteness. Still, it seemed to Joe that the additional tutoring changed nothing.

Throughout Chicago, municipal crews were cleaning and watering the main thoroughfares regularly, to prepare for the opening of the Exposition on May 1. Old buildings were being repainted; parks had been reseeded and replanted with young trees. A festive mood seemed to prevail. But men in the business community knew that clouds were lowering. More banks were in trouble, whispering of possible closure. Prices of shares were sliding downward. Already there were hundreds of unemployed men adrift in the streets.

Although this disturbed Joe, little of it touched his household. Ilsa was cheerful and busy, looking forward to the opening day. One morning Joe came to the breakfast table to find her immersed as usual in her newspapers. After they kissed, he took his seat and he asked, "What are your plans today, my dear?"

With a teasing smile, she said, "Shall I tell you? What kind of a mood are you in?"

"Good enough to withstand anything. It looks like a lovely day."

"At noon I'll be dining with Ellen and Jane." Ellen Starr and Jane Addams, her friends from the Hull House settlement.

"This afternoon we're all attending a discussion program on prostitution and the double standard."

"I see." He didn't want to be annoyed with her, but he was. He saw no point in women upsetting the status quo by delving into radical or unsavory issues.

"By the way—" She reached for a newspaper. "I read in the *Inter-Ocean* that

Stead is coming to Chicago." Joe consulted his pocket watch and quickly poured more tea. "Mr. Stead, the English journalist. The reformer."

"I know who he is. Stead the busybody."

"Perhaps he can do some good in Chicago, Joe. You know this is one of the wickedest cities on earth. Gambling, thievery, murder—" She touched another of the papers in front of her. "Just last night, a young woman was fatally stabbed on State Street. No purse, no identification—and there are no clues to the killer. Is it any wonder we lead in the nation in the number of criminal arrests? Chicago is fearfully corrupt. The aldermen—what do they call them?"

"The gray wolves."

"Yes—well, they've all but published their prices for a vote, or a city franchise. Stead may do some good."

"I can certainly predict one of the first things he'll do. Condemn the saloons. Every self-appointed savior of mankind includes that in his program. We'll have the reformers after every brewery in town, wanting to close them down. Frankly, I wish you'd stay away from Miss Addams and Miss Starr, and especially that harpy Frances Willard."

"Joe, Mrs. Willard is a fine moral person. The Women's Christian Temperance Union advocates moderation, and there is nothing wrong with—"

"Oh yes, there is. Because first it will be moderation, then prohibition. The word has been bandied about before."

"I won't have you saying things about the W.C.T.U. that aren't true. The organization works in many social areas, worthy ones. Child labor. The welfare of unfortunate young women lured to the streets—I'm proud to contribute money to that effort."

"Money earned from beer sales, don't forget."

"Perhaps my activities can wash away some of the taint, then."

Joe flung his napkin down beside his plate. "Damn it, woman, that's uncalled for."

Contrite, Ilsa rushed around the table and threw her arms around his neck. "You're right, I'm sorry. I just don't want you to run over me, I have opinions of my own. But I have no right to be mean about it. Forgive me?"

"Always." He kissed her warm cheek, mollified.

In the carriage on his way to the brewery, instead of opening a folder of technical articles he'd torn out for quick scanning, he reflected on Ilsa's continuing dislike of his business. She certainly was not alone. And her attitude remained perfectly understandable in the light of what had happened to her father. Yet he continued to resent it. He especially resented it because the climb to his current prosperity had been long and difficult, and sometimes even physically dangerous.

Did she have any real sense of all he'd gone through to achieve success? He told her a lot about his daily affairs, and he had never lied to her. But he sometimes spared her feelings by keeping certain information to himself. For instance, to build Crown's, he had done much more than slave over formulations, ingredient price lists, sales ledgers, architect's blueprints, label designs, payroll books. In the early years he'd worked himself to complete physical exhaustion every day for months at a time. What's more, the brewing trade could be dangerous.

□ □ □ □

Going after anything worthwhile in life entailed risk, of course. A man of ambition and courage didn't let that stop or delay him. A man accepted the dangers, the element of chance. If he didn't, he won nothing.

But there *were* dangers. For example, brewery workers were routinely crippled by rheumatism, sometimes turned into living gargoyles, because they worked for years in dampness and cold.

During the first month of operation of the Crown bottle house, Joe and his foreman were trying to correct an equipment problem one morning, when suddenly a man reading a gauge shouted that pressure was shooting up too fast.

"Shut everything down," Joe screamed above the clank of the conveyors. At that moment, the first bottle burst. Ten more exploded, and another ten, shooting shards of glass everywhere. Joe was nearest the part of the line where the bottles were bursting. Had he not been wearing his spectacles he might have been blinded. As it was, both lenses were starred with cracks, and his exposed face was lacerated. The foreman was on his knees, a palm over his left eye, blood oozing between his fingers.

Weeks later, the foreman came back to work. He had a new glass eye that perfectly matched the other. Joe paid for everything.

Sometimes the hazards arose not from accidents, but were a consequence of human frailty, human avarice. When pasteurization and refrigeration made possible long-distance shipping of bottle and keg beer, Joe conceived a plan to market his product where there were many Germans but few breweries. South Carolina and Texas were among his first targets.

In Austin, shortly after he opened his third Texas agency, a saloon owner showed him a competitor's price sheet. Joe saw instantly that the numbers were ridiculous; no one could sell keg beer that cheaply. The owner shrugged off Joe's questions and insisted that he meet the sheet prices if he wanted the establishment to serve Crown's.

Joe asked to see the price sheet again. He studied it silently. Then he said he'd think about it, and asked if he could have the sheet. The owner didn't object. On the street in the hot dusty sunlight, Joe looked at his thumb. It was smudged with ink.

He made inquiries and passed money around in local print shops. No one was helpful. Finally, he found a printer in a dirty little shop on an alley, a man obviously hurting for business. Joe questioned him hard. The printer finally admitted it was he who had printed the sheet for the saloon owner the previous week. He confessed because Joe offered him half again as much money as he'd gotten for the original job.

So Joe's suspicions were right, the sheet didn't come from the competing brewery. He carried the sheet back to the saloon owner and told him to eat it.

The man shouted threats. "You're lucky I don't put the law on you," Joe said, and walked out. That night, someone fired three bullets through the flimsy door of his hotel room. Fortunately, at the time, he was sitting on the commode behind a door at the end of the hall, paying the price for eating the town's highly spiced food. He had never told Ilsa.

Just five years ago, he had gone to St. Louis, to call on Adolphus Busch. He wanted to buy six cars from Busch's subsidiary, the St. Louis Refrigerator Car Company. About fifty years old, Busch was two or three inches shorter than his guest, rather heavy around the middle, with long wavy hair and a mustache and goatee that gave him a distinguished air.

He received Joe in an opulent office in his mansion, known as Number One Busch Place. At first Busch was cordial. He recognized Joe as a shrewd and aggressive competitor. He said, yes, certainly, he'd be happy to sell the refrigerator cars at a friendly price. Then he rang for his butler, who brought a silver tray bearing delicate goblets and a bottle of Mr. Busch's fine French wine.

Joe drank some wine to be polite. Quietly, Busch proposed that the two of them agree on a fixed price for barrel beer in territories where they competed head to head. Joe politely said no.

Busch asked him twice more, with increasing petulance. His queerly hooded eyes lost all pretense of friendliness. After Joe's third refusal Busch stood up so violently, he knocked the silver tray off the desk. The bottle smashed, the fine wine gurgled away.

"You son of a bitch, I'll drive you down, you and all the other sanctimonious sons of bitches who haven't got the sense to throw in with me. Get out of my house, God damn it, right now. *Right now!*"

Joe had been a particular target of Busch's enmity ever since. Crown's was repeatedly attacked in selected districts with low prices that could only guarantee a loss for Busch. Joe's response was always the same. Drop his own prices slightly, and personally call on his accounts to reassure them and ask them to ride out the war. Busch always grew tired of selling his beer at a loss, and prices went up again. But Joe was never foolish enough to think that the king of St. Louis had forgotten, or ever would. It was just another hazard of the trade.

Though he and Ilsa had lived together many years, she didn't fully understand the price he paid for the family's comfort and happiness. The many prices . . .

"Mr. Crown? We are here."

Nicky Speers stood on the curb, holding the carriage door open. Joe saw the fountain, the statue of Gambrinus. "Sorry," he said, jolted out of his reverie. The folder of articles slid off his knee.

While he gathered them up, it struck him that alcohol was the only issue in their marriage that had never been resolved, only smoothed over, suppressed, a hundred times and more. It was the one issue with the power to divide them. The one issue that could threaten what they had worked together to build.

He left the carriage, no longer savoring the April sunshine or the balmy air. Ilsa was right, he needed to get away. He felt one of his dark moods coming on.

But he couldn't outrun the issue, it was forever there, a canker, a worm in the dark, gnawing. It didn't bode well. He tried not to think about that either.

18

Paul

SCHOOL WAS TORTURE. A repetitive, soul-deadening routine of recitation and memorization. Daily subjects included reading and literature, grammar and spelling, mathematics, and rudimentary science instruction. Mrs. Petigru loved to quote the science text *Our Bodies and How We Live*, which bore on its title page the words REVISED AND APPROVED BY OFFICIALS OF THE W.C.T.U. To Paul it seemed as though half the book was devoted to attacks on the harmful effects of tobacco and alcohol.

Drawing was included on two days each week. It consisted of copying illustrations from books onto a slate. Mrs. Petigru liked to stand at Paul's elbow, gazing down at the mess of white lines and cloudy-white erasures while she murmured, "Hopeless. Absolutely hopeless."

Paul's mathematics exercises consistently received a failing grade. Mrs. Petigru wrote notes all over his papers, disparaging the pencil smudges, his poor handwriting, the generally unsatisfactory nature of his work.

She badgered Paul about his appearance almost every day. Ordered him to straighten his shirt, tie his shoelace, comb his hair in the lavatory. "You are a sloppy boy. I noticed it the first time I saw you, and it immediately told me all I needed to know about your capabilities. Disorderly appearance—disorderly mind."

He had been struggling with the English of a Buffalo Bill dime novel each morning and afternoon on the streetcar. Mrs. Petigru saw it on his desk, snatched it up, reviled him for bringing trashy literature to school, and dropped it in a wastebasket.

And all because his uncle was a German brewer.

Reading exercises were similar to the ones he was doing with Mars. Pupils were called forward to read a passage from *McGuffey's Sixth*. One day the selection might be a passage from *Hamlet*, full of words impossible for him to understand or pronounce. ("Have they *heard* of Shakespeare in Germany, Paul?") It might be a rhythmic, eerie poem called *The Raven*. ("Speak up, Paul, have you lost your voice?") His turn came again with a famous speech to a Virginia convention made by the American patriot Patrick Henry. " 'The war is inev-inev—' "

"Inevitable," said Mrs. Petigru, with a soulful sigh of resignation. A nasty pupil named Maury Flugel tittered.

Paul struggled on syllable by syllable. " '—inevitable—and let it come. I repeat, sir, let it come. It is in vain, sir, to exten—uh—' "

"Extenuate. That word is pronounced ex-ten-u-ate. When are you going to learn, Paul? We're all hopeful it will be soon."

The whole class laughed.

Mrs. Elsie Petigru was his enemy. But he was unfamiliar with the ways of American schools, and didn't know what to do about it. Tell Uncle Joe? No, he didn't want his uncle immediately deciding that he fell short, unable to live up to the expectations of the family.

One morning at recess a boy from the class approached him shyly and asked him if he wanted to shoot marbles. Paul almost whooped for joy. He said he had no marbles of his own. The boy eagerly shared his sack. A bond was sealed.

The boy was Leo Rapoport. Short, round-faced, with black eyes and a funny lump of a nose. He was a full head shorter than Paul, but he seemed more like a little old man than a thirteen-year-old.

Leo had a kindly and merry disposition, Paul discovered. Yet, mysteriously, he too was an outcast. One day in the lunchroom he explained why:

"My pa's a Unitarian, but he was born a Jew. Mama's R.C."

"What?"

"Roman Catholic. Fish-eater. Papist." Leo was philosophical. "It's a pretty bad combination, a Unitarian and an R.C. It means you're liable to get beat up twice as hard, twice as often. Can't do much about it."

"Tell me more about your mother and father," Paul said.

"They sure aren't rich, like your uncle. Mama's a very high-class lady, though. She gives piano lessons."

"What does your father do?"

"He's a drummer."

"With a band?" Paul was excited.

Leo laughed. "Nah. Drummer means a peddler. Pa travels nine states. He sells ladies' corsets. Hot stuff." Leo rolled his eyes. "I could bring some pictures maybe."

"Yes, why not?"

Leo also had valuable advice:

"Don't ever make old Petigru mad. If that happens she takes her ruler out of the bottom drawer. It's this long—this thick. She uses it on your hands. Last October, on a dare, Dora Gustavson went into the boys' toilet and pulled her bloomers down. Someone snitched, I think it was Maury Flugel. Petigru used the ruler. Dora couldn't do her penmanship exercises for a week."

As the days grew longer, Paul hurried every Saturday to finish whatever jobs Aunt Ilsa asked him to do. Then, with her permission, he hopped on a car to explore the city. Sometimes Leo joined him. Leo had been born in Chicago. Indeed, he'd never been anywhere else, except to a beach in Indiana once for a summer picnic. Leo knew a lot about the city. If he didn't know something, Uncle Joe did. From them, and from his own sharp observations, Paul was getting an education about the history and character of a great metropolis.

Che-cau-go was an old name, he learned. Nobody was sure of what it meant. It might have meant "wild onion," it might have meant "bad stink." Over the years, as a village grew up around an early trading station on the prairie beside the lake, and a town followed the village, and then a sprawling city, a profusion of somewhat more relevant names followed. There was Slab Town, because of all the slab-sided wooden buildings, and the Garden City, because of the passion of early residents for laying out spacious homesites and planting trees and pretty shrubs and flowers. There was Porkopolis, because of meat packing, and Gem of the Prairie, no explanation needed. But for all its modernity, little more than a generation ago Indians had walked the street. It made Paul's hair prickle to think of standing where red men had trod.

Almost a million people crowded Chicago now. There was no sign of the growth stopping or slowing down, and there wasn't even a trace of the great fire of 1871 that had razed the business district, gutted four square miles, done over $200,000,000 in damage, driven more than one hundred thousand from their homes, left two hundred and fifty dead, and certainly many more dead but uncounted in charred hovels and incinerated buildings. Uncle Joe and many other Chicagoans spoke of events in the past in terms of "before the fire" or "after the fire."

Chicago had started to rebuild almost immediately after the fire. Buildings in progressive new styles now rose everywhere. A railway elevated above the street ran to the South and West sides, and plans were being drawn to bring it to the center of town. This downtown was a pandemonium of buggies, wagons, cable cars, horsecars, and pedestrians, all hurrying madly all the time. There was no significant shade for the teeming streets, only telegraph and telephone wires casting meager shadows, but there were thriving theaters, and large stores like Field's, and Elstree's. There were splendid hostelries, like Mr. Potter Palmer's internationally famous eight-story Palmer House on State Street, destroyed twice and rebuilt more splendidly each time.

Chicago had landmarks. Old ones, like the Water Tower north of the river, which the fire had spared; new ones, like the ten-story Auditorium Building at Michigan and Congress, where the symphony orchestra performed. It had many solid residential areas—neighborhoods of Irish and Bohemians, Poles and Scandinavians, and of course Germans, who predominated on the *Nordseite*, where the Crowns had moved first when they left Cincinnati. There were also slums, and disreputable areas ruled by a criminal element. One of the worst was the Levee, centered down at Twenty-second and Dearborn. Paul stayed out of those districts.

There were fine areas of mansions belonging to the newly rich—you couldn't find many old rich in a city so young—and it was in one of these, lower Michigan Avenue, that the Crowns lived. The most prestigious address, however, was Prairie Avenue, down around Eighteenth Street. Here lived the Pullmans, the Fields, the Armours. Aunt Ilsa told Paul that some Prairie Avenue residents called Potter Palmer a traitor for moving away and building his present castle on North Lake Shore Drive.

Chicago was a forest of advertising signs. A thousand saloons displayed the universal emblem, a foaming beer stein. Some of these signs bore the Crown insignia, and the name. Paul was able to inform Leo that his Uncle Joe supplied the signs free if the establishment carried the brewery's product exclusively.

Chicago was at all hours a raucous choir of street vendors. Pushcart men sold pins and pears, little girls sold matches, little boys sold papers, older girls sold hot ears of corn from tin boxes, and perhaps, Leo hinted, perhaps they sold themselves. The streets resounded with the chant of the old clothes man who wore six coats and a teetering stack of ten hats; the squeal and shriek of the scissor grinder's wheel spitting sparks like a firework; the bellow of the newsboy hawking something called an extra; the clank of the cart of the rag-and-bottle man. No section, even Michigan and Prairie avenues, was without a daily horde of peddlers.

There were silent vendors as well, sickly sallow creatures who wore gaudy placards strapped on, front and back, and shuffled with slow exhausted steps from block to block. Sandwich men, Cousin Carl called them when one of them passed the house. At supper the family discussed sandwich men. Uncle Joe said they were the lowest of the street sellers; the dregs. Joe Junior called them "the downtrodden," with a look at his father.

Chicago was a pall of coal smoke, a wind reeking of raw meat, a miasma of floating river garbage made all the worse by the stench of human and animal waste. Chicago was noise, dirt, poverty, bright lights, an exciting vigor, a sharp sense of danger. It reminded him greatly of Berlin, and despite the horrors of school, he fell in love with it.

Leo Rapoport had a dog, Flash. A tan mongrel with scraggly short hair. Sometimes Flash was waiting for Leo when the last bell rang, and sometimes he followed him to school in the morning. One day in April, Paul sat on the concrete wall waiting for Leo as he now did every day. He saw Leo coming briskly along the sidewalk with Flash romping at his heels.

"I don't know what's wrong with him today, Paul, he's acting up. Maybe it's spring. Go home, Flash. Flash, go."

Flash ignored the command.

Reluctantly, Leo and Paul headed for the building. Somehow Leo didn't close the door quickly enough, and Flash darted inside. He ran up the wooden stairs to the first floor, his claws tick-ticking on the worn yellow-brown wood. Students hurrying to their rooms laughed and pointed.

"Flash, go home," Leo exclaimed with a dramatic gesture toward the stairs. But Flash's antics amused him, the dog capering and leaping and pretending to a ferocious growl. Leo started to giggle. He kept pointing and demanding that Flash go home, but made no effort to catch him. Soon Leo and Paul were both laughing, inexplicably convulsed by the diversion.

Suddenly a classroom door opened with a bang.

"In the name of heaven, what is going on out here? Whose beast is this?" Mrs. Petigru demanded.

Flash barked.

She kicked him. Paul detected a change in Flash's growl. It was distinctly rancorous.

Flash crouched with his head near the floor. Mrs. Petigru tried to kick him again. Flash snarled, snapped, seized the hem of her skirt in his teeth. There was a loud *rrrip* of fabric.

"Oh, look at that, *look!*" Mrs. Petigru exclaimed. Leo fell against the wall, hanging onto Paul, laughing helplessly. Mrs. Petigru's face contorted. She grabbed Leo's ear and twisted. Leo stopped laughing, and let out a howl.

"You nasty little mongrel, is this dog yours? Someone get the principal at once."

Transformed, Flash was baring his teeth and growling low as he slowly circled Mrs. Petigru. Paul tried to straighten up and stop laughing. He let out a last, rather weak guffaw.

"You, you're just as bad," Mrs. Petigru cried. Her hand shot to Paul's ear. "I have no more patience with you." She twisted. "None!"

Paul heard doom in her voice. Their relationship had taken a new, dire turn.

Mr. Relph and a male teacher managed to corner Flash and drive him down the stair and out. Leo ran along calling, "Good boy, good Flash, go," in a quavering voice.

The principal telephoned Leo's mother and Paul's uncle that afternoon. After school, Mr. Mars was sympathetic to Paul's plight, but could offer no advice beyond, "Tell the truth, it's the honorable way."

Uncle Joe didn't arrive home at his usual time. This prolonged Paul's suffering. Finally, Uncle Joe stomped into the house at twenty past nine, apologizing to Aunt Ilsa and pleading difficulties at the brewery. He looked grim.

"We've kept supper warm, Joe."

"First Paul will come with me to the study."

Once there, his uncle's charge was simple. "Explain yourself."

Paul did his best. He said that Flash was his friend's dog, that he'd been frisky and ran past them into the building by accident, and the two of them had just gotten carried away, laughing. "I know that it was wrong. I am sorry."

"That's all you can offer in your own defense, sorry?" Uncle Joe scowled. "I'm sorely disappointed in you, Paul."

Paul hated the feeling of having let down this powerful man who had been so kind to him. He mustn't confirm his guilt with complete silence. "Sir, may I tell you something?"

Uncle Joe's reply was a curt nod.

"I do not think it was so bad, not so terrible, except for Flash tearing her dress. Mrs. Petigru is not a nice woman. She—" He swallowed. "She may be a good teacher, but a nice woman, no. She doesn't like Germans. She doesn't like beer." Uncle Joe leaned back in his chair, startled.

"She doesn't like me, either," Paul went on. "She punished me by twisting my ear so hard I thought it might bleed. That is the truth, Uncle."

"Well, even the principal said your teacher was a strict disciplinarian. Strict is all right, cruel isn't."

Uncle Joe fixed him with a stare that left no doubt about who was in control.

"This time we'll wipe the slate clean. I can see that perhaps it had a funny side to it." He raised a cautionary finger. "But you were wrong to rebel—laugh at the teacher's discomfort. Don't do it again. You're in America now. Ways are different. It's your duty and responsibility to fit in. Let's have supper."

Uncle Joe left the room first. Paul followed him, no longer hungry. He'd disappointed his uncle after all.

On Saturday morning two weeks before the great opening day of the Exposition, a knock at the door dragged Paul out of bed at half past five in the morning. He stumbled to the door and was surprised to find Joe Junior there, already dressed.

His cousin shut the door and leaned back with an amiable smile. "Been meaning to tell you, I think it's great that you got your teacher's goat the way you did."

Paul was flustered. "Thank you."

"Ragged her good, did you?"

"I would say so. Definitely." He was delighted by his cousin's interest and approval.

"What are you doing this afternoon?"

"Pete has work for me outside, I'm not sure how much."

"Tell him you can't do it today. Make it up tomorrow. The brewery closes at noon for a warehouse inventory. Meet me there and I'll show you a few sights. Little corners of Chicago you'll never find on your own." He winked.

Paul was speechless.

Assuming a vaguely fatherly air, Joe Junior crossed his arms. "Well, old man, what about it? Will you come?"

"Of course. Sure."

"Swell." Joe Junior dodged out the door and hurried off down the hall.

Paul found his cousin piling up sacks of hops on the brewery loading dock. The spring afternoon was mild and clear, with a pleasant breeze blowing out of the south. Unfortunately such breezes always picked up the stink of sewer waste and garbage in the Chicago River. Paul could even smell the cattle, hogs, and sheep in the Union Stock Yards, miles away.

"Just about ready," Joe Junior said, heaving the last sack onto his shoulder. He carried it inside and returned. "There's someone I want you to meet." He shouted something into the gloomy warehouse.

In a moment a burly bald fellow walked out. He was an impressive, not to say forbidding, man with huge shoulders, a shining pate, glittering eyes.

"Benno, say hello to my cousin Paul Crown. Paul, this is Benno Strauss."

Paul's skin prickled. The infamous Benno. He'd heard Uncle Joe rail against him at the dinner table. Benno Strauss led the socialist-anarchist faction at the brewery.

Benno shook Paul's hand. Paul's grip was strong but Benno's was mighty. To Joe Junior, Benno said, "This the one?" Benno's English was guttural, rough.

"Right, this is him."

Benno regarded Paul with a long, speculative gaze. It wasn't friendly. Finally he said, "Okay."

Paul was mystified. The cousins started for the steps leading down from the dock. Benno said, "You getting much out in Pullman, Joey?"

Joe Junior grinned. "Plenty."

At last Benno smiled. He had large irregular white teeth. Paul thought of a tiger he'd seen in the Berlin zoo. "Well, I am going to visit a couple of young ladies this afternoon. *Huren,* but clean. I thought maybe you want to come along. Me, I like to see the workers getting what they need."

"Thanks, got other things to do," Joe Junior said. "Come on, Paul."

Benno pulled at his crotch. He looked at Paul without a smile.

"Teach him good," he said to Joe Junior as they left.

Paul had never expected to visit a place as lonely and sad as a graveyard, but that's where Joe Junior took him after they drank some beer and ate the free lunch in a saloon on Clark Street, then walked south to Harrison Street, west to Desplaines Avenue, and through a gate. "What is the name of this place?" Paul asked as they walked along a winding road between marble monuments.

"German Waldheim Cemetery. The fancy, respectable cemeteries wouldn't bury a lot of dirty immigrants, so this one was started. What I want to show you is over there, beyond the chapel."

He strode across the bright spring grass and around the cream-colored chapel to an elaborate monument of impressive size. A male figure—a workingman, Paul surmised—reclined in a pose that suggested death, while a female in a robe and cowl reached behind her to place a wreath on his brow; at the same time the woman seemed to be striding forward defiantly. A date, 1887, was carved into the monument and, at the base, a legend.

THE DAY WILL COME WHEN OUR SILENCE WILL BE MORE
POWERFUL THAN THE VOICES YOU ARE THROTTLING TODAY

There were many bunches of flowers at the foot of the memorial. Some were withered, others fresh. Joe Junior locked his hands behind his back and gazed at the sculpted figures with an intense, almost reverent expression. Sunlight falling through newly budded trees threw a pattern of light and shadow on his face.

"Paul, you have to promise me something. Promise not to mention this place when we get home."

"Of course, but why?"

"Because Papa would kill both of us."

"Then why are we here?"

Joe smacked a fist into his palm. "Because somebody's got to teach you. Just like Benno said." There was blue fire in his eyes. "This is the Haymarket memorial. The woman with the wreath is Justice. Which is something the martyrs never got, except here."

"But what is the Haymarket? Who are the martyrs?"

Joe Junior pointed to the base of the monument. "Sit down."

The Haymarket (Joe Junior said) is a big public square north of here on Randolph Street, between Desplaines Avenue and Halsted Street. Randolph widens there, so it's always been a good place for farmers to bring their fruit and vegetables and set up an open-air market. The Haymarket is the place this terrible crime happened.

Chicago had been boiling with labor trouble for years. Then, in 1886, February, it exploded. The men at McCormick's reaper factory walked out. All they wanted was fair pay and the eight-hour day. McCormick said go to hell, and started hiring new workers, scabs.

Workers at other companies struck, even some at Pullman had the guts to go out. For a few weeks everybody thought the factory bosses would be smart, put in the eight-hour day, end the trouble. Benno admits he was telling audiences at rallies that by May day, the great workers' holiday when all the red flags wave, red for the blood of the downtrodden, the eight-hour day would be the rule.

I wasn't there for any of this, you understand, I was still little; I heard all about it from Benno. He was working at McCormick's then. He was one of the strikers.

The first of May came and the strike was still on. The leaders called a meeting out on Black Road, close to the McCormick plant. Four or five thousand showed up, pretty angry after three months with no job, no pay envelope, no food for their little ones. The speakers worked them up as usual. Benno spoke that afternoon. He didn't expect it would get out of hand, the speakers were just supposed to whip up the workers so their nerve wouldn't buckle. But it did get out of hand. The quitting bell rang at McCormick's, the gates opened, and a sea of scabs started to flow out. The strikers went wild. They ran like the wind and surrounded the plant, driving the scabs back inside, sending the plant guards to the gun cases.

The police showed up in patrol wagons, and on horseback. Even so, the crowd wouldn't disperse. Benno and some others rallied them for another run at the gate. The workers beat on the gates and screamed for the blood of the scabs. The guards opened fire through slits in the wall. The police closed in behind. Six strikers were shot and killed. The mob broke and ran. That riot was over.

August Spies was editor of the labor paper *Arbeiter Zeitung*. Most of the strikers, in fact most of the workers in Chicago, were German, and still are. They read papers and listened to speakers in their own language.

The day after the McCormick riot, Spies printed pamphlets and wrote an editorial. The message in both was the same. "Take arms! Protect yourselves!"

A protest meeting was called for Tuesday night, May 4, in Haymarket Square. About dusk, people began to gather. The sky was dark, a lot of clouds, thunder muttering, like God knew what was going to happen and was setting the stage. Soon there were about a thousand in the square. A block away, in the Desplaines Avenue station house, companies of police were strapping on revolvers and polishing their extralong billy sticks made out of hickory.

Before the meeting started, the crowd had to shift out of the square, move north, squeeze into Desplaines Avenue to find a platform for the speakers. All they could find was an empty produce wagon. August Spies spoke standing in the open bed, under a sky ready to rain down buckets. Lightning was flashing and flickering, Benno said. He was near the wagon.

Albert Parsons spoke next. A good man, the son of a general who fought on the Reb side in the war. Then came Sam Fielden, an Englishman, a Methodist, and devout, they say.

Mayor Harrison was on the fringe of the crowd; he had plenty of nerve, old Carter. He decided there wasn't any problem, any danger—any need for the police to march on the listeners—this came out later. He went to the precinct house and said so. One police officer had other ideas. Inspector John Bonfield. He hated unions. He took over.

He ordered his men out. They formed in a column and came marching up Desplaines, long billy clubs swinging, hands on their revolvers. They met the crowd and pushed, squeezing people closer and closer together. Rain was pattering down. Still nothing happened.

A police captain shouted an order for the crowd to break up. From the wagon Fielden shouted that they wouldn't, the meeting was peaceable, violating no law. A great big roar went up, and just then someone threw the bomb with the lighted fuse over the heads of the crowd. No one knows to this day who threw it, or from where.

The bomb exploded at the head of the police column. Seven officers died, sixteen were hurt. The police broke ranks, crouching to shoot, wading in with swinging clubs. The rain pelted down. God flashed the lightning every other second, Benno said, and the coppers showed no mercy. The riot was over in five minutes.

It was a crime, that bomb, I wouldn't deny it. But what followed was a worse crime.

The next day Albert Spies and his assistant editor, Schwab, were arrested. Parsons surrendered. Fielden was arrested, along with four more suspects—a carpenter, a printer, a house painter, and a beer wagon teamster, like Benno became later.

The trial was a circus. The police couldn't offer even one piece of evidence to prove that one of the eight men had thrown the bomb, that one of them had made it, or any of them had touched it, or knew anything about it. They were guilty because they'd made speeches, at the Haymarket and before. They'd given the bomber the *idea*. Stirred him up—drove him to the brink. For that, the prosecutor, Mills, wanted the death penalty.

Each defendant made a closing statement for himself. Parsons praised the justice and fairness of bombs and dynamite. He said they were equalizers. He also claimed the jury had been threatened, even bribed. Didn't do any good, minds were already made up, the eight had been tried and convicted in the papers. After the verdict, Judge Gray sentenced seven of them to hang. Neebe, the beer wagon teamster, got fifteen years.

It took a long while for the wheels to grind but finally, in November '87, they hanged Spies. They hanged Parsons. They hanged Fischer, the printer, and Engle, the house painter. Louie Lingg, the man from the carpenters' union, he beat them. Someone smuggled a dynamite cap into his cell before the hanging. He put it in his teeth and bit it and blew his own head off.

That left two condemned men, Schwab and Sam Fielden. The governor had had enough; he commuted their sentences. The city was still wild with fear. Businessmen kept cleaning out the gun shops. A bunch of rich people donated six hundred acres on the lake shore to the U.S. Government, trading the land for a promise that the government would put soldiers there to protect the plutocrats from bombers. That's why we've got Fort Sheridan.

Nothing much has changed in six years. Mrs. Parsons, the widow, she tries to speak about the trial, the injustice of it. Every time there's a meeting with Mrs.

Parsons on the program, the police arrest her the minute she steps to the podium. Disorderly conduct. The plutocrats can't stand hearing the truth about what they did, or what they are.

John P. Altgeld always thought the trial was a farce, the hangings a scandal. He wants to pardon the two men left in jail. So a lot of people want to lynch him, just like they lynched Parsons and the rest. My own father hates the idea of a pardon for those two men. Even pardons won't make a difference. It's too late. There's a score to be settled.

"And you thought we had free speech, didn't you?" Joe Junior thrust his hands in the pockets of his pants, standing in front of Paul with legs apart; a position of power, authority.

"There's another monument to the Haymarket, up in the square. A bronze statue of a noble Chicago copper with his hand raised. I'll be damned if I'll show you that, you'll have to see it on your own. Let's go." Grim-faced, Joe Junior wheeled away. He strode rapidly toward the winding road, in and out of sun and shadow. Paul ran after him.

Just outside the cemetery's iron gates, Joe Junior grabbed Paul by the shoulders. "Remember, not a damn word. Can I trust you to keep quiet?"

"Yes, Joe."

"About everything you see, everything I tell you?"

"Yes, absolutely. But I still do not fully understand—"

"Because Mr. Joseph E. Crown, Esquire, is a damn capitalist, that's why."

"Is that bad?"

"*Bad?*" Joe Junior guffawed. "Everything Pop believes in—everything important—is wrong. For instance—there's no union at the brewery. Unions protect the rights of workers, but Pop's dead against them."

Paul was silent. He didn't want to endanger the tenuous camaraderie between them. Yet he was confused and even a little angered by Joe Junior's animosity toward Uncle Joe. He decided he had to say something.

"Joe, you are very smart, I'm not so smart. But I would say that if your father believes in wrong things, those wrong things have certainly built a fine house, a fine life for everyone."

"Listen, kid. What we've got on Michigan Avenue is show. A lot of trappings bought with the sweat of poor workingmen who spend their whole lives in dirt and poverty just so men like Pop can wear fancy suits and live in big houses."

"Yes, I know about poor men, poor districts, in Berlin I lived in one. But—"

"I'm talking about *here*. Right here in Chicago." Joe Junior grabbed him by the arm. "I'll show you."

They went to a section Joe Junior called the Nineteenth Ward, on the same West Side. It was a district of narrow crowded streets, small dingy shops, ramshackle cottages, each with its wooden box of ashes and refuse out in front. The cottage yards were tiny. Half-naked children played in the bare dirt.

The sidewalks were worm-eaten planking broken through in place after place. Side streets were dried mud, unpaved. Down one of them, Paul saw pushcarts, heard the peddlers shouting, the shrill housewives haggling. Horse and dog dung and decaying garbage fouled the air. He had seen slums in Berlin, but this one was worse.

"Working people," Joe Junior said, waving at open windows where torn lace curtains blew. "Forced to live like this. Any system that allows it is rotten, ready to fall, it—oh, my God."

"What is it? What's wrong?" Joe Junior had blanched and stepped back abruptly.

"Hymies," Joe Junior whispered, pointing to the next corner. Paul counted five good-sized boys arguing among themselves. They carried ball bats and bottles.

"What did you call them?"

"The Hymies. It's a gang. One of the worst. The old peddlers around here are always getting beaten up and robbed because they're Jews, so the gang goes out and gives it to anybody they find, for revenge. Now before they spot us, let's turn around and walk slowly to—oh, Jesus. Too late. Run!"

He spun and dashed away. Paul ran after him as yells and oaths came from behind. In a moment Paul risked a look. The gang boys were chasing them full tilt. One, dark-haired and leading the rest, bowled into a shabby old man in the street, knocking him down. No one stopped.

Joe Junior darted across the street in front of an ice wagon. The horse reared and whinnied. The driver whipped it furiously and screamed curses at the cousins. Arms pumping, Paul looked back a second time. The gang leader was grinning. He knew they were catching up.

"Here, this way!" Joe Junior hauled him into a narrow passage with shanties on the left, a board fence on the right. He groaned when he saw a pushcart blocking the other end of the passage, at the next street.

Paul spied something and dug in his heels.

"Joe, grab that barrel. Pull it over here."

"Why the hell—?"

"Do it, do it, then climb up!"

They manhandled the old barrel under the low eave of a deserted shanty with a peaked roof. Joe Junior scrambled onto the barrel, then to the roof, with Paul right behind. Paul pushed his cousin up and over the peak to the sloping side away from the passage. They lay on their bellies with their faces against tarpaper shingles. The gang poured into the passage, laughing and yelling. Suddenly, making a low strangled sound in his throat, Joe began to slide.

Paul flung his left hand over the roof peak and grabbed Joe with his right. Joe slid halfway down, his legs dangling below the eave. Paul ground his teeth together, sweating and wincing against the pain in his shoulder and arm. Out of sight in the passage on the other side, the gang was angry. *"What's going on?" "Where'n hell are they?"*

"I'm slipping," Joe Junior whispered. His weight threatened to tear both of them off the roof.

"Hang on," Paul whispered back. "If we fall they'll hear and that's the end."

"But—"

"Be *quiet.*"

"They must be runnin' like the wind, the little bastards," one of the gang yelled. "Come on, let's keep going. When we catch 'em we'll skin 'em."

Paul couldn't hold his cousin any longer. He let go and Joe Junior slid off the roof, landing with a crash in a pile of discarded chicken crates.

Paul dragged himself back to the peak. At the end of the passage, he saw the gang tip the pushcart over and pummel the helpless man who owned it. Then they ran on, out of sight.

Shaking and short of breath, Paul climbed over the peak and slid down the roof, landing in the passage. Joe Junior staggered into sight around a corner of the shanty, picking chicken feathers from his hair.

"Your plan saved the bacon," he said. Another expression that mystified Paul. "I confess it, I'm not quick enough to come up with something like that."

"Joe, excuse me, I think we should stop talking and get out of here while we can."

"Right. Good thinking."

They hurried out of the passage the way they had come in. Paul was still trembling from their narrow escape. But it had won something for him, something he wanted badly. Joe Junior's admiration; the beginning of a friendship.

They rode a horsecar toward the downtown. Relaxing on the hard wicker seats, bathed in the warm spring air blowing through the window, Paul risked another important question.

"Do you really not like your father? Aren't you proud of him? He has done well in America."

Joe Junior put his elbow on the window sill. Shadows of telephone poles flitted over his face. "Sure, he's done well—according to his rich pals."

"But, Joe, he came over here by himself, then he fought for the slaves and Abraham Lincoln. Aunt Lotte told me."

"I know he did. I know all about it. But after the war, he changed!"

Joe Junior turned toward his cousin, intense. "Joe Crown is what they call an exploiter. He exploits the working class. Takes advantage of them for gain. Hell, he'd exploit me the rest of my life if I let him. He'd bury me in the brewery in a collar and fancy cravat. Think I want to be like him? Run that God damn place after he's gone? No, sir. Never." He smacked the window sill.

After they crossed the West Branch of the river they left the rattling car. On Adams Street at LaSalle, Joe Junior walked him past an unusual nine-story building, the headquarters of the Home Insurance Company.

"This is a pretty amazing building. It was put up five or six years ago—first of its kind. There's a steel-beam skeleton inside. It bears most of the load. That means the outside walls don't have to be so heavy. If a building is constructed that way, it can go up to twenty, maybe even thirty stories. They call them skyscrapers."

"*Wolkenkratzer.* I heard the word in Berlin. They came from Chicago?"

"Right."

"Who paid for this amazing building, plutocrats?"

Joe Junior laughed and punched Paul's shoulder. "Score one for you, kid.

Listen, I can love Chicago and still hate the leeches and parasites who live here, I guess."

They strolled along through the crowds, enjoying the sunshine. Paul thought about his cousin and Uncle Joe. He had a curious feeling that maybe Joe Junior wasn't telling the entire truth. Maybe he did admire his father—or had at one time—but couldn't admit it anymore. *What do you suppose caused such a terrible rift? Was it really just those evil capitalist-plutocrats?*

"Blast," Joe Junior said, stopping suddenly. "Broke my shoelace." He looked down the street. "I can buy a new pair in Elstree's."

He took Paul into an elegant four-story building on the corner of Adams and State. He bought laces at the notions counter, handing his five cents to a large lady who gave the boys a hard stare. In dusty clothes, exuding a powerful aroma of sweat, they hardly looked like typical customers of such a fine, well-lighted emporium. The clerk motioned to a floorwalker, who followed Joe and Paul to the State Street entrance.

"Elstree's started here, it's a Chicago family," Joe Junior said, speaking loudly to be heard above the clang of bells on horsecars and the general racket of the street. "Now they're in New York, San Francisco, I don't know where else. Last year there was a big scandal when the store sold some women's coats and two customers died. Turned out the coats were sewn in a sweatshop infected with smallpox. No one prosecuted the Elstrees, naturally. That's what I mean by exploiting poor people."

"Yes, I see. How do you know such things?"

"Oh, certain people keep track, don't worry."

Joe Junior consulted a clock in a jeweler's window. "Hey, it's half past four. Come on, we'll hop a cable car down to Fifteenth and walk over to Prairie. After what we went through this afternoon, I'd say we deserve a peek at heaven."

"What are you talking about now?"

"Someone really special. I'll introduce you."

Paul asked who it was but his cousin was already running into the street, narrowly avoiding a speeding cycle with an enormous front wheel. The man perched on the high seat veered and nearly ran down two pedestrians.

On quiet and shady Prairie Avenue, in a district of homes even larger and more splendid than the Crowns', Joe Junior loitered by a hydrant near the corner of Fifteenth Street. "Our neighborhood's okay, but this one is the real swank. Even though old man Palmer moved up to North Lake Shore Drive, there are still plenty of millionaires left."

He pointed to the mansion across the way. "That place belongs to Mr. Mason Putnam Vanderhoff III. Pork Vanderhoff, the packer. We aren't waiting for him, we're waiting for his daughter. Her name's Juliette. She plays lawn tennis at three o'clock every Saturday if the weather's warm."

"I thought your girl's name was Rosie."

"It is. Julie's my friend. She's also the most beautiful creature you ever laid eyes on."

"And you meet her out here?"

"Have to, old Pork hates foreigners, and Pop especially. Not sure why. Mrs.

Vanderhoff's on some committee of women for the Exposition, but she kept Mama off. She won't speak to Mama."

"Then how do you know this girl?"

"I met her last winter, at the public ice skating in Lincoln Park. We—hold on."

He dodged behind the trunk of a sycamore, which was hardly wide enough to conceal a fence rail. From the north, clipping along down Prairie, came a small driving wagon, shiny and black, with no top and a cut-down front for easy entrance. The driver was a young woman in a smart tennis dress, white linen with a narrow red stripe and great puffy leg-o'-mutton sleeves. She wore a vivid scarlet flannel tam at a rakish angle.

As the stylish little vehicle approached, the wind snapped the young woman's skirt and Paul caught an arousing glimpse of black stockings above pointed white linen oxfords. He noticed a tennis racquet on the seat beside her.

Joe Junior jumped from behind the sycamore, stuck his two little fingers in his mouth and blew a piercing whistle.

"Julie. Over here."

The girl swung the pony to the near side of the street and reined to a stop, raising dust. "Why, Joey Crown, what a nice surprise." She flashed him a smile. Paul hoped he wasn't gawking. He'd never been in the presence of anyone so supremely rich before. In Berlin, tennis was a game enjoyed only by a small segment of the elite. He supposed that was also true in America.

"Just in the neighborhood," his cousin said. "Thought I'd say hello. You going to skate again next winter?"

"Of course, are you?"

"Wouldn't miss it. How was your tennis game?"

"Fine, but I got very tired after two sets. Mama says that's to be expected if you're a girl, but I wish it weren't so."

Now she was gazing at Paul, who stood in his cousin's shadow, entranced by the girl's striking looks. Miss Vanderhoff was about his age, and rather slightly built, with delicate fair skin and large luminous gray eyes. Her inky black hair beneath the scarlet tam was thick and shiny. She had fine even teeth, and, more important, her smile seemed warm and natural.

Joe Junior noticed the looks passing between the two of them. "Oh, 'scuse me." He executed a little bow that made her laugh. "Madam, may I introduce my cousin, Paul Crown? Paul, Miss Juliette Vanderhoff. Paul's been living with us since Christmas. He's from Germany. Guess he qualifies as a greenhorn." There was the slightest pause. "He's okay."

"How do you do, Paul?" The girl was reaching down to shake hands. He tingled at the cool dry touch of her fingers. He had trouble collecting himself to answer.

"Very fine, thanks." His voice sounded like a frog's croak. Mortifying.

She didn't seem to notice. "Are you planning to stay in America?"

"Definitely, I am making it my country." He was aware of his accent: heavy, foreign. She probably found it comical.

"Then welcome," she said. "Do you ice-skate?"

"Oh, yes. I don't have skates here"—he had never owned a pair in his life— "but in Berlin I skated often, and very well."

He didn't mean to lie and boast that way, he was just thoroughly addled by her beauty.

"Then we'll see each other at Lincoln Park when the lagoons freeze next winter—"

"Miss Vanderhoff! Your mother is asking for you."

The shout made her jump. A manservant in livery was standing at the front door of the Vanderhoff mansion.

With a sigh, Julie said to Joe Junior, "Mama probably recognized you." To Paul: "Her upstairs sitting room is there, in front. I must go."

Julie turned the pony's head into the street. "Happy to meet you, Paul. Till winter, Joe." She waved.

"Till winter," he said, his hand raised. She might be just a friend, but Paul saw that his eyes were adoring.

Joe Junior nudged him. "Didn't I say we'd catch a glimpse of heaven?"

"You're right, she is beautiful."

"But completely out of bounds, so don't get any ideas, kid." His cousin was joshing him again. Yet there seemed to be a note of regret in his voice.

As they walked south on Prairie Avenue, Paul realized that his mouth was dry and his pulse still racing. Something surprising and incredible had happened there in the shade of the sycamore.

He was in love.

"I can hear the old gears grinding in your head," Joe Junior said. "What about?"

"I am thinking about a job. I wish I had a job instead of a desk in that school. If I had a job, I could save some money. With money I could buy a pair of skates."

Joe Junior's eyebrows shot up. His mouth started to curl. Before he could speak, Paul burst out, "If you laugh at me I'll hit you."

Joe Junior slung his arm around Paul's shoulder and gave him a brotherly squeeze.

"I won't laugh. I know how it feels. Unfortunately she doesn't care two pins about me, except as a friend. Maybe you'll have better luck."

In bed that night, Paul had a troubling thought. Now that a friendship was developing between him and his cousin, he supposed he'd stepped across an invisible line. He had taken sides.

Against Uncle Joe.

Well, what of it? Uncle Joe was the one who'd sentenced him to that school. His cousin was treating him almost like an equal. That made the difference.

19

Joe Crown

ONE AFTERNOON a week before the opening of the Exposition, there came to Joe's office one Oskar Hexhammer. Joe knew him chiefly by reputation, although they had been introduced once, by a mutual acquaintance, in the rooms of the exclusive Germania Club on North Clark Street, of which all three men were members.

Hexhammer was about thirty, prematurely bald, with thick black hair that stuck out like wings above his ears. He was slender, wore eyeglasses, and projected an attitude of absolute authority.

He had arrived in Chicago less than ten years ago, and had quickly set about establishing himself as a leader of the most conservative German element. Evidently he'd come to America with an inheritance, which he used to start the *Chicago Deutsche Zeitung,* one of the city's many German-language newspapers. He was its publisher and chief editorialist.

Joe didn't subscribe to the paper. He found it parochial, one-sided, and dull. It seemed to survive chiefly on municipal advertisements, which the city government always placed in German as well as English. Its circulation wasn't even close to that of Hermann Kohlsaat's *Abendpost* or Anton Hesing's *Illinois Staatszeitung,* a paper Joe read regularly. Fiercely abolitionist when it was founded, the *Staatszeitung* purveyed opinions that agreed with Joe's. On the issue of the eight-hour day, it held that workingmen would be "happier" working ten hours, because they would otherwise have two extra hours to spend in idleness, which could lead to domestic disharmony and even to crime.

Although Joe was annoyed by Hexhammer's insistence on seeing him without an appointment, he shook the visitor's hand and invited him to sit down.

"*Wie geht's mit Ihnen, Herr Crown?*" The visitor had a recognizable accent. Berlin. Snobbish Berlin, at that.

"I prefer to speak English, Mr. Hexhammer. What can I do for you? I'll appreciate your being brief, we're always busy around here."

"I trust you can spare fifteen minutes in the furtherance of German *Kultur.*"

Joe smelled a financial solicitation. He leaned back, touching the tips of his fingers together so as to partially hide his face. "Please be more specific."

Hexhammer polished his spectacles with a starched handkerchief. "Certainly. I am sure you'd agree with the premise that in the fatherland, where you and I were born, the people enjoy a more civilized, refined style of life than they do here in America."

Joe groaned inwardly. Here was yet another apostle of the notion of superiority of all things German.

"Not necessarily," he said. "I remember my homeland with great affection, but I prefer this country. I love its democracy, its energy, even its vulgarity. I love that it isn't wedded to the past, but looks always to the future. I love the concept that all men stand on the same starting mark, with only their individual ability and ambition limiting how far they can go. I love the welcoming spirit of America. Just in December, my nephew—"

Hexhammer interrupted. "You love the idea of mixing with Bohemians, or Poles? Dirty Irish—all the dregs of the earth?"

Joe laughed. "I was told that you were a secret aristocrat. It's true."

Hexhammer wasn't amused. "Some would make a similar charge about you, sir. You decided that a home on the *Nordseite,* among your own, wasn't sufficiently prestigious. You chose to move down to Michigan Avenue."

"Where I live, and why, is my affair. For your information, our first house was simply too small. My address does nothing to diminish my regard for my native country, her people, or her traditions."

Joe was outwardly calm. But he was upset by the suggestion that others might think badly of him because he'd moved from the heavily German North Side district five years ago. Joe's good name mattered to him.

"Let me be even more specific, Mr. Hexhammer. Our family belongs to St. Paul's Lutheran Church at Superior and Franklin—you know it, I assume."

"Of course."

"It's the oldest Lutheran church in the city; it goes back to 1848. Germans organized it and the congregation is still predominantly German. Some Sunday school classes are still taught in the German language. Further, my wife and I donate regularly to the hospital of the Alexian Brothers, founded by monks from Aachen, and also to the German Hospital on Lincoln Avenue. When I was first able to support charitable works, I gave all that I could to the Schwabenverein, to help that club erect the Schiller monument in Lincoln Park. Is that enough respect for heritage, Mr. Hexhammer?"

"Certainly, excellent."

"Then what are we discussing?"

The visitor cleared his throat. "Are you aware of the formation in the fatherland of the Pan-German League?"

"I know a little about it. A band of superpatriots, isn't it?"

"Nothing so distasteful. Although a civilian organization, the League is a logical and highly important extension of our government."

"My government is in Washington. But go on." Joe's hand dropped to his vest. He began to tap and rub the polished boar's tooth.

"The League has very specific goals. It favors a higher state of preparedness for the army, a larger and more powerful navy with a global capability, an expanding domain of overseas colonies, and of course armed vigilance in regard to our mortal enemies, France and the British Empire."

Joe shook his head. "I can never understand why the Kaiser hates England when his own grandmother, Queen Victoria, reigns there. I was shocked when he said that his withered left arm was a taint from his British blood."

"A perfectly correct and appropriate remark, in my opinion. However, to return to the League—it is another of its goals which brings me here. The German diaspora is now worldwide. Wherever Germans are settled, the League strives to promote our language and culture."

"Back to German superiority, are we?"

The visitor missed or chose to overlook the sarcasm. "For good reason, sir. We are the people of Beethoven, after all. The people of Wagner, and Goethe." Hexhammer leaned forward; lowered his voice. "I am connected to the League's overseas directorate. Closely connected." *What a pompous ass,* Joe thought. *Am I supposed to cower and tremble?*

"Mr. Hexhammer, before we continue this, please answer one question. If the *Kultur* of the fatherland is so consistently above that of America, why are you here instead of back there?"

"I thought I made that clear, my friend. As Germans it is our duty to influence the political and social course of the country in which we reside. To do this we must begin with the children. To this end, the League is promoting formation of a totally new *Turnverein,* to be called the Kaiser Wilhelm Royal Turnverein of Chicago."

The last few words faded to an indecisive mutter; Joe Crown was regarding the visitor with a skeptical scowl.

Hexhammer collected himself. "You do believe in Friedrich Jahn's principles, do you not? A sound body and a sound mind?" Early in the century, in Germany, Jahn had created a movement, and a passion, for physical culture. It led to immigrants founding *Turnvereine,* gymnastic clubs, all over America.

"Indeed yes, I've always encouraged my youngsters to play vigorously in order to stay healthy."

"Are they enrolled in a regular club program at present?"

"No. They were in one when they were small."

"Then I suggest that you enroll them in our new club. With a founder's donation of at least one thousand dollars. Your children will thus be part of an elite corps for the propagation of German values through physical training."

"Mr. Hexhammer," Joe said, "I very much object to anyone coming to me and saying I must spend my money this way or that way. Furthermore, when I choose to make a contribution, I decide on the amount."

"But it's your duty as a Ger—"

"Please don't harp on my duty. I know my duties. They don't include contributing to this particular bit of jingo patriotism."

Hexhammer recoiled in his chair. Earlier he'd removed his gray gloves and laid them in his lap. Now he began to twist them savagely.

"That's a very curious attitude for a man who professes to love his native land. It's a puzzling attitude for a businessman who—may I say it?—depends on the good will of German people."

He paused while that sank in.

"Word travels quickly in this town, sir. I wouldn't want your reputation blackened. Or your beer sales diminished."

Joe Crown rose. He walked slowly around the desk and stood over Hexhammer. "This conversation is over. Leave my office."

Hexhammer squirmed out of Joe's shadow, sidestepping toward the door, twisting his gloves. "I think you'll regret this. You are not a good German."

"Perhaps you're right. I'm an American citizen, after all. Get out, please."

Hexhammer slammed the door. Joe sank back into his chair. He'd done the right thing but he was fully aware that the young publisher had a certain influence among the mossbacks in Chicago. The threat to brewery sales bothered him in one important respect. He held himself personally responsible for the welfare of every man on his payroll. That welfare depended on the success of Crown's from week to week and month to month.

Well, he would never lay off even one man because of falling sales, he had decided that long ago. He'd spend himself to bankruptcy first. He wasn't being noble. A decent man just conducted his business that way.

He feared he wasn't finished with Hexhammer. More precisely, that Hexhammer wasn't finished with him. He tried to put it out of his mind while he signed a stack of letters Zwick had typed that morning.

20

Paul

ON THE GREAT DAY, a faraway roll of thunder woke Paul before dawn. He wanted to go back to sleep. He turned on his left side. He forced himself to yawn. He turned on his right side. No use; his mind was racing with thoughts of the Exposition. An entire day free of Mrs. Petigru!

In the metal heating pipes that snaked through the house, he heard rattling; a distant ghostly voice. Though it was still dark, Louise would already be in the kitchen. Aunt Ilsa too. Aunt Ilsa had announced *Frühstück* for half past six. Manfred didn't like the change in routine and had let it be known in the kitchen, behind Aunt Ilsa's back. Manfred disliked anything that he hadn't planned and endorsed personally.

Someone knocked. He leaped out of bed, stumbled through the darkness to whisper, "Who is it?"

"Fritzi. Are you awake?"

"No, still asleep, can't you tell?" Fritzi giggled. "What do you want?"

"Open the door. Please." Sighing, he turned the knob.

A strong scent reminiscent of fruit overpowered him. He couldn't see Fritzi's face, only the silhouette of her long curls and ankle-length nightdress against the glow of a dim light down the hall.

"I didn't mean to wake you, Paul." He grumbled something noncommittal. "I'm so excited, I can't sleep."

"I woke up too," he admitted.

"What do you want to see most at the fair?"

"Everything."

"I want to see the painting of Ellen Terry."

"Who is that?"

"Paul, where have you been? Ellen Terry is one of the greatest actresses in the whole world."

"Ah."

A long silence ensued. Fritzi rubbed her bare toe on the fine hall carpet. "Well, I guess I'd better go comb my hair or something."

"Yes, probably."

"I'll see you at breakfast then." He was quite unprepared for her sudden lunge forward, or the kiss planted on his cheek. She whirled around and sped to her room, curls flying.

Stunned, he closed the door and leaned against the wall in the dark. He touched his face where Fritzi's lips had pressed. His fingers came away sticky. He sniffed them. That was the scent; some sweet night cream she was using for her complexion.

Things were going too far with Cousin Fritzi. She was a nice person, lively and clever, though she did tend to wear you out with her chatter and her imitations. Obviously she considered him more than a relative. She had romantic designs. He'd suspected it for quite a while but hadn't wanted to admit it.

The kiss changed everything. He mustn't lead her on, even slightly. Cousins couldn't become attached and, besides, he had someone else in mind. Someone older, whose ravishing eyes and hair and figure he'd dreamed about more than once. He needed to discourage Fritzi in a way that would be conclusive but wouldn't hurt her. He must think about that.

Not today, though. Today was a celebration. The only person in the house who didn't share the feeling was Joe Junior. He always spoke sourly about the Exposition. How would he behave at the opening ceremonies?

Paul switched on the electrics and began to wash and dress as the first light was breaking over Lake Michigan. It was May 1, 1893.

Everyone came to breakfast except Cousin Joe. Uncle Joe was in his regular place, though he had to leave shortly for a second, more important breakfast with dignitaries at his club. He only had a small plate of herring and a cup of black coffee in front of him.

Uncle Joe looked grand in a frock coat with satin-faced lapels, an ascot scarf of dark red and black stripes, striped gray and black trousers. When Aunt Ilsa came in with a platter of sausages, he said, "Where is Joe Junior, may I ask?"

"He has a terrible stomachache. He asked to be excused today, and I agreed."

"Very well, let him stay home. We don't need the company of a spoilsport. If he wants to go to the fair later, he can pay for it himself."

Thunder boomed. Uncle Joe frowned at the threatening sky visible from the window nearest him. "I hope we won't have a storm to ruin the outdoor program. At least President Cleveland is already in town. We have a new President, Paul, elected last November."

"I remember seeing his picture as I traveled here. Many—ah—*Plakate?*"

"Posters," said Aunt Ilsa.

"Yes, thank you."

Aunt Ilsa and Louise bustled about, serving mountainous platters of food. "Eat, children, it will be a long day for all of us." Manfred glided through the dining room twice, his stern eyes registering his disapproval. In the middle of the meal Carl excused himself for the toilet. He came hurtling back and collided with Manfred.

"If you please, Master Carl! Watch where you're going."

Uncle Joe coughed, a gentle but clear statement that Manfred's tone was too harsh. Manfred flushed. Paul said, "It wasn't his fault, Mr. Blenkers, he couldn't see you from around the corner."

"Oh, I see, thank you for enlightening me, Master Paul." Manfred stared at Paul, then marched out haughtily.

Paul didn't need this latest incident to tell him that Manfred had an intense dislike of him. Perhaps just by arriving, existing, he'd disrupted the household order that Manfred had established. The steward would never be a friend but Paul didn't much care; he put Manfred in the same category as Mrs. Petigru.

A violent storm broke as Uncle Joe, wearing a tall silk hat, departed for his breakfast reception. Rain beat on the roof and sluiced down the windowpanes in torrents; for a while it was impossible to see Michigan Avenue. Fritzi broke into tears, exclaiming that everything was spoiled.

Soon after breakfast, while the storm was raging, Paul knocked softly on Joe Junior's door. "Come in." He was startled to find Cousin Joe sitting up in bed in his nightshirt, with a book. He looked perfectly healthy.

"Joe, I am sorry you're sick."

"Just a bellyache."

"You really can't go?"

"I don't want to go. Mama understands. You go on, I know you want to see it. I just don't like the whole idea—crammed in among a lot of nabobs. You can give me a report tomorrow."

"Yes, I will," Paul exclaimed, reprieved.

"Shut the door behind you. Thanks." Joe Junior's eyes were already on his open book.

Almost miraculously, the rain abated, the storm clouds blew over, sun broke through to bring steam from the drenched streets. By the time Nicky Speers drove the family to the Exposition at half past nine, the weather looked fine.

All the way to the grounds, Fritzi complained that her corset hurt. When she and Aunt Ilsa walked, they tilted forward slightly because of their stiff binding garments. Just the night before, Fritzi had done an exact and hilarious imitation of that walk, which she called "the kangaroo bend."

Streets leading to Jackson Park were choked with carriages, buggies, horse-drawn cabs, people on foot. Uncle Joe met the family at the main gate, anxiously motioning for them to hurry. Buffeted on every side, they followed him. Paul could hardly keep from gaping at the buildings, blinding white in the sunshine, and magnificent.

Their seats were special but not comfortable. They sat on hard bleachers erected at the foot of a great wide stair on the east side of the Administration Building. On the stair itself, a heavily decorated platform held a full orchestra, a large choir, and all the dignitaries whom Uncle Joe pointed out. The President of the United States, Grover Cleveland. Vice President Adlai Stevenson, who was from Illinois. Mayor Harrison. Governor Altgeld. Three special guests from Spain —the Duke of Veragua, a lineal descendant of Columbus, his wife, and a woman identified as the Infanta Eulalia, the king's daughter.

The opening ceremonies began at fifteen past eleven. The orchestra played a Wagner overture. This was followed by prayers, choral anthems, and several speakers whose verbosity made Paul and Carl and Fritzi fidget and squirm. East-ward, toward the lake, thousands packed the esplanades on both sides of the shimmering Grand Basin. Uncle Joe said between three hundred and five hun-dred thousand people were expected today.

Everyone rose to applaud the President after he was introduced. Mr. Cleve-land was a burly, strong-jawed man with a forceful voice, but Paul didn't listen to much of what he had to say. The English words were long, the sentences compli-cated; and his eye was constantly distracted by the incredible sights all around him. White buildings of great beauty and symmetry; broad avenues; lagoons and reflecting pools; statuary of every description.

About twelve-thirty, the President concluded his remarks. Wild applause broke out—perhaps out of gratitude. On either side of the Grand Basin and in the intersecting avenues, the crowd quickly grew quiet again. Uncle Joe leaned for-ward intently. "Watch, everyone. He's ready."

President Cleveland stretched his hand toward a gilded telegraph key in front of him. His voice boomed and echoed. *"As by a touch the machinery that gives life to this vast exposition is now set in motion, so in the same instant let our hopes and aspirations awaken forces which in time to come shall favorably influence the welfare, dignity, and freedom of mankind."*

He pressed the key.

The orchestra leader's baton struck the downbeat. As the first notes resounded and the massed choir sang, fountains throughout the grounds erupted with foam-ing columns of water, flagstaffs miraculously unfurled the banners of America, Spain, and other nations, streamers dropped from every rooftop, drapes fell away from a giant gilded statue of the Republic rising from a pedestal at the east end of the Basin.

Chimes began to ring, steam whistles to sound from a fleet of electric lagoon launches built to ferry visitors through the waterways of the fair. Guns boomed from a naval vessel anchored offshore. From a white peristyle behind the statue of the Republic, two hundred white doves burst from their cages and flew up-ward. Aunt Ilsa said, "Do you know this piece, Pauli? The 'Hallelujah Chorus.' The composer, Mr. Handel, was a German. From Saxony. Isn't it thrilling?" He had to agree that it was.

As flags, fountains, and streamers declared the fair officially open, the roar of the crowd drowned out Handel's music. Fritzi grabbed Paul's sleeve, jumping up and down and sobbing emotionally. Uncle Joe slipped his arm around his wife while trying to remove something from his eye with a large hanky. Aunt Ilsa looked quite handsome in a smart little hat, black felt with blue and black ostrich plumes. She carried a tightly rolled parasol—Fritzi had a smaller one—and had lightly touched up her face with rice powder and rouge. Her dress was cinched at the waist, with a short train and dust ruffle. Her petticoats rustled in a pleasing way.

Carl gaped, as awestruck as Paul. The boys wore smaller versions of Uncle Joe's fine suit, bought specially for the occasion. Paul had never been dressed so splendidly, though he didn't like the confining starched shirt collar. Much as he hated it, he supposed it wasn't half as bad as the torture inflicted by female garments.

The Handel chorus ended. The orchestra struck up "America." Consulting his program, Uncle Joe said, "This is the end. Paul, what do you think? Quite impressive, isn't it?"

"Yes, sir."

"Try to convey that feeling to your cousin sometime."

"Papa, can we go?" Fritzi asked, bouncing up and down on the riser.

Aunt Ilsa grabbed her. "Be careful, you'll fall."

"Oh, Mama, I can't stand still, I'm too excited. I want to see the picture of Ellen Terry as Lady Macbeth, where is it?"

"I must look in on the brewery exhibit," Uncle Joe said. "Twenty-four of my competitors are displaying their products. I want to be sure Crown's compares favorably. I'll go now and meet you in half an hour. Perhaps then we should visit the German exhibit. I saw the wrought-iron gates when they were installed last week. They're spectacular."

"No, let's go to the Krupp gun," Carl said.

Aunt Ilsa said, "There's also a German village on the Midway."

"Yay, the Midway," Carl said, hopping up and down like his sister. "I want to ride the wheel, can we ride the wheel, Papa?" At school everyone had been talking about the giant revolving wheel with gondolas spaced around it. Paul couldn't imagine what it would be like to ride such a device into the sky.

"Paul, do you have something you want to see most?" Uncle Joe asked as they worked their way down to the foot of the bleachers. "Perhaps Sandow the strongman? He's another good German."

"Well, sir, what I would like best really is the Buffalo Bill show." Cody's encampment was set up just outside the grounds; the show would play until the Exposition closed in the autumn.

"Capital idea. Carl said you wanted to see it in Berlin and could not. I'll buy tickets for later in the summer. Here's a thought. We could celebrate when you finish the school year successfully."

"Thank you," Paul said with a stricken expression.

"Come, everyone. We must decide on a place to meet."

The avenues were packed; progress was slow. The Crowns paused to admire the huge statue of Christopher Columbus, his sword upraised, his flag unfurled behind him. A well-dressed but sickly-looking woman approached. Aunt Ilsa smiled and said, "Nell, good day to you."

The woman looked away and passed by.

Fritzi tugged her mother's sleeve. "Mama, who was that?"

"Mrs. Vanderhoff."

"Why wouldn't she speak?"

"I don't know, but it isn't the first time. Don't worry about it."

Vanderhoff? A relative of the girl from Prairie Avenue? Was she here? Perhaps he'd see her. Why on earth would anyone snub Aunt Ilsa, the kindest of women?

Aunt Ilsa stopped at a building of unusual design, with a dramatic entrance of concentric arches finished in gold leaf. Quite breathtaking, Paul thought.

"That is the Transportation Building, children," Ilsa said, her guidebook open. "Mr. Sullivan designed it."

"Who's he?" Carl said, bored.

"Louis Sullivan is a Chicago architect. He and his partner, Mr. Adler, are quite advanced. Some call Mr. Sullivan a genius."

Uncle Joe joined them after he'd seen the brewery exhibit. "Our presentation is fine. Fred's diagrams of the brewing process are simple but effective. I'm pleased." That seemed to be his mood as they continued to stroll. "Isn't this fair a marvelous accomplishment? Before Congress chose Chicago over those other cities, all the skeptics said we couldn't do it. Couldn't deliver an exposition of this magnitude, and on time. But we showed them!"

They turned into another avenue. In the distance, Paul saw the huge iron wheel revolving. The Ferris wheel, named after its inventor. Tiny figures rode inside the wooden gondolas around the rim of the wheel.

Uncle Joe said, "You've been very quiet about your wishes, Ilsa. What would you most like to see?"

"The Women's Pavilion."

"Sorry, that's the one place you'll have to visit by yourself. I have never seen the need for a special monument to the female gender, and I don't now."

"Of course you don't. But I must tell you, Joe, I plan to attend the Women's Congress when it convenes at the Art Institute. I shall go to as many of the sessions as time allows."

"All right, but please stay off the barricades. They're already too crowded with reds and freethinkers and these so-called new women. Now, shall we all take a vote? Where to first?" He patted his coat. "I have some special passes that will speed us into most of the exhibits."

"The Ferris wheel?" Carl cried.

"Not that one, I'm afraid. They say it's going to be the very biggest attraction."

They settled on the Krupp gun, exhibited in a special Krupp pavilion on the lakefront. Krupp's of Essen was a fine old German firm, even Paul knew of it. The pavilion was a miniature Prussian fortress, complete with turrets and battlements. The gun was eighty-seven feet long. One of its projectiles weighed twenty-three hundred pounds. It could be fired a distance of sixteen miles, said the Krupp engineer in attendance.

Carl was thrilled and impressed and couldn't stop asking questions. Uncle Joe seemed disturbed by the exhibit. As they were leaving he said, "Is that Germany's chief boast these days, war weapons? Is the fatherland showing off its strength like some street bully? If so, what does that say? Nothing that I like to hear."

Next they went to the Fine Arts Building, to find the portrait of the actress Ellen Terry, painted by a Mr. Sargent. Fritzi stood enraptured for five minutes, clasping and unclasping her hands and sighing, until Uncle Joe snapped his gold watch shut and said, "Time to go."

They trooped to the Midway Plaisance, a broad east-west avenue stretching for one mile across the north side of the grounds between Fifty-ninth and Sixtieth streets. Here all the lighter diversions had been segregated.

They admired the Blarney Castle from Ireland, then walked through the narrow passageways and keyhole gates of the Streets of Cairo, which was populated by women in veils and swarthy men in robes and red fezzes. It was an exotic, faintly wicked exhibition, and its general raffishness failed to charm Aunt Ilsa. Nor did she smile when Uncle Joe said, "Perhaps when you're visiting the Women's Pavilion, I'll attend a performance of that dancer, Little Egypt. The men at the brewery are all talking about her *danse du ventre.*"

Carl whispered to Paul, "It means she dances with her belly, I heard it in school."

They ate an early supper at the German Village, in preparation for standing in line for the Ferris wheel. They sat under gay lanterns at an outdoor table, in the looming shadow of the Wasserburg, a replica of a moated fifteenth-century castle. A German band played familiar songs while the family ate *Nudelsuppe* and *Kücken mit Spargel.*

They waited nearly an hour for their ride on the wheel; actually two wheels, with thirty-six gondola cars mounted between. In the darkness of the spring night, the colored lights of the Midway Plaisance and the Exposition lit the sky with a great glow.

Finally their turn came. With others, they climbed into a forty-passenger car with big glass windows and comfortable swivel seats. Fritzi shrieked when the wheel jerked and the car rose, swaying, then stopped again while the car below was loaded.

"The wheel is two hundred fifty feet across, I read that," Carl said.

"With another fifteen feet of base," his father said.

"Fifty cents is awfully expensive for a short ride," Fritzi said.

"Oh, do be quiet, everyone, and look," Aunt Ilsa said. "Have you ever seen anything so beautiful?"

She leaned forward in her chair and pressed her gloved palm to the glass. A spectacular vista of twinkling lights spread beneath them, running more than a mile to the south.

Aunt Ilsa made a joyful little sound, part laugh, part gulp, and squeezed Paul's hand.

"Pauli, can you believe your eyes? Was there ever a more magnificent sight?"

"No, never," he whispered as the car rose and swayed. His face was bathed in the colors of the magic twinkling lights. The panorama below symbolized the almost limitless wonders of the new scientific age brought to its fullest glory.

In America.

Exhausted, they said little as Nicky Speers drove them back to Michigan Avenue at eleven o'clock. Paul looked for a light under Joe Junior's door and saw none. Tomorrow, then.

Unintentionally, he arose late. A schoolday! He dashed downstairs and barely had time to cram a roll in his mouth and wash it down with milk. Joe Junior had already left to catch a tram to the brewery. Uncle Joe refused to let his son ride with him in the landau, fearing an appearance of favoritism. It wasn't until a quarter of nine in the evening that Paul trailed his cousin to his room.

"Well, tell me. What did you think of it?"

"Joe, don't get mad. I thought it was pretty fine."

"Oh, you did?" His cousin stared at him. Paul's stomach knotted. Suddenly Joe Junior grinned. "Hell, I didn't expect anything else. I expected you'd be taken in. All that show. All those fancy names for it. 'The New Jerusalem.' 'The White City.' Maybe the buildings look beautiful to you, but it's just white paint over cheap stucco. There's another side to that fair, Paul. Things you need to know."

"What things?"

"Maybe I'll let Benno tell you."

Paul's hands were sweaty with excitement.

"When?"

"Sometimes there are Sunday labor picnics, out in the country. I might take you to the next one. If I do, can you keep quiet in front of Mama and Pop? Fritzi and Carl?"

Paul's heart was beating fast. His cousin was drawing him into his confidence; trusting him with a dangerous secret. Like a true friend. He shot his hand into the air.

"Silent as a statue, I promise!"

Paul ran to his room, flung himself on the bed, elated. But only briefly. He clasped his hands under his head and lay gazing at the ceiling. The secret, the confidence, was already bothering him.

By saying he'd go with Joe Junior whenever asked, and then keep it a secret, he'd made a kind of pact with his cousin. A pact weightier than mere friendship between boys who were relatives. It could cause trouble. He spent a restless night, full of worry and guilt over disloyalty to his aunt and uncle.

Scarcely a month was left in the school term. Paul was failing. Failing every test; failing his handwriting exercises; failing his recitations at the blackboard. Mrs. Petigru took delight in announcing his poor marks to the class.

Mrs. Petigru kept him after school to inform him that she would have to hold him over.

"Sorry, I do not understand."

"I refuse to promote you to a higher grade. Your work's completely unsatisfactory. I'll keep you here and you will repeat the whole year. Perhaps the second time, a few grains of knowledge will penetrate that thick German head."

He reeled out. Stay with Mrs. Petigru another *year?* Never. He'd jump off a building. He'd swallow poison.

He tried to think of a way out. His mind was blank. And he was too ashamed of his predicament to tell Uncle Joe or his tutor.

Around the house, Fritzi was driving everyone mad with her imitation of the portrait of Ellen Terry. She'd made a crown of gold paper and borrowed a shawl from her mother to simulate the kimonolike sleeves of Miss Terry's gown. Paul and others would unexpectedly come upon Fritzi posing in a corner, or in the middle of the staircase, wrapped in the shawl, the crown raised above her head with both hands while she gazed heavenward with an ethereal expression.

Carl snorted and called her dizzy. She threatened to hit him, which merely egged him on. "Dizzy, dizzy, dizzy," he chanted, dancing around her. Uncle Joe found them rolling on the carpet, pulling hair and punching each other.

He boxed Carl's ears severely, and ordered Fritzi to stop the imitations. Fritzi ran sobbing to her room, which vexed Uncle Joe even more. In fact he seemed grim and short-tempered lately. When Fritzi came to supper red-eyed, he delivered a stern lecture.

"Please stop that sniffling. I am tired of theatrics in this house. I won't go to the German-language theater, it's too old-fashioned, but I occasionally enjoy a play in English, you all know that. I do, however, have a low regard for persons involved in putting on plays. The stage is a disreputable, godless calling. Any man or woman foolish enough to take it up deserves to be rejected by society. And they usually are. Please pass the mashed potatoes."

After that evening, a new gravity seemed to prevail at the supper table. Uncle Joe was subdued, speaking quietly to Aunt Ilsa about "the gold standard" and "shares" and other mysteries. One night, unable to restrain his curiosity, Paul politely asked whether there was any special reason for so much talk of financial matters. There certainly was, Uncle Joe said, going on to explain that since May 5, prices of shares in large companies had begun to fall off sharply. "European investors are pulling millions of dollars out of American banks. Illinois Trust is in trouble, the Chemical National too. I fear it's the panic many people predicted."

Joe Junior said, "What do you expect, Pop? The system's corrupt."

Aunt Ilsa looked pained. Uncle Joe struggled to contain himself. "Thank you for enlightening us. We surely respect your wisdom and experience as a student of economics."

Joe Junior's jaw clenched and he turned red. He attacked his food with stabs of his fork.

Still, Uncle Joe wasn't so downcast about the panic that he completely lost interest in other things. He took Paul and Carl to a Saturday afternoon baseball game between the Chicago White Stockings and the Providence Grays. He drove the landau himself. Their destination was Congress Park, out on Congress Street at Loomis.

Paul sat beside his uncle on the coachman's seat. Carl was amusing himself in back by monotonously singing a song called "Slide, Kelly, Slide," over and over.

"I wish Joe Junior could have come with us," Paul said.

Expressionless, Uncle Joe watched the street traffic. "You know he's working today. Not that it matters. When he was smaller, he loved coming with me to a game. No longer."

Congress Park was a fine place, with a cycling track on one side and lawn tennis courts on the other. A high brick wall surrounded the playing field. Uncle Joe said the park held ten thousand people, but it was only half full this afternoon. They went through a turnstile and climbed a stair to Uncle Joe's private roof box. It had four comfortable armchairs and weather curtains which had already been drawn aside and tied.

Both teams were on the field, practicing hitting and catching. The field was brilliant green, sending the aroma of freshly cut grass all the way up to the box. A few picture-perfect clouds lazed in the sky. In the aisles, vendors hawked beer, sausages, roasted nuts.

"The beer is Crown's," Uncle Joe said with pride. "I know Bill Hulbert, the coal merchant who's president of the team. That helped with the selection." He smiled.

"I don't know the rules of the game, Uncle."

"I'll try to explain them. I've loved baseball for many years. In the camps during the war the men played a lot of ball. I played, though never well. Back in '69 I saw the first professional team in America, the Cincinnati Red Stockings, for only a nickel. When I sit out here on a beautiful day like this, I'm happy. I'll admit that inside, a part of me frowns and says, *Joe, you ought to be working.* That's a German for you. Always a little guilt under the smile. Some don't even smile." But he did.

Carl began to sing "Slide, Kelly, Slide" again. "Carl, after the fiftieth time that song is annoying. Desist." He said to Paul, "Mike Kelly was one of the greatest players the White Stockings ever had. His position was right field, just there. He led the league in runs scored in '84, '85, and '86. King Kelly, they called him. Off the field he was a wastrel, a carouser. But you had to like his play. Look out, they're taking the field."

He pointed out the manager of the White Stockings, Cap Anson. "Used to play first base. He knows the game, but I don't like him. He hates the colored people. At one time there was a fine Negro player in the league, Fleet Walker of Toledo. Anson refused to let the White Stockings play Toledo because of that. It drove Walker out of the game."

Soon a man in shirt sleeves, the umpire, shouted, "Play ball," and the game began. Uncle Joe patiently interpreted the plays, and Paul began to catch on. Providence took an early lead, three runs to one. This brought a black youth off the bench; Paul hadn't noticed him before. The black boy wore a White Stockings jersey. He ran to home plate and did a kind of shuffling dance. The crowd cheered and whistled.

"That's Clarence, the team mascot," Uncle Joe said. "Anson makes him do that cakewalk step at every game."

Carl said, "Cap Anson calls him the pickaninny."

"Carl, don't use that word."

Several Chicago players surrounded Clarence. The boy stood patiently while the white men scraped their knuckles back and forth through his kinky black hair. "That's for good luck," Uncle Joe said. "They mistreat the boy, make fun of him because he's colored. Anson's idea. For this we fought and bled thirty years ago?" Blood had rushed to his face.

By the seventh inning, when Uncle Joe left the box for refreshments, Providence still held on to its lead. Carl put his foot on the rail of the box, which he couldn't do when Uncle Joe was present.

"They need Billy Sunday. Used to be the utility outfielder. Fastest man you ever saw. Ran like a scared deer."

"Did he quit?"

"Yep. God called him to be a preacher and Pop says he answered the call. Personally, I wish he'd kept plugs in his ears."

Uncle Joe returned with some smooth pale wursts of a kind Paul had never seen. Each was wrapped in a soft roll. "These are new. They're called frankfurters. You can guess where they originated. Try one. Here's a sack of peanuts too."

In the first half of the ninth inning, a surprise home run by the home team's catcher drove in runners from second and third base. The crowd cheered when the pitcher struck out the last Providence batter in the second half, ending the game. Uncle Joe leaned over the box rail, applauding and shouting, "Hurrah, well done!"

The light was fading in the west. The White Stockings leaping and hugging one another on the green grass cast long shadows. Paul was stuffed with snacks, warmed by his uncle's friendship, happy to be with boisterous Carl. A perfect afternoon.

Sleepily jouncing in the carriage, he felt grand. The euphoria lasted until they trooped into the kitchen from the stable. Louise had her head bowed over the stove; she didn't greet them. Aunt Ilsa pulled something from her apron. Her face was grim.

"This came today, Joe. It's the letter you wrote to Charlotte."

Uncle Joe took the soiled and wrinkled envelope. On the front, stamped in red, was a single word. VERSTORBEN.

"Deceased? How could it be? What happened?" With a look of anguish, he turned to Ilsa. *"What happened?"*

"I suppose we will never know. Possibly it was the illness Pauli has talked about."

Paul was shaken too. There was a choking lump in his throat. Uncle Joe snatched off his straw boater and hit his leg. The edge of the brim cracked.

The letter fell from his hand. Tears flowed down his face. Ilsa put her arms around him. No one said a word.

Uncle Joe took them to the Exposition a second time—again without Joe Junior. They began with an afternoon performance of Eugene Sandow, the world-famous strongman. Afterward, Uncle Joe went backstage to greet a young man he later identified as Florenz Ziegfeld, son of Dr. Ziegfeld, founder and president of the Chicago Musical College. Young Florenz booked most of the bands appearing at the Exposition. He was Sandow's manager in America. Uncle Joe seemed to know every Chicago German of substance or accomplishment.

In the evening, they attended a concert by Mr. Theodor Thomas and his Chicago orchestra ("He's from Cincinnati originally," Uncle Joe said.) The program consisted of music by the German composer Richard Wagner. Aunt Ilsa said Wagner was a genius, and a credit to all Germans, but the slow, heavy music made Paul squirm.

He much preferred the music they heard at an outdoor bandstand, just before the fireworks. Liesgang's Chicago Band and its guest conductor, Mr. Sousa, played stirring martial airs, including "Marching Through Georgia," which Herschel Wolinski had played aboard ship. Poor Herschel, where was he now? Paul really didn't believe they'd meet again.

□ □ □ □

On a Thursday evening at the end of May, Uncle Joe packed a grip and caught an evening train for the South. By a stroke of luck there was a labor picnic the following Sunday. A political-cultural day, Joe Junior called it. He politely asked his mother if he and Paul could go for a hike in the country. Aunt Ilsa told them to be careful and to return before dark.

Their destination was a place called Ogden's Grove, beyond the city limits. "Why do they hold it so far away?" Paul asked as they rattled along on the horsecar for the first stage of their journey.

"So the bluenoses won't yell about Sunday beer drinking, and the Chicago coppers won't snoop. Even if you don't listen to a single speech, these are great affairs. I met my girl, Rosie, at one of them last year."

"You know a lot about socialists. How did you learn?"

"Not in school, that's for damn sure. I listen to Benno and his pals. I read everything I can find. Karl Marx. A Frenchman called Proudhon. Bakunin— Russian—the first man to say the old order had to be overturned by revolution. I read a lot of articles by Prince Kropotkin, from the Russian nobility. He lives in London now, like any ordinary person. Even translated, the foreign stuff's hard going, I don't understand a lot of it. So I read this, too." From under his shirt he pulled a newspaper printed in German. *Die Fackel. The Torch.* "It's a special Sunday edition of the labor paper, *Chicagoer Arbeiter-Zeitung.* If Pop caught me with it he'd have my hide."

"Then why do you read it? Just to make him angry?"

Joe Junior sat up straighter, his lips in a hard line. "That's a dumb question. I read and hang out with these people because Pop and all the men like him are wrong, their ideas are wrong, they're oppressors of the poor."

"But you wouldn't kill them, would you?"

The horsecar was slowing its already plodding pace for the end of the line. Joe Junior rested his elbow on the sill and watched a straggle of small cottages passing by. "You ask a hell of a lot of questions."

"I want to learn."

Joe Junior whirled and pinned him with a look.

"So you can pick the right side?"

Paul resisted the prodding. "To *learn,*" he said again.

His cousin searched his face as if expecting to find signs of truth or falsehood there. All at once the tension drained from him, he relaxed, and slipped his arm around Paul's shoulders, giving him a squeeze.

"All right, that's fair. Just make sure you always question the right people."

They hopped off the car where the macadamized road ended. Before them was a double-rutted stretch of sunlit dust, heavily shaded by large old trees. In a field to his left Paul saw cows grazing, and a barn needing paint.

They trudged for a mile and then Paul heard music. An oompah band; a tuba, maybe two or three smaller horns. They came to a rickety wooden arch with a faded sign at the top. OGDEN'S GROVE. Back in the trees Paul saw trestle tables with little gauze tents protecting food, and people mingling, and a few dancing a schottische on the grass. Children chased each other through patches of sunlight and shade.

In the grove, Joe Junior introduced Paul to people so quickly, he didn't have time to fix names and faces in his head. A few things registered. The families were generally not well dressed; there was a lot of patched clothing. Some of the men were almost sinister because of heavy beards and long hair. One of them reminded him of the Russian journalist, Rhukov. He was surprised by the great number of infants and youngsters, and by nationalities represented. Not merely Germans but Swedes, Bohemians, even a pair of Englishmen.

Throughout the grove, faded red flags were planted in the ground. "Red for the blood of the oppressed," Joe Junior said. "Red for the Internationale, and everybody who's died for the cause." He snatched two sour pickles from a brown crock and replaced the lid. "Here's something to keep you from starving. Let's find Benno."

They found him on the other side of the grove, arguing with half a dozen men. Benno spied them, broke off and hurried over, grinning. His teeth looked huge beneath his flowing guardsman's mustache. "Hey, looka here. The pupil. Glad to see you again. How's he coming, Joey?"

Joe Junior tilted his hand back and forth. "*Langsam. Langsam.*" Slowly.

"Your name's Paul, ain't that right? Old Joe's nephew?" Paul said yes. Benno scratched his nose. "And how long you been in this country?"

"Since Christmas, that's all."

"You speak the language okay. He speaks the language okay, don't he, Joey?" With a smile, Joe Junior nodded. "Pretty well."

"My aunt in Berlin taught me some of it before I came over."

"Got you." Sunlight brought a sheen of perspiration to Benno's bald head. "Well, drink some beer, kid, it's free. There'll be speeches after while. Very instructive, so listen close. See you later." Benno returned to his friends, all of whom were regarding Paul with suspicion. "Nah, he's okay, I know him," Benno said to them.

Paul and Joe Junior stuffed themselves with sausages, homemade bread, and beer from an unmarked keg. It was dark, bitter brew; definitely not Crown's. Who had paid for the beer and food?

"We have a couple of patrons among the rich," Joe Junior said. "You won't ever find them at these affairs, but they make their presence known in other ways."

Benno and some others shoved wooden boxes together to improvise a platform. Three speakers addressed the crowd of people sitting or lying in a great semicircle on the grass. The first man, from Poland, had such a thick accent Paul could scarcely understand him. The second, introduced as Mr. Parkin-Lloyd, "one of our leading socialist comrades from England," tried to explain and embellish some theories of the writer Karl Marx, whom Joe Junior had mentioned. Paul knew nothing about this Marx and found the Englishman boring.

Benno took the platform as the final speaker. He started with a denunciation of the fair. "They're puttin' on this thing, this circus, to show off what capitalists make from the sweat of workers. You think they're celebrating the great American democracy? Okay, tell me—opening day, how many niggers was invited to sit on the stage with the U.S. President? Not a damn one, that's how many. How many darkies helped plan that fair? Not a one. They're free people but the white oligarchy, it locked 'em out. Something else. They got a building in Jackson Park, I read about it, I wouldn't ever go look at it except maybe to spit on it—there's gold all over the doorway. Yes! For decoration! So much gold, it'd feed and clothe hundreds! That building, that whole fair, cost *millions.* And there's more out of work every day with this panic the rich bankers started. It's a rotten disgrace."

He called for "propaganda of the deed" to demonstrate their "solidarity." He called bombs and pistols "the best friends we got." He shouted for "retribution" and "violent overthrow of the system" and, chillingly, "the heads of the pluto-crats."

"They squeezed blood out of us for years, okay, we take theirs!" He flung his arms straight up over his head. "Right in the streets of Chicago!"

He let his arms fall to his sides.

"Comrades—I thank you."

Benno received the loudest ovation of the day.

He jumped down from the boxes and startled Paul by coming straight over to him. "Okay, what y'think? Are you hearing a message?"

"I hear it, Herr Strauss. I don't know if I like it so much." Benno scowled but Paul wouldn't retreat; this man was speaking hate against Paul's family. He screwed up his nerve and finished, "I don't know if I like the idea of taking blood in the streets."

"How else you think we're gonna win?" Joe Junior drifted up to them. "Hey, Joey, get busy. This one's backbone ain't stiff enough yet."

Benno's huge paw slammed down on Paul's shoulder. "Get clear on this, kid. You can't stand around saying maybe it's this way today, maybe that way tomor-row. Got to choose. Sooner or later in the class war, everybody's got to choose."

"Take sides against my uncle, is that what you mean?"

Benno stared at him. "Yeah."

"You don't like my uncle very much."

Benno's first response was a shrug. "Like ain't got nothing to do with it. Truth is, I don't think Joe Crown's a bad man deep down. He wouldn't rob his mother of her last crust of bread. But he cares a lot more for property than the rights of us workingmen. Also, he's stubborn, like most Dutchmen. A bad combination." Benno formed a huge fist under Paul's nose. "Makes him like a rock about certain things. We got a national union. A national program—"

"Which Pop opposes one hundred percent," said Joe Junior.

"Right, right. Could be trouble; we come pretty close to it two, three times already. What I'm saying, kid—you can't sit on the fence. You only find one kind there, yellowbellies."

His hand clamped on Paul's shoulder. The thick strong fingers hurt.

"You got to choose your side, absolutely. If you don't learn nothing else today, learn that."

21

Joe Crown

HE SAW THE RED DIRT ROAD winding south. He heard the jingle of bits; the creak of horse furniture. The column moved through the hot morning with a strange dreamy grace.

He saw the wooden sign stuck in the ground at the roadside. Crudely cut, like an arrow, it pointed ahead.

HELL FIVE MILES
COME ON YANKS!

The column kept moving. Dust rose up, but the hooves of the horses at walk made so faint a sound, it was like a murmur in the blood. Leading the patrol, Captain Ehrlich was laughing and chatting as though at a picnic.

Turn back. Don't go down this road, I know what's waiting.

No one heard him. Or, if they heard him, paid no attention.

The column was passing through thick woods pierced by golden shafts of summer sun full of slow-swirling dust.

Suddenly an old Negro in ragged clothes stepped from a stand of myrtle at the roadside. Sidearms were whipped out of holsters. Captain Ehrlich raised his hand. "Hold fire, I don't see a weapon."

The old black man snatched off a crushed straw hat. *"That's right, Cap'n, nothin' to hurt you. I'm Erasmus, your friend. Sign back there, it mean what it say. They's bad people up ahead."*

"Soldiers?"

"Some. Mos'ly old men, boys from 'round here. But they blood-mad to kill some of you Yankees. They got plenty of guns. Don' go on, turn back. It be bad for you when night fall."

He heard the old man's plea clearly. Saw Captain Ehrlich in profile, full of stern courage. "Thank you, Mr. Erasmus, but we have orders to advance. We'll be watchful."

Listen to him, Ehrlich. I know what's waiting. Don't go down the road!

"Don't. Don't . . ."

"Sir? Are you all right?"

"Uh? What's that?"

"You cried out something fierce."

Drenched in sweat, shivering in darkness, he didn't know where he was.

Then he felt the stiff plush seat under his legs. Heard the clickety sound of the express speeding on to Cincinnati. Saw streaking past the window the lights of a lonely farmstead. The conductor was a black bulk looming against the dim lantern that swayed above the door to the vestibule.

"Cried out? I'm sorry. Bad dream."

The conductor grunted and went on.

Joe leaned his forehead against the glass, joyfully realizing he was on the southbound train. Awake, and not imprisoned in the familiar dream of the road in northern Mississippi. A dream that had gripped him for years and wouldn't let go.

Joe Crown owned a large block of shares in a textile factory at Millington, a small town in the sand hills of South Carolina formerly known as Company Shops when railroad maintenance work was done there. He also owned a winter estate in South Carolina. It was of substantial size, located on a dirt road six miles west of the Atlantic Ocean and an hour's horseback ride south of Charleston. Some Yankee carpetbagger had built it after the war, and named it Royalton. When Joe bought it he rechristened it Chimneys. He'd ridden through the entire war with the Union cavalry, all the way down to Savannah and up again through the Carolinas, where General Judson Kilpatrick and his horse soldiers laid waste to great swaths of land. "I named it Chimneys," Joe said about the winter place, "because we left little else standing in that beautiful state when we passed through."

He couldn't have been more grateful to be taking one of his business trips, temporarily free of the turmoil in Chicago, where the papers were full of news of solid companies collapsing, share prices still tumbling. If he admitted it, he was also glad to be free of the situation in his own household. Paul was settling in well, doing all right in school or at least not reporting that he wasn't. Carl had taken to him, and Fritzi had lost her heart. But Joe Junior seemed colder, more embittered about all the things Joe stood for, than ever before. As if merely by existing, being himself, Joe was an offense to his oldest boy.

It was the influence of that damnable Benno, he was sure. Reinforced by the privation sweeping the country along with the panic. The last newspaper he'd read before leaving contained a long, grim article about "suicides among the despairing poor."

Joe couldn't help contrasting his nephew with Joe Junior. Whenever he did, he was washed with guilt, because he found his son wanting. Sitting by himself in the darkened car, he was drawn into the past, to a virulent, explosive quarrel two years ago. The quarrel that seemed to create the permanent gulf between father and son.

Even now he shuddered to recall it. The shouting. The accusations—all brought on when Joe Junior came home with a letter of dismissal from his third school, an expensive private academy. There were high standards for pupils from the Crown house; high expectations. Joe Junior had been unable to fulfill them and, later, aware of this, he'd openly flaunted them by courting failure. The letter he brought home put the match to the fuse; the explosion came after fifteen minutes of acrimony behind tightly closed doors and windows in the airless study. Joe Crown had done something rare then. Lost his temper completely. Responded to some sneer, some shout from his distraught son, by striking him across the face with his open palm. Striking him so hard the white marks of his fingers showed like stigmata for five or ten seconds . . .

Suffused with shame, guilt, he'd whispered an apology. Not for the harsh things he'd said about Joe Junior's failure, but for the blow. A decent and responsible father didn't strike in anger.

The apology seemed to do no good. Joe Junior's eyes were like blue flints. Nothing had been the same between them since that night.

The train arrived in the hilly city he had left in 1871 with his wife of two years. After many earnest talks, he had convinced Ilsa that it was smart for him to quit Imbrey's in Cincinnati. The old breweries were family owned, leaving little room for a newcomer to advance. And the Chicago fire of '71 suddenly threw the whole commercial scene of that growing city into chaos. Joe sensed an opportunity. Ilsa finally agreed that he should seize it.

Since '71 they'd returned to Cincinnati only for short visits with Ilsa's relatives, most of whom were elderly. Joe Crown loved the old city on the Ohio. Loved the splendid Roebling bridge that now connected it to Kentucky. But Cincinnati never would, never could match or even compete with the rude burly giant on Lake Michigan. That was home.

He had about two hours before the connecting train to Columbia and Charleston departed. He decided to walk awhile. The war memories were gripping him strongly again, as they did from time to time, always with little or no warning. A vigorous stroll might help him throw off the spell of the past.

Outside the depot a dreary rain was starting to fall. Joe nearly stumbled over a young man, twenty or so, sitting cross-legged against a pillar with a cap held out. Joe's face darkened at the sight of the beggar's dirty blue blouse. A Union infantry blouse. On the left breast hung three medals, cheap tinplate things, resembling no medals he'd ever seen. Probably bought at some novelty shop.

"You're too young to have worn that coat."

"It was my uncle's," the beggar whined. Here was one of those spiritual cripples who refused to stand up and help themselves. So far as Joe could see the fellow was perfectly sound and whole. "Forty-second Ohio Infantry, Brigadier James A. Garfield—"

"You disgrace the uniform by begging in it. Take off the blouse, I'll buy it."

"What the devil—?"

"Here's five dollars." Joe flung bills into the outstretched cap. "Now take it off and give it to me, before I cane you with this stick."

The beggar slid the money into his pants pocket. He tottered to his feet, muttering, "Crazy damned Dutchman." But he quickly rid himself of the garment, which Joe rolled up under his arm.

In a saloon across from the depot he ordered an Imbrey's lager. He blew off some of the head, tasted, smacked his lips.

"Still as good as ever," he said to the barkeep.

Reaching down to the floor, he passed the uniform to the man, together with a dollar. "Get rid of this for me, please. Don't ask questions, just burn it."

Joe stood very straight at the bar, one shoe with a gray spat on the brass rail, and let the heaviness of memory, the pull of that incredible holy war of thirty years ago, possess him once again.

It was a phenomenon he couldn't explain to others. Not to Ilsa, and certainly not to the children. Only men who had fought in the war could understand.

A heavy gloom settled on him. Although he knew the probable consequences, he was powerless to push it back. He didn't like delays, or changes in routine. But this one, like similar ones in past years, was inevitable.

He walked back to the depot through the drizzle, reclaimed his grip, and exchanged his South Carolina ticket for another that would take him to Tennessee.

22

Paul

ON A SATURDAY MORNING in early June, Paul went to the Exposition alone.

A week of school remained. At the end of it, he supposed, Mrs. Petigru would send home a letter to his aunt and uncle, to say he would be held over. Until now he'd been pretending all was well. He hadn't even told Cousin Joe about his troubles.

Uncle Joe was still traveling in the South. He had telegraphed Aunt Ilsa to say that it might be as much as two weeks before he returned. Some kind of expansion at the textile mill was being planned. He had to attend meetings with architects and contractors.

Paul asked his aunt's permission to go to the fair because he had a dollar fifty cents saved from the small sums she paid for chores around the house. He'd pondered for a week before making the decision to go. He hadn't forgotten Juliette Vanderhoff; by wintertime he must have ice skates. Carl had gone with him to A. G. Spalding's store one day after school. Skates were currently off the shelves because it was summer, but a helpful clerk said a fine pair of racers—crucible steel heel and toe plates, steel runners polished and nickel-plated, straps of russet leather—would cost two dollars twenty-five cents. Paul felt sure he could earn that much by the first freeze. He would see the fair while he had the chance.

He took a crowded yellow and red tram to the Fifty-seventh Street entrance, and from there walked a few blocks south to the Buffalo Bill encampment. He stood outside for a while, running his hand up and down the rough wood of the palisade. He could hear the morning performance in progress. Wheels creaking, hoofs pounding, Indians war-whooping, revolvers blasting—and spectators clapping, whistling, stamping. With a shake of his head he turned away, wondering if he'd ever see the show.

He walked briskly to the booths at the Sixty-third Street entrance, bought his

ticket and passed through the turnstile. He wandered in and out of the splendid
white buildings without any special plan, simply letting one exhibit after another
surprise and enthrall him. In the Agriculture Building he marveled at a cheese
weighing twenty-two thousand pounds. In the Mines and Mining Building he
saw the world's largest gold nugget, 344.78 ounces, according to the sign.

Joe Junior had informed him that, among hundreds of dull pictures and sculp-
tures, there were some spicy ones hanging in the mammoth Fine Arts Building
and its two annexes, so he went there next. In room after room, the walls were
crammed from floor to ceiling with framed canvases. And Joe Junior was right,
there were nudes. Standing nudes, reclining nudes, large nudes, small nudes,
nudes observed from the front and from the rear. There were plump buttocks and
large breasts with rosy nipples. In every one of the paintings, the most intimate
area was hidden by the model's hand, a drape, some grape leaves.

Paul's face grew flushed and he got an erection from looking at the pictures. In
front of the most voluptuous ones, he stared fixedly until he could imagine the
face of Miss Juliette Vanderhoff. The guards gave him disapproving looks—there
were no other unescorted young people in the galleries—and a matron who
passed by as he was creating another fantasy muttered something about "cor-
rupting our youth."

Leaving the building, he decided he would buy a bit of lunch, a glass of beer,
and headed for the Midway. He avoided the exotic offerings of the Persian Coffee
House, the Chinese Tea Garden, the French Cider Press, and chose instead a café
with no national allegiances, near the west end. He took a small outdoor table for
two, under a striped umbrella. The table stood next to a low picket fence separating the café from the street.

The sun was hot, filtering through airborne dust with a fierce white glare. Paul
sat in shadow, glancing into the passing crowds between bites of sausage. His
head started to throb. He knuckled his eye, blinked several times. When he
opened his eyes, he started. There was a man standing next to his table on the
other side of the fence. A man silhouetted in a corona light. A man sprung from
nowhere.

"Can I believe my eyes? The Berlin boy. Taken any art lessons?"

He was speaking German. His hair was longer, hanging over his collar like hair
in a religious painting. Everything else was the same. The long, white, starved
countenance. The glowing dark eyes behind the gold-wire spectacles with tiny
round lenses. The shabby derby, greasy cravat, long duster. The cigarette hovering near his lips, held by yellowed fingers. Where had he come from? Out of the
ground? Out of the sky? Paul remembered thinking the first time that his eyes
were the eyes of Death.

"What are you doing here, Mr.—?"

"Rhukov."

"I remember."

"Permit me to ask the same question of you." Rhukov stepped over the fence,
pulled out the other chair, sat down. "Waiter. Beer."

After those two words in English, Rhukov returned to German. "You left Berlin.
What scared you out, the generals rattling their swords? The distasteful thought

of conscription? Or were you lured by Buffalo Bill? Did you decide to chase the cowboy show as a life's work?"

Rhukov puffed his cigarette, waiting. Paul pushed his plate aside.

"My uncle lives here. He brews beer. I always planned to come to America." Stretching it there, wasn't he? But Rhukov made him nervous, defensive, even though he had an inexplicable liking for the odd young man.

The waiter brought Rhukov's beer in a glass with a Pabst crest. He tipped with a three-cent piece. "When did you make the crossing?"

Paul answered, then described a few of the circumstances.

"Out of Hamburg, you say? And you weren't struck down? You've got a guardian angel, my friend. There was an epidemic."

"I heard."

"Eight thousand, ten thousand dead before the autumn frosts came to stop it. The Hamburg politicians tried to ignore the epidemic for a while. Hush it up. Nothing wrong here, they announced, strolling past corpses still drooling and dribbling out of their dead mouths and dead asses." He threw his cigarette on the ground.

"Well, who expects anything else from those in power? Politicians, prime ministers, princes—all the same. Pack of jackals. Swine at the public trough. Lie, rob, kill their mothers to keep their office or their throne. You'll get used to it when you're older. Either that or you'll stand on a chair and hang yourself."

He shook two cigarettes from a crushed paper pack. Paul took one, Rhukov struck a match and lit both. Paul took a puff and doubled over, hacking.

"You hate it," Rhukov said.

"I do. I wanted to be polite."

"That's crap." He snatched the cigarette away and tossed it over the fence into the street.

"Rhukov's rule number one. Do nothing that you hate. It shortens your life." He tilted his head back and drank the rest of the beer. "Waiter. Another."

"Here also," Paul said, although the heat and dust and this astonishing reunion were making him a little groggy.

Rhukov paid for both beers, waving aside Paul's protests. "Do you like America?"

"Except for school."

"School! What do they teach you?"

"Nothing I want to know. I'm doing terribly."

"But otherwise happy?"

"Very happy."

"I'll ask you again in five years."

"You still haven't answered my question, Herr Rhukov. What are you doing here?"

"Same as before. Hunting a few stories."

"You must like the job."

"Oh, certainly. The free and glamorous life of the roving journalist! Bedbugs and body lice. Sleeping in doss houses. Bedding elderly whores because they don't charge so much. Alternatively, risking a bullet in the back from a crazed husband. I eat well, though. Truly. I get a shave and then I haunt the hotels.

There's always a banquet. War veterans, temperance societies, electric motor salesmen, homeopathic physicians, clergy exhibiting reformed whores. Always plenty of leftovers waiting to be thrown out. I know how to talk to the busboys. I'm at home with the lower classes. So here I am, searching for glimpses of the future. Plenty of those to be had. Not as pretty as some like to pretend. Seen the Krupp gun?"

"Yes."

"Scary. How about the exhibits from my own beloved country?" Paul shook his head. "Christ, how can you miss them? Mother Russia is a huge presence here. One of the largest. Finish your beer, we'll have a look."

They walked to the Russian state pavilion, one of many located inside the vast Manufactures and Liberal Arts Building. Rhukov led Paul to a display of exquisite bronze miniatures of animals and peasant groups.

"Don't they look happy, the precious little things? You can't smell them, you can't feel the anguish when the crops fail, there's not a back broken by years of toil. The serfs are bleeding out their lives in poverty, children are starving, and Tsar Alexander has decreed that every ruble paying for this romantic bullshit— every Russian display at this circus—shall come straight from the imperial treasury. Does it ever slip into his feeble brain that he might spend the same money to succor his own people? Never. Well, the clock's running down for the Tsar and rulers of his ilk. Certain men are laying plans and building bombs. The world is coming to an end, Berlin boy. The world as we know it. The birth of the new one will be bloody. You'll see it in ten years. Or less."

Paul thought of Benno Strauss. Despite the heat, he shivered.

Rhukov hurried them out of the pavilion. "I can't stand a big dose of this. I have to search out antidotes. Something that faintly suggests a little measure of humanity. A spark of enlightenment—a grain of progress. You've seen the Electricity Building?"

"Not yet."

He yanked Paul's arm. "We'll remedy that immediately."

In the Electricity Building at the south end of the Lagoon, they stood before Edison's Tower of Light, a shaft nearly eighty feet high, studded with electric globes of all sizes and colors. They flashed in constantly changing patterns and rhythms.

"Truly marvelous, isn't it? A few years ago I was ignorant of inventions like this. I didn't realize the nature, the magnitude of what's rushing toward us like a locomotive with the throttle wide open. In my first year trying to scratch out a living with my pen, I had an experience that opened my eyes. It happened in Vienna, in a great amusement park, the Prater, heard of it? For a few pennies they sold electricity. You paid your money and gripped two handles which gave you a jolt of this new thing *electricity*. I felt an incredible force tingling through my hands, racing up my arms and through my body. In an instant, I knew the future was coming, couldn't be escaped. New ideas crashing upon us, science digging the floor from under us, everything tumbling, thrown about, rearranged —an apocalypse, and not wholly political this time. It's here, boy—it's here at this fair, if you can search it out. You think this tower is spectacular? I'll show you something you truly will not believe. Down this side aisle, follow me."

The aisle was dim, flanked by small booths with uninteresting exhibits. Rhukov pointed to a signboard on the left.

THE AMAZING TACHYSCOPE
See Pictures That Actually
MOVE!

Pictures that moved? How could it be?

The booth itself didn't look promising. In front of some drab draperies, between drooping palms in pots, stood a large rectangular box with a wooden step in front. It was about Paul's height. A metal piece much like a stereopticon viewer was attached to the sloping front at eye level. There was a coin slot. Paul wondered about the price; he only had a few cents left.

Alternately dubious and seduced, he followed Rhukov into the booth. Two men were talking at a table in the corner. The men strolled over to greet them. "It's the journalist again," said the heavier of the two. "Good day, sir."

Rhukov switched to slow, less than clear English. "Good day to you. My friend here—" Paul tried to look adult and thoughtful. "He doesn't believe your sign."

The man chuckled. "Skeptic, is he? We've seen plenty of those. Lad, this gentleman is Mr. Ottmar Anschütz, owner and perfecter of the Tachyscope. Which is very much worth the modest price of a dime."

"What sort of pictures does it show?"

"My boy," said the inventor—actually it was *mein* boy; he was another German—"have you seen the animals at Hagenbeck's Zoological Circus on the Midway?"

"No, sir."

"There is in the performance an elephant whose name is Bebe. Inside my Tachyscope, Bebe moves and performs just as realistically as in real life. The pictures in the machine were taken in the Tiergarten."

"In Berlin? I'm from Berlin."

"I suspected as much from your accent." Anschütz fished a coin from his checkered vest. "Step up, I will treat the young skeptic to a viewing."

Paul stood on the step and leaned into the eyepiece. He saw only darkness. At his elbow, the other man, the heavy-set American, was saying, "Mr. Edison was supposed to have his machine, the Kinetoscope, on exhibit here. It's similar, but they didn't get it ready in time."

"Watch closely," Herr Anschütz said. The coin dropped in the slot. Inside the box machinery whirred and clicked. A sudden flash of white light dazzled Paul.

He grabbed the box, almost falling off the step. In the viewer he saw a grainy picture of an elephant with a fanciful little ballet skirt around its middle, prancing, sidestepping, *moving* back and forth over a stretch of grass that might have been the Tiergarten but was unrecognizable to him.

Paul hardly dared to breathe. The movement seemed jerky, as though interrupted at very short intervals by the flashing light. Never mind, it was astounding, greater by far than the lifeless still photographs he'd tacked up in his room on Müllerstrasse. This was a moment like Rhukov's in the Prater, light pouring out of the eyepiece like blinding flashes of revelation, *flash, flash,* another, and another, and another . . .

Moments later, groggy, he stepped down from the Tachyscope. "Sirs—Herr Rhukov—that is the most astonishing, incredible—wait. Where is he?"

The others turned. Herr Anschütz pulled a face and shrugged. The American said, "He was standing right there. I saw his silhouette against the flashing lights on the Edison tower. I turned to speak to Herr Anschütz—no more than a second or so—and when I looked again—gone."

Paul smelled smoke from a strong cigarette and thought he saw a blue wisp of it dispersing in the air. In Berlin, Rhukov had disappeared with the same eerie abruptness. But this phenomenon was overwhelmed by the miracle of the Tachyscope.

Herr Anschütz walked off to speak to a young couple hesitating outside the booth, possibly wondering, as Paul had, whether to spend their money. Paul said to the American, "Do you know all about this machine?"

"I know something. I have my own studio of photography."

"How does the machine work?"

"Well, you are not looking at pictures that actually move, merely at separate still pictures which create that illusion when they're flashed at a rapid speed. Inside the cabinet there's a revolving drum. The pictures of Bebe are mounted on the drum sequentially. The flashing light is the excited gas in a pair of Geissler tubes. It enhances the effect."

"I've never seen anything so lifelike. It's amazing. Wonderful."

"Good for you! I knew you were a smart youngster the minute I spotted you."

A strange little man. He wore a nondescript suit and a string tie. He came up to Paul's shoulder. He had a potbelly and a salt-and-pepper mustache so bushy and unkempt it nearly hid his mouth.

His hair needed barbering. His eyes were huge behind spectacles with thick round lenses. He had the pale skin of a mole or some other creature of the dark. He wasn't forbidding, or menacing, as the vanished Rhukov could be. He was just—odd.

Except for his eyes. The spectacles enlarged them, making them all the more arresting. The eyes looked as if they could reach into your head, seize your very brains, and twist them until you were convinced of whatever the man wanted you to believe. Like Rhukov's eyes, they had a power.

"But, sir, do you think these moving pictures will ever be more than a—uh—"

"Novelty?"

"A novelty, yes, I think that's what I mean."

"Of course I do. They'll be entertainment, my boy. Entertainment and education of such a scope and scale, you can't imagine. Someday moving pictures will be shown on giant screens in great auditoriums, for the amusement and edification of all. Pictures like these speak a universal language. They'll sweep the world. It may take a few years, inventors are still struggling to perfect a projection machine. But it will come, make no mistake. It will come just as the new century's coming. Rooney says so."

"Rooney?"

"Wexford Rooney. Here's my card." He fished in one pocket, then another, finally found it in a third.

"That's the address of my present studio. North Clark Street. Drop around if you ever need a camera, or want instruction, or just a little chatter. I photographed up and down the country during the late unpleasantness." Paul looked blank. "The Civil War. Been in the trade ever since. Drop around."

"I will, it is a promise. I have one more week of school, then I will come."

"Fine, just fine. Can't find enough willing converts. Nine tenths of the world consists of Doubting Thomases. Plain fools." He flipped Paul a coin. "Take another look at Bebe, my compliments."

He stood back with his thumbs in the armholes of his vest and a pleased look on his face. Paul bent over the Tachyscope with the white light flashing, flashing into his eyes, into his bones and his soul, making the miracle part of him forever.

On the tram ride home, Paul patted his shirt pocket a dozen times, to be sure he hadn't lost Rooney's card.

He had always thought the still photograph, as exemplified by the lost Kodak and his picture cards, to be the greatest of all miracles of the new age. He was wrong, he had seen something that leaped a thousand miles beyond. He was euphoric when he ran into the kitchen at half past five, and nearly bowled over Louise, the cook.

"*Gott im Himmel*, what's got into you?"

"Is Aunt Ilsa home?"

"No, gone out with Fritzi and Carl."

"Joe Junior?"

"Upstairs."

He was panting when he knocked on his cousin's door. Joe Junior had just come from the bath. He was wearing a suit of ventilated summer underwear, light gray, which he'd unbuttoned to the waist and pushed down to his hips. Damp hair clung to his head. He was toweling water from his flat muscular chest.

"What are you so damn excited about?"

"Joe, I must tell you what I saw at the fair."

Joe Junior scratched his crotch and perched on the edge of the bed. "Little Egypt."

"No, no—a machine! A marvelous machine." He sat beside his cousin, struggling for the English to describe the miracle.

"I could learn to make such pictures, Joe. I always wanted to draw but I have no talent. This talent I could learn, it employs machinery."

"If it's so great, how come everybody isn't talking about it? I never heard of it."

"But—"

"What does it have to do with anything? What does it have to do with lifting a burden from some workingman's back?"

Silent anger flared in Paul. Could his cousin talk of nothing but poor people? Joe squeezed Paul's shoulder and delivered grown-up advice with a smile.

"I'd forget it. Call me when it's supper, will you? I need a nap."

◻ ◻ ◻ ◻

Paul quickly forgave his cousin. Hadn't Rooney said the world was full of unbe-lievers? It was the easy thing, to scoff. That night he sat on his bed, his glance flying back and forth between the board with the photographic postal cards and the calling card in his hand.

It was a very poor card. Old, grimy, bent at the corners. The printer's ink had smeared. Still, it seemed a magic key to a magic door. On the other side of that door, if he could believe Rooney, he could learn about photographs and how to make them. And then, perhaps, learn more about the pictures that moved.

One more week until school was over, then he'd have free time, he could go. Being held over in Mrs. Petigru's room no longer dominated his thoughts. He pinned the card carefully on his board and stood gazing at it.

One week. How would he ever endure the wait?

Before school on Monday morning, he shared his exciting discovery with Leo Rapoport. Like Cousin Joe, Leo was unimpressed. Called the invention "cracked." This, he explained, meant the same as crazy.

Leo had other things to talk about. "Sit down," he whispered. Paul sat on the low cement wall at the edge of the schoolyard. After swift looks both ways, Leo opened his battered school bag of brown duck. He took out a wad of folded sheets with printing on them.

"Finally my old man threw out last year's sales sheets. Lamp this stuff, will you? Just don't wave it around. I'll stay on guard."

On guard against what? Paul unfolded the sheets, and quickly leafed through the pages, which were identically designed. Above blocks of feature and price information, three quarters of each page was given over to a full-figure engraving of a beautiful young woman wearing an item from Mr. Rapoport's line. Every girl was incredibly voluptuous, with enormous bulging breasts, vaguely erotic pout-ing lips, a slight forward tilt to the body affording a peek into a gorge of cleavage. There were sheets for plain undecorated corsets and fancy French corsets with silk embroidery; lightweight four-hook summer corsets and high-hip corsets dar-ingly cut to reveal more flesh. The wickedest pictures showed the woman's foot on a chair or stool, to display an expanse of forbidden inner thigh.

"These are for buyers who work for stores, not for the ladies who wear the stuff," Leo explained. Suddenly he grabbed Paul's sleeve.

"Look out, here comes Maury Flugel. Hide those, quick. If he sees 'em, he'll snitch."

Paul shoved the folded sheets into the left pocket of his linen school jacket, pushing them out of sight without glancing down. Maury arrived a moment later.

Fists on his hips, he said, "I seen you two reading something. A yellow-back dirty book? Come on, Leo, be a pal, let me see."

"You're no pal, you're a snitcher," Leo said, shoving him. Leo marched toward the schoolhouse door. Paul was right behind. As he neared the doors he checked his left pocket. He was horrified to see that a corner of the folded bundle had popped out, very noticeably. His heart raced. He didn't touch the sheets until he was inside and the double doors hid him from Maury.

In the cloakroom he turned his jacket inside out, making sure the printed sheets were entirely hidden, and then hung the coat on the last hook at the end.

Just before morning recess, Mrs. Petigru called Paul to the desk to say the letter to his aunt and uncle would be ready on Thursday, and he was to deliver it, she would telephone that same night to make sure he had. The bell rang. Pupils rushed to the cloakroom for wraps; outside it was overcast, with a strong wind blowing. Paul started to go.

"Stand there, young man, you are not excused until I say so." The room was empty when she finally gave him a curt wave. "You may go."

He rushed to the cloakroom. His coat had been disturbed. He stabbed a hand into the pocket holding the sales sheet. It was empty.

He took Leo aside in the yard; told him of the disaster. They knew the culprit. There was nothing they could do without starting a fight, risking exposure if one of the teachers broke it up.

When they returned from recess, Mrs. Petigru was seated at her desk, spots of color burning in her white cheeks. Her eyes raked the room, alighting on Paul. He had seen Mrs. Petigru angry, but never like this.

In a low tremulous voice Mrs. Petigru addressed the class. "At the end of recess I found something lying on this desk. Something unfit for young people. Something filthy, vile, and obscene." Her left hand dropped to a drawer. Slid it out. She laid the folded sales sheets on the desk blotter and quickly covered them with her right hand, fingers splayed. Sweat ran down inside Paul's collar. Mrs. Petigru shut the drawer. The sound was loud as a pistol shot. Her wrathful eyes found him again.

"Paul Crown, come up here."

Maury Flugel snickered, but everyone else was rigid with fear. They recognized a special fury in the teacher.

Paul walked forward and stopped beside the desk, standing as straight as he could. Between Mrs. Petigru's spread fingers, he could see that on the back of a sales sheet, someone had printed in block letters PAUL C.

Mrs. Petigru stared him down.

"Whose are these, Paul?"

He kept his voice level, as strong as possible. "I see my name on them. They are mine."

"Where did you get them?"

He couldn't say *From Leo.* Nor could he say something like, *My uncle's house.* He gave the answer she would believe.

"I bought them from a man at a beer garden."

"More of that fine German morality, eh? What is the matter with you, what sort of person *are* you? These are only fit to be burned. That's what I'll do with them. I've given you my best, Paul. I've pleaded, struggled, helped you conscientiously. And how do you thank me? You bring beer-hall filth into my classroom."

With each phrase, she grew louder. Little bits of spittle flew from her lips. "You're a good-for-nothing. What's more, you're stupid. That thick German head of yours. You can't learn anything."

Something gave way in him. He blurted, "I could learn something if I liked it."

"Oh, indeed?" Leaning back, she folded her arms. "Such as? Loafing? Besotting yourself with beer, amusing yourself with smut?"

"That is not fair, I did not ever—"

"Be still! Now, step back from the desk one step. Put both your hands here." Behind him, Paul heard a girl utter a strangled, *"Oh."*

Paul swallowed, stepped back. He leaned down, placed his palms on the blotter. In the classroom, someone's foot scraped.

"Mrs. Petigru, those pictures are mine, I brought them."

"Sit down, Leopold Rapoport. I detest liars. You can't right one wrong with another. Paul, spread your fingers."

He obeyed. Mrs. Petigru opened the center drawer and took out her long thick ruler.

23

Joe Crown

THE TRAIN FROM CINCINNATI carried him deep into western Tennessee. He stepped down from his car at Henderson Station, a trim genteel figure in a white suit and dark cravat. The stares he drew from depot loungers were no different than those any well-dressed stranger would attract in any small town. Yet he feared his guilt was splotched on his face like a birthmark.

He hired a buggy, stowed his grip under the seat, and wended his way south and east, toward the river: Pittsburg Landing and Shiloh Church.

It was pretty country, just as he remembered. Rural, with only here and there a farm in what was otherwise dense woodland. Flimsy wooden bridges spanned creeks and ravines on the dirt roads; he remembered that, too, from thirty years ago, the eve of battle, when he was twenty . . .

Shortly after dawn on the morning of April 6, 1862, the Union Army lay at rest, preparing breakfast. No one anticipated hostilities, least of all General Grant, who was somewhere on the Tennessee River in a Union gunboat. After its triumphant capture of Fort Henry and Fort Donelson, the Army was slowly pushing south toward Corinth, a strategic rail junction in northern Mississippi. The Army was still essentially amateur, and it showed. Picket lines were poorly maintained, cavalry patrols carelessly scheduled. Contempt for the enemy led to a lazy overconfidence.

So they were taken by surprise that peaceful Sunday when the young soldiers of the young Confederacy came howling and smashing out of woodlands to the south.

The 5th Ohio Cavalry was flung into action that morning to try to prevent a rout. Joe remembered the frightened boyish faces—he assumed his was no different—as the 5th Ohio charged around the Union infantry, jumping fences, trying to shoot, while Reb shells landed with ferocious detonations and geysers of blown-up earth . . .

In his rented buggy, Joe arrived at the weedy and deserted battlefield late in the day. At sunset he found the familiar oak woods where the 5th had engaged the Rebs to save the Union infantry from being flanked on the right on that long-ago Sunday afternoon. Joe had ridden behind Major Ricker, on the regiment's left. He remembered well that breakneck charge, the smoke so thick you could hardly see an enemy ahead, let alone a comrade next to you. Standing in the cool evening shade of a huge oak that still bore battle scars, Joe swallowed and felt his eyes mist as he remembered with pride all the young voices screaming their brave defiance during the charge. The senior officers had started the yell, which outdid any vaunted Rebel yell he heard later . . .

An orange fire like the heart of a steel-making furnace suffused the western sky. Joe Crown leaned against the ball-pocked oak, lightheaded, his face chilly as the wind cooled his sweat. How young they were that beautiful Sunday, which became another night of rain. How ardent and heroic both armies were, until they saw, for the very first time, hundreds and hundreds of dead men with bodies bullet-riddled, limbs blown off, or heard at midnight, in the drenching rain, the screaming of amputees in the hospital tents . . .

In the storm that night, Joe had patrolled the perimeter of their encampment. A glare of lightning showed him a figure creeping through the trees, moving away, a pack slung on his back. Joe immediately pulled his sidearm from under his rubber poncho. "Halt. Halt or I'll shoot."

The soldier froze. "Walk back here to me. Hands in the air," Joe commanded.

Above the noise of the rain, he heard the man's shoes crackling and squishing on soggy ground. He sensed the man near him. Heard his rapid breathing. Another lightning bolt forked down, painting the fugitive's face.

"*Private Linzee!*"

Joe saw the boy's face in memory, wet with tears as well as rain . . .

Hans Linzee was eighteen, an apprentice wheelwright from Hamilton, Ohio; a good soldier. He spoke English with an accent. He was a shy, sensitive boy, and a favorite of Joe's because of his artistry. Linzee carried a paintbox and brushes and a block of special paper in his kit. Did the most remarkable small studies of landscapes, encampments, soldiers at rest. Linzee had enormous promise; Joe wanted to encourage him to look beyond the wheelwright's trade after the war and develop his talent.

"Linzee, what are you doing out here?" Joe slipped the revolver under his poncho. There was no danger. "Were you running away?"

Miserably, Linzee said, "Yes, sir."

"I can't let you do it. I don't give a hang for the rules, it's for your sake. If you got away it would ruin the rest of your life. You would hate yourself. I would rather shoot you down for desertion."

Joe tugged gently at the boy's sleeve. "Come with me, there's a little bit of shelter under that tree." The rain still struck them there, but not so fiercely.

Joe squatted down. "Now, Hans, I want you to tell me why you started to run."

"I was back in the woods, relieving myself," Linzee said in a faint voice. "There I stumbled upon a body without a head. There were farmyard hogs eating the neck stump—oh, sir, oh, sir, this war—*es ist furchtbar*—terrible. I hate this war."

"With good reason. But you've never let it affect you before. You mustn't now, you're one of my best soldiers."

"Thank you, but I have no more heart for it. Will we fight tomorrow?"

"Yes, I'm sure of it. General Grant and General Sherman won't tolerate a defeat."

Linzee burst out crying. *"Mein Gott, Herr Leutnant—ich habe Angst. So viel Angst!"*

Joe cradled the boy like an infant. He was precisely two years older than Hans Linzee. "So are we all. Every man jack in this Army is frightened. If he isn't he's crazy. Rest now. Rest and collect yourself. There's nothing to fear tonight."

He continued to soothe the boy while the downpour soaked them both.

The Confederate general Albert Sidney Johnston fell at Shiloh in the Sunday battle. Thousands of others, lesser lights, fell too. Close to twenty-five thousand men in all, from both sides; ten times the number killed at First Bull Run. Joe's prediction made in the midnight rain came true. Sunday's stalemate and near defeat became a qualified Union victory on Monday; the Confederates under Beauregard slipped away toward Corinth.

It was after Pittsburg Landing that Joe Crown began to hate the war, as passionately as he had once favored it. He hated the dirt and confusion. The randomness of suffering and death. The heavy hand of mischance. He hated the way it reduced decent, honorable young men like Hans Linzee to cringing cowards. Everything in his nature cried out against the seemingly senseless disorder that prevailed so much of the time. The only way he kept his faith and courage up was by thinking of the cause. The Union. An end to black servitude. But it was hard.

Linzee came to him a few days later, his spirits seemingly restored. *"Herr Leutnant,* I thank you for saving me from myself, from disgrace, the other night. I will make you a special gift." Joe smiled and waved and said it wasn't necessary. "Oh, yes, definitely, it is," Linzee replied. So Joe said all right.

And then, in Mississippi, he found himself on a winding red dirt road.

May 1862.

Led by General Halleck, "Old Brains," the Union Army was crawling south from the rail junction of Corinth, which General Beauregard's entrenched commanders, Generals Van Dorn and Bragg, had abandoned at the end of May.

Brick-red dust swirled in powdery clouds from the twisting road as the horses passed. Detachments of the 5th Ohio were searching for enemy ambushes, enemy stragglers; twice they'd exchanged fire with Rebel horsemen.

The day was sultry and still. Lieutenant Joe Crown's dark blue blouse was unbearably hot. He smelled his own unwashed body as he bent his head to avoid low festoons of Spanish moss.

Leading the patrol, his commanding officer, Captain Frank Ehrlich, was laughing and chatting as though on a picnic. Ehrlich ran a hardware store in civilian life, in Lebanon, up the pike from Cincinnati. He had a grade school education. In Joe's opinion he wasn't qualified for his command; too disorganized, and, for a

German, inordinately lazy. But Ehrlich had a brother in the Ohio legislature. The 5th was riddled with appointments won by influence.

Not that the rank and file was much better. Very few of the troopers had useful experience with horses. Most were townsmen—storekeepers, schoolteachers, office clerks—not trained to the saddle like the men in the Southern cavalry.

In the van, sitting stiffly and heavily on his McClellan saddle, Captain Ehrlich gradually sank out of sight as he rode into a depression where a creek ran. Joe watched him come up the other side, near a wooden sign crudely cut like an arrow pointing ahead.

HELL FIVE MILES
COME ON YANKS!

The thick woods seemed peaceful enough this hot morning. But the sign silenced conversations, and the men were soon darting nervous glances into gloomy thickets.

After a quarter of a mile the road leveled again. Captain Ehrlich was pointing left. Joe jogged ahead to join him. An old Negro had stumbled from a heavy stand of myrtle.

Revolvers were drawn. Captain Ehrlich raised his hand. "Hold fire, I don't see a weapon."

The black man clutched his old straw hat to the bosom of his patched and faded work shirt. "That's right, Cap'n, nothin' to hurt you. I'm Erasmus, your friend. Sign back there, it mean what it say. They's bad people up ahead."

"Soldiers?"

"Some. Mos'ly old men, boys from 'round here. But they blood-mad to kill some of you Yankees. They got plenty of guns. Don' go on, turn back. It be bad for you when night fall."

Frank Ehrlich looked stern, fearless as he said, "Thank you, Erasmus, but we have orders to advance. We'll be watchful."

Ehrlich raised his hand again and signaled for the column to move forward. Joe Crown rode by the old sad-eyed Negro crushing the straw hat to his chest. He was seized by a terrible foreboding.

They camped off the road that night, beside a rushing creek where the men bathed in the dark. A cook fire was lit, but the officers warned the men to approach it only when absolutely necessary. Joe felt they shouldn't have built a fire at all, but the men had gone thirty-six hours without hot food and Captain Ehrlich insisted.

Joe sat well away from the fire, gnawing on a piece of salt pork. The only sounds were the purl of the creek, the calls of night birds, the splash of bathers. Yet he was uneasy. Constantly searched the dark woods beyond the picket perimeter. Were unseen Rebs moving out there . . . ?

"Sir?" Joe looked up. It was Linzee. "This is the gift I made," he said, smiling proudly. Joe was astonished to see a white china shaving mug.

"Where on earth did you get that?"

"At the crossroads store, yesterday. The storekeeper didn't want to sell it to a Yankee. I showed him my rifle. Then he begged me to take this, for nothing."

With a ceremonious flourish of his left hand, Linzee turned the mug around, revealing a painted side. Joe laughed with surprise and delight. Some men stretched out nearby turned to look. The firelight flickered on a painted king, fat and jolly and robed in red, sitting on a gold throne wearing a jeweled crown nearly as large as his head. Exquisitely lettered, the word CROWN was painted above the figure, and the word *Rex* below.

"Hans, I am overwhelmed. It wasn't necessary to do this, but I thank you, I'll use it proudly."

One of his sergeants, reclining, called out, "Hey, Lieutenant, can we see?" Joe nodded to Linzee, who turned around.

"Too dark, move a little closer to the fire."

Joe listened; he thought he heard unusual small sounds blending with the creek noise. "No, I don't think you should—"

While he was speaking, Linzee stepped two paces nearer the fire. He was brightly lit, grinning happily. The bullet hit the back of his skull and blew away his brow and eyes, spraying Joe with a fan of blood.

Linzee fell sideways into the fire. His blood made a hissing sound as it splashed onto the coals. The men were running, away from the fire. More shots rang out. Captain Ehrlich was shouting, taking charge. Joe was shaking. He had something in his hand. Astounded, he saw the shaving mug, which had evidently flown from Linzee's hand as he fell. Joe didn't remember catching it.

"Take cover," Captain Ehrlich shouted, jumping to the fire, kicking and scattering the wood to put it out.

"Captain," Joe screamed, "get back before—"

Guns in the darkness volleyed again. Frank Ehrlich danced like a marionette whose strings were jerked. His eyes dimmed to death while his rubbery legs gave way, throwing his body on the ground near the fire. Joe was rapidly stepping backward, slapping his holster, dragging his revolver out. A hard blow struck his left arm.

When he glanced down, he saw his wool sleeve glistening. When he realized he'd been hit, it started to hurt. He dragged his Colt from the holster, waved it over his head and shouted for his men to pour their fire into the sector of the woods where the Rebs were hiding. Soon the noise of Union small arms fire filled the night. After five minutes of this, feeling faint, Joe shouted, "Cease your fire."

His left arm hung at his side, leaking blood down the back of his wrist and off his fingers to the sandy ground. He stepped on something that cracked and broke under his boot sole.

A piece of broken china.

He didn't remember dropping the mug. The pieces were scattered near Hans Linzee's body.

"Lieutenant, listen! They're gettin' away . . ."

He heard galloping horses, fading away south. Joe shoved his hot revolver into his belt, steeled himself and pulled Linzee's uniform blouse off him, then his undershirt. It was bloody, but it would serve as a tourniquet.

He called for assistance. One of his noncoms ripped the undershirt into strips and knotted them tightly, one after another, above Joe's wound. He told his men to tear down tree branches, light them for torches. He thought the danger was past.

Lightheaded, he walked around the campsite, assessing the damage. Ehrlich dead. Linzee dead. Four men wounded, two of them badly.

He stood for a bit looking down at Linzee's stripped torso; the pale soft chest with little flabby breasts and no hair. Linzee's right hand was almost touching a piece of the shattered mug. Joe turned away.

He took himself down to the creek bank and there, with heavy brush to shield him, he cried. If anyone saw him, they respected his grief.

At the end of five minutes he straightened up, weak and sick of soul, but able to function again because he must. He climbed the bank on shaky legs. His head buzzed. Like Linzee at Pittsburg Landing, he wanted to quit. It was out of the question. Ehrlich was dead, Joe was in command, he had wounded men, he must find a field hospital. He went about the disrupted campsite marshaling his noncoms, helping to bury the dead and rig litters for the wounded.

Before they left the campsite at dawn, he picked up the pieces of the mug and dumped them in his saddlebag, then led the retreat north along the road, holding his throbbing arm tightly against his side.

He was never the same man afterward.

A field surgeon wanted to amputate his injured arm but Joe refused. Smashed the bottle of anesthetic whiskey out of the surgeon's hand with his right fist as the surgeon leaned over the wooden examination table.

His superiors commended him and brevetted him to captain, officially replacing Frank Ehrlich. He returned to duty with his left arm wrapped in a sling. A year later he was brevetted to major, and then, in Georgia, six months before the war ended, to full colonel.

In some mystical way still not fully understood, the wound he took, the flowing blood, washed out the deepest part of his Germanness. The Civil War to save the Union baptized him an American, forever. . . .

The war affected his life in another way. It transformed his liking for order into a passion that ruled him. *Ordnung.* His soul-deep need to impose rational patterns on his life through his control of it, and whatever touched it. He had thought about this many times before, but never with such a burst of insight, perfect understanding, as came to him now on the darkening battlefield. *Ordnung* was his cause, and his creed; the forces of order, reason, civilization, against the ever-present, constantly threatening forces of chance, anarchy, chaos.

Ordnung was the reason for his battle with Benno Strauss. It was the source of his struggle at home. Joe Junior was drifting willfully or accidentally into confusion. He saw this with a clarity never experienced before. Perhaps he could carry on the battle more effectively now that he understood it more fully. Thank heaven his nephew wasn't like his boy. Joe doubted his ability to wage war on two fronts at the same time.

He roused himself from the reverie and realized the lateness of the hour. He shook the reins lightly over the back of the old buggy nag. The leather springs creaked and the rear axle squeaked as he left the somber shadows of the battlefield. On the way back to his inn he passed the little Shiloh Meeting House, whitewashed logs all pale and innocent in the gloaming. To have a church of God give its name to a great slaughtering field . . . wasn't that remarkable?

Weeds grew up around the meeting house. The wind stirred them, a rustling whispering sound, like fallen men sighing goodbye. Joe Crown hurried the buggy up the rutted road as the night came down. He did not look back.

Some mornings later, he walked out the door of the State Hotel in Columbia, South Carolina. It was a fine June day, the twenty-seventh. A black youngster sold him a paper. Joe stepped to the curbstone and scanned the headlines.

Yesterday the stock market had hit the bottom of its month-long sell-off. Everyone in the saloon bar, the prosperous gentry of Columbia, had been discussing it last night. The word used in the paper was "crash." How much worse could it possibly get?

Very much worse. He spotted a smaller story, out of Springfield, Illinois.

ALTGELD SIGNS PARDON

Three Haymarket Conspirators
to Be Released at Once

"A Grievous Wrong Is Righted,"
Illinois Governor Declares.

Joe's oath made the newsboy jump. "Sir? You say somethin'?"

"I said damn it. I said damn it to hell, and back again." He threw the paper in the gutter.

There was even more in store. When he finished his day's business and returned to the hotel, the clerk reached into a pigeonhole and handed him a telegraph message.

His eye flew first to the signature. Ilsa had sent the wire, which was short.

PLEASE COME HOME. PAULI EXPELLED.

24

Paul

UNCLE JOE walked into the house at half past five on Thursday, the twenty-ninth of June. He handed his grip to Manfred and struggled out of his bedraggled coat as he climbed the stairs without speaking. "He's having a bath," Aunt Ilsa advised Paul in the kitchen a few minutes later. "You are to come to the study at a quarter after six."

Paul nervously watched the grandfather's clock in the hall and knocked the instant the clock hand moved. When Uncle Joe summoned him in, he was surprised and relieved to see Aunt Ilsa seated next to the open window, by the end of the desk. A light breeze was blowing the curtains.

Three walls of the room had shelves filled with handsomely bound books from floor to ceiling. Over half the volumes were in German. Uncle Joe had put on a fresh shirt without a cravat. He pointed to the empty chair in front of him.

"Take a seat. Tell your story."

Paul did so, neither minimizing his actions nor embellishing Mrs. Petigru's cruelty. He never once glanced away from his uncle's eyes during the brief recitation. His heart was pounding, his stomach hurt, but outwardly he was composed. A gargantuan effort.

At the end, Uncle Joe removed his spectacles and dangled them over the side of the chair. Aunt Ilsa pulled a handkerchief from her sleeve and dabbed her upper lip and forehead.

"I believe you, Paul," his uncle said. "Your words have the ring of truth. Also, what you say doesn't fundamentally contradict the events described in the principal's letter." He tapped the letter on the desk behind him; Paul hadn't noticed it before.

"He acknowledges Mrs. Petigru punished you more harshly than was merited. Let me see your hands."

Paul held them out. Faded purple bruises marked his fingers and the backs, to his wrists. She'd beaten his hands so hard, he hadn't been able to bend his fingers without severe pain for three days afterward.

"Can you move your fingers freely?"

"Oh, yes." He flexed them. "I'm fine now." He darted a warm look at Aunt Ilsa. She had telephoned Dr. Plattweiler for a liniment prescription, which had helped.

"Good. Regrettably, the principal concludes his letter by saying he must stand behind the authority of his teachers. You can't continue in that school. You warned me you weren't suited for study, and it seems you were right. Perhaps plunging you so quickly into an American system was unfair. In any case, your aunt and I have discussed and agreed on the next step. I will discharge Mr. Mars tomorrow, with a month's extra salary, and on Monday you will start work at the brewery."

Paul was speechless. Uncle Joe said, "Ilsa, if you will leave us, I will discuss the particulars with Paul."

She acquiesced with a little nod and kissed her fingertips to Paul as she walked past. The doors rolled back, rolled shut. Paul's heart was still beating fast. A few weeks after his arrival, the prospect of working in the brewery had been attractive. Now something more fascinating was luring him. How to tell his uncle?

"Now that your aunt is gone, I can speak more frankly." Uncle Joe picked up the principal's letter. "This truly saddens me. Not the charge of bringing obscene material to class, that sounds frivolous in the light of your description of the drawings, where they came from, a salesman's bag. It's admirable that you tried to shield your friend. But I find nothing else admirable in what you did. I had great hope for you, Paul. Great hope. For weeks, for months, I discover, you have been failing. You never spoke up. You said everything was fine."

"I did not want to disappoint you, Uncle."

"What do you think you have done here?" He threw the letter on the desk. "I can't understand how you could get such poor marks. Germans are good thinkers. At least you could have passed your mathematics, Germans are always good with figures—"

His voice was shaky, something uncharacteristic of him. Paul recognized that his uncle was in a high temper. He waited tensely while his uncle cleaned his spectacles with a pocket handkerchief. That seemed to calm him; his color returned to normal.

"The brewery—" he began.

"Sir, may I please interrupt?"

"What is it?" His uncle didn't like it.

"At the Exposition, I saw something marvelous. A machine showing pictures that appear to move." He described the dancing elephant.

"Exactly when was this?"

"Saturday last. I went by myself. Oh, but Aunt Ilsa gave me permission—"

"I've heard of this machine but I haven't seen it. Continue."

"At the—ah—*Marktbude*—"

"Booth."

"Yes, thank you, there I met a gentleman who operates a studio of photography. He knows how the moving pictures are made. His name is Mr. Rooney." From his shirt pocket Paul took the precious card. His uncle examined it with an unreadable expression. "I said I was interested, I would like to learn to make such pictures. He invited me to visit. He said he would teach me. Could I not ask him for a job? One day—" Paul's face glowed. "One day, I might learn to make pictures for the machine I saw."

Uncle Joe thrust the card back. "I believe in welcoming and adopting worthy inventions, but I see no useful purpose in the one you describe. Of what earthly good are pictures of an elephant dancing? I haven't bothered to see that machine because it's a toy. A novelty. Make a career of it? I'm sorry to say I find that proposition slightly ridiculous."

Trying to suppress his anger, Paul pressed his fists on the knees of his knickerbockers till the knuckle joints were white. "All right, Uncle, I won't talk any more about the machine. But Mr. Rooney's studio is a regular business. I suppose he makes all kinds of photographs."

"That is a very low trade in my estimation. In these times very chancy, too. People out of work won't waste money on photographs. But they'll buy a few glasses of beer—it makes them feel better."

"Uncle, please, I beg you, at least let me call on this gentleman and ask whether he might employ me."

"No."

"*Ich protestiere!*"

"You protest? You are in no position to protest, young man. You have shamed this family. You will go to work at Crown's next Monday. Your hours will be six in the morning until four-thirty, six days a week. No Sunday work. I pay a very good starting wage. Ten dollars and a quarter per week. That's as much as a dollar more than my competitors offer. Certain men in my employ choose to ignore the fact, but it's true. Further, I don't pay good wages because someone forced me, I do it because it encourages hard work and loyalty. Since you live with us, you won't have to spend anything for rent or food, you can save everything you earn. A great advantage."

With that pronouncement, Uncle Joe leaned back in his chair. Paul seethed. He felt rebuffed. Pushed away like an annoying child who knew nothing.

"Monday, six sharp. Now if you'll excuse me, I have some bills and correspondence that require attention before supper."

He had turned back to the desk before Paul reached the sliding doors.

25

Joe Crown

ON THE FIRST DAY he returned to the brewery, Joe saw large numbers of men loitering in the streets. Gaunt-faced men, gathered on corners that had been empty before the panic struck.

He turned from the carriage window and rapidly scanned several newspapers. The pardon was still a major issue, and much of the nation felt as he did about the freeing of Fielden, Neebe, and Schwab. A New Jersey minister proclaimed from his pulpit, "Illinois stands discredited for the three A's—Altgeld, aliens, and anarchists." Only the liberal fringe of the press praised the governor's decision.

Altgeld was finished politically, that was certain. It was fit punishment for someone who would free convicted terrorists.

A more important issue than the pardon was the state of business. Share prices hadn't rebounded even slightly. Scores of solid firms were closing. The papers were filled with rumors of giant railroads, the nation's bellwethers, going into receivership.

In the wake of the collapse, the issue of bimetallism, unlimited coinage of silver as well as gold, was polarizing the nation. For twenty years the Western silver producers had argued and lobbied for a bigger market for their product; a market guaranteed by the government. Western farmers wanted a greater supply of dollars for loans, more dollars than were available with the recent decline in the world's gold production. The U.S. Treasury's supply of gold was dwindling.

Overseas investors had lately expressed great uneasiness about the possibility that debts owed to them would be repaid with silver. They wanted gold to guarantee all debts. On the day the market crashed, the government of India had abruptly suspended its coinage of silver, sending a message, and a shock wave, to United States financial centers. Despite the air of crisis, Joe remained a gold-standard man. He considered the Western silver crowd a pack of selfish primitives out to wreck the economy.

As soon as he arrived at his office, Stefan Zwick asked to see him.

"Sir, I hate to bear bad news. Deliveries and shipments were down last week by eight percent, as against the week before."

"Figures, please."

"Yes, I've just gotten them together." Zwick handed Joe several inked ledger sheets. He quoted their contents from memory. "Last week, ten thousand, six hundred and forty barrels, as against eleven thousand, five hundred eighty-three the week before. A drop of nine hundred forty-three barrels, reflected in a corresponding drop in sales and reorders by certain accounts."

"Any explanation?"

"I'm afraid it's Oskar Hexhammer. He wrote a scathing editorial in the *Deutsche Zeitung.*"

"You know I never read that rag. What was in the editorial?"

"Mostly a lot of German jingoism. But Hexhammer cited you by name, as a native German unwilling to support the new *Turnverein,* or German culture generally."

"What a fatuous lie."

"Nevertheless, I believe it hurt us."

"Is there any pattern to the losses to support that statement?"

"Very much so. The losses are concentrated entirely in Chicago. They occurred at family establishments. The beer gardens in the German neighborhoods. Sales to accounts in other areas are steady."

Joe shook his head. "What do you do with a destructive fool like Hexhammer? Except hope he'll go away."

"I fear his influence among older beer drinkers won't go away."

"Well, don't concern yourself, it's my worry. Leave the figures. I'll have a meeting with Dolph Hix. Try to find some ways to increase our tavern promotion to offset the losses. We'll survive this. As I tell anyone who will listen, in bad times like these, an inexpensive glass of fine beer is medicine for melancholy."

But it was a poor start for the day.

By midmorning the temperature soared above ninety. Shortly before eleven a pipe broke in the brewhouse, causing a six-hour shutdown and the loss of the entire contents of the huge copper kettles.

In the afternoon Joe struggled to work in the confusion created by two loutish men prying at his office baseboards and knocking holes in his wall to install a telegraph wire and terminal for faster communication with present and future agencies. The hammering, the plaster dust, the profanity, the incessant complaining of the two who seemed ungrateful to have decent jobs, vexed him greatly. When he went into the brewery later, and ran into Benno, his tongue got away from him.

"Well, Benno, you got what you wanted. Your martyrs set free."

Bare to the waist, Benno was manhandling a keg onto a hand truck. His torso glistened. He held the keg still with his foot.

"They wasn't ever guilty, Mr. Crown."

A sweat drop fell from the end of Joe's nose. His shirt felt like some kind of rubber garment, stuck to him. "Then I trust you're satisfied."

"Well, sir—respectfully—not yet. We got to deal with what the union wants from Crown's, and the other breweries."

"What you have at Crown's at present is all you'll get. I treat my men well. Better than most are treated."

"Sir, I grant you. But we got certain very important demands—"

"Don't make them on my time. Get to work."

A smile, half rue, half respect, played over Benno's face. "You are a rock, Mr. Crown. A hard rock. That's good in a man, I admire it. But we will crack you."

"Get out of my way." Joe pushed him against the brick wall. He stormed off, leaving Benno in a state of astonishment that quickly became anger.

Ilsa said her prayers on her knees beside the bed. Joe lay rigid, hands nervously tapping his stomach. All windows in the bedroom—not American guillotine windows but the good European kind that opened out—had been flung wide to catch any night breeze. But there was none. The starched lace curtains hung limp. The distant stars simmered in a haze.

Ilsa climbed into bed, rolled onto her left side to face him. She insisted on wearing her flannel gown to bed despite the heat. A heavy fold touched his hand where it rested between them.

"You are very quiet tonight, Joe."

"A lot on my mind."

"How do you expect Pauli will do in the brewery?"

"It's Paul. How many times have I said that? He chooses to call himself Paul."

"He'll always be Pauli to me. Pauli is a German name, he is a German boy. I can't think of him any other way. Little Pauli from Berlin who fainted on my oriental carpet."

Joe knew better than to argue the point. "He took it well when I told him, he's a courageous lad. He's intelligent, and quick, his school problems take nothing away from that. He should do well if he shuns the troublemakers." He chewed his lip for a moment.

"On that subject, I have a confession. This afternoon I lost my temper with Benno Strauss. An argument over the Haymarket pardon. I laid hands on Benno. I pushed him."

On Michigan Avenue a carriage went by, a lonely sound in the night. "I knew there must be a reason you were so quiet. I'm very sorry it happened."

"No sorrier than I am. I regretted it the moment I did it. Unfortunately that was a moment too late."

"Will there be trouble because of it?"

"Impossible to say. We're going through terrible times. Stefan told me that down on the Levee, the aldermen are feeding their out-of-work constituents with free lunches at the saloons. Hundreds of them. On the telephone this afternoon, a man I trust told me that George Pullman plans to retrench. Wage cuts, perhaps layoffs. Pullman is a major employer in the city. It will have a huge impact. Hungry men are desperate men. Their unrest can be contagious."

He uttered a long sigh. "Sometimes I wonder how much strain the system can stand."

"Or this family," Ilsa said.

He found her hand in the dark and held it tightly. He lay awake long after she fell asleep.

26

Joe Junior

AS HE LEFT THE BREWERY late on Friday, Joe Junior started sneezing. He hoped it didn't mean illness. On Sunday he planned to go out to Pullman again, and he was wound up tight about it. Rosie was always hot, but lately they'd been frustrated by circumstances.

Just last week, all they'd done was hold hands, and grab a few feels, and kiss with tongues; it was her time of the month. The Sunday before that, her parents had hovered in the house all afternoon, giving them no time alone. That kind of thing made him cross, and huge and tight in his groin. Sodden dreams relieved it only a little.

His father always objected to his going to Pullman. Joe Crown disliked Rosie, although he'd never met her. He disliked her because she was a Bohunk; a lot of Germans looked down on people from Bohemia. He never criticized Rosie out loud—that would have proved him a snob—but he made his opinions known with looks and pointed questions whenever Joe Junior mentioned her.

Of course his father objected to everything he did these days, and vice versa. It was hard to realize that they had once been close. He'd remembered that when Pop took Paul and Carl to the White Stockings game. He'd actually wanted to go along. Sure, he was working at the brewery, but he could have gotten out if Pop had asked.

That day, once again, he'd been angry with his father, and jealous of Paul. The anger was particularly stinging because, when he was small, Pop had taken him to ball games often. In those days the White Stockings were playing at Lakefront Park, at Randolph and Michigan; you could see blue water and whitecaps from the stands. Joe Junior had fine happy memories of the two of them whooping and cheering for the Chicago team.

Everything changed after he was thrown out of his last school, the *Bayerische Akademie*, a good, dull German school on the *Nordseite*. When Pop received the letter saying Joe Junior was dismissed from the *Akademie* for bad behavior, he and Pop had their most violent argument, full of shouting on Pop's part, excuses and humiliated anger on his. That day, for the first time, his father struck him in the face.

Nothing had gone well since then, if he excluded meeting Rosie; and he wasn't even sure of the permanence of that relationship. At the brewery, he was secretly worried about rising antagonisms, Benno stirring up trouble with pronounce-ments, threats, that grew more reckless as conditions in the country got worse. Joe Junior sided with Benno most of the time, but he feared a moment when Benno might test him by demanding he take part in some act of violence. Some "propaganda of the deed."

All of his fears and resentments seemed to be connected to his father in one way or another. But in rare private moments, he could admit the anger masked something else. He thought of it as a stone in the deep well of his heart. A stone of sadness about Pop; a stone of loss that he would never raise into the light for anyone to see. Not even Mama.

All of this was boiling in him that Friday afternoon.

He came swinging past the corner of Michigan and Nineteenth in the dusty yellow light of a summer day. His shirt was stiff, and smelled of sweat. He'd been shoving kegs all day. He carried an old sweater slung over his shoulder; it had been cool and damp when he left home just as it was getting light this morning. Paul would be leaving home at the same time starting Monday. Joe Junior was secretly glad Paul had failed in school and was going into the brewery. It made them closer.

In the side yard, Carl was tossing a football with two boys whose skin was the color of milk chocolate. They belonged to the old-clothes man who drove his wagon through the neighborhood once a week, collecting discarded garments, and even paying a few cents if one was particularly fancy. He saw the wagon parked in the alley behind the stable.

He waved to Carl and the colored boys and cut through the garden, where he came upon his sister. Near the stone angel, Fritzi was swaying and dancing to music only she could hear. Her eyes were shut. She still wore the black crape armband she'd put on when one of her idols, Edwin Booth, passed away. He noticed a long scratch on Fritzi's nose, not there yesterday.

She heard his shoes scrape on the paving stones of the path, stopped her dancing and ran to him. He bent down for a kiss on his cheek. Fritzi made a face.

"Phew. You need a bath."

"I'm going to have one. After I rest a little." He sank down on one end of a stone bench, and sneezed.

"Are you sick, Joey? There's nothing worse than summer grippe."

"I'm fine." He wiped his nose with his pocket bandana. "Where'd you get that scratch?"

"School. Molly Helfrich said you were a red. I pulled her hair and she hit back. But I won." He laughed. "Are you a red, Joey?"

"I think so. I'd say I was a socialist, but not an anarchist."

"Why are you? Because Papa doesn't like it?"

"Sure, I can't have Pop telling me what to think, can I?" Though he smiled, he meant it.

After reflecting a moment, Fritzi said, "Is Paul a red?"

"Not yet."

"Do you like him?"

"Yes, I like him fine."

"Are you bosom friends?"

"Friends," he corrected. "That's all."

"Mama spends an awful lot of time helping Paul. Fussing over him."

"You have to expect that, he's still getting settled here."

"I guess I don't mind. Not too much anyway. If it was anyone else I'd be spitting mad."

He laughed again, and tousled her hair, "Ah, love!"

"Joey Crown, if you say that again, if you laugh at me, I'll kill you. I'll *kill* you!"

"Now, now, I'm not laughing. Not your dear brother."

He put his arm around her, and they walked that way into the house.

Shortly after he finished bathing and dried off, he heard the faraway jingle of the telephone. He wandered downstairs and met his mother, who had just come out of his father's study. Mama's face was drawn and unsmiling.

"Supper will be very late. Your father telephoned. He is at the county jail. The police locked up Benno Strauss this afternoon."

"Benno." He thought about it. "I didn't see him all day. I figured he was making deliveries."

"I don't know why he's in jail, your father didn't explain. He's in a fury."

The family didn't sit down to *Abendessen* until a quarter after nine. Pop had come in at five past the hour, banging doors, stomping upstairs with uncharacteristic noise.

"I will explain why I am so late," he growled as he served himself mashed potatoes. "Benno Strauss left work at noon without permission. He went to the lakefront, downtown. There, he and some forty others held a parade, with signs. Ostensibly the purpose was to plead for jobs. Most of the marchers were unemployed. The police tried to remove them—"

"Probably so the tourists wouldn't see what's really going on in Chicago," Joe Junior muttered to Paul.

"The demonstrators resisted and they're all behind bars. Benno's bail cost me thirty-five dollars. Cook County Jail is a vile place. I hope I never have to set foot there again."

"I don't quite understand," Mama said. "Benno isn't unemployed, he has a good job."

"Which he clearly doesn't value or appreciate." He speared a piece of Mama's German pot roast, dry and tough because of the delay. "I suppose he marched out of sympathy. Most of those arrested belong to some damned union or other, excuse my language."

Mama said, "Given how you feel about Benno, I'm a little surprised that you bothered to help him at all."

"It's the principle. I had to help an employee. Benno Strauss could have stayed there and rotted for all I care. Joe Crown's worker, though—he had to be helped." He speared another bite. "Heed this, Paul. When you start your job, see that you stay away from Strauss."

Joe Junior liked to see his father off balance this way; it seldom happened. He winked at his cousin. "Oh, there are worse teachers than Benno. I guess you had one of them in school."

His father had his fork halfway to his mouth. He dropped it to the plate, a loud clatter. "You keep your comments to yourself, young man. You know very little, you chose to scorn schooling. All you've been taught, you've learned from a pack of socialist rabble rousers."

"Well, I don't blame Benno for demonstrating. I sympathize with anybody who's out of work because of men like—"

"Who are you to sympathize? Who are you to judge? You have a soft life, you don't know the real meaning of hunger, hardship, desperation—"

"Oh, here we go," Joe Junior sneered, turning slightly in Paul's direction. "Now we'll get the story of the brave hard-working immigrant boy."

Mama jumped up. "That is shameful, young man. Shameful and intolerable. Go to your room."

Openmouthed, he stared at her. Standing up to Pop was one thing, but opposing Mama was something else entirely. Seeing her angry, her hands shaking noticeably, stunned and unnerved him.

"Joseph." Her voice dropped. "I said go. Obey me."

He threw his napkin on the table and left, saying nothing, looking at no one.

Half an hour later, he was sitting on the edge of his bed, in a terrible state of confusion.

A soft knock startled him. Mama came in before he could speak.

"Joey, I am sorry I raised my voice to you. Unfortunately you provoked it." He turned his head.

"Please look me in the eye. Why do you delight in provoking quarrels with your father? He isn't a wicked capitalist, he is a man of strong character who has worked hard to make a success of his life."

Somehow he couldn't frame a coherent answer.

Mama's skirts swished softly. At his side, she touched his brow. Her fingers were gentle, warm. "*Liebling,* tell me. What is it?"

He flung himself off the bed, away from her. He shoved his hands in his pants pockets and stared out the window at the lights of the mansions on the other side of Michigan.

"He wants to control everybody. He wants to control me. But he left Germany because he didn't want to be controlled, not by poverty, not by a rotten system that was growing worse—" He spun to face her. "He's said all that, Mama, I've heard him. He came here, made his own way. He was free, independent, nobody bossed him—"

"Nonsense. He had many bosses along the way. Bosses at the ice company, bosses at Imbrey's. He had scores of superiors in the Union Army."

"But he always knew where he wanted to go and he kept going, he didn't let anyone order him to turn in some other direction. All I want is the same chance. Don't you understand?" *Damnation* . . . he felt tears. Weak little boy tears he couldn't hold back.

Mama moved near to him again. "I do, but I have a question, very important. More important than your wants and wishes, Joey. Do you love your father?"

"What difference does that make?"

"Please don't shout."

"All right, but I'm not going to take over his damn business, which is what he wants. I'm the oldest—he expects it."

"Oh, no. No, Joey. Perhaps he expected that at one time. Or at least he had hopes. But I'm certain that he no longer—"

"It doesn't matter, I'd never do it." The shameful tears kept flowing. He beat his fist against his leg. *"He can't tell me what to do."*

Mama took that with her usual composure. Said quietly, "But that is his nature, Joey. To organize everyone, every aspect of his life, and ours. If that is a flaw, we must accept it."

"Not me. Never."

She drew a long breath, as if resigned. She exhaled and her bosom settled.

"All right, you have spoken your mind. Now it is my turn. It makes no difference how you feel, he is your father. So long as you live under this roof, he is entitled to respect. You will apologize to him."

She strode to the door. The electric fixtures lit her eyes in an odd way, making them glint like hard gemstones. She pulled the door open.

"You will do it now. He's downstairs, in the study. Waiting."

Most of the lights were out on the lower floor. The house felt like a mausoleum, and great shadows of chandeliers and furniture heightened the feeling. With a dry tight throat, he walked to the study doors. Tapped gently.

"Pop?"

"Come in." His father's voice had a flat, remote quality.

He rolled the doors back. Joe Crown wheeled around at the desk, a pen in his hand, the usual papers and letters in various neat stacks behind him.

It took all of his nerve to meet his father's eye.

"I apologize for my words and my actions at supper."

"Accepted, thank you," his father replied with a quick little nod. "I too regret things I said. It was a difficult day, Benno's arrest upset me greatly."

Joe Junior had an impulse to step across the carpet, fling his arms around his father, hug him, say he understood. He hovered on the point of it for a breathtaking moment and then something—too many memories; too many reprimands in the past; too many *orders*—shattered the feeling. He felt awkward, standing there. His father sensed it. Gestured with his pen, tried to smile. It was a poor, tired smile.

"You may go to bed, son. I have much work left here."

"Yes, good night, Pop." Quickly he wheeled and shut the doors. He leaned there in the darkness, exhausted; shuddering. Something had changed tonight. Tonight he'd confessed his deepest anger to his mother, and found she had no way to ameliorate it. The significance of that frightened him. He could never go back to the way it was when he and Pop went to ball games, because the anger was deep, and there was no remedy. Maybe this evening they had all recognized it for the first time.

As he climbed the shadowy stair, the anger came surging back. He'd apologized because Mama wanted it, that was the only reason. Paul would start at the brewery on Monday. It was an opportunity. He'd really work on Paul. Win him over to his side. He'd fix Pop for causing him all this pain.

Halfway upstairs, another huge sneeze burst from him. He leaned against the banister, teeth clicking, severely chilled.

27

Ilsa

SHE SPENT a long wakeful night beside her husband. Joe had sunk quickly into sleep, perhaps to escape memories of the evening.

This gloomy night when her husband and her son had let their terrible feelings erupt seemed to epitomize the unraveling of a summer that had promised to be rare and magical, this summer of the Exposition.

Ilsa's first disappointment had come long before opening day. She had very much wanted to be on the Board of Lady Managers of the Exposition, because the board represented a step forward: women doing important work on behalf of women. Ilsa had enough money, and certainly sufficient social standing, to qualify for a board seat.

But someone blackballed her in the nominations committee. Later a friend told her it was Nell Vanderhoff. Her husband, Pork Vanderhoff, and Joe Crown had once been on reasonably good terms. Never close, but polite in their relationship as businessmen. Then one summer, at the brewery's annual picnic, there was an altercation. Vanderhoff sometimes paid a visit to the picnic because his company supplied all the meats. Ilsa hadn't attended the picnic that year, and Joe said very little about the particulars afterward. But he swore Vanderhoff was the aggressor, although ultimately, who did what made no difference. The relationship turned to ice. The following year Crown's bought its picnic sausages from another packing house.

Ilsa had attended programs presented by the Congress of Women during the month of May, as she'd told Joe she would. The Congress met at the Art Institute on Michigan Avenue, in newly refurbished spaces rechristened the Hall of Columbus and the Hall of Washington. Ilsa had listened to Lucy Stone, frail and tiny but still a fiery speaker, declare again that forcing women to be homemakers, and only homemakers, was "a band of steel on society." She'd heard others argue the opposite—that child rearing and household arts were the highest expression of woman's character, and her chief purpose. She'd applauded her friend Jane Addams, who spoke on the positive good that could be worked in domestic service by women who brought to the job not merely a physical presence but true dedication and a measure of training, the kind of training Miss Addams's settlement house offered in its programs for its poor clients. And Ilsa had taken Fritzi to one of the presentations by famous actresses, this one a historical sketch of women on stage read by Madmm Modjeska.

But it wasn't the same as it could have been, had she been allowed to help plan the Women's Building; helped judge the competition among female architects that led to the selection of a neoclassic design by Sophia Hayden, trained for her profession at M.I.T.; helped determine the size and content and placement of the exhibits inside. On opening day, instead of traipsing around the grounds with her family, she'd have been seated on the platform when Bertha Palmer and her committee dedicated the Women's Building. She'd have been there with Mrs. Altgeld and Mrs. Adlai Stevenson and other distinguished women from all over the world. She knew Joe would have been proud, despite some of his primitive views about the role of women.

She never said a word to him on opening day. She loathed self-pity and complaining. Still, the hurt lingered.

And there was the matter of Pauli's expulsion.

Pauli was a smart boy, exceptionally smart in his way, but formal schooling was wrong for him. Further, he had gone through months of abuse and humiliation from a bad teacher at school. A woman who despised Germans. And she had pushed him into it.

When he was expelled, Ilsa reluctantly agreed with Joe's decision about the brewery. It was the only proper decision, but not a good one. Since hearing it in the study, Pauli had behaved like someone defeated.

Worst of all, of course, was the argument this evening. Joe Junior's apology solved nothing, repaired nothing. She had insisted on it because it was the decent thing, but she knew without hearing it that the apology would be hollow. Joe Junior's rebellion was understandable. He was energetic, impatient, bright—all the characteristics that made young men assertive.

Ilsa was sure her husband and son loved each other, although in moments of heat they might seem irreconcilable foes. What worried her now, to the depths of her heart, was the feeling that a wider chasm had opened between them tonight. So wide that father and son might never be able to build a bridge, reach one another, let love rule again.

In the night, she found herself turning on her side, toward Joe, as each had a habit of doing for comfort. Her hand stole out and touched the hair over his left ear gently, brushing it with the lightest of caresses.

"Joe, Joe," she whispered. *"Bitte—bitte! Lass nichts schlimm geschehen."* For a second or so she didn't realize she'd resorted to her native language.

The plea was not to him alone; it was an appeal that flew far beyond the walls of the bedroom; rose up high to something unseen, unknowable, in which she still believed. It was a spoken prayer; a reflection of the deteriorating state of the family; a measure of her desperation.

Please, please! Don't let anything bad happen.

28

Paul

PAUL WAS SHAKEN by the overt enmity between his uncle and his cousin. He'd known it was there, but never guessed how frightening it was in its ferocity.

On Saturday morning when he went into the kitchen for a refill of his breakfast coffee, Aunt Ilsa was working with bread dough again, pounding and kneading it with violent blows and pokes. Her expression upset Paul. She was not someone who scowled often.

About eleven, Mr. Mars called, for his final wages.

He and Paul walked in the garden, where one path led through the outer wall of shrubbery to the side yard. Carl was romping with some new gadget, a stick with a string and a four-blade rotor on top. Paul and the tutor watched Carl wind the string on the stick, then give it a yank. The rotor and stick lifted into the air and hovered for a few seconds, defying gravity. Then the toy fell.

"The Pénaud helicopter," Mr. Mars said. "Twenty-five cents. There are millions in the toy boxes of American children. They were invented in France, didn't you have one?"

"I didn't have store toys, mine were carved or made at home."

Carl wound the rotor and released it again, clapping as it flew higher this time. Just an hour before, Aunt Ilsa had punished him for tinkering with her Black Forest cuckoo clock. Carl had removed it from the wall and taken it apart to see its workings. He put it back together but it no longer ticked or said "Cuckoo." For this Aunt Ilsa had given him a new list of chores, without pay. It didn't seem to dampen his enthusiasm. Paul wished he could recover from trouble as quickly.

Mr. Mars walked to the praying angel and sat on the nearest stone bench. He fanned himself with his broad-brimmed felt hat. "This is a sad day for me, Paul. I will miss tutoring you. You're industrious, and smart. If the subject interests you," he added with a wry smile. "I predict you'll do well when you find your calling in life."

Resentfully, he thought, *I found it. Uncle Joe said it didn't amount to anything.*

"What will you do, Mr. Mars?"

"Aye, me. Continue as before. Tutor the bratty little daughters of pretentious nabobs. Teach them French. Teach them poetry. Teach them—and know they'll forget every bit of it."

"I won't forget. I am thanking you, I have better English now."

"Well, let's not exaggerate. You have English which is improving. I won't forget you either."

They shook hands. Paul stood on the street corner watching Mr. Mars hurry away, the hem of his long green and blue plaid coat flapping in the summer air.

□ □ □ □

Outside the schoolhouse Paul said goodbye to Leo. He'd arranged the meeting by leaving a note on Friday, the last day of school. The principal's assistant, a homely young woman, had been very nice about it. She made no reference to his expulsion.

The schoolyard was empty, scoured by a summer wind that bounced a tin can noisily over the gravel and blew Paul's uncombed hair to and fro. The tail of his striped summer shirt hung out. He ran toward Leo when he appeared at the corner with Flash, and explained about going to work at the brewery.

"So we say goodbye for now, Leo. But I will see you again. I'll come to your flat, you gave me the address."

Leo blushed. "Don't come, we're moving. Pop got fired. Nobody's buying corsets, I guess. Pop's pretty busted up about it . . ."

Sad-faced, he scratched Flash behind the ears. "I'll send you a new address when we get one."

"Good, it's a promise."

They hugged each other.

Leo never sent the address.

Late in the day Paul stood in front of the window of the shop on North Clark Street. He put his nose against the glass again. Dark, empty space. He couldn't believe it.

On the glass in thick red tempera, someone had painted FOR RENT.

On a stepladder, a man with a toothpick in his mouth went about his work, unhooking chains that held a faded sign. ROONEY'S TEMPLE OF PHOTOGRAPHY.

"But where is he?" Paul asked, holding out the card.

The man took the toothpick out of his mouth, leaned the other way and spat a big squirt of tobacco juice on the sidewalk. "Who gives a damn? He was a lousy tenant, Rooney."

"When did he move?"

"He didn't *move*, I threw him out. Tuesday. Christ, he was five and a half months in arrears, I carried him long enough."

"But please tell me, where has he gone?"

"Try a park bench. Try Cook County Jail. The little son of a bitch had a swarm of creditors chasing him. Rooney don't pay his bills. Not regular, anyway. He can't leave off with the ponies, that's his trouble."

Paul didn't understand the reference to ponies. As he turned away from the painted window, the man unhooked one chain on the sign. Paul stepped to the curbstone, crushed the card and flung it in the gutter with the other trash.

On Monday he woke early, long before daylight. Like the morning he went to the rail yards to see Buffalo Bill's train, or the opening day of the Exposition. He'd slept restlessly.

As he lathered his face and shaved and dressed, he was conscious of the need to hurry. He was to see the brewmaster, Mr. Friedrich Schildkraut, at six sharp. In any fine brewery, the brewmaster was God, and that was true at Crown's. Uncle Joe had emphasized this when he lectured Paul at Sunday night supper:

"We are a successful business in large part because of Fred Schildkraut. There is no one else I would trust with his job—I was brewmaster myself until my other responsibilities got too large. I hired Fred away from Pabst in Milwaukee at three times his old salary. He understands many things about brewing far better than I do. Mechanical refrigeration, for one. In the early days a brewmaster wasn't much more than a superior cook, but now he's the keystone of the whole enterprise. The brewery is Fred's life, which is good for me, but bad for his wife and four boys. When we're in a peak period, or he's confronted with a problem, Fred will stay two, three, four nights without going home. I try to persuade him to leave, he refuses. He works all night until he falls asleep at his desk. Fred expects you at six o'clock. I'd be punctual. I'd be a few minutes early. Fred is a Catholic. Very devout. Don't use any bad language in front of him."

Cousin Joe wouldn't be going with him to the brewery this morning. His case of grippe had grown worse on Sunday. Aunt Ilsa put him to bed with fever. So Paul had to tiptoe through the slumbering house alone, to the dark kitchen where he picked up the lunch in a paper sack Louise had left for him.

A horsecar took him within two blocks of the brewery. He felt sleepy and gritty-eyed. His face was raw from the razor; shaving was still a relatively new experience.

It had been drizzling for ten minutes. The deserted streets glistened. A light mist or fog was congealing in the damp air as he walked to the employee gate at the south end of the brewery block. A cobbled alley ran from the gate, parallel with Larrabee Street, into the heart of the brewery. The mist coiled slowly along the ground, hiding the foundations of the fortresslike buildings. Somewhere machinery clanked; steam hissed. There was not another workman in sight.

An old watchman sat in a small booth, reading a paper by lantern light. Paul knocked on the glass. The watchman shuffled out.

"Hello, my name is Paul Crown. I am to work here."

"Yes, I was told. Pass on."

"I am to see Mr. Schildkraut."

"Second floor, front building. Down the alley, turn right. The door to the *Bierstube* should be unlocked, Fred came in half an hour ago."

He walked away from the booth into the dark maw of the alley, the black buildings rising like medieval keeps on either side. This was to be his life now. His entire life. He had no purpose, only this job pushed on him by his uncle.

Bad feelings buffeted him as he trudged over the cobbles. Uncle Joe had no sympathy for his wishes, all he cared about was numbers, sales, having things his way. He'd found work he might do, enthusiastically, as a career and Uncle Joe scoffed at it. Paul understood Cousin Joe's rebellion.

He stopped and gazed up at the brewery buildings. A few lonely lights gleamed behind opaque windows. The machinery clanked. The air smelled rich with brewery smells, not at all appetizing. God, why was he here? Maybe he didn't belong in America. How the baker of Wuppertal would laugh if he saw him now.

Calm down, it may not be forever, this job. There's one advantage. A very important one. When winter comes you will certainly have ice skates.

Concentrating on a vision of Juliette Vanderhoff's face, he walked on into the brewery.

Friedrich Schildkraut's office was a corner space like Uncle Joe's, but at the rear, overlooking the alley and the manufacturing buildings. Light showed beneath the closed door. Paul ran a palm over his unruly hair and knocked.

"Come in, young man."

The office was darker than Uncle Joe's, and more disorderly, strewn with flasks and thermometers, little muslin sacks of grain and hops, diagrams, blueprints, technical papers in German. Amid the litter, a small gold-lettered sign confronted the visitor. F. SCHILDKRAUT, BREWMASTER.

On the wall behind the desk, a bleeding Christ hung from a wooden cross. Nearby was a framed photograph of a bearded man. Schildkraut noticed Paul studying it.

"Louis Pasteur. A great friend of beer, as it turned out, although Pasteur began his researches principally to aid the winemakers in France. So they might compete with German brewers." Schildkraut's lips twitched; it could hardly be called a smile. "Sit down, please."

As soon as Paul sat, the brewmaster stood up. He was a tall, austere man, about forty, with a long jaw that tapered to a blunt chin, and thick hair yellowing to gray. His left arm ended at the elbow; sleeve and cuff were neatly pinned up with a safety pin. As a young man, Uncle Joe had told Paul, Schildkraut lost his arm in a dust explosion in a malthouse.

The pendulum of a wall clock ticktocked noisily. From his intimidating height, the brewmaster looked down at Paul. "What do you know about beer? Do you know what this is?" Schildkraut said, without giving him a chance to answer the first question. From the desk he snatched a funnellike metal device, badly dented.

"No, sir, I don't."

"This is what we call a swimmer. Filled with ice, it went into the beer to control the fermentation temperature. That was before refrigeration. In the days of underground cellars, and cooling caves. The days when lager couldn't be brewed all year round, but only as long as a supply of river ice lasted." He tossed the swimmer on the desk.

At the window, he scowled at something he saw below. He pivoted suddenly and barked at Paul like an army drillmaster. "Do you know where the term 'lager' originated?"

"From the German *lagern?*"

"Of course. *Lagern.* To lay down. Deposit. Store. After fermentation, lager rests in a cool place for two to three months. Do you know whether lager is bottom or top fermented?"

"No, sir."

"The bottom—unlike English brews. It was never possible to brew lager in America until the early decades of this century. Before that, legend has it, every yeast culture died before it completed the long journey across the Atlantic. Then came clipper ships, making the trip in three weeks or less. The yeast survived. I see we shall have to teach you almost everything. Especially since your uncle indicated to me that you might make a career of it."

Paul's neck prickled. "Sir?"

"Didn't you hear me? Your uncle said you might develop an interest in brewing as a life's work. We have tried to direct young Mr. Joe that way, without success. I am very happy to hear there may be another opportunity for—"

Paul interrupted by standing up. The brewmaster scowled.

"You wish to say something?"

"I do, Mr. Schildkraut. My uncle was kind to get me this job, it is time I had one. But I have never said I wish to be a brewer all my life. I am not certain."

That was a lie. A necessary and politic lie, but a lie all the same. He was certain he didn't want to be a brewer. He'd seen the elephant dancing . . .

"The truth is, sir, I came to America to decide what I want to be, not—well, not to be told what I must be. People in America, they are free to choose. That is the reason I came here."

Slowly Friedrich Schildkraut lowered his right hand to the back of his swivel chair. He gripped it with long tapering fingers. He leaned forward. *He is furious, I will be discharged before I start.*

"Good! You have backbone. There is no place for a weakling in a brewery." Schildkraut actually smiled. "We'll do our utmost to convince you it's a worthy profession. I don't mind telling you that Mr. Crown feels you have a lot of promise."

Schildkraut was far more relaxed all at once, less forbidding. "We'll teach you everything. We'll start where the beer starts, in the malthouse. We do our own malting, we don't buy from outside. Some of your tasks will be onerous and exhausting. Our mash vessels are direct-fired, not heated by steam. You'll spend several months stoking the fires. You'll clean equipment. You'll go home so tired you'll want to weep. But you'll learn a noble trade. Just don't fall in with the wrong crowd here."

Schildkraut circled the desk and laid his good hand on Paul's shoulder. "We have at least one employee who belongs to the exalted, glorious National Union of United Brewery Workmen of the U.S., A.F. of L. Mr. Benno Strauss." He spit into a desk-side cuspidor.

"Benno and his friends are agitators. Don't listen to them. Young Master Joe has a tendency to do that, it's leading him astray. The fact is, while there's breath or strength in your uncle, or in me, we won't permit a socialistic trade union at Crown's. Or the devil-inspired eight-hour workday. Men who are idle an extra two or three hours a day are susceptible to extra temptation. We'll never have it. Never."

Light sweat had popped out on Schildkraut's forehead. But his grip relaxed. "This way," he said, stepping toward the door with the bearing of a soldier. "I'll take you personally to the malthouse and get you started."

Paul nodded compliantly, but he was churning inside again. What had he gotten into? Was this a brewery, or a battleground?

Part Four

JULIE

1893–1894

We advocate the thorough education and training of woman to fit her to meet whatever fate life may bring. Not only to prepare her for the factory and the workshop, for the professions and the arts, but more important than all else, to prepare her for presiding over the home. It is for this, the highest field of woman's effort, that the broadest training and preparation are required.

> 1893
> Mrs. POTTER PALMER at the dedication
> of the Exposition Women's Building

29

Julie

ON THE FIRST SATURDAY MORNING of September, Mrs. Vanderhoff was combing her daughter's hair.

This weekly ritual took place in Julie's dressing room. Julie's unbound hair hung below her waist. Hair the color of coal. Hair shiny as a pool of spilled ink. Hair that was Juliette Vanderhoff's pride and glory, because her mother had taught her it was so. Mrs. Vanderhoff had taught her daughter many things about women, their dispositions and afflictions, their duties as refined young ladies, then prospective brides, then mothers, then great hostesses.

Nell Fishburne Vanderhoff, younger of two sisters born in Lexington to the Kentucky Fishburnes, was five feet tall and compactly built. Once, youthful and blooming, she might have had the charm of a bisque doll. Now, in her forties, she merely looked breakable. Lines of exhaustion were scribed deep in her face. Great brown shadows surrounded her eyes. Her skin resembled pale yellow marble with blue veining. Her hands often trembled, though not this morning.

Julie had observed her sixteenth birthday on May 28. Her figure had matured sufficiently for her to wear women's fashions, such as this morning's expensive gown of peach silk. It had been cut and sewn at Redfern's, the New York City branch of the fashionable London couturier.

She sat motionless, gazing at herself in a large oval mirror while Nell plied the comb and brush. She couldn't enjoy the ritual as she once had. She felt too old. Again this morning, a tantalizing memory of the boy she'd met months ago disturbed her composure. Joey Crown's cousin; the German boy.

Their meeting on the street had been brief, yet she remembered him. His broad shoulders and strong, honest face. His brown eyes, large and shining with a curious liquidity that left her seething with improper thoughts, emotions, to which she dared not put words. He had a perfectly terrible accent, but his smile flashed quickly, and it was genuine. There was about him a forthrightness, a lack of pretension she never found in young men of her age and social class.

Perhaps she imagined all this because he was an immigrant, with a certain exotic aura. Perhaps none of what she saw in him, save for the physical features, was real. She didn't care, she had taken a liking to the boy. She wished they could become better acquainted.

□ □ □ □

Nell Vanderhoff worked the hairbrush downward in a few more swift strokes, and the ritual was finished. She laid comb and brush aside; then, reaching from behind to touch her daughter's cheeks, she regarded Julie's face in the glass.

"I have never seen your cheeks so red. Too much time in the sun, playing tennis."

"I love tennis, Mama."

"You overdo. Just as you overdo skating in the winter. Excess in either one is bad for the complexion, the circulation—the entire constitution. I've told you repeatedly, Juliette, girls and women are delicate. You must expect it. Deal with it. Guard yourself rigorously against the ravages of weather, of nerves, of—"

"Oh Mama, I just don't understand how fresh air can be bad for you."

"Nevertheless, that's the case. Dr. Woodrow will confirm it—and please don't be obdurate and suggest that you know better than a doctor trained at clinics in Switzerland. You grow more willful every day. It must be your age. A passing phase. Let's hope it passes quickly, because dealing with it exhausts me. It simply shreds my nerves to bits."

She drew her hands back while continuing to look into Julie's eyes. Her expression was always the same: sorrowful, disappointed, yet with flickers of anger. It always pierced Julie with guilt, a certainty that she'd failed, been found wanting, as her mother's only child.

"Mama, you know I never want you to feel bad because of me."

"I hope so, dear. I hope so."

The physical and emotional health of Mrs. M. P. Vanderhoff III were constant concerns in the family. Neurasthenia—prostration of the nerves and brain—was a recurring complaint for Nell. Many women of her class and upbringing were afflicted with it, but Nell's was an extreme case, even Dr. Woodrow admitted that. Julie's mother suffered from excruciating headaches, and problems with digestion and elimination. She often flew into shrill rages, or sank into long periods of morose silence. She spent many hours, sometimes days, in her bed, with the room darkened.

She read periodicals incessantly, hunting for new nostrums. She flogged poor Dr. Woodrow to find and prescribe new cures. One month an iron tonic, the next a compound of rhubarb, or camphor, or mustard. She took sulphur baths; she wrapped herself in kelp. She forced Woodrow to bring his surgical implements to the house and bleed her. Regularly, these cures restored her energy and spirits. Just as regularly, gloom and suffering returned, and the cycle repeated.

Nell had taught her daughter that such suffering was woman's lot. That it was a result of the female nature and humors, and that Julie must not expect her life to be any different from her mother's. Julie hated the inevitability of that, but it did seem to be true. She too was plagued by headaches, as well as profound and sometimes prolonged black moods in which she wanted to do nothing, see no one. Nor was she unusual. Many of her young female acquaintances were devastated by ills ranging from a high nervous state to a perpetual head cold, stomach gripe, catarrh, and the depression attending woman's monthly curse. Julie had the idea that the health of young American women was generally bad, and wondered why it should be so.

On the positive side, her health problems diminished whenever she exercised regularly and vigorously. In this she had to strike a balance, because Nell opposed sports for young ladies.

Julie folded her hands in her lap and again gazed at herself. Her cheeks were indeed sunburned, but the color deepened even as she watched. She had a powerful, uncontrollable, slightly wicked longing to see the German boy again.

Common sense quickly pricked that bubble. What she wanted was impossible; could never happen. The German boy belonged to the Crown family. Mama and Papa hated the Crowns, all of them.

Well, what did it matter anyway? He probably didn't remember her, she'd probably made no impression that afternoon they met.

The sad thought quite ruined the rest of the day.

30

Paul

AS FRIEDRICH SCHILDKRAUT had predicted, he learned. Because of the performance Schildkraut demanded from his men, he learned quickly.

He learned the process, beginning with the soaking of the brewer's barley in the malthouse until it germinated properly. Then it was kiln-dried, cleaned, ground, stirred into water in the great copper kettles. Cooking released the sugars, allowed the draff to settle to the bottom and left the wort. After cooling, the wort was boiled with the hops, the resulting mash cooled again, quickly, and piped into a fermenting tank where the yeast worked, transforming sugars into an alcohol content between four and five percent, depending on the formulation. Each batch, each beer, was the result of painstaking attention to ingredients, temperatures, cooking times, cooling times, fermentation and storage times. The senior men at Crown's were always writing in their thick brewers' books. No wonder Germans had taken to the profession; it required a total dedication to detail.

Paul oiled and wiped the brewery machinery; helped with repairs. He worked on the huge mills that handled five hundred bushels of malt in an hour; on the pneumatic malters that regulated moisture and temperature of the germination bed; on the Baudelot coolers that lowered the water temperature with a mix of water, ammonia, and brine. In the subbasement, he stoked the fires under the brewing kettles.

He didn't mind the hard work. He was putting money aside every week. In a month he had enough saved in a jar to pay for skates as soon as Spalding's restocked the shelves. Juliette Vanderhoff was always there to remind him that the drudgery had a purpose.

The job toughened him; thickened his legs; built up his arm muscles. His beard was tougher too. He was still growing; changing; rushing swiftly to manhood.

He soon learned something else at the brewery. His earlier feeling had been right. He didn't want to be a brewer all his life. There had to be a way to explore the new world of photography; there had to be someone else to teach him its techniques, now that Rooney had dropped from sight.

As Schildkraut had predicted, he went home at night completely exhausted, muscles in arms and legs and back hurting hellishly. Sometimes he was so tired he nearly nodded off at the supper table. Once when Paul lifted his head with a start, realizing he'd dozed between bites, Uncle Joe gave him a quick, pleased smile.

Finally Spalding's stocked its winter equipment. Paul bought a splendid pair of racers like the ones the clerk had described to him. He was moving steadily toward a meeting with Miss Vanderhoff, but there was more to the preparation than just buying skates. Every night, when all he wanted to do was sleep, he drove himself through forty-five minutes of knee bends and other leg exercises. Joe Junior said learning to skate meant toughening your leg muscles and especially your ankles. He would fall into bed in pain, but it was soon relieved by visions of Juliette Vanderhoff's delicate skin, rich ebony hair, lithe rounded body.

On a warm Sunday in late September, Uncle Joe took all the family but Joe Junior to the Buffalo Bill Wild West and Congress of Rough Riders show. Paul's cousin went out to Pullman to see his girl that day.

Uncle Joe had booked one of the best front-tier boxes. Paul could barely sit still, watching a performance he'd only been able to dream about in Berlin. Colonel Cody, white-hatted and noble as ever, charged up and down on Isham, blasting blue glass balls to bits as assistants threw them into the glare of huge arc lights.

There was a surprise in the much-anticipated Deadwood Stage number. The coach made a slow circuit of the arena and the mustachioed driver stopped here and there to point to a spectator—who was thus invited into the coach for the rest of the act. Paul almost collapsed when the driver pointed at him.

He scrambled over the railing with his aunt and Fritzi and Carl calling encouragement. He squeezed between a fat woman and a man who smelled of hair oil. As the coach rattled and swayed around the arena, the mounted Indians swooped down on it, brandishing lances and uttering bloodthirsty cries.

A volley of pistol shots announced the arrival of Buffalo Bill and his cowboys. They quickly chased off the Indians and sent the coach around the arena once more, to discharge its delighted passengers at their seats.

Afterward, Paul shook his uncle's hand and thanked him effusively. "You're welcome," Uncle Joe said, already glancing elsewhere. He rushed away to greet an acquaintance leaving the show with his family.

Uncle Joe's reserve puzzled him. When Joe Junior came home that night, Paul spoke about it.

"You mean you don't understand the reason? Come on! You're still Pop's nephew, but now you work for him. You're part of his property. Maybe you pal around with Benno—"

"I am not pals with Benno, I do not like that man."

"Makes no difference to Pop. You're on the other side of the fence. Not a union man, but the next thing to it. Nothing you can do about it, either. So watch your step."

Joe Junior had been shifted to the bottling house, so Paul didn't see much of him during regular working hours. Usually they met during the thirty-minute break for lunch. While they ate, Joe Junior would expound his theories of labor and capital, which Paul assumed he'd gotten from Benno Strauss. In the evenings, after supper, Joe Junior would occasionally drift into his room to press a book on him.

"Part of your education, you've got to learn these things, Paul."

There was an American philosopher, Thoreau, whom Joe Junior loved because his writings encouraged disobedience of unjust laws. There was a novel called *Looking Backward*, by Edward Bellamy. "A man falls asleep and wakes up fifty years later, in 1957, and the world's a perfect socialist utopia."

Joe Junior wanted him to read a local reformer, Henry Demarest Lloyd, an editor at the *Chicago Tribune*. "A real hell-raiser. He wrote a great book about the coal mine owners downstate who locked out their men because the men made a few basic demands. The miners practically starved. Lloyd's just written a new one, it's even better. *Wealth Against Commonwealth.* You know about Charles Darwin, don't you?"

"Heard of him, that's all." Paul was vigorously doing his knee bends while Joe Junior lounged on his bed.

"Darwin had this theory that in the animal world, only the strongest survive. All the capitalists—the mercantile aristocracy, Lloyd calls them—they like to think it applies to them. They imagine they can chew up little men and spit them out because that's how nature works. Lloyd crucifies them. That's pretty radical for a newspaper editor who works for plutocrats."

"I would think he would lose his job."

Joe Junior grinned. "Except for one thing. Lloyd married the publisher's daughter. I'll get you his book as soon as you finish these," he said, pointing to the small stack on the floor next to the bed.

Paul also read more newspapers, picking up old ones left around by the brewery workers. He didn't understand many of the terms in the front-page dispatches and editorials, so he bought a cheap pocket dictionary.

Soon he perceived a pattern in the simpler prose of most daily journalism. Workingmen were almost universally hated, or at least considered dangerous. Paul saw that Joe Junior, for all his exaggeration, his antagonism toward his father, was perfectly correct about one thing. Chicago, and America, was riven by a struggle. Workers against owners, owners against workers. The struggle was full of poisoned words, hatred and, often, violence.

Before he switched off the lights, Paul would sometimes sit gazing at the stereoscope picture of the lady Liberty, and wonder whether all she represented was as peaceful, pristine, and fine as he'd once believed.

□ □ □ □

One sunny noontime he and Joe Junior went up to the brewery roof to eat wursts and bread from their paper sacks. Louise packed two sacks every day except Sunday. The sacks were the only evidence that Paul and Joe Junior came from a special, favored household.

Benno Strauss and a half dozen of his cronies were already on the roof with their tin lunch pails. As usual, Paul felt daring to be up here with the socialists, in defiance of his uncle and Schildkraut.

Benno was always friendly to Paul. If they chanced to meet in the brewery, he would offer some gruff greeting like, "Joey teaching you good, kid?"

"Quite a lot," Paul would answer. He really didn't know yet how much the instruction was worth, and he wasn't sure what to think of Benno. Benno was certainly fearsome to look at. And strong. Yet he was a blow-hard. Even those who liked him said so behind his back.

Benno and his friends were eating and talking loudly. One man peered over the roof coping and made rude comments about the well-dressed customers enjoying dinner under the trees in the *Biergarten.*

Paul and Joe Junior were sitting a short distance from Benno's crowd. Benno was eating his enormous sandwich of salami and onion and garlic on black bread with the ferocity of a bear crunching the bones of prey.

The moment he finished, he broke into someone else's conversation and took over, as if by right. "When I was in Paris in the winter of eighteen and seventy-one, we wasn't so lucky about food. Before the siege was all over and the enemy marched in, we was dining on broiled cat and roast rat. Believe me, I was happy to see the God damn Germans all over the place; we could slip around at night, cut some corporal's throat and steal a knapsack to fill our bellies."

Skeptical, one of his friends said, "You were happy to kill Germans, your own people, when they captured the city?"

"My *own people* was in Paris. The brave ones who set up the Commune in the spring of '71. The Germans, they were just a pack of imperialist dogs."

Another friend waved good-naturedly. "Ah, blow it out, Benno. You were probably dead drunk with some chippy the whole time."

"Listen, I went to bed *and* went to the barricades. Wasn't ever no time Strauss couldn't fight one minute and fuck the next."

The men laughed; so did Paul and Joe Junior. Benno heard them. "Yeah, you better believe it's true, you babies."

"Benno, let's talk serious," another of his friends said. "We've let up on the boss lately. Do you think that's right?"

Paul and his cousin shot looks at one another.

"Nah, it ain't right, but I've had things on my mind. We got to start pressing him again. Demand nine hours a day. Also one apprentice for every fifteen men, not twenty. Even if we ain't got the union, that's what the union wants."

Paul walked over to the group. "Mr. Strauss, may I ask a question, please?"

"Sure, tell me what's on your mind."

"I have asked questions of other people about this union of yours. I was told the union wants a maltster to be paid sixty dollars a month. My uncle pays seventy-five. Doesn't that make him a good boss?"

"Nah, don't be fooled. Your uncle pays a little more here, a little more there, but he saves a lot more by keeping the sheep happy, keeping the union out. Stupid question."

Paul's face reddened. "I am only trying to educate myself. To find out what is right—"

"Hey, Paul," Cousin Joe called. A warning.

No longer genial, Benno lumbered to his feet and jabbed Paul's chest with his thumb. "The union is right. Socialism is right. Your uncle, he's wrong because all the capitalists are wrong. Look at what they're doing to this town!" Benno slashed his hand toward the vista of rooftops, the river, the hazy silver lake to the east. "Hundreds of men out there ain't got jobs. They got empty bellies, their wives and little ones are starving too—who cares? And the moment that *gottverdammt* fair closes, you'll see ten times as many on the streets."

"Benno," someone said in a low voice. Benno's odd oriental eyes flicked toward the rooftop door. A nondescript little man in a checked suit sauntered out, working his teeth with a gold pick.

"Afternoon, boys. Fine day. Enjoy it, we'll have all that blasted ice and snow soon enough."

There were a few muttered greetings, but they weren't cordial. The newcomer's name was Sam Traub. He had a desk in the main building, he came to work every day, but his salary was paid by the United States Government. Tax laws required a revenue man on the premises of every brewery. Joe Junior said Traub was considered a spy for Uncle Joe and Mr. Schildkraut.

"Why you worrying about the weather, Sam?" Benno said. "You're always cozy at the boss's fire, ain't you?"

His friends laughed. Traub too, but Paul detected an undertone of anger. "Ah, Benno, why the hell don't you go back to your own country if you don't like this one?"

Benno hooked his thumbs in his belt, enjoying himself. "Because we got to reform this one."

"Don't count on it. The coppers and Judge Lynch, they'll reform you first. Good thing, too."

"Sam," Benno said, "fuck you."

Two of his cronies applauded. Traub snatched the gold pick from his mouth. "Leave it to reds to ruin a man's digestion." The slam of the stairway door was loud as a shot.

Benno chuckled and sat down on the coping. "Told him good, huh?" He stroked one side of his mustache with an index finger; noticed Paul frowning.

"Something wrong with you, little boy?"

"Just another question."

"Spit it out."

Paul knew he should keep quiet, but he wanted to know. "You talk, you're always saying you have this plan, that plan, but you keep your job here—you draw your wages. You even let my uncle pay to free you from jail—"

A thrill of fear went through him as Benno got up and stalked toward him. "Are you saying we're a bunch of talkers—blow-hards?"

"I'm saying—"

Benno grabbed Paul's shirt and leaned close, spewing fumes of garlic and onion. "You got the wrong idea, little boy. Joey?"

Joe Junior jumped to his feet, almost like a dutiful soldier.

"We got some more educating to do here. Can you and him get out of the house on Sunday?"

"Sure."

"Then bring him. Come out about eleven. Catch the train that leaves the Illinois Central depot at six past the hour."

"Bring me where?" Paul said.

"Indiana," Joe Junior said. "The dunes."

"We'll show you the revolution ain't all talk, little boy."

Gray sky swept down to meet gray water churned to whitecaps. The bitter wind reddened Paul's cheeks and put a flat unpleasant taste in his mouth. During the relatively short train trip Cousin Joe had told Paul that the men they would meet weren't socialists, they were avowed anarchists.

They got off the I.C. at a small rural station, then trudged two miles north to this desolate stretch of lake shore. They found Benno with five friends, none of whom Paul recognized from Crown's.

Benno was the only imposing one in the group. The others resembled school-masters who never went outdoors, or weak-eyed clerks grown round-shouldered from their toil. Two of the men had spectacles; one had a lens painted black. Another's uncombed yellow beard reached below his waist. All were shabbily dressed, two in suits and derbies, two in odd combinations of patched pants, jeans coats, cheap wool caps. The poorest of the five wore castoff army clothing: a caped overcoat, dark blue, and soiled light blue trousers with a yellow stripe. Hardly a heroic lot, Paul thought. It renewed a suspicion that Benno Strauss was a fraud.

Shivering, he and his cousin stood with Benno, slightly apart from the others. Joe Junior stamped his feet. "Christ, I'm freezing. Wish they'd hurry it up."

"Shut up, we got to get it just right," Benno said. A stocking cap covered his bald head. Its frowsy pompom shook in the wind. "They're pretty near done."

Benno's five associates were hammering unpainted siding and squares of roof tarpaper onto a small shanty which they'd knocked together on the first dune, in sight of the breaking waves. The purpose of erecting such a structure in this deserted place eluded Paul.

He blew on his hands and stamped his feet as his cousin was doing. "When did you start putting up the shanty?"

"This morning. We come out on the six o'clock train."

"Do you come here often?" There was evidence to suggest it. Pieces of charred wood lay in three different hollows on the sheltered side of the dunes.

"Once a month, sometimes more." Benno pulled a small paper notebook from his coveralls, then a pencil stub. He wet the pencil lead on his tongue and wrote.

In front of the shanty, which had neither a door nor windows, the man in the old army greatcoat waved to Benno. His shout got lost in the wind. Benno waved back, then said, "In case Joey ain't told you yet, what we're doing out here is training. Sharpening the tools we'll use to drive the plutocrats down. Get what we want."

The men began scattering from the vicinity of the shanty, all except the one with the black spectacle lens. Crouching over an old valise, he took something from it and pushed it through a small hole left open in the side of the shanty. Then he dropped to his knees, and Paul saw a spurt of smoke near the hole. The man leaped up and ran after the others, as though the Devil was behind him. Benno swept a big arm around each of the boys.

"Down, quick!"

They threw themselves forward, and just as Paul's cheek hit the sand a detonation blew the shanty apart.

The echo of the blast seemed to last a long time. Gradually the sounds of wind and surf replaced it. The last bits of the shanty tumbled down from the sky. A smoking section of tarpaper skated away over the dunes like a drunken bat. Paul was horrified.

"Have a look," Benno shouted as he ran forward through the sand with a speed and grace surprising for a man of his age and bulk. Paul and Joe Junior followed. "God, I didn't expect this," Joe Junior panted. "Last time they had just a few sticks of dynamite, they lit them and threw them—"

Everyone crowded around the shanty site. The anarchists were laughing and congratulating themselves.

"That crater is three feet deep," Paul said.

"Look again, it's four or five," a man said. Another German; his English was so wretched, Paul barely understood him.

Benno scribbled in his little notebook, excited. "We don't do this for sport," he said to the visitors. "We study the damage, the way dynamite blows things apart. Propaganda of the deed, it's a lot more than words."

His eye fell on Paul. "I ain't trying to scare you, but you better believe this. If your uncle don't give us what we want without blood, then blood is what we'll give him. Him and all the rest."

Joe Junior stared at Benno with a strange, pained look. Surely he couldn't hate his own father enough to want to do him harm, Paul thought. Surely he still loved him a little . . .

"Exactly what did you use to blow it up?" Paul asked.

"Regular commercial dynamite. Anybody can buy it. You could. You know what they say about dynamite. Very democratic, it makes everybody equal."

His friends whooped and clapped. Benno relished the reaction. Then, abruptly, he grabbed Paul's arm and twisted it.

"Get this straight, too. You better never say a word about what you saw. Not to nobody. Huh, Joey?"

"That's right," Cousin Joe said.

"You don't have to be with us," Benno said. "Don't even have to like us. But if you talk about us, it'll go hard." Benno shook him. "*Verstanden?*"

"Yes, I understand. I won't talk." Benno released him.

A blackened shrub at the edge of the blast pit sent off a curl of bitter smoke, quickly blown away. Paul was genuinely frightened. He believed Benno's threats now; every one of them.

□ □ □ □

On the return train ride they said almost nothing to each other. Joe Junior rested his cheek against the dirty window, lost in a reverie. And not a happy one, Paul was sure. On the way out he'd acted cocky about introducing Paul to his dangerous friends. Now he seemed genuinely shaken by the demonstration. He'd seen what Benno could do to Uncle Joe.

Back at Michigan Avenue, they went straight to their rooms with only a murmured goodbye. They didn't discuss what they'd seen, that night or afterward.

On October 28, the day before the Exposition closed, Mayor Carter Harrison, Sr., answered a knock at the front door of his mansion on Ashland Avenue. A gregarious and popular man, Harrison frequently found well-wishers and job seekers on his doorstep.

It was no well-wisher this time, but an unemployed man named Prendergast, who believed Harrison had schemed to bar him from a municipal job. Prendergast fired a pistol three times. The mayor bled to death in fifteen minutes.

"Madness," Uncle Joe said next evening. "There are wild men in the streets. The socialists and anarchists foment this sort of outrage."

Joe Junior's response was a sullen stare. For his part, Paul thought Uncle Joe might be right.

Autumn's vivid hues, the glowing skies and flaming trees, gave way to the monochrome of impending winter. The sun was a faint lemon-colored disk behind racing dark clouds, and then one day it was hidden altogether.

It couldn't turn cold fast enough for Paul. Maybe there would be snow and ice by Thanksgiving Day, a holiday unknown in Germany. The great President Lincoln had established it in 1863, to celebrate the survival of the Union and the victories of its soldiers.

North wind stripped leaves from the trees on the Crown property. When Paul had time, he helped Carl gather and burn them on the curb at Nineteenth Street. The smell of smoldering leaf piles was a new one, sweet and sad and unforgettable.

Joe Junior never helped with such chores. He called Paul a fool; didn't he already work like a mule at the brewery? Hoping he wasn't completely serious, Paul stood up for himself:

"I don't mind. I still have many kindnesses to repay in this house." Although he felt a little less warmly toward Uncle Joe than he had when he arrived, he meant it. Joe Junior just shook his head in that superior way of his, and walked off. Except for occasional raggings from his cousin, however, Paul's speaking his mind didn't seem to have any adverse effect on their growing friendship. For that Paul was thankful.

When the Exposition closed, Benno's prediction came true. Thousands more were laid off. They roamed the streets in gangs. Benno and his friends at Crown's railed at the plight of the unemployed, but Paul thought they were secretly pleased. As though all the suffering would help the cause and hasten the outbreak of class violence. In his pocket dictionary Paul found a word to describe Benno and his friends. He'd first seen the word in a newspaper. The word was "cynical." They were cynical men.

But he no longer held the foolish belief that they were harmless.

31

Joe Crown

IN NOVEMBER 1893, Joe Crown had a welcome visitor from New York. An old friend he'd met through the Republican Party, in which they were both active.

Carl Schurz was twelve years older than Joe. He was also, indisputably, the most famous American of German ancestry. Born near Cologne, he had plunged into the rebellion of '48 while a student at the University of Bonn. He'd emigrated to America in the 1850s, settled in Wisconsin, and there involved himself in the new and idealistic Republican Party.

Already a practicing attorney by the time war loomed, he helped secure Lincoln's nomination for President, briefly held the post of Minister to Spain, and returned to his new homeland in 1862 to lead Union troops. He fought at Second Bull Run, Chancellorsville, Gettysburg, and mustered out with the rank of major general.

He turned to journalism and was owner-editor of the *St. Louis Westliche Post* when he was chosen to be a senator from Missouri, the first German-born citizen ever to hold office in that high chamber. Now he was a journalist again: chief editorial writer for *Harper's Weekly,* and traveling through Chicago on one of his fact-finding trips.

Schurz was a lanky, scholarly man with a great ruff of graying hair sticking up from his head. His alert darting eyes seemed magnified by the small round spectacles he wore. He was well loved by the Crowns, and Ilsa welcomed him warmly to the house on Michigan Avenue. All the children were dutifully presented once again; Schurz had a favorable comment about each, and was especially attentive to young Carl, who had been named in his honor. Fritzi giggled and flirted shamelessly, then offered to do an imitation of the guest. Schurz was amused but Ilsa immediately said no. Throughout all this, Joe Junior was polite but silent. His father didn't fail to notice.

When Paul was introduced, Schurz said, "I applaud your choice of America as a homeland. I made that choice, as did your uncle. Three wise men, eh?" Ilsa laughed too loudly, and Schurz beamed; he had a sense of his own importance.

The family and the visitor consumed a huge meal at one in the afternoon. Then Schurz and Joe retired to the study, and over drinks—Heimat dark beer for Joe, schnapps for Carl—they discussed the state of the nation and the world. Being Republicans didn't mean they always agreed. Joe had been one of hundreds of thousands of Union veterans unswervingly loyal to President Grant despite accusations of malfeasance and incompetence that tarred him in the last years of his presidency. Schurz had led the anti-Grant faction.

Other issues embroiled them in friendly argument as well. Reform of the spoils system was one. Schurz was an advocate of civil service, but Joe saw it as just more government interference. Another issue was Cuba. The island ninety miles off the Floridas had excited the interest and aroused the anxiety of Americans for years.

Joe and Schurz didn't disagree that Spain had a bad record of repression and misrule in its island colony. They agreed that the Cuban effort to throw off the yoke of Madrid was right and proper. The struggle had begun in the early 1870s, when a strong band of exiles, the Cuban Junta, operated out of a boardinghouse in Manhattan, raising funds for filibustering expeditions.

The so-called Ten Years' War between Spain and her rebellious colonists sputtered on until the dismal Treaty of Zanjón in 1878. But freedom was a potent idea. There remained in New York a powerful cadre of refugees formally organized as the Cuban Revolutionary Party. The rebels worked from a storefront near the New York piers. The leaders were an old soldier, General Máximo Gómez, and a young journalist and ideologue, José Martí, who'd been sent to a Cuban rock quarry at fifteen, punishment for revolutionary activity.

It was Martí who had lately led the campaign for *Cuba libre.* Now, in the autumn of 1893, the campaign was stalled again. The depression had closed many of the East Coast cigar factories and sweatshops. Unemployed Cuban cigar workers had no money to give to the revolutionists.

"And a good thing, too," Schurz said in Joe's study. "If Martí's invasion plans can't be funded, perhaps they'll wither away."

"You oppose the overthrow of a tyrannical regime? You're against liberty?"

"I am against imperialism which wraps itself in the flag, Joseph. There is a strong faction in this country which delights in doing that. It is a faction growing more vocal and influential all the time. A faction, I fear, that secretly craves expansion not of American liberties, but of commercial markets for American goods."

Joe said, "Bosh," and tossed off the rest of his beer. "This country should do everything in its power to free Cuba. If necessary, we should provide armed assistance."

"How can you argue that way? What if the fatherland chose to export *its* style of government, with the army willing to fight to guarantee success of any such venture overseas? Don't laugh, the military clique in Berlin is strong. Ideas like that are afloat in the Chancellery."

"It isn't the same thing, not at all."

Schurz stretched his long legs toward the bright fire in the hearth. "If you say so. I'll not drive a good host to the point of anger." He raised his small glass of schnapps. *"Prosit."*

Joe said, "This Cuban situation won't go away, you know. Martí and his men have wide support. Some of the biggest newspapers in New York are backing them. Sam Gompers, the only union man who isn't half mad with power and red ideas—"

"I know, I know." Schurz raised a placating hand. "Let's not try to resolve the question here. I'd like to take a walk."

From the window Joe said, "It's very cold. The sky's threatening."

"I need the air."

So, bundled in heavy overcoats and bowler hats, mufflers, and gloves, they walked in the bitter gray afternoon to the dark, whitecapped lake.

"How is your business, Joseph?"

"It has come back satisfactorily." He described the problem caused by Hexhammer's editorial. "In bad times people want their beer more than ever. He didn't reckon on that."

Joe led the way along a path beside huge blocks of granite abandoned after some unsuccessful construction job. The waves struck the other side, showering icy water on their hats.

"The labor situation, however—that's another matter. Pressures are building up in the brewery. I can feel them even though I seldom see evidence. That damned Eugene Debs and his new union are part of the cause." Joe referred to the giant American Railway Union, created during the summer from many smaller railway brotherhoods, largely through the effort of a labor leader from downstate Indiana.

Schurz said, "I've not met Debs yet. They say he's a good man—even a saintly man." Joe snorted.

"Does he have a large following in Chicago?"

"Not among my friends. He's a socialist, and makes no secret of it."

Joe stepped up on a block of granite in which someone had chiseled a ledge. He looked out at the lake, vast, cold, forbidding.

"I have a more personal problem at the brewery. There's a radical faction, and my older boy, Joe, hangs out with them."

Schurz's cheeks gleamed pink from the wind. The two friends stood side by side on the ledge, gloved hands in pockets. "Joseph, lest you forget—I was one of those radicals in '48."

As if he hadn't heard what Schurz said, Joe continued. "I'd discipline Joe— take him out of the brewery at once—except that I fear it would push him into their camp. He's a smart boy in many ways, but in others, stupid. I hope to heaven he'll come to his senses as he matures. Sometimes, quite frankly, I almost don't recognize him as my own child."

He turned, confronting the dark skyline of the city. They had walked quite far; he could see above the granite blocks the ten-story Auditorium Hotel at Congress Street and, immediately north, the fine Studebaker Building.

"It's twenty years since I came to Chicago—thirty-six years since I arrived in this country—and I hardly recognize either one. I don't know what to make of the world today. Electric lights. Telephones. Pictures that come like magic from Eastman's little black box. Everyone madly wheeling on cycles—why, they're even talking about buggies driven by engines, not pulled by horses; can you imagine? They're writing articles about contraptions to fly in the sky!

"Look at the city, what do you see? Workingmen, fairly paid, decently treated, spitting in the faces of their employers. Settlement houses where those who would destroy society are made welcome—allowed to spout their vile ideas from public platforms—and applauded for it! There are clubs and colleges for women —women who belong in the kitchen, and the nursery—Carl, what's happening?"

"Age, I think. Advancing age is happening, to you, and to me."

Joe Crown swore. It was an infrequent occurrence, but when he did it, he did it well, in blistering, jaw-bending, polysyllabic German.

Schurz maintained a sympathetic silence. Some men grew archly conservative as age claimed them, and undoubtedly his friend was one such. It could never diminish Schurz's affection. Joe Crown was a fine man. He was honest in the conduct of his business; he was a caring father and a devoted husband. Schurz didn't have to approve of his friend's political or social views in order to understand the pain he was suffering because of them.

Joe's wrath abated. He looked sad, even baffled. Gently, the visitor said, "These fears you have about the brewery—do you honestly think you will have trouble?"

"If they continue to oppose me—if they push their demands—yes. The depression just makes the reds more reckless. They want to show they can succeed with their programs, while honest businessmen are failing."

"You don't fear violence, do you? Surely not."

"It's entirely possible."

"Well, I pray it never involves your son."

"Who knows? He's turned his back on me."

"Young men are often at odds with their fathers. It seems to be a necessary part of growing up."

"Necessary? The scorn he has for all I've tried to give him? All I can offer him? Oh, no."

Joe Crown's hat blew off suddenly. Agile, he leaped down from the ledge and caught it as it bounced away over the frozen brown earth. Putting it on, he blinked suddenly, and stuck out his tongue to taste something in the air.

Schurz felt it too. He peeled off a mauve glove, and touched his cheek.

"Snow."

"Yes." Down from the north, where the sky was slate-colored, tiny snowflakes sped, growing fatter every moment.

"A sure sign of winter, Carl. Perhaps Joe Junior will give us a few months of peace. He revels in the outdoors in the winter. He loves to ice-skate. My nephew bought himself skates too, he showed them to me just yesterday. He wanted to know how soon the lagoons in Lincoln Park would freeze. Come along, we should be getting back."

32

Paul

LOW ON THE HORIZON, huge as a house, the winter moon turned the ice pale gold. Wind rattled the tree limbs above the bank where Paul sat lacing his skates with fingers half numb. Close by, Joe Junior trotted in place, hugging himself, sailing little clouds past the moon each time he exhaled. It was five-thirty in the morning.

"This is insane, Paul. You don't know how to skate."

"If I cannot skate, I cannot meet her. You said so."

"I also said it won't matter a damn if you do meet her, Vanderhoff despises Germans, Bohunks, Irish—the whole lot. He's got a special hate for Pop."

"I don't care, I am going to meet her. Help me up, please?"

Cousin Joe put his hand down and Paul took hold, struggling upright on his skates. Lincoln Park lay desolate and empty in the moonlight.

With his left skate Paul took a three-inch step on the ground. His legs were strong but his ankles still wobbled dangerously. Another three-inch step slid his right runner to the edge of the frozen lagoon.

"I don't know whether that ice is thick enough," Joe Junior said. "It only froze night before last."

"Even so, I must try."

Paul's cheeks felt like raw meat. His woolen winter coat seemed thin as newspaper. He tugged the stocking cap down over his tingling ears, and pulled on wool mittens. He inched his left skate onto the ice, then his right. His left ankle rolled over. He fell down.

"My God, this will never work."

"Help me up, Joe. I will learn to skate."

"And die in the attempt." But Joe Junior gave Paul his hand again. He maneuvered effortlessly on skates.

Paul swayed, barely holding his balance. "Please, give me a push. See if I can skate a little way."

Joe Junior pushed the small of his back. Paul glided forward about three feet, the blades rasping in the silence. Far away, a train wailed. The sound rose up toward thousands of white stars.

"I'm moving, I am skating," Paul cried. With a whoop, he windmilled his arms. He fell down. This time he got up without assistance.

"Sit down, Joe, rest, I will practice by myself."

"If you do, we'll be here till Christmas." Joe Junior skated to the bank and there sat down facing the lagoon, hugging his knees to keep warm.

Paul slid his right skate forward and fell down.

He got up and tried again.

He fell down.

Soon his rear hurt. He kept trying. He fell down seventeen times before he managed to skate ten feet, out toward the center of the lagoon. The moon, rising higher, changed color from gold to bone white. The ice crackled under Paul's skates.

"Joe, look, I'm staying up, I am learning how," he called. He pushed off and sailed on toward the middle, the ice crackling more and more noisily under the blades. Frigid air raked his raw face. He laughed, delighted, sailing along—

The ice broke. He dropped into black water, hearing Joe Junior yell as he sank.

His clothes dragged him down. The freezing water terrified him. But he'd always been a fair swimmer, and he was strong. He touched the lagoon bottom, flexed his legs, kicked upward. He lifted his right hand over his head and found the ice. It broke the moment he grasped it. *Oh, God, I'm done,* he thought, sinking again.

Something took hold of his arm, arresting his descent. Joe Junior, precariously balanced on ice that was creaking and threatening to break, pulled him halfway out by main strength.

Then the ice collapsed. Both of them floundered in the water, their thrashing throwing silver drops in the air. Joe Junior had presence of mind; he knew which side of the widening hole might have the thickest ice. There he managed to climb out. He pulled Paul out after him.

"Christ, what damned foolishness," he gasped. Then he laughed. "You're a sight." Paul's soggy wool cap was cocked over one eye.

"You are also."

They both laughed.

Paul's teeth started to chatter. "This is enough for one night," his cousin said. "We'll go to the brewery, the night watchman will let us in. We can dry off before we start work."

Paul followed his cousin toward the bank, managing to skate rather than walk. "But I am coming back tomorrow night."

"I'm afraid you mean it."

"I am going to meet her, Joe. You don't have to come with me while I learn."

"You expect me to stay away and let you drown? A dead capitalist or two wouldn't bother my conscience, but a dead cousin—that's different."

Joe Junior nudged him. "There she is."

It was a Sunday afternoon. December; very cold. But the sun shone. From a large public pavilion on the lagoon's east side there drifted the jaunty melody of "Grandfather's Clock" played on a hurdy-gurdy.

Despite the temperature Paul felt warm. Perhaps it was due to nerves and excitement. The ice was crowded with skaters, boys and girls, families with children, some skating slowly, others speeding, darting in and out. Even so, it was impossible to overlook Juliette Vanderhoff. She was inside a smaller pavilion on the near bank. The pavilion was dark green, with a brick hearth and chimney in the center. A log fire blazed. A sign hung on the eave facing the lagoon.

LINCOLN PARK SKATING CLUB
—Members Only—

Warming herself in the pavilion, Juliette Vanderhoff stood out because of her cape and wide hood of scarlet velvet. Seven or eight young men surrounded her, laughing and chatting. The young men all had a sleek, prosperous look.

"We must go over there," Paul said. "You can remind her we met this summer."

"All right, but you've got heavy competition. A bunch of swells."

"Swells?"

"Rich boys. Don't worry, what can you lose?"

Everything, Paul thought.

They stepped on the ice. Paul skated fairly easily now; nights of practice had steadied him and given him confidence. "Hey, Julie, hello," Joe Junior called as they clattered into the club pavilion, scraping their blades on the rough flagstones. He shouldered a couple of her admirers aside. "Do you remember my cousin Paul?"

Paul snatched off his cap, ready to say something. He could think of nothing. The gray eyes, the lovely warm smile bewitched him. Her thick black hair shone within her hood.

"Why yes, the German boy." The word *boy* crushed him. She held out a black-gloved hand. "How nice to see you again." They shook hands. She said to the others, "This is Joseph's cousin, Paul Crown."

Paul was aware of the looks the young men were giving him. A tall, smirky blond fellow slapped him on the back. "Hello, Dutch. Julie, shall we skate again?"

"I suppose." She smiled at the blond boy, though she seemed to be casting a hopeful glance at Paul. "Paul, this is Strickland Welliver II. He's our club speed champion."

"Watch my smoke," Welliver said, very smug. He touched Julie's arm in a possessive way. *Hurry, think of something.* If he didn't, Welliver would sweep her off; his chance would be lost.

"Miss Vanderhoff, I think you had better come with me first," he said, struggling equally with his English and his nerves. "There is a park police officer who wishes to see you."

Strickland Welliver said, "A what?" Joe Junior almost choked.

"Police officer—isn't that how you say it?" Paul gestured toward the crowded lagoon. "Just over there. If you will come with me—"

Fearing she might slap his face, he nevertheless took hold of her arm. Her gray eyes probed his, curious, surprised, then pleased.

"All right. Excuse me, Strickland—Joe—all of you."

She followed Paul out of the pavilion into the sunlight.

They skated.

They glided around the lagoon, moving with the flow, counterclockwise, toward the pavilion where the organ grinder finished "The Bowery" and swung into a quick-time version of "Old Black Joe." Julie's cheeks were bright pink. She skated with short, crisp strides, her upper body seeming to float without effort or direct connection to her legs. Paul was tense, fearful of falling.

Julie shielded her eyes. "Where is the officer? I don't see him."

"Well—" Paul couldn't stand it. He twisted to a stop. She bumped into him.

"Oh," she said softly, pulling back but still standing close. They were the same height. Their condensing breaths mingled. This close, her gray eyes seemed enormous. Between his legs, he ached.

"Miss Vanderhoff, I have a confession. There is no officer. I did it to get you away."

"That's very ingenious. Audacious—"

"But if there *were* an officer, he *would* wish to see you because—" He gulped and risked everything. "You are *sehr schön*—I'm sorry, I'm nervous—you're beautiful."

"Why, thank you, Paul." She didn't seem angry; touched, rather. She glanced back at the club pavilion where Strickland Welliver was watching them, gloved fists on his hips.

"You're a most unusual young man. Polite, but very clever."

"I am not so young, Miss—"

"We've been properly introduced, you must call me Julie."

"Julie." The music of it, on his tongue for the first time in her presence, almost drove him out of his mind. "You called me a young man—well, I'm not so young. I am sixteen."

"So am I. My birthday is May 28."

"Mine is the fifteenth of June."

"Then I'm older. Let's see—eighteen days older. So you'll just have to do whatever I say." There was a teasing light in her eye. "Paul—I have a confession also." She waited until two men skated past. "I knew there was no police officer. But I was happy you invented one."

Clouds of her breath touched him, faintly sweet with clove. Her scarlet cape brushed his coat; for a moment he felt the soft mass of her breast. His head pounded.

"Paul."

"Yes? *Yes?*"

"Shall we skate?"

She sensed that he was inexperienced, and skated slowly. He kept pace, mercifully with no falls. Her acceptance of his crude trick overcame some of the initial awkwardness between them.

Joe Junior skated by, backward. His red face crinkled in a smile. He waved and kept skating backward, somehow missing people without looking at them.

"You speak English very well," she said.

"Thank you. I have studied hard, on my own and with a—*ein Hauslehrer.*" Mortified, he mumbled, "I don't know the English."

"Do you mean a teacher? A tutor?"

"That's it! I had a tutor! Thank you."

They skated.

"Are you working at Crown's brewery now?"

"Yes. Sunday is my day off."

They skated.

"I like your cousin Joe. I consider him a good friend. He's very intelligent. He reads a lot, doesn't he? Some of his ideas are rather alarming, but I always enjoy hearing them. I wish I could see more of him. I'm afraid my father is very—well, disapproving of people who haven't been in this country as long as our family. The first Vanderhoffs came to Connecticut before the Revolution."

"You have to do what your father wishes, I suppose."

"True. In this day and age daughters are expected to be dutiful."

They skated.

"I thought I might not get away from home this afternoon," she said. "My mother is bedridden again. Quite sick."

"Oh, I'm sorry."

"Thank you."

"Was it sudden?"

"Oh, no. Mama suffers from a recurring condition called neurasthenia. Extreme prostration of the nerves and brain. Her spirits sink very low. Sometimes she won't even speak for days. It upsets me awfully, but Dr. Woodrow says it's perfectly normal for women. My Aunt Willis who lives in New York says that's nonsense, but Father doesn't believe her. He hates all of Aunt Willis's ideas. She visits twice a year, he hates that too."

"Do you like your aunt?"

"Very much, although some of her ideas are awfully bold. She reminds me of your cousin."

They skated.

"How do you like America?"

Since the exposure of his little ruse, he felt he could be truthful with her. "I don't like it as much as I thought I would." He smiled. "But I'm liking it better now."

A man skated by, doing a slow expert Dutch roll, moving forward and back and forth laterally at the same time. He was a man of middle height, wearing a derby, a long scarf of dark blue plaid, expensive pigskin gloves, a turtleneck sweater under his double-breasted tweed suit. Paul wouldn't have paid much attention but for one other touch. The man had a monocle with a long ribbon.

He seemed interested in Julie. Paul stared at him. The man smiled and abruptly skated off to the left. Paul quickly forgot about him.

A roast chestnut seller pushed his little wheeled stove along the bank and cried his wares. The hurdy-gurdy pealed out "Daisy Bell," a hit song of last year; you heard it everywhere. Fritzi said it was inspired by the cycling craze.

Julie looked at Paul. He looked at her . . .

"Watch out, you young idiot." A fat nursemaid barely managed to lurch out of the way, dragging along a child on tiny skates. Paul made a violent move that threw him into the bank, where he crashed.

Julie had the skill to stop herself just where the ice ended. Humiliated, Paul scrambled up, brushing off his pants. "I'm afraid I'm not a very good skater."

"You said you skated a lot in Berlin."

"You remember that?"

"Of course."

"Juliette—that—it was another tale. I wanted to—to—*ach*. I can't think how to say it."

"Is the word you want 'impress'?"

"Yes. Impress. I wanted to impress you."

With a kindly smile, she laid her glove on his arm. "You have."

Blond Mr. Strickland Welliver II came hurtling out of the blaze of the sinking sun, calling to her while he executed a flawless figure eight, "Are you going to hang out with him all day?"

"No, Strickland, don't be impatient." She whispered to Paul. "If you like I'll give you some skating pointers next Sunday."

"Yes. Wonderful!" But how could he live through six whole days without seeing her?

"Goodbye, Paul. Thank you."

She squeezed his hand and skated away, pursued by the blond young god, Strickland Welliver.

On the crowded cable car clanging south on State Street, Paul blurted his secret to his cousin.

"I love that girl. I have fallen in love with her."

"You're crazy."

"No, I am in love."

"Then, my friend, you are in trouble. She may fancy you, but if Papa Pork finds out, he's liable to take a cane to her, and you too. Didn't I tell you old man Vanderhoff hates foreigners? He hates anybody who isn't a blueblood—and that means us."

Paul was dreaming deliriously of Julie's eyes, inky hair, fair round bosom; he scarcely heard the warning.

33

Elstree

HE SKATED SLOWLY. The pickings were poor this afternoon. Which was unfortunate, since the circumstances were ideal. He saw no one he recognized, other than Vanderhoff's daughter, who had gone.

He let the more vigorous skaters pass, the better to survey possible choices. Dusk came down, drear and bitter. An old caretaker set kindling alight in iron barrels placed around the lagoon. Reflections of flames danced on the skater's monocle.

It was perhaps foolish of him to wear a monocle, since it drew attention. But he liked the aura of gentility it created. You could look at it another way, too. If others fixed on the monocle, and remembered that, they would forget his face. Yet there remained an element of risk, which he enjoyed. It lent spice to these outings.

He thought of the Vanderhoff girl, Juliette. She had been skating with a young man with blue eyes, reddish-brown hair, and a sturdy physique. He was jealous of the boy but reasoned that even if Miss Vanderhoff had been unescorted, he couldn't have spoken to her. She might have remembered him.

Unlikely, but she might. He had been presented once, three years ago, in the dress circle foyer of the Auditorium, to which Vanderhoff and his affected Southern wife had dragged their daughter for an evening of symphonic presentations of the music of Wagner. "Juliette," her father said, "may I introduce Mr. William Vann Elstree III? His family owns the department store where your mother prefers to shop—to the chagrin of Mr. Marshall Field."

He vividly recalled Juliette's youthful prettiness that night. The gown she wore —virginal white, matching the aigrettes in her incredible black hair. Her breasts had been budding then. The memory turned him hard as he skated.

How he'd love to see that black hair unbound, spilling down her white nakedness. See whether she was as luxuriantly hairy in other . . .

Ah, why speculate? He took risks, but he didn't court the impossible.

Still, he had trouble getting her out of his thoughts.

He removed his gloves and warmed his hands at one of the fire barrels. Sweat coated his face. But not because of the flames.

Custom House Place from Harrison to Twelfth Street was the most elegant vice district in Chicago, and one of the most famous in America. It was an area seemingly unaffected by the worsening depression; Elstree made the silent observation as his hansom pulled to the curb in front of the Society Club. For a cold Sunday night, activity on the street was brisk. Other cabs, and plenty of foot traffic.

Most of the establishments on Custom House Place catered to a better class of clientele; there were a few dives, but they were kept under control by the other owners. A gentleman could come here with a relatively high degree of safety. Still, he never took chances. He carried a little plated hideout pistol, always.

The seven-foot doorman of the club, a mahogany-colored man with a long white beard, ran down the broad steps and opened the hansom's door. "Good evening, sar. Welcome back."

Elstree jumped out and paid the driver. He had changed to evening clothes. White tie; tall hat; a short cape; gloves. He looked smart.

"Good evening, John." Everyone called the doorman John the Baptist. The owners of the club said he was a Parsee from Calcutta. He wore a faded livery, something from a theatrical costumer's, embellished with a blue silk sash which held a sheathed dagger. "Circus night again."

"Yes, sar, got a crowd already. Going to be a fine show. Almost ready to start. Hurry on in."

Elstree climbed the steps under the flickering gas lanterns—no electrification here as yet—and knocked at an ornately carved door.

Another man in livery admitted him to a foyer furnished and lit with the restrained taste of a fine home. The only raucous note was sounded by a parrot in a cage hanging in a stand. The parrot whistled, cocked his head and screamed, "Welcome, welcome, welcome, mister."

"Hello, friend. Right on the dot, aren't you?" From a parlor to Elstree's right came a small, delicately built woman. She was at least sixty, handsomely gowned in grandmother gray. She shook his hand. "We're glad to see you."

He handed his cape, hat, and gloves to the footman without looking at him. "Thank you, Sue. Are we in the upstairs parlor?" Little Sue, who was white, owned the brothel in partnership with Big Sue, who was black.

"No, the billiard room in back. Had to move the table out. Overflow crowd. I brought in a girl from the Levee for this circus. Down there they call her Beefsteak Bert. She's a big person. A small one wouldn't be able to stand the gaff."

Little Sue winked, the first violation of her grandmotherly persona. Elstree chuckled.

"The usual charge tonight?"

"That's right, seventy-five. We'll add it to your tab. Go right on back, they're still serving champagne." At the Society Club, that was the only drink regularly offered. Whiskey or beer had to be ordered by the customer ahead of time, at exorbitant prices.

Elstree walked quickly down the dim hall, which was papered in a maroon fabric flocked with a pattern of large lotuslike flowers. In the smoky room at the end of the corridor, gentlemen were sitting and standing with champagne glasses. He heard growling. The crowd shifted and he saw a coarse little man with a stubbly beard hanging onto a rope leash. At the other end of the leash was a huge tawny boxer dog.

Elstree stopped when a door opened in an alcove to his right. A booming voice greeted him. "Look who's here. Bill! By God, now we got some class."

"Kindly don't shout my name, Sue," Elstree said, although the billiard room was so noisy, it was doubtful that anyone had heard. He stepped into the alcove. Big Sue, a three-hundred-pound woman, wore a black bombazine dress with long sleeves and a high collar concealed by a three-inch choker of diamonds. She gave off sweet waves of perfume.

"How's your health?" she asked. Big Sue was always cheerful and friendly, and while he didn't care for niggers of any stripe, he had to admit she was a successful businesswoman.

"It'll be much better after I spend a few hours here."

With a twinkle, Sue said, "How's your wife?"

He seized her chin, pinching and twisting. The pain made her grimace, showing all her even white teeth.

"Don't get saucy. You know what I do to girls who are saucy with me. There are two standards in this world, Sue. One for wives and one for husbands. Keep it in mind."

Elstree gave her chin a final pinch, making her gasp softly. He sauntered away to the billiard room.

Heads turned when he walked in. A couple of acquaintances greeted him, but not by name. Nor did he use theirs. He found a chair, took a glass of champagne. A side door opened. Several of the guests exclaimed and clapped.

Out walked Beefsteak Bert, a woman of about thirty with long dirty blond hair and shoulders like a steelworker's. Her satin wrapper was decorated with sequined peacocks. She simpered and curtsied to the crowd, then loosed the belt of her robe and let it drop.

More applause. Elstree joined in, a freshly lit Cuban cigar jauntily held in his teeth. Beefsteak Bert put her hands on her knees and, coyly glancing over her shoulder, bent forward and pushed out her enormous white rear. The handler could barely hold onto the dog, whose frantic clawing threatened to rip the carpet.

Through the cigar smoke Elstree had a sudden unexpected vision. Dizzying as strong drink, it banished thoughts of the coming show. The vision was Juliette Vanderhoff—far more desirable than the debased whore, but just as naked.

34

Paul

SHE SWEPT EVERYTHING from his mind. His nagging dissatisfaction with Crown's because he knew the career he wanted, but didn't know how to take it up or learn it. His worry and guilt over disappointing Uncle Joe a second time when he left the brewery—almost an inevitability now. The simmering antagonism between his uncle and his cousin, both of whom had claims on his heart. And the old question, seldom out of mind: had he really found his home, the place he belonged for the rest of his life? Not so much this particular house on Michigan Avenue, but Chicago; America? None of this seemed to matter now. He was racked by longing and fear of loss, consumed by furious storms of jealousy of those in her circle—parents, friends, anyone—who dared to keep her from him, or intruded on the lovesick thoughts he wished, hoped, prayed she was thinking about him.

The following Sunday it rained. Even so, he traveled all the way up to Lincoln Park. He found the lagoon melting, the pavilions empty. For nearly an hour he skulked up and down the street near the mansion at Fifteenth and Prairie. But he saw no sign of Julie.

When he got back to the Crown house, he couldn't find Joe Junior. He wandered to the stable. The English coachman, Nicky Speers, was currycombing Uncle Joe's prize carriage horse, a beautiful bay named Prince.

"Nicky, have you seen Joe?"

Speers rubbed the horse's muzzle affectionately. Prince tossed his head and blubbered. "Young Mr. Joseph doesn't confide in me, but I strongly suspect he went out to Pullman."

"Have you met his girl?"

"He sneaked her in here one night for five minutes. A Bohunk, she is. Pretty thing. Fine strapping figure, though there's something bloody cold about her, too. Hand me the brush, please. Righto, that's a good lad."

It wasn't until after the evening meal that Joe Junior returned. Through the half-open door of his room, Paul heard his cousin stride along the hall, whistling. A few minutes later Paul knocked at his door. Joe Junior called for him to come in. He was stripping off his shirt. There were three short parallel scratches on his back.

"I looked for Julie at the park this afternoon."

"When it's this warm? Paul, my boy, you are love-struck. Badly."

Paul sank down on the bed with a glum nod. "You saw your girl today, I suppose."

Joe Junior winked. "Yes, sir!"

"Will I meet her sometime?"

"Never in this house. If I brought her around, Pop would raise hell, same as Pork Vanderhoff will if he finds out about you. Rosie's old man, Tabor, joined the Railway Union that Gene Debs started last summer. Three or four miles of spur track come into the Pullman works, so Debs organized there. King George Pullman hates that. Rosie's ma worries about it because they live in the company housing."

"But you had a good time today."

"The best. Rosie isn't one of these delicate society girls. The kind that imagines babies come from heaven, or faints at the sight of a couple of dogs doing what's natural. You may have that problem with Julie."

"Oh, I wouldn't think of—"

"Come on, sure you would, you're a man, aren't you?" Paul's face was red. Thoughtfully, Cousin Joe added, "Julie's a peach, but I think she's proper. At least the Vanderhoffs raised her to be proper. So don't be too disappointed if she —well—holds back." He laid a sympathetic hand on Paul's shoulder. "Know what I mean?"

"Yes. But I don't think you are right about her. Anyway, she will be my girl."

"Sure. Sure she will," Joe Junior said with a certain false heartiness. "Listen, I'm worn out. Tomorrow's a workday."

Paul said good night and walked back to his room. Joe Junior's remarks about Julie left him anxious and troubled again.

The Crowns observed many German traditions but ignored others. Always, in the homeland, the fir tree, the symbol of Christmas, was put up on Christmas Eve. The Crowns brought in their tree, and decorated it, two weeks earlier. Uncle Joe liked the anticipation and the festive look the tree created. But he never permitted the candles to be lit until Christmas Eve, and he personally hung the pickle as any good German father did. With everyone else out of the room, he hid the small cucumber-shaped glass ornament on the tree as cleverly as he could. A reward of one gold dollar went to each of the younger family members who found it without touching the tree. A year ago, Paul had found it first, in less than a minute. Joe Junior had refused to take part, claiming he was too old.

The Crowns went to church often during the Advent season. There were many special services. Paul had always enjoyed Christmas music, and last year the anthems and carols had seemed joyous, triumphant, beautiful beyond belief. This year he found church—indeed, the whole celebration—an annoying distraction. He found everything a distraction except the young woman looming so large in his life.

Even so, on Christmas Eve, he got sudden goose bumps when the choir and congregation at St. Paul's sang *"Stille Nacht"* in the soft glow of the candles illuminating the sanctuary.

Back on Michigan Avenue, they lit the candles on the tree and toasted the season with spicy mulled wine. Uncle Joe lifted his cup to Paul.

"This is a most important anniversary. A year ago we gained a new member of this family. May the coming year be even better and even happier for you, Paul."

"I thank you very much, Uncle."

"Pauli. Our Pauli," Aunt Ilsa said, giving him a great hug and kiss and managing to spill some of the mulled wine on her fancy holiday skirt. For a moment or two Paul felt that yes, perhaps he was where he belonged.

Christmas fell on Monday. Uncle Joe and Aunt Ilsa were again generous with their gifts. Paul received several shirts, two pairs of corduroy knickerbockers, and a silver-plated comb and brush set, obviously expensive since each brush had a raised Crown insignia on the back. Paul's prize gift was a fancy bicycle suit—sack coat and knee-length pants—of fine cassimere wool in a brown pincheck pattern. He was delighted. He only wished he could have given a gift to Julie somehow.

By Wednesday of that week, half the household had colds. Half the brewery workers, too. At noon Saturday, Paul was sent home from Crown's with a fever.

The delivery wagon from Frankel's meat market was tied at the hitching block nearest the rear entrance on Nineteenth. Paul dragged himself into the kitchen, which was deserted except for Frankel's delivery boy, a gangly older youth with an enormous spit curl arranged to hide some of his prematurely bald head. The delivery boy wore a voluminous tan duster that reached to his knees.

"Say, pal, I got a problem," he said. "Where's your cook? I been hunting all over, I can't find her."

"Louise was sneezing and coughing last night, she went to bed. I suppose she is resting in her room."

"Then I got to speak to the lady of the house."

"She will be out all day. Or so she said this morning."

"Jesus, that is a problem." The delivery boy scraped the nail of his little finger up and down a crevice between two front teeth. He flicked something off his nail and said, "I'm supposed to pick up a list, special order, for New Year's."

Without thinking much about it, Paul said, "Why don't you go up to Louise's room on the third floor? Knock softly, so you don't wake her if she's sleeping. If she is awake, I expect she will give you the list. Go up the back stair there, behind the pantry. On the top floor it is the second door on your left."

The older boy thanked him, calling him pal again, and disappeared.

Paul hung the kettle on the hob to boil. He craved a strong cup of tea with milk. A few minutes later he walked from the kitchen to the short hall just beyond. The hall was relatively dark. From there he observed the delivery boy standing in front of the decorated tree, admiring it.

Before Paul could make his presence known, a voice boomed from the second-floor landing. "You down there. What are you doing?"

"Just having a glim at your tree, pal."

Manfred Blenkers rushed down the stairs. "I have seen you before. What's your name?"

"Jimmy Daws. I'm from Frankel's."

"We don't allow tradesmen in this part of the house. Get out at once."

Manfred Blenkers made the word tradesmen sound like a filthy epithet. Though Manfred was the absolute monarch of household affairs, Paul thought this was going too far. He walked out where they'd see him.

"I sent him upstairs, Manfred. He was searching for Louise, to take a special order for Monday. I said it was all right to go to her room so long as she was awake."

"*You* gave this person leave to roam around the house?"

"Yes, what is wrong with that?" Paul resented the prosecutorial tone.

"Listen," the delivery boy broke in. "I went up the back way, I talked to her, I got the list and came down the front way. So what? You're makin' a hell of a fuss over nothing."

"Don't curse in this house or I'll see that you're fired, you guttersnipe. Remove your dirty boots and your dirty self from these premises, instantly."

Midway through that, Paul decided he couldn't put up with any more. He screwed up his nerve and stepped forward. "Mr. Blenkers, you have no right to badger him like that."

"What? What are you saying to me?"

Somewhere above, there was a gasp. Paul saw Fritzi crouching behind the rail of the upper landing.

"I am telling you, Mr. Blenkers, he needed to see Louise, I told him where to find her. What is the harm?"

"Your uncle will decide that when he comes home."

"If you want to tell him, go ahead. I will tell my side, we will see who comes out best."

Paul said it calmly, looking straight at the steward, who now had a vaguely wounded expression. The delivery boy was nervously tapping the front of his long tan coat with his right hand. His left hand was deep in his pocket, as if he were holding his belly because it hurt.

Manfred recognized that his authority had been breached. With a lot of hand-waving, he cried, "All right, enough, leave, both of you!"

He marched noisily up the stairs. Grinning, Paul bobbed his head toward the kitchen and the delivery boy followed him out. As the door shut, Paul heard Fritzi's delighted laugh, and clapping.

The kettle was spouting steam. Paul lifted it off the hook with tongs, put it on a decorated tile to cool. Jimmy Daws was giving him a long stare, indicating that judgment by an older, superior person was in process.

"Thanks for helping me out with that spook. I've locked horns with him before. I'd as soon slit his throat as look at him."

Paul didn't imagine he was serious. "Manfred is all right, but he acts like he is a general. Nobody likes him very much. Do you want some tea?"

"Can't stand the stuff. Got to go. More stops to make. Tell you something. I don't ordinarily make friends with Dutchmen. In your case I'll make an exception. Shake, pal."

They shook. Jimmy Daws kept his left hand in his pocket. He walked out and Paul brewed his tea.

When the family sat down to the evening meal, Aunt Ilsa immediately spied something and put her hand to her mouth. One of the display racks in the cabinet of gold-edged Bavarian china was empty.

"The largest platter is gone. The most valuable piece." She rushed to the cabinet. "There is also a small plate missing. No, two!"

Paul remembered the delivery boy with his hand in his pocket, as if he were holding something under his long tan duster.

Aunt Ilsa excused herself, pulling a handkerchief from the waistband of her skirt as she left. Paul felt wretched.

He pushed his plate aside, appetite gone. "Uncle Joe, I think this is my fault."

"No," Fritzi exclaimed from across the table. Everyone ignored her. Paul explained what had happened. "I sent him upstairs. I did not expect him to be a thief."

"Why would you?" That was Aunt Ilsa, back again, touching her hanky to her puffy reddened eyes. Stepping behind Paul's chair, she patted his shoulder. "You're a trusting person, Pauli. You did what you thought best. Don't I always say people are more important than things?"

"Truly, it isn't Paul's fault," Fritzi said. "Manfred was ordering the delivery boy around as though he was dirt. Paul was brave. He spoke right up to Manfred."

"I don't doubt Manfred deserved it," Uncle Joe said. "He's an excellent servant, but sometimes he can be a miserable—" He broke off as Helga came in with a dessert tray; plump pears, small *Meringetorten,* newly baked Christmas *Springerle.* Uncle Joe shot warning looks around the table. No one spoke.

Paul almost broke a tooth when he bit the hard sweet anise-flavored *Springerle* impressed on top with a Christmas tree design. He wasn't paying attention to the cookie; he was shooting appreciative glances at Fritzi. She gave him a huge, dreamy smile in return.

She does not know I have a girl . . .

Well, he would say nothing to Fritzi about Julie. She had stood up for him; how could he hurt someone so loving and loyal?

His sickness lingered. His temperature went up. Delirium gripped him for two days. Then the fever broke in a shivery burst of sweat. Aunt Ilsa changed his bed linen personally, and insisted he rest at least three more days.

Fritzi came in almost hourly. Did he want hot milk? Did he want her to sneak out and buy some Nick Carter novels? Did he want to read one of her many books of dream interpretation? Tennyson's *Idylls of the King?* Her theatrical scrapbook? "I have wonderful new pictures of Richard Mansfield and James O'Neill." Did he want to hear some imitations, and if so, who—?

"I'm fine, Fritzi, thank you, I don't need anything. Thank you also for defending me."

"Cousin Paul, I have to warn you about something."

"What's that?"

She leaned on the end of his bed, whispering. "This is dreadfully serious. Nicky Speers told me." Fritzi loved theatrics; she could turn the most trivial conversation into melodrama.

"Told you what?"

"Manfred has it in for you. He told Nicky you shamed him. Usurped his authority."

"You-what?"

"Usurped. It means to steal, take over. Manfred doesn't forgive anyone who does him dirt. You'd better be careful."

"I will."

"I mean for a long time."

"I'll remember. What about you, though? You stood up for me."

"He'd better not fool around with me! I'll speak to Papa and Papa will fire him."

Paul decided she wasn't acting; she was a brave girl. No, a young woman. In January she'd celebrate her thirteenth birthday. She was growing up, though not filling out. Even though Aunt Ilsa said it was not a proper subject to discuss in front of boys, Fritzi often complained about her flat bosom. She didn't seem to find any subject improper.

"Now before I go—" She dug her hand into her apron pocket. "I brought you this little hand bell. Ring it if you want anything. Even in the middle of the night, I'll come in a trice."

"Yes, thanks, I will ring." The moment she went out he put the bell under the bed.

He yawned pleasurably, forgetting his cousin and her warning in favor of dreaming and scheming over Julie. How was he going to see her after skating season? See her alone? That was the challenge facing him now.

He'd think of something, he was determined. Just let her father try to stop him.

35

Joe Crown

ON THE SATURDAY NIGHT of the robbery, Joe Crown had telephoned Abraham Frankel at home.

Frankel was stunned, and outraged. No, Jimmy Daws had not come back at the end of the day. "*Ach,* I should have fired him weeks ago. I knew he was *ein schmutziger Abschaum.*" A dirty scum. "Oh, Herr Crown, I am so sorry. I will repay you for your loss."

"Not necessary," Joe said. "Ilsa is grieved, but things are just things, she'll recover. This delivery boy—do you know where he lives?"

"In the slums, that is all I can tell you. He would never give an address. He bragged that he lived in a large flat, in a very fine block, but I knew it was a lie. Jimmy was always spouting lies to glorify himself and his background."

Joe filed a police complaint, without result. It was impossible to find a thief who was determined to hide himself in the criminal warrens of Chicago.

36

Julie

NEW YEAR'S MORNING, Nell Vanderhoff was combing Julie's hair.

The ritual was particularly important today. The first of January brought one of the city's premier social events, which the Vanderhoffs always attended thanks to Nell. Her family, the Fishburnes of Lexington, were part of Chicago's elite community of Kentuckians, and so was the hostess whose house they would visit this afternoon.

Julie felt wonderful this morning. Since the start of the skating season, her health problems had disappeared. Vigorous exercise in the bracing winter air wasn't the sole explanation.

Julie's reflection in the glass triggered a familiar complaint from her mother. "Your cheeks are too red again. Much too red. I wish you wouldn't spend every Sunday afternoon at the skating club. Some bad people congregate in Lincoln Park. When Strickland Welliver called last week, and you were still upstairs, he told me as much." Julie's gray eyes flickered with anger. "Young Joe Crown goes to that club, doesn't he?"

"Oh—sometimes." She let it trail away as if to suggest a mere acquaintance with Joe.

"You must not associate with him. The slightest hint of it would send your father into a fury."

"I know, Mama. I've never understood why Papa despises the Crowns."

"Many reasons. They're foreigners. They speak with horrible accents."

"Not Joe, he—"

"There is more to it, much more," Nell interrupted. "Some years ago, your father overheard Joe Crown, Sr., making vile and insulting remarks about those in the meat-packing business. As if a mere brewer were somehow superior to Philip Armour, and Gus Swift, and your father."

"I've heard this, Mama. But no one will ever tell me what Mr. Crown said. What remarks did he make?"

"Your father only gave me the gist of them, and I refuse to repeat even that much. You must accept my word that your father's anger is fully justified."

Nell reached down to grasp Julie's shoulders with tiny veined hands. The older woman's breath was faintly tainted, like air from a sickroom. "I'm quite serious, Juliette, you must have nothing to do with that family. If you love and respect your father, you will certainly—"

Julie jumped up. "Oh, Mama, why is everything always put that way? If I love you and Papa, I'll do this, I'll do that. I don't know Mr. Crown, but young Joe is a fine person."

"I don't believe it. I've heard from reliable sources that he harbors radical ideas. That he's practically a socialist, and torments his father with it."

"It may be, but I like him."

Nell stepped back, separating herself from her daughter.

"That is disappointing."

"I'm sorry. But I'm sixteen, almost seventeen, I have ideas of my own. That doesn't mean I don't love you or Papa."

"Disappointing," Nell repeated. "What I'm saying, Juliette—if I must be so plain—it hurts me."

Please, don't do this again.

"Mama, you know I'd never—"

"I must go and lie down. My heart is beating too fast."

Oh, don't . . .

"I'll send one of the girls to help you with your corset. We mustn't be late to Bertha's."

"Mama," she cried out, vainly. The door to the hall closed.

Julie sank down, lacing her hands together until they turned white. Why did Mama always have to use the weapon of her fragile health? It was the one weapon Julie could never turn aside, because part of her remained the dutiful daughter. Wanting to please; wanting to be loved . . .

She remembered the awful argument over education last year. Aunt Willis, her mother's older sister, had attended Oberlin College for two years after the Civil War. On one of her visits, Aunt Willis succeeded in persuading Julie that young women needed and indeed were entitled to the sort of higher education men received. As an example she cited a famous local woman, Miss Jane Addams of the Hull House settlement. Miss Addams and her female associates were successfully helping Chicago's poor and creating a model for others to emulate, and Aunt Willis said they were able to do it only because they were educated. Enlightened, that was the exact word Willis used.

After several discussions of the subject with her aunt, Julie announced to her parents that she wanted to attend college. Julie's father, a profane man, cursed his sister-in-law right at the dinner table. Nell Vanderhoff said she would consider her daughter's request, although the statement was accompanied by a hurt look. Next day she locked herself in her bedroom, prostrated with one of her spells.

Willis left a day later. Nell was still in her room. Three more days passed;

anguished days for Julie. On the fourth day she went to her father and said she'd reconsidered, she really didn't want to go to college after all.

What had changed everything for her was the German boy.

She often thought of him that way, *the German boy,* because he was eighteen days younger. But he was hardly a boy. He was strong, and very nearly a mature man.

He was quiet. Never assertive over trivial matters. Some might mistake that for slowness, or timidity. An error. In their Sundays together, Julie had come to understand that Paul was quiet in order to listen; observe; learn.

Not that he lacked spirit, or ambition. He had plenty of both. He'd talked several times of the excitement of a career in the new field of photography.

He had a kind way about him; an essential decency. Kindness, intelligence, strength—it was a wonderful combination of traits, she thought as she dressed. In her eyes the German boy had no flaws. She was in love with him.

And he probably didn't even suspect her feelings. How she melted at his touch; almost swooned every time he circled her waist with his strong arm as they skated.

Because of him, she constantly dreamed of an idyllic future. Yet there was an element of dread in the daydreams. What would happen if it came to a choice between Paul and her family? She didn't want to hurt her mother. But she couldn't give up the German boy . . .

In this state of confusion, Julie left in the family carriage, with her parents, at half past one o'clock. Their destination was the home of Mr. and Mrs. Potter Palmer, 1350 Lake Shore Drive, called by friend and enemy alike the Palmer Castle.

In the depression of 1893, some sixteen thousand firms had already gone bankrupt. Over fifty had capital of more than a million dollars. Great industrial complexes such as the Pullman Works had laid off large numbers of men, reduced the hours of those remaining, and slashed wages 30, 40, 50 percent. It was said that in the tenements and hovels of the unemployed, children stayed in bed all day because it was the only way to keep warm and survive the winter.

That hard world never intruded at Palmer Castle; even its doors symbolized its impregnability. There was not a single outside knob or handle. There were no keyholes or visible locks.

With its eighty-foot tower and sawtooth battlements, the Palmer residence did resemble an English castle. Potter Palmer and his wife had personally designed the house, and they were presumed to be responsible for the odd, rather displeasing choice of exterior materials—Wisconsin granite with contrasting inlays of Ohio sandstone.

When the Vanderhoffs arrived, the porte-cochere was crowded with vehicles driven by men in an array of liveries, all of them ostentatious. The Vanderhoff carriage was sizable and expensive, yet insignificant compared to the huge victoria just ahead in the line. Nell pointed to it. "The Pullmans are here!"

Mason Putnam Vanderhoff III grunted. If Nell was an elf, Pork Vanderhoff was a giant; a great round-shouldered hulk of a man, six feet six inches tall. His weight was always somewhere between 270 and 280 pounds, a considerable part of it on deposit in an impressive paunch.

Pork had dewlaps and small gray eyes that never seemed to rest. Despite middle age, his hair was still black as an Indian's. He wore it combed straight back and sleekly oiled. People said he was much the handsomer of the two brothers who controlled Vanderhoff's and its various products distributed under the "Big V" label. Israel Washington Vanderhoff—I.W., he was called—was the guiding financial genius, while Pork directed production and distribution. I.W. lived in New York. Three times divorced, he relentlessly pursued young actresses and took the pledge and a water cure at least once a year.

Pork's size was a constant burden. He had to stoop to enter rooms or sit comfortably in carriages. Like their afternoon host, Potter Palmer, he was a shy, silent man when he was among people he didn't know, although in other circumstances, to Nell's embarrassment, he could be loud and extremely profane. Many of Chicago's industrialists were retiring men. Some, like Marshall Field, whom Pork knew from the exclusive Commercial Club, refused to come to social functions at all. Field's wife Nannie always attended in his stead.

"By the bye, Mason," Nell said, nervously adjusting her hat, "I received a letter from Willis yesterday. She will be here in the spring for her usual visit."

"Oh, God damn it to hell and back, why can't she ever get sick? I despise that woman. She's the next thing to a harlot. She'd kiss a nigger if given half a chance."

Julie winced because she loved her wild and undisciplined aunt. The father of the Fishburne sisters had passionately hoped for a male child. When fate denied his wish, he insisted that his firstborn be named after him. Thus Willis. It was a fine Southern tradition, the bestowing of honored family names on girls. But the girls then had to cope with the resulting confusion for the rest of their lives.

The carriage moved forward. Palmer footmen jumped to open the door. In a moment the Vanderhoffs were disposing of their wraps in the immense octagonal entrance hall. The hall soared up three stories, its walls hung with Gobelin tapestries, its mosaic floor of Italian marble hard and noisy underfoot.

Christmas greens perfumed the mansion. Distantly, a string orchestra played above the babble. There was an enormous crowd. All aflutter, Nell said, "I must locate Bertha. Come with me, please, Juliette."

"I'll try to find some of the fellows," Pork said. By fellows he meant his approximate equals in commerce and social standing. "God damn hot in here already." Nell rolled her eyes. Pork lumbered off and was soon jawing at the owner of the *Tribune*, Joe Medill, a former mayor. He and Pork were staunch Republicans.

Medill, over seventy now, was acknowledged as a founder of the party. Some said he had named it. A Canadian by birth, he had arrived in Chicago from Ohio in the 1850s, and bought a small interest in the *Tribune*. He'd become a close friend of Abraham Lincoln, and promoted his nomination when the Republicans held their 1860 convention at the Wigwam in Chicago. Nell Vanderhoff was deferential to Joe Medill only because he was important. As a Kentuckian from a conservative family, she never forgot that Medill had been not only a fiery abolitionist but a confiscationist, wanting Southerners stripped of their property after the war. On that score, happily, Mr. Medill was defeated by the gentler policies of his friend, the murdered President.

Nell nodded to Medill as she passed him. She gave a wave and smile to his wife Katharine, for whom she had greater tolerance. Katharine was just slipping away from her husband to join a group that included Samuel Insull, the British-born president of the Chicago Edison Power Company. Mr. Insull was an austere, even prissy man, balding, with pince-nez glasses. He was about thirty-five and one of the town's most eligible bachelors. Nell had idly mentioned this to Juliette once, and had terrified her.

There was an aura of celebrity about Mr. Insull because he had been closely associated with Thomas Edison for a time. In England, he had helped organize the highly successful Edison subsidiary, thereby earning a promotion to the post of confidential secretary to the great man, in America. Pork Vanderhoff, himself an aggressive businessman, had spoken of Insull in awed tones more than once. "One God damn smart limey. The fellows say he's got a few pints of Jew blood in him. A real self-promoter."

Eventually Edison's partners, and even his family, found Insull just too precocious and ambitious, and forced his demotion. Edison personally helped his protégé find another situation. The inventor saw the Midwest as a good market for electricity, so Insull was presented as the ideal man to head the new Chicago Edison Company.

Many electric companies served the city at the time. Available generators could only deliver electricity to an area of about four square blocks. As equipment improved, Insull quietly and steadily absorbed other companies and expanded his own power lines. "That man has put out the candles and lamps all over Chicago," Pork said. "He'll do it all over the county, you watch."

Nell was alert to Mr. Insull's reaction to the arrival of Katharine Medill. He gave her a formal bow but didn't accept the hand she held out to him. "He doesn't like newspaper people, he thinks they're busybodies," Nell whispered to Julie. "I'm surprised Bertha got him here at all. He never takes a drink and goes to very few parties." Observing Insull's haughty airs, Julie thought that hostesses probably didn't want to invite him, unless they had unmarried daughters.

"Shall we look for Bertha in the drawing room?" Nell said. Julie followed obediently, and as they moved on, she saw several McCormick children, grown now, as well as Nettie McCormick, the fragile but reputedly tough widow of the poorly educated Virginian who had built a commercial empire with the reaping machine he first tinkered into existence in the 1830s.

Cyrus McCormick had moved to Chicago in 1847, opening a small plant to centralize manufacturing of his reaper. The reaper revolutionized farming from the Kansas plains to the Russian steppes. It was the foundation of the enormous McCormick fortune, but McCormick invented many other farm machines; during his later years, he or his deputies had been in court constantly, prosecuting or defending patent infringement suits. Lincoln had once won a case against him. There was spilled blood in his history, too: the strike at his plant that led to the Haymarket riot.

Circulating in the crowd brought Nell and Julie near a stocky silver-maned gentleman with sparkling blue eyes and an impressive domelike forehead. Nell swiftly veered off to confront him with hand held out.

"Potter."

"My dear Nell. And Julie. How charming you both look. Happy New Year. Thank you for coming."

"Would we miss it? Never, dear man. Where on earth can we find Bertha? There's such a crush—"

"Just in there, with our special guest from New York. The authoress." Potter Palmer spoke to the Vanderhoffs in a friendly and relaxed way; because of the Kentucky connection, he knew them well. He had a bond with Pork too. Palmer was an Eastern Yankee who had sensed and seized an opportunity when Chicago was young. So had Pork, from Connecticut, and Field, who was from Massachusetts, and Armour and Pullman, both New York State men.

Like them, Palmer had been born in the 1830s. He made fortunes in real estate, Civil War cotton, and then retailing. For some years R. H. Macy's had annually sent representatives to study Palmer's dry goods store, which was famous for its bargain sales, lavish window displays, and absolute dedication to customer satisfaction. Marshall Field and his partner Levi Leiter had built their own fortunes by buying out the Palmer store.

"I never have time for fiction, but I presume you know the lady's work, Nell," Palmer continued to Nell and Julie, gently guiding them by their elbows to urge them on; others were waiting for a moment of his time. With a nod at Julie, he added, "It's too racy for young girls, I'm advised."

With a simpering smile, Nell said, "Perhaps if I knew the lady's name . . ."

"Did I neglect that? Mrs. I. J. Blauvelt."

"Oh dear, really?" Nell fanned herself with a hanky. Julie felt several degrees warmer. Mrs. I. J. (for Isobel Judith) Blauvelt wrote the sort of novel meant to be smuggled under the bedcovers and read with flushed cheeks and palpitating pulse. Her books had about as much literary merit as a flour sack label, but no one cared. Mrs. Blauvelt herself was roundly condemned. "She crosses the frontier of prurience under the flag of naturalism" was the charge of one cleric. Her latest, *The Spangles of Society,* had nevertheless sold tens of thousands of copies.

Julie loved Mrs. Blauvelt's books, which she bought surreptitiously, or borrowed from acquaintances. They had a soothing sameness. The heroines were always chaste, always rich—and always had their virtue imperiled by fortune-hunting "cads" or "old roués." Some poor but upright young man—a muscular deck steward; a snappy-talking journalist; a poet of unrecognized genius—came along toward the end to propound life's true values and pull the heroine from the cad's clutches, into a blissful final chapter of sunsets, doves, and flower-covered cottages. The stories were set in glamorous locales. A European spa; Saratoga in racing season; the mansions of Newport and New York. No Terre Haute, Laramie, or Palatka, Florida, for Mrs. Blauvelt's thrill-hungry readers.

In her liking for the cheap and racy novels, Julie joined a legion of women of all ages, shopgirls to grandes dames. What a coup to have Mrs. Blauvelt here! For a few moments, she quite forgot about Paul.

Mother and daughter squeezed into the packed Louis XVI drawing room, the first of its kind in Chicago. It was a vision of gold and white, with specially commissioned wall and ceiling Frescoes depicting riotous roses and chubby pink cupids in flight. "Ah, there she is," Nell exclaimed, waving. "Bertha!"

"Dear Nell," said Bertha Honoré Palmer, gliding to embrace her friend. She never rushed; she was confident others would wait for her. "How lovely to see you. And Julie. Have you met Judith? Come, you must."

Mother and daughter followed the woman who had bestowed upon herself the title of "the nation's hostess"—not without some justification. Bertha Palmer was intelligent, a social leader with strong opinions and a vigorous program of philanthropy. She had important ties in the East. Her sister Ida was the wife of Fred Dent Grant, oldest son of the former President.

She was also wonderfully assured and attractive, Julie thought. Somewhere in her forties, she had striking dark eyes and handsome features. For today's reception she had chosen a lavish gown of her favorite color, blue, and put tiny pink rosebuds among the diamonds sparkling in her hair.

"Yes indeed, I hit him with my parasol," said the stout blond woman to whom Bertha led them; she was standing at the center of a dozen female admirers. "Three times! I won't let some cheap journalist insult me. Not five minutes into our interview, he blandly asked if I consider my work to be trash. *Trash?* This is the age of new writing! The new realism! I am an artist!" Julie knew that was true, but not as it was meant. Mrs. I. J. Blauvelt was a former circus performer who had left the high wire to take up the pen, and thereby gotten rich.

Members of her claque murmured and applauded her statement. Nell and Julie were introduced. "How do you do?" Mrs. Blauvelt said, visibly annoyed by the interruption of remarks about herself. She had a jaw like a horse, and eyes like agates. Her bosom was fashionably full; she looked much too heavy for the high wire.

"We were discussing Gene Field, the fellow Isobel thrashed," said an elderly woman, who Julie thought was a McCormick. She got the various McCormicks mixed up, but she believed this was the wife of Leander, Cyrus's brother and partner. "His column may be popular, but I for one find him insolent."

"At least one can understand his English," another woman said. "That dreadful Irish dialect of Dunne's is incomprehensible." This was a reference to Finley Peter Dunne's Mr. Dooley, a mythical Chicago saloon keeper who dispensed philosophy and political opinion through a column in the *Evening Post.* Julie found Mr. Dooley droll, but she didn't dare tell her parents. Pork Vanderhoff hated what he called "shanty Irish," and everything about their culture.

Julie liked the *Daily News* "Sharps and Flats" column by Eugene Field—no relation to Marshall—even more than she liked Mr. Dooley. Field hated pomposity and convention. Pork of course "loathed" Mr. Field. And Julie's mother had once said, "How is it possible—how is it *remotely* possible for a man who writes verses beloved by children"—Julie had memorized and recited *Little Boy Blue* early in her school career—"to be so sarcastic and disdainful of those he knows are his betters?"

Mrs. Blauvelt's voice brought Julie out of her reverie. The author had resumed her autobiographical monologue of self-congratulation. At one point she compared herself to Gustave Flaubert and Émile Zola. She saw incipient boredom on the faces around her and immediately marched off to seek new listeners. The little group dissolved.

Nell was waving to another acquaintance, but Julie didn't want to spend the afternoon trailing after her mother, so she contrived to slip away as Nell rushed in the other direction. She wandered by herself through various rooms of the mansion. The Spanish music room, the English dining room, the Moorish passageway leading to the ballroom where the orchestra played.

The ballroom was undeniably the focus of the party. Almost a hundred feet long, it was packed with guests helping themselves to eggnog and Madeira, chicken salad and escalloped oysters and other delicacies spread on long buffet tables. Various painted ladies and gentlemen gazed down from railed picture galleries at either side of the room. The small white-tie orchestra sawed away on a balcony at the far end. Great blazing Tiffany chandeliers lit the scene, whose splendor matched anything Mrs. Blauvelt might have imagined.

Julie sampled the eggnog and wistfully wondered what Paul was doing this afternoon. Enjoying himself, she hoped. Alas, he'd never be invited to the Palmers'. She wished she were with him.

She gazed around until she saw people she knew slightly. Charles Yerkes, the traction king, and his beautiful second wife, Mary Adelaide. Julie didn't want to talk to them. Papa couldn't stand the man. He said Yerkes had served time in prison for some kind of stock fraud. In Chicago he controlled a network of construction, operating and holding companies, and though Julie had no head for business, nor any interest in it, she had ridden Mr. Yerkes's defective cars, and knew of his gouging fares. Yerkes ignored all complaints. When the issue of overcrowding was raised, he'd replied with a sneering remark printed in all the papers: "It's the straphangers that pay the dividends." Julie's father said of Yerkes, "If you're going to be a God damn crook, you owe it to your loved ones to keep it a secret."

She worked her way around Mr. and Mrs. Yerkes, nodding and smiling when Mary Adelaide greeted her. She spied her father among a group of men and women intently listening to another gentleman. She didn't recognize the speaker; she saw only his back.

She circled through the crowd till she had a view of his face. Then she recognized him instantly. It was George Pullman, an imposing man in his sixties who wore a full and impeccably trimmed imperial.

George Mortimer Pullman was another of Chicago's giants; another who had left school early, like McCormick. He had started as a cabinetmaker in upstate New York, but his mind ranged to much larger objects and concepts.

His fortune, his huge manufacturing plant, and the ideal workers' town he built nearby all sprang from one invention. In the late 1850s, Mr. Pullman had remodeled two day coaches of the Chicago & Alton line, installing his patented fold-away upper berths hinged to the sides of the car.

Passengers liked the prototype sleeping cars, but the railroads were skeptical and overly cautious. After Mr. Pullman perfected and patented a collapsible lower berth in 1865, he had to finance his own prototype car, *Pioneer*, which proved too large for existing stations and underpasses. But he wouldn't change his design, which the public loved, so the railroads eventually surrendered to the

Pullman Palace Car Company, and rebuilt their depots and their overpasses. Mr. Pullman had also invented the dining car, and the chair car, and the car with vestibules. Papa thought Pullman overbearing, but he was acceptable because he voted Republican.

Mr. Pullman was speaking to his group without pause, as if expecting no interruptions. His gestures were broad, theatrical. The man did indeed radiate an unpleasant arrogance.

Julie slipped in among the listeners, near Pullman's wife Hattie. Pork gave his daughter a fishy blink of recognition and thoughtlessly twisted the tip of his little finger in his right ear, as if to dislodge wax.

"They bay at me like a pack of hounds because I reduced employee wages. I did it simply because orders have been reduced. But I am castigated for making no similar cuts in the salaries of company officers and foremen. There you have a total lack of understanding of commerce and the American system."

"How do you mean, sir?" someone asked.

"You don't grasp it? If I cut the wages of my executives, I face the possibility of mass resignations. That would leave me with only a skeleton management when prosperity returns. Maintaining salaries for the upper echelons is imperative. So is continuance of our dividend. The public expects eight percent on Pullman shares, so we pay eight percent. It's a matter of confidence."

"They're simply vile, these people who hurl accusations at George," Hattie Pullman declared. "We even have some malcontents who continue to draw Pullman wages."

"People who hold jobs and still speak against the company?" said a gentleman. "I can't believe that."

"Absolutely true," Pullman said. How smug he was, Julie thought. "However, I'm not without resources in that regard. I have a network of—let's call them observers. They help me root out the worst agitators. When I discover one, his lease in the town of Pullman is canceled."

"It's only just," Hattie said. "George invested hundreds of thousands to build a model town. A town in which all that's ugly and discordant and demoralizing is eliminated."

Julie hesitated but then raised her hand. "Mrs. Pullman, may I ask a question?"

Hattie Pullman froze. "If you wish, Miss Vanderhoff."

"Really, it's more a matter of not quite understanding something. The newspapers say that one of the complaints about the town of Pullman is that rents haven't been reduced, even though wages of the renters have." Actually she never read the papers; she'd heard about it from young Joe Crown.

She made her statement with an innocence that anticipated a friendly reaction. She thought she was being logical, straightforward, and fair. She merely wanted the facts from Pullman himself. She was altogether unprepared for the stunned stare from her father, the withering look from Hattie Pullman, or the scorn and fury of the great man himself:

"Miss Vanderhoff, must I count you among those ill-informed persons who know nothing about business? Pullman the manufacturer and Pullman the landlord are separate and distinct centers of profit. Do not confuse the two."

"But it doesn't seem entirely right that—"

"Juliette, where's your mother?" Pork said loudly. "We must move on. George —Hattie—friends—a happy New Year to you all."

"And to you," George Pullman said, without feeling. He glanced at Julie; it was the kind of look he might have given someone who was unclean and odorous.

In the carriage, everyone was silent. Nell dabbed her eyes with a handkerchief. When Julie leaned forward to touch her mother's hand, to explain that she'd really meant no harm, Nell drew her own hand away with a wounded look. She rested her forehead against the side window and shut her eyes. At home, she went to her room without speaking.

Julie paced her bedroom, increasingly distraught. The door crashed open.

"Papa—"

"Don't say anything. Not a damn word. You shouldn't have spoken to Pullman that way. Everyone will hear about it. Didn't you see them staring before we left?"

Julie's nerve broke. Tears came. "It was a fair question—"

"Not from a refined young woman, God damn it. Your place is one step to the rear, listening and looking pretty. You dishonored your mother this afternoon. She's in bed again, prostrate."

That night, in the darkness of the bedroom, Julie slowly sank into a darkness of her own.

She fought it, recognizing it for what it was; the onset of a condition similar to Nell's; a state of depression and immobility that could last for days, or weeks.

She understood her feelings were probably a guilt reaction to the uproar she'd caused with one question. Understanding didn't help her fight off the despair. Paul was forgotten. She pulled the covers over her head and drew her knees against her bosom and clenched her hands, and hid.

Why not? Women were afflicted with delicate nerves; this kind of suffering was inevitable. Mama said so.

37

Paul

ON A WARM MARCH DAY when the snow was melting, Paul paced the aisles of McClurg's bookstore, a Chicago landmark located in an old brick building at Monroe and Wabash. The store smelled deliciously of book paper and leather bindings and the coffeepot kept hot on a gas ring near some rocking chairs in a rear corner. Cousin Joe said it was called the Saints and Sinners Corner; many of the town's literary figures rocked and read and argued there. A man sat there now, with an open book. Paul had said hello nervously the first time he passed by. The man gave him a cheerful reply.

Paul wondered if he was someone famous. The man was in his early forties, long and skinny. He slouched in the rocker, one leg thrown over the arm. He had pleasant, regular features, eyes as china blue as Cousin Joe's, thin straight hair on his balding head, a large mole on his left cheek. His wrinkled sack suit was an atrocious plaid, brown, yellow, and green. A dented black derby lay underneath his chair.

Paul paced up one aisle, down another, fretfully. He took care to go quietly at the back of the store, so as not to disturb the man reading. When Paul came near again, the man looked up suddenly, noticing something. His eyes flickered a warning.

A second later Paul heard thumping footsteps. "Young man." He spun around. It was the prissy clerk who'd eyed him when he walked in. "You're wandering as if you're lost. Do you wish to purchase a book?"

Nervously, Paul grabbed the nearest one. "I'm waiting for a friend, is that all right?"

"It depends. Are your hands clean? If not, kindly don't touch the stock."

Hastily Paul replaced the book. The man in the rocker called out, "Say, Simpkins, I spotted a snake back here."

"A snake? My God, where?"

"Over in that corner." The man got up; he was tall, slouching, round-shouldered. He pointed. His nails were badly bitten. "I saw it crawl behind that empty crate."

"We've never had a reptile in here—" The clerk rushed to the front, rushed back with a broom. He held it in front of him like a rifle as he crept toward the crate. The man in the corner winked at Paul.

The clerk kicked the crate aside. Nothing there, except dust and a spider's web.

"Mr. Field, is this another of your practical jokes?"

The man had an infectious smile. "Call it a necessary distraction."

"To what purpose, may I ask?"

"Simpkins, don't act so damned snotty. This is McClurg's, not a finishing school. The purpose was to stop you from badgering innocent customers like this young lad. Have you forgotten a bookstore's for browsing? That is its heavenly purpose. If you can't remember that much, go chase snakes."

Simpkins marched off, livid. He glared at Paul as he passed. Still amused, the tall man sat down again. "I'll have to speak to General McClurg about that worm."

Paul approached the rocking chair. "Allow me to thank you, sir."

"Sure, Dutch, and I'll tell you how. Buy the *Daily News*. Don't read anything else."

Paul decided the nickname Dutch didn't sound so bad if someone said it in a friendly way. "Do you work for that paper?" he asked.

"I write for it. Field's my name. Go on, look at all the books you want. The worm won't bother you again."

"Thank you. I am waiting for someone. She's very late."

"Well, let's hope she hasn't stood you up." He went back to his reading.

Paul didn't understand "stood you up," unless it meant Julie wasn't coming. He hadn't seen her for six weeks. Nor had Cousin Joe. He was going crazy with worry and longing. He hoped he hadn't made a terrible mistake last night, paying one of the Vanderhoff stable grooms fifty cents to smuggle a note into the house. "I will," said the groom. "But she may not read it right away. She ain't been well."

"She's sick? What is wrong?"

"I hear it's female complaints."

He paced again, twisting his cloth cap. He was still in his work clothes. He'd let his hair grow long, almost to his collar, over the mild objections of Aunt Ilsa.

She isn't coming, it's all over, I don't know what happened, I'll never see her . . .

The tiny bell at the front door whirled him around. A girl was silhouetted in a blaze of midday sunshine. Outside, dirty snowbanks were melting.

He recognized her, elated. She hurried down the aisle, darting looks at the clerk and another customer. His heart pounded.

She didn't look well. Her skin was very like the color of new-fallen snow. Great bluish shadows around her eyes subtly changed their color, dulling the sparkle he remembered. Paul took her gloved hands in his.

"Are you all right?"

"Yes, fine."

"You got the note."

"Yes, and no one knows about it except the man who brought it."

"He told me you have been sick."

She glanced away. "A nervous condition. I'm getting well." It might be so, but she seemed to lack the jaunty confidence that he thought was part of her nature.

"Why aren't you working?" she asked. "It's Saturday."

"I begged a few hours off. The brewmaster likes me, he didn't object. I had to see you. Julie, the ice on the lagoon is gone."

"The skating club's closed?"

"Days ago. We must find another way to meet every week. That is why I wrote the note. Do you cycle?" Surely she did; everybody was cycling. America had a mania for it.

"I do, but Mama doesn't like it. She feels it's vulgar. Why do you ask?"

"Because I have a plan. You must start cycling in Lincoln Park. You can rent a wheel there, I have already inquired. I will pretend to be your cycling instructor."

At that she gasped. "My—?"

"*Lehrer.* Your teacher. What name shall I have? Leopold? Thomas? Sammy? Thomas, that sounds respectable. Thomas the expert wheel man. My teaching, it's—uh, *zuverlässig*—" He struggled for the English. "Reliable?" She nodded approval. "Reliable, with utmost courtesy at all times." He bowed, pulling faces, trying to cheer her. The clerk sidled along the next aisle, whisking a feather duster over the books while he attempted to eavesdrop.

"I will come on Sundays. I can stand outside your house, respectfully, and you can join me there. I will wear clips on my knickerbockers. You can point me out to those inside. My humble attitude. You can even appear to pay me. I'll return the money."

She laughed. "Oh, Paul. I don't know what to make of you and your schemes."

"I like to get things done. If not one way, then another."

"You're scandalous."

"Oh, no, I don't make a scandal—never. I will always protect your honor."

"You misunderstand." She touched his hand; let her gloved fingers drift across his skin. "I like your daring."

"Ah. Daring. *Wagemutig.* Now I see. Thank you." He grinned. He felt like one of those daredevils he'd read about, the ones who illegally plunged over the Niagara Falls in a barrel. He felt himself plunging, just like them.

"I want to see you, I have to see you." Now it was his turn to touch her, fingers gently closing on her sleeve. "I cannot stop. Ever."

She seemed to take heart from his words. Her expression changed, more resolute all at once. He saw the young woman of strong will and bright temperament with whom he'd skated that first day.

Softly, she said, "Nor I."

The prissy clerk was staring, not a yard away across a book bin. He tap-tapped his duster on the spines. Paul stepped between Julie and the bin, blocking his view. He leaned close to whisper.

"*Ich liebe Sie, Juliette.*"

"What did you say?"

He blushed. "I don't have the courage to say it in English."

"I think I know what it means. I feel—the same thing."

"Then please, let me pretend to be your cycling teacher."

"Oh yes. But I don't think it's wise for you to come to the house. I'll tell my parents that I heard about you from a friend who belongs to the Saddle and Cycle Club. That you come well recommended, with good references. Mama will fuss, but I think I can deal with her. I'll do my best."

"This will be on Sundays."

"Yes, Sundays."

"Soon?"

"We can start tomorrow. I'm so glad you sent the note. You're brave, Paul. Brave, and sweet—" She was close to tears, but there was happiness, too. "Will you say the words again?"

"*Ich liebe Sie.*"

As if the limit of his patience had been reached, the clerk opened his mouth to say something. Paul tugged Julie's arm. The reporter, Mr. Field, was watching, amused. He reached into his vest for a little notebook and pencil.

Outside, they felt a lake wind. They stood in the balmy sunshine with cool drafts from the wet snowbanks blowing over them. Paul's heart was thundering.

"Will you say it to me?"

"*Ich liebe Sie, Paul.* If I knew a thousand languages, I'd say it in every one. I love you."

He was in heaven. The Lorelei singing on her great rock in the Rhine couldn't have made sweeter music. He knew his life had been changed forever.

Part Five

PULLMAN

1894

If ye be ill, or poor, or starving,
or oppressed, or in grief, your
chances for sympathy and for succor
from E. V. Debs are one hundred
where your chances with G. M. Pullman
would be the little end of nothing
whittled down.

> 1894
> EUGENE FIELD of the *Chicago Daily News*

Unless you take decided action at once
the riot and rebellion will be entirely
beyond your control and much property
and blood will have to be sacrificed.
. . . I pray God to guide you and show
you the terrible volcano on which we
stand.

> 1894
> Message from a Chicago businessman to
> President Cleveland

38

Joe Junior

THROUGHOUT THAT WINTER, Joe Junior spent less time with his cousin. Paul no longer needed his services as a go-between at Lincoln Park. He and Julie were smitten; they hardly noticed anyone else.

Joe Junior questioned Paul about his plans to see Julie when spring came and the club pavilion closed. Paul grinned and said he'd already concocted a scheme. Joe Junior congratulated him but warned his cousin again: "You damn well better not let old man Vanderhoff find out."

Joe Junior didn't mind being relieved of duty as Cupid; he had his own girl to think about. Visiting Roza Jablonec required a trip of almost ten miles out to the model town of Pullman, founded in 1882 as a residential community for five thousand workers at the Pullman Palace Car Company. To reach the town, he had to take a horsecar line part way, then change to another.

He didn't mind the ride because he didn't mind being alone with himself. He usually carried a book in his pocket. He liked the solitary pleasure of sitting and reading; always had. He liked sports you could enjoy by yourself. He wasn't like Carl, he didn't like playing on teams.

Riding the horsecars south on a Sunday, he would sometimes imagine in vivid detail how it might be that day if he were lucky. Rosie on her back, groaning, pushing herself up beneath him, crying out for him to go into her faster. Then again, it might not happen. It all depended on whether Rosie's parents, Tabor and Maritza, went out for a while. Joe Junior and Rosie always made love in the house. Their first attempt to do it elsewhere, in the haymow of a livery barn, had ended in discovery by the owner, and flight, moments after Joe took his pants down. Another time, in some shrubbery out in the country, a hornet had stung Rosie twice. That ended the search for a bower of love remote from Pullman.

He didn't always think of sex on his Sunday morning trips. Sometimes he read and reread difficult passages of some book, until he understood it. Sometimes he speculated about the future of the country, or about his family. Pop, who would never lift his heavy hand from the backs of his employees, his wife, his children. Never curb his lust for control of everything that touched his life. Never change.

And sometimes he would think about Cousin Paul. Paul was a good kid. Young, though. Deplorably green. And a dreamer, a stargazer. Paul thought America was better than the old country. Better than any other place on earth. He thought that in America, nobody schemed and cheated and killed to get what they wanted.

Nobody bought off politicians. Nobody treated the ordinary working stiff as a pawn, a chip in a big-money game controlled by a very few players.

Joe continually tried to enlighten his cousin. It didn't seem to take. And although they'd come to like each other, the cousins argued a lot. Once they'd had a real blowup. After work Joe Junior sometimes stopped at Donophan's Pool and Billiard Hall on Lake Street. Donophan's was a noisy, smoky place, popular with a working-class crowd. And they didn't serve Crown's beer, only Budweiser from Busch of St. Louis.

At Donophan's, Joe Junior sometimes played a friendly game of billiards with someone else. He also shot pool alone, against himself, his past performance. Paul asked questions about the game, so Joe had invited him along one night. He chalked his cue, handed another to his cousin, and said, "This isn't a contest, remember. I'm demonstrating."

He racked the colored balls. Paul broke them. He couldn't get the feel of the cue. They played rotation and Joe sank all but one. After three more equally lopsided games, they stepped up to the brass rail of the bar and ordered nickel steins of beer. The pug-nosed bartender eyed them.

"How old are you boys?"

"Old enough," Joe Junior said. "Just get us the beers, will you?"

"All right, all right, keep your pants on."

Joe Junior rested his elbows on the scarred mahogany. "I'm spending a dime so we can have the free lunch."

"But if you paid for it, it isn't free."

"That's right."

Paul shook his head, perplexed. "America."

They walked down the bar to the plates laid out on soiled white napkins. There were slabs of rye bread, hard-boiled eggs, salted fish, pickles, a bowl of sauerkraut. Joe Junior ate two mouthfuls of the kraut and handed the fork to Paul, who broke off a bit of fish. Someone else asked for the fork—it served the entire bar—and Paul gave it to him.

The pug-nosed barkeep served their beer. Paul blew foam off and tasted. "It isn't as good as ours."

Joe Junior laughed. "Spoken like a faithful wage slave."

"Joe," Paul said, serious all at once. "I have read about the trouble at the Pullman factory. What will happen there?"

"Not a damn thing, if anyone's counting on fair play from the bosses. They're like all the rest of the capitalists in this country. You'd find out if you'd read some of the—"

"I know, I know. The books. Right now I'm studying a new English grammar I bought."

"You won't find the truth in there."

"You talk so much about the truth, but what is it?"

"Something you don't want to hear. You don't want to hear that our glorious freedom isn't what it's cracked up to be. You're free, all right. Free to exploit anyone who's weaker. Free to make little kids slave on dangerous machines in a filthy dark factory. Free to grow up a slave yourself."

"Suppose I work in a factory that's as bad as you say. I am free to quit, isn't that true also?"

Joe Junior's laugh mocked him. "Of course. You've got all the freedom in the world to walk out, starve in the streets, wear rags—die. You think we're so special here? We're not. This America you've cooked up is just in your head, Paul. A fantasy. You think every man who works hard and sticks by the rules will end up rich as Pop? The hell he will. A few get to be bosses and they rig the game. They rob and cheat and run your life! *That's* the truth."

Paul was silent, frowning. "Joe, answer this. If America is no better than anyplace else, why do so many people risk everything to come here? Why did I come here?"

Joe Junior threw an arm around his cousin's shoulders. "I won't answer the second question, kid. But I've got the answer to the first one. We have a man in Chicago named Mike McDonald. Big Mike. He's a gambler. He's rich. He runs a joint called the Store, at Clark and Monroe. He also runs the aldermen and politicians in the Democratic Party. Big Mike has a saying. 'There's a sucker born every minute.'"

"What does it mean—sucker?"

Joe Junior picked up his stein and drained it. "Somebody who believes anything you tell him."

Paul slammed his stein on the bar. High color rushed to his face. "You think that is what I am? Well—"

"Now wait, I—"

"—thank you very much." Paul took his foot off the brass rail and stalked away.

Joe Junior chased him; caught him near the front door. "Hey, don't get sore. I wasn't calling you a name, I was just trying to explain. Tell you the truth. You asked."

"The truth *you* see. I see something else. I see all the people on a ship looking up at the great Liberty statue in New York Harbor, hoping she guards the doorway to a better place than the one they left. I was one of those people."

Joe Junior sighed. "All right. Let's leave it. I didn't mean to make you feel bad." He offered his hand. "Pals?"

Paul relaxed. The color went out of his cheeks. "Sure. Pals." They shook. They walked up Lake Street, arms linked. That ended it for the night. But of course it didn't settle anything.

April came. America was still in the strangling grip of the depression. Ordinary people felt powerless—somehow controlled from afar by forces they couldn't defeat or even understand. There was much talk of "bosses" and "trusts" and "gold bugs"—distant, sinister cabals manipulating the economy and playing with the lives of poor men, never caring whether they lived or died.

In Ohio, one Jacob Coxey of Massillon had organized several hundred of the unemployed with the intention of leading them on a protest march to Washington. Coxey was a farmer, a devout Christian, Populist, Civil War veteran, and genuine small-town eccentric; he'd named his youngest child Legal Tender Coxey.

A small corps of journalists followed "General" Coxey's Army as it tramped east through cold spring rains. Spirits didn't seem daunted by the weather or sore feet, the reporters wrote. A small musical aggregation called the Commonwealth of Christ Brass Band played tunes for marching and singing. A favorite was a parody version of "After the Ball."

> After the march is over,
> After the first of May—
> After the bills are passed, child,
> Then we will have fair play.

Doubtful. Very doubtful, Joe Junior decided.

On the twenty-eighth of April he would be eighteen. He had reached his physical maturity; he would always have the small, slight frame inherited from his father. But his shoulders, arms and legs were thick with muscle. The palms of his hands had grown hard from toil. With the unconscious arrogance of the young, he thought of himself as a man.

That April the man of almost eighteen was unlucky in Pullman two Sundays in a row. Tabor Jablonec went out but his dowdy wife Maritza stayed home.

Tabor was a worried man, like most everyone who worked for George Pullman. Consequently he drank. To get a few glasses of cheap red wine, he had to walk over to the neighboring village of Kensington. By decree of Mr. Pullman, there were no saloons for workingmen in his utopian town. One small bar in the seventy-room Hotel Florence, named after Pullman's favorite daughter, served drinks to managers and executives, but the drinks were priced so high, hourly workers couldn't afford them. Mr. Pullman believed that men who sweated all day were less efficient and productive if they drank at night.

Tabor Jablonec had reason to drink and to fret. He was a carpenter in the Pullman repair shops, where cars were received, refitted, and sent out again. Pullman's cars could be found on three quarters of the trackage in the United States, but not one car belonged to the railroads. The company operated the cars on contract, hiring its own conductors, porters, chefs. It collected a fee of two cents a mile for repair.

At the start of 1894, Tabor's hourly wage had been reduced 20 percent, and another 15 percent in late February. After the second cut, Tabor added up the sums he owed his landlord and others, drank half a bottle of red wine on his lunch hour, and did something he'd never done before, or even contemplated. Standing in front of the desk of his foreman, Castleberry, twisting his cap in pale scarred hands, Tabor protested the latest cut.

Castleberry replied in a way that was condoned, even encouraged, by those at the highest levels of the company. He stormed from his chair, knocked Tabor to the floor and cursed him, calling him, among other things, a "dirty ungrateful shit of a Bohunk." The foreman warned Tabor that one more complaint would cost him his job. As it was, Tabor was punished with a month's layoff and felt lucky.

"Why don't you move out of Pullman?" Joe Junior had asked once when Tabor was sitting idle at home. "You shouldn't stay here, paying these rents, letting them abuse you."

Tabor replied in his heavy accent, "I got to stay if I don't want to be out for good. When the company calls men back to work, anybody who ain't renting in Pullman goes to the bottom of the list."

Joe Junior's only comment was a muttered, "Jesus." Which earned him a look from Rosie's mousy mother. Maritza Jablonec counted on her Lord Jesus Christ to set Mr. Pullman on the path of righteousness. If not in this life, then the next.

Roza Jablonec's father was a slightly built man with brooding dark eyes and a high rounded forehead that reminded Joe Junior of pictures of Daniel Webster. Unfortunately that image was marred by a receding chin and a small, weak mouth. Tabor's only child had inherited his best features, but she'd gotten voluptuous lips and breasts and a strong chin from her otherwise ordinary mother. Rosie was a year and a half older than Joe Junior, which was part of her attraction.

He had met her in the country, at Ogden's Grove, where he'd taken Paul. The occasion was the first of those political-cultural outings to which Benno invited him. On that hot and dusty Sunday in the autumn of 1892, he was profoundly awed by the radical nature of the crowd, the bold and lawless pronouncements in the speeches. He wondered whether police wagons would thunder into the grove any minute to halt the subversive proceedings. To counter this anxiety, and his nervousness among strangers, he drank a whole growler of beer, and then another, before the entertainment started.

Rosie was third on the program. It wasn't her father who'd fetched her along to the gathering, but Joe Junior didn't know that at the time, just as he didn't know her name, or anything about her, except that she excited him the moment he saw her. As she stepped up on the platform improvised from crates and boards, she lifted her skirts to show her bare ankles. There was applause, chiefly from men, to compliment her face and figure. Her talent as yet was an unknown quantity.

Roza Jablonec had wide hips and heavy peasant legs. Her hair was dark brown, thick and wavy. Her full, billowy chest was the kind so in fashion with women and girls. For the picnic she'd covered her bosom with a high-necked blouse of coarse white material. Her dark skirt had felt flowers, gaudy and obviously homemade, sewn around the hem.

Joe Junior was lounging against a tree not far to the left of the improvised stage where Miss Roza Jablonec was introduced as a young singer of promise. Benno belched fumes of onion and garlic and nudged him. "I wish she'd promise me her tits. Beauties. Put your head between 'em, you could smother. A lovely way to die, ain't it?"

A bowlegged white-haired man with an accordion sat on a nail keg at a corner of the stage. Joe Junior learned sometime afterward that the accordionist was the father of Rosie's only girlfriend; he was a Pullman worker more angry, less fearful, than Tabor. The daughter had invited Rosie to the outing, and she'd told Tabor and Maritza she was going on a picnic on the lake shore.

The audience lying about on the yellowing grass grew quiet. The singer clasped her hands in a stiff artificial pose and began to sing "Ta-ra-ra Boom-de-ay." Done fast, and loudly, it hid certain flaws which quickly became evident in her second number, "My Sweetheart's the Man in the Moon." Her voice was sweet but thin; and even Joe Junior's untrained ear could hear that she frequently sang off-key.

No matter; he found her spectacularly attractive. Not so much her physical attributes, though they were fine. It was a kind of raw aura that he sensed; a wantonness she communicated by cocking her hips, tossing her wavy dark hair, flirting her round dark eyes at men in the crowd.

It was late in the afternoon, and some of the bachelors in the audience had drunk a lot of beer. While the young woman was still singing, Joe Junior heard a lewd proposition yelled out from the rear of the crowd. Then a fat man tipsily waved his beer pail and shouted, "All right, dear, that's enough, let's hear the next turn."

The accordion player's fingers produced a last pitiable squeak from the box. The girl stopped singing in mid-phrase, looking at the audience with dismay that quickly turned to anger. With never a conscious thought about it, Joe stepped forward.

"Shut up, give her a chance, where's your manners?" he shouted.

The fat man was startled; embarrassed. Behind Joe Junior, one of the men from Crown's snickered. "Same place as her talent. *Abwesend.*" Absent. Joe Junior made a large, clumsy gesture, trying to show the young woman that she should resume her song.

Her eyes fixed on his. A fleeting warm smile smoothed the anger from her face. She nodded slightly.

He nodded back. The accordion picked up the tune.

Sweaty and tumid, he clutched the tin growler in both hands while she finished the ballad. There wasn't much applause, but at least there were no boos or catcalls. Joe Junior clapped hard, ignoring Benno's smirking friends. He rushed to the end of the stage just as the girl jumped down with her skirt lifted in both hands.

She stumbled as she landed. He was there to catch her by the shoulders, prevent a fall. She gasped, a burst of breath, and for an instant leaned her big soft breasts against his shirt. She must have felt something herself, for she gasped again, and her eyes grew large. Some force, some highly charged linkage, leaped between them, in both directions, without a word.

He let go of her, stepped back, and struggled to find his voice.

"My name's Joe. I liked your song."

"My name's Roza."

"Roza, that's pretty. It's like Rose."

"You're pretty nice yourself. Meet me in ten minutes. Let's go for a walk."

Well away from the grove, safely concealed in dappled shade of yellow and scarlet leaves, she braced against a tree and lifted her skirt and underskirt. He tugged her drawers down and with his head pounding, touched her great dark bush. She laughed and licked his lips with her tongue.

It was his first time, but not hers, he suspected. She made it simple and, quick as it was, bliss.

□ □ □ □

He began to see her regularly in Pullman. He called her Rosie and she liked that.

She wasn't a studious girl, or smart in the conventional sense. She never read books. Yet somehow she'd learned a lot about life and developed a clear if hard-edged philosophy, especially about her father:

"Papa was born poor in Bohemia, he grew up poor, and it scarred him for life. He'll never make trouble at the factory, he'll let them shit all over him so long as they pay him every week. I learned a big lesson from that, Joey. I learned what comes first. It's being somebody, having connections, so they can't shit on you. That's one part and here's the other. You have to be somebody with a dollar in your pocket. The more the better."

"I don't think that way, Rosie."

"I know, I piped you out pretty fast. You're all tied up with fine fancy ideas that won't keep you warm or put a beef roast on the table, that's why we ain't going to stay together. What's it matter? Fucking's good enough for now."

It was easier for her to say it than for them to accomplish. Two Sundays in a row, she and Joe Junior had no chance to be alone. But it didn't discourage him. If anything, it made him all the more annoyed—and determined.

On April 22, six days before his birthday, he boarded the horsecar as usual. The weather was balmy and bright, the kind of a day for stealing squeezes and kissing a girl's ear until she succumbed and lifted her skirts.

On the long ride he tried to keep his mind off the private places of Rosie's body that he'd enjoyed before and urgently needed to visit again. He drew from his pocket a paper-covered book with the title printed in minuscule type to make recognition at a glance impossible. The book was a translation of *Talk Between Two Workers*, by the Italian anarchist Enrico Malatesta.

Benno had loaned it to him. It violently damned the owners of property—men like Pullman and Joe Junior's father.

> Do you not know that every bit of bread they eat is taken from your children, every fine present they give their wives means the poverty, hunger, cold, perhaps even the prostitution of yours?

Pop wasn't that bad, he knew. Yet Joe Crown did belong to the class Malatesta hated, and he shared many beliefs with men who were much more ruthless.

He shoved the book into his pocket, unwilling to read more and spoil the morning. He spent the rest of the ride thinking of how much he wanted his girl.

Tabor Jablonec and his wife and daughter lived in one of Pullman's brick row houses reserved for married workers. These dwellings were distinctly inferior to the homes on Foremen's Row and didn't quite represent the ideal that Mr. Pullman and his management advertised. Rents were high and so were the rates charged for water and gas, which the town bought from the city of Chicago, marked up and then resold. Despite the wage cutbacks, the company was main-taining utility prices at predepression levels.

When Joe Junior knocked and Rosie let him in, she put a finger to her lips. "We got company." Swearing to himself as he entered the kitchen, he forced out the usual polite words when he met the visitor. She was a woman of about thirty-five, rather small, plainly dressed, with hair drawn back in a bun. A squarish jawline suggested an uncompromising disposition. She shook Joe's hand vigorously when she learned who he was.

"I know your mother quite well. She's one of our favorite helpers at the settlement house. We'd have her there all the time if we could get her. Will you give her my regards?"

"I will, sure," he said with a smile. Now he was fascinated rather than annoyed by the visitor. He wondered what the founder of Hull House was doing in Pullman, seated at a flimsy table with sheets of closely written foolscap in front of her.

Rosie's mother explained. "Miss Addams is learning about how we live." Maritza's English was better than her husband's, her accent less noticeable.

"And I can state the answer in one word. Badly."

So saying, Jane Addams folded her papers and put them in her reticule. She explained to Joe Junior, "In view of the extreme privation brought on by the economy, I was asked to compile figures for the Chicago Civic Federation. What I'm finding is disgraceful."

"I know it's terrible here," Tabor said. He was seated with his elbows on the table, his palms against his temples. "When a man sweats hard and don't get drunk—when he's got a wife who helps, and saves—when he works ten years for the same bosses and still can't get out of hock, there is something wrong."

"I would quit," said Miss Addams. "At the very least, I would object, forcefully."

"I did it once, I got in bad trouble."

After Jane Addams thanked the family and left, Tabor put on his cap. "Going to Kensington for a while." Maritza nodded without comment, provoking more silent curses from Joe Junior.

Maritza Jablonec sat in the tiny grubby parlor, darning threadbare socks and union suits all afternoon. Rosie and Joe stayed in the kitchen and talked. He managed to slip his hand up under her dress a few times. Out of sight of Maritza in the parlor, he licked Rosie's open lips and let their tongues caress. That was worse than not touching at all.

About four-thirty the kitchen door opened and Tabor stumbled in, followed by two other men who worked at Pullman. One was a spindly fellow Tabor introduced as Link Randolph, the other a dour paunchy man called Dice Harrod. Link was carrying a brown pint bottle of whiskey, nearly consumed.

He was ranting. "Born in a Pullman house. Fed from the Pullman shop. Catechized in the Pullman church. When you retire, the Pullman pension is your ticket to the poorhouse. When you die you probably go to the Pullman hell. They pretend to give us everything and they take everything away, even our self-respect. They take what comes out of our toilets, for Christ's sake."

Maritza covered her mouth. Joe Junior said he didn't understand the last remark. "Sewage, sewage. King George takes it for fertilizer on his truck farm. *Bastard!*" He threw the empty bottle against the wall. Bits of brown glass tinkled to the floor behind the stove. Maritza stared forlornly at her stained wall.

Dice Harrod scraped a match to light a stubby cigar. Through puffs of smoke, he blinked like a frog on a lily pad. "What are you going to do about it, Link?"

"I'm going to join the committee."

"What committee?"

"The one that's being organized to go to the bosses and demand they put our wages back where they were before the cuts."

Dice Harrod blinked. "Did I hear you? Did you say demand?"

"That's what I said. This week or next, we're going to do it, you can count on it."

Joe Junior noticed Maritza shooting worried looks at her husband. Dice Harrod puffed away. "Jesus, that's awful dangerous, Link. You step out of line, you know what happens. They'll get back at you."

"I don't care anymore, God damn it."

"Dangerous," Dice Harrod muttered again, shaking his head. "Who else is on this committee?"

"Never you mind, it's a good strong group."

"But you're a member."

"God damn right."

"How about you, Tabor?"

"No! I'm interested, but I don't get messed up with stuff like that."

When the men left, Maritza said, "Dice is right, Link shouldn't do it."

"Yes, Dice is right. It's the company view, but he's right," Tabor agreed. Joe Junior wanted to speak, but he didn't. Instead, he leaned close to Rosie's fragrant hair. It smelled like roses; he'd bought her a special bar of scented soap for ten cents. She used it only on Sundays.

They went outside. With the kitchen door standing slightly ajar, he backed her against the wall. He lifted her hair aside with his right hand and gently licked her ear.

"I counted on getting a birthday present today."

"Don't worry, I'll save it," she whispered back, clamping her legs tight together and wiggling herself against his hand. Her underdrawers were wet. He was so hard he hurt.

Next time he visited, Rosie told him Link Randolph had been fired, and handed an eviction notice by the Pullman real estate division.

"Dice Harrod was one of their damn spies. For once Papa was smart, he didn't take Dice Harrod's bait."

Five hundred strong, "General" Coxey's Army reached Washington and marched up Pennsylvania Avenue, the leader himself carrying the petition for a federal public works program to help the unemployed.

At the Capitol, Coxey was instantly arrested when he trod on a lawn said to belong to the government. One of his followers tried to dash through police lines and was smashed back by fists and billies. The mounted police who had followed the demonstrators charged their horses at them, clubs swinging. The "army" scattered and disbanded as if it had never existed.

At the brewery there was frequent and heated discussion of Coxey's march. Some thought it was valiant, others thought it hopeless from the start. Benno had the strongest opinion. He enlightened Joe Junior at quitting time, in the little room lined with lockers Joe Crown provided for his men.

"Marching don't get nothing accomplished. Waving some piece of paper in Washington, that don't either. I'll tell you what they should have done, they should have taken along some dynamite."

On May 6, Joe Junior again set out for Pullman, burdened with a sense of probable defeat. He hadn't been intimate with Rosie for weeks. This Sunday proved no exception. Tabor invited him to Kensington, to a mechanics' hall where an overflow crowd of Pullman workers was expected. They would listen to a special speaker, Eugene Debs of the American Railway Union. Joe Junior decided he might as well go along since Maritza had made known her intention to spend another afternoon at home. Rosie looked piqued, at her mother and at him.

Joe Junior had never seen Debs, only pictures in periodicals which usually accompanied attacks on his socialistic preachments. He couldn't have been more surprised at the man's appearance. He expected a rough, truculent person; a Benno Strauss from down the road in Terre Haute, Indiana. Instead, he saw a lean, clean-shaven, balding man who might have been a bookkeeper. Debs was six feet tall, about thirty years old. It was a hot afternoon but he wore a perfectly pressed tweed suit and hard white collar. His shoe tips gleamed. From an earlier base as secretary-treasurer of the Brotherhood of Locomotive Firemen, he had worked to implement his vision of all railway unions united in one, for their common good. The A.R.U. now had almost three hundred thousand members. Its recruiting argument was persuasive. If a man joined the A.R.U., he was protected should the bosses try to play one brotherhood against another to break a strike.

Debs spoke for half an hour, without notes. After two minutes, Joe Junior was impressed; after five, he was mesmerized.

"I have moved quietly around the town of Pullman these past few days," Debs said. "I have talked, and asked questions, but mostly I have listened. I came away with one indisputable conclusion. If, after working for George M. Pullman for years, you are laid off, and then, two weeks after your work stops, you find yourself ragged and hungry, what can we say but this. George Mortimer Pullman stands revealed as a self-incriminated robber. He has no humane interest in you, he has only pretended to have it. His paternalism is the same as that of a slave-holder in regard to his human chattels. That is why I urge you to stand behind your committee tomorrow. Keep your courage high, your purpose clear before you, and you will carry the day."

"What committee now?" Joe whispered to Tabor.

"Same one that got Link Randolph fired."

"What are they doing?"

"I don't know nothing about it. I don't want to know."

Debs strode down to the edge of the platform and snatched off his spectacles, the better to rake his gaze across his audience of plain, tired, impoverished men. "I conclude with one final thought. Remember that the American Railway Union stands with you. Our philosophy is simple. When one brother is assailed, all others go to the rescue. In this contest, labor will stand by labor. Count on it."

Men jumped up, whistling and applauding. Joe Junior clapped loudly. The floor of the hall shook with the impact of boots and shoes stamping approval. Tabor glumly shook his head.

"That kind of talk will get you fired. Come on, I need a glass of wine."

Joe went along to the saloon, but after one drink of the cheap dago red he couldn't stand any more of Tabor's whipped-dog attitude. He asked whether Tabor planned to go home.

"Not right away." Tabor signaled for another glass. Instantly, Joe Junior saw a way to turn this to advantage.

Back in Pullman an hour later, he said to Maritza, "I'm afraid Mr. Jablonec is getting pretty far under the weather over in Kensington. It was an exciting meeting, people all worked up. Mr. Jablonec had already drunk several wines when I left."

"Oh my, where is he, Fanucci's?"

"Yes. He wouldn't leave."

"I'll have to walk there and bring him home. Rosie will fix you a bite of supper."

He returned a grave nod as she rushed to find her shawl. From her chair at the kitchen table, Rosie treated him to a rapturous smile.

Joe Junior and Rosie tumbled violently into her narrow bed. In the times they'd been together, he had never seen her throw off her clothes so fast. He poked into her with all the speed and fury of long deprivation. He exploded inside her in less than a minute, and left her writhing and calling for more. He rested forty minutes and took her again, slower, with more heat and more sweat and more wild cries from her panting mouth when they climaxed together.

Afterward, propped on his elbow and fondling her white breasts, he said, "I hate going home after I see you. I hate living on Michigan Avenue when there's so much fear and hunger out here."

Rosie laughed. "You don't want to go home to Michigan Avenue? I'll trade places in a wink."

"You don't understand that it feels bad to eat off plates with gold rims when people are out of work? Starving?"

"I don't care how it *feels*, I want to eat off plates like them. I want to *own* plates like them."

"Those, Rosie. Plates like those. How are you going to better yourself if you can't talk right?"

They'd joshed about this before. "It ain't grammar lessons they're after from girls like me, Joe," she would say. This time she reached down for him, and squeezed. "I got ways."

He rolled over on his back and gazed at the water-stained ceiling. A locomotive whistled somewhere. In the corner, a short candle burned in a dish. The gas had been turned off for nonpayment of the bill.

"I wish you wouldn't make fun of things I believe in," he said. "Maybe you wouldn't if you understood them better. I could give you some books about—"

"For God's sake, no books! You read too much yourself. That's why you're always stewing about poor starving people when you ought to be happy you got a warm safe bed to sleep in, plenty to eat—folks with a nice bank account. I wonder why you're so messed up?"

"Maybe the name for what I feel is conscience."

"Maybe the name for it's crazy. Besides, I get a feeling a lot of this labor stuff is hot air."

He rolled toward her again, little reflections from the candle showing in his eyes. "It isn't."

"Is that right. Well."

"Don't laugh at me. You'll see."

"Will I? When?"

He started to answer, then flushed so deeply the color spread to his neck. "I don't know, yet. But when the time's right, I'll strike a blow to help the cause. I'll strike a blow."

"Oh, Joey, don't talk like that, it's stupid. If you start believing it—"

"I do believe it."

"—you'll get yourself killed, and that's stupid. Throw your life away for some idea out of a book? Not me."

"Rosie, let's not fight."

"I ain't fighting, I'm just telling you, I take care of me first."

He leaned over, kissed her roughly. "I'll take care of you too. Maybe I'll buy you some gold-rimmed plates for a wedding present, how about that?"

The tension broke; she laughed. "Don't bullshit me, Joey. There are two kinds of girls, the kind men marry and the kind they screw. I'm the second kind, I got no stupid notions the other way. I know what I am. What kind of girl. A girl who learned to fuck and likes it. That's all right, I can use it to get a nice life, a nice flat, nice clothes. I never expect you to propose marriage, Joey. If you did I wouldn't say yes; I got bigger things in mind."

She ran her hand down to his groin and closed it on him.

"I ain't talking about this, either. Now come here, I'm ready again. Mama won't be all that long coming back from Kensington. Put another one of those things on. I don't want babies, yours or anybody's. I'm going to get up and out of this dirty place or die. I'm going to eat off some man's plate with a little gold rim even if you won't."

On May 7, a three-member grievance committee went to Pullman management to ask for reinstatement of regular wages. The executives listened with apparent sympathy and then restated the company's position. Times were bad. Orders were down. Wage cuts were not 40, 50, 60 percent, as alleged; they averaged 19 percent. Further, Pullman was building cars at a loss to keep the shops open, and at least part of its work force employed.

The meeting ended amicably. Word quickly circulated in the community of Pullman that the three committee men who had approached the company were for the moment satisfied.

At midweek, each of the three received notice of an indefinite layoff.

On Friday, May 11, exactly at noon, thirty-one hundred men of the Pullman Palace Car Company put down their tools and walked out. They demanded lower rents in Pullman, cancellation of the wage cuts of 1893, and immediate reinstatement of the three committeemen.

Not all Pullman workers joined the walkout. Tabor Jablonec was among those who stayed. "I didn't expect nothing else," Rosie said to Joe Junior when she told him.

Tabor's loyalty didn't help him. On Monday, management laid off the remaining three hundred workers indefinitely.

39

Julie

AUNT WILLIS FISHBURNE arrived during the second week of the Pullman strike. She never stayed long when she visited. She observed what she called her three-day rule. "After three days, fish and visitors quickly begin to stink." Three days were quite long enough for driving Vanderhoff half out of his wits, but not nearly long enough for Julie.

Aunt Willis would soon celebrate her forty-eighth birthday. Unlike her sister Nell, she was a tall woman, with austere features. A long jaw; a long nose; sunken cheeks. She wore her gray-shot hair mannishly clipped and unadorned. Not for her the fuzzy curls, fat buns, heavy chignons of fashion.

Willis's thinness was the kind sometimes called stringy. Her bosom was minimal. She resembled a woman from some back-country plantation in the South, where life was hard and generally unhappy. Until you noticed her eyes. They radiated warmth and mirth and cynicism by turns. They were windows through which you saw fireworks displays.

Aunt Willis arrived on Prairie Avenue in a depot hack. She spent longer than necessary chatting with the cabman, returning to him some kind of flask he'd evidently shared. She was dressed, as usual, in a costume designed to shock. Full oriental trousers under a short skirt and tailored tunic, low-laced shoes and red silk stockings with a diamond design.

Willis had studied the doctrines of Mrs. Amelia Bloomer of Seneca Falls, New York, the liberated woman who had pioneered hygienic dress in the 1850s. Once enlightened, Willis never looked backward. She scorned the layers of Victorian crinoline, the frills and flounces, the brutal bustles lashed in place. She said they caused a repression of normal and healthy female spirits.

Julie's aunt was an authentic black sheep. She had run away from her Kentucky home when she was barely fifteen. A boy was responsible. A boy her parents loathed, Nell had confided to her daughter. There was more to it, however. Of all the Fishburnes, Willis had been the one infected by the disease of abolitionism.

As a girl, she read escaped-slave narratives and memorized whole pages of

Mrs. Stowe's inflammatory novel. She began to pay attention to conditions around her. This new interest put her at odds with everyone else in the Fishburne household. "I remember scenes, terrible ones," Nell said. "She railed at Father about the evil of slavery, the madness of secession. She stood on a chair and pulled off her underdrawers because they were cotton, and cotton came from the slave South. To this day my sister won't wear cotton underthings, only silk." Willis had become an embarrassment Nell tried to conceal from the world.

Fortunately Willis lived in New York. There she worked for causes that made her sister blanch. She consorted with whores at street missions, in order to put an end to their sexual exploitation. She wrote pamphlets demanding changes in one-sided divorce laws. She openly embraced free love and told Julie that a woman had a complete and absolute right to control her own body. No doctor had the right; no politician or prelate had the right; no *man* had the right—though they were always trying to assume it.

Two years ago Willis had lost the latest of her three husbands, each of whom had contributed to her state of financial independence. Nell preferred not to hear a syllable about any of them; the first was a radical, the second was dissolute, and the third was a Jew.

Willis's first husband, the Reverend Chauncey Stone Coffin, was twenty years her senior. From his father he had inherited his Unitarian faith, as well as several millions from the family's New England-based shipping line. He was a leading figure in the crusade for abolition and Negro equality. Willis met him in Chicago during the war. She was living alone and supporting herself with menial jobs, throwing herself into humanitarian work every free moment. She changed dressings and carried bedpans as a helper at St. Luke's Hospital, where Union and Rebel wounded sometimes lay side by side. She went twice a week to Camp Douglas, the prisoner compound out on Cottage Grove, there helping to write letters for illiterate Southern boys, or just talking to them, holding their hands, sharing their pain at being locked up by fellow Americans hundreds of miles from home and loved ones. Toward the end of the war, the Reverend Coffin toured the prison camp, met Willis, and began his courtship.

He pursued her for two years, while she was attending Oberlin College after the war. At last his entreaties persuaded her.

The Reverend's passion for black freedom and punishment of Southerners knew no bounds. Unfortunately neither did his passion for female members of his audiences. On one of his speaking tours after his marriage, he was discovered in a hotel room in St. Louis, embracing the altogether naked wife of a local church deacon. Willis heard about the affair, and Coffin left her a million dollars in return for secrecy and a quiet divorce.

She married her second husband, Loyal McBee, a few years later. He was an actor who succumbed early to the most dangerous temptation of his trade, drink. His talent was too meager for anything but secondary roles. He couldn't keep a penny in his pocket, but Willis loved him madly and completely.

Their marriage lasted four years. On tour in *Julius Caesar,* he was playing Cassius to Mr. Booth's Marc Antony in Detroit. He left the theater after a matinee, found a saloon, emerged an hour later and fell in front of a horsecar. His neck was broken. He died instantly. Not until a week later did Willis learn for the first time that Loyal's family owned a huge flour mill in Rochester, New York, and had given him half a million dollars in a trust fund he couldn't touch so long as he was in the disreputable profession of acting. Willis inherited the money.

Simon Mordecai Weiss was her most recent spouse. Weiss was a merchant prince; or, more correctly, an aging king when Willis met him.

Weiss had risen from his father's junk trade to become America's reigning monarch of wholesale hardware. He always had dirt on his knuckles or a smear of grease on his cheek; he examined major purchases for his inventory personally. He was a wonderfully kind man who had married and divorced two previous wives, both of whom he found greedy and vapid. He and Willis met by chance at a lantern slide lecture on the African interior presented by Mr. Henry M. Stanley, the journalist who thrilled the world by locating the lost Dr. Livingstone on Lake Tanganyika in 1871.

Willis and Weiss happened to have tickets for adjacent seats, and struck up a conversation. Willis liked the old man before she ever knew who or what he was. Two weeks later, he presented her with a simple and honest proposition. If she would marry him, and live and travel with him, engaging him in lively and intelligent conversation for the remainder of his life (it was her bright, rather tough manner which had captivated him), he would make her his sole heir. He had no family.

During his proposal he confessed that he had a weak heart and didn't expect to live more than five years; he was seventy-seven at the time. Actually he lived fourteen months. The day after he died, his attorneys came to the widow with two different offers from competitors of the deceased. Weiss had often said he expected her to sell the firm after he passed on: she was too lively a woman to spend her life learning about bolts and screws and angle braces. She negotiated cannily, the rival bidders raised their ante several times, and she finally sold to the man who offered five and a half million. She cried every day for a month after she buried the kind and thoughtful Weiss.

Willis had never deliberately sought wealth in any of her husbands. Often she wondered if that was why wealth had found her.

Despite her advanced views and her involvement in less than respectable causes, Willis retained many of the virtues of a Southern woman. Unless hectored or outraged by stupidity, she was considerate of others, excepting of course boors and complete fools. Her brother-in-law qualified for both of those categories, but because he was family she tried to hold her tongue in his presence.

She wasn't always successful. What seemed mere common sense to her was often unthinkable to her brother-in-law and Nell. Hence she usually managed to outrage them at least once per visit. This time it happened at supper on her first evening in Chicago. She finished her demitasse and lit one of her small dark brown cigars.

"On the train I was reading about Mr. Pullman and his differences with his workers. He sounds dreadfully arrogant. I hope the strikers hold out until they're treated fairly. I hope they bring Pullman to his knees."

"You would," Pork muttered. Nell flashed him a look—*Won't you keep the peace? This will be over in three days. I know she's crazy but she's my sister.*

Julie's father seemed unresponsive to the signal. Julie herself was fidgety. She wanted to get Aunt Willis alone. Tell her about Paul. Ask her advice.

Willis tapped cigar ash into her saucer. Nell tried to hide her disgust. Julie's mother looked especially peaked under the bright electric chandelier. Willis noticed.

"Are you not feeling well again, Nellie?"

"Well, I've been in bed for several days—"

"On the advice of that doctor with the choirboy face, I suppose."

"Dr. Woodrow."

"Who cares what his name is? Anyone who prescribes bed rest in the dark when the sun is shining is a quack." Willis waved her cigar.

Nell looked like a hurt bird. "You wouldn't call him a quack if you were afflicted. God made you a rarity, sister. A healthy woman."

"Sister dear, that's nonsense. I'm healthy because I live a healthy life. No encumbering garments. No sickrooms. Vigorous walking every day. Plenty of good food and drink—"

"And men," Vanderhoff blurted.

Julie's hand flew to her mouth. But the anticipated storm didn't break. Willis smiled at her brother-in-law.

"True enough, Mason. I've had three splendid husbands. But I've decided I'll never marry again. First, finding a man to match the others would be hard. Further, in this modern age it isn't necessary, one doesn't have to wear a ring to enjoy the opposite sex."

Nell gasped. "Willis, that's filthy."

"Oh, I suppose you think so. I forget we're rather in the middle of the Dark Ages here."

"You mean here in Chicago," Vanderhoff said. "Here on the prairie. In the provinces."

"That's it exactly, Mason," Willis replied with her sweetest Southern smile. Julie wanted to giggle. She loved Papa, but it did amuse her when something inflamed him and he puffed up like a toad.

Anticipating a shopping expedition with Aunt Willis the next day, Julie spent a restless night and woke before daylight. She and her aunt spent most of the day in Elstree's and Field's and the other large stores, then went to supper at the restaurant of Willis's choice, the English Chop House. It was a racy, disreputable place on Gamblers' Alley, popular with sporting men, painted women, big-bellied pols and fast-talking journalists. Amid dark woodwork, breathing air that was one part tobacco smoke, one part frying grease, one part whiskey fumes, Willis was at home.

"All right, tell me about it," she said when they were seated and she'd lit another cigar.

Julie's gray eyes widened. "About what?"

"Come, do you think I haven't noticed the changes since I was here last? Your cheeks are full and red, but your eyes have a haggard look. Young women lose sleep over young men."

She stretched her hand across the table to squeeze Julie's.

"Tell me."

Julie eagerly let it tumble forth—everything about Paul Crown, who was part of a family the Vanderhoffs loathed.

"You've been seeing him, however." Willis gave it the slight inflection of a question.

"Every Sunday. Now that it's good weather, we go cycling in Lincoln Park. He pretends to be my instructor. He's very brash and daring. I think I love him, Aunt Willis."

Willis was quiet for a moment. "How old are you, Juliette?"

"Why, you know that, you send me a beautiful present every year. On the twenty-eighth of this month I'll be seventeen."

"Yes, I do know that. But to mention it aloud is pertinent. You're young. It's possible this infatuation will pass."

"It won't. Besides, I've read enough to know that not so many years ago, girls much younger than I fell in love, married, had children by age fourteen or fifteen."

"Yes, but they had good reason. They could expect much harder, and shorter, lives. They needed to hurry, you don't. You have so many advantages—so much to look forward to. All I am doing is cautioning you. Be very sure."

"I am."

Willis looked at her steadily for several seconds. "All right, then. If it's true, and it holds true, don't say you *think* you love the boy, declare it."

Julie swirled her little silver spoon in the melting dessert ice. "What about Mama and Papa? They would hate him. But I'd die if I had to stop seeing him."

"Then don't."

"Oh, yes, that's how I feel. But what would I do if they found out?"

"Defy them."

"Defy—? Oh, Aunt Willis, I don't know if I could do that. I don't think I'm prissy, or too proper, but I love Mama and Papa. I want their respect and approval. Their affection—"

"Which they ration out according to how you behave."

Julie looked away. Her aunt had judged it correctly.

"I appreciate your feelings, child. You're a dutiful daughter, and a decent person. Regrettably, in this world decency can be a handicap. Furthermore, your mother—my flesh and blood—has filled your head with falsehoods about your frail health, weak nerves, general lack of stamina. You mustn't believe any of it. It's part of the prevailing absurdity about womankind. Take the old shibboleth that women must lie down and be invalids once a month, regular as clocks. Ridiculous. Girls are taught all the wrong things by society and their mothers. Beautiful hair is more important than a beautiful brain. The chief function of a female is to be ornamental. Except of course when she is busy being a brood sow."

"Aunt Willis," Julie whispered, covering her mouth.

"Dear, there's nothing shocking about plain truths, plainly stated. A woman is born with intelligence and character. More than your average man possesses. A woman is capable of more important and meaningful things than prettily decorating a house like a doll. Do you know the drama by Mr. Ibsen, about the woman named Nora?"

"No. I've only heard Ibsen's name. People say he writes dirty plays."

"Naturally. People have a stock of handy shopworn accusations to hurl against anyone who sticks his head up with a new idea. Henrik Ibsen is a powerful dramatist. A genius. For a man, he knows an astonishing amount about our sex. A woman needs a purpose, Julie. A mission she believes is important. That and a glass of fine Kentucky bourbon, a bracing swim, or a vigorous lover will cure almost anything that ails you. Still—setting all that aside—I know you face a different, more immediate issue because of this boy. Namely—whose life is it? Your mother's, your father's, or yours?"

Troubled, Julie studied her hands. She knew the brave answer to the question. She just couldn't bear to confront the consequences it conjured.

Aunt Willis seemed to understand. She covered Julie's hand with hers. On every finger she wore a ring with a different stone.

"Don't doubt yourself. You have the courage to take the right road, if you'll only believe it. To do it would undoubtedly cause you pain for a while, but you'd survive. You'd make your stand successfully."

"I hope so."

"I made mine in Kentucky. I survived."

"You've never told me much about that."

"Ah, haven't I?" Willis leaned back, half closing her eyes. A strange dreamy expression made her almost beautiful for a moment. Her voice grew soft.

"It's a short enough story. Kentucky was a state riven in two. The Fishburnes were secesh. Billy Boynton's people were loyalists. *Poor* loyalists. Mudsills. I didn't care. I packed a few things in a bundle, shinnied down the rain pipe and ran away. I had six days and nights with Billy before he mustered in."

"Did you marry him?"

"No, I did not. No minister would have performed the ceremony without a paper certifying that we had parental permission."

Julie was awestruck. "It must have taken such courage—you were only fifteen. Did you ever—?"

She waited while the mustachioed waiter laid down a silver tray bearing the bill. "Did you ever regret what you did?"

"Not once. Those six days and nights with Billy Boynton were among the happiest I've ever known. I wouldn't trade them if they offered to make me Empress of China."

"What happened to your young man?"

Willis put out her little cigar in a crystal dish, twisting and crushing it with force. "Shot and killed at Chickamauga. Here, I'll pay the bill. It's time we went home. Just one more thing."

She touched her niece's hand again.

"If this love affair becomes too difficult for you to bear by yourself, think of me. Come to me at any time if you need a haven, or a friend."

40

Paul

UNCLE JOE continued to condemn the Pullman strike loudly and often. So did all the newspapers that came into the house; Paul read these slowly, laboriously, always with a small English grammar and his pocket dictionary close by. The newspapers were so fiercely against the strikers that he began to wonder whether they had secret ties with Mr. Pullman. He recalled Cousin Joe talking of the rich conspiring against the poor. In the one-sided accounts there certainly seemed to be evidence of it. No one could be as selfish, irresponsible, depraved, lawless as the papers described the strikers.

The strike, and its opponents, raised doubts which Paul resisted. He didn't want to be reminded of the baker of Wuppertal. Didn't want to believe his cousin's dark assertions about America—the repeatedly proclaimed "truth." But the doubts were there, and they intensified every day.

On a hot evening in June, after work, Joe Junior persuaded Paul to accompany him to a meeting before they went home. It was a Saturday, the day after Paul's seventeenth birthday.

"Gene Debs is giving a speech tonight. He's a terrific orator, you need to hear him."

Paul was very much afraid he knew the message already. For the sake of friendship he agreed to go, though all he really wanted was to get home and sleep and hurry the coming of Sunday afternoon.

After they left the brewery they had supper in a saloon, then went on to Uhlich's Hall in the 400 Ashland block. The drab old auditorium was hot, and nearly full, when they climbed the gallery stairs. Paul was uncomfortable about being with this crowd, surely all socialists. Most of them were poorly dressed, with the rough look of day laborers.

Cousin Joe said, "Debs's union has been in convention here for five days. Everyone's wondering whether Debs will make a big announcement. Support the strike. See all the reporters down there?" He pointed to a railed section on the main floor; it was packed.

Promptly at seven, a man walked onstage. He introduced himself as George Howard, vice president of the American Railway Union. With some oratorical flourishes, he presented the chief executive, Mr. Debs. Long applause, whistling, foot-stomping, greeted Debs as he walked out from the wings. Paul thought Mr. Debs the radical looked more like a monk mistakenly dressed in a wool suit, white shirt and cravat.

When the applause subsided, Debs stepped to the podium. He spoke without notes.

"Gentlemen, I come before you to announce a decision reached by the executive board of your brotherhood. To speak personally for a moment, many of you know I have been reluctant to press forward with open support of the Pullman strikers. I am still reluctant."

His voice reached the rafters, and even stirred Paul. "It is true that the American Railway Union has become very large in a short time. But we remain a young and untried organization. Say what you will about the Pullman Palace Car Company"—a few scattered boos—"no rational man can deny it is a company with great financial resources, and powerful connections at the highest levels of local and national government. For that reason alone, I have been unwilling to recommend that we mount an action to show our solidarity with those who bravely struck for their rights."

Paul leaned close to his cousin. "What does he mean, action?"

"A sympathy strike by this union."

Debs lifted his head; his gaze swept the gallery. "For five days we have met here in convention. We have listened to tales of the abuse of workingmen at Pullman, abuse totally inconsistent with the morality of a modern, civilized country. We have acknowledged the continuing naked intransigence of the Pullman management. That management doggedly proclaims there are no issues to negotiate. With blind eyes and deaf ears and hearts devoid of Christian compassion, the Pullman Company turns away from its own employees who are starving and suffering for the sake of—what? Exorbitant or unreasonable demands? No! A subsistence wage!"

Joe Junior hunched forward. "I think he's going to do it."

Debs paused to sip water from a barrel glass. When he'd drunk about half, he put the glass away and gripped the sides of the podium. Seconds passed. Uhlich's Hall was so quiet, Paul heard a floorboard squeak when someone shifted his foot.

"Gentlemen—for all the reasons just stated, I have set aside my reluctance." Someone whistled; others whooped. Swiftly Debs raised his hand for quiet. "I will not oppose, and indeed I endorse the action of the executive board of your brotherhood. Here is their decision, reached after long and careful deliberation. If, within ten days, the Pullman Palace Car Company does not agree to arbitration in good faith, then the American Railway Union will commence a boycott of all Pullman operations."

There was a flurry of movement among the reporters on the main floor. One man in a straw hat scrambled for the aisle. Debs said sharply, "Just a moment. Hear the rest." Protesting, the reporter sat down. His colleagues shushed him.

"During the boycott, the brotherhood will refuse to handle or service Pullman cars regardless of which line is carrying them. We will use no violence. We will stop no trains. We will simply stay our hands. Our effort will be peaceful, conducted with a high sense of honor. We will treat the corporation better than it treats its own people. But we will stand fast, and maintain the boycott until such time as arbitration begins."

Slowly Debs looked around the hushed hall. He had them straining to hear; even Paul, who had slowly, almost unconsciously been pulled into the spell of the man's oratory.

"That is our message to the world. In these dark and difficult times, we can do no less than support our brave brothers in American labor. I can and will do no less while I draw breath. Thank you, and good night."

The A.R.U. vice president, Howard, jumped up from his seat to lead the ovation. Joe Junior shot to his feet and, somewhat reluctantly, so did Paul. Debs held the podium and seemed to sway, as if spent. His eyes roved around the hall. A faint, tired smile was his only acknowledgment of the clapping and stomping.

Reporters pushed and shoved out of the press enclosure, trying to reach Debs. Men from the audience reached him first, pummeling his back, pumping his hand. As Paul and his cousin worked their way up the aisle, Joe Junior was exuberant. "This is it, we'll see action now."

"You are probably right."

"Why so glum? Don't you care about the strike?"

"I suppose I should, but—"

"You can't think of anything but Julie, is that it?"

Paul tried to smile. "That seems to be so."

"Well, you'll have to think about something else now. The boycott changes everything. It's dynamite."

As the two left the hall, Paul wondered if his cousin was aware of the word he'd used. Pictures flashed in his head. The sand dunes. The shanty blowing up. Benno Strauss laughing . . .

Bad pictures. Were they harbingers of worse to come? He hoped not.

Two shiny Fleetwing safety cycles leaned against the trunk of the sycamore. On the other side, in dappled shade, Paul and Julie rested on the new grass. Her right arm, in white, and his left, in a starched shirt with sleeve pushed up, lay close together, touching.

They were meeting two hours later than usual today, four o'clock; Aunt Ilsa had delayed Sunday dinner because of a special reception following morning worship at St. Paul's. Pastor Wunder was introducing a new assistant, recently ordained.

When Paul heard about this early Sunday morning, he ran all the way to Prairie Avenue and lurked near the Vanderhoff mansion until the family drove off to church. Then he went swiftly along Fifteenth to the rear of the property, where a short path led from the sidewalk to the side door of the stable.

Seven melon-sized whitewashed stones lined each side of the path. Theirs was the second on the left as you faced the stable. Paul had picked out the stone after Julie said that using the servants to smuggle notes in and out would inevitably lead to discovery.

He slipped a note under the message stone and patted the earth to smooth it. Julie always checked the stone before she left home. He was out of breath and sweating when he got back to the Crown house. No matter. To miss seeing her for a whole week would be unbearable.

Their meeting place was the bicycle rental stand near Fisher's Beer Garden at the northern edge of Lincoln Park. He arrived twenty minutes early. She arrived on time. "Yes, I found the note."

They clasped hands, squeezed, then separated with guilty smiles.

She wore a smart new cycling outfit. Low shoes of white canvas, white leggings with a knee-length overskirt, a fitted white bolero jacket, a gay sailor hat with a broad ribbon of emerald satin. In Paul's eyes, no one, any place, any time, could have looked more beautiful.

They pedaled south on a road that curved through the heart of Lincoln Park. The park was full of pleasant summer sounds. Children romping. Cyclists tinkling their bells. The whack of a soundly hit baseball, then cheering. At the south end of the park they turned around, pedaling back to Fisher's, where they dismounted and left the road. Paul and Julie chose their spot, on the lake side of the big sycamore. In the beer garden the German band blared *"Die Wacht am Rhein."*

From the pocket of his lightweight linen coat Paul took a small square block of drawing paper and a piece of brown chalk. He tried to sketch her as they talked.

He brought up the strike. "I don't know much about it," Julie responded. "Papa says the strikers should be arrested. He says the ringleaders should be shot. I don't think he means it."

"No, but the subject seems to get people very hot. My uncle speaks the same way."

"Rich men," she said with a shrug. "They think alike. Let me see, please."

Embarrassed, he showed the sketch. "Bad as ever. I try, but I have no talent. I want to make pictures with a camera. Perhaps even the kind that move, that would be the most exciting."

"I've heard about those. Papa saw a demonstration at the Exposition. He said the pictures were useless and trashy."

"Oh, no, I don't think so." He tossed the mawkish sketch aside. "What if you could photograph truly important things? Sights that no ordinary person would ever have a chance to see? Presidents, or kings, or cannibals? Egypt, or China, or the high slopes of some great mountain like the Jungfrau? What if you could photograph wars? It would be like a history book springing to life before your eyes. That wouldn't be useless or trashy."

"No, it certainly wouldn't."

He leaned back against the tree. "It is work I could give my whole life to, Julie."

"You'd leave your uncle's business?"

"Yes, I am already tired of the brewery. The pay is good but I have no real interest in making beer, just drinking it." She laughed. "I want to photograph. Of course I have to learn how to do it. At the fair I met a man who would have taught me but his shop closed, I don't know where he went."

"There must be another way. You'll find it. I think you can do almost anything you want with your life."

She was beautiful beyond belief. Her forehead gleamed. Her lips were soft and pink. The heat put a silver dew on her upper lip. His head filled with chaotic thoughts of nakedness, locked limbs, soft ardent cries. He slipped his left hand over hers.

Reacting to his touch, Julie turned to him, the black strands of her hair blowing and tossing over the puffed shoulders of her jacket. "Please, Paul. We mustn't."

He didn't let go. "I am feeling bad, Julie."

"About meeting this way?"

"No, because I have to be polite, when all I want is to hug and kiss you."

"We can't start that. We don't dare. I might not be strong enough to stop."

He scrambled to his knees. A pair of male cyclists bowled by on the road. Paul gave them a glance, then bent forward and kissed her.

They'd kissed on the lips twice before, chastely. But this was June; full summer, with heat in the earth, and in the air, and in their blood.

He pressed his mouth against hers, feeling her cool lips quickly grow warm. Somehow her mouth opened. Somehow their tongues touched. She uttered a little cry and hugged him around the waist, her cheek flat against his starched shirt.

He stroked her shining hair, not caring who saw them. "I want more than just to meet this way. Please allow me to speak to your father. I will make him understand my intentions are good. He will forget his bad feelings toward my uncle—"

"No, he won't, and you mustn't say a word. If you spoke to Papa he wouldn't allow me to see you again, ever. We'd lose even these few hours."

"But I can't stand this too much more, I want to be closer. Feel," he said in a burst. Still kneeling, he drew her to him so the stiffness was cushioned on her breasts.

Eyes closed, she hugged him harder, and made a little sound of passion in her throat.

"I can't have only secret meetings the rest of my life, Julie."

"Oh, I can't either, but—but—" She started to cry.

He embraced her and stroked her dark, glossy hair again. "Then what are we going to do?"

"I don't know!"

He moved away when her sobbing grew louder. He'd already been more forward and intimate than decency allowed. He touched her tear-reddened face. Held it between his palms. Bent again to kiss her tenderly, comfortingly, beneath the rustling sycamore leaves . . .

"Hey. Hello there."

The cry wrenched them apart. Paul looked for the source. He saw a fancy red tandem cycle on the curving road, a tail of dust spurting out behind it. The young woman on the front seat peered over her shoulder from beneath a straw hat. Because of the dust, Paul couldn't immediately make out her features, or those of her blond escort. Julie recognized him a moment before Paul did.

"Oh God, Paul."

It was her rich friend Welliver.

41

Ilsa

IN THE AUTUMN of 1889, two young women named Jane Addams and Ellen Starr had sublet the second floor of a run-down mansion at the corner of Polk and Halsted streets. Mostly working-class people lived in the building, but memories of the mansion's first owner, a real estate mogul named Charles Hull, remained. The place was Hull House forever.

Hull House not only advised the poorly educated people of the neighborhood on practical matters of diet, child care, sanitation, managing a small budget, but also initiated programs to expand and enrich the mind. Chamber music groups performed at Hull House. Authors read and discussed their works. Painters gave demonstrations and instruction. Professors lectured on aesthetics and history and literature. Controversial speakers presented their social programs.

But Hull House reached out far beyond the immediate neighborhood, into the homes of Chicago's wealthy and influential women. There the purpose was to spread the truth about the plight of Chicago's poor.

Miss Addams and her friend Miss Starr were in certain ways typical of females of their class and generation. College-educated, they saw a life of purpose and good works as incompatible with marriage.

"When I completed my degree at Rockford Female Seminary," Miss Addams told Ilsa shortly after they got acquainted in the late 1880s, "I expected to travel and idle the years away in meaningless pursuits like many another young woman of comfortable circumstances. I toured Europe twice, and during the second trip I had an experience at a brewery in Coburg, Bavaria. I saw young women trudging back and forth from five in the morning until seven at night with huge casks of beer on their backs. The beer was hot. They were carrying it to a cooling house. The beer often spilled, scalding them. Disfiguring them for life, perhaps. Still they trudged. Fourteen hours a day, for one and a half marks. Thirty-seven cents. It was a terrible epiphany. I am not a saint, Ilsa. I am not spiritual, I view myself as a practical woman. But I knew in Coburg that I needed a lifetime mission, and that it had to be a mission of helping women in my own country who were beaten down by toil into a condition of hopelessness."

Before that conversation ended, Ilsa Crown pledged herself to work for Hull House. She knew her husband would object. The settlement had a somewhat radical cachet. She didn't care. In this, Joe would have to bow to her feelings as a modern woman.

In the troubled spring and early summer of 1894, Jane Addams convened groups of affluent women who supported her and urged them to use their influence in the matter of the Pullman strike.

To a group of seven gathered around her parlor table on a Monday in late June, the day before the A.R.U. boycott was to begin, she showed a page of *Harper's Weekly*. "Here the strikers are characterized as 'blackmailers and brigands.'" She held up a *Tribune*. "Here is 'Dictator Debs' leading 'the Debs Rebellion.' To the press they're all monsters. Yet I was out at Pullman again yesterday, and I'm convinced that the strikers are largely peaceable and decent people who have been abused by their employers."

"Will the boycott go on as scheduled, Miss Addams?" Ilsa asked. No matter how close the friendship, no one ever called her Jane.

"I fear so. I spoke with Wickes, the vice-president charged with labor relations. He repeated the company position. There is nothing to negotiate. Nothing to arbitrate. But there's worse news. As you've no doubt read, in anticipation of the strike widening into a boycott of all Pullman cars, the General Managers Association is bringing in one of its own, John Egan, to take charge. The G.M.A. represents the twenty-four railroads headquartered or terminating in Chicago. John Egan is general manager of the Chicago & Great Western. He's opened offices and his men are already on the streets, looking for recruits."

"Recruits for what?" a woman asked.

"A force of special deputies. They will be sworn in and used to move the trains Mr. Debs's brotherhood refuses to handle. They will confront the pickets."

"Is that not a legitimate response?" Ilsa wondered aloud. "Or at least to be expected? The Attorney General in Washington, Mr. Olney, sits on the board of several railroads, and favors the owners. Would he not logically employ such tactics?"

"That isn't the issue, Ilsa. The G.M.A. is recruiting the worst element. Toughs, pickpockets, traffickers in women—any bit of scum that can be scraped up, armed, and issued a temporary badge. I ask all of you to speak to your husbands. Let them speak to officials they may know at the various railroads, or in government. Order must be maintained. We must not see a reign of lawlessness in the name of capitalism."

Ilsa did raise the issue with Joe at the supper table. He scoffed:

"What's wrong with preparing to defend yourself against a rabble? Nothing. If matters get out of hand, the authorities should call for federal troops. Altgeld is so pink, he would probably refuse any request for state—Fritzi! For the last time, put that away at the table."

She had been trying to pass around her latest treasure. It had cost her an entire dollar, saved from her allowance. The dog-eared autograph card was one of those traditionally handed out by legitimate theaters so patrons could get signatures of starring actors. What made it special was the autograph of the young player who had written his name in a large flamboyant hand. J. W. Booth.

With a mournful sigh, Fritzi slid the card into the pocket of her embroidered apron. As soon as her father's head was turned, she made a head scarf out of her white linen napkin. She held it under her chin and cocked her head this way and that, acting out some role.

Vexed, Ilsa snatched the napkin off her daughter's head. Carl concentrated on fitting the tines of two forks together so they would stand up in a V, balanced. He was trying not to snicker.

"I'm entirely behind the G.M.A.," Joe Senior declared. "That infernal Debs is building a personal empire on the backs of his dupes."

"Pop, that's ridiculous," Joe Junior said.

"You think so?"

"Yes, and I support the strikers." From the breast pocket of his corduroy jacket he pulled a long white ribbon. Joe Crown tugged his half glasses lower on his nose and peered over them.

"What the devil is that, may I ask?"

"The Railway Union is passing them out to members and friends. Debs wants his people to be easily identified in a crowd, so no one frames them for some trumped-up criminal act. The ribbons show solidarity, too."

"Not in my house. Nor at the brewery."

"I'm sorry, Pop, this is a matter of conscience." Joe Junior started to tie the white ribbon around his left sleeve.

"Stop." Joe Senior shot his hand out, palm up.

"Give it to me, Joseph. Now."

"Pop—"

"*Now.*"

Their eyes locked. Joe Junior's will broke. He dropped the ribbon in his father's hand. Joe Senior crumpled it and whisked it out of sight.

"You may finish your supper."

Ilsa sat like a stone, fearing to move, possibly worsen things. She knew young Joe was furious with his father's iron discipline; probably more furious with himself for bending under it . . .

"I don't care for any more," Joe Junior said. "I want to be excused."

"Go!" Joe Senior waved. "You spoil my digestion anyway, you and your radical nonsense."

"Joe, please," Ilsa said. "Some of what your son is telling you is quite true." Joe Senior dropped his hand to the boar tooth on its gold chain. "Miss Addams is of the opinion that the Pullman strikers are by and large peaceful. They—"

"Miss Addams, Miss Addams—frankly, Ilsa, I'm sick of hearing the opinions of an aging spinster who has no grasp of reality."

"Oh, that's unfair," she retorted, her own anger rising. Joe Junior got up, muttered "Excuse me," and walked out. Pauli looked troubled. Carl's forks fell apart with a clatter. His father glared. Carl wilted.

Joe Crown tossed back the last of his stein of dark Heimat beer. The stein was finely etched with the family emblem. "No wonder his mind's poisoned against law and order. There are more anarchists in this city than in St. Petersburg."

Ilsa controlled her anger with great effort. "Wearing a ribbon isn't such a terrible—"

"It represents anarchy. It shames this family. I won't have it. That's the end of it."

Fritzi, Carl and Pauli were all watching with strained expressions; Carl actually looked frightened. For the sake of harmony, peace at the table, Ilsa reined her conscience and suppressed her anger.

"Everyone eat, please."

She too had surrendered. She didn't like herself for that. Or her husband for forcing it.

The following day, Tuesday, after some further consideration of all Jane Addams had said, Ilsa decided she had a duty to convey it to others, no matter what Joe thought. She would do what she must, and say nothing to him.

Although modern devices such as the telephone made her nervous, she nevertheless rang her neighbor on the south, Mrs. Sophie Pelmoor, to explain the strike from the workers' perspective. Mrs. Pelmoor hung up on her.

Surprised and dismayed, Ilsa made six other calls to acquaintances around the neighborhood. The reaction varied from indifference to outright wrath. Emmeline DeVore, whose husband owned a small insurance company, denounced the message, and then the caller:

"We don't need your kind in this neighborhood, Mrs. Crown. Go back to the *Nordseid* or whatever you call it. Better yet, go back to Germany."

Next morning Pete the yard man discovered that someone had thrown eggs at the house during the night. Joe Senior marched out to look. He stood with his hands on his hips and his lips pressed together. Then he said, "Ilsa, I ask you politely to stay away from those harpies at the settlement house. We don't need this sort of thing. My business does not need this sort of thing."

Ilsa didn't reply. Nor did he wait for an answer. He assumed she'd obey him. When he and everyone else had left for the day, she hid herself in her room and cried.

That wasn't her usual way of reacting to difficulties. Ilsa despised weepers; women who used tears as a crutch, a shield, a weapon of persuasion. But there was one night years ago, vividly remembered, when she had cried as if the world was ending . . .

In Over-the-Rhine, north of the Miami Canal, she and Joe were struggling newlyweds. One spring Saturday in 1870, Joe's employer, Herr Imbrey, gave him something the Crowns could never buy for themselves: a pair of tickets to a concert by the Maennerchor, Cincinnati's oldest and finest singing society.

For the special evening Ilsa decorated her hair the only way she could afford, with a sprig of lily of the valley picked wild. After the concert, hand in hand, she and Joe walked to Weilert's on Vine Street and took a small table in the garden. Overhead, paper lanterns swayed in a strong breeze. On the white lattice behind her husband hung a lithographed portrait of Mozart. In the garden all was noise, merriment, punctuated by the dominant huff of the tuba in the little band.

Joe was struggling hard these days. He spent every free hour at the Young Men's Mercantile Library on Walnut, digging bits of knowledge from books on business and finance, stuffing his head with them in preparation for making his way on his own. Ilsa was wildly in love with her young husband. With his tenderness, his essential kindness, he had opened a whole world of physical intimacy to her. And she enjoyed it—which she would not have dared admit to her mother.

Still, one large cloud troubled their horizon. She and Joe had not yet conceived a child. They wanted one desperately. Several, in fact.

Joe ordered two lagers from one of the jocular waiters. The beer made him expansive, and a little garrulous. In the din of music and voices, he leaned forward, grasping her hand. "Is there any news?"

"Yes, but I'm afraid it's the same as last month." She averted her eyes during this. It was not proper to speak openly of such matters, even to your husband. "I don't know what's wrong with me, Joseph." She burst into tears.

"Nothing, nothing's wrong, dearest," he exclaimed, jumping up to comfort her and in the process knocking over his chair. Bending down, he hugged her. Nearby patrons stared. "We must try again. We'll succeed, I'm sure of it."

He righted his chair and sat down.

"We'll succeed because we must. Life and work amount to nothing without a family. Families are the glue of life, Ilsa. Our only immortality. The salvation of the world."

Ilsa apologized for her tears. But they were real, and there would be more before the long struggle ended and she conceived the child who was born and christened Joseph Junior in 1875, six long years after their marriage. No friend or physician could explain the delay, or why a similar problem didn't occur with Fritzi and Carl, both of whom were conceived and delivered with relative ease.

The long wait for a first child had a profound effect on the Crowns. It deepened their feelings toward their offspring. In its way it was responsible for the intensity of Joe's anger at his older son. The anger was the other side of the coin of love.

Ilsa's tears on the morning in June were salutary; they mitigated her feelings of failure, though they didn't banish them. She had failed Miss Addams, antagonized Joe and her neighbors, and behaved in a way she deemed both ineffectual and, at the crucial moment, cowardly. She dried her eyes and took refuge in her regular duties.

Ilsa followed the weekly routine handed down by generations of dogged and efficient *Hausfrauen*. Monday was washday. Tuesday, ironing. Wednesday was devoted to darning, an almost undetectable repair of a garment being another of those hallmarks of the superior homemaker. Thursday was theoretically a day of rest, in preparation for cleaning the whole house on Friday, and baking for the coming week on Saturday. This was Wednesday, so the late morning found her in the rocking chair in her sitting room, with her strongest spectacles, her marble and wooden darning eggs, her pincushions bristling with needles, her caddy of spindled threads of all colors, and her basket of undershirts, drawers, stockings resting on the floor beside her footstool.

At noon Joe telephoned from his office with a gruff apology. She apologized too. She asked about Joe Junior and Pauli. Yes, they had both reported for work as usual, there seemed to be no further signs of a revolt. Perhaps their son had calmed down, Joe said. Ilsa silently doubted it.

"However, I have issued an order banning any display of white ribbons on these premises. Fred Schildkraut will discharge any man who wears one."

"I see. Is that all?"

"Yes." A considerable pause; then he cleared his throat. In a voice full of strain, he closed the conversation with his usual, "I love you," and rang off.

The A.R.U. action against all Pullman cars had started on schedule on Tuesday, June 26. So far there had been no fights or demonstrations by unruly mobs. Eugene Debs continued to insist the boycott would be peaceful. But the newspaper owners and editors remained almost uniformly hostile. A *Tribune* lying on a stand near Ilsa's sewing table headlined Mr. Debs as THE CHAMPION OF ANARCHY, and mocked him in the subheadings:

"Six Days Shalt Thou Labor"—Bible.
"Not Unless I Say So"—Debs.

Hearing loud footsteps on the stairs, she laid aside the suit of Joe's summer underwear she'd been patching. Fritzi bounded in from school. Next week summer vacation began; she would be at home and underfoot all day.

"Mama, I want to recite something for you."

"What is it?"

"We have a new pledge to the flag. Miss Jacobs says it appeared in a magazine."

"Yes, but that was almost two years ago," Ilsa nodded.

"Starting in September we're to say it every morning." Fritzi appropriated Ilsa's footstool, jumped up on it, clapped a hand over her heart. "I pledge allegiance to my flag, and the republic for which it stands. One nation indivisible, with liberty and justice for all."

Ilsa responded with the required applause. Fritzi jumped off the stool and curtsied. Then she dug in the pocket of her pinafore.

"Look what I found, Mama. It's a note. I think it belongs to Paul. He must have dropped it."

She held out the crumpled notepaper, a delicate powder blue.

"If it's Pauli's, we should not read it."

"Oh yes, you must, Mama."

Humoring her, Ilsa smoothed the paper and tilted it toward the sunlit window. In recent years she'd begun to experience annoying difficulties with reading. The note was not too troublesome. The sweeping feminine hand was large, the message short.

> P.—
> Sunday as usual.
> "How I love thee!"
> J.

"Could the initial possibly stand for Juliette Vanderhoff, Fritzi?"

"I'm sure of it, Mama."

"He is still seeing her."

"Where do you think he goes every Sunday afternoon? It's just sickening."

Ilsa should have been amused by Fritzi's jealousy, but she wasn't. She knew Pauli had gone ice-skating with the Vanderhoffs' daughter during the winter, Joe

Junior had let it slip once several months ago. Ilsa had even discussed it with her husband:

"I pressed Joe Junior and he admitted Pauli is wildly infatuated. Do you think he will get over it?"

"Probably. He's young. He'll certainly get over it if Vanderhoff finds out. That stupid ass is liable to come after him with a horsewhip."

"Joe Junior has made Pauli aware of that. Pauli doesn't care. Young lovers think they're immortal."

"Yes, don't they," he murmured, taking her hand . . .

Ilsa returned the note to Fritzi. "It would be best if you put this back where you found it—no, I have a better idea. Drop it near Pauli's door. That way he'll be sure to find it, and no harm done."

"Well—all right." Fritzi didn't like the idea. She handled the note as if it had a bad odor, and left.

Outside, evening clouds—swift-moving, dark gray—began to hide the sun. Ilsa rocked slowly, meditating as the light faded. Soon she sat in darkness relieved only by the glow from street lamps. She prayed Pauli's youthful fling would work itself to a conventional end. If that should not be the case—if he was truly serious about the girl—the Vanderhoffs would intervene, and it would mean heartbreak for him. Heartbreak, or something worse . . .

42

Paul

IN THE PAPERS and in conversation, the Pullman boycott became the Pullman strike. Paul couldn't avoid reading or hearing about it. At Crown's they talked about little else.

After work every day, Joe Junior insisted they stop at Uhlich's Hall, which had become the headquarters for Debs and his men. The atmosphere was best characterized by the word bedlam. Union men argued and made announcements; journalists loitered and scribbled notes; breathless runners raced to the telegraph office every few minutes. When Paul asked an official what all these runners were doing, the man explained that the A.R.U. sent a hundred or more telegrams every day, to other locals of the brotherhood.

"We got to brace 'em up. Make sure they hold firm without resorting to violence. Gene won't tolerate that."

"Bet he will before it's over," Joe Junior said after the official left. "There's no other way to win."

It was at Uhlich's on the night of June 28, with the boycott two days old, that the cousins saw Mr. Debs storm out of the conference room where his executive committee sat in continuous session.

Debs's vest was buttoned, his cravat neatly tied; rolled-up sleeves were his only concession to the hot weather. His expression said there was bad news.

A couple of reporters left their table. Debs said to them, "I was just on the telephone. The G.M.A. has ordered that any man who won't handle Pullman cars will be fired."

"What are you going to do, Gene?"

"Stand fast. What else?"

After a few nights, the men at Uhlich's Hall began to recognize Paul and Joe Junior. And Debs took notice of them. One evening when runners were scarce, he asked the cousins for help; Joe Junior leaped at the chance to tear off to the telegraph office, shouting for Paul to wait where he was. An hour later he made a second run. The cousins got back to Michigan Avenue at half past ten. Aunt Ilsa was in the kitchen, in her nightrobe. She'd been anxious about them, and wanted to know where they'd been. Without hesitation, Joe Junior said, "No place special. Just walking. Talking. It's a nice evening."

Paul couldn't believe his cousin would lie so baldly to Aunt Ilsa. She seemed to accept the explanation, though not without a comment:

"I suppose it's all right, you are young men. Strong. But I hate to think of you in the streets with all this strike trouble. You must be careful."

"Sure, Mama," Joe Junior said, hugging her.

"Go to bed, please, tomorrow's a workday."

They hurried upstairs. Paul had trouble going to sleep. With that lie, it seemed to him that Joe Junior's relationship with his parents had taken a new turn; a bad one.

Next evening, a heavy rainstorm depleted the number of men at Uhlich's Hall. Joe Junior and Paul were there, wet but faithful. Joe Junior was sent to the telegraph office, and Paul sat wishing someone would ask him to run.

The hall was unusually quiet. One reporter dozed at his table. A man was chalking numbers on a large blackboard set on an easel.

EST. TONNAGE LAST WEEK—40,000
EST. TONNAGE THIS WEEK—10,000

The night before, when they'd seen the blackboard for the first time, an official had explained that many long-distance trains were made up with a combination of freight and Pullman cars. The blackboard tallied freight tonnage in and out of Chicago; the boycott was having an impact.

The door to a back room opened and Debs came out with another man. There was a savory aroma of frying bacon. The reporter woke up. "Anything new, Gene?"

Debs shook his head. The reporter collected his umbrella and shuffled out. Paul yawned but suddenly grew alert when Debs spoke to the other man in a familiar language. After a short conversation the man put on his cap, walked up the aisle and out. Paul realized he was the last person in the hall, though men were still meeting in the conference room; their shadows moved on its frosted glass window.

Debs waved to Paul and started for the back room. Curious, Paul jumped to his feet. *"Herr Debs? Sprechen Sie Deutsch?"*

"Ja, seit vielen Jahren. Ich hab' es von meinem Vater gelernt. Französisch auch. Er ist aus dem Elsass, am Rhein, gekommen." Debs had said he spoke French as well as German, his father had taught him. His father came from Alsace, near the Rhine River.

"You're German?" he asked, still in that language.

"Yes, sir."

"And that young chap I sent off with the wire—who is he?"

"My cousin. I am waiting for him."

"He should return soon. If you have an appetite, come on back, I'm frying some eggs and bacon." Paul followed him eagerly.

The room in back was an improvised bedroom and kitchen. There was a cot, and some books piled on a crate beside it. There were stacks of Chicago newspapers on the floor, and writing materials on a rickety table. On a small claw-footed stove in the corner, a bacon slab was sizzling and blackening in a skillet. Debs quickly lifted it out with a fork and dropped it on a plate. He took some eggs from a paper sack, broke them and pushed at the transparent whites with a wooden spoon.

"Clear those things from the table, make yourself comfortable," he said, still in German. He had a pleasant, gentlemanly way of speaking. He hardly seemed satanic, as the newspapers portrayed him. Paul took to him at once.

Debs gestured to the frying eggs. "My wife Kate is a superb cook, but I'm not so bad myself. I worked at the stove a lot, helping my mother, when I was a boy in Terre Haute. Do you cook?"

"No, sir."

"It's useful to know how. When you travel as much as I do, you get tired of hash house food. I always try to stay at a boardinghouse where I can use the stove. Two nights ago, when we had quite a crowd in here, I fixed steaks and asparagus with a vinaigrette sauce. I'm afraid eggs and bacon is the best I can do tonight."

"Anything will be fine, sir. I have worked all day, it's been a long time since our noon meal."

"Where do you work?"

"Crown's brewery. The owner is my uncle. My name is Paul Crown."

"Very pleased to meet you, brother Crown." Debs shook his hand. "I've drunk Crown lager a time or two. Excellent stuff. Are eggs over all right?"

"Certainly. If I may say so, you speak German very well."

"My father was never a wealthy man, but he was rich with learning. He came to America in 1849, penniless, and taught himself English. Every evening, he read great authors aloud to our family, often in the original language. I heard Goethe and Schiller in German and, in French, the greatest of them all, Victor Hugo. My middle name is Victor because my father admired him so."

"How did you come into this union work, may I ask?"

"Very gradually. I quit high school when I was fourteen and took a job in the Terre Haute railroad yards, cleaning grease off the trucks of freight engines. A year later I stepped into a cab as a fireman for the first time. I learned how it feels to work all night, freezing one minute, broiling the next, shoveling coal for very little money, with no protection against injury or sickness, no matter whose fault. I made a bad decision, leaving school so early. But work was a great teacher in its own way. So was Appleton's Encyclopedia; I read every word." Deftly he slid the eggs from the skillet onto plates, then halved the bacon with a knife. The aromas made Paul ravenous.

Debs put the plates on the table and served two cups of coffee. "My greatest, most profound teacher of all was Hugo. Have you read *Les Misérables?*"

"No, we didn't have French novels in our home in Germany."

"Too bad. I advise you to read that book. It's the story of a poor starving fellow who's hounded all of his life for stealing a loaf of bread. The story tells you everything you need to know about the way the world runs. That is, the way the world runs unless and until men stand up for their rights—justice. Victor Hugo is probably the reason I became a union organizer."

They heard the street door open and close, then footsteps in the main aisle. Paul went to the door. "Here we are, Joe."

Joe Junior was soaked, and astonished to find Paul sitting at a table sharing food with the leader of the Pullman strike. Debs formally introduced himself. Then he broke two more eggs and dropped them into the skillet with more bacon.

It was inevitable that they talk about the strike. Joe Junior said he supported it. So did Paul, though a little less fervently.

"Arbitration is the best way to improve the lot of workingmen," Debs said. "I've never been strong for strikes, but if a strike does become necessary—if the owners absolutely refuse to bargain—then the strike must be peaceful. No law-breaking, no bloodshed. Violence is always wrong. What's more, if you employ violence, you lose public sympathy. You endanger the very cause we're all working so hard to promote."

Paul looked at his cousin. Joe Junior kept his eyes on his plate.

When they left the hall, the rain had stopped. Joe Junior walked along the wet and deserted streets with his head down and his hands in his pockets.

Eating eggs and bacon cooked by Mr. Debs gave the strike new importance. Paul read every inch of newspaper copy, however slanted. He borrowed papers at the brewery, even picked them up from trash barrels.

The strike was biting deep into the commerce of Chicago. Freight tonnage continued to drop. The papers stepped up their cries for action against the strikers, and the General Managers Association maneuvered to promote it by putting forth a new argument. The railroads were public institutions. The A.R.U. was therefore attacking every American citizen.

Under the direction of the G.M.A. strike manager, Egan, rail lines began to make up their trains differently. Pullman cars were coupled to freight trains that didn't usually have them, or to short-run locals carrying commuters to the suburbs. Mail cars were coupled behind Pullman coaches, thereby proving the strike was interfering with government property.

Aided by Chicago's chief of police, Brennan, the G.M.A. continued to recruit special deputies to protect railroad property and move the mail. A lot of them were street toughs, but many were railroaders: engineers, firemen, brakemen.

The United States Attorney General, Richard Olney, made a hurried trip to Chicago to assess the situation. Uncle Joe spoke of it at supper:

"Olney's a Boston man. Very conversant with railroad law because he holds directorships on the Atchison, the CB & Q, and at least one other. He'll settle this."

Eugene Debs at Uhlich's Hall saw it otherwise:

"The G.M.A. is intriguing to bring Washington into it. It wants the boycott viewed as a confrontation between union men and the federal government."

The strategy worked. President Cleveland declared that the mails must go through. "If it takes every dollar in the Treasury, or every soldier in the U.S. Army, to deliver a postal card in Chicago, that postal card will be delivered."

Weather reminiscent of Turkish baths settled on the city. Days of white haze, Lake Michigan smooth and bright as a sheet of tin, no breeze stirring. Smells of garbage and sewage fouled even the best streets. Fights broke out at the brewery.

In the midst of this, on July 2, Monday, the government acted. Judge Peter Grosscup of the Chicago federal bench issued an injunction restraining Debs et al. from interfering with the mails, interstate commerce, and the conduct of business of any of twenty-three railroads the injunction named.

The cousins were at Uhlich's that night, when Debs emerged from the conference room to address a large crowd. Paul thought Mr. Debs looked thinner and noticeably worn.

"The gauntlet is down," Debs said to the hushed audience. "Never before in history has the process of injunction been perverted to apply to workingmen making an honest and lawful protest. This injunction denies us the right to picket. It specifies that any such activity is a felony. For all such alleged crimes, we are denied trial by jury. Judges will determine punishment. And what judge can you name who is friendly to our side?" For the first time, Paul heard rage in Debs's voice.

"Do you see the position into which they have maneuvered us? If we obey the injunction and await a court test of it, months from now, the strike is broken. If we don't obey, the law is broken."

A loud call from the gallery: "Then what's your next move?"

Debs wiped his forehead with a handkerchief. He managed a smile. "Why, we're going ahead. The executive board has voted to call a general strike of all railroad brotherhoods, everywhere."

Amid the tumult of cheers and foot-stamping, Paul and Joe Junior left the hall. Paul's cousin was jubilant. It was Paul's turn to be silent. Little by little, the strike seemed to be slipping toward the violence Mr. Debs so abhorred.

On the roof next day, the temperature must have been over ninety. The roof was deserted except for Paul. His forehead dripped sweat. The heat sapped him. His mood was sour.

He hadn't seen Julie for three Sundays in a row. The Vanderhoffs were home; he knew because he'd loitered outside the house one night. Had Julie been seized by another of her illnesses? She'd told him about them, but never in detail.

She only spoke of "blinding headaches" or "feeling gloomy for days." He was reminded of Aunt Lotta's moods. Julie said hers was an inescapable "female problem," common to all women. Was that true?

He had no appetite for the wurst and bread in his lunch sack. He unfolded a *Tribune*. The front-page headline leaped at him. **THE STRIKE IS WAR!**

A man came out the door at the head of the stairs. Sam Traub, the tax agent. He too had a newspaper. He spread one sheet on the coping next to Paul. Traub's cravat was tightly and carefully tied, held in place by his buttoned vest. There was a translucent coat of talc on his cheeks. He looked cool and dry and waxy.

Traub took a small apple from his pocket and cut it in half with his clasp knife. He munched the apple and leafed through the remaining pages of his paper.

"Here's another one gone 'count of this damn weather. Makes seven so far." He showed Paul.

MRS. ELSTREE SUCCUMBS

Arrangements Pending for Spouse of Department Store Heir

Her Sudden Death Attributed to Heat

Paul swabbed his neck and face with his bandana. He wasn't surprised that people were dying.

To the southeast he noticed a rising plume of black smoke. "What is that?"

"Bet you it's more freight cars. Six or seven burned at Blue Island last night."

"The strikers are burning freight cars?"

Traub gave him a sly smile. "Not exactly. The special deputies tip 'em over and torch 'em. Makes the strikers look bad. It's what the damn reds deserve."

"Oh, I don't think so, Mr. Traub."

"What do you know? You're a greenhorn, brand new to things in this country. I'd advise you to keep your nose out of it."

Paul gazed at the black and sinister banner of smoke. Bombs, fires, threats, special police—*mein Gott*, it was all going the way Cousin Joe predicted.

The strike is war, said the *Tribune*, and so it became. Copies of the injunction were nailed to telegraph poles all over the city. Federal marshals presented a copy to Debs, who accepted it calmly. Less calm were two thousand protesters who gathered for a mass meeting at the Blue Island yards of the Chicago, Rock Island & Pacific line. Arnold, the chief federal marshal, arrived with a squad of lawyers and deputies. He read the injunction aloud amid curses and catcalls, then ordered the crowd to disperse. The protesters refused, shouting threats. Rocks and bottles flew. Arnold and his men fled. On Independence Day, a Wednesday, four companies of the 15th Infantry from Fort Sheridan marched to the lake front and encamped. President Cleveland had answered the call for federal troops.

That night, mobs roamed. Almost fifty freight cars burned in the Illinois Central yards. Rail traffic was disrupted by switches thrown and signal lights changed. Trains were stoned by strikers protected by darkness.

General Nelson Miles arrived to command the U.S. troops. He established his headquarters at Michigan and Adams, in the Pullman Building. Business leaders and newspaper editorialists were relieved and happy.

At the brewery, Joe Crown had set aside a large room as a lounge and wash area for his men. Individual wooden lockers lined one wall. Since the start of the heat wave, Paul had kept a second blue work shirt in his locker; a shirt he could wear all day, and sweat out, and hang up to dry overnight.

Sometimes the room was crowded and noisy at the end of the day, sometimes not. At the close of work on Thursday, Paul pushed the door open and heard someone singing. He recognized Benno's voice before he saw him.

Benno stood at the wash trough. The shoulder straps of his overalls were down on his hips, and his work shirt was unbuttoned to the waist. He was swabbing his chest with a wet rag and singing to himself. There was no one else in the room.

Paul nodded to Benno and went to his locker. Benno stopped washing himself and grinned. "You don't look so happy, Mr. Pauli."

"It is hot as hell. I'm tired."

Paul opened his locker, pulled off his shirt, and began to dry himself with a towel.

From his locker Benno pulled a twist of wax paper. "Want a licorice?"

"No thank you, I am not hungry."

Benno shrugged, raised his hand to put the licorice back on the shelf. Somehow he dropped it. He bent over and something fell out of his shirt, landing on the sweating concrete between his heavy shoes.

A blued revolver with a white ribbon tied around the barrel.

They looked at each other. Benno shot a glance at the door. Men were coming. He snatched the revolver and jammed it under his shirt. He buttoned the three lower buttons and pulled up the straps of his overalls. He walked over to Paul. He was no longer smiling.

Benno laid a huge fist on Paul's shoulder.

"You seem like a nice boy, Pauli. Smart. So I'll go easy, just a warning." But he didn't go easy. He closed his fingers on Paul's shoulder until there was pain. In the hall the voices, the weary laughs and complaints of day's end were louder.

"You didn't see nothing in here. You say otherwise, to your uncle or anybody, you won't have no job for a long time. Maybe you won't have no arms and legs, either, *versteh?*"

"Yes," Paul said, as calmly as he could manage. He didn't want to cower in front of Benno Strauss. On the other hand, there was no reason to be stupid and antagonize someone so big and determined.

"Good. Smart," Benno said.

The outer door banged open. Half a dozen men trooped in. Benno was instantly transformed. He gave Paul a huge grin and a slap on the shoulder, as if they'd been bantering. Then he greeted the others. Paul quickly changed his shirt and left.

Warning or no, there was one person he had to tell. After supper he drew Cousin Joe into the garden. Above the trimmed shrubbery, the sky of the summer night glowed red. In a few words, Paul described the encounter with Benno. His cousin surprised him by saying:

"Yeah, I saw it too. He showed it to me. There are four others in the brewery carrying hideout pistols. Four that I know about."

"He *showed* you?"

"Right. He took me aside in the wagon yard day before yesterday. He said, 'You're a good soldier, ain't you? We can count on you, can't we?' "

"Count on you for what?"

"I don't know, he didn't explain, just looked at me and then walked off." Joe Junior stared at his hands. "I'm on Benno's side but I never thought there'd be guns inside the brewery after Pop threw them out."

"Benno gave me a warning, Joe. He didn't say it exactly, but I know what he meant. That he would hurt me or kill me if I—what is the word you use sometimes?"

"Ratted?"

"Yes. Ratted."

Joe Junior nodded. "He warned me too."

Paul shivered. "He had an ugly face. The strike is getting ugly. You were right about—" He couldn't seem to think of the English. *"Gewalt."*

"Violence?"

"Yes."

Joe Junior looked at him under the ruddy sky. They heard distant firecracker sounds which might have been gunfire. They heard a police wagon careen past the front of the house, horses galloping, gong ringing.

"Joe."

"What?"

"Can Benno count on you?"

His cousin's vivid blue eyes picked up reflections from the lighted windows of the mansion. "I don't know," he said again. "I think Pop's on the wrong side, Pullman's side, the side of the plutocrats. But I don't want to kill anybody."

"I don't either."

They sat on the stone bench in front of the praying peace angel. Their shoulders touched. Neither moved. The silence lengthened, betokening a shared fear.

43

Rosie

ON THE SUNDAY NIGHT before Judge Grosscup issued his injunction against Debs, Rosie's beau had left Pullman about half past eight, after eating supper with Rosie and Maritza. Tabor wasn't there. Another of his Sunday disappearances. To a saloon, Rosie assumed.

It had been a frustrating day. No time to be alone with Joey, nothing but some kissing and groping his crotch and going half crazy because she was all hot and wanting him more than usual.

Supper was the familiar poor fare. Bread four days old when her mother bought it, and a miserable thin stew made of beans, a couple of boiled potatoes, and a few chunks of lamb with a faint odor of spoilage. The stew, the hot airless rooms of their little house, the anxiety hanging like a fog in Pullman, put her in short temper, thinking of how, and how soon, she could escape from this God damned trap.

She needed singing lessons to train her voice. She had to find a man to pay for those. She needed a ticket to New York City. From the same man, or maybe another. After she met Joey Crown, she'd harbored some silly dreams of marrying him. They didn't last long. He didn't have money to pay for music lessons or a train ticket. He could barely afford a little bar of rose-scented soap.

She admired Joey in a lot of ways. He was brainy; read books she couldn't understand if she tried her hardest. Under her tutelage he'd become a skillful lover, ardent, but tender if the moment or her feelings required it; he never hurt her. Unfortunately some of his ideas were stupid. Who but Joey would turn down a chance to run a brewery, be rich and never worry about the next dime, or anything?

Tabor came in noisily, his cheeks sweaty and pink with heat. He was excited, which wasn't typical of him. Whatever had happened, he didn't look the same. He was almost the handsome father she remembered and worshiped from childhood. The father who took her rowing on the lake in a rented boat. Brought her corn-husk dolls or paper sacks of hard candy when he should have spent the money for a new cap to keep warm in the howling winds and blizzards of the savage Illinois winters. The father who'd always been eager to play games. Checkers, jacks, rummy, skat, with Mama joining in.

"Guess what, guess what! I got a job!"

Maritza rushed in from the parlor. "What did I hear? What are you saying? You already have a job, Tabor, you're just waiting to be called back."

"This is a special job, extra. Two dollars fifty cents a day. Look, it's okay. Before I took it I ran over to Castleberry's house."

Maritza put fists on her hips. "And what did your foreman say about it?"

"Why, he said it was just fine, the company would like it, it would look good on my record when I came back."

"What kind of job is it, Pop?" Rosie already had an ominous suspicion, based on things she'd heard around Pullman.

He patted the left pocket of his shirt. "Special deputy. I get my badge and gun tomorrow."

"You're scabbing?"

Tabor looked hurt. "Rosie honey, that's a nasty word. I'm going to help guard railroad property. Break this strike that's ruining things for all of us."

Rosie's mother twisted a soiled gray handkerchief in her raw-knuckled hands. "Tabor, you don't know anything about guns, you mustn't do it."

"Listen, it's a big honor."

"Papa, Papa—two dollars and fifty cents a day and a chance to get killed is no honor. Don't do it, don't make us all mad at you."

"Girl, mind your tongue."

"Listen to her," Maritza said. "Listen to me. I beg you, don't do this crazy thing."

"What the hell's wrong with all of you? We'll get some money in the house and it'll go good on my record, Castleberry said so."

"Pop, please listen. You know what I think—people should do whatever earns a dollar and to hell with anything else—"

"Roza!" her mother exclaimed.

"—but this time the money don't matter. Turn it down. Tell them no, it isn't worth the risk. This strike don't matter either. Who wins, who loses—it's all a game of marbles. You got to look out for yourself. Always. I don't want you hurt even a little, Papa."

"That's good of you, Rosie, you're a good and loving daughter, I appreciate it." Tabor's eyes had a shiny look, moist like a spaniel's.

"Then tell them no."

"Yes, Tabor, please," Maritza pleaded.

With a guilty look at his wife, then Rosie, Tabor said, "Can't. I signed the paper."

"Oh, Pop."

What a weak, wrongheaded man he was. She hated herself for loving him so completely, faults and all. Thank God a person had only one father in a lifetime.

44

Paul

SMOKE THICKENED in the skies over Chicago. Paul smelled it through the open windows of his room. He smelled it in the cars riding to and from work. Sometimes he even smelled it inside the brewery. At night he had trouble falling asleep because of the stench. It reminded him of Benno and his gun.

He would avoid trouble by obeying Benno's warning; keeping quiet. Cousin Joe's situation was more dangerous. He'd been marked as a confederate if Benno needed him. For Cousin Joe to defy his father with words and looks was one thing. An overt act was altogether different. His cousin understood this. He was tense, withdrawn; he no longer smiled or bantered with Paul.

Fifteen rail lines coming into Chicago were partially or wholly shut down. Stalls in the Water Street produce market had been empty for nearly two weeks. Lines of boxcars waited outside the city, their cargoes of grain and vegetables softening and putrefying. In the stockyards, carloads of meat stood on sidings. The meat turned gray and bred maggots and dripped a foul water from the boxcar doors. The rotten smell blew from the yards and mingled with the pervasive smoke.

Larger and angrier mobs were abroad every night. More soldiers were being called from Michigan and Iowa, Colorado and California, even though the governor had wired President Cleveland twice to demand withdrawal of federal troops. Altgeld asserted that only he had the authority to ask for soldiers, and he hadn't exercised it.

The President's reply to the governor was silence, an insulting rebuff; an assertion of national over state power.

More soldiers arrived. More deputy marshals took to the streets and rode the few trains still operating. Workers at the brewery talked uneasily of a phrase going around among soldiers and deputies. "Shoot at the dirty white ribbons."

Firemen and switchmen, telegraphers and engineers joined the strike without authorization of their brotherhoods. The G.M.A. announced that effective Saturday, July 7, armed militia would ride every mail train leaving the Union and Dearborn Street depots, and the depots of the I.C., Rock Island, and Northwestern lines. Every soldier would carry a hundred rounds of ammunition, to repel persons attempting to interfere with commerce.

Shoot at the dirty white ribbons . . .

On Friday afternoon before the latest G.M.A. decree was to take effect, Paul was called from the bottling house to his uncle's office. Uncle Joe was barricaded behind his usual pile of unfinished work. He looked small and tired. He was reading something on a ragged piece of heavy brown paper, a scowl on his face. He folded the paper and shoved it into a drawer. His smile of greeting was little more than a twitch of his lips.

"Paul, I have an errand for you. It really falls into Dolph Hix's department, but he isn't here, and neither are the other two sales agents. The task requires a touch of diplomacy."

"Sir?"

"*Diplomatie.*"

"Ah. Thank you."

"You can show me how you handle jobs that call for something more than a strong back. Office jobs, for instance."

Oh no, I am not going to replace Cousin Joe. He had to tell his uncle where his true interest lay. He'd done it once and Uncle Joe had dismissed it. He must try again. But not now.

"I assume you know what's meant by a red light district," his uncle said.

"*Ein Bordellviertel?* I do. There were many in Berlin."

"There are many here. I just learned that one of my accounts, the Canadian Gardens, has added a wine room upstairs. The words 'wine room' are code. A signal that customers may purchase not only beer but—well, you understand. I managed to get the owner of the Gardens on the telephone. He calls himself Toronto Bob. Every cheap crook and whoremaster in Chicago gives himself some sort of flashy name. When I accused Bob, he laughed and didn't deny anything. I told him I was suspending deliveries. I won't sell Crown's beer to an establishment that traffics in women. But I want my ornamental tap handles back."

He reached behind him to find one. Paul had seen them in taverns, and in the

Stube downstairs. Lovely and tapering, they were turned from solid walnut, painted with the Crown symbol, and lacquered. A ring of solid brass trimmed the end that attached to the tap.

"These are expensive. Three dollars twenty cents apiece. For that you can get three excellent pairs of shoes, with change left over. I want the tap handles from the Gardens, and I also want the sign outside. It's metal, but not so big that you can't carry it." Many breweries distributed signs without cost. Most were cut in the shape of a stein, brightly painted and lettered with the brewery's name.

"Here is the address. It's south of Van Buren on Clark Street, in Little Cheyenne. That's a disreputable area. Not as bad as the Bad Lands, south of Taylor, or, God forbid, the Levee. In those districts the police patrol in pairs. But Little Cheyenne is bad enough. I want you to be careful."

"I will, sir. But I roamed the bad sections of Berlin many times." And the west side of Chicago, where the gang had chased the cousins. "I can look after myself, Uncle."

Uncle Joe tilted back in his chair, giving him a long look.

"I believe that. I want to test my judgment."

As Paul went out, Uncle Joe opened a drawer, unfolded the note written on brown paper, and smoothed it on the desk blotter. The scowl was back on his face.

Uncle Joe hadn't exaggerated about Little Cheyenne, a section named for a wide-open railroad town in the West. A shadow seemed to lie on it; a shadow of poverty, and dirt, and dissolution.

Paul hurried along the plank sidewalk on Clark Street, among loitering bums and a few heavily painted women. The music of a melodeon dinned from a concert saloon. Nearly every establishment had something to do with selling spirits, unless it was a pawnshop.

A grizzled tout motioned to him from a doorway. "Come on into Candy Molly's, lad. Fifty cents for a good time, and a free peppermint stick too."

Paul shook his head, kept walking amid the human flotsam drifting on the sidewalks. No one bothered him. He was big now, sturdy, and he walked with a confident stride. He wasn't afraid of the inhabitants of Little Cheyenne, he was fascinated. He wished he had a camera to snap a few photographs.

Two blocks below Van Buren, over on the east side of the street, Paul spied the metal sign in front of the Canadian Gardens. Soot had darkened the painted golden beer and snowy foam, the familiar brewery emblem, and the large CROWN'S in bold red script. He crossed, noticing all at once that he was being followed by a boy of nine or ten. A boy with a vulpine face and ragged clothes. Paul took him for a pickpocket and glared at him. The boy sauntered away after making an obscene gesture.

Toronto Bob's Canadian Gardens was a large ground-floor room with a low ceiling, a long bar lit with trumpet-shaped electric fixtures, and tables scattered about on sawdust. Except for the reek of its spittoons, and the impoverished look of its few customers, it wasn't too unpleasant. At the rear, a weary-looking girl about Paul's age was escorting a fat man up a stairway.

Paul stopped at the near end of the bar. The barkeep was a one-eyed bantam of a fellow wearing a black patch. As Paul began explaining his errand, the barkeep interrupted him.

"I knew this was comin'; Bob tole me. You can get up on a ladder an' take the sign down yourself. As for the tap handles, you can see they're gone. I don't know where the hell they are, you'll have to speak to Bob. He ain't here."

"Can you tell me where to find him?"

"Jesus, you don't want much. Bob left five minutes ago. Said he was dropping his Kodak off at Rooney's, to see if Rooney could fix it. It jammed or something. You might catch him there."

Rooney? "Sir, please—where is this Rooney's?"

"End of the block and turn left. It's the shop two doors past Wampler's, the red light hotel."

The side street was narrower, dirtier, darker. Tenement buildings leaned in from both sides, as if about to fall. Paul looked up at a strip of sky, bright blue, with summer clouds. Somehow very little of the light penetrated down here.

He stepped over the remains of a dead cat. He felt someone was watching him, but there was no one in sight except a lone tout picking his teeth under a sign for Wampler's Hotel. Paul hurried by with a glance into the dingy lobby. A stout woman with blacking around her eyes beckoned.

He forgot the seedy surroundings the instant he saw the shop. Over a dusty show window hung a gaudy sign not yet weathered or dirtied. On a cream-colored ground, red circus lettering with a gilt shadow edge proclaimed:

ROONEY'S TEMPLE OF PHOTOGRAPHY

Beyond the flyspecked glass on a wrinkled drape of plum velvet lay several box cameras. One was a duplicate of the ruined Kodak he'd lost over the rail of the *Rheinland.* A small pedestal displayed four lenses. A placard offered USED CAMERAS, another PHOTOGRAPHIC PORTRAITS.

Excited, he looked deeper into the shop. It was dark save for a faint light in back. He went in. A small bell on a spring arm over the door jingled. There was a powerful aroma of chemicals.

"Coming, who is it?" There was a click; a weak electric globe in the ceiling lit up the shop. Paul almost clapped for joy. It was the same little man!

Cracker crumbs hung in his salt-and-pepper mustache. His thick lenses shone with reflections of the ceiling fixture. He wore a stained smock.

"Yes, can I help—? Why, stars! I know you, don't I?"

"You do, sir. We met at the Exposition. You showed me the machine of moving pictures. You explained how it worked."

"So I did, so I did." The little man snatched off his spectacles. Even unmagnified, his dark eyes were as penetrating, hypnotic as Paul remembered. "Gave you my card. You said you were interested, but you never came around."

"I did, sir. The shop was closed, they said you had moved." *For not paying the rent.* He recalled a cryptic reference to ponies. He still didn't understand it.

"Well, yes, I did, that's right," Rooney said quickly. "Wanted a better location. I have a lot of carriage trade, you know." A better location in Little Cheyenne? Carriage trade? Paul doubted it.

"Tell me, how did you track me down?"

"It is a happy accident." He explained.

"The barkeep told you straight, Bob Hopper was here. But that was ten minutes ago. I don't know where he went."

"I see. Then I suppose I had better go—"

"Here, wait. Since you're an enthusiast of the photographic art, I can give you a very favorable price on a camera. Care to look around? By the way, the name's Rooney. Wexford Rooney."

"I remember."

"What's yours?"

"Paul Crown."

"German." It wasn't a question.

"Yes."

"I'll call you Dutch."

There seemed to be nothing he could do to avoid that nickname.

"Let me show you around, Dutch."

Wexford Rooney, whom Paul judged to be in his middle fifties, never stopped talking during the next half hour. He moved with a funny stooped walk, as though years of hunching under the black camera cloth had put a permanent curve in his spine.

He proudly exhibited a long display case holding cameras, lenses, other apparatus Paul didn't recognize. Judging by the accumulated dust, no one had opened the case in some time. On the wall above hung a hand-lettered card.

> Secure the shadow ere
> The substance fade.
> Let Science imitate
> What Nature made.

At the center of the room stood a huge camera on a tall tripod, a black cloth draped over it. The barrel lens pointed toward a round velvet settee, an array of head clamps, three classical columns of varying height, a replica of a small footbridge. "I can offer you a wide choice of backgrounds if you'd care to have a portrait made," Rooney said. "Permit me to demonstrate." He shoved a stool near the back wall. Standing on it, he could just reach several ceiling rollers mounted parallel. He snatched at a ring and pulled one down. "Sylvan forest." Pulled another. "Majestic mountains." Another. "South Seas palm hut." Another. "A fashionable conservatory." The backdrops, painted on canvas, were crude and, Paul thought, uniformly bad.

Rooney hopped down, dry-washing his hands. "Very artistic, don't you think?" He didn't wait for an answer. He snapped a switch to light an electric bulb at the head of a narrow stair. "More space up there. I rent the whole building and sublet the second floor to a merchant who sells cheap novelties. A philistine. But he pays regularly, thank God. Third floor's another studio. With a huge skylight. Part of the roof's usable as an outdoor studio."

"Very fine, sir. Very splendid."

"Right," Rooney said, and snapped off the light. "Now you might like to see some of the pictures I made during the late unpleasantness. Come into the back and sit down."

Paul followed Rooney toward the rear. "I'm just having my supper. I know it's early, but my last portrait appointment canceled." Had there really been an appointment to cancel? It didn't matter. Paul had taken a liking to the odd little man, so pale and molelike.

Rooney led him into a small kitchen and eating area with a linoleum floor. The electric light from the ceiling was dim. On the table lay Rooney's meal: a bowl of tomato soup on which a skin had formed, two crackers, a cup of tea. Rooney reached around to snap off the electric light in the shop. "Saves a penny or two. Sit down, Dutch, please."

Paul took one of the two chairs. "Want a cup of tea?" While Rooney put a kettle on a gas ring, lit it and turned up the flame, Paul had a chance to look around. A flimsy curtain on a wire partially hid a cot in an alcove. A half-open door gave a glimpse of rectangular metal trays and large brown glass bottles on a worktable.

On a homemade shelf attached to the wall he noticed a sepia-tinted photograph of a pretty child posed in an idealized way, head tilted to one side, hands clasped and tucked under a round little chin. The child was three or four, with wistful dark eyes, plump cheeks, hair hanging to the shoulder in curly ringlets. Because of the sailor collar and tie, Paul decided the child was a boy. The oval picture frame was cheap yellow metal, rust-pitted. Unlike most of Rooney's possessions, it was free of dust.

Gravely, Rooney said, "It's my son, Wexford Junior. An only child. He died when he was four. A terrible accident. I was to blame."

"I am sorry, Mr. Rooney."

"Thank you." He gazed at the portrait. "Oh, I loved that little boy. How I looked forward to teaching him my profession." Paul sat very still. Rooney gave a sniff, and a toss of his head, like a dog trying to shake water off its coat.

The teakettle whistled. Rooney honked into a handkerchief and vigorously wiped his nose. It seemed to restore his spirits. He poured hot water into a cracked mug, then swished a corroded silver tea-leaf holder through it. He put the mug in front of Paul.

"Where are you from, Dutch?"

"Chicago now. But I came by train and boat from Berlin."

"Berlin, always heard it was a magnificent city. I was born in Charleston, South Carolina. A lot of Irish settled on our southeast coast, did you know that? Would you guess I was a Southerner? Of course not. Lost my accent years ago. I'm not even positive I'm Irish. I was an orphan. I went north at an early age. I had no connections, I wanted to learn a trade."

He rummaged in a cabinet, pulled out an album, brought it to the table. He opened it to a cardboard-mounted photograph, faded and brown, that showed him as a young boy. He was already thick-waisted. He was standing beside a closed wagon, shaking hands with an older man. The man was short and slightly built, neatly dressed in a cravat, duster, and straw hat. The man was in profile; he had a nose like a saber.

"That's me with my mentor, Mr. M. B. Brady. A genuine Irishman. Maybe not the finest photographer in the short history of the profession, but I count him the smartest. I started as his apprentice, sweeping the floor of his studio on Pennsylvania Avenue in Washington. He taught me everything. How to frame portraiture. How to handle glass plates in the dark. How to coat them with the collodion emulsion. How to get where you wanted to go when the military officers said no. He taught me everything except how to turn a penny. A number of us worked for him, taking the war photographs, and we're all forgotten except him. He allowed only one name on those pictures. Brady."

A fly walked around the rim of his bowl of soup. Rooney saw only the past. "I'll say this for Mr. Matthew. He had a vision. No, an obsession. He wanted to photograph what had never been photographed before. Battlefields. We went to the war zone in closed wagons like the one you see, equipped with everything—cameras, plates, drape cloths, chemicals. The soldiers couldn't imagine the purpose of such a vehicle, they called it Brady's What-Is-It Wagon. We worked with artillery shells bursting in the sky and dying men screaming in the hospital tents. Nobody had ever seen such pictures before. Here, look for yourself."

He showed Paul a horrific photograph of dead bodies piled in a trench and flowing over the top.

"Took that at Petersburg."

He showed the next, a startling, eerie image of gutted buildings, vacant windows, in a vista of rubble with no visible sign of human life. Black as obsidian gravestones, the buildings leaped out in contrast to a white sky.

"This is Richmond, after it burned and the Reb flags came down. You're looking at history, Dutch. A moment of human history preserved—frozen—for eternity." Paul's spine prickled. It was magic, but the real world too. This was drawing and painting with a camera. This was what he wanted to do with his life.

Rooney turned the page. The new picture was that of a youthful officer, stiffly seated with his campaign hat in his lap. "Oh, I remember this boy. Wanted a portrait for his sweetheart. A sniper killed him at Brandy Station, one week before his twenty-first birthday. The boy never gave me his sweetheart's address. I kept the plate, Brady didn't want it." He touched the innocent face. "He was a lovely brave young man—" He lifted his glasses and dashed something from his eyes.

He closed the album. "After the war, I went home afire with the power of photography. I settled on the coast below Charleston, little town of Beaufort. I married a young woman from there. Old family. Indigo, then rice, then cotton. Heavenly voice she had. Sang in the church choir. Wexford Junior was born. I opened a small studio. I loved the trade but there was no money in it. At least I couldn't find any. Then the tragedy occurred. The drowning. Alice blamed me, and rightfully. Things deteriorated. A few months after our son's funeral I knew we were finished. I packed a valise and told Alice I was leaving. She wept but she wasn't really hurt, she was glad it was over. I don't blame her. I paid too much attention to my trade, to light and composition, not enough to bankbooks. Or taking care of my little boy. I was and I remain an impractical man." He peered sideways from behind his spectacles. "We all have our demons. You're too young to know."

He drank some tea. Once again his spirits improved noticeably. He spoke of photography revolutionizing society:

"Think of a courtroom trial. Evidence presented clearly, graphically, for the jurymen to see. Goodbye to the lying, perjuring witness whose falsehoods send some poor wretch to the gallows. Photography is honest. Oh, it can be made to lie. But it must not."

He spoke of a journalist named Jacob Riis, in New York, who had published a book about slum conditions and illustrated it with his own flashlight pictures. *"How the Other Half Lives,* that's the name of it. I'd like to show you my copy but regrettably I had to hock it. In New York they're clearing slums, rewriting building codes, founding charitable societies because of Jacob Riis. Wasn't his text that did it, it was those photographs of starved whipped people staring out of rooms with dirt walls where they lived four and five to a bed." Paul could almost see the room.

"We talked about Edison and his moving pictures, didn't we? Now if you want to speak of revolutionary—that's revolutionary."

"I want to learn to take photographs, good ones like yours."

"Well, without false modesty I say you're looking at the best teacher in Chicago. Come around any free hour, if I'm not here I'll be back soon. I'll teach you to load the film, work the shutter, handle the chemicals—everything. I'll teach you the craft, and the art—why, I'd be delighted."

With a brimming heart, Paul said, "I would like that very much."

"Capital! I'll expect you in the near future. The very near future."

"Thank you. I have a job six days a week at my uncle's brewery. But I will find the time somehow. Now I really should be going."

"All right, but come back, Dutch. Please come back."

With that odd stooped walk, Rooney escorted him through the littered studio and saw him into the street with a wave. Paul watched Rooney through the dirty window as he shuffled to the back and yanked a curtain on rings, pulling it across to hide the sad little kitchen, and himself.

Never mind the poor surroundings; he was thrilled by the prospect of learning all that Mr. Wexford Rooney could teach. He had to leave the brewery, that was certain now. He needn't do it immediately, he could wait until he learned the fundamentals and Rooney said he was equipped to seek a job in the profession. Then he would break it to Uncle Joe as gently as possible. For the present, he'd share his exciting secret with Cousin Joe and Julie, but no one else.

Abruptly, he remembered why his uncle had sent him to Little Cheyenne. He couldn't recover the tap handles tonight, but he could certainly borrow a ladder and take down the Canadian Gardens sign. He pivoted around to head for Clark Street—

Stopped.

Motionless under the pale white globe of the red light hotel were four ragged figures. They barred the sidewalk from wall to curb. Two of the loungers were Paul's age; one was a mulatto with skin the color of a fancy yellow shoe, and the other an emaciated towhead. A third, he judged to be about twelve. The one nearest . . .

There wasn't any mistake. It was the boy with the vulpine face.

Waiting for him.

The four spread across the sidewalk. Above, Paul heard a woman. "Gonna be a show, Gert. Come watch." He saw two whores squeezed into a second-floor window.

The boy sidled toward him. "Not so cocky now, are you? Pretty fancy clothes you got there. Any money in the pockets?"

Paul's heart thumped. He shot a look backward. Rooney's was dark as a grave; no immediate help there.

Paul stepped off the curb into the gutter. The boy on the outside countered the move, blocking him again. Sewer water trickled around Paul's shoes. He could hear the whores chatting up above.

"I did not come here to look for trouble."

"Listen to him," said the mulatto. "Another God damn greenhorn off the boat."

"A Dutchman," the towhead said, marching up to him. "My granddad taught me about Dutchmen. He fought with Stonewall. Granddad said the Dutchmen at Chancellorsville ran away. Flying Dutchmen, Granddad called them. Ain't that funny?"

Paul tensed for a feint, intending to slam past them, knock down one or two if he could, and outrun the rest. The towhead's face reddened.

"Hey, you fucker. I said, ain't that funny?" He slapped Paul, then grabbed Paul's left ear and twisted. Paul punched his stomach.

Towhead staggered. "Stand clear, Davey, I'll take him," the mulatto said, pulling something from under his shirt.

Paul lowered his head and set his feet to hit again. But the mulatto was faster. His yellow fist swung in a long hard arc. Paul saw the length of pipe only a second before it smashed his head.

He gave a cry and slumped to his knees in the gutter. Water soaked his shoes, his pants, his shirt cuffs as he tried to brace himself. He heard a grunt from the mulatto; a rush of air. The pipe struck the back of his skull, smashed his jaw into the gutter, made him bite his tongue savagely. He tasted the blood gushing in his mouth, and slid forward in the gutter, prone, one hand groping for a hold on the slimy curbstone. That was all he remembered.

45

Joe Junior

ABOUT HALF PAST EIGHT that night, someone knocked at the door of Joe's room, startling him. He was lying down, still dressed, the room dark, watching the flicker and pulse of red light in the sky.

He went to the door. It was his mother. She seemed tense.

"So dark in here. That smoke is terrible. You should close the windows."

"Too hot, Mama."

"Your father wants to see you in the study."

He went downstairs feeling like a condemned man suddenly yanked from his cell and told that his sentence wasn't imprisonment after all, but immediate hanging. He was sweating when he knocked for permission to enter.

Only one lamp was on in the study, the desk lamp with its shade of green banker's glass. The windows were closed, as if that would shut out the reality of rioting and burning.

His father's face was drawn. Despite the heat he wore his vest and his detachable shirt cuffs too. He'd been late coming home; only Joe Junior, his mother, brother and sister had eaten together. Paul was missing for some reason.

"I have a serious question to ask you, Joseph. I expect and demand an honest answer. I could ask your cousin, but he isn't here. More pertinently, however, I ask you because you are my son."

Nervously: "Sure, Pop, ask."

His father reached to the shadowy desk. Between thumb and middle finger he showed a folded square of brown kraft paper.

"Today someone at the brewery put an anonymous note in my office. I believe I recognize the writing as Emil Tagg's. The note says Benno Strauss is carrying a pistol at Crown's. Which is expressly against my orders. If I asked Benno, he would lie. Emil bears him a grudge because Benno attacked him, so Emil isn't entirely reliable either. I am asking you. Have you seen any such weapon?"

Joe Junior's head rang. The floor under him seemed to tilt back and forth. Here was a line clearly drawn, and he had to retreat from it, or step over.

"Joe, I am waiting."

Good soldier . . . can I count on you? His head hurt. His father's posture changed, signaling his intention to stand.

"Young man, I order you to answer me."

Yes, God damn you, you order me, you order everybody . . .

"No, sir. I haven't seen anything like that."

"Why are you sweating?"

"It's hot as hades in here."

Joe Crown stared at his son for what might have been as much as a half minute. Then, curtly, he said, "All right, thank you, you may go."

In the entrance hall, Joe Junior grabbed the banister and rested his forehead on the cool smooth wood, eyes closed. His heart was hammering. He'd done it. Taken the step. Sworn his allegiance to the other side. He felt giddily proud of himself.

A half hour later, he heard the telephone bell downstairs. Someone answered on the second ring. Probably Manfred, who usually took all calls unless he was out of the house.

He went to the window and leaned on the sill, staring at the red sky. Had he done enough for Benno with his lie? Discharged his obligation? God, he hoped so. This was deep stuff; more dangerous than he'd ever dreamed.

Sounds from the stable caught his attention. He sat on the sill, holding the window frame with one hand while he leaned out. Stretching, he could just see the stable roof, and a portion of Nineteenth Street to the west. He watched the Crown landau wheel out of the stable, Nicky Speers on the box, popping his long whip. There was a flash of his father's silver goatee at the window, then the carriage was out of sight.

He ran to the hall and started downstairs. The telephone bell jingled again. He bumped into Fritzi coming upstairs in her white cotton nightgown, a book under her arm.

"Why did Pop go out? Something wrong at the brewery?"

"I don't know, but he was all excited. I heard him whispering to Mama, about Paul. I hope Paul isn't hurt or anything . . ."

Manfred appeared. "Mr. Joseph, the caller is asking for you. A young woman." The steward always made it evident that he disliked this kind of disruption of routine.

Joe Junior patted his sister—"Go on to bed"—and hurried to answer.

He wasn't ready for another shock. But he got one.

"Joey? 'S that you?"

"Rosie?" Her voice was faint and scratchy at the other end of the wire. The telephone he'd answered was located in the short service hall leading to the kitchen. The hall light was turned off. He kept his voice low. "Where are you?" The Jablonecs couldn't afford telephone service.

"Min Slocum's, her folks got the only phone on the street." He couldn't believe this was his Rosie, always so strong.

"You sound scared to death."

"I am. I'm scared to death for Pop."

"Why?"

"All hell's broke loose. Did you look at the sky? A neighbor told Ma there's hundreds of boxcars burning in South Chicago, the yards of the Panhandle line. People are running up and down, it's crazy. The worst is, Pop's going on duty tomorrow morning, right where they're expecting trouble."

"Going on duty? I don't understand what—"

"Scabbing! Pop's scabbing, he signed on to be one of the special deputies."

"Oh Jesus. Oh my God." He slumped against the wall. "Why in hell did he do that?"

"For the money, two and a half bucks a day. The Pullman bosses say it's all right, they say it shows loyalty."

"He's sold out his friends, for Christ's sake. He could get killed. Of all the stupid—"

"Joe Crown, I know all that, I don't need lectures and sermons, I need you. There's a repair train going out at ten o'clock, with soldiers and deputies to take it through. Pop's one of the deputies. The strike people are going to stop the train at the level crossing at Loomis and Forty-ninth. Pop's pretending he isn't scared but I know different. I love my pop, I have to be there to see he don't get hurt. But I don't want to go alone, please come with me."

"Rosie, it's a workday, I don't think I—"

"Joey, you son of a bitch, I never asked nothing of you before. I been good to you, Joey—" She was close to crying. "You can't weasel out, you got to help me this once."

He ran his palm down his sweating cheek.

"I'll be there, nine-thirty." He slammed the earpiece on its hook.

46

Paul

HE CAME BACK TO PAIN. He was lying on the floor, some kind of hard pallet. Eyes closed, he slid his tongue forward. His lower lip felt fat as a sausage. It hurt. So did his tongue. The flat metal taste of blood filled his mouth.

A man spoke. "He's waking up, Ella."

Paul tried to assess the extent of his injuries. His belly and ribs hurt, and the back and side of his head, where the pipe had struck. He remembered the second blow driving him into the gutter, but nothing else.

His right eyelid worked, his left didn't. "Wait, it's all caked with the blood," a woman said. He heard water slosh. A dripping cloth pressed against the closed lid. Tepid water trickled down his face. He could open both eyes.

Against a mottled brown sky he saw splashes of color, hundreds of them. Rose red, yellow, white, ultramarine, fiery orange. He blinked, and things fell into perspective. The brown was a water-marked wall in a dirty stale-smelling windowless tenement room. The colors were scraps of felt and silk in shoe boxes, lying on a table among packets of wires and a few finished artificial flowers.

"Lad, you're a sight," the man said. He was stout, with a pink cherubic face and curly white hair. His wife behind him was pale and lean as a straw. Paul heard children's voices.

The man crouched down beside Paul and held up a small framed mirror. Paul grimaced at the reflection. Purpled eyes. Huge lower lip. Brown blood still caked on his temple.

"They left you in the alley behind the hotel. I was out looking for work and I found you as I was coming home. It's raining hard." Paul heard it. "I brought you in. I am Marcus Mantville. This is my wife Ella."

"I'm Paul. Thank you." Every word was an effort. He tried to sit up. The top of his head throbbed. He touched it and felt more dried blood.

"Careful, you've a big laceration there," Mantville said. "You are German, am I right?"

"Yes, from the city of Berlin. I came here two years ago."

"Do you live nearby?" Mrs. Mantville asked.

"I live on Michigan Avenue with my uncle, Joseph Crown. I came down to Clark Street on an errand for him."

"Well, it's a vile neighborhood. We've been here six months, we've learned," Mantville said. "You shouldn't walk home in your condition. We have no telephone. Give me the address and I'll send my boy Judson to your uncle's, to fetch him."

They helped Paul to an outer room. It had one window opening on a large air shaft with similar windows on every side, below and above.

"I apologize for the poor quarters," Mantville said. His son Judson, eleven or twelve, had already left. Mrs. Mantville bade Paul sit at the deal table, which was the main piece of furniture, apart from an old sofa with the legs missing at one end. In a corner stood a rusty wood stove. In a wall niche above, a coal oil lamp gave feeble smoky light.

Paul glanced back to the windowless room. He saw four thin pallets of striped ticking. No beds. No toilet.

A brown-eyed girl of perhaps four stood at a respectful distance, shyly watching him. She held something in the crook of her elbow. "I am grateful to all of you," Paul said. "I'm sure my uncle will be here soon."

Mantville pulled up a chair and took from the table drawer a churchwarden pipe, which he packed and lit. The tobacco smoke improved the smell of the flat.

"Were you carrying any money?"

Paul felt his pockets. "About thirty cents in change, that's all."

"They took it, of course. Lord, I hate this sinful neighborhood. We had no choice but to move here, or a place like it, after they threw me out of Pullman."

"You worked at the factory?"

"Nine years. I thought it was a wonderful opportunity, else I wouldn't have come all the way from Philadelphia. I'm a cabinetmaker by trade." Mantville uttered a sad laugh. "I was. After I made my protest, I was discharged, and blacklisted. I can't get a job anywhere that's decent. So we do sweat work here." He pointed his pipe at the artificial flower materials in the next room.

"What did you protest?"

From the wall Mantville brought a small cheap picture frame. Under the dirty glass was a large, elaborately engraved check from the Pullman Palace Car Company. It was paid to M. Mantville, in the amount of four cents.

Paul handed it back. "I don't understand."

"That's my paycheck, lad. The paycheck that drove me to demand my rights." Mantville rubbed a finger over the glass. "Each job at Pullman is rated, with a fixed minimum and maximum wage per hour. A cabinetmaker was rated at seventeen to nineteen cents. The company also sets prices for individual piecework. A man is supposed to do enough piecework in one hour to earn within his hourly range. Not more, and not less. Our section, building new coachwork for the latest Pullmans, developed a team spirit and expertise that made us quite fast, even as we kept the quality right up to the mark. We began to make a penny more per hour. Then two. When we reached three pennies, it threw the bosses into a panic. The job rating was dropped to ten to twelve cents. Piece prices were dropped in proportion."

"That's terrible."

"Indeed yes. What you see here, the check I didn't cash because it was hardly worth it, was my pay for two weeks. Twelve days of ten hours each. My gross earnings under the reduced rates were nine dollars, eleven cents." Ella Mantville started to cry. She covered her eyes with her apron.

"Of course we lived in the town of Pullman then. The company deducted for rent, water, gas, even three dollars a year to use the library. What remained after two weeks of work is what you see. Four pennies. Don't think this was a rare check, checks like it were common. I've seen many for two pennies, even one. A lot of the lads framed them."

Cousin Joe had told Paul a lot that was bad about Pullman, but he'd failed to grasp the vicious reality behind the words. Words couldn't capture misery like this.

The little girl moved nearer. Shyly leaning against his leg, she offered something for his examination.

"See my dolly? It was my Christmas present. St. Nicholas brought it."

The doll was a rail spike. The doll's skirt was newspaper. The doll's hair was a few strands of old knitting wool. Paul's heart broke.

"It's a pretty doll," he said, touching it. Forgotten were his aches, his anger over the beating, the humiliation of being whipped physically; all that was left was outrage.

Like a tidal wave, something was rushing, moving in him. Joe Junior was right. *And the baker of Wuppertal . . . ?*

Uncle Joe was polite but gruff when he came up the unlit stairs of the tenement to find his nephew. He thanked the family, and shook Mr. Mantville's hand, but he didn't linger or make idle conversation. To Paul it seemed that his uncle's face had a look of strain. In the carriage, riding home through heavy rain, he asked about the tap handles and the sign.

"I couldn't find that fellow Toronto Bob to ask about the handles, Uncle. I was on my way back to the saloon to take down the sign when I was set upon. Please let me go back tomorrow, I want to finish what I began."

"No, I believe you did your best. Dolph Hix returns from the road in the morning, he'll take care of it."

Uncle Joe turned to watch the passing street. Terrible conflicting feelings warred within Paul. He could never repay Uncle Joe for all his kindnesses; the food, the shelter, the concern—even the misguided effort to educate him. At the same time, his uncle endorsed the actions of a man like Pullman who bled his workers and would even insult a man with a paycheck of four pennies. Four *pennies.* Paul wasn't a Benno Strauss, but now he could understand why men who were downtrodden and desperate talked of bombs as their only recourse.

"Paul." He started. "Are you hurting? You're very quiet."

"It's that family, Uncle. They were kind. They are good decent folk. They're starving. It isn't fair."

"Life isn't fair."

"All the man did—his only crime—was to speak up when the Pullman Company cut his pay."

"Oh, I expect there's more to it. Probably he was associating with the radical elements. The agitators."

"How can you say that, Uncle? You don't know."

"I have experience to guide me," Uncle Joe said, rather sharply. He began to twist the boar's tooth on his watch chain. Paul turned away, biting his lip as he gazed at lighted shop fronts passing in the rain.

Uncle Joe touched his arm. "I'll send around a sum of money to help them. A hundred dollars. I'll do it because they helped you. I don't have great sympathy for their plight, however."

"Sir—with respect—I think you should."

"See here, you really don't know a thing about it. Poor people usually live the sort of lives they earn, and deserve."

"I do not believe that."

Uncle Joe leaned on the head of his cane. "You are starting to sound like your cousin. It disappoints me, Paul. I gave you more credit."

Paul looked away again. The carriage lurched and bounced over a street railway track. Paul clenched his teeth. His bruised body hurt, but there was a worse inner pain. Neither he nor his uncle said anything else on the ride home.

Paul and Uncle Joe entered the house about half past nine. Paul convinced his aunt and uncle that he didn't need Dr. Plattweiler, but Aunt Ilsa decreed that he must rest at home at least one day, possibly two, before returning to work. Uncle Joe disappeared into his study without comment.

Paul threw his soiled clothes down the galvanized laundry chute. In the bathroom he washed his face with hot water, a painful process. He donned a robe over his nightshirt and sat while Aunt Ilsa dressed the cut on his scalp. His aunt wore her nightrobe and slippers. Her hair was in a single long braid.

He slipped under the duvet, feeling better. She patted him. "You must be starving, Pauli. Stay awake for a little, I will come back to remedy that."

She reappeared in a half hour with a large tray of wursts, hot bread and beer, then gave him a final hug and left.

He was drowsing when Joe Junior knocked softly and entered the room.

"I just got home. God, who decorated your mug that way?"

"It's quite a story, I'll tell you if you want. What have you been doing?"

Cousin Joe sat on the bed. "Just walking for a couple of hours. All hell's broken loose. Altgeld ordered out the militia today. Five regiments. In the morning there'll be fourteen thousand armed soldiers in the city. Nicky Speers was out too, he says the mayor's issued a proclamation banning assembly by 'riotous persons.' Listen, something else—important. I won't be at work tomorrow."

"Neither will I, your mother forbade it."

"I'm playing hooky. Not for fun, either. I'm doing something for Rosie. If anybody asks, tell them you don't know where I am. Which will be the truth, because I'm not telling you."

"Sure, Joe."

Joe Junior wiggled his fingers. "Now give. Who banged you up?"

Paul told it as quickly and concisely as he could. At the end, his cousin shook his head. "Christ on the cross. I've heard about those two- and four-cent checks. Never saw one, though."

"It changed my mind," Paul said. "Those poor people changed my mind. I am for the strike one hundred percent."

"You mean it? You're with the strikers no matter how Pop feels?"

"Yes. I won't deny it's hard to say so. Uncle Joe has been good and kind to me, I'm not angry with him. It's Pullman I'm against."

Blue eyes sparkling, Joe Junior threw his arms around Paul, hugged him, slapped his back. "Good for you, kid. Good for you!" Paul tried not to gasp or groan aloud in his cousin's rough embrace.

"We need white ribbons," he said. "If we can't wear them in this house, we can wear them other places."

Grinning, Joe Junior headed for the door. "I'll look for some. But remember— tomorrow you don't know where I've gone."

"Right, no idea," Paul nodded.

The door closed.

Feeling that the day had been a kind of watershed, Paul put out the light, rolled on his side and let drowsiness dull his physical pain. For the painful guilt induced by turning his back on Uncle Joe there was no remedy.

47

Joe Junior

ROSIE CLUTCHED his sweaty hand. "This way, I hear the train." He heard it too—the hoot of the whistle, the low steady chug of the locomotive. The tracks were a block ahead on Forty-ninth Street.

Initially Joe Junior and Rosie had missed each other for ten minutes, caught in the swirl of men and women and youngsters, maybe three hundred, four hundred, all converging on this one level crossing. The crowd raised clouds of saffron-colored dust from the street. It sifted into Joe Junior's hair and fell on Rosie's damp skin like a fine ladies' powder.

Around his left arm, above the elbow, he'd tied the white ribbon. He'd rescued it from his bureau drawer, where he'd hidden it. In the morning's excitement he could almost forget the way his father had humiliated him over the ribbon. He saw many more white ribbons here.

Near the tracks they hauled up short behind noisy men and women standing three and four deep. Already the crossing gates had been torn down, broken to kindling. Children waved pieces as souvenirs.

The crowd flowed onto the tracks. Joe Junior and Rosie were repeatedly jostled and shoved. He squinted to the right, north, the direction of downtown. He glimpsed blue-clad men from the Illinois National Guard riding the cowcatcher of the locomotive, which was about a block away, chugging slowly, squirting steam.

Guardsmen sat on the roof of the engine cab too, faces shadowed under their campaign hats, rifles on their knees. They were basically civilians, probably nervous. The United States had fought no war for almost thirty years.

"I wonder where Pop's at," Rosie said. She craned up on her toes. Her red and white gingham dress, faded from laundering, stuck to her in wet patches under her breasts and arms. A damp butterfly place marked the center of her back.

A Guard officer on the cowcatcher waved his hat at the mob. "Clear the track. We're authorized to fire if you don't clear the track."

A lanky boy threw a stick. "Fuck you, scab." The Guard officer batted it down before it hit him. The mob flowed along both sides of the train, screaming, "Scabs, scabs, dirty scabs."

The train chugged on toward the level crossing. The mob inevitably gave way before it. But men and women ran along both sides of the train, throwing stones, sticks, bottles. Rosie bobbed up and down on her toes. "Where are the marshals, Joey, do you see them?"

He pointed. "There, second car."

"Do you see Pop?"

"Not yet." It was hard to see anything clearly in the rising dust.

The train consisted of four gondolas and a caboose. The second gondola carried a huge swivel crane, rusty red, with a heavy chain and a great iron hook swinging from it. Most of the marshals were on this car; men in vests and derbies, pistols displayed prominently, tin badges winking. Joe Junior searched their faces, hunting Tabor. He caught his breath.

"I know that marshal. The one with something silver in his lapel. It's a damn delivery boy who stole some good china from our house." She paid no attention.

The gondola carrying the crane and the marshals squealed and creaked through the Forty-ninth Street level crossing. The delivery boy from Frankel's butcher shop wore an old derby, and he hadn't shaved in a while. He twirled his blued revolver like some Western pistoleer. His tin badge flashed and so did the silver object pinned to his lapel. Joe Junior identified it suddenly. "Godamighty, he's wearing somebody's silver soup spoon." At the brewery he'd heard that a lot of the deputy marshals were stealing what they could, wherever they could.

Straining on tiptoe while she held his arm for balance, Rosie still wasn't interested. The gondola passed; the delivery boy's eyes touched Joe Junior's and slid on, without recognition.

"There's Pop," Rosie cried suddenly, "there, on the next car." She jumped up and down, pointing. Behind the gondola with the crane came one with stakes along the sides to hold a load of rails. Tabor Jablonec and three other marshals were sitting on top of the rails. Tabor wore overalls. His tin badge was pinned to the bib.

"Oh God, Joey, he's all right. Pop. Papa! Over here." She yelled and waved. Tabor spied her as the car rolled through the crossing. He waved. He blew on his fist and polished his badge for her.

The last two gondolas went by, laden with crossties and kegs of spikes; and finally the caboose. Joe Junior felt an enormous relief.

Then, about half a block south, the wheels of the locomotive shrieked and grated on the rails and threw off sparks. The work train jerked and stopped. Rosie squeezed his hand so hard he thought she might break his little finger.

"What's wrong, is anything wrong?"

Through drifting dust, he saw another big knot of people flowing onto the tracks down about Fiftieth Street, blocking the train. "They're all around the engine, they aren't moving."

Both of them heard a Guard officer yell, "Out of the way or I'll give the order to shoot." Someone threw a green bottle that arced high and splintered against the forehead of a guardsman sitting on the cab roof. Blood spurted. The soldier fell backward and tumbled off the side of the cab. Joe and Rosie heard shouts and curses, as if the mob was attacking the wounded man.

People began to pound on the locomotive, the sides of the cars. Someone fired a round. Several guns went off, quick, smacking sounds, like giant firecrackers. Joe Junior flung his arm around Rosie, drew her close to protect her even as he silently cursed Tabor's stupidity. She beat his chest with her fist. Tears welled from her eyes. "Why'd he get mixed up in this, why?"

A dozen more rounds were fired. A man cried, "They're shooting innocent people!" A woman screamed.

"They hit Jebbie, they shot my boy!"

The mob went wild.

Men and women who had been harassing the marshals and guardsmen with nothing worse than oaths and a few sticks, grabbed at the nearest legs and yanked. Guardsmen fought to keep from falling off. The bravest in the mob tried to board the train. Joe Junior's heart hammered. People were shoving, shouting, screaming; rocks and bottles were flying again, and there were more of those firecracker noises.

"Rosie, come on, this isn't safe." He tugged her waist. The deputy marshals formed lines on both sides of the first two gondolas. Arms extended, teeth gritted against their own fear, they fired into the crowd.

People fell; there was more screaming. On the locomotive and back on the caboose, guardsmen were yelling orders no one could hear. One, and then several, and then all of them opened fire off both sides of the train, creating a deadly crossfire. Joe Junior saw at least three men fall, and two women.

Rosie tore away from him, shoving and kicking her way through the panicked mob. She was hysterical, screaming as though Tabor could hear her. "Pop, Pop, get down, hide yourself."

He ran after her. A man tried to gouge his eye with a thumb, for no apparent reason. Joe Junior seized the man's shirt, kicked him in the crotch, threw him out of the way. People were going crazy. Rosie was going crazy, her screams clear and shrill among all the others.

He jumped up on a broken crate beside the tracks, just long enough to spy Tabor Jablonec. Tabor was still on his feet on the gondola, white with fright. He discharged his pistol into the crowd while bullets from his own partisans buzzed around him. Joe Junior ran on, trying to catch Rosie. Just then he saw Tabor rise on the toes of his dusty shoes with a startled expression. Tabor dropped his revolver and seized his chest. Under his hand, in the middle of his overall bib, blood spread. He pitched off the stalled train, hit the gravel and rolled.

"Oh, Pop, oh my God, oh Jesus in heaven," Rosie screamed as she fought her way to the crumpled body. She knelt and dragged her father's head up into her lap.

Joe Junior reached her. She was weeping and frantically stroking Tabor's face. "Oh God, oh Jesus Christ, Papa, why did you have to get mixed up with the bastards?"

"Rosie," Joe Junior said, ducking down again as bullets buzzed. He touched the sweat-soaked back of her blouse. She ignored him, rubbing her father's arms and legs, as if trying to put life back into him.

He smelled the waste of Tabor's body then; Tabor's eyes were already closed. "Rosie, he's dead, leave him. We'll find a wagon and come back and—"

"I won't," she screamed. A bullet buzzed between them. Joe Junior flinched and averted his head but she didn't seem to notice. Desperate, he crouched down and struggled to get his arms under the vile-smelling corpse of Tabor Jablonec.

She realized what he was doing. *"No!"*

"Rosie, come on, we've got to get away."

The shout, its force, pierced her hysteria. She staggered along beside him as he half walked, half ran with Tabor's body in his arms. He went north, to Forty-ninth, away from the popping guns, the screams and lamentations of the wounded and bereaved. A block east on Forty-ninth he laid Tabor in the hot shade on the west side of a livery barn.

Rosie dropped to her knees again. Joe Junior stared at his palms. Bloody. Tabor's blood had leaked all over his shirt and even stained the white ribbon. Rosie's empty hand sought his.

"Why did he get mixed up with them, Joey?"

Joe Junior shook his head, his big blue eyes burning. "He shouldn't have done it. He should have known he was on the wrong side."

Losing control again, she leaped at him, scratching his face.

"Shut up, God damn you, I can say it, you can't, not you or nobody else. Get away from me with your damn preaching!"

"Rosie, I'm sorry. You need help to move him—"

"I don't need nothing from you. You and your loony ideas about right and wrong—who cares? Who gives a shit? Right and wrong don't buy shoes and clothes. You're just like he was that way, you'll never have two nickels to your name either. You'll probably get killed too. Get away."

"Rosie, I just want to help with—"

"Get away. Stay away. *God damn you, leave me alone, I don't ever want to see you!"*

He stared into her wild hate-filled eyes. He started to speak, but saw it was hopeless.

He walked away quickly, around the corner to the front of the livery, and in through the wide front door. On a chair tilted against the side of a stall, the stable hand sat reading a ten-cent Deadwood Dick novel.

"Come outside, hurry up. There's a girl whose father's been shot. She needs help."

The stable hand, a burly boy of fifteen with a humped back, gave him a dubious look. But he ran outside and around the corner anyway. Joe heard him exclaim, "Oh, miss—Lordy. How bad's he hurt?"

"He's *dead*, open your eyes, *look* at him!"

Joe Junior walked rapidly toward the east. Distantly, perhaps at the Fiftieth Street crossing, a single shot resounded. Then silence. Street dust drifted in the noonday light. The dust made his hair white as an old man's.

He doused his head and bathed his hands in a street trough for horses. He pulled his shirttail out for a towel. He didn't know whether to discard the bloodied shirt or keep it on. Either way he'd attract attention. He kept his shirt.

He walked all the way to Michigan and Twentieth, taking close to an hour. He knew that if he tried to board a car looking as he did, he'd be thrown off, or arrested. As it was, a hardware merchant saw him coming, dodged into his store and began cranking his telephone. A few blocks later, a foot patrolman stopped him. Joe Junior darted past, giving no explanation, and outran the patrolman only because he was middle-aged, with a sizable load of fat.

He crept into the warm, still house by the back way. In the kitchen Louise Volzenheim was shelling peas. She nearly fainted at the sight of him.

"Master Joe, what is all that blood?"

"There was an accident, my girl's father was killed. It's his blood."

Louise couldn't speak, it was too horrifying. With a numb feeling he climbed the stairs in the silent house. He ran water in the bathtub and soaked, cleaning the dried blood off his hands and arms.

He couldn't save his shirt. But he untied the blood-spotted white ribbon and carefully laid it on his bureau.

The moment his mother came home, he told her.

She clasped him to her breast and rocked him back and forth. "Joey, Joey, it could be you lying dead."

"But it isn't, it's Rosie's father. The dirty scabs killed him, and more besides. Ten, twenty, I don't know how many."

"We must send flowers for the poor man's funeral, it's the least we can do."

"I guess you're right," he said, feeling a curious sense of completion, a deadness. Rosie's screamed words of banishment would be in his head forever. "I won't be going to the funeral myself. I may never see her again."

"I don't understand."

"It doesn't matter, Mama, just let it go. Please?"

He told the story again at supper. His father insisted, after stating that he'd be docked two days' pay. One for the actual hours missed, the second for the act of truancy. Joe Junior was too exhausted to be angry.

Fritzi was agog as she listened to him. Carl too. Paul sat with both hands in his lap, saying nothing. At the end, Joe Junior could feel himself shaking a little. He glanced down at his palms. They were cleansed of blood, yet he saw stains. Always would . . .

"Joseph," his father said, smoothing a palm down over the point of his fine silver imperial, as if that way he could also smooth out some inner turmoil, "I hardly know where to begin to express my feelings about this matter."

Joe Junior's blue eyes seemed to enlarge, burning again.

"I am deeply shaken by the risk you took. I could have lost a beloved son. I suppose it was noble of you to try to aid that young woman. But she endangered herself recklessly, and you also. I am sorry for her father, though I never met him, or the young woman either. At least he died on the right side of the quarrel."

Joe Junior clenched his fists under the table. A vein in front of his left ear stood up in relief. His father saw. In a gentler voice, he said:

"I withdraw what I said a while ago. I won't dock your pay. You were wrong to leave work without permission, but I think you have absorbed enough punishment for one day."

Ilsa murmured, "Oh, thank you, Joe."

Joe Crown folded his napkin. "Please go to bed, son. Try to rest, put it out of your mind."

"I never will, Pop. Not as long as I live."

"That's rather theatrical."

"It's how I feel," Joe Junior said.

Their gazes locked. Redder in the cheeks, his voice low and strained, Joe Crown said, "You'll excuse me, I have work." He walked out of the dining room buttoning his coat.

"Come to my room later," Joe Junior whispered to Paul as they left the table a few minutes afterward.

"Rosie's through with me," Joe Junior said, closing the door behind Paul.

"That's bad, I am very sorry."

He tried to shrug it away. "I knew there wasn't any future with her, she told me often enough. She's after someone who can throw barrels of money at her."

There was a bleak silence, then Paul said softly, "They are terrible men, those soldiers and deputies."

"Murderers. Nobody in the crowd had anything but rocks and sticks." He walked to the bureau, and from the second drawer he pulled the bloody ribbon. "This is his blood on here."

"Martyr's blood," Paul said.

"That's right." Joe Junior rummaged through another drawer, and produced his clasp knife. He made a loop of the ribbon, and cut it in two.

"Here."

Paul laid the piece of stained ribbon on his left palm, and touched it with his right index finger. "Damn them. Damn them to hell." His eyes were full of glistening tears. For the first time that day, Joe Junior smiled.

48

Joe Crown

SOMETIMES, YEARS LATER, if he was in a dark mood, or hunting for simple answers, he would look back and blame Stead. William T. Stead, the English reformer, and his book, *If Christ Came to Chicago,* which Ilsa was reading that fateful Sunday night.

Of course, Stead was only the match. Joe's increasingly short temper was the fuse; his temper, and a mounting sense of pressure, encirclement. Events of that hot week of July 1894 were the powder that exploded and led to devastating consequences in the family.

It was a curious and unsettling Sunday to begin with. There was young Joe's brush with death at the level crossing; the papers reported fourteen fatalities and many more injured. The father of the Bohemian girl from Pullman was one of the dead.

All Sunday morning young Joe moved about the house silently with a strange blank look on his face. The boy was obviously feeling shock, and pain, so Joe said nothing provocative, hoping to promote a swift healing process. He did notice that Paul shadowed Joe Junior almost continually throughout the morning. They seemed inseparable.

Although Paul had failed to accomplish his mission in Little Cheyenne, Joe Crown realized he could hardly blame his nephew, given the attack by hooligans. And Paul was clearly a hero to his younger cousins. At Sunday dinner, Fritzi several times lauded Paul's "bravery." It seemed to embarrass him, and cause him to eat faster than ever. An hour later, Joe Crown walked by the open doors of the sitting room and heard Carl whistling and exclaiming over the story, which Paul was evidently retelling at Carl's request.

In the afternoon, Joe Junior left, saying he needed to walk. He was dressed more neatly than usual, and he advised his mother that he might be gone until supper. This wasn't his typical behavior. Joe supposed the shooting had chastened him. The change, though precipitated by a tragedy, was not unwelcome.

Paul and Carl went outside to play ball, giving him a chance to catch up on the newspapers. Every paper carried similar headlines.

THIRSTY FOR BLOOD!

Frenzied Mob Bent on Death and Destruction!

Anarchy Is Rampant!
Mobs Apply the Torch!—Flames Make Havoc!
Unparalleled Scenes of
Riot, Terror and Pillage!

He crushed the paper and flung it aside. The chaos and bloodshed were inspired by reds and their chief agent, Debs, there was no doubt in his mind. The Debs boycott menaced the orderly progress of commerce, and physically threatened all decent people who only wanted to get on with their daily lives. The troops ought to crack down harder; fill the jails with the strikers if necessary. He'd permit no such breakdown of discipline at Crown's.

His reaction to events in the city set him on edge. By the time he went to bed he was in a foul mood.

The house was again unbearably hot, and so was he. His nightshirt was white muslin with pearl buttons down the front, and collar and cuffs trimmed with piping of claret-colored silk. Though it was a lightweight garment, meant for summer, he felt as if he were wearing three fur overcoats.

Ilsa was worse off. Her muslin gown, cut in the Mother Hubbard style with enormous full-length balloon sleeves, had tight wristbands and a high collar trimmed with fine torchon lace. Ilsa was lying with her head against the bolster, reading. He noticed that it was Stead's book, which he'd written after his investigations of vice in the city. Published in February, the book had sold thousands of copies, and continued to sell. The mere sight of it was enough to make Joe crosser.

There was no breeze in the bedroom, only a soggy stickiness to the air. Uncomfortable and sweaty, he climbed into bed next to his wife. A moth flew frantically around the electric lamp at the bedside. In the clear globe, the filament blazed blindingly.

He pulled up the starched sheet. A few seconds later he kicked it off. He dragged the hem of his nightshirt up to where it just barely covered his private parts. From a side table he snatched a paper fan imprinted with the brewery's name and the Crown device. He fanned himself furiously. Ilsa gave him a worried glance and turned a page.

A moment later she said, "Here is something you might find interesting."

"Nothing written or spoken by that sanctimonious meddler interests me."

"My dear, you mustn't close your mind. Mr. Stead expresses some quite unexpected opinions on saloons."

"Oh?" he said, more sarcastically than he intended. "Does he want to blow them up instead of just padlocking them?"

"You're unfair. You haven't read so much as one word of—"

"Nor do I intend to. Will you please turn off the light so I can go to sleep?"

In her own way Ilsa was quite as stubborn as her husband. She propped the book on her stomach. "Not until I read you a paragraph from the chapter entitled 'Whisky and Politics.' Mr. Stead clearly distinguishes between family saloons and those he terms indecent."

"Ilsa, I'm not interested in the views of a man who condemns the way I make my living."

"Wait, he doesn't condemn—"

"I refuse to listen. Good night."

He rolled over, away from her.

He lay there tense for about a minute. Then came a dreaded signal; Ilsa closing the book with a gunshot snap.

"And I will not be hectored and dismissed like some servant, Joe Crown."

Something in him leaped like a racehorse at the bell. Something in him was eager to quarrel. He rolled back toward her. "Damn it to hell, woman—"

The argument, steadily more heated and incoherent, lasted twenty minutes. She fell asleep crying. He fell asleep on his right side, his back to her, scrupulously avoiding any contact as he lay there rigid with anger.

Next morning, when Dolph Hix returned to the office, Joe sent him to the Canadian Gardens. In an hour, Hix telephoned to say he had the sign, but the tap handles were gone. Toronto Bob professed to know nothing about it. "He probably destroyed them in retaliation for pulling our beer out."

Red-faced, Joe said, "Then just bring back the sign, no more delays." He slammed the earpiece on the hook.

At half past ten he was at work with his door closed. He tore up a third sheet of Crown Brewery stationery, threw it into the basket and pulled a fresh one from the desk drawer. He was struggling to write a note of apology to Ilsa, to accompany two dozen yellow roses he'd ordered from Eitel the florist, for delivery before the end of the day.

He inked his pen in the well. *My dear Ilsa—*

That was as far as he got. There was a loud knock; Stefan Zwick bounded into the office before Joe could say anything.

"Sir, I am very sorry to—"

"I told you, no interruptions!"

"I know, sir, but I felt I had to report a situation occurring outside."

Joe noticed a sheet of yellow foolscap in Zwick's hand. A sheet with names written on it.

"Tell me."

Stefan Zwick coughed and shifted from foot to foot in front of the desk. "Sir, we have—uh, a labor demonstration. A work stoppage."

"A *what?*"

"Stoppage, sir. Eleven men have walked off the job for one hour, in sympathy with the Pullman boycott. Schultheiss from the cooperage. Chester Amunnsen from—"

Joe's fist struck the desk. A pile of papers slipped off the edge, falling like limp white birds. "And Strauss? I'll wager he's at the head of it."

"Yes, sir, he does seem to be in charge. He's taken three other teamsters out with him. I have the complete list here." Zwick offered the yellow sheet.

"When they come back, give them notice."

"Sir, they haven't left the premises. They're gathered at the front gate."

Joe rushed to the window. He swore in German when he saw Benno and the others lounging around the fountain. The men were laughing and joshing as if on holiday. Each wore a white ribbon on his sleeve. Schultheiss the cooper struck a sulphur match on the buskin of King Gambrinus to light a cigar.

"The God damned effrontery. They're picketing on my property."

He dashed for the door. Benno Strauss had at last stepped over the line on which he'd scraped his toe insultingly for months. Joe stormed down the stairs and out through the *Bierstube*.

Mickelmeyer the headwaiter veered to intercept him in the open-air garden. Mickelmeyer looked boiled in his black swallowtail coat, cravat, white apron. A couple of the strikers saw Joe and stopped their chatter. Benno was seated on the street side of the fountain. He swished a hand in the water and continued to talk cheerily.

"I am glad you came down, Mr. Crown," Mickelmeyer whispered. "Those men will be a terrible interference with our noontime trade."

"Oh, no." Joe strode to the gate. "All of you get off the fountain!" He grabbed the nearest man, little Wenzel from the malthouse. He flung him sideways so violently, Wenzel almost struck his head on the brick wall flanking the gate.

Benno looked around. A slow smile; then he stood up, rubbing his palms on the legs of his coveralls. Joe looked for bulges that might reveal a hidden pistol. He saw none.

"Explain yourselves," he demanded. "Why did you walk off the job?"

Still with that infuriating smirk, Benno said, "I guess you got a pretty good idea, Mr. Crown. Some of the other trades, they're going out too. The bakers, a few butchers—all good Germans," he added, relishing the thrust.

A painful pressure was building in Joe's head. He heard men coming up behind him through the *Biergarten*. On the roof he saw workmen watching. He thought he recognized Joe Junior among them.

Wenzel made a great show of dusting and arranging his shabby coveralls. For a small man, he was courageously defiant. "We're putting you on notice, Mr. Crown. We're in full support of the railwaymen, and we'll stay out for one hour every day till King George Pullman surrenders."

"You are telling me this is a union action, then?"

Benno shook his head. "The United Brewery Workmen got no part in this. We organized it amongst ourselves."

"You *organized* it? It's damned anarchy," Joe said, rising on his toes. Even so, he was shorter than Benno, always at a disadvantage. "Get back to work or you're finished at Crown's, all of you."

That brought uneasy looks from some of them. Benno's expression grew grave.

"Threats ain't going to work this time, Mr. Crown."

"Don't mess with him, sir," someone else exclaimed. Sam Traub, the tax agent, was standing immediately behind Joe, with Fred Schildkraut. "Call the black maria. Picketing's a prison offense, the injunction says so."

"Fuck you, scab," Benno said. "We ain't picketing, just resting."

He sat down again.

The fountain splashed. Aloof, King Gambrinus gazed at white thunderheads gathering in the east. Benno crossed his ankles and folded his arms. Joe's face was by now scarlet.

"You're through, Strauss. I carried you too long. All of you are through. Discharged, immediately."

"If that's the way it's gonna be, you owe us wages for—"

"I owe you nothing. Get off my property."

At that moment a hack clattered up North Larrabee Street from the direction of downtown. Two businessmen stepped out. While one paid, the other eyed the scene of confrontation. The strikers had spread themselves on either side of the fountain, barring entrance to the beer garden.

"Stefan?" Joe said without looking around.

"Here, sir."

"You'd better telephone the precinct."

At the gate, Mickelmeyer said, "I refuse to wait that long." While Zwick ran into the brewery, the headwaiter strode forward and took hold of the nearest striker.

"Get out of the way of our patrons."

"Take your fucking hands off him," Benno shouted. The man Mickelmeyer was holding kicked him in the shins. Mickelmeyer roundhouse-punched him, spilling him into the fountain. Benno reached behind him, under his shirttail. A blued pistol glinted. A pistol with a soiled white ribbon tied to the barrel . . .

Joe went for the gun, clamping both hands on Benno's wrist. Benno smelled of rank sweat. His clenched teeth were inches from Joe's eyes. Benno was powerful as a maddened gorilla, but Joe had his own strength, pumped up by tenacity. Benno jerked his gun arm one way, then the other. Joe held on, though Benno was nearly wrenching his shoulders out of their sockets.

The worker in the fountain floundered and spat water. Traub pushed him back in and held his head under till Mickelmeyer dragged the tax agent away. The businessmen jumped back in the hack and waved the driver on. Through all this, Benno kept trying to free himself. When he couldn't, he kicked Joe's leg with his steel-toed work shoe. Joe swore, stumbled backward and fell.

Streams of sweat ran down Benno's bald skull. His nostrils were huge, his eyes dehumanized by wrath. He flung out his gun hand, aiming at Joe, who was flat on his rear on the brick walk. Joe stared into the black muzzle, visions of Mississippi flashing in his head . . .

Dizzy, breathless, Joe scrambled to his feet.

"Give it to me, Benno. You don't want murder added to your crimes."

"Uh-uh, Mr. Crown, you don't get this piece. And you better keep your distance, or God damn me, I'm gonna—"

He didn't finish, because Joe launched a looping right-hand punch into Benno's midsection, which was hard as a washboard. Benno swayed and yelled, "Dirty cocksucker!" Fred Schildkraut ran in with a bung starter which he whipped down on Benno's gun wrist. The gun fell into the fountain with a splash.

The workman named Schultheiss rushed to Benno's aid. Mickelmeyer knocked him back with one punch, pounded him to the sidewalk with a second. Wenzel and another striker leaped on Sam Traub and tore his coat. Joe felt drunk, wildly out of control; he threw another punch at the middle of Benno's face. Benno's nose wasn't as tough as his gut. It spouted blood, all over the snowy front of Joe's shirt.

Cupping both hands under the drip of blood and snot, Benno cursed him steadily and savagely while men on the roof clapped and cheered, for which side no one could tell.

Sam Traub opened a clasp knife and tried to slash another striker. "Sam, stop it," Joe shouted. A whistle pierced the noon heat. O'Doul, the foot policeman who patrolled the area, came lumbering down Larrabee as fast as his corpulence would allow. Though almost sixty, O'Doul was still tough and fairly agile in a fight. He drove two of the strikers off with whacks of his hickory club.

"Wagon's coming," Sam Traub cried. Joe heard the racing horses several blocks off, then the clattering bell. Benno didn't have to warn his comrades. They ran in both directions along Larrabee.

Benno lingered.

Joe grasped the rim of the fountain and leaned over, head down. His mussed hair dangled in front of his sweating forehead. His heart beat too fast.

"Crown." Angrier than Joe had ever seen him, Benno shook a bloodied finger. "You ain't heard the end of this, you capitalist shit."

He ran south, flicks of blood flying from his nose and speckling the sidewalk.

Joe reached into the fountain, grabbed the pistol and flung it. The gun sailed in an arc, landing in the street, shiny with diamond droplets of water. If Benno saw it at all, he didn't come back for it.

"Who belongs to that piece?" O'Doul demanded.

"Strauss," someone said.

"I'll be needing it for evidence." O'Doul stepped into the street and pocketed the pistol.

Joe pushed graying hair off his forehead. Straightened his necktie. Leaned over the fountain a second time, cupped both hands and dashed water on his face. Listening to the rising clangor of the bell, he stared at his distorted reflection. He despised the man he saw; the man responsible for the violence. Benno Strauss was anarchist trash, and Joe had allowed him to control matters until reason was abandoned, order destroyed. That the situation had required desperate measures didn't change his feelings. He felt defeated.

Defeated . . . by events that seemingly were out of control.

A wurst on black pumpernickel and a stein of cold Crown lager at his personal table under the linden tree calmed him a little. The police wagon picked up three of the fleeing strikers. "Sorry to say Strauss wasn't among 'em," O'Doul reported.

Joe thanked O'Doul and promised he'd be at the precinct house shortly to file charges. When the patrolman left, Joe asked Mickelmeyer to summon his clerk.

"Stefan, sit down." Zwick took a chair in the dappled shade of the linden. A lake breeze stirred the leaves and changed the shadow patterns on his face. His employer said, "We have a bad situation here. I'm sure Benno and the others will feel vindictive. I hope they realize reprisals will only bring them more grief. But we mustn't count on it. If we err, it must be on the side of caution. Change all the locks in the brewery."

"All, sir?"

"Every single one."

Zwick made a note on the little pocket pad he carried. He asked no further questions. Benno owned a full set of keys to the loading dock and connecting doors into the brewhouse and refrigerated storerooms. Joe Crown always trusted his men.

Zwick tapped his pad with the point of his pencil. "We should be able to accomplish this by Friday, sir."

"By six o'clock tonight, Stefan. Pay whatever it costs. But get it done. Get it done."

Two wagons from Lorenz Brothers, Locksmiths, arrived at half past one. What seemed like a regiment of rude and noisy men swarmed through Crown's, cutting new chain, snapping new padlocks, setting new bolts, testing new keys. A major part of the racket seemed concentrated outside Joe's office.

In the middle of the afternoon, the yellow roses arrived. Joe finally finished his note to Ilsa. Too short, and poorly phrased; the right words simply weren't there. After Zwick sent off the roses and the note with a teamster who'd stayed on the job, Joe called his clerk in again.

"I've had another thought. Tell George Hoch to buy a pistol of some sort. Tell him the company will pay for it."

George Hoch was the brewery's night watchman. He'd held the job for twelve years. He was thorough, attentive to his rounds, but he was, as Joe recalled, sixty-seven years old. In his entire career George had never dealt with any intruder more menacing than a rat or a youthful prankster. If there was trouble of a serious nature, Joe realized, he couldn't and shouldn't rely solely on George. He would have to hire an agency such as Pinkerton's. They could send a younger, tougher man to guard the premises at night. If necessary, more than one.

Shortly before the day shift went off duty, Joe asked Stefan Zwick to find his son and his nephew. In ten minutes they were standing before his desk. Both of them looked hot, tired, apprehensive.

"By now everyone knows what happened this morning. It was an unpleasant incident, but it's over. I am not asking for your opinions of the illegal walkout, I expect I already know them. I am asking each of you to give me a pledge. A pledge that you'll say nothing to Ilsa, or Carl and Fritzi. There is no need for them to worry, I want their feelings spared. You shouldn't have any trouble agreeing to that, either of you."

He let the words sink in, then said, "Paul?"

"I pledge."

Joe shifted his gaze to his son. His hand dropped to the boar's tooth on its chain. A little sharply, he said, "Joseph? Your answer?"

"I'll keep quiet." A second later he blurted, "For Mama's sake only."

"That's all I ask. Thank you both, you may go."

They walked out without looking at each other. When Paul shut the door, Joe propped both elbows on his desk and held his head and thought, *What next?*

49

Joe Junior

TRUDGING TO UHLICH'S HALL after work, Joe Junior said, "I wish the whole blasted brewery had walked out. I didn't know about it, I was up on the third floor of the brewhouse, puttying in a new window."

Paul shrugged. "Nobody told me either. I guess Benno doesn't know I'm with the strikers."

Joe Junior took his half of the bloody white ribbon from his shirt and tied it in a buttonhole. Paul pinned his with a safety pin. A strolling policeman scowled at them.

"We should have the courage to wear them all day, Paul."

"I know. But Mr. Schildkraut would take them, and report us. We still have to live in your father's house. I don't feel good about it, but that's how it is."

Joe Junior was silent awhile. He couldn't remember feeling so glum.

The strike wasn't the only reason. He missed Rosie. To lose her the way he had left a residue of mingled pain and humiliation.

On the Sunday after Tabor's death, he'd decided he should pay his condolences to the family. He had cleaned up and prepared himself mentally. He was standing at the car stop when he realized he was really going out to Pullman in hopes of seeing Rosie; hearing her say she hadn't meant a word.

But she had, and he knew it.

When the horsecar was still a block away, the bell had rung twice; the driver had seen him waiting on the corner. That was the moment Joe Junior realized the futility of what he was doing. He turned abruptly and left.

He'd spent the rest of the afternoon along the lake shore. Even walking briskly, with a clean onshore wind blowing over him, made him feel no better . . .

A lumber wagon with creaking axles passed the cousins, then a rattling hansom. Joe Junior said to Paul, "You know, Pop made it worse today. It was only supposed to be a stoppage, for an hour. To show solidarity. He turned it into a mean fight."

"You think Benno will hit back?"

"If he does, there'll be a real muss, bet on it."

He feared what might happen in the next few days or weeks. Events were rushing on toward some huge, unguessable conclusion. As he'd done many times since that Saturday, he pictured Tabor Jablonec falling, bleeding; he'd never seen a man die before. It was harrowing. He didn't want to watch anyone else die. He hoped Benno wouldn't instigate trouble. Wouldn't ask his question again.

"Can I count on you?"

□   □   □   □

At Uhlich's Hall, Gene Debs spoke to reporters about the violence.

"I haven't changed my position, I never will. A man who commits violence in any form, whether he's a member of our brotherhood or not, should be promptly arrested and punished and we should be the first to apprehend him. We must act as law-abiding citizens, or not at all."

With a weary air, he trudged off to the conference room and shut the door. Shadows of men passed back and forth on the frosted glass window. Joe and his cousin heard contentious voices. Nearer at hand, one of the reporters muttered to a colleague, "He's done for. The whole strike's done for. Just a matter of time."

The cousins left, dispirited.

It did seem to grow worse for the strikers. The A.F. of L. executive board refused to express solidarity with "Dictator Debs." A few more brewers and bakers walked out in sympathy, and then some cigar makers, but massive arrests of strikers on criminal charges rapidly weakened the resistance. Freight tonnage out of Chicago increased every day. Uhlich's Hall was broken into, desks rifled, papers seized. Gene Debs and three other union officials were arrested on indictments from a special grand jury. His father and Fred Schildkraut and Sam Traub and all those like them were elated.

At the end of work on the Thursday following Tabor's death, Joe Junior went to his locker for his cap. He wouldn't wait for Paul tonight; at noon his cousin had told him he had to stay in the brewhouse until a batch finished at eight o'clock. Joe Junior didn't care, there was no longer much point in running to Uhlich's Hall.

As he was shutting his locker he noticed a white paper lying at the very back of the shelf. A folded note. The hair on his neck started to prickle. He waited until two older men left the room, then quickly opened the note.

LAKE ST BRIDGE 5:30, <u>URGENT</u>

He'd never seen the big slanted handwriting before. But he knew whose it was. He slammed the locker and ran out, filled with dread.

He leaned on the railing of the Lake Street bridge spanning the north branch of the Chicago River. A smell of garbage and human waste rose off the water. In places the river sprouted thickets of masts; vessels tied up at piers of lumber yards or commercial warehouses.

A coal barge passed under the bridge, tooting its whistle. Silver-gray clouds alternately hid the sun and revealed it as a fiery white disk. Whenever the clouds thinned that way, the river's surface glowed with greasy rainbows.

Nearby, the clock tower of St. Meinrad's Catholic Church rang six. Joe Junior decided he'd wait ten more minutes. He gazed at the fouled river and watched a dead dog float by, trailing a streak of blood black as oil.

"Don't turn around. Don't use my name. Don't say nothing."

From the corner of his eye he saw Benno's profile, and a torn straw hat protecting his bald head. Benno settled his elbows on the rail like a friend stopping to chat. He was haggard, yellowish bags showing under his queer Oriental eyes.

"They changed the damn locks at the brewery."

"I know."

A squad of federal infantry went marching by, red-faced and perspiring in their blue cravanette uniforms. The sergeant shouted cadence.

Benno talked softly, with a genial smile. "It's time for you to be a good sojer like those boys. Time for you to help the cause."

Joe Junior's mouth dried out. "What do you want me to do?"

"Hey, just a little something easy. Find a certain key tomorrow. Sneak it out with you at quitting time. When it's dark, but before ten o'clock, unlock the door of the bottling house. Leave it open. That's all."

"What are you going to do?"

"Gonna show your pop that he can't fire honest workingmen just for standing up for trade union solidarity."

"Show him? How?"

Benno thumped the rail. "Propaganda of the deed. I said we'd strike a blow, nobody believed me. You din't believe me."

He remembered the Indiana dune, the dynamite blasting the shanty into the sky. He was trembling, but he had to speak. "I won't help you if it means hurting anybody. I won't be a party to murdering anyone. If you mean to plant a bomb where men are working, I just won't—"

"You can quit worrying, because we're gonna strike our blow where it won't hurt nobody, just wreck a lot of equipment. The bottling house—the pipes running to the brewhouse—at night, when it's shut down. Cost your old man plenty, but no lives lost, I don't want that neither. The coppers and sojers on my tail with a noose? Hell no."

Joe Junior digested that. It was bad, but not as bad as he'd feared it might be. "Can you promise me you won't try anything at the brewhouse?" The brewhouse had a shift working throughout the night.

"Sure, Joey. Swear to God." Benno held up his right hand.

"How will you do it?"

"You leave that to me. Part of it is, we got to make sure old George Hoch's on his rounds someplace else." He waited a moment. "What d'ya say, Joey?"

His stomach hurt. "I say it's hard, what you're asking is hard. The brewery is still my father's property."

"*Property.*" Benno blew a big gob of spit over the rail. "Bullshit. Property is the curse of the world."

"Maybe, but he's put his life into that place."

Benno's voice dropped. "You saying you ain't going to help us after all? Jesus, what a turn. You said you were with us. All along you said that. What are you, a liar? I thought you was a man, thinking for yourself. Nah. You're a baby."

"Damn it, Benno, don't say that."

"How else should I say it, Joey?" Benno answered with a sweet smile. "Have you got balls, or were you just fucking with us?"

Joe Junior rubbed his mouth with his knuckles. He saw his father's stern eyes. Saw Rosie covered with her father's blood.

Propaganda of the deed. He'd studied the literature; convinced himself it was the best way to deal with a rotten and unjust system, wasn't that true? He couldn't let consideration for his family's property paralyze him. He had to think of the importance of striking a blow, sending a signal to Joe Crown and all his plutocrat friends . . .

He could do it with no one getting hurt.

"Joey?"

"All right, yes."

Benno laughed. "Good. Knew we could count on you."

"Don't be so damn cheerful, I've got to figure out *how*."

"Sure, Joey, take your time."

Joe Junior watched a hog's carcass float by, turning slowly among a garnish of melon rinds. He rubbed his fingertips against his palms. "Mr. Schildkraut keeps spare keys on a board on his wall. Each key on its own hook. His office is never locked. I could get the key when he goes downstairs to the *Stube* for his dinner. He always goes right at noon, you can set a clock by it."

"Just don't get caught."

"You think I want to go to jail? No more than you do." He was a little calmer, thinking it out, convincing himself. "Don't worry. I'll have the door unlocked by ten."

Benno draped his arm across Joe Junior's shoulders. "You got the stuff after all."

He sneaked into the house and pleaded a bellyache so he wouldn't have to speak to anyone, eat supper, risk a show of guilt before the fact. He knew he wouldn't sleep that night and he didn't. Lying awake, he kept seeing images of his mother. It had to be done, sometimes men had to take a strong, even dangerous stand. He prayed to heaven she'd understand and forgive him if she ever found out.

The night was humid and still. As he brought the key to the lock, his hand shook. Sweat made the key slippery. It dropped and landed in the alley with a clink loud enough to be heard on the moon.

He darted looks up and down the alley that ran parallel with Larrabee Street, separating the bottling house and the main section of the brewery, where scattered lights shone. At the second floor front, a shadow passed between a window and a lamp. Mr. Schildkraut, working late again. Back here, where he skulked with the key, there were no lights at all.

Because he knew the daily routines of his father and Fred Schildkraut and most of the other men in the front office, it hadn't been hard to pinch the key while Schildkraut dined in the outdoor garden. He carried a brewer's book, as though he'd come into the office building on some work-related errand. Stefan Zwick appeared in the hall and bumped into him just seconds after he stole out of Schildkraut's office with the key. Joe greeted Zwick, waving the brewer's book, and hurried to the stairs.

At the door of the bottling house, he listened. All quiet. Old George Hoch, the watchman, had walked through this part of the brewery twenty minutes ago. He wouldn't return until his next circuit, around eleven. When old George came shuffling across the alley to inspect the rear buildings, Joe Junior hid behind some bales of straw in the carriage yard on the southwest corner of the property, beyond the bottling house. He found one buggy there, the horse with a feed bag on its muzzle. Schildkraut's horse and buggy.

The horse nickered as he was crawling behind the straw bales. Moments later, the watchman poked his head into the yard. Joe Junior reached for the stolen key in his pocket, clutching it so hard it cut his palm.

Old George withdrew from the yard and ambled away, humming . . .

Joe Junior took a firmer grip on the key and poked it into the keyhole. He experienced a fearful moment when it wouldn't turn. Then, with a click, the door unlocked.

Gaining confidence, he slipped around the corner, along the north wall of the building, until he was almost at the back. There he sat down to wait. He rested his head against the bricks and closed his eyes. It was too late for regret, or retreat.

He had to relieve himself. He tried not to think about it. With a start, he raised his head. Someone had hissed or whispered.

He clambered to his feet. Against the lights of the office building, he saw two men silhouetted in the alley. He could discern the curve of Benno's bald head. The other man was unrecognizable.

He called out softly, "All clear." Benno and the second man vanished into the bottling house. What were they using? Dynamite? An infernal machine? How long would it take to place it? Need he stay? Somehow he felt he should.

Pressure in his bladder worsened. He endured it as long as he could, then braced his left hand against the bricks and unbuttoned his pants. The stream sounded like a waterfall.

A grime-coated window to his left showed a faint light inside the bottling house. Perhaps they'd lit a candle to aid them.

Then he heard something that caused him to panic. Footsteps in the brick drive across the alley. This time the silhouette was that of a man in a summer boater, with a cane. The man was whistling "Daisy Belle," the bicycle song.

Schildkraut going home.

Would he see the dim orange light moving behind the window? Joe Junior wanted to throw himself in front of the window, hide it with his body . . .

Apparently the angle was wrong; Schildkraut didn't notice. He passed out of sight behind the bottling house, bound down the alley for the buggy park, whistling his tune. Joe Junior rested his forehead against the bricks. If this was the practice of anarchism, it was a very frightening business.

He caught his breath. The footsteps had stopped.

Rigid, he watched the corner of the building. Schildkraut reappeared. Perhaps his senses had belatedly registered some detail amiss. Schildkraut looked both ways, and back at the office building. Still visible in the alley, he raised his cane. Poked the door of the bottling house. It swung in, the hinge squealing.

Schildkraut jumped forward, disappearing. The firefly light went out. "Who is that?" Schildkraut called. "Come forward, show yourselves." Joe Junior ran toward the corner by the alley, arms pumping. Inside he heard others running, and Schildkraut continuing to call out. Then came sounds of a struggle and a strident voice he didn't recognize:

"Benno—the fuse!"

Joe reached the bottling house door. A huge roar and a sheet of flame blew him backward across the alley. A flying brick struck his forehead and everything went black.

Firelight and smoke. Screams and shouts. He opened his eyes.

The bottling house was in ruins, most of its north and east walls blown down. Bright flames were consuming conveyor and crowning equipment that was twisted like metal spaghetti.

A huge beam pinned his lower legs. A heap of brick and mortar chunks covered him nearly to his neck. Men raced back and forth between Joe and the blaze. They didn't even know he was there in the wreckage.

A round-shouldered man appeared against the leaping fire, waving a silvery pistol. It was old George, the watchman. "They were all trapped inside. They're dead. Mr. Schildkraut, Strauss, some other man. All dead. Oh my God, my God, my God."

50

Paul

THAT SAME FRIDAY NIGHT, weary, Paul went to bed soon after supper. Cousin Joe had been absent for the meal; no one seemed to know where he'd gone, and Uncle Joe was cross about it.

Paul tossed restlessly for a while, thinking of Julie. He was anxious to see her, to tell her of his incredible good fortune in finding Mr. Rooney again. He dozed off and had slept perhaps half an hour when he was jolted awake by a heavy weight crashing onto the bed in the dark.

"Carl! What the devil are you doing?"

"Something bad's happened. Papa left a while ago, and Mama's awake and upset. She won't say anything except that Papa got a call from the brewery. What's it mean?"

"How should I know? I have been sleeping. Ask your brother."

"He's still gone."

"This late?"

"Uh-huh. Paul, I'm scared." Carl Crown would be twelve years old in November. Physically he was a young ox, but this night his voice had the thin high-pitched sound of a boy half his age.

"I'm sure there's an explanation, nothing really wrong. You'd better go back to bed."

"Could I stay here for a while? I don't mind the dark. I'll be quiet."

"All right, if you'd feel better."

Carl sat in the corner chair, which creaked. Paul couldn't go back to sleep.

□ □ □ □

Sometime around midnight, a huge commotion erupted downstairs. Voices; heavy footfalls. Paul and his cousin ran into the hall to see people rushing up the stairs. First Nicky Speers, with Cousin Joe lying in his outstretched arms like a stricken Christ Paul had once seen in a Catholic Pietà. Cousin Joe's face was bloody, and gray dust coated his skin and hair and clothing. His left shoe was twisted at a bizarre angle.

Nicky hurried past, followed by Uncle Joe; the same dust covered his fine black suit. He didn't even look at Paul and Carl. Aunt Ilsa came next, wearing her nightrobe.

"Aunt Ilsa, what has happened?"

"A terrible accident at the brewery. Some sort of infernal device in the bottling house. Three men have been killed, and Joey was hurt, we don't know how badly yet. Please go to bed, both of you."

She hurried on. Paul and Carl stared at each other. The door of Cousin Joe's room closed.

The house was in an uproar for most of the night. Outsiders arrived. The first was Dr. Plattweiler, wearing a fine clawhammer coat but no cravat. Carrying his satchel, he stumbled up the stairs.

When the doctor left, Fritzi forced herself into Cousin Joe's room. Her mother put her out a minute later. She and Paul and Carl whispered in the hall. Yes, Cousin Joe was all right; just some bad scrapes and bruises and a wrenched ankle.

"But I've never seen Papa in such a rage. What did Joey do?"

No one knew the answer.

Two police detectives in suits and derbies arrived about half past one. Uncle Joe met with them in the study. They were gone by two, but fifteen minutes later a reporter from the *Tribune* rang the bell. When Manfred answered in his nightshirt and robe, the reporter managed to slip past him into the foyer. Uncle Joe ran from his study and wrestled the reporter out the front door, cursing him. Paul and Carl and Fritzi peered down from the second floor landing, utterly confounded.

"Whatever has happened," Paul said, "it must be a terrible thing."

He was up at half past six, to brew a cup of tea. Yawning, Louise Volzenheim came out of the pantry. "I have not packed a lunch. You're not to go to work today. Mr. Crown is shutting down all but essential operations."

Paul sank onto a stool. Manfred came in, belting his satin robe. Paul looked at the cook, then at the steward. "Can anyone tell me what happened?"

Louise looked away. Manfred spoke. "I'm not reticent about saying it. A building blew up. Two anarchists were killed. One was that vile fellow Strauss. Another victim was Mr. Crown's brewmaster. Master Joe unlocked the building for the bombers, or so Dr. Plattweiler confided before he left. I don't know whether he did it alone or in collusion with some of his radical friends."

He fixed an accusing eye on Paul.

□ □ □ □

About seven, Louise prepared a breakfast tray for Cousin Joe. Aunt Ilsa, still in her nightclothes, asked Paul to take it to him. His aunt moved and spoke in a dazed way. He had never known her to look so sad.

He climbed the stairs with the tray. Silver domes kept the sausages and bread warm. A white china pot spouted steam and the aroma of strong coffee. The few lights burning on the second floor cast soft pools on the carpet. After the commotion of the night, a dispiriting silence had settled on the house.

He pulled up short at his cousin's door; from inside came Uncle Joe's loud voice:

"I am not going to file charges against my own son and have the whole damned story dragged through the courts and press. But make no mistake. I hold you responsible for this atrocity. For Fred Schildkraut's death."

"Pop, I only unlocked the door. Mr. Schildkraut came along at the wrong time."

"I'm damned if you can shift the blame so easily."

Paul edged closer to the door, trying to keep the cutlery on the tray from rattling.

"Benno promised me no one would be hurt. He said he just wanted to damage some machinery. That's the God's truth . . ." Cousin Joe's voice trailed off, utterly lacking conviction.

"And you believed Benno? You *believed* a lawless lying red anarchist? *Christus bewahr uns!*" Christ save us. "I have read about dupes of the reds, but I never imagined I'd have one in my own family. How could you let yourself be seduced? Poisoned by that filthy lawless crowd?"

"*I didn't mean for anyone to die!*"

"But they did, you can't bring them back, and you can't escape the guilt, it's yours forever. May God forgive you. I can't."

Paul gasped when the door opened suddenly. Uncle Joe stormed out, his shirt collar hanging askew, two vest buttons in the wrong buttonholes—Paul had never seen him so disarrayed. Uncle Joe shouted at him.

"Have you been eavesdropping?"

"Sir, I was asked to bring this tray for—"

"Give it to me!"

"Sir, Joe is my friend, I would like to speak to—"

"I said leave this!" His uncle was shouting like a wild man. He grabbed the tray. Paul let go, but Uncle Joe didn't have a good grasp. With a huge crash of shattering dishes, clangs of silver domes falling, the contents of the tray splattered the wall. The broken china pot gurgled coffee onto the carpet.

Uncle Joe yanked the door shut behind him. "Stay out of there, I order you. After what he did, he's not to be visited, or entertained, by you or by anyone." He stormed down the stairs. "Manfred! Helga! Where are you?"

In his room, Paul determined to see his cousin no matter what his uncle said. He waited an hour, made sure the upper hall was clear, everyone else downstairs, then stole to the door of Joe Junior's bedroom. After a quick soft knock he slipped inside.

"Are you all right?"

"No bones broken. I'll make it. But Pop didn't believe my story that Benno promised no one would get hurt."

"I believe you."

"You're the only one." To Paul's astonishment, there were tears in his cousin's eyes. "Get out of here," Joe Junior whispered. "No need for two of us to be tarred and feathered."

More shocks were in store. Late in the afternoon, Paul picked up a note from the message stone at Vanderhoff's. Julie couldn't meet him the next afternoon. No explanation. Could it be another illness? Or woman's eternal affliction? Julie had once hinted that, when it came, she went to bed for one or two days, as expected of members of her sex.

The prospect of not seeing her depressed him even further. So did the Crown house when he returned. It had been transformed. It might have been *eine Aufbahrungshalle;* a funeral home. A three-foot black wreath with a large bow of black silk hung on the front door. Swags of black crepe covered the tops of picture frames and mirrors throughout the downstairs.

Abendessen was a ghastly affair. No one wanted the food Louise had cooked. Aunt Ilsa was red-eyed and drawn. Uncle Joe had a black armband on his shirt-sleeve. Carl and Fritzi wore them too. Uncle Joe spoke sharply to Paul.

"You will wear an armband like everyone else. Get it from Manfred. This household is in mourning for Friedrich Schildkraut. We pay no respects to the scum responsible for his murder."

Ilsa twisted her napkin. "May Joe Junior come down to eat?"

"He may not. Send his food up to him. I want him to sit in that room until he comes to a full appreciation of what he did. It isn't merely thousands of dollars of property destroyed, it's human life. He is—what do they call it in the courts? *Ein Teilnehmer.* An accessory."

"Oh, dear heaven—" She was on the point of tears again. "Joe, you can't mean that. He mustn't be penned up like an animal."

"Why not? He behaved like an animal, let him suffer like one. There is no way he can atone for the loss of a fine upstanding man like Fred, no way under God's blue sky. He is guilty. I have ordered Manfred to keep his door locked so he can contemplate that fact."

Paul was stupefied. Treat your own son like *ein Knastbruder?* A jailbird? If ever he hated his uncle, it was then.

He got his black armband from Manfred, who continued to look at him as though he were some kind of viper. Fritzi caught him in the back hall. "Come out in the garden, I'll tie it for you."

Outside the air was heavy, with mutters of summer thunder in the distance, and flickers of heat lightning. Fritzi looped the black band around his arm and knotted it. Suddenly she leaned close, her breath warm as she whispered:

"Joey needs to talk to you."

"Your father's locked him up."

"Talk through the door, after everyone's asleep."

More conspiracy. It alarmed him. But he couldn't abandon his cousin. "All right."

Fritzi kissed his cheek impulsively. "You are wonderful." He said goodnight and hurried from the dark garden.

About half past eleven he crept along the hall. His nightshirt brushed against his calves. The landing light cast a soft-edged circle on the carpet. Otherwise the upstairs was dark.

He listened for sounds of anyone stirring. All quiet. Reaching the door of his cousin's room, he whispered, "Ssst. Joe. Here's Paul."

He heard a muffled scraping as his cousin dragged himself to the door. "Is it safe to talk?"

Another swift look up and down the hall. "I think so."

"I'm going to leave, Paul."

"*What?* Cousin—"

"Don't argue with me. You think I'm going to stay here when my own father calls me a criminal?"

"He was upset, he surely didn't mean—"

"Oh yes he did. Yes, he did. I'm going to get out for good. You've got to help me."

"How can I? This door is locked. I don't know where to find the key."

"I'll leave by the window. You've got to put up a ladder. With this splint, I daren't risk a jump. There's a big ladder in the stable, hanging on pegs, opposite the stalls."

"I have seen it." He didn't want to be the cause of more trouble in the household. But he knew where his loyalty lay. Uncle Joe condemned Paul's cousin cruelly and unfairly . . .

"Paul? Will you do it?"

"Yes, of course."

"You'll have to fetch the ladder without Nicky seeing you. It may be hard."

Perhaps impossible. When Nicky was well, he often went to the taverns at night if he wasn't needed. But he was in bed this evening, in his partitioned loft above the stalls, stricken with a severe case of summer grippe. He might be laid up for several days. "I will think of something."

Of course, why not? Wasn't he *ein scharfsinniger Junge* from Berlin? What a bitter joke. His head was empty as a sieve.

"Do you know when they're burying Mr. Schildkraut?" Joe Junior asked.

"Tuesday morning. Crown's will be open only half a day Monday."

"That means there will probably be visitation at the funeral home tomorrow night, and Monday night too. I'll go Monday night. I'll get my bundle ready."

"Are you going far away?"

"To the end of the earth, that's how far I'd like to go. I don't want to hurt Mama, but Pop's forced it. He can take the blame this time."

The brewery closed at noon Monday. Paul rushed home and found Nicky hanging about in the kitchen, still sniffling and sneezing and feverish. It was unlikely that he would be driving tonight.

With this in mind Paul scouted the property. He loitered in the alley, then strolled around to the north side of the stable, studying a window in Nicky's quarters in the loft. Could the corner of Nineteenth and Michigan be seen from the window? He thought so. The plan became clear.

He pleaded a stomachache and didn't go to supper. He stayed in his room, trying to read a tale of a plucky messenger boy written by one Mr. Horatio Alger. He couldn't absorb three words. He paced up and down, lifting the lace curtain every few minutes. About seven, as a purple summer dusk was enveloping roof-tops to the east, he saw the landau leave the stable, turn the corner and speed north along the lighted avenue.

His aunt and uncle would be at the funeral home until perhaps nine o'clock. The journey back from Evanston would take at least a half hour. By nine it would be almost totally dark, but he must go then even if it was not. With dismay, he saw hundreds of sparkling stars in the heavens. He'd have preferred a cloudy night.

He left his room at ten minutes before nine. On the landing he bumped into Fritzi. Already in her nightdress, her hair falling loose around her shoulders, she was clasping a Scott novel to the scalloped lace and ribbons on her flat bosom.

"Where are you going, Paul?"

"Just for some air."

"Take me with you. I can't stand this place—all those black decorations—and Joey locked up. Wait two minutes, I'll put on my shoes and—"

"No, Fritzi, I want to walk by myself."

"But—"

"*By myself.*"

He ran down the stairs. From below, he looked back and saw Fritzi gripping the newel post with a small white hand. "Another time," he called softly. It didn't help. She turned her back and disappeared.

The downstairs was silent. Louise was away tonight. So was Mrs. Blenkers; she'd gone to visit her sister, who lived on the west side. He had carefully ascertained all this during the day.

He stole into the kitchen, dark now, but still fragrant with the smell of a spicy rabbit stew served for supper. A block of light slanted across the tiled floor from a door standing partially open. The door led to a small room adjoining the pantry. It served as a kind of sitting room for Manfred until he went off duty and retired to his quarters upstairs.

Paul took hold of the chopping block to steady himself and peeked in. Manfred sat on a wooden chair. His reading glasses had slipped down his nose. His chin rested on his chest. His newspaper had fallen on the floor. Paul wiped his upper lip and crept past the oblong of light.

From the garden he glimpsed a figure at the window of his cousin's room. He waved, then stepped through an opening in the hedge to the alley. Earlier, he'd collected twigs and rags and stuffed them in the bottom of an empty nail keg from the cellar, then filled the keg with kindling from the scrap wood pile. He'd hidden the keg under a cardboard box against the wall of the stable.

He lifted the box and reached behind the keg. His fingers closed on smooth glass. A small bottle he'd filled with kerosene, also from the cellar.

He uncorked the bottle, dumped the kerosene over the kindling and rags, and tossed the bottle in the fragrant grass without a sound. The night was full of humming rustling noises. The air smelled of summer leaves, the lake, the inevitable stinking fumes of Chicago's manufactories.

He carried the keg around the stable to Nineteenth Street and there looked toward Michigan. The dark chute of Nineteenth narrowed into the west. Above it a band of smoky orange still shone at the horizon.

Paul hurried toward the corner. There he set the keg on the curb under a rustling sycamore. From the window of the stable loft, Nicky Speers could see it —if only he would.

He broke the first two wooden matches trying to light them. He struck the third and tossed it into the keg. The kerosene flamed up with a whoosh. The light tinted the sycamore leaves as he ran back to the stable and threw himself against the wall near the alley.

He waited for any sound of response. There was none. Just when he thought he'd planned stupidly—failed—he heard the window go up. Nicky uttered an oath. A moment later he came pelting from the stable's front door in his night-shirt, carrying a bucket of water.

While Nicky ran to the burning keg, Paul darted into the alley and opened one of the stable's folding doors. He found the ladder, hauled it off its pegs. It was ten feet long and heavy. Thank God he had strong arms and shoulders. Even so, he was breathing hard by the time he reached the side of the house. Joe Junior already had his splinted leg over the sill.

"Watch out," he called, and tossed something. Paul dodged the bundle of belongings stuffed in a pillowcase tied with a bandana.

He positioned the ladder. Joe Junior worked around backward, holding tight to the window frame while he placed his unsplinted foot on the top rung. He climbed down one rung, another. On the corner, Nicky Speers shouted an alarm. Because of a tall hedge, Paul couldn't see him, only a ruddy glare. *Hurry,* he thought, steadying the ladder with both hands. Somewhere a door opened. Then, someone running . . .

Stepping down to the third rung from the bottom, Cousin Joe was first to spy him. "Look out. It's Manfred."

He came charging at them along the side of the house. Paul shouted, "Run, Joe," and leaped between Manfred and the ladder. Joe Junior hopped off the second rung, letting out a groan as he landed. "Run," Paul cried again, and threw himself against Manfred's legs. They tumbled in the dewy grass. Manfred's thrashing heel slammed Paul's jaw, and not by accident.

"Mr. Joseph!" Manfred shouted in a drillmaster's voice, as if that would stop everything. Prone in the grass, Paul saw his cousin's face as a white blur in the starlight. Joe Junior snatched up his bundle and fled to the alley, gone.

"You devil. You damned sneak!" Manfred hauled Paul to his feet. "What have you done?"

Manfred shook him. That was enough. Paul kicked his shin, then knocked his forearm down. "Let go of me, who the hell do you think you are?"

"Someone with more loyalty and honor than you." But Manfred stepped back and dropped his hands. He wiped them on the bib of his kitchen apron. Like so much else, it bore the coronet of Crown embroidered in dark thread.

"I was dozing, but I thought I heard someone in the kitchen. I should have known it was you. You've been acting suspiciously, it's been all over your face today." Manfred sneered. "You make a terrible criminal."

Nicky Speers appeared through a gap in the garden hedge. He was barefoot. "Bloody pranksters—hello, what's all this?"

Manfred ignored him. "Wait till Mr. Crown gets home," he said to Paul. "Wait till he hears what you've done."

Paul sat in the study awaiting the return of his aunt and uncle. Manfred had turned on lights and posted himself on a chair outside, like a jailer. Paul tried to stay calm.

Finally he heard a door close. Then voices, low at first, but quickly louder, one of them shearing off into a sobbing cry, as Aunt Ilsa ran upstairs.

The door was thrown open. Uncle Joe knew everything; it showed in his eyes, and the pinkness of his cheeks, and the diamonds of sweat in his beard.

Paul stood and squared his shoulders. He'd grown several inches taller than his uncle, but it hardly made a difference. In his anger, Uncle Joe was a Goliath.

"My son has run off, with your connivance and assistance—it's unbelievable. We gave you shelter, your aunt and I. We gave you the affection of a family. We encouraged you, saw to it that you had a good job, with a future. This is our repayment?"

"Sir—"

"Where is my son? Where has he gone?" Joe Crown's shout stirred ornamental glass pendants on a table lamp. They tinkled like fairy bells.

"Uncle Joe, I cannot tell you. He did not confide in me."

"Get to your room until I decide what's to be done. I should lock you up, too."

"As you locked him up? You drove him to what he did."

Something slipped in his uncle's head. *"Gott verdamm' dich!"* He slapped Paul across the face, full palm, making Paul's head snap to the side.

Paul recovered and drew a long, deep breath. He was white. "It won't be necessary to lock me up, Uncle. I will stay or leave, as you please."

He was convinced he had been absolutely right to aid his cousin. And yet he couldn't help feeling a traitor. How hateful that he wanted to cry like a child. He fought the feeling as he walked out of the study, past Manfred Blenkers standing with his arms folded, smiling.

51

Joe Junior

HE WENT TO PULLMAN after all, out of desperation.

The model town was back to normal. Though it was close to midnight, many lights showed in the rows of brick houses. Sounds drifted from windows. A man and woman laughing low, intimately. A baby fretting noisily, gasping shrieks of hunger. Someone playing a piano exercise. Someone's dog barking . . .

After several futile minutes on Rosie's doorstep, he hoisted his bundle and knocked at the house immediately adjoining. A short, slight man of middle years answered. He gripped the doorframe, blocking the entrance with a pugnacious stance. He wore a faded nightshirt and carpet slippers. From the color of his face, the pertness of his nose, Joe Junior suspected he was Irish.

"How do you do, sir," Joe Junior began.

"What is it you're wanting this time of night?"

"I'm a friend of the Jablonecs. Their place is shut up tight. No one answered my knock. Can you tell me where they are?"

"Gone. Evicted. This housing is for workers. After the mister was killed there were no workers in that family."

"And Rosie—she went with her mother?"

The man wrinkled his nose. "Nobody can say where that one went. A wild girl. Hard as they make 'em. She left the day after the funeral. Ran off. Mrs. Jablonec collapsed, the poor thing. You could hear her caterwauling at all hours. Say, lad, don't I know you?"

"Possibly, sir. Rosie was a friend, I sometimes came to call on Sundays."

"That's it. Well, you'll have to hunt far and wide to find her now. She never told her poor mother anything, so my Kitty says. One thing sure. That girl's headed for perdition. Can't tell you anything more."

"All right, sir, thank you."

The door shut. The light in the front room went out and Joe Junior was left in the looming shadow of the row houses. He hadn't harbored any great hope of Rosie's taking him back, but he'd thought she might offer him temporary refuge —let him lie low for a day or two, in case Pop put someone on his trail.

He gazed up at the sky, a thousand stars swimming in heat haze. The vastness, the loneliness paralyzed him. A distant train went whistling through the enormous night.

He fought his sadness, his sense of loss and isolation. His dread. He was strong; why should he fear what lay out there?

He picked up his bundle and tramped to the corner. There he halted to get his bearings. He chose a street running west. Somewhere a bell tolled midnight.

52

Pork

TWO BLACK TROTTERS pulled the handsome Studebaker carriage, one of four that Pork Vanderhoff owned. The driver stopped in front of the Crown brewery at a few minutes before 10 A.M. on Thursday, the second day following young Joe Crown's disappearance. Pork of course had no knowledge of that yet.

Pork stepped from carriage to curbstone with a heavy gasp and eyed with distaste a statue of some oafish Teutonic king at the center of a bubbling fountain. He had already put in three hours at his headquarters on South LaSalle Street; in the Vanderhoff packing empire the day began at 7 A.M. and continued until work was done, even if employees trudged home at midnight. As Pork often confided to his cronies, his success, built on drive and sweat, was a prize to be guarded and preserved, especially after generations of family failure in the same trade. "I don't love the money for itself, but I love what it stands for. And I love the game. The getting of it. Outfoxing, outdealing, outthinking the rest of them." In that respect—the worship of success—Pork shared something with the rich German brewer he'd come to see.

The sky promised another sunless but hot day. Pork shifted his leather portfolio from one hand to the other in order to examine his fingers. They were sooty from the carriage ride. Chicago's familiar pall of coal smoke stained the sky, just as Chicago soot stained skin and clothing.

Pork's huge paunchy body moved toward the gilt-lettered doors of the brewery offices like a whale in the sea of wringing-wet air. He didn't ask to see the proprietor. Rather, he stated that he would see him, at once. No, he had no appointment. A flunky ran upstairs, ran down again with Joe Crown's clerk, and in a few moments Pork was seated before the owner's desk.

He saw many things of which to disapprove. The German flag brazenly displayed. A desk bereft of a panel of bell buttons, which Pork considered the sign of a progressive industrial firm. Pork's LaSalle Street headquarters was elaborately wired with signal bells, each with a slightly different sound; he could summon one of his many underlings merely by pressing a particular button.

What he disapproved of most was the man staring at him with the sort of stare Pork could only deem unfriendly. He vowed to remain civil while he stated his case.

He was frankly shocked by Joe Crown's appearance. He remembered the brewer as robust, despite his relatively small frame. This morning he was shrunken; sapped, somehow. His face had a mealy and haggard cast. The damned anarchist bomb, no doubt.

"Hello, Joe. Thank you for consenting to see me. Sorry to hear about the disruption of your production—oh, and I believe there was loss of life also. Regrettable. At least the back of the strike is broken, and that devil Debs is facing prison. Have you read the latest freight tonnages?"

Joe Crown dropped his hand to his watch chain and rubbed some kind of animal tooth hanging there. "Yes."

The silence crashed. Pork squirmed in the chair. It was too small. All chairs were too small, except those specially built for him.

"Joe, you and I have not seen each other for some time—"

"That's true. You sold our restaurant excellent meats for several years. I've always regretted the incident that ended our relationship, though frankly I have never understood why it occurred. I do know that you subsequently blackballed me to keep me out of the Commercial Club. A friend told me the stated reason. Too foreign, you said. I sounded too German—I didn't speak good English. My English is as good as yours."

Pork's forced cordiality had already evaporated. "Sir, I'll tell you straight out. I am not accustomed to—"

"May I ask you to state your business?" Joe indicated an open window, through which came the racket of a steam drill and carpenters' hammers. "We are rebuilding the bottling house. We are under great strain here. So please come to the point. What do you want of me?"

I was right, he's detestable. Arrogant as always.

Pork unsnapped the catch on his portfolio. "This." He placed a folded sheet of notepaper on the desk.

Joe Crown picked it up and read it as Pork continued. "Written to my daughter Juliette by someone who is your ward, or at least a relative. Note that he wrote endearments at the bottom. In the German language."

Joe Crown handed the note back. He was pink with annoyance. Pork had scored a march; taken him by surprise. "How did you come by that note, may I ask?"

"A young man of my daughter's acquaintance, a fine chap named Strickland Welliver, chanced to see Juliette and your relative together in Lincoln Park. They have apparently been meeting secretly on Sundays. Welliver wrote me a letter about it. Due to the press of business it failed to come to my attention until this week. I immediately set a watch on Juliette, as well as on the grounds of my home located on Prairie Av—"

"I know where you live. Go on."

Pinpoint sweat drops glistened on Pork's dewlaps. "This person and my daughter have evidently worked out a system for sending and receiving private messages. The note was found under a stone at the rear of my property. One of my grooms spied on the young man as he trespassed to place it there."

Like a fine tragedian, Pork manipulated the moment. He reached for the note, a star sapphire big as a dime flashing on his little finger. He thrust the note into the portfolio, closed the brass latch, sat back. The visitor's chair creaked.

"I have ferreted out the boy's name. I forced Juliette to reveal it. Well, force is perhaps too strong. She gave me the name the moment I confronted her. She has lately displayed an uncharacteristic defiance—the result of the unwholesome influence of my sister-in-law, whom you don't know. I also place equal blame on this boy. Paul Crown."

"Paul is my nephew. He arrived in this country two years ago. I haven't been pleased with his behavior of late. That isn't the issue, however. What am I supposed to do about this revelation?"

"Order your nephew to stay away from Juliette. Cease and desist with these dirty little notes and clandestine meetings. How do I know what filth he's written in a foreign tongue?"

"Oh, it's nothing a high-minded man like yourself would object to, Vanderhoff. Quite romantic, actually."

"You're toying with me, sir. Now listen—you tell your nephew that I'll have him arrested and horsewhipped if he comes near my daughter once more. I won't have her tainted by association with some mongrel German immigrant."

"Vanderhoff, my nephew observed his seventeenth birthday last month. He has lived more or less independently for some years, and even though I have reservations about his character, he is more mature than many twice his age. I hold him responsible for his own actions. I'll not defend him or protect him. You may speak to him if you wish. He works here. In the malthouse at the moment. My clerk will be happy to direct you."

Damned insufferable kraut! Pork wouldn't tolerate it. "Sir, get this clear. I am not going to muck about in a dingy brewery, confronting a common workman on the subject of my daughter."

Crown shrugged. "Suit yourself. If you won't speak to Paul directly, I can't help you. Good morning."

"By God, Crown, you can't dismiss me like this!"

Joe Crown pushed himself up from his chair like some savage beast arising from slumber, and came around the desk. Blanching, Pork heaved to his feet and began to back away. His breathing was rapid, almost painful. A sharp chest pang made him wince.

"Get out, Vanderhoff. You made a fortune in a nasty trade and it turned you into a pompous ass. I don't like you, and I don't like your insulting language. Walk down those stairs before I throw you down."

To his everlasting shame and rage, Pork obeyed.

How right he was to hate Joe Crown, as he had ever since that fateful Sunday afternoon five years ago. It especially galled him that he'd liked Joe Crown when he was a customer—well, at least respected him despite his foreign birth. They were strongly alike in some ways. Both ambitious, dedicated businessmen, tough and canny and therefore successful.

Pork's wholesale division turned a fine profit purveying sausages and sliced meats to restaurants, including Crown's *Bierstube*. As a favor to a good customer, he supplied the same items at cost for the brewery's annual picnic in August. As a matter of good will, Pork always visited the picnic for an hour or two.

On the August afternoon in question, hellishly hot, Pork drank too much Crown lager in a short time, and was soon compelled to wobble to a stinking outhouse set up at the edge of the picnic grove. As he was relieving himself, he heard Joe Crown's voice through the thin wooden wall. Crown was chatting with someone, about his past:

"My first offer of an apprenticeship in Cincinnati was a good one but for one thing. My prospective employer was a butcher, who had a substantial packing operation on the side. Killing and selling the parts of dumb animals is a dirty, bloody business, Fred. I suppose I'm a hypocrite since I enjoy eating meat, and someone must supply it. But I don't consider it pleasant work, or clean, though I'd never say such a thing to a supplier like Mason Vanderhoff."

Pork stood with his forgotten member in hand, quaking with wrath.

"Brewing, now—brewing's a fine trade. When people drink beer they're happy. Brewing is also a good German occupation. That's why I decided to cut ice for much lower wages, in hopes of working myself into a brewery." Crown's voice was slowly fading. *"I absolutely did not want to be a butcher. They're held in low esteem in America and Germany too. Around the world, in fact."*

Pork couldn't tolerate it. He rushed outside, forgetting his open fly, and chased Crown, who was strolling arm in arm with a man he recognized as the brewmaster. Lurching into a sunny glade, Pork came at Crown from behind, seized his shoulder, and threw a punch.

Joe Crown defended himself. He felled Pork with one blow. Sat him on his rump in the dirt, a humiliation never to be forgotten or forgiven.

"I don't know what this is all about, Mason, but I don't take kindly to being attacked without warning. I trust I didn't hit you too hard. Let me help you up."

He reached down with his right hand. Pork spat in his palm.

They never did business again. In the autumn of that same year, Joe Crown's name came up for membership in the Commercial Club. Pork's vote kept him out.

Recalling the picnic always put Pork into a state. For most of the ride downtown, he kept yanking at his knotted cravat, fighting for breath in the hot interior of the carriage. The pain in his chest was gone, but not the other, deeper pain. Joe Crown's insulting words expressed a shameful truth. The truth that drove Pork on and on, to earn more, amass more, display more . . .

The Vanderhoffs had been among the pioneer settlers in the Connecticut colony. Several generations of Vanderhoff men had raised hogs, slaughtered them, and cured the hams, shoulders, and sides in the smokehouse of a farm in the woods above the fine little town of Darien. Some of Pork's earliest memories—perhaps he was four or five—consisted of images of the abattoir in the woods; the killing barn where his father worked.

Pork knew very well why the Joe Crowns of the world scorned the butchering and packing trades. Pork's own memories explained it: the ramshackle barn, the soil of its floor crusted over with dried blood and offal residue, the iridescent green flies and audacious rats that ran even in daylight. His first playthings were hog bones; Mama could afford no other toys.

When he started to school, he was already too stout. The Vanderhoff family ate poorly, so diet was not the cause; rather, something in his physical makeup.

The stench of the family trade was always on his clothes at school. That and the stigma attached to the trade kept him from having good friends. Within a short

time, his classmates gave him the nickname he never escaped; the name that
defined his bulk, and eventually his trade. Pork.

Although the killing barn was well hidden in the woods, it continually made its
presence known. Hook-beaked, leather-winged carrion birds were always roost-
ing and sailing above the trees. The little stream below the farm was fouled and
clogged by the blood and parts Pork's father regularly dumped. From time to
time irate selectmen from the town came to call, claiming that children who
drank the water downstream had fallen ill. Pork's father listened and did nothing.

Pork's father had lifelong pretensions to refinement which his son inherited.
He also had an impractical daydreamer's nature, and a propensity for failure, like
all the generations of Vanderhoffs before him. Pork sneered at daydreaming. "A
theory has no value at the bank," he liked to say.

In the carriage, Pork kept sinking into the hateful pool of remembrance. He
thought of his poor defeated mother, whom he'd loved devotedly. Once when he
was little he'd stood at her knee watching her put on her only pair of shoes. It
would never leave him, the sight of her dirty sock sticking from the burst toe of
the shoe, the plaintive sound of her voice. "When you grow up, you'll work hard
to buy Mama some nice shoes, won't you?"

"Oh yes, Mama," he'd wept. "Mason will work for you. For Mama. For Mama."

Like the Chicago tycoon slightly above him in reputation and riches, good old
Phil Armour, who boasted, "We use all the pig but the squeal," Pork Vanderhoff
had fled the hardscrabble region of the Northeast for a greater opportunity that
seemed to glimmer in the West of the young nation. Pork and his brother Israel
Washington Vanderhoff, six years his junior, first ran a packing operation on a
flatboat on the Ohio River. In that period Pork developed a curious and defensive
pride in his work. He liked to boast that he could cleave the skull of a prime hog
with an ax, and heave it into the boiling kettle for debristling, faster than any
other man or boy. He frequently won bets on it.

His emaciated brother I.W. turned out to be something of a genius with mathematics, money, and real estate. By age twenty-one he was also a confirmed
drunkard. During the Civil War, I.W. convinced his brother to sell mess pork
futures at forty dollars a barrel, anticipating a price drop at war's end. After
Appomattox the price went down to eighteen dollars a barrel. They had their first
clean killing.

The Vanderhoff brothers followed Phil Armour and Gus Swift to Chicago.
There they built their business, capitalizing on technological advancements that
could enrich packers smart enough to seize upon them. Armour was the leader in
this; the first to hang carcasses on hooks on a powered chain that moved them
speedily and efficiently through the plant. He pioneered the centralized shipping
of pork, mutton, and beef from a major rail hub. The German lager beer makers
installed refrigeration equipment well before the packers had it, and again, Armour the innovator seized the idea, recognizing a way to convert slaughtering
and packing from a seasonal to a year-round trade, not dependent on cold
weather or a supply of expensive purchased ice.

Pork Vanderhoff had walked in blood and animal brains since boyhood. He had
dumped thousands of tons of heads and feet and tankage in any available creek or

river. He had paid two dollars a cartload to subhuman drones who hauled the refuse away to the prairie and buried it. He'd encouraged his wayward brother into bouts of sobriety, seeing to it that he took the water cure at least once, and often twice, annually. He still relied on I.W.'s financial acumen and a natural charm that stood him in well with the wives of Manhattan bankers; I.W. had been forced to move to New York after a sordid and potentially violent sexual incident with a foreman's wife in Chicago.

As a result of the brothers' success Pork acquired not only wealth but an aristocratic wife from one of Kentucky's noblest families. He fathered a lovely daughter who would marry well and bear fine grandsons. He was respectable and well regarded by his fellow businessmen. He pleaded with his male friends not to call him Pork—Nell fairly raved when she heard the name spoken—but somehow it stuck, perpetuated by newspapers, his employees, and no doubt his own appearance.

Pork Vanderhoff controlled a veritable empire of processing and distribution. Enormous pens in Kansas City. Subsidiary plants for utilization of the by-products. America ate Vanderhoff hams and sausages, buttered its toast with oleomargarine with a base of Vanderhoff steam-rendered lard, took its Saturday night bath with soap made with Vanderhoff tallow, glued its wallpaper and furniture joints and envelope flaps with Big "V" Brand glues. Six thousand refrigerator cars shuttling between the Atlantic, the Pacific, and the Gulf bore the Big "V" insignia. Out of this success had come important friends, civic honors, memberships in exclusive clubs, status and standing in Chicago, the Republican Party, the nation.

He hadn't achieved all this so his daughter could marry some damned foreign upstart. He would separate Juliette from this pernicious influence forever.

He hit on the scheme the moment he emerged from the elevator. Gleeful, he stepped into his opulent paneled office, which predictably renewed his sense of strength and control.

Nell had chosen the dark teakwood furniture. In the corners, Wall Street and Board of Trade tickers juttered and spewed tapes. Opposite the desk, beside the door, a full-length likeness of I.W. surveyed the office from an ornate gilt frame. The portraitist had executed his commission wisely, removing the splotches from I.W.'s cheeks and reshaping the beetlike nose. It was a manly, no-nonsense picture of Republican rectitude.

Around the walls, spotted between large framed chromos of various Big "V" plants and marshaling yards, hung mounted heads of elk, boar, grizzly, none of which Pork had shot, or even hunted. He liked to imagine he had, though.

At his desk he examined messages and telegrams that had arrived since his departure for Crown's. Nothing urgent, and only one message that needed to be dealt with before the end of the day. This was a lengthy telegram from Mark Hanna of Ohio, once again promoting Bill McKinley for the Republican presidential nomination two years hence. Hanna requested a substantial donation to the party war chest to help counter the continuing agitations of the free silver crowd.

Pork decided to send a draft for two thousand. He was a confirmed gold bug.

He hated the free silver radicals. Only last week, over supper, he had told dour red-whiskered Phil Armour, "Those men will have to be dealt with as crushingly as the damned Southerners who rebelled against this country."

He stabbed a bell on the thirty-button panel at the right of his desk and heard it ring in the bullpen beyond the heavy carved door. He leaned back in his huge chair, more relaxed. He was vastly pleased with his solution to the problem of Juliette. Further, he knew how to implement it over her objections. The strategy had worked before, and would work again.

His chief clerk, Roswell, knocked and hurried in. "Mr. Vanderhoff," he murmured, his pencil poised, his pad ready, his mind blanked to receive its master's imprint.

"Steamship schedules," Pork barked. "New York to Europe, now until the end of the year. Get me anything you can on the resorts and spas, too. Only the finest. I want to make the arrangements at once. Perhaps yet today."

"A vacation, sir?" Scribbling, Roswell at the same time managed a sycophantic smile.

"That's right. Mrs. Vanderhoff and myself are taking Juliette across the water. It will be the start of my daughter's grand tour. I will bring Mrs. Vanderhoff home after a month or two, but Juliette may be abroad for as much as a year."

Pork was tense as he awaited the encounter with his daughter that same evening. He tap-tapped the thick yellow envelope on the blotter. The envelope bore the emblem of Thomas Cook's, and the address of its local office.

Pork's study at home was a smaller replica of his lair on LaSalle Street. The walls bore specimens from the taxidermist, including a splendid blue-water shark and a prettified, largely imaginary rendering of the old family place at Darien.

A sixteen-button bell panel was within easy reach on the wall behind him. It was no mere affectation. He regulated the household by means of those bells. Nell, with her delicate Southern sensibilities, had for more than a decade refused to utter a word to any of the servants except the chief steward. Hence the bells. The enjoyment of riches was not all pretzels and candy, Pork often said to himself.

The ticking clock showed half after eight. He'd already set up the fiction of an all-night card game—he loathed cards; it was I.W. who was a wizard at determining other people's hands sight unseen—and he would be leaving as soon as he concluded this interview. The thought of the person with whom he intended to spend the night made him reach under the desk and rub his crotch.

Well trained, Juliette knocked softly before she entered. Pork's heart brimmed at the sight of her. Despite her recent streak of rebellion, which he now understood, she was a lovely young woman, a daughter to delight any father. All the more reason to separate and protect her from the young foreign brute who surely intended to vandalize her body. Pork prayed the desecration had not already taken place.

"Julie, good evening." He beamed.

"Papa." She sat in the side chair, her smile, alas, more perfunctory than his.

Still, he kept up the front. "How fetching you look tonight. That's a new summer outfit."

"Thank you, Mama bought it for me." Her shirtwaist was a dusty pink, like autumn roses, with a tiny figure in it. A smart turn-down collar, plain white, set it off. The skirt was gray grenadine, the open-mesh leon weave allowing the matching pink lining of taffeta to show through most attractively.

Still, clothes didn't entirely make the girl. He noticed a nervous agitation of her fingertips where they rested on her knee. Unbecoming fatigue circles around her gray eyes, too. A thought struck him. He must check the latest listings of telephone and telegraph charges for the household. He didn't want his daughter communicating with that damned subversive Willis for advice.

From a humidor Pork extracted a Cuban cigar, tubular, green, eleven inches long. He fancied Cuban cigars. For that reason he'd given a thousand dollars to the Cuban freedom organization in New York. He didn't give a curse for its principles, he just didn't want all the finest cigars to be smoked by a lot of royalistic queers in a palace in Madrid.

Julie coughed delicately. Blasted female sex! Nell did the same thing when he enjoyed a cigar in her presence. He put the cigar in a crystal ashtray from which the smoke could rise straight up. With a sly-fox grin, he pushed the Cook's envelope across the desk.

"A present for you, my dear."

The envelope lay in the pool of light cast by his green-shaded banker's lamp. Julie's gray eyes darted to it. Of course she knew the significance of the name Cook's.

She said nothing. Pork announced his plan for their grand tour. It was part of his scheme to pretend to absolute ignorance of the trashy German boy.

When he finished, Julie said, "It sounds lovely, Papa. But I don't want to go away. Not for a year, or even a month. I have too many interests here."

Sparkling beads of sweat were collecting on Pork's dewlaps again. "What are they, pray?"

"Reading. My music—"

"My dear. English books are available on the Continent, I do believe. Pianofortes are not unknown in France, or Italy, or the Netherlands—why, those places are almost civilized, I hear."

More provocatively, he added, "They ice-skate and cycle over there, too."

He watched closely. She didn't bite at either of the hooks. First came a shake of her head; her thick black hair glinted like the wing of a raven in sunshine. Then:

"Papa, there is no other way to say this but straightforwardly. I won't go. I don't want every moment of my life planned for me."

"Juliette! That sounds ungrateful."

"I don't mean to be ungrateful. I appreciate the thought, the expense of what you have in mind. I just don't want to go to Europe right now." Her voice grew stronger. "I am grown, after all. Many girls are married and raising children at seventeen or eighteen. So I think I should have some say about the matter."

Pork's very soul rebelled. Women had no *say*. Why, he hadn't even mentioned the trip to Nell. She would fall in line, that was a given.

His sapphire ring glowed and glittered as his fat hand reached out to stroke the Cook's envelope. "Don't be so stubborn, Juliette. Read the material in here.

There's a tentative itinerary for the first ninety days. A description of the deluxe suite of staterooms I've already booked on the Cunard line's finest—"

"I'm sorry, Papa," she interrupted. "I won't go."

My God, this infatuation is deep, and dangerous. He'd presumed it could be disposed of quickly. Now he wasn't sure. He unsheathed the weapon he'd been saving.

"I will not relay your reaction to your mother just yet." Julie's gray eyes flashed with bitter comprehension. "Your mother very much wishes to take this trip. You know as well as I do what may result if you continue to balk. You know the precarious state of your mother's nerves. Do you want to be responsible for a collapse? Or, God forbid, something worse? If you deny her this, and something dire happens, it will all be on you."

With a soft cry, Julie bolted. She held the edge of the open door, as if about to faint. Her tear-streaked face showed above the puffed top of her sleeve as she looked back.

"That's so cruel."

"All on you," Pork repeated loudly. "On you."

She shut the door with a crash.

He leaned back, positively aghast at the little scene just concluded. Her "infatuation" deserved a much stronger label. It was an adolescent love-madness, of the kind parental guidebooks warned against. That nephew of Crown's must be a devil of a seducer.

Still, as his shock passed and he accustomed himself to realities he hadn't suspected before, he felt a little better. He had observed Juliette's pained and guilty look at the moment she left the room.

She was correct about her physical maturity; she had many of the traits of a woman five or ten years older. Inwardly, however, she was still immature, with all the turbulent emotions of girlhood. It was understandable that she might fall in love with someone completely unacceptable, and be whipsawed by her feelings for him.

At the same time, she had been strictly trained to revere and obey her parents. And to touch the quick of those filial emotions, he had drawn his sharpest knife. One set of emotions could be pitted successfully against the other. It had worked before. It would work again. He would be patient.

He rang the bell for his coach and was soon carried away up Prairie Avenue on a cresting wave of confidence.

Pork spent the night at a shabby cottage in the weedy wilds of Touhy Avenue. But the cheap surroundings were, in fact, as delightful as a Turkish harem because of the occupant of the cottage, an aspiring soubrette named Liza. Liza toured with Midwestern theatrical troupes of dubious reputation and accomplishment. He had once sneaked into McVicker's to see her when she had a minor role in a light comedy. She was a poor actress onstage. But she was a spectacular performer in bed.

The following morning, Friday, he went directly to LaSalle Street at a quarter of seven. His clerk Roswell greeted him on the threshold, looking frantic.

"You'd better go home immediately, Mr. Vanderhoff. Your wife is in hysterics."

Pork rushed to Prairie Avenue. He found Nell in her quilted robe, her hair standing up at all angles, ranting through the house. She fell on Pork and beat his chest with tiny fists.

"She's gone, I don't know where she is, her bed's still made, she must have left during the night, where is she, what's happened? My God, I'm in ruins, call Dr. Woodrow before I lose my mind."

53

Paul

PAUL HAD BEGUN to feel like a stranger in the Crown household. Uncle Joe and Aunt Ilsa were polite, but that was all. Paul could still hear suppressed wrath in his uncle's voice, and a deep, soul-searing sadness in Aunt Ilsa's.

The Tuesday night following Joe Junior's departure, Paul had worked up courage to speak to his aunt in her sewing room. He clumsily tendered his regret that Cousin Joe was gone and asked her forgiveness for the part he'd played. She said yes, it was her Christian duty to forgive him. But her words sounded empty. He couldn't blame her.

Fritzi was grieving. She didn't accuse him in any direct way, but neither did she chatter and joke with him. She seemed sorry for him, but she didn't seek him out as she had before. Carl gloomed about the house, but he appeared to be the least affected. Maybe he wasn't old enough to understand fully what had happened. Maybe he had an innocent belief that his brother would soon come trooping home. It was evident to Paul that no one else believed it.

At work he spoke only when necessary. In every spare moment he read newspapers. Not so much for information as for distraction.

The Chicago strike was broken. Railway workers who had supported the Debs boycott by deed or word were finding severance slips in their pay envelopes. Withdrawal of the federal troops had begun; the soldiers were boarding cars for California, where labor unrest had broken out in Sacramento and Oakland. The following Monday, Eugene Debs was to go before a judge for a hearing on charges of contempt filed after he ignored the injunction. Debs had retained a shrewd and pugnacious lawyer named Clarence Darrow, an Ohioan who had come to the big city some years ago. It was something of a scandal when Mr. Darrow resigned an excellent position as general counsel of the Chicago & Northwestern Railroad to defend a rabble-rouser routinely characterized by editorial writers as "an utter madman," "known syphilitic," or "a felon richly deserving of the hemp." But then Darrow wasn't a typical career-minded lawyer, Paul deduced. Some of his inflammatory statements were quoted. "The country is ruled by business, and business is legal fraud." "Justice is like the amount of sugar or salt on your table—regulated by the money you have."

Paul had tacked the piece of white ribbon among his postal cards on the board in his room. The bloodstains had turned brown. The ribbon seemed foolish and pathetic now that the strike was melting to a memory and the light of capitalistic reason and order was returning to the dark city.

He hated the fact that a decent gentleman like Mr. Schildkraut had lost his life. But was Cousin Joe the sole culprit? Benno and his accomplice had planted the bomb. And couldn't it be said that Uncle Joe bore some of the responsibility? To place all of it on Joe Junior was damnably wrong, and Paul was still convinced that he'd been right to help his cousin escape. He just wished that the other people he'd come to love didn't hurt so much, didn't blame him so much. He wished that he didn't hurt so much either.

Uncle Joe said nothing. Nothing about his son, and nothing about any decision regarding Paul. By Thursday Paul could no longer stand it. At noon, leaving his lunch sack unopened, he went to the office building. Typewriting with two fingers, Stefan Zwick watched as he raised his hand to tap on his uncle's door.

"I wouldn't if I were you."

"Mr. Zwick, I must."

He knocked. A growled monosyllable gave him leave to come in. He stepped only far enough into the room to shut the door.

"What is it?"

"Sir, I hate to interrupt—"

"Which is precisely what you're doing."

Paul reddened but stood his ground. "I have so much wanted to ask—is there any news of my cousin?"

"None. I'm in contact with the police every day. I've also hired a private agency. They too have failed so far. Joe Junior has seemingly vanished from the city of Chicago."

"Uncle, please believe I'm sorry. I did what he wanted. I helped him when he asked."

Uncle Joe held his pen as if it were a spear he was about to hurl at his visitor. "No," he said, "you took a stand against your aunt and me. You can't absolve yourself with a show of contriteness now. Please get out, I'm busy."

When he reported for work on Saturday morning, a Negro boy stopped him at the gate.

"This here's for you, sar." He handed Paul a folded note.

"Are you sure?" There was nothing written on the outside of the note.

"Yes, sar, wasn't no trouble to spot you. You was described just perfec'."

"Described by whom?"

"A real pretty young white lady. I had my shoeshine box outside the Northwestern depot an' she come up an' tol' me what you looked like an' paid me a whole dollar to bring that an' find you."

Paul unfolded the note. His lips went white.

Radigan's Hotel & Cottages—north
of Waukegan. This afternoon—
PLEASE!! YOURS ALWAYS.

At four o'clock he was slumped on a green plush seat on a northbound local of the Chicago & Northwestern, staring out the window at telegraph poles and small suburban farms shuttling by.

He'd get in more trouble for leaving work without telling anyone. Somehow he didn't care very much. The note had a clear urgency about it, and his standing with Uncle Joe could hardly be worse.

He got off the train at the sleepy Waukegan depot at the foot of a steep hill on the lake shore. He rented a red safety cycle for twenty cents and set off north along tree-lined Sheridan Road. After pedaling several miles into open country, he was close to the Wisconsin state line. To the left of the macadamized road he saw a weathered sign—RADIGAN'S—swaying on chains. A lake wind raising whitecaps blew the sign hard.

Behind the sign stood a white frame house with cupolas, a widow's walk, weather vanes, and lightning rods. To the rear, laid out in a U, were a number of small square cottages built to resemble the house but without its porches or gingerbread.

Stiff and dusty, he climbed off the wheel and walked it up the dirt drive leading to the cottages. He understood what might be happening, yet couldn't altogether believe it. The prospect was thrilling and frightening at the same time. What he was doing was foolish and dangerous.

One of the cottage doors opened. Someone in white waved a handkerchief.

His heart soared with happiness. He couldn't get up the dirt drive fast enough.

He parked the cycle outside the cottage. He ran to the door and threw his arms around her and kissed her damp cheek. She'd been crying. Happy tears, he hoped.

She kneaded his shoulder and kept repeating his name as she drew him inside.

"You got the note—" she began.

"I did, I just don't understand—"

She stopped his words with sweet-scented fingers on his lips. "Last night I ran away. I had to see you, by ourselves. I took the train and rented a little trap at a livery. I've put it in the barn so no one will notice it from the road."

"Julie, in the name of heaven—you left home? Why?"

"I love you, Paul. I love you so much, and Papa wants to separate us."

"What? Has he found out?"

"Oh no, I don't think so, it's just the devil's own timing. He and Mama want a grand tour of Europe. They're insisting I go with them." She was calming down, brushing tears from her eyelashes. Light fell through a small lace-curtained window at the rear; a sun halo radiated around her black hair.

Paul noticed details of the cottage. Linoleum flooring. A throw rug. A cheap library lamp hanging from the ceiling, its glass shade and oil font etched with flowers.

The large iron bed was finished in white enamel, with brass knobs on the corner posts. Nearby was a matching white commode, the doors shut to hide the china pot. The mirror above, tilted forward slightly, was speckled from age. It reflected a wavy image of the lovers as they sat side by side on the bed, touching, hugging.

"Don't go if you don't want to," he said.

"I told Papa I wouldn't. He said Mama had her heart set on the trip. He said it would devastate her if I refused. He said it might kill her. Whenever they want something they use Mama's health to make me do it. I've thought about leaving home permanently, but what would I do? Be a shopgirl? I don't know how to do anything for myself."

He clasped her hand in both of his. "You got here, didn't you? How did you find this place?"

"I was here once before, two years ago. I was coming back from Wisconsin with Mama and Papa. Our carriage broke down and we spent the night."

"But how did you get in this time, by yourself?"

"By offering the clerk a bribe. Aren't you glad? Say you're glad. If you don't it'll break my heart—I love you so."

She pressed her palms to his cheeks and kissed him. His arms slipped around her. They tumbled back on the hard bed, her travel-dusty shirtwaist of white lawn rumpling under his hands. He threw his left leg over her hip and kissed her deeply. She gave a low moan, pushing herself into him, stroking his face.

"I want you so, Paul. It's been so long since I've seen you—"

"And so much has happened." He kissed the damp corner of her lips, her nose and eyes. "I've so much to tell you."

"Later, sweetheart." She kissed his throat, tugged at his waist.

"Julie, I must not take advantage of you—"

"Oh, don't say that," she exclaimed, laughing and crying too. "I'm begging you to love me. Why do you think I compromised myself by doing this? Please don't refuse me. Make love to me while we have a chance."

They kissed again, his hand on her breasts, touching and then kneading gently. Julie petted his ear, ran her tongue over his cheek, becoming aroused. "I'm not experienced," she whispered. "Mama refuses to discuss—men and women." Paul's hand worked under her skirt and petticoat, stroking the cotton stocking on her inner leg. "She says the whole subject is improper. What little I know is hearsay."

"Don't worry, it doesn't make any difference—"

Braced on his elbow, he gazed at her tear-reddened face. The most beautiful he'd ever seen. This encounter in a cheap room on the windy lake shore sealed a permanent change in his feelings, his life, his fate.

"I love you, Juliette. Always. Eternally."

"Then do love me, Paul." She raised her arms. "Now."

The wind shifted around to the northwest in one of those abrupt changes common to the region in summertime. They could hear and feel the wind creaking the cottage as they lay naked in each other's arms, soft, warm, satiated, under a coarse starched sheet and a down comforter. All the light had gone out of the day except a splintered gleam of the sun setting behind the poplars bordering the property.

She said, "Are you hungry?"

He laughed. "Food is the last thing on my mind. I've so much to ask you. So much to tell—"

"Well, if you do get hungry, I brought a hamper. I filled it in Waukegan this morning. There's cheese, some bratwurst, a loaf of bread, a bottle of Mosel wine the shopkeeper almost refused to sell me because of my age—it'll be too warm, I suppose."

"You are more capable than you allow yourself to believe, Miss Juliette. To rent this place—stock it with food—wine, even—"

"It's because I fear they'll make me go away and I won't see you for a year. A lot can happen in a year, Paul. People can separate forever. They can forget."

"Never. I love you. *Immer*. Always."

They kissed, and touched, and began slow, languorous lovemaking a second time. She was less shy, less hesitant. She embraced him with an eagerness that tore the climax out of him in such a shattering way, he slept for a half hour afterward.

She slept too, nestling in the crook of his arm. They slept as comfortably as old married people. Or so he mused in the drowsy delirium of his joy.

In the dark, he struggled into his shirt and pants. She put on her skirt and white shirtwaist with nothing underneath. He helped button the shirtwaist in back. He felt oddly but happily domestic.

He opened the curtain at the front of the cottage, noticing only three windows lit in the hotel. A buggy with large yellow wheels was parked by the porch, the horse tied to the hitching block. The rush of waves against the rocky shore beyond the road was a soothing sound.

Julie had matches. He closed the curtain, pulled down the library lamp and lit it. They feasted from the hamper. The Mosel wine, though warm, was nectar. Julie looked soft, fulfilled, as she munched black bread he'd sliced from the loaf with his clasp knife.

"I must tell you what's happened. Cousin Joe is gone."

"Joey? Where?"

"No one knows. He ran away." He described the events leading up to it. She was astonished, but even more so when he described his role in it, how it was discovered, and how the family reacted.

"Oh, Paul, I am sorry." She stroked his face. "You had to help him when he asked, you hadn't any choice."

"That is what I thought."

"Poor Joey. Do you think he's gone for good?"

"I have that feeling, yes." He paused. "You are the second runaway I've associated with this week." His attempt to lighten the conversation failed. He cleared his throat for the dreaded question. "You are going back, aren't you?"

"I don't know. I have courage, Paul—sometimes. But not often enough."

"Courage is like a muscle, I think. You must use it."

She laughed, patting him. "You're a bright young fellow. I'm glad I fell in love with you. You'll go far."

Julie said she'd sent a telegraph message to her Aunt Willis night before last, while she'd been agonizing about this clandestine meeting. She'd asked permission to come to her aunt's home if she needed a refuge. Her aunt's housekeeper had telephoned by expensive long distance, saying Willis had left for Paris a fortnight earlier, with a traveling companion. "The housekeeper never said so right out, but I could hear what was in her voice. The companion is probably a new man. My aunt has the courage I don't."

"You do have it," Paul insisted, kissing her unbound hair.

She wasn't persuaded.

"Now we must talk about tomorrow," he said. "We will have to tell lies about our absence."

He hated lying to anyone. But, for Julie, discovery would be serious. She was a female under the age of consent. She had lost her virginity, the evidence was on the sheet beneath them. He would receive the blame—he'd take it, gladly—but she would suffer the taint.

"Truly, we must think up the very best—"

"Not now, Paul. In the morning. We won't spoil this night with worry. Hold me. Give me courage."

They made love once more, and fell back to sleep.

Someone was drumming.

Paul bolted up. He'd kicked the comforter off. He was frozen. Julie muttered into her pillow, still asleep.

"Julie!" His voice was low, hoarse. He took hold of her shoulder to rouse her. He recognized the drumming for what it was. Someone pounding on the door.

"Juliette? We know you're there, answer."

He shook her. She still didn't waken. Outside, the man said, "Use the God damned ax."

Paul just had time to leap out of bed and pull on his pants as the blade cleaved through the door with a splintery crash. A groping hand twisted the knob. A second ax blow knocked the door from its top hinge. There were four—no, five men outside, crowding in. One was a huge round-shouldered hulk wearing a fedora.

The lanterns flashed. Boots rapped on the linoleum. Julie sat up naked. She was mute with terror. Paul yanked the sheet over her.

Her glazed eyes focused. Bright silver badges gleamed on vests. Strident voices overlapped.

"Juliette. Oh my God. Deputy, arrest him, for Christ's sake, she's a minor."

"Don't blame me for this. She booked the room with a false name." That was a bald man with a waxed mustache and suspenders over a collarless shirt.

One of the men wearing a badge grabbed Paul's shoulder. Paul knocked the hand away. The man cuffed his face.

Paul struck at the man and missed. He fell on the throw rug, his behind hitting hard. The deputy kicked his leg, his ribs, while the hulking man shouted at the bald man. "You knew she was under age, Radigan. You took the bribe anyway."

"Stand up, you pile of shit." One of the lawmen manhandled Paul to his feet. Julie cried, "Oh, don't hurt him."

"Be quiet," her father shouted. Another deputy with a tinplate badge snapped handcuffs on Paul. The hotel owner whined:

"I took the twenty so she wouldn't be suspicious, Mr. Vanderhoff. She signed a phony name in the book but I recognized her from the time before. I did right, I telephoned you, didn't I?"

"Hours later. Christ, you can smell the rutting." The hulking man struck Paul across the face. "You little son of a bitch, I'll see you imprisoned for the rest of your natural life."

He lunged to his daughter and pushed her off the bed. She used the comforter to hide herself. The hulking man grabbed a bull's-eye lantern from one of the deputies and passed it over the sheet. "Oh God, look. The damage is done. The damage is done."

"See here," Paul cried out. "You have no right to come in here and frighten her—"

"Don't talk to me of *rights,* you God damned foreign scum, you fucking seducer." Vanderhoff thrust the bull's-eye lantern forward as if wanting to set Paul on fire. One of the deputies pulled him back.

"Mr. Vanderhoff, hang on, let's follow our plan. Get him into the wagon."

"What are you going to do?" Julie said. She was on her knees behind the bed, trembling.

"Take him across the line to Cook County," the deputy said. "Throw him in jail. When some of the hopheads and bugger boys get hold of him, he won't soon forget it."

Another deputy snickered. "He'll be ready for the nut farm when he gets out."

"If, if," the first one said.

"Stop congratulating yourselves," Vanderhoff snarled. "Put him in the damn wagon."

A deputy pushed Paul outside. The night air raised gooseflesh on his bare chest and arms. Under the newly risen moon, two horses hitched to a closed wagon breathed transparent vapors into the chilly air.

He had no thought for himself, only for her. He looked back toward the dark cottage; called out, "Julie? Remember what I said. You're stronger than—"

Vanderhoff seized his arm. "Shut up." He flung Paul against the wagon. "You'll never see my daughter again."

Paul's eyes, usually so mild, shone like moonlit ice. "*Es fliesst noch viel Wasser den Rhein hinunter!*"

"What garbage is that?"

"An old proverb. A lot of water will yet flow down the Rhine."

Livid, Vanderhoff screamed, "Lock him up before I beat him to death!"

The deputy jabbed Paul with a truncheon. "In the wagon, Dutchie. Where you're going they don't serve no beer or sauerkraut."

"But they like fresh meat," said his colleague, generating laughter. "You'll wonder why you ever set foot on the fucking boat."

The doors of the wagon slammed, hiding the moon. A chain clinked; a padlock snapped in the hasp. Paul huddled on a hard bench, shackled hands between his knees, in total darkness.

54

Julie

SHE DRIFTED in a strange twilight state. Her body was weightless. That seemed natural, and correct.

She had no concept of time. Faces came and went at the periphery of vision, gliding over her, large and a bit misshapen, like painted balloons.

"I hope you are resting. Dr. Woodrow mixed a special prescription. You must drink more of it now."

She recognized the voice, the face. Her mother. She felt pressure against the back of her nightgown. Lifted, she sat up part way. A hand resembling a little bundle of dead twigs brought a glass to her lips. She drank of the sweet syrupy liquid and sank down again with a tired sigh.

Fairy lights winked distantly. She recognized candles, each surrounded by four spikes of light that formed a luminous star.

Her mother's frail hand descended from the darkness, stroking the long black hair.

"It's so beautiful. You're such a beautiful child. I can't have some coarse ignorant foreign boy despoil such beauty. Papa told me the truth. Oh, I cried. I was beside myself, like a madwoman. You're damaged goods. We will have to live with that, what else can we do? But we will take certain steps, as if it never happened. Dr. Woodrow has already made sure there will be no child. No one outside this family will know it happened. There are ways to deceive a bridegroom. That's for the future. Now you must rest. Rest and let Mama heal you. A woman's health is everything. Nothing else matters."

Presently another face floated above her. She recognized Papa, jovially flourishing a thick yellow envelope.

"Don't forget this, Juliette. We'll have a splendid holiday, the three of us. But first you'll spend a month in Cleveland. Dr. Woodrow's recommendation. There is a fine establishment called the Mountjoy Hospital for Orthopedic and Nervous Disorders. The largest number of patients are women suffering from neurasthenic prostration. A month of rest, in complete seclusion—you'll be ready and eager for Europe."

That brought a new face into her thoughts. It was twice as vivid as the ones slowly circling and drifting and bumping each other in the twilight where the candles burned. This face was young, strongly cut. The hair was brown, with reddish glints. The eyes were blue, kindly, trusting. The sight of it brought cascades of sensation, emotion. Memory of kisses, caresses, their bodies together. Fear of separation. Loss. Threat—

"Paul? Where are you?"

"Dr. Woodrow, Dr. Woodrow," someone cried in the twilight, stridently.

Dr. Woodrow's huge head appeared, angelic. There was curly blond hair dusted with gray at the ears. There were cheeks like ripening apples, and a pink bow mouth. He smiled and patted her hand. "Now, now."

"Is it a crisis?" said her mother somewhere in the dark.

"I believe so."

"What do you recommend?"

"Bleeding. It's restorative."

She began to thrash, and cry, "No." They didn't seem to hear. Someone grasped her hands and pulled them above her head, out of sight, exposing her wrists. Papa sat on her ankles.

There was a rattle and clink of metal things. Disembodied hands carried a twinkling silver basin past her eyes. It floated over her like some bright fantastic airship, and disappeared.

"Now, now," Dr. Woodrow said again, stroking her black shiny hair.

Scissors cut each sleeve of her nightgown. She struggled to no avail. Rubber tubes were tied and knotted around her upper arms. Dr. Woodrow donned white muslin gloves. Hands brought a silver tray into view. A sparkling tray of silver instruments with sharp points or blades for bleeding.

"It's salubrious," said Dr. Woodrow, his lips pursed and pink like a lover's. "You'll hardly feel it."

He selected a twinkling scalpel.

She screamed.

55

Paul

HANDS GROPED on his leg. Half asleep, Paul fancied it was some bug, a larger specimen of the ones crawling in the moldy straw-filled mattress.

His eyes cleared. A feeble gaslight beyond the bars illuminated a moonface with bloodshot eyes, a mouth of rotten teeth. The face hovered close to his. The hand groped higher.

"Crazy Tom's asleep, pretty boy. Come down to my bunk and be nice to Swede. If you do I'll give you a plug of my chaw tobacco. But you got to chew something else first." Swede giggled.

Paul knocked his hand away. "Let me be, I want to sleep."

"Oh yes?" Swede grabbed Paul's ear and twisted viciously. "It don't pay to be snotty in jail. Word gets around. You'll turn your back and drop your drawers in the shitter, then some boys will pay you for your snottiness in a way you won't like."

Paul felt busy mites in his hair, his armpits. He wriggled and scratched. Before the deputies dimmed the gas for the night, Crazy Tom, an inebriate and apparently a frequent guest of the county, had sat on the stool in the corner with his shirt off, scratching the vermin until blood ran in the hair on his chest.

Swede fondled his neck again.

"I said leave me alone, damn you."

"All right, pretty boy. I will for now. Just keep watch on your behind."

Swede gave Paul's buttocks a pinch, giggling again. His forehead and thinning hair sank from sight. Swede slept in the lowest bunk. Paul had the one on top; the middle one was empty. The cell contained bunks for six. Crazy Tom snored in the bottom one on the other side.

Fending off the old man called Swede had been Paul's burden for almost twelve hours. He was exhausted by it. He rolled toward the wall and covered his face with his elbow. He was so weary and ashamed, he wanted to die.

Late in the morning the police wagon had brought him through the gate of Cook County Jail, most of whose granite-walled cells had no windows. The jail reeked of human waste in metal buckets and tobacco juice spat onto the granite floors. The slimy coating was treacherous.

Paul's cell block was a bedlam of shouts, oaths, obscenities. The cells had been unlocked from four in the afternoon until six. During those two hours he'd been allowed to roam the corridor. Up and down, up and down, shuffling among the dregs of the city. Some of the men eyed him, others tried to touch him; some whispered things he tried not to hear.

For supper the guard had brought tin plates of cold gray corn bread squares. Paul bit into a piece and found a nest of wiggling white worms. He gagged into the reeking toilet bucket; Swede and Crazy Tom found it very amusing.

The cells adjoined the women's block via a connecting door that was kept open. Soon after everyone was locked up for the night, the women began to weep and shriek. "Hey, screw. Screw, fuck you. No, fuck this. Put your head up this. Ha-ha, ha-ha, ha-ha . . ."

Footsteps approached. The night guard peered in. "Sleep tight, ladies." He raked his truncheon over the bars. Crazy Tom started and yelled. The guard laughed and went on.

Paul fought to maintain his courage, but it was hard. *This is America? You came all the way across the ocean to experience this?*

And Julie . . . what had happened to her? Had her father punished her? He feared for her safety.

Shortly after guards woke the inmates in the morning, Paul was pulled from his cell and escorted down a flight of stairs to a granite-walled room with no windows, a cheap electric fixture in the ceiling, a wooden chair in the middle of the damp floor, a steam radiator hissing.

Two detectives wearing stiff collars and sleeve garters welcomed Paul with smiles he immediately distrusted. "Sit down, Dutch," said one detective while the other shut the door and shot the bolt.

The radiator gave off so much heat, Paul was immediately bathed in sweat under his coarse jail shirt. The heavier of the detectives took a wide-legged stance in front of Paul's chair.

"This is a sweatbox. Do you know what that means, Dutch?"

Paul shook his head.

"We work in teams in here. Each team does one hour on, one hour off. That way, we can keep you here till you tell the truth. You won't eat, you won't drink, you won't sleep, you won't piss, you'll sit there and sweat." He leaned over to shout. "Why did you kidnap her?"

"You are fools, I did not kidnap—"

"Don't call names in here, you kraut son of a bitch. You're in police custody. In Chicago, U.S. of A. Hal? Give him a tap, so he'll mind his manners."

A shot-loaded sock hit the back of his head. Driven forward, he fell off the chair. The other detective kicked him as he fell.

Paul groaned and scratched the granite floor. He shut his eyes.

"None of that, you shit bag. Get up." The older detective grabbed the waist of his trousers and yanked. Paul was forced to scramble to his knees, then to his feet.

The detectives threw him in the chair and yelled their questions. Did he have a criminal record? Did he belong to socialist or anarchist cells? Did he have clap? A history of kidnapping and raping young women? No matter how he responded —denial, or what passed for a scornful laugh—it didn't satisfy them. He took blow after blow of the shot-loaded sock.

His skin gushed sweat. He felt that every ounce of fluid in his body must be boiling away. The detectives didn't seem to mind the heat.

For perhaps the thirtieth time he denied the kidnapping charge. Before the detective could hit him again, someone banged loudly on the door.

Annoyed, the older detective said, "Keep your pants on out there. Hal, get that."

The door creaked. Then:

"Ease off, boys. This one's bailed out. Clean him up and bring him downstairs."

The lawyer was a natty little fellow in a derby and velvet-collared overcoat. Paul wondered why he wore the coat in warm weather. The lawyer's name was Kaspar Gross. He took charge downstairs, showing Paul where to sign the various papers. Then he shook Paul's hand vigorously and congratulated him, as if it were some great honor to be released from Cook County Jail.

Paul was still barefoot, though he'd been allowed to keep his coarse gray prison shirt and pants. He lurched down granite stairs into a courtyard. Above it, an opalescent square of sky boiled with thunderclouds. In the center of the yard was the Crown landau with the top raised.

"Glad you're safe," Nicky Speers called down from his seat. "Better climb in, it's starting to rain." Heavy drops began to plop in standing water. Paul opened the carriage door to discover his uncle seated with both hands resting on the silver head of a cane.

Uncle Joe's face was unreadable. Paul dropped onto the leather seat opposite him and pulled the door shut. Uncle Joe rapped the cane on the floor and the carriage swung out of the courtyard into Dearborn Street as the rain came down.

"I will take you home before I go to the brewery," Uncle Joe said in a husky voice, as if he were trying to rein in enormous anger. "You smell like a sewer."

"That's what it is in there, a sewer."

"Vanderhoff lost no time in informing me of what you did. He tried to reach me yesterday but I was in Milwaukee on business. He telephoned me at home after midnight. Fortunately I was downstairs, and your aunt was sound asleep when the call came. I couldn't locate the attorney until this morning."

"I am still very grateful."

The statement made no visible impression. "Is that dried blood in your hair? Did they abuse you?"

"They questioned me hard. I will be all right. If you will only listen to my side, Uncle—"

"Go ahead."

"Juliette asked me to meet her at that little hotel in the country. I love her. She loves me."

"That's completely immaterial." Paul was terrified of his uncle's cold voice. It was more like a judge's than that of a blood relative. "Vanderhoff agreed to drop charges in return for a pledge of silence from our family. A criminal action against you would result in a trial, and the press loves nothing better than a courtroom circus involving prominent people. Vanderhoff desperately wants to avoid that. I don't want a scandal either. We didn't have to bargain long. Vanderhoff did require one additional condition. That you never again see or communicate with his daughter."

"I can't give that kind of promise."

"It isn't necessary that you do. I gave it for you."

"Uncle—!"

"Kindly keep quiet. Your aunt has suffered quite enough lately, I won't tell her the truth about this shameful affair, and neither will you. Here is our story. You were loitering in a tavern on Saturday night. You drank too much beer, got into an argument, and the police were summoned. You refused to leave the tavern peaceably so the police used force. Hence your bruises. You were detained in jail until Kaspar Gross got you out. There, you've made liars of both of us."

"But the explanation is good. I don't want Aunt Ilsa to think badly of me."

"Think *badly?* You helped our son run away. Don't ask for miracles."

Paul wiped the back of his hand across his lips. "Will she believe the story?"

"I think so. She is convinced that alcohol affects people adversely. The older she gets, the more she hates drinking, even drinking beer. It's better that she think you got drunk, she can accept that. She'd die if she knew you violated an innocent young woman."

Paul slumped in the corner. After all the sweating, he was cold. Uncle Joe gazed out of the landau at the rainy morning, the inevitable traffic clog of horsecars, drays, private vehicles. "I don't know what's become of this family, everything is crashing down about us. At supper the very night you were away with Vanderhoff's daughter, Frederica brazenly announced her intention of becoming an actress."

Frederica. He never used Cousin Fritzi's full name.

"An actress—can you imagine? She is thirteen years old! How could I explain to a girl her age that actresses are regarded as harlots? I simply said she would do no such thing. She disputed that, strongly and vociferously. Thirteen years of age, well bred, and she disputed her father. She said if I objected, she'd do what Joe Junior did. Leave."

He shook his head, as though burdened beyond the limits of his strength. The rain hammered the carriage top. "Crashing down," he murmured again. "My son ran away with your connivance. You dishonor the family with your immoral behavior—"

"Uncle Joe, it isn't immoral, we love each other. We want to marry."

"Spare me, Paul, the idea's preposterous. The age of majority in this country is twenty-one. Until you reach that, you can't marry without consent. Furthermore, you don't have the slightest appreciation of the meaning of the word 'love.' You don't know the responsibility it demands. Or the respect. That is clear from your sordid behavior.

"By all that you've done this week, you force me to a painful decision. You will pack your belongings and leave our house. Please do so before I return home tonight. Your job at Crown's no longer exists. Henceforth you will have to make your way on your own."

"But I don't have any place to—"

"You have acted very independently up till now. You have lived on the streets of Berlin. Crossed this country from New York to Chicago alone. I have every confidence that you can take care of yourself. Find a place."

Uncle Joe sounded like a different man. Bitter; cruel. Paul's vision was momentarily blinded by tears.

"Uncle Joe, I can't believe—"

Uncle Joe struck the carriage floor with the ferrule of his cane. "You had better believe me, Paul. The decision is made."

Paul shut his eyes and leaned into the corner, trying to hide how heartsick he was. His uncle didn't look at him for the duration of the trip to Michigan Avenue. "Around to the back, Nicky," he called as they arrived.

There Paul opened the door and climbed out. Huddled in his slicker and oilcloth hat, Nicky Speers flicked the whip over the team. The landau pulled away while the summer shower streaked Paul's face with rain.

The Crown mansion had the air of a mausoleum. Helga Blenkers told him his aunt had already left for the morning. He stumbled upstairs to his room.

Hour after hour rain poured down from a black sky. The streets were awash. Despite the gloom, the blow Uncle Joe had dealt him, he found himself regaining a little strength. Maybe he'd been through so much, he just couldn't hurt any more. He bathed, shaved, and stretched out on his bed for a blessed nap.

He awoke about half past one and remembered what he must do. He put on fresh drawers, a shirt, knickerbockers snatched from a closet hanger along with a jacket. He counted his money from the bureau. Three and a half dollars.

In fifteen minutes he packed a selection of clothes in his valise, leaving room for his souvenirs. Pack-rat Pauli. Well, it was true. The board was overflowing. He could take only the most important things. A paper White Stockings pennant which he carefully rolled around the stick and tucked down into the side of the valise. An engraving of the beautiful Lillian Russell torn from an illustrated weekly folded and slipped inside his English grammar. Though the valise was already bulging, he stuffed in the globe and stand.

He put a rubber band around all of his postal cards except one—the painting of *Brauerei* Crown with flags flying from its towers. That he ripped in half and threw on the bed.

His fatigue-ringed eyes lingered on the last treasure tacked to the board. The stereopticon view of New York Harbor. He no longer believed its promise as completely as he once had. He thought of leaving it behind.

He wasn't quite ready to do that. He pulled the tack and held the card a moment, pensive. Then he put it in his pocket.

Aunt Ilsa came rushing in. Her eyes were puffy again. She flung her arms around him.

"Oh, Pauli, Pauli, how can this happen? He telephoned me five minutes after I got home. That was an hour ago. I have been arguing ever since, trying to dissuade him. He's a good man, don't doubt it. But he's angry. Angry and wounded. There have been so many blows in one week—"

"That much I understand."

"I pleaded with him, I begged as I've never begged. Anger is a human failing, it can be forgiven, but this goes too far, that's what I told him. We do not shun our own family. But he's just in a fury—" She was sobbing with her hands over her face. "He won't even—allow you—to stay one more night."

Paul put his arms around her. She smelled of lilac water. He kissed her cheek. He loved her and always would.

"I must help you find a place for the night—"

"No, I can do that. I'm grown up, Aunt Ilsa."

"That's very true, but—"

"I've lived on the streets a long time, please don't worry." He already had a destination in mind. It had been there the instant he awoke.

She saw on the bed the ripped halves of the brewery postal card. She hugged him again. "*Ach, du lieber Himmel. Es tut weh.*" There is such pain.

"I will take care of myself, I will be fine."

"You can't simply disappear, Pauli. You must let us know where you are. Come back to visit."

"Of course I will." Did she really think he would ever step inside his uncle's house again?

The rain was slackening. It was time to go. He felt a little unsteady as he opened the closet for his corduroy jacket.

He remembered something in his bureau drawer. He slipped into the jacket, opened the drawer, fastened the spotted white ribbon to his lapel with a safety pin.

"Fritzi will want to say goodbye," Aunt Ilsa said.

"Of course, if I see her." He didn't plan to hunt for her; he was anxious to be away from this house of unhappiness. "Goodbye, Aunt Ilsa."

He kissed her cheek once more, picked up his valise and walked out.

He was not going to crawl out of the dark mansion like a felon. He took a firm hold on his bag and marched down the staircase boldly, even a bit noisily. With a false appearance of confidence, he strode toward the front door; the same door through which he'd tumbled, frozen, starving, but full of hope, so many months ago.

Someone stepped from clotted shadows on the far side of the entrance hall. Manfred. Elegant in a starched white shirt, perfectly creased gray trousers, brilliantly polished shoes, the leather bib apron he wore for morning chores.

"Well, well. Leaving us, I'm told. Back to the potato fields of your homeland?"

"It would please you."

"That's true," Manfred said. "This household is like a fine banquet into which you brought the smell of cabbage soup."

"Manfred—" Paul drew a breath. "If you were younger by twenty years, I would knock you down."

Manfred paled and stepped back.

Paul wheeled and went out.

A silver afternoon; a silver sky. Strong light in the west promised better weather, but it was still raining.

He started along the sidewalk, unaware of his disarrayed state. He'd put on the pair of corduroy knickerbockers that had a small rip at the knee. His left sock was falling down over his shoe.

As he reached the corner of Nineteenth, Fritzi came sprinting through the garden, calling his name.

"Paul, don't leave. This is all Papa's fault, he's bad."

"No he isn't. Truly."

"I hate him."

"Oh, you mustn't. Promise me."

She sniffled. "All right."

"Good. Goodbye." He stepped off the curbing.

She ran beside him, shoes splashing puddles, throwing mud on her skirt and his bare leg above the drooping sock.

"You can't go away from us, this is your home."

He stopped and swung around to look at her.

"I thought so. I came thousands of miles because I believed it. I was wrong. If I have a home at all—which I often doubt—this is not it. I have to look elsewhere."

"Paul, don't go, we love you!"

"I love you, *Fritzchen.*" He flung both arms around his skinny cousin, a crushing hug. He wanted to cry again. The moment passed.

"Goodbye," he said for the second time.

He hoisted his grip, knocked off a little gob of mud clinging to it. He waved and left her standing by a puddle while the sky wept silver tears.

When he arrived in Little Cheyenne, the sky was growing dark. The storm had burst again, with frequent lightning and thunderclaps. Torrents of rain sluiced through the gutters. Paul hardly noticed how soaked he'd gotten. He hurried past Wampler's red light hotel to the door of the Temple of Photography.

His knocking fought the rumbling sounds in the sky, the rushing floods in the gutter. He knocked harder. Presently a key rattled. The door opened.

"Mr. Rooney?"

"Who—? Dutch! What a surprise!" He noticed Paul's valise.

"I have left my other job, sir. I have left my relatives, to make my way on my own. I'm eager to learn the science of photography."

"And the art, don't forget the art."

"Of course. Will you allow me to come in?"

"By all means! This is a joyous moment. You must dry out, you look a perfect mess. Pants ripped, socks falling—"

Paul laughed. "Oh, I always look this way. Not proper for a German, people say. Somehow I can't help it. Please don't worry; otherwise I am a good, neat worker."

Rooney laughed too. "We shall find out."

Paul stepped over the threshold, certain that he had left one world forever and was entering another, better one. A world in which he might at last find a sense of purpose and belonging, no more *der Aussenstehende*, the outsider, living by the sufferance of a tyrant. In this new world he'd make the home he longed for. With Julie.

56

Pork

IN OCTOBER the Vanderhoffs arrived at Wiesbaden.

It was high season, the fashionable month to take the waters at Germany's most celebrated health resort. That made no difference to M. P. Vanderhoff III. He was already sick of the tour. They had exhausted themselves ogling the castles along the banks of "Father Rhine." They had trudged through Goethe's house in Frankfurt, Baedekers in hand. Now they moved into a three-bedroom suite at a majestic old hotel on the Wilhelmstrasse promenade, hard by the *Kurviertel*. The cure quarter.

The atmosphere at the spa was elegant and festive. In the spacious rooms of the *Kurhaus* one might meet and mingle with an international celebrity clientele, on a footing of perfect equality. A maker of vitreous china lavatories from England could chat with an Austrian duke. A New York traction king—or a Chicago sausage maker—could feel at home with a Polish prince. Pork enjoyed this comfortable democracy of the rich and well placed.

But for the most part he found Germany, and all of Europe, too old and therefore too backward. Too self-consciously quaint. Too—there was no other word for it—*foreign.*

Not far from the *Kurpark,* at the *Trinkhalle,* one found the most famous of Wiesbaden's twenty-six medicinal hot springs, the *Kochbrunnen.* Nell and Juliette slept late each morning, but Pork, unable to break old habits, rose before six, dressed, and strolled briskly to the *Trinkhalle* along linden-lined avenues. He took this walk wearing spats, a silk topper and a Prince Albert with wing collar and four-in-hand.

Punctually at seven the *Trinkhalle* band began to play martial music. Pork sat at a white iron table within view of the steaming, snorting spring. He tipped lavishly, so one or another of the smartly uniformed attendants could be counted on to rush him his first glass of the medicinal waters. This he quaffed with visible disgust; it was warm, and salty.

At Wiesbaden one always consulted a private physician before starting a health program. Pork's physician, an austere man named Dr. Stollknecht, ordered Pork to drink four glasses of the damnable water before returning to the hotel for his breakfast of one soft-boiled egg, one breadstick and black coffee. The regime seemed to be having a beneficial effect on his elimination, but not his disposition. He was sick of starving. He was sick of salty water. He was sick of *"Die Wacht am Rhein."* He wanted to go home.

His impatience was exacerbated because he had nothing to do in Wiesbaden. The hotel reading room routinely included two or three people devouring Mr. Hope's *Prisoner of Zenda.* Pork wasn't interested. He never read novels.

He was equally bored by other forms of culture. He dozed through performances at the Royal Opera House, or the *Lieder* recitals and turgid Schiller dramas to which Nell dragged him.

Most spa clients at Wiesbaden entered into lively discussions of world events. This year the topics were colorfully varied. They included the prospects and character of the new Tsar, Nicholas II; the possible fate of the Jew officer, Captain Dreyfus, accused of selling state secrets in France; the enormous armed might of Japan that was crushing China in the war in the Far East. Since Pork was neither a student of public affairs nor a good conversationalist, he wanted no part of such talk. Instead, after his breakfast, he usually went off by himself to sightsee, allowing a driver to take him where he would in the nearby Taunus Mountains. One day they drove up to the Hill of Nero. There Pork ate a lonesome noon meal at the restaurant, then returned through the dark green forests. So still and primeval were they, so sensuously fragrant with crushed leaves and fecund soil and all the other sweet rotting scents of autumn, that Pork gazed from the moving carriage and imagined himself a creature with horns and goat legs, chasing and rutting on plump German wood nymphs who practiced every sort of delicious indecency—cheerfully.

That afternoon Pork visited another establishment quietly recommended by the hall porter. It dispensed no medicinal waters, only beer and champagne served by pink-nippled country girls in transparent chemises. Pork found it marvelous for his health anyway.

One of the few positive aspects of the tour was Juliette's condition. The stay in Cleveland, the sea crossing, and the initial weeks on the Continent seemed to have achieved their purpose. Pork's daughter was docile and quiet. She seldom spoke unless addressed, although now and then she did utter some sharp retort or criticism, always about something small and unimportant. There were occasional outbursts of crying, too. Pork found it paradoxical that these reassured his wife.

"It's typically female behavior, Mason. She is well and normal again."

In Frankfurt, Nell had bought Juliette a little dog, a Pomeranian, from a recommended kennel. His name was Rudy. He showed his high spirits by constantly running, jumping and yapping. Pork detested him. The dog didn't like him either. The day Rudy arrived, he lifted his leg and peed on Pork's best suit, right in the sitting room of their suite. Pork began carrying a rolled-up copy of *Leslie's;* there were no further incidents. Julie seemed to enjoy having a pet. She even smiled occasionally when she picked Rudy up and petted him.

The end of the first week at the spa was marred by a visit from Willis. She came by train from Paris, accompanied by a young man she'd met in New York. He was a tower of flesh, six feet six or seven, with shoulders that belonged on some heroic statue in a park. He laughed a lot, and drank two or three liters of Franconian wine at a sitting, without being the worse.

His name was Boronsky. Willis said he was Russian, and a poet. Pork suspected he was a Jew, and a fortune hunter. Certainly he was too young for any woman who cared about her reputation. That of course excluded Willis. She and Boronsky were full of enthusiasm for a new edition of *Salome* by that fellow Wilde who sported a sunflower in his lapel, the one who went around preaching art for art's sake. This particular book contained depraved illustrations by some Englishman named Beardsley.

After supper one evening, Boronsky read several of his own poems. Pork found them incomprehensible as well as suggestive. He walked out in the middle of the fourth one.

Willis spent two afternoons with her niece. She returned from the second outing irate. She said to Nell in private, "I saw the incisions. I made her push up her sleeves and show me. Sister or no sister, if you ever bleed that girl again, I'll have the law on you."

"Dr. Woodrow recommended it. Besides, it was done weeks ago. We were only trying to make her well."

"Oh, splendid. Why didn't you carve an idol and dance around it, too? Why didn't you kidnap some children and cut their hearts out by moonlight?"

"Willis!"

"That hellhole in Cleveland sounds barbaric. I'd take Julie away from here tonight, but for the fact that she's a decent, honorable, thoroughly misguided girl you and your husband have terrorized into believing nonsense. She thinks she owes you something merely because you're parents. Because of an accidental meeting of Mason's sperm and your—whatever it is you offer down there. Christ knows, it must be primitive."

Nell almost swooned. She rushed out and Willis packed and left on the seven o'clock local for Frankfurt, accompanied by her burly paramour.

Pork heard a report of the outrageous conversation that night as they prepared for bed. "Maybe it's a blessing she left," Nell said. "Maybe we'll never see her again."

"It would be wonderful," Pork said, struggling into his nightshirt. "But nobody's that lucky."

The following Wednesday Pork visited the *Kurhaus*. A string quartet was playing Haydn airs in one of the public salons. The chess rooms were busy. The *Kurhaus* was the spa's international meeting place, but Pork was now interested in the reading rooms. He had lately discovered copies of several overseas papers, including the *Chicago Tribune.*

Browsing a copy four weeks old, he came across a startling social item about Joe Crown. The brewer had closed his Michigan Avenue mansion and taken his wife and children to his estate in Carolina, intending to remain there for the foreseeable future.

Smugly, Pork concluded that his swift action against Crown's nephew was responsible for the retreat. Before leaving home, he'd also heard that Crown's elder son, the radical, had run off. Pork was delighted to see the arrogant little man suffering. He only wished Joe Crown's exile could be permanent.

Juliette was in bed with her monthly distress when the unexpected meeting occurred.

Dr. Stollknecht joined Pork for breakfast that morning. He piled into a gargantuan portion of eggs, wurst, and breads while Pork, rather miffed, picked at his health plate. Despite this, they had a pleasant and lengthy conversation about racial purity. Pork found the physician quite the most agreeable, sensible German he'd ever met.

Pork said he viewed contamination of American blood by ex-slaves and immigrants as a potential disaster. Dr. Stollknecht agreed. Inferior blood could destroy a nation. He believed governments facing such a threat should intervene. Ruthlessly, if necessary.

They shook hands and parted. Swinging his cane in the mild October sunshine, Pork went for a stroll in the spacious *Kurpark*. He sat on a stone bench beside the lake and watched two stately swans swim by, followed by two amusing cygnets. He was still sitting there when he got a start. A man was bearing down on him along the path; an American—and what's more, a Chicagoan.

"Mr. Vanderhoff? Good morning. William Vann Elstree." The man removed his monocle and held out his hand. The amazed Pork shook it. An armband of black crepe was tied around Elstree's left sleeve.

"Yes, of course, I know who you are. Won't you sit down? This is an honor. An unexpected pleasure."

Elstree took a seat. He drew off mauve gloves and laid them beside his stick.

He fanned himself with his homburg. Pork's tiny eyes darted sideways, to William Elstree's jaw. Certainly the man was not handsome. But he radiated charm and, more important, the power only wealth conferred.

"You and your family are taking the waters, I hear," Elstree said.

"That's true. I guess Americans make their presence known pretty quickly." Pork added another of his gratuitous ha-ha's. Elstree responded with a smile and a nod. Pork said, "How do you happen to be here, may I ask?"

"Oh, the same reason. The waters. But you and I meeting this way—that's purely accidental."

Somehow Pork doubted the statement, though he couldn't have said why. Elstree might have learned that the family was at the spa by reading the papers. The peregrinations of touring Americans, especially notables, were reported throughout Europe. Mrs. Astor was at Bruxelles for the week, Mrs. Vanderbilt would arrive in Florence on Saturday . . .

"Mr. Vanderhoff."

"Sir?"

"Since we've chanced to meet like this, allow me to raise a subject that's been on my mind lately. I hope you won't be offended."

"No, no, why should I?"

"Oh, there's a reason. Perhaps you'll say I'm unseemly, given the relatively short time that has gone by since the death of my wife Marguerite. She passed away this summer, in Chicago. Heatstroke."

"I read about it. Tragic, tragic. My condolences."

"Thank you." Elstree gazed at light cirrus clouds in the autumn sky. "I am still in mourning, and will be for some months."

"That's fitting. Please continue."

The shoulders of Elstree's finely tailored suit slumped a little. "Where to begin? Marguerite and I—well, do you mind very much if I'm candid?"

"No, no," Pork exclaimed, eager to please this man whom he secretly considered one of his betters. The Elstrees had been rich a lot longer than the Vanderhoffs.

"Marguerite and I did not have the most loving of relationships in recent years. Personal differences."

"They happen. But you maintained the marriage—"

"Oh, of course. That's only decent."

"I agree."

"Mr. Vanderhoff, you're here with not only your wife but your attractive daughter."

Startled, he said, "That's true."

"As you know, I have met her."

"The Auditorium, wasn't it?"

"Exactly." Elstree smiled, charming and warm. "From the first, I admired her beauty, and what I perceived to be her intelligence. I'll be frank, sir, and I hope you won't condemn me. Before I embarked on this tour I spent some weeks in retreat at the family place on Long Island. Southampton. There I found an image coming to mind frequently. I experienced a not inconsiderable embarrassment and guilt over it. You see, when Marguerite died, I pledged myself to think of no one else for a suitable interval. A year or more."

Pork was stunned, already leaping ahead to what this rich gentleman might be suggesting.

"Go on, sir. Say what's on your mind."

"Thank you. It's simple enough. When the proper amount of time has passed, I'd like your permission to call on your daughter."

Pork sat back. What an incredible stroke of luck. Elstree came from one of Chicago's finest families. He was uniformly regarded as a kind and modest man, well mannered and well spoken. Furthermore, he was a Princeton graduate. Pork hardly dared think of what a catch he would be for Juliette.

"Mr. Vanderhoff?" Elstree looked worried, possibly interpreting the silence as rejection.

"Oh. Excuse me. I'm just taken aback."

"Not angry, I hope."

"No, no. It's quite a surprise, that's all. I'll be candid with you in return. Your request is welcome. Very welcome. Juliette's mother would be pleased if you called. I'd be honored. For some time now, we've been—ah—concerned about the caliber of our daughter's male acquaintances. Hoping for something more— substantial for her future."

Elstree smiled warmly then. "I'm happy to hear you say it. I must remind you, though. I'm forty-four years old."

"No problem at all," Pork exclaimed. "A sensible woman prizes maturity in a man."

"But it's fair to ask whether your daughter would object to my interest."

"Certainly not. Furthermore, her mother and I have all the authority in such matters."

"As it should be," Elstree murmured. Again he smiled.

What a boon, Pork thought. What an amazing, marvelous, totally unexpected boon. Then panic seized him. Just as quickly as it had surfaced, this prize catch might swim away. He stabbed his hand inside his Prince Albert for a silver case.

"We must get better acquainted. Would you care for a Havana cigar? May I call you Bill?"

Elstree said Bill would be fine. He took a cigar. They chatted pleasantly for over an hour.

Part Six

LEVEE

1895–1896

Photography is a marvelous discovery, a science that has attracted the greatest intellects, an art that excites the most astute minds—and one that can be practiced by an imbecile . . . What cannot be taught is the feeling.

1856
French photographer GASPARD FÉLIX TOURNACHON ("Nadar")

I don't know about your mayors, but God has forsaken this part of Chicago.

1897
Evangelist DWIGHT L. MOODY, in the First Ward

57

Paul

"I'LL TEACH YOU," Wex Rooney said that first night. "Give you a place to stay. I'll share whatever scraps and snips come to the dinner table. But you'll have to find work, I can't offer a job with pay. I can barely scrape up money for myself."

"Done," Paul said.

"One thing more. I don't care what you call yourself outside, but around here, it'll be Dutch."

He lay on a straw pallet, under an old blanket of blue wool marked U.S. Army. He'd pulled the blanket up to his chin. The loft was damp and cold. Above, beyond the loft skylight, the full moon shone behind flying clouds the color of wood smoke. Earlier it had rained. Drops on the skylight sparkled like diamonds.

Dutch. He hated the name. Never mind that there was an explanation for calling Germans Dutchmen: *Dutch* was easier to say than *Deutsche*. He'd chosen an *American* name, Paul, and he didn't want someone pushing another on him, not even Mr. Wex Rooney. How could he stop Wex from calling him that?

It occurred to him that maybe he shouldn't try too hard, given Rooney's generosity. He was starting out to create a new life for himself, he could stand to be Dutch for a while. Maybe Wex would grow tired of the name, or forget it.

A new life, that was the most important thing, after all. He had a glorious opportunity here. A chance to master a new, modern trade for the new, modern century that was coming. He would apply himself to learning everything Wex Rooney could teach. He'd prove Cousin Joe's bitter views of America were wrong; the predictions of the baker of Wuppertal, too. And when Julie came home from her grand tour, he would win her somehow—even over the objections of her mother and father.

He regretted losing the family with whom he'd felt so comfortable, but he had to start over. If America had robbed him of a family, he must remember it had also given him Julie.

In the morning he asked Wex Rooney for a tack and permission to affix something to the wall of the loft. Near his pallet on the floor, where he could see it as soon as he awoke or before he fell asleep, he tacked the stereopticon view of New York Harbor, with the Lady Liberty still beckoning to him.

Rooney's Temple of Photography was in Chicago's First Ward. The ward had been enlarged in 1890, Rooney said, and now ran west from Lake Michigan to the South Branch of the Chicago River, and south from the river to Twenty-ninth Street; Thirty-first Street at the extreme southwest corner.

The huge ward held most of the city's corporate offices, finest hotels, big department stores. The Crowns lived in the First Ward. So did the Vanderhoffs. So did dangerous thieves and killers, depraved prostitutes and pimps, and some of the crookedest politicians in America.

South of Van Buren Street, the First Ward sheltered Chicago's worst vice districts, including Little Cheyenne, where Rooney's temple was located, and the Levee, a section even more notorious. As a destination for thrill seekers, the Levee had boomed after Mayor Harrison came out strongly for catering to every desire of visitors to the 1893 Exposition. Even though "Our Carter" had been assassinated in untimely fashion, his open city stayed open, and thrived.

Paul went to the Levee, and elsewhere, in search of work. He trudged the streets in snow and sleet, frigid sunshine, keening winds that numbed the face and raked the skin raw. He answered classified advertisements. Climbed dark stairs to shabby offices where dull-sounding jobs were already filled.

"It's the depression, we haven't recovered yet," Wex said. "Then too, winter's a slow time. Did you notice all the streetside cribs on the Levee? Had their shutters closed, didn't they? Come spring, those shutters'll be open. Gents will be strolling and driving by on balmy evenings, eyeing the stock. When good weather comes, and more whores are working, other jobs open up. Don't be discouraged."

Wex Rooney's prices were low because most of his customers were poor. Newlyweds who couldn't afford anyone better for a wedding portrait; parents who wanted cheap photographs of their children to send to relatives in the old country. Wex was not good with small children; he brought out the worst in them somehow. They balked at obeying his instructions. They stained his prop seats with fingers sticky from candy. During one grim session, a brat suddenly threw up all over the settee, the floor, and Wex's trousers. It was soon clear to Paul that Wex's considerable talents didn't provide a decent living even after years of experience. He was always scrambling for the rent money; always pressing his second-floor sublet tenant for a little in advance; always embarrassed by certain commercial jobs in the shop.

One such job was the printing of large photographs of attractive young women, for posting outside concert saloons in the vice districts.

"There's more saloon than concert to those dives," Wex reluctantly explained when Paul asked about the pictures. "You occasionally find a besotted professor pounding the ivories, but you'll always find a slew of females dignified by the title waitress. What they're waiting for are suckers to buy drinks that're mostly colored water. The girls—'girl' being a term for any waitress under eighty-five—work on commission. Some of them have faces fit to stop clocks, as the saying goes. So the owners lure customers off the street with more fetching visages. Like these. In this batch, two of the ladies are actresses in respectable touring troupes. Three are deceased, I've been using their pictures for years. The others I don't know about; photographers trade them for favors, equipment, that sort of thing."

"You mean these women aren't employed by the saloon displaying their pictures?"

"Unfortunately, that's what I mean."

"Mr. Rooney—with respect—you told me that photographs shouldn't lie."

"These pictures don't lie, it's the owners doing the lying! I'm the fellow in the middle. The fellow who doesn't like to starve. Now be off, I've got to deliver the prints to Hannegan's before six."

Wex and Paul didn't starve, but the food Wex brought home was poor in quality and meager in quantity. Soup bones barely fit for a dog. Turnips; bundles of tough, stringy greens. Their bread came from stores where poor people lined up to buy stale loaves baked days earlier.

In the small back room where they ate, Wex regularly dusted the photo of his son. Paul speculated about the little boy's death. A deplorable accident, Wex called it; an accident for which he blamed himself. He said no more, and Paul felt he shouldn't ask questions.

In January, at the end of his second week of searching, he got a job as a sandwich man, wearing boards advertising a cheap café. Uncle Joe had called sandwich men the dregs of street vendors. Paul couldn't be choosy.

The café owner said Paul had to walk the streets ten hours every day. For this he would be paid three cents, less than a quarter of his daily wage at Crown's. His first day on the street, a sleety rain was falling. He had no mittens, only his cap and jacket for protection. People in cafés and passing carriages ignored him. He was sneezing and shaking when he got back to the Temple that night.

Wex was upset. "You can't keep that job, you'll die of influenza."

"I can do it," Paul insisted.

And he did. At the end of each day he was required to return to the café and store the signboards. On the third evening he found the owner in conversation with an older man, corpulent and poorly dressed.

"This is my brother-in-law Solly, he was laid off his regular job today. I got to give him the boards. Here's what I owe you, and a little extra."

Shocked, bitter, half sick, Paul carried home his splendid earnings as a sandwich man. Ten cents.

Judge William Woods sentenced Eugene Debs to six months for contempt. In January 1895 Debs began serving his term at the McHenry County Jail out in Woodstock. The reason for this, the papers reported, was overcrowding in the Cook County facility.

Paul felt sad for Mr. Debs, who had impressed him as an honest and principled man. He pitied all those who had bravely gone to the barricades against Pullman and lost their homes, their jobs, even their lives, for nothing. With the help of the government in Washington, the railroads had won.

Thoughts of the futile strike reminded him of Cousin Joe. He wondered if they would ever meet again. Sometimes he had a dark premonition that his cousin might be dead.

He found a second job. Cleaning toilets and emptying spittoons in a noisy restaurant on Van Buren, the Brass Bull. The waiters, older men in greasy black tail-coats, were hostile to anyone new or weak. Paul had only one friend, a tubby middle-aged dishwasher named Murmelstein. The waiters called him Sheeny Sam.

One night at closing time a waiter who constantly complained about poor tips turned on Sheeny Sam without provocation and started a fight. Two other waiters joined in. They pushed Murmelstein's head into the big zinc tub of wash water.

The owner and the other waiters formed a ring, laughing and making jokes. Murmelstein waved his arms frantically. Paul saw that it would be foolish to jump in against so many tormentors. He ran into the darkened restaurant, picked up a small table and flung it against the plate-glass window.

The waiters released Murmelstein and raced into the dining room. The owner cornered Paul. "What the hell did you do that for?"

"So you wouldn't drown Sam."

"You little son of a bitch, what do you care about some kike? Get the fuck out of here. I'll keep your pay to settle up for the window."

Wex began to teach him. The sessions took place at night, after Paul came back from his job-hunting rounds, or his brief periods of employment. Even if he was exhausted to the point of stupor, he insisted he was alert, ready, enthusiastic.

"In the 1850s, the very earliest days of the photographic art," Wex told him, "a French genius who signed his work Nadar said that photographic theory can be taught in one hour, the basic technique in one day. What can't be taught is the art. Keen observation of subject and conditions. Composition. Imagination. I can quickly give you all you need to know about the technical aspects. As for the rest, either you will develop the skills, the art, from within yourself, or you won't. On that point I have already formed an opinion."

"Sir?"

"In photography there is a term you'll hear frequently. The latent image. It is the invisible image formed on a surface coated with a light-sensitive material, the emulsion, when the emulsion is exposed to light. You can't see the latent image at that stage but it's there, ready to be brought forth by the development process. By analogy I find—I sense—a latent image within you. You have a sharp eye. A quick mind. Most important, from our first meeting at the Exposition, I have comprehended a great eagerness to learn everything about this marvelous art of the modern age.

"In photography, of course, you need no fine hand for drawing. You draw with light, which has its own mysterious power to form images, and with your creative spirit. That is the latent image. Talent. It will be my task, my challenge, my joy, to develop the image—bring it into the world—let its fruits be seen by others."

He turned slowly to gaze at the sepia-tinted picture of the pretty child with curly hair.

"I'll do it for you as I'd have done it for him."

Paul sat totally still. For the first time he understood Wex's kindness and generosity. He understood the role he was playing in Wex's life. He'd been playing the part unwittingly for days.

Well, he would continue to play it, gladly.

□ □ □ □

Night after night, Paul's head was filled with facts, names, events. Louis Daguerre of Paris, who had perfected the earliest photographic process; it had borne his name ever since. Sir John Herschel, an Englishman, responsible for coining the terms "photography" and "positive" and "negative." Frederick Scott Archer, inventor of the process of suspending light-sensitive crystals in wet collodion on glass plates.

Wex explained that all Matthew Brady's field operators had used the wet-plate process throughout the Civil War. Hence the need for the lightproof wagon. "You had to coat the plate in the wagon, make your exposure, then jump back inside to process it immediately. The first dry plates I saw came over from Liverpool about 1865. Crystals of silver bromide in a dry gelatin base. By 1880, thanks in large part to Eastman, the process was perfected and the wet plate was gone."

Equipment too had undergone evolutionary development, Wex said, illustrating with a boxy *carte de visite* camera from the 1850s. "It makes small multiple exposures on a single plate. You just slide the plate holder to a different position, thus. This camera mechanized the business because studios could hire dolts to operate it. Soon every celebrity wanted a portrait on a *carte*—a paper print pasted to a cardboard mount of standard size. People collected them by the millions. Cardomania, that's what they called it."

Wex had amassed thousands of old photographs of all types. Some were posed by models to tell an allegorical story, like "The Two Ways of Life"—gentleman sinners on the left, the redeemed on the right. Paul thought the sinners, lolling with plump bare-breasted women, had much the better part of it.

Some of the photographs were sentimental. "Fading Away," which Wex said was a big seller in the late 1850s, depicted an ethereal young woman expiring in bed while family members looked on with attitudes of piety and grief.

He owned carton after dusty carton of daguerreotypes in velvet-lined, leather-covered cases; some were framed in mats of hand-painted glass. He had blurry calotypes and cheap tintypes raggedly cut from master plates with shears. Paul grew numb staring at so many faces.

"Do you know these people?" Paul asked.

"Not a one. Most of them are dead, I suppose. But they're all *here,* that's the point of it, don't you see? Long gone, they're still here, their look, their essence— their *moment*—preserved. These"—he rattled a box of tintypes—"only a fool would look at them and call them exciting or meaningful in and of themselves. These are insignificant people, forgotten, as you and I will be forgotten someday. But the *idea* in these, Dutch—history captured; time stopped; death defeated— that is exciting. That is magnificent. That is the miracle."

He showed Paul boxes of yellowing scenic postcards. "There is still quite a rage for these."

"Yes, I collect them."

"My partner and I formed a company to produce cards." He tapped a tiny line of type under a photograph of a pretty Oriental girl posed with a parasol, a blossoming cherry tree in the background. EXCELSIOR ART-PHOTO CO., CHICAGO.

"We hired operators. Sent them around the world. The Acropolis, St. Petersburg, the Alps, Australia, the Holy Land. For six years we had a thriving business."

"What happened?"

Wex sighed. "I'm too trusting. I kept my eye on the artistic side and paid little attention to my partner—or his business practices. One day he absconded with our entire bank account. I believe he's living with some doxy in South America, but I could never afford to hire detectives to prove it."

Despite such defeats, Wex remained an enthusiast. "New lenses, new shutters, new emulsions, new papers—the field is changing every minute of every day. Mr. Eastman, the dry-plate manufacturer in Rochester, revolutionized photography when he found a way to put his emulsion on a paper base. Clever coot, Eastman. Do you imagine he designed his Kodak in order to sell more cameras? No, sir—to hell with the cameras, he'll practically give those away. He wants the cameras *used*. He wants to sell *film*."

Exciting and helpful as they were, lessons and demonstrations could teach only so much. One Sunday during a February thaw, Wex dusted off a pebbled black Kodak camera and said, "There's been enough theory, you must start to practice. Suspend your search for work for a day or two. The weather's good, I want you to go into the streets for snapshots."

Paul said he didn't know or understand the word.

"Comes from hunting. A hunter making a fast shot is said to snap it off, never certain he'll hit the target. It's the same with this type of camera, there's no way to see what the lens sees. You aim, hope—and snap."

He demonstrated, doing a waggish little dance step around the floor. "Snap, snap, snap!" He stopped dancing and held out the Kodak. "This model is two years old but it takes excellent pictures. No one has been battering down my door to buy it. It's yours, to keep."

Paul took the camera in both hands. There was a smile on his face, bright as day breaking. It made Wex laugh and rumple Paul's hair affectionately.

"My star pupil."

Paul snapped all over town. He brought home pictures of horsecars (blurred); manhole covers (nearly unrecognizable); pushcarts (recognizable, but spoiled by unfortunate composition). He took six shots of the Crown mansion, from different points on the other side of Michigan Avenue. Wex disappeared into his darkroom, where he developed and printed the snapshots for Paul.

"Not much imagination, but the technique's all right," he said as he cut the damp prints apart with a scissors and hung each on a wire with a wooden clothespin. "Except for trying to stop the motion of trams. Can't be done with a cheap lens and shutter. Why did you take so many views of this house?"

"I used to live there."

"Oh." Wex picked up another print. "These are the real disasters. Look at the two pushcart peddlers. Because of the position of the camera the men appear to have telephone poles growing out of their heads. Where was your eye? Your concentration?"

"I'll do better," Paul promised, severely let down.

"All right, but there's more. The subjects you chose—my God, they're dull.

Those peddlers might be zombies. Couldn't you animate them with a little chatter? Try again. Bring me something that won't make me yawn."

He went out the very next morning. The sun was high in a clear sky, all the dirty snowbanks had melted, water was rushing in the gutters with a sound that promised spring. It was so warm, it might have been May. He set out for Clark Street but pulled up suddenly at the sight of three garishly rouged women sunning themselves on the steps of Wampler's red light hotel. He recognized the oldest, the stout one with a red butterfly painted on her mouth. She'd come out in slippers and a worn satin robe that revealed a canyon of cleavage. It took him only a second to gather his nerve.

"Hello, ladies, how are you today?" He strode up to them, smiling.

The youngest of the whores was skinny and long-nosed and had a bitter air about her. She blew cigarette smoke at him. "Fuck off, squirt. I don't take on babies."

"Aw, Floss, I've had customers younger'n him," said the second, a girl of incredible homeliness who nevertheless had pretty green eyes. "Least I think so. How old are you?"

"I am eighteen. That is, almost."

"Well, come back later, we don't start work till four or five. We're up all night, f'Christ's sake."

"Ladies, ladies," Paul said quickly, "I am not here for—ah—the usual purpose. I would like to take your photograph."

"Oh, that's one of those snapshot cameras, I seen 'em in a magazine," the homely one said, interested.

For the first time, Butterfly spoke to Paul. "And I seen you someplace before, Junior. Who are you working for, the coppers?"

"Oh, no, I live at the shop just down there."

"Empty Pockets Rooney," said the bitter one.

"Mr. Rooney. I am his student."

"Student of what, how to go hungry?"

"Aw, leave him be, Floss, he's okay," the homely one said.

"Don't be too sure," Butterfly said. "Why would anybody with a grain of brains want a picture of us?"

Paul was about to lose his chance. His mind raced. He said to Butterfly, "I recognize you also, you watched when I was attacked and beaten on this sidewalk by four ruffians."

"Yeah, now I remember." She was less suspicious. Paul smiled his warmest smile.

"I gave you a show that day. You owe me a picture, I think."

Even the bitter one was amused. "Ain't he a sly little pisser."

"Awright, why not?" Butterfly said, shrugging and heaving her massive body off the stoop. "Stand up an' primp, ladies, we're gonna get real artistic with Junior."

Paul began to snap. The whores fell into the spirit of it, striking exaggerated poses, cocking their heads and their hips, coyly drawing their robes open for a glimpse of knee and thigh. A peddler of cutlery stopped his cart to watch, and then a drayman from a brewery that competed with Crown's. When Paul finished twelve exposures and thanked the women, the homely one exclaimed, "You can't stop now, we got to get the boss out here." Soon Paul was photographing the whores in company with the red-nosed proprietor of Wampler's, and then with his pale, round-shouldered desk clerk, and then even his poor bedraggled cook, a toothless Negro who looked to be ninety. Paul snapped another fifteen pictures before he said that he really had to go.

"Awright, Junior, but you got to bring us girls a picture apiece," Butterfly said.

"I will, I promise."

"Floss is right, you're okay for a little pisser. Come back some night an' we'll fix your water pipe." She gave him a large wet kiss that left a scarlet stain on his cheek. The other two whores kissed him too. The bitter one twitched his penis through his pants and whispered, "I'll bet the girls go for you, Dutchie." He hurried away toward the Temple, happy but rather overwhelmed by it all.

Wex rendered his verdcit:

"Fine, these are fine. Too much light, see how their facial tones bleach out? But you surely got some lively expressions out of those soiled doves."

After a moment's reflection, he went on. "I think my original speculation was right, I think you may have the knack. But you want to be more than a mere mechanic. Don't waste time reading all the photo journals that pile up around here. They're good for privy paper, that's about all. While you're learning to handle the camera, study some novelists. The ones with an eye for the arresting detail. Balzac. Zola."

Wex rummaged among his books and found three Zolas with yellow paper covers. "The philistines say he's dirty, but philistines never like anything daring or profound."

In a week, Paul read through *The Dram Shop*. He followed it with *The Human Beast*, then the sexually arousing *Nana*. Prompted by Wex, he read and reread Zola's rich set pieces describing Parisian crowds, theaters and hotels, black locomotives hurtling across the countryside of France. He saw what Wex was getting at. Zola was like a human camera that sorted and captured aspects of the truth, but never softened that truth, or hid it.

When Paul delivered the printed snapshots to Wampler's Hotel, the whores oohed and exclaimed. Floss, the young one, produced a nearly full bottle of stale champagne and they all drank and toasted Paul the great photographer. Butterfly again offered to give him a romp. Paul declined with effusive thanks. He staggered out of Wampler's with a buzzing head. The stale champagne made him run to the toilet and throw up, but nothing could mar his delirious feeling of success.

Though chiefly a photographer of scenes and portraits, Wex wasn't parochial. He was excited by the sort of photography demonstrated when they met at the Exposition. Photography that conveyed motion.

He told Paul about Eadweard Muybridge, an Englishman commissioned to take scores of pictures of a favorite trotting horse owned by the former governor of California, Leland Stanford. "The gov wanted to prove that a running horse had all four feet off the ground at certain times. He put a lot of money on it. Muybridge's pictures won the bet for him."

Wex owned all eleven volumes of a work of Muybridge's called *Animal Loco-motion*. It contained hundreds of plates of animals and human beings, male and female, in various attitudes of walking, running, leaping, stooping, climbing. Paul found the photographs astounding.

Wex dipped into another closet and produced a curious drum with slits in the side. A series of Muybridge's horse pictures were mounted inside the drum, which sat horizontally on a spindle. When the drum was spun rapidly, Paul peered through the slits and saw a marvelous effect. The separate still photographs blended into one image. The horse appeared to gallop.

"It's called a zoetrope. Child's toy. Didn't you ever have one?"

"No, sir, not in Berlin."

"Well, enjoy it. Better blow the dust off."

Paul took it to the roof. There, in the chilly sunshine of a cool Sunday, he lay on his side with his head beside the spinning drum. The slits moved so fast, the drum seemed to vanish.

While the magic horse *ran* . . .

As the weeks passed, he learned more about his mentor. Wex indeed seemed to have no talent whatever for making or keeping money. But then, Paul decided, money wasn't the reason you should love photography, or make it your career.

Wex was a heavy drinker of whiskey, especially, though not always, at night. If he had no customers or commercial jobs, he'd drink in the daytime. Paul guessed he bought whiskey with money he should have spent for warm clothes or better food.

The whiskey relaxed Wex's tongue. Slurring his words, he would make reference to "my many flaws." Or talk about "my ruling passion, which is utterly beyond my control, and which contributed to the demise of my happy home down in Carolina." After those words, he gazed for a long time at the sepia-tinted portrait of his boy.

Trying to cheer him up one night, Paul said he didn't see evidence of too many bad habits. Wex gave him a sideways look from behind his glasses.

"You will. Warm weather's coming. Sporting weather. That's a perilous time for me, Dutch."

Saying that, he poured himself another hooker.

In the middle of February Paul found a new job. General helper at a low dive called the Lone Star Saloon and Palm Garden. It was located on Whiskey Row, the west side of State Street, down near Harrison, and catered to a seamy trade of white men, black men, and young toughs Paul suspected were professional pickpockets.

The Lone Star's proprietor was a small, coarse man named Mickey Finn. He said he was Irish and came from Peoria. He kept a bung starter in his belt. On Paul's first day he threatened to use it on three quarrelsome customers. "I put out men's eyes with this," he told one. "I'll do the same for you if you don't shut your lip."

Finn was proud of a large brown bottle stored under the bar. The bottle contained a milky liquid with which he spiked the drinks of certain unwary customers. At midnight, the end of Paul's second day, Paul waited nervously in the storeroom while his employer rifled the pockets of four men laid out on the filthy floor. Finn handled them roughly, turning them back and forth like meal sacks. Alarmed, Paul said, "Won't they wake up?"

"Not with them knockout drops in 'em. Finn's Number Two Cocktail. Nothin' like it. Soon as I'm done, you haul these bozos outside and drag 'em away from here. A block or two's good enough. It's your last job every day."

He noticed Paul's expression. "What the hell's wrong with you, kid? Can't understand the king's English? What I want you to do is—"

"I heard, Mr. Finn. I don't like this kind of work. I quit."

"Come here, you kraut bastard," Mickey Finn screamed, tearing the bung starter from his belt. Paul was already out the alley door and gone. He was a long time falling asleep that night. Cousin Joe was right, a lot of his vision of America was turning out to be foolish fantasy.

One day in late February he followed his routine of combing the classified advertisements in day-old papers he was allowed to pick up in the lobby of Wampler's Hotel. Today he had a copy of the *Inter-Ocean*. He found no suitable jobs mentioned, so he leafed through the news and social pages. One item made his heart leap.

Vanderhoffs Return
From Grand Tour

Farther down the three-inch story he read, *The gracious and charming Miss Juliette Fishburne Vanderhoff remains abroad for an indefinite period.*

He crumpled the paper, threw it, and then kicked it. If she loved him, as she professed, wouldn't she have come back as soon as possible?

No, he was being unfair. He didn't know the circumstances. Some emergency must be keeping her in Europe. Perhaps she was sick again and had to recuperate. But he wouldn't find out for a while. He must wait.

He would, no question. The waiting would be painful, but it would be worth it. Julie would come back to him. He was certain.

58

Joe Crown

EARLIER IN THAT SAME WINTER, a morning in January, Joe Crown rode to the Atlantic Ocean from Chimneys, his great house a few miles from the South Carolina coast, astride a spirited gray. Gray had been a despised color for a horse in the Union cavalry. This gray, Old Stonewall, was a beauty.

Joe had risen at four after a troubled sleep with many wakeful periods. He'd slept poorly for weeks, an experience he'd had before. Too much to think about. Too many problems. He felt old. Prey to every kind of sour and pessimistic thought about private and public matters.

He had stolen downstairs, lit a lamp, and read for the second time an elaborate booklet describing the Habsburg School, a private academy for boys of German parentage. It promised a great deal. Heavy emphasis on deportment and social graces, a strong curriculum, of which science was an important part, and a program of team sports. It was located in Westchester County, New York, on the border with Connecticut.

That was its principal drawback in Joe's opinion. He had spent virtually all his life in America in the Middle West. He subscribed to its attitudes and shared its myths: the Middle West was more open, friendly, democratic, while the East was closed, haughty, a place where money manipulators hatched schemes to victimize the public and arrogant social cliques held themselves above common folk because of "old blood." A few years ago a little popinjay named Ward McAllister, who pretended to lead and speak for New York City's four hundred best people, had sneered at the idea of Chicago's ever having a similar high society.

Still, the East had undeniable advantages. The finest universities were located there, as were private academies such as the one he was considering for Carl. The Habsburg School promised consistent stern discipline for its pupils, a powerful appeal. Joe Junior and then Paul had come to disastrous ends in Chicago schools. He didn't want his bumptious younger son to go the same way.

Undecided about the school, he had left the booklet on his desk as day was breaking. He dressed upstairs; Ilsa had already left their bed, presumably to cook. In South Carolina the winter thus far had been warm, so he put on a loose white shirt of cotton with full sleeves tightly cuffed at the wrists, and twill trousers stuffed into riding boots.

In the dining room he took coffee and a warm baking powder biscuit laid out on the sideboard by Delphine, the wife of Ford. They were the year-round house couple, blacks native to the state. Good, religious people, both able to read and cipher as well as any white person.

Sunlight, and sounds, streamed in through the open dining-room windows.

Birds warbling. The ring of iron on iron, in the distance. He remembered the lightning-blasted tree out by the road. Orpheus LaMotte, his tenant farmer, had felled the tree in the autumn and split fireplace logs from it every few days.

Joe found he had no appetite for the biscuits and no desire for the strong coffee. Thoughts of Joe Junior were rushing in, filling him as they always did with a terrible anger and a terrible ache, hopelessly tangled. Often he awoke in the middle of the night with his son's bright blue eyes shining in the dark of his mind. So wrathful; accusing . . .

But who was to blame for what had happened? Joe Junior! And Paul, who had abetted his son's flight. There was no question.

In the stable he saddled Old Stonewall and trotted him into the looping drive of crushed oyster shell in front of Chimneys. The great house had two stories, finished in white oyster-shell tabby. A massive whitewashed chimney rose at either end. A wide piazza behind white columns spread across the entire front of the mansion. Joe waved goodbye to Ilsa, who had just emerged from the separate kitchen building behind the great house. He thought she looked tired and not a little despondent. She returned his wave.

He booted the gray down the wide road beneath giant live oaks whose branches time and weather had shaped into a graceful arch over the road. He guided the gray with taps of his boot heels; he hadn't ridden a horse with spurs since he took off Union blue.

The ring of metal on metal grew louder. Near the end of the tunnel of trees, Orpheus LaMotte was at work with his maul and iron wedge, splitting foot-long rounds of the tree trunk. He wore his usual plow shoes, drill trousers, and a patched shirt of jeans cloth already sweated under the arms. Orpheus had been born in Carolina in 1855, ten years before the Union Army brought freedom's Jubilee. After Appomattox, he had taken the last name of his master on an Ashley River plantation named Resolute; the master had been killed sometime during the war. Orpheus and his wife Lydie and three attractive daughters lived on the property in a house he had built room by room, with help from other blacks in the neighborhood.

"Morning, Mist' Crown," he said as Joe reined up. Orpheus had a large, ugly nose and pitted cheeks, but perfect even teeth and a smile like sunshine.

"Mist' Carl, he was already at my house rompin' with Prissy 'fore I come over here. That all right?"

"Of course, if he doesn't knock her down."

Priscilla LaMotte was Carl's age, a tomboy. Slightly built, she could beat him in a footrace but couldn't outwrestle him. Carl loved playing with Prissy, and today his tutor wasn't coming from Charleston. Mr. Ungar rode his swaybacked horse to Chimneys on Mondays, Wednesdays, and Fridays.

Joe waved and trotted on. The road became a sandy track through palmettos and pines. He followed the salt wind eastward, toward the marshes, the sea oats, the sunrise.

He wanted to be alone, to think. He left behind at Chimneys essentially the same insufferable mess that had driven him from Chicago. Joe Junior gone—his nephew gone too, as proper punishment for his defiance and ingratitude. Joe had moments of regret about ordering Paul to leave. The regret was hurtful, so he never permitted it to last long. A man made up his mind, then lived with the consequences.

But other problems persisted. Fritzi wouldn't stop nattering about her determination to have a career on the stage. Carl was rapidly growing taller, more mature. He'd be thirteen in the autumn. Could the rebellion of adolescence be far away?

Ilsa smiled less. She said he had been too hard on all the young people—still was too hard on those left behind. Both Fritzi and Carl had been jerked away from their regular schools and hauled off to South Carolina for the winter, there to keep up with their studies as best they could with the help of Mr. Ungar, the young gentleman tutor from Charleston. Mr. Ungar was a German; his parents had come from some village near Munich. Ungar himself lacked the relaxed and easy disposition of most Bavarians. He was smart, but he was superior and sharp-tongued. Carl and Fritzi couldn't stand him.

Old Stonewall stepped smartly along the cart track between the dunes. Joe heard the ocean. Above the dune line, radiant light filled a cloudless sky. The air smelled salty and warm.

He guided the gray between dunes to the white beach, which was hard, and wide, and gently laved by a purling surf. The beach was empty as far as he could see in either direction. A shrimper's boat stood offshore with its nets down. Otherwise man and horse had all of creation to themselves.

A pelican sailed over on light air currents. Another plunged into the sea, then floated on its belly, presumably digesting a fish. Clam holes in the sand squirted water as the gray trotted by. Tiny land crabs ran from the hoofs.

Joe Crown loved the Low Country of Carolina. It had a beauty unlike any other place. He liked the South generally, and this was true despite his service in an army dedicated to killing its sons. A year ago he'd opened an agency in Atlanta, shipping barrels of beer from Chicago in his own refrigerator cars. Crown lager had done well in the city Sherman burned. Joe was now thinking of expanding in Charleston and developing, if he could, one or two tied houses there; he had three in Atlanta. A tied house was a saloon serving beer from only one brewery.

He did experience a certain irksome discomfort when doing business in Charleston, or anywhere else in the state—this despite his strong positive feelings for Carolinians, whom he found some of the kindest and most gracious people he'd ever met. Many, like Ungar, had German forebears. The various German states and principalities had shipped boatloads of settlers to the colonies through the port of Charleston.

Warm and courteous, Carolinians were at the same time insular; provincial in the extreme. They worshiped their ancestors to the point of enshrining them. He suspected they were even worse snobs than were the old families of the Northeast. It didn't matter whether a Carolina dynasty was rich; in fact, most were dirt-poor thirty years after the war. It only mattered that it was old and bore a distinguished name.

He dismounted to rest the gray. He tied the rein to a driftwood log, pulled off his boots and stockings, and walked barefoot in the cold surf. He must think about going back to Chicago soon. He could trust the brewery to run itself for a month or so, with frequent telegraph messages to and from the owner. But eventually his nature compelled him to return to make sure everything was up to standard. This time he didn't look forward to it. He was growing disenchanted with Chicago, a political sewer increasingly controlled by a band of boodlers, the aldermen, who openly sold favors. Financed by silent partners, they set up dummy companies, then handed municipal traction and utility franchises to those companies for one purpose—to sell out for an exorbitant price when a legitimate group wanted a franchise in the same part of town. No one blinked. No one cared.

Joe's own First Ward was headquarters for the worst boodlers—Alderman Coughlin, a shanty Irish pol allied with Kenna, a saloon keeper. Of late the damned governor, Altgeld, was openly working with the Democratic organization controlled by Coughlin and Kenna. The purpose, it was said, was to conspire against the Eastern wing of the Democratic Party, whose leader was President Cleveland. Everyone knew why Altgeld was lined up with the crooks; Grover Cleveland had gone over his head and sent the troops to quell the Pullman strike. Altgeld wanted revenge.

The governor and the Chicago boodlers were making noises about supporting the free silver radicals. Unlimited coinage of silver was an issue certain to split the Democratic Party. For the first time, Joe was thinking of doing something he'd never done before. Voting Republican.

He was disgusted that he'd been forced to such an extreme position. Just another demonstration of the depths to which Chicago—America—was falling.

Ah, but wasn't he a fool to fret about chaos and disorder in Chicago, and the country, when the same conditions existed in his own household?

He rode back to Chimneys two hours later. Only moments after he walked Old Stonewall into his stall, the stable door crashed open. There was Ilsa, in a state.

"Joe, go to the cottage, quick. Prissy's badly hurt."

"What happened?"

"She and Carl were playing rough on the porch. Carl threw her too hard, she fell against the window, the broken glass slashed her."

Joe touched her briefly as he ran past, into the morning light and down the side road, a quarter of a mile to the whitewashed house of Orpheus and Lydia LaMotte.

Orpheus saw him coming and hurried to meet him. On the porch, Lydie was bending over Prissy's limp body. One of the sleeves of Prissy's dress was torn away. Blood glistened on her arm and soaked the blanket on which she lay. Carl stood in the sand near the porch, eyeing his father with a frightened expression.

"She's cut bad, Mist' Crown, but it weren't Carl's fault," Lydie said as Joe ran up on the porch.

"The devil," he growled, kneeling. Prissy's eyes had a foggy look; she was awake, though obviously in pain. The gash on her arm was six inches long, and deep. When he probed it gently, the girl cried out.

"It needs to be sewn up. Calhoun Manigault at Green Pond is the nearest doctor. I've never dealt with him but I'm sure he can take care of this. Lydie, you keep her comfortable and keep that wound clean while Orpheus and I hitch up the buggy."

Orpheus LaMotte's sweating face grew anxious. "Sir, Dr. Calhoun—he don't treat the colored."

"Let me worry about that."

Dr. Calhoun Manigault's surgery was a room built on the side of his large cypress-wood house. Squat little chickadees bustling about near the stoop flew away as Joe tromped up the steps and knocked.

Manigault was a handsome, paunchy man of middle years, with a mane of white hair that gave him a distinguished air. "Come in, please, sir, what may I do for you?"

Joe pointed to the buggy. Prissy was sitting up, supporting herself with her unbandaged arm. "The girl had an accident, her arm needs stitching."

Manigault wiped his hands on a small towel he'd brought to the door. In a low voice, sharing a confidence, he said, "I'm sorry, but I don't take Nigra patients. Seven miles north of here, you'll find a—"

"I'm not going seven more miles, Doctor. She's bleeding badly."

Manigault squinted from behind his square wire spectacles. "You're a Yankee."

"Yes, I own Chimneys."

"Ah. Crown. I've heard of you. Well, I'm sorry, Mr. Crown, I do *not* treat colored."

Joe stepped closer and gripped the bleached gray doorframe with his left hand. He was almost a head shorter than the doctor.

"Understand me," he said. "You'll treat that girl or they'll be treating you in a Charleston hospital. You may be laid up for weeks. How do you feel about that?"

Manigault averted his gaze. With a wave of the towel, he said, "Bring her in."

On the ride back to Chimneys, Prissy sat beside Joe on the driver's seat. Her head lolled onto his shoulder. She wasn't quite asleep, but Manigault had given her a teaspoon of some opiate to relieve her pain. He'd done a decent job of cleaning and stitching the wound. And he had charged fifteen dollars; robbery. Joe paid without protest.

Dr. Calhoun Manigault was an exemplar of the worst side of the South, Joe thought as the buggy rolled along; one of those who were stubborn about that past in which they'd been defeated in war and humiliated in peace. They perpetuated fictions to defend their actions and absolve their guilt. At meetings of the board of the textile mill in which Joe held shares, or at banks and clubs in Charleston, he still heard a lot of cant about the blissful antebellum days. How "our darkies" had been far happier than Negroes living in the slums up North— never mind that in the slums up North, they were free. Not fairly paid, or decently treated. But *free.* Joe had looked deep into the wounded eyes of enough Carolina blacks, including his tenants Orpheus and Lydie, to know that what the white Carolinians said was a lie.

Even now, thirty years later, the wounds of the war still festered. All over Dixie, the embittered whites were using the law to deprive free black men like Orpheus of their hard-won rights. Baffling new literacy tests, poll taxes, property requirements for voting. There were black schools, and black townships, and black balconies in churches once again. There were black toilets at the railway depots, with stern warning signs about observing the rules of separation.

Like many another Northerner, Joe wasn't ready to accept a black youth as a suitor for his daughter, or even a neighbor on Michigan Avenue. But he would readily have invited the best of them—a lawyer, a musician, the prominent young educator Booker T. Washington—into his home, for conversation or dinner, without hesitation. He considered this attitude liberal as well as morally correct.

Prissy's head bumped gently on his shoulder. Although her eyes were closed, her brown hand with its white palm found his. Joe needed but one hand for the reins of the plodding horse. He held Prissy's hand and thought about Carl, and made up his mind.

With Prissy returned to the house of her parents, and Ilsa reassured that she would be fine, Joe was finally able to retire to his study about two o'clock. A thick envelope of memoranda and letters had arrived from Stefan Zwick yesterday, brought down to Chimneys by a horseback messenger.

He'd no sooner opened the envelope than a fiendish cackling and howling came through the open window. He batted the gauzy curtain aside and stuck his head out. Fritzi was capering on the front piazza, tearing at her hair and screeching like a goblin. *"Take the rope from my neck! Take it away!"*

"In the name of heaven, stop that!" He flung his leg over the sill and climbed out. From a table of white-painted wicker, his daughter plucked a small paper-covered book. Some kind of play text, he saw.

"Papa, I'm practicing. I'm Henry Irving in *The Bells.*"

Last year Joe and Ilsa had taken Fritzi to see the celebrated English actor perform his most famous role, Burgomaster Mathias, the slayer of an elderly Polish Jew who passed through the burgomaster's village in a sleigh. Haunted by guilt, and the sound of sleigh bells, in the third act Mathias went convincingly mad before a thrilled audience.

"Well, I can't abide the noise. I am trying to concentrate on work. Give me that, please."

"Papa, I paid a lot for this prompt book in Chicago. A whole fifty cents! Please don't—"

"I said I'll take it." He grabbed it away, stepped around Fritzi, and stomped into the house through the main door.

Ilsa rushed into the airy central hall from the dining room. "Joe?" Without answering, he wheeled into the study and kicked the door shut behind him.

One crisis after another; was there no end? He was in a fury. He hated the feeling, the weakness it represented, but it was uncontrollable. He looked at the prompt book in his hand. He'd intended to keep it for an hour and then return it. Suddenly it was a hateful symbolic object. He flung the book into the grate and set fire to it with a match.

Late in the afternoon, as the winter sun was setting, Ilsa quietly entered the study. Joe was sitting motionless at his rolltop desk, his eyes seemingly focused somewhere beyond the litter of brewery correspondence. After a moment he glanced up. He noticed Ilsa had put on a shawl over her shirtwaist.

"Will you come take a walk with me?" she asked.

"Yes, that's a good idea. I have something to say."

"Fritzi would like her book if—"

"Her book's gone." He pointed to the black ash in the grate.

"Oh, Joe," she said, shaking her head. The simplicity of her condemnation angered him all over again.

He and Ilsa walked down a path of crushed oyster shell behind the great house. The path ran beside a high hedge of crepe myrtle, bare and severely trimmed back for the winter; then it curved to the edge of a sloping bank. Below the bank, reeds extended west for more than a hundred yards. Beyond lay the water of the tidal marsh, its sun-struck surface shining like the bottom of a copper pot.

Ilsa took his hand and pressed it against her side. "You have something to say, but I will speak first. Joe, I want to tell you something you know already. There is too much trouble in this family."

He tried to disengage his hand. She gave a small, wry smile, as if to say his reaction was expected. She didn't let go.

"Are you blaming me?"

"Stating a fact. Come on, walk, don't be so stubborn."

They continued their slow course along the path. It led to a point of land hooking out toward the water. At its widest place twenty yards from the point, foot-thick limbs of a gigantic live oak shaded both the land and the marsh. Ilsa leaned against the trunk.

"Our son left us, who knows for how long? I have faith that we'll see him again someday, but that doesn't make it easier to bear. Little Pauli, who came to America with such great hopes, he's gone too; I hope it isn't as far. We mustn't drive Fritzi away. Or Carl."

"Fritzi's full of this damned lunacy about stage acting—"

"I think it's just a passing phase. All girls go through them."

"How can you be so sure it's a phase?"

Ilsa patted his face, gently, without reproof. "I am her mother. You are many things, but that's one thing you can never be, my sweetheart."

The endearment surprised and disarmed him. All at once his anger softened. From the pocket of the old frock coat he'd put on for the walk, he pulled one of the expensive Havana cigars he'd begun to favor lately. He bit and spat the end, then struck a match on his boot.

"All right, I take my share of the blame for everything that's happened lately. More than my share."

"No, you mustn't—"

"Let me finish, please, it's my turn. I try to act in good faith, according to what I was taught, and what I believe. I make decisions that way. Carl will attend that school in the East. He needs the discipline, to settle him down. I will explain that to him tonight."

"So," Ilsa said, suddenly cool. "Only the husband decides, is that it?"

"What's wrong with you? It's always been that way in the country we came from, and here too. It's been that way in our marriage."

"Indeed it has, but the world's changing. Women are changing."

"I'm too old," he said with a dogged shake of his head. "I was raised a certain way and it's the only way I know."

"Yes, yes. *Ordnung*. Well, my dear Joe, it's time you took a different path, this one is leading you astray. You must—oh, what's the English for *anpassen*?"

"Adapt."

"Yes. When a savage storm rises—one of those hurricanes that sometimes strike this coast, let us say—the trees bend. Even the strongest bends in order to survive. Because God always sends the storms, Joe. Always."

"You're asking a lot of a man my age."

"What on earth does age have to do with it?"

"If you don't understand, I can't explain. I've made the decision about Carl."

"Without consulting me."

"Have it any way you want it. It's done."

He flung the cigar down and walked away from her, back toward Chimneys.

Ilsa sent word by Delphine's husband Ford that she was tired and wanted to rest rather than eat supper. Fritzi and Carl hardly spoke during the meal. Afterward, Joe wanted a schnapps in the study. Ford brought it to him.

"Be anything else, Mr. Crown?"

"Yes, please ask Carl to come here."

Shortly the boy's footsteps sounded in the hall. Joe twisted the key that raised the wick in the desk lamp, brightening the room. It would probably be decades before electricity or a gas utility reached this far into the Low Country.

Carl Crown entered and stood with his hand on the doorknob. The boy's height and stocky, powerful build showed that he was maturing rapidly.

"Carl," Joe said, keeping an even tone.

"Father."

"Did you see Prissy tonight?"

"Yes, sir. I told her I was sorry."

"As well you should. You played too roughly. Prissy's a girl, weaker than you. You're much too careless about your strength, Carl. I know it isn't intentional, but we must cure it. In the fall, you are going to a new school, in the state of New York. They emphasize scholastics, but they emphasize gentlemanly deportment, too."

He showed Carl the booklet and explained several of the points it contained. Throughout, Carl stood straight and silent as a little Prussian soldier. When Joe was finished, Carl made the one comment his father wanted and expected:

"Yes, sir."

Joe hugged his son and kissed him good night. Carl left quietly. For a few moments Joe was content. At last he was restoring a measure of order to his world.

He rang a hand bell. When Ford arrived, Joe ordered a second schnapps. This surprised the black man. The master never drank two in an evening.

"Ford, have you seen Mrs. Crown?"

"Sir, Delphine said she took pillows an' things to the spare bedroom. Told Delphine she was feeling poorly, she'd sleep better there."

"I see. Thank you, Ford. That's all."

When Ford was gone, Joe slumped in his chair. He regretted he'd quarreled with Ilsa, but he was still angry with her. Ilsa had changed. He'd sensed it before, but tonight he felt it as a crushing certainty. He loved her, of course. He prized her intelligence, her backbone. Yet those very qualities were leading her on to areas in which women had no place. She experimented with new ideas too freely. They'd patch up the quarrel, he had no doubt of that. Ilsa had a boundless ability to forgive. But the larger issues still loomed.

Despite her protest that it was irrelevant, he *was* growing older, in mind and in body. He would be fifty-three on the last day of March. He hated the stiffness he was already feeling in his bones and joints. Further, he didn't understand some of the crazy trends and doctrines blowing through the world. He was still a modernist in regard to inventions, technology, but he didn't like the intellectual and moral atmosphere the new science was creating, at a speed impossible to cope with . . .

He finished the schnapps. His head buzzed. Some profound crisis was brewing in his life. He had heard that it often happened to men his age. They walked out of the house one night and disappeared forever. They tossed over a wife of thirty or forty years, married a woman half her age, and flung themselves into a pathetic parody of youth complete with hair dyes, garish suits, and fatherhood at sixty. The idea horrified him.

In his mind he saw a fearful image. The iron wedge Orpheus used to split his logs. The wedge hammered deeper and deeper into the heartwood, so deep it could never be dislodged until the thing into which it had been driven split asunder. Was he driving an iron wedge into his marriage?

Or was Ilsa?

He sat up a long time, worrying. Toward midnight, a storm began to rumble somewhere over the Atlantic. He shut the downstairs windows. To the east, sheets of white light shot across the sky.

As he climbed the stairs, incredibly tired, he heard the rain, and more thunder. He changed into his nightclothes, turned down their bed, hesitated and pulled the coverlet up again. He stole across the varnished pine floor of the hall, turned the handle stealthily, and crept into the room, and the bed, where Ilsa was sleeping. He hardly made a sound.

After an extended silence, she said, "I am awake."

He rolled toward her. They reached for each other, embracing. Lightning burst outside, flashing through the slits in the closed shutters. They held each other tightly.

"I'm sorry," he whispered. And again, "I'm sorry."

"It's all right," she said, though he wondered if she believed it. "Did you tell Carl?"

"Yes."

"How did he take it?"

"Better than I expected. Maybe he doesn't like our home anymore." The bitter thought had come suddenly.

Ilsa was quiet for another interval. "I saw that a new packet from Stefan had arrived. Was there anything from the detectives?"

"The weekly report. Nothing in it, as usual. What do they have to go on but a physical description that could apply to ten thousand young men? It's a vast country, Ilsa. If he chooses to obey the law, as I hope he will, who will notice him? Certainly not some local police department."

"Then you think he's gone for good?"

"Ilsa, don't—"

"Answer me, Joe."

"Yes, I think he's gone for good. I'm sorry. I take the blame."

59

Paul

WEX TAUGHT HIM how to expose an Eastman dry plate in a big tripod camera, process it, and contact-print the negative plate by locking it in a frame with a sheet of printing paper, lugging the frame to the roof, and timing the exposure in the winter sunshine. Paul's first such plate was a simple head study of his mentor; Wex had taken off his spectacles and managed a fey grin. After nervous moments on the roof—too much time? too little?—Paul carried the print downstairs, washed it, fixed it, and hung it up with clothespins.

He stood in front of it, cocking his head one way and another. The mustached old pixie grinned back at him from the dripping sheet. Paul swelled with pride. He had *made* this picture. Taken it—finished it—everything. Suddenly he clapped his hands, grinned, shuffled his feet in a joyous little dance, like a black boy he'd seen dancing for pennies on a street corner. His worries and disappointments seemed altogether trivial at this moment of discovery and self-esteem. Truly, it was a blessing to live in an age of miracles.

Three stalwarts of the First Ward Democratic Club hired Wex to photograph them for the club headquarters. The Democrats controlled the ward, and much else besides, and Wex had a solid relationship with them. He had a particular loyalty to the two bosses, an alderman named Coughlin and a saloon keeper named Kenna.

The three who called on Wex were underlings. Loud-spoken, and dressed in fancy clothes that managed to look cheap. Paul didn't like them, but he recognized the significance of their swaggering airs. They had power in the city.

Wex blandly named his price—five dollars each. The pols yelped, swore, started to walk out. Wex laughed.

"Why are you so het up, boys? You know the club can afford it. Most of your cash comes from City Hall boodle, and there's plenty of that, I hear."

The pol who spoke for the group said all right, five smackers apiece was a deal. *Smacker;* dollar. Paul filed that away in his growing lexicon of slang.

Wex took more than a half hour posing and photographing each of the politicians; he was a perfectionist about his craft, if about nothing else. At the end of the session the leader said, "Send the pictures around fast as you can. Alderman Coughlin's wanting a new one of himself. If these turn out good, we'll put in a word."

The unexpected profit of fifteen dollars, half in advance, elated Wex. "Dutch, let's take the night off. There's something I've been yearning to see for months. Now we can afford it, without a guilty conscience."

"What is that?"

"Mr. Edison's flicker parlor. We'll have oysters at the Palmer House first."

In a narrow space at 148 State Street, the latest invention of the Wizard of Menlo Park could be enjoyed for five cents per view. It was snowing heavily when Paul and Wex walked in from the slushy street. Wex's glasses were speckled with melting snow. It dripped from his old cracked shoes.

Despite the weather the parlor had four customers, including a respectable middle-aged woman wearing good clothes. Wex flung his arms out like a happy child. "Isn't this something? They say Edison plans to spread these parlors all over America."

They stepped up to the ticket counter. A pedestal nearby displayed a metallic bust of the great inventor. Behind this stood ten cabinets, back to back in two rows of five, each cabinet about three feet high and two feet deep. Although the walls of the Kinetoscope parlor were a bilious brown, management had provided plenty of electric light as well as a rail in front of each row of machines, for the comfort of patrons leaning forward over the eyepiece.

The man selling tickets was well dressed, in a suit, stiff collar, and string tie. Wex said, "Are you the manager, sir?"

"The owner. This is a parlor franchised by the Edison Kinetoscope Company."

"How long are your films?"

"Approximately twenty seconds. A quarter permits you to see five."

"What, a whole nickel for each?"

"You can't expect genius to work for nothing. The Kinetoscope's a fabulous invention."

Wex bought two twenty-five-cent tickets and handed one to Paul. Moving away from the counter, Wex ticked Edison's bust with a fingernail. "Fake," he whispered. "Bronze paint on plaster."

Paul's pulsebeat quickened as they approached the cabinets. "These are the machines Mr. Edison didn't deliver in time for the Exposition?"

"The same."

Wex looked at the pictures in one row of Kinetoscopes, Paul the other. Edison's subjects were inoffensive, not to say dull. Paul viewed "Organ Grinder," "At the Barbershop"—watching haircuts was not his idea of excitement—"Shoeing Horses," "Trained Bears," and "Sandow the Great." The last was the most appealing. The famous German strongman was posed against a plain dark backdrop, clad in a garment resembling a large diaper. It afforded an impressive display of Sandow's flexing arms and quivering biceps.

When Wex finished looking into his five machines, he returned to the counter. "Sir, I'm in the photographic profession myself. I'd like to see inside one of those machines." The owner balked. Wex argued and finally pressed a half dollar on him.

"Well, all right, I suppose Mr. Edison can't spy on me from New Jersey."

As soon as the other customers left, marveling at what they'd seen, the man moved one of the cabinets, unscrewed the back and removed it. Wex knelt, enraptured. Paul peered over his shoulder at a loop of film that appeared to feed continuously over geared rollers.

After several minutes Wex stood up. "Thank you, sir, most enlightening." He tipped his cap and they went out. The snowfall had stopped. "Despite the incredibly dull subjects, that box is the miracle of the age. Temporarily."

"Why do you say that?"

"Because the picture is too small. Because only one person at a time can view it. What's needed is a machine to *project* the picture. Throw the image onto a wall, or a special screen, for an audience. A large, *paying* audience. Those journals that come into the shop say inventors are working frantically on projector designs, and that includes Edison—though he makes no secret of having little faith in the worth of the process. I say just wait a few years, everything will change. No more dingy rooms like that one, there'll be special theaters. And crowds to fill them. Something so wonderful can't possibly fail to catch on." Wex's spectacles flashed under a street lamp; he was almost dancing in the slush.

"Still, Mr. Edison's not only a mechanical genius, he's a true promoter. He's taking advantage of the novelty and selling Kinetoscope exhibition rights for entire states, nothing less. Owners of the rights can then lease the machines to other individuals, or open parlors of their own. It takes a deal of cash, I hear."

"How new is this parlor?"

"Opened in May, last year. Damn poor timing. It got lost in the hullabaloo of the Pullman trouble. For months hardly anyone knew it was here."

"I wonder if the owner is making money on his investment."

"I should hope so. Say, that's a fine English word, 'investment.' You're learning a deal of them, aren't you?"

"Trying. I study my grammar and dictionary every spare minute. And I don't think in German anymore. Well, almost never."

"All the better for you when you become a citizen."

That night Paul had a dream about the Kinetoscope pictures. In slow, dreamy images, the great Sandow, tall as a house, flexed arms as thick as oak trees to show biceps bigger than boulders. At his feet, thousands of pygmy spectators applauded. In the morning Paul awoke with a new excitement and enthusiasm.

Those are the pictures I want to make. If Wex is right, one day they'll be popular with millions. If I were a camera operator who took such pictures, I could afford to be a husband, and it would be fine work, too. Why, I might go all over the world! . . .

An unhappy thought stole away his excitement. If he did what he was imagining, he'd have to abandon the man who'd taken him in and taught him. That wouldn't be easy—if he could do it at all. It was a problem he didn't want to think about.

At last, on a raw windy day in late March, he found a good job. Driver of a delivery wagon for the Illinois Steam Laundry Company.

The laundry was owned and run by one Albert Grace. Mr. Grace had a round jowly face, dressed well, and had the air of a man who sold religious goods or something equally proper. During his interview, Paul was asked a few short questions. The rest of the time Albert Grace talked.

"I run a necessary business," Grace said. "Provide an important service. I have dozens of accounts, and this laundry is the favorite of every one of them. If you take this job, you are on the front line for the Illinois Steam Laundry Company. When you deliver and pick up, you are the embodiment of Albert Grace. That's a very high responsibility."

At the end of twenty minutes of monologue Mr. Grace shook Paul's hand and said he was mightily impressed by Paul's grasp of English. Considering Mr. Grace's lofty pronouncements, Paul was astonished to learn the truth about the Illinois Steam Laundry Company when he began work. To be sure, the laundry supplied dining-room and bed linens to a few of the lesser downtown hotels. But the bulk of its business came from a long list of customers in the First Ward. The Illinois Steam Laundry Company handled the linens of whorehouses.

The laundry's principal territory, the Levee, ran from Eighteenth Street down to Twenty-second, between Wabash Avenue on the east and Clark Street on the west. Originally confined to a couple of blocks on State and considered a subsection of Satan's Mile—Van Buren to Twenty-second—the Levee had lately grown and now eclipsed all the other vice districts: Little Cheyenne, Little Hell, the Bad Lands, Coon Hollow, and the formerly preeminent Custom House Place. Albert Grace's laundry occupied a three-story building on Wabash near Twenty-fourth Street. This was convenient to the place considered the social heart of the Levee, Freiberg's Dance Hall on Twenty-second.

Picking up and delivering with the laundry wagon began another dramatic education for Paul. Although Uncle Joe had often railed against the vice thriving in Chicago, Paul had never guessed the staggering size of the trade. He was astounded at the number of individual cribs, fancy bordellos, concert saloons, dance parlors with women available in upstairs "wine rooms." Their names teased the imagination. The Chinese Delight. The Dark Secret. Mother Maude's. The "Why Not?" Many of them ran day as well as night shifts. The depression continuing to grip the country seemed to have little effect on the demand for illicit sex. Every morning, after just a few stops on his assigned route, Paul's wagon was so stuffed with linen, he had to throw his full weight against the rear doors to latch them. He loaded and unloaded the wagon four, sometimes five times between seven in the morning and six at night. At first he simply couldn't believe there could be so much rutting going on in so many places.

A Niagara of spirits flowed through the vice dens. Thousands of barrels of beer were served, but not one came from Crown's. Organized thievery was an important sideline in many of the places. Gambling thrived in neighboring pool halls, handbooks, craps and faro rooms. Everything contributed to the Levee's booming prosperity, but sex was the engine. Scores of legitimate businesses such as newsstands and delicatessens, dry cleaners and breweries, furniture stores and carpet dealers—and laundries—used black ink, or red, according to the rhythms of the whorehouse trade.

Paul quickly learned that the trade had connections to City Hall, police headquarters, the local precinct house. It was no secret; people talked and boasted of it openly. There were even links to swank residential sections miles away. Mr. Grace, his wife and seven children had recently relocated to one of these, Evanston. From a fine home in that totally dry enclave, the Graces donated to all the significant German charities in the city, always making sure their generosity was mentioned in the papers. Mr. Grace had been born Albrecht Gerstmeier, in Silesia, a fact undetectable from Grace's precise English. It made Paul laugh to think of the thousands of stained sheets and pillowslips on which the respectability of the Grace family rested.

During his first weeks he met hundreds of girls. He ran into them, warm and sleepy and waking up with a champagne cocktail, at noon or later. He chatted with them while they ate steak and eggs for breakfast at three or four. The Levee was a rainbow of girls: immigrant girls from Bohemia and runaway girls from farms downstate; Polish girls and Irish girls; shiny black girls from Alabama and tawny brown girls from the faraway isle of Jamaica; even some Chinese girls and red Indian girls. There were girls in purple tights and girls in red harem pants; girls in little-girl shifts trimmed with blue lace and girls who showed everything in Mother Hubbards of black fishnet; girls in corsets with garters and pink stockings and girls in high-collared velvet gowns suitable for attending church. He met girls who'd been to college and girls who couldn't read; girls who were Lutherans, Baptists, Catholics, African Methodists—or agnostics or atheists after a childhood of hell-roaring exhortations against sin.

A few of the whores were almost grannies, but most were shamefully young— lured in by the ropers and controlled by cadets, the Levee's name for pimps. Some of the whores were thick-witted and crude, as ugly inside as out. Others were merely adrift, or frankly in the trade to put something aside for old age. A few entertained hopes of some rich customer's falling in love with them. A sad and vain hope, Paul thought.

Paul was young, energetic, and almost always cheerful. He had rough good looks and a convivial disposition, and his color improved now that he was out in the weather all day. Most of the whores and madams liked him, so he got acquainted with a lot of the stock quickly.

One of his favorites hailed from a farm near Ottumwa, Iowa. She weighed over two hundred fifty pounds and was therefore called Slim. Paul enjoyed talking with her over a cup of afternoon coffee, and her employer, Madam Elaine, didn't seem to object. Madam Elaine was graying and regal, with the face of a choir singer and the vocabulary of a drayman. "Drink all my coffee you want," she told Paul. "But if you waste Slim's time when she has a customer, or try to fuck her for nothing—then, my little lad, I'll cut off your cock with a dull cleaver."

Unfortately Slim saw more in Paul than an occasional social visitor, and she began to leave boxes of candy on the hall table, marked with his name, if she was busy. One day he found the candy in a heart-shaped box, with a note. Slim said she'd risk the wrath of Madam Elaine and meet Paul somewhere if he wanted to make love to her. For nearly a week he agonized over the best way to tell Slim that he appreciated her generous offer but could not accept.

He was spared when he came in one morning to find that a customer had slashed her with a razor after an argument. She'd been taken to the emergency hospital, where she died. Her body was shipped to Iowa in a special large coffin paid for by Madam Elaine. Madam Elaine was shaken by great racking sobs the evening Paul accompanied her to buy the coffin. "She was such a God damn good girl. The crazy fucker who cut her is a dope fiend. He's going to suffer for what he did, I've put the word out. He'll get what he deserves, a new mouth under his chin and a swim in Lake Michigan, may his shriveled rotten soul burn and stink in hell forever."

The ice in Lake Michigan began to melt and crack apart, piling up in huge blocks on shore. Sleet storms gave way to rain. Paul smelled spring behind the eternal Chicago miasma of stockyard offal and horse manure.

Driving morning and afternoon and sometimes into the night for the laundry, darting in and out of houses and dens with his canvas hamper of linens overflowing, he had plenty of offers to sample the stock. He always declined politely, with an improvised excuse. He didn't fancy himself morally superior. He just wanted to be loyal to Julie, and he didn't want clap. So he didn't whore around. Nor did he drink, except for one or two daily lagers. Going out of his way to find a place that served Crown's was a small gesture of loyalty to the family.

One evening after work, in a hard rain, he stood outside the mansion for a quarter of an hour. The windows shone with warm electric light. Familiar figures moved back and forth: Helga Blenkers; Fritzi, hopping and spinning with her arms flung wide in another of her theatrical fantasies.

He watched Uncle Joe's landau return from the brewery. For an instant he wanted to dash across the rain-lashed street. Catch the carriage. Pound on the side. *"See here, I'm part of this family. Can't we patch this up?"*

Instead, he walked away, with bitter thoughts of his uncle's turning him out. He'd make his way without the family's help, counsel, money, or affection. He'd find affection of his own. Affection, and a true home.

With Julie.

That spring he was a street boy again.

He was no longer an innocent. Berlin had taught him much at a young age, and he saw the dirty, dangerous side of the Levee. But the district had an undeniable excitement and energy, and he wasn't intimidated by the residents. Cautious but friendly, he never judged anyone's morals too severely. He acquired a tougher look but didn't strut or consciously attempt an air of bravado. He didn't cock a cigarette in his mouth for effect; he tried Dukes and Caporals a few times and coughed too much. But he carried himself with quiet authority. The panhandlers steered away from him and never directly solicited a handout, though he sometimes gave them a penny or two. His favorite was a spindly, dignified old gentleman with the poorest of clothes but the finest of manners and diction. His name was Shakespeare. The first time Paul handed him a coin, he clasped it tight in his fist, struck a pose and declaimed: "A kind overflow of kindness! *Measure for Measure,* act the fourth. For your kindness I owe you a good turn! *Much Ado,* act the first." Paul enjoyed the old man so much, he began to search for him in order to give him something. On one occasion he watched a patron come out of a saloon and ignore the genteel panhandler's appeal. Shakespeare shouted after him, "I am not in a giving mood today! *Richard Third,* act the fourth. Fuck you, brother."

The grifters with their three-card monte stands never bothered Paul because they never mistook him for a rube, and the cadets working the sidewalks never solicited him.

Then there were the pickpockets, some as young as eight or nine. One afternoon on Twenty-second Street, he felt something lightly brush his left pants pocket. He whipped his hand down and caught a wrist the color of dark honey.

Paul jerked the thief in front of him; he was a tan boy, part white, part Negro, with delicate features and filthy clothes that were falling apart. The boy looked starved. He was, at the most, ten.

The feral boy tugged and wrenched to get free. Paul's grip was too strong. "Listen, I work around here, why the devil are you trying to rob me?"

"He don't give a hang where you work," said an unseen speaker behind him. "He's one of Dummy's boys." The voice belonged to a colored bootblack in neatly pressed pants and a vest. Much darker skin than the pickpocket's. He was standing tensely at the corner.

Remembering a word Joe Junior had taught him, Paul said to the pickpocket, "I don't like being marked for a sucker. Do you hear?" The boy flung his head back and spit on him.

"Mean little son of a bitch, ain't he?" said the bootblack. "Millard Fillmore's his name, can you feature it? I s'pose he didn't have any name at all when some slut whelped him. He'll kill you for a dime."

Paul figured the pickpocket expected a few blows, or worse. Give him a surprise, then. With his free hand he reached into his pocket. "A dime, is that all it takes? Here are two. Buy a glass of milk and some sausages. Use the rest for a bathhouse and a haircut. You'll feel a lot better."

And with that he let go.

The stupefied pickpocket stared back and forth from Paul to the coins. Then he grinned; half his teeth were a diseased dark brown. He tossed the coins up and caught them.

"Thanks, Dutchie." He dropped the coins in his pocket and produced a long clasp knife. He opened it with a snap and flourished the blade, six or seven inches long.

"Go on, do as you're told, Mr. President Fillmore," Paul said. "And stop trying to frighten your elders."

Fillmore grinned wider and snapped the knife shut. "You got some balls, Dutchie. See you later."

"My Lord, you took a chance," said the bootblack, fanning himself with his hand. "Dummy's boys are killers."

"Dummy?"

"Dummy Steinbaum. He trains and runs the gang. Starts 'em at seven years. Uses a dressmaker's dummy with a coat or dress on it, an' little bells that tinkle if the boy's careless."

Paul climbed to the seat of his wagon and drove away. That was his only direct encounter with the pickpocket gang of Dummy Steinbaum, an organization that numbered between thirty and forty members. On his rounds a few days later he heard that Millard Fillmore had told his mates he'd personally cut up any of them who dared to steal a penny from the German laundryman.

Every week Paul put a little money into a bank savings account. By mail, from the great thick pulp paper catalog of Sears, Roebuck & Company of Chicago, he began to buy items for a new wardrobe. He shopped by mail because all the whores said that unless you could afford luxury goods, you could do no better. The catalog masthead claimed as much with its boldly printed slogan: CHEAPEST SUPPLY HOUSE ON EARTH.

Sears sold through its enormous office and warehouse on North Division Street. Paul bought a sack suit of good French corduroy, gray; the bottom of the coat had the popular round cut. Price, $7.95. He bought a fancy duck vest, single-breasted, with polka dots; $1.05. He bought a pair of gents' high-top front-laced balmorals, commonly called bals, in calfskin, with needle-point toes; $3.75. He bought a shirt, detachable celluloid wing collar and celluloid cuffs and a striped cravat. He topped it off with a dressy young man's derby; $1.50.

"Quite the sport, aren't you?" Wex said, amused, when Paul showed him the clothes from the large carton delivered by the express company. "You'll be trigged out just right for the track."

"What track?"

"The racetrack. Washington Park. Hawthorne. Heard of them, haven't you?"

"I don't think so."

"You're probably not interested, either." Wex sniffed the warm wind blowing through the propped-open skylight. "They'll be operating soon, thank God."

Frowning, Paul remembered searching for Wex the first time. He recalled a puzzling remark about Wex's being fond of "ponies." If Wex was betting on horse races, that might explain the perpetual poverty of the temple of the photographic art.

Wex noticed Paul's frown. "I know, I know, gambling's a terrible habit. Told you I had demons." The next seemed torn out of him. "The horses cost me Alice, my studio, everything. Because they cost me the life of my boy."

Paul drew the new derby from its round box. Doing that allowed him to collect his thoughts and reply carefully. "I have wanted to ask about him. I thought it wasn't my place."

"It isn't. I've never told anybody. Never been close enough to anybody. Let's go in the back. We'll sit down. Where I can look at the picture."

I have loved horses (Wex said) ever since I was raised up in Charleston, South Carolina. Charleston had a racecourse long before there was such a thing as the United States, did y'know? A respectable place it was, too. Highly favored by the gentry.

So I was cursed early with the love for a fast horse. And I soon felt the need to put down a little money to show my faith in the speed, and the heart, of a fine animal. If you don't understand the rage to gamble, to plunge all in order to win all—if you've never caught the fever, as some men call it—then I can explain neither the feeling nor the cause, for the first is like the wildest form of love, and the second is beyond comprehension. At least mine.

Now across the sound from the little town of Beaufort, where I lived after the war with my wife Alice, and had my studio, and saw my son come into the world, there lies a wild, largely unpopulated barrier island by the name of Hilton Head. It was named for the navigator who found it, Captain Hilton.

On Hilton Head the wind blew lonely, and a few impoverished plantation operators came slinking back after the war, and a great many colored freedmen wandered about, confused over their new rights and new status.

A certain amount of trading in staples went on between Beaufort and the whites and blacks living isolated on the other island. It was the old colored man who swept my studio, Germanicus by name, who brought me word of the fabulous horse on Hilton Head. A sorrel horse, strong as Hercules and more red than brown; red as glory, they said, its mane and tail lighter, something like honey tinctured with a few drops of blood. This marvelous horse had incredible speed and was owned by a freedman named Alammelech Smalls, Lam for short. Lam Smalls had a reputation as a proud man; proud to be free at last and proud to be proud instead of ashamed of his black skin. In that year soon after the Jubilee, no wonder he named the great horse Liberator.

On the same island, there was also this ruined planter who had lost virtually everything. His great house had been looted and smashed down to a hovel. This gentleman's name was Colonel Prospero Drayton.

Colonel Drayton had a fast horse, a black stallion. He hated the idea that the nigras were free, he hated what he called their uppity pertinacious ways—and so you won't be surprised that he conceived a monstrous hatred of Lam Smalls, and Liberator, as soon as he heard of Lam's bragging about the sorrel's speed.

Naturally a race was arranged. The word went out through all the Low Country. There was no question that I would go over on that Saturday, in my little sailing skiff, with oars aboard in case the wind failed. I wanted to see the spectacle. Most of all, I wanted to wager the contents of the studio cash box on Liberator. This I never said to my wife in so many words, but she understood; she was angry, as always.

On the morning of the race the sun came up with a peculiar dead white color, the air was heavy and still, and Germanicus, who spoke the secret slave tongue of Gullah, most of which I could understand, said to me, *"Mester Waxfud, uh debbil ob uh stawm cawmin dis daay, moy bone dun tall me. You battuh be cahpul crossin' duh woyd wawtuh en duh small bowat."* I failed to heed a word, though Germanicus knew the good and bad humors of that coast far better than I, who had been away for many years. And also, I had the fever to bet on the race.

My little boy, Wexford Junior, was at that time four and a half. Bright as a polished pebble. Knew all his letters by sight. Talked like an ancient philosopher —an astounding vocabulary. And pretty, pretty as an angel.

Little Wex wanted to see the great race too. Alice objected, for Port Royal

Sound is a large body of water, with strong tidal currents. Nevertheless, against my wife's protestations, little Wex went with me into the skiff. Our passage to Hilton Head was swift and easy, for a nor'east breeze had sprung up, and I could sail virtually without effort or thought. Little Wex and I were mightily excited when we beached and secured the skiff on the mucky shore of Hilton Head. I noticed a certain dark gray hue arising on the northeastern quadrant of the horizon, but I was too flushed with the fever to care.

The race was scheduled for noon. Colonel Drayton's cousin Midian was up on the stallion. Lam Smalls himself rode Liberator. I put everything, one hundred eleven dollars, on the sorrel and the former slave. Precisely at twelve the starting pistol shattered the silence. Liberator immediately sped ahead by a length, then two lengths—even a majority of the whites cheered the magnificent effort. Then, inexplicably, Liberator took a fall. Went down sidewise, bellowing in pain.

Simple mischance, nothing more. Midian Drayton raced to victory, and the colonel flung his whiskey bottle against a rotting store front and laughed like a madman. Lam Smalls was all right but Liberator was not, both forelegs had snapped.

Broke, and not wanting little Wex to see the beautiful sorrel put down, I hurried away to the beach with my son. Already the wind was up, blowing grits of sand in our faces. Small scallops of white water showed on the ocean and the sound. I made ready as fast as I could, because the northern sky was now very dark. I should not have put out from the beach then, but I thought I could make it across in time.

We made excellent progress, even in the heavy chop. I talked constantly to my son, with the cheerfulest smile I could muster, for I saw he was frightened by the keening of the wind and the smacking of the waves. We were three quarters of the way to our destination when the full storm struck.

The skiff capsized, a madness of water and foam, above which I managed to hear the thin little wail of my boy. I had his hand clasped tightly in my right fist, and my left flailed out to seize the gunwale of the overturned boat. The tide was flowing in, the breaking storm behind it, and the poor child was sobbing, though we were both so wet, constantly dashed and half drowned by waves, no tears could be seen.

I held on that way for five or ten minutes, blown steadily inland, toward one of the many small bumps of land too small to be called an island. My wrists felt fit to break, my arms were afire with pain, but I held on, crying things like, "We're all right, Wex, hold fast to Papa, we're going to make it."

Another huge wave broke over us. And suddenly this awful feeling—

(Wex raised his right hand, fingers spread, and as he looked at it, the horror showed.)

Nothing there. He'd let go, or I'd let go, or we'd been sundered by the last wave—not a hundred yards from a scrap of ground where we could have survived.

I went as mad as Drayton, shouting my boy's name. Now the lightning came. The thunder crashed. If he'd piped a reply, how would I have heard? If I'd let go of the overturned skiff, I'd have died myself. With the salt spray burning my eyes, I searched everywhere for his curly head, a waving fist—

Gone.

The storm threw me half senseless onto that bit of land, that bitter refuge of sand and wind-lashed sea grass. I stood on braced legs and yelled his name into the storm—"*Wex! Wex!*" There was no answer.

The storm blew out at four o'clock, and a beautiful golden sun sparkled the waters, which were calm again. A shrimperman who'd laid up in some inland channel during the blow came down toward the ocean and saw me, and took me off in the dory he towed behind the larger boat. Seventeen days later a small Negro girl gathering oysters at low tide found my son's decomposing body, in the marsh not far from Beaufort.

That's the story of how I gambled and lost more than money. Alice never forgave me. It was the end. The end of my marriage—my studio—

The end of the man I might have been, had I not had the fever.

Do you want to know the worst part? I still have the sickness, God damn my soul. Explain it if you can.

(Wex lowered his head into his hands.)

I can't.

At length Wex recovered. Spoke calmly again. "There you are, face-to-face with my demon. And he never leaves me be. I still go to racetracks."

Paul brushed the brim of his new derby, which he'd set carefully on the cleanest spot on the table. "Well, I might go sometime, to see what it's like. I'm very sorry about your son."

"Thank you, Dutch. I feel better for having got it out in the open after so long." He rubbed a finger back and forth under his nose. "Now perhaps you understand why I take such pleasure in having you here. Teaching you what little I know—"

"It isn't little, it's very much."

"All right, we won't argue. It's your turn for confession. Your mood's been a lot sunnier this last week or so. Care to say why?"

"I am working, I have money—"

"And that's why you bought those new duds?"

"To look more American, yes."

Wex rolled the tip of his tongue in his cheek. "That's all?"

Paul flushed. "Well—no. I've met a girl. I think she wants me to take her out."

"What about that society girl in Europe?"

"I know, I shouldn't look at anyone else. But I do get lonely—"

Wex sidled around the table and threw a companionable arm over Paul's shoulder. "Go on, it's all right to have a date with this other one. You're young, it's spring, and just because you take her out for fun you don't have to marry her."

"That's right, I don't," Paul said. He was smiling again.

Paul had flirted innocently with a lot of the young women who worked eleven-hour shifts in the heat and steam and damp at the laundry. Only one seriously caught his fancy. She was seventeen, and though she certainly couldn't qualify as a beauty, he found her attractive. About five feet tall, she had a mass of red curls and a pert rump even a shapeless gray skirt couldn't hide. She had a large well-proportioned bosom, too; it seemed even more prominent because she was small.

She operated a steam mangle, ironing the bed and table linens of customers who paid extra for the service. Her round glasses were perpetually fogged. Her name was Nancy Logan. She brought a carrot cake to the laundry one Tuesday, saying she'd baked it for him. Her interest was clear.

After the discussion with Wex and another day or two of agonizing, of weighing Julie's remoteness, Wex's advice, and his own pent-up need, he invited Nancy to go roller-skating the following Sunday.

It turned out to be a wonderful warm day. The breezy outdoor rink, roofed in green slate with walls of white-painted lattice, was crowded. He and Nancy skated separately awhile, then with his right arm around her waist. A calliope blasted out tunes of the moment. He wore his new outfit, with derby. She'd pinned a sprig of artificial orange blossom to her seriously out-of-date bustle.

Nancy pressed against him at every opportunity. Her breasts touching his sleeve aroused him. He felt mortally guilty, and at the same time he enjoyed it. He tried to be more careful about keeping space between them.

Nancy was from Indiana. "I had to move out because ma and pa had thirteen of us kids, and the farm can't produce enough to feed everybody. I came up on the Monon line from Reelsville a year ago last month. I almost didn't get out of the Dearborn Street depot alive."

"Why not?"

"There was this young fella, standing around and picking his teeth with a silver pick. After I asked directions at the newsstand, I noticed him watching me. I started for the door and he headed me off, all smiles. Not a bad-looking fella, but nothing special either. Tall, skinny, with a spit curl here." She traced a corkscrew on her forehead with her little tan glove. Her description stirred something in Paul's memory, but he couldn't get hold of it.

"He asks me if I'm new in Chicago, I say yes, I came to find work. He grabs hold of my arm and says he might be able to help. Might be able to find me a room, too. He smiles a big smile and says his name's Jim. Something about that smile—something about him that I can't explain to this day—it scared the life out of me. I ran out of the depot with my grip. I ran eight or ten blocks before I had nerve enough to look back. He wasn't anywhere in sight. I never saw him again, and I'm thankful."

"You did the right thing. I will bet he was a roper from the Levee."

"What's a roper?"

"A man who loiters in train stations trying to round up young girls for"— reddening, he sought some tactful English—"illicit purposes."

"Oh my Lord. You mean they want girls for the places we work for? Houses of ill repute?"

"That's right. Young girls are picked up, then locked in a flat somewhere. Then they are—ah—Nancy, are you sure you want me to continue?"

"Yes!"

"The imprisoned young women are—ah—outraged by one or more men, over a period of several days." Her green eyes grew huge. "It's called breaking in. So I am told," he added hastily.

"Lord. I was lucky, wasn't I?" She snuggled against him. They skated slowly among older couples and young men showing off solo. The calliope began "Tell Them That You Saw Me," a sentimental hit everyone was humming.

"Want to know something?" she said without looking at him. "I'm awful glad I met you. I really like you."

"I like you also, Nancy."

"Hope you don't mind me speaking up. I'm pretty bold about important things. Guess it's the farm. There's a lot of plain talk on a farm. I mean, animals are right out in the open all the time, doing what animals do."

"Yes, I understand," he said, awkwardly; he was aroused again.

They skated to "Over the Waves."

"Dutch, I need to ask you something. Have you got a regular girl?"

Julie's eyes haunted him. "Yes, Nancy. But she's a long way from here. All the way across the Atlantic Ocean."

"Did she leave you?"

"Not exactly. Her parents didn't like me, they took her on a trip."

"Do you miss her?"

"I do."

"Will you get over it?"

He couldn't answer. She read his face. "That means no. Hell. My bad luck."

She picked up his left hand and turned toward him, letting him watch for other skaters. The metal-shaded rink lights set her eyes to glowing like jade. "All right, you were honest, and if that's the cut of the cards, what can I do? Here's a proposition. You can love her and me too. So come on, let's go to my place. It's just one room, but it's private."

"Nancy, I don't think—"

"I'm strong for you, Dutch. Awful strong. I won't try to take you away from her. I promise."

He tasted the spring air. He savored her nearness. His body was raging. Without a word, he led her from the floor of the rink.

"Oh my God," he said, bolting up in the narrow bed in Nancy's mean little room on Jackson, within sight of the West Branch of the river.

"What's wrong?" She threw off the sheet and clambered to her knees. The light of a spring moon through the small window silvered her belly and thighs. In the shadows her nipples looked like black cherries.

"I am so slow—"

"Not with me you aren't," she said, flicking his privates gently, in a teasing way. They had made love twice, each of them pouring into it a need of a different kind.

"I'm talking about the roper. The one you met at the station. I think I know him." He described the delivery boy from Frankel's and the theft of some of Aunt Ilsa's fine china. "His name was Jimmy too."

"Jim, Jimmy—there must be thousands in this town."

"Not tall and thin, with a spit curl here."

She clasped his hand as it came away from his forehead. "Well, if it's him, I hope you never meet him again, once is enough for anybody. There was something bad about him. Something awful. Lord, I'm cold all at once. Think you can do something about that?"

60

Jimmy

HE WAS BORN James Aloysius Daws, in one of the poorest Irish patches on the West Side. His mother, Bert, insisted her son was legitimate. Insisted he had a father. Jimmy never saw him. At least in later life, he couldn't remember him.

When he was small, they moved in with his Uncle Francis, on Grand Avenue, west of the river. This was an original Irish neighborhood from which the Irish were moving as soon as they could better themselves. Practically every week the neighborhood received a new detachment of dagos fresh off the cars from New York. The dagos moved in with relatives who had already taken over the hand-me-down houses of the departed Irish. The Irish who stayed behind, unable to afford a nicer neighborhood or the suburbs, were silently scorned by the older Italians and mistreated by the younger ones. Jimmy soon added dagos to the list of people he hated.

He hated his relatives, too. Uncle Francis had a wife sterner than most nuns, and eleven children. Even at four and five, Jimmy had to punch and kick ferociously to protect his few inches of sleeping space on the floor.

He assumed that his mother had some kind of regular job during those years, but she never talked about it, then or later. Uncle Francis was a bellman at the Palmer House. Most of his wages came in the form of tips. Sometimes he brought home next to nothing, and when that happened he went off to mass, muttering that God would provide. Which was a stupid way to look at it, Jimmy decided. All you had to do was notice the raggedy clothes Uncle Francis and his family wore, or the pitiful food they ate. No better than slops at a workhouse.

Uncle Francis was the one who turned Jimmy against God and the Catholic faith, forever.

Uncle Francis was devout to the point of mania. He had a favorite article of punishment, a piece of quarter-inch lumber. Nothing Jimmy ever felt on his scrawny ass hurt as bad as that flat board in the hand of Uncle Francis.

His uncle beat him for impertinence or for slothfulness, but he beat him most often for transgressions involving the Church. Uncle Francis ordered his children, and Jimmy, to attend the 9 A.M. children's mass every Sunday morning. The priest always gave a little homily about obedience, usually couched in some story about meek and mild bunnies, forgiving jackasses, and other animals and attitudes wholly foreign to Jimmy's experience.

Uncle Francis had spies in the parish who reported any truancy at the children's mass. After just a very few homilies dealing with long-suffering bluebirds who got a reward in bird heaven, Jimmy became the family truant. When Uncle Francis beat him, Jimmy's mother never protested. How could she when she was living on her brother's charity?

Uncle Francis's doddering parish priest seemed to encourage this sort of inducement to piety. Or at least the old fool never objected within Jimmy's hearing. Jimmy quickly learned to hate priests and their whole clerical rigmarole.

When Jimmy was six and a half, another incident magnified his hatred of his uncle. Some of the Italian boys cornered Jimmy one afternoon and demanded he empty his pockets for them. All the boys were older and bigger.

Jimmy feinted one way, ducked the other way, and ran. He thought Uncle Francis, when he returned from the Palmer House, would congratulate him on his speed and cleverness in avoiding a beating. Instead, Uncle Francis, who once again smelled of the saloon, went into a rage. He led Jimmy out behind the cottage and lectured him on the unmanly sin of cowardice. Then shouting, "Dirty yella brat, got a yella streak this wide, I'll get rid of it once fer all," he whaled Jimmy with the quarter-inch board.

The accusation of cowardice had so humiliated and scarred Jimmy that, as such incidents sometimes do, it sank deep into his being. So deep as to be almost buried. Years later, he never realized that it influenced half the things he did to demonstrate nerve, to prove he didn't have that streak down his back.

The charity of his uncle's household was considerably less than a blessing. Still, Uncle Francis's rickety cottage provided a measure of security. Jimmy realized this most keenly when, with no warning, the security was snatched away. As Uncle Francis walked home one night, he was set on by a gang of toughs. Later the police determined they were all members of the A.P.A. The American Protective Association, an organization devoted to baiting Catholics and, it was hoped, driving them out of America. The police found Uncle Francis in the gutter with blood and brains running out his nose. He lived six hours. The household disintegrated.

Jimmy's criminal career began soon afterward. He accompanied his mother to fine stores. She wore the same large hoopskirt each time. Outside the store, careful not to be observed, she pushed Jimmy under the skirt and hoops. He duck-waddled into the store in the dark, bumped by her legs, tickled by her bloomers, terrified of discovery.

In the store, Bert slipped various articles through a slitted pocket in her skirt. Jimmy stowed them in larger pockets specially sewn inside her petticoat. Later Bert pawned the articles for whatever she could get.

It provided a modest living for about a year. Then one day, store detectives in Field's swooped down on Bert, and the next thing Jimmy knew, his mother disappeared into the women's wing of the Bridewell.

Leaving him to begin his real education, on the streets.

□ □ □ □

Jimmy was living under a pile of wood at a lumberyard when he chanced to fall in with three colored boys, very tough and smart. Instead of beating him or cutting him with their big clasp knives, they took a liking to him. He became their pupil.

Soon he was slipping zinc torpedoes onto the rails just before a streetcar passed. When the explosion set the passengers to gasping and screaming, Jimmy jumped aboard and snatched one or more handbags. He was lean and he was fast. He was never caught. The colored boys insisted he split the loot with them, but he didn't mind; a few cents were always left over for a stale roll and a cup of coffee. At age eight he was earning his way.

Bert Daws left the Bridewell at the end of four months. She took up residence at Number 441 South Clark Street, a three-story brownstone whose opulence astonished her son. The place was a palace. Other women lived there too, occupying more than twenty comfortable bedrooms. The landlady, Mrs. Carrie Watson, was soft-spoken and refined. She wore diamond chokers, carried perfumed lace handkerchiefs, and drove around Chicago in a white carriage with fancy yellow wheels that Jimmy hated. She sent regular donations to the Catholic church across the street from her brownstone and to a synagogue nearby. Jimmy had a cot in a cozy space behind the bowling alley in the basement.

At Carrie Watson's, electric lights twinkled all night, every night. Wine was served in silver buckets. Carriages and hacks bearing well-dressed gentlemen arrived and departed frequently. One evening a chuckling chef from the kitchen showed Jimmy an upstairs peephole and helped him stand on a stool to look. In the room beyond, Jimmy saw one of Mrs. Watson's ladies writhing underneath a gentleman. Neither was wearing a stitch.

He realized what went on at Number 441. He decided that his mother must be doing that sort of thing too. He wasn't shocked. Not in the least. People did the thing all the time, he'd learned that early. And Bert wore nice clothes again. He slept warm at night after the bowling pins stopped clattering. Mother and son were eating regularly, fine food prepared by two Negro mammies. Just the table scraps would have been a banquet to Uncle Francis. Jimmy thought it very smart of his mother to make her way at Carrie Watson's.

It didn't last. Bert got into a vicious fight with another woman. Jimmy never knew why. Mrs. Watson said Bert was responsible and turned them out. They moved to a succession of smaller, grubbier bordellos. Finally, one night when Jimmy was ten, gunshots changed his life forever.

The establishment in which Bert and Jimmy were living at the time was the lowest form of brothel, a panel house. A panel house was designed to relieve customers of a lot more than their pent-up passions. The layout was standard. Between every two bedrooms was a smaller chamber, called an operating room. It had a common wall with each bedroom. In these two walls, usually paneled in dark wood on the bedroom side, or papered in some monotonous pattern that lulled the eye, there were hinged or sliding panels that opened from the operating room. In each bedroom, the bed and the one visitor chair were placed with precise calculation. When the guest was busy and the lady was jumping and shouting—panel house women were coached to feign passionate noise to conceal the occasional telltale squeak of a hinge—the operator reached through the opening and rifled the gentleman's pants hanging on the chair or the end of the bed. Sometimes the operator used a long pole with a hook for a difficult extraction.

Jimmy earned a regular wage manning an operating room. He was adept with the hook. The madam of the panel house was considerate enough to assign him to an operating room on a floor below his mother's.

The night the shots rang out, he ran upstairs and found Bert leaning against the wall of her bedroom. A pudgy black whore who was her friend was shaking her arm, sobbing, "Bert, don't shut your eyes. Bert, wake up."

Bert was sagging, clutching her middle. She was wearing her gaudy silk wrapper with peacocks embroidered on it, as she always did when she worked. The blue ground of the wrapper looked black where blood was soaking through. The wall panel was wide open, the hinged part swung back into the operating room. The guest chair lay on its side.

Under the flickering gaslight, Jimmy ran to Bert with a cry. He flung his arms around her and held her. Feebly she caressed his hair. Pronounced his name once. Then she sagged and slid away. He decided later that she had died at that moment, in his arms. Ever afterward he remembered the sight of his own blood-smeared hands.

Her slayer, some drummer, had detected the attempted theft of his valuables. He had already been hauled off by the coppers when Jimmy reached Bert's room. The madam paid the coppers well for that kind of quick action.

The madam said she'd pay for an inexpensive funeral but, reluctantly, she would have to ask Jimmy to leave now that Bert would no longer be working productively.

At age ten Jimmy went onto the streets for good.

He did all right; he was no chump and never would be. He made few mistakes. Those that he did make taught him something.

He blacked boots on downtown corners, in good weather and bad. He suffered through winters when the sleet struck your cheeks like nails. Winter in Chicago had its own survival methods. You enrolled in a public night school and pretended to study. Actually you sat in the back and dozed, thereby staying warm for a couple of hours.

Jimmy was a striver. Nothing much got in the way of that, and certainly not the faith into which he'd been baptized. He regularly stole from poor boxes in Catholic churches around the city. His favorite was the poor box at Saint Stanislaus Kostka, because by stealing at that church, he was doing dirt to a Polack congregation, and he disliked Polacks.

He disliked Germans too. No, that was too mild. He hated them like rat poison. Down on Roosevelt Road there was a predominantly German church, St. Francis of Assisi. One of Jimmy's few serious mistakes occurred there.

After hanging around St. Francis of Assisi for a day or two, he was struck by a new and inspiring thought. Instead of coins from the poor box, he ought to swipe something of substantial value. He settled on an obvious and logical choice, the golden monstrance brought out by the priests to display the host.

Church ritual afforded him a fine opportunity to steal the monstrance. This was during forty-hour devotions. The monstrance remained on the altar the entire time.

The priest always began the devotions, but since the ritual lasted through the night, naturally the priest had to sleep. Parishioners organized among themselves to be sure that at least one person was always in a front pew, awake and alert. Jimmy concealed himself in the back of the church, hoping that one of the watchers would be too tired to stay awake.

Around three in the morning, it happened just that way. Jimmy crept past the pews one by one, snatched the monstrance from the altar, jammed it under his coat, and ran.

Exhilarated, dreaming of his newfound wealth and the way his reputation would grow because of his feat, he took the monstrance to Glass the pawnbroker.

Glass laughed at him.

"Are you pulling my leg, Jim? Do you think I can put this in one of my showcases with a price tag? Do you think I can *sell* this? Fence this? I'm not *katholisch,* but I know what it is. Everybody knows. You're a stupid *goy,* I always gave you more credit. Think before you steal! Are you going to return this, or shall I do it?"

Mortified, Jimmy tried to sneak the monstrance into St. Francis of Assisi that afternoon. Unfortunately the sexton caught him and summoned the mealy-faced old German priest.

Holding tight to Jimmy's arm, the priest shouted at him in guttural English. "Are you a Catholic?"

"I am, what's that got to do with—?"

"It compounds the crime. Not only are you a blot on society, you're a disgrace to your faith. Even Our Lord Himself couldn't save you. You are going to hell, boy. You are going to hell."

Jimmy, twelve at the time, gave him a smirk. "Nah, Father, I been there already. Been there and back."

Then he rammed a knee in the old man's testicles.

The priest cried out and collapsed against the sexton. Jimmy fled down the aisle.

After that he hated Germans more than ever. He never forgot the lesson Glass expounded, though.

As he grew up, how he appeared to girls became more and more important. If a fellow didn't look tough, flush with cash, smart as the next joe or a little smarter, it was for damn sure he'd go through life being ignored by all the desirable girls. Didn't matter if a fellow *was* any of those things—might be a lot safer, in fact, if he *wasn't.* But the *appearance*—that was crucial. If the girl fell for the surface appearance, you were on first base; if she didn't, you'd never make a score—hell, you were the strikeout king. Thus from a more or less normal interest in girls came his twisted way of courting them; his propensity for lying about what he was, what he had, and most everything in his past.

He had jobs of all kinds and occasionally tried to improve himself with a respectable one. He never lasted. Honest jobs gave him no chance to get ahead fast, to make money without effort. Sometimes thievery cost him the job, sometimes his explosive temper or his outspoken dislike of the foreign-born, whether employers or co-workers. Jimmy hated strange accents, whether they belonged to wops, krauts, kikes, dagos, or niggers from down in Dixie. He knew he might be a bastard, but by Christ he was an American through and through. He loved his country, it was a land of opportunity.

Delivering meat for Frankel's was one of those respectable jobs that didn't last long. It had taken him into some fancy homes, but that merely aroused his anger by reminding him he wasn't getting ahead fast enough. After picking up fine china at the Crown house on Michigan, fearing prosecution, he'd decamped from Frankel's without giving notice.

He had worked at a variety of jobs since then. Busboy, bouncer, general helper at a dancing academy where he got free lessons because the proprietress liked his cheeky ways. He worked as a special deputy during the Pullman strike, and when that ended, as a roper for a large crib on Clark, south of Taylor, in the Bad Lands. He liked being a roper, especially when he was allowed to join the crew at the break-in flat. It amounted to rape, but that was the job. Very enjoyable.

He kept the job until he caught a dose of clap. He figured a little blonde from Rock Island had given it to him. He'd roped her at the depot and participated in her break-in. She kept screaming that she was a virgin. A joke; virgins didn't give you clap. With the permission of the madam, who didn't find the girl satisfactory anyway, Jimmy called on the dishonest little tart in her mussy room and punched her up, until she wailed for mercy.

Her caterwauling enraged him. He kept punching her. Rolling her off the bed and punching her. Hauling her up by her hair and punching her. Punching her while she crawled on her knees toward the door, through a slick of blood that gushed from her nose. He kicked the small of her back. She snapped forward, her head cracking against the door. Then she sagged sideways and flopped on her back, white and still.

"Aw come on," Jimmy said with a nervous snicker. "Don't spoof me. Open your eyes, I won't hit you again."

Nothing.

"I said wake up, you bitch." Again he grabbed her hair, dragging her up. Blood dribbled from her nose onto her small white breasts. Jimmy let her fall with a thump.

He put his nose near her mouth. Cold; no breath. A foul odor rose from her relaxing body. "Aw Christ."

He raked his hands through his hair, his eyes wet with fright. "Aw Christ, *Christ amighty.*"

The madam was furious. Disposal of the body was his responsibility. "Then stay out of this house. For good."

He hauled the corpse to the river at night, in a stolen wheelbarrow. The dead girl was in a coarse sack that had once held unmixed cement. Fortunately her body was light. He dragged the sack into a lumberyard on the West Branch; he'd previously spent a whole five bucks so the night watchman would leave the gate padlock open on the hasp.

At the lumberyard pier, terrified of discovery even in a deserted neighborhood in almost total darkness, Jimmy weighted the sack with pieces of pipe, tied the neck with wire, and slid it into the river, which shone like oil under the moon. He staggered away, leaving the wheelbarrow. In the alley outside the lumberyard he dropped his pants, sick with the runs.

By the end of the week his terror had abated, replaced by a sense of superiority and strength only murder could convey. A few days later, one of the cadets who worked with the madam sought him out. He and the cadet had done each other favors.

"Bad news, Jimmy. That little chippy from Rock Island? Her brother's deputy police chief. He's in town raising hell. They found her, y'know."

"I dint know."

"It was in the papers. Thing is, there'll be heat now. You better get away from the crib trade, and stay away, for a good long time. Hide yourself someplace where the bulls ain't likely to look. Get into something respeckable." That was how he said it, *respeckable*.

So Jimmy Daws got into something respeckable and thereby met Paul Crown again.

61

Paul

THERE CAME to the Temple of Photography another of those flashy dressers common in the First Ward. The man was built so massively, he might have been a brother of the late Slim. He introduced himself as Toots Tilson. "From the committee."

Paul showed Toots the cane-bottomed visitor's chair next to the dusty display case, then ran upstairs and knocked at a door. Wex came out wearing his canvas apron with many pockets, and his rubber gloves. Downstairs, Toots sniffed and said, "Jesus, that's some toilet water."

"Sodium thiosulfate," Wex said. "Hypo. I'm working in the darkroom tonight."

"I won't take long. I come about the insurance." Toots pointedly stared at Paul.

Wex mumbled, "Dutch, will you excuse us?" Paul left. Later, in the kitchen, he and Wex shared some rye bread, sticks of celery, and two brown bottles of Heimat.

"That man sells insurance?" Paul asked.

"Figure of speech. Coughlin and Kenna came up with the idea, and everybody likes it. If a contributor to the fund gets in trouble with city hall, or the cops, the fund hires attorneys for him. Even stands bail. Goes to the wall for him, in other words. I started paying in a few years ago when I was doing some, ah, special business."

Paul sat with his elbows on the table, waiting.

"Ah hell," Wex said, "I suppose I don't have to keep it secret from you." He jumped up and returned with a large cardboard folder of the kind used to mount a photo. The cover had a gold curlicue border, cheaply done, flaking off.

"I took this picture behind locked doors. Printed it myself. I sold about three hundred copies, two dollars apiece. I did it solely to promote the art of photography, you understand. Some sprout of sixteen, seventeen, got hold of one and showed it to his papa, who happened to be a church deacon. The dirty philistine went to the papers. Next thing I know the coppers are charging me with purveying obscenity. I spent two nights in the lockup. But that was all. A lawyer hired by the fund sprung me and got me off without a trial. I was stuck with a devil of a lot of pictures, though. Go on, take a peek. It's called The Pearl."

Paul opened the folder. The large print showed a hinged clam shell, six or seven feet wide, lying amid some beach props he recognized. The top half of the shell was folded back. Standing in the shell was a young woman, posed with one hand near her startled rounded mouth, and another suggestively covering her intimate parts.

The girl was voluptuous, with dark hair and eyes. She wore a garment resembling a white satin union suit, ornamented with a satin sash. Paul could understand why the picture had gotten Wex arrested. Material like this was sold from underneath a counter.

Wex tore off a chunk of bread. "Work of art, isn't it?"

"Oh yes, definitely," Paul lied. He closed the folder. "So that gentleman, Mr. Toots"—he had trouble saying the odd American name—"wanted your payment for the fund?"

"Yes, and I haven't got it."

"What did you do?"

"Same as I've done before. Worked out a trade. It'll clear my account for six months. The Bath—Alderman Coughlin—wants a new portrait of himself for his family. He's vain as a peacock. Those three pols who were here before recommended me, so Coughlin's coming to the studio a week from tomorrow, five o'clock. Get home early that day to meet him. You never know when you'll need a friend, or a favor, down on the Levee."

"Greetings, lad. John Joseph Coughlin's the name."

He crushed Paul's hand in his big paw. Six feet tall, Coughlin was built like an iron worker. His neck was thick and red, his shoulders broad. His chest and stomach formed a single corpulent curve. He wore his oiled hair in a high thick pompadour. Impressive sideburns reached an inch below his ears. His upswept mustache points glistened. His nails were manicured and polished, and he smelled of talc. He was carrying something flat wrapped in brown paper.

"Happy to meet you, sir. I'm Paul, Mr. Rooney's assistant. He's waiting for you back there, if you'll come along."

Bathhouse John Coughlin was no more than thirty-five, but he had a fearsome reputation. On the way home from a magic lantern lecture about the Great Fire,

Nancy Logan had warned him. "Alderman Coughlin runs the gray wolves at City Hall. Hasn't an honest bone in his body, they say. Don't let him entice you into a bad way of life, you're a smart fella. Kind and sweet, too. One of these days you'll want to carry that other girl home to a little cottage. You be careful."

Wex had told Paul that the alderman was proudly, flamboyantly a product of Conley's Patch, an enclave of Chicago's poorest Irish. He'd begun his working career as a rubber at a Turkish bath on Clark Street, but he was ambitious and soon moved to the Palmer House, whose baths were famous throughout America.

He next bought a bathhouse of his own on East Madison, then a second one in the Brevoort Hotel. He still operated those, as well as a saloon called the Silver Dollar; he was a free-silver Democrat.

But Coughlin's real business was Chicago—the control of it from City Hall and the dispensing of its municipal favors in return for boodle. He'd been elected to council for the first time in 1892 and overwhelmingly reelected two years later. People who disliked him said he insured his victories with flying squads of thugs who kept opposition voters away from the polls. Wex said that when Coughlin allied himself with saloon keeper Michael Kenna, nicknamed Hinky Dink, their control of the First Ward had become unassailable. Although Hinky Dink Kenna was temperamentally different from the Bath, as political operators they were equally shrewd and tough. Hinky Dink had a majority of First Ward election judges in his pocket. He could turn up an unlimited supply of voters bearing names from gravestones. "The Hink brings in his repeaters from as far away as Lake County," Wex said. "No secret about what he pays, either. Fifty cents a vote, plus all the sausage, bread, cheese, and beer you can swallow."

Coughlin dressed like a nob. A nob with debatable taste, but still a nob. To be photographed, he'd chosen a frock coat of shiny black silk with an ostentatious metal star pinned to the lapel. It said *Alderman.* He complimented his outer coat with a shirt of bright green silk, a sky blue cravat, and an ivory silk vest adorned with yellow flowers. His spats matched the flowers.

"Here's Mr. Coughlin, sir," Paul announced. Wex popped from under the black camera cloth and rushed forward to pump the Bath's hand.

"Alderman. What a pleasure. Sit right down. Do you have any suggestions about the portrait? Any particular pose in mind?"

Coughlin's choirboy face grew thoughtful. He pulled out a handkerchief and dusted the corner of a garden bench Wex had spent half an hour positioning in front of three Doric columns. Wex grew red with embarrassment.

"Nuh-uh," the alderman said when he finished dusting. "Except I want it to have dignity, it's for Mary and the wee ones."

"Dignity. My feeling precisely. Something completely befitting your station—"

"That's the ticket, pal." Beaming, Coughlin yanked up the tails of his coat and plumped his rear on the bench.

Wex had donned an ankle-length brown duster for the session. He tripped on it twice, which showed Paul how nervous he was. He ordered Paul to move a reflector two inches to the left, then back to the right one-half inch. This went on for fifteen minutes. After a further delay for polishing the camera lens, and another for adjusting Coughlin's pose, and another for apologetically taking a comb to a wayward oiled curl on his subject's head, Wex squeezed the bulb to make the first exposure.

"We need Rembrandt lighting," he said after stepping back. "High and from the side." He was sweating mightily. So was his subject. The Bath gestured in an officious way.

"Lad, fetch that package lying yonder. Rooney, let's hang this up on one of these here columns. Some might call it commercial, but what's wrong with that? Make money, I say. Make money and live long."

Paul gave him the parcel. The Bath unwrapped a yellow sign with strong chocolate lettering.

CLEANLINESS GIVES HEALTH
HEALTH IS RICHES—HEALTH IS LIFE
THERE'S HEALTH IN COUGHLIN'S BATHS!

"Oh, fine, very dignified," Wex said. Coughlin preened. "Dutch! Fetch a hammer and nail."

And so it went, an hour and a half of fussing and adjusting, with occasional interruptions to expose a plate. Finally the Bath consulted a huge silver turnip and said he had to go. He pumped the photographer's hand. "Swell, just swell. We'll take care of your insurance payment, don't worry."

"That's wonderful of you, Alderman, thank you."

Coughlin peered around the dusty rundown studio. "Looks like business could be better."

"Yes, sir, very much so."

"I'll pass the word downtown. If the aldermen don't want pictures of their wives, maybe they'll send their girlfriends. Call on me anytime you need a favor. That goes for you too, kid. That's what my job's all about. Service and prosperity. Prosperity and service."

He tipped his hat and blew out of the shop like a prairie cyclone.

Wex fumed over the prints that came out of the darkroom. "These are disgraceful. These are an insult to the profession. Look at that advertisement. 'Cheap' isn't the word. I can't think of a word bad enough."

In one print the Bath's eyeballs were rolled toward heaven in a saintly way. The sign fairly screamed its message. Paul couldn't help laughing. Not Wex. "God, the prostitution. If he has a scintilla of taste, he'll hate these."

On his way to work Paul delivered the package of prints to the Silver Dollar saloon. A day later the postman brought a note on parchment notepaper with an elaborately engraved heading.

HON. J. J. COUGHLIN
Alderman
Residence, No. 165 Van Buren Street
Committees:
Finance • Health • Wharves & Public Grounds
Harbors • Viaducts & Bridges
Streets & Alleys (South)

The note quickly conveyed the alderman's reaction.

Swell pictures!! Washington Park opens up next week. My horse First Ward will run. Be my guests in my box won't you. Yrs admiringly,

Coughlin

The following Monday, Paul asked for Tuesday afternoon off. Albert Grace fiddled with a pencil for a minute to make him nervous. Then he said he'd allow the absence because Paul had proved himself dependable and a hard worker.

"But your pay will be docked."

Washington Park's grandstands, clubhouse, and landscaped grounds occupied an eighty-acre site at Sixty-first Street and Cottage Grove. Warm sunshine blessed the opening day. Paul and Wex rode the South Side Elevated, trying to stay as far from open windows as they could. The engine burned soft coal and threw off clouds of soot.

The El let them off near the track entrance, in the midst of a large and festive crowd. Paul wore his gray cord suit and carried a Kodak from the shop. Wex looked flushed and sweaty. Earlier Paul had seen him stuff a roll of bills in his coat. How he came by the cash Paul couldn't imagine.

On the crowded esplanade, a young man with blond, center-parted hair tried to press handbills on them. Waving him off with an oath, Wex seemed extraordinarily nervous. Overwrought, almost. No wonder he called horse racing his demon.

For splendor and spectacle, Washington Park's opening day could hardly be matched. Chicago's well-to-do were arriving in huge four-in-hand coaches. Coaching was the rage among the rich, Nancy said, and Paul believed it. He'd never seen so many fine vehicles in one place.

"Meet you inside," Wex said, rushing off without explanation. Paul followed the line of gleaming victorias and phaetons and tallyhos through the gates. Plumes bobbed on the blooded horses. Tiny silver bells jingled. Metal and leather had been polished and rubbed to perfection. Well-fed men and women packed the coaches, waving to the less fortunate. The biggest vehicles had benches on top; those too were filled.

A few gentlemen chose to arrive alone, on thoroughbred horses with docked tails. On winding paths around the clubhouse, the gentlemen made their mounts pace, sidestep, kneel to the unwashed who pressed against the railings on each side. Presently the gentlemen seemed to grow bored. They dismounted one by one. Grooms led the animals away to stables.

Wex came hurrying back with a newspaper sticking from his pocket. "All right, let's hunt up our host." Paul fell in step, glancing at the paper. It was devoted to horse racing.

Located at the front rail of the center grandstand, the Bath's box was one of the largest and best, with nine chairs and additional room for standing. Other guests were already seated. As Paul and Wex stepped in, Paul noticed several cardboard boxes stacked in one corner.

The Bath greeted them boisterously. "Glad you boys could make it, hope you brought plenty of cash." His infectious laugh boomed. He worked Wex's hand up and down like a pump handle.

"Handsome outfit you're wearing, Mr. Alderman," Wex said after he freed himself.

"You like this here combination?" The Bath fingered his dove gray lapel. His shirt was pink, his cravat and spats white, his waistcoat dark green with a white check. "I call 'em my racing colors. Come along, meet the gang."

The first to be presented was a tiny dour man, five feet tall and about Coughlin's age. Everything he wore was black except his stiff-bosomed shirt. He chewed an unlit cigar and regarded the newcomers with the chilliest blue eyes Paul had ever seen.

"This is my associate Mr. Michael Kenna. Hink, meet Wexford Rooney and his helper, Dutch. Forgot your last name, Dutch, sorry. These are a couple of first-class artistes, Hink."

"Pleasure," the dour man said, not shaking hands. He then sat down and ignored them.

"Over here—" The Bath moved to a tall, powerfully built man. "My pal from Twenty-second Street, Colonel Shadow. Heck, give him his whole due—R. Sidney Shadow the Third. Of the Denver Shadows. Great old pioneer family! Puritan stock from Maine. This man's a genius, boys. He's an inventor, a showman— you're gonna hear plenty from him."

Wex said, "I recognize your name, Colonel. You're in the picture business."

With a stately bow, the man offered his hand. "Correct, sir." The colonel's voice was a marvelous instrument—stentorian, yet seductive as a preacher's. "Call me Sid, won't you? Permit me to introduce my nieces, Miss Waterman and Miss Akers."

Two young women curtsied and giggled. One was dressed like an admiral, with a yachting cap, the other like Sherlock Holmes, with a deerstalker. Both wore a lot of scarlet lip rouge.

People were filling the stands and the landscaped infield. A brass band played. The sky was a fine light blue. Spring breezes fluttered the grandstand flags and the plumes of ladies hats, and riffled the silks of the jockeys parading their horses for the start of the first race. "Ooo, Sid, they're almost ready to go!" Miss Waterman cried. If she and the other "niece" were related to the tall man, Paul was President Cleveland.

Flushed again, Wex made a darting move toward the gate of the box. "Is there time left to wager?"

The Bath eyed the horses. "Just—if you hurry. First Ward isn't up till the third race. In this one I'd lay something on Tinker's Dam. Keep your bloomers on, girls; that's d-a-m, it ain't dirty." He laughed louder than either of the squealing tarts. Wex bolted from the box.

"Dutch, how about taking a snap of us?"

Paul gladly obliged the alderman, first posing Coughlin with his arm around the tarts, then enlarging the group and leaning back over the rear rail to get them all in. Kenna wouldn't stand up for the photograph. He sat, chewing his cigar and reading his racing form. He was either the shyest man in the world or the most arrogant.

Wex came back and crowded into the last shot. The horses were in the gate. A bell rang, everyone in the stands jumped up, yelling, and for the next two and a half minutes programs were brandished and kerchiefs waved while sunlight flashed on the lenses of expensive field glasses. A horse named Prince Hal won the race. Tinker's Dam came in sixth in the field of seven. Wex tore up his tickets.

Paul was fascinated by Colonel Shadow. If Wex was something of an Irish pixie, Shadow was a granite statue. His features were craggy, his jaw line long and powerful. He dressed in elegant Western style: tooled calf boots, twill trousers, a spring overcoat of smooth black wool melton. His shirt was cadet blue; the pointed ends of his cravat flowed down over the front. His sand-colored sombrero was the match of that worn by Buffalo Bill in his Wild West show. It had a band of russet leather embossed with Indian designs. Altogether, Colonel R. Sidney Shadow the Third was an imposing personage, though quite pale, as though he stayed indoors too much.

"Excuse me, Colonel," Paul said, "do I understand correctly, you are in the picture business?"

"That's right, son."

"The moving pictures," Wex said. "The flickers."

"The rage of the coming age," Colonel Shadow intoned. "What's your name again, sir?"

"Wexford Rooney. I am a photographer."

"Fine! This is your assistant?"

"Paul Crown, sir. Everyone calls me Dutch."

"Dutch. Fine." They shook. The colonel flipped back his overcoat to reveal a scarlet satin lining. He handed cards to Paul and Wex. The cards bore his name and the words CHICAGO LUXOGRAPH COMPANY, together with an address.

"I'm proud to say I'm the inventor and holder of the patent on the Luxoscope peep show machine. We're in five Midwestern states already and expanding at a furious rate. I'm also working on a Luxograph projection system."

"Wonderful," Wex said with a distracted air. "I'd like to hear all about it. But the next race is coming up. Excuse me."

He left and Paul took the empty chair beside the colonel. Excited, he said, "I first saw flicker pictures at the Exposition. It was thrilling. Do you really believe such pictures will be shown on large screens someday?"

"Absolutely. Where do you come from, Dutch? Germany?"

"Yes, Berlin. But I am a Chicagoan now."

"Interested in our infant industry, are you?"

"Very much. I like all kinds of photography. I am studying it with Mr. Rooney. But I'm fascinated most by the moving pictures." *Fascinated. Chicagoan.* He hoped Colonel Shadow noticed his effort to use those big words; Paul wanted to impress him.

"Smart," the colonel said. "That's the future. I'm not satisfied with earning pocket change from a film, I want to earn thousands. That's why we're rushing to perfect a projector, and a camera to go with it. So keep your eye on us." His hands framed a banner in the air. "Luxograph Pictures. Big as life—bright as day —and better than Edison's."

Laughing, the Bath said, "The Wizard ain't gonna like that, Sid. Neither will all the shysters he keeps on the payroll so he don't get his designs stolen."

"My projector will be original, patent-protected," Shadow said. "Mr. Thomas Alva Edison had better start to realize he can't have the whole pie to himself."

Paul wanted to ask about opportunities in Shadow's business, then felt a stab of guilt. As if he was betraying Wex just by being interested.

Bugles announced the next race. Wex rushed into the box with more tickets. "I bet on Evangeline to win."

"Hmm, I dunno," the Bath said. Evangeline finished last.

Moments after the race was over, two young men walked into the box. Paul had seen one of them before—the blond with his hair parted in the middle. He pulled handbills from the stacked boxes, then tapped his companion on the shoulder.

Facing away, scanning the crowd, the other young man didn't turn around immediately. When he did, Paul got a shock. It was the delivery boy who had stolen the Crown china. And, very likely, the roper who'd tried to trap Nancy.

He looked much more prosperous than he did when he was working for Frankel's. He wore a derby, high stiff collar, plaid suit, gleaming brown shoes with needle-point toes. His darting eyes showed that he recognized Paul.

Shadow noticed the exchange of looks, though missing its meaning. "These are my two assistants, Mr. Lewis Kress and Mr. James Daws. Lew and Jimmy."

Lew Kress shook hands first. He had a hangdog air, and a thick Southern accent. "Pleased to meet you-all." Jimmy Daws stepped forward, his brown eyes thoughtful. He shook with Wex, then Paul.

"Hullo, pal. Been a long time."

"You know each other?" Shadow said.

"We have met," Paul said, leaving it there.

Jimmy Daws slapped his shoulder. "Yes we have. 'Deed we have. Glad to see you again."

"All right, enough damn sociability," Shadow said with a gruff laugh. "You're not here for sport, you two. Get rid of those handbills."

Lew and Jimmy filled every available pocket with wads of them. Paul noted the word "Luxoscope" in circus type, along with many exclamation points. The assistants started out the gate at the same time. Jimmy biffed Kress on the shoulder. "Jesus, watch it." Though he was smiling, his eyes were anything but friendly.

Kress stepped back. "Sorry."

Jimmy tipped his derby to the group and left, reserving his last attention—a swift, speculative look—for Paul. Despite the hot sun beating into the grandstand, Paul felt a chill.

The Bath's horse, First Ward, placed in the third race. Wex won twenty dollars. Then he lost it all on Saratoga Boy in the fourth. Saratoga Boy stumbled and had to be dragged off the track in a canvas sling.

Wex dug down and found a few more dollars. He left the box with a harried expression. Paul was asking himself whether it would be dishonorable to speak further to Shadow. He very much wanted to.

Lew Kress and Jimmy came back for more handbills. Jimmy chatted and joked with the tarts. Kress tried to interject a remark. Jimmy shushed him, with all the deference he'd give a bothersome fly. Kenna leaned over to whisper in Coughlin's ear; he was chewing his cigar and scowling like a gargoyle. Coughlin slapped his back. "Ah, don't worry yourself, Hink, I'll take care of that bozo. He'll vote the way he oughta vote, or he'll need crutches."

Colonel Shadow acted bored with the nieces. Paul thought that if he didn't seize the opportunity, it might never come again. He slid over to the chair beside the colonel.

"Sir? I would very much like to work with flicker pictures. I would like to learn how to photograph them. Do you by any chance have a position?"

"I thought you worked for Rooney."

"I stay with him, but my job is delivering laundry. Mr. Rooney knows my interest."

Shadow relaxed. "I don't have anything now, but keep in touch, you never know. I like young hustlers with ambition. My boy Jimmy, he has a ton. Kress, though—he's a disappointment. Jimmy chews him up like a soggy biscuit. Must be that damn Dixie upbringing."

A minute later Paul's neck prickled again. The two helpers had come back. Jimmy Daws was leaning against the rear rail of the box, arms folded.

Watching him.

Wex's luck was bad the rest of the afternoon. At the end of the seventh and final race he threw his remaining tickets away. "Dutch, let's go home." He shook hands all around. "Ladies. Mr. Kenna. Colonel—I truly want to hear more about your enterprise."

"Anytime. You have my card." Shadow shot a look at Paul.

"Alderman Coughlin, thank you, it's been a grand afternoon." Wex's face said otherwise.

"So long, Dutch," Jimmy said to Paul as he and Wex moved to the hinged gate. "Maybe we'll see each other again."

"Very possibly," Paul said.

"Till then." Jimmy tipped his derby.

Jimmy's presence at Shadow's would make it a less desirable place, but Paul couldn't let that stop him.

On the El, Paul confessed he'd asked Colonel Shadow about employment. "But I would hate for you to think I was disloyal to you."

"Ah, forget it," Wex said, waving. "You're honest and I appreciate it."

The car rattled over the tracks. Soot blew in, speckling Wex's hair.

"Listen, Dutch, I'm proud you were my pupil, even for a while. I've known all along that you'd move on. It's the living pictures you fell in love with first— wasn't I the one who showed them to you? I saw the light in your eyes when the elephant danced. If you can sign on with a man like Shadow, do it. Don't feel guilty, or look back."

"That is very generous of you."

"Sure," Wex said with a shrug and a wan smile. "A man who loses can afford to be generous, can't he? He isn't risking anything."

Paul tried to continue the conversation but Wex wasn't interested. He sat with his chin in his palm, gazing at the buildings passing by, the streets and weedy lots below.

Communing with his demon? Paul wondered sadly.

Wex's unselfishness lifted a burden from Paul. The future shone with a special new brightness. He couldn't wait to tell Julie of all he'd learned from Wex, and of the even more exciting possibility of learning the moving picture trade. When would she finish that damned trip and come home to him?

On his rounds next morning, he asked Madame Camille, owner of the Pleasures of Paris, whether he might use her telephone. Because she liked him she said yes. He'd already delayed this call too long. He tapped his foot nervously while waiting for the line to connect.

"Crown residence. Manfred speaking."

Paul roughened his voice and muffled it with his sleeve. "Mrs. Volzenheim, please."

Manfred grumbled. There was a lengthy silence.

"Here is Louise. Who is that?"

"Louise, don't say anything, it's Paul."

"Master P—"

"No! Not my name. I implore you, just listen. Tell Aunt Ilsa I telephoned. Only my aunt, not my uncle. Tell her I'm safe and well, she mustn't worry."

"Are you here in Chicago? Please, everyone will want to know—"

He interrupted. "Is there any news of Cousin Joe?"

"Nothing. Not a whisper. It's so sad, both of you gone, everyone so un-happy—"

"Uncle Joe must be happy."

"Oh, I don't believe that's true."

"We hold different opinions there, Louise."

A girl in a pale pink wrapper came sauntering down the hall, smoking a little cigar. Teasingly, she pulled her robe open to show herself, then leaned against him, licking his cheek and his ear. Paul made shushing sounds.

"Yes, hello? What is going on there?"

"Nothing, I'm in—a place of business, it's busy."

"Never too busy for you, lovey," the girl whispered, rubbing his pants. Laughing at his discomfort, his scarlet face, she sauntered away.

"Remember, only tell my aunt."

"Not Fritzi, or Carl?"

"Aunt Ilsa can decide."

"Will you telephone again?"

"Not for a while. Thank you, Louise. I miss you. Goodbye."

When Paul dragged in from work that night, Wex's mood was, if anything, deeper and darker. He spoke with a slur as he served bowls of bean soup at the table.

From his coat pocket he took a brown pint bottle, one-quarter full. He uncorked it, tilted his head back, drank, and put the bottle on the table. He looked at Paul like a guilty child.

"I lost altogether too much money at the track. I'll need another extension on the rent. I don't know if the landlord will allow it again—" A long sigh. "I told you mine is a poisonous disease."

Gently, Paul said, "Then why don't you stop?"

Wex wiped his mouth. Stubble showed; he hadn't used his razor today.

"That's a thought, isn't it? Absolutely right, too. I must stop. If I don't, then you and I will be looking for a roost in some tree in Lincoln Park."

So it was that bad, that desperate. He'd had no idea.

Wex gestured with the bottle. "Eat your soup. There's more."

"Thank you, I'm not very hungry just now."

"Demons," Wex mumbled, gazing at his son's photograph. "Everywhere."

"Yes," Paul said. He envisioned the eyes of Jimmy Daws.

62

Jimmy

ON THE FIRST DAY of April 1895—before he met Paul at the racetrack— Jimmy observed his twentieth birthday. He was gainfully and, he hoped, safely employed with Colonel R. Sidney Shadow. Jimmy had started with the colonel about five weeks after the murder of the little blond tart, and his terrified abandonment of the whorehouse trade.

Jimmy worked at the colonel's peep show joint on the corner of Twenty-second Street and State, west of Freiberg's Dance Hall and opposite Buxbaum's Marlborough Hotel. Freiberg's was one of the busiest dives on the Levee. Men paid twenty-five cents to get in, forty cents for every highball for themselves or for the girls (highballs the girls drank were seltzer water lightly tinted with ginger ale). If a girl made an arrangement, she took her customer across the street to the Marlborough. Ike Bloom, who owned Freiberg's in partnership with his brother-in-law, also had a financial interest in the hotel, where the price of a hot mattress was two dollars per half hour. Bloom received a cut of every dollar. It was a sweet arrangement. Everything on the Levee was an arrangement, as Jimmy knew very well.

Jimmy had met the colonel by chance, at Freiberg's. Shadow came in for a romp because his ladyfriend had her monthly complaint. At the long bar they fell into casual conversation. Shadow must have liked something about Jimmy's looks and cocksure attitude, because he started to question him. Did he need work? Was he single? There were no questions about his past. Finally Shadow asked him to drop around next morning to talk about a job.

That was in the late fall of last year. By then Shadow's establishment had been open for several months. Jimmy had passed it several times. All the window glass was opaqued with paint. Above, on the building, two big signs in bright primary colors shouted to both streets:

Colonel R. S. Shadow's
LUXOSCOPE PARLOR
The MIRACLE of the Era!—Pictures That MOVE!
—Suitable for All Ages—
No Charge for Admission

By a dusty cash register at the front of the peep show parlor, Sid Shadow interviewed his prospective employee. He was straightforward.

"I currently have another helper, Mr. Lewis Kress. Lew was a student at some jerkwater divinity school down South. Unfortunately he was dumb enough to fool with the daughter of the Episcopal rector and put a little bun in her oven. He left his studies rather precipitously." Jimmy came to understand later that Shadow's vocabulary could be more formal and elegant when he wished it to be.

The colonel paused to draw on a long cheroot. The flavorsome aroma was one of those little symbols of the success Jimmy craved and intended to have someday.

"I'm telling you about Lew Kress for a reason, Jim. If I hire you, I want you to consider Lew your enemy. It's good for the business."

"I—Colonel—gee—I don't get that."

"It's simple," Shadow said. "Let's suppose I own two bulldogs. Let's suppose I pit them against each other. It isn't as reckless as it sounds. I might lose a dog in a scrap, but I might gain a champion money-winning throat-tearing fighter. Now do you get it?"

Jimmy grinned. "Yes, sir. I sure do."

The ground-floor Luxoscope Parlor had ten bulky peep show machines, five on each side of a wide aisle. The machines operated on the flip-card principle they shared with a competing machine called the Mutoscope. Edison's Kinetoscope used a continuous strip of film instead of cards, but the effect in all the machines was similar: the illusion of motion from a sequence of rapidly flashed stills.

Shadow's machines featured subjects such as the Lake Michigan surf rolling in, or a horse-drawn fire engine careening through an empty street (that cost thirty dollars to arrange, Shadow said). There were novelties: a man sneezing uncontrollably and shattering vases and china; a comical black mammy baking a pie with many attendant mishaps of spilled sugar and scattered flour.

The colonel complained that most of the card sequences were too tame. He intended to introduce racier subjects. Mild as the current ones were, he said, a lot of people, including most ministers, considered the flicker pictures an invention of the devil. Lucky they never got into the back room.

Above the parlor on the second floor, Shadow occupied rooms with his common-law wife, a pale, busty blonde named Mary Beezer. The two assistants shared the remaining space. Almost the first thing Jimmy did after Shadow hired him was inspect their rooms. Lew Kress had the larger one, with windows overlooking State Street. Jimmy would be forced into a dark cubicle with no windows. That evening, he announced to Mr. Lew Kress that they would exchange.

"See here, I been with the colonel since he opened," Lew said. "You-all can't do this."

The instant Lew protested, Jimmy kicked his shins, flung him against the wall, then showed him the blade of a knife.

"Let's get straight, Lewie," he said to the trembling Southerner. "You move out and stay out of my way, or you'll make me mad. You don't want to do that." Smiling sweetly, he patted Kress's cheek with the flat of the knife.

Lew Kress cleared out of the large room in a half hour.

Jimmy's work for Shadow consisted of tending the peep show cash register, watching to make sure patrons didn't damage the machines, guarding the special back room, and sometimes passing out handbills in other parts of town. Lew Kress passed them out on the Levee because Jimmy didn't want to be humiliated by bumping into acquaintances while doing such menial work. In addition to all this, he found he could earn extra money when Bathhouse John or Hinky Dink issued a call for troops at election time. He considered himself a loyal Democrat, so why not?

Jimmy didn't plan to stay with Colonel Shadow forever. You couldn't get rich working for somebody else, and Jimmy was ambitious for wealth and for the kind of power wielded by the Levee kingpins. Until he was sure the death of the little blond tart was forgotten, however, and until he decided where to move for the biggest opportunity, he'd stay.

Actually he was fairly happy, first of all because Shadow's Luxoscope Parlor was in the heart of the Levee. When a gent came to the Levee and went on a tear, the term for it was "going down the line." Jimmy went down the line so often and enjoyed it so much, he had no desire to work anywhere else.

Second, he liked the business of flicker pictures. It had glamour and a zesty air of lawlessness, especially in the curtained back room. Yet it had a highbrow, scientific air about it. Jimmy had attended parochial school for only four years. He hated his studies, and the nuns showed him the gate after he beat a weaker pupil to a bloody ruin in the schoolyard. Mother Superior said he was an incorrigible, whatever that meant. She said he had a violent temper. Jimmy could read, of course, but he did it with difficulty, confining himself to spicy stories in the *Police Gazette,* or *Mixed Drinks: The Saloon Keeper's Journal.* So it pleased him to be involved with something brainy like flicker pictures. Mr. Thomas A. Edison himself was involved with them. Everybody had heard of Edison.

Finally, he liked his living quarters; the nicest he'd ever had. He enjoyed the constantly changing view of State Street, the musical rumble of the South Side El running by, and the other, more provocative noises he could hear by resting his forehead against his side of the colonel's bedroom wall. Listening to Shadow and Mary excited Jimmy. He loved sex. With his fear about the dead tart abating, he loved life.

Which was a wonder, considering how bad a lot of his had been up until now.

□ □ □ □

In the cellar Shadow maintained a workshop. There he tinkered relentlessly, building and rebuilding his big, boxy flicker projector. So far it had failed to work right. Shadow showed Jimmy the workshop the day after he started. The large room had concrete walls covered with yellowing white paint and patches of mold. There were spiderwebs in the ceiling corners, pieces of unfinished lumber lying about. There were toothed gears of various sizes, hand tools and rubber belts, perforated strips of film, and a whole lot of drawings with measurements and arrows all over them. Many discarded drawings were stuffed in a box in a corner. An electric bulb with a crudely cut tin shade hung above the main workbench. There were oil lamps for extra illumination, and a damp, unpleasant smell. *Like a grave must smell,* Jimmy thought.

Shadow tried to explain the workings of his planned projector but Jimmy didn't get it. He told Shadow he'd been stuck with terrible teachers who short-changed him when it came to understanding machines and "science stuff."

He silently congratulated himself on a good, weepy speech. Shadow seemed a little disappointed.

As the weeks passed and he proved himself by roughing up and ejecting a couple of unruly customers, he was additionally charged with maintaining good relations with the beat patrolmen and fly cops who dropped in occasionally. Through them, and through regular visits to the precinct house to deliver the sealed brown envelope Shadow sent every week, Jimmy regained his nerve and lost all fear of being prosecuted for killing the little tramp and floating her in the river.

Colonel Shadow paid off the local precinct house for a very specific reason. The back room. There, an eleventh machine showed a card sequence called "A Chinese Dream."

Jimmy watched it a dozen times in his first couple of weeks on the job. Every time, it stiffened him so bad, he had to relieve himself on his own. In the forty-five-second sequence, a dreamy-eyed little Chink girl danced wearing nothing but some veils. Through them, you could clearly see her tits, the ends round and dark as summer buckeyes. If you were especially sharp-eyed, you might even catch a glimpse of something dark and tantalizing between her legs. That was why Jimmy, or sometimes Lew Kress, guarded the back room so diligently. To see "A Chinese Dream" cost three dollars, and required a special notched slug for the slot.

Jimmy once asked Shadow whether he'd personally photographed all the still shots of the dancer. He knew the colonel made most of the pictures for the machines in front.

"You bet, kid. Mary was up in Detroit visiting her sister. The sequence took seven hours. Afterward I fucked that little lotus blossom up one side and down the other. She loved it, pleaded for more. She was out of her mind from opium."

A thrilling shiver raced up Jimmy's spine. He admired Shadow—his shrewd business sense, his cool ruthlessness. In his own sphere Shadow was a winner. Maybe not a big winner, not just yet; but he would be. The colonel soon became a model for Jimmy, who had similar ambition. He intended to be a winner by the time he was the colonel's age. He'd never permit himself to be turned aside from that goal; never be distracted by the maunderings of priests, or the naggings of a wife, or the pleas of any brats he fathered, because he wasn't going to father any. And if he should father one by accident he'd never stick around. Anyone who let things like the law, or scruples, get in his way was a chump.

Shadow worked under enormous pressure that he put on himself. Jimmy thought it stupid, but it was a fact. The colonel frowned a lot and never stopped to chat when he was busy, but suppertime was different. Then, when Mary served him beer or sometimes a shot of whiskey, he'd stop scowling, drop his airs, and grow talkative—as if making up for the rest of the day. One evening when Jimmy was relaxing too, and feeling curious, he asked Shadow how he'd earned the rank of colonel.

"Why, I awarded it to myself, kid. Just like I gave myself a high-class name. You don't want to be too honest in this world, it doesn't impress anybody."

Jimmy was agog. "Are you saying your name ain't Shadow?"

"I confess!" Shadow clapped his hand over his heart. "Actually it's Sigmund Seelmeister." He said this with great relish. As a second glass of beer arrived via Mary, he went on to explain that he didn't come from a fine old family of Denver pioneers with Puritan origins in Maine; he'd been born on a pig farm near Evansville, Indiana. He'd run away at age eleven to get free of a stepfather who beat him all the time. "Ran away from the smell of pig manure, too. Even thinking about it still makes me puke." Shadow said this with his shirt hanging out of his pants, one tooled boot propped on the kitchen table, and his tall glass of beer close by.

As a runaway, he'd worked where he could, mostly as a roving farmhand.

"I did it for three years. It was dull as a Presbyterian hymnal, and it broke your damn back, too. Then one Saturday night, with a week's pay in my pocket, I bought a ticket to a traveling show in Logansport, Indiana. Professor Martin's Minstrels. I went wild for what I saw on that stage—the music, the dancing—it was a whole new experience. I hung around the theater door afterward and hit it lucky; they needed a hired boy for scut work. That night I said goodbye to sweet corn and hay baling and chicken shit forever.

"I was a big kid. Only fourteen, but I could handle the hardest work they gave me. For six months I shifted scenery, took the wardrobe trunks to the depot, delivered them to the hotel in the next town—that kind of stuff. But I kept after Professor Martin to try me out in the show. I had a good singing voice if I do say so, and I knew how to use it; I was singing hymns in church at age four. I was limber and quick on my feet, too. Finally the troupe lost a man and the professor said yes. I played one-night stands with Martin's Minstrels for almost six years, blacking up every night, warbling coon songs over the footlights, telling coon jokes, and dancing the cakewalk—" His right hand was raised above his head, waving a phantom tambourine.

A curious, dreamy smile came to his craggy face. "I loved it. I loved the applause, even when it was just hicks clapping. I never got over the excitement of whipping up an audience. Listening to them stomp and cheer for a show you put on for them . . ."

His hand came down. "After six years, though, I knew I was going nowhere. Then I had another stroke of luck. I met Mary. I was twenty. She came to the show in some jerk town in Missouri. She had this sparkler on her hand, a wedding ring big as my thumbnail, which just whetted my appetite, don't y'know. Of course she also whetted my appetite with her fabulous tits."

He gulped the rest of his beer and belched. "I guessed right away that she was hot for a romp on somebody else's sheets. I was right, she was married to this two-hundred-pound feed and seed merchant with a problem. No iron in his naval gun. She came up to me after the show and said she loved my performance. Then she said, 'I'll bet you give good performances wherever you are.' She didn't have to draw pictures. I took her back to the hotel room, screwed her for three or four hours. She made a hell of a lot of noise, enjoying herself for maybe the first time ever. It didn't surprise me. Big men are big all over, know what I mean?"

At this point Mary entered the kitchen and overheard. She put her hands on her hips. "Sid! Are you telling that story again?"

"Bet your life. I've seen tits and I've seen tits, but these are grand prize winners." He grabbed them to demonstrate, then pulled her into his lap.

"You wicked devil." They both laughed uproariously, and she gave him a long wet kiss on the mouth. Jimmy sat there agape.

"I quit the show and Mary and I knocked around on the road a few years. I sold things, we didn't starve, but I missed something, and I didn't know what it was till I discovered these little pictures that move." His gaze drifted dreamily again. "Ever heard the word 'epiphany,' Jim? Fine English word, epiphany. I had one. Just like seeing Martin's Minstrels in Logansport. Magical . . ."

"That's enough jabber," Mary said, bouncing off his lap. "We'll be dead of starvation if I don't get something on the stove."

So Jimmy didn't find out how Shadow had jumped to the raffish profession of the flickers. Nor did he ask later. He really didn't care so long as he got paid.

Of girls he now had a plentiful supply. For all his pastiness and skinniness, he was excellent at maintaining appearances. Thanks to the free lessons he was a good dancer. He'd developed a pretty good line and used it to advantage. One relationship early in the year had lasted over two months, an unusual length of time for him. This was with a girl named Rosie French.

Rosie had moved up from Pullman after her pa was killed during the strike. She was an amateur whore, not allied with any house. Nor did she enjoy the protection of a cadet. It was a dangerous way to do business on the Levee, but Rosie was tough. He admired her.

She in turn admired his ambition. She had ambitions of her own, she told him. She intended to be a music hall soubrette in New York, thereby making herself available to rich men from the audience. She'd go East as soon as she had enough cash put by. Jimmy didn't know a lot about legitimate forms of entertainment, but he had a pretty good ear for music. After listening to Rosie sing "Where Did You Get That Hat?", he decided she didn't have much of a chance of becoming an artistic success. She'd have to keep on performing on her back, too. At that she was accomplished.

Rosie had a temper that was almost the equal of his. After a stupid quarrel over something trivial, she ordered him out of her room. He threatened her with a beating and she countered by jerking a little silver-plated hideout pistol from under her mattress.

"Bare knuckles may work on some poor sisters, Jimmy, but they won't work with me. Lay one hand on me and I'll empty this in your face."

For the first time in memory, Jimmy lowered his fists in front of an adversary. He even grinned sheepishly and tried to hug her. She wouldn't have it. She locked him out.

Strangely, he found himself drawn back to her despite that kind of treatment. He found her room vacant. An old crone on the floor below said Rosie had left for New York. He felt bad for days. Rosie was a piece of work. He'd liked her more than he realized. He missed her.

In the spring, before he met Paul again, Jimmy joined Bathhouse John's campaign flying squad for the first time. It was exhilarating work, and Shadow was glad to have him do it because it solidified the colonel's relationship with the ward bosses.

Night after night before the city elections, the Bath marched through the streets of the First Ward leading his Democratic Fife and Drum Corps. Sometimes there were five or six hundred in the torchlight parade, men and women and youngsters too. At every saloon, the Bath bought beer and put in a word for his favored candidates. His flying squad policed the route of march. Silenced any opponents foolish enough to heckle; tore off their lapel badges or campaign hatbands, and if that didn't work, mussed them up. They ripped opposition posters from walls and telegraph poles, ran off anyone attempting to paste up new ones, and generally established the supremacy of the Bath and the Hink in the election process.

Election day activity began early. The bars opened at 5 A.M. so that the extra voters Hinky Dink brought in could be fueled to amiability by six, when the polls opened. Regrettably, at that hour the bars had to close for the day.

A few minutes after six, Jimmy boarded an already crowded tallyho hired by the Bath to carry his flying squad around the district. Twenty men rode inside and on the coach, all of them partially or completely drunk. Throughout the day the coach careened from polling place to polling place, summoned by telephone or foot messenger by election judges who thought the opposition was showing too large a turnout, or voting dead names, a prerogative the Democrats jealously preserved for themselves. Usually the sight of the Bath's tallyho swaying to a stop and spilling its crew of toughs was enough to assure an opposition retreat and a return to favorable conditions at the polling place. Sometimes the Bath himself was present, the pockets of his black overcoat bulging with coins. Dimes in the left one, quarters in the right. He handed them out to voters with disarming innocence.

Jimmy had a thoroughly fine time that day. He bashed a few heads and satisfied himself once, with a randy little whore, standing up in an alley. After dark, the outcome of the election assured, everyone got drunk again. Whores from all the Levee establishments gave away their favors. Jimmy looked up the tart he'd poked earlier. They drank and frolicked most of the night.

Yes, sir, Jimmy thought when he woke up around ten next morning, the Levee was the center of the universe. Who cared if you were sick and hung over? Who cared if the pain in your head was fierce enough to pop out your eyeballs? This was the place to be, the Levee, and those who didn't go down the line and savor its glamour and excitement and aura of power were poor ignorant fools.

Not long after the election, in that same spring of '95, Jimmy ran into the kraut kid at Washington Park.

What a stunner. For a few seconds he was ready to bolt. He hung on, kept his nerve, and when the kid didn't say anything about the stolen china, actually acted friendly, Jimmy relaxed.

He was mightily puzzled, though. What was somebody who lived in a fancy house doing in a box at the racetrack? Who was the little fat man, Rooney? He asked Shadow. Turned out Rooney was a photographer, and the kraut kid was some kind of assistant.

For a few days Jimmy worried that the kraut might contact the police after all. But no detectives showed up. Lucky again. Within a week the incident was fading from memory.

After his first altercation with Lew Kress over the rooms, Jimmy never had cause to lay hands on him again. But they argued a lot. Jimmy's habit of bragging about the possessions and accomplishments of his family irked Lew, though of course all three—possessions, accomplishments, family—didn't exist. He just felt compelled to talk about them as if they did.

Down in the cellar, Colonel Shadow continued to slave away, putting together brass gears and belts, lenses, and scrap wood to make a rectangular cabinet on spindly tripod legs. Things still weren't going well.

"By God I'm not going to let this whip me, I'm not going to lose out," Shadow said one night when Mary Beezer was preparing stew in the flat for all four of them. The colonel was sitting in his undershirt under the wan electric lights, cigar dangling from his hand. His pomaded dark hair, which varied in color from week to week, hung in strands over his forehead. "The flickers, the living pictures —I don't give a damn what you call 'em, they can make us a pile if we can show 'em in a regular theater."

"What kind of subjects would you photograph?" Lew Kress asked. "Different from the ones in the machines?"

"Lew, are you stupid? Of course I'll make different pictures. Our camera will go anywhere—" He chewed his cigar. "That is, if it's light enough and I can get the God damn thing to work."

"Are you boys hungry?" Mary placed bowls of stew on the table. The stew contained a few peas and a lot of boiled potatoes in last Sunday's chicken gravy.

"You take this dustup down in South America," Shadow said. "It's a natural."

"Britain's dispute with Venezuela over the border of British Guiana," Lew Kress said. Jimmy didn't know what the hell the little show-off was talking about.

"Right!" Shadow smacked the table. Mary Beezer jumped forward with a cry, grabbing his stew bowl as it teetered on the edge. Jimmy got a nice peek at her creamy white tits. He rubbed his erection under the table while Shadow carried on.

"The limeys are talking about sending in warships. That's a God damn violation of our sacred Monroe Doctrine. Suppose there's real fighting. Suppose we get tough. Send in the Marines! Show the flag! Blow the fuckers up! If we could photograph that and show the pictures here—everywhere—Jesus Christ, they'd be rioting for tickets!" Again he hammered the table.

"We've *got* to be in the marketplace soon. We've *got* to have a complete camera and projection system ready by this time next year. That's the goal, boys. That's the ramrod up our ass. Let's eat."

Occasionally Jimmy was called on to render stern service for the colonel. One summer night with the Levee afloat in rumors of yet another anti-vice crusade, he was browsing through the *Police Gazette* when a little man with a thatch of curly red hair mixed with gray came in furtively. The man whispered that he'd heard there was "something special" in the back room.

Jimmy noticed a bulge in the coat pocket of the man's shiny dark suit, but he didn't think it was a gun. More like a book. He took a chance.

"Yeah, it's called 'A Chinese Dream.' Real hot stuff. Costs you three bucks. And you got to wait until those two chumps are gone." He gestured to a pair of men cranking machines.

"I'll wait, gladly. Many thanks, laddie." The man had a queer accent. Scotch burr, Jimmy thought.

In a few minutes both customers left. Jimmy collected the money, handed the little man the special slug, and led him to the back. The man was sweating heavily. "Enjoy yourself," Jimmy said, and pulled the curtain shut.

He leaned against the wall and lit a smoke. He listened to the slug rattle down the slot, heard the crank turning, the photo drum clicking . . .

"The Lord preserve us!"

Jimmy ripped the curtain open. The little man was holding a small black book with gilt-edged pages. He shook the book at the Luxoscope. "These pictures are filth. I was told, but I refused to believe it."

"Who the fuck are you, some copper?"

"The Reverend Gypsy Kinross. I came to the Levee to witness its sins and abominations for myself."

Jimmy had heard the name Gypsy Kinross. An evangelist, running some kind of Holy Roller campaign in a hall uptown.

Enraged by the man's trickery, Jimmy swung and knocked Kinross to the floor, then kicked his legs apart and gave him one in the crotch. The evangelist cried out.

"Christ save me!"

"He better, nobody else will!"

Jimmy dragged the evangelist out the back door to the alley and proceeded to beat him.

Hands held out, pleading, Kinross tried to crawl away. Jimmy wasn't through with him. He unbuttoned his shirt and took off his St. Christopher medal, which he wore on an extra-long, extra-strong chain. Not for any religious purpose, however. He whipped the chain over Kinross's head and around his neck. He crossed his hands and pulled.

"You breathe one damn solitary word about this place or what you saw, I'll track you down and kill you, if I have to drag you from a pulpit to do it. Get me?" Kinross could only respond with gagging sounds while he plucked weakly at the chain.

"Okay, good."

Jimmy leaned forward and spat in Kinross's face.

Then he pushed Kinross over on his side, taking care to maintain a good hold on the chain. The links had torn Kinross's throat and were spattered with blood. Jimmy unwound the chain, wiped it on his pants, and slipped it over his head. He went inside and slammed the door. His knuckles hurt like hell. They were bruised and bloody. But he felt like a king.

In the morning Shadow noticed his injured hands. Asked what had happened.

"A little trouble. It was nothing."

The incident with Gypsy Kinross never reached the papers. Nor did any policeman come to inquire.

On a hot day in August, Jimmy was hanging over the cash register, licking a paper cone of shaved ice soaked with lime flavoring. Lew Kress was perched on another stool, poking with a screwdriver at a gearbox. He wore spectacles and his usual hangdog air.

Jimmy finished the shaved ice and threw the twist of paper in the general direction of a trash can. He missed it but didn't bother to pick up the paper. It lay there leaking green ooze while he opened a long clasp knife. He began to clean his nails.

He heard a horse and wagon in the street. Looking out the door, he saw a delivery vehicle painted with the words ILLINOIS STEAM LAUNDRY COMPANY. The driver walked in, wearing just a sleeveless singlet with his pants. No wonder; the whole city was frying.

"Well good Lord, looky here."

"How are you?" said the kraut. "Remember me?"

"Sure. Crown." Jimmy held out his hand. "Daws."

"Yes, I recall. From the racetrack."

Lew waved his screwdriver limply. "Kress."

"Hello, how are you?"

Jimmy supposed he owed the kraut something for unwittingly helping him snatch the china, and keeping still about it later. It didn't make him like the kid's accent any better. It was thick as a sausage.

"What you doing pushing a laundry wagon?" Jimmy asked. "I thought you worked for that photographer."

"Not exactly. He's my friend. He teaches me photography. May I ask—is your employer here? The colonel?"

"Should be coming down those stairs any minute. On his way out."

As predicted, Colonel Shadow soon appeared, dressed for the street in his sombrero and flowing cravat. Mary clung to his arm. She'd dolled up with big scarlet patches of rouge. The kraut tried to cover up his soaked singlet as he introduced himself.

"Yes, kid, I remember you," Shadow said pleasantly.

"I would still like a job in the picture business, sir. Would you perhaps—?"

"No, I'm afraid not. Two boys are all I can afford." He tipped his sombrero and went out. Mary followed, trailing a cloud of toilet water that masked the smells of dirt and sweat around the cash register.

Jimmy balanced the knife point on the ball of his middle finger. "Get rid of one of us, maybe he'll take you on."

Lew Kress nearly dropped the gearbox. He was white as a piece of uncooked fish. It delighted Jimmy, who flipped the knife in the air and watched it come down and embed itself in the counter, humming.

The kraut didn't smile at Jimmy's little joke, just nodded. "I'll see you again, Daws."

"Right. So long." He pulled the knife out of the counter and cleaned another fingernail.

Paul Crown's shoulders glistened like sunlit glass as he walked out. He mopped his chin and neck with a blue bandanna, then climbed aboard the wagon and shook the reins over the swaybacked horse. The wagon creaked out of sight. Jimmy reached under his collar and absently fingered the holy medal chain.

Delivery man, huh? Not much of a job. Maybe the best a foreigner could get. But he lived in that fancy house, so why was he reduced to hustling laundry?

It occurred to Jimmy that maybe the kraut *didn't* live in the fancy house anymore. Maybe there was a falling-out at home. Whatever the explanation, the kraut struck Jimmy as a straight-ahead guy. A guy with plenty of sand; not easy to push around. This was a considerable concession from someone who had a fierce dislike of Dutchmen generally.

Of course, even if the kraut did land a job with Shadow—which really wasn't likely, Kress would probably be here forever—it wouldn't buffalo Jimmy. If the kraut, or anyone, disputed Jimmy's authority or otherwise troubled him, he'd do what he always did. Hurt them.

Simple as that. He was no chump.

63

Joe Crown

WHEN SUMMER CAME, the long days and the heat, conversations with Ilsa seemed to grow shorter and cooler. Often there was contention, even if their discussion didn't begin that way. The first time Joe was fully aware of this, they were sitting alone, she with her darning, he with papers from the brewery, after the children had gone to bed.

"Joe."

"Yes?"

"Louise took a telephone message this morning."

Annoyed by the interruption, he tilted his head down and peered over his spectacles. "Is there something unusual about that?"

"It was Paul."

He sat in stunned silence while she described the message. "He asked that I not tell you he called. Louise said he was polite, but she could hear anger in his voice."

"Then he shouldn't have bothered to—"

"Joe, please. I've worried myself to exhaustion about him. About both boys. You wonder that Paul's angry? You banished him like a peasant who dares to disagree with a king."

He flung his papers on the floor. "That analogy is ridiculous. Let's be very clear. I don't wish the boy ill—sickness, anything like that. But I gave him all I had to give, and he repaid it by abetting Joe's flight from this house. I'm supposed to be grateful? Forgiving? I am sorry, no."

He rose, stooped to gather the papers. "If you'll excuse me, I think I'll work in the study."

She didn't reply. Her eyes were on her darning again. He walked out, his face dark as a boiled beet. He deliberately gave the door a good slam.

They lay in bed, not touching. It was two weeks later. All the windows were raised. Again there was no air stirring; summer's sticky heat imprisoned Chicago.

She said, "Are you awake?"

"I am."

"You didn't tell me about the detective report today."

"The usual. Nothing."

"Oh dear Lord. I'm so worried. Not a letter, not even a postal card since he left. He might be injured. Even—"

She was unable to finish.

"Ilsa, let me reassure you about one thing. Whatever else he is, our son is a strong, competent young man. I despise his political ideas—the way he was so easily influenced by someone like Benno. But I never for a moment minimize the good character you developed in Joe as he grew up. If he's silent, it's because he chooses to be silent, not because he's come to harm."

"Then are we wasting our money on the detectives?"

"Yes, I think we are. It's shamefully expensive to keep them searching week after week. But I'll do it as long as you want, though I don't hold out much hope of success."

"Then cancel the arrangement for a while. I assume we can hire them again."

"Anytime."

"All right. Let them go."

He reached for her hand, tentatively, shyly as a new suitor might. She twined her fingers in his, squeezed, sought his chin with her other hand, kissed him.

It was a brief pause in the upward spiral of tension between them. He hoped it would last. But three nights later, with the temperature still in the eighties at eleven o'clock, the telephone rang downstairs.

□ □ □ □

Joe Crown knelt in the street. A crowd of neighborhood people surrounded him. Someone had led the sobbing widow away. His landau with top down was tied to a hitching block nearby. He'd sped across town to North Halsted Street in response to the call. He was still wearing his carpet slippers, and his nightshirt was tucked into pants with suspenders. He felt as if he'd put on three fur overcoats; his face streamed with sweat.

A sick bile filled his mouth as he looked at the small nondescript man lying on the wooden sidewalk with his head at a crooked angle. Blackish blood mixed with brain matter was coagulating underneath his skull. Huge flies were darting and buzzing near the blood. Natty in a white summer suit, Dolph Hix stood behind his employer, a sick look on his face.

"There ain't nothing you can do, Mr. Crown, it was an accident," said the police patrolman who'd come when a frantic neighborhood boy ran to the precinct to report a man falling off a roof.

Joe stood up slowly, feeling pain in his joints, an ache in his belly. "I'll pay for his funeral and burial. Everything the best. Someone please tell his wife."

"I will," Dolph Hix said. "If she'll talk to me."

Joe retreated to the steps of the tenement and sank down with hands pressed to his temples. Dolph Hix had been working the customers at a saloon two blocks farther north. He'd been freely buying Crown beer because the saloon was well run and had a large, steady clientele. The owner presently bought from three breweries, but Joe wanted the saloon as a tied house for Crown's. The man lying there half covered with someone's motheaten blanket had apparently enjoyed one free beer too many, stumbled home to his flat, gone up to the roof for relief from the heat, and somehow fallen.

Dolph Hix came over to his employer. "I didn't see him leave the place, Joe. There are witnesses who say he was *blau.*" Germans had a whole range of expressions for degrees of intoxication. Dolph Hix wasn't German, but he'd learned the expressions at the brewery. The most extreme stage, falling-down drunk, was tersely indicated by the word for blue.

"Staggering, then," Joe said; he wasn't pleased.

"Yeah, his wife should have kept him away from the roof. I hope you don't blame me for—"

Joe silenced the sales agent by reaching out to grip his arm. "No, Dolph, you were only doing your job."

But he knew someone who would blame *him.*

"It isn't my fault," Joe shouted, in the kitchen two hours later. Ilsa had been waiting up for him; she had brewed a pot of coffee because he said he couldn't sleep. Her hair was in a long braid, draped over the shoulder of her heavy robe.

He'd explained what happened and said he would pay reparations to the widow—the couple had five children—but it didn't mollify her. The tragedy ignited her wrath in a way he'd seldom seen. They'd been arguing for fifteen minutes.

"You can't evade responsibility, Joe. Your employee, Dolph Hix, was buying beer for everyone. You admitted it." Ilsa looked wan and old, and without warning she began to weep. "That poor man. Just like my papa. Killed by *jenes verdammte Zeug!*"

That damned stuff, she called his beer. "Ilsa," he said, in a tone of warning.

"It's your fault, Joe Crown. God forgive you—you and your awful business that destroys men's lives."

She ran out. He stood trembling with the mug of hot coffee in his hands. Suddenly he whirled and threw the mug against the wall, coffee and all.

He'd narrowly missed Ilsa's plaque with its platitude about a contented household. Coffee ran down the wall beneath it. Shards of crockery lay scattered on the floor, the stove, even the butcher block.

The hell with it, he thought, Louise can clean it up tomorrow. He slept on one of the downstairs sofas that night.

He paid for a fine funeral for the dead man, and for a choice burial plot. He wrote a letter of condolence, never acknowledged. Because the accident had struck Ilsa with such force, he put Dolph Hix and his two junior sales agents into different jobs, traveling for the brewery, checking on the out-of-town agencies. He took away their rolls of cash and forbade them to buy free drinks in saloons.

After a ten-day road trip, Dolph closed Joe's office door, slumped into the visitor's chair, and said Bo Stone, one of the junior men, was quitting. Then he said he'd like to do the same thing, but he was loyal. "Loyal and sore. A hell of a combination, Joe."

At home, Ilsa didn't speak of the accident again. She didn't apologize for what she'd said in the kitchen. Forthcoming on any other subject, she maintained her household routines and family conversation with no apparent change. But when Joe tried to tell her of Dolph's new duties, her response was a steely silence.

After a few weeks he returned Dolph Hix and the remaining assistant to their former positions. He reinstated their expense accounts and then hired two more men as junior sales agents. He didn't tell Ilsa. Never before had he withheld brewery news as important as this, but he decided it was definitely necessary this time.

64

Joe Junior

HE KEPT WORKING his way West. It was his intention to see the Pacific Ocean. There was no one telling him which way he had to go, no one issuing orders except for short periods when he hired on to earn money.

He did carpentry, dug drainage ditches, trekked across the autumn fields of Illinois. He shoveled snow on a street crew in St. Louis during the winter of '94–'95. He'd always been physically strong, but he was smaller than many young men his age, so he felt compelled to work twice as hard to prove his worth. As he approached his nineteenth birthday in April of 1895, he realized he'd never grow much bigger. Sometimes people termed him a runt good-naturedly. To compensate for his size, he let his beard grow again. He kept beard and mustache trimmed but full. His beard reached his chest.

His skin was darker from all his time outdoors. His hands were powerful and scarred in a couple of places from little accidents with an axe or from a fistfight when someone called him runt derisively. In one altercation on a carpentry job site, his opponent grabbed a piece of two-by-four and smashed him across the face. His broken nose gushed blood, and healed with a crooked little bump in the middle.

Long hours and the agony of strained muscles didn't bother him; exhaustion helped him sleep, in fact. Helped ease the memories of his family, Rosie, Benno. He thought a lot about Benno's death. He decided it had been stupid and futile. He wasn't soured on the cause of the laboring man. To the contrary, he was one of them; their cause was his, despite his father's efforts to make him feel like a pariah because of it. He still believed walkouts were good weapons. Strikes too. But bombs? Stupid.

It was at night that he missed his home most. Missed his brother and sister, and Paul, and especially his mother. She'd be worried about him. Sometimes he suffered intense guilt over that.

When it came to his father, his emotions were tangled. He harbored bad feelings toward Joe Crown; yet in a strange way he hadn't expected, he also felt a renewed kinship. Because he was independent now. Following his own plan, not someone else's. His father had done that as a young man, then failed to understand that his son must do the same thing.

He went west through Missouri to Kansas City as the snow melted and the ground softened and the sun stayed up longer, felt warmer every day. He made enough to get by, and when he'd accumulated a few dollars, he thanked his boss and started west again. He didn't live comfortably, but he never starved. Occasionally on a Saturday night he even enjoyed a woman. A few moments of heated pleasure, then a tip of the cap, and no looking back. There were no Rosies to remember with a sense of loss and regret.

In Kansas City jobs were scarce. He worked for two weeks as a sandwich man, carrying boards. One day he happened upon a ball field where Negro teams played. He hung over the low board fence for a couple of innings, the only white face visible. He savored the crack of the bat, the cheers from the black folk in the stands. He reveled in the smell of the grass, the dust around the bases. He remembered White Stockings games he'd seen with his father. It made him sad.

He also remembered a conversation about sandwich men. Pop had called them the dregs. And here he was, one of them. It made him laugh.

When the sun set and he took the boards back to the café, the owner asked him as usual for the route he'd followed. The owner was an Irishman who'd emigrated from County Wicklow twenty years before. He'd spoken bitterly of signs that had greeted him in America. *No Irish need apply.* Joe Junior mentioned that he'd lingered a few minutes near the colored people's ball field.

"You did that on my time? You dumb little shit, we don't cater to niggers. We don't let 'em in the door. You're fired."

He heard there was work in Kansas, so he crossed the wide Missouri on a three-cent ferry. A farmer hired him to string barb wire for several days. Barb wire had changed the whole agricultural picture on the Western plains, the farmer said. Before barb wire came along in the 1880s, homesteaders who laid out crop fields and pastures had only hedgerows of Osage orange, or wooden fences that rotted out or broke easily, to keep stray cattle off their land. Barb wire changed that forever.

The farmer also told him the level of the land in Kansas rose almost thirty-five hundred feet between the Missouri and the Colorado border. Joe Junior was excited about that. If he walked even one mile, he was climbing toward the mountains; the only significant geographic barrier between himself and the legendary California sunshine, the Pacific shore.

Moving west, he passed through forests of oak and hickory, and over a flat plain that was rising invisibly beneath his feet. In the small towns he began to see Indians. Kaw, sometimes called Kansa, and Osage, and Pawnee, wearing ordinary farm clothes and looking singularly peaceful. No one in Kansas feared the savage nomadic Comanche any longer; they were beaten.

The Indians lived in permanent villages. They hunted as well as farmed. They had marvelous deep-chiseled brown faces, and he knew Cousin Paul would have thrilled to see them.

The bluestem prairie ("Once," a man told him, "the bluestem stood here tall as a walking man—sometimes tall as a man riding horseback.") gave way to a more desolate landscape of low-growing buffalo grass and weather-stunted cotton-woods straggling along creeks hardly worthy of the name.

Then came Abilene, Dickinson County, on the east-west railway. Abilene had been a boomtown when the long Texas cattle drives ended there. Now it was a faded, dusty little place, with only a few rundown hotels and saloons open in the section called the Devil's Addition that had once been a hell-raiser's paradise. There were a few real cowboys left, but they were old men. He talked to one who sat in a rocker on the porch of the dilapidated Drover's Hotel on Texas Street, south of the tracks. The old cowboy wore a leather vest and ancient leather chaps over patched jeans. His shirt collar was black with grime. It must have been a year since anyone had trimmed his long, matted gray hair. He had cheap yellow false teeth, which accounted for his name, Ivory.

And he had a fund of spine-chilling stories about night stampedes, and Comanche raids, and the glorious young whores who flocked up and down Texas Street in the old days, tempting a man to Hell with every conceivable variation of sex. Joe Junior listened to him for a whole afternoon. As he rose to go, he mentioned that he needed work.

"That way." Ivory jerked a thumb in a general westerly direction. "The winter wheat harvest. Plenty of able-bodied young men needed." Joe Junior thanked him. As he turned to go, the old cowboy's eyes were already closing.

□ □ □ □

Leaving Abilene, he traveled into the wheat lands. The hard red winter wheat germinated in the spring and was harvested in the warm months by sweating men who looked small beside their huge machines.

The machines, called headers, traveled slowly through the ripe fields. The header's revolving reel mechanism swept the grain across a sicklelike mowing blade. The loose heads fell onto a flat collection table, then rode sideways and upward on a moving belt. The stalks dropped off the side, into a wagon whose driver matched his pace to the machine. The header was an enormous, ungainly piece of equipment; so heavy it had to be pushed from behind by a team hitched to a trace bar. But the wagon could go directly to the threshing site; no extra men were needed to gather and stack the wheat in shocks for transportation later, as was necessary with older machines. Joe Junior's first work on a crew was driving a mule team behind a header.

His boss was a wheat farmer named Edgar Jeter. He hadn't a single bunkhouse or shed for the sizable crew working his four clanking rattling headers. The food Jeter's wife laid out was slop. After two days, Joe spoke to Jeter out by his chicken coop at sundown.

"We ought to have some running water. Use of your well—"

"Well's for the family. Try the creek."

"It's a mile from here, Mr. Jeter."

"So? You're healthy. Hike."

"We don't even have a privy."

"Take care of that when you're down at the creek."

"Mr. Jeter, maybe the rest of your crew will put up with these conditions. But I've had some experience with labor organizations."

"What are you, a red? Shut your mouth or you won't get paid."

"No, I won't shut up. You have a responsibility. A duty to give your men basic decent—"

The fist big as a rock came flying out of the sunset glare. Joe Junior landed in the dust. Jeter loomed above, throwing a malevolent black shadow on him.

"Get the hell off my land or I'll break you in two pieces. I won't have a God damn red socialist agitator working for me."

Joe Junior picked up his knotted bundle of belongings in the stubble field where the crew was allowed to camp and walked west in the starlight.

He found work on other farms, roundabout little towns with musical names. Mentor, Groveland, Redwing, Pretty Prairie. The harvesting season was at its height, hundreds of crews swarming in the fields.

He joined a crew working for one of the Mennonite farmers in Ellsworth County, Bruno Cherry by name. Mr. Cherry was in his late forties. He'd come to America in 1873 with his bride of three months, all the way from the Ukraine. The original family name was Chermochev.

Cherry was a strapping, talkative man. He spoke excellent, almost biblical English, with scarcely a hint of accent. His beard was as long as Joe Junior's and nearly the same color, although gray in places. Quite without warning, his left eye would wander inward, as if to contemplate his nose for a while. He was a hard master, but honest and considerate. He had built a sturdy bunkhouse for the itinerant crews that worked his two thousand acres twice a year. Food was plentiful and good.

"Originally ours was a North German family," Cherry said. He talked to Joe Junior and others during rest periods in the field, when Mrs. Cherry drove the water wagon out to the big headers. There was no foreman to prevent such intimacy; Cherry bossed his hired crews personally.

"Many Prussian Mennonites went to the Ukraine in the latter part of the eighteenth century. Mennonites always seek and find the richest land," he said with a smile. "In the Ukraine our sect created large and successful farming colonies. Then, twenty-two years ago—1873—there came a decree from the Tsar. All able-bodied men were to be conscripted into the army. Mennonites will not fight wars. We hold that human life is sacred. Hundreds of young men left. I was one."

Joe Junior liked Cherry, just as he liked Cherry's stout wife and three daughters, all of marriageable age. None had found the right suitor; Mennonites couldn't marry outside their religion. They were plain people. Their clothes were simple, even coarse. Their square, two-story house was devoid of ornamentation except for lightning rods and a cast iron weather vane. The exterior was a drab gray, relieved only by white shutters. Throughout the interior a great many oil lamps provided warm illumination. At night the house shone like a golden Christmas tree. Joe Junior couldn't imagine that electric lines would ever reach this far into the wilderness.

Cherry and his Mennonite friends husbanded their land in a way that was new to most of their neighbors: they let certain sections lie fallow every second year. The fallow fields gathered a whole season of the sparse Kansas rainfall and stored it for the next year, Cherry explained. To the surprise of many, but not the Mennonites, that second-year crop was typically big.

Bruno Cherry saw that Joe Junior wasn't like most of the other harvesters. They were either illiterate men who'd never known anything but farm work, or stuck-up college boys spending the summer earning money. The family invited Joe Junior inside their house for supper more than once. Mr. Cherry loved to discuss the past of his adopted state.

"Soon after I came here, we had more than ten years of wonderful rain. People from the East rushed to buy land. Then the great blizzard of '87 struck. The suffering, privation—beyond description! After the snow melted, there came years of drought. People no longer saw a future here. Two hundred, three hundred thousand left the state. I saw many a wagon returning East with a slogan painted on the side. 'In God we trusted, in Kansas we busted.' "

Two of Cherry's daughters giggled effusively, an opportunity to cast admiring looks at Joe Junior.

Cherry was concerned about the welfare of families presently working the land. "We have to seize and shape our future, the big moguls in the East won't help. That is why Kansans created the new political party."

With a nod at the oldest daughter across the table, Joe Junior said, "How does that work? Miss Rebekah told me Mennonites won't swear allegiance to any government, only to God." Rebekah blushed. Her sisters stabbed her with looks of jealousy.

"True," he said.

"So you never involve yourself with politics—"

"Not true in my case. That is the reason I'm shunned by some of my brethren. Called a damned heretic." Mrs. Cherry averted her eyes. "They mean damned in the most literal sense, you understand. I can't help it. A man grows and changes however he must. A man answers the voice of God that he hears inside him. I'm certain that was true of the first leader of our sect, Father Menno. He defied the very church of Rome that ordained him. Tore away from it completely, for doctrinal reasons—a damned heretic if ever I heard of one," he said with a laugh.

"Further, the Christians from whom our sect sprang, the Anabaptists of the sixteenth century, were not so unworldly. They were in fact ardent reformers. Resisters of oppression. Righters of wrongs in the world of commerce, and in society. Following that example, I have stepped off the narrow path and engaged myself with this new movement. It grew out of the Grange, the Patrons of Husbandry. You know it?"

"No, sir."

"A cooperative of farmers trying to solve mutual problems. We study the writings of social thinkers. Social moralists. Edward Bellamy. George's *Progress and Poverty*."

"I've read Henry George!"

"Splendid. But do you believe him? Do you believe wealth rightfully belongs solely to those who create it, never to any who hire the land out to others, and feed off their sweat and suffering?"

"Yes, I believe it," Joe Junior said, enthralled. Here was a man as passionate in his way as Eugene Debs, or Benno Strauss in his less violent moments.

Cherry leaned back. "Where did you come from, Joseph? You don't tell us anything about yourself."

"No, sir, there isn't much to tell. Mrs. Cherry, would you pass the biscuits, please?"

Supper was over. Mrs. Cherry and the daughters were quietly clearing dishes, washing them in a basin, drying them, with more glances at the young visitor, who was listening to Bruno Cherry explain that from the Grange had come the Kansas People's Party, organized at Topeka five years ago. Soon it had been renamed the Populist Party, spreading like a prairie fire in a dry season. The Populists put up slates of local candidates, then state candidates; now they were thinking nationally.

"Our demands are simple and fair," Cherry said. His eye wandered as he ticked off points on his fingers. "The eight-hour work day throughout America. For elections, the Australian ballot, which is secret. An income tax under which everyone pays in proportion to his income—the rich more, the poor less. We want full suffrage for women. We want the government to strip control of railroads, telegraph and telephone companies from the greedy sharks of the East. Above all, we want free silver at the ratio of sixteen to one."

He shook his head. "It's easier to say than to do. We are locked in a hard and vicious fight. The Eastern papers call us mad dogs. In some quarters our candidates are jeered. Jerry Simpson, once a sailor on the Great Lakes, was a candidate for Congress in 1892. His Republican opponent laughed and pointed out that he was so poor he couldn't afford socks. Exactly, said Jerry Simpson, it was one reason he was running for Congress. Sockless Jerry Simpson is in Washington. Sockless Jerry was reelected last year."

"Do you plan to run anyone for President?"

"In the next election we would like to nominate Mr. William Jennings Bryan. He stands with us on free silver and many other issues." Cherry's eye wandered back into place. "So now you know what we do in Kansas when we aren't breaking our backs to earn a living."

"I'd like to hear more, Mr. Cherry."

"Truly? That's splendid. I will take you to the county seat on Saturday night. You will hear a speech from one of our best, Mrs. Mary Lease. 'The Lady Orator of the West.' Yelling Mary, some call her." He gave a rumbling laugh. "Yelling Mary. It fits. You'll see."

Torches blazed in the public square of Ellsworth. All around Joe Junior were men and women with lean, worn faces. Faces hungry for honesty, starved for justice, eager to hear gospel. From the back of a farm wagon Mrs. Mary Lease gave it to them. She was a handsome woman with a ringing contralto voice.

"We no longer have a government of the people, by the people, for the people; we have a government of Wall Street, by Wall Street, and for Wall Street. The great common people of this country are slaves, and monopoly is the master!"

Yelling Mary was the wife of a Wichita apothecary and the mother of four, he'd been told on the buggy ride into town. "And she's a lawyer, too." Cherry was proud, as if describing a local athletic hero.

"Our laws are the output of a system which clothes rascals in robes and honest men in rags. Two years ago we were told to go to work, raise a big crop. We went to work. We plowed and planted. The rains fell, the sun shone, nature smiled, and we raised that big crop. And what came of it? I'll tell you what came of it. Eight-cent corn! Ten-cent oats! The politicians said we suffered from overproduction!"

A roar of rage went up in the square.

"Overproduction! When statistics tell us ten thousand little children starve to death in the United States every year! When scores of young shop girls are forced to sell their virtue on city pavements for the bread their pitiful wages deny them!"

Mary Lease raised her fists above her head.

"This is my message to you. It's time we raised less corn. It's time we raised less wheat. *It's time we raised more hell!*"

Shouts, shrieks, whistles, Indian whoops. Someone shot off a pistol. Red-faced with excitement, Joe Junior clapped as hard as the rest. Here was a political party standing for everything he believed. A party of people armed with principled anger, not dynamite. That night he was baptized in the boiling waters of Populism. That night in Ellsworth, Kansas, he was born again.

When the harvest ended, it was time to go on toward the Rockies; the valleys of California and the Northwest; the shore of the Western ocean. He said goodbye to the Cherry family. Mrs. Cherry wept. So did two of her daughters. Bruno Cherry gave him an extra five dollars he could ill afford.

"No arguments, Joseph, you are a good worker. You're a good young man. We can't baptize outsiders into our faith but if we could, you could marry Rebekah or Hester or Miriam and I would be happy. I say it again, you are a fine young man. Your parents must be proud."

A shadow seemed to float across Joe Junior's vivid blue eyes. As if making a joke, he said, "I doubt it. They're far away from here. They don't know much about me anymore. They don't even know where I am."

"You must rectify that," Bruno Cherry said, stern as an Old Testament prophet. "It is unjust and unkind to let them worry and wonder about you."

Joe Junior was taken aback. Riven by guilt, he hoisted his bundle over his shoulder and set off on the sunny road winding over the prairie through the wheat fields.

In the village of Black Wolf on the Smoky Hill River in the northwestern corner of the county, his guilt grew too heavy to bear. Cherry was right, he shouldn't punish his mother with worry. His father's feelings didn't enter into it.

It wasn't hard to find an appropriate token. Three dried grains of wheat, the heads of the stalks, picked up from a roadside where they'd fallen.

He purchased an envelope at the Black Wolf general store. At the postal window in back, he borrowed a pencil and a scrap of paper on which he wrote the words *Joe Jr.* He put the paper inside the envelope and immediately changed his mind. He removed the paper, sealed the envelope with the wheat grains inside. He cocked his hand to the left, so that his writing slanted that way. He wrote *Mrs. I. Crown* on the outside, and the address, then stepped up to the wicket to buy his stamp.

65

Ilsa

ILSA LAY IN BED, feverish, felled by a severe case of summer grippe. Her flannel gown was soaked with sweat. The sheet pulled up to her waist felt as oppressively heavy as a winter duvet.

She hated sickness. She equated it with weakness, or punishment by the Almighty for some sin clearly visible to Him if not to the sick person.

Ilsa knew her sin. Failure to hold the family together. Even, possibly, her marriage. From the night the man fell to his death, drunk on Crown beer—the night she started a new argument despite the old unbreakable deadlock on the subject dividing them most deeply—she had felt Joe slipping away from her.

On a lower shelf of her bedside stand lay a book she hadn't opened in some time. The *Proceedings* of the Women's Congress of 1893. Almost tremulously, she opened it and turned the pages. Speech after speech, all on "the woman question," as it was called.

How vividly the images of certain speakers reappeared in her imagination. She could hear their proud, fearless declarations, to which she'd given close and sympathetic attention, knowing all the while that her Joe would be angry with the speeches, and the speakers, and with her for listening to them.

She turned a page. Miss Frances Willard, the pillar of the Temperance Union. *"The greatest discovery of the nineteenth century is the discovery of woman, by woman."*

Another page. Mrs. A. J. Cooper, an eloquent Negress of Washington, D.C. *"Not until race, color, sex, and condition are seen as accidents, and not the substance of life—not until then is woman's lesson taught, and woman's cause won."*

Lucy Stone, one of the staunchest of the early crusaders. Now old, tiny, and frail. But still full of fire. *"The idea that woman's sphere is at home, and only at home, has been like a band of steel on society. But the spinning wheel and the loom, the taking care of the house and children, could not and cannot supply the needs or fill the aspirations of women."*

The next page brought her to the hottest zealot she'd heard: Laura DeForce Gordon, an attorney from California. *"All through the ages there has been a system of repression, suppression, and oppression toward women. The conservative, repressive training of the home has abetted and supported it. So have the religious teachings of the various churches. It is an attitude, a pattern of behavior, that is incomprehensible, wicked, and no longer tolerable in any respect."*

Such brave words. She'd been set afire by them, convinced they marked the way of the future.

She closed the book and ran her hand over the fine leather cover stamped in gold. Perhaps the new ideas weren't so good after all. Perhaps they were thrust forward too aggressively. They didn't sustain her now. How could ideas, however worthy, heal the raging anxiety of her heart? Or convince her it didn't matter? How could ideas compete with the love of her husband, which she felt she was losing?

A knock at the bedroom door startled her.

"Mrs. Crown?"

"I'm awake, Helga."

"The morning mail arrived. There is a letter, addressed to you."

"Please, bring it in."

Joe rushed home from the brewery in response to her telephone call. Sitting by her bedside, he turned the envelope one way and then another, studying it. Ilsa's face glowed. "He's alive, Joe. He sent the grains of wheat to show us. He must be out West."

"How do you know they came from him?" Joe held up the envelope. "This isn't his handwriting."

"Of course it is. He tried to disguise it but he can't fool me. I'd be a poor mother if I couldn't recognize my own son's hand."

"Well, I'm not convinced." He stood up, looking warm and uncomfortable in his wrinkled white summer suit and vest. "I don't recognize the writing and I don't believe you do either; you just say it because you want to believe it."

"Of course I want to believe it! Is it wrong to want him back? I do. Is it wrong to believe he's well and will come home someday? I do. Is it wrong to think he sent this to tell us not to worry? No."

Joe responded to her anger impassively. He laid the envelope on the bed. "Well, if it is from Joe, he sent it to you, not to me. You must excuse me now, I still have a lot to do this afternoon."

Bending, he kissed her briefly on her perspiring cheek. He smiled at her and waved as he went out. She wasn't fooled, not by any of it.

She picked up the envelope with its unusual contents—its signal; its token of Joey's survival. She pressed it against her gown, between her sagging breasts. The truth was in her husband's eyes. A certain—*distance*, altogether new. A growing resentment. She had lost her son. She had lost her nephew Pauli. Now she was in danger of losing Joe, and she had no remedy for it. Being herself—kind Ilsa, dutiful Ilsa, Ilsa always prompt with the meals, Ilsa who kept the house immaculate—that was no longer good enough. That couldn't help her any more. She associated with the wrong women. She espoused the wrong ideas. She spoke too forthrightly. She'd forgotten a wife's proper place. She couldn't go back even if she wanted to.

66

Julie

AT THE END OF THE SUMMER of 1895, Julie sailed home from Europe with her little dog Rudy. She'd lost fifteen pounds. Her face was chalky. She had a nervous, distracted air, and she seldom smiled.

She'd finished the tour much as she'd begun it; like a sleepwalker. Pork Vanderhoff had arranged for Cook's to book all the hotels, all the railway tickets, all the excursions in old cities, all the guides who shuffled her about from cathedral to palace to spa to the inevitable tourist shop where the guide coincidentally seemed acquainted with the proprietor. On these junkets—everywhere, virtually, except to her bedroom—Julie was accompanied by a dough-faced nurse-chaperon her father had hired after interviewing a dozen candidates. The chosen woman was Belgian. She had six sisters, all but one a nun. She felt she'd misspent her own life with a husband, and talked about little else.

Julie arrived in Chicago no wiser, no stronger of will, than she had been when her father and mother shipped her off. No wiser, no stronger—but fully as resentful.

The very day she came home, she ran to the whitewashed message stone by the stable. It was gone; all the stones were gone. Dug out, the soil raked and smoothed for narrow flower beds. She felt abandoned. For a moment she almost hated Paul.

Two weeks later, with Pork and Nell absent from the house, she rang Ilsa Crown on the telephone and invited the somewhat startled lady to be her guest for tea.

On a chill, blustery, rainswept September afternoon the women met at a table secluded behind artificial palms in the fashionable Rose Café of the Hotel Richelieu on Michigan.

"It is very kind of you to invite me," Ilsa said with a polite smile. She was a woman of obvious warmth and excellent manners. A woman without pretense or, apparently, any need for it; she made no attempt to minimize her accent. Julie couldn't understand her mother's continuing hatred of Mrs. Crown.

Ilsa continued, "We have seen one another at public functions but have never been introduced. Is there some special reason you wished for us to meet?"

"Yes, I confess there is." The bald waiter glided to the table with his order pad. "Tea for both of us, Victor. A plate of finger sandwiches, too."

"Very nice," Ilsa murmured. Victor left. On a small dais across the room, a string trio scraped away at "I Don't Want to Play in Your Yard."

Julie found it hard to smile, but she did. Her cheeks were white as the napkin she was twisting in her lap. Cramps were torturing her. She'd fought her way out of bed to keep the appointment. It was the first day of her monthly trial.

"Have you any word of your son, Mrs. Crown?"

"No. The police have largely abandoned the case. We have used a firm of private detectives, with no success."

"That's so sad."

"Yes—well—one must bear it. I have faith that Joey is alive and well, perhaps in the West." She made no reference to the envelope with its token of wheat.

They chatted of less painful things while waiting for their tea. Ilsa mentioned the renewed outbreak of war in Cuba; the rebels had resumed their fight for independence several months ago. Julie said she knew little about world affairs. Ilsa asked her opinion on possible candidates in the 1896 presidential election. Julie said she had no opinion. Literature, then? Had she read *The Prisoner of Zenda?* Yes, in Europe; she'd enjoyed it immensely.

What about Mr. Crane's *Red Badge of Courage,* just published? Julie said she wasn't familiar with the book. Ilsa explained that although it wasn't a smashing best-seller, it was earning the praise of a small number of discerning readers, and of many critics who hailed it as a little masterpiece. "I've not read it yet myself," she said. "I can't pry our copy away from Joe."

Victor arrived pushing a silvery trolley. He poured Earl Gray from a pot heavily decorated with silver grapes. Julie toyed with a tiny triangular sandwich from which all the crusts had been cut. "I've only heard of the book. My mother's friends told her it was ugly. We usually have nothing in the house but romantic novels. Mama prefers them."

"I see." Ilsa was unfailingly polite, but Julie could tell that she had disappointed her guest. A cramp made her catch her breath. She pushed her cup and saucer aside. Even the soothing tea refused to go down easily.

"Mrs. Crown, may I speak candidly?"

"Of course, my dear."

"I invited you here to ask about your nephew."

"Pauli?" Ilsa seemed to sag a little. "I'm afraid Pauli moved out of our house some time ago. Shortly after Joe Junior left. Pauli's departure was a direct consequence of that. I was aware that you were acquainted with Pauli, of course." She had the decency to stop there, with no reference to Radigan's Hotel.

The cramps kept coming. They were so terrible, Julie almost gasped aloud. "I really did care for him, Mrs. Crown. I still do. Do you know his whereabouts?"

"Regrettably, I don't. Nor does anyone in our household. I had a telephone message from him several months ago. I believe he was in Chicago at the time, but he didn't say so. I've heard nothing further. Of course"—she paused as if reluctant to complete the thought—"there is always the possibility that he has returned to Germany."

"Oh, no, he wouldn't, not when the two of us felt so strongly about one another." Julie bowed her head and put her hand to her eyes. "He wouldn't."

"My dear, I didn't mean to upset you. I personally think it unlikely that Pauli has left the country. It's just that we lack information, so we can't entirely discount the idea."

Julie took her hand from her tear-streaked face. Victor rushed to the table, alarmed by his customer's distress. Ilsa Crown assured him all was well. As soon as he left and the ladies at nearby tables stopped staring, she reached across the table to clasp Julie's hand.

"Juliette, I think I failed to realize the depth of your feeling. Pauli was—is—a wonderful boy. I am so sorry I don't know where he is."

"I wonder why he's left no messages for me."

"It could be that he doesn't know how. I have the impression your parents would not welcome any communication from someone named Crown."

"He'd know how to get in touch if he wanted to, there are ways. Paul's clever."

Ilsa sat stoically, saying nothing. Julie's chin came up. In spite of her acute pain, she managed an air of brittle cheer. "Well, at least we have settled that question, haven't we? Paul's gone. And he didn't say where I might find him. Nothing to be done, is there?"

Nell took her daughter aside the following Monday, into the mansion's music room. Ferns and green plants growing in great stone urns beneath a skylight filled the room with a woodsy aroma. Julie sat at the grand piano, idly picking out a scale. Nell paced back and forth, mysteriously cheerful and excited.

"Your father wants me to break the news, he said it's time."

"What news, Mama?"

"There is a gentleman who wishes to call on you, Juliette. A gentleman with serious intentions."

Julie's head snapped up, her eyes huge as some trapped forest animal's. The chatter and bustle of servants came softly through the open doorway.

"Who is it?"

"A very eligible widower. You've met him, although perhaps you don't recall him well. His name is William Vann Elstree."

"The department store family?"

"Yes. His wife passed away over a year ago, in the prolonged heat wave. He declared his feelings in Wiesbaden and asked your father's permission to call. We insisted he wait a suitable interval and he was most agreeable."

Feelings of terror and confusion churned through Julie. Nell rushed to the piano, hands clasped joyously. "Mr. Elstree is somewhat older than you, but he's a model of courtesy and gentility. So well bred, well mannered—"

"Mama," Julie began, preparing her defense.

"And of course he's enormously wealthy."

"Mama, I don't wish to quarrel with you, but—"

"We simply can't go through this again, Juliette. I'll not tolerate it. Nor will your father." All at once Nell smiled sweetly. "If you aren't yourself, if you're slipping again, perhaps we need to consult Dr. Woodrow—"

"No!"

"—possibly consider another month or two at the Mountjoy Hospital in Cleveland—"

"No, Mama, no!"

Nell began to chafe Julie's hands, stroke her thick dark hair. "Then do be more rational, dear. And please, please, don't think me unkind. What I want most in the world are two things. Contentment for this household and for you. I want to see you wed to the right kind of man. I want that before I go to heaven."

Julie cried; she couldn't stop. But Paul was *gone*, what did it matter? "All right, Mama. All right. *All right.*"

"Are you saying Mr. Elstree may call?"

"Yes, Mama, he may call, why not?"

Nell stepped back; triumph put a glow in her eyes. "Thank you, my dear. By saying that you make me exceedingly happy. I think you will make yourself happy in the bargain."

Nell patted her hand once more, then left the room. Her step was brisk. She was smiling.

67

Paul

IN CUBA, fighting between the insurgents and Spain raged across the island. In Germany, a canal opened from the North Sea to Kiel Harbor on the Baltic. In the Transvaal, relations between the Boer farmers and the British government worsened. In England, the aesthete Oscar Wilde, linked to a male lover, launched a court action against the lover's father, the Marquis of Queensbury. In Russia, Tchaikovsky's *Swan Lake* ballet had its first complete performance, in St. Petersburg. In France, the brothers Auguste and Louis Lumière perfected a machine capable of both exposing and projecting sequential pictures on a moving strip of celluloid ("I imagine your friend Shadow's agog over that," Wex remarked to Paul. "Yes, and feeling the hot breath of competition on his neck, too."). In America, football players at Latrobe, Pennsylvania, took money to play "professionally," Secretary of State Olney invoked the Monroe Doctrine against Britain, a Dublin-born musician named Victor Herbert conducted the famous 22d Regiment Band (formerly Gilmore's), the "Silver Wing" in Congress asserted its independence from the regular Democrats, and a gentleman named King C. Gillette announced his invention of a new-style "safety" razor.

But in Chicago in that autumn of 1895, world events, national events, everything, paled beside a sensational murder trial. One Herman W. Mudgett, residing in an ornate three-story house on Sixty-third Street under the assumed name Dr. H. H. Holmes, was accused of as many as fifty murders and mutilations within the past three years. Police investigators tore apart "Holmes's Castle," and every newspaper described and diagramed its labyrinth of rooms where, it was discovered, killing and torture—and madness—had reigned amid the comings and goings of unsuspecting neighbors.

Wex and Paul rushed down to Sixty-third and Wallace on a Sunday, as many other enterprising photographers were doing. They took pictures of the exterior of the fantastic wooden house with its towers and numerous bay windows blocked on the inside with sheet iron. After spending all day at his job, Paul worked for hours every night, helping Wex print and mount the souvenir photos. Wex hired three neighborhood boys to roam the downtown hawking them. Sales were poor; too many competitors had the same idea.

In the midst of this, an emergency took Nancy Logan from the laundry. At harvest time, Nancy's mother fell off a McCormick reaping machine she was driving and broke an ankle and a hip. "Ma will be laid up for months. Somebody's got to cook for the men." Paul carried Nancy's grip to the Dearborn Street station.

"I don't mind leaving the laundry," she admitted. "Or Chicago, it's a hard town. Dirty and dangerous—all this mad doctor stuff, it's scary. I'll miss you, though. If I hung around I might make you forget that other girl. I'm stubborn when I want to be." A few tears came.

"I'll probably marry some dull farmer boy from down home. But I'll always be in love with you."

Nancy jumped up on tiptoes, holding both his arms tightly. "I'd do anything for you, Dutch. If you ever need help, come find me. You better kiss me before I bawl."

At least twice a week Paul walked by the Vanderhoff mansion in the chilly autumn twilight. He saw no sign of Julie and assumed she was still abroad. He continued to daydream of a job with Colonel Sid Shadow while continuing to practice still photography.

Wex criticized the pictures harshly, often sarcastically. Refusing to be whipped by it, Paul kept shooting. Finally he developed and printed a portrait he liked: a street woman in a head scarf standing beside a pushcart of wilted flowers. Light from above fell onto the left side of her face, illuminating her skin like a plain cut by dozens of dry creeks. The light flecked her left eye, and the effect was a telling sadness; a silent story of resignation to poverty and failure.

"That's good," Wex said when he saw it. "In fact it's better than good. You're catching on. You've developed an eye. It'll serve you just as well with the living pictures, I suppose," he added with one of his characteristic sniffs.

During October, equipment began to disappear from the Temple of Photography, a piece at a time. Then Wex sheepishly asked Paul for a small loan. Though Wex didn't say so, Paul assumed it was for the back rent. He brought the money home from the savings bank without a question. The second time Wex asked, assenting to it reduced Paul's small account to zero.

A collector came around on the first of November; Paul heard loud voices behind a closed door. The collector stormed out. A day later, in a trash box, Paul found some slips with odd names penciled on them. Wex wasn't paying overdue rent after all, he was placing bets. The season meetings in Chicago had ended, so he must be wagering at tracks somewhere else. Perhaps down South. Paul asked one of his good customers, Madame Camille, whether this was possible.

"Honey," the madam said, "wonderful inventions like the telegraph and long-distance phone wires are good for a hell of a lot more than saying happy birthday, granny, how's your lumbago? You mean to tell me you've never been in the betting parlors around here?"

"No, they don't use laundry, I don't know about them."

"Keep it that way. You go in those joints regularly, you're on the road to the poorhouse."

So the disease that afflicted Wex hadn't abated. It saddened Paul. He said nothing. He owed Wex a lot. He trusted him to pay back the loans.

One evening over a typically meager supper, Wex said, "Dutch, when did you arrive in this country?"

"The ship docked in New York on the first day of June, three years ago. Why do you ask?"

"Citizenship. After five years you're entitled to go before a district or circuit judge and declare your bona fide intention of becoming a citizen. For you that means year after next. Wait two more years, you can take the oath."

"Oh yes, I've already considered it. There are terrible things in America, which I never expected. This mad doctor and his butchery—never did I hear of such crimes in Germany. But there are wonderful things here too. A chance to work in an exciting trade, for one. With that, and an American wife, I'll want to be a citizen."

"Is Vanderhoff's daughter home yet?"

"I don't think so. I have passed by the house a few times without seeing her. I haven't telephoned or written letters. I don't want to embarrass her. I also don't want to visit the county jail again. I'll get in touch, don't worry."

Wexford Rooney the photographer was not entirely unknown to the city's better element. He had a reputation as a good journeyman, if not a very suave or polished one. So he got the occasional wedding assignment, or did group portraits of the members of a lodge.

His political connections were not solely with the Democrats of the First Ward; he knew a few minor Republicans too. When a society photographer was suddenly taken ill, one of the Republicans sent for him to photograph a Saturday afternoon reception being given by Mr. and Mrs. Potter Palmer. The guest of honor was Marcus Alonzo Hanna of Ohio, said to be the gray eminence of the Republican Party; the man who would name the Republican candidate for President next summer.

Wex was in a transport of excitement. He nicked his face three times shaving. He was ironing a shirt as Paul left for work. When he came home in a hack at dusk, his attitude was quite different. He seemed glum, nervous. Paul was sitting at the table in back with a bottle of Crown lager and the *Tribune*. He was puzzled when Wex didn't speak, only nodded, and then began to putter at the stove with his back turned.

"How did it go?"

"Oh, fine, fine," Wex said, still facing away. "Mr. Palmer tipped me extra. I must get right to work developing and printing the pictures tonight."

"Did the guests treat you well?"

"Oh yes, they were very kind. Very posh crowd."

"Mr. Rooney. Something went wrong. What is it?"

Wex turned then and removed his spectacles, looking sad.

"I saw someone you know. The young lady."

Paul jumped up. "Julie? She's back?"

"She returned in late summer. I asked to be certain."

"Tell me how she looked."

"Oh—beautiful. Very beautiful, just as you said. She's a proper young woman. Well behaved."

A silence then; another anguished look at his pupil. "She didn't attend the party by herself."

"Of course, I would assume her parents also—"

"That isn't what I mean. She had an escort."

Paul lowered the beer bottle to the table. "I don't believe you."

"I'm sorry, it's true. She came with William V. Elstree, the department store heir. He's a widower now." He sniffed. "Not a young man."

"She must have gone with him for convenience."

"I wish it were so, Dutch. I made a few discreet inquiries about that, too. I wish I hadn't."

"Tell me the rest. You must."

"The young lady's being seen with Elstree at concerts and levees more or less regularly. I have one exposed plate showing them together."

"Oh my God. What happened? *What happened?*"

"I don't know. I didn't want to tell you. Wouldn't hurt you for anything. Wouldn't have said a word, but it struck me that you had to know. Maybe—" He flushed, then finished while looking in the other direction:

"Maybe you should stop thinking about her. It looks like the young lady has sailed off on some new course."

□ □ □ □

A few minutes after eleven, Paul walked out of the darkroom with a developed glass plate. He examined it by electric light. Once a negative image had seemed strange and foreign to him. Now it was as familiar as the taste of beer or the texture of black bread; his eye and mind instantly translated the spectral reverse images. Tones of gray in her dress; the skeletal white of his dark formal suit. The man had his arm around her. Each of them held a fluted glass with something in it. Paul tilted the plate, studying her black teeth.

She was smiling. He hurled the plate across the room.

It struck the stove and shattered loudly, raining down its daggers and chips of glass. Paul wiped his hands on his canvas apron as Wex bounded from the dark-room. He saw the damage and groaned.

"It slipped out of my hands."

"Which one was it?"

"My girl."

Wex gave him a long stare, eyes red and huge behind his spectacles. "All right, can't be helped. Accidents happen."

"Yes, they do," Paul said. He'd never felt such pain, not even when his own family turned him out.

Wex went to bed at midnight. Paul pried the crown off a new bottle of his uncle's beer and sat under the kitchen light, drinking. He drank another bottle after that, and another. Trying to solve the riddle.

What had caused her to change? Had she lied to him all along? Tricked him? How could that be, after all their declarations of love, hers just as fervent as his? How could it be after their pledges of undying devotion? And that night at Radigan's . . . did he mean no more to her than a one-night experiment?

"It looks like the young lady has sailed off on some new course . . ."

How could it be?

He telephoned the Vanderhoff mansion next morning. He asked for Miss Vanderhoff. "Who is calling, please?" He gave his name to the male servant. "She is not here." He asked to leave a message. "Sorry, that is not possible." The servants had been rehearsed. The wall was up.

68

Joe Crown

IN NOVEMBER Joe had the misfortune to encounter Oskar Hexhammer again, this time at the rathskeller of the Germania Club. The rathskeller was a large, dark, comfortable room with oak paneling and white tablecloths. All around the walls, stuffed and mounted heads of bison and boars and stags with splendid antlers contemplated eternity with glass eyes.

When Hexhammer walked down the stairs, the place was empty save for Joe, who was waiting for his hops supplier; he'd scheduled a noon meeting while they ate. A full stein of dark Heimat beer sat on the bar in front of him.

He was in a foul mood. His supplier was already fifteen minutes late. While waiting, Joe had been mulling his dissatisfaction with the brewmaster he'd hired after Fred Schildkraut's death. Heinz Freising was competent but riotously disorganized, which Joe blamed on his Bavarian upbringing. Freising was always cracking jokes around the brewery. Joe had nearly decided to replace him.

Now here was Hexhammer, making straight for him. He was still publishing his *Chicago Deutsche Zeitung,* which lavished praise on anything emanating from the fatherland or the lips of the Kaiser. He'd made no further editorial attacks on Joe or his brewery. The two men saw each other occasionally at this club, German restaurants, social functions, but always at nodding distance. Joe was customarily the one who nodded first, out of politeness. Hexhammer always accompanied his nod with a smirk, as though expressing some fancied superiority. The damned ass.

"Well, Joe. *Wie geht's mit Ihnen?*"

"Fine, Oskar. You?"

"Oh, splendid. How's business?"

"We're shipping at record levels. We expect to close out the year at seven hundred and forty thousand barrels."

"Ah."

Joe was silently amused. He hadn't realized a single syllable could carry so much disappointment. "Buy you a beer, Oskar?"

"Is it yours?"

"Naturally."

"How dare I refuse?"

Joe signaled. "Carlo, draw one for Mr. Hexhammer." He wished his supplier would appear. Two other men he knew slightly came down the stairs, laughing and talking. Joe felt all the more trapped.

He tried to steer the conversation to neutral subjects. The talented Baltimore team that had won the National League pennant in the fall. Hexhammer said he knew nothing about baseball, it was a crude American game. Young Mr. Crane's remarkable Civil War novel, then? "I read it but I loathed it. English is such an ugly language. The classic poetry in the language you and I were raised with— that is true art."

Joe's annoyance grew. He fingered the boar's tooth on his watch chain; pulled out his watch and snapped it open. The damned supplier was now twenty-two minutes late.

Hexhammer then began to praise Kaiser Wilhelm's statesmanship, especially his decision to force Bismarck out of office a few years ago. The chancellor had opposed the buildup of a two-ocean navy, which the Kaiser craved, having read and reread Admiral Mahan's book on sea power like some new holy writ. The Kaiser in turn hated the treaty Bismarck had secretly negotiated with Russia in 1887. So did Hexhammer:

"In eighty-seven, when Bismarck addressed the Reichstag, he made a magnificent statement: 'We Germans fear God and nothing else in the world.' Then he spent an hour justifying that damned cowardly treaty."

Joe looked again toward the empty stairs. "Cowardly? I saw it as a shrewd move to promote peace. Russia standing with France—two of Germany's traditional enemies allied—that would be very dangerous."

"Nonsense. Bismarck became an old lion, Joe. Openly opposing his sworn leader. The Kaiser had a duty to discharge him."

"And that was his reward for serving twenty-eight years, steadfastly, according to what he believed best."

"He spread dissension! He looked backward, like every old man. The Kaiser looks to the future. Creation of a new German empire. Peacefully, one hopes, but if not, then forcibly."

"Oskar, you sound like a warmonger. Whatever you think of Bismarck's policies—and as an American, I disliked many of them—"

"Yes, we all know where your loyalties lie."

Fuming, Joe plowed on. "—he was and is one of the great men of Europe. One of the great men of this century. A colossus."

"No, no—an old lion. There's a new generation rising in the fatherland that devours old lions. It's lucky you're in this country. I think you became an old lion some time ago."

Joe nearly threw his beer in the man's face. Fortunately, at that moment his supplier came tromping into the rathskeller, hailing him. Joe signed the chit for the beer and swiftly left the bar to greet his guest.

The encounter with Hexhammer stayed with him, vastly upsetting. In the final moments of the argument his head had throbbed. He was losing control. Control of himself, his family, his whole ordered existence. What it augured for the future —the unforeseeable dangers, failures—frightened him.

How could he regain control? Fire the brewmaster? That was a start, but it wasn't enough. What, then? Where and how could he take command of events in a demonstrable way, so as to shore up his crumbling faith in himself?

69

Paul

PAUL STRUGGLED to lay a waterproof cover on the laundry hamper. Wind whipped his scarf back and forth across his face. The delivery wagon was tied near the service entrance of the Sherman House, on the Clark Street side. Someone in a cap came rushing around the corner from Randolph, head down against the rain. He bowled into Paul. Handbills flew.

Paul dove to retrieve some from under the wagon horse. "Never mind, nobody wants any today."

The mournful statement made him look up. He recognized the hangdog face under a dripping bill cap. "Hello, remember me? We met at the racetrack and at Colonel Shadow's arcade."

"Yes." Lew Kress stuffed wet, bedraggled handbills in the pockets of his wool coat. He stepped into the lee of the laundry wagon and blew on his bare hands. The November rain was cold, falling hard.

Paul said, "A poor day to advertise moving pictures, it seems."

"Isn't it. I hate this damn job. I hate this town. I should go home."

Paul focused instantly on what Lew Kress had just said. "Home, where is that?"

"Little town in South Carolina. Branchville. Never heard of it, have you?"

"No, I have not. I'm sure it's pleasant. Why don't you go?"

"I'll tell you why. I can't afford a train ticket." He stepped against the building, turned up the collar of his shabby coat, looking miserable. "Money's like water to me. I can't hold on to it. I have this—terrible passion for the whores. I spend every cent on them."

"And it's only the rail fare that keeps you in Chicago? What is the amount?"

"Second-class, it's eleven dollars and fifty cents. More than I'll ever be able to save. Look, I'm soaked and frozen, I'm going."

Paul grabbed his arm. "I'll get it."

"What? What did you say?"

"I said I will get the money for your ticket. It will take a while, but as soon as I have it I will find you at the arcade." Paul drew a breath. "I want your job."

"This job? You're crazy."

"No, the job will suit me."

"Shadow can be a son of a bitch. A slave driver. Do you know what that means?"

"I think so."

"And that Jim, he has a mean streak, I'd never turn my back on him."

"Even so, I want the job. I want to learn about the living pictures. I will pay your way to South Carolina."

"Why, good Lord—" Skepticism gave way to a kind of joyous babble. "You're a real gentleman, you are. Straight talker, too. All right, it's a bargain." They shook right there in the downpour. "You come 'round as soon as you've got the money, hear? Can't be too soon to suit me."

He waved as he rushed off. For the first time in weeks, Paul forgot the terrible shock, the terrible sense of defeat caused by the news about Julie. He laughed and did a little capering step on the sidewalk.

Chicago was a crossroads; everyone of importance came through, rushing between the oceans. Men with new political ideas, new business schemes, new inventions. That was why Paul and Wex found themselves shivering on the street on another miserable day, the twenty-ninth of November; the day after Thanksgiving.

The night before, a near blizzard had blown through. High snowdrifts lined both sides of Michigan Avenue; wagon traffic had churned the center to brown slop. Low-hanging clouds laid a gray murk over everything, including the few spectators scattered along both sides of the avenue.

"Why are we doing this?" Wex asked rhetorically. He crossed his arms and slapped his ribs with hands encased in patched mittens. He didn't smile, didn't seem himself of late, and had offered no explanation.

"We want to see the race. You told me it was the first such race to be held in North America."

"I'm sure there'll be another. In better weather."

Paul smiled, though his face was stiff. His nose was numb, his shoes were soaked; his socks felt like wet rags. They'd been waiting more than an hour. Several of the new "motor wagons" were scheduled to race north from Jackson Park over a fifty-four-mile course. The storm had obviously delayed everything.

Another half hour passed. Wex said he needed a drink to warm up, nothing was worth this kind of torture. Overlapping the end of his complaint, Paul heard a faint noise. "They're coming!"

To the south, a strange vehicle came chugging out of the mist, followed by another. "Motor wagons." They resembled horseless buggies with small engines mounted in the rear. The second was nearly a block behind the first. On they came, weaving and sliding on the treacherous ice underneath the slush. Two more vehicles appeared. All four drivers were muffled to the eyes. There was a spatter of applause from both sides of the boulevard.

Paul spied a small German flag painted on the second motor wagon. "Benz!" he yelled. "Come on, Benz!"

Wex exclaimed, "My God, they must be doing eight or nine miles an hour, can you believe it?"

The second motor wagon passed by. The engine noise from the two laggards grew louder. Wex identified one as an Electrobat but didn't recognize the other. "The papers announced eight or nine entries. The snow must have knocked out the rest."

Just then, across the street, Paul spotted a familiar figure; a young man wearing knickerbockers, a heavy coat, a bright red watch cap and matching mittens. Paul waved. "Carl! Over here!"

Carl Crown dashed across Michigan in front of a police wagon flinging up slush from its wheels. He snatched off his cap, his cheeks were nearly as red. Paul introduced Carl to Wex, who shook hands, then started trotting in place to warm his feet.

"You've gotten so tall, Carl. How old are you now?"

Carl was grinning, genuinely happy to see Paul. "I was thirteen this month. I'm home for a week's holiday. I'm in school in New York. Damn far away. The headmaster's a damn old son of a bitch."

Paul chuckled at Carl's new worldliness. "Otherwise it's all right?"

"Oh, not the studying. But I'm learning football. I love that. What about you?"

"Oh, things are excellent. I have a good job. Mr. Rooney is teaching me photography. Next I want to learn about the living pictures. The flickers."

"I heard they're dirty. Mama said Pastor Wunder preached about them. A real hellfire sermon."

Slapping his sides, Wex said, "The living pictures are a new, vital part of photography, and photography is the art and science that can enrich the world. Thrill and entertain millions. Educate them—"

Carl was obviously nonplussed, so Paul interrupted the lecture. "Tell me, how is Fritzi?"

"You know her, Paul. Crazy. Right now she thinks she's the lady of the camellias. She saw some foreign actress—"

"Helena Modjeska," Wex said. "She played Chicago last month."

"That's the one. Fritzi imitates her all the time. Every night she dies nine or ten times at least. It's sickening."

"Have you heard from your brother?"

Carl shook his head. "No one can find him. I guess he's gone for good. Sometimes when his name just comes up by accident, everybody stops talking and Mama looks ready to cry." He touched Paul's arm. "I wish you'd never left."

"I do too. Sometimes. I hadn't any choice."

Carl tugged his cap on. "Guess I better go home. Pop gave strict orders I shouldn't stay too long."

"It doesn't surprise me," Paul said. He and Carl hugged each other.

"Luck, Paul."

"To you also. Study hard, you need to be smart in this world." Carl jumped the curbside snow pile and was soon lost in the dark gray mist of morning.

"Big lad," Wex said. He took off his spectacles and wiped away condensation. "I'm definitely leaving. I need a whiskey."

"But how will we find out who wins the race?"

"I know someone at the *Tribune.* I'll telephone later."

They walked west from Michigan to a small tavern with fogged windows. They went into a vestibule, warmer than the street. There Wex paused, his nose shining like a glass strawberry. "Listen, I just want to say this so you're clear about it. I know you're keen to learn about the flickers. You're free to move out anytime there's an opportunity. I encourage it, I won't feel bad. I take that back, I will, you're good company. Let's go in, warm up with drinks, I need to talk to you about something else."

"What?"

"Why—ah—" His gaze darted away from Paul's. "Never mind, it isn't important."

With the inner door open and soothing warmth flowing out, Wex again stopped abruptly. "Do you have any money on you?"

"Forty cents."

"Good, I'm temporarily short."

With a worried expression Paul followed him into the tavern.

That night, shivering under two thin blankets in the loft, he couldn't sleep. His thoughts fixed on Shadow, Lew Kress, his own financial predicament. He had no money saved, he'd loaned it all to Wex. What could he do about that ticket?

In the weeks that followed he found no ready answer to the question. Then, on Monday night before Christmas, he returned home from the Steam Laundry as usual and found a wagon parked in front of the Temple. Two draymen were carrying out furniture and equipment and loading it in an open wagon.

It was a cold sparkling night of stars and wind. Wex stood in the street, bareheaded, hands in his pockets, gazing up at the Temple sign. Paul hurried to him. "Wex, what's going on here?"

Wex wouldn't look at him. "Eviction. My things are going into storage. The locks will be changed tomorrow morning."

"But why?"

"Because the rent is once more in arrears. Four months this time. The landlord called in person. Told me he had a new tenant with good credit. Tore up my lease right in front of me."

"Is that legal?"

"It's legal when I can't pay for a lawyer to fight it."

"What about Mr. Coughlin's insurance fund?"

Wex shook his head. "The Bath said he was sorry, but the fund's for people in trouble with the law. He sent me to a man who makes loans at usurious rates. I signed a paper that'll bleed me till I'm a hundred. It was the only way I could pay to move the goods and store them."

Paul was upset. "I thought there was enough money for the rent. I loaned you all I had."

Wex seemed to shrivel inside his coat. "I paid two months. But I owed for six. I hoped for a quick stroke of luck. I wagered the rest, my money and yours, at various tracks down South."

"By telephone and telegraph?"

"Oh, you know how that's done?"

"I found out. How much did you lose?"

Wex gazed at the chilly stars, as though hoping some deity might descend to rescue him.

"Everything."

"All of my savings?"

"Yes, I regret to say."

"How could you do that?"

Wexford Rooney wheeled on him. "Who are you to take that tone with me? You're just a youth. I am fifty-seven years old! Do you think I like this? That it makes me proud? I'm a weak man, Dutch. Many creative artists are weak. You expect me to be a good, perfect German. Well, God damn it, I'm not German, and I'm not perfect."

Wex swung away to stare at the workmen carrying out his largest camera and tripod. His sparse hair blew in the night wind. A laughing whore and her customer hurried into Wampler's Hotel. For a moment Paul wanted to hit Wex Rooney in the face. Then he saw how old, small, defeated he was, facing the winter, facing the merriest season of the year with all his goods, cameras, reflectors, lens boxes, piled up higgledy-piggledy in the overloaded wagon.

The drayman in charge adjusted his earmuffs and gloves. "No more this trip, we'll be back in the morning." They drove off toward the gaudy glow of Clark Street.

"So tomorrow we are thrown into the street," Paul said.

"Dutch, I'm sorry. I'm sorry I cursed you, and even sorrier that this happened. I suspected it was coming, I wanted to warn you. A dozen times I started to tell you, but I couldn't do it, I'm a coward. At the end of the week I will be leaving town. I am forced to take a position elsewhere. I applied for it through a classified several weeks ago, when I saw the end coming. I'm going to a large photographic studio, as a general helper and artist in charge of color tinting. Look, it isn't Shakespearean tragedy," Wex said, with a glimmer of his old pixy smile. "I won't starve. Neither will you. It's time you moved on anyway, we discussed that. Perhaps Shadow will take you on. Do you need a letter of reference?"

"No, that isn't what I need. I hope this place you're going is good. Is it New York or some other large city?"

"Would that it were so." He sighed. "Charleston, West Virginia."

"Where is that?"

"Nowhere. It's nowhere," Wex said, so faintly Paul could scarcely hear it.

Standing in the bitter air, gazing at the Temple's dark facade, Paul realized how much the place meant to him. How much this cantankerous, weak, strange, contradictory, idealistic, impractical old man meant to him.

"Is there any food inside?" he asked.

"Nothing."

"Well, come on, I still have thirty cents. We can have sausage and rolls and coffee for supper."

Wex fell in step like an obedient child.

Light snow was falling through gaps in the roof of the train shed. Paul had put Wex's two cheap valises into the second-class car. He knew Wex couldn't afford a tip for a porter.

The Baltimore and Ohio conductor cupped his hands around his mouth. *"Boooard!"*

"I hate this," Wex said.

"Please give me the studio address. You promised to write it out."

"Yes, I have it." He put a scrap of paper in Paul's hand. "You forgive me?"

"For what? We're friends. I can never repay you for all you've done."

"Oh God." Wex flung himself on Paul and they embraced. "I'd be proud to have a son like you. Proud." Hugging the old man, Paul managed to tuck five dollars into his pocket; money he'd begged as a salary advance from Mr. Grace's payroll clerk.

Steam hissed. The bell rang. The anxious conductor motioned his last passenger to the steps. "I'll write to you when I know where I'm staying," Paul promised.

Wex jumped to the lowest step. "I'll write you too. Someone has to be your conscience. You're too fine a vessel to be wasted. Goodbye, Paul, goodbye, goodbye—"

The train swayed off into the winter night. Falling snow melted on Paul's face. He had felt alone like this on the pier at Hamburg. He had felt like this an hour after Uncle Joe cast him out.

Later, he walked past the Temple and stopped to tug at the padlock and chain on the front door. He trudged on, carrying his small valise of clothes and mementos. The globe and stand, the paper flag, a packet of souvenir postcards wrapped with an elastic, the stereopticon card.

He was too proud to approach one of the madams, tell her he had no place to go, ask her to let him sleep in some corner. He prowled the alleys of the Levee until he found a discarded wooden packing case with one end broken open. He crawled in and slept there.

In his dreams, the baker of Wuppertal appeared. Vindicated, he was laughing at Paul and his misery and stupidity.

He awoke at daylight, nearly frozen. The Steam Laundry opened its doors at five, so he sneaked in early and cleaned up in the room allocated to male employees. His hands were so stiff, he could barely hold his straight razor. Shaving without shaving soap, he scraped and reddened his face. Some of the girls noticed. Paul said it was the winter weather.

The next few nights he slept wherever he could find shelter. The first night back in the packing case, he awoke to find a rat chewing on his shoe. Another night he fled the packing case ahead of a snarling wild dog intent on sampling his leg.

At the end of the week he settled up with Mr. Grace's pay clerk for the money advanced to him and gave notice.

Albert Grace heard of this and was waiting for Paul at the end of the workday. Grace was no longer the blustering autocrat, he was a penitent. Everyone on the routes loved Paul, business had risen noticeably because of his steady and diligent attention to his duties. The owner wrung his hands and asked if some thoughtless action on his part had precipitated this abrupt departure. Paul said no. Grace begged him to reconsider, assuring him that a fine career in laundry was his for the asking. Paul thanked him and said his life was taking a different direction. That same night he stored his valise with Madame Camille. At midnight, in the yards of the Monon Railroad, he jumped aboard a freight and huddled in the corner of a boxcar as the train rattled south to Indiana.

He staggered over the hard ground at daybreak. He'd jumped off the Monon at Greencastle. A sleepy depot agent gave him directions. He walked all the miles from there to Reelsville.

A white fog enveloped the world, muting sounds. Trees looked like strange constructs of wire, tortuously shaped. Winter had folded and frozen the land into solid waves of mud, with a dusting of snow in the troughs. His stumbling feet snapped off dead cornstalks as he crossed the fields. His forehead and cheeks burned. How could he be so warm in December? He had a good idea.

He wanted to lie down. He lifted his left foot and placed it ahead. He lifted his right foot and placed it ahead. The horizon tilted. He waited till it settled, then went on. He was reliving the trek to Chicago, with a different purpose but the same determination.

Three pigs squealed and ran as he entered the dooryard. He fell against weathered siding, rested a moment, then stumbled along the side of the house in the cutting wind.

Lamplight shone behind a bleached gingham curtain in the window of the back door. Paul knocked on the glass. He leaned his forehead on the siding and shut his eyes.

Someone lifted the window curtain. The door opened. Her voice, stunned, bewildered, rolled over him like a blessing.

"Dutch. What are you doing here?"

He opened his eyes but could barely focus them. "Nancy. You said once you'd help me if I needed it. I need help now. I need to borrow money. I need eleven dollars and fifty cents, exactly . . ."

70

Rosie

ROSIE WENT TO NEW YORK in the spring of 1895. She'd saved the money in Chicago, but as it turned out, she didn't have to spend it. She screwed a railway conductor twice, in an empty Pullman compartment, and he wrote a slip for a full refund of her coach fare. Till she died, she'd never forget the garlic on his breath, or the smell of his wool uniform.

When she left the New York Central depot and plunged into the giant, thundering, clangorous, stupefyingly crowded city, she was excited as never before. Lugging her cheap floral-printed suitcase, she asked a policeman for directions and went directly to the only street she knew, the Bowery. It was downtown; she'd read that it was the heart of New York's theater district and a thoroughfare high-class gents visited for special entertainment.

She was disappointed when she saw the Bowery. The theaters were few and rundown. They presented variety bills and were squeezed between shooting galleries, dime museums, Turkish baths, hotels that advertised "night, day, or by the hour." There were no gents visible, either, just ratty bums with bottles in paper sacks.

A tout sidled up to her. His clothes smelled like vomit and his breath was worse. "Want some smoke, girlie? I know a place to get it."

"I don't use no dope. Get the hell away from me or I'll find a copper."

He called her a cunt, but he left.

Music issued from many of the dives she passed. One piano had a mandolin attachment, which made the professor's frenetic playing sound like hammers on an anvil. Men in evening dress spieled in front of the dime museums. In the midst of the drays, hansoms, and pony carts rolling through piles of horse shit, there came a gaudy open-air wagon full of well-dressed people rubbernecking and looking properly shocked. The side of the wagon said *BROADWAY SIGHT-SEEING CO. The Safe Comfortable Way to See New York's Street Life.* A guide standing up in the front blared his commentary through a megaphone.

A bum wobbling next to Rosie threw his empty wine bottle at the wagon.

"Ga'damn slummers." She sure wasn't in the middle of the high life. As she drifted along, tired and hungry, her hopes sank.

In a dim-lit café she bought a stale roll and coffee for two pennies, and at that point her luck improved. She was accosted by a handsome middle-aged man with a drink-blotched face. By nightfall she had a bed in a two-room flat on the top floor of a tenement. The bed and the flat belonged to the man, whose last name was Stopes and whose first name was Buck, short for Buckingham.

Stopes was crazy for female flesh, the younger the better, and Rosie didn't mind surrendering in return for a temporary haven. At least Stopes was clean. And he spoke like an educated man. His quarters, unfortunately, demonstrated that he was unable to use his intelligence to rise high, except in his building. The upper floors of a tenement always housed the poorest people; she knew that from Chicago.

The flat had no electricity. No closets. Instead of a sink, a faucet poked through one wall, with a catch basin on the floor underneath. The tenement roof was a sort of park and promenade for all the residents. Many similar roofs separated by narrow air spaces formed a street above the streets; a regular turnpike for sneak thieves, bill collectors, rent dodgers. Rosie had seen some pretty miserable places in her young life but never one as filthy, dark, and depressing as this. She intended to get out at the first opportunity. She didn't mention this to her benefactor, of course.

Buck Stopes called himself an "impresario." She'd never heard the word. He said it meant he produced entertainment events. She was excited until she discovered his productions were limited to illegal fights pitting a fox terrier against fifty to a hundred rats in a zinc-lined pit surrounded by benches, inside a carefully guarded warehouse entered from an alley. Spectators who enjoyed this sort of thing—it was rather out of vogue, Stopes admitted—bet on the number of rats the dog would kill in a certain amount of time.

Stopes's terrier, Boss Tweed, was named in honor of the late politician, leader of a ring of grafters that had embezzled thousands, maybe millions from the New York City treasury. Rosie made it clear to Stopes that she would never attend one of his little sporting events.

Stopes couldn't make a living from them; his regular job was barking for Nagle's Dime Museum. P. T. Barnum had been the first to make a great success of such a museum, and the many imitators were still popular. At Nagle's, the bedazzled bumpkin from out of town could see all kinds of curiosities, human and mechanical. The chess-playing Egyptian Enigma, a painted pharaohlike figure with a gold headdress, operated from inside by a dwarf named Archie. The Panoramic Man, said to display on his totally tattooed person a complete capsuled version of human history, from Adam and Eve forward. The Limbless Wonder, and Henrietta the Four-Legged Hen, and the Bearded Boy (Archie, switching roles with a clever disguise). The star attraction was Professor Quine, the Man with the Miracle Throat; four times a day he smashed a bottle and a water tumbler and a sheet of glass and chewed and swallowed fragments of all.

Down in the cellar of Nagle's there was a large papier-mâché grotto. For an extra nickel, male customers could enter and enjoy "The Living Picture Gallery." On a tiny stage, three women, all unattractive and overweight, posed and postured for a few minutes in full-body see-through tights, while the professor of the establishment performed airs on his violin. Stopes offered to get Rosie into the Gallery but she declined; she wanted to work someplace with a better class of customers. A place that might offer a chance at a singing job.

"Hell, babe, I don't blame you," Buck Stopes said. "You've got the looks for it. You should make the rounds in the tenderloin, up on Sixth Avenue. Some of the dance halls like the Haymarket are real poison pits, but some are okay. Stitch Meyer's Alhambra at Sixth and Twenty-ninth, that's one of the best."

The Alhambra Dance Hall was a two-story building with an Arabian Nights look outside and inside. To Rosie's surprise, Stitch Meyer saw her in his office five minutes after she walked in. Meyer was a short, tough, red-haired man who wore a gold wedding ring and the neat, conservative clothes of a banker. He interviewed Rosie with the office door shut and never laid a hand on her or uttered so much as one suggestive word.

"You're a pretty girl, I can always use a pretty girl as a waitress. I'll describe how things work in the Alhambra and you can decide if you like it, or not. We got a dance floor downstairs—"

"Yes, sir, I saw it."

"Tables, good eats, a fair drink for the price. There's entertainment, three shows a night. Nothing real smutty. Basically this is a meeting place. Respectable gents from uptown, or Westchester, or across the Hudson in Jersey, they come here for a little relaxation. A little pleasure. They come to meet attractive young ladies. What goes on after a gent meets a young lady at the Alhambra ain't my affair. I get my percentage from the food and drinks and the admission charge of fifty cents—that's for the gents, ladies come in free."

"I see."

"Also, we don't allow no close dancing, not on the floor. If a gent wants to dance close with a lady, they go into one of those little curtained rooms at the sides. In other words, the Alhambra ain't like some of the dives in the district. I know what men will do even if they're married, so I give 'em a respectable place to do it."

He leaned back and clasped his hands over his vest of brocaded gold satin. "How does that sound?"

"It sounds okay, Mr. Meyer. You're straight with me, I'll be straight with you. What I really want in New York is to be a singer."

"Well, I don't hire no waitresses to double as singers. Maybe we'll try you out in the show sometime, but not until you been here awhile. To start, it's just two dollars a week, but you keep every cent in tips. That can add up. Oh, yeah, this is important. You're not to interfere with the ladies who come in every night. If some gent fancies you, makes a private arrangement, all right, it's your affair, and his. But I don't allow my girls to be out there competing with the regulars. I hire you to work for me. Fair?"

"Fair."

Stitch Meyer's grin showed a number of gold and silver teeth. "Swell. Want to start tonight?"

□ □ □ □

Stitch Meyer's Alhambra was warmly lit, cheerfully noisy, usually crowded because of its reputation as a safe place. Rosie found her employment there profitable and congenial. Not her last stop in life by any means, but an excellent way station. She wished Joey Crown could see her in her fringed red dress; or Jimmy, who'd been a terrific lover but frighteningly scrambled in his head. Wouldn't they think she was something, her hair neatly pinned up, her face rouged, her bare arms and cleavage perfumed? Wouldn't they think she was really coming up in the world?

She was scrupulous about following orders. If she flirted with a customer, it was done quietly, almost coyly. Even so, just the first week she earned twenty-eight dollars from four late-night liaisons, without incurring the displeasure or even the notice of the management.

She made friends at the Alhambra, too. Professor Spark, who led the little trio of piano, violin, and cornet, listened to her sing one night after closing and said she had "promise" but "needed formal training." She sensed that what the professor meant—they were all called professor, these piano pounders—was that she didn't sing very well. No matter; singing on the bill at some famous place like Tony Pastor's on Fourteenth Street was only another rung, not the top, of the ladder. She could barely *see* the top of the ladder, it reached so high into the white clouds where the walls and turrets of a rich man's golden mansion gleamed.

One of the variety acts at Stitch Meyer's was a five-member kick line of female impersonators. The best of them, Fanny Hawkins, took to Rosie right away, and she to him. The night they met, Fanny confided that his real name was Franklin, which he hated.

Fanny Hawkins was on the stout side, but stoutness was quite popular with gentlemen. He wore a wig of long blond curls, knew how to apply makeup artfully, had china-blue eyes and soft skin virtually without body hair (Rosie saw him almost naked in his dressing room many times). In Rosie's view Fanny was more beautiful than Lillian Russell; his masculinity was virtually undetectable.

Fanny befriended Rosie and steered her away from rough or tightfisted customers whenever he recognized them. He listened to Rosie's plans for herself—a singing career leading to marriage with a wealthy man, age not a factor. As a new and loyal friend, Fanny declared that Rosie was sure to make it.

By the first week in December, she was already a little restless at the Alhambra. Too many months had gone by with only tips and trips to the mattress in a nearby hotel to show for it. One Wednesday night Rosie came in at her usual time. Outside a snowstorm was brewing. It was a typically boring evening until half past eleven. Then, just as Fanny and his colleagues concluded their specialty dance on the small stage, Rosie heard a commotion at the front door. Serving a crowded table, she craned to see what it was all about.

Stitch Meyer was effusively greeting a new arrival. A tall, pink-faced fat man with jowls. He wore a beautiful gray overcoat with a black fur collar and carried a shimmering black topper under his arm. Melting snow glistened in his dark hair. He seemed to be recognized by quite a few patrons, whom he hailed as "sport" or "old fellow" in a deep, booming voice.

Meyer personally escorted the fat man to a choice table. Professor Spark rushed to shake his hand, bowing as if he were royalty. Fanny was at the bar, sipping from a beer stein. Rosie worked her way through the crowd with her serving tray, handed her order slip to the barkeep, then ran down to the end to speak to Fanny.

"Who's that swell? Everybody but me knows him."

"Everybody south of Forty-second Street," Fanny agreed in that mellow contralto voice of his. "That's—"

But Stitch Meyer took care of it, leaping to the stage, raising his hands for quiet. "Ladies and gentlemen, the Alhambra is honored tonight by the presence of one of its favorite guests. Right down here in front, America's musical man of the moment—the nonpareil composer and showman—Mr. Paul Dresser. Paul, take a bow."

The genial fat man heaved to his feet and waved. A pinky diamond flashed on one hand. His suit and satin cravat with sapphire stickpin were as fine as his overcoat and silk hat. He was wearing a special holiday vest of red satin with green piping and little gold bells sewn on. Rosie's heart raced at the sight of such elegance. But the man's name meant nothing. She said as much to Fanny.

"Aw, come on. Paul Dresser? He wrote the biggest song hit of the year. 'Just Tell Them That You Saw Me.'"

"Sure, I know that one." She'd heard it all over Chicago and New York, a tearful ballad presumably sung by a young woman who'd wrecked her life on the rocks of passion. Street organs cranked out the tune. Newsboys whistled it. She'd seen a large souvenir lapel button bearing the title. "Just tell 'em that you saw me" was a catchphrase of the moment.

"Half a million copies of the sheet music and still selling," Fanny told her. "I don't know when Dresser writes them, he's in bed with a woman most of the time."

"What woman?"

"Any one he fancies. He's got plenty. I'd get on the list but I'm afraid he'd be disappointed when he pulled down my bloomers." Rosie laughed. Fanny lit a short thin cigar. "They say he's had clap, but who knows? If ever there was a man could help you get what you want, it's Broadway Paul."

"Say, Rosie, these ain't gonna keep till sunrise," the barkeep yelled. He shoved a tray of drinks to the front of the bar.

"Be right there, Kippie. Oh, Lord, Fanny—how do I get him to notice me?"

Fanny had no ready answer. As Rosie rushed to serve her customers, she could hardly keep her eyes off the songwriter, whom she guessed to be around forty. He'd ordered a bottle of the finest house whiskey, and in two minutes she saw him toss off two shots and pour a third. His face grew all the redder.

"Say, Paul, play us something," a customer from a nearby table called. People applauded, whistled. The composer affected a shy modesty, shaking his head. The applause grew louder, helped by Professor Spark's rapping on his upright piano and gesturing to the stool he'd just vacated. Still maintaining that reluctant air Rosie spotted as a complete fake, Dresser stood up. A woman waved her blue kerchief.

"Paul, play us some of that fast new stuff."

Dresser lost his air of good humor. "That raggedy-time coon crap out of St. Louis? Not me. I know what the public wants. The heart ballad. The home song."

Renewed applause endorsed his sentiment. Dresser glided through well-wishers at the front tables; for a fat man, he moved with exceptional grace. Money—talent—a fancier of women—what could she do to attract his notice?

Dresser spun the top of the piano stool to lower it. Rosie was in the shadows where a narrow balcony projected above the bar. Grabbing one of the balcony posts for courage, she called out, "Play us your hit, Mr. Dresser, that's what I want to hear."

Dresser put his hand above his eyes. "Who said that?"

Rosie stepped forward, out of the shadows. "I did, Mr. Dresser."

Over the heads of the crowd he looked her up and down. Thighs, hips, tits, face. He broke into a huge smile and bowed from the waist.

"I must always honor the request of a pretty young lady."

He whirled around and sat. With his right hand he ran up the keyboard, from bottom to top, a glittering arpeggio. More applause. He shot his cuffs; the shining pinky stone flashed. He began to play and sing in a not unpleasing voice.

> "Just tell them that you saw me,"
> She said—"They'll know the rest.
> Just tell them I was looking well, you know.
> Just whisper if you get a chance
> To mother dear, and say,
> I love her, as I did so long ago . . ."

He sang it all, to the end, looking not at the piano keys or the rapt listeners, but at her.

At half past twelve Rosie changed clothes in the dingy little room assigned to the waitresses. With her cheap cloth coat over her arm, she hurried down the hall, her legs trembling. Earlier, Dresser had slipped her a note asking her to stop at his table. When she did, he said he'd "squared things" with Stitch Meyer. Meyer didn't like the forward way she'd called to the composer. "But since it was me, he didn't fuss too much."

Dresser told her she was free to leave the Alhambra two hours before closing; he had squared that too.

He was waiting by the main entrance. He took Rosie's coat. Through the patterned glass of the double doors she saw a hansom at the curb in the falling snow.

"This is very exciting, Mr. Dresser. Where are we going?"

He held her coat. When she'd put it on, he stepped in front of her and slid his hand around her waist. He caressed the sumptuous curve of her rear.

"Dear, there's only one way for someone as fresh and pretty as you. Uptown."

He withdrew his hand. Rosie buttoned her coat. Dresser set his silk topper on his head and gallantly offered his arm.

They spent the night in Dresser's suite at the Gilsey House, a swank hotel on Upper Broadway. Rosie had never seen fancier rooms, felt cleaner sheets, or smelled fresh roses in a bedside vase. Dresser was an ardent and accomplished lover. After the second time, they talked for an hour. Next day Rosie bid Buck Stopes goodbye without seeing him; she just removed her things from the tenement while he was at Nagle's.

She hailed a cab to take her away from the Bowery. Dresser had given her money, a whole tenner. Not as any sort of payment, he said most emphatically, just as a little gift to a charming person who had for the moment won his heart.

71

Paul

PAUL WENT TO SEE SHADOW on a foggy Saturday, less than twenty-four hours after Lew Kress left town. It was December 28, 1895.

Jimmy Daws was on duty in the peep show parlor. Paul asked for the colonel. "Upstairs." Surly as ever.

He did find the colonel upstairs, though in an unexpected position. R. Sidney Shadow III, in shirtsleeves, was lying on his back under the kitchen sink. He was cursing loudly and fluently while attempting to repair a pipe dripping water on his face. His big wrench was greasy, and there were smears of grease on his knuckles, his ears, his chin, his shirt collar, his suspenders.

He heard Paul come in; his eyes were on a line with Paul's shoes. He crawled out, almost whacking his head. He shoved a pan under the sink to catch the unrepaired drip and grabbed a towel.

"Colonel, I am sorry to interrupt your work—"

"Don't apologize, kid. This is no damn job for a gentleman. What can I do for you?"

"Since it is almost the end of the year, I thought I would ask once more about a position."

"Jesus, are you a mind reader? Greetings, oh swami!" He salaamed. "One of my boys blew out of town yesterday."

"Is that so? What an unusual, um, I don't know how to say—"

"Coincidence. Sure is. But that's life. Come into the office, we'll talk." Shadow pounded on a closed door next to the stove. "Mary? Wake up. Let's have some coffee in here. Two cups."

Shadow interviewed Paul in a windowless room barely large enough for two chairs and a small rolltop desk. Piles of drawings, blueprints, technical journals, were stacked on every horizontal surface except Shadow's chair; Paul had to clear his to sit. The disorder would have sent Uncle Joe into a rage.

Shadow asked Paul a few questions. When he came over from Germany. His background. Paul hedged a little. Without directly saying he had no relatives in

Chicago, he created the impression that he'd been pretty much on his own since he arrived.

"What happened to your pal Rooney?"

"He had to leave town. Financial difficulties."

"You were staying with him, weren't you?"

"Yes, he taught me a great deal about still photography."

"Interesting geezer, Rooney. A little strange—" He made a corkscrew motion with his index finger. "A little disconnected, if you know what I mean. But I liked him."

"Yes, a very good man. He treated me well."

"Mary, come in," Shadow called. Paul turned to see a buxom, smiling woman with a cup and saucer in each hand. Shadow introduced her as Mary Beezer. She greeted Paul pleasantly as she handed them coffee. The cup that passed in front of Paul's nose on its way to Shadow had a strong aroma of whiskey.

"Mary makes a damn good cup of coffee," Shadow said. "Throws in two eggs, like the Swedes do. Thanks, Mary. I think I've got Lew's replacement here."

"Oh, that's a break." Mary flashed Paul a smile of exceptional, even embarrassing friendliness. Then she left. Shadow took a long swallow of coffee.

"So you really want to learn the living picture business."

"More than anything, sir."

"First you need to know a few things about the way I work." In his resonant voice, he delivered a short oration about pitting one bulldog against another, perhaps to gain a champion fighter. Paul found it bizarre. Was Shadow referring to him and the other helper, Daws? He thought it wiser not to ask. But the strange speech worried him.

Shadow outlined his duties. Paul said he could handle them. Shadow told him what he'd make. Four dollars a week and board. "And we don't punch clocks around here. We work when it's necessary, as long as it's necessary."

Paul blinked, swallowed, and said, "Fine."

"Then that's it. Welcome." They shook hands. Paul was elated.

Shadow led him through the kitchen, casting a hateful look at the dripping sink, and showed him to the stairs. "Where are your things?"

"I have only one valise, stored with a friend."

"Go get it. When you come back, Jimmy'll show you where you bunk. Glad you're with us, Dutch—they call you Dutch, don't they?" Without allowing Paul a chance to answer, he went back into the kitchen, muttering, "To think that a gentleman from a fine family is reduced to being a fucking plumber."

An hour later Paul was back with his valise. Jimmy locked the front door of the peep show parlor—there were no customers—and led him upstairs to a door opening off the landing.

"This here's yours."

Paul tossed his valise on an iron bed jammed between narrow unpapered walls of lath. There were perhaps eighteen inches of space on either side and two feet between the end of the bed and the wall. A light bulb with a paper shade hung from the water-stained ceiling. The room had no furniture except the bed and a crate standing on end as an all-purpose bureau. He might have been back on Müllerstrasse.

Jimmy leaned against the doorjamb, arms crossed. "Mary cooks, but she don't make the beds."

"I'm used to that, I've done it most of my life."

"Come on, I'll show you my room."

Paul switched off the light and followed him across the landing to a large room with windows. "This is mine. When I came to work here it belonged to Kress, but I took it away from him."

Jimmy stared hard as he said it. There was a moment between them; Paul felt it strongly. If he swallowed this, accepted the arrangement, Daws would have him whipped.

He ran his tongue under his upper lip. Gave a snap to the brim of his cloth cap, pulling it down near his eyebrows.

"You live here and I live in a closet?"

"That's it, yeah."

"I don't think so."

He walked out, returned with his valise, threw it on the floor at Jimmy's feet. "I'll take half this room."

Jimmy looked stupefied, then enraged. Paul spread his feet, braced for a rush. "Dutchie, I don't like what I just heard. You better not give me trouble."

"I won't if everything's fair. This is a big room. I'll move the other bed in, it can go over there, each of us will have plenty of space."

"What happens if I say no?"

"Then we will settle the question some other way." He curled his fingers into fists. Jimmy took note.

Paul waited, palms damp, stomach tight. He didn't know whether Jimmy would fold or jump him. Jimmy himself seemed unsure. He shifted his weight from foot to foot, checking Paul up and down. Paul had turned eighteen in June but looked older. There was an evident toughness about him. It showed in his stance; the way he held his head, thoughtfully chewed his lip. Jimmy took a while deciding what it all meant.

Finally he smiled, in a way Paul thought insincere. "Fishy," that was the American word.

"All right, Dutchie. You helped me out once, I guess I'll give you a break. But remember where you stand around here. I'm the number one boy. The head nigger. You stay out of my way, we'll get along fine."

Paul tipped his cap. "*Danke schön.* And you stay out of mine."

Shadow's peep show arcade was considerably less elegant than the Edison parlor up on State Street. The lighting was poor. There were no comfort rails for the viewer to lean on. No well-swept floor, just sawdust. Also, Shadow's subjects were considerably more racy; clearly aimed at a male clientele looking for slightly illicit thrills.

There were animal pictures. "Rats and Terriers!" "Fighting Cocks!" There was "Pass the Bottle!", a rowdy saloon scene in which a man bought and gulped a bottle of beer. "Knock 'Im Dead!" was a simulated prizefight performed by overweight draymen Shadow had hired by the hour. Paul noted Shadow's propensity for exclamations. He talked the same way.

"Opium Joint!" had a cast of three, recruited from a local Chinese laundry. "Whee Paree!" and "Spanish Señoritas!" featured high-kick dances badly performed by Levee whores. While the prudish might have railed against the dances, the women were actually fully clothed, down to opaque tights under their short skirts.

Signs of haste were evident in all the sequences. The performers were not good. But the lighting and composition struck Paul as excellent, and the simple magic of motion was enough to entrance him, whatever the flaws.

On Tuesday night, New Year's Eve, Shadow closed the parlor at six o'clock, declaring that only saloons and whorehouses would have customers that night.

He pulled down the shade on the front door while Paul swept up dirty sawdust and spread a new layer. Strands of dyed hair straggled over Shadow's forehead. He was already weaving noticeably. Mary Beezer had left on Sunday; her mother was ailing down in Richmond, Indiana, where Mary grew up.

"I gave Jimmy the night off. How about you, Dutch? Going out for some drinks? Maybe a woman?"

"I don't think so, Colonel."

"I don't feel much like it myself. Come upstairs, we'll have a cup of cheer to celebrate." Paul smiled and followed his employer, who appeared to have already taken several cups of cheer. Men ran by in the street. There were pistol shots. The Levee was starting to celebrate.

In the kitchen, Shadow opened a cupboard. The middle shelf held an astonishing number of full and partially full whiskey bottles. He pulled one down, with two large tumblers. On a sideboard stood the pitiful Christmas tree Mary had put up. A skimpy pine, eighteen inches high, nailed to a wooden crosspiece and decorated with popcorn strings, tinsel, and three small ornaments. Every time Paul saw the little tree, memories of the spectacular Crown tree arose to sadden him.

Shadow poured a full glass for each of them. He kicked the pipe under the sink. "Finally fixed the infernal thing."

"Yes, I noticed. A good job."

"Sure, I'm a man of parts. Know what that means? A jack-of-all-trades, but higher class." He pulled his chair out with the toe of his tooled boot, then sat down and drank half his whiskey.

Paul took a sip to be polite. Shadow waved him to a chair. "I'm self-educated, y'know. I can fix or build anything. I can sell, I spent a few years on the road peddling this and that. I can sing, tell jokes, do a pretty good coon shuffle; I was with minstrel shows for a while." Paul was agog. "Man of parts! Trouble is, till now the parts never fit in one box. Wait here."

He lurched into his messy office and returned with a smudged schematic pencil drawing of a rectangular machine filled with gears, roller hubs, parallel lines of arrows following a convoluted track. "This is the box. Shadow's Luxograph projector. Know why I'm so crazy to make this work?"

"Why?"

"Because I love shows. Any kind. Jugglers tossing Indian clubs. A darkie choir clapping and swaying this way, swaying that way. Our new battleships, white as your ma's wedding dress, sailing into New York Harbor with every flag flying. Shows!"

He drank again. "A line of eight blond ponies high-kicking in a variety hall, that's a show. Big girls with fuck-me eyes, legs this thick around, red stockings, black fringe cut low to show plenty of tit. A show!" He banged the table.

"Or how about a President of the U.S. of A., standing up to swear his oath? A show! Some poor sucker climbing the steps of a gallows for carving his sweetheart into eight pieces—a show! An orphanage burning down—fire horses and wagons to the rescue—a show! A Sioux war dance—a show! Buffalo Bill on his big white horse, blasting blue balls out of the air, bang, boom, bam, a show! Earthquakes! Typhoons! Brigades of Chink soldiers marching at the Great Wall, a show! Dear old Queen Victoria waving a hanky to ten thousand subjects, hello there lovey, bend over and kiss my tiara—the whole world's a fucking extravaganza, and I'm the man to bring it home and show it to every poor bastard who'll never see it for himself. Another little drink?"

Paul shook his head. He felt like the snake charmer who couldn't look away from his cobra. *Hypnotisiert!* Mesmerized.

"I'm dead serious, Dutch. The flickers can fill halls as big as the Chicago Auditorium, I know it. And a camera—*my* camera—can go anywhere for scenery, oddities, big events. I'm going to film disasters, elections, coronations. Why, I'll film a fucking Turkish harem by paying off the eunuchs! I'll come out with the world's hottest pictures! Ninety-eight Turkish delights, photographed while the sultan's off putting the old sausage to wife number ninety-nine! I'll tell you something else I'll film, Dutch. War. Yessir, the bloody fields—the courage and the carnage! I'll film right up front, where the bullets buzz, I won't be hanging around the tents of sissy officers five miles in the rear."

Despite the slurred words, the ranting that reminded him a little of Rhukov, Paul was excited. How often he'd touched places on the wooden globe old Frau Flüsser gave him in Berlin. Touched them, wondered about them, yearned to see them, knowing he probably never could. Here was the way.

Shadow poured another full glass of whiskey. "I can do it, kid. I have a feeling for audiences—what they like and what they'll choke on. You know that songwriter from Terre Haute, Dresser? Writes those big hits that sell thousands of copies? I read something he said. 'I write for the masses, not the classes.' Well, I'm going to make flickers for the masses, not the classes. Bring on those wars! Nothing'll race the heart and click the turnstiles like some good old American boys larruping a bunch of fucking heathens with dark skins."

He leaped up, making Paul gasp. From the seat of the chair Shadow jumped to the kitchen table, waving his glass so forcefully, the remaining whiskey flew all over.

"Hail Columbia, here's to Uncle Sam! The red, white, and blue! We're coming to get you, world! With the greatest invention of modern man! The rage of the age! If you don't think so, kiss my ass!"

Paul burst out laughing, and clapped. Shadow swayed, dangerously close to stepping off the table.

"You understand, kid, I can tell. Lew and that other dummy—nuh-uh." He swayed more violently; shot out a hand. "Help me down before I fall down, f'Christ's sake."

Paul helped him. The man was incredible. He was greedy, he had a foul mouth, he had no scruples. But he had a vision. A magnificent vision Paul could see, understand, embrace, because it spoke to everything he'd ever longed for, every fool's dream he'd thought impossible. Creating pictures. Seeing the world. Fitting into life. Knowing your purpose, your place. *Belonging* . . .

And here it was, all of it, here in a cheap, malodorous kitchen in a scabrous, rundown flat above an arcade that showed filthy pictures in one of the lewdest districts of America or, probably, the universe.

Hurrah!

With Paul's help, Shadow relaxed in his chair. His head immediately lolled forward on his chest. Somewhere in the streets, a brass band struck up "Auld Lang Syne."

The whiskey glass dropped from Shadow's hand and rolled noisily over the cracked linoleum. He snored. Paul threw his arms over his head in silent joy.

Seeing the vision.

Paul lay awake long past midnight, fingers laced beneath his head. It was more than three years since he'd come to Chicago. Three years in December. So much had happened. So many changes. Uncle Joe and Aunt Ilsa, Cousin Joe, the brewery bombing and Benno's death. Most of all Julie, whom he couldn't, wouldn't surrender now that the whole world was opening to him.

He knew she still loved him. Being seen in society with a rich man must be something her parents forced on her. She'd admitted she wasn't strong when they played on her sense of family duty, on the guilt they'd nurtured in her since she was small.

Come spring, when he was on his feet, he'd find a way to reestablish their relationship. He'd declare his love again. Take her back, make her his, forever.

72

Rosie

Paul Dresser was besotted with her. He moved her into the Gilsey House, insisting she didn't have to work, at least not for a while. He bought her new clothes at the Broadway stores, chiefly Lord and Taylor's; most of his wardrobe came from a fine Broadway emporium for men, Brooks Brothers. At Park and Tilford's grocery he bought wicker hampers full of wines and cheeses for wild naked picnics in and out of bed in his suite.

She learned a lot about him fairly quickly. That his real name was Johann Paul

Dreiser, Jr. That he'd been born into a large and devout Catholic family in Terre Haute. "I turned out to be the wild roving one. I do have one brother, Thee— that's short for Theo—who bangs around a lot writing for newspapers."

He told her this while they were nestled in his huge soft bed with tall carved bedposts. They fell into the habit of drinking champagne and talking in bed late at night, between what Paul called going to the races. He had an enormous appetite for the races. He always knew what he wanted, this little trick, that little specialty. He was conscious of his bulk. They seldom made love in the missionary position; he was a considerate man.

When Paul was fifteen, his father, whom he bleakly described as a religious fanatic, sent him to St. Meinrad's Seminary in southern Indiana. The school prepared young men for the priesthood. "I spent more time in the local variety house than I did in class. I lasted two years. I was already singing for my friends, playing the piano or pipe organ, telling jokes, taking pratfalls. So I joined up with the Lemon Brothers, a minstrel troupe. I developed my act and I went to the races with at least one young lady in every town we hit. I wrote my first song when I was with the Primrose Minstrels. 'Where the Orange Blossoms Grow.' Very forgettable, I assure you."

Terre Haute was his base until 1880, when he left for good at age 23. But he still listed it as his place of residence. There was a big wide sentimental streak in this fat man who loved drinking and womanizing.

Rosie learned plenty about New York from Paul; far more than Buck Stopes had been able to teach her. Paul really was a king on Broadway, at least that part of it involving entertainment, Fourteenth Street to Forty-second, which was all that interested her. When the winter weather allowed, she'd tuck her gloved hands into the expensive fur muff he'd bought her and they'd stroll his favorite street. He pointed out great homes, like the Goelet mansion at Nineteenth— "You'll see peacocks in the old lady's garden when it's warm." They dined in top hotels like the Bartholdi and the Broadway Central. He showed her the impor- tant theaters: Keith and Proctor's, Koster and Bial's Music Hall, the fabled Tony Pastor's on Fourteenth—yes, he'd played there, several times.

From the comfort of a hansom cab he showed her Miner's New Theater on the Bowery, where he'd made his debut on the New York stage in '91. "I was billed as Paul Dresser, eccentric comedian and vocalist. I knocked around a lot of theaters, singing, dancing, doing straight parts in farces. During the day I com- posed. 'I Told Her the Same Old Story.' 'Just Take a Seat, Old Lady.' Songs you never heard of. I laid siege to this town for four years until I finally broke down the walls. It's a tough town, but if *you* are tough, and stick to it, you'll break through."

"Where do I start?"

"Miner's has a pretty good amateur night every Friday. We might practice a couple of numbers and try you there—something wrong?"

"I was living with a man on the Bowery when I met you. I moved out and didn't tell him. What if he shows up?"

"It'd be a long coincidence, but what if he does? I'll be there, I'll look out for you."

Gazing at his smiling, confident face, she believed him.

□ □ □ □

One night they dined at the posh Hotel Metropole, up at Forty-second. Over game hen and champagne, they discussed philosophies of love. Rosie found it easy to be open with Paul:

"I've had some bad times. Some bad men. It taught me things. Hurt them before they hurt you, that's my motto."

"Present company excepted, I hope."

"Don't tease," she said, fondling his cheek.

"It's a smart philosophy, if not the kindest I've ever heard," he said. "I suppose I take the same approach with most women. Not you, you're different. So's another girl I've never mentioned. A girl back in Evansville who calls herself Sallie Walker."

"It isn't her real name?"

"No, Annie Brice. She thinks Sallie Walker is classier. Sal's a real lady. A straight shooter. I've had hundreds, and she's the one I can't get out of my system. Fine thing for me to tell you, isn't it?"

"No, Paul, the two of us—we understand each other. That's why we'll always be friends."

He squeezed her leg under the table.

"I'm feeling very friendly right now. Hurry up and finish your dinner."

Paul was always busy because sheet music was a growing business. He explained to her that hundreds of selections were racked and sold in department stores and music shops for fifty cents apiece. Stock was changed almost daily.

He introduced her to his partners, Pat Howley and Fred Haviland, founders of the music firm of Howley, Haviland, which occupied several floors of an office building on West Twentieth near Broadway. Two blocks south was the headquarters of the distinguished Oliver Ditson Company; Paul said the district was rapidly becoming the capital of America's sheet music industry. "Couple of blocks north of here, there's a stretch my colleagues have started to call Tin Pan Alley. Listen to all the pianos going strong on a summer afternoon with the windows open—you'll know why."

The Messrs. Howley and Haviland were drab, courteous men who looked more like bookkeepers than musicians. Flamboyant Paul was a special kind of silent partner. The outside man, they called him. In addition to writing songs for the firm, he hunted for new composers with promising material, wheedled and charmed variety hall artists into performing new H&H songs, even passed out money to the padrones of the Italian organ grinders to assure that important numbers would get repeated plays on important street corners.

About this and almost everything else in his life, he was ingenuously candid with Rosie. Yes, he'd had syphilis. He swore he was now cured. He continued to chase women, probably would never stop. This signaled Rosie that her time as his lover wouldn't last forever, though maybe friendship would. And he would be a powerful friend to have.

Rosie honestly liked Paul Dresser, which was unusual; with few exceptions she loathed the men who gave her sex. Paul was exceedingly generous, always handing out small loans to this "old fellow" or that "old sport" along the Rialto. He was boisterous, jovial; a popular companion of men as well as women.

He wrote religious anthems, patriotic numbers, minstrel ballads—anything saleable by the firm. He was a hard worker when the mood was on him. Sometimes he stayed up all night in the hotel suite, composing on a small pump organ of oak veneer with fancy brass trimmings. The remarkable instrument was hinged to fold up, and slipped neatly into a box that resembled a large sample case. It weighed only twenty-eight pounds, easily portable.

He had a curious, private streak of sentimentality. The first time she came upon him working at one of his "heart songs," bent over the organ keyboard, tears, real tears, were pouring down his cheeks. She retreated quietly, so as not to disturb him. Here was a man unlike any other, she thought, amazed.

Paul organized her debut at Miner's on the first Friday in March 1896. She sang "Daisy Belle," followed by "Just Tell Them That You Saw Me." Paul personally wrote the piano arrangements, suiting them to her limited vocal range.

She was trembling and terrified as she huddled in the wings, waiting her turn —third on the bill of eight acts. She followed the Four Singing Newsboys and a blackface comic who proved unpopular. His feeble jokes drew no response— except a sudden outcry from the gallery. *"The hook, give him the hook."* Dozens took up the cry, stomping as they yelled.

The hook resembled a long shepherd's crook. Paul had warned her of it, saying some ill-tempered stage manager at Miner's had originated it years ago. She saw it used right here. The stage manager ran out with it and actually pulled the hapless comic offstage by the neck.

Rosie trembled her way through her two numbers, watching the professor in the pit wince at several of her flat notes. But she drew sustained and enthusiastic applause, and a number of lewd invitations were shouted over the footlights. In the third row, wearing a feathered and wispy pink boa, Fanny Hawkins applauded wildly and whistled through his teeth. The response was a tribute to Rosie's looks, not her singing voice. She didn't win any of the prizes, not even a measly one dollar for third place.

Paul consoled her in bed at the Gilsey House. They were naked in the dark, warmly nested under two down comforters. Heavy drapes were drawn over the windows to shut out the lights of the Rialto, still shining at half past two in the morning.

"About tonight," Paul said, touching her bare thigh. "Don't be too down. Remember what I said about hanging in."

"I do. I will."

"That's a girl. Ready to go to the races?"

She laughed. "Sure. I can't get over you." They'd gone to the races twice since eleven o'clock.

"More champagne first?"

"I better not. I love it, but it makes me dizzy."

"Makes you chatter like a magpie, too," he said, chuckling.

She giggled. "I know, but with you it don't matter."

"For God's sake, girl. Keep on using bad grammar, you'll never get where you want to go in this town."

"Don't be sore, Paul. I keep trying to talk right. A boy I liked a lot, he told me the same thing."

"Smart boy."

"He was rich. But there was no chance he'd marry me. I liked him." She screwed up her courage. "I like you, too, Paul, I really do. We're sure a lot alike, ain't we?"

"No. I don't say ain't." It was a gentle joke. He patted her cheek. "You want another drink?"

"No."

Beneath the comforters he stroked her legs. "I'm going to be dead on the level with you. There's another girl I'm seeing right now."

She was hurt, but she hid it. "I guessed. You ain't—haven't been here so much at night lately."

"I'm glad you're understanding about it. You know I'm not a marrying man."

"Oh, I know that, yeah."

"We need to find you another place. I'll help you out with cash till you're on your feet. It wasn't a very promising start at Miner's, but I still think we can get you a singing job. I'll throw in a lesson or two. Introduce you to some people. But before I do—pay attention, this is serious—you need to make a few improvements. First, start calling yourself Rose. Rose French. Rosie has a cheap sound."

"Rose? Rose. Sure. From this minute on—absolutely. Oh, Paul—" She rolled against him, against the soft, lardy warmth of his paunch, his hairy legs. "You're a good man. Have all the women you want."

"As if I could stop."

"We're friends, ain't—?"

"Aren't."

"Aren't we?"

"Always."

73

Paul

PAUL CAME TO THE FLICKERS, the living pictures, at a watershed; a time of creative explosion. Peep show machines, whether built with film loops or flip-card drums, were losing their novelty. The Edison Kinetoscope Company had tried to boost sagging sales by introducing the Kinetophone, a cabinet with long flexible listening tubes and, inside, an Edison phonograph. Pictures were roughly synchronized to tinny music. The Kinetophone failed.

In New York, Philadelphia, Paris, London, inventors and promoters rushed to perfect a projection system for living pictures. One was announced almost weekly —the Kineopticon or the Panoptikon; the Phantoscope and the Eiodoloscope; the Animatograph, the Biograph. Paul was baffled by the names, and the differences, although Colonel Shadow seemed to have some grasp of them. At first Paul couldn't guess how he managed it. Then he took notice of the size and content of the twice-daily mail deliveries. Into Shadow's seedy establishment came string-tied bundles of overseas newspapers; letters from correspondents on the East Coast and abroad; cheaply printed technical journals; celluloid film stock from Rochester, New York, accompanied by explanatory notes from Mr. Eastman himself.

The colonel shared every new development, usually at supper. Mary listened with a kind of bemused politeness, Jimmy Daws listened because he had to, and Paul listened avidly, trying to glean kernels of understanding from the complicated technical talk Shadow spewed forth at dizzying speed.

Most developments in the field excited the colonel, but not all. In Paris in December, two brothers named Lumière had unveiled their Cinematograph projection system to an invited audience of one hundred. "Oh, God damn those frogs," Shadow groaned when he read the news in a month-old London paper. At the stove, Mary clucked sympathetically. Paul was sitting at the table. Jimmy was on duty downstairs; as soon as Paul ate, he'd relieve him.

"Sid, don't work yourself up," Mary said. "It hurts your nerves."

"How can I help it? These two bozos showed thirty minutes of film. Twelve different subjects! 'Workers Leaving the Factory.' 'Three Monsoors Playing Cards.' 'Sea Bathing in the Mediterranean'—Jesus, Jesus, they're ahead."

The colonel looked terrible, Paul thought. Not only pale from winter confinement but haggard from worry. He'd been in the cellar workshop all day. His patched blue work shirt was stained with varnish, sprocket grease, glue, and some unidentifiable substances.

"Here's the worst," he said. "They showed the pictures in some basement at a place called the Grand Café. The first crowd got in free. After that they sold tickets—one franc to see the whole show. The first day they took in thirty-three francs. *The next day they took in over two thousand.* It's been that way ever since. God damn it anyway," he cried, crushing the paper and flinging it over his head.

"Sid, honey, please."

"They're beating me to market! And they aren't the only ones." He held his head with both hands, uttering a string of harrowing oaths.

Mary dished out a passable *Rippchen,* which she'd cooked in Paul's honor. Paul complimented her. She smiled provocatively. Shadow ate his meal in record time, even faster than Paul, and tossed off two shots of whiskey with it. He threw his napkin on the floor and departed for the cellar in a rush.

Paul went down to the parlor. He told Jimmy about the colonel's state. Heading for supper, Jimmy rolled a cigarette. "I can't figure why he gets so fired up. It's just another business like his minstrel shows or the patent medicines he sold."

"No, this is much more important to him. Much more important to the world, too. It may be the very greatest—"

He cut it off there. Jimmy was gone up the stairs, uninterested.

□ □ □ □

Paul roamed the city, passing out handbills or illegally pasting them on walls and telegraph poles. Better-dressed people usually wouldn't take them; if they did, they threw them away as soon as they saw what was being advertised. Could you blame them? How could the pictures attract a broad audience if you had to go into a bad neighborhood to see them? How would they prosper if preachers damned them as lewd? Which, in the case of "A Chinese Dream," was true. Paul had watched it several times. He recognized the technical merit of the photography and managed to separate that from the erotic content. Shadow's picture wasn't meant to be artistic, it was meant to arouse. It did.

When he wasn't on the streets, Paul sat at the register and kept an eye on the poor working men, the floaters, the occasional harlots, who constituted the parlor's trade. If business was slow, he tore through technical journals Shadow had discarded, studying the engraved diagrams, trying to fathom the jargon.

Sometimes he thought about the artistic rather than the technical aspect of living pictures. On a couple of warmer days, he took his noontime sausages and beer up to the big roof of the building and sat in the chilly winter sunshine studying the light, wondering why some kind of picture couldn't be photographed here. There was plenty of space for improvised scenic backgrounds like those Wex had used. Maybe he'd suggest the idea to the colonel if there was a good opportunity.

He thought about Wex, too. Hoped he was getting along all right in West Virginia.

He thought about Nancy. At the end of his first month with Shadow, he addressed an envelope to her in Reelsville and put a dollar in it. He sent a dollar every two weeks thereafter.

One night when Jimmy was watching the parlor and Shadow seemed calm at supper, Paul asked if he might see the workshop. The colonel reacted like a child asked to open his toy box. "Sure you can, kid, come on."

Paul had to bend to keep from bashing his head on beams above the narrow stair, as did the colonel. The workshop smelled of oily rags, sawdust, mold. Once the walls had been painted white, but large sections had peeled off, leaving scabrous gray patches. Neither the dirt nor the damp nor the ungodly clutter of plans and materials bothered Paul. To the contrary, he felt privileged, as though he were a visitor in the cave of some great sorcerer.

In one corner, fixed to a tripod obviously homemade, there was a rectangular wooden box with a hand crank and a hole for a lens in the narrow, front side. "This is it, Dutch. The Luxograph. Means writing with light."

He picked up a smaller box from the worktable. "This is the magazine. Lightproof. Holds fifty feet of Eastman celluloid negative. You have to load it in the dark, but you can load it in the camera anywhere." He opened the hinged side of the camera, showing Paul how the smaller box fit behind the lens. He closed the camera, rotated the crank on the side.

"You get eight frames per turn, two turns per second. In other words, sixteen frames a second, same as the Lumière Cinematograph. Mr. Edison's sticking with forty-eight frames. Now tell me, do you really understand the principle of this thing?"

"I believe so." Paul drew a breath. He must speak carefully; make no mistakes. "Film in the camera moves to the lens, and away from it, one frame at a time. At the lens a frame is exposed like a snapshot. The film is standing still then. While the film moves to allow the next exposure, light must be kept out. This is the purpose of the shutter mechanic—no—" He struggled a moment. "Mechanism. The shutter mechanism. The same idea applies when the film is shown. Still pictures are flashed one at a time. But the frames go by so fast, the eye is tricked, it sees continuous movement."

"Dutch, that's not half bad. I read in a book that it works because of a principle of optics; it's called persistence of vision. If you flash a light, then put it out, the eye sees the light for a tenth to a twentieth of a second afterward. Same thing with flicker pictures. Your eye holds one picture till the next is in front of you, and it all seems continuous. Not only does Daws not understand any of it, he doesn't give a shit."

"Well, sir, you know what I think. I'm keen on every bit of it."

A grin spread over Shadow's pale, blotchy face. Paul had passed the examination.

"You know, kid, the great Mr. Edison's fooled around with living pictures for eight or ten years. I mean Edison in the person of his helper, Laurie Dickson. Dickson does all the work in Room Five. Room Five, that's the flicker room. The Wizard of Menlo Park, who doesn't work a hell of a lot at Menlo Park anymore, has a locked room for every one of his major projects. I know because Mary's favorite brother Benjamin—Benjy—bummed around the country as an itinerant carpenter for years. He was in Jersey when the Wizard built his big new lab. Benjy did some remodeling work at Glenmont, too. That's his fancy mansion."

"Is that how you first heard about the flickers?"

"Yeah, from Benjy. At least once a year, sometimes twice, Mary's old lady gets sick. She's eighty-two now, sound as a gold dollar, but she gets sick like clockwork. Mortally ill. Ready to meet her Maker. It's how she whips Mary's old man into line. And the kids—twelve, counting Mary—they all rush home for a week, everybody sits around and eats pie and cries into their hankies and then Mary's ma pops out of bed, rises from the dead, good as new till the next time. In 1890 it really looked like the old lady was ready to cash her chips and leave the game. I was on the road, peddling. You wouldn't believe some of the stuff I sold. Medusa hair-growth salve. Five dollars for a jar this teeny, and absolutely God damn worthless. Anyway, I said to Mary, this sounds serious, I'll go to Richmond with you. Wouldn't you know, the old game hen rallied like always. But while I was stuck in Richmond, I listened to Benjy talk about Room Five. Edison doesn't think much of the living pictures, he just fools around with 'em because he can afford it. He can afford anything, whether it pays or not. He's got a picture studio on the property at West Orange. The roof's nothing but big shutters that can open to let in more light. The whole building pivots, like a swing bridge, so it can follow the sun all day. All that just to tinker!"

"He made his own peep show machines, didn't he?"

"One of his subsidiary companies did. Now he's working on a camera. From what I hear, his camera isn't practical. It's driven by a battery-powered electric motor. Too complicated, too costly—most of all, too heavy. Pick up the Lux-ograph."

Carefully, Paul folded the tripod, lifted it and rested it on his shoulder.

"Light."

"God, you're eager. Forty-eight pounds isn't what I call light. But it isn't as heavy as an elephant, either. At forty-eight pounds the Luxograph can go any-where there's a picture worth taking. All you have to bring to it is a sharp eye and a steady hand on the crank. Somewhere in this mess I've got thirty feet of ruined film. Want to see how to load it?"

"Yes!"

Shadow laughed. "Guess I didn't need to ask."

The companion to the camera was the Luxograph projector, also unfinished. Crank-operated, it resembled a child's coffin standing on end. Inside was a com-plex arrangement of rubber friction rollers, gears, and sprockets that moved the perforated film through a metal gate, holding each frame behind the projection lens for an infinitesimal moment before jerking the next into position. Shadow was proudest of a glass cell he'd designed into the space between the arc light and the film gate. "Film's flammable as hell. Water in the cell damps down some of the arc light heat. There may be some picture distortion, but not enough so people would ask for their money back. I hope."

He turned off the workshop light and wiped his hands on his shirttail as they went upstairs. "You want a beer?"

"Certainly, thank you very much." It was turning out to be a momentous evening.

In the kitchen, Shadow brought a brown bottle of Crown's from the icebox and fetched a bottle of Kentucky bourbon from the cupboard. Mary called sleepily from the bedroom.

"Be in soon, sweet. G'night."

Shadow filled his glass to the rim. Paul pried the crown off the bottle. "*Prosit,* Dutch." Shadow drank an alarming amount in one gulp. "That camera downstairs is all I need to start supplying pictures. But I'll have to build a projector for every location that might show 'em."

"What sort of locations would they be?"

"Variety theaters. But I'm also thinking I could have my own places, maybe using abandoned stores. Wouldn't need much to try it. Just a few benches or chairs, plus a good white wall. If I made money with one, I could expand. I could have store shows in every town of any size. Operators would have to be trained to run the projectors, but I'll have that problem anyplace I go."

The man's vision was amazing. Perhaps he wasn't a genius like Mr. Edison, but he had imagination and a grasp of practical things, especially making money. Paul said, "That is a very ambitious plan."

"Yeah, but down the road aways. Variety halls are first. Even that's risky. So far I've put three hundred and twenty-nine dollars into building one projector. How I can recoup enough money when the pictures will be sharing the bill with ten other acts I'm not sure. Also, I haven't got so much as one good picture for demonstrating the projector when it's ready. I know there's a way to make it all work, but I haven't figured out every angle. It keeps me awake nights. When I'd rather be dreaming of Mary's milky thighs."

"You say you have made no pictures?"

"A couple of short ones—a few seconds. Not enough for a variety bill. They'd want ten, maybe fifteen minutes' worth."

"Could I help you make more? I have been studying the roof of this building. It's very large. As the spring comes, there will be much more sunlight. We could film a little picture with a story. I read that they showed a story picture in Paris."

"Yeah, I saw that. In my opinion, people don't want to see stories."

"But if we made one or two, you would have something to demonstrate."

Shadow flung a boot on the table. Gave Paul a long look. "You're right. If you get any ideas, jot 'em down. I'm glad I took you on, kid. You've got plenty of the old git-go. That's American for drive—push. Jimmy, he's different. He's a tough apple, but he's short on ambition. I mean the useful kind that earns you last rites in your own warm bed instead of a prison cell. Jimmy wants the green stuff but he doesn't want to work for it. Not in any way that calls for thought, or lasts longer than five minutes. Now don't get me wrong. I've bent the law more than a few times. But make a habit of it and someday they'll build a hang noose just for you."

After a pause, Paul said, "Colonel, I have wondered—did you like appearing on the stage?"

"For a while. Then it got boring. Same blackface every night. Same bad jokes and coon songs—" He jumped up, did a fast shuffling dance, struck a pose. When he sat again, he almost fell off the chair. It didn't keep him from pouring more whiskey.

"The minstrel shows taught me plenty. But peddling was a lot more profitable. I told you I sold some awful stuff. Farmer Brown's Family Recipe Pep Tonic— 'the drink that makes wives content.' Nothing but grain alcohol, coloring, and cayenne. One old coot died after downing two pints, his heart gave out while his cock was still going. The town fathers hauled out the tar barrel for me. Fortunately I'd already decamped on the midnight local. Then there was my cultural endeavor. The Little Library of Ribaldry, twenty-two handsome miniature volumes containing some of the world's juiciest—well, you get the idea."

"It is a long way from minstrels and peddling to the pictures. Was it Mary's brother who inspired your interest?"

"Right. I'd been looking for the big one, the big chance, all my life. Seemed like I was never going to find it. I was pretty discouraged. Then I had another piece of dumb luck."

"What?"

"Mary's ma got ready to die again."

Just last year it was (Shadow went on). The old lady had her semiannual seizure. It looked serious, same as it had back in 'ninety. All the Beezer brothers and sisters sent frantic telegraph messages—"This is it, this time she's really going." Mary was truly busted up, though. I had to go along to buck her up.

Like I said, I was feeling pretty low. I'd opened this parlor in June of 'ninety-three. No, I didn't lay out the place, or manufacture the machines, a man named Eppleworth did. I think he stole someone else's machine design—all the flicker people steal from each other—but I never had the opportunity to ask. Eppleworth got shot to death on State Street six weeks after he opened. Bystander in a stickup. I was sick of peddling, I saw an advertisement, I scraped up every penny and I bought the joint on contract from Eppleworth's widow.

We dickered a lot. At first she wouldn't budge on the price. Like Mary when I met her, Bessie Eppleworth was a lot younger than the old geezer who got himself plugged. I thought of an inducement that might persuade her to lower her price. I talked it over with Mary. She didn't like it much but she said all right since it was business. Bessie Eppleworth signed the sales contract on the last night of our blissful week at Toronto and Niagara Falls. She bought the tickets, the rooms, the wine—everything but the marriage license. I think she hoped I'd ante up for that. Not me! That trip was strictly business, I wouldn't have married her no matter who paid for it.

I had big plans for the parlor. Big dreams. I was stupid. This is a bad neighborhood, and Chicago has two other parlors in better locations. From the start I barely made enough to buy groceries, buy coal, pay the light bill, and keep a few cents in my pocket. So I wanted to get away, think things over. That's another reason I went back to Richmond with Mary.

It sure as hell wasn't a vacation in paradise. Richmond, Indiana, is nothing but a bunch of hay-binders and dirt-kickers. After the first twenty-four hours I was out of my skull with boredom, just like the first time. I excused myself from the premature wake and strolled downtown to a saloon, where I fell into conversation with the one customer who didn't look like a hayseed. Fancy suit, good manners. He introduced himself as C. Francis Jenkins, but I should call him Charlie. He was in town for his sister's wedding.

Charlie Jenkins was some kind of clerk in the Treasury Department in Washington. On the side he fooled with inventions and wrote these Jules Verne-type articles about sending voices and pictures through the ether with no wires, don't ask me how. I told him I tinkered and built things too, and was pretty good at it, so we hit it off.

I told him I owned a peep show parlor. No future, he said. Big pictures projected on big screens to big bunches of people, that's the future, he said.

How can you be so sure? I asked.

Well, he said, he couldn't give me any solid proof just yet. But he and a man named Tom Armat, a real estate broker in Washington, they'd formed a partnership and staked everything they had. They'd bet the farm on pictures.

He explained how it happened. Couple of years before, some gent named Tabb had wandered into Armat's office on F Street. He knew Armat slightly, knew he was always looking for opportunities. Tabb was high on Edison's Kinetoscope, in fact had a deal to take several machines to the Cotton States Exposition in Atlanta and make a big splash in the South.

Armat couldn't see any future or profit in a picture machine watched by one person. But he did like the basic idea. He'd been out to the Columbian Exposition here and spent hours looking at the Anschütz Electric Tachyscope. I did the same thing. (Paul said that he had too.) Armat saw a future for the bigger pictures thrown on bigger screens. He was convinced the public would go wild for them.

Back in Washington, Armat signed up for some classes he thought would help him understand the flickers. That's where he met Charlie Jenkins, at the Bliss School of Electricity. They got to be pals very fast. They *both* were onto the idea of projected pictures. So they went into partnership to build their machine.

Jenkins and I spent hours in that saloon over the next couple of days. I got a quick education. Armat and Jenkins already had one projector finished. It was big and noisy. It jerked the film too hard, so the picture shook and jerked too. Gave you a headache in thirty seconds, Jenkins said. Also, the film wore out fast. Broke all the time.

Jenkins said his partner had solved the problem. Figured out a loop system to ease the tension, bring slack film down so the sprockets only jerked it a few inches at a time, and the rest of the roll wasn't strained so much. That was a lightning bolt of an idea. That was genius.

Armat and Jenkins took their machine to the Cotton States Exposition, but it turned out that projected pictures weren't any more popular than Tabb's Kinetoscope parlor, in fact Jenkins and Armat had a riot on their hands as soon as they turned out the lights for their first show. People screamed and ran, they thought it was a trick to corner them in the dark for pickpockets or rapists. I've never had too favorable an impression of the intelligence of Southerners.

They were pretty discouraged, but they wouldn't give up. They knew that people had to be *sold* on living pictures, had to *decide* flickers were the rage of the coming age. Charlie and his partner were still convinced it would happen. Charlie convinced me.

He'd brought one of the Atlanta projector machines to Richmond by railway express, and a couple of his short flickers, to amuse his family and the wedding guests. Another bunch of keen thinkers, that crowd. They didn't care for anything he showed them. But I did. God, I'll never forget. He invited me to his hotel room. He pulled the shade, shoved a big pile of drawings off the bed—he was working on refinements for the projector—and showed a little film called "Annabelle the Dancer." Sort of a cousin to "A Chinese Dream," but clean. The picture was practically life-size on the window shade and the wall on either side. That's when I knew Jenkins was right, Armat was right, and Edison was a dumb, egotistical old fool spoiled by all his publicity. There in that hotel room in crappy little Richmond I had a vision. I saw the new century in all its glory. I shook the hand of C. Francis Jenkins, called him a great man, which he is, and thanked him for unveiling the future.

The rest of the story is simple. At the hour the Jenkins wedding was scheduled, with a long wet reception to follow, I again excused myself from the continuous premature wake for Mary's ma and went back to the hotel. I paid an old darkie bellman five dollars, practically all the money I had, to pinch a duplicate key from the front desk and then stand watch in the lobby.

I spent almost four hours copying Charlie's drawings. When the darkie rapped on the door and said Mr. Jenkins was back, hoisting one in the saloon, I put everything back in order, decamped quietly down the back stairs, and disappeared into the night.

And that, kid, is how R. Sidney Shadow got into the flicker business to stay.

Shadow leaned back with a smile. "I was off to a fast start, which just about put me even with all the bozos who got in before me. One of my big worries now is patent infringement. I've made a few modifications on the projector, but small, like the water cell. I'm praying Jenkins and Armat won't catch up to me until I have enough money to hire good lawyers."

From the bedroom came Mary Beezer's muffled voice, imploring. Shadow stood up. "I think Mary needs a little attention. See you later."

He bumped into the wall while opening the bedroom door. Steadied himself and peered around at Paul.

"I think you've got the makings of a picture man, Dutch. I think you've got the stuff. Don't let it swell your head."

On a bright, windy morning in March, pelted by soot and cinders from the rumbling El half a block to the east, the Luxograph Company created its one-minute extravaganza, "Her Burglar." Paul had composed a short scenario, writing in pencil on three small cards; Shadow had edited and rewritten it.

On the sunlit roof Mary sat on a stool in front of a large canvas square tacked to a frame. Jimmy had painted the canvas to resemble bricks. Cursing and complaining the whole time, he had done a sloppy job; the mortar lines were wavy.

Colonel Shadow turned up his coat collar, pinned up the front brim of an old sombrero, and crouched behind the Luxograph camera. He'd braced the tripod with wood blocks so that the camera would remain steady on the scene to be played in front of the fake wall. Mary held an open book, an experience wholly foreign to her.

"Here we go, Mary, start reading," Shadow called, beginning to crank.

"God damn it, Sid, I'm trying, I've got some damn cinders in my eye."

"Stop that, I'm reading your lips. *Burglar!*"

Jimmy stole into the scene. Mary had fashioned his domino mask by cutting holes in a navy blue bandanna. Jimmy looked altogether natural in the role.

He crouched behind Mary, menacing her with upraised hands. Mary heard something, jumped up, terrified, and threw her book away. The book accidentally hit Jimmy's head and bounced off. "Watch it! That hurt."

"Keep it up! Keep it up!" Shadow exclaimed, cranking. "Burglar, grab her." Jimmy seized Mary's wrists with more force than was necessary.

"*Policeman!*" Paul rushed into the scene, wearing one of Mary's wide belts and a toy star from the five-and-dime. Shadow had given him an old rusting Army Colt revolver, unloaded, which he brandished as he collared the villain. Jimmy raised his hands but his scowl said he didn't like this part.

Mary batted her eyes, threw her arms around Paul's neck, kissed his cheek. Paul postured in a heroic manner, then snagged the burglar by the collar to lead him away.

"All right, stop, film's run out. Good job, everybody."

Paul ran downstairs to open the parlor. Shadow developed the film himself.

That night, in the musty second-floor sitting room, Mary hung up a bed sheet while Paul and Jimmy wrestled the Luxograph projector from the cellar. With the arc light blazing, Shadow cranked, and there upon the sheet, the images only slightly warped by the water cell, "Her Burglar" sprang magically to life.

Paul clapped and rocked back on his stool, laughing. "That's wonderful."

"Yeah, ain't it?" Mary said, stretching out her hand to find his in the dark. Somehow her hand landed in his lap. Paul presumed it was accidental but then she kept it there, with embarrassing results.

"I don't like bein' hauled to the clink," Jimmy said between puffs of his cigarette. "Next time I'm the good guy."

Shadow shut down the machine and Mary withdrew her hand after another squeeze. The room light came on. "It looks good," the colonel said. "But it's just a silly story. Is that what people want out of flickers, or do they want reality? That's the bug that keeps biting me, boys and girls."

Mary said, "I love stories."

"Not dumb ones like that," Jimmy said. "Gimme the real stuff."

"Why not both?" Paul asked. "The flickers can do anything. You said so yourself, colonel."

"I'll think about it," Shadow said.

Late in March the colonel rushed to New York on an overnight train. Another new competitor, American Vitagraph, was presenting its first program at Tony Pastor's New Fourteenth Street Theater.

"Stuart Blackton and Al Smith showed twenty minutes' worth," Shadow reported glumly after he dragged back to Chicago. "Waves on the shore of Long Island. Broadway cable cars. Fire engines. In the last fifty feet, a Lehigh Valley Railroad train called the Black Diamond Express came busting out of some tunnel. Half the people jumped out of their chairs, screaming. It's the real thing they want. Real thrills. The flickers are never going to tell stories and make it pay."

The last evening in March, a Tuesday, Paul was first to eat supper. As usual, he ate fast. When he wiped up the chicken gravy with a last piece of bread, Mary was amused. "Almost don't need to wash 'em when you get through."

He went downstairs to relieve Jimmy, who whistled and did a little dance step on his way out. "You're feeling good," Paul said.

"Mary's baking me a cake tomorrow. She's a peach."

Paul's spine prickled. "Tomorrow is your birthday?"

"Yeah, April the first. Hey, what's wrong? You look like you just got kissed by the bearded lady in the freak show." Paul ran a nervous hand through his unruly hair. "Come on, Dutchie, spill."

"I was just thinking about an old German superstition. Nothing important."

Scowling, Jimmy walked back to the register. "What kind of superstition?" No reply. "*What superstition?*" Jimmy grabbed Paul's shirt.

"Let go, I'll tell you."

Jimmy's cheeks were red, his chest heaving. But he let go. "Give," he said.

"It's just an old superstition, mostly among church people. They say April first is the day Judas was born. They say it's unlucky."

"Hah. Some joke."

"Jim, I'm truly sorry I blurted it out, I wasn't thinking."

"And I better never hear it again. I'll show you who's lucky and who ain't, you just watch."

He stalked out. The door at the head of the stairs closed loudly. Paul brooded on his careless mistake. *Gott, solch ein Zorn!* Such a temper . . .

Years later, when certain events occurred between them, Paul remembered the night of March 31, 1896. He was sure that was the time Jimmy conceived a hatred of him. He was sure there was something fateful about Jimmy's birthday after all.

In New York, at Koster and Bial's Music Hall, Herald Square, the Edison Vitascope System premiered on the evening of April 20. Miserably, Shadow read about it in a newspaper.

" 'Sea Waves.' 'Umbrella Dance.' 'Kaiser Wilhelm Reviewing His Troops.' 'A Boxing Bout.' They used *two* projectors—no waiting while the film was changed. That's not all. Four of the flickers were in color! Created a sensation. Do you realize what was involved? Every single frame tinted by hand—"

He crushed the paper and threw it under the sink. "Edison, that fraud, gets gallons of ink, and it isn't even his machine. He bought out the inventor."

"Who's that, hon?" Mary asked.

"Tom Armat. The one who used to be in real estate. He's a flicker tycoon now."

The name Armat sent a thrill of alarm through Paul. Thomas Armat had been in partnership with C. F. Jenkins, the man whose drawings the colonel had copied. If Armat had made a deal with the Edison interests, Shadow had therefore stolen from Edison, and Edison was notorious for protecting his patents the way a tigress protected cubs. Edison kept entire law firms on call.

"Sid," Mary said after thinking it over, "there's just one answer. You have to get your pictures on a variety bill too."

"I have a fish on the line. Finally. He's coming over Thursday. We'll show him 'Her Burglar.' "

To the Levee came Mr. Ishmael (Iz) Pflaum, owner-manager of Pflaum's Music Hall on South State. Mr. Pflaum was a huge St. Nicholas figure with a white fan beard. He carried a little pocket notebook filled with numbers and dollar signs.

Pflaum plumped himself into the best chair in the sitting room, in front of the hanging bed sheet. Mary nervously placed a snack of hot wursts with German mustard on the little table at his elbow. Paul served the guest a growler of beer fresh from Freiberg's. Jimmy had been banished to the parlor.

Mary switched off the light. Shadow cranked the Luxograph. Paul hunched behind him, nervously shivering despite the heat thrown off by the arc. There was Mary, reading. Jimmy crept into the scene. Iz Pflaum's hand found the wursts and carried one to his mouth every few seconds as if propelled by a motor. But he never took his eyes from the glowing bed sheet. At the end, with the lights on, the snack plate was empty.

"Sid—" Mr. Pflaum ran his tongue over his teeth with a squishing noise. "I'll take it. The machine there."

"You'll—? Why, Iz, that's swell. Just swell! I do have a minor problem."

"I don't like problems. I don't like people who gimme problems."

"I'm sorry, Iz, but this projector is the prototype. Not for sale."

"Then build another one. I gotta have it soon or we don't do business."

"This instrument cost thr—four hundred and fifty dollars, materials alone. For a new one I'd need an advance."

"How much?"

"A hundred dollars?"

"Seventy-five. Come by tomorrow, we'll draw up the papers. You furnish five minutes of flickers, I'll show 'em as chasers."

"As what?"

"That's what they call 'em at Koster and Bial's, chasers. At the end of the bill, after the midgets, the magician, the chorus girlies, and the Jap acrobats, you chase the audience out with pictures. That's all they're good for, clearing the house."

Paul wanted to argue that. It wasn't his place. He decided Iz Pflaum was a greedy, ignorant man of no imagination.

Pflaum put on his bowler and lumbered to the door. "One more thing. That little story was nice but I want real-life subjects. Only."

"Certainly, Iz, we'll deliver, that's the only kind of picture I want to make. 'Her Burglar' was an experiment. Reality, that's the stuff. I'll have our camera operator start filming immediately."

"You got a regular operator to take the pictures?"

"Of course I do. Right here." Shadow put his arm around Paul, who tried not to fall over.

"Mr. Crown is young, Iz, but he's highly talented."

Paul stood there with his mouth shut. *Besser stumm als dumm.* Mr. Pflaum grasped his hand and wrung it. "Very good, happy to know it. I didn't realize you were this far along, Sid."

"That's all right, Iz, most people don't realize Chicago Luxograph is such a thriving firm. Let me show you down the stairs. Some of the treads are broken. The carpenter's been due here for weeks . . ."

After the colonel and Iz went out, Paul and Mary laughed and hugged each other.

Mary had a delicious aura of warmth and beer. With a quick glance at the door, she caressed his cheek. "You had a big one in the dark the other night."

"Mary, you embarrass me. You're the colonel's wife."

"Ah, not legally. I could be your girl at the same time."

He thought fast. "I guess I'll be too busy, I have just been promoted."

She laughed again. "Paul, you're a sketch." She kissed him, quickly but ardently, with her lips and her tongue.

Thus on that evening, fate in the person of Ishmael Pflaum decided forever the direction of the Chicago Luxograph Company, and Paul's life.

□ □ □ □

Twenty miles southwest of Chicago, under boiling gray clouds, they set up the camera. They pushed the claw legs into the gravel ballast between the rail ties. The precious Luxograph sat in the middle of the right-of-way belonging to the Wabash, St. Louis and Pacific—"The Banner Railroad."

Paul was extremely tense. Storm wind out of the blackening northwest bent waist-high cornstalks in the fields on either side of the track. A stutter of thunder made the two wagon horses prance; Mary had trouble controlling them from the driving seat. She clutched her straw bonnet. "It's going to be a devil of a storm, Sid, you better hurry."

Shadow paced up and down the track with loping strides. He revealed his inner state by his hunched shoulders, the crow's feet around his squinted eyes, the way he snatched his gold watch out of the pocket of his frock coat and nearly dropped it. "Four minutes. The Cannonball's never late unless there's a blizzard, a derailment, or a bridge washed out."

Everyone wanted sensational locomotive footage on their flicker programs, including Iz Pflaum. The New York Central's Empire State and the Lehigh Valley's Black Diamond were already drawing crowds. Sid Shadow aimed to please his client with the crack train of the Wabash line.

Paul turned his cap so the bill pointed backward. The wind plucked and pushed at his faded blue shirt. He'd tucked his pants into heavy work shoes. It seemed appropriate attire for a camera operator; racy, modern . . .

"He's waving! He's waving!" Shadow exclaimed, dancing up and down.

"Sid, he's waving!" Mary shrieked.

"I see him waving!" Paul cried.

About a half mile to the north, standing on a trackside storage box, Jimmy Daws was signaling with his hat. Paul chewed his lip. Pieces of cornstalk, twigs, and other debris whirled by. Dust clouds spun. A streak of lightning forked down to the horizon. Thunder followed almost at once; the storm was close.

Over the top of the camera Paul spied a dot of white light. It rapidly grew larger. Shadow said, "Just remember, crank steadily. I'll hang on to the tripod. For God's sake don't lose your nerve."

Paul felt the ground vibrate. Faintly at first, then more and more strongly. Jimmy jumped off the storage box, moving back from the track and possible danger. The headlight glared. Hellish horns of vapor and dust spurted from under the iron locomotive hurtling toward them.

Fat drops of rain began to splash Paul's face. But he was oblivious of the storm. There was only the train, and the task, and the knot in his belly . . .

"Lens cap, lens cap!" Shadow screamed. Paul yanked it off.

"Start cranking."

Paul cranked, counting one-two, one-two silently, timing his two cranks per second. The rails hummed. The earth shook. The whistle of the Cannonball howled. The engineer saw them. The headlight grew big as the sun. Right below it, on the round front plate of the locomotive, Paul recognized the line's painted emblem, an unfurled flag.

The Cannonball kept coming. Growing huge. Filling the world . . .

One-two, one two . . .

"Keep cranking, keep cranking," Shadow breathed. "Oh my God, this is sensational! Spectacular!"

The whistle screamed.

Lightning flared.

Thunder exploded. *One-two, one-two* . . .

Rain fell harder. Paul's arm and wrist ached from cranking; his back ached from crouching. He wanted to throw the Luxograph over and jump. If he didn't, they'd be crushed. He could now read the slogan painted in the center of the emblem on the front of the locomotive. "Follow the Flag" . . .

He kept cranking.

"Sid, you're gonna be killed." Mary's hysterical voice was faint in the roar of the train and the storm. The Cannonball grew taller and wider, coming on like one of those prairie cyclones he'd read about. He thought of Julie; of all the things he'd left undone in his young life. *ONE-TWO, ONE-TWO, ONE-TWO, ONE-TWO,* someone should make up a song; sing it at his funeral . . .

"*Now!*" Shadow screamed, and jerked the tripod.

Paul jumped to the left, without looking. A great roaring suction of air tore at his shirt and cap. He fell into the cornfield, gasping.

The Cannonball passed.

Shadow stayed on his feet with the camera and tripod on his shoulder, just beside the track. "My God, we got it, I think we got it." He was nearly as hysterical as Mary.

The mail and freight and passenger cars shuttled by. Paul scrambled to his feet, drenched by the sudden heavy rain. His trembling lessened. He'd stood fast. He'd got the picture.

"Here, cover up, I've got a hat," Shadow said, handing Paul a folded newspaper from his coat pocket. Paul unfolded the paper and started to lay it over his head. He noticed a headline.

MISS VANDERHOFF ENGAGED.

To Wed Prominent Clubman
W. V. Elstree III.

August Wedding Date Announced
by Parents of Bride-Elect.

Part Seven

FLICKERS

1896 – 1898

Such a bustle and a hurry
O'er the "living picture" craze,
Rivals rushing full of worry
In these advertising days.
Each the first and each the only,
Each the others wildly chaff,
All of them proclaiming boldly
Theirs the first A-Kind-O-Graph.
But it is a wonder really,
How the constant flood of life
O'er the screen keeps moving freely,
Full of action, stir and strife.
'Tis far from perfect in its movement,
'Tis very hard upon the eyes;
The jolty wobble's no improvement,
Smooth-running films a great surprise.
Still successful beyond reason,
'Spite of all its erring ways,
Holding first place in the season
Is the "living picture" craze.

1896
British Journal of Photography

74

Joe Crown

"WHAT ARE YOU READING, Joe?"

He twisted onto his left shoulder to let the glow of the bedside lamp fall on the book's gold-stamped spine.

"The Red Badge of Courage," Ilsa said. "You've read that before."

"Twice. It's a powerful book."

"Some of my friends say it's too realistic, they stopped after a few pages."

"I agree, it isn't a woman's book. What of it?" Joe felt testy. The damp, windless night made the house an oven. His linen nightshirt, the lightest he owned, was sweated through. The summer had arrived early; it was only June. Much of the city was sleeping easier now that "Bluebeard" Holmes had been hanged for his crimes in May. Joe Crown wasn't sleeping easier, and it had nothing to do with Chicago's infamous mass murderer.

"Young Mr. Crane has never been to war, isn't that right?" Ilsa said.

"But you might believe so. He has imagination. By God, he does. If we've finished the conversation, Ilsa, may I continue to read?"

She wiped her forehead with a crumpled handkerchief; the movement of her hand hid the hurt on her face.

"Yes, Joe, certainly. I wouldn't disturb you for the world. Good night." She turned away from him.

Hostile feelings toward Ilsa had been stirring within Joe for over six months. He believed himself to be the one who had been misunderstood. Wronged. So he didn't take her hand in his and gently suggest, as he might once have, that they search for ways to break down the barrier arising between them.

He read for another hour. Young Crane's powerful tale called to something in his blood. In memory he heard bugles and drums. The tramp of foot soldiers, the gallop of cavalry, the laughter and singing by the camp fires at night . . .

For all of war's dirt and travail, which Crane compellingly captured, a war gave a man an enemy he could attack and defeat according to certain rules. Joe Crown had no such enemy. But he devoutly wished for one.

In this year of 1896 America was demonstrating her new status in the world by asserting her power in the Western hemisphere. Late in December of the preceding year, she'd faced down the mighty British empire.

Great Britain had sent three warships to blockade a port in Nicaragua in response to a quarrel over some debt Britain claimed she was owed. Washington accused Britain of violating the Monroe Doctrine. Congress threatened mobilization. The mighty British empire backed down almost at once.

This left America's jingo element—politicians whose districts included shipyards or military posts; professors and bureaucrats who worshiped Admiral Alfred Mahan's writings on naval power; newspaper publishers whose circulation needed a boost; outspoken patriots such as New York City's young activist police commissioner, Theodore Roosevelt—without a cause.

Then, fortuitously, there came on the scene General Valeriano Weyler y Nicolau, Spain's newly appointed governor-general of Cuba, charged with putting an end to the outbreaks of rebellion in the back country.

General Weyler's first tactic was institution of the policy of *reconcentrado*. Reconcentration. Relocation of the population of the rural provinces into detention camps far from their homes. These were the country people who had sheltered and protected the roving bands of freedom fighters—the rebels who attacked and destroyed government forts and property, then vanished back into the villages, indistinguishable from peaceful farmers.

Weyler said he was moving the provincial people to commodious cottages with ample food and adequate sanitation. The dispatches of foreign journalists told a darker story. Weyler was crowding hundreds, thousands, into ill-lit barns and warehouses infested with rats and vermin. With no provisions for sanitation, and little or no food. Children began to starve and die. Adults who protested began to disappear. Correspondents in Havana began to hear horror stories of atrocities in the compounds. A new name appeared in their telegraphed stories. Butcher Weyler.

In New York, to fuel their hot circulation war, Mr. W. R. Hearst of the *Journal* and Mr. Joseph Pulitzer of the *World* capitalized on the plight of the Cubans. The columns of both papers overflowed with titillating dispatches about "young Cuban amazons" shot down and decapitated, elderly nuns "outraged," heroic priests "roasted alive" by Weyler's troops. *Reconcentrado* gave the yellow press exactly what it wanted.

Joe Crown joined the protest against Spain and Butcher Weyler. He put on his best G.A.R. suit of indigo blue wool flannel and sat with hundreds of his fellow veterans at a rally of four thousand people in Central Music Hall.

An eighty-piece platform band played martial airs by John P. Sousa. Speakers waved the rhetorical flag, denounced the Spanish dictators, and threatened war in retaliation for atrocities. Joe was thrilled. Here was a new cause.

He did recognize that the growing national fervor for *Cuba libre* wasn't entirely idealistic. American investors had sunk as much as fifty millions of dollars in railroads and sugar mills on the island. The labor leader Sam Gompers denounced Spanish tyranny in fine-sounding phrases, but you had to remember that he represented the cigar makers' union. Joe himself had a liking for an occasional cigar of fine Havana leaf, already in short supply.

Still, did it matter that commercial interests were tied up with the new patriotism? Did it matter if America went to war for sugar and tobacco? The Cubans were downtrodden, Spain was in the wrong, Weyler was a beast.

If war came, and it well might, could he take part? How?

□   □   □   □

Outwardly, Joe Crown's life had an appearance of calm. The brewery was prospering. A new brewmaster, Samuel Ziegler, was proving highly satisfactory. The two children were no more fractious than usual.

Fritzi, fifteen, was doing well in her studies, although she continued to make frequent and annoying references to her coming career as a stage actress. She had discovered Shakespeare and went about constantly with a script, playing Portia or Beatrice, Desdemona or Lady Macbeth.

Carl, home from the Habsburg School, was growing taller, broader in the shoulders. He was a powerful boy. One afternoon he batted a ball from the side yard all the way across Michigan to the front door of the Heindorf mansion. It cost Joe two hundred fifty dollars to replace the stained glass panels.

Joe Junior, fortunately, was no longer a subject of bitter contention between Joe and Ilsa. Every few months Joe brought up his offer to rehire the firm of private detectives. Ilsa always said no, it wasn't necessary, the wheat stalks in the envelope had convinced her that her boy was safe and well. In December Joe had nodded agreeably and then, on his own, reengaged the detectives for two months. With no results.

He spent a lot of time at White Stockings games, taking Carl with him. He enjoyed the fresh air and excitement but often recalled, with sadness, how pleasurable it had been with young Joe Junior at his side. Or how much Paul had enjoyed his first game. Sometimes Joe would search around the ballpark, hoping he might spy his nephew in the bleachers. He never did.

He found himself willing to leave his desk at the brewery on almost any pretext. Early in July he had a fine excuse when the Democrats convened at the Chicago Coliseum to nominate a presidential candidate. A month before, in St. Louis, Marcus Hanna had maneuvered his forces and called in markers to give the Republican nomination to Governor William McKinley of Ohio.

A lifelong Democrat and contributor to the party, Joe Crown went to the convention. He arrived as the doors of the Coliseum opened in the morning and stayed in the crowded gallery until the day's session was gaveled to adjournment. Puffing away on Cuban cigars, he disgustedly watched the Illinois delegation down on the floor. Governor John Altgeld was seated there, constantly whispering to his allies in the silver wing. Among them Joe recognized Michael Kenna; Altgeld whispered to him often. *Damned conspirators,* Joe thought, blowing out the match with which he'd lit a new panatela.

Belatedly, he noticed a woman in a flat-crowned straw hat seated directly in front of him. He tapped her shoulder. "Excuse me, does this cigar bother you?"

"Oh no, I like the aroma."

"Really. That's fairly unusual for a woman. Thank you."

He smiled. She smiled, turning slightly in her seat. She had eyes of deep blue, friendly and intelligent; dark red hair showed under her hat brim. He was aware of a shapely bosom that a prim Gibson girl shirtwaist couldn't hide. She was a woman of early middle age, not beautiful but certainly handsome. That night, in bed, Ilsa snoring lightly beside him, he pictured the woman's face for a long time.

Silver was the great issue at the convention. With the value of gold increasing and that of silver declining, farmers continued to suffer under laws that said debts contracted with paper money must be repaid in gold. The agrarian West cried that such treatment was unjust and destructive, while the commercial East continued to fight for the gold standard and control of the money supply. Joe, being a conservative businessman, stood squarely with the gold wing.

But there were powerful and popular men among the opposition. One of the most notable was a former congressman and newspaper editor born in Salem, Illinois, but now a resident of Nebraska, William Jennings Bryan. Bryan, the free-silver Populist, was a reigning star of the Chautauqua.

The Chautauqua institution from upstate New York was the Prometheus of American life. It brought the fire of culture—educational and inspirational speakers, musical performances, lantern-slide lectures—to the backwoods and the prairies. It did so by scheduling its attractions on a circuit of tents and town halls said to number twenty thousand. Bryan was a special favorite of Chautauquas in the Bible Belt and the Cotton Belt, the Cyclone Belt, the Corn Belt—rural America.

Joe often discussed party politics with German business acquaintances who were Democrats. In the past year Bryan's name had come up often. Following an unsuccessful bid for a Nebraska Senate seat, he had been delivering and polishing one speech on the Chautauqua wheel. It was even referred to as "The Speech." In the press it was praised for its form and eloquence, if not its content. Joe wanted to hear "the Boy Orator of the Platte," if only to judge "The Speech," and the man, for himself.

Already the money issue had caused trouble at the convention. Nebraska had rival delegations, gold and silver. Before the convention opened, officials on the national committee voted to seat the gold delegates. A floor fight reversed that and gave Nebraska's seats to the silver delegation, which included Bryan. Joe witnessed the floor fight from the gallery. That the wise heads on the national committee were outvoted by a pack of loud, rude farmers made him fume.

On a hell-hot July day, the convention began debate on the currency plank of the platform. Joe stripped off his coat and lit another cigar. In the seat ahead, by herself once again, the handsome woman tilted her head without looking around. Acknowledging the smoke and, perhaps, his presence.

The galleries were packed. So were the aisles. As many as twenty thousand jammed the hall; it had been widely advertised that Bryan would give his free-silver speech during the debate. Joe hoped it would fail to win an enthusiastic response.

Ben Tillman, the wild-eyed politician from South Carolina, was the first proponent of free silver to be recognized by the chair. Senator Hill of New York argued for the gold standard, then Senator Vilas of Wisconsin and former Governor Russell of Massachusetts. Finally the Honorable Mr. Bryan was introduced.

The galleries rocked with prolonged applause and cheering. The leonine young man from Nebraska took the podium with an expression and a stance obviously well rehearsed. The handsome redhead leaned forward expectantly. Joe again found himself noting and admiring the fullness of her bosom. *Damned odd behavior for a man my age,* he thought with a wry amusement.

Bryan was over six feet tall, with a powerful jaw, dark eyes, and a flow of long dark hair swept back from a high forehead. He was, as best Joe could recall, thirty-six.

"Mr. Chairman and gentlemen of the convention," he began, hushing the hall with a voice deep as the lower organ registers; it could have been the voice of a famous tragedian or a pulpit spellbinder.

After a few words to acknowledge the delegates and guests, Bryan said, "My friends, I would be presumptuous indeed to present myself against the distinguished gentlemen to whom you have listened if this were a mere measuring of abilities. But we are not engaged in a contest between persons. The humblest citizen in the land, when clad in the armor of a righteous cause, is stronger than all the hosts of error. I come forward as a plain person, to speak to you in defense of a cause as holy as the cause of liberty. It is the cause of humanity."

The huge Coliseum was virtually silent. Bryan knew how to throw his voice to the farthest seat, the highest rafter, without apparent effort.

"We say to you that you have made the definition of a business man too limited in its application. The man who is employed for wages is as much a business man as his employer. The attorney in a country town is as much a business man as the corporation counsel in a great metropolis. The farmer who goes forth in the morning and toils all day is as much a business man as the man with a seat on the board of trade who bets upon the price of grain."

It was these small businessmen—these pioneers, Bryan called them—for whom he pleaded. Eastern interests had forced these little farmers and merchants into a conflict they didn't want, but were prepared to fight.

"We do not come as aggressors. Our war is not a war of conquest. We are fighting in the defense of our homes, our families, and posterity. We have petitioned, and our petitions have been scorned. We have entreated, and our entreaties have been disregarded. We have begged, and they have mocked us. We beg no longer. We entreat no more. We petition no more. We *defy* them!"

Joe rocked back in bewilderment as a great roar erupted. Floor delegates jumped to their feet. So did men and women throughout the gallery. The handsome woman held her hands over her head as she clapped. Joe glimpsed her ecstatic face as he applauded politely. *What the hell is happening here?* he thought, both in reference to the demonstration and to himself.

Bryan let the tumult continue for a minute or so. Then he held up his hands. The floor and the galleries began to quiet down at once.

Bryan pitched his voice low, in preparation for what Joe sensed would be a climb to the final peak of the speech. Bryan spoke of McKinley, calling him a decent and well-intentioned man who had enjoyed wide popularity and approval until three months ago. Then there was a shift:

"No personal popularity, however great, can protect from the avenging wrath of an indignant people a man who will declare that he is in favor of fastening the gold standard upon this country."

Now the volume rose; the tempo quickened:

"You come to us and tell us that the great cities are in favor of the gold standard. We reply that the great cities rest upon our broad and fertile prairies. Burn down your cities and leave our farms, and your cities will spring up again as if by magic. But destroy our farms, and the grass will grow in the streets of every city in the land."

Another ovation.

"If they dare to come out in the open field and defend the gold standard as a good thing, we will fight them to the uttermost. Having behind us the producing masses of this nation and the world, supported by the commercial interests, the laboring interests and the toilers everywhere, we will answer their demand for a gold standard by saying to them—you shall not press down upon the brow of labor this crown of thorns. *You shall not crucify mankind upon a cross of gold.*"

Bryan stepped back one pace. He rested his fingers on the podium and lowered his chin to the bosom of his shirt. He shut his eyes, sending a signal that he'd finished. A silence ensued.

Then—pandemonium.

Delegates stormed the platform, hauled Bryan down and hoisted him to their shoulders. Band music blared, barely heard in the din. Bryan's coat was torn. His white handkerchief was snatched and ripped apart for souvenirs. He bounced dangerously on the shoulders of delegates trying to carry him through the crush in the aisles. In the galleries, people yelled and clapped and tossed hats in the air.

Even Joe Crown was shaken. It was a powerful speech. A momentous speech. He knew it would change the course of the convention.

"Magnificent. Just magnificent, wasn't it?" He realized the handsome redhead was speaking to him.

"Very accomplished," he said, forced to shout.

"I must have some air, I feel faint."

"Yes, I too. Permit me to go with you. I'll go first, those stairs are jammed."

He fought his way down ahead of her, half dizzy with heat, wondering what in God's name he was doing, but not stopping, not hesitating for one moment. Outside on the pavement where spectators without tickets marched up and down with Bryan for President banners, the woman fanned herself with her straw hat. Joe helped out by fanning her with his fedora.

"Thank you, thank you." She clutched his shirt-sleeve. "I believe we've heard a speech that will go down in history. I believe we've heard the next President, don't you?" The crowd surging out the doors crushed her against his vest. He felt the bump and press of her bosom. "The hall is unbearably hot. I must have some refreshment. There's a little café across the way. I noticed it earlier. Won't you join me?"

Her face was inches from his. Her dark blue eyes probed with an easy candor. He saw in them a frightening image of himself saying yes, with all but certain consequences.

And he *wanted* to say yes . . . "Thank you so much, I can't. My coat's still upstairs. Also, I am due to meet someone." How lame it sounded.

She withdrew, the heat in her lovely eyes cooling quickly. "Yes—well—I understand, of course."

She walked through the crowd and crossed the street. He watched her straw hat bobbing till it disappeared in the doorway of the café. He turned back into the Coliseum, groping for a cigar in his vest, hurrying away as fast as he could from the monstrous abyss of contemplated adultery.

□ □ □ □

The Democratic convention nominated William Jennings Bryan for President, on a platform of unlimited coinage of silver.

Joe Crown's conversion to Republicanism dated from that day. Bryan was calling the rural poor to wage a class war. He wanted the kind of blood that flowed in the Pullman strike to flow again in every city and village and crossroads in America. He spread the poison that had ruined Joe Junior. Joe Crown had a certain nostalgic sympathy for the Men of '48, but he was no revolutionary and never had been.

He wrote a draft for three thousand dollars and sent it, together with a long letter pledging his support, his time, and more money, to Marcus Alonzo Hanna, the Republican kingmaker. In due course he received a warm reply from Hanna, welcoming him to the Republican fold and promising him invitations to campaign functions involving such party notables as the Honorable Mr. Schurz and the Honorable Mr. Roosevelt.

Joe never saw the handsome woman again. Thank God she'd never told him her name or address.

75

Paul

AUGUST 29. The last Saturday of the month. Fifteen minutes past noon. Paul had been standing on the curbstone on East Huron Street, across from St. James Church, since fifteen minutes before eleven, when fine carriages with liveried drivers were already unloading wedding guests.

Newspapers had printed the date and the time of the ceremony, half after eleven, weeks ago. And for weeks he'd argued with himself, wanting to stay away. Ultimately he couldn't. The yearning to see her was too strong.

Mary said St. James Episcopal was an old church, the swankiest of all the Protestant churches in the city. Paul had dressed carefully, to look respectable and as neat as possible. He'd put on his black Sears tennis shoes with corrugated rubber soles; very comfortable for long days on his feet. His bibless overalls were dark gray duck with leather knee pads, heavily scuffed. His shirt was lightweight Penang cloth striped vertically, blue and white, a ninety-eight-cent extravagance. To hide some of his face he'd bought a cheap flannel baseball cap in the flat-topped Chicago style. Stitched across the front were the words "White Stockings."

He loitered in the shade across from St. James for more than an hour, while organ music pealed from the church. The doors were open to catch any breeze.

Both bride and groom must have entered by a side or rear door; he never saw them until the service ended and the triumphant music from *Lohengrin* burst forth, sending the carriage drivers scattering to their vehicles.

Guests spilled from the church and down the wide steps, forming ranks three and four deep on either side. Cries of excitement went up as the bridal couple came out and dashed down the steps.

Julie wore a shimmering white gown. Her face was a blur amid bobbing heads, waving arms, flying rice thrown by gentlemen in morning coats, women in long dresses and enormous wide-brimmed hats. Paul saw the girl he loved as no more than a snapshot image, gone almost the instant he spied her. She ducked into a large carriage parked at the foot of the steps. On its door gleamed a golden shield design with an unfamiliar symbol in each quarter section and a knight's casque surmounting the whole.

The groom stopped briefly to smile and clasp the hand of a male guest standing halfway down the steps. Elstree was older—middle-aged—but Paul already knew that.

As the guest carriages began to depart, Paul stuck his hands in his pockets and walked away. At that moment he hated William Vann Elstree, wanted to do him physical harm. Elstree had denied him Julie. He imagined her soft arms around his neck that one sweet night at Radigan's. Then he saw her with her new husband in the bridal bed . . .

He cursed under his breath. He grasped a lamp post to steady himself and shut his eyes. Something hard whacked his knuckles. A sweaty-faced Chicago policeman with a long billy was glowering at him.

"No loitering. I catch you at it again, you'll enjoy a night of city hospitality." Paul nodded and hurried away from the copper. His knuckles hurt. He walked south, toward the Levee, filled with bitterness, despair.

Still, he had the prospect of a good career; Wex Rooney and Shadow together had given him that. He could have a lot of girls, except the one he wanted. Hadn't Magda at *Die goldene Tür* told him it would be so? *"Life has a funny way of pulling tricks like that, Pauli . . ."*

He would go on. Life might play tricks, but it demanded you endure them; that was a basic duty you faced every morning when you awoke. If your dreams turned to dross, if your family banished you, if you lost the person you loved, and all hope of finding your heart's true resting place . . . you went on.

But God, it hurt.

76

Elstree

THE PRIVATE RAILROAD CAR *Pride of Petoskey* hurtled east in the late summer dark, attached to the crack overnight express of the New York Central. The huge car had been built by Pullman, under the direction of Elstree's father. The name came from the popular summer community where the Elstrees had once maintained a home. With the social compass swinging wildly from year to year—now Newport, now Saratoga, now Tuxedo—the family had given up Michigan for the newest summer gathering place of the haut monde, Southampton Village on the south shore of Long Island. Elstree looked forward to spending his honeymoon at the family's estate on the ocean.

He smoked a small cigar while he lingered over a demitasse of dark, bitter coffee. Coffee prepared, as were all things in his life, exactly as he ordered. He sat at the four-person dining table in the open area toward the rear of the car. On either side he could see himself in profile. To his left, in the window with its half-height curtains, the image was sharp. To the right, across the aisle, there was a dimmer, muddier reflection in a panel of the highly buffed rosewood used throughout the car.

From behind him came the soft swish and clink of Melton's hands in the galley dishpans. Melton was cleaning up after the wedding supper served while the train sped across northern Indiana. Melton was sixty-two, black; he slept in a narrow bunk adjoining the galley. Under the bunk a generator juttered away day and night, providing the soft electric light from the car's elaborate fixtures.

The forward section of the car consisted of a large bedroom and separate water closet. Occupants of the bedroom entered or left by a door at either end. All doors on the car could be key-locked. The rabble riding trains to which the *Pride of Petoskey* was attached had no access to Elstree's private world of convenience.

He was growing impatient. He took his monocle from his eye and polished it with a linen napkin decorated with the family crest, white on white. He laid the monocle aside and finished his coffee. Then he moved to one of two large swivel chairs bolted to the floor through a Persian carpet of muted design. Like all good Victorian domiciles, this small apartment on wheels was crowded with chairs, both leather and plush, ottomans, expensive little taborets, rubber plants and potted palms, cigar stands, china dogs, small bookcases, wicker hampers for magazines and papers, even a compact pipe organ.

Elstree saw none of it. His eye remained fixed on the door to the bedroom. Juliette had locked herself in there directly after she finished her slice of white wedding cake frosted with a strawberry glacé. It was assumed she was preparing herself for her husband. Did this take the better part of an hour?

Melton appeared. He was arthritic and inclined to hobble. "Mist' Elstree sir, will you be requiring anything else tonight?"

"No, Melton, thank you. Splendid dinner."

" 'Preciate that, sir. A privilege to serve you, as always. Once again, congratulations. I'll retire now."

"I don't hear the mutt anymore." Juliette had insisted on bringing along her damned dog Rudy. He'd yapped all through the meal, locked up in Melton's cubicle.

"No, sir, he's sleepin' in his little basket. I like havin' him in there with me."

Elstree waved at cigar smoke floating around his head. "Raise one of those windows about an inch, will you? In the morning, you may knock with coffee about eight."

"Yes, sir, Mist' Elstree. I'll take care of everything."

Melton raised the window; the noise of the train and rushing air grew louder, and a draft rapidly dispersed the cigar smoke. Melton disappeared. Elstree's gaze was on the rosewood door again. From where he sat, he could count the small square inlays that created a Grecian urn in the center panel. A hundred and forty-six. He'd already counted them twice.

He adjusted his patterned silk robe over the knees of his lounging pajamas. His carpet slippers were velvet, embroidered, like his robe and pajamas, with the family crest. He crossed his legs; uncrossed them. He fought a yawn. The day had been long and tiring, as he'd expected. It had also been disconcerting, which he hadn't expected. Juliette's mother had raised a suspicion that continued to bedevil him.

The morning ceremony at St. James Church had proceeded without incident. At the altar, flanked by gigantic arrangements of roses and lilies, orchids and artificial orange blossoms, Elstree and his nineteen-year-old bride said their vows. At the conclusion, he planted a chaste kiss on Juliette's cool lips, virtually without a response.

From the church, the bride and groom, relatives, and invited guests returned to the Vanderhoff mansion. There were three hundred guests, the absolute capacity of the house. The reception could have been held in the ballroom on the second floor, but Nell Vanderhoff wouldn't have it. Snotty little Ward McAllister, who originated New York's "Four Hundred" phrase, derided Chicagoans for their upstairs ballrooms.

Furniture from the mansion's main floor had been put in temporary storage in a warehouse to create space for the wedding buffet and silver champagne fountains. While Maestro Theodor Thomas and a half dozen of his finest string players serenaded the guests from a corner of the conservatory, everyone gorged on oysters and littleneck clams, caviar with toast points, cold asparagus and cold sliced pheasant, Camembert cheese and Turkish coffee, strawberries dipped in chocolate, and a dozen other uncommon delicacies. Nell Vanderhoff had banned pork in any form.

Nell hovered near her new son-in-law during the early part of the tedious three-hour affair. Elstree acknowledged that Nell was a rich woman, and socially important, but he didn't like her. First, she was sickly; she made a career of her illnesses and discussion of them. Further, she presided over the reception with an objectionable false sweetness. She told Elstree how lucky he was to marry her daughter. "Throughout Juliette's whole life, I've taken special care of her beauty, and particularly her hair."

"Yes, it's lovely," Elstree agreed, looking around.

"Juliette is an unsullied child, William." Nell's voice was pitched low. "Completely unsullied. Please take that into consideration."

"Oh, yes, Mother Vanderhoff, I will."

Twice more during the reception Nell sought him out to repeat essentially the same message, to be certain he understood. Or at least he assumed that to be her purpose, until the third time, when a sudden suspicion assailed him. She used a certain word once too often.

Well, he thought as he stared through the window at the featureless dark of Ohio, he'd have the truth out of his bride before he exercised his rights. This determination showed in the set of his mouth, the gleam in his eye as he sat smoking another small cigar and counting, counting the rosewood inlays . . .

The *Pride of Petoskey* swayed and clicked over the rails. Air blowing through the partially open window rattled the palm fronds. Still, when it came, Elstree clearly heard the sound he'd been awaiting. The turn of the key on her side of the door.

Inviting him in.

He was stiff with expectation. He wanted to see her shiny black hair unbound; see her slim body bared for his eyes. But first he must clear up the suspicion planted by Nell's use of that one word three times.

Elstree seized the twenty-four-karat gold handle of the rosewood door. He wrenched it down with a motion both rough and urgent.

How lovely she looked. How lovely, and shyly frightened, standing by the foot of the double bed they would share.

She'd washed her face clean of rouge and powder. She smelled fresh, of lilac water. She hadn't yet removed all her clothes. Under a sheer robe of peach silk he saw her pink brocaded corset, trimmed with lace at the bodice and ribbons at the shoulders. Her legs were stunningly shapely in mauve stockings; on her right knee was a white garter. Color rushed into his cheeks.

"My dear, you're an altogether ravishing bride." He bent to kiss and inhale the warm scented curve between her throat and shoulder. She pulled away.

Annoyed, he too stepped back. She'd brought her champagne glass to the bedroom, he noticed. There it stood on the dressing table, among her cosmetic pots. Empty. Had she drunk it for courage?

"Dear Mrs. Elstree," he said. "You look troubled. On this night of all nights? It shouldn't be."

"Bill, before we—Bill, there's something I have to confess to you."

Like a goblin, sickly little Nell loomed in his imagination. Her ugly red lips repeatedly mouthed the word "unsullied."

"A guilty secret? You? I can't believe it."

"Please don't joke. This is difficult enough."

"All right, then, out with it."

Julie turned away. Raised a brocaded window blind. She watched a few lonely lights, a country hamlet, flash by. He watched her anguished reflection in the glass.

"My mother wanted me to deceive you about something. I mean deceive you here, tonight. I don't know how she proposed that I do it, I never listened to her scheme, I shut out the words whenever she tried to explain . . ."

Icy with outrage, a sense of being a victim, he said, "Continue."

To her credit, she squared her shoulders and hugged the silk night robe across her bosom and looked straight at him with her stunning gray eyes as she spoke. "I've had—a previous experience. I'm not what the romance novels would call—"

"*Unsullied?*"

His ferocity stunned her. Her hand flew to her mouth.

"*Well?*"

"Yes, that's what I had to confess to you. A man expects certain things in the woman he marries. You've been so gentle and considerate, so decent throughout the courtship—" Rather smugly, Elstree smiled. "I can't be dishonest about—what you're getting."

Elstree had chosen Juliette Vanderhoff because she was one of the most stimulating females he'd ever met. Not stimulating in a cheap way, like some of his tarts from the Levee. Her attraction lay in her youth, freshness, chaste air. A large part of his reward for the whole tedious courtship, dancing attendance on her whining mother, her stupid parvenu father, was this moment when he would be the one to take her virginity.

Which was nonexistent.

He struggled to control his raging emotions and maintain a calm tone.

"Who was this man?"

"It isn't relevant, Bill." She took a deep breath. "I'm not going to reveal that."

He almost hit her. "You understand this alters our whole relationship."

"I should think it alters it for the better. Honesty is always—"

"*Honesty?* I don't give a God damn for honesty. If you're secondhand goods, you're no better than a street whore."

"But it was only once."

"Once or a thousand times, it's all the same. I no longer have any reason to treat you with respect. Take off your clothes."

"Bill—William—please. You've been so gentle and kind all these months—all the time I was making up my mind—I thought you'd understand."

"Oh, I do." He shed his robe and flung it down, then clawed open the knot of his pajama trousers and let them fall. "I understand fully, you gutter bitch. Now will you undress yourself or shall I do it by tearing those things from your back?"

Elstree reeled out the door. Blood streaked the right side of his face, leaking from a wound at the hairline. When he'd tried to have her a second time, rolling her onto her belly and pulling her up into position, she'd groped for a lady's mirror, smashed it, and fought him with a scrap of silvered glass.

He'd knocked the mirror fragment out of her hand. She'd jumped off the bed, cracking him on the forehead with the stool from the dressing table. For a few seconds he was too groggy to fight back. She shoved him to the door and pushed him out.

He stood shivering in the sitting room area. He was naked, bleeding at the temple; a large bruise was already purpling over his right kidney, where she'd kicked him, crying out that she wouldn't be used again the way he used her the first time. He couldn't believe it. Couldn't believe their wedding night had degenerated into a physical struggle, consummated by what amounted to rape.

The train clicked and rattled; the car rocked. His hand groped for the clean starched cloth Melton had laid on the dining table. He swabbed blood from his face, then threw the stained cloth under the table and returned to the rosewood door. She'd locked it.

"Juliette, unlock this door. I'm your husband, I demand you let me in."

"I don't know what you are. You're not what you led me to believe. I thought we'd have a calm life, if nothing else. What a dreadful, awful mistake. You're some kind of wild animal."

He beat on the door. "Let me in."

"And have you do what you did before? Oh no," she sobbed.

He pounded the door with both fists. She had cheated him, deceived him, denied him the respectable virgin-wife he wanted for a showpiece. She was a fraud, her damned old mother was a fraud . . . he found himself almost baying with rage, cold and naked in the swaying car.

"Mist' Elstree?"

He whirled; Melton's head was poking from the galley. The cuff of a worn flannel nightgown showed where Melton's black hand clutched the galley curtain.

"You damn nigger, what are you looking at? Get back in there—no, wait. Where's the dog? Bring me the damn dog." He lurched to the window nearest the bedroom door, twisted the catches, wrestled the window all the way up. A typhoon of night air blew in.

Trembling, Melton brought Rudy out on his little sapphire-studded leash, a wedding present from Elstree to Juliette even though he loathed the animal. The Pomeranian recognized Elstree and wagged. Elstree grabbed the dog, jammed it under his arm, quickly looped the leash around the dog's body.

"Now go to bed and don't come out for any reason or I'll flay your hide."

Melton bowed his head and retreated behind the curtain.

Elstree ran back to the window. God help him, he was stiff as an iron pipe again. And shocked to see the discoloration of the kidney bruise. He'd never imagined the girl had such backbone. But then, she'd been defending herself; his lovemaking had not been exactly gentle.

The next time would be less so.

He raised his voice to be heard above the roar of wind and track noise. "Juliette? Are you listening?"

The wheels rattled and banged; the locomotive's mournful whistle sounded twice.

"You'd better let me know you're listening, I've got your shitty little dog right here in my arms. Speak, Rudy." He gave the Pomeranian's neck a vicious pinch. Rudy yelped. "Did you hear him? If you did, tap on the door."

She tapped the door.

"That's better. Now you listen to me." Rudy started to writhe in his hands and kick frantically, trying to scratch free of his captor. Elstree held him tight. "I'm standing by a window. It's open. I'm going to put Rudy out the window and hold him there. If you don't let me in, I swear I'll drop him. There's only one ruler in this marriage, and it isn't you, you slut."

No answer.

Elstree grasped the dog's neck with both hands and thrust him through the window opening. "I'm holding him outside now. One more second and I'm going to throw him under the wheels."

The key turned in the lock of the rosewood door.

Trembling with the excitement of victory, Elstree yanked the dog back inside and slammed the window. He practically threw Rudy to the other end of the car. Yelping, Rudy flew into a leather chair, peed all over the chair cushion, then jumped to the floor and raced up and down, barking.

Elstree laughed. This felt good.

He opened the door and grinned at the sight of his young wife, her body rounded into a ball under the satin bed sheet, her black hair tangled over her shoulders, her gray eyes watching him with something close to mortal terror. The right eye was already puffy.

"Now that's better, Juliette. Submissive. Like a proper female. Like a proper whore."

He shut the door and gave her a moment to drink in his bloodied face, his bruised belly, his mammoth erection. Then he jumped on the end of the bed.

Outside, the Pomeranian ran up and down, chewing at a cigar stand, peeing again . . . frantic. He crouched under the dining table, trembling, making whimpering noises. Another sound, not dissimilar, came from behind the rosewood door.

77

Rose

BY THE LATE SUMMER of 1896, Rose's intimate relationship with Paul Dresser was over. But they remained good friends and still slept together occasionally. He'd helped her find a small and affordable furnished flat on East Eighteenth Street. Following his advice, she now called herself Rose French and had a small bank account in that name.

Also at Paul's urging, she'd begun to read regularly. Mostly the gossip newspapers and women's magazines. From them she was gaining a knowledge of fashion and learning how to recognize and find inexpensive imitations of French styles at the department stores.

She worked hard to purge grammatical lapses from her speech. It made her feel better about herself. She owed a lot to Paul, including her job at Tony Pastor's New Fourteenth Street Theater. Paul had spoken personally with Mr. Pastor, "the king of variety," and helped her prepare two songs for an audition. Now she was "Rose French, the International Soubrette." Fourth from the top of the bill, typically just above the trained-dog act or the balancing artist who performed headstands and handstands on barrels and chairs, and just below a team of Irish comics, Jewish comics, blackface comics. Sometimes Mr. Pastor himself topped the bill, warbling sentimental ballads and humorous numbers he had composed.

Pastor ran two shows a night for his chosen audience of tourists and ribbon clerks, their frumpy wives and gap-toothed brats. The burly, mustached Pastor, a refugee from the circus, had cleaned up the traditional variety bill to encourage family patronage. There was never so much as one racy song or skit in his theater, and prominently on the doorkeeper's booth backstage was a placard warning the artists not to take the Lord's name in vain on the premises.

Despite the moral constraints—they were only superficial anyway—Pastor's was an exciting place to work. It was in the heart of New York theater, just off Union Square on the north side of Fourteenth Street, near Third Avenue. The famous Academy of Music was a short walk to the west, and outside the Morton House on Union Square, in warm weather, you could mingle with a flock of unemployed male actors who hung about hoping to pick up odd jobs, onstage or offstage. That section of the block was affectionately called the Slave Market.

Pastor's theater was a handsome, well-kept house tucked into the first floor of an office building of red brick trimmed with white marble. White Corinthian columns decorated its portico, and bevel-glass doors and white marble floor tile enhanced its lobby. The imposing proscenium arch featured a large bas-relief of the goddess Terpsichore.

The building itself was owned by New York's Tammany Society. Many an evening Tammany's most important sachems, sleek portly men with glittering finger rings and sly eyes, would lounge in unsold boxes, courtesy of Pastor, who was a pal to all of them.

Of late, to clear the house, Pastor's had begun showing a short program of the new living pictures at the end of the bill. This was in direct response to similar programs at Koster and Bial's on West Twenty-third. Rose found the flickers a mildly diverting novelty, but nothing more. She was far more interested in the prosperous gentlemen who occasionally bought a five-dollar private box.

Rose's act consisted of fast and slow numbers. "Clementine" and "Annie Laurie." "Little Brown Jug" and "Old Folks at Home." "Just Tell Them That You Saw Me" was always good for a big hand. For her finale she did a military medley that closed with "Maryland, My Maryland," a song that drew a standing ovation if there were some old Rebs out front.

Even at a house as successful as Pastor's, however, Rose's pay wasn't enough to support her as stylishly as she wished. Her salary covered the rent but not the little extras. Lace garters. Dark red pumps. Bottles of good wine. She earned money for the niceties by sharing her favors with those gentlemen in the five-dollar boxes who sought her out afterward. An insurance broker from Rahway, New Jersey. The owner of a farm implement store in central Indiana. Married men, most of them. Dull and harmless, but smart enough to catch on to small hints she made when she was intimate with them. Most left twenty or thirty dollars in the morning. Left it on the empty pillow if she was still asleep, or tucked it in her garter if she got up to brew coffee. She did that for the ones she guessed to be very well off.

She took their money, but only as a gift, an appreciation. She wasn't a whore—and would have fought anyone who said she was—because whores had no chance of attracting the *right* gentleman. One who was rich and well-bred, who wanted a pleasant, steady arrangement in New York and was willing to pay for it.

So far that paragon hadn't shown up. She was beginning to feel discouraged. That was her mood as she walked through noisy, bustling Herald Square toward the Howley, Haviland offices on West Twentieth Street one warm and cloudy afternoon in August.

She had dressed with care; she and Paul were having supper before the first performance at Pastor's. Her light summer dress was a respectable gray, set off by a white jabot trimmed with lace. Her summer cape was black taffeta, accordion-pleated. Her hat, worn with a rakish tilt toward her left ear, was black-dyed straw with fans of gray taffeta on top. With white kid gloves, a black silk umbrella, and shiny black shoes, she was a picture of respectable young womanhood.

To the music of several pianos pounding at once, Rose climbed the stairs to the lately expanded offices of the music firm. Howley, Haviland was booming, as was the sheet music business generally. For people still mired in the lingering depression, a fifty-cent piece of music was cheap entertainment if they had a piano at home.

Howley, Haviland had added a full-time song plugger to its staff to demonstrate the firm's latest numbers at lodge halls, political clubs, and the piano departments of large stores. The firm had also branched into publishing of a different kind—*Ev'ry Month: An Illustrated Magazine of Literature and Popular Music*. Price, ten cents. The magazine included theatrical reviews, information on the latest styles, gossip about members of the Four Hundred, all written by Paul's younger brother Theo, with an occasional assist from an outside hack.

Paul made no secret of the reason he'd urged that his brother be hired: "He's quick. Been a news reporter, a good one, in Chicago and other places. But he's never made more than pocket change from writing. Probably never will, either. He's happy to be in New York, drawing a regular paycheck. Theo's kind of stiff but he's a good sort, we've always gotten along. He helps me with a lyric once in a while. I like having him around."

Theo was about twenty-five, fourteen years Paul's junior; Rose thought him a homely, buck-toothed, gangling fool. But he was a regular writing machine and turned out all the copy necessary to surround the centerpiece of every issue of *Ev'ry Month*—an insert of three or four Howley, Haviland songs.

"Three numbers for a dime instead of a dollar and a half," Paul said. "That's why the magazine's a hit."

□ □ □ □

The office was musical bedlam, as usual. Paul came out of his cubicle to clasp her hand, kiss her on both cheeks, and tell her she looked smart. From another cubicle Theo sidled forth. Rose said hello, striving to keep from showing her distaste. She could hardly hear his shyly mumbled greeting. A simp if ever there was one.

Paul pulled some sheets of yellow foolscap from his back pocket. "Here's the copy for the Reflections column. I made one small change."

Theo blinked like a nervous owl. His fingers were long, white, trembly. Over Theo's shoulder, Rose was startled to see a pair of intense blue eyes staring at her from behind the glass of the plugger's booth. The pale young man in the booth had thick black hair full of cowlicks; his pallor made his eyes all the more vivid. He couldn't have been more than eighteen. He wasn't the regular song plugger.

Obviously taken with Rose, he smiled. She lifted her nose and turned her back.

"What did you think of my short story, Paul?" Theo was saying.

"Haven't read it yet. You know I'm against fiction in the magazine, Thee. But my partners outvoted me. You having any luck with that lyric?"

"None," Theo said dolefully. "I'll keep working on it. Good day, Miss French." He shuffled away.

Paul put his arm around her. "I'm trying to write a new home number, about the place where Thee and I grew up. It's a great idea but we haven't pulled it off. Thee's been working on the verse for three months. I have just the beginning of a chorus—"

Leading her into his office, he played a few notes one-handed and then sang. "Oh, the moonlight's fair tonight along the Wabash—so on. It's still rough."

"It's pretty, Paul." That was about all she could say; she didn't think a song about a place where farmers slopped pigs and shoveled cow shit could ever be popular. He was just letting his sentimental side show again.

"Have a chair for a few minutes, Rose, then we can go."

Rose took off her gloves and sat decorously on the wooden chair. Every office at Howley, Haviland had a large window into the central reception area. Thus, conscious of eyes on her again, she glanced over to the plugger's booth. There was the frail young man, staring and grinning. He wore a red-and-white-striped shirt and sleeve garters.

She didn't mind men being friendly, but not with a man like that. Correction— boy. She gave him a scowl and looked the other way.

Paul finished his work, squeezed into his smart tan coat with black velvet lapels, snatched his topper from the coat tree, and they were away to supper.

Crossing the reception area, she glanced into the plugger's booth. The kid was gone, leaving a great litter of printed songs, music writing paper, pencils and erasers on the top of the upright. Thank God she didn't have to make eye contact one more time. She hated Jews.

After supper, Paul said he'd be at her flat soon after the second show at Pastor's. "For a little warmth and comfort," as he put it. Rose was pleased. She was feeling hot, and not from the weather.

After the second performance, a pleasant surprise was waiting for her in her small but well-maintained dressing room—a large wicker basket brimming with yellow roses. She searched for a card, found none. She rushed through the back-stage area to the doorkeeper's cubicle.

"Zachary, when did those flowers arrive?"

"During your turn. Wasn't no delivery boy, either, a gentleman brought 'em. Must have seen your first show."

Another out-of-towner looking for a companion. Still, it was an unusual approach. "What did he look like?"

"Don't remember his face, it wasn't anything special. But he sure had swell clothes. An evening suit, topper, cane—the works. He was a real polite gent. Well-spoken. I asked if he wanted to leave a card; he said, 'Perhaps another time.' That word 'perhaps,' it struck me. Around here it'd be 'maybe.'"

"Yes," Rose said, suddenly excited. Back in her dressing room, she counted the yellow roses. There were twenty-four.

She said nothing to Paul about the flowers. After they'd been to the races once and were lying pleasantly spent in the airless dark of her flat, she remembered something.

"Say, Paul, at the office—who's the kid in the plugger's booth?"

"Our new plugger. Business is getting so good we need two. His name's Harry Poland. I heard him down at Nigger Mike's, in Chinatown."

Rose had been there. The actual name of the saloon was the Canton Café, and Mike Raines, the proprietor, was actually a bearded, swarthy Russian Jew with an unpronounceable name. Because of his dark complexion he'd gotten the name Nigger Mike. All his waiters had to sing; it was a condition of employment.

"Funny-looking Jew boy," Rose said.

"Yes, but a nice kid. Good voice. When I found he could play as well as sing, I hired him right away. He's a pretty damn good musician. Self-taught, like me. He wants to compose. When I interviewed him, I told him the pay was nothing, but if he wrote something, we'd look at it. Maybe even publish it. I thought he'd say go to hell but he said sure, it was better than giving songs away for tips every night. Only problem with Harry, he likes that raggedy-time crap. I told him to keep that opinion to himself."

Paul reached for the champagne bottle on the floor next to the bed. Tonight he was pouring into a tumbler, not a fluted glass. He'd been pounding the bottle harder lately, she'd noticed. Paul always had a good appetite for drink, but now he started earlier in the day and consumed more.

She wondered if he was afraid of something. Afraid he'd never have another hit as big as "Just Tell Them"? Afraid of that fast-time, raggedy music, played mostly by Negroes? She'd heard it once or twice. She kind of liked it.

"Well," she said, "that Harry was sure looking me up and down today."

"Maybe he's stuck on you."

"After one look?"

"With you, Rose—" In the dark she heard lip-smackings, gurglings; Paul quickly downing his champagne. "With you, it's possible. Roll over here to Papa Paul . . ."

□ □ □ □

Rose found that every visit she made to Howley, Haviland only intensified the interest of the young song plugger. He popped out of his cubicle to greet her, to introduce himself with a combination of shyness and nervousness. He must have said "I'm Harry Poland" on six different occasions. She never encouraged him, always high-hatted him with a sniff or a quick turn away, but it didn't faze him. He kept following her, dancing around and waving his arms like a scarecrow on fire. His energy and enthusiasm wore her out. His perpetual smile had a jolly, infectious quality, but she wouldn't have admitted that aloud. At supper one night, Paul advised her that Mr. Harry Poland was definitely love-struck.

"Well, he'd better find himself some nice Miss Rebecca, because Rose isn't buying."

Laughing, Paul said, "I told him. He said he didn't care. He's writing a song for you. On his own time."

"Jesus Christ," she said, so startled her oyster fell off her tiny silver fork.

Paul sighed. "You've got to keep working on your vocabulary. What if you're invited to a really swell party someday? You can't get away with saying 'Jesus Christ, Mrs. Astor.' "

On a September evening about seven o'clock, with heavy rain falling on Manhattan and a north wind blowing the cold melancholy breath of autumn through the streets, Rose climbed from a hansom and ran for the doorway of Howley, Haviland. She wasn't performing this week; Pastor had booked a different singer, one Irish Tessie. Tessie was built like a wrestler, and her contralto voice was poor, but she was loved because she encouraged the audience to sing along. She had the number two spot. Mr. Pastor had relinquished the top of the bill to the Four Cohans. Rose's favorite was young Georgie, who was a smart aleck but quite a hoofer.

With her evening free, she was to meet Paul for supper. Climbing the dark, narrow stair, she heard a piano banging out a march. Probably one of the firm's new military numbers.

Howley, Haviland closed at six but the main doors were unlocked. Two cubicles were lighted. In one, buck-toothed Theo was blue-penciling typewritten copy. In another—with his back to her, thank God—Harry Poland was furiously playing the march. Rose slipped into a reception chair, hoping to remain unnoticed until Paul showed up.

Light from the street fell through the rainswept windows in the front offices. It cast shifting watery patterns on the walls. Sad patterns, out of key with Rose's mood. During the two weeks of her last engagement, roses had come from her anonymous admirer every third or fourth night. Always by a delivery boy; he hadn't returned personally since the first time. Next Monday night she'd be back on the bill. She was full of anticipation.

A desk lamp flashed on Theo's spectacles as he sat up and stretched and yawned. When he noticed her sitting in the half dark, he stepped into the reception area and switched on the light.

"Hallo, Rose. I didn't see you there at first."

"Where's Paul? He's late." She was furious. The sudden glare of ceiling lights immediately stopped the music in Harry Poland's cubicle. He swung around on his stool and grinned and waved.

"Paul went up to the Broadway Hotel to see a singer about some of our new numbers. Said he might be a little late. Anything I can get you? Coffee's still on the gas ring."

"No thank you, Theo."

"Back to work, then. Tonight I'm the Prophet." For *Ev'ry Month*, Theo wrote columns under various pseudonyms including the Prophet, the Cynic, and the Optimist. Soon his typewriter was clicking away slowly. What a ninny.

"Miss French?"

Oh God, she'd been dreading this. She turned toward him with studied hauteur. "Mr. Poland."

"Won't you call me Harry?"

She didn't answer.

"Say, if you've got a second, step in here." He had an accent. A European Jew accent, she supposed; she didn't know much about such things. It wasn't heavy. Maybe he was taking English lessons.

"Mr. Poland—"

"Oh, please. I've been working on a song of my own. Just the melody so far. Won't you come listen a minute?"

His bright blue eyes and unquenchable smile battered away her resistance. If she didn't do it, he'd keep on wheedling and begging. She walked to the door of his cubicle.

"Please, sit," he said, fairly dancing with excitement. From a straight chair he scooped a stack of Howley, Haviland sheet music and threw it on the floor with a bang. He adjusted the chair carefully at one end of the piano, then with those quick jumpy movements of his, adjusted it again. He gestured to the seat like a cavalier doffing a plumed hat. What a blockhead.

But she sat down.

Transported with joy, Harry Poland planted himself on his stool, frantically leafed through the thick stack of songs and music paper jammed on the piano rack. He found the sheet he wanted. A single page, covered with music notations and many eraser smudges.

"Listen, I hope you like this." He laced his fingers together, cracked his knuckles, adjusted one cuff, then the other, and started to play.

It was a pretty tune, she had to admit. Melodic but with a certain liveliness, although he played it at a slow tempo. He played it once, jumped back to the bridge and played the last part again, finishing pianissimo. Punctuating the end of the song was the bang of Theo's shutting his door.

"Well?" Harry Poland said. She could hear the quiver in that single word.

"It's nice," she said, about the same way she would have said, Oh, there's a fly on that wall. "How much is it worth?"

Baffled, he repeated, "Worth?"

"How much money will it make?"

"I don't know that, I just know I like it." Harry bravely smiled. "Know the name of it?" He thrust the paper at her. She saw the title block-printed at the top, unnoticed before:

ROSIE.

"I haven't worked on a lyric yet, my English ain't—isn't so good. But soon I'll try, and then—Miss French! What did I do?"

Standing, she threw the paper at him. "You insulted me. Don't you know my name? It's Rose, Rose French, it isn't Rosie. You wrote this for somebody else."

"No, for you! Rosie is the right name. Rosie is what you are, even if you don't call yourself that."

"Listen—"

"It has a ring—Rosie. It has your sparkle."

"You little kike, you must be drunk. Kindly don't speak to me again. Keep your cheap Jew songs to yourself, I'm not interested."

With her heels beating a rhythm like the march he'd been playing, she banged across the wooden floor of the reception area. Why the hell didn't the Messrs. Howley, Haviland and Dresser throw the little sheeny into the street where he and his pushy, raggedy kind belonged?

At the main doors she glanced back. Theo was peering from his window in a puzzled way. Harry Poland was hunched on his piano stool with a stricken look. No more jumping around. No more smile. Good. Maybe he'd leave her alone.

Paul came tramping up the stairs and met her on the landing. He wore his usual fine evening suit, with cape. His tall black silk hat glistened with raindrops. "Rose, what's wrong? You look awful."

"Oh, I had another conversation with that new plugger."

"Is Harry bothering you?"

"I cooled him off." She took his arm at the head of the steep stairs. "I think he got the idea that I don't like Israelites. Let's go."

No flowers arrived the first night she was back at Pastor's. Nor the second. Unworried, she counted the hours until the third evening of performances. None then, either.

By Saturday night she was despondent. Whoever he was, he'd given up. Found someone else to tweak his fancy, and probably his cock.

Coming offstage after a distinctly limp performance at the second show, she bumped into old Zachary, the doorkeeper. He was practically dancing with excitement. "He brung another basket. Jumped out of a cab, rushed it to the door, said to tender his apologies, he'd been detained in Chicago several weeks. 'Tender'—'detained'—did you ever hear such grand speech?"

"Get out of my way," Rose said, already past him.

This time there were three dozen white roses in a big wicker basket. And a shiny white satin bow tied to the handle. And a card.

With a name.

W. V. Elstree III.

78

Joe Crown

IN THE AUTUMN of 1896, Joe Crown was a man consumed by a single conviction. Bryan had to be defeated. Governor McKinley—the Major, the G.A.R. liked to call him—had to win the election and bring to America the sanity of the gold standard, the benefits of protective tariffs, and the end to the threat of grass roots revolution.

Because McKinley's wife was in poor health, he declared he would wage what he called a front-porch campaign. He would speak to partisans and well-wishers only from the porch of his white house in Canton, Ohio. Marcus Hanna and his Republican operatives scheduled special excursion trains to Canton seven days a week, while party stalwarts stumped for the candidate elsewhere. Joe met one of these roving spokesmen at a reception in Chicago early in September. Mr. Theodore Roosevelt, the police commissioner of New York City.

The evening gave Joe his first close look at Roosevelt. Though he was only thirty-eight and several inches shorter than six feet, he dominated the roomful of older and richer men. He didn't smile in the conventional way; rather, he seemed to clench his jaws, open his mouth to expose a mass of white teeth, then hold the pose. He wore pince-nez on a ribbon and a large lapel badge resembling a gold dollar. Around the edge were the words IN GOD WE TRUST, IN BRYAN WE BUST.

In his youth, it was said, Roosevelt had been sickly. You would never know it. He was stocky as a sequoia; his burly chest and thick arms seemed about to burst out of his suit. A disciple of what he called the strenuous life, he'd retreated to the Dakota Bad Lands for a while after his first wife died. There he'd punched cattle, dealt with some tough characters who called him "Four-eyes," and written a book about ranching. He was a meteor in the Republican sky and he knew it.

Roosevelt addressed the gathering from a small dais. His speaking style tended to be declamatory, his voice shrill. It put you off until his charm and the heat of his conviction won you over. After the speech, Joe introduced himself. He and Roosevelt took cups of whiskey punch. Roosevelt took one sip, no more.

On the subject of Bryan, he was a tiger:

"I am absolutely appalled at his ability and willingness to inflame hatred directed at those who are well off. I can describe the people who respond to those appeals. Whether through misfortune or misconduct, they are people who have failed in life."

Roosevelt's blue-gray eyes fixed on Joe as if daring him to disagree. Joe put down the thought that Roosevelt's remark was unforgivably snobbish. He said, "I wouldn't hazard a guess about that. It's the silver issue that changed me from a Democrat to a Republican."

"A commendable outcome, whatever the cause. We must stop that man, Mr. Crown. I'm devoting everything to the task. I'll be back in the Midwest next month on a whistle-stop tour. My friend Cabot Lodge is going on the hustings. So is Carl Schurz."

"If I may change the subject just a moment, Mr. Roosevelt—"

"Hah." Roosevelt had a way of bursting out with that. Not a laugh, exactly; more of a verbal explosion. "Too formal. Call me Theodore, I'll call you Joe."

"I'd be pleased, Theodore. I want to ask whether you think there'll be war with Spain."

"I fervently hope so. I put Butcher Weyler on a par with Bryan. Another madman to be suppressed. Looking at the larger picture, I believe American interests must be served. The sphere of democracy must be expanded. I've been a frontiersman, you know. I've experienced the salubrious effects of a challenge. The old West is gone. Six years ago our own Census Bureau declared the frontier closed, and historians such as Francis Parkman concurred. But Americans need a frontier. In Cuba we have one. Cuba calls out to stern, vigorous men with empire in their thoughts. I think war is entirely probable. When it comes, I intend to be there in some capacity."

The whiskey punch heated Joe's face. The fumes of fine Havana leaf being smoked by many of the guests was intoxicating—a plutocrat's incense. "I'd like the same thing," he said.

"Hah! Capital!" Roosevelt appraised him. "You're not too old. Not too old by any means. Let's talk about it further when I come back in October."

Next morning at the brewery, Joe wrote another draft to the Republicans, this time for five thousand. He compulsively discussed and praised young Roosevelt at home. One evening at supper, he brought up Roosevelt's attitude toward Weyler. Ilsa held her forehead. "Joe, Joe—not again."

"What do you mean?"

"This constant talk of Roosevelt, Roosevelt—*es ist eine fixe Idee.*"

"An obsession? You're making it a crime to praise a man of intelligence and strong character?"

"No, but you do it so often, frankly it's a little tiresome."

"Perhaps you find everything I do tiresome."

"Joe, stop. That isn't it at all." Seated at the side of the long table, Fritzi nervously traced patterns on the crocheted tablecloth. Ilsa continued, "I don't like this Mr. Roosevelt and his kind rattling the sword all the time. Why should we contemplate a war in Cuba?"

"Because the Cubans are fighting for freedom."

"And the sugar trust would like us to fight for their cane fields. Miss Addams says—"

"Miss Addams! Now there's a real obsession. One we can do without."

"Joe, I wish you wouldn't constantly ridicule my friends. They are educated, caring women whose opinions—"

"Are impractical and unrealistic."

"You don't even let me finish!"

"—totally unconnected to the world of reality."

"Are you saying that about me also, Joe?"

"If you agree with them, yes."

"Well, isn't that fine. The last time you saw Oskar Hexhammer, you said you called him a warmonger. Now *you* sound like one."

"The Cuban matter is different. American interests demand—"

"Oh for heaven's sake, spare me!" Ilsa exclaimed. She ran out of the dining room while Joe and Fritzi stared at one another.

The Republicans conducted their campaign almost as if they were crusading against the anti-Christ. Every party loyalist with oratorical ability took to the rails and the roads. Roosevelt stumped Michigan, Indiana, and Illinois in October, storming into the Coliseum for a rally on October 15. There he appeared before a spellbound audience of some thirteen thousand people. As a heavy donor, Joe Crown sat in a reserved section, two rows from the speaker.

Roosevelt inveighed and sweated, gestured and pounded the podium for two hours. Bryan and his followers were the philosophical heirs of the blood-maddened leaders of the Terror that had nearly destroyed France. Bryan's ally, Governor Altgeld, had pardoned criminal assassins. Bryan's operatives included the most dishonest politicians in Chicago.

At the end of the address the hall went wild. *"Teddy! Teddy! Teddy!"* The Republicans shouted and paraded as loudly and fervently as the Democrats had for the Boy Orator of the Platte. Joe left the Coliseum with a better feeling. Not all of the country had slipped into radical insanity, thank God.

In October the Republicans also resorted to use of a medium condemned by preachers and scorned even by that lowest of social classes, actors. Three days before Roosevelt's triumph at the Coliseum, Hammerstein's Olympia Music Hall in New York introduced a new short film from the American Biograph Company titled "McKinley at Home—Canton, O." With the candidate's full cooperation, it presented a reenactment of Governor McKinley's being informed that he'd received the nomination. Money from the campaign war chest was secretly used to strike extra prints for showing all over the Midwest. There the picture was called "Major McKinley at Home."

Joe couldn't bring himself to sneak into the Columbia Theater downtown to view it. That was the proper conservative attitude. Still, if even one disciple of Bryan's would see it and then stop reading Count Tolstoy, comb and cut his hair, and vote for the Major, who cared how disreputable the means of persuasion?

Down from his retreat at Bolton Landing on Lake George in New York State came the aging Carl Schurz, to speak in Chicago in the closing days of the campaign. He attracted only a fraction of Roosevelt's crowd.

Joe and his friend Schurz dined at Schlogl's German restaurant after the speech. Joe repeated Roosevelt's statement that war with Spain was likely in the next year or two. He repeated his wish to take part. "Perhaps an Army commission?"

"I can't help you, Joe. I'm no longer in government. Haven't been for years."

"Come, you have hundreds of friends in Washington. Influential people. And there'll be a Republican administration."

"Why not ask your friend Joe Cannon? Since Uncle Joe was reelected three years ago, he's become one of the most powerful men in the House. Write to him."

"I did, last week. But I'm also asking you. I look at this the way Grant and Sherman looked at a battle. The objective is to win. You don't go in with one regiment if you can call up a whole army corps."

"You're still speaking to the wrong man. Morally and intellectually, I am against this nation's trying to impose its political will, or its commercial dominance, on smaller and weaker countries."

"Why, Carl? Expansionism is an avowed principle of the party. A plank in the platform. It's also the prevalent mood of the people."

"The prevalent aberration. It makes the Republicans nearly as despicable as Bryan."

"Opinions aside, we'll probably have to fight. All the papers say so."

Schurz snorted. "They're engineering it. Hearst, Pulitzer—that lot."

"Even so, if war comes, I want to serve. And I'll ask you for whatever help you can give. I've never asked a favor before."

Schurz was silent a moment. "How does Ilsa feel about this?"

"She's opposed. Adamantly. Like you, she's opposed to a war. That's immaterial, however."

Carl Schurz gave his friend a long, quizzical stare. Then he laughed. *"Hartnäckig Deutsch!"*

"Stubborn? Yes. A privilege of old age. Will you help me?"

"Of course. I can oppose a war, but I can't ignore friendship. I will do all I can, for old times' sake."

79

Paul

IZ PFLAUM showed "The Wabash Cannonball" on a Tuesday night, after the variety bill. Paul, Shadow, and Jimmy were squeezed into a booth rigged from curtains at the back of the house, praying the prototype Luxograph projector wouldn't fail. Mary fidgeted in the last row, just in front of them.

Iz Pflaum personally introduced the picture, stepping before the curtain in a suit of tails. He warned the sparse audience that any person with a feeble constitution should hold tight to his or her seat or, alternatively, leave.

This produced snickers and jeers. No one rose to go, however. In the booth, Shadow threw the switch and crossed his fingers. There were gasps and cries as the improvised cloth screen lit up with an image of an onrushing train.

The Cannonball grew and grew, seeming to hurtle straight for the audience. Now the cowcatcher detail was clearly visible—the flag emblem above it—even the railroad's painted slogan. "Oh my God!" Mary exclaimed as patrons jumped from their seats and kicked and pushed and screamed in the aisles, frantic to escape. Three were unable to leave because they fainted.

"That was sensational, did you see how it emptied the house?" Pflaum said after he'd revived the three faintees with sal ammoniac and they had all staggered out.

Shadow said, "But that isn't the sole purpose of—"

"Great chasers, Colonel. I want your pictures—minimum of ten, within one week. I'll lease the projector, you train my nephew Herk to run it. See me at eleven tomorrow, we'll write up the contract."

The four members of the Luxograph group went back to the Levee and, to celebrate, drank far too much beer.

Next morning, with an aching head, Paul asked Shadow, "Where will we get all these pictures so fast?"

"We'll make 'em, for Christ's sake. Why do you think I hired you and Jimmy, as fucking ornaments? Stop frowning, kid. These are what I call happy problems. We're on the way. We'll have Iz Pflaum yelling so loud for Luxograph pictures, he'll pee his pants—and open his wallet wide."

Never in his memory had Paul spent such a frantic week. While Mary tended the peep show parlor, he and the colonel and Jimmy rushed from one end of the city to the other in a rented wagon. They photographed "Summer Shower in Jackson Park" and "Troops Drilling at Fort Sheridan." They photographed "The Elevated Rounding a Curve" and "Professor Milo's Dancing Dachshund." On the roof, using the fake brick backdrop, they photographed "A Packet of Sneeze Powder," with Mary doing the sneezing. She had a nice comic talent, Paul thought; she also performed quite gracefully for "Dance of the Butterfly Maiden," a completely respectable effort in which she wore a three-layer costume and showed nothing more titillating than her knees.

With Jimmy and a Levee damsel as the players, they filmed "Lips Aflame," a direct imitation of one of the biggest Edison hits, forty-two feet of continual kissing by Broadway actors May Irwin and John Rice. Out in Elgin they photographed "At Work in the Watch Factory," and on Clark Street, "Here Comes the Trolley." As Paul set up the camera beside the tracks, Shadow ran to press money into the hands of two policemen who had stopped all other traffic but the approaching streetcar. On the curb, Jimmy was chatting up a couple of racy-looking girls, telling them what a great dancer he was. "Get over here, Daws," Shadow shouted.

Jimmy ambled into the street looking resentful. Shadow stamped his boot. "Move your ass! I don't pay you to line up your pussy willows on my time."

Scarlet, Jimmy said, "You want me to crank?"

"Dutch'll do it, he's steadier. You hold the tripod down. Now, f'Christ's sake, *now*, here comes the God damn streetcar!"

□ □ □ □

The first bill of chasers was a hit, even though they were shown from a single projector with a two-minute wait between each one. Iz Pflaum asked for more— five new pictures every second week. And where there was one opportunity, there were sure to be others. Shadow leased the peep show parlor to a couple of middle-aged entrepreneurs from the Levee. He personally pulled the cards from the machine showing "A Chinese Dream" and closed the back room. He wanted no coppers or vice crusaders interfering with his vision—a new, larger photographic empire in which penny-ante pornography had no place. He reincorporated as the American National Luxograph Company.

Riding the tide of opportunity, Shadow drove himself and his employees to unprecedented effort. He found a commercial studio that could handle roll film. He set them up to process his negatives and strike prints. Still, there weren't enough hours to travel to locations to shoot one-minute actualities, as the colonel had taken to calling them, and at the same time build a second projector in the cellar because he had a line on a variety house in Indianapolis that had heard of Pflaum's success and wanted to match it.

Throughout the summer and early fall, Paul lived in a constant haze of exhaustion. He slept four hours a night, five if he was lucky. They staggered out at six every morning to film until the light disappeared at dusk.

At one or two in the morning they drew up lists of possible film subjects. "Parade of the Wheelmen." "Park Police, Mount and Drill." Paul had read about a Lumière film, "Grand Canal, Venice," shot from a gondola, and "Niagara Falls Gorge," an Edison subject filmed from the observation car of the Niagara Gorge Railway. From these came "On the Lagoon," a pleasant glide over the sunlit waters at Lincoln Park. To forestall protests from Jimmy, Paul said he'd man the oars while Jimmy cranked the camera at the prow of the rowboat. Jimmy himself came up with one subject—"Making Soap Bubbles"—which Shadow said privately was pretty simpleminded, but which audiences enjoyed and applauded. Shadow's genius was responsible. On the roof on a windless day, he'd set his camera so that the sun made the bubbles glisten and shimmer. For a man self-trained, he had a remarkable eye. But who in the world could have trained any other way for this new craft?

Paul learned by observing his ruthless and profane mentor. He tried to imagine what would make a good, pleasing backdrop, then introduced the factor of motion. He lay awake when he should have been sleeping, visualizing camera setups.

Competitors were resorting to short reenactments of current stage plays. This prompted Paul to think of Fritzi and the authors she admired. At one of their late-night brain sessions, he put forth the word "Shakespeare?" almost diffidently, and Shadow went wild. "I don't like stories but that guy's in a class by himself. I heard all about him from actors I know. Let me think, let me think." He massaged his temples. "What's the show where the darkie kills his wife?"

"I believe it's *Othello*." Jimmy folded his arms and looked away.

"We'll try it."

They recruited a black man, William Soames, who did janitor work at several Levee barrooms. Soames was about forty, sweet-natured and shy but command-

ingly built, with wide shoulders and powerful arms. Shadow also hired a neighborhood whore named Katie Favors, a little thing with blond curls. At first she
wasn't keen about associating with a colored man, but she changed her mind
when she heard the purpose was creation of one of those new flicker pictures.

On the roof, wearing a dressing gown to which Mary had stitched ropes of
secondhand Christmas tinsel, the Moor from Chicago nervously chatted with the
equally nervous Desdemona from the whorehouse. Katie Favors wore a pale gray
nightgown with a lace-edged collar that left her white throat bare. She actually
looked quite fetching in it; almost innocent, Paul thought. The backdrop was the
brick wall repainted with Arabian Nights arches. The sole prop was Paul's bed.

"Choke her!" Shadow cried as they started to crank.

"I don't want to hurt you, Miss Favors," William Soames said as he gingerly
put his right hand on Katie's neck. He bared his teeth; she fluttered her eyes.
They swayed back and forth rather tentatively. Finally Soames pushed his victim
onto the bed. She clutched her forehead and expired.

Shadow stepped back. "Terrible. For Christ's sake, Willie, you act like you're
handling a china doll. This bitch betrayed you. Got in the kip with some other
fella—right, Paul?"

"Well, he thinks so. Actually—"

"You're burned up about it, Willie. Shake her around! Roll your eyes! Snarl!
Film costs money. Make it right this time or you don't get paid."

With that inspiration, William Soames delivered a performance that made everyone applaud. He choked Katie Favors with both hands and whipped her from
side to side so forcibly, she uttered blue oaths in a strangled voice. William rolled
his eyes and gnashed his teeth as instructed. A gob of spit formed on his lower
lip, sending Shadow into ecstasy. Then Katie Favors gave it extra effort, doing a
series of leg jerks and bodily convulsions on the bed before breathing her last.

When Paul stopped cranking, William Soames knelt beside Katie, chafed her
hands, and apologized for treating her so roughly. She sat up, rubbing her red
neck. "Oh, that's okay, a little lotion will take care of this. I got into it myself.
Kinda fun, wasn't it?"

When "The Death of Desdemona by William Shakespeare" showed at Pflaum's
for the first time, it created a sensation. Women hid their eyes and cried out. Men
jumped on their seats shouting, "Lynch that dirty nigger!" Frightened but proud
too, the mild-mannered Soames had to be smuggled out a side door.

The constant rushing about, passing out bribes to get into places that would
otherwise have barred them, thinking up subjects, working against the deadlines
Pflaum imposed, created an atmosphere of perpetual crisis that only a young
man, or a driven older one like Shadow, could survive. For Paul it helped dull the
memory of the scene outside St. James Church, and the accounts of the reception
afterward, which the newspapers had printed in hurtful detail. He wore himself
out purposely, and as the days passed, some of the pain abated.

But not all. Nor would it, ever.

Gradually, and quite without any conscious plan, Paul became the senior member of Shadow's crew. The colonel asked questions of Paul but not of Jimmy.

When Paul and Jimmy helped in the cellar, building the new projector, Jimmy malingered—went out for a smoke or rested—whenever he could get away with it. He just wasn't interested. Paul, sensing that Jimmy resented their changing status, marveled at the contradictory behavior of human beings. Jimmy engineered his own loss of favor, and he blamed someone else.

When the colonel jumped on a train to lease his second projector in Indianapolis—a third was half finished—Paul took charge of filming for two days; they didn't dare fall behind. He and Jimmy bought their way into the baseball park, and from a position near the White Stockings bench filmed the home team losing to its opponent. The stands were filled with people wearing McKinley or Bryan badges and ribbons. Once again Paul found himself doing most of the work. Jimmy spent a lot of time leaning over the rail of a box to chat up a homely but well-dressed woman with a large bosom.

As the game ended and the shadows lengthened, they folded up the Luxograph tripod and boxed their gear in the silent, empty park. Paul said, "You don't like this job much, do you, Jim? Why do you stay?"

"Got to, I'm out of circulation for a while yet."

"What does that mean, circulation?"

"You wouldn't understand. Let's say I'm staying till I find something better."

"How could any job be better than this?"

"This nickel-and-dime shit? Jesus, Dutch, you're strange." Then he nudged Paul, grinning. "Hey, did'ja see that woman? She's married, it's her husband who has the box over there. He couldn't come today. She says he don't give her much of what a woman needs. I'm gonna tell Shadow I got a bellyache, can't work in the cellar tonight. I'm taking the lady out to dance, and then I'll take her to Buxbaum's Hotel and dance her a different way. Till she's in heaven."

Paul knelt to latch the box, keeping his face turned to hide his dislike of the bragging, and the braggart.

On the sunlit porch, Mrs. McKinley sat in a large wicker rocker. The porch door opened. Out stepped the Major, followed by a second gentleman. Whistles and applause from the audience greeted the appearance of the candidate.

"That other one's McKinley's secretary, George Cortelyou," Shadow whispered from the next seat.

The Major examined telegrams informing him of his nomination. Appearing pleased, he returned the telegrams to his secretary and took off his hat. Out of his pocket came a large white handkerchief. Paul sat spellbound in the dark, the silver images flickering on his face.

The Major mopped his brow and cheeks. The picture flashed off, leaving a blank screen. A scalloped velvet curtain dropped from above. The auditorium lights came on, the applause sputtered out, and the audience rose to leave.

"Major McKinley at Home" had lasted slightly more than one minute. Election day was Tuesday. Presumably the film would be withdrawn after that. Paul and Shadow had come back to see it a second time, to study the technique. There wasn't much technique to study. The camera shot from a fixed position on McKinley's lawn. Still, the reality fascinated Paul.

Shadow too; as they went up the aisle he said, "That's the genius of flickers,

Dutch. Actuality. Faces and places never before accessible. That French outfit did 'The Coronation of the Czar of Russia.' Edison's bunch did 'Arrival of the Chinese Viceroy at the Waldorf Hotel.' Everybody's into actualities."

"I wish we could have filmed that picture."

"Not a chance. It was a Biograph deal all the way. The candidate's brother Abner has shares in the company. So does ex-President Harrison. The owner of this theater's a Republican. Maybe we should have done our own version of McKinley—" Shadow was eyeing a well-endowed cashier who had just come out of her booth with a tin cash box. "Found some gent who's a ringer for the Major, set him up at a nice white house on the North Shore and called it Canton—listen, excuse me. Don't tell Mary where I went."

The colonel swooped over to the cashier, bowed, and flourished his sombrero, then began to whisper. The cashier giggled. He took her arm. Paul walked home alone, amused by Shadow's cheerful immorality. It was odd that he could overlook it in the colonel and despise the same trait in Jim Daws. He wished Jimmy would get back into circulation, whatever that was. Was he hiding from someone? Paul wouldn't have been at all surprised.

William Jennings Bryan had stormed back and forth across the hustings like a Nebraska cyclone, thrilling thousands with his delivery of The Speech. William McKinley sat on his porch in Canton and let others stump for him. Including a surrogate—a *Doppelgänger* on a strip of celluloid yanked through a lighted box one frame at a time. No one could say to what extent the election was influenced by repeated showings of "Major McKinley at Home" in large cities for almost three weeks before November 3. Only the outcome was unequivocal. Bryan lost by six hundred thousand popular votes. America returned control of both the Senate and the House to the Republicans. Respectable folk could sleep soundly again. The dragon of bimetallism was slain.

November brought dark clouds and chill rain. Paul and every other Chicagoan smelled winter on the wind.

Shadow's mad pace never slackened. He reeled from camera to cellar to railway station with a glazed eye. He dashed from city to city, hunting for picture outlets, haggling over deals, fighting off competitive companies doing the same thing. The biggest was Edison Vitascope, headed by the team of Raff and Gammon, men who had expertly marketed Edison's peep shows nationally.

Shadow placed a third projector in a variety house in Louisville and contracted for a fourth in Milwaukee. He rented an empty haberdashery in Peoria with the intention of running his own store show. He explained to Paul that he'd hire a local operator-manager at a low salary, and all the profits would belong to the company. Assuming people showed up. The variety houses already drew substantial audiences, and Shadow received a small percentage of every ticket sale when his films were showing. But it might not work out so favorably in locations without vaudeville acts; the ledger for Peoria might be decorated with red ink. But he wanted to try:

"You rest on your heels, you get no place. And this company is going someplace, believe me."

"I do," Paul said.

For the local audience, they filmed "His Honor, The Bath" in December. It was a crisp winter day, with diamond-hard sunlight; the day of the First Ward Ball at the Seventh Regiment Armory.

Presided over by Coughlin and Kenna, the Ball was the principal fund-raising event for the spring election campaign. Everyone who did business in one of Chicago's vice districts had to buy tickets. All night long gamblers and cadets, madams and their stock, would socialize in the midst of balloons and confetti, dance on a waxed floor, drink and engage in other pleasures in private boxes furnished with greens, patriotic bunting, advertising placards—and curtains.

The Bath turned up outside the Armory in the special wardrobe he'd chosen for the night's festivities, due to begin at eight. Paul wished for film that would reproduce color, because the Bath was a peacock spectacle in a tailcoat of billiard-table green, a dove gray waistcoat, lavender trousers and necktie, pink gloves, yellow pumps, and shiny black top hat.

Shadow introduced his crew. The Bath peered at Paul, then Jimmy. "I've met you lads before."

"At the racetrack," Jimmy said.

Paul said, "We met the first time at Rooney's Temple of Photography."

"Right you are. New field for you two, huh? Pictures that jump around all over the place. I love this modern stuff. Put 'er there." They all shook hands.

Following Shadow's direction, Paul set up the Luxograph to film the alderman striding back and forth in front of the stone wall of the Armory. There was constant interference as wagons arrived and stevedores unloaded cases of beer and wine. "Ain't it grand?" the Bath said with a theatrical wave at the wagons. "Democracy at its best, right, boys?"

"Keep walking, Alderman, please," Shadow called through a small megaphone, which Paul had never seen before today. He thought it ostentatious, but that was Shadow. For this occasion the colonel had put on his finest white sombrero, frock coat, and flowing tie.

The Bath smiled and bowed to the lens, one hand over his paunch, one hand in back. Paul cranked until the film ran out.

"Boys, this was a pleasure." Once again the alderman shook hands all around. "I'll be in the front row at Pflaum's first time you project it. Here's a ticket to the Ball for each of you. Some tickets for free drinks also."

Paul shook his head. "Thank you, but I'm tired, sir. I don't think I'll attend."

"Yes you will, the Ball is something to see," Shadow said, waving his megaphone. He was expansive after several sips from the flask Coughlin had cheerfully shared. "You'll have a hell of a good time and remember it fondly. Assuming you don't catch the clap."

Shadow was right, the Ball was something to see.

By half past seven o'clock, several thousand people packed the Armory. By ten, when Bathhouse John and Hinky Dink led the grand march around the floor, the revelry was well advanced. Paul had run back to his room; he'd put on his best clothes and slicked his hair lightly with Macassar oil. He stood now with a stein of beer, bemused by the spectacle.

Pimps had turned out in everything from tails to garish suits. Young whores wore costumes of every kind: wooden shoes and yellow braids, American Indian tunics and warbonnets, ball gowns and wedding gowns. A geisha with white face gave him a long wet kiss and whispered that tonight she did it for free. He patted her inky black hair, piled high with pearl pins. "Thank you. Later."

Waiters fairly ran with trays of beer steins and whiskey glasses. Dancers whirled around the floor, throwing themselves into the waltz and the schottische and the polka. Every hour a new musical aggregation took its turn on the stand. The object was volume, not a sensitive performance. Bernhard's German Band came on at midnight. By then Paul had drunk a lot of beer. He went to the gent's downstairs. To reach it he passed through a dim area beyond the brewers' booths, and came upon a couple copulating standing up.

Returning upstairs, he ran into a little blonde tart named Tippy, whom he knew from his laundry days. They hugged and greeted each other warmly.

Tippy had a certain winsomeness he'd always liked. They held hands, and he stole a few kisses after he refilled their beer steins.

When Bernhard's group struck up a polka, Tippy clapped her hands. "Paul, do you know how?"

"Yes, my aunt taught me at Berlin beer gardens, years ago. But I am not very good."

"Never mind, come on."

Jimmy, wearing a cheap plaid suit, happened to be strolling by with a Levee girl named Fat Marie, who lived up to her name. He heard the exchange. With his eye on Paul, he said, "Hell, Marie, I been a polka champion since I was knee-high. Let's show 'em."

"Oh Lord, Jim, not a contest," Paul said, trying to laugh him out of it.

"What's wrong, afraid you'll look like a chump?"

Paul flared. "Hell no, I am not afraid." He swept an arm around Tippy. "Let's go."

"First one to drop's a dirty dog," Jimmy said. He rushed his dazed partner to the waxed floor and swung her into the rhythm of the oom-pah band.

Paul and Tippy followed them quickly. The little blonde laughed in a giddy way, gripping Paul's hand and waist tightly. Couples flew by, one of them Jimmy and his partner. Fat Marie was sweating, dark red from forehead to jowls.

Paul danced Tippy around and around, faster and faster. It felt like riding on a great wind gust. Tippy hung on delightedly. They whirled and dipped, whirled and dipped . . .

Suddenly, behind them, Jimmy shouted, "*Oh, Christ!*"

Tippy gasped. "He fell."

Paul stopped abruptly and led Tippy to the side of the floor. Jimmy had gotten up and was leaning on Fat Marie. Then he limped to the nearest box and leaned against that, resting his right ankle on his left knee and rubbing it. Fat Marie touched his arm sympathetically. Jimmy yelled at her. Paul couldn't hear the words in the din. He didn't need to hear them. Jimmy's eyes said everything.

"Shall we quit?" Tippy asked.

Good sense prompted a yes. But he was feeling the Dutch courage of the beer, and resentment of Jimmy. "No. We dance."

He awoke the next morning in Tippy's bed, a dreadful taste furring his mouth. Immediately there flashed into his head a memory of Jimmy's eyes when Paul and Tippy were finishing the polka. Jimmy's angry eyes.

That night in their room, Jimmy said, "I'm not going to forget how you showed me up in front of everybody. Then you went right around the floor to celebrate."

"Jim, I want to offer an apology. I had drunk a lot of beer—"

"Fuck you, I don't need your apologies. From now on we do the work but we ain't friends and never will be. Got it?"

He rolled over and pounded his pillow. Paul lay back, glumly thinking, *As if we ever had a chance of being friends* . . .

Paul wrote several letters to Wexford Rooney in care of general delivery, Charleston, West Virginia. Early in 1897 he finally got a reply. It contained some news.

> In certain respects life is treating me less harshly than before. Notably, I have found a room at the boardinghouse of a Mrs. Lucille Suggsworth. She is a person of intelligence, fine culinary skills which most of her cloddish guests fail to appreciate, and a warm caring disposition. Lucille was widowed last year. We are close companions, if you get my drift.

The letter contained some complaints.

> My servitude at the Nu-Age Photography Salon of Charleston is, as I feared, a dreadful experience. I seem to have inherited all the screaming, puling, vile-tempered tots whose idiot parents want them immortalized for posterity. Yesterday one of the little wretches—a mere four years old—sank her tiny choppers into my wrist as I attempted to adjust her pose. God save me from the rabies!!
>
> To make it worse, I am then required to finish the printed portraits of these midget monsters by color-tinting their precious little lips and cheeks. I'd sooner black their eyes and shade out a few teeth—the uglier the result, the more true to life!
>
> I lack adequate words for my general surroundings, save to say this place is a cultural Sahara. The chief intellectual subjects discussed in Charleston include the secret tippling of the pastor and the characteristics of family pets and farm animals. Pray for my sanity.

The letter contained the inevitable admonitions.

> In all that you do in your newfound career in living pictures, remember above all one watchword. Honesty. Honesty!!
>
> I hope sincerely that you will soon declare your intent to become a citizen. This is a great land—nay, unequaled—and I say that in full knowledge of all the moral, legal, and general shortcomings of us Americans and our system. I say that knowing the Red Man is raped of his land, the

Black Man is rapidly being deprived of all of his hard-won rights—even the White Man is often made to feel a pariah if he hails from the wrong part of the globe and speaks with a queer accent.

Still, there is unrivaled opportunity, and a matchless idea behind America, which, while far from perfectly implemented as yet—if it ever will be!—still beckons us on. Surely you will heed me when you realize these words come from one who was never able to capitalize upon that opportunity for himself. Yet I believe in it. So do not shun or discard the idea of becoming a citizen, even though some aspects of life here have been bitterly disappointing.

Yours ever,
W. Rooney

Paul laid the letter aside. Wex might be disappointed too. Paul would stay in America while learning as much as he could of his new craft. But citizenship? No; since he'd lost Julie, that was something in which he no longer had any interest. What the baker of Wuppertal said about America seemed ever more truthful.

In February 1897, the world's champion heavyweight fighter, James J. Corbett, went into training for his title defense against Bob Fitzsimmons. Gentleman Jim would meet the challenger on March 17 in Carson City, Nevada. For weeks, everyone with a drop of sporting blood had been talking of little else.

"It's a shame we can't buy a train ticket, go out there and film it," Paul said one evening at supper.

Shadow said, "We weren't privileged to be invited. We didn't present the right credentials." He rubbed his fingers together, feeling invisible money. "Enoch Rector's Veriscope company got an exclusive license to film the fight." He wrapped a string of Mary's overdone spaghetti on his fork and sucked it into his mouth with an audible *snap*. "But don't worry, we'll do it too."

"Huh?" For once he had Jimmy's attention. "You just said—"

"What we are going to film, boys, is what I call a counterpart. I've already rented a site. A farm out near Wheaton. I've been to the Chicago River piers scouting potential look-alikes. I've located our Corbett but not our Fitzsimmons. I'll find him, I still have three weeks."

"You mean we're going to fake a picture?" Paul said.

Shadow seemed affronted by his tone. "Who sets policy around here, you or me? Don't think our American National Luxograph is the only one doing it. I had a letter from Sig Lubin in Philadelphia. He's planning the same thing. Rector's pictures will be shown exclusively at one Chicago theater. What's Iz Pflaum supposed to do, sit by and weep? He's a steady customer—he deserves a fight picture too. We'll make our version accurate and truthful, one hundred percent." Shadow banged the table.

Leaving Paul speechless and Jimmy amused.

In April, twenty days after the fight and a week before the scheduled premiere of Rector's authentic version, they traveled to Wheaton with a wagonload of equipment and lumber. They built a shaky prize ring in a field. Late the next day, while Jimmy, Paul, and the colonel were stringing the ropes, the two stevedores showed up. One seemed slow-witted; the other smelled like a wine cask when he exhaled.

The following morning, in the farmer's barn where they'd all slept, the stevedores donned tights and gloves. The men bore only a slight resemblance to engraved portraits of Corbett and Fitzsimmons, though the man chosen to represent the challenger was, at least, partially bald.

The camera was lifted to a platform on stilts beside the ring. Shadow fussed and yelled as if this were the actual fight, with the outcome unknown. Under an elm tree not yet budded, Mary patiently guarded the hamper of cold beef sandwiches and bottled Apolinaris water bought to keep the combatants refreshed.

This time Shadow personally manned the crank. Paul sat on a stool at the front corner of the camera platform, a copy of the *Tribune* in hand. He'd read the long Carson City dispatch half a dozen times and marked it for emphasis. Jimmy stood by in a striped shirt and cloth cap. A silver referee's whistle hung from a lanyard around his neck. The farmer and his son were playing handlers of the two fighters; Shadow had coached them on the use of water buckets and sponges between rounds.

Shadow began to crank. "Action. Start reading, Dutch."

"*Round one. Gentleman Jim danced lightly from his corner, while the Cornishman seemed to lurch and shamble into the fray. Fitzsimmons swung a punch, which missed. Corbett stung him with a left jab.*" The stevedore, whose hair had been blacked for the Corbett part, dutifully jabbed. The bogus Fitzsimmons staggered. Paul thought of Wex's charge about honesty. His conscience writhed.

"*Another futile blow caught the air and nothing more. Then the champion replied with still one more rapierlike jab . . .*"

So it went, round by round, with pauses to reload the camera and rest the actors.

In the actual fight, during the fourteenth of fifteen scheduled rounds, Jim Corbett had carelessly dropped his guard, and the battered Cornishman had slammed a left hook into his gut. The punch, ever after called a solar plexus blow, flung Corbett on his back for a full ten count, costing him the championship. They finished filming the counterpart of the knockout at ten past one in the afternoon. They congratulated each other and celebrated with a gallon jug of low-grade whiskey.

American National Luxograph's "exclusive" pictures of the Corbett-Fitzsimmons fight ("A Dramatic Representation") opened at Pflaum's in late April. Although the official Rector pictures were also showing, Shadow's eighteen-minute highlight version did fine business, more than satisfying Iz Pflaum.

And further disillusioning Paul:

"Doesn't the public know the difference?"

"Sure they know the difference," the colonel said. "You miss the point, kid. They don't care. Any picture is still a hell of a novelty to most people."

"Well, as you reminded me when I first spoke out of turn, this is your business. But I must say what's on my mind. I don't think we should do such representations. We should go where something is happening and bring back the real event, not an imitation."

Mary had finished eating and was buffing her fingernails. Jimmy speared three more pork sausages on his fork. With heavy sarcasm, Shadow said, "Do you happen to recall that we weren't invited to Nevada?" He repeated his money-feeling gesture.

"But there will be places where we can go, and we should. You said so yourself, the night I was hired. I was impressed."

"Were you." Shadow studied his helper with a grudging amusement. "You really believe we should never produce a staged film?"

"Unless it's clearly a play or a little story. If that's foolish, I'm sorry, it's how I feel."

"God, Dutch," Jimmy said. "You're always putting on your damn airs."

"Wait, let's follow this," Shadow said. "Dutch, I'm sure I was sincere when I made that speech, though I frankly don't remember too much of what I said. I still believe the Luxograph can and should go anyplace. Trouble is, right now we can't afford to go a hell of a lot farther than the county line. We're stretched to the limit. Every penny that comes in goes out for raw stock or materials to build another projector. These representations—fakes, you call 'em—they're income. And I tell you again, everybody's doing 'em. Smith and Blackton at Vitagraph filmed some hick waterfall in Passaic, New Jersey. They're showing the picture up and down the East Coast and calling it Niagara Falls. The crowds go wild. From what I read, nobody so far—not one damn person—has shot up a hand and said, 'Oh, gentlemen, wait, wait, isn't that Passaic? I'm leaving!' If people believe a fake's real, and the fake's easier, who's hurt?"

"Who? I don't know. But honesty is hurt."

"All right, we'll send you and Jimmy and the camera to real places around the whole damn world, when we can. *When we can*—those are the words to remember."

Paul said nothing. Shadow looked spent; great dark rings showed under his eyes. This was no time to press a philosophy of pictures. Perhaps Shadow did believe in the right one and just couldn't afford it, as he said.

Shadow yawned. "Mary, could I have more coffee? I have to get downstairs but first I have to wake up."

"What are you doing, working on the new projector?" Mary asked.

"Yeah, the one with more capacity. Paul, you want to help me again?"

"Sure."

Jimmy's eyes didn't conceal his feelings. What was the American expression? Bad blood. Paul couldn't deny it was there. Bad blood between them.

Mary brought the colonel's coffee and resumed her nail-buffing. After a few seconds, she suddenly threw the buffer on the table. "Oh God, Sid, I forgot. Did you look at the afternoon mail?"

"When have I had time? I'm lucky to find thirty seconds to run to the crapper."

"There's an important letter for you. At least it looks important."

"Yeah, who's it from, Her Majesty Queen Victoria?"

"It's from the Edison Manufacturing Company, in New Jersey."

Shadow blanched. "My God. What do you suppose they want?"

"Maybe the great Mr. E. knows about your work, maybe he's impressed and wants your autograph."

"Mary, this isn't funny." Paul had never heard Shadow's voice so hushed or seen him so unnerved. "Where's the fucking letter?"

80

Julie

ON A JUNE MORNING in 1897, Julie and her husband took breakfast on the marble terrace of Belle Mer, the summer residence Elstree's father had built in Southampton Village. It was situated between the intersection of First Neck Lane and Dune Road to the west, and St. Andrew's Dune Church, where services were held in the summer months.

Though it was only half past eight, the day was already sultry. The sky was overcast. Throughout the gardens and glades of their five acres, birds sang. Below the sloping lawn, beyond the dune and their private beach posted with NO TRES-PASS! signs, the ocean, the wonderful sonorous ocean, rolled in from the other side of the world.

Julie wore a morning robe of quilted satin, too heavy for the season. Her little dog Rudy nestled in her lap. Elstree had dressed in his own bedroom, appearing in white flannel trousers and his scarlet coat denoting membership in the exclusive Shinnecock Hills Club, where he golfed. This morning he had a ten o'clock bridge game at the Southampton Club, for the usual two cents a point.

Elstree looked tanned and fit. Julie, on the other hand, was pale, with purple shadows under her eyes. Somehow nothing would erase them, not even sleeping ten to twelve hours a night. Her black hair hung to her waist, combed and brushed and prettily secured at the midpoint by a white ribbon bow. She wore her hair long all the time, except when some social occasion required her to put it up. It seemed a way to make a silent if bitter statement about her life: "*I am a rich wife of whom nothing is expected save obedience, social graces, a pleasing appearance, and the delivery of one or more babies, preferably male.*"

He had been at her a lot on that subject recently. Verbally and otherwise. She'd already miscarried once, in her third month. After she awoke from the opiate the doctor had administered, the darkness in her mind lasted for weeks. Crying spells, visions of Paul, hours in bed in the daytime with all the drapes drawn. She grieved for the poor nameless babe she'd lost, yet a certain part of her thanked God the child would never have to know a father like Bill.

Without taking his eye from his *New York Times*, Elstree rattled his gold-rimmed coffee cup on the gold-rimmed saucer. A serving girl with a silver pot jumped forward from her station at the nearest French door.

When the girl retreated, he said, "My dear, is there any news? I calculate it's about time for—"

"No," she broke in. "Again this month, no change."

And God forbid that there should be, with this new thing hanging over us.

"You know how eager I am for a son. Ideally, more than one. Isn't it true that problems such as we're experiencing generally arise with the wife?"

"I'm not a medical expert, Bill." *And you're a man, flawless, therefore ready to blame every deficiency on the woman. Just like all your fine male friends.*

"Well, I really wish you'd consult a specialist. I'm sure there are excellent ones in the city. Shall I look into it?"

"No, I will." *I'd sooner be dragged over red-hot rocks than give you a child. I won't be your brood mare.*

Since the nightmare experience in the private railroad car last fall, she had at least been spared further brutality. Without actually apologizing, Bill said his behavior that night was due to the tensions of the wedding, and an excess of champagne, which always induced a bad reaction. A month later he told her he would be more comfortable in a separate bedroom, and he assumed she would be also. When he had needs, or was impatient for her to conceive, he visited her for an hour. He hadn't hurt her even slightly since that first night. Yet he still could intimidate her with his eyes, because she knew the furies that could rise behind his composed, rather ordinary face.

Her hand moved back and forth, stroking Rudy. The oval-cut diamond of her engagement ring glittered. *How do I approach him about the new problem? How do I even begin?*

For an hour before breakfast she'd worked to stiffen her nerve, telling herself the matter was too important to ignore. Then the tug of depression would undermine that conviction. The depression was powerful and sly. She personified it as a predatory animal crouching in a corner of her soul, waiting to attack when she was weakest.

She slipped her hand in the pocket of her robe. Touched the notepaper. She took strength from it. She mustn't let the matter pass.

"Listen to this damned nonsense," Elstree said. He shook the paper to show his displeasure. Below the massive marble rail of the terrace, the pruning shears of Henry Prince clicked away. Henry Prince was a Shinnecock Indian; a short, stout man with black curly hair and a nose and mouth suggesting a Negro ancestor or two. He had been born Prince Henry, a tribal name, but had decided long ago that reversing the names would make him more acceptable to wealthy employers. Henry lived out by the Shinnecock Reservation with his wife and two boys. Unlike most of the other Indian cabins scattered in the pine flats, Henry's property was free of weeds and broken windowpanes.

Elstree read aloud. " 'The reign of the Nero of the nineteenth century, King Weyler the First, must be ended at all hazards.' Isn't that a lot of damned rot?" He threw the paper on the green wicker table. Henry's broad brown face appeared between the marble balusters, on a level with Julie's slippers decorated with silver thread. Henry gave her a wink and a smile. Among a staff of twenty-two, he was her only friend. She sometimes went by herself, in a buggy, to take a hamper of food to his family. She went when Bill was at one of his clubs or staying in town. She knew he wouldn't approve.

Elstree reached for his cup, expecting it to be full; it was. She said, "Who were you quoting, Bill?"

"Joe Wheeler, the Reb cavalry general. He was one of the last to give up after Appomattox. He's been in Congress for years. Represents some district of wool hats and rednecks down in Alabama. I've always thought him one of the more sensible politicians from that part of the world. Until this."

"Weyler is the governor of Cuba?"

"Yes. I'm a Republican but by God I don't support intervention in Cuba. Let Weyler hang all the revolutionaries and peasants down there, who cares? If we listen to Wheeler and the other jingoes—if we interfere—we'll be in a damn war that would be catastrophic for business. Drown us in blood. Blood happens to be the same color as red ink."

Julie was sadly amused by his ferocity. William Vann Elstree III took no active role in management of the family stores, merely spent the enormous income generated by them. Yet he liked to pose as the field general who designed the chain's grand strategy. On their wedding night he'd called her a fraud. He was no less of one.

Julie's hand crept to her pocket again. Her mouth was dry. The strong coffee set her stomach churning. Henry Prince's shears clicked on as he worked his way toward the end of the terrace. Two other men were thatching the green lawn with rakes.

Elstree looked closely at his wife. "You didn't hear half of what I said about Joe Wheeler. What's wrong, pray?"

The folded notepaper in her pocket burned hotter than her fear. She glanced behind her. The serving girl had gone inside.

"Bill, who is the person who uses the letter *R* as a signature?"

"I'm afraid I don't know what you—"

She took out the paper and held it up. The abrupt movement sent Rudy bounding off her lap. "I found this note signed *R*. The handwriting is a woman's. The note confirms a time for supper at Rector's in town." Elstree stared. Her courage, not great to begin with, rapidly shrank. "I presume the note's yours. The servants can't afford Rector's."

"Where did you find that?"

"On the floor beside the liquor stand in the library. Dropped accidentally, I imagine."

"Please give it to me." He held out his hand and snapped his fingers. "Please."

"Am I not entitled to an explanation?"

"No. Give it to me, Juliette. Now."

The best she could do to show her anger was to drop the note on the table between them. Elstree's chair creaked as he snatched the note and stood up.

"Bill, are you seeing someone in New York?"

"You have no right to ask me a question like that."

"I think I have every right. I'm your wife."

He walked around the table and put his soft, manicured hand on her shoulder, gently. It terrified her.

"My dear, understand this. Men are men, with well-defined rights and privileges. Wives are expected to make allowances."

"I see. Is this what they're calling a double standard, Bill?"

"I don't know what they're calling it, sweet. I know it's the way I live, and I don't propose to change."

"Well, you'd better, Bill, or I—"

Elstree's smile chilled her to silence. He closed his hand on her left wrist firmly enough to hurt. He bent to her left ear as if to kiss it. "Don't threaten me. Don't you ever threaten me. I live my life as I please. You're my wife, you'll inherit my money, what else do you want?"

Then he kissed her on the cheek. "After bridge I'll be taking a train into town. If you need me tonight, it's the Princeton Club, as usual."

"Will they take a message while you're at Rector's?"

He dropped his pale hands to his sides. With a terrifying stare but perfect politeness, he said, "Goodbye, dear." And stalked off without a backward look.

Julie went up to her room, locked the door, turned off the two electric lamps with fringed and pleated shades, closed the drapes, and lay in bed past noon.

Belle Mer was a forty-room house, copied by its architect from a French country palace. Julie and her husband had been in residence since early June. After their honeymoon on the estate last fall, they'd wintered in Elstree's townhouse in Chicago. In January and February they were in Palm Beach. In June Elstree's private railroad car brought them from Chicago to Long Island.

Of all the places, Julie preferred Long Island. She loved the rough moorlands running east to Montauk. The wind-twisted trees, the ponds, the grazing sheep and cattle, the tar-paper huts of the fishermen, the small unpainted clapboard houses of the potato farmers. The farther you traveled in the direction of land's end, the more lonely and barren the prospect became. The wind and sky, the bluffs and beaches so empty and primitive, mirrored her loneliness. A dilapidated windmill stood at Montauk, its vanes slowly turning in the sea wind. You might have thought yourself in the Old World, where trolls hid in deep woods and princesses died of unrequited love . . .

Southampton Village, the center of Southampton Township, was altogether different. It was social and snobbish. The first of the moneyed elite had moved there around 1875. Members of that founding group who were still alive considered themselves quite special. Mrs. Goodhue Livingston of Old Trees, for example. She had a small coterie of female friends of similar status and longevity in the community. People called them the Dreadnaughts, and it was apt. Like gray battleships, they ruled the social seas and patrolled for interlopers. On the one occasion Julie had been invited to tea by Mrs. Livingston, the old lady said to her, "If you can get past the foul-smelling duck farms at Riverhead and Quogue, and the equally noxious Tammany Democrats who've built at Hampton Bays, this is really quite a little paradise we have here. We intend to keep it that way, for ourselves."

Julie quickly understood that she didn't belong to the charmed circle, and might never. She was the daughter of a man named Pork, whose Connecticut origins had been forgotten and whose credentials were not yet recognized in the

East. For Bill it was different. He mingled easily and was accepted by other clubmen and their wives, some of whom had roots in Chicago. Julie supposed her rejection was in part caused by her age, or perhaps by the air of sadness she feared she projected without wanting to. As she sank deeper inside herself, it really didn't seem to matter.

When the Elstrees had returned from Palm Beach in March, Nell had called on her daughter at least twice a week. She gushed over the splendor of the Elstree townhouse. She praised Julie's decision to marry such a fine man. Nell's step was energetic during these visits, her eyes bright as a bird's at a feeder overflowing with seed. Julie had made her extremely happy. Julie had restored her health. And Julie's unbound hair—oh, how glorious that was! Nell took it as a symbol of her daughter's newfound appreciation of all her mother had done for her. Willful children did come to their senses, didn't they?

Nell's happy state was briefly disturbed when Pork had his accident in late March. At the packing plant, he took a tumble on a floor slippery with blood and broke his ankle. Forced to lie at home for two weeks, he conducted business from his bed and complained endlessly. He returned to work sooner than Dr. Woodrow wished, and the ankle failed to heal properly. He resorted to a crutch and installed an inclined stair elevator at the mansion on Prairie Avenue; seated on it, he could ride up and down the great central staircase in relative comfort. He continued to complain.

Pork was slow to heal; still hobbling when the Elstree servants packed forty-six crates, cartons, valises, and hatboxes for the couple's summer sojourn at Belle Mer. Nell wept when Julie said goodbye. "Caring for your father is such a burden. As if I don't have enough of them already."

Still, she didn't forget her daughter. Hardly a week passed without some expensive little gift arriving on Long Island by express. A stuffed bird; a brooch; a gold box for pins. Tokens of a mother's regard for a child who had finally seen the beacon light of duty.

Julie followed a screening hedge of bayberry near the inland edge of the property. It was early afternoon. During the time she lay in her dark bedroom, the sun had broken through, although it had a peculiar yellow cast, more like autumn than summer. The first mosquitoes were out, clouding around her neck and face.

On the other side of the hedge she heard a small motor running. She passed through a break in the bayberry, knocked and stepped inside the shed building. It smelled of soil and mold and the menhaden fertilizer sold in coarse bags by the factory across the Island. Henry Prince looked up from the wheel on which he was sharpening his shears.

"Henry, will you drive me to Montauk? I'd be grateful for the company."

"Ready in five minutes, Mrs. Elstree."

Though Henry always maintained proper decorum with his employer's wife, he and Julie were close, for reasons neither had ever expressed. Indeed, Julie couldn't fully explain it to herself. She just found Henry's broad face and flat nose and dark brown eyes likable, and the man himself trustworthy.

Henry drove the little buggy east along dirt roads that became more narrow and rutted every mile. They plunged into Hither Woods, a woods so deep and overgrown, she half expected to see the trolls she'd imagined.

But the destination, Montauk Point, was worth the struggle. Henry tied the buggy at the foot of the slope crowned by the hundred-foot-high lighthouse. As he packed his corncob pipe he said, "I'll wait here if you want to roam awhile."

"Yes, I do." Julie clambered down. The sea roared loudly. Her long hair tossed and snapped around her shoulders. A northeast wind had come up, pushing black cloud banks ahead of it. Westward, the sun was all but hidden in summer haze. The kerosene-oil light in the lighthouse was flashing.

"Might be a nasty storm there," Henry said with a nod seaward. "The roads will be mire if it rains."

"I'll only walk a little while," Julie promised, and ran up the hill. The wind off the Atlantic almost tore her shawl from her shoulders.

Circling the lighthouse, she saw the keeper high above. He waved to her; she waved back. She leaned against the eastern side of the lighthouse, gazing at the wild waves foaming and crashing.

Julie knew she wasn't one of the so-called new women who defiantly proclaimed one standard, and only one, for both sexes. She was married. Not happily, but she'd spoken the vows. Still, she could come here, to the lonely light where the wind moaned and the waves burst into huge white fans of spray, and she could speak the truth in her heart.

Paul, I love you. I'll never love anyone else, no matter whose name I bear. God as my witness, I'll escape from this maze I walked into because of my own cowardice. It may take months, or years, but escape I will.

And then I'll find you.

About once a month Julie visited her uncle in the city. I.W. Vanderhoff lived in baronial splendor in a four-story townhouse on upper Fifth Avenue, where telephone and telegraph lines spiderwebbed the sky above the street and farmers drove herds of pigs to market amid the hack and carriage traffic.

Uncle Ike was a scarecrow, an old tosspot and womanizer, but Julie warmed to his very lack of respectability. "I wouldn't fit in with that snotty crowd," he said in reference to Southampton. "Two glasses of bubbly and I'd pinch some old dowager's bottom."

Julie played rummy with Uncle Ike. His card sense nearly always defeated her. So the game proceeded somewhat by rote, simultaneously with conversation. During a game in late July, Uncle Ike scratched his beetlike nose and said, "Juliette, how's this fellow of yours? Does he make you happy?"

"Uncle Ike, will you discard?"

"I gather that means he don't." Uncle Ike had never quite forgotten his country origin. He was so magnificently rich, he could flaunt it. He liked that.

"Bill Elstree's quite the clubman," he went on. "Bit of a rake in days gone by."

"Play," Julie said.

Uncle Ike cocked his head, taken aback. "My, this ain't the Juliette I used to know. You sound hard, child."

"Things change, Uncle Ike. People change. That's all I care to say. Will you please play?"

□ □ □ □

That was one of the rare days. A day when she felt secure and confident; possessed of a measure of that courage Paul always said she had within herself, if only she'd reach down and find it.

But then there were the other days. The days of female complaint, when savage pains drove her to bed. The days when she thought fearfully of Bill and the violence latent within him. Days when the bestial darkness crouched in its corner, waiting to leap and devour whatever scrap of contentment she'd found . . .

Amid a run of the dark days, she saw Aunt Willis again.

It was early August. Elstree had left for the race meeting at Saratoga. "Telegraph me at the Grand Union Hotel in case of emergency. I'll be away two, perhaps three weeks."

Julie wondered whether R might also be registered at the Grand Union. She'd considered hiring a detective to follow Bill, in hopes of discovering R's identity. Then she decided that she really didn't want to know.

Elstree's trip to the Monte Carlo of America turned out to be well timed. It allowed Julie to see Aunt Willis in New York without risking a confrontation between her aunt and Bill. They met in Willis's suite at the Waldorf and rode in a hansom to Delmonico's for luncheon.

Willis was bone-thin and grayer, but otherwise unchanged. She was full of enthusiasm for her new passion, collecting art. "I've chanced on a wonderful painter named Claude. Claude calls himself an impressionist. It's a curious term, but it defines his work exactly. Some of my tasteless friends say Claude paints with dribbles and dabbles and dots. What of it? The work's beautiful, very evocative. I've bought three paintings and I'm negotiating on a fourth. They'll never be worth anything, but I don't care."

She spoke of her longtime friend Miss Clara Barton, who had founded and still headed the American Red Cross. Six years ago, Willis had rushed to the flooded coast of South Carolina in the wake of a killer hurricane, there joining Miss Barton's relief contingent. She'd worked for days on skimpy rations and little sleep, until fever overcame her.

"If there's a Cuban war, Clara swears she'll go," Willis told her niece. "The woman is seventy-six years old, I've never seen such grit and stamina. She said she'll take volunteers. 'Well, here I am,' I said to her. *Cuba libre!*" Willis whacked the table so forcefully, the maître d' rushed to see if one of his waiters had dropped something.

Willis examined her niece critically. "You're peaked, Juliette."

"I suppose I stay indoors too much."

"No taste for the beach out there?"

"Not really. I walk a lot, but mostly on dark days."

"Dark days. I see."

At Julie's suggestion they ordered a house specialty, Long Island duckling. The waiter brought a silver stand and opened a green bottle of Riesling that Willis had selected. From her reticule Willis drew a small package wrapped in silver foil. "Mr. Kipling's latest. *Captains Courageous.* You must read it."

"Thank you, I will, I have plenty of time. Bill's playing cards and betting on horses at Saratoga for a few weeks."

Her aunt squinted through smoke rising from her little cheroot. "You're not getting on with him, are you?"

Julie's impulse was to deny it and spare herself a long, probably pointless discussion. Then she recalled the silent vow she'd made at the lighthouse. She'd never be able to resolve her problem if she hid it forever.

"No, I'm not. I think there's another woman." She described finding the note signed *R*.

Willis sighed. "Dear me." She reached across to clasp Julie's hand. "I know the discovery must have hurt you terribly. Are you absolutely sure about it?"

"When I confronted Bill with the note, he refused to tell me her name, but he didn't bother with a denial. He said men and women live by different standards, and I had to accept it."

"Oh, that old cant. Please pay attention to what I'm going to say. You are *not* required to suffer simply because he gave you that huge diamond and dragged you in front of a parson to repeat a few trite words. I recommend that you find the evidence against him. Hire a good lawyer. One who will know detectives to put on the case. That's the best advice I can give you. No matter what it costs, in cash or stress on your nerves, divorce the cheating bastard. He doesn't deserve a fine person like you."

Julie toyed with her salad fork. "It's easy to talk about it. People do divorce, but it's always a scandal and a disgrace."

"It would be much more of a scandal and disgrace for my sister than for you. And you'd get your freedom. Besides, people soon forget."

Julie was silent. Willis squeezed her hand again. "You have perfect justification, child. And you have the courage, if you'll only use it."

Julie's face clouded with an odd look, very much like that of a child contemplating something both appealing and frightening. "That's what Paul said."

"Paul. He's the boy you loved?"

"Paul Crown. Yes. I still love him."

"Where is he?"

"I don't know."

"What are you going to do?"

"I don't know," she repeated with a forlorn shrug. The dark mood was lowering. Julie wondered whether it was a condition one of those new alienists could treat and cure. How she wished it were. How she wished for so many things . . .

"Will you be staying long in New York?" she asked.

"I'm sailing back to England Tuesday. I have met this young musician. A cellist. Half my age, but he gives the most incredible performances with his instrument."

Julie looked at her aunt to see if she'd made a lewd joke. Aunt Willis's face might have been cast out of concrete.

"In the concert hall, child. The concert hall. Whatever did you think I meant?" Then she winked.

□　□　□　□

The next time Julie played rummy with Uncle Ike, she said, "Do you know any lawyers here in the city?"

"I know the usual weasels, vultures, and bloodsuckers, you bet. Why?"

"Could you put me in touch with one who handles divorce?"

"Divorce? Honey, that's dirty business. You have to catch the other party with his suspenders down, right while he—"

"Yes, I know that. I need a lawyer who won't object to soiling his hands."

After a long silence and a keen look, I.W. said, "See what I can do."

At her next visit, he had a name for her. Rubin Silverjack, Esquire; office on lower Fifth Avenue. She was seated in Silverjack's consultation chair by the end of the week.

Rubin Silverjack, Esquire, resembled a sincere and pious priest. He was in his forties, conservatively dressed. Julie felt Uncle Ike had made a terrible mistake until she looked closely at Silverjack's fiery black eyes.

Silverjack leaned back in a well-oiled swivel chair and tented the tips of his fingers together. "Please relax, Mrs. Elstree. This discussion will be entirely confidential."

"Thank you." Julie's mouth was dry as sand.

"You say you believe your husband is committing adultery with another woman."

"I have good reason to believe that, yes. He—" Shame put scarlet in her cheeks. She forced herself to go on. "He also hurt me physically on one occasion."

"Please describe that. If it isn't too trying."

Haltingly, she did. Silverjack reached into a waistcoat pocket. A gold toothpick gleamed. He hid his mouth with his left hand while he worked the toothpick. When she finished, he said, "Were you badly hurt?"

"Yes. I was frightened for my life."

Silverjack meditated a moment. "I'm afraid that will do you no good, except to give you the determination to go ahead. The divorce law in New York State, as in practically every other state, is narrow and explicit. Outrageously one-sided, in the husband's favor, I might add. Only if there's a provable adulterous relationship with another woman do you have grounds. Were you aware of all this?"

"No." She could barely be heard.

"You will need to catch your husband in a compromising situation. That's often a costly and very time-consuming procedure, though I have excellent connections for arranging surveillance."

"How long do you estimate it would take?"

"It might take a week, or a year." Julie was stricken. She didn't want to wait so much as a day. She feared her husband. She covered her eyes. Just as her hope was vanishing, Silverjack said, "There is, however, a second way."

He reached to a lower drawer and handed her a clean white handkerchief. He must have a supply for distraught clients. The gold toothpick reappeared while she blew her nose and dabbed her cheeks dry. The twisting motion of Silverjack's right wrist was snaky, vaguely indecent.

"You may keep the handkerchief, Mrs. Elstree. I know this is trying, I'll be as brief as I can. There are certain females willing to accept money for going on the witness stand and enacting the role of the other woman. They're willing to perjure themselves and testify that they have slept with the husband. They are expert at giving particulars. The judge knows it's a charade but it permits him to favor the wife. The husband knows it's a charade but it's his word against that of the witness, who is well coached to withstand badgering during cross-examination. There are two women in particular whom I employ. Both are actresses with —shall we say troubled histories? Each can convey injury, wrath, whatever the scenario demands. I beg you not to look so shocked, Mrs. Elstree. The strategy is used again and again to rescue wives from intolerable marriages. It works. Until the statutes are reformed, nothing else will."

Again he leaned back, fingertips together. "I also know a few judges. That helps."

"Mr. Silverjack, are you saying that in order to be free—"

Hand upraised, he stopped her. "To be free in the quickest and most expeditious way."

"But you're saying I have to break the law."

"Become an accessory to fraud. Yes."

"No, I can't possibly, I—"

And then she thought again of that night, her wedding night, riding the *Pride of Petoskey* to New York. She remembered Bill's striking her repeatedly. Holding her in a grip that left bruises on her body for weeks. The longer she delayed, the greater her risk . . . and her suffering.

"All right, Mr. Silverjack," she whispered. "Do whatever's necessary. I put the case in your hands."

"Thank you for your confidence, Mrs. Elstree." Rubin Silverjack's eyes were alight with excitement. He no longer looked like a gentle priest. He looked like some eager and gloating prelate from the Spanish Inquisition.

She rushed back to Uncle Ike's townhouse in a hansom cab. She was feeling jubilant. "He took the case!" She flung an arm around I.W.'s neck and kissed him. "Thank you."

"Want to play some cards to celebrate?"

"I would love that."

In the middle of their last game, the telephone in the next room gave its loud ring, something like a combination of a fire bell and a ratchet. Uncle Ike jumped up. "Be right back."

Five minutes later he returned, obviously shaken. "That was the long-distance wire. Your mother. The way I get it, your pa was riding that stair elevator up to his room to take a nap. The mechanism jammed and threw him off the seat. He fell down twenty steps. He's in a coma. He may not live."

At seven-ten in the morning on the fifteenth day after his accident, Mason Putnam Vanderhoff III died. He had never regained consciousness.

The long death watch had been a time of anguish for Julie. She sat at her father's bedside every day. He never woke; never recognized her. Even prepared for his death, she was overcome with grief when Dr. Woodrow pulled the bed sheet over Pork's face. She and Nell were standing at the foot of the bed. "I'm so sorry," the doctor said. Nell began screaming and pounding the footboard with her fists.

Julie mourned for her father even as she rehearsed the initial steps of her escape from her husband. Before she left for Chicago, she'd telephoned Silverjack to explain what had happened and to tell him to go ahead with any arrangements he needed to make.

"Shall I file the complaint?"

"I want to tell my husband first."

"That isn't your responsibility, Mrs. Elstree. Considering what you said about him, I'd advise you against it."

"Mr. Silverjack, it's something I must do myself."

"As you wish."

Nell was inconsolable and barely coherent whenever Julie tried to speak with her. In its way, her mother's distraught state was a blessing. It was as if an extra obstacle big as a boulder had been rolled out of Julie's path.

Alone in her bedroom in the Chicago townhouse, she slept fitfully the night before the burial. And at St. James Church she scarcely heard the Episcopal priest deliver a forty-five minute eulogy to her father. Over four hundred had gathered to listen. The Palmers and the Armours, the Swifts and the Pullmans, the Fields and the McCormicks, and all the lesser kings of Chicago commerce.

It rained all the way out to Graceland, a prestigious cemetery stretching north from Irving Park Road to Montrose; here Chicago's notables could be buried among their peers. Julie rode with her husband in his clarence, the largest and most expensive of his four vehicles. It had cost almost four thousand dollars. He'd chosen it for the funeral because it was finished entirely in black lacquer, except for a delicate horizontal stripe of dark gray.

Elstree kept his arm around Julie, murmuring condolences she hardly heard. Her stomach ached. Her head hurt. She vowed not to weaken. She had set today as the day to speak, and she meant to be free.

The cortege entered Graceland Cemetery from North Clark Street. At the grave Nell sobbed uncontrollably as the priest prayed over the ostentatious coffin. With its silver finish and rose bosses, the coffin struck Julie as feminine. It had been selected by her mother in a moment of semi-lucidity. Pork would have hated it.

Julie wondered what Nell would do when she learned of her decision. Fall ill again? Disown her, probably. No matter; she didn't want a penny of her father's fortune. Or Bill's. Only freedom, and Paul.

Uncle Ike put his arm around her as the coffin disappeared into the grave. He smelled of gin. He stepped over to Nell, leading her away like a father comforting a shattered child. Elstree touched Julie's sleeve. "Come," he said softly.

Julie's stomach throbbed and burned. Her face was pale as eggshell behind her black veil. The coachman held a black umbrella over them as they went up a slippery path to the line of hearses and carriages.

The door of the clarence closed with a firm, solid sound. Julie leaned back and shut her eyes a moment. Elstree began, "You bore up splendidly, dear. I know how trying—"

"Bill. Bill," she repeated, in a whisper. She flung herself around to face him. If she waited, hesitated, she was lost.

"Bill, I'm leaving you. I want a divorce."

He stared at her. Stared long and hard. Her hands started to tremble.

The traces jingled; the clarence lurched forward on the graveled cemetery road. Elstree laid his black topper on his knee and peeled off his black gloves. "Have you discussed this with a lawyer?"

"Yes. In New York. Rubin Silverjack is his name. He specializes in cases like mine. I mean to be free, Bill."

"I'll reply to that with one word. Never. Whatever your reasons, your objections to this marriage—never."

"Please, Bill, have the decency to be honest. You consort with other women, that's no secret."

"I don't deny it," he said agreeably.

"Then think of how you've treated me, since the very day we were married."

"Treated you very handsomely, I should say."

He reached out to grasp both her hands in his large, strong left hand. Somehow, clamped around her black gloves, his hand reminded her of a white spider. She wanted to hit it. Hit him . . .

"Divorce is something I simply won't contemplate. In our circle it ruins a man's reputation. When a wife files, it insults and demeans the husband, because it brands him an adulterer. Publicly. You don't understand the way society works. One can do anything so long as it's private. I'll block you at every step, Julie."

"There are ways around it. I'll use them, I swear."

"Julie, Julie," he said. "How old are you?"

"I was twenty in May, you know that."

"And I'm twice that, and more."

"You remind me of it often enough."

"To remind you of my greater experience. The wisdom that comes with years. Let me call on that now, to forestall this crisis. Let me advise you. Forget this scummy attorney. Forget you ever uttered the word 'divorce.'"

"But I don't love you, Bill."

"Whatever does that have to do with it?" His smile was puzzled, almost boyish. "If you persist with this behavior, I'll commit you to an institution. All it takes is my word. My signature on a few papers drawn up by my attorneys and certified by cooperative physicians. I can do it in a day if you force me. Mental institutions are hell holes, even the finest of them. I'd be sad if you made me send you away. But I'll do it."

The clarence creaked through the rain, falling harder now; the world outside was hidden. "Bill, that's horrible. Cruel. You smile and say things like that—what kind of man are you?"

"Why, a concerned man. A husband. Until such time, if any, that I decide otherwise."

"So you can be free anytime you want, but I can't?"

"You understand perfectly," he said with a benign smile.

She fell back against the maroon plush cushion, sick with defeat. Elstree slipped his arm around her, held her tighter than necessary, letting her feel the dangerous power in his arm.

"Really, now, it's best that you collect yourself. You must be composed for the reception at home, your poor mother can't handle the many callers without your help. We'll say no more about this. We'll forget it completely. I'm sure you didn't mean a word of it. It's been a trying, trying day."

81

Shadow

THE BRIEF and polite letter from the Edison Manufacturing Company of West Orange, New Jersey, asked Colonel Shadow to call on the inventor at his estate, Glenmont, within sixty days. There was a promise of "business news you will find highly important," but no explanation. The signature was that of Mrs. M. Edison. Shadow had read that the inventor and his second wife worked closely together, supervising Edison's various enterprises and subcorporations.

Shadow didn't make the trip until the deadline had almost expired. The reason for his procrastination was fear. Thomas Edison was a worldwide legend, worshiped by schoolchildren and virtually awarded sainthood by the press. He was the "Wizard," the self-taught genius who had lit America with his incandescent lamp, his power systems to deliver that light over wide areas, and his manufacturing techniques to make the light bulb cheap and easy to produce. In 1877 his astounding phonograph had brought all manner of sounds from a revolving cylinder. He had dozens of patents on communications devices ranging from telegraph instruments to stock tickers. He belittled his own amazing creativity with a saying of his own devising. "Genius is one percent inspiration and ninety-nine percent perspiration."

He was, in short, a man to make the spine weaken, the knees quiver, and the brain reduce itself to something resembling fruit preserves. Shadow delayed as long as he dared. Then he brushed up his best clothes, packed a valise, put on his sombrero, and kissed Mary goodbye as if for the last time.

Two days later he arrived at the front door of Glenmont, a mansion with a great stone veranda, innumerable chimneys and roof gables. It was situated on ten or twelve gorgeously wooded acres in the Llewellyn Park section of West Orange, allowing Edison easy travel back and forth to his plant. Shadow guessed the house must have twenty or thirty rooms.

He'd hardly slept last night, rolling around in his bed at a cheap hotel. Shaving, he'd nicked himself twice with his straight razor and stanched the blood only after heavy applications of styptic. His hair was pomaded, his cheeks were lightly powdered, and his heart was pounding like hell.

When he rang the bell, multiple chimes sounded inside. He was admitted by an English butler, who took his card.

He waited beneath a glittering chandelier. Directly in front of him rose a mammoth staircase. At the first landing, where it divided, multicolored light streamed in through stained glass. In a matter of a minute or two, he counted seven other servants running about. He was awed by the opulence. Also shamelessly jealous.

The butler returned. He ushered Shadow to a large corner sunroom and said Mr. and Mrs. Edison would join him shortly.

The room was hot; many large windows let in the sun. Large and small green plants in clay pots crowded all but the very center of the room. When Shadow sat down in one of several comfortable chairs, he was startled by a pair of eyes regarding him malevolently. The eyes were glass, in the stuffed head of a fanged tiger whose skin had been stretched for a rug. With the toe of his boot Shadow pushed the head to one side so that the tiger was looking at something else.

A maid came in rolling an elaborate wooden tea cart with a silver service and bone china cups. She lifted a silver dome to show him a plate of tiny sandwiches with the crust trimmed from the bread and invited him to help himself. Before she left, she straightened the rug. The tiger was staring again.

The Edisons kept him waiting only a few minutes. Mrs. Edison came in first. She was a pleasant, stout woman of middle years who shook his hand firmly and said, "Hello, Colonel, I am Mina Edison. This is my husband Thomas."

And there he was, the famous Wizard with the rumpled suit, familiar white hair, and pug-dog face. Shadow's hand shot out as if propelled by a piston.

"An honor, sir. If I might say—the greatest honor of my life."

"Yes, thank you," Edison said diffidently; no doubt he'd heard it thousands of times during his fifty years. "Please sit." He had a loud, raspy voice.

Mrs. Edison took a chair between Shadow and her husband. "Tea, Colonel? We import it from London."

"Very fine, thank you," said Shadow; he hated the stuff.

"Milk or sugar?"

"Any way you want to fix it, ma'am." Mrs. Edison gave him a puzzled look, then added a dollop of milk and a half teaspoon of sugar. "I hope this is satisfactory."

Shadow sipped the nauseating drink. "Ambrosia." He didn't know how he'd choke down the rest.

Abruptly, Edison said, "Mina will sit with us in case I have trouble hearing or understanding you." Every American who could read knew the story of Edison's deafness. As an enterprising boy of twelve, a regular little Horatio Alger type, he was a candy butcher on Grand Trunk Railway trains shuttling around Michigan. One day he was trying to reboard a train with a stack of papers to sell in the aisles along with his candy, peanuts, and other oddments. The train was departing. He had no hand free. He yelled for help. From the platform of the last car a conductor pulled him aboard. By the ears. Soon he was suffering headaches. Then came a slight deafness, which gradually increased, though as Shadow understood it,

Edison still had partial hearing. At least he didn't walk around waving a damn ear trumpet.

Edison laced his hands and rested them on his dark gray vest. He had a slight paunch. The suit he wore was fine goods. "You may be perfectly candid in Mina's presence," he said.

"Thank you, sir."

"I am a plain man, Colonel. I was born in one plain town, Milan, Ohio, and raised in another, Port Huron, Michigan. My father was a plain man also. He manufactured shingles. Later he sold grain and feed. My education was received at my mother's knee, and at the reading tables of the Detroit Public Library, between trains. As a lad, my best friends were telegraph operators and railway conductors. Plainness—plainness everywhere. It prevails in my life today. I have my work, my wife and six children, my reading, an occasional walk in the woods. All I need. Here too, we live plainly."

Oh yes? Shadow thought. *I wish I lived in a palace this "plain," you fucking fraud.*

Edison sipped a little tea from the cup Mina handed him. "I will be plain while speaking with you, Colonel."

"Delighted, sir. It's always the best way."

"You may not think so when you hear my message."

Shadow sat absolutely still.

"Mina, I can hear him adequately. You may leave us. Please thank Cook for the refreshments."

She bowed out without a word. Double doors were rolled shut. Shadow felt compelled to seize the initiative, otherwise he might be sitting here till dark. "Your letter mentioned business, sir. Is it about the flickers I produce? Have you by chance seen them?"

"I have not. I have heard about them." Edison's face and rough voice revealed nothing. "I invited you here for a friendly discussion of the picture business in general. Are you a rich man, Colonel?"

Startled, Shadow said, "Not yet, sir. But I have hopes."

For the first time Edison smiled.

"Well, if you continue to use elements of my designs in your projectors, you can forget your hopes, because the American National Luxograph Company will cease to exist." From an inner coat pocket he whipped out a blue-covered document. "I present you with a complaint which will be filed in the federal court. I am suing you, your partners, distributors, employees, heirs and assigns, on fourteen counts of infringement of the patents of the Edison Manufacturing Company.

Shadow sat there with his mouth open as wide as the stuffed tiger's.

"You stole my designs, Colonel. The designs on which I collaborated with Mr. Thomas Armat."

"No, no, Mr. Edison! I don't know Armat. I consulted with his partner Charlie Jenkins, that's all."

"Consulted? And he allowed you to become privy to every last detail of his work? Somehow I doubt that, sir. However, the particulars of your thievery don't concern me, only the result. I have entered into a business arrangement with

Thomas Armat, who is, as you say, the partner of Mr. Jenkins. Therefore you have stolen from Armat, from me, and from the Edison companies."

Shadow had a sudden and painful urge to go to the toilet. He turned the brim of his sombrero rapidly in his hands. "You really mean to take me to court?"

"Yes, and you'll be left with nothing, my lawyers will see to it. They have wiped out stronger men than you. You shouldn't have threatened my position of leadership in a prestigious and expanding field."

"For God's sake, sir, can't we settle this some other way?"

For the second time, Edison smiled.

"Why, yes, of course we can. That's why I invited you to discuss matters in person. We can settle it out of court if you agree to pay me a royalty on every projector you sell or lease, and every cent you take in from your films. These amounts will be subject to verification by my auditors. I will have the absolute right to examine your books at any time. Shall we get out our pencils and do some figuring, like gentlemen?"

Shadow mumbled, "I don't have a pencil."

Edison reached to another inside pocket. "Here. I always carry two at meetings like this."

The light waned and the shadows of the potted plants grew long. They negotiated for over two hours. Shadow felt he would have a terrible accident if he didn't get to the water closet soon. Mercifully, Edison said:

"We're finished. Thank you, sir. My attorneys will draw the necessary papers for signature."

Shadow jumped to his feet; a mistake which severely agitated his bloated bladder. "You're a hard bargainer, Mr. Edison."

"Yes, but this way you'll stay in business and you'll prosper. Honesty is always the best policy. When you are dealing with the Edison Manufacturing Company, it is the only policy, because the alternative is bankruptcy."

He offered his hand. "Thank you for coming so far to see me. We will go forward together. May I say you have an excellent speaking voice, Colonel. Strong and vibrant. Shall I show you out?"

"I can find my way," Shadow answered. Glassy-eyed, he staggered to the entrance hall, nearly falling over a large Chinese umbrella jar.

"Son of a bitch," he whispered, relative to Mr. Edison as the butler let him out. He ran down the driveway, frantically hunting for a suitable tree.

"Hardfisted, greedy son of a bitch," Shadow muttered, this time as he waited for the local at the depot. "And every God damn schoolboy thinks he's a fucking angel. A kindly old inventor tossing his blessings to the public out of sheer goodness. Jesus."

And what a reversal he'd come upon! For years Edison didn't give a damn about the idea of a flicker projector, and said so. Now you'd think he'd invented the business, just because certain segments of the public would pay to see living pictures. What the Wizard had said and done to him was outrageous. But he wouldn't interfere with Shadow's business now, that much was assured.

Soon Shadow began to smile a little, and then to chuckle. He found himself changing his view of Thomas Alva Edison. The old coot wasn't so bad. Those involved with flickers always said he was a promoter, and they were right. He knew what he wanted, he fought hard for it, but Shadow would have done the same. He decided he and Mr. Edison were alike. Bandits.

Except, of course, Mr. Edison was a fucking genius on top of it.

All those little schoolboys and schoolgirls sighing over pictures of the kindly old inventor leaning his head on his hand would never know the dark side of the truth. Ah, well. Such was life.

82

Fritzi

IN THE LATE SUMMER of 1897, Fritzi's parents took her on a trip to New York State. Papa needed to confer with a businessman in White Plains about opening a Crown agency somewhere in Westchester, and Mama and Papa needed to confer with the headmaster of Carl's school about his poor grades and his football injuries. Not injuries to Carl, but the injuries he inflicted on others when he bucked the line or ran for a touchdown.

Papa installed them in a suite at a resort hotel on the shore of Long Island Sound, near suburban Larchmont. Fritzi begged off from the first day's activities. She assured Mama that she'd behave properly, and saw them off in a rented buggy.

During the morning she sunned herself on the rocks overlooking the Sound. She daydreamed of the magical places and personages hidden in the haze to the southwest. The famous playhouses of New York's Rialto. The matinee idols.

Daydreams were Fritzi's antidote for life in Chicago. She had turned sixteen in January and was still humiliated by a flat bosom. Hardly a day passed that she didn't think of her older brother, and of Paul. She missed them terribly.

In Chicago she had only one beau, a young man she tolerated out of supreme desperation. Miles Pilbeam was his name. He attended her church. His "sport" was checkers. He read calculus texts for enjoyment. Her private name for him was Miles Pea Brain.

Around noon, growing bored, she walked down the shore. The breeze was strong. Waves broke into white water. A few venturesome sailboats pitched steeply into the troughs. She passed a number of run-down residences, then came to a large, rambling white building that reminded her of her own hotel.

Only one person was sitting on the wide veranda, in a rocker. A tiny elderly woman wearing shiny black silk, and a black shawl, and a black scarf tied under her chin. On a plaid lap robe tucked around her legs lay a closed book. She was rocking and gazing at the Sound.

Fritzi minded her manners; smiled and nodded to the old lady. Only when she'd walked twenty feet beyond did the shock hit. She turned and rushed back with a wildly beating heart. She crept up the broad sand-scoured steps as if they led to an altar.

The old lady must have been seventy, or more. But no one who loved the theater could mistake the features, even blurred by age. The strong chin, the popping blue eyes remembered as so lively on stage. Fritzi had read that other famous players called her Duchess, out of respect and fear. She inspired fear now, even though she was just rocking and smiling to herself, perhaps recalling some especially good performance.

"Ma'am? Excuse me."

"Yes, child, what is it?"

"Beg pardon, aren't you"—she clutched the porch pillar, fearing she'd swoon —"Mrs. Drew?"

The old woman was pleased to be recognized. Mrs. John Drew had trod the boards, and managed the Arch Street Theater in Philadelphia, for many years. She was the first woman to operate her own acting company. She was a legend. And here she sat, in Larchmont, small and tired.

"That's correct, my dear. Louisa Drew. What's your name?"

"Fritzi Crown. Frederica."

"Do you live in Larchmont? I live in this hotel. It's for old people. My family placed me here for my own good when I retired." She said it without recrimination.

"I live in Chicago. Oh, but I've seen you on stage. I saw your final tour with Mr. Jefferson, in *The Rivals*."

"Joe," the old woman murmured, smiling. She brushed at her forehead, as if to smooth aside a loose wisp of hair. All of Mrs. Drew's hair was hidden by her shawl; not a strand showed. She kept brushing.

Fritzi held fast to the pillar and managed to say, "I want to be an actress. I want it very much."

"Is that so? Do you have talent?"

"I believe I do. Others would have to judge."

"But you have the desire."

"Oh, yes."

"I don't know how I should advise you in that regard." A frail hand indicated the water. It was a perfect stage gesture—minimal, but it fixed Fritzi's attention, which was its purpose. "Waves and actors. They are so very much alike. They come for a little time, rise to separate heights, and travel with varying speed and force. Then they're gone, unremembered."

Her blue eyes, so bright in her old face, pinned Fritzi like a specimen.

"Do you appreciate what I'm saying?"

"Yes, I do."

"And still you're determined?"

"Very determined."

"Then go forward. It's a profession full of heartbreak, doubt, and betrayal, but noble withal. There's no calling to equal it." She stretched out her hand and touched Fritzi lightly in a sort of benediction. Mrs. Drew's fingertips felt like dry paper.

"Bless you in your endeavor."

The screen door banged open, propelled by a young man in white flannels. The white line of a part exactly bisected his dark hair. His chin was deeply dimpled, his teeth almost perfect. Fritzi judged him to be her age, or a little less. He didn't seem like a boy, though. With his satanic good looks, he more closely resembled a roué in a stage melodrama.

"Mum-mum, are you all right out here? Not too chilly?"

"No, no, fine," Mrs. Drew said. The boy fussed and rearranged her shawl, then the plaid lap robe on which lay the forgotten book. "Miss Fritzi, this is my grandson Jack. He's with me this summer. Jack has done some acting. His mother, my daughter Georgie, is an actress. His father Maurice Barrymore is an actor—"

"Maurice Barrymore? Oh, I've seen him." Fritzi felt she wouldn't remain upright and conscious five more seconds. Maurice Barrymore was worshiped by women for his handsomeness and powerful stage presence. This boy, Jack, nearly matched his father; he too inspired woozy thoughts of D'artagnan, moonlight, stolen kisses.

"Jack, this is Miss Crown. From Chicago."

His dark eyes flashed with contempt for so plain a creature. In a bored voice he said, "Charmed." He picked up Fritzi's hand and kissed it. Then he went back inside the old people's hotel.

Mrs. Drew bid Fritzi good afternoon. If Fritzi's feet touched the pebbled sandy shore on the walk back, she didn't remember. Her path was straight ahead, and clear as a May morning after rain.

Until this day, she'd had doubts aplenty. They were strengthened every time Papa spoke in opposition. But suddenly what Papa believed, what he said about actors and the theater, didn't matter. Joe Junior had left. Cousin Paul had left. If it became necessary—if Papa forced it—she could leave too. After this morning, this magical morning, there was no other course.

83

Joe Junior

HE WORKED HIS WAY west a day, a week, a month at a time. Hard physical labor, outdoors, among ordinary, often illiterate men.

He wore his beard long again, long and thick as a G.A.R. veteran's. His skin was dark tanned leather. Between jobs he knew privation, hunger, homelessness. Yet he thrived; the life agreed with him. The majestic land west of the wheat prairie rewarded him with beauties beyond belief. And with repeated discoveries of a truth: the old human wickedness and cupidity hadn't been left behind by the pioneers.

His hardest work was within himself, and it was constant. The effort to purge himself of painful feelings of loss and anger; of homesickness, and a desire to punish. Some memories he refused to part with. Memories of Fritzi, whose exuberance seen through the lens of distance was no longer annoying but endearing. Burly Carl, who'd forever be stronger than he knew, and infinitely lovable. Cousin Paul, whom Joe Junior had grown to care for nearly as much as he cared for his brother and sister. Strongest of all was his love for his mother. That was why he kept sending her the little tokens of his pilgrimage with no destination. From Denver he dispatched a small sparkling half of a geode in a sturdy wooden box. The expressman adamantly wanted him to mark his name and address on it; at least a general delivery. Just as adamantly, he refused. She'd know the sender.

He hiked and hitched rides on boxcars through the Rockies and the Sierra, descending from the latter into the flat Central Valley of California. He thought it remarkably like Illinois, but enhanced by spectacular mountains behind him and lower, gentler ones ahead. Though sparsely settled, the Central Valley seemed a rich place for crops. He learned that little rain fell, except in a short season in winter, but mechanical irrigation systems were coming into use.

He found wheat growing in the valley of the San Joaquin, presented himself as an experienced hand, and celebrated the Fourth of July by starting the harvest. He worked with migrants like himself, Irishmen, and a large number of Hungarians.

He moved on and spent a few weeks weeding in sugar beet fields so long and wide, the boundaries were lost in haze. Here he encountered dozens of Chinese laborers in straw coolie hats. The only Chinese he'd seen before were in photographs or inside some steamy hell of a laundry in Chicago. Neither he nor the Chinese could understand each other, but they communicated all the same, with laughter and gestures.

Working his way southwest, he was a gandy dancer for a while, tamping new ballast along a spur of the Southern Pacific. At night he shared a coffeepot or a whiskey demijohn with other railroaders. He said he wanted to see Los Angeles. They warned him that working men weren't welcome there if they had pro-union sympathies, as he clearly did. The local Chamber of Commerce and a powerful paper edited by one Colonel Otis were promoting their city as California's union-free haven for business. He continued on anyway.

In Los Angeles he bathed in the Pacific and stood with his arms flung wide, tasting the salt wind from the Orient. He imagined he could smell exotic fragrances from the lands below the horizon.

All during these travels, even as far back as Colorado, if he wasn't too dirty and there was enough money in his jeans to allow him to squander a day, he'd visit a public library. Sit at a table and read for hours. He no longer wasted time on the political theorists to whom Benno had introduced him. He was delving deeper, out of some need he couldn't articulate or even wholly understand. He was trying to read great works, to glean from them great and worthy ideas that might have some application to his rootless life. A life whose purpose, if any, still seemed ill-defined.

He read from the Bible and he read the great English poets. He did it because he wanted to; there was no Joe Crown Senior driving him. No pedantic teacher saying his choices were foolish—*"How can you be so witless, Master Crown? Perhaps you belong in another school."*

The library, any library, was a school he could love. When the librarians didn't order him out because of his wild looks or stink of sweat, he went to school until they locked the doors at night. He began a personal chapbook, nothing more than a cheap school exercise book from a general store. In it he wrote phrases and quotations that seemed to have special depth or importance. Only after some months, one day while he was leafing through the many pencil-scrawled pages, did he realize that a pattern could be detected in the passages he'd chosen.

From the gospel of St. Matthew he'd copied a few words spoken by the master to the third servant in Christ's parable of the talents. The third servant had buried his one talent in the ground for fear of losing it while his master was away. The other two servants invested their talents, which increased. They were praised by the master when he returned. The third servant expected praise and received a rebuke.

From blind John Milton's *Areopagitica* he copied *I cannot praise the fugitive and cloistered virtue, which never sallies forth and sees her adversary.* From Shakespeare's *Measure for Measure,* an admonishment by the Duke: *Thyself and thy belongings are not thine.*

There were others. And he came to understand why he collected them. He wanted to strengthen his courage to protest when he saw some terrible wrong done to common workers, of which he was one. Chicago, Pullman, Benno, his mother, even his repressive father, had together kindled some fire in him. The words written down haphazardly were meant to remind him that genuinely great men of the past, great thinkers, believed such a fire mustn't stay hidden in the dark of the heart but should be brought forth to ignite action and redress wrong.

He released the fire willingly but not without cost. Twice he was badly hurt by beatings, and he was tarred once, near Ventura, when he told an owner he was paying slave wages.

So there were regrets when he ached and bled and could hardly stand after a beating—yes, plenty of regrets then. But there was no regret about heeding the messianic call he heard.

He was, in short, becoming a troublemaker.

Not everywhere. Not on every job. Sometimes it wasn't necessary. Occasionally men were paid fairly, treated decently. In Riverside, in the amazing and colorful orange groves he'd read about, he helped pick the winter crop of Washington navel oranges on the estate of a man named J. M. Chance. He never saw this owner, but the man housed his pickers in spartan but clean barracks, with privies and ample running water, and he fed them well.

Riverside was one of many small towns platted and touted to visitors and speculators in a great Southern California land boom of the 1880s. Promotion of the sale of building lots in these new towns was underwritten by the giant railroads, he came to understand; they hired writers to pen rhapsodic books about California, to lure customers from the East and convince them to settle on "America's Mediterranean Coast." The more settlers, the more business for the railroads.

The boom had largely collapsed, but the towns remained, struggling on. Redlands, like Riverside, was another center of "the groves." It looked surprisingly prosperous, with several business blocks, a large hotel, and a railway, the East San Bernardino Valley line, passing through. Joe Junior knew that many of the recent arrivals in Southern California were from the Midwest; Redlands, he was told, had been developed largely by Chicagoans.

He was in Redlands in the extremely warm summer of 1897. He hired on to pick a crop of the Valencia oranges that ripened in the summer. The large grove belonged to an Englishman with a title. Joe Junior worked among a lot of Mexicans imported from over the border; dark, warm-eyed men who smiled even in the fearsome heat and spoke a musical language he picked up a little at a time. There were a few Chinese too. These Chinese seldom spoke. They never smiled. A Mexican who knew English told Joe Junior the Chinese were at the bottom of the heap, constantly abused. Thousands had been driven out of little Chinatowns all over Southern California because white workers wanted their jobs. White labor hated greaser labor but hated Chink labor even more. Joe Junior saw this when the red-haired freckled boss of the picking crew yanked a ladder out from under a Chinese youth. When the young man hit the ground, the white boss kicked him several times. For God knew what offense.

On his fourth morning in the Redlands grove, Joe Junior discovered dark flecks—some kind of tiny dead insects—in the breakfast gruel brought to the open field where the workers slept, together with blue-enameled pots of coffee already grown cold. He spat out a mouthful of the gruel and protested to the crew boss.

The answer to his complaint was simple and curt. "You don't like the food, pack up. You'll lose the pay posted to your account."

"Even if I quit, you haven't any right to keep—"

"Shut up." The crew boss, a head taller, wrapped a hand around Joe Junior's small wrist. The clasping fingers felt like an iron jail shackle. "You complain any more, we'll have a real hard go, you and me. It won't take much to smear a runt like you all over the ground."

He flung Joe Junior's arm loose. "What are you, some college boy out here on a lark? I seen you writing in that copybook. What's in it?"

"I don't think you'd care for it," Joe Junior said and walked away. He knew this job would end as some others had.

That afternoon the crew boss started abusing another Chinese. God damn slant-eyed son of a bitch, he called the man, whose queue was white where it hung down beneath his conical straw hat.

The crew boss slapped the Chinaman's face, hard. Old and frail as he was, the little fellow fought back. Pumped two determined but feeble punches into the belly of the white man's shirt—just the excuse the crew boss needed. He threw the old man to the ground, seized his pigtail and dragged him a few yards, for the start of what he termed a real hard go.

From the top of his ladder, Joe Junior looked around. Every other picker was bent to his task. The Chinaman wailed as the crew boss kicked and pummeled him. Joe Junior uttered a soft sigh. There was always a wonderful fragrance in the groves. The orange blossoms were gone, but there was still a thick sweetness, because oranges were inevitably crushed underfoot, or surreptitiously broken open with a thumbnail for juice. It was an odor Joe Junior had grown to love. He wished he didn't have to leave it.

I cannot praise the fugitive and cloistered virtue, which never sallies forth . . .

The elderly Chinese screamed louder. There was an audible snap as a bone broke. Joe Junior quickly climbed down from his ladder.

Forty-eight hours later, he walked—stumbled—into a small general store across from the Redlands railway depot. The backs of his hands bore ugly bruises. His lower lip had split open and had stopped bleeding only after he held a rag to it for a long time. His right eye was shut, caked with blood and eye matter. The lid was swollen, the flesh around it dark.

The little store was hot, dusty, silent. Open bins of nails, rakes and hoes in a barrel, burlap sacks of chicken feed in slanting sunbeams from the front window, reminded him of still-life groupings. He tapped his hurt knuckles on the counter, lightly. A small, round-shouldered man with a sour mouth came from the back room.

"I'd like to buy a souvenir. I haven't much money."

The storekeeper cleaned his spotless hands on his spotless white duck apron. "Who did your face that way?"

"A man out at the Dorset groves. He was beating one of the other pickers."

"Beating a white man, or a Chink?"

"Does it matter?"

"Sure does."

"I can't see why."

The storekeeper withdrew slightly from his side of the counter. "Are you one of them red agitators? Seems we get a few more in the groves every season."

"I don't belong to any labor organization, if that's what you mean." *Not yet.*

"You're an Easterner."

"Chicago."

"Same thing. East of the Sierra." He dried his hands on the apron again. "You come out here, buy up our land, and think it gives you a right to tell us how to do everything. Me, I was born in Los Angeles when it was dust and a few adobes. Now it's real estate developments and sight-seeing trains and all you damn Easterners telling us how to do it."

"Maybe you need telling. Maybe you're uncivilized out here."

The storekeeper spat a gob of silvery spit. Joe Junior heard the ting of a hidden spittoon. He should have known this neat man with the neat string tie and thin, oiled, carefully combed hair wouldn't spit on the floor.

"You just keep that up, you'll get hurt again."

"I expect that's true."

"I mean hurt *bad.* The worst. Go to San Francisco, that's where they tolerate your kind. Reds. Now do you want to buy something or not?"

"I want to buy a souvenir for my mother."

"Here's a popular item." From a shelf behind him he took a small replica of an orange crate stenciled with dark blue letters.

SOUVENIR
From the Famous Groves of
REDLANDS CALIFORNIA
"Where the Sun Shines All Year"

"That's candy in the crate," the storekeeper said.

"I wouldn't have guessed real oranges. How much?"

"Fifteen cents."

"That sign on the shelf says ten cents."

"Haven't had time to letter a new one. You want it or don't you?"

Joe Junior paid for the souvenir and walked out. He found the post office, used the desk pen to ink the address on the little crate, then bought a stamp.

"We send a lot of these from here—" The clerk stopped, taking notice of Joe Junior's mauled face. "No sender address?" Joe Junior shook his head.

He wandered over to the depot and sat on the lid of a platform toolbox, enjoying the healing sunshine on his face. He pulled the bedraggled chapbook from the knapsack sewn together from four old bandannas by a kindly farmer's wife near Merced. Leafing through the pages, he wondered if the writers of these various passages knew how hard it was to follow advice, not merely dispense it. He felt weary and defeated then; and it didn't help when the stationmaster stepped outside and ran him off.

He walked out of Redlands at dusk, heading north.

84

Paul

PAUL WISHED Jimmy would make good on his threats to quit. Sharing a room with him had never been pleasant, but now it was an acute strain. Jimmy knocked about at all hours; occasionally he brought in a girl. On those nights, Paul's salvation was a bed sheet partition he and Jimmy had rigged on a wire.

In countless small ways, Jimmy continued to show his dislike of Paul: Paul's quickness of mind, his willingness to work, his zeal to master every part of the business. Shadow didn't help matters. He never bothered to conceal his increasing regard for Paul, and usually introduced Paul as his assistant while Jimmy remained "my helper."

It seemed to Paul that Jimmy didn't belong in the picture business, or in any other reasonably honest enterprise. Jimmy was greedy and short on scruples. Why he didn't take up one of the more lucrative occupations common on the Levee Paul couldn't understand.

And then Jimmy fell in love.

One night in January of 1898, he brought home a voluptuous blue-eyed goddess of a girl. Not to bed her but to show her off at the supper table.

Jimmy's girl was seventeen, perhaps eighteen, and Jimmy was extremely nervous as he introduced her. Miss Honoria Fail. She said she preferred Honey. Her voice was high and small, a child's voice in a body that was anything but childish. She had an ample Lillian Russell figure. Her straw-colored hair was piled high and pinned. And she wore white gloves.

"Where did you meet this young pup, Miss Fail?" Shadow asked. "Not in this neighborhood, I hope."

"Oh no, sir, we met at Pflaum's Music Hall. My Aunt Maureen took me there specially to see the living pictures. She was afraid to go alone, she's a maiden lady. I'd never seen them either, I got very excited. Afterward, in the lobby, who should we see coming out but Aunt Maureen's friend Sally Phelan. They stepped away to chat. That's when Jim and I became acquainted." Miss Fail smiled prettily. "I don't s'pose I'd have listened when Jim spoke to me, except that Aunt Maureen was way across the lobby, sympathizing with Sally for the loss of her husband right after Christmas. Jimmy was pretty fresh." She giggled. "He marched right up, told me his name, and said he made the very pictures they were showing inside. I was so impressed! When he asked for my address, my knees got all watery. I knew I shouldn't do it, but I gave it to him."

"Her number, too," Jimmy said. "Her folks have two telephones in their house."

Honey Fail giggled again, blushed, and sought Jimmy's hand for reassurance. At supper, she talked a lot about her priest and her church on the South Side.

Light snow was falling when Jimmy fetched Miss Fail's muff in preparation for taking her home on the trolley. Gravely, she shook hands all around. "Colonel Shadow. Mary. Paul. So happy to meet you. I hope I'll see more of you, I will if Jimmy asks me back, it's so thrilling, this business of yours."

"My sentiments exactly," Jimmy said, putting on his derby. He sang out a cheerful good night and with visible pride escorted Honey Fail to the stair.

When they'd gone, Shadow said, "I can't get over this. For once the little squirt shows some interest in something."

"I'd say the lovebug's bit him," Mary offered.

Shadow loosened his flowing cravat. "Jim had better be careful. He'd better not try taking liberties with that little morsel."

"Is she someone special?" Paul asked.

"Kid, that pretty little piece is only the daughter of one of the most powerful aldermen in the city. A man on a par with the Bath and Hinky Dink. Francis X. Fail, from the South Side. Hot Stove Fail, they call him. Because he'll steal anything, even a red-hot stove. But he draws a line between civic boodling and morality at home. He's a devout Catholic. Five daughters. The oldest is twenty-three, and I'm told every one of the little darlings is a virgin. If there's one who isn't, I pity the son of a bitch responsible if Alderman Fail finds out."

So it was that Jimmy Daws stayed in the colonel's employ with an improved attitude. He complained less. Sometimes he actually pretended to like the work. Honey Fail came to supper at least once a week, discussing her sisters, her priest, her parish, and the flickers—"So thrilling, the most exciting, marvelous invention ever!" She was dim-witted in a harmless, innocent way. Paul liked her enormously.

On Wednesday morning, the sixteenth of February, Paul bolted out of bed when the colonel shouted, "Oh my God!" on the other side of the wall between the bedroom and the kitchen. He dragged his pants on, then his singlet. Jimmy continued to snore away. Paul tiptoed across the freezing floor barefoot and tapped on the kitchen door. Shadow was sitting at the table, wearing an old velvet robe with a hole in one elbow. Mary was rattling the blue enamel coffeepot at the stove. Gardens of sparkling frost flowers bloomed on the windows.

Paul noticed Shadow's boots, wet and dripping on a newspaper. He'd already tramped through the drifts for his morning *Tribune*.

"Dutch, there's big news. I mean the biggest. Look." He showed the front page.

EXTRA!

3:30 A.M.

MAINE IS BLOWN UP IN HAVANA HARBOR.

American Battleship Destroyed
By a Terrific Explosion
Said to Have Occurred on Board.

MANY ARE REPORTED AS EITHER KILLED OR HURT.

All the Boats of the Spanish Cruiser *Alfonso XII*
Are Sent to the Assistance of the
Officers and Crew of the Wrecked Vessel.

"How can it be? She sailed there on a friendly visit." Paul had read every word of every recent dispatch from Key West and Cuba. The *Maine* had left a berth in the Dry Tortugas and steamed to Havana almost three weeks ago.

"Oh sure, perfectly friendly," Shadow said with a roll of his eyes. "But there's all that fighting still going on. Maybe our consul, that old Reb Fitzhugh Lee, had some notion about showing the Spaniards the heavy guns on a U.S. warship, did you stop to think of that?"

"Even so, the papers said the Spanish officials gave the American sailors a reception that was"—he pulled the English word out of his memory—"cordial."

"They fucking blew her up. That's cordial?"

"Is there proof the Spaniards did it?"

"Hell no, it just happened. But the spics are responsible, I'd put money on it."

"When exactly did the ship sink?"

"Around nine-thirty, nine-forty last night. The telegraph dispatch says she was at anchor, everything quiet. Then—bang! I'm with Mr. Hearst, we should whale the tar out of those fucking Spaniards and throw 'em the hell out of this hemisphere."

Mary's slippers scuffed on the linoleum. She sat down next to Shadow with brimming cups of coffee. Her cleavage was white as milk, and not adequately hidden by her red robe. She dabbed her eyes. "Those poor sailor boys. How many were lost?"

"Nobody knows yet. Maybe two hundred."

"Oh my God, Sid, that's awful. Think of the grieving mothers and wives."

Suddenly the atmosphere changed. Shadow dropped the paper. His eyes gleamed.

"Think of the picture possibilities."

The *Maine* disaster came at a time when America was in no mood to be tolerant of the government in Madrid. Earlier in February, Enrique Dupuy de Lôme, Spain's ambassador to the United States, had sent a personal letter to a Spanish newspaper editor who was in Cuba gathering material. Somehow the letter fell into the hands of the revolutionary junta in New York. The junta passed it to the eager editors of William Randolph Hearst's *Journal*. A facsimile of the letter appeared on the front page, together with a translation. President McKinley was characterized as *weak* and *catering to the rabble* by supporting Cuban independence, however reluctantly. He was *a low politician desiring to stand well with the jingoes of his own party*. Hearst's headline writers called it THE WORST INSULT TO THE UNITED STATES IN ITS HISTORY.

As details of the *Maine* disaster came in, there was little else on Chicago's front pages.

EXTRA! EXTRA!
TWO HUNDRED AND FIFTY-THREE ARE DEAD.

Wreck of the Battleship *Maine*
Is the Worst Disaster That Has Ever Befallen
the Navy of the United States.

CHICAGO BELIEVES IT TREACHERY.
PATRIOTISM ON ALL TONGUES.

Spain Must Prove Innocence.

SPANISH DONS SHOW THEIR TEETH.

Made Threats of War to General Lee
When Told the *Maine* Was Coming to Havana.

Commander Knew He Was in Danger
of Treacherous Attack But Duty
Obliged Him to Face It.

WAR SPIRIT AT CAPITAL.
ALL THE OFFICIALS ARE ASTIR.

Roosevelt Regrets That Entire Fleet
Is Not Now at Havana.

PRESIDENT MCKINLEY ASKS PATIENCE.
AN INQUIRY HAS BEEN ORDERED.

Whether the Battleship Was Sunk
by Spanish Treachery or by Accident
Will Be Ascertained by Naval Experts.

When Facts Are Known They Will Be Dealt With
As the Dignity of the Nation Requires.

READY TO GO TO CUBA!
SEVENTH REGIMENT ILLINOIS NATIONAL GUARD
AGAIN RESTORED TO FULL STRENGTH.

Irish Boys Receive the News with Enthusiasm.
Say They Would Be Glad to See Service.

Two days after they saw the first *Tribune* extra, Shadow nailed a two-foot flagpole to a wooden base he'd knocked together. The pole was cut from a thick dowel, with a newel post knob mounted on top. Paul rushed out for a small can of gold paint and slapped it on the pole while Mary completed a small replica of the Spanish flag. American flags were easy to find; they were being hawked on street corners all over the city, together with cardboard-mounted photographs of the *Maine* before she became sunken twisted metal in the shadow of Morro Castle.

They shot the picture on the roof on a freezing, windy day. Shadow set up the fixed-focus camera to frame the bare flagpole but not the stand. Jimmy grumpily manned a brazier improvised from a skillet resting on bricks. In the skillet Paul ignited kindling and lumps of charcoal, then spattered kitchen grease on the fire to create smoke.

Shadow told Paul to take the crank, then dropped to his knees beside the stand, out of camera range. "Smoke, give me smoke!" Jimmy worked an old fireplace bellows. Mary waved a pillowcase over the brazier, forcing the noxious clouds of smoke toward the pole and driving Jimmy into a fit of coughing and tears. "Jesus, Jesus, that's awful."

"Shut up, work that bellows!" Shadow tugged on a pulley line Paul had rigged. The crude Spanish flag rose to the top of the pole. "All right, here we go!"

"I'm ready," Paul cried, cranking.

Shadow's bare wrist and powerful hand shot to the top of the pole; in the finished picture it would look like the hand of a giant. Mary had basted the flag's grommets with just a few threads. Shadow seized the Spanish ensign and with one jerk ripped it down.

"Still cranking?" he shouted without looking around.

"Cranking."

Shadow snapped the American flag to the pulley line and ran it up. Jimmy wildly pumped the bellows. Mary madly waved the pillowcase. The winter wind caught the stars and stripes and snapped the flag out straight.

"That's beautiful!" Paul exclaimed. "Perfect."

And when the audiences at Pflaum's saw the one-minute flicker called "America's Answer to Despots!", the response was riotous—people spilling into the aisles, people shouting and brandishing fists, people standing on their seats, cursing the spics and baying for war. Iz Pflaum feared he'd have to phone for a police wagon.

In the kitchen, they broke out the bourbon and the bottles of Crown's to celebrate what was sure to be a big money-maker. Even Jimmy was proud of the little picture. Shadow waved Mary's compliments aside. "Nothing compared with what I have in mind. A real extravaganza. We'll start buying and making the props tomorrow."

The final death toll in Havana harbor was two hundred and sixty-eight. The yellow press thundered "Remember the *Maine!*" Masses of Americans suddenly took up the banners only the jingoes had carried heretofore. On March 8 and 9, Congress speedily passed a fifty-million-dollar war appropriations bill. McKinley signed it, although he was known to be unhappy about the prospect of a war and unenthusiastic about taking any stance that would provoke one.

A Naval Court of Inquiry convened to investigate the sinking. The issue could be framed in a single question. Was the disaster caused by a Spanish mine or by spontaneous combustion in a coal bunker? At the end of March the inquiry board delivered its report to Congress. The *Maine* had probably been sunk by a submerged mine, set by persons unknown.

The red line on the war fever thermometer took another upward jump. Assistant Secretary of the Navy Roosevelt said war was inevitable, and the President ought to show some backbone. Hundreds of thousands of common and ordinary Americans endorsed that view, as did some uncommon ones, among them Buffalo Bill Cody and the retired outlaw Frank James.

On the roof, Colonel Shadow created his extravaganza called, with less than stunning originality, "Remember the *Maine!!!*" The added exclamation points were the colonel's personal creative touch.

He and his assistants built a wooden frame; a large rectangular box without sides. They fitted it with a heavy canvas lining that Mary sewed. Into this lining they would pour water (Havana harbor). On one of the long sides they tacked a cardboard backdrop, which Paul painted with a blue watercolor wash and Jim decorated with clouds made of drugstore cotton.

At the lower edge of the backdrop, near the waterline, they pasted pictures of buildings with tile roofs, cut from postcards of Lisbon, Portugal. A cardboard-mounted magazine engraving of El Morro was positioned at one side. Mary fashioned a few skimpy palm trees from wire and brown and green crepe paper. These were poked into holes in the backdrop so that they appeared to be growing in front of the buildings. Paul thought the effect was ludicrous and would fool no one. Shadow cheerfully predicted it wouldn't matter a damn, and would he please keep such comments to himself?

Jimmy sawed small rectangular blocks of wood. Mary cut out a large cardboard-mounted photograph of the *Maine*. They'd bought three of these from street vendors; the extras were insurance. Using carpet tacks, Paul fastened the picture of the *Maine* to one of the wooden blocks. To smaller blocks he nailed smaller postcard cutouts of shrimp boats. ("Do they have shrimp boats in Havana harbor, Colonel?" "Dutch my lad, do you think the uneducated wops and polacks who just got off the boat and wandered into Pflaum's will know the fucking difference?") To the shrimp boats Mary attached fine sewing thread, which would allow them to be pulled through the water.

With all in readiness, they waited for a sunny, cloudless morning, then rushed to the roof in a state of nervous excitement. Paul carefully laid four pinches of gunpowder on top of the wooden block to which the *Maine* cutout was tacked. Then, behind the backdrop, he placed a bottle of alcohol, a long wire with the tip wrapped in cotton, and matches.

Shadow rubbed his hands and surveyed the arrangements. Jimmy was again fanning the charcoal brazier with the bellows. "We're going to need more smoke than that." Shadow fished in his coat and handed Mary a cigar. "Light up."

"Sid, I don't smoke."

"You do now. It's for art, remember."

"Oh God, I'll die." Shadow ignored her.

Paul emptied bucket after bucket into the canvas liner until the water was even with the bottom of the backdrop. "Tie down the battleship," Shadow ordered.

Holding two bent pins, Paul stuck his arm into the water, to his shoulder. He planted the pins in the bottom of the canvas, like fishhooks. The effect was quite nice; threads running from the pins to the battleship cutout kept it bobbing gently. He hoped water wouldn't leak out too rapidly through the pinholes.

"Here we go, I'm cranking!" Paul fancied that people a block away heard Shadow. The colonel seemed to equate screaming with creativity.

"*Smoke, God damn it!*" Jimmy worked the bellows like a madman. Mary puffed and exhaled, puffed and exhaled.

"*Shrimp boats!*"

Paul crouched at one end of the tank, unwrapped two threads from a nail, and pulled two cutouts across the tank in back of the *Maine*.

"All right, they're out of range, let 'em go."

Paul ran to the rear of the tank. Shadow kept demanding more smoke. Mary was moaning and swaying. She looked sick but she kept puffing. Working fast, Paul immersed the cotton end of the wire in the alcohol, then lit it. He thrust his arm through a prepared hole in the backdrop, praying the burning cotton would find the pinches of powder.

With a flat report, the *Maine* blew up.

"Oh my God, sensational!" Shadow screamed and immediately stopped cranking. He grabbed Mary's waist with both hands and waltzed her around.

Mary moaned, "Oh, Sid, stop, stop or I'll puke." She reeled to the cornice, sat down and held her head.

They turned the *Maine* cutout on end, rigged new threads, and restarted the smoke. Paul was responsible for pulling the battleship down into the water, bow first. He'd worked a little too fast setting the hooks for new threads, and the canvas had torn. The water level of Havana harbor was dropping rapidly as the *Maine* "sank." Shadow assured them the effect was so fantastic, no one would notice. "Trust me, trust me."

Paul went to bed that night wondering if all people in the living picture business were crazy. If so, he was now a crazy person himself. He laced his hands under his head and reflected on how much he enjoyed it. In fact, he was coming to love it.

"Remember the *Maine*!!!" created a sensation in the trade and block-long lines at Pflaum's Music Hall. Although clearly recognized as a fake, and presented without music, it thrilled audiences. Paul went back to Pflaum's three times, to sit in the silvery flickering dark and ponder.

Every trick and deception in the picture was unbelievably crude. Only a small child or an idiot would think the cutout ships and backdrop real. Yet there was undeniable magic up there on the thirty-foot screen. The scene *lived* because it *moved*. The water rippled in the sunlight—never mind that the *Maine* sank after 9 P.M. on a winter night. The smoke billowed across the frame, and the cutout ship vanished under the water with an abruptness that was startling.

At the end of the footage, a card Paul had lettered repeated the picture's title: the exhortation to remember. Audience reaction never varied. People howled, stamped, pounded and sometimes damaged Iz Pflaum's seats in a patriotic frenzy.

Paul was still dissatisfied. He compared the *Maine* picture with the film of the hurtling Wabash Cannonball. One was a trick and a cheat, one was honest and real. People were not so stupid; they saw the differences and when the novelty of living pictures wore off, they would begin to object to anything fake. How very much better it would have been for the Luxograph camera to have been on the esplanade of Havana harbor that night.

Of course it was impossible to predict a disaster. And the sinking of the *Maine* couldn't possibly have been photographed with existing film because of the darkness. But what about some larger event, spread over a long period? Many Americans thought there would be war; indeed, they were actively promoting it. If war broke out, why not take the Luxograph camera there and film real action?

The possibility excited him. Hadn't Shadow preached that very thing, the night he hired Paul and drunkenly sat him down to listen to a visionary speech about the spectacular possibilities for living pictures?

Of one thing he was sure. If the living pictures continued to depend on fakery, never sought to depict real places and events, Iz Pflaum's prediction would undoubtedly come true. Flickers would remain chasers in cheap vaudeville houses forever.

□ □ □ □

Colonel Shadow had no time to discuss such philosophical niceties with his help. He was overworked and harried as a result of the sensational box office for the faked picture. He dashed around the Midwest, signing up fourteen new theaters to exhibit Luxograph programs; six of the theaters belonged to the prestigious Orpheum Circuit. These already had Edison projectors, but Shadow had signed his agreement with the great man and thus was free to supply pictures without fear of retribution. He could also continue to open his own store shows, with Luxograph projectors, in other cities. This he did in Cincinnati and Milwaukee, hiring a manager-operator for each.

In Chicago he frantically searched for additional real estate. He rented an old livery stable half a mile south of the Levee headquarters and took out a bank loan to install woodworking equipment. He hired a middle-aged Swede named Gustav Wennersten, an expert carpenter who was slow to speak but marvelously quick to understand the design and construction of Shadow's projection machine. Gus Wennersten took charge of building new projectors. Paul helped him when he wasn't filming for Pflaum's and Shadow's growing list of outlets. Jimmy did some of the heavy work for Wennersten—shifting and sawing lumber, nailing the cabinets together—though he did it clumsily and with loud complaints. After two weeks Gus Wennersten had enough of Jimmy. He said he would quit unless he could hire a qualified assistant. Shadow stormed and cursed and said he'd go bankrupt, but allowed Gus to hire a man as cheaply as possible.

Then a new problem arose. The manager of Shadow's store show in Peoria was remitting suspiciously small sums every week. One week he sent nothing. Shadow wired an old pal who lived near Peoria, a man he'd known in his minstrel days. The man telegraphed back to say he had covertly observed the colonel's store show on four successive nights. Each night there was a reasonable crowd; ten or fifteen people at each of the first two showings, five or six at the last one. Shadow scribbled some computations on a sheet of paper, came up with a total, and asked Jimmy to take the train to collect what was owed. Jimmy came back two days later with a satchel full of money and the backs of his hands badly discolored.

"I had a real good talk with that chump, Colonel. I showed him the chain on my holy medal, but that didn't impress him so we got serious. I dunno how he'll explain black-and-blue marks and a broken arm to his wife and three kids, but if you want to keep him on, he won't cheat you any more, 'cause I promised to call again if he did."

"Excellent work. I will keep him, he's a good man if you disregard his cupidity. I trust the trip wasn't too tiring?"

"Nah," Jimmy grinned. "It was a pleasure."

All of them continued to work sixteen, eighteen hours a day. One evening when they were hurrying through supper at ten-thirty, Shadow stuffed half a bun in his mouth and said, "Mary, you're starting night school on Monday."

"I am starting what?"

"A bookkeeping course. I'm up half the God damn night writing down all the figures. It's time to distribute the load among all the toiling bees."

At the stove, where she was frying thick slices of ham, Mary pointed to her iron skillet. "I'm going to distribute this load on your damn skull, Sid. I hated school."

"Mary—" Shadow took a generous swig from his bottle of whiskey. "If you don't help me out, I'm going to lose my mind and probably hang myself."

"Oh no, not Sid Shadow, Sid Shadow told me nothing would stop him from making his million."

"I don't want to argue, I'm starved. We'll go to bed and talk it over."

She gave him a look as she brought the skillet to the table with a towel wrapped around the iron handle. "We're going to discuss this in bed?"

He ran his hand over her rear while she served the ham. "The way I'm feeling, we may have to discuss it three or four times."

Mary actually blushed. Jimmy snickered. Paul had grown used to the blue language and he laughed too.

Leaving Paul and Jimmy to wash and dry the dishes, Shadow and Mary went into their bedroom and closed the door. Soon the springs were squeaking. On Monday night Mary put on her best hat and went to night school.

April came. Again Spain refused to heed United States demands for independence for Cuba. President McKinley was increasingly pressured to take a strong stand and intervene. He remained reluctant. The yellow press hammered at him. Members of his administration openly criticized him. Little by little he gave way. On April 11 he sent a message to Congress, saying in part, *I ask the Congress to authorize and empower the President to take measures to secure a full and final termination of hostilities between the government of Spain and the people of Cuba . . . and to use the military and naval forces of the United States as may be necessary.*

Congress responded with a joint resolution demanding freedom for Cuba, and instructing the President, as commander in chief, to employ appropriate military force to carry it out.

On April 20 McKinley signed the resolution into law. A state of war existed between America and Spain.

In addition to all his other duties, Shadow was again rushing to the cellar to perfect the new camera with improved capacity. He'd been talking about it excitedly for months, but hadn't pushed to finish the work. Now the swift, almost dizzying expansion of the American National Luxograph Company drove him to it. They still had to film new subjects regularly, and the new camera could be a significant help.

Gus Wennersten came over from the other facility and solved a couple of small but vexing design problems. Jubilant, Shadow gave Gus a twenty-dollar bonus and proudly announced to his little family that the camera was ready.

It would hold four hundred feet of cellulose nitrate film negative in a separate lightproof magazine mounted on top of the main body of the camera. After exposure, the film was fed to a take-up reel in a second lighttight magazine, this one attached to the camera back. Above and slightly behind the crank was a footage meter of Shadow's own design. A meter was necessary because several subjects could now be filmed with a single magazine.

On the evening after the war declaration hit the papers, Paul asked the colonel if he could spare a few minutes to discuss an important matter.

"For you, Dutch—anytime. Let's take a stroll." Shadow fired up a long cigar. They walked in the direction of Freiberg's, where the professor was hammering "Animal Fair" so loudly the music could be heard for blocks. Electric signs painted Twenty-second street with gaudy colors.

"What's on your mind, kid? I can't raise your pay. God knows you deserve it, but I'm pressed to the absolute fucking limit at the moment."

"No, it is not about wages." Paul stopped on the curb, raised his chin, and looked the colonel in the eye.

"I would like you to give me the new camera."

"Got an idea for a longer picture, have you?"

"In a way. I would like to take the camera to Cuba."

"*Cuba?* Oh sure, why not? Hell, let's take it to the moon while we're at it. Did Mary scramble your brains for breakfast?"

"Colonel, please hear me out. I want to follow the American soldiers for our picture company. If they go into battle with the Spaniards, there will be opportunities to film scenes that are completely new and amazing."

"Dutch, that is the God damn craziest, most risky idea I have ever—"

"American Mutoscope is sending a man."

Shadow jerked the cigar from his mouth. "What did you say?"

"American Mutoscope has planned for weeks to send a cameraman from New York. I read it yesterday in one of the journals. Vitascope may go as well. We're an important, growing company, just like those others. We can't be left out."

"Do you know what you're asking?"

"I am asking for the new camera."

"Crap on the new camera, I'm talking about *you.*"

"Yes, I know there might be dangers. I am willing to chance them. I go back once more to the night you hired me. You spoke long and with feeling about the living pictures. What they can do and should do. Show the wonders of the world. The drama. Now's the time, there's no drama bigger than war. You said that too."

"I know, but I don't remember! Listen, Dutch. I like you. I don't want to send you off and see you come back on a stretcher, full of greaser lead. Isn't necessary. We did all right with the two pictures we made on the roof."

"Not the real thing, sir. Cameras can bring back the truth. It's our—our duty."

"That's the line I've been hearing from you ever since we faked the prizefight in the country. Where'd you pick up these big noble ideas?"

Paul was red-faced. "Mostly from Mr. Rooney. He said a camera could lie but it must not."

"And you're not scared to pack up and pole off to Cuba? They're going to be shooting real bullets down there."

"I am scared, certainly. But I am excited too. I felt exactly this way on the pier at Hamburg, waiting for my ship to America. People on the pier warned me I might die during the crossing. I knew it was possible but it didn't matter, I had to board that ship. I had to cross the ocean to this country to look for a home. There was never any other choice for me."

"Dutch, you're a funny kid. You have ambition, but that isn't all. Something else pushes you, I can't figure out what." Shadow scratched his long jaw. "Cuba, huh? War footage."

"Never before seen in all the world, Colonel."

Shadow stared beyond the Levee lights to some large and shining hill of gold, a sizable part of which he might bank if scenes of real battles were exhibited at Pflaum's and his other licensed theaters and store shows . . .

"You'd need help. Jimmy would have to go with you."

"He won't like that."

"If I order him, he'll go."

"Or quit."

"Maybe, but my guess is he won't. He's still chasing Fail's daughter. She still thinks his work is so thrilling." He fluttered his eyes. "I don't think she's allowed him to peek at her little treasure just yet. He wants that so bad it hurts. Marching off to war would impress Miss Fail. It might get her to drop her bloomers when he comes home safe. Hell, maybe even before he leaves. If I had ten silver dollars this very minute, I'd bet it all that Jimmy'll go."

"Then you will give me the camera?"

"If you're willing to risk your ass, I'll risk the new camera, film stock, your expenses—the works. Let's go in here to Freiberg's. I'll buy you a beer and a steak. Lord, think of it. American National Luxograph goes to war! Did I really have that big idea when I was drunk?"

"Absolutely. That's why I wanted to work for you."

"I decided when I met you that you had the stuff. Damn if I wasn't dead right."

He put his arm around Paul in a way that was almost fatherly, and they passed into the smoky blaze of the dance hall. "What do you say I print up some calling cards? Paul Crown, Operator—no, wait, we'll use your nickname too. Paul 'Dutch' Crown—I like that. Sounds"—his hand cut a slashing figure in the air—"adventurous. Plenty of grit. Real American, too. Dutch Crown, Chief Operator, American National Luxograph Company. That's big, I like it."

85

Joe Crown

"I WISH you wouldn't go," Ilsa said. "How can the brewery get along without you?"

"Easily. Stefan and my brewmaster, Sam Ziegler, can handle everything between them, at least for a limited time."

Joe dipped the paddle and the canoe glided across the Lincoln Park lagoon known as Swan Lake. After church and another of Pastor Wunder's excruciatingly long sermons, Ilsa had insisted they make this little excursion. Canoeing had never been one of her passions, so it puzzled him. Until now.

"But Joe, I still feel—"

"Ilsa, we're officially at war. I have served before, I can serve again. It's my patriotic duty."

He rested the paddle on the knees of his gray worsted trousers—too heavy for the unexpected heat of this April afternoon. His face gleaming with sweat, he tilted his straw boater forward to shade his eyes. Ilsa had given him the hat for Christmas. He told her it was wonderful. Secretly he thought it foolish for a man his age.

She dabbed her upper lip with a lace handkerchief. "There may be an element of patriotism in it. But I think you're doing it chiefly because you're so unhappy at home. Unhappy with me."

"Now wait, I deny—"

"Be so kind as to let me finish this time. At a certain age, men rebel. That is well known. I know my personal objections to spirits and beer have angered you, and I'm deeply sorry. I wish I could say to you that I renounce what I believe in order to make your life happier. I can't do that. Maybe twenty years ago, yes, but not now. I am the person I have become, for good or ill."

"A marvelous wife, I've always said it and I stand by it."

"Thank you, but I know you take exception to the way I feel about this war."

"You and your friends."

"Yes, Miss Addams is likewise adamantly opposed to it. But that plays no part here. Or it shouldn't. Truly, I'm thinking of you. And the business." He looked at her skeptically. "You have made an enormous success, Joe. You are expanding as never before. Six new agencies this year alone."

"Seven. Last week I bought a piece of property in Omaha."

"Nebraska now! Aren't you proud?"

"Certainly."

"You have everything a man could want."

"Oh yes. Everything." He threw the paddle on the thwart in front of him. "I have a son at private school whom I seldom see. I have a daughter foolishly determined to enter a profession whose members are considered riffraff, at best. I have another son who might have dropped off the earth—"

"No! Remember all those little things he's sent. The orange candies from California—"

"They were addressed to you, not to me. Then there is our nephew, totally lost to us—"

"Pauli didn't choose to leave our house, you banished him. I must constantly remind you of that."

He ignored her flare of anger. "Well, if this is what I've worked for—if I am a man with everything—I pray to God I'm never forced to experience having nothing."

He snatched off his boater and dragged his sleeve across his dripping forehead. "It's too damned hot out here, we're going back."

▫ ▫ ▫ ▫

The following Tuesday night, April 26, Joe left for Washington on the Baltimore & Ohio. He'd bought a Pullman berth but when the porter asked if he wanted it made up, he shook his head. He sat up all night, staring out the window with his seat lamp extinguished. The vast American night streaming past was as dark and unfathomable as his own life in this, his fifty-sixth year.

Rain was falling when he arrived in the capital. He checked into his room at the Willard Hotel, a haven for generals and politicians and lobbyists since before Lincoln's time. From there he telephoned Joe Cannon's office on Capitol Hill. He'd previously telegraphed him to announce his visit. They met for a noon meal of bean soup, soda bread, and beer in the dark and smoky Old Ebbitt Grill on H Street. Uncle Joe looked more like a hayseed than ever. As he noisily spooned up soup, Joe asked how he'd been.

"Busy." Uncle Joe scratched his scraggly beard without dislodging several bread crumbs. "This chairmanship of Appropriations, it's a damn important job these days. Right after old Bill asked for four million for the Navy and I helped him get it, he called me in again. On a Sunday! 'Uncle Joe,' he said, 'I've decided I need another fifty million right away, in case we really do go to war.' I'm a good Republican, he's a good Republican, so I said, 'Mr. President, consider it done.' I got the bill written up right away and he got his money."

"Yes, but I read that you didn't consult all the members of your committee, and some of them were furious."

"So what? I don't just sit on my ass, I *run* my committee. If the other boys don't like the way I do it, they can go to hell and go home."

Before they parted with a strong handshake, Uncle Joe whispered, "I know why you're in town. I put in a word with old Bill."

Joe's appointment at the Executive Mansion wasn't until eight o'clock. Late in the afternoon, as a spring shower started, he dodged through the fast traffic on Pennsylvania Avenue to call on young Roosevelt. Thirty days ago, Joe had sent a tender-of-service letter to Secretary of War Russell Alger. He had then written Roosevelt, Uncle Joe, and Carl Schurz, asking each for a letter of endorsement and support. One of Alger's clerks returned a polite note saying two letters had been received—Uncle Joe hadn't bothered—and Joe's offer was being given careful consideration; he would be interviewed. The clerk enclosed a White House appointment card with the time inked on it.

Just as he'd done with Cannon, Joe had telegraphed ahead to invite Roosevelt to supper. The assistant secretary of the Navy kept him waiting only ten minutes. The shower had turned to a rumbling storm; rain beat the office windows. Electric lights were on. They flashed on Roosevelt's eyeglasses as he bounded from his desk.

"Joe my friend. Welcome to Washington." They shook hands. "You're seeing President McKinley?"

"Yes, tonight."

"Then we should pop along for supper soon. Please have a seat while I clean up one or two matters." Roosevelt yanked a pen from a heavy inkstand and attacked a pile of memoranda, scowling over some, muttering comments over others.

Joe glanced around the office. One wall held a map of Asia with a large red Maltese cross marking Hong Kong. A red circle ringed Manila in the Philippine Islands, another Spanish possession. In December Commodore George Dewey had steamed out of San Francisco to go on station with the Navy's Asiatic Squadron. Dewey was thought to be under orders to attack Manila in the event of war, and it was expected the Filipinos would welcome such an attack. They had their own burgeoning liberation movement.

On an easel in a corner was a large matted photograph of an iron warship. Roosevelt noticed Joe studying it. "Yes, that's the *Maine*. I keep it as a reminder of the indignity done to us by the Spaniards."

"Have you reached a final count of lives lost?"

"Two hundred sixty-eight." Roosevelt clenched those tiger teeth. "Tragic. So was the loss of the vessel. Sixty-seven hundred tons. Four ten-inch guns in armored turrets fore and aft. Additionally, six-inch guns and four torpedo tubes— and even at that, she was rated a second-class battleship. We have newer, larger ships, but the *Maine* was a real beauty."

"Spain has a lot to account for," Joe said.

"Damned if she doesn't. The commander in chief has finally come around to that view. I don't refer to him as Wobbly Willie any longer." Then abruptly he said, "I'm finished here. We can go. But I must stop a moment in the signal room."

Joe waited in the office, listening to the melancholy sound of the rain. When Roosevelt returned, he was frowning.

"Dewey is steaming under secret orders. For days we've had no signal from him. Now there's a report through Madrid of an engagement having been fought in Manila Bay. The report includes the words 'heavy losses.' Hearst and some others will be jubilant about that. Not I. I'll have to come back here as soon as we've dined."

The rain was stopping, replaced by a mist. Pennsylvania Avenue was still jammed with hack and carriage traffic hurtling along in both directions. Roosevelt took the lead, striding into the street at terrific speed. Joe was in excellent condition but had to push to keep up.

"We're forming a volunteer cavalry regiment, have you heard?" Joe hadn't. "Westerners, mostly. Expert horsemen and marksmen. In fact it was a German who suggested the idea to me. Baron von Sternburg. He came up to Sagamore Hill for some shooting a few years ago. I'm very excited."

"You mean you'll go with this new unit?"

Roosevelt grinned. "I've been appointed second in command under Leonard Wood. We'll muster in San Antonio. My boss, Secretary Long, is having pups, but I'll be blasted if I'll miss this fight. So much is at stake. Including a much-needed opportunity to shake the stick at the country where you were born."

"Germany? Why?"

"Because Kaiser Bill, whom I like very much personally, is not our friend in the Caribbean. Nor in Asia for that matter." Joe wanted to ask for amplification, but music caught their attention. Martial music, cranked out by a hurdy-gurdy man coming toward them in front of Willard's. Roosevelt wagged his stick in the air and hummed a few notes. "Damn catchy, isn't it?"

"I've heard it a lot, but I don't know what it is," Joe said.

"Sousa. New last year. 'El Capitán' was positively my favorite till he wrote this one. 'The Stars and Stripes Forever.' Isn't that a grand and appropriate name? It sums up the spirit we're all feeling."

With his thumb, Joe rubbed the underside of his wedding ring on his right hand. *I'm not so sure I feel it. What if Ilsa's right? What if I'm only running away from the disaster I seem to create in the family? What if I'm running away from her?*

Over the first course, small cakes of finely chopped and seasoned crab from the waters near Baltimore, Roosevelt explained his concern about Germany.

The preceding November, in response to the murder of two German missionaries in Shantung province, the Kaiser had dispatched his Asiatic Squadron under Admiral von Diedrichs and landed five thousand men on the China mainland.

"Then, same month, we had the nasty little incident with Herr Lüders, closer to home. Port-au-Prince, Haiti. Lüders is a German national. Owned a livery stable down there. Got into some sort of muss with the local government and they expelled him. Well, the German minister, von Schwerin—can't stand him; one of those arrogant sorts—von Schwerin demanded reinstatement of Lüders and a reparations payment to him amounting to twenty thousand dollars. While this was going on, two of the Kaiser's training ships showed up and anchored in the harbor at Port-au-Prince. I tell you the rest in confidence—with great regret. The Haitian president inquired through channels whether United States naval help was available. He was told it was not. The decision was made over my head. The money was paid, Lüders was allowed to reenter Haiti, and I'm sure Kaiser Bill's little demonstration of power made him very smug."

Roosevelt pulled off his eyeglasses, the better to convey his seriousness. "I am frankly fearful of our friend the Kaiser. His policy is expansionist. He believes in the doctrine of a two-ocean navy. It's my theory that he's maneuvering in this hemisphere because he wants a coaling station in the West Indies. One day, soon or late, we'll have to show our aces and call his bluff. That may cause suffering for decent German-Americans whose only feeling for their homeland is an understandable, nonpolitical affection. People such as yourself."

It was a new thought, and dispiriting. Yet not all that new either, he realized a second later, when he recalled the unpleasant arguments with Oskar Hexhammer.

"So you really think we face a challenge from Germany, Theodore?"

"I do unless the Kaiser changes course. Which is another compelling reason for a demonstration of American resolve and strength in Cuba." He noticed Joe's plate. "You've hardly touched your meal. What's wrong?"

"Not hungry. Anxious about tonight, I suppose."

"You're due over there when?"

"Eight sharp."

"At least it'll be quiet. I hate that place during the day. Supplicants, applicants, tourists roaming wherever they please, poking at the Tiffany screens and bouncing on the ottomans in the East Room—we have to do something about that. *After* we fry the hash of Generalissimo Weyler," Roosevelt added with another of those canine grins.

Striving for his best military posture, Joe marched into the Executive Mansion. In front of the tall, colorful Tiffany glass screens in the vestibule, he presented the appointment card to a guard, who said, "Staircase on your left."

Upstairs, in the corridor of the East Wing, an elderly doorkeeper stepped forward. "Good evening, sir. Please have a seat, the President will be with you soon." He pointed to a closed door. "In there, the Cabinet Room. It's his informal office."

The doorkeeper trundled down the dim hall lined with scarred wooden benches and chairs, presumably for all the job and favor seekers who packed the mansion at busier times. Joe polished his small bronze lapel badge with his suit cuff. He'd worn it because he knew McKinley too was a G.A.R. loyalist.

He fingered the boar's tooth a while. A young man came out of an office, whistling. He wore a suit of summer linen and a straw hat with a ticket in the band marked Press. He looked up from his little notebook to give Joe a stare, then went on to the creaky stairs, whistling. The new Sousa march again.

A door opened nearby. A clerk beckoned. "Mr. Crown? If you please."

And thus Joseph Crown, immigrant and citizen, entered into the presence of the highest officer of the land. His head swam with excitement.

The Cabinet Room resembled the boardroom of a seedy bank in a country town. Old portraits of unfamiliar men hung on the walls. The furniture was dark, heavy, ordinary. Beneath a large but tarnished brass chandelier, William McKinley, twenty-fifth President of the United States, had established a small work area at one end of the conference table. Spread before him were pens and inkstands, a large stained blotter, a holder for stationery.

McKinley rose quickly. He looked better in person than in his pictures, which emphasized his blunt, blocky chin, his thickening jowls, his sleek hair. He had a warm, forthright air, lively gray eyes, a smile that seemed genuine. He shook Joe's hand energetically.

"Mr. Crown. Welcome, sir. Your fine products are well known here, even to those of us who are abstemious."

"Thank you very much, Mr. President." Joe found his nervousness abating. The situation was not unlike that on a battlefield. Once in combat, you were much too busy to worry about death.

Two men stood behind the President, one in full uniform and braid. McKinley turned to them. "May I present Secretary of War Alger and General Miles, commanding general of the Army. Gentlemen, Mr. Joseph Crown, of Chicago."

"How do you do, General, Mr. Secretary." Joe knew quite a lot about Nelson Miles, and almost nothing about the civilian. Miles was a big, sturdy man in his late fifties. He had a ruddy face and a splendid mustache curved like the horns on a Texas steer. Though not a graduate of the U.S. Military Academy, he'd worn Army blue since the war and had fought successfully against Rebs, Comanches, and Apaches.

Miles greeted Joe enthusiastically, Alger with reserve. The secretary was slightly older than the general; a fine-boned, graceful man. He was a lumber tycoon and a former governor of Michigan. A pure white mustache and goatee hid most of the lower part of his face. His eyes lacked warmth. He had a folder on which Joe could see his own name written large.

"Do sit down and let's get to the matter," McKinley said. "We have less than sixty days to organize the most massive military expedition in the history of this country."

General Miles said to Joe, "Sixty days because that brings us right to the start of the rainy season, and yellow fever."

McKinley turned to Alger. "Do you have Mr. Crown's tender-of-service letter, Russell?"

"Right here, Mr. President." Alger slid the folder across the table. McKinley took out Joe's letter, scanned it quickly, turned it face down. Next he studied a number of rectangular cards and letter-size sheets clipped together in the file. Joe recognized his own medical and pay cards from the war, as well as field reports he'd written.

"An admirable record here, Mr. Crown."

"Thank you, sir."

"Fifth Ohio Volunteer Cavalry. Cincinnati boys." The President closed the folder. "What prompts you to step forward to serve your country again?"

"I have had experience, this land has been very good to me since I emigrated many years ago, my brewery is doing well and I can easily absent myself for a while. Altogether, Mr. President, I believe I am qualified. Further, I believe in this war—in America's taking up the burden of liberating less fortunate peoples. And I have read, sir, repeatedly, that men are needed."

"God knows that's true," Miles grumbled. The President frowned at the invocation of the Deity. He was known to pride himself on being a Christian gentleman; no intoxicants, no swearing, no immoral behavior. Miles missed the reaction completely and continued: "When the war resolution came down from the Hill, we had approximately twenty-six thousand troops in the peacetime Army and slightly more than two thousand officers, chiefly out West. You can imagine the difficulty of mobilizing in two months."

"Yes, I can certainly—"

Alger interrupted. "Are you fit for duty, Mr. Crown? No health problems?"

"None that I am aware of."

"Cuba is a pesthole in summer. We would require that you have a medical examination."

"I will do it at once, if that's the only thing barring me from consideration."

"Not the only thing, sir. Not quite." Alger's smile was small and supercilious; Joe much preferred General Miles and the President, although the secretary probably thought himself superior to both.

The President said, "You stand favorably in our eyes, Mr. Crown. I have received strong endorsements of your character from Representative Cannon of Illinois and Assistant Navy Secretary Roosevelt, who as you know will be taking a volunteer commission soon. I have also heard from the Honorable Carl Schurz. Mr. Schurz does not support the action of this government in Cuba"—Alger touched his nose, an eloquent and disdainful gesture—"but his regard for you, and your qualifications, could not be higher. I see a rare opportunity in your application."

The last remark mystified Joe. McKinley glanced pointedly at Miles, who said, "The President's correct, your qualifications are outstanding. If your health matches up, you would stand an excellent chance of receiving a commission. First, however, we must satisfy ourselves in regard to one crucial question. Would you be willing to serve under a former Confederate?"

Joe was so surprised, he couldn't answer immediately. Alger leaned back and folded his arms, amused. "An Alabama Reb likewise named Joe," he said.

Nettled, General Miles said, "The secretary refers to Congressman Joe Wheeler. He too is desirous of serving his country. He will be commissioned major general of volunteers."

"You know his war record, I presume," Alger said.

"I know he graduated from West Point but changed sides. He led Confederate cavalry through the whole war."

"Indeed he did, right down to the final hours, when he was chasing Jeff Davis through the Carolinas, hoping to escort him to some safe haven. Davis was apprehended in Georgia before he could escape, then the Federals caught Wheeler."

"I personally wrote the order sending Wheeler to prison at Fort Delaware," Miles said. He gave an ironic laugh. "Now here we are, eagerly sanctioning his return to Union blue."

Alger rested folded hands on the table. "We are doing the same for our consul general in Cuba, Fitzhugh Lee. Robert E. Lee's nephew."

"I know Mr. Lee's background," Joe said, perhaps too brusquely, but Alger's condescension grated.

If the secretary noticed, he didn't react. "Mr. Lee has also accepted a commission as major general of volunteers. It probably wasn't as hard on him as joining the State Department, to work for the brother of General Sherman."

McKinley took charge. "There we are coming to the heart of it, Mr. Crown. The reason for the question. You see, in this war we have something beyond an opportunity to restore freedom to Cubans who have been unduly oppressed and abused by their Spanish masters. I do not minimize the moral worth of that, not in the least. But I also recognize a high opportunity to unite the men and women of America as they haven't been united for thirty-three years. The blue and the gray, together. That's why we ask you to search your conscience. You fought against the Confederacy. Could you now submerge any lingering feelings of hatred and serve with men who rebelled against the Union? Men who bear at least a marginal responsibility for the deaths of your friends and comrades?"

Joe didn't want to sound pompous or insincere when he replied. At the same time he wanted to speak his heart. He said, "Mr. President, I fought for freedom then, freedom for the Negro. I would be privileged to fight for freedom for Cuba now."

Alger said, "Yes, but under Joe Wheeler?"

"Fighting Joe Wheeler had an outstanding reputation. I don't know the man personally, but I know how highly he was regarded. He was at Shiloh and so was I. After more than thirty years, we surely—"

Alger interrupted. "Is it yes or no, Mr. Crown?"

Joe laid his hat on the table. His heart thundered in his chest. "Yes, Mr. Secretary." He quickly turned toward the others, a small but clear suggestion that he was dismissing Alger. "Yes, General. Yes, Mr. President. Are those answers satisfactory?"

McKinley jumped to his feet for one of those vigorous handshakes politicians reserved for favored constituents.

"Eminently, Mr. Crown. Eminently!"

At last Commodore George Dewey signaled Washington. Early on May 1, his Asiatic Squadron had entered Manila Bay. Six United States ships in line, commanded by Dewey from his flagship, the armored cruiser *Olympia*, had defeated seven Spanish vessels likewise coming out in line. The battle began at 5:41 in the morning, with an order that catapulted the commodore into overnight fame: "You may fire when you are ready, Gridley."

The American fleet destroyed a total of ten Spanish vessels and captured the Cavite navy yard without serious damage to any United States ship. Dewey became the hero of the hour. Newspapers put his engraved portrait on front pages. Songwriters rushed to compose ballads. Politicians called him presidential timber. America rode a cresting wave of triumph.

So did Joe. Nine days after his return from Washington, following delivery to the War Department of the results of his medical examination in Chicago, he received a letter from Secretary Russell A. Alger, informing him that he would be commissioned brigadier general of volunteers.

86

Paul

THE WAR DEPARTMENT asked for a hundred and twenty-five thousand men; a million wanted to join, even though there was a gold rush drawing thousands up to the Yukon.

The yellow press exulted. Flags and bunting appeared on public buildings, glowing in the sunshine, rippling in the wind. Concert bands and symphony orchestras substituted marches for waltzes and concertos. A few antiwar voices were heard, but the protesters were damned in the press, even threatened with lynching. What kind of patriotism could you expect from socialist college professors from New York and New England, and shorthaired women who endorsed free love?

A sudden panic engulfed the East Coast. Somewhere in the Atlantic, Admiral

Cervera's Spanish naval squadron was roaming. Savannah and other seaboard cities demanded protection against invasion. The Navy sent some of its creaky old monitors, which looked like the original one that had fought the *Merrimac.*

When Shadow informed Jimmy that he and Paul would be leaving for a war zone, Jimmy's face purpled, but he didn't explode until he was alone with Paul.

"He said you're the one who sold him on this damn lousy scheme. Are you nuts?"

"Come on, it'll be an adventure. Maybe the adventure of a lifetime."

"Not if some spic shoots me. You may be going by yourself."

But Jimmy didn't make good on that threat either, for the reason Shadow had predicted:

"I told Honey about the damn trip. She practically wet her pants." He mimicked her high voice. " 'Ooo, Florida. It's so warm, a regular resort.' I told her we weren't going to hang around the fucking beach, we were going to Cuba. Bullets! Fighting! I said I damn well didn't want to go. Big mistake. She said she wouldn't look up to me if I shirked my duty. Jesus Christ. She's got to *look up to me* before I can get her down on her back. You crazy kraut," he said with a shake of his head and a malevolent glare.

On the first of May, Sunday, Paul and Jimmy prepared to leave for Tampa, where the Army was marshaling. They packed camera, tripod, reflectors, and stands in two wooden crates whose estimated freight charges very nearly had Shadow gibbering. Each crate carried a black stenciled legend.

FRAGILE!
Moving Picture Equipment
property of:
AMERICAN NATIONAL LUXOGRAPH CO.,
Chicago, Illinois, U.S.A.

How much equipment they would be able to transport into Cuba Paul couldn't say.

Shadow gave him a packet of fifty calling cards, produced by the cheapest job printer the colonel could find. All the cards used Paul's nickname as well as his given name. Mary got hold of one of the cards and foolishly showed it to Jimmy, didn't he think it looked nice? That night in their room, Jimmy jabbed the card under Paul's nose. "What's this Chief Operator shit?"

"Not my idea. Ask the colonel." Paul pulled off his shirt, tired and ready for bed.

"Ask the colonel, huh? Sure I will. If I can find five minutes when you aren't kissing his ass."

Paul wheeled and grabbed him by both shoulders. "If you don't like the card, stay here, God damn it."

He expected Jimmy to throw a punch when he laid hands on him. Instead, Jimmy's jaw dropped. A feeble smile crept onto his face. "Leggo. C'mon. Jesus, Dutch, I didn't know you had a temper. I never saw you mad before."

"Keep this up, you will see it all the time." Paul stormed past the hanging sheet, yanked it across the wire and lay down to rest.

Rest? He was taut as a violin string. He heard Jimmy grumbling and swearing in his part of the room and was suddenly, unexpectedly reminded of Jimmy's birthday. April first.

The day of Judas.

They were to leave on Tuesday morning. The night before, Jimmy went out with Honey. At supper Mary surprised Paul with a gift. A braided straw hat with a wide and rakish roll brim and a ribbon band of royal blue.

"Can't have our chief operator looking shabby down there with all those generals," she said with a warm look. Shadow mumbled agreement.

Paul was touched. "It's a fine hat. It will keep the sun off very well."

"I have another for Jimmy," Mary said. "Not as nice, but I couldn't leave him out."

"I'm glad you didn't. It will save me a lot of trouble."

Shadow said, "Bad blood between you two." The very words that had leaped to Paul's mind months ago.

Paul nodded. "Sometimes. Not this trip, I hope."

No one offered encouragement on that point.

After supper Paul went to the cellar, where the colonel kept paint for lettering the company name on projector cabinets. He took the can of red enamel and a two-inch brush upstairs and carefully painted a red dot on the globe, at a spot Shadow had identified as the approximate location of Tampa.

He replaced the paint and returned to pack a small grip. All at once he grew sad. This wasn't a home. It was just a room—cheap, dingy, squalid. Would his home always be like this, the place he was at the moment, nothing more?

He pulled down the stereopticon card, yellowing badly now. He knew Joe Junior had told him the truth, America wasn't quite the paradise dreamed of by immigrants. At least part of what the baker of Wuppertal had said was right. Still, one of his dreams in Berlin had been realized, and at times it all seemed an unfathomable miracle, meeting Wex Rooney, then Shadow, and finding another miracle enfolding all three of them. The miracle of photography. Which was just one of countless miracles of a new age coming . . .

He was embarking on a great adventure; despair had no place in it. He looked at the card one last time and put it in his grip.

Next morning, the third of May, Shadow and Mary saw them off at the depot. Honey Fail came with Jimmy, which helped curb his anger, as did the new straw hat Mary had given him. He recognized that it wasn't as fine and expensive as that of the chief operator, but he seemed mollified by someone showing him even the slightest generosity.

Paul looked smart in a belted jacket and his new hat. On his shoulder he carried a canvas bag, homemade, containing a spare lens and a magazine of Eastman raw stock. Shadow didn't like to trust expensive film to overheated baggage cars, though he had to take the risk with additional magazines that were being shipped to Florida from Rochester. Shadow had advised his helpers that he'd booked the smallest available rooms at the Tampa Bay Hotel, headquarters for the American expeditionary force.

The colonel shot his linen cuffs and gripped Paul's arm. He had to speak loudly because of the depot din. "Dutch, I'm counting on you and Jim to bring back tremendous pictures."

"Just don't get in the way of those Mauser bullets," Mary cried. "I read they buzz like bees." Clinging to Jimmy's arm, Honey Fail uttered a little squeal of fear. Jimmy patted her hand, looking wan.

Shadow turned away to greet an *Inter-Ocean* reporter he'd wheedled into covering the departure of the only Chicago picture makers going to the war zone. Shadow looked very much the captain of a great enterprise in his tawny frock coat, tooled boots, and sombrero. Jimmy and Honey put their foreheads together, whispering and touching. Two older men, companionably drunk, wandered by singing, *"Dewey, Dewey, Dewey, he's the hero of the day. And the* Maine *has been remembered in the good old-fashioned way . . ."* Mary took advantage of the distractions and flung her arms around Paul's neck. She sweetened her farewell kiss by sticking her tongue in his mouth.

The train conductor shouted his all-aboard. "Well, here we go," Jimmy said.

Honey hugged him. Excitement pitched her voice higher than ever. "Oh, you're so brave. Go down there and thrash those dirty greasers."

"No, no, they're only supposed to film them," Shadow exclaimed. "I want pictures, not a couple of corpses." Jimmy looked sick.

The Atlanta-bound train departed a minute later. Jimmy was already inside the second-class car. Shadow ran alongside the steps of the vestibule and shouted at Paul in the billowing steam.

"You're carrying the expense money. For God's sake don't squander it, but don't stint on the telegraph, either. I want regular reports."

"Right, Colonel."

The train gathered speed. Shadow ran faster. "I trust you, Dutch. You're in charge. Keep your eye on Jim, keep him in line. Keep your head, bring back the goods, one day you might be my partner—"

He stopped as the train rushed on. He raised his right hand high. Paul barely heard him cry one last word.

"Luck."

Paul settled next to Jimmy on a thinly padded seat. Jimmy untied his four-in-hand, a concession to Honey's presence, and stuffed it in his pocket.

A vendor came through with a tray of fruit, packets of nuts, dime novels, and playing cards. Jimmy bought a Nick Carter and an apple. He attacked the apple with savage, crunching bites.

Paul laid the canvas bag at his feet and pulled a *Daily News* out of his side pocket. A local politician had addressed a war rally at the Auditorium. *With this noble crusade to expand our influence and extend the blessings of liberty to our suffering Latin brothers, America comes of age, and truly enters the world for the first time . . .*

I could say the same, Paul thought, buoyed up by the morning's excitement, the noise and motion of the train, the mixture of anticipation and dread of the unknown awaiting them in Florida, and beyond.

They slept, or tried to sleep, sitting up. They left the train for quick snacks in shabby station lunchrooms, sometimes bringing tin cans of strong black coffee back aboard. Jimmy complained endlessly.

The train hurtled down through the midlands, imperiously clanging and wailing to announce its coming, streaming smoke as it passed. They crossed over the mighty Roebling suspension bridge spanning the Ohio at Cincinnati, where Uncle Joe had lived when he came to America. On white-fenced horse farms in Kentucky, blooded mares and stallions raced beside the train, outrunning it before galloping off again to sunlit pastures. Then came Tennessee; limestone cliffs, lacy waterfalls glimpsed in dark grottoes, timbered mountains seen from steep grades and occasional single-track switchbacks. As they chugged through the southern part of the state, Jimmy asked a peculiar question:

"You think we're gonna make any money on this trip?"

"It isn't an expedition to make money. Well, perhaps for American National Luxograph it is, but not for us. Unless you count our pay."

"Count it? Most of the time I can hardly find it. Down in Florida I aim to pluck up some extra. Fellow on the Levee said there'd be plenty of hicks in an army camp. Fair game."

Jimmy leaned back and crossed his arms. "And fair warning to you, Mr. Chief Operator. Once in a while I may not be around when you need me."

"Look here, we have an assignment to—"

"Ah, dry up with that crap. I'll do my job. But I'll take care of a few others on the side. You keep quiet about that." He punched Paul's shoulder, feigning friendliness. "Be a pal."

Disgruntled, Paul looked out the window.

"Jesus, you Dutchmen are pious bastards." Jimmy pulled his straw hat over his eyes and stretched out to sleep.

In the early dawn Paul woke up suddenly when the train stopped with a jerk. He'd been dozing with his head against the glass, and the window raised a couple of inches. Outside he smelled a cool fresh morning. He heard crickets and frogs. He saw a small depot.

Then he heard shuffling feet, voices shouting orders. A lantern hanging above a signboard showed the name of the stop. CHICKAMAUGA STATION.

Soldiers from Camp Chickamauga piled aboard the train; young recruits in tall khaki hats, blue cravenette blouses, red bandannas tied around their necks. They wore clean leggings and carried clean white blanket rolls. About twenty of them came into Paul's car and found seats among the half dozen civilian passengers. A runty sergeant with a leather patch over his left eye was in charge. He settled his men, then took a seat by himself. He was asleep when the train pulled out.

Morning brought them to Atlanta. Bright sun shafts speared down between the roofed platforms. Paul yawned and scratched at the stubble on his cheek while taking note of swags of red, white, and blue bunting wrapped around the wrought iron roof pillars.

He heard music. A brass band playing "A Hot Time in the Old Town Tonight." A small crowd had come down to see the troop train pass through. An idea clicked in his head. In the vestibule, he cornered the conductor.

"How long is this stop?"

"Forty-five minutes."

In the coach he shook Jimmy to wake him. "We're going to shoot here. Wait for me."

He ran back to the sleepy sergeant, who listened to him and immediately said no. But Paul insisted.

"You must accommodate us, we're the American National Luxograph Company. Surely you've heard of the biggest name in the moving pictures?" The sergeant didn't dare say he hadn't. "This is for the war effort. Hundreds of thousands will see you and your men on theater screens. You will all be proud."

Twenty minutes later, Paul and Jimmy created a sensation by setting up their camera on the platform. They filmed the recruits marching past, then reset the camera to photograph them boarding the cars. Paul wasn't sure he had enough light in the platform area, but if the pictures came out, they would be marvelous.

Jimmy said he'd rather be sleeping.

In a switchyard near the depot, the coaches were transferred to a locomotive of Florida's Plant System. Soon surprising new landscapes were flowing past the window. Great oaks bearded with Spanish moss, fields, and raw hillsides of rust-red dirt. Ragged farmers paused behind their plow mules, tiredly staring at the soldiers who waved from the train.

One young recruit took out a mouth organ and began to play "The Stars and Stripes Forever." The music made Paul forget how long and tiring this journey was. It buoyed his spirits.

This will be a fine experience. I'll learn a great deal, and when I'm safely back in Chicago, then I'll worry about what comes next. But not before.

Lord, how he wished that future could involve Julie. Well, nothing to be done there, she was lost to him. He could move on. Probably he should. As always, the Germans had a proverb for the situation. *Andere Städtchen, Andere Mädchen.*

Other towns have other girls.

The train chugged on, scribing the sky with sooty smoke. The soldiers complained about the rifles they would be issued. Old Springfield carbines that used conventional black powder. The standard rifle of the Spaniards, a Danish-made Krag, was designed for the new smokeless powder.

"Hell, that's a death sentence," one soldier said. "If a sniper don't show smoke from his muzzle, how do you know where he's at? He can get you 'fore you can say jack robinson."

At a country depot in Georgia, eight young girls jumped out of buggies and farm wagons and swarmed into the train, begging for souvenirs—brass buttons, rifle cartridges. Many of the young soldiers obliged.

Into Florida, the hamlets became fewer, poorer. Shanties of scrap lumber built right beside the tracks housed whole families of Negroes who stared at the train with dark and melancholy eyes. Longhorn cattle grazed on weedy land in pitiless sunshine. Paul had long ago rolled up his jacket and thrown it on the wooden rack above the seat. He stank from a lack of washing. The whole car stank. His skin was slick from humidity. Wiping it with a soggy handkerchief did no good; he felt slimy again right away.

The sergeant with the eye patch had commandeered a double seat at the front end of the car. With the conductor's help he'd found a piece of wood for a card table. Playing poker, he began to relieve his young men of pocket money.

The mouth organ started up again. A soldier with a strong baritone voice began to sing in a maudlin, mocking way.

> "Just before the battle, Mother,
> I am thinking most of you . . ."

A Chicago song, Paul remembered. Fritzi played it on the piano on one of those happy evenings soon after he arrived, when he sat contentedly by the fireplace, the melody drifting in from the music room. Uncle Joe said a Chicago man had written the song at the time of the Civil War, when Uncle Joe rode a cavalry charger, and thousands of boys as young as these boys in blue, as young as himself, perished.

Others joined the singer, all of them loud but not mocking the sentiment as the first man had.

> "While upon the field we're watching,
> With the enemy in view."

Scowling, Jimmy pulled off his straw hat and fanned himself.

> "Comrades brave are 'round me lying,
> Filled with thoughts of home and God,
> For well they know that on the morrow,
> Some will sleep beneath the sod."

Jimmy jumped up, leaned over the back of his seat. "Shut the hell up. Let's have some quiet!"

Paul said, "Jimmy, sit down."

The soldiers broke off. A couple of them stood. Jimmy whacked his straw hat against the seat cushion. "I'm trying to get forty winks, I don't want to listen to a lot of shit about death."

"Sir, your language," said a commercial traveler across the aisle.

The one-eyed sergeant rushed back from his seat and braced Jimmy. "Mister, these brave boys are goin' to war, they've got a right to holler. I can't say you've got the same right, I don't see any sojer suit on you."

"Fuck you, runt."

The sergeant whipped his fist up. Paul flung himself past Jimmy and spread his arms, a barrier between them. "It's hot in here, everyone is tired, we don't want trouble."

All the soldiers were on their feet, ready to fight. Jimmy turned pale as the foolishness of his challenge sank in. The sergeant swiped his mouth with his hand. To Paul he said, "Awright, but he better keep still." He thrust his chin in

Jimmy's face. "Hear that? Keep still, or you're liable to leave the train real sudden. Ass first out one of them windows."

Off he went, shooing his men to their seats and clucking like a fretful mother. The few civilian passengers looked scornfully at Paul and Jimmy. Paul felt hot with shame. "My turn to sit by the window," Jimmy growled. Paul didn't argue.

Late at night, with the oil lamps trimmed low, Jimmy snoring lightly, the coach quiet save for the repetitive clicking of the trucks on the rails, something compelled Paul to dig into a pocket of his coat for one of the cheaply printed business cards. By tilting it toward the swaying lamp at the front, he could read it.

PAUL ("DUTCH") CROWN
—Chief Operator—

So once again he was a new man. Once again he was reborn.

And once again he was hurtling into a darkness whose boundaries, whose heart, whose secret traps, he couldn't see or even imagine. Once again there were wonderment and eagerness, a sense of inevitability, and more than a trace of dread. The Americans had an expression for going to war, facing its dangers. They said you were going to see the elephant.

He slept fitfully on the bumping, jerking train. He kept the card, the proof of this newest sea change in his life, protectively curled inside his palm. Once or twice when he awoke, he drowsily recalled who he was, and where, and marveled.

Dutch Crown.

Age twenty; twenty-one next month.

Going to see the elephant . . .

87

Ilsa

ON THE NIGHT before Joe went to war, Ilsa ironed his underwear.

She worked in a room high in the house, under the eaves; a room set aside solely for ironing. Normally two laundresses who had been with the family for years came in every Saturday to do the week's work. This batch Ilsa felt compelled to do herself. As if the act could imbue the garments with some protective magic.

That very afternoon she'd rushed to Elstree's to buy the underwear. Seven suits, each with shirt and ankle-length drawers. The underwear was made of summer balbriggan, dyed gray and vented all over with small drop-stitch openings. Although it was expensive, the clerk assured her it was the finest, and coolest, gentlemen's underwear available. He pointed out the ribbed cuffs of the shirt and drawers, the fancy collarette neck, and the small pearl buttons.

Ilsa feared for her husband in the dews and damps of the tropics, and she felt partly responsible for driving him there. She would do anything to protect him, to bring him back safe and whole.

The granite facade of Elstree's was decorated with patriotic bunting, as were most of the businesses along State Street. From a five-and-dime came the music of a piano. Sousa's "El Capitan." She peered through the window and saw a man in suit and vest hammering the keyboard on a dais at the front of the store. A dozen adults and several children stood around the dais, clapping and marching in place. Much of Chicago, and the nation, was infused with a patriotic fervor, as if the war would be a great lark. Joe acted that way, fairly skipping around the house, humming and singing to himself.

But not every American cheered the pronouncements from Washington, the recruiting leaflets and posters, the bands and parades—in one of which Joe had marched with his G.A.R. unit. Pro-war feeling was strong in the Middle and Far West, less strong in the East. There, a few professors, artists, writers, editorialists, were beginning to speak against the jingoes, in and out of the administration.

Ilsa knew of this opposition because Joe had received a long letter about it from Carl Schurz. Joe's friend was vehemently against military adventurism in Cuba, or anywhere else. He was trying to organize formal resistance of some kind. Which disgusted Joe. He had a large file box of Carl's letters he'd saved over the years. This latest one he threw away.

Ilsa's friend Miss Addams was deeply concerned about the war. She'd discussed it at Hull House last week, during one of her informal teas with Ilsa and like-minded women who supported the settlement house.

In 1896, Miss Addams had reminded her friends, she'd taken another of her spiritual pilgrimages, this time to an estate called *Yasnaya Polyana,* located some hundred miles outside Moscow. Here lived the celebrated literary genius Count Leo Tolstoy, who had abandoned the world's luxuries and amenities to don peasant garb every morning, work in his own fields all day, and, through this spartan program, strengthen and expand his Christian vision of a better world.

"Count Tolstoy absolutely believes the state, any state, to be anti-Christian," Jane Addams said. "Therefore the true practitioner of Christianity must reject the state and all its policies. Follow the count's doctrine to the limit, and you must inevitably conclude the Spanish war is immoral."

She shook her head gloomily. "The count's a saintly man, few would question that. Still, saints can be too high-minded for the day-to-day realities. Fine principles and preachments sometimes aren't enough when evil winds are blowing. In this very neighborhood, the jingo talk is doing something bad to the children. They used to play simple games. Now they play war. They don't 'free Cubans,' they 'kill Spaniards.' The count could lecture on a soapbox down in the street and they wouldn't stop. And their parents wouldn't stop buying all that bunting—all those little flags. War can have a beautiful, seductive face. People revel in the passions it permits. One can understand it easily enough. It's the predatory spirit in all our natures. It lies so near the surface, ready to burst forth, spread its destruction—"

She stopped. The women were glancing uneasily at one another. Ilsa said, "My husband's friend Carl Schurz writes of wanting to organize a formal opposition. If such a group was created, I don't believe I could join it, for personal reasons. Could you join?"

Miss Addams seemed smaller all at once. "I don't know. My reputation as a radical is bad enough already. And the work of Hull House must go on. My becoming a member of Mr. Schurz's group might create so much new enmity, hostility, that our income here, the contributions that support us, could be reduced to nothing. So I don't know," she repeated in a bleak way. "I tend to think that, like you, I would hold back."

Ilsa said nothing to Joe of this discussion. She didn't even intimate that she'd taken part. If she opposed the war openly, then she opposed him. And she wouldn't do that, now his decision was made and the papers signed by the military authorities.

It was cowardly, her silence. She knew that. But she'd lost her son. She'd lost her nephew. She couldn't stand to lose her husband's love as well.

Ilsa had laundered all seven suits of underwear and hung them up to dry during supper. Joe had eaten hurriedly, pleading the need to check through the items he'd laid out for his valise. She nodded to agree but he didn't see; he was already gone from the dining room.

She had helped Helga wash and dry and stack the dishes. On her way upstairs she stepped into the large family room, to the small whatnot formerly in Pauli's bedroom. She'd moved it downstairs and placed on it some of the anonymous tokens she was certain Joe Junior had sent to her. The little candy oranges in the miniature crate had a slightly brown cast. On top of the whatnot rested half of a roughly spherical geode, its tiny quartz crystals winking and sparkling like the suns and moons and planets of some fairy universe.

Where is he? she wondered as she touched the rough, sparkling cavity. *Dear God, let him be safe—happy—even if I never see him again.*

She had begun her ironing at a few minutes past nine. She was still at it when a downstairs clock faintly chimed ten. The ironing room was hot and sticky. She'd opened both small round windows, but no air was stirring in the May night.

Perspiration gathered on her chin as she worked. Occasionally a drop fell. She ironed with relentless zeal, finishing each garment perfectly, folding it, then pressing it lightly again so that it would pack well. Though she sometimes felt rebellious about the duties her German upbringing forced on wives, tonight she did this mundane work with a furious energy.

Why does he have to go? she thought as she swept the iron back and forth. Of course she knew. He was a patriotic man, a man of principle. The war of the rebellion had been a major experience in his life, a crusade undertaken with high moral purpose. There was something of the same spirit moving in him now.

But there were other motives. In recent years his loving heart had clashed too fiercely with his Germanic passion for authority, order, control, with calamitous results for the family. And his sense of guilt must be a terrible burden. All of this military preparation might be his attempt to overcome the guilt feelings, regain control of his disordered world, put it back together, and prove that his beloved *Ordnung* was not altogether destructive.

Ilsa also believed Joe was disappointed and bored with the ordinary flow and detail of his life at home. Which meant he was disappointed and bored with her. He was certainly angry with her, even though he tried to mask it. She'd argued her principles, her opinions, too often. Especially on the subject of his business.

She could find only one small consolation in what was happening. Better a blue Army uniform for her dear Joe than another woman.

Yet even that thought wasn't overly reassuring. Joe was not setting off for some G.A.R. encampment, some jolly outing with old veterans who told lies by a camp fire and whose greatest risk might be drinking too much and falling down. Her Joe was putting on a uniform for another war.

There would be shooting and killing. Men maimed for life, or dumped into hastily dug graves, never to come home to loved ones. A mischance—standing in the wrong spot at the wrong moment, turning left instead of right on some jungle trail—any of a thousand things done in the haste of war could bring the fatal bullet. Take him away from her forever. The ultimate loss, beyond her power to bear . . .

And there was nothing she could do about it. Nothing except sit on the hard stool, in the heat, under a glaring electric bulb, ironing his underwear with love and stubborn devotion.

Part Eight

TAMPA

1898

Now, Senator, may we please have war?

1898
Assistant Secretary of the Navy THEODORE ROOSEVELT

HOW DO YOU LIKE THE *JOURNAL'S* WAR?

1898
Hearst newspaper headline

88

Dutch

IT WAS ALMOST DARK when the train chugged into Tampa. Long vistas of mean unpainted houses lined shabby streets of rutted sand. Here and there fronds of scrawny palm trees stirred in damp wind off Tampa Bay. Paul kept yawning. He was worn out, famished, and dirty.

The train stopped in the middle of a downtown business block. A small depot could be seen on a nearby corner. All the soldiers left the car. Leaning out, Paul saw the other passenger coaches emptying similarly. Mounted men and supply wagons struggled through the sand as night came down. The conductor stuck his head in the door. "Next and final stop will be the hotel. Five minutes."

The train went across a railway and wagon bridge spanning a river, then through palmetto groves and another area of ramshackle houses lit by dim street lamps a block apart. Jimmy said, "God, what a sorry-looking burg." Paul agreed. The mighty United States Army appeared to be mustering in a backwater of civilization.

Then the train passed through elaborate iron gates onto a siding. Jimmy sat up, grinning. Paul looked out and was amazed to behold an Arabian Nights illustration come to life.

He was gazing at the spectacular Tampa Bay Hotel.

Henry B. Plant, founder of the Plant System of railroads, shipping lines, and hotels, had built a magnificent winter resort on the west side of the Hillsborough River. The hotel was sited on a six-acre tract riotously planted with palms, orchids, dogwood, bougainvillea, orange trees, lemon trees, lime trees, grapefruit trees, banana trees.

The main building, long, rectangular, and five stories high, was made of dark red brick. An enormous silver onion dome rose from each corner and, in between, minarets crowned by silver half-moons. Moorish arches framed the doorways, and smaller ones ornamented the guest room windows above. Verandas wide as two lane-streets, ablaze with multicolored electric lights and embellished with wooden gingerbread, ran all around the building. Couples strolled; men in uniform took the air in white wooden rockers. Through the car window came muted laughter and band music. The floodlit minarets shone brighter than the misty moon. Paul's first thought was, *I have to buy a picture postcard of this place, otherwise no one will believe it exists.*

Jimmy, too, was impressed. "How many rooms in this place?" he called to the conductor.

"Five hundred and eleven. Looks like a sultan's palace, don't it? Wait till you get a glim by daylight. They got a dozen tame peacocks wandering around."

"Peacocks? I never seen one of those before."

"The hotel's usually closed this time of year, but Mr. Plant, he's a patriot, he opened it right away when Washington said they needed it. You boys are looking at headquarters for the Fifth Army Corps."

As they toted their grips up the aisle, Paul stopped to ask another question. "How large is Tampa, sir?"

"Fourteen, fifteen thousand, counting the spics—the Cubans—in West Tampa and Ybor City. Now that the soldiers are here, population's probably double. They're camping everyplace. You boys staying at the hotel?"

"Yes. We are moving picture camera operators."

"Well, you're damn lucky you're bunking here instead of in the open with the sand fleas and no-see-ums."

Paul hurried to catch up with Jimmy, who was already out of the car and happy for a change. "My God, Dutch, there's women all over the place."

"Time for them later. We should get our equipment from the baggage car."

"Oh, right, I forgot, you're in charge now." Paul spun around.

"Look here, I'm tired of your sneers."

"Too bad. As long as I'm on this rotten job, you better not order me around like some dinge from the cotton fields. Because if you do—"

"If I do, then what?"

"I'm not saying. Just don't push me. Don't be a chump and things'll be okay."

"I will try to remember that." Paul pivoted and walked toward the head of the train, fighting his anger. He should buy his so-called assistant a return ticket to Chicago immediately. He'd get along better doing all the work himself.

He had two of the crates off the baggage car and resting in the sand when Jimmy came straggling along, whistling. Paul curbed the impulse to hit him.

Colored porters in livery brought four-wheeled carts and tagged the crates for transfer to the hotel's baggage room. Paul tipped them, then asked, "Where do we register?"

"There, sir." The black man indicated doors at the near end of the building. "The west entrance is for train passengers, the one at the east end for carriages coming over the bridge. Go straight in, down the long hall to the rotunda, you'll see the desk."

They followed a gravel path to the veranda and saw a multitude of different uniforms, and attractive young women in handsome gowns; women with tawny skin and ravishing black hair. Jimmy said, "If that's Cuban sugar, I want some."

"On your own time," Paul snapped.

Inside, a great long hallway stretched to the rotunda, where tiny figures could be seen. The hall was decorated with tall carved chairs, Chinese jars, small statues, miniature potted palms. Doors to several parlors stood open. In one, ladies were playing cards; in another, officers and a civilian were using writing desks. The doors of these public rooms were rich mahogany, with inlaid satin panels.

Paul was so awed by the rotunda, he snatched off his straw hat as if he'd entered a cathedral. The rotunda was perhaps seventy feet across; finely carpeted, brilliantly lit with electrics. The walls were hung with tapestries, large paintings, mirrors of rose-tinted glass. Granite columns supported an open gallery on the second floor.

The rotunda was crowded. Men and women in evening attire; Navy officers in cool white duck mingling with their Army counterparts, who wore the heavy blue better suited to Alaska. A few officers were dressed in more casual khaki; several of them carried Western-style sombreros. Could they be part of the 1st Volunteer Cavalry, the regiment of cowboys, socialites, and college athletes he'd read about? The commander was a Colonel Wood, an experienced Indian fighter.

He noticed two grim-faced officers emerging from a doorway marked Telegraph Office. A long bulletin board was set up against one section of the wall, papered with news clippings, telegraph messages, a miscellany of official orders and documents. One of the officers pinned a yellow telegraph flimsy to the board. Even with that, the scene was festive, not warlike.

At the desk, Paul slid his card over the green marble. The clerk, middle-aged and brusque, said, "The Luxograph Company. Your rooms are ready. Fifth floor. Floors two and three are reserved for senior officers or those with families. The daily rate is four dollars, which includes meals but no extras such as spirituous beverages. The reservation form says we are to bill everything to your company in Chicago."

"Yes, correct," Paul said as he signed the register. Jimmy was leaning on the marble counter, watching women. Some were stout, quite gray, and escorted by older officers. But any number were unattached. A few, matronly, wore the uniform of the Salvation Army. The younger ones were the kind they'd seen outside, attractive girls from Tampa or perhaps Cuba itself.

Paul nudged his partner. Jimmy took the pen and managed to splatter ink on the otherwise clean page. The clerk said, "You will find the dining room that way, at the end of the east corridor, through the Solarium and to your left. You're too late for regular service this evening, dinner is promptly at six. But food is available in the gents' rathskeller downstairs or in the Oriental Annex. The Annex is between this building and the boat house on the river. During the day the floors of the Annex are taken up so you may bathe in our pool."

Jimmy's response was an amazed "Sweet Jesus and Mary." The offended clerk pinged a silver bell. Another black porter—there seemed to be scores—loaded their valises on a small handcart and took the room keys. The man was sixty or so, with tired brown eyes.

"Elevator this way, gen'mun."

They passed a short Japanese officer in a colorful uniform talking to a civilian wearing a frock coat. The civilian was jotting in a notebook. Both men were smoking strong-smelling cigars. Paul was surprised to find he liked the aroma. The main elevator was near the grand staircase. Others were located at each end of the long corridor, the porter told them. The open cage was beautifully done in gilded curves and scrolls. "Handsome work," Paul said.

"Otis," the porter said. "Mr. Plant, he buys the best."

The car brought them up to the fifth floor, and another equally long hall. The porter stopped to show them a closed door. "This here's your bathroom. One bath for every three guests, you won't find 'nother Florida hotel with that kind of comfort." He stepped to the next door and unlocked it. "You first, sir," he said to Jimmy.

Even Mr. Plant's smallest guest room, though appallingly hot, was well appointed with an Oriental carpet, a single bed with spotless linen, and a dressing table. A small bedside table held an upright telephone and a paper fan imprinted with the name of the hotel. The room was lit by a ceiling fixture with three electric bulbs, and two more on the dressing table mirror. The room had a radiator and small fireplace, neither one needed tonight.

"Put my bag on the bed, boy." Head averted, the porter did as Jimmy ordered.

Paul asked if Tampa weather was always like this. The porter assured him it wasn't. Temperature and humidity were much too high for May; things would improve. Paul supposed it the usual cheery propaganda of a resort. Jimmy fanned himself. "Before that happens we're liable to fry up here."

Jimmy followed along to Paul's room, which was identical. "Here, and thank you." Paul handed the porter twenty-five cents. The man smiled and thanked him warmly. As the porter left, Jimmy said, "Damned if I'll pay a nigger extra to do what he's supposed to do."

Paul sailed his straw hat onto the bed. "Are you hungry?"

"Nah. I want to look over some of that cunny downstairs."

"Suit yourself." Paul unbuttoned his sticky shirt. "We should unpack the crates first thing in the morning. Start filming as soon as we can."

"Yeah, sure, okay. Knock on my door. If a woman answers, leave." When he got no smile from Paul, he said, "Just don't make it too early. Seven, seven thirty—"

"Six."

"*Six?* You may be up then, but not me. I'll see you when I see you." He walked out. A moment later Paul heard him lock his door and go down the hall.

Paul washed in the separate bathroom. He combed his unruly hair with water, put on a fresh shirt, and set out to explore. He took the stairs instead of the elevator. At the landing between the gallery and the rotunda he passed a wall mirror wide enough for half a dozen ladies and gentlemen to examine their appearance, full length, at the same time.

At the newsstand he picked up a free brochure about the resort and bought a colored picture postcard showing the main building. He said to the clerk, "I would like to try a good Tampa cigar."

"I recommend these, *Guerra y Diaz*. Factory's in Ybor City. Only five cents apiece, but excellent Cuban leaf and wrapper. Are you a regular cigar smoker?" Paul said no. "Don't draw the smoke down into your lungs, savor it in your mouth and then exhale, you'll find that very satisfying."

Paul went down to the lower level, where he found the barber shop, the masseuse, the ladies' mineral water baths, the office of the house physician, and finally the place he wanted, the rathskeller. There was an entrance from the corridor, as well as a stairway coming directly from the floor above. Slow-swirling smoke and the click of billiard balls came through an arch near the bar.

He picked up a menu and was surprised to find Armour beef and Big "V" pork sausages listed. The barkeep said Armour, Swift, and Big "V" all had branch plants in Florida. Vanderhoff's was in Ocala.

Paul asked for a lager. Out of the pipes came a foaming stein of Extra Pale from the Florida Brewing Company of Tampa. He ordered a lamb chop with stewed tomatoes and kidney beans plus a side dish of hot chowchow, an American pickle relish he'd grown to like. "And then nougat ice cream and black coffee, please."

"Take any table. The waiter'll bring it."

He chose a small table in the corner. The beer was all right, but no match for Crown's. Even exiled, he could admit that his uncle brewed a superior product.

His food came, and as he ate, he read the brochure. Plant had opened the hotel in 1891, at a cost exceeding two million. Another five hundred thousand had gone into furnishings "personally selected by Mr. and Mrs. Plant during an extended tour of Europe." Suites cost seventy-five a day.

He tossed the brochure aside in favor of his *Guerra y Diaz.* He asked the barman for a cutter, snipped the end. He struck a match from a ceramic matchbox holder and lit up. Prepared for unpleasant consequences—coughing, choking, retching—he drew a little of the smoke into his mouth and rolled it around. Careful not to inhale, he let the smoke dribble out. He found its scent and warmth mellow and satisfying; there was a slight sting inside his mouth, but nothing worse.

He put the cigar between his teeth and gently bit down. Leaving, he glanced at the backbar mirror. He liked the man he saw. With the cigar, that man possessed *eine grosse Reife.* A greater maturity. Definitely.

He would buy more cigars in the morning.

Outside the air was sweet but oppressively damp, blurring everything with a haze. The hour was growing late, the pathways less crowded. He strolled in the direction of the boat house. There, the brochure had informed him, guests could embark on a scenic cruise of the river in "electric launches of the latest design."

He wandered past dark tennis courts and stopped a moment at the Oriental Annex, a large and brightly lit pavilion from which came dance music. Melodic and a trifle sad, the waltz reminded him of Julie. He left.

In his room he unpacked his clothes, the stereopticon card, and the paper flag. He propped the card against the mirror and laid the flag in front of it. To this little display he added the souvenir postcard of the hotel.

He undressed and tried to sleep. Even naked, it was difficult in the heat. Finally he drifted off but he awoke promptly at five minutes before six. It amused him to think that even a slumbering German seldom forgot punctuality.

When he knocked at Jimmy's door, there was no response. He knocked again, harder. Still nothing. Considerably annoyed, he bought two cigars downstairs, left the hotel and caught a trolley across the Lafayette Street bridge. The morning was gray and steamy. In the daylight the town was even more dreary and primitive than it had seemed when they arrived. It was also far busier. Main streets were clogged with four-mule wagon traffic and menaced by mounted dispatch riders who traveled at the gallop regardless of pedestrians in their way.

Soldiers were abroad on the plank sidewalks. Most wore the standard uniform of heavy blue flannel. Some were Negroes, Paul was surprised to see. The black soldiers stayed together, noticeably apart from the whites.

In a small café decorated with American and Cuban flags, he ate a quick breakfast of mush and strong coffee. The counterman, a swarthy fellow with an accent, was loudly warning two customers that Spanish warships would bombard Tampa at the end of the week, after which enemy infantry would land and ravage the town. One of the listeners said, "Hell, Emilio, that's only the ninth or tenth invasion rumor in the last two weeks. When I see some greaser coming after my missus with his pants down, *then* I'll grab my gun."

As Paul left, he noticed a little drift of sand inside the doorsill. Tampa, Florida, was indeed a strange new experience. It was heat, it was stickiness, it was tropical vegetation, but above all, it was sand. Still, he liked being here. It was exactly the kind of experience he'd dreamed of as a boy in Berlin.

He smoked a cigar as he walked. Almost every store window displayed one or more gaudy placards. BUY FROM TAMPANS WHO "REMEMBER THE *MAINE!*" FIFTH ARMY SOLDIERS WELCOME HERE! SPECIAL DISCOUNTS TO OUR BRAVE BOYS!

A reflection slid along the dusty rectangles of glass, moving at his exact pace. Mr. Dutch Crown. With cigar. He liked the image more and more.

He located the Plant System freight office in the depot at the corner of Polk and Tampa. The crate of film from Eastman was waiting. He signed for it and arranged delivery to the hotel. A half hour later, he found Jimmy enthroned in a rocker on the front veranda, looking like a carefree vacationer. To Jimmy's left, at the main entrance, an Army sentry relaxing in a rocker casually saluted every second or third officer who entered the hotel. The sentry needed a shave and yawned a lot.

Jimmy had large dark circles under his eyes. When Paul asked what he'd done last night, Jimmy winked. "I don't got to tell you ever'thing, do I, mister boss?" he said in a mock Negro accent.

They unpacked their equipment from the baggage room. By ten the film had arrived, and they set up the Luxograph camera on the lawn in front of the hotel. Paul paced back and forth, his straw hat shading his eyes as he planned his first shot—a long view of the veranda.

The camera drew a crowd, which included two military men. The taller had showy ribbons on his blouse, a tropical pith helmet, a swagger stick. He introduced himself as Captain Lee, Her Majesty's military attaché from Washington. The other officer wore high boots, a plain khaki uniform, and a billed cap. On the front of the cap was a small white roundel with a red dot in the center. He was introduced as Colonel Yermoloff, "attaché from the Imperial Russian Embassy."

Paul said, "My name is Dutch Crown and this is my associate, Mr. Daws." Yermoloff clicked his boot heels and bowed. He had a tiny graying goatee and a cool, remote air. His thickly accented English consisted of "How do you do?"

Colonel Yermoloff tugged a small folding Kodak from the pocket of his blouse and wandered off to make snapshots of several hotel peacocks parading their elegant tail fans on the lawn. Captain Lee asked questions about the camera, which Paul answered politely. Jimmy stood by, smoking cigarette after cigarette and ogling every woman in sight.

A man in a linen shirt and white flannel trousers came striding up the path from the tennis courts, racket in hand. The sleeves of a white sweater were tied around his neck. He stopped to greet the attaché. "Top of the morning, Arthur." His clear, strong speech left no doubt that he was American.

"Hallo, Dickie. Have a good match?"

"Yes. I won."

"Here's one of these film chaps. Mr. Crown, have you another moment?"

"Certainly." Paul was eager to meet people, and the captain's deference said this man was important.

"We have any number of journalists gathering in Tampa, but here is certainly the most famous and distinguished." The American laughed in a deprecating way. "Allow me to present Mr. Richard Harding Davis, currently representing Mr. William Randolph Hearst and his *New York Journal.* You're familiar with Mr. Davis's byline and his books, surely."

"Indeed yes. I am honored, Mr. Davis. *Soldiers of Fortune* is a wonderful, exciting novel. I read it last year."

Captain Lee smiled. "You and half the world. This young chap's name is Dutch. The other gentleman is his associate, Mister—I'm very sorry, I didn't—"

"Daws," Jimmy growled.

A strikingly handsome man of about thirty-five, Davis was impeccably polite to Jimmy as well as to Paul. His handshake was hard and strong.

Affably, Davis said, "Are you picture fellows trying to put us poor pen-and-ink men out of work? Two of you in the hotel, and I hear at least two more are on the way."

"You mean another company besides ours is already here?" Paul was alarmed.

"Right. Fellow named Bill Paley. Came in on a dispatch boat last week. Been filming at Key West for a while. Stout man—big as a barrel. You can't miss him."

"Nor his airs," Captain Lee said with disdain. "Overbearing sod, Paley."

"Now Arthur, don't be too hard on him. He's in poor health." Davis said to Paul, "There's a reason I know about your competition. My employer, Mr. Hearst, hired him personally. Paley and I have no formal relationship, but our pay comes from the same pocket. Paley usually makes films for the Eden Musée, that's a dime museum on Twenty-third Street in Manhattan."

"And you say there are two more companies due to arrive? Can you tell me who they are?"

"American Biograph's one. I'm not familiar with the other. You can understand my general lack of interest, Dutch. I wrestle with nouns and adjectives all day and all night, but you fellows just turn that crank."

Amused, Captain Lee stepped away to watch the antics of the Russian attaché. Yermoloff was running around in a crouch, chasing the agitated peacocks who wanted nothing to do with him or his camera.

Davis rested his racket on his shoulder. "German, are you? I mean originally."

"Yes, I arrived at Ellis Island six years ago."

"Your English is good. What's the name of your company?"

"American National Luxograph of Chicago."

"Going with us all the way to Cuba?"

"I hope so. It's my intention to apply to the military staff for battlefield—ah—"

"Accreditation."

"Thank you." Paul liked this man. "Does anyone know where the Army will attack the Spanish?"

"General Shafter probably knows. Or General Miles, if he ever shows up. The general staff doesn't bother to inform us working types about plans. We're reduced to listening at keyholes and eavesdropping on bar conversations. One day I hear the objective will be Santiago, the next it's Porto Rico."

"Can they not decide?"

"Not yet, my boy," said Captain Lee, who had returned a moment ago. "We are at the mercy of Admiral Cervera and the Spanish flotilla."

"Our Navy's out there chasing Cervera," Davis explained. "But they can't seem to find him, or his ships. Until they know where he is, no troops will sail from this port. I personally think—just a minute, there's a gentleman I need to see."

"Who's that, Dickie?"

"Crane. Up there on the veranda. Excuse me, will you? Happy to meet you, Dutch. We'll talk again." He walked briskly toward the hotel.

Paul and Captain Lee watched the handsome journalist bound up the steps to greet a younger man in a straw boater and soiled white duster; a man who looked as raffish and lethargic as Davis was smart and energetic.

"They say Dickie's pulling in three thousand per month from Hearst," the captain mused in a vaguely envious way. "Plus expenses, of course. He gets additional fees for whatever he writes for *Harper's Monthly*. He's a lot richer than that rum chap he's chatting with. A lot more civilized, too. Mr. Crane is a nonconformist. One might even say renegade."

"I'm afraid I don't recognize the gentleman."

"Stephen Crane? Made quite a to-do with his Civil War novel."

"That Mr. Crane! *The Red Badge of Courage*. It's marvelous."

"I wouldn't know, I seldom read fiction. I never read any that's obscene. His first book was some filth about prostitutes. And there are people who call him a genius! I find him abominably rude, arrogant, and desperately in need of a bath. Don't waste your time, Mr. Crown. Good day."

All this conversation bored Jimmy. He was lying on the grass now, lazily smoking a cigarette and studying the rows of guest-room windows.

"Jim, shall we get to work? The light's good, I would like to start cranking."

"Sure, okay." Jimmy stood up and brushed himself off, but he took his time. Paul stepped to the camera. He noticed Jimmy running his eye along the rows of windows again.

In the next few days Paul and Jimmy dashed about with the Luxograph camera, photographing subjects Paul hoped would please Shadow and excite audiences. Standing ankle-deep in the surf at Old Tampa Bay, they filmed "The First Artillery Bathing Its Horses." The colonel could add one or more exclamation marks, as he pleased.

On a dismal stretch of sand and low palmettos northeast of town, they filmed

"Second Infantry Practices Entrenching Drill." In pine woods, in pitiless heat, they filmed maneuvers of a thousand-man cavalry column—some squadrons galloping, some trotting, all kicking sand in the faces of the struggling camera operators. While the scorching sun flashed and winked from steel sabers, Jimmy once again threatened to quit. It was becoming a habit; Paul paid no attention:

"I have a different idea here, help me. Come on, damn it!"

Jimmy slogged after him, to a place where four sizable palmetto logs lay scattered about. They dragged the logs together and crisscrossed the ends, building a low breastwork. Paul crouched with the camera just behind this structure while a detachment of the cavalry gleefully charged straight at him, splitting in half only at the last moment. Jimmy knelt six feet to the rear of Paul, clenching his teeth in terror.

The riders streamed by on both sides, very close, but they were good horsemen and there was no mishap. Paul raised the camera and straightened the tripod. "If this footage develops without damage, it will be *sensationell.*"

Jimmy pulled a cigar from his shirt. "Well, you could've had a sensational funeral. This is getting pretty damn dangerous."

"You had any spic stuff yet?" Jimmy asked that night in the rathskeller as they slumped over the bar with beer and a plate of cheeses.

"I don't need girls"—a lie; the ache was becoming fierce—"I need alligators."

"*Alligators?* I wouldn't go near one of those leather-hided fuckers. What's got into you?"

"This telegraph message was on the bulletin board when we came in. The colonel wants pictures of Florida alligators. We must find one."

Jimmy finished his beer. "You go on to bed and think about alligators, I got somebody waiting to smoke my cigar. See you tomorrow."

Troop trains rolled into Tampa every day, bringing new detachments. Paul and Jimmy roamed the encampments, searching for likely subjects. The first camp had been set up on the Tampa Heights, vacant scrubland about a mile above the center of town, but that site had been filled very quickly. Now the Army was bivouacking new arrivals in DeSoto Park and Ybor City, Palmetto Beach and Port Tampa, nine miles away on the bay. Some units were stuck in Lakeland, thirty miles east. The newest camp was in a park on the west side of the hotel.

Civilians were pouring into the city too. The Plant line shifted its entire Sanford office staff—Paul and Jimmy photographed the arrival at the depot—and began hiring black day laborers from as far away as Ocala. There came also, inevitably, those who saw opportunity in supplying familiar wartime amenities. Tent saloons sprang up in the poorer sections, wherever there was a bit of space. Most had whores or gambling available. There was little interference; licensing laws in Tampa were loosely written and enforced. Paul didn't think Iz Pflaum would show scenes of low life, so he wasted no film.

Lines of idled boxcars, many giving off the stench of spoiling food, stretched thirty miles north because the two railroads serving Tampa, Plant's and the Florida Central & Peninsular, were the bitterest of competitors. The Plant System wouldn't allow Florida Central freight on its right-of-way. Worse, Plant owned the single track from the city to the port on Old Tampa Bay. Jimmy thought they should film some of the boxcars, but Paul thought them ugly, and of little interest, and vetoed it.

Both railroads were promoting excursion fares throughout the state. Eight dollars bought a round trip ticket from Jacksonville. How could you *not* afford to go and admire America's brave men drilling for war? On a single weekend the two lines brought in more than twenty thousand sightseers; Paul and Jimmy photographed some of them pouring off the bunting-covered cars.

Paul found tips on possible subjects and caught up on the latest news by whipping through the *Tampa Times* in his insufferably hot room after a day that typically lasted eighteen or nineteen hours. The paper told him that municipal facilities were grievously overtaxed; the water system had to be supplemented from wells owned by local companies. But Tampa residents were overlooking the crowds and the inconveniences because they were bathing in a river of new money. Retail business had never been so good. Newsboys made an unheard-of thirty dollars a week, lemonade and peanut vendors as much as fifty.

While officers were attending fancy balls at Plant's hotel, civic groups entertained enlisted men at picnics. Every church had its gospel concert, ice cream social, and strawberry festival where soldiers could meet young women under proper supervision. Ladies' prayer circles baked hundreds of cakes. So did the United Daughters of the Confederacy. High patriotism was in the air; America was coming together again in the crucible of this war.

There was no trouble between soldiers and the citizens of Tampa until the volunteers began arriving in large numbers. The *Tampa Times* observed that the experienced troops, the regulars, behaved well, but certain volunteers were intent on carousing and starting brawls, mostly in and around the new saloons, brothels, and gambling hells.

About ten days after Paul and Jimmy arrived, the famed evangelist Dwight L. Moody returned, having conducted a revival in Tampa only weeks before. He brought Ira Sankey, a celebrated organist. In a public park, Moody and Sankey and a third luminary, Oliver O. Howard, the general turned preacher, conducted day and evening services. The Luxograph team took the camera there one afternoon.

O. O. Howard was reading Scripture when they arrived. A prominent Civil War veteran, Howard had lost his right arm at a place called Fair Oaks, but had remained on active duty until the surrender. He'd been awarded the Medal of Honor, or so Paul was told by a magazine sketch artist named Remington, a man with a burly frame and short, thick legs who seemed a likable, Falstaffian sort, at first.

Remington was sketching Howard from the back of the crowd, where Paul and Jimmy had set up the camera. Paul noticed that most of the crowd were soldiers, mainly Northern. While Jimmy cranked, Paul walked back to Remington, who had his foot on a stool and his sketch pad on his knee. Paul asked Remington why the local folk were boycotting the service.

"After the war, Howard ran the Freedmen's Bureau. He started a college for the colored up in Washington. He can wave his Bible and preach about peace and brotherhood, but down here he's still a damn Yankee nigger-lover."

The service ended as the sun was dropping behind the palms. Mr. Remington closed his sketch pad and came over to examine the camera. He wasn't impressed. He called the living pictures "a business for rag pickers and other New York kikes."

Paul protested that Colonel Shadow wasn't a Jew, nor was Mr. Edison, but what did it matter if they were? Remington looked affronted and left. Whenever Paul met him in the hotel after that, Remington merely nodded, without smiling.

Paul drank a lot of beer and wolfed a lot of wursts in the rathskeller, but seldom had time for a proper meal. By the end of his second week in Tampa he was losing weight. Sometimes he left his room before daybreak, forgetting to shave. It hardly mattered; smooth-cheeked or scrubby, the heavy humid air made him feel dirty either way. The hotel was bedlam, filled with high-ranking officers, their wives and children, and a growing number of journalists.

Paul continued to down a stein or two of beer in the rathskeller before tottering up to bed each night. He was now aware of a clear and rigid hierarchy among the journalists. Lowest were the camera operators like himself, Jimmy, and the porcine William Paley of the Eden Musée, whom Richard Harding Davis had mentioned. Paul had seen Paley from a distance on several occasions. He wanted to strike up an acquaintance with him but never seemed to find the opportunity.

Above the lowly representatives of an ill-defined and poorly regarded novelty medium were the newspaper reporters largely unknown outside their own editorial rooms. One step up were those with nationally recognized bylines. John Fox, Frederick Palmer, George Kennan. E. F. Knight of the *London Times*. The sketch artist for *The Century* and *Harper's*, Frederic Remington, whom Paul disliked. At the apex of the pyramid were the two whose writings had made them internationally famous. Mr. Davis and Mr. Crane.

Both were journalists of the greatest repute. There the resemblance ended. As Captain Lee had suggested to Paul, Mr. Davis stood for society and the salons, Mr. Crane for the street and the slums. Crane hobnobbed with colleagues and ordinary soldiers, Davis with the generals and the admirals. Davis was uniformly friendly, never haughty. But everyone, including Davis himself, probably, knew there was a chasm: Richard Harding Davis alone and resplendent on one side, and on the other, the legion of the lower-paid, led by the writer some of them called Saint Stephen.

One evening, late, Paul dragged himself up from the rathskeller to the rotunda. It was quiet; only a few couples drifting through and two Army lieutenants examining messages on the board. Walking toward the elevator at the east end, he entered the Solarium, a large room with tall windows, white wicker chairs, tropical plants in fancy urns. A man was seated there, alone, reading a *Tampa Times*. It was Paley.

Weary as he was, Paul thought this an ideal moment to introduce himself. He approached. After a few seconds Paley closed his paper and deigned to notice him. Paul was shocked to see the man close up. His eyes had a sickly, sunken look, his skin a yellow cast.

"Mr. William Paley? I have wanted to meet you. My name is Crown. I am a camera operator like you."

"Oh, yes, I heard there was another one in the hotel. Who do you work for?"

"The American National Luxograph Company of Chicago. Our president is Colonel Sidney Shadow."

"Never heard of him." Paley gave a dyspeptic belch, without covering his mouth. His breath was terrible.

"But he is licensed by Mr. Edison."

"So is the Eden Musée, young man. So are a dozen others. Now if that's all—"

"No, please, I would like to buy you a glass of beer downstairs. I thought we might exchange ideas. I know you are very experienced."

Paley threw his paper on a wicker table. "I have no time to teach novices, and I sincerely doubt I can learn from one. Good night."

He left the Solarium with a slow, wobbly step. Obviously he was ill. Even so, the rebuff rankled. Paul felt small, stupid, and definitely the outsider.

Next morning he awoke before daylight, as usual. His room was on the sunny side of the hotel, and at the end of each day the temperature seemed to be a hundred. At night the room hardly cooled at all. He was sweating as he collected his razor, soap cup, and brush from the accumulating clutter on the dressing table and headed for the bathroom.

He shaved, dressed, and ate breakfast in the mammoth dining room with its ninety-foot dome and high windows, each framed by an elaborate mahogany arch. By half past seven he'd dragged Jimmy from sleep by repeated knocking. While Jimmy ate breakfast, Paul loaded their equipment into a rented wagon. Before nine they were driving along a sand road straggling its way toward the Bay, to film more drills. Suddenly Jimmy pointed. "Holy mother. Look!" Shadow's alligator was sunning itself on the bank of a scum-covered lagoon beside the road. It was a great leathery specimen, twelve to fourteen feet from snout to tail.

"At last," Paul exclaimed softly. "He's perfect." He stopped the wagon.

Anxiously eyeing the gator, Jimmy tied the horse to a shrub. Paul stepped quietly toward the lagoon, carrying the camera. He unfolded the tripod and set the legs in the sand without a sound. After checking the reading on the footage meter, he started cranking.

The gator sensed the interlopers. It roused, opened its huge long jaws crowded with sharp teeth, and started to move.

Toward the camera.

Jimmy ran for cover behind the nearest palm. "Dutch, pack it up, that thing'll eat you alive!"

Paul kept cranking. He could feel his heart leaping in his chest. The alligator advanced in a slow, almost stately way, dragging its whitish belly, leaving a trail of disturbed sand and pine straw as it drew closer.

Paul tilted the tripod forward with one hand to keep the gator in the frame. It kept coming.

Paul set the camera down and let go of the crank. Hopping on one foot, he managed to tear off a shoe and throw it. The shoe bounced on the gator's snout. The gator ground its belly in the sand and stopped.

Little half-round eyes fixed on Paul with a baleful stare. Gingerly, Paul hoisted the tripod and carefully put a foot behind him. Took a step backward. Another.

The alligator opened its jaws . . .

And turned and rushed to the lagoon, leaping through the scum crust with a great splash and sinking from sight.

"Godamighty, that was close." Jimmy was sweating heavily. "You got balls. If that thing had put its lamps on me, I'd have peed my pants."

"One minute longer, me too." They both laughed in a rare moment of camaraderie.

Paul checked the film counter. He'd gotten seventy-five feet if it all came out. In terms of tension and fear, he'd paid dearly for every foot. It cost him a shoe, too.

He remembered the moment in Indiana when he'd thought the Wabash Cannonball would run over him. He'd felt the same panic then, the same elation afterward. The moral was apparent. If you wanted exciting pictures, you had to take risks. That was why Jimmy would never last in the business.

Later that afternoon, wearing a new pair of shoes charged to the company, he walked over the Lafayette Street bridge with a small wooden crate under his arm; the first two 400-foot magazines of exposed negative. He'd packed them in excelsior and painted warnings about fragility and heat on the crate.

At the depot, the commercial agent helped him fill out papers for a C.O.D. shipment to Chicago. He watched carefully while the agent wired on the shipping tag. Using the agent's paste pot, he fastened a hotel envelope to the crate. On the sheet of stationery inside, he'd indexed the subjects, using the meter numbers.

He went next to the Western Union office on Franklin Street, where he laboriously printed Shadow's name and address on a blank, then the message.

SENDING SENSATIONAL FOOTAGE EXPRESS COLLECT.

He wet the tip of the pencil stub on his tongue. He hesitated only a moment before signing Dutch.

Paul soon came to recognize the most important officers headquartered at the hotel. Notable among them was a small, frail man who seemed to go everywhere at a rapid lope. General Joe Wheeler was one of several ex-Confederates wearing blue again. Another was the former United States consul from Havana, General Fitzhugh Lee, a big Santa Claus whom everybody liked as they did Wheeler.

The commanding general of the expeditionary force, General William Rufus Shafter, was accorded proper respect, but few cared for him personally. The general's nickname was Pecos Bill. He had a distinguished record as a Civil War officer and an Indian fighter, but the reporters said he'd changed considerably since those days. Now sixty-three, he weighed approximately three hundred pounds. His uniform was big as a tent and fit badly. His graying hair and walrus mustache always looked unkempt. Whenever he moved, or even stood still, he breathed hard and noisily. His aides trailed him closely, as if he might topple over with a heart seizure at any moment. The reporters said Shafter was too old and too fat for the exertions of a summer campaign in the hot latitudes.

One evening when Jimmy was roaming again, Paul went down to the rathskeller. He'd become a regular customer; he liked the room because it attracted a comfortable crowd. Lieutenants and captains drank there, and once in a while a major, but the high brass preferred small private parties or spent the evenings in conference. So far he hadn't seen a general or even a colonel downstairs.

Tonight was the exception. He found himself near a colonel. His face seemed familiar, but Paul couldn't identify it.

The colonel was having a cup of coffee and complaining loudly to a couple of juniors. "Of course it's a government conspiracy, and politically motivated. The intent is to punish me for my convictions by keeping me in Florida, out of the action."

The junior officers made sympathetic noises. Paul finished his beer and went upstairs for a stroll. Only then did the speaker's identity register. His face and huge leonine head had appeared on Democratic posters all over Chicago two years ago.

He asked questions next day to confirm it. Yes, Colonel William Jennings Bryan was serving with a regiment of Nebraska "silver soldiers."

Bryan was nearly invisible in the hotel. That wasn't the case with a flamboyant lieutenant colonel named Roosevelt, of the 1st Volunteer Cavalry. The regimental commander, Leonard Wood, was a veteran professional. But his second got the attention.

One morning as Paul was setting up the camera to photograph flamingos in a large reflecting pool on the grounds, Lieutenant Colonel Roosevelt came striding along, wearing khakis and a blue bandanna with polka dots. Paul had seen similar bandannas on other men in the regiment the newsmen variously called Wood's Wild Westerners, the Cavalry Cowpunchers, Teddy's Terrors, or the Rough Riders.

Roosevelt greeted Paul with a toothy grin and a booming hello. He stopped to watch Paul adjust the tripod feet. Jimmy had gone off for a new film magazine.

Roosevelt pointed to the name stenciled on the camera. "That's you, American Luxograph?"

"Yes."

"I know a little something about this picture business. The American Biograph contacted me two years ago, shortly after President McKinley posed for them in Canton."

"Right, sir. Your estate in New York, I saw the footage."

"Fascinating, these flickers. They reach and influence so many. Or they have that potential. Too bad their moral tone isn't higher."

"Colonel, if I may disagree—that's a false impression. I admit that until now, most of the subjects have been—excuse me, I still have trouble with my English —in German I would say *alltäglich*. Is there a word 'trivial'?"

"Indeed so."

"The pictures have been trivial, but that will change. Serious films, films of actual events such as this war, will change it."

"I like a man who's an optimist. And perhaps you're right. After all, the flickers helped Bill McKinley win." Looking thoughtful, Roosevelt polished his silver-wire spectacles on his sleeve. "What's your name, lad?"

"Paul Crown. Everyone calls me Dutch."

"Well, Dutch Crown, look me up if I can assist you in any way. Any way at all."

They shook hands. Roosevelt had a crushing grip. As he strode off, Paul was keenly skeptical of his friendliness. In the rathskeller it was said that the colonel had strong political ambitions and actively sought publicity.

Thinking that, Paul was wryly amused. What a cynic he'd become at the old age of almost twenty-one.

Officers around the hotel talked with a fair degree of candor. There might be music and dancing and gaiety at night, but there were problems, horrendous ones, discussed all day.

Freight cars now blocked the rails for fifty miles north. Other boxcars sat idle on sidings as far away as Columbia, South Carolina. The cars contained vital arms, ammunition, food. But the Quartermaster Department couldn't unload the cars and quickly route their contents to the proper storage sites because the department had no way to determine whether the shipment was for the Commissary Department, the Ordnance Department, the Engineer Department, or the quartermasters themselves. There were no bills of lading, no explanatory paperwork of any kind; nothing but the same painted legend Paul had seen on every car. MILITARY SUPPLIES—RUSH! The materiel needed for the expedition could be sorted and routed only by a search of individual cars, an effort requiring thousands of man-hours.

Paul heard complaints about the vile food being supplied by government contractors, and the ineptitude of War Department purchasing agents who were sending men to the tropics in clothing more suited to the Yukon gold strike. One night in a ground-floor salon, he heard Roosevelt hold forth in front of a small crowd of officers and civilians.

"Criminal, that's what it is!" Roosevelt pounded a fragile table; a piece of porcelain statuary almost toppled. "In the 1st Volunteers we refused to accept those blue hair shirts. We procured our own khakis, at our own expense. If Secretary Alger doesn't like it, he can court-martial us. But first I'll knock the damned teeth of the damned little runt down his damned throat, you can count on that, boys."

His listeners clapped and gave several supportive huzzahs. He certainly knew how to work a crowd.

The War Department was derelict on many fronts. Through sheer mismanagement it had thus far failed to spend its latest fifty-million-dollar appropriation for modern equipment—Krag-Jorgensen rifles, the new smokeless powder.

Port Tampa represented another potential disaster. Paul and Jimmy drove out there one day to survey the picture possibilities. It was hardly worth the bother. From a freight yard at the end of the single track owned by the Plant System, two spurs ran to twin wooden piers extending some three thousand feet into Old Tampa Bay. There were three tracks on the south pier, one on the north. The Plant line boasted that the piers could handle two dozen oceangoing vessels at one time. The British attaché, Captain Lee, told Paul that one dozen was more realistic. And thirty to thirty-five ships would be required for the expedition. Further, the channel was difficult; narrow and no deeper than twenty-three feet. The largest transports drew eighteen feet. There were only four pilots with enough experience to handle such ships in the local waters.

Four regiments of Negro regulars had been sent to Tampa. Two infantry regiments, the 24th and the 25th, and the more exotic 9th and 10th Cavalry; the famous Buffalo Soldiers, who had policed the Plains and protected white settlers since the Civil War.

The volunteers from Southern states and a majority of Tampa citizens didn't like the blacks. There were incidents; taunting matches, fights with fists, rocks, barrel staves. Then, out in Lakeland, where the 10th was camped, a trooper from the regiment asked for a haircut at a barbershop and was refused. The black soldier protested and argued. He was driven out of the shop by the white owner's invective and by threats from several customers.

Soon after, a band of men from the 10th came marching down the center of the main street. They pulled their pistols, blew out the barbershop window, and shot up the street. Before they were disarmed and taken away under guard, a white bystander lay dead.

"And he was just watching," Jimmy said. He was in sympathy with the locals.

Late one afternoon he and Paul were taking a short rest in rocking chairs on the front veranda, having spent the whole day in a fruitless search for exciting subjects.

Jimmy had a *Tampa Times* and began to regale Paul with excerpts from an editorial. He mispronounced most of the larger words: *"Enrolling the Negro in the Army has made him forget his place. Negro soldiers have made themselves offensive to the citizens of Tampa. They insist on being treated like white men, and display a pronounced insolence when they are not. The white officers in charge of the Negroes have done nothing to curb this arrogant behavior."*

He lowered the paper. "Bang on the target, wouldn't you say?"

"No. Why should black men loyally serving their country arouse such fury?"

"Jesus, Dutch, are you ever gonna understand America? Niggers are one step from slavery and half a step from apes."

"Is that it? They were slaves before your great Civil War, and everyone thought them poor low creatures who could only be field hands and housemaids, and even though the North won that war, people still feel the same way about the Negroes? That's stupid. They didn't choose to put on chains and do menial work, did they? Anyway, my uncle said the war freed them and made them equal with all other—"

"Uh-uh, forget that. Free, maybe. But equal to a white man? Never. A nigger isn't fit to stand in a white man's shadow."

"But the Negro soldiers are Americans! They wear the same uniform as the white soldiers do. They stand the same risk of dying. They should be entitled to the same decent treatment."

"You say that too loud, some of these Florida crackers'll fit you with a tar overcoat or a hemp necktie."

"Come on. That is ridiculous." Paul rocked a moment or two, thinking. "We should film some of the Negro cavalrymen, they'd be interesting subjects."

"Oh sure, let's do that. And the first time they show the pictures at Iz Pflaum's, the micks and the bohunks'll tear out the seats and burn the place down. Nobody wants to see coon soldiers, for Christ's sake. Right here it says the Army practically has to threaten white officers with court martial to get 'em to command one of those units. They should put the damn niggers up front, to save the white boys."

"How can you say such a thing?"

"Because I'm a white man, and I look after myself. Anybody who gets in the way of Jim Daws when Jim Daws is looking out for himself—he's in for it."

That night Paul was sipping beer at the rathskeller's crowded bar when a chunky young man wearing a checked cap approached him. "Excuse me, you're Crown, aren't you?"

"That's right."

The stranger offered his card. "Billy Bitzer. American Biograph, New York. Thought I should say hello."

Billy Bitzer was older than Paul by perhaps five years; a neatly dressed fellow with a squarish, likable face. He laid his cap on the bar. "Another beer? My treat." He signaled the barkeep. "I figure we may need to help each other in Cuba. We sure won't get any help from the newspaper boys. They don't think much of us."

"So I have discovered, though Mr. Davis is very friendly."

"You're German," Bitzer said as the beer arrived. "Me too." He blew off some of the head and took a long drink. "I hear old Paley gave you the snob treatment."

"How do you know that?"

Bitzer leaned back, resting his leather elbow pads on the fine mahogany bar. "He's been telling people that some young pup accosted him in a pushy way. Knowing Paley, that means you were polite and he was his usual snotty self. Bill Paley's a prick. Maybe if we're lucky he'll get sick and go home."

"He already looks terrible."

"Used to demonstrate and sell X-ray machines. He claims his sickness is related to that. I like to be charitable when someone's had tough luck, but not if they're nasty. Want another beer?"

"Yes, I'll buy this one."

"What's your first name?"

"They call me Dutch."

"Put 'er there, Dutch." They shook hands. "Pals united against pricks like Paley. Sounds like a lodge. Let's drink to it."

They drank to it. Presently Paul ordered a round and they drank to it again. They took to each other immediately.

They talked about girls. Bitzer preferred the ones in New York; Paul thought the Cuban girls of Tampa looked very passionate and desirable. They talked about beer, agreeing that the local stuff was to be consumed strictly for its effect, certainly not for its quality. They talked about cameras. Bitzer was envious of

Paul's because his from the Biograph Company had one drawback that canceled out many good features.

"Runs on storage batteries. Almost two thousand pounds of them. I bitched in New York and they said, 'Billy, you don't want to go, we'll pay somebody else.' I sit on my kiester for hours just waiting for a teamster willing to haul all those crates. Your Luxograph sounds like a honey. Maybe I should steal it."

He winked and waved for refills. They parted soon after, exchanging garrulous vows of friendship and promises of future revelry.

With four steins of Florida Brewing's Extra Pale sloshing around inside him, Paul was more than a little unsteady riding the elevator to the fifth floor. As usual, stepping from the cage was like going from a small hot closet to a large hot oven. He'd gotten used to sweating all day outdoors, and all night in the hotel.

He tried to insert his key in the keyhole and kept missing. A door opened far down the hall. A man darted out of a room next to the staircase, clapping a derby on his head. Smoke trailed from a cigarette in his other hand.

The man was quite tall and thin. Smartly dressed, with a neatly trimmed beard. He flashed a look along the hall, saw Paul, and then, without any reaction, stepped quickly around the corner to the stair going down.

Paul's room key had fallen from his hand, unnoticed. Was he drunk? Somewhat. Was he insane? Definitely not. The face had leaped out with burning clarity. Vivid dark eyes. Gold-wire spectacles with round lenses no bigger than pennies . . . anywhere in the world he would recognize the man he'd first met in the Berlin rail yards.

But the man leaving hurriedly was barbered, well-tailored; *clean.*

Paul forgot his key lying on the carpet and ran down the hall, noting the number of the room from which the man had emerged. He took the stairs in pursuit. At every landing there were tantalizing aromas. A trace of gents' cologne; a hint of talc . . . Mikhail Rhukov gave off odors, but not that kind.

On the ground floor he saw no sign of the man. He dashed by a couple of startled Navy men, straight to the rotunda. The night clerk was sleepy and cross.

"I am Mr. Crown, five eleven. Can you tell me the occupant of room five thirty-six? It's very important."

The clerk opened his mouth to say no. Paul slid a dollar across the green marble. The clerk covered it and drew it smoothly to his pocket, then turned the morocco-bound ledger a hundred eighty degrees. He leafed through the pages slowly. He glanced at the pigeonhole rack, connecting a name with a number.

"It's the wife of an American officer who's encamped with his men at Tampa Heights."

"Thank you. One more question. Upstairs, very briefly, I thought I saw a friend. Possibly he's a guest. He's Russian, his name is Mikhail Rhukov."

"Spell the last."

Paul did it as best he could. The clerk again turned pages.

"We have no one by that name."

"Are you sure? He speaks English with an accent heavier than mine. You would remember him."

"I would, and I don't."

"But I saw him, there can't be any mistake. Mikhail Rhukov—?"

"We have no Rhukov from Russia, Romania, Bulgaria, Switzerland, or any other address in Europe. That's all I'm going to tell you. This hotel protects the privacy of its guests. We have many celebrities who stay with us in the winter season."

Paul turned away, wondering if he had really mistaken one man for another. Or seen the human equivalent of a desert mirage.

No, absolutely, he wasn't that besotted. It was Rhukov. Scrubbed up; sartorially transformed—but *Rhukov.*

If an Army officer had put his wife in the hotel but returned to his camp every night, Paul could readily imagine why Rhukov had left in such haste. But that answered none of the other questions hammering in his head.

Where had he come from? Where had he gone? Where was he now?

What devil's miracle had transformed him?

From that night, Paul devoted his few free moments to the mystery. It remained unsolved. No employee he questioned recognized Rhukov's name or description, but that proved nothing; he'd already learned that the staff was not overly forthcoming about guests.

Several of the journalists thought the description sounded familiar but couldn't identify the man. They were unanimous about one thing. He wasn't Russian. One man insisted he was English, a second countered with Canadian, a third said that whatever he was, he had only stayed for a day or two.

Paul telephoned other, cheaper hotels across the river. Nothing. One day when he and Jimmy were away, filming, the wife in room 536 checked out and a young Navy ensign moved in.

It was dead end. Whatever the explanation, the clean Rhukov had vanished as suddenly, inexplicably as the dirty one.

May wore on. Several times, Army horses or mules broke loose from their corral and stampeded through the downtown, terrorizing citizens. Paul and Jimmy were never in place at the right moment to film one of these equestrian rampages. Instead, they photographed "Blanket-Tossing A New Recruit" and "Cuban Refugees Awaiting Rations." Hundreds of these refugees had come to Tampa via Key West.

Next came "Friendly Enemies," a baseball game between a Tampa team and the Irish of the New York 69th Volunteers. Crane was in the bleachers, shouting profane and sarcastic comments when either side made a mistake.

If Crane was a genius, his appearance belied it. He was a man of average height with straw-colored hair, a sallow face, and a large mustache. His duck trousers and white shirt were grimy. He smoked a pipe and, every inning or so, left his seat for a bottle of beer. Toward the end of the game, when the 69th had fourteen runs to the home team's one, Paul and Jimmy moved the camera to shoot a few frames of Mr. Crane the baseball fan. People seated around him wondered about the attention; he looked like a dirty idler. When Crane saw the camera, and Paul cranking, he tipped his straw hat in a sardonic way, stuck out his tongue, and laughed uproariously. Paul suspected Shadow wouldn't like the footage, no matter how famous the subject.

Because it was taking a long time to organize the troops and the attack convoy, picture subjects became fewer and, in Paul's estimation, duller. They were reduced to "A Trolley Ride Through Tampa" and "Morning Washup of the 1st Florida Volunteers." Florida had raised twenty companies, but Army regulations stipulated that a regiment was twelve companies, so eight had been sent home. Paul wished the whole lot had been sent home. He and Jimmy filmed the Escambia Rifles of Pensacola, a scruffy, loudmouthed lot. Several of them mocked Paul's accent to his face. For a change Paul was the one ready to fight, Jimmy the one who dragged him away. "Bad odds," Jimmy said later. He was correct. There were a lot of farmers in the Florida companies; big, with sunburned necks and strong arms.

That night at the hotel, Paul got two more shocks, the first while he was riding the elevator downstairs for a meal and beer.

The crowded car stopped at every floor. On the second floor a foreign officer stepped in. He wore khakis and the familiar red-dotted roundel on his cap. A military attaché Paul hadn't seen before.

Then his spine crawled. *Yes I have.*

He'd only glimpsed the man's face—could see nothing but the back of his head as the car descended—yet he was almost positive. When the car opened at the ground floor, he hung back. The attaché stepped away briskly, in profile a moment. Yes! There were the gray eyes that chilled the otherwise ordinary face. There was the hook-shaped dueling scar on the left cheek. He had never forgotten the lieutenant with the gold cigarette case in the Berlin rail yard.

A reporter he knew slightly stepped off the car with him. Paul said, "Do you know that officer?" The attaché was bowing to kiss the gloved hand of an American officer's wife.

"Sure. Captain von Rike. German embassy, Washington."

His past seemed to be gathering around him as if some great climax was brewing; something personal, beyond the war and his insignificant role in it. He felt unseen forces rising like storm winds; forces he could neither identify nor comprehend. They were driving him inexorably *zu einem Wirbel*; to some vortex, some whirlpool. And an unknown end.

The second shock came in the rathskeller, not long after he found Mr. Crane in the middle of an argument. Mr. Crane was faced off against another reporter. Crane's straw-colored hair straggled over his forehead to his brows. His soiled shirt lacked a collar. There were six empty beer bottles lined up at his elbow.

His adversary was a reporter named Sylvanus Peterman. He worked for the *New York Journal,* but he was never seen with Davis, the *Journal's* star, and only seldom with the other men, two or three dozen, whom Mr. Hearst had sent to Tampa to handle the lesser chores of receiving editorial instructions, writing minor stories and fillers, sketching, transmitting copy, paying bills. Paul had heard that daily telegraph charges for the Hearst organization often exceeded a thousand dollars.

Peterman was plump, pale, well dressed; he wore shell-rimmed glasses and smelled of toilet water. Though no older than Crane, he was already going bald.

He combed his pomaded hair sideways to hide his bare skull. Most all the reporters disliked him. Crane looked as though he wanted to strangle him.

Paul edged closer. Peterman was saying sententiously, "Kipling put it admirably. *'Take up the White Man's burden, send forth the best ye breed—'* "

"Oh, not that shit," Crane said through the smoke from the cigarette hanging on his lip. "Freddy, another bottle."

" *'Go, bind your sons to exile, to serve your captives' need.'* "

"Oh, shit, shit! Freddy, God damn it, step lively, I can't listen to this sober."

"Crane, what's wrong with you? Where's your perspective? If we don't civilize and democratize the backward colored peoples, who will? We must develop these new markets—occupy new lands if necessary. We're the leaders of the world now. We are a conquering race!"

The fresh bottle arrived. Crane laid his cigarette on the bar and took a long swig. He raised the bottle. "I salute you"—a wet, phlegmy cough hunched him over for a moment—"salute you, brother Peterman. Or is it brother Hearst?"

"You can sneer all you want, I'm proud to work for a true American visionary who—"

"Shut up and answer the question I asked you five minutes ago. Just how are you and wild Bill going to accomplish this magnificent conquest if the recipients don't want it?"

"What a hypocrite you are. How can you take money from the *World?*"

"Easy. I don't send the paper any pandering copy."

"How very noble. But you forget, Mr. Pulitzer and Mr. Hearst believe what I'm saying."

"Bullshit. Mr. Hearst and Mr. Pulitzer don't believe anything but the circulation numbers. Now answer me. How are you going to spread and enforce your great American gospel? With whips and chains, while shooting red, white, and blue rockets out your ass?"

"You're disgusting."

"And you jingo boys make me sick." Crane hurled his cigarette at the nearest spittoon and missed.

"So self-righteous," Peterman snarled. "You and your filthy novels and your arrogance. Always mocking the traditional values. Trampling on them like some damn pagan. Decent Americans won't have it—and we're the majority!"

"Then almighty God help us, brother Peterman, because no one else will. I've had my dose of propaganda for the night. Get out of here before I knock you down with a fart, that's all it would take."

He turned his back.

Sylvanus Peterman swept his eye along the bar, past Paul, various journalists, a pair of second lieutenants trying to contain their anger. He stalked to the stairway with a martyred air.

"Fill me up again, Freddy," Crane shouted, waving his empty bottle. It slipped from his hand and smashed behind the bar.

The barkeep said, "Mr. Crane, maybe you've had too much."

"Too much is never enough. Is Joe Pulitzer's money good in this rat hole, or isn't it?"

"You should eat something—"

"Absolutely. Tomorrow or the next day. Plenty of time." The hacking cough bent him over again. He gripped the bar with both hands until the spasm passed.

Sighing, the barkeep snapped the crown off another bottle, set it in front of Crane, then began cleaning up the glass with a broom and pan. Leaning on his elbows, Crane rolled his head blearily from side to side. He noticed Paul standing at his left.

"I know you. The camera kid. You tried to preserve me for posterity at the ballpark."

"Good thing you did, Dutch," Freddy said. "At the rate he's going, he won't be around long."

"Up yours," Crane said cheerfully. "What's your name, camera kid?"

"Dutch Crown. American National Luxograph Company of Chicago."

"Graph this, graph that—every one of 'em's a graph. Damn things'll never catch on." He put a new cigarette in his mouth, or tried. On the first attempt he mashed the end against his lip. "Buy you a beer?"

"Fine, thank you." Freddy drew a Florida Brewing Extra Pale. Crane raised his bottle for a toast. Paul did the same with his stein.

"Let's drink to absént love. Have you got an absent love, Dutch?"

Paul said softly, "I do."

"Mmm. Mine's Miss Cora Stewart. Proprietress of the Hotel de Dream, Jacksonville. If there is a sporting house in America more tasteful and well-mannered, I don't know it. Salud. To Cora."

"Prosit. Cora."

They drank.

"Not much to do around here, is there?" Crane said. "Not much to write about. I'm bored silly. I've been working on another short story."

"I greatly admire your writing. I haven't read *Maggie,* your first, but the *Red Badge*—if you wrote nothing besides that, I would say your mark is made."

"Thanks. Thanks very much." He seemed tired all at once.

"May I ask a question on another subject?"

"Sorry, I don't know a thing about Joe Pulitzer's girlfriends or bowel habits."

This was a strange, compelling man, Paul thought. But very self-destructive. Crane kept the cigarette dangling from his mouth, squinting through the blue smoke, to nowhere.

"It's nothing like that. Recently, in this hotel, I thought I saw an old acquaintance. I saw him at a distance, on the fifth floor. I wanted to hail him but he hurried off. Now I can't find him. His name is Mikhail Rhukov. Like you, he's a journalist."

Crane shook his head. "Maybe if you describe him—"

"Tall, very slender. Has a beard. When he smiles, his teeth seem whiter than piano keys." Crane straightened up, blinking. "His spectacles are small. Lenses no bigger than this." Paul showed a circle, thumb and forefinger. "He's very outspoken."

Crane drew the cigarette from his lips and dropped it on the floor and stepped on it. "What did you say his name is?"

"Mikhail Rhukov."

"Then he has a twin. You described Michael Radcliffe. He's a journalist. But he's an Englishman."

"Englishman?"

"Do you have a hearing problem? The man you described is Michael Radcliffe. Very upper-upper type. If he wasn't born in Blighty and bred up at Oxford or Cambridge, I'll pay you a thousand dollars. As soon as I get it."

"A British journalist—how can it be?"

"I dunno, kid, but it is."

"I described him to several of your colleagues. A few seemed to remember him, but no one knew his name."

"He was registered in the hotel only two nights. Came over by steamer to Charleston, then took a coaster to Fernandina and a train here. We drank champagne at this very bar, then continued at one of the tables. We got on damn well. We talked for hours. I believed everything he said about himself, but at the same time a voice in my head was yelling fire, fire! He was all that he seemed, but he was something more. Have you heard of Otto Hartstein, Lord Yorke?"

"No."

"One of the two great press lords of England. Michael Radcliffe's a roving correspondent for Hartstein's *London Light*. The flagship paper. He's married to Lord Yorke's only child, Cecily Hartstein. Talk about career insurance."

Radcliffe? England? Married? No Russian accent? Paul was reeling.

"Do you know why he left the hotel, Mr. Crane?"

"Well—" Crane coughed and as soon as he recovered, lit another cigarette. He was scrutinizing Paul warily now, his eyes clearer, his concentration intense. "Some affair of the heart. Or at least the bedroom. It involved a lady who was in the dining room regularly for a while. On her left hand the lady displayed large and expensive engagement and wedding rings."

"Mr. Crane, I must find this man. I must see if he is Mikhail Rhukov."

"You say you're his friend."

"Rhukov's friend, yes, absolutely."

"I'll beat the hell out of you if I find out you're lying." Crane took a puff of his cigarette. "He rang my room just before he checked out at ten minutes past three in the morning. The next afternoon he called again and I forwarded his bags. I watch the bulletin board for him. Telegraph messages, instructions, little murmurs of affection from his wife. It's professional courtesy. I'm sure he'd do the same for—"

"Please. Where is he?"

Their eyes locked. Crane's hard gaze made Paul squirm.

"Some flea pit in Ybor City. I'll slip you the address. Freddy? A piece of paper. And another beer. Make it snappy."

89

The General

JOE MET his immediate superior an hour after he stepped from a Plant line Pullman at the hotel. A note waiting at the registration desk informed him of the meeting. It would be held not at the headquarters of the Cavalry Division, about a mile away, but in a hotel parlor. He threw his belongings into his small two-room suite on the third floor, splashed water on his face, and went downstairs via the main staircase. He was in full uniform; heavy blue frock coat with a brigadier's star on the shoulder strap; dress sword buckled on.

The opulence of the hotel continued to astonish him. In the busy rotunda, near a bronze of Little Red Riding Hood and the wolf, he asked a bellman for directions to the parlor. It was located in the long hall leading to the east entrance.

At the telegraph office he quickly wrote a message to Ilsa, saying he'd arrived safely. Then he hurried down the corridor. Outside the parlor he nervously passed a hand over his hair, then his imperial. He knocked; a soft voice bade him come in.

Even in this small room, Mr. Plant had spent a great deal of money. There was an intricately carved fireplace mantel; a lacquered Japanese cabinet inlaid with pearl flowers and butterflies; a reading stand with a mammoth atlas. At a large table covered with a green cloth sat Major General Joseph Wheeler.

Joe was startled when General Wheeler jumped up to greet him. A superior officer usually stayed seated. Joe presumed Wheeler was demonstrating Southern courtesy. He had a reputation as a fine gentleman; unpretentious.

"General Crown. I am so glad you're here. I saw your orders several days ago. I have been so anxious to meet you."

"And I, General Wheeler." They shook hands.

Wheeler was a small and sprightly man, shorter than Joe. He weighed no more than a hundred pounds, and was in his early sixties. His mustaches were neatly pointed; his white beard would have suited Rip van Winkle. His blue coat with the two stars seemed too large. It bagged, and Joe noticed many papers stuffed in the pockets. A black slouch hat, not regulation, rested on the green tablecloth.

"Please, sit down," Wheeler said. "I can't offer you anything stronger than water. At least it's the bottled kind."

"Thank you, sir, I'm not thirsty."

They sat opposite each other at one corner of the table. A window was open to the front veranda. Soft music drifted in; a concert band was playing "La Paloma." Couples passed back and forth under the colored lights. Both the men's voices and those of the women were pitched low, and there was intermittent husky laughter. Laughter that hinted at secrets; intimacies behind locked doors. Joe could understand. In him, too, something roused in the sweet hot dark of the May night. A certain tension, excitement, spiced by the danger of impending war . . .

He asked permission to light one of his long Havana cigars. Wheeler graciously said, "Of course." What a deceptive man, Joe thought as he struck a match. "Fighting Joe" resembled a retired planter, or perhaps a schoolmaster living comfortably on an inheritance. He certainly did not look like a man who'd been a vigorous combatant in the Congress for nearly twenty years. Every other year he was reelected in his Alabama district with virtually no opposition.

"I'm happy to have you with the Cavalry Division," Wheeler said. "As you know, your command is the 2d Brigade, consisting of the 1st and 10th regulars and Colonel Leonard Wood's peculiar assortment of volunteers. Think you can handle regular troops?"

"I did so in the late unpleasantness, General. At least they were regulars by the time it was over."

"Indeed, wasn't it so on both sides?" Wheeler said with a melancholy smile of remembrance. "My question was mostly rhetorical. You wouldn't be sitting here in that uniform—or at least you wouldn't be in my command—if I didn't think you were up to it. You have an outstanding war record."

"Thank you, sir. But I have to return the compliment. Yours is legendary." Wheeler chuckled, and waved in a deprecating way. But his cheeks were pinker.

"Fifth Ohio Cavalry," he said. "I commanded the 19th Alabama Infantry."

Joe nodded. "I know, sir. We may have met at Shiloh, but we were never introduced."

"No, no we weren't, were we." Wheeler laughed hard this time. "Our side might have claimed the victory if we'd held on to the advantage we gained the first day. My poor lads fought four separate engagements before dark. They had grit, but they weren't cut from granite. The worst fight was at the Hornet's Nest. Advancing against Prentiss's infantry, Hickenlooper's artillery . . . those who survived were utterly spent. They had the heart to fight on, but not the strength. And the next day you Yanks brought up your reinforcements. Crittenden, Nelson, Lew Wallace . . . a day after that, our retreat turned into a rout. We damned near ran back to Corinth, Mississippi."

Joe was suddenly and eerily transported. He heard old drums tapping; old bugles calling. Saw shot-pierced guidons tumble, to be lifted again by another hand . . . "I had some adventures in Mississippi myself," he said. "Some misadventures."

"Ah, but wasn't it a high time, General Crown? A high time, and an unparalleled experience."

"War is a better experience in memory than in fact, I've decided. But you're right, nothing in my life has ever matched it."

The distant band played "Marching Through Georgia." Wheeler went to the window and quietly closed it. "I hated the end. Jeff Davis clapped in irons, and abused. I was thrown in that damned Fort Delaware, smack in the river, in a cell five feet below water level. Wet all the time. We ate kitchen scraps and garbage. Only twenty men at a time were allowed to the sinks, and only at night. Sometimes five hundred waited in line. Inhuman."

"As bad as Libby and Andersonville, I imagine," Joe said. Wheeler flashed him a sharp look. "And our own prison camps in the North."

"I was lucky, I was paroled after only two months. July of 'sixty-five. I had made up my mind to survive as long as necessary. Attitude helps a man, and mine helped me. I feel I pulled through because I was God damned, excuse me, if I was going to be laid in my grave by rotten Yankee food, Yankee vermin, and Yankee discourtesy."

"I was never imprisoned, but I tried to have the same attitude. It helped me then, and it's helped me in civilian life." Joe paused. "May I have leave to ask a question? I suppose you're tired of hearing it, but I'd like to know how it feels to be back in Federal blue again. Strange?"

"No, Joe—may I call you Joe?"

"By all means."

His eyes were merry as a boy's. "You know, it feels like I've hardly been away. Like I went on a three-week furlough and just came back to my own colors, refreshed and ready. I'm proud to be serving here. After I was freed from prison, and the sting of loss began to abate, I realized we had to reconstruct the country from both sides. I've worked for that in Congress. Telling Dixie to quit waving its old shot-up flags and mouthing its surly slogans and get to work building its railways and factories. Many opposed me, some cursed me, one or two even took shots at me, but I was right. I have a son in this corps, Captain Joe Wheeler Junior. I'm proud he's with me, with us, under the old flag. Just as I'm proud you're here. Blue and gray together—maybe we can make some sense out of the mess Alger and his clerks have handed us. Well, sir. I've kept you too long. If there is nothing more—"

"One thing, sir. As soon as possible, I'd like to know the brigade's resources, in detail. Numbers of men, wagons, horses, mules. An inventory of weapons, ammunition, food. Exact numbers."

"You shall have it all, by tomorrow afternoon. I like a man who's precise."

"I don't know any other way to live, General. Or any other way to succeed, regardless of the enterprise."

Wheeler liked that too. Joe rose and gave a smart salute. Wheeler returned it, more casually. Joe held the door for his superior. Wheeler left the parlor at a lope, jamming his black fedora on his head as he vanished down the hall.

Joe found the rathskeller and ordered a local beer. His presence seemed to change the atmosphere in the long, darkly paneled room. Laughter stopped. Conversations grew muted. While he sipped from his stein, he noted the rank of the officers present. No one higher than captain.

So that was it. The top brass stayed out of this place. It was all right with him; the beer was pale thin stuff. He left three quarters of it in the stein and, upstairs, washed out the taste with a glass of iced tea from a table where the pitchers were continually refilled. He liked iced tea. He drank gallons of it on his trips to South Carolina.

He strolled outside to listen to the last of the concert, which was taking place near the west end of the front veranda. A second lieutenant told him the band was that of the 33d Michigan Volunteers.

Joe's eye fell on one of the listeners, an attractive Cuban woman who was shamefully young for the attentions of a man his age. He assumed she was a refugee with money; no other class of Cuban could stay at Plant's hotel.

The young woman was stocky; some would say plump. She wore a tight white dress with a red dust ruffle, and a white shawl with long fringe. Her bosom was large and round, reminding him of Ilsa's in her youth. A tall comb with mother-of-pearl inlays was tucked into her shining dark hair, which she'd gathered in a bun at the back.

The young woman must have sensed him watching. She turned around suddenly. Blushing, Joe smiled. She smiled too, then looked away. When the concert ended, she went into the hotel by way of the west veranda, on the arm of a slender man in the uniform of the Cuban refugee forces. It pleased Joe that the young woman had acknowledged his interest without anger or visible contempt for his age.

Joe went up to bed, feeling good, anticipating a sound sleep. He liked Fighting Joe Wheeler; they would get along. As the President had remarked in Washington last month, perhaps the Civil War was finally over.

In lieu of reveille in the hotel, orderlies knocked on doors at 5 A.M. For the first few days Joe thought the early rising would kill him, considering the long hours he immediately began to put in, meeting the officers in his command, attending conferences with Shafter, Wheeler, and the other generals, familiarizing himself with paperwork and procedures at Division Headquarters, studying and memorizing the inventories of men and materiel he'd requested. But soon he began to feel more alert and vigorous than he had for a long time.

He continued to be amazed by the hotel, which he heard referred to as Plant's Folly. Why had H. B. Plant, known to be a canny businessman, put such an opulent establishment in such an unlikely location? Joe supposed he'd gambled that people wintering in Florida would flock to his place from older resorts on the East Coast, ignoring the drabness of Tampa itself. Apparently Plant's guess had been right. In any case, Joe developed a liking for the strange Moorish barn. It gave an odd festive tone to a war that would inevitably turn nasty, as wars always did. It provided a spacious and convenient base for the Fifth Army Corps. And at night it was more cheerful than any other camp or headquarters in his memory.

He was uncomfortable in the hot parlor and bedroom of his suite, but he liked the bustle of the rotunda and enjoyed relaxing and smoking on the verandas. He liked the band music, and the presence of such notables as Richard Harding Davis, world famous for his reporting and for his stories of Gallegher and Van Bibber. The *Harper's* artist Frederic Remington conducted a daily salon in the hotel, and there were constant rumors that the great Hearst was about to arrive on a chartered yacht, though he never did.

Of greatest interest to Joe was the young genius Crane, whose Civil War novel he so admired. He was eager to meet Crane and compliment him. One evening he chanced to encounter the author coming along the corridor from the rotunda. Joe stepped up and said hello, and instantly smelled whiskey.

Pallid and slovenly, Crane weaved on his feet and looked beyond Joe's shoulder while Joe was praising him. At the end Crane mumbled something unintelligible and staggered on. Joe was affronted and disappointed. Great talent didn't come in attractive packages, it seemed.

At the first convenient moment, Joe tucked a bundle under his arm and slipped away from the hotel between meetings. It was steamy and scorching outside, temperature in the upper eighties. He broiled like a lobster in his uniform.

A desk clerk had written directions for him. He went part way by trolley, then trudged through sandy streets in West Tampa until he came to a large white tent with a wooden sign in front.

REFUGEE THRIFT SHOP
—All Welcome—

The tent was empty; no one was prowling its crude racks of secondhand clothing, shoes, utensils. A stout woman with beautiful olive skin and a harelip greeted him in broken English. He slipped the brown paper package onto the plank counter.

"I'm donating these. Seven suits of gents' summer underwear. Balbriggan, very fine goods. Never worn."

Joe found some of his fellow officers congenial, others obtuse or enslaved to regulations; a very few were actively unpleasant. It had been much the same thirty-five years ago. The aide assigned to him from the senior staff, Lieutenant Tyree Bates, was quiet and intelligent. A nine-year veteran. Joe wryly assumed Bates's chief responsibility was to compensate, if possible, for the inadequacies or ignorance of a politically appointed general.

Nothing in Bates's behavior suggested this, however. He observed proper military courtesy at all times. When Joe asked a question, Bates either knew the answer or had it in minutes, without the faintest hint that Joe should have known it already.

The most interesting study, perhaps, was the commanding officer, General William Rufus Shafter.

Though he was Wheeler's age, he had none of Wheeler's vigor. He rolled and wheezed when he walked. His hair was a gray mop, seemingly resistant to any comb. His walrus mustache always needed a trim. He was clumsy, slovenly, and wholly unconcerned about the niceties of social behavior. Perhaps he'd spent too many years in barracks in the lonely Southwestern deserts.

The general's bulk presented practical problems. He needed a special oversize chair for staff conferences, for instance. Joe was skeptical of Shafter's ability to withstand the rigors of battle in the tropics.

On the positive size, Shafter was a strong-minded, not to say opinionated, leader. Few subordinates argued with him or even expressed a slight disagreement. Shafter's receding chin could be characterized as weak and flabby, but there was nothing weak about the flame in his blue eyes. It could boil a man down to nothing in seconds. When he was frustrated, which was often, he resorted to a frontier vocabulary.

Joe discovered this when he and Lieutenant Bates accompanied Shafter and the other generals, their aides, and a couple of the attachés on an inspection tour of the lamentable facilities at Port Tampa. They rode nine miles in a dingy day coach drawn by a Plant switch engine, then proceeded from the yards on foot.

Plant had originally dredged only a shallow channel suited to small coasting vessels. In the bay, riding on greasy gray swells amid clouds of gulls hunting garbage, Joe counted twenty-two merchant vessels, some very large. The government owned no transports; all the ships had been rented from private lines whose owners had gutted them, installed bunks and horse stalls on the lower decks, and stripped the upper decks of most of the passenger amenities.

On the twin piers, noisy work gangs were laying extra tracks beside the original four, but it would be of little help. The piers had no cranes or hoists for loading cargo. The engineers had previously concluded that each pier would accommodate no more than two large transports at one time, and the dredged channel no more than six or seven. Everyone feared the confusion at embarkation.

A number of civilian tents were scattered along the piers; deadfalls, ready to relieve the departing soldiers of a few extra dollars. The whole dismal scene, including the bay crowded with Navy cutters and torpedo boats, local fishing vessels and private yachts adding to the traffic, quickly sent Shafter into a stormy funk. He grew short of breath and had to sit on a packing case and fan himself.

"God damn Henry Plant, what was the stupid son of a bitch thinking when he laid his tracks in the center of the piers instead of next to the water? The God damn stevedores will have to haul every last item an extra fifty feet to load the ships. Extra work, wasted time—gentlemen, sometimes I think we should dynamite the fucking War Department to blast it into the real world."

"General, please don't excite yourself," one of his aides whispered.

"Let me be, I'm fine, just help me up. Let's retreat, gentlemen, I can't stand the sight of this fucking place one more minute."

Standing next to Joe, the German military attaché rolled his eyes. Since their introduction a few days before, Captain von Rike had sought Joe out at every opportunity, wanting to speak German with a *Landsmann*, a countryman, or show off his excellent English. The attaché was a Prussian, of medium height, perhaps twenty-five years younger than Joe. He was trim, with widely spaced gray eyes and light freckles on both cheeks. A hook-shaped scar disfigured the left side of his face. He'd gotten it during a student duel, he had informed Joe proudly. Joe couldn't decide whether he liked him.

The following night the attaché showed up on the veranda where Joe was smoking a cigar and listening to the music. The band this evening came from a regular regiment, the 11th Infantry. Its demonstrative bandmaster flourished his baton like a saber. He was apparently well known in the Army—his name was LaGuardia—and his band was much better rehearsed than were bands from the volunteers.

Joe intended to wait until the end of the concert, then stroll or take a ricksha ride in hopes of catching another glimpse of the young Cuban woman. It irked him when von Rike sat down in the next rocker, immaculate in his white ducks and black jackboots.

Captain von Rike polished a monocle on his sleeve. "I inspected several of the regiments today. I have never seen such careless, carefree encampments." He fitted the monocle in his right eye. "Where is the rigor, my dear general? Where is proper discipline?" He lit another cigarette from his flat gold pocket case; he smoked incessantly.

Joe considered the attaché's challenge and gave a considered reply. "Americans tend to reserve the discipline for the engagement."

"Yes? They will suddenly and magically discover it when the shooting begins? Begging your pardon, General, I am doubtful. Victories are built on discipline that is ingrained by months, not to say years, of training."

Von Rike smoked with his hand inverted and the cigarette held between thumb and index finger. Pink and white lights along the eave glittered on the convex curve of his monocle. "And this hotel! A headquarters with a luxury menu? Peacocks and lawn tennis? Nightly dancing? I find it wholly unprofessional." He inhaled smoke again, quite satisfied with himself.

Joe finally decided he didn't like the attaché. "Captain, are you saying you like to suffer *before* as well as during the battle? I can arrange it."

"Oh?" Von Rike was confused; he had no grasp of subtle mockery.

"Yes indeed. Let me give you several tins of our newest ration. What our War Department describes as canned fresh beef. It's unsalted. Ghastly. Some sharp contractor foisted it on Washington."

Von Rike still missed the sarcasm. He frowned. "*Was bedeutet* foisted?"

"Persuaded them to take it. Perhaps by deceit, or passing a bribe or two."

"Ah. *Bestechungsgeld*. Bribe. I see!"

"I'm joking with you, Captain. The stuff isn't fit to eat."

"But good for building character, *ja?* We Germans—true Germans—" Joe absorbed the thrust; fought a rush of annoyance. "We would swallow and suffer in silence."

"Then you'd never make an American, I'm afraid."

"Certainly not. It is not my desire."

Under the smiles, the exchange had grown sharp and unpleasant. Joe stood up. "It's late. Will you excuse me?"

"Of course, General. We'll talk another time."

I hope it won't be soon.

He walked swiftly to the nearest door into the hotel. He could feel von Rike's eyes burning on his back. *Prussians,* he thought. *All the same, they never change.*

At the iced-tea table he helped himself to a tall glass. He carried it outside by another door and stood in a patch of shadow, puffing a cigar and sipping. The chat with von Rike had put a cloud on the evening. The regimental band didn't improve matters with its closing number, an arrangement of "*Vesti la giubba.*" Joe hated Italian opera, which he considered an insult to the genius of Richard Wagner.

Joe finished his tea, his cigar clenched in his jaw. He noticed General Shafter and his wife talking with another couple. After a moment the general moved on, rather like a shambling elephant.

And then Joe saw her. She was wearing the same close-fitting white dress; perhaps she'd left Cuba with only a few belongings. The dress was stunning, clinging to her breasts, which showed brown and full above the round neckline. She was again on the arm of the man from the refugee forces. Disappointing.

A civilian to whom he'd been introduced stood a little way to his left, jotting notes on a pad. He'd recently come up from the naval station at Key West. He was a journalist, but he also had some connection with Miss Barton of the Red Cross, whom Joe had seen around the hotel. Her chartered hospital ship, the SS *State of Texas,* was anchored in Old Tampa Bay.

"Beg your pardon, Kennan, do you know that young woman up there on the porch? The one in white."

"I know her slightly," Kennan replied. "One of the exiles. Estella Rivera is her name. Attractive, isn't she?"

"Very much so." Joe hesitated before the next question. "Is that her husband?"

"Her brother. He's with the rebel forces. I'm told their father is still in Havana. An old gentleman who believes the Spaniards are perfectly right to . . ."

Joe didn't hear any more. His head buzzed. He took fast nervous puffs on his cigar. *You're too old, furthermore you're married,* said the cautioning voice he'd come to despise. He paid no attention.

He bade Kennan good night, stepped onto the veranda, and buried his cigar in a sand urn. He smoothed the buttoned front of his double-breasted dark blue frock coat. He would introduce himself to the young woman. He would invite her to the Oriental Annex to dance. There was some force rushing in him, insisting on it. He wasn't too old . . .

On the arm of the slender man in uniform, the young woman went toward the arched entrance to the hotel. Joe swore, so audibly that the Austrian attaché passing by gave him a stare. Estella Rivera paused; turned slightly. Over her shoulder, she sought Joe's eye.

And smiled.

In a moment she was gone.

She'd known he was there! She'd been looking for him too. Elation sang through Joe Crown. He felt transformed; like a man of twenty again. He was certain he could dance half the night and never tire.

And he would, with Señorita Rivera in his arms. It was inevitable now, the hell with consequences. He only hoped there might be a few, of a sort he found himself wanting very keenly.

90

Dutch

TO GO TO YBOR CITY he put on the best clothes he had, with a few new embellishments. He thought he'd better. The man he'd seen at the hotel wasn't the grimy, disheveled Rhukov of old.

Paul was being frugal in Tampa—a necessity, given Shadow's grudging twenty-cent per diem for incidentals. But he was a journalist of sorts, and as a group, the journalists were dropping a lot of money into Tampa cash registers. Most had decent expense accounts, so they ate and drank with little regard for the cost and were always buying natty clothes. Paul followed their example. Using his carefully hoarded daily allowance, he bought a new shirt of blue chambray, one dollar at Davis Brothers, the best men's store. To this he added tan elastic suspenders with nickeled buckles, fifteen cents; the suspenders matched his duck trousers, which were a popular color called dead grass. As a last extravagance, he chose a washable tie of blue, pink, and brown madras cloth, seven cents. All this together with his straw hat, made him feel presentable, even a little rakish, as he set out.

He found the place with no trouble. Tin numbers were tacked to the siding at the foot of a stair on the windowless side of a corner building on Fourteenth Avenue. The corner's ground floor was occupied by *Mantiquería Estefan,* a grocery.

A man in an apron was carefully sweeping the wooden sidewalk that already looked clean. His bushy black hair and heavy mouth blended oddly with his sand-colored skin. There were many Afro-Cubans in Tampa, Paul had discovered. The man smiled and greeted him in Spanish. Paul said hello in English. Someone yelled, the man dropped his broom and dashed inside. *"Al instante, Señor Estefan!"*

Paul walked around the corner to the stair, which was in shade. A hot wind was blowing. He took off his straw hat and the wind immediately arranged his hair into its usual disarray. The top button of his shirt was undone, and his madras tie hung crookedly.

He climbed the stairs to the solid unpainted door weathered to a dishwater gray. He knocked. Inside a man grumbled. Paul was startled to hear a woman's voice too. The man called out.

"Crane? That you? Hell of an hour to come calling."

The voice made Paul's flesh crawl. It was Rhukov's. But as everyone at the hotel had sworn, the accent was definitely English.

"Blast it, Crane, will you answer?"

"It isn't Mr. Crane, it's Paul Crown, from Chicago. Looking for Mr. Michael Radcliffe."

Muffled voices conferred. Bare feet approached the door. A bolt shot back. The door opened. Mikhail Rhukov stood there naked and white as a fish.

"God save us. It is you. Come in, old chum, come in!"

The flat was a single large room with a few pieces of inexpensive furniture, a sink, a small single-door ashwood icebox, a rumpled double bed in a sleeping alcove. In the bed lay a slim, attractive young woman who had covered her lower body with the sheet, leaving her round brown breasts on display.

Still bewildered, Paul said, "How are you?"

"Top-hole. Couldn't be better. Stevie Crane obviously trusted you enough to give you this temporary address. Sit, won't you?" He indicated a chair next to a small deal table by an open window with gauzy curtains blowing, then snagged white duck trousers from the back of another chair and slipped into them. "I am absolutely agog, Paul. Why are you in Tampa? Good Christ. Not in the military, I hope?"

"No, a new profession. I am a photographer."

"You mean a journalist, like me?"

"Of sorts. I operate a camera. I film living pictures for theaters in the North."

"A camera operator! Of course. Magnificent solution!" He applauded. Paul didn't understand until his friend said, "You're still drawing. Only it isn't an ill-proportioned mess of scribbles any longer, I expect the pictures are actually recognizable."

Paul laughed. "Well, I hope so. Excuse me, I am unsure about something. What shall I call you?"

"Radcliffe. Now and forever, Michael Radcliffe. Took it from a book I found in the British Museum. Family name of the earls of Sussex. Couldn't be more English—in the old times, Queen Elizabeth's day, it was Ratclyffe." He spelled it. "I prefer the more modern version. Here, I'm being a wretched host. Can I offer you a lemonade? A soda?"

"A beer if you have one."

Michael opened the icebox and pulled out a bottle of beer with a Spanish label. He poured himself a tall glass of lemonade.

"Why are you staring?"

"Because you are transformed, Mr. Radcliffe."

"Michael."

"All right—Michael. I still can't believe it."

"Please do believe it." He extended his left hand to show a wide gold ring with an intricate weave of tiny gold wires between the raised rims. "Married, too."

"Yes, I heard that." He couldn't help darting his eyes to the bed.

"Luisa? A dear friend, that's all. I have a strong and frequent need for the kind of friendship Luisa provides. Should you ever feel a similar need, I can assure you Luisa is a kind, caring, accomplished professional." The brown girl smiled. "The half-breed chap who works for Estefan can always find her. Just telephone the grocery and ask for Tomaso."

He moved to the bed, sat next to Luisa and spoke in Spanish while gently caressing her right breast. She gave him a nod and an agreeable smile. "I asked her to go out for some air. We two must have a good solid chat."

Luisa bounded from bed, her large black bush fully in view as she pulled items of clothing from under the bed. She kissed Michael and ruffled his hair, then leaned over Paul and gave him a chaste kiss on the forehead.

When she'd gone, Michael opened a cabinet and took down a water glass holding cigars. "They make them down the street. Perfectly splendid smokes—have one?"

"Thanks, I will."

Michael chuckled. "Well. The waif has certainly grown up."

"It's true. I have changed in many ways. I have a nickname now."

"Fancy that! What is it?"

"Dutch."

"Not very original. But it suits." They sat a moment, puffing and relinking themselves in these surprising surroundings.

"I want to ask the question you asked me," Paul said. "How did you get where you are? I don't mean Florida, I mean the splendid state of your clothes. The English you speak so well—"

Michael waved the cigar, leaving blue traceries. "Quite simple, really. I got tired of *poor*. Poor is disgusting. Poor means no one takes you seriously. No one invites you to a proper dinner or introduces you to important personages. No one likes the way you smell—even in some dirty pub in the East End of London, they won't sit next to you. This is hardly a surprise to either one of us, I'd known it forever. But in London four years ago—a year after I saw you in Chicago—my tolerance of *poor* ran out. I was still spewing my usual sour opinions, a thousand words at a time, but fewer and fewer editors were having any. I realized I wasn't a young man any more. I was steadily sinking. One night when the city was experiencing some bloody awful weather, a revelation came to me. I was sleeping in the only accommodations I could afford. A space under the Tower Bridge. Rain pouring down like bloody hell. I was feverish. Self-diagnosis, I couldn't afford a doctor. It must have been a high fever because I was sleeping blissfully soaking wet. I woke with a bobby shining his lantern in my face. 'Move on,' says he, giving me a nudge with his boot. Move on? *Where?* The Savoy? Windsor Castle? I couldn't afford to *move on*. I didn't have a farthing. My last four articles had been rejected on Fleet Street. Too liverish and impolite to be read by the gentlefolk. In a flash, I understood that I could *move on* to but one definable destination—death. Finis. The end. The Thames was handy. Or I could hop over to the nearest railway station and jelly myself under the wheels of a locomotive. Any number of options! But I had years to live. I wanted more women! I'd come to adore fish and chips! I left Tower Bridge, and that very night, while I wandered wet and sick, in places I can't remember, the heavens opened and gave more than rain, they gave the answer. I must sell out."

Pumped up with pride and mirth, he thumped the table. "And I did! From that moment, I relaunched my life in a new direction. I began immediately to gentrify myself. I obtained a razor and soap from the Salvation Army. I burgled a jumble shop with poor padlocks for a new wardrobe at no cost. I pinched newspapers—outran the old blokes selling them on corners—and through the advertisements I located a position. Night dishwasher at Claridge's Hotel. My English was adequate—the vocabulary, the grammar—but the accent? Unacceptable! Thanks to working below-stairs at Claridge's, however, I was eventually able to rectify that. Took elocution lessons twice a week from a poor old actor who hung around the Covent Garden pubs. He was a master dialectician but too drunk to get parts any longer. I myself drank only cold water or hot tea. I didn't squander my wages on whores, it was either free goods or nothing."

He sighed. "I don't mind telling you, there were some long, dry, difficult spells. But I finally escaped the wretched doss house where I lived for months. Got a cheap bed-sitter in a vile neighborhood. But it was mine so long as I paid the rent. I began to write a novel in the style of Walter Scott, having no real interest in it but hoping it would make money. Please don't ask to read it, I burned the manuscript when the Goddess Prosperity smiled. That was approximately two years after my awakening under Tower Bridge."

"Somewhere in there you married the daughter of a publisher?"

"Yes indeed. And I was sent over here by my father-in-law's paper to trail around after Captain Lee and write colorful prose about him and this noble war —if we ever have it. As you've undoubtedly seen, everything so far is confusion, heat, and ennui. One can send only so many cables describing the Florida orange trees. There's a lot of marmalade in England, from much better oranges."

He inhaled his cigar. "I'm still confused on one point. How did you spot me?" Paul described the moment in the corridor. "Ah. I don't recall seeing you, though perhaps I did. Truthfully, I didn't want to see anyone, I wanted to get the hell away from there. I was, as you might suppose, entertaining a lady."

"Married," Paul said, grinning.

"Indeed yes. Right at the climactic moment of our third romp in as many hours, the telephone clanged. Her idiot husband was in a dive in West Tampa. He'd drunk a lot of cheap dago wine and he thought it might be ripping to pop across to the hotel and exercise his marital rights before he crawled back to his camp. I certainly didn't want to meet him, I'd glimpsed him once or twice before. The brain of a gnat but the stature of a great ape. And on his hip, a sidearm like this." He measured a long pistol barrel in the air.

"Since Her Majesty's military attaché is doing little but playing tennis or boringly describing Sandhurst to anyone foolish enough to listen, I felt I could take a short French leave without unduly arousing my editors. I kissed the hand of my damsel and advised her that if she wanted no further attentions when her spouse arrived, she should lie there and plead an attack of neurasthenia, a popular affliction among the fair sex. I sincerely hope the strategy worked. I'll never meet dear Margo's spouse in Cuba, you can count on that. You won't find me anywhere *near* the fighting. Imagination will create battles more vivid than the real ones. It did for Mr. Crane, why not for your humble and obedient?"

By now, Paul couldn't contain his laughter. "You haven't changed, not at all."

"Don't let my secret out, dear boy."

"I just can't get over this. I hear everything you say but I don't know how it could happen. There are fairy tales where the frog changes to a prince—this is one, Mikhail. Sorry. Michael."

The thin curtains blew. A seller of flavored sodas passed in the street, shouting in Spanish, then English. Michael studied the end of his cigar reflectively. Paul's was down to a stub; it was fine mellow leaf, the smoke soft and soothing on the tongue.

"Possibly you're right," Michael said at last. "But it wasn't a kiss that transformed the frog, it was a free ticket."

Quite by chance (Michael said), an acquaintance of my elocution teacher had a theater seat he was unable to use. He couldn't sell it because it was a different sort of ticket, a regularly reserved seat for a series of special matinee performances at the Independent Theater Club. Not the usual West End tripe, but plays of content. Provocative works. What they're calling the theater of ideas. The club performances are given at the Royalty, a splendid little venue on Dean Street, in Soho. They are always on a Sunday afternoon so that theater people can attend. Of course there are other subscribers. One of them chanced to be sitting in the seat next to mine in the stalls. She remarked on the absence of its usual occupant. I remarked on his indisposition. I introduced myself as Michael. She introduced herself as Cecily. She was smartly but plainly dressed. Far from a beauty.

My new acquaintance was pleasant but rather shy. She grew quite flushed when I invited her to accompany me to the stalls bar at the interval. She drank a lemon squash and said little. After the performance we strolled a short way together. As we were shaking hands, exchanging farewell pleasantries, I impulsively invited her to refreshments at the J. Lyons tea shop in Piccadilly. Mind, I knew nothing about her beyond her first name, Cecily. I was simply lonely. No, suffering! I hadn't been with a woman in four or five days.

The second invitation produced no false modesty. She came, without hesitation. I would have preferred to swank it at the Café Royal, but I barely had enough cash to pay for a pot of Lapsong Suchong and a plate of scones. We had a lengthy chat about theater, books, political issues. She was obviously well educated and very pleasant company, actually. As we stepped out of J. Lyons, another impulse seized me. I invited her to my bed-sitter in the Brompton Road.

Again, she came. And not unwillingly. She had her knickers off in a trice. At approximately half past seven in the evening, I took her virginity. Thirty-one years old and still untouched, can you imagine? Overprotectiveness will damage a woman far more than riotous sex, that's my opinion.

We indulged ourselves a second time. We dressed and I escorted her downstairs to search for a cab to take her home. It was a nasty night. Thick fog. She took me in her arms and kissed me, then she told me her full name. Cecily Hartstein.

Not *the* Hartstein? Oh, yes, the same. I hid my wonder and terror as best I could, saw her into the hansom, and prepared to flee the country.

I didn't move with sufficient dispatch. Late next morning a messenger brought a curt letter from her father, commanding me into his presence at eight o'clock that night. A driver would be sent. With manacles and other devices of persuasion in case I balked, no doubt. The poor, silly, grateful young woman had blathered all to papa.

I thought of doing a bunk right then, but it was too late. I felt sure her father would have legions of thugs watching the railway stations to thwart any such attempt. I was in such a state, I forgot to ring Claridge's to inform them the Monday night dishes would have to be washed by others. I said to myself, it is the end of Rhukov.

Of course it turned out that it was not the end.

Otto Hartstein . . . Otto Hartstein is a Jew from Dublin. Talk about a minority! Father a rag-and-bone man. Real Dickensian stuff. Grubbing around with trash and old marrow bones was all right for people in novels, but not for little Otto. Little Otto wanted better. I gather he was a lonely lad, his only real companions the books he could borrow or steal. He left the family business at a tender age, sailed across the Irish sea, and went to work as the floor-sweep in some provincial newspaper in the Lake District. Within nine years he owned it. He was twenty-two. The rest, as they say, is Fleet Street history.

Lord Yorke's minions arrived on the dot. No weapons visible. All very civilized —for the nonce. I was hauled out of West London, eight or nine miles into the country, to this magnificent domicile with a crest on the iron gates and a name carved in the granite lintel of the front door. Claddagh House. Claddagh—in Gaelic, friendship. Precious little friendship I'll get here, I thought. Probably a heated poker up the arse, followed by submersion in his duck pond in a weighted sack.

I was conducted to a dark, dank hall lit only by a hearth that would sleep six. The butler retired and His Lordship looked at me a long time. Then he said, "Brandy?" To my astonishment I heard myself say, "Surely."

The drink settled me. Put my mind, what was left of it, back on the path of reason. As I saw it, Papa had three choices. One, he could kill me or have me killed or, perhaps worse, permanently maimed, but I didn't think he was completely out of his mind; thus I reasoned he would reject that alternative.

Next, he could pay me off, which he attempted to do. It was a staggering sum. But I remembered Cecily's ardent groans of joy in my cheap little bower of love. So I looked the old man in his cocked eye—I didn't know which was the right one, and found later I'd picked wrong—and I said, "Lord Yorke, there are not enough pounds sterling in creation to reduce me to such base behavior. I refuse your indecent bribe. You never uttered it, I never heard it."

"You're a foreigner," he said. "Are you a Jew, like me?"

"No," said I. "Russian originally, but I have written for newspapers and periodicals all over the world, what's it matter?"

From that moment, I had him. Hartstein is a fierce old bird, but no fool. After all, no one had as yet taken his only child off his hands, and here was someone who might. And he was a journalist!

So there it was. He could kill me, buy me, or embrace me in the bosom of the family.

He embraced me.

It's worked out remarkably well. Cecily is a plain creature, but she has a handsome full figure, always something I like in women, and she has a sharp intellect. She's kind, runs an excellent household, and she is forgiving. With a man like me, forgiveness is important.

Of course there were a few strings the pater tied on me. No philandering in London. Attention to better grooming and tailoring. Less use of what he terms indecent language. Importantly, a new name, on the Anglo-Saxon side.

His Lordship deposits forty thousand pounds per year in my personal account. I work for his flagship paper. My title is reporter, but I'm treated like the little prince. I still write the occasional authentic Rhukov piece, bile and brimstone, but now they pay attention. The earls and viscounts and their sweet-smelling mistresses, the Whitehall hacks and their dull wives, the diplomats who take the credit and their clerks who do the work—I have discovered they don't run the other way if you speak well, dance well, have a proper wife with the proper connections. They read you! They haul you into the study for brandies and a closed-door tête-à-tête. They ask your opinion on armaments, or tariffs, or the opposition candidate. Who's lumbering whom? Who's bedding what bit of fluff? Who is dealing secretly, and will it possibly cause a war? I sold out for all that.

And I adore it.

Doors swing open without my touching them. I see dazzling possibilities for the future. Management of my own paper. Many papers! But underneath— Dutch, you're sworn to secrecy now—I am still the same vicious, sarcastic, distrustful reprobate I always was. Isn't that a magnificent arrangement?

Don't scorn me too severely. You're no innocent yourself. You're smoking cigars. You're in a disreputable trade.

I saw the way you looked at Luisa's lovely bare ass.

After Michael finished and put on a shirt because it was growing cool in the shadowy room, he asked Paul for equivalent information about himself; the intervening years since the Exposition.

Paul held nothing back. He tried to speak calmly, factually, but it was hard; there was too much disappointment. He told Michael of his hopes for a permanent home in America, with the Crowns. He told of being cast out; of finding and then losing Julie. An emotional story, it was a little tangled in the telling. But Michael understood, nodding from time to time. At every mention of Uncle Joe, he looked disturbed. Paul couldn't imagine why.

At the end, he spoke of the baker of Wuppertal, whose words now seemed prophetic.

Michael shook his head, said quietly, "Such dreams . . . crushed by two fierce blows, the girl and your family. Possibly the girl couldn't help what happened. But your own family? Throwing you out like a dog that misbehaved on Mama's carpet—"

"I would say it was my uncle's carpet."

There came the curious disturbed look again.

Paul stared out the window. A soft tropical dusk was descending, purple clouds shot through with amber lights. A sudden flash of green filled the sky, Ybor City, the darkening room. A moment later, everything normal again, Paul couldn't imagine it had been real.

"You were so happy when I saw you in Chicago," Michael said. "I'm truly sorry. You didn't find everything you hoped for in America."

"No. Only a little. Well, I was warned. By a man I met on the pier in Hamburg. He'd been here for ten years. He was going home in disgust. I can't deny I've met some wonderful people—" He thought of Aunt Ilsa and Wex Rooney; Fritzi, Carl, Cousin Joe. The cheerfully dishonest Shadow and his Mary . . .

His uncle's face appeared. He banished it.

"Julie most of all," he said.

Another pause. "Going to stay?"

Paul looked up; accepted another cigar from the glass. He snipped it with Michael's gold cutter and struck a match on the sole of his boot. A cool detachment seemed to come with the flavorful smoke. It was the first time anyone had asked the question.

"I don't know. I have learned a splendid trade here, one that I love. But I do read the journals, I know the pictures are a growing business in many countries. I think making pictures will take me all over the world someday. I could live in many places." He hadn't expressed that thought before, either.

"Even your homeland."

"Yes, why not? It would probably be no better, but it would be familiar. Truthfully, I've not thought much about it till this moment."

But he knew he would be thinking about it more. In the unlikeliest of places, Ybor City at dusk, a seed had been sown.

He stood up. "I should go."

"Yes, Luisa's probably irked with me. I asked her to sit and wait in the Flores Cantina just up the street. On the other hand, she may have earned a few dollars in the interim, she's enterprising. I'll go a block or two with you." He slipped into a pair of rope sandals, opened the door of a chifforobe in the corner and pulled out a thick, knob-headed walking stick. "Luisa taught me that a solitary stroll in Ybor in the evening can be dicey if you chance to meet the wrong people."

All the electric lights were burning in the grocery on the corner. Tomaso was once again brooming the dirt-free sidewalk. He waved to Paul and Michael. Michael saluted him with the walking stick. A brindle dog was jumping in circles in the street, chasing sores on its tail.

"I'm very glad we met again, Pau—Dutch, forgive me. I shan't forget your name too many more times, I promise. And we'll definitely see each other. Crane telephones the grocery if there's anything I should know. Also, I may sneak back to the hotel for a personal look around. I can't deprive my editors of cabled copy for too long. And you and I can have a serious chat on what this war is about. If anything."

On a dusky corner he offered his clean, pale, manicured hand. "I'll turn back. Here's to Cuba."

"To Cuba. I am very happy for you, Michael. I like this new personage you've become. But meeting him for the first time—it was a shock."

Soberly, Michael said, "You might prepare yourself for another. Are you familiar with the high-ranking American officers?"

"General Shafter. General Wheeler. I don't know them all. I haven't filmed them, they are always attending meetings. Besides, I don't know any way to make such a picture interesting."

"I've studied the whole staff roster. My friend, you need to be aware of something." He laid a hand on Paul's shoulder.

"There is a brigadier general from Chicago. Undoubtedly he's stopping at the hotel. He volunteered his services just as Wheeler did. Crane told me he's a brewer. His name is Joseph E. Crown."

91

The General

HOW QUICKLY it all came back. The salutes; the protocol; the familiar bugle calls sorting each day into a series of small, manageable boxes. *Ordnung.* Comfortable, pleasing—the essence of his German soul.

The disorder in Tampa did not please him. It infuriated him. True enough, most of it originated in Washington. But its consequences were felt cruelly by those trying to organize the largest military expedition ever sent outside the United States.

The tangle of freight cars remained an enormous headache. Separate components of one man's individual field ration—tinned meat, hardtack, bread—had to be found in separate cars miles apart, identified only with that legend Joe and all the others on the staff came to hate. MILITARY SUPPLIES—RUSH!

The commercial ship lines leasing transports to the War Department wanted a top dollar for vessels stripped down so drastically as to be almost unlivable. The owners argued that this was necessary to reduce the cost of repairs and refurbishment once the war was over. Secretary Alger's men in Washington had done the negotiating and contracting, but it was the Army that had to wrangle with individual captains.

General Shafter's strategy was summed up in one word. "Hurry." He wanted to strike into Cuba, overrun as many Spanish positions as he could before rain and yellow fever became significant threats. Secretary Alger seemed to do everything possible to nullify the strategy. A telegram from Washington changed the general orders every day or so:

First the Army was to land in force at Cape Tunas, on Cuba's south coast, resupply the rebel forces of General Máximo Gómez, and return to the ships. This was quickly countermanded in favor of a major landing at Mariel, its objective the capture of Havana. Then Commodore Winfield Scott Schley's Flying Squadron found Admiral Cervera's flotilla in the harbor of Santiago de Cuba. Commodore Schley reported three armored cruisers, three destroyer torpedo boats, and the battleship *Cristobal Colon* trapped at their anchorage. This produced more telegrams, and a new objective—Santiago harbor, its forts, and the town. Attacking Havana would be delayed until the autumn.

Next the Army command was confronted with the problem of capacity. It was discovered that the War Department hadn't contracted for enough ships. No more than twenty thousand men could be transported, instead of the planned twenty-five thousand.

"Do you know what this means?" Wheeler fumed when he conveyed the news to Joe. "They'll transport mules for the wagons, horses for the artillery caissons, and enough mounts for officers. But the troops in our division will have to fight dismounted. Roosevelt was just in here, shouting and cursing, I thought he'd chew the carpet before he was through."

Joe shook his head. "What an infernal mess."

"You can thank Alger's damn Yankee procurement clerks. They are experts, all right. At stupidity."

So all during the last days of May, frantic conferences were held, orders were written and rewritten, papers were shuffled and reshuffled, telegrams contradicting the telegrams of yesterday—which contradicted telegrams of the day before—were posted nightly on the rotunda bulletin board.

The furious and often futile activity soon exhausted Joe and put him in ill temper. He would snatch a meal in the dining room if the workday ended before eight, or have a cold snack and a bottle of the abysmal local beer sent to his room if it ended at ten or eleven, or later, as it frequently did.

He avoided the public rooms where the officers gathered to drink and argue.

The German attaché had developed a leechlike attachment, continually trying to corner him to spout the latest gospel from the Chancellery on Wilhelmstrasse, Berlin. *"Napoleon taught a great lesson. A nation that is proud of its nationhood is a nation that conquers." "Creation of the new unified Germany is the most important political event of this century." "Formerly, the fatherland was merely a stage. Now it is the principal actor."* And on and on. Joe detested the thought of his native land falling into the hands of men such as von Rike and the Kaiser, who was proving himself a headstrong, arrogant, potentially dangerous leader.

One day, on horseback, Joe rode to the encampment of the 1st Volunteer Cavalry. It adjoined Division Headquarters on the hotel road. As he neared the camp entrance, he saw a man crouching behind one of those newfangled motion picture cameras, cranking away to photograph a squad of soldiers. In front of some coconut palms, the soldiers were demonstrating the manual of arms. Rather sloppily, too.

Joe touched his boot heels to his mount and moved closer. He reined up near the coconut palms. The corporal in charge of the squad fell all over himself to salute. Joe snapped off a return salute and barked at the man bent over the camera.

"You, there. What's your name?"

The cameraman turned around. He was young, and wearing a checked cap with the bill backwards. Joe had never seen him before. Pulling a card from the pocket of his duster, the cameraman said, "Billy Bitzer. American Biograph, New York."

Joe reached down from the saddle and took the card. "Well, Bitzer, this area is the camp of Colonel Wood's regiment. The colonel has issued specific orders—no cameras allowed anywhere near the Rough Riders. It interferes with drill."

"I heard that. I don't like it much," Bitzer added with a cheeky smile.

"Doesn't matter. You'll obey the order. Carry on, Mr. Bitzer."

Joe reined his horse around and cantered up the sandy road. The Army didn't need such men hanging around. Didn't need its deficiencies paraded on screens in low-class variety theaters. Things were bad enough without that.

Joe had now been in Tampa for two weeks. The initial excitement of returning to uniform was fading somewhat, though he continued to enjoy hearing subordinates address him as general. He liked the impressive sound of it.

He rediscovered aspects of Army life he'd forgotten in the glow of happier memories; the inflexible military mind, for one. He came up against this in an officer on Shafter's staff, Major Rollinson Gilyard. Gilyard was a career soldier, with experience on the Plains. But he hadn't gone to West Point. Behind his back, brother officers said this drove him to excess. Gilyard constantly whittled a point on perfection, and every man under him felt its jab.

Joe's personal orderly, Corporal Willie Terrill, warned him. "I advise the general to stay away from Major Gilyard. He don't like anything 'less it's by the book, and sometimes he don't like the book, either." Willie was a stout, deeply tanned soldier; a regular. His mother was a Cherokee Indian.

Major Gilyard was of medium height, round-cheeked, pink and pale; almost an albino. His searching eyes were magnified by strong spectacle lenses. He complained about sloppy salutes, the polka-dot neckerchiefs the Rough Riders wore instead of the regulation red, the linen duster Joe Wheeler favored in place of a blue frock coat with braid—everything. Joe followed Corporal Terrill's advice and avoided him as much as possible. Sometimes it wasn't possible.

On June first, the day General Miles finally arrived from Washington, Joe received an inspection report on *Percival*, a freighter of the White Arrow Line scheduled to transport half the 9th Cavalry. The report came through Gilyard and had been initialed by him. Joe jammed on his hat and carried it straight back.

"Major, this report is completely unsatisfactory."

"I'm afraid there's nothing to be done, General." Gilyard's eyes seemed to swim like large pale fish behind the bowls of his glasses. "The contract with White Arrow was drawn and approved in Washington."

"I don't care. This report says the men of the Ninth will be transported in refitted cargo holds on the two lowest decks."

"Yes, sir. Segregated from the white infantry companies that will also be aboard. The Negroes will exercise on the main deck, port side, the white men to starboard. A line of demarcation will be painted on the deck to separate—"

"I'm talking about conditions below decks. If our soldiers are going to be penned up like hogs, at least there should be light and air in the pens. According to this, the hull of *Percival* has been repainted, portholes and all. In other words, the portholes are sealed. That must be corrected. I'm going out to the ship and speak to the master."

"With all respect, General, in case of an unsatisfactory report, regulations require a formal written complaint first, with copies to the appropriate War Department desks. Only then—"

Choleric, Joe broke in. "What if we're ordered to embark tomorrow? And is there a regulation to explain why we stupidly allow things like this to happen? Good day to you, Major."

"General, I most respectfully urge you not to—"

Joe slammed the door of the parlor, cutting off the rest.

From his valise stored under the bed, Joe took his old wartime revolver, which he'd kept oiled and wrapped up all these years. The leather of the cartridge belt was brittle and cracked but otherwise serviceable. He loaded the Colt and strapped it on beneath his frock coat. The civilian masters were rough seafaring men, and some were said to be quarrelsome.

He made the nine-mile trip to the port on horseback. From a distance he spied Captain von Rike and his counterpart from the Imperial Navy, Commander Paschwitz, taking photographs with snapshot cameras. All the foreign attachés busied about with cameras, taking dozens of pictures for their respective governments. Perhaps the most earnest was Major Shiba of Japan; he carried two and snapped everything from wagon axles to flagpoles.

Joe tied his horse to a picket pin from his saddle bag, stepped around a massive pile of ammunition boxes, and boarded a small steam cutter at the stairs. The cutter carried him out across the bay to *Percival*, whose master, one Captain Squires, greeted him at the gangway with a scowl.

Captain Squires was about forty. He hadn't used a razor for days. He wore bell-bottom pants and a singlet with holes in it. He ushered Joe to his untidy cabin, which smelled of stale bedding and sweet gin.

"I can't say this visit's welcome, General, we're pretty God damn busy around here. Can we make it short?"

"Certainly, Captain, if you cooperate. I want to see the bunk space below."

Squires scratched broken fingernails on his stubbled face.

"Why, something wrong with it?"

"There's an unsatisfactory report on the readiness and fitness of the accommodations. Specifically, I understand the portholes are sealed."

"Can't do anything about that, she was just repainted."

"I'll see for myself, please."

Squires took Joe's measure while rolling his tongue inside his lower lip. "Maybe my mate's available to show—"

"You show me, Captain Squires. Personally."

Squires found a battery lantern. They tramped down iron stairways to a dark hold. Joe coughed and covered his mouth; the mixed smells of paint and powerful disinfectant were strong enough to asphyxiate a mule.

"Hold that lantern up, please." Grumbling, Squires complied. The light revealed tightly arranged tiers of bunks four high. The bunks were new, raw pine lumber full of splinters and poorly put together.

"These are wretched."

"What's it matter? Just gonna be a bunch of niggers sleeping down here."

"Excuse me, they're American soldiers." Joe strode down the aisle to the hull where the circles of portholes were dimly visible, like a string of full moons on a foggy night. He tried to force one open, but it was rusted inside and painted over outside.

"Captain, see that these are opened and scraped clean of paint. Every one of them."

In the dark aisle, Captain Squires looked like some unclean troll in a cave. "Impossible. Haven't got the time, or the men. Besides, there's not one damn word in the contract about portholes."

Joe pivoted back to the hull. He unbuttoned his frock coat, reached down and drew his Colt. He raised it to shoulder height, stretched out his arm, steadied, and fired three shots. The porthole burst outward. The detonations rolled and clanged through the hold.

The strong smell of powder drifted. Outside, sunlight sparkled on the swells. Above decks, men were running and shouting. Joe held the hot revolver away from his body as he walked back to Captain Squires.

"There, Captain, I opened one of them. You do the rest. If you don't, I'll come back, and we'll have another discussion. It won't be so friendly."

"You meddling old bastard, if you think I'm going to—"

Joe whipped his left hand behind Squire's head and jerked it forward. The muzzle of his revolver rested on the point of the captain's chin.

"Yes, I think you're going to, Captain Squires, and you'll do it promptly and properly. Now show me the way to the stairs, there's a rotten smell in here."

□   □   □   □

Joe stood in the stern of the little Navy cutter as it sped away from the *Percival*. He felt marvelous. Youthful; confident—full of himself. He had exceeded the limits imposed by regulations. Had behaved, in fact, like a boy swollen with bravado and a careless feeling of immortality. The brave, eager volunteer of long ago . . . before he saw the elephant.

He held his hat under his arm and let the hot wind ruffle his silvery hair. As the cutter raced toward the Plant pier, he seized on another, equally compelling reason for his buoyant spirits. He'd made up his mind about something. Tomorrow night, Saturday, he would speak to Señorita Rivera.

92

Jimmy

THE RED LIGHT of sundown glared on the brass balls hanging from the single stem. The familiar symbol jutted from one end of a painted sign.

I. MELNICK
Buy—Sell—Pawn

Smoking a long slender panatella, made locally, Jimmy stood with the sole of his left shoe propped against the wall of a business block directly across the street. A spic lawyer in a suit and derby came out of first-floor law offices. As he locked the door, he gave Jimmy a stare. Jimmy glowered right back. The man started, then walked rapidly in the other direction.

The shop on the opposite side of Nassau Street was narrow, just a single display window and a door beside it in a recessed entry. The door had a wire grille behind the glass. Jimmy had been in West Tampa earlier in the week. He'd spotted the store, then the item in the window that would make a swell present for Honey in Chicago. A delicate little necklace of gold or, more likely, gold plate, strung with short gold-link chains, each with a tiny red or green glass stone at the end. The tent card beside the necklace announced a price of eleven dollars. Lot of fucking nerve the sheeny had; it probably wasn't worth half that. Jews, they were all alike. Bloodsuckers.

He'd returned twice more to pipe out the pawnbroker's routine. It never varied. As the neighborhood grew deserted, Melnick, a short, frail husk of a man, pulled all the merchandise from the window and lowered a shade. The second night, Jimmy brought a short pry bar under his coat. When Melnick left, he drifted to the empty alley behind the shop. The door resisted the pry bar. Jimmy had broken open enough places to suspect the reason; an iron bar inside, dropped into brackets flanking the door. To get in that way, he'd need a fire axe. Which was out, because of noise.

The sun fell lower, tinting the clouds, shooting red rays along Nassau Street but leaving the locked-up shops and offices in deepening shadow. Jimmy swatted a gnat pestering his neck. He spat disgustedly when he saw the bloody smear on his fingers. He wiped his hand on the pale stucco of the wall behind him. He was sick of this town full of bugs and snotty Army officers. Sick of the smelly, sticky Southland and its mush-mouthed citizens. Sick of his partner—the whole she-bang.

He couldn't deny he'd done all right in the money department. He'd made several little forays inside the hotel and twice had come away with a sizable reward for his daring. He'd pawned some of the loot at another shop like this one, only across town, Ybor City. He used the proceeds to entertain himself with whores, of which there were plenty, with more arriving on every train. Still, they weren't the same as the beautiful, devout Catholic girl in Chicago. He supposed he was being a chump, falling for her, but he'd heard such a thing could happen.

As soon as this stupid war was over, he'd have what he wanted from Miss Honoria Fail—without marrying her, that was out. All he had to do between now and then was keep his hide in one piece. Let his dumb and eager partner take the risks, he'd wait and play the hero in Chicago. Take Honey's cherry, and say goodbye to Shadow and this nickel-and-dime picture business. There were plenty of better, faster ways to make a dollar. Ways that didn't rub your nose in "honesty"—or even the pretense. He'd been raised with those, he'd go back to them. By now, he was sure, all danger of being connected with the tart's murder was past.

Abruptly, he stood up straight. Over in the pawn shop, the Jew was leaning into the display window, pulling the merchandise. The man was no more than a blur—he'd already turned off his electric lights. He was following his routine exactly.

Climbing into the window, he drew the shade down. In a few seconds he'd be out the door with his keys. Jimmy slung his cigar into the street, took off his straw hat, and pulled the holy medal and long chain over his head. He slipped the chain in the left pocket of his seersucker coat.

The shop door opened. Jimmy was already striding across the street, shooting looks both ways. A couple of drunks were hollering in front of a cantina one block west, otherwise it was quiet. The sun was nearly level with the earth, painting the building fronts a deep scarlet. With his back to the street, the pawnbroker was locking up in the dark alcove.

He was having trouble with his key. Muttering, he didn't hear Jimmy's stealthy approach. For a second Jimmy stared at the funny crocheted skullcap fastened to the small man's hair with hairpins. Then Jimmy tapped his shoulder.

"Excuse me."

The man gasped and whirled around. He had a triangular face and the eyes of one perpetually suspicious and put upon. He'd been chewing a cinnamon stick, a pleasant smell.

"Are you open?"

"What's it look like? I'm closed, come back Sunday."

"But there's a piece of goods I really need to buy for my girl. Tomorrow's her birthday."

"Closed!" the man said testily. "Shabbat." Whatever that was. "Go away. Come back Sunday morning, then I'm open."

"Jeez, sorry I came too late," Jimmy said in a mild way, stepping back.

Melnick nervously fumbled his key into the keyhole. The door was still slightly ajar. Like a cat jumping, Jimmy launched himself and slammed his hands against the pawnbroker's back.

The man knocked the door open as he fell in. Jimmy jumped inside after him, but left the door ajar for light. The shop smelled of sawdust on the floor, dusty sheets draped over the display cases.

"Please, mister—" Staggering to his feet, Melnick held up his hands. "Don't hurt me. I done nothing to you."

"I know, but I want something you got here."

"What is it?"

"A necklace, with little red and green stones. You had it in the window."

"It's locked up in that case. I'll get it, you can have it, just don't hurt me."

"Now you're being smart. But what if you decide to blab to the coppers later?"

"I won't, I swear."

"All right, then, go get it."

Melnick stumbled through the dark shop toward the ghostly draped cases. Jimmy watched the man's head turn slightly toward the rear of the shop. On guard, he dropped his hand into his pocket to clasp the holy medal and chain. Melnick moved sooner than he expected, fairly hurling himself toward the back door. "Fucking little kike," Jimmy snarled, yanking the medal and chain out of his pocket.

The fleeing pawnbroker looked over his shoulder and stumbled. On his knees, he heard Jimmy coming for him and yelped, "No!" Jimmy threw the chain over the man's head, jammed his knee in his back, yanked hard.

"You shouldn't have tried to double-deal me," Jimmy said, applying more pressure with his knee and his hands. "You brought this on, y'hear me?"

The pawnbroker's head lolled forward and his body began to sag against the chain that was wet with oozing blood; the little man was past hearing.

Jimmy choked him a while longer, then let him go, let him fall. And smiled. Deep down, he had to admit he'd been nervous about snatching the necklace and leaving the Jew alive. Secretly, this was the outcome he'd wanted. The feeling of power was so heady, he almost felt drunk.

Jimmy shot a swift look at the front door. Everything quiet. He left the pawnbroker sprawled in the sawdust while he pondered a problem. How to find what he was after? He chewed his lip a few seconds. He located the light switch but didn't turn it on. He closed the front door, shot the inside bolt, and pulled the window shade. Then he switched on the lights.

Melnick was a disgusting sight, his eyes open and his stinking bowels too. Jimmy worked fast, ripping the sheets off the locked cases one after another. He spotted it in the third case, lying in its long velvet-lined box. He tore off a piece of sheet, wrapped it round and round his hand like a white boxing glove, held his breath, and hit the glass one hard blow with his head averted. Seconds later, he had the necklace box in his pocket and the lights off again.

He lifted the iron bar from the brackets and went out through the rear, tucking the holy medal down into his shirt.

In excellent spirits, he strolled toward the hotel. His fiercely beating heart was slowing down. It had been much easier to kill a second time. And they'd never connect him with the death of some cheap kike pawnbroker, why should they? He began to whistle that new Sousa march, "The Stars and Stripes Forever." He felt safe. Much safer than when he went to ground in Chicago after he put the girl in the river.

He lit another panatella and smiled again as he reflected on a fine evening's work. How he wished he could describe it to Dutch, who thought he was so damn smart. Dutch thought that if you broke your back, hustled your ass—were *honest*—life would shower you with its rewards. What did a kraut off the boat know about it?

Thinking of Dutch reminded him of something else. His partner was Shadow's boy; Shadow's favorite. While Jimmy had no intention of staying in the picture business, the favoritism galled him. Sometimes he really wanted to show Dutch his holy medal and chain. Prove to him that all those rewards he stupidly worked for could be snatched away in a space of two or three breaths.

Nah, don't be a chump, he said to himself as he walked along in the damp dark that had fallen on Tampa, hiding its ugliness. No reason to go crazy. He didn't hate Dutch Crown that much.

Not quite.

93

Dutch

ON THE SAME FRIDAY that Jimmy Daws went to West Tampa and General Joe Crown paid his visit to the *Percival,* Paul returned from Ybor City in a state of shock from Michael's last revelation. At the hotel, he went straight to the noisy, crowded rathskeller.

Billy Bitzer hailed him from a table. Bitzer had a pitcher of beer and a plate of sausages and sauerkraut in front of him. Paul sat down and asked his question in what he hoped was a casual way. "Sure," Bitzer said, "there's a brigadier named Crown on Wheeler's staff. He ran me out of the Rough Riders' camp couple of days ago. Tough old turkey. Joseph E. Cro—"

With a glass of beer halfway to his mouth, he made the connection. "Crown. Are you two related?"

"Distantly. We are related distantly."

"You sound like you don't care for him."

"Please, may we not pursue it further?"

"Whatever you want, pal. Join me in some dinner?"

"Another time. I have no appetite."

He hardly slept that night. Very early the next morning, he slipped a note under Jimmy's door to say they wouldn't film until noon. No explanation.

It was still dark when Paul stationed himself in a plush chair in the rotunda, with a newspaper. He chose the seat carefully. It was partially screened by a palmetto growing in an urn, but still gave him a view of the staircase and the corridor leading to the elevator. He would go unnoticed unless someone was looking directly into the shadows where he sat.

At half past six, three officers came down in the elevator. There was no mistaking the face and bearing of the senior man with the brigadier's star. No mistaking the posture, the assertive stride, the brushed hair silvery as steel. Paul raised the paper in front of his face. His hands were cold. When the three had gone into the dining room, he jumped up, flung the paper in a basket by the reception desk, and fairly ran to the veranda.

He found it hard to breathe in the damp, pale dawn. The sky was streaked flamingo pink to the east. The lawn was soaked with dew. He started walking, paying no attention to where he was going.

What should he do? The Tampa Bay Hotel was huge. Huge, and overflowing with guests and visitors. If he stayed alert, didn't eat in the dining room—and if he had a bit of luck—he could probably avoid his uncle.

Or should he make his presence known to Uncle Joe? Take the first step toward a mutual forgiveness, a possible reconciliation? The voice of family, common blood, said yes, powerfully.

But his uncle had banished him. What if he was rejected a second time?

He reentered the hotel by the east door and took the stair immediately inside up to his room, which was littered with his growing collection of mementos. Through the window came a distant blare of bugles and the sounds of the hotel waking. He sat on the edge of the bed. Shut his eyes and brought his thumbs against his forehead. The pressure helped him think.

He remembered the pain of his banishment from the mansion on Michigan Avenue. Then he thought of his cousin. Rash and headstrong as he was, Joe Junior's only real crime had been caring about the downtrodden. He'd foolishly allowed himself to be influenced by Benno, and men had died. But never intentionally would Joe Junior have been a party to that.

But his father treated him as if the opposite were true. As a consequence Joe Junior was lost to Paul. Lost to his mother, his sister and brother, because of Uncle Joe's rigidity, stupidity. And Paul had no home in Chicago, no place in America where he truly belonged.

He recognized that his uncle had been kind to him until the trouble came. Paul genuinely admired much about Uncle Joe. His bravery in coming to America alone; his idealism in fighting to free the *Negerin* in the great war. His remarkable and successful drive to riches and position afterward.

But Paul could never condone what Uncle Joe had done when he was opposed.

Fixing on that, he beat down the strong yearning for reconciliation. Scoffed at it, till it withered.

Go to Uncle Joe? . . .

No; he would not.

94

The General

SHE WAS SEATED ALONE at one of the small white tables. She knew he was watching; had been watching while he tensely circled the dance floor several times.

The music and heat in the Annex dizzied him a little. How beautiful she was in her clinging white dress with the red ruffle. Waiting for him . . .

Him.

A sudden guilt held him motionless near the main entrance. *You must not do this. You must not betray Ilsa.*

He swept the thought away. Stronger influences—the imminent war, distance from Chicago, renewed confidence in his own vigor, her beauty—overran his conscience. He smoothed the front of his uniform blouse and moved toward her with a quick, decisive stride.

"General, good evening. Are you feeling all right?"

The sudden voice startled him. He spun to his right. He hadn't noticed Major Gilyard before. Gilyard was also sitting alone. His magnified eyes regarded Joe with a certain suspicion.

"Yes, Major, I am, why do you ask?"

"If I may be forgiven, sir, you look pale."

"Haven't been sleeping well, that's all. This hotel may be pleasant in the winter, but right now the rooms are damned hot."

"No arguing there, General. I hope your rest improves, sir."

"I'm sure it will, thank you so much for your concern," Joe said, and strode off.

She saw him coming. Her eyes, dark brown and glorious, grew larger and larger as he approached. Reaching her table, he bowed like any self-conscious swain of twenty. His eye chanced across the stunning deep cleavage above the neck of her gown. He felt himself blushing.

"Señorita Rivera, I am General Joe Crown."

"Good evening, General, I know who you are," she said, smiling. Her English, though flavorfully accented, was perfect. Suddenly, again, he was ashamed; she couldn't be older than twenty-five.

"Would you care to sit?"

"I came over to ask if you would do me the honor of dancing with me."

"I'm sorry, no."

"Señorita, forgive me if I offended—"

"Not at all. When I fled Havana last year, I made a vow that I would neither sing nor dance again until the revolution drove the Spaniards out forever."

"Well. Commendable idealism." How many in the hall were staring? Gossiping? She was so lovely, it made no difference. "I wonder, then—would you care to stroll in the garden?"

Her smile returned. She had a splendid full red mouth. "A very pleasant suggestion." Rising, she unintentionally brushed his blue sleeve with her bosom. He felt like a planet flung out of orbit, falling through space.

In the garden, on the dark paths where other couples strolled, she took his arm.

"I notice your brother isn't here this evening."

"A special meeting was called by General Shafter. Some problem concerning the rebel forces. Almovar was with them in the mountains until last month. He was on the staff of General Calixto García."

A silence ensued, becoming more awkward as it prolonged itself. Desperate, Joe said, "I have wanted to make your acquaintance for many days now, Señorita." Then, a rushed afterthought: "Your brother's too, of course."

"Oh, certainly." Her irony was dry; almost undetectable.

"You say you fled Havana—"

"After a fierce family dispute. The Riveras have lived in Cuba for more than a hundred years. Our father is an importer of sherries and riojas and other fine wines from the homeland. He believes in the queen, and in Weyler—Spanish supremacy, in short. It's to be expected, he's Castilian, seventy years old. Age, wealth, and breeding make a strong brew. A man drinks it, he's almost certain to become *conservativo*. Are you familiar with that word?"

"Intimately," Joe said, a little surprised at his own irony, which she missed. "You and your father fell out, then?"

"Yes. Both Almovar and I quarreled with him, in a very bad way. We quarreled over this war, and also over our older brother, Ernesto. Ernesto left university two years ago to fight with the rebels. He died on the *trocha.* It was a very grisly death."

"Once again, I apologize. I don't know that word you used."

"*La trocha.* The trail. It's a cleared space in the jungle, rather like a shallow ditch. A hundred fifty, two hundred meters across—eighty kilometers long. *La trocha* is a barrier meant to contain the rebels. The first one was built during the Ten Years' War, from Móron all the way down to Júcara. For a while it was abandoned. When Weyler arrived, he repaired and reactivated it, then built a second one from Mariel, slightly west of Havana on the north coast, to Majana in the south."

She went on to explain that the *trocha* was not merely a trench, but a fortified barricade. Trees felled during the ground clearing were piled up along both sides —"A barrier of trunks and roots wider than a boulevard, and much taller than you, General." At intervals of a half mile to a mile, small forts, blockhouses, and watchtowers kept the jungle on both sides under observation.

"Wherever *la trocha* is not manned, there are bastions of sharp stakes, strung with a cat's cradle of barbed wire. On the western *trocha* Butcher Weyler introduced small artillery and electric lights. But that isn't the end. He planted bombs, each with its spiderweb of trip wires. One of the wires caught Ernesto as he was crossing the *trocha* with a dispatch from General Antonio Maceo. The bombs are designed to fragment—pierce their victim with many small pieces of iron. Wounded, Ernesto was a feast for *los cangrejos*. Land crabs. They live near the coastal waters and scavenge in the dark. But they will come into the light if there is bloody meat. Many are the size of saucers, some even as large as this." In the glow from the veranda lights, her silhouetted hands spread to the width of a dinner plate.

"Gruesome creatures," she went on. "They click and clack their pincers, and they leave nothing on the bones. You never want to meet *los cangrejos*, General. You especially never want to meet them if you are unable to defend yourself. They will devour the flesh while the victim is still alive. Providing the victim is helpless. Ernesto was helpless."

"*Mein Gott,*" Joe whispered. "*Das ist schrecklich.* Horrible. How did you learn of this?"

"A lieutenant inspector came along on horseback shortly after sunrise. Ernesto was not yet dead, but he had no chance to live. The crabs were still feasting. The lieutenant scattered them with pistol shots. Then he fired a bullet of mercy into what was left of our poor brother. Ernesto was carrying identification with his dispatches. The lieutenant was more decent than some, he wrote to our father. Ernesto's death precipitated the quarrel."

"How so?"

"Our father said the tragedy was entirely Ernesto's fault, because he valued freedom above his own life. Almovar and I could not abide that. We packed and left our father's house the next day." Estella Rivera's voice was low and bitter. Joe was stung by similarities to events in his own family.

At a bend in the path where the shrubbery grew thick and tall, she paused. The floodlit minarets and domes shone silver in the sky, but in the garden Joe and the girl were immersed in darkness. Estella's white kerchief shone faintly as she touched it to her upper lip. "Now, General—"

"Please call me Joseph, or Joe."

"Joseph, then. I have said enough about my history. Tell me something of yours."

The darkness and her sweet light scent, a little like almonds, a little like tropical flowers, aroused him. In a husky voice he said, "What I have to tell you is, I think you're the handsomest young woman I've ever seen. The most desirable—" His left hand clasped her right shoulder; his right clumsily groped her bosom. At the same time he leaned forward to kiss her. She twisted her head and he kissed only the corner of her mouth.

"Don't, you'll shame us both. Yourself for the attempt. And me for wanting it."

Startled, humiliated by his foolish behavior—feeling his age—Joe stepped back. His hands fell to his sides. Once more she stunned him: "Come to my room. We'll have privacy there. Four twenty-five is the number. Come in ten minutes."

She whirled and ran off in the dark.

The dance band in the Annex played "Animal Fair," with much boisterous, rhythmic clapping as accompaniment. Joe staggered to a bench and sat down. Was he rejected, or invited? He didn't know.

He stole along the fourth-floor hall, feeling like a burglar. On the main staircase he heard a man and a woman coming up, chatting and laughing. He darted into an alcove, flattened his back against the wall. The voices receded, a key clicked, a door closed.

He peeked into the corridor. Empty. He rushed down the hall; found the door. One soft tap and she let him in. She'd changed to a dark red silk wrapper with a high neck.

She had a single room, smaller than his but decently appointed, and just as hot. She indicated the chair. "Please, Joseph, sit down. Would you be more comfortable without your jacket?" While he took off the heavy uniform blouse, she opened the closet. "I have a half bottle of an excellent Spanish red. The last of the supply I brought from home. Would you care for a glass?"

"I would, thank you. I'm normally a beer drinker, I brew beer, you see—in Chicago—but yes, wine would be fine."

She poured a generous drink in a barrel-shaped hotel glass, but took none for herself. She sat down on the bed and crossed her legs gracefully. She was very assured and composed for a woman so young. Well educated, obviously; heartbreakingly beautiful . . .

"I thought we might talk," she said. Though she was friendly, she was clearly setting limits. This intimacy was for conversation only. The bed was for sitting, nothing else. It made him want her all the more.

He drank a little of the rich, fragrant rioja. "Talk? Certainly, I'm interested in more about your history. But first I must tell you something. I thought about concealing it. I find I can't." He twisted the ring on his right hand. "I am a married man."

"Why, I knew that the first time you looked at me. I knew it before I saw your ring. But thank you for your candor. It confirms my impression that you are a good, honorable man. Now what did you want to ask?"

"Your background. Havana—"

"I was born and educated there, initially in a convent, later in a private academy."

"It must have been difficult for you and your brother to leave."

"Not under the circumstances, no. Quite easy."

"But you left your father."

"It was our duty to resist the government at this time. He would not."

"How do you feel about him now? If he's still a loyalist, doesn't it make him something of a traitor?"

"To me and my brother? Joseph, Joseph, there's wisdom in your face, is it only a mask? Blood flows stronger than the strongest river, always. We quarreled with our father, Almovar and I, but it was a quarrel with his foolish attitudes, not with his essence. Not with his soul. You do not cancel the word 'father,' reject all its weight, all its importance, by saying you reject the cloak it wears at a particular time. The slogans it proclaims. The error into which it stumbles. We'll go back to our father when the war's won and Cuba is liberated. No doubt he'll hate a new regime. Perhaps he'll hate Almovar and me, he's old and stubborn. Certainly we will never change his feelings about Ernesto. But we'll love him all the same. What person would forever abandon a parent, or any relative, for harboring the wrong views? For being misguided? Making human mistakes?"

Joe's hand grew slippery on the glass. "I did."

That gave her pause. "You? Oh, Joseph. Tell me how it happened."

"There's more," he said, the words suddenly unstoppable. "I drove out a second person, my nephew, because he helped the first one—who was my son."

"Joseph. No wonder there is sorrow in your eyes. Is that why you ran away to war?"

"No, absolutely not, I—"

He cleared his throat. His eyes met hers again. In a small voice he said, "Perhaps. After it happened, after I sent both of them away, relations with my wife—she is a very fine woman, you understand—but things between us—" His chin sank. His shoulders slumped. He raised the tumbler an inch; a tiny gesture.

"Deteriorated. Perhaps I did run away from it."

She left the bed and knelt at his knee. Her bosom pressed his leg but this time there was nothing erotic in the contact. She reached up to stroke his damp forehead with fingers surprisingly cool and dry. "Catholics go regularly to confession. It purges pain and cleanses the heart and thereby calms the mind so it can find new paths. Tonight I'll hear your confession, Joseph."

"I'm a Protestant, Estella."

"Not tonight, not here with me. Wait! I see a mule rearing up in those handsome eyes. I won't allow it. Tell me everything."

Kneeling like a supplicant, she squeezed his hand, which, most curiously, was shaking. He felt like the supplicant. She took the tumbler of wine and set it on the dressing table.

"Everything," she said.

All the rest of the night, midnight until morning, he sat on the straight chair under the electric lights mounted in the ceiling. He removed his tie, then his shirt and singlet; sat bare-chested, his suspenders down on his hips—again, most curiously, without embarrassment. It seemed natural to sit that way and talk with her. Perfectly easy and comfortable.

She picked up one of the paper fans supplied by the hotel. She returned to her place on the bed and fanned the air between them, cooling them both a little. The slow rhythm of the fan seduced him; helped him talk.

The monologue that poured out of him was about boyhood, Aalen, Cincinnati, and Chicago. About Ilsa; the war; the struggle to build Crown's. About his children—how he loved them and how they rebelled. Even dear Fritzi with her silly ideas about entering the lewd profession of acting.

He spoke in detail about Joe Junior, driven out; and his nephew Pauli soon after.

"In our family I established certain rules—"

"You drove your son out because he broke your *rules?*"

"Estella, you don't understand. In business, rules are absolutely necessary."

"Your family is not a business. Life is not a business."

"Don't look at me that way. I'm a human being, I have my own beliefs—strong ones."

"I presume the same can be said of your son. It can be said of my father. Or of any person."

"You're confusing me. My life, my *whole life* has been built on the principle of order. *Ordnung,* that's how we Germans say it. With my own hands, and that principle, I created my success. Wealth—"

"Buttressed by these rules which everyone must obey, or lose your love?"

"Stop that, for God's sake. Stop it!"

She went to him again; caressed his damp neck with her dry, cool hands. She added a jot of rioja to what was left in the hotel glass. He drank without looking at her. He drank all of it. In a few moments the confession resumed.

He talked of his need to offer himself to the Army again, at all hazards, because he believed in America and its cause, but also because he thought he'd die in Chicago if he didn't. He described the quarrels with Ilsa, which seemed to grow more frequent after Joe Junior and Pauli left. "She has all these radical women for friends, she's taken in by their ideas."

"Wrong ideas, you believe."

"Absolutely. She doesn't see it. She says I'm the one who's wrong."

"Ah. A woman with backbone. A woman who speaks her mind. Another rule broken. I can see this woman. She is not docile. If she were younger—if, for example, she couldn't abide her father's political views—there's no telling what she might do. Temporarily exile herself in a foreign country, perhaps."

He gave her a fierce look. She stroked his hand, speaking softly. "Tell me the rest."

He described the death of the man who fell from the roof. His increasing resentment of Ilsa because of the blame he felt she placed on him. Blame for the death; blame for the loss of their son and their nephew. Estella listened attentively, now and again murmuring a word or two, English or Spanish, he couldn't be sure. He sat there under the three electric bulbs and he poured out words, thoughts, feelings, he'd never shared with anyone.

At the end, exhausted, he slumped in the chair.

"A remarkable story, Joseph. I heard many fine things in it. I think you understand now, if you have not understood before, who was in the wrong when your son left, and your nephew. It isn't my place to give you advice. Nevertheless I shall, because I learned the habit from the nuns who taught me as a girl. They were fine women, but inclined to bossiness." She smiled.

"Repair the damage with your wife the moment you return home. Repair it with your son and your nephew as well."

"It's too late, the boys are gone."

"No, as long as they are alive somewhere, you have the opportunity. Find it. Seize it, or you'll never again be a whole man, you'll keep hunting another war, another reason to leave your wife, your home, your calling, and underneath it all, your remorse."

He stared at his veined hands. He looked at the mirror of himself and saw mistakes, and folly, and hated the image, but she forced him to confront it . . .

the night's confession had forced it. His eyes explored and silently adored her face.

She laid the fan aside and sat calmly, accepting the scrutiny. There was a powerful, silent current surging between them. An understanding of a physical hunger for each other, an awareness of their isolation in the privacy of a hotel room in the middle of the night. Somehow, inexplicably, Joe felt he'd already taken her, known her intimately.

It wasn't enough:

"I want to love you, Estella. There, in the bed."

"I want it too, Joseph. But we will not."

"You refuse me?"

"It breaks my heart but, yes—tonight I refuse you."

"What if I should insist?"

"Joseph, don't pretend. You aren't that kind of man. Furthermore, you can't make the rules for everything."

He reached for his singlet on the floor beside the empty barrel glass. "Then I'd best get out of here."

"Yes, I think so. It's almost five."

When he was dressed, she held his arm and walked him to the door. She touched him with her body, her mouth scant inches from his, still breathing out that fascinating exotic mixture of scents. "I want to give you my own confession before you go. If you weren't married, I would take you to that bed this instant. I'd love you very hard, a long time."

Her red mouth came up, warm and sweet, in a protracted kiss of parting. His heart beat like thunder.

"You are a good man, Joe Crown. We'll not see each other again."

In the hall he took a few steps, then turned back for another kiss. The key clicked on her side of the closed door. Dragging his blue frock coat on the carpet behind him, he walked away.

Next morning he presented a note to the clerk at the rotunda desk. "This is for your guest Señorita Rivera."

"Rivera, Rivera." The man riffled some cards. "General, I'm afraid she's departed. For Key West, she said."

"Have you a forwarding address?"

"She left none, I'm sorry. You might ask her brother."

But he wouldn't. *She knew*, he thought, profoundly sad and grateful. *She knew last night that together, we were in danger. She saved us from ourselves, and lifelong shame.*

But that was not the only way she saved me.

95

Elstree

IN THE DARKEST HOURS of that same early Sunday morning, hundreds of miles away in New York City, Elstree stretched his legs in a plush armchair. The chair was one of several good pieces he'd bought when he moved Rose from Eighteenth Street and set her up in a better flat.

Red and yellow electric signs on Sixth Avenue tinted the wallpaper between patches of shadow. He heard her taffeta skirts rustling. Once he'd thought it a sensual sound. Not tonight. And she couldn't break herself of certain old habits. Buying cheap perfume was one. The odor sickened him.

An elevated locomotive hooted somewhere to the north, coming downtown. The shadow of her gloved hand appeared on the wall, moving toward the switch.

"Don't turn it on. You've given me a monstrous headache."

"Well, I'm so sorry about that. I'm so damn sorry. What am I supposed to do?" She was half defiance, half tears.

"Rose, please shut up a minute and let me think."

"Who are you to order me like that?" Her tone was weaker than her words. She sank down on the creaking bed. Removed her suede gloves and then her hat, a little straw adorned with artificial violets, a satin ribbon bow, a spotted veil. Beside her lay one of the new-style flat purses, called pocketbooks. She always wanted to look smart and she always failed, because taste was not something she'd been taught as a child and thus carried through life unconsciously, like physical grace.

Julie had taste. Everyone in his circle had it. De rigueur. Consider the clothes he'd chosen for an evening less than fully formal. Patent leather button shoes in the low-cut summer style. Linen spats and clocked socks. Midnight blue dinner jacket with matching silk bow tie; a white piqué waistcoat. Everything was conservative, smart, and expensive.

They'd returned in a hack from a very late supper at Delmonico's. Rose was back at Tony Pastor's on Fourteenth Street, third from the top of the bill. "Rose French, the International Soubrette." He'd seen her too often and had come to hate her third-rate voice. Her looks had besotted him for a while, but he couldn't explain how that cheap allure had persisted so long. He supposed it was because he was sometimes a fool over women far beneath him in all respects except sexual appetite; and hers was gluttonous.

The elevated shunted by, light from its cars flying over walls and ceiling. Elstree felt a patter of cinders in his hair. He reached behind him and slammed the window. "Christ, this place is dirty all the time."

"Who rented it? Not I, Billy."

"God damn it, don't call me Billy." He rapped the ferrule of his stick on the floor. The stick was fashionable malacca, with a heavy, crooked handle.

Giving him a wary look, she untied the laces of her fingertip cape and laid it aside. Elstree stroked the stick, back and forth, with a circle of thumb and index finger. "Let's discuss this little surprise you've sprung on me, Rose. How do I know it's mine?"

"You damn well better know, I haven't been with nobody—anybody else. And sometimes you aren't too careful."

The stick flashed up, an accusing pointer. "*We.* I am not the only one culpable. If indeed there's really any culpability here."

"You try to make me feel low with those words I can't understand."

"Culpability. Responsibility. Is that clear enough for your dim little brain?"

"You listen to me, you bastard. There is plenty of *culpability* here. Feel my belly."

"Don't be disgusting." He was enraged. He wanted an heir, but not from a tramp. He fought an impulse to strangle the wretched creature; punish her for presenting him with this hateful irony.

Rose was pouting. "You like to feel me well enough before we fuck." She snatched off her bonnet and threw it on top of the cape. "I'm telling you, Bill, this is real. I know because I went through it once before."

"Who was it, that greasy bucket of lard Dresser?"

"No, someone else, it doesn't matter. And don't call my friends names."

Elstree sighed. "Well, I shouldn't be surprised by this. Before I sent you the flowers the first time, I suspected you weren't exactly the virgin lily of the variety stage. But that's what I grew to like—a certain well-used quality. Your repertoire of tricks. Much more interesting than your repertoire of songs." He sang a few words of "Maryland, My Maryland" in an off-key falsetto.

"Christ, you're cruel."

He laughed and smoothed his hair. In the hot glare from the electric signs, a stone on his finger ring flashed. "Once, as I recall, you said you liked cruelty at certain times."

"I said a lot of things, once. So did you."

Elstree rapped the ferrule again. In the flat below, someone yelled a complaint. "All right, what is it you want?"

"I want help. You got me in a fix. I'll have to give up my career for a good long time."

"Your career. That's hardly a loss, especially to audiences. I'll pay whatever it costs to get rid of it. But I won't pay a penny more."

"What—what if I won't do that?"

In a reasonable voice, he said, "If I'm the father, it's my choice. I don't want the little beggar."

Rose paced to the bay window and back to the bed. "Bill, I can't do it. The first time, I lost it natural, after seven weeks. But I'd already found one of those men with dirty nails and no diploma. Turned out I didn't need his help. Then last year a friend of mine, a dancer in the line at Tony's, she went to his place out on the marsh at Throgs Neck to get rid of one. She bled to death." She rubbed her arms in an agitated way. "Not me. Not me."

Elstree took out a small cigar; scraped a match on his shoe. In the spurt of light, his face looked calm; ordinary except for the monocle in his right eye. It seemed to be a hole in his skull; an open furnace door with a raging fire inside. He blew on the match. The fire went out.

At the last moment, distracted by anger, he didn't light the cigar. He tossed the smoking match on a throw rug near his chair. "You and your friend must have picked the wrong man."

"Doesn't matter, I won't do it. I'll have the baby, and I want five thousand—no, I want ten—till I get my figure back, and my career."

"Lying on your back and spreading your legs is your real career, Rose. That's the career for which all women were intended."

"I've met sons of bitches, but you're the worst."

Elstree stood up and reached into his trouser pocket for a money clip, silver with a small diamond set in. The clip carried hundred dollar bills only. He dropped two on the bed.

"That's for expenses. Get rid of it, get on with your life, and don't bother me again."

"That's it? You just dismiss me?"

"I'd like to part cordially, but it's up to you."

"Bill, you may be able to fob off whores and society girls this way, but you can't do it to me. I'll raise hell."

He felt heat in his face. "You had better not."

"Fuck you, I will, I'll get lawyers, I'll make noise, I'll smear your name everywhere. I'll go out to Long Island and find your pure little wife and—"

He hit her a slashing blow with the malacca stick. She staggered back, striking her knee against the bedpost. He dropped the stick and pushed her onto the bed.

He jumped on her, pinning her right hand with his left while he punched her face. His ring tore her cheek. He knelt hard on her and hit her again. Hit her, hit her . . .

Finally, he stopped. Blood smeared her cheeks and drooled out of her nose. He'd loosened two of her lower teeth. He disliked having to put her down this way, it was messy and upsetting, with no thrill in it. Somehow, women always drove him to something like this at the end of a relationship.

She rolled from side to side, crying and moaning softly. He retrieved his stick and top hat and snapped on the ceiling light. At the mirror, he saw he'd gotten her blood on his fine white scarf, a lovely piece of Chinese silk. The scarf was ruined.

Angry, he whipped it from around his neck and used it to clean his knuckles. Then, reasonably presentable again, he threw the scarf on the carpet.

He looked at Rose on the bed, snot and blood running down her chin, hateful eyes following him as he moved. She lay on her side, like a child curling up to protect itself from an abusive parent. What an idiot he'd been to entangle himself with her.

Still, she was such a pathetic sight, it inspired a certain pity. He took out the diamond studded clip and dropped another hundred beside the first two. Her lips peeled back over her teeth in a way that reminded him of a cornered cat.

"Goodbye, Rose. Don't ever try to see me again."

He pivoted, reached out with the stick and used the ferrule to flick off the lights.

He walked quickly down two flights and into Sixth Avenue, deserted at this hour near dawn. Under the elevated trestle, manholes trickled steam into the glow of the electric signs. He stopped by a trash barrel, drew the apartment key from his waistcoat and disposed of it.

He walked with his cane resting on his shoulder. A great dray piled with fragrant cabbages rolled by. He waved and called a greeting to the driver. At a cross street he saw a faint graying above rows of East River tenements. He must find a hack to his club. Breakfast service began at half past six.

He imagined the taste of an omelet; a grilled small steak, crisp fried potatoes; the double-shot eye-opener. He'd enjoy himself, just as he was enjoying himself in the cool bracing air of morning. The eastern sky was turning from gray to soft coral, but the north-south streets were still dark. He began to whistle.

Suddenly he realized what the tune was. "Flowers That Bloom in the Spring, Tra-la." One of Rose's numbers. How appropriate. He kept whistling it as he strolled on, disappearing where the morning light didn't reach.

96

Joe Junior

THEY ATE QUIETLY, sparingly, on Sunday night. Not because the food wasn't good or plentiful. Ehling Sieberson, the crippled shingle weaver, his widowed daughter Anna, and her son Thorvold had plenty of flesh on them; Anna set a fine table. Joe Junior had discovered this repeatedly during the two months he'd lived in the attic of the small house on Rucker Hill in Everett, trading his chore work —tasks that could be done only by a man with all ten fingers—for his bed and board.

Tonight Anna had served salt herring and thin slices of smoked local salmon; potato cakes and a steaming bowl of parsnips; her fine, crisp *flatbrød;* head cheese, cardamom cookies, strong coffee, and caraway-flavored *akvavit.* Everyone drank the strong coffee except Ehling, who downed the *akvavit* as if it were no more potent than well water.

The mood was somber and their appetites smaller than usual because Joe Junior, his friend Julius Rahn, and several others were going to walk into the shingle factory in the morning, present a short list of demands to the general manager, Mr. Grover, then walk out and picket until the demands were satisfied, or they were jailed. What they planned to do was dangerous. That was why no one spoke of it, until Thorvold, age ten, brought it up. Thorvold, called Thor, was a stout boy with eyes so blue, he might have been Joe Junior's son.

"What time will you go in the morning?" Thor asked. Joe Junior put down his fork and smoothed his beard in a thoughtful way.

"Why, the regular time, I suppose. Half past six. Julius will be here in a while to discuss it."

"Can I come down with you and watch?"

"You may not, eat your supper," said his mother. Anna Sieberson was a fair-faced, blue-eyed Norwegian woman, seven years older than Joe Junior. She had a broad, full bosom, strong arms, a small mouth with thin lips that spoiled her otherwise pretty face. But smallness and thinness didn't affect the warmth of that mouth, he'd learned.

When Ehling was in one of his rare good moods, he liked to compare his daughter to the sturdy and beautiful rhododendrons growing all around the house on the hillside. "Only strong plants can survive here. The fog, the damp, the gale winds—the rhododendron withstands them all. Anna is like that."

Anna's husband, Lars Prestrude, had been a shingle weaver at the Smiley Shingle Company, one of several such companies down on the waterfront. One night two years ago he'd fallen over in his chair just before bedtime; a heart seizure. Anna took back her maiden name after she buried Lars, using the five dollars sent by Grover at the factory. If Lars Prestrude had died as a result of an accident on the job, Grover wouldn't have sent a penny, or even a note of condolence. By the self-protective reasoning of the bosses, to give the slightest aid or recognition to the family of a man who died as a result of a job accident would implicate the owners. The bosses in the Pacific Slope lumber and shingle industries would have none of that. It was one reason for the planned walkout.

Now, at the table, Anna exchanged a look with Joe Junior. In his there was affection, in hers, entreaty. She said she loved him, and he knew she wanted him to propose marriage. Despite warm feelings for her, he couldn't do it, although a part of him would have liked to settle down with her, enjoying her goodness and the ardor he'd discovered the first time she stole to his cot in the attic. Old Ehling was going deaf, couldn't hear the cot's pings and creaks that night, or any of the nights that followed.

But if he settled down with Anna, he would be surrendering to the bosses, what they represented, what they did to their men—or didn't do, in the case of the shingle weavers. He'd be turning his back on his conscience and his inner calling, whose outward manifestation, regrettably, was too often failure. Still, he had to go on.

Thor wasn't satisfied with his mother's answer. He spoke again to Joe Junior. "Will there be trouble tomorrow? The police?"

"Julius assures me the chief and his men will be on the scene by noon," Joe Junior said. "Later, I guess, we may be visited by some of the saloon derelicts Grover hires to discipline anyone who causes trouble."

"Men like that, they're the ones who killed Daniel Ivars," Anna said. "I told you what they did to him."

"Trouble," Anna's father said with a snort. "Course there'll be trouble. I've told people all my life, shingle weaving isn't a trade, it's a battle."

Ehling Sieberson was a round-shouldered man of fifty-three. He looked ten or fifteen years older. His face had the pasty pallor Joe Junior associated with shingle weavers; it was the badge of their perilous occupation. That, and their hands. On Ehling's left hand only half a thumb remained, and no fingers, just stumps at the knuckles. His right hand had a full thumb and index finger, and three stumps. Ehling Sieberson was a sour and defeated man, no longer able to work at his trade. He survived in modest comfort only because his late son-in-law, Prestrude, had received a small inheritance from an uncle in Wisconsin.

Ehling's pronouncement silenced the table again; very little was said during the rest of the meal. When Ehling was finished, he took his *akvavit* glass to his chair in the parlor; he was expert at carrying a glass with the two fingers of his right hand. Crossly, Anna sent Thor to his schoolbooks. Joe Junior said, "I'll help wash dishes."

She turned her back. "Go outside and smoke your pipe. It's a pretty evening, make the most of it." Then suddenly she whirled around. "We could have such a happy life together. You'll throw it all away."

"Anna—" He touched her; she recoiled. "It isn't that I don't care for you, I do. But I have to go tomorrow. I have to stand with the others."

"You and your damn conscience," she said. "Go on outside, Joey, leave me alone."

He left her with her hands in the dishpan and sunset light through a small window catching the tears on her plump cheeks.

Everett, Washington, was a growing community; over six thousand people, most employed in, or dependent on, the lumber industry. There were nine shingle mills, seven sawmills, and a pulp mill. The town had electricity and telephone service; the former hadn't yet reached the hill, and the Siebersons couldn't afford the latter. You could count on at least two things in Everett, westerly winds blowing from the Orient and the snarl and whine of saws in the mills that worked a night shift.

The Sieberson house was small, impeccably clean, and largely alone on Rucker Hill above the town. There might come a time when the richer element would want homes up here, because of the view. At present, the nearest residence was a poor shanty a quarter of a mile away.

For all its isolation, the house was pretty, sided and roofed with different widths and varieties of shingles, some of them made by the Smiley Shingle Company, whose large rambling factory Joe Junior could easily see down below on the waterfront. Anna Sieberson was the person responsible for softening the starkness of the hillside location. She'd planted spirea, blooming white now. She'd carefully sited beds of rhododendron, whose fluted flowers, rose and pink and white, were just opening in their spring glory. The family had put in a vine maple just where the road from the lower hill straggled past the house. The maple's springtime leaves were a spectacular red.

Joe Junior leaned on the rail of the narrow porch that overlooked the rhododendron beds, the town, Port Gardner Bay on Puget Sound, and long Whidbey Island, where the Olympic Mountains rose, hiding the Pacific to the west. *This is such a beautiful place to be so full of greed and pain,* he thought. This was the wheat farms and orange groves all over again. Pullman in a setting suitable for the greatest of landscape artists.

It was a clear, cool evening, not quite summer yet. The air grew steadily sharper as the sun sank and the Sound turned from slate gray to indigo in the changing light. Three fishing trawlers were bearing north, going home. A tug churned south, drawing two large rafts made of pilings. A valuable cargo of new lumber was stacked on each, secured by chains.

Joe Junior had come to love the peculiar beauties of this coast. When he awoke in the morning, he could look from a circular window on the attic's east side and see the snowy peaks of the Cascade Range; watch the slow transformation of the forests of pine and Douglas fir on the near slopes—the inky color of the night changing to the rich dark green of day. Near marshy places on the shore, where eelgrass grew, the lapping water sometimes looked red as wine. On a Sunday outing Thor had shown him a piece of the branched red algae people called sea rose. It was found nowhere else, Thor said.

He relished the special aromas of the place. Salt and seaweed, tarry creosote on the dock pilings, freshly cut lumber, wood smoke from the mills burning sawdust and scraps.

Seattle was about thirty miles south of Everett. On a sunny day in April, Joe Junior had observed his twenty-second birthday there. He'd spent several hours sitting on a wharf watching tug skippers maneuver lumber rafts to a railroad pier.

He didn't like Seattle, it was a madhouse because of last year's Yukon gold strike. Every day Northern Pacific trains dumped new arrivals into the already overcrowded streets. There were no rooms, cheap or expensive. Every leaky vessel on the Pacific Coast was touted as a fast, comfortable ship to Alaska. Prices were higher than the mountains.

In Seattle, as throughout most of the West, there was a lot of enthusiasm for the war with Spain; so much that Joe Junior had taken to calling this the Jingo Coast. War fever had spread despite a strong populism in the state; in 1896 Washington had gone for Bryan and free silver, although of course the lumber barons had foamed and ranted against the "Popocrat" as though he were Satan. Much of this had been told to Joe by his friend Julius Rahn, a thirty-two-year old shingle weaver who so far had lost only the tip of his left little finger.

Hating the greed and clatter of Seattle, and having no desire to risk death in snowy mountain passes as the price of searching for gold in Alaska's rivers, Joe Junior had drifted up to Everett, seat of Snohomish County. The town had been settled about thirty years ago, and Julius Rahn said John D. Rockefeller had an interest in the company that had done much of the real estate development; there was a Rockefeller Street downtown.

Joe Junior packed his pipe, lit it, and sucked the sweet rum-flavored tobacco into his mouth. Although he had certainly learned to live without contact with his family, he missed them. It had been too long since he sent his mother a little package, he must do that soon. Thor had given him the perfect idea. An acorn-size nugget that seemed to sparkle with flecks of gold. It was iron pyrites, sold in souvenir stores. Fool's gold. But it was pretty.

He thought of his sister with her mimicry. Burly little Carl, whose knockabout clumsiness made him smile as he recalled it. Carl was probably not so little any more.

And cousin Paul, where was he? Still in America, or back in Germany, perhaps disillusioned like many another immigrant? It wouldn't have surprised him.

Sometimes Joe Junior even missed his father. This was such a moment. During his wanderings he'd come to realize that in comparison with other bosses, Joe Crown wasn't such an ogre. More generous and fair with workers than most, in fact. If he ever saw his father again, he wondered if he'd have the nerve to admit that many harsh things he'd said in the past were wrong. Joe Junior didn't believe in letting yourself be injured or killed by the enemy, but neither did he believe any longer in the usefulness of dynamite, the virtue of "propaganda of the deed."

Well, it was an unprofitable speculation, given the situation here. In less than twelve hours the sun would rise and he would stand with the other shingle workers down at the factory.

Perhaps because this part of America was so fair and clean, the greed and repression he'd found made him sadder than usual. The pattern was familiar. The bosses owned mayors and town councils. They owned governors, legislators, and judges. They supplemented the salaries of sheriffs and deputies, who did their bidding. They dominated the press and the pulpit. They defended their right to form combinations in their own interest, but denied working men the right to organize to defend theirs.

He'd seen a lot of the country by now; met a lot of Americans. Mostly, the poor were good, except for the few who turned on the others and robbed or killed them out of rage and desperation. Mostly, the rich were bad, because their preoccupation was the constant defensive war to protect their businesses, their bank accounts, their *property* . . . always with the same results for the worker. You were shorted in your pay packet. You were cheated at the company stores. You were fired if you objected; arrested, beaten, or maimed if you tried to organize.

Working men out here knew of Gene Debs; he was a revered leader and socialist. But his doctrine of peaceful protest and negotiation wasn't popular. "This is a God damn dangerous trade, shingle weaving," Julius Rahn said when they were planning tomorrow's action. "You can't be soft and work them saws ten hours a day. We got no patience with sitting down at a table, jawing and jawing for weeks. Where does it ever get a working stiff? No place. Strike quick and strike hard, that's the motto around here."

So they chose to walk, not talk.

The lumber coast had known a brief period of labor agitation a little more than ten years ago, Julius explained another time. The Knights of Labor, the great idealistic organization founded in 1869 with the purpose of joining every worker in America in a single brotherhood, had appeared in the Pacific Northwest in the mid-1880s. One of the goals of the Knights was the reduction of the mill workday from twelve hours to ten.

A bloody confrontation was expected once the issue was joined. To the astonishment and fury of other bosses, a respected lumber magnate, Cyrus Walker of the Puget Mill Company, granted his men the ten-hour day almost at once, preferring that to a long, ruinous strike. In less than a year, after a few small and relatively peaceful strikes at other mills, the whole Pacific Slope combination gave up and established the ten-hour day.

After winning that battle, the Washington State Knights went through a series of internal power quarrels and disappeared. When the depression of 1893 came, volume dropped, mills closed, jobs were fewer; men would accept any wage. In the last couple of years, however, the industry had started to revive. Jobs were becoming plentiful again.

But working conditions weren't getting any better. Joe Junior discovered this when he answered a newspaper ad and was hired as a utility man at the Smiley Shingle Company, at one dollar five cents per ten-hour day. With a six-day week, this brought him the munificent monthly salary of twenty-five dollars twenty cents. Even a skilled weaver like Julius only received a dollar forty per day; a little better than thirty-three dollars a month. One of the demands to be presented tomorrow was a daily increase of ten cents. Another was advance notification of layoffs that were now announced with no warning, the moment orders fell off.

The general manager, Abel Grover, who interviewed Joe Junior, said nothing about layoffs. He spoke of a dollar five cents a day as though it were the wealth of Midas. A gruff, deeply religious man, Grover had a little lecture prepared for new employees:

"I'll tell you what kind of man we like around here. A serious, thrifty, industrious man. A reasonable man who understands that we try to improve working conditions to the extent our balance sheet will allow. But we don't want union stuff—bums from the deadbeat class who do nothing but attack corporations and capital."

Grover answered Joe Junior's sole question—yes, there was a Mr. Smiley; James Lincoln Smiley II. He lived far away in San Francisco, as did a number of other Pacific Slope lumber barons. Smiley had a princely house in the Nob Hill district. He visited the mill once or twice a year. Later Joe learned that when Smiley sailed up Puget Sound in his yacht and docked in Everett, he met only with Grover and the section supervisors, never with the workers. Julius Rahn had seen Smiley often in ten years but had never exchanged a word with him.

"It don't surprise me," Julius said soon after he and Joe Junior got acquainted. "Around here they talk about 'the price of labor' same as they talk about 'the price of shingles' or 'the price of oxen.' We ain't human beings, we're things, store-bought and sold when, as, and if it suits Mr. Smiley and all the rest like him."

Joe Junior had been put to work with a broom, his chief task being the cleanup and removal to the burning yard of the incredible quantities of cedar sawdust generated each day. What he saw, particularly on the upper floor where the weavers worked, almost beggared belief. The first time he went up there and stood slack-mouthed amid the swirling sawdust and the screaming steel saws, he thought he'd ventured into some torture chamber devised by barbarians.

Each shingle weaver sat in front of a pair of spinning ripsaws mounted in a metal table. A chute device fed chunky blocks of cedar to the left side of the table. The weaver pushed the block against the left saw with his left hand and the teeth peeled off a rough shingle. In some mills, Julius said, a weaver had a quota of fifty shingles a minute. At Smiley's it was fifty-five. Floor supervisors circled constantly, counting.

The instant the shingle was split from the block, the weaver reached over the left sawblade to grasp it. He did this by instinct, never watching, because at the same time, his right hand was manipulating the previous rough-cut shingle on the right-hand saw; trimming it, or slicing out knots. This done, he threw the finished shingle into a chute to the right of his table. The shingle slid down to the packing stations on the first floor. The weaver's hands flew over and around the blades, each hand doing a separate task fifty-five times a minute. The weaver worked in a constant cloud of sawdust spun off by the blades, and for protection wore only a water-soaked sponge on an elastic, covering his nostrils.

"If the blade don't get you," Julius Rahn said, "the cedar asthma will."

On Joe's fourth day, while he was sweeping on the lower floor, he heard a scream from overhead. Only a couple of packers bothered to look up from the work of bundling shingles. Joe watched a blood-splattered shingle slide down the chute and then, scrawling a bloody line, an index finger severed at the middle knuckle. One of the packers snatched the finger and tossed it into Joe Junior's waste barrel and went on working.

When a weaver was maimed too badly to work, he was discharged without any extra compensation. And if he died as a result of a factory mishap, the management neither acknowledged his death nor contributed to a fund to help the widow. As Joe Junior had learned from Anna and Julius, that would admit the bosses bore some responsibility. The position of the bosses was clear and simple. When a man took up the trade of shingle weaving, he did so knowing the hazards of employment. That was the main reason they were walking out in the morning; like all the other shingle mills, Smiley's wouldn't admit to an iota of guilt if an accident left a man without work and maimed for life.

Repacking his pipe in the cool evening air, he heard Thor ask Anna a schoolwork question. She answered with a harshness not typical of her. He noticed a flash of white on the road that wound along Rucker Hill. Julius Rahn said his hair had turned white during his first year in the factory.

Julius climbed the porch steps and joined him at the railing. "How are you, Joey?"

"All right. You?"

"It's worse than we thought down there. Matilda's awful upset. I left her crying."

"How do you mean, worse?"

Julius Rahn buttoned the upper buttons of his black and red plaid mackinaw. Joe wanted to go inside for a sweater but he didn't; Julius was too upset.

"About three this afternoon, Abel Grover paid a call to my house."

"For God's sake, Julie, why?"

"To plead with us to call it off tomorrow."

"How does he know about it?"

"Hell, he's got plenty of spies on the floor, don't think he ain't. Grover offered me two hundred dollars. I wouldn't take it. I could sure use it, though." He sounded sad.

"Why would the general manager try to—?"

Julius interrupted. "Do you know Weyerhaeuser?"

"Heard his name. Another German immigrant, like my pop. He's important in the lumber trade in the Midwest, isn't he?"

"Important? In lumber, Fred Weyerhaeuser's like old man Carnegie in steel, or Rockefeller in oil. For months I been hearing that he's sniffing around here. He wants to expand from St. Paul, and there ain't but two places he can go, the South and the Northwest. They say he hates the hot weather and the nigger beating and the backward ways of the South, so he ain't going there. Something else. There's a new outfit in town, the Coast Lumber Company. I think it's a front for Weyerhaeuser. They got men looking at shingle mills to buy. The Bell-Nelson mill. Ours too."

Julius Rahn looked at Joe with pale gray eyes full of wrath. "Grover used a lot of two-dollar words this afternoon. After he left, I wrote down as many as I could remember. I thought everybody should know what he said before we walk out."

Julius produced a wrinkled piece of foolscap and, with difficulty, read from it in the failing light. "Grover said Mr. Smiley was *desperately anxious to preserve an appearance of labor harmony*"—he tilted the paper and squinted—"'cos anything else would *surely create a negative impression in the mind of any prospective buyer. So we will be doubly hard on agitators. Let them all be warned.*"

Joe Junior heard Anna gasp. He turned around. There was no one in the dim rectangle behind the half-open door.

Carefully, Julius Rahn put the paper back in his pocket. "That's the message, Joey. 'Let them all be warned.' I'm making the rounds, every one of the others." It sounded impressive; there were, counting Julius, only nine.

"What I'm telling them is, you don't have to go through with it. You don't have to be there. I don't want nobody to get killed."

Joe Junior's stomach hurt. "That's good of you, Julie. I'll be there anyway."

"Hoped you'd say that. If we don't stand up together, we'll be down forever. Well, got to leave, going to Erickson's next." He pulled a cloth cap from his coat and settled it on his white hair. "Cold wind, ain't it? Damn westerlies never let up. Just like the bosses, huh?"

He said it without smiling. Joe Junior laid his hand on his friend's shoulder. "Don't worry."

"Naw, not me. See you in the morning."

"In the morning. Try to get a little sleep, will you?"

The answer was the tap-tap of Julius's shoes on the wooden stair. At the bottom he called out, "Oh, I forgot. We'll meet at the regular starting time."

"The regular time." Joe Junior waved. Julius was quickly gone in the dark that lay on the road.

He went inside and shut the door against the chill. The gas mantles were trimmed low. Ehling had gone to bed. The kitchen was cleaned up. It was so still, he could hear faint wind outside. He trudged up the narrow stair. No light showed beneath Anna's closed door.

She wasn't in her room, she was in the attic, in his narrow cot, under a down comforter and a wool blanket, naked. She turned the brass key and extinguished the oil lamp he used for reading. Not a word passed between them before they made love.

Anna had thick, strong legs. She clasped them high around his waist with a power and urgency entirely new. She bit his lip and flung herself up against him in rising rhythm, as if to show him what he was throwing away by his decision to go with the others.

Her white-blonde hair was undone and got tangled between their mouths as they kissed. Her face was wet with salty tears he tasted when he kissed her eyes. Her climax was long, with loud sounds he'd never heard from her; as if she was in beautiful pain.

When their bodies were cooling and they snuggled together, his muscular arm around her shoulders, her head tucked in the hollow of his neck, she made her last plea, as Abel Grover had done to Julius:

"Joey, I love you, don't go down there in the morning. I told you about Daniel Ivars, one of the ringleaders the last time they tried to organize. They kicked and beat him, then they lifted him over a saw blade and lowered him down. They knew just how to do it, so it'd hurt the most. He lay bleeding and screaming the rest of the workday and no one dared stop and help him, or run for a doctor, Grover forbade it, no doctor could set foot on company property without his permission. Daniel Ivars bled to death around four in the afternoon. Like all the rest, his widow got nothing from the company."

Her hands were at his face, each caress another plea: "They might do something that awful to you. Don't go."

"I have to, Anna. I have to go."

"Oh God, oh God, I love you so, you crazy stupid man."

She slept with him until around three in the morning. Each was restless; now and again she'd seize him and hug him. She was a fine woman. He wished he loved her as much as a man should love a wife. He loved his work more. Or it needed him more, perhaps that was a better way to put it.

She stole out of the attic while it was still dark, so old Ehling or Thor wouldn't discover her moral lapse—as if they didn't suspect already. At 6:15, warmly dressed in a gray wool cap and a mackinaw of green and black plaid, he quietly left the house.

He went down the porch stairs to the vine maple and there breathed deeply before he stepped into the road. The sun was still behind the mountains. But there was enough light to see the layout of the town. There was enough light for him to find his way down to the Smiley Shingle Company.

97

Dutch

ON THE LAST MONDAY in May, the thirtieth, the hotel was full of talk about a Jewish pawnbroker found murdered in his shop. Police were investigating. The *Tampa Times* suspected "someone from the gambling and saloon crowd which has followed the Army to our city like the biblical plagues of yore. It is also possible the culprit belongs to a certain bad element in the Army itself, notably the aggressive colored men."

Late in the morning, Paul left Jimmy idling at the hotel and again walked across the river with a small wooden crate containing two more magazines. He feared the colonel would find most of the footage dull. There were the now-familiar scenes of soldiers drilling, playing ball, erecting tents, scouring mess kits. Most of the rest was scenic material. Sailboats in the Bay. Palms swaying in sea breezes. Some of the local beauties, who were not so beautiful, tossing a beach ball and frolicking in their neck-to-ankle bathing costumes. There was only one sequence Paul considered unusual and exciting—a demonstration of one of the four rapid-fire Gatling guns that would be taken to Cuba.

Several correspondents had gone out to the beach to watch the demonstration, including Sylvanus Peterman, the humorless jingo whom Crane had christened "the worst of Hearst." Crane himself showed up a few minutes later, slack-jawed and sleepy, wearing jeans pants and a sweated-out shirt of red silk. He greeted Paul with the animation of a hospital patient.

Billy Bitzer was setting up a few yards from Paul and Jimmy, William Paley and his assistant an equal distance in the other direction. Shirtless, Bitzer hailed Paul with a smile and a wave. Paley took no notice of his colleagues. He wore a suit black and heavy as an undertaker's. Sweat dripped from his haggard face.

Davis wasn't present, so of the reporters, Michael Radcliffe was the sartorial king. The temperature was near ninety, but Michael looked perfectly cool in his spotless white linen suit, colorfully striped scarf cravat and white felt homburg. His knob-headed stick was tucked under his arm. Michael shook Paul's hand, and Jimmy's when Paul introduced them. "Swell-looking suit," Jimmy said with a grin. "Cost much?"

"Enough." Michael had an immediate and negative reaction to Jimmy, Paul saw.

As the young men readied their camera, the Gatling gun arrived, pulled by artillery horses. The gun had a crank and a ring of ten rifle barrels mounted around an axle. The crank, sights, and loading hopper were protected by an iron shield above the gun mount, and by a smaller iron apron below.

"Ever seen one of these?" Michael asked. They said they hadn't. "The gun was developed by Mr. Lincoln's minions during the American Civil War. Of course you know war departments. They move with the speed of mastodons. Takes them only a century or so to decide a weapon is useful and should be widely adopted."

Jimmy wandered away to adjust the tripod of the Luxograph. Michael continued to his remaining listener. "Do you recall my telling you I paid to experience jolts of electricity at the Prater in Vienna? How I felt the apocalypse through my hands that day? I had a similar, equally powerful reaction the first time I saw one of these guns operating. Science is piously promising to fill man's horn of plenty in the next century, but I'll tell you what it's really doing. It's opening the gates of hell."

Smiling balefully, he strolled off to a patch of shade.

Noncoms led the horses away, unchained the limber from the gun's trail, then wheeled the gun so that it would fire almost due north along the beach. The target was a coconut palm just above the high-tide line. The tree tilted steeply toward the water, its fronds almost directly above the breaking surf.

The reporters and three cameras were ranged in a semicircle on the shore side of the gun. A young first lieutenant of infantry stepped in front of the gathering.

"Gentlemen, allow me to introduce myself. Lieutenant John Henry Parker, 13th Infantry. General Shafter has placed me in command of the Gatling Gun Detachment going to Cuba, presumably because I learned a little something about artillery at West Point." He raised his eyebrows and smiled self-deprecatingly.

"There have been several modifications to the gun since it was invented by Dr. R. J. Gatling, a physician, in 1862. This particular gun is the 1895 model, the latest. So long as the crank is turning, the ammunition hopper is kept full and no round jams, the piece will fire continuously. The recommended rate is six hundred rounds per minute, though the gun is capable of even faster speeds." Jimmy let out a long, two-note whistle.

"The gun employs a gravity feed of the Bruce type. During the demonstration you will see that the rounds go directly from the box into the loading hopper. I should also point out this cross-hair sight on the left of the muzzle, and this pointing lever with which the gunners can accurately control the elevation and direction of fire. You gentlemen with cameras may start them if you wish, we are ready to begin."

Paul was already cranking. Paley had a problem and there was a five-minute delay. Bitzer lit a cigarette. Paul took a cigar stub from his shirt pocket and enjoyed it until Paley announced he was ready. Lieutenant Parker cracked out orders to his men, who suddenly moved quickly, ripping off box covers, dumping the contents, turning the crank. The barrels projecting through the shield began to revolve and stutter.

The sound was unnerving; a deafening *brrr* that sent chills through Paul. The opening in the shield was large enough for the gun to move back and forth horizontally about fifteen degrees. While the barrels revolved, the bullets chewed across the trunk of the palm tree from left to right, right to left, back and forth, blowing bark chips and splinters in all directions. It seemed only seconds before Parker yelled "Cease fire!" and the gun stopped its deadly drumming. A silence crashed over the watchers, broken only by the sibilance of the surf. Then came a cracking and a grinding as the palm toppled into the blue water with a great loud splash. The trunk had been cut through at a height of about three feet. The splintered stump was smoking. Behind Paul, Jimmy said, "Jesus, ain't that something? One guy could mow down a whole gang with that thing."

"Gentlemen, that completes the demonstration," Lieutenant Parker announced. "If you have questions, I'll be happy to answer them."

Paul checked the footage counter and capped the lens. Michael strolled over, swinging his stick. "There it is, chaps—the future. War is no longer a cricket match for a bunch of nice fellows whose mums taught them to be mannerly above all things." Paul could agree. He'd never seen anything so destructive at short range.

Sylvanus Peterman ran down the beach, rudely pushed another reporter aside, and crouched by the fallen tree. He caressed the splintered end of the broken trunk, moist-eyed with excitement. Jimmy walked up behind him, equally admiring of the damage done by the Gatling. "Couple of bloodthirsty sods, Peterman and your friend," Michael remarked.

"Jim's my helper. I wouldn't go so far as to use the other word."

At the freight office Paul filled out papers for another collect shipment. As he left the depot, Paley of the Eden Museé climbed down from his wagon with a box similar to his. Paul said hello. Paley didn't reply, just threw him a hostile look as he rushed inside.

A familiar tightness was building in Paul. He could relieve it by calling the grocery in Ybor City and asking Luisa's whereabouts. Hot as it was, he decided to walk a while, hoping it might drain off some of his tension.

On Franklin Street he bumped into Dick Davis coming out of the popular and expensive Maas Brothers dry goods store. In defiance of the weather, Davis was wearing his best professional costume—a dark blue coat and gray riding breeches tucked into polished black knee boots. His soft gray fedora had a white puggaree draped down in back. A case for field glasses hung on his right shoulder. He was carrying a gift box wrapped in foil paper. On his way to some fancy function, Paul assumed.

Still, Davis had time to stop and give him a smile. "Hallo, Dutch. Surviving in this blasted town?"

"Barely, Mr. Davis."

"We all feel that way. Worst place I've ever seen. Orange trees, sand fleas, and derelict houses in an ocean of sand. The locals won't like the copy I'm writing about it."

"Is there any word on departure?"

"Nothing. How's your picture making?"

"I've used up Tampa. I'm ready for Cuba."

"You and the rest of us. Take care." He jumped into a waiting carriage. The black driver shook his long whip over the horse and the carriage rolled off. The expense account of the famed R.H.D. must be huge indeed.

Paul walked aimlessly, with no destination. Soon he was on Pierce, headed north on the shady side. It was no cooler there. He bought a tin cup of lemonade from the bucket of one of the many street sellers. It tasted like sweet soup heated on a stove. God above, when would they get out of here?

After ten or twelve blocks, he turned east, into an increasingly shabby section. Presently he was on Liberty, the western fringe of Ybor, biting off the end of a fresh cigar and thinking seriously of searching for Luisa at once. He was distracted by loud laughter from an alley between two stores, each with dual signage, English and Spanish. To the left was a *Farmacia;* on his right *Quincalleria Jonas*—Jonas hardware. At the drugstore hitch rail, a sorrel mare with a U.S. Army saddle was standing with her head down. Outside the hardware store tools pitted with corrosion stood in open barrels.

In the shadowed alley, four soldiers in blue blouses were tossing a fifth into the air with a blanket. Paul had photographed blanket-tossing in the camps. He thought it a silly but harmless form of abuse of new recruits. But an alley was a strange place for . . .

The soldiers whipped the blanket aside and let the victim fall. He was a black man, his holster empty, his sidearm nowhere visible. Bloodstains on his brown fatigue blouse were very visible.

Landing hard, he gave an involuntary cry. In a few seconds he tried to rise, pushing with his hands. An overweight sergeant kicked him. The sergeant was white. So were the others.

"Here, leave him alone," Paul shouted, running into the dim alley. Three of the soldiers were young men; farmer types with red sunburned skin and an undernourished look. The sergeant was older, with pendulous chins and a face round and white as a cream pie. He snaked his revolver out of its holster.

"I wouldn't mess in this, boy." He brought the gun up and straightened his arm. The muzzle was level with Paul's eyes. "You listening? You better."

"This nigger went where he shouldn't of," one of the others said. "He tried to sit down next to a white woman at the drugstore fountain."

"Looks like you beat him half to death for it," Paul said while his brain busily calculated the odds against him.

"Hey, he's some kind of foreigner, Cheat," a third soldier said. "A kraut or suthin'."

Sergeant Cheat drew back the hammer. "Yeah, well, mebbe I'll blow that funny accent right down his throat. Boy, d'ya know who we are? Jacksonville Light Infantry of the 1st Florida. This here's our home state. Our territory. Don't fuck with us."

Volunteers. He might have guessed. He felt taut as a wire, not wanting a bullet but not wanting to run, either. On the ground behind the four, the black soldier was groggily rousing. When he took in the situation, his hand shot out, grabbing the sergeant's boot, tripping him.

The sergeant fell on his face. The revolver went off. In the narrow alley the shot resounded like a thunderclap. Paul had already flung himself out of the way.

Cheat's bullet tore through the dirt, raising dust. Paul slammed into the wall of the hardware store, the force of it snapping his teeth on his tongue. He tasted blood as he reeled around to the street, yanked a shovel with a long wooden handle from one of the barrels. Holding the shovel in both hands like a fighting staff, he jumped back into the alley. Blood drizzled out one corner of his mouth.

Sergeant Cheat was on his knees, grappling with the black man for the revolver. From the sidewalk someone yelled, "What the devil's goin' on?" One of the Jacksonville soldiers stepped behind the black man and booted him in the small of his back. Paul bowled into the other soldiers with the shovel held in front of him. Two of them went down.

Cheat yanked hard on the revolver and got possession of it. Holding the barrel, he struck the black soldier a vicious looping blow to the head. The black soldier pitched over, unconscious.

"Cheat, we'll be in the guardhouse, we don't run outa here," one of the soldiers panted. Cheat squinted at Paul crouched with the shovel, then at townspeople collecting at the mouth of the alley. He spat at Paul. The gob missed Paul's cheek but struck his shirt. Cheat led a running retreat down the alley and over a board fence, out of sight.

A woman in a bonnet stepped into the alley and shielded her eyes. "Oh, never mind, it's just one of those coloreds." She and the man with her moved on. The crowd dispersed. Paul's heart began to slow down.

The black soldier lay with eyes closed, his bleeding cheek resting in the dirt. He wasn't a very handsome specimen; he had a jutting jaw, an ugly, misshapen nose, a back-slanting forehead. Paul knelt to make sure he was breathing, then returned the shovel to its barrel and went into the hardware store, where he asked for a telephone.

"Drugstore," the man said, avoiding his eye.

Paul crossed the alley. The drugstore's marble soda fountain was up front. Its four tall wire stools were empty. At the back, where peculiar odors seeped from white apothecary jars, the little black-haired druggist was energetically dusting a large glass teardrop containing bright red liquid.

"There's a soldier hurt outside. Can you telephone the authorities for assistance?"

The white druggist went on dusting the teardrop in its silver stand. "Phone's out of order."

The druggist was perspiring. Instantly, Paul understood. He stalked back to the screen door, disgusted.

In the alley, he squatted and lifted the injured man, who groaned again but didn't waken. Though leanly built, the soldier was heavy. Paul bore him on his back, staggering a couple of times. He draped the man across the saddle of the cavalry horse, having assumed they belonged together.

He untied the rein and led the horse through the streets. Every block or two, he checked the man's pulse and breathing. He led the horse all the way up to Tampa Heights, to the camp of the 24th and 25th Infantry Regiments; the nearest black units. The camp was neat and orderly, its grid of sandy streets marked out by rows of white tents. A trooper directed him to the dispensary tent.

He described the incident to a black orderly. The orderly pointed to a cot and lowered some insect netting around it. Then he hurried off to find a physician, who turned out to be white.

The doctor examined the soldier and found nothing more serious than the bruises and abrasions produced by the beating. He made a note of Paul's name and where he was staying, and thanked him. Paul left the camp and paid five cents to ride the trolley down into town. Although he was bedraggled—even more unkempt than usual—the conductor didn't bother him. Like the other passengers who got on or off at different stops, Paul was white.

He thought of telephoning Tomaso at the market and asking about Luisa's availability.

Another time. He was too damn tired.

Next morning, a few minutes after six, a knock woke him. He tugged on his pants and was surprised to find a white cavalry officer standing outside; a lean, tall man, middle thirties, with blue eyes, bushy brows, and a downturned mouth that gave him an air of extreme severity. The man's posture was so correct, his uniform so neat, his boots so clean, Paul made an instant judgment. *If I were a soldier, I would not want to serve with this man, he'd be too difficult.*

"Crown?"

"Yes."

"First Lieutenant Pershing, 10th Cavalry. May I come in?"

Paul rubbed his eyes as he stepped back. The lieutenant shut the door, flicked the strap of his campaign hat from under his chin, and took the hat off. Paul started to gesture to the chair, then realized it was piled with clothes ready for the laundry. His blue chambray shirt lay on the floor under the dressing table. Almost every horizontal surface was covered by items of his souvenir collection. Pershing's blue eyes whipped over the disorder and didn't like it.

"I'll take only a few moments of your time," he said. His features were strong, if humorless; a prominent nose, large ears that lay flat to his head. He stood with his boot heels apart, as if at parade rest. "Doctor Long, who serves the 24th, gave me your name. I'm advised that you assisted one of my men yesterday."

"If you mean the Negro, yes, I did."

"I'm here to thank you. Corporal Person is a member of the troop that I command. The regiment was informed of his situation last night. The doctor said Person will be up and about later today. I caught the local train from Lakeland at 4 A.M. and I've just seen him. We're tracking the men who beat him. You reported that one was called Cheat?"

Paul raked his dark hair, all tangled from sleep. The lieutenant's sentences seemed to fly at him like bullets. "That's the name I heard. Sergeant Cheat. He boasted about his unit, the Jacksonville Light Infantry of the 1st Florida."

"All I needed was that confirmation. We'll have him arrested within an hour. The Negro regulars are having a lot of trouble with these damned redneck volunteers. I hate for it to happen to Person, he's a fine soldier. I hate for it to happen to any man in the 10th. I've learned to respect and admire our black troops. They try harder than most because the Army is their ticket to a decent life."

Then there was a noticeable break in the rhythm of Pershing's speech; a pause as he studied Paul's reaction. "That isn't what you expected me to say, is it? I'm very much aware that it's a minority view. I recently did a short tour at the Military Academy, as a cadet tactical officer. Went there from service with the 10th at Fort Assiniboin, Montana. My former post didn't make me popular. When

I told my cadets of my high regard for black troops, the cadets started calling me Nigger Jack. Behind my back, mostly. Sometimes they softened it to Black Jack. That name I don't mind. Now, Mr. Crown, a request. If you can, please go up to Tampa Heights before the day's over. Corporal Person very much wants to tender his thanks to you."

"I believe I can go, I set my own schedule."

"Are you a newspaper correspondent?"

"A camera operator for the American Luxograph Company of Chicago. The moving pictures." The lieutenant looked vaguely disapproving.

"I gather from your accent that you're German."

"Yes, Swabia, and then Berlin."

"I have German roots myself. The family was Alsatian originally. The name was Pfoershing in the seventeen hundreds." He shot his hand out. "You're a very decent chap. Thank you again for helping one of my men."

They shook hands. With crisp movements, Lieutenant Pershing donned his campaign hat and snapped the strap under his chin. Once more he looked at the litter of souvenirs and laundry. He started to say something but reconsidered and about-faced. He didn't walk out of the room; he marched.

In the yellow light of the dying afternoon, Paul rode the trolley again. Evening fires were burning throughout the camp; cooks were tending their kettles and seeing to their stocks of dishes and cutlery stored in boxes and crates nailed to trees. The smells were pleasant, except for that of the latrines.

The black troopers lay napping in their tents, or sat reading in the shelter of big heavily sprung army wagons. On a sandy diamond, some of them were playing a noisy game of baseball. The white officers had a small enclave to themselves, with camp chairs arranged under a giant live oak draped with Spanish moss. A table made of citrus crates held copies of New York newspapers and popular magazines. An officer reading *Harper's Weekly* took his pipe from his mouth and looked curiously at Paul.

He found Corporal Person on the cot where he'd left him. Behind the insect netting Person was sitting up, playing a solitaire game laid out on a copy of the *Police Gazette*. Nearby on another cot, a soldier more amber-colored than black thrashed and groaned.

A sheet covered Person's lower body. His muscled chest and shoulders were shiny in the heat. A long bandage was wrapped around his head; crinkly gray hair showed between his ears and the bandage. A knife scar several inches long ran from the middle of his right cheek to his jaw. When he saw Paul, he broke into a grin. He had large teeth and a smile bright as a searchlight.

"You got to be the German fellow who pulled my hash out of the fire."

"I brought you here, if that's what you mean. Paul Crown is my name. Everyone calls me Dutch."

"When I woke up this morning, I thought about you. Didn't know your name so I gave you one. Heine. Heard another German called that once, he didn't seem to mind. Dutch is a name for one of them fellows with wooden shoes who lives in a windmill."

"You mean a Hollander. It's a confusion Germans can't straighten out. I've quit trying. Call me Heine if you want."

"Good. Everybody needs a nickname or two. Only man I know who don't have a proper one is the sarge over there." He pointed to the groaning man. "Sergeant Leander, all he's got is a terrible case of the Tampa trots."

"Do you have a nickname?"

"Ott. Short for Othello. My brother's Duff, short for Macduff. My sister's name is Filia, from Ophelia. Our daddy was a Pullman car porter, y'see. Had lots of time to read during the night. He was partial to poetry, especially Shakespeare. After President Lincoln and General Grant brought the jubilee, and pop was allowed to learn to read, you couldn't stop him. Pop used to say he hated to take time from books to earn a living. Man's never lonely with a book in his pocket, he'd say. Books gives a man ten thousand friends. Some are smart, some are funny, some are just pleasant for passing the time, but they're all good. Me, I ain't as smart as my pop but I still read a lot. Here, I'm forgetting my manners. Pull up that stool, sit yourself."

In the street, a long file of mounted troopers passed at a walk. Their lieutenant, like Pfoershing-Pershing, was white.

Paul asked, "How'd you get in that fix yesterday, Corporal?"

"Hey now, you helped me out, let's keep it Ott, all right?"

"Fine," Paul said.

Ott Person seemed a gentle man, easygoing, yet he had an unmistakable toughness. Under his right arm, along his ribs, Paul saw another scar, a long, horizontal pucker that might have been made by a bullet, or an Indian arrow.

"Tenth Cavalry's camped way out in Lakeland. I was sent in with dispatches for General Shafter at the hotel. Rode thirty miles on horseback, delivered the pouch, and thought a drink of soda water would taste good. I didn't want to ask at the hotel, place gives me the jitters. Too fancy. I rode across to Tampa and spied that drugstore. I went in, said 'scuse me to a nice-lookin' lady and sat down on the stool next to her. Those Florida boys came in a minute later."

The blaze of his grin disappeared. "They dint take kindly to me bein' there, sitting by a white lady. Lot of that feeling in this town. Tell the truth, there's a lot of it wherever we're posted."

They exchanged some facts about themselves. Ott had been raised in Philadelphia and had run on the streets until he was eighteen, old enough to enlist. Paul said he'd been a street boy in Berlin. Ott grinned.

"Knew there was something made me like you right off."

"And you like the Army?"

"I most surely do. I guess I been an American longer than you, so let me explain something. In this here country we got equality, but some's a lot more equal than others. In the Army it's a mite better. There's travel, and some self-respect, even some danger now and again to prove a man's worthy. My brother Duff, he thinks I'm crazy. When I was on leave last month, Duff said he'd never go to war for a damn bunch of white folks. 'I got no country to fight for,' he said. 'I got no rights here.' I told him, 'Duff, you're wrong, you're dumb as a mule. We got some rights. Not enough, but more than Poppa had before the jubilee, and I keep chipping away to get a few more.' That may be why I walked into that drugstore yesterday. I knew it was a white man's place.

"Anyway, Heine, I try to b'lieve in this country spite of all the bad things it's done to people of color. I don't know of a better country, and I've read on the subject. Things do improve. Sometimes hellish slow, but they do. A hundred years ago the Person family dint have a last name. The Persons bent their backs on a cotton farm in Chatham County, Georgia, right along with a dozen others whose granddaddies were snatched from Africa. I 'spect there'll be a lot more changes, time another hundred years have gone by. If I didn't b'lieve it, I'd gather all my uniforms in a pile and set fire to 'em. Then I'd go home and tell my brother Duff, 'Hey, you're right.' But I don't b'lieve like Duff does, and I ain't ready to give up hope. Not just yet."

Paul consulted his pocket watch and said he had to leave. Ott Person swung his bare feet off the cot, keeping the sheet on his middle. "They say I can go back to my troop in the morning. We'll be off for Cuba one of these weeks and I may not see you if things get hot down there. But if I do see you, and you're in a fix, remember this. I owe you for helping me. I always pay what I owe, you won't have to ask twice."

"Thanks, Ott, let's hope it won't be necessary. So long."

"So long, Heine."

Troubled, Paul trudged a sandy road under widely spaced street lights. What kind of country was it that asked a man to wear its uniform, then spat on him? Americans bragged that theirs was a nation of liberty and law. Were the liberty and law only for an elect of white men? It seemed so.

At the hotel gate he paused to listen to a regimental band playing "After the Ball." The music flowed into the dark gardens where couples were strolling and laughing in a way that made a single man feel sad. "Julie," he whispered. "Julie."

Don't do that, it's over. She's gone.

He realized he'd wrapped his hand around one of the wrought iron bars of the gate. Clutched it so hard, there was a small bleeding cut on his palm. He couldn't stand celibacy any longer, he was going to have to telephone Tomaso.

The frailty of human flesh kept him from it. He caught the sickness of the town, the "Tampa trots," from food, dirt, bad water, the tent where he visited Ott Person—who could say?

He'd never felt so miserable and helpless. He had a lot of bad thoughts. He was a speck of common clay, meaningless in the great scheme of the universe. His wishes and hopes counted for nothing.

Jimmy was considerate enough to look in a couple of times a day, though he made a lot of tasteless jokes about Paul's plight. When he visited on the second night of Paul's illness, he seemed unusually cheerful. Paul asked whether he'd done any filming on his own.

"Ah, jeez, I couldn't. The crank jammed. Sand or something. I took it to a photo shop, it should be fixed later this morning." It was a lie. Who in Tampa would know how to repair their kind of camera? But Paul didn't have the energy, or the evidence, to accuse Jimmy.

□ □ □ □

On Monday, June 6, feeling better, he went down to the rathskeller about noon. He paused at the bottom of the stair for a check of the customers. He was determined not to meet Uncle Joe if he could avoid it.

Bitzer was finishing his lunch at a table. "Hey, Dutch, glad you're well. Getting any good pictures?"

"There isn't too much to photograph in my room, I'm afraid."

"Not much left to photograph outside, either. I wish we'd get going."

Paul agreed. He left the Biograph man mopping up gravy on his plate and surprised the barman by ordering iced tea in a tall glass. He was sipping it when Crane came in, looking as bad as ever.

"Hallo, Dutch. Heard you were down with the local quickstep."

"I was, but I'm much better. Care for a cigar?"

Crane shook his head, ordered whiskey, and packed his pipe. "There was another break-in last night, did you hear?" Paul shook his head. "Burglar got into the room of some major from Michigan. Stole about forty dollars and a gold watch chain. I expect it's the same enterprising boyo who's been working the joint for a week or so."

"There have been other robberies in the hotel?"

"Four."

"I haven't heard a word about it."

"You've been sick. Furthermore, you're not supposed to hear. The manager isn't eager to have it known that Henry Plant's palace of pleasure entertains sneak thieves. I only heard it when I was in bed with one of the tasty colored girls who clean the rooms." Crane tossed off his shot of whiskey. "Kid, you look like a bee stung you. Why are you surprised by some measly breaking-and-entering jobs? You round up hundreds of high-paid military types for a great and noble crusade like this, thieves are bound to follow along with the whores and saloon keepers and other practitioners of free enterprise."

"Yes, I suppose that's true," Paul said in a strained way. His scalp was crawling. He saw a face, and felt unnerved the rest of the day.

At supper in the rathskeller, he sat alone at a table by the wall. Jimmy breezed in about half past six, heading for the bar. Paul had an impulse to hide from him. Reluctantly, he waved.

Jimmy ambled over, full of good cheer. He hung his derby on a wall peg and sat down. The derby was golden brown, with an elegant silk band and the brim curved slightly downward at front and back. Very nobby.

Brand new.

"So you're back on your two pins, huh?"

"I am, thanks. You sound happy."

"Top of the world."

"I looked for you all afternoon. I examined the camera. It seems fine."

"Yeah, the shop fella fixed it good as new."

Easy to do, since there was nothing wrong with it.

A bit testy, Paul said, "We've not gotten much film."

"Hell, you've been in bed."

"But where have you been?"

"Here and there," Jimmy said with a shrug. Paul stared. Jimmy winked. "Ah, you know. Chasing local cunt. Hot stuff, Dutch. I keep telling you to try it."

Paul laid his small silver fork on his plate of bluepoint oysters in the shell. His revived appetite had abruptly vanished. He suspected something other than women was responsible for Jimmy's good spirits. On the train coming down, Jimmy had said he intended to make money from the trip.

Abruptly, Paul jumped up.

"Jesus, are you sick again?"

"Yes!" Paul darted from the table, into the billiard room, where there was a separate door to the lower corridor. A close call; Uncle Joe was at the bottom of the stairway, talking steadily and seriously with a major and a captain. Paul left hurriedly.

Tuesday, the seventh of June. The pressure had built to an intolerable level. Late in the morning he telephoned the grocery and asked for Tomaso. Luisa came to his room about half past eight. She took one look and exclaimed, *"Ay, Dios mio! Qué cuarto de cochinos. ¡Incréible!"*

"What did you say?"

"I said this is incredible. This a room for pi—uh—like a barnyard." She giggled. *"¡Semejante junco!* Such junk. Where are we supposed to make love, on the ceiling?"

Mortified, Paul grabbed his straw hat and a new pair of brown canvas leggings, bought as protection against snakes and spiders said to be common in Cuba. He stood sheepishly with the hat in one hand, the leggings in the other, because there was no place to put them. Politeness made Luisa cover her pretty mouth, but her laughter was too strong to be contained. "Jesus save us, sweet, what *is* all this?"

"Souvenirs. I like to collect things from places I visit."

"Well, you have certainly done a magnificent job," she said, hands on her hips. It forced him to see everything he'd accumulated in Tampa. Postcards of the beach. Postcards of shrimp boats. Postcards showing interiors and exteriors of the hotel. Three sand dollars and a dried starfish. Conch shells. A stuffed baby alligator. Four coconuts, two carved into Indian faces. A miniature wooden crate full of orange-colored candy balls. Six pieces of driftwood in assorted, presumably interesting, shapes . . .

And of course, on the dressing table, the paper flag and the worn stereopticon card.

"I have never seen such a a large—how do you say? *Museo?*"

"Museum?"

"Yes, such a large museum in such a tiny space. What are you going to *do* with all of this, *querido?*"

"Crate the best pieces and send them to Chicago."

She started to slip out of her dress of bright yellow silk. "Do you live this way at home?"

"This is my home. This or another place like it."

She stopped, with the dress just above her fine brown breasts. She wore white muslin drawers, knee length and trimmed with lace, but nothing above.

"Hotel rooms?"

"Hotel rooms, furnished rooms—it doesn't matter."

"How remarkable," she said in a soft, almost grave voice. "You are different, dear Paulo. I have never met a person like you."

"Now you have. Any place with a door and a window, a light and a bed, is home enough for me. The important part's the bed."

He didn't want her to see the lie, or the pain, as they undressed and met warmly in each other's arms.

Luisa was ardent; tender and amusing by turns. But she kept track of time. She was gone by 10 P.M., slipping his money into the bodice of her yellow dress and giving him a deep and sweet farewell kiss. "I like you, Paulo. You're a fine and gentle lover. Be safe in Cuba, and go home safely afterward."

The door closed with a soft click. He flopped on the bed with his hands under his head, his eyes on the ceiling. He didn't want to look at the pathetic collection of junk. That's all it was, cheap junk, gathered in a stupid attempt to fool himself into thinking he had belongings, and therefore belonged somewhere. He didn't. His long search for a home was *Idiotie*. Idiocy. Unintentionally, Luisa had forced him to confront the truth he'd tried to hide for a long time. Unintentionally, he'd confessed to her.

This is my home. This or another place like it. There is nothing else.

He fell asleep, a quick slumber of forgetfulness. Half an hour later he was jolted awake by noises in the hall. Doors slamming. People running. The ratcheting sound of the elevator cage shutting. My God, was there a fire?

He jumped from bed, pulled on his drawers, yanked the door open. All along the hall, soldiers and civilians were scurrying with grips and canvas field bags. Crane bolted from his room several doors down, suitcase in one hand, books in the other.

"Stephen! What is it?"

"Orders to sail. Posted a few minutes ago. Admiral Sampson has shelled the Santiago works into silence, and Washington's signaled Shafter to Cuba. Better pack and get downstairs or you'll be all night paying your bill."

He hurried to the main stairway. Paul threw his shirt and pants on and rushed next door to Jimmy's room. He knocked and called out. No answer.

He tried the knob. The door opened. He switched on the lights. The room was hot, the window closed, the bed still made.

Cursing, Paul ran to pack.

Crane was right, it was hell getting out of the hotel. In addition to standing in the cashier's long line, he had to find a porter, strike a bargain, give the man four dollars, and Shadow's address. The porter promised to box and ship all the souvenirs in Paul's room. He'd packed only the paper flag and the stereopticon card. He half suspected the souvenirs would be dumped in some trash bin.

What did it matter? Luisa had dragged the truth into the light. There would be many other rooms, many other places to collect souvenirs—and dozens of dots of dark red enamel to be painted on the wooden globe Mary was keeping for him. That was his life now. The life of a gypsy who had no home, and never would have one.

98

Ilsa

ILSA'S DAYS AND NIGHTS were filled with worry.

She worried about Pauli, who had surprised her with a souvenir postcard a few weeks ago. The card had been mailed from some hamlet in Georgia. It showed a grove of peach trees. What in heaven's name was Pauli doing in Georgia?

She worried about her son. The silence of weeks had become the silence of months; many months. It would soon be a year since the last token arrived; the little crate with the orange candies, placed carefully with the geode in front of the mirror of her chiffonnier.

She prayed she'd hear from Joe Junior again soon. Although she never would have breathed it to Fritzi or Carl, or loved them one whit less, there was a truth all mothers knew. There was a mystic specialness about the firstborn. She prayed that one day, she would embrace her firstborn again.

Most of all she worried about Joe. She missed his physical presence; they'd never been separated for such a long time. She desperately feared for his safety. The fighting would begin soon, the papers said. When the Americans invaded Cuba, Joe's nature wouldn't allow him to hang back to protect himself. He'd ride or march in the front rank, leading his men. It was a source of pride for her, but a source of dread, too.

Even if Joe escaped physical harm, she feared the distractions of war, especially an excitement she could no longer provide. A certain calm settled over the best of marriages late in life, all her female friends said so. She and Joe had discussed it once, in bed, and he'd rebelled against the very possibility. Had used strong words to characterize the kind of middle-aged existence he didn't want. *Geistlos;* dull. *Langweilig;* boring. Soon after the discussion he began to write letters to Carl Schurz and others, offering his services to the military.

So Ilsa had another fear connected with the war; an ill-defined but potent fear of younger rivals. The newspaper dispatches spoke of Cuban women, handsome and refined, living in exile in Tampa. At night Ilsa peered into an oval mirror in her bedroom and saw dozens of new, unattractive lines.

As soon as Joe had arrived in Florida, he'd telegraphed to let her know. His next communication was a five-line letter on the stationery of the Tampa Bay Hotel. It had come ten days ago. Since then, nothing. What—or who—was distracting him?

A final, extra layer of anxiety was added by Ilsa's growing distrust of the war itself. She had never said it to Joe explicitly, but she wasn't a jingo, and she deplored those who were.

Support for the war continued to be strongest in the Midwest and the West. In the East, more heavily populated by Democrats and free thinkers, resistance was formidable. The war was being denounced as commercial imperialism concealed by patriotic slogans and windy pronouncements about American ideals. Ilsa read that the distinguished president of Harvard, Charles Eliot Norton, and others were planning a June meeting at a place in Boston called Faneuil Hall, to organize some kind of anti-imperialist league. Not to oppose the war outright, but to keep it a war of liberation rather than a war to grab new territory and thereby create new markets for American business.

Important persons were speaking out in support of such a league. Ex-President Cleveland, the philosopher William James, labor leader Samuel Gompers. Andrew Carnegie, who had earned all the money he needed for ten lifetimes and was now an apostle of peace, joined the movement.

Her dear friend Miss Addams continued to withhold her name, and her allegiance, for the reason she'd explained before. "The organizers have pleaded with me by mail and by telegraph but I simply can't do it. I must have community support. I must keep these doors open."

There were millions who saw nothing wrong with a war to gain territory and expand American influence. One was a young Indiana lawyer, Mr. Beveridge, reputed to be an orator as powerful as Bryan. Beveridge had started crisscrossing the country with his message of American duty and destiny, and he was rising like a bright evening star on the national horizon. Long excerpts from his speeches ran in the Chicago papers: *The trade of the world must and shall be ours . . . American law, American order, American civilization will plant themselves on those shores hitherto backward, bloody and benighted.*

"What rot," Miss Addams said one gloomy, rainy afternoon at Hull House. "That young man is making a career of wrapping himself in the flag."

"He surely is," Ilsa agreed. "But it isn't hurting him. Mr. Beveridge's speeches have won him great favor with the Indiana legislature. He's likely to be chosen to go to the Senate."

"No matter, it's rot. How dare he suggest we take on the care of new colored populations? We can't successfully help or deal with our own—and we've had more than thirty years to try."

"Do you think Mr. Beveridge really believes what he's saying?"

"Why not? Men who delude others begin by deluding themselves."

That night, while a summer storm raged outside, Ilsa sat at her desk and wrote a draft on her household account for one hundred dollars. She put it in an envelope addressed to Hull House, along with a note asking Jane Addams to see that it got to the right people in Boston, anonymously.

Then she dropped to her knees beside her bed. While the rain hammered the silent, lonely house, she clasped her hands and bowed her head.

She prayed to God to bring Joe back to her, whole in body and still loyal in heart. She prayed to be cleansed of the guilt she felt because of her loathing for the war. Rebellion might satisfy a militant "new woman," but it couldn't soothe a guilty *Hausfrau.* It was the old conflict; she'd been raised to be dutiful and retiring, not outspoken. Could she ever tell Joe about the donation?

Her room was black as the rainy night enfolding the house. She clasped her hands so tightly they hurt, talking to someone else now.

Joe, I don't know whether it's right or wrong, this war. Could it be both? Do we ever know such things?

I am sure of one thing only. I will die if something happens to you. You can be a jingo all your life if you'll just come home to me.

99

Dutch

PAUL REACHED PORT TAMPA with the crated equipment at midmorning. Three gray iron vessels were tied up; others were waiting in the channel. Army siege guns on each pier guarded the approach. Switch engines were shunting livestock and coal cars through the yards to the pier spurs. Soldiers poured off the cars, their clothes flecked with coal dust or cow dung. Carrying white blanket rolls and outmoded Springfield rifles, they formed up in the heat to await their ships.

"Don't lose sight of these boxes. I'll pay you another ten dollars once we stow them aboard," Paul said to the burly black drayman he'd stolen from another customer at the hotel by offering him thirty dollars—ten more than he asked.

"Which ship's yours?"

"All the civilians are supposed to travel on the headquarters ship, *Segurança.* It'll be too crowded, I want to go some other way." That was because a substantial part of the crowd would consist of generals, of which his uncle would certainly be one.

He had to search for Jimmy. For all he knew, his partner might have gone back to Chicago without telling him. He plunged into the mob on the pier. Wagons, artillery caissons, horses, bands, civilians shouting and waving from the windows of four Plant Line sightseeing cars—it was an incredible tangle. In the midst of it, his collar open and his jowls dripping sweat, General Shafter sat at a desk made of orange crates, alternately screaming orders and profanity at his aides.

Paul's way was barred by a regimental band playing "The Girl I Left Behind Me." He wriggled and slid between the musicians. "Excuse me, let me through, must come through." As he fought his way, he stepped in a horse turd.

He hopped on one leg, shaking the dirty shoe in the air. He lost his balance and lurched against a man in jackboots and a spotless uniform of white duck. Before he could apologize, the man snarled, "Kindly be more careful, *mein Herr.* You spoiled my picture." He'd been taking a snapshot of one of the docked transports.

Paul recognized him, of course. "I am extremely sorry, Lieutenant—"

"Captain. Captain von Rike. Military attaché from the embassy of His Majesty, Emperor Wilhelm the Second." He adjusted his black fatigue cap with the red-dotted roundel in front. "And you, sir?"

A moment's hesitation. "Dutch Crown."

"Crown. There is a general named Crown on the staff of General Wheeler."

"Is that so? No relation."

"You are a civilian correspondent?"

"Something like that. If I damaged your camera, I'll pay for the repair."

The politeness surprised and mollified von Rike. Obviously he had no memory of their previous encounter in Berlin. He was a little more cordial when he said, "That won't be necessary, I ruined only one picture. You are German?"

"Yes. My family's Swabian."

"I am Prussian." As if no one could tell. "I am always happy to see a country-man, from whatever region. If this *verdammt* expedition doesn't sink into the sea from sheer disorganization, perhaps we'll have occasion to visit further. Chat about the fatherland. Great things are on the horizon for the German empire. *Guten Tag, mein junger Freund.*" Von Rike clicked his heels and strode off. He walked like a man who owned the earth.

Five minutes later Paul found Jimmy.

It was accidental; he was passing a crude yellow pine building, one of several forming what people called Last Chance Street. Soldiers and civilians stood in a line that snaked to the door of the building. Jimmy came out a side door, snugging his derby on his head.

"There you are!" Paul cried, dashing up to him.

"Where else would I be? If you want a drink or a girl before we sail, better get in line."

"No time, we have to find a ship. Come on."

They started off, Jimmy grumbling as usual. "Screwing Honey had damn well better be worth it, I—hey, hold up. I'm hungry." He stopped where three black women had set up large umbrellas and were frying chicken pieces on small clay stoves. Jimmy bought a drumstick. The woman wrapped it in a twist of brown paper. "Much obliged, Mammy. You want any, Dutch?"

"No thank you."

"God, you're a sore ass this morning."

"I worked all night getting our gear down here. Where the devil were you?"

"Enjoying myself. You ought to try it some time. You krauts are too fucking stiff-necked."

Paul walked away. He didn't need this. This heat, this noise, this dirt, this bedlam of snare drums and fifes and cymbals and trumpets, ships' whistles and bells, hallooing civilians waving hankies and little flags from the sightseeing cars, heavily burdened stevedores cursing and grunting as they staggered through the sand to gangplanks of the docked ships. He didn't need the tension, the worry. And he especially didn't need the companionship of an untrustworthy oaf who had very probably added robbery to his accomplishments in Florida.

□ □ □ □

The bow of a dilapidated freighter loomed. She was at least four hundred feet long. Paul stood in her shadow, staring up at her painted name. *Yucatan.*

"Crown? Dutch Crown? Over here."

Colonel Roosevelt jumped from the lower end of the gangplank. If he hadn't been quick, the stevedores would have run over him. Tenacious as ants, they labored up the steep incline with naked backs bent under a barrel or crate.

Roosevelt's khakis were sweated through. Heat misted his eyeglasses. There was black dirt in the creases of his forehead and throat. "You look a bit lost," he said to Paul. "Any way I can be of assistance?"

"I need two places on a ship."

"Correspondents are assigned to the headquarters ship."

He thought quickly. "I've photographed all the officers. I want to get pictures of ordinary soldiers, not generals, while we're at sea."

"Regular soldiers. Hah. Good idea. Very democratic. There are two of you?"

"And our equipment."

"Bring it aboard."

"You have room?"

"No, we'll be tight as sardines in a can. But two more won't make much difference. Did you ever see such a damned mess as this pier? General Shafter is an imbecile. Criminally negligent in my opinion. Some regiments are assigned to three ships, some don't have any. The rail cars for our regiment never arrived, so we jumped on some coal cars. This ship was in the harbor when we arrived. I went out and claimed her and brought her in and we've held her against all boarders. The commandants of the 2d Infantry and the 71st New York both insisted the ship was theirs. They ranked me but I blocked the gangplank and politely disagreed. They were furious. Said they'd bring me up on charges. Hah! Let them! They'll have to wait till the war's over. Fetch your gear, Mr. Crown. Fetch your partner. The armada will sail on the first favorable tide. We're going to war, my boy."

With great glee, he thumped Paul on the back.

"To war!"

Paul found Jimmy again, and the drayman. The three wrestled their crated equipment aboard *Yucatan.* "Sure won't be any God damn pleasure trip," Jimmy said, fanning himself with his new derby.

For once Paul agreed with him. Heat devils shimmered in the air. *Yucatan's* gray metal deck fairly sizzled, radiating the heat like a griddle ready for a chef. From an open hatch came the neighing of officers' horses and the powerful smell of droppings. On the pier, General Shafter was lunging about, his uniform blouse cast aside, his great drooping belly sweating through his undershirt as he hectored and pushed stevedores bodily to hurry them.

Twenty minutes before *Yucatan* was scheduled to warp away from the pier to allow another transport to come in, Paul found he was out of cigars. He worked his way down the gangplank and ran to Last Chance Street. There he bought a small box of cheroots at three times the normal price. As he started back to the transport,someone hailed him. Michael Radcliffe, immaculate in his white suit. Instead of the heavy walking stick, he carried an ebony cane with a filigreed gold crutch handle. He seemed oblivious, impervious, to the disorder and dirt of Port Tampa.

"Got your ship, have you?" he asked Paul.

"Yes, right there."

"Not going with the rest of us press fellows on *Segurança?*"

"I want some shipboard footage of the Rough Riders. Their vessel is the *Yucatan.*"

"I'm sure Colonel Roosevelt will be delighted to have the publicity." Michael strolled along with him, swinging his cane. "I've been brooding about your situation. Your various disappointments in this country. Have you had any further thoughts on the subject?"

"None. Too busy."

"Well, I have one. Consider another venue. London. Despite clever propaganda to the contrary, not all the geniuses reside in America. A few days ago I suddenly recalled a gentleman who's becoming quite well known in Britain. He too is a Paul. Robert W. Paul of Hatton Garden. He was some sort of engineer or instrument maker before he became fascinated with the very gadget that's captured you. Robert Paul invented a projector called the Theatrograph. He produces and exhibits pictures like those you're making for this bloke in Chicago. Like your chap, he employs a camera operator. Perhaps he'll need another, he's doing well and expanding rapidly. Furthermore, he has competitors who are doing the same thing. Even Lord Yorke, my esteemed father-in-law, has expressed interest in the moving pictures. And let me assure you, he does not waste time speculating about profitless ventures. With your experience, I'm certain a place could be found for you. I'll gladly assist you with contacts. You would be doing work that you like, and you could live anywhere. Your original homeland, if that's what you fancy. Why not? One place is as good as another. I know, I've seen most of them. I think at heart you're a wanderer, like me. I must have sensed that on the day we met. Christ knows it wasn't your artistic talent that impressed me."

Paul laughed, but he couldn't say a word; Michael's idea was too new and startling.

They were at *Yucatan's* gangplank. Soldiers crowded the rail high above. Jimmy was squeezed in among them, motioning for Paul to hurry. Hands were scurrying all over the ship, readying her for departure. Her whistle blasted.

Michael laid his elegant stick on Paul's shoulder and gave it a tap. "Think about it! It could be a fine opportunity. Solve all your problems. Give you a fresh start. If you're interested, I'll pop off a cable or two. Assuming we all get out of the bloody Cuban jungles alive."

He strolled away swinging the cane. The filigreed gold crutch handle winked in the sunlight like some priceless nugget, some promised treasure, of a new Eldorado.

Yucatan's lines were cast off, her engines started. She warped away from the pier, maneuvering slowly until she was in the channel. There she anchored to await orders to form the convoy.

The ship rode low in the water. She was rated to carry six hundred men, but she'd boarded almost a thousand: all the Rough Riders, two companies of 2d Infantry regulars who'd managed to squeeze past Roosevelt's barricade, and their band.

Jimmy and Paul went below to inspect their quarters—two bunks among hundreds. The stench from oil and horse shit and sweating bodies was overwhelming.

"I'm not sleeping in this rat hole," Jimmy snapped.

"I don't like it either. I heard we're allowed to camp on deck if we can find room."

"Let's go. If we can't find room, I'll make some. Throw a couple of these farm boys over the side."

It wasn't necessary. The deck was filling up fast, men spreading blankets, pinning the corners down with gear, but Paul and Jimmy found two places up near the anchor hawser. It reminded Paul of his days and nights on *Rheinland.*

The ship stank all the more when the evening's ration was served. It consisted of biscuits, canned beans, canned tomatoes, and the malodorous "canned fresh beef" purveyed to the Army. There were loud, profane complaints, and many rations thrown into the bay.

As the sun set, a better mood prevailed. The band from the Second set up on the wooden cover of a cargo hatch and played "The Star Spangled Banner." The bay sparkled with silver highlights. Fluffy tropical clouds tinted orange lazed in the western sky.

Jimmy wandered off in hopes of finding a dice game. Paul leaned on the grayed teak rail, watched the clouds and pondered Michael's proposition. It was startling, but far from absurd.

Think about it!

Indeed he would.

When dark descended and the hazy stars shone, Paul settled himself on his blanket with his head resting on his valise. He expected to be asleep when the convoy sailed.

He awoke with the morning sun in his face. Jimmy was next to him, snoring. The ship wasn't moving.

He picked his way among sleeping men until he found an officer of the Second leaning on the rail, forlornly gazing at the water of Tampa Bay. The Bay looked gray and greasy; garbage floated everywhere.

The officer said that during the night, sailing orders had been canceled. Washington had received a signal about two warships sighted in the Nicholas Channel, off the north coast of Cuba. The ships flew Spanish colors. Although the convoy would have a United States Navy escort for the last part of its voyage, the War Department refused to risk an attack on unarmed transports. The ships would stay in Tampa Bay until Washington said the danger was past.

While they rode at anchor, Colonel Wood enforced strict discipline in his regiment. Daily inspections were held at seven in the morning and five in the afternoon. Gambling was banned. Even so, Jimmy managed to find a game of craps or euchre every night, and win some money.

One evening he found Paul smoking a cigar at the rail. Jimmy was flushed and excited; he'd won fourteen dollars. "Say, there's something I've been meaning to show you." He knelt over his grip, opened it, and pulled a long, thin box from the bag. "Put your lamps on this, pal."

He snapped the box open, revealing a velvet lining and a gold-plated necklace from which little imitation rubies and emeralds dangled.

"Beautiful," Paul lied. "Did you get it in Tampa?"

"Yep. Cost me eleven bucks. For the first time, Jimmy Daws, esquire, pleads guilty to being a chump over a girl. Wasn't for Honey, I'd have bought a return ticket 'long about the time we hit Atlanta." He put the necklace back in its case and slipped the case into his grip. Then he leaned over the rail, hands clasped as he gazed at the rippling scarlet water. "This is gonna be my first and last war. I'm going home and set myself up as my own boss."

"Doing what?"

"Making money. But I haven't done too bad down here. Better'n I expected."

"You made money in Tampa? How?"

"Oh, different ways. Cards. Craps. You know."

Yes, Paul thought, *I think I do.* But he didn't call Jimmy a liar. He would need Jimmy's help in Cuba. Even if he was a thief.

Paul couldn't imagine a group of men more interesting than the 1st Volunteer Cavalry. The regiment included cowboys from the wild West and star athletes from the finest Eastern colleges. Roosevelt told him that Sergeant Ham Fish, a college man who rowed for Columbia, was the grandson of President Grant's secretary of state. Private Charlie Younger's father was Bob Younger, who'd ridden with the James gang. The commander of "A" Troop, Captain Bucky O'Neill, was the current mayor of Prescott, Arizona. He was also a former lawman and reformed gambler, nicknamed Bucky for "bucking the tiger" in high-stakes games.

It was a curious mixture, and the senior officers were visibly proud of that. It was also a regiment without horses for the enlisted men. One evening Roosevelt said in a jocular way that he'd just heard a new name for the regiment. Wood's Weary Walkers.

Paul laughed but Roosevelt grew sober, gazing at the ships at anchor with their cabin windows glowing, their running lights twinkling. "This is a momentous expedition, Dutch. I thrill to be part of it. If we succeed—the Spaniards can't prevent it, only the incompetence of our own high command—we'll score the first great triumph in what will be a world movement toward democracy."

Paul said nothing. He still had no clear and certain opinion of this burly socialite. Roosevelt loved sweeping pronouncements. He wanted personal publicity. Yet he seemed honest; and no snob. Which of several Roosevelts was the real one?

The colonel took off his spectacles and polished them with his polka-dot bandanna. "While we have a moment, permit me to ask a question that's been nagging me."

Paul knew what it was. He was instantly tense.

"Are you in any way related to General Crown of division staff? I suppose two men having the same name can't be considered a great coincidence. But two men from Chicago with the same name and German backgrounds? That's stretching it a bit."

Paul watched a gull sweep over copper-colored wavelets. The sun dropped under the horizon and there was that startling flash of green he'd seen before. The silence lengthened.

"Well, Dutch, what about it?"

"Colonel, I'll tell you the truth. I am related. But my uncle and I are estranged. I've not informed him that I'm traveling with the expedition, and I don't believe he knows. Please keep that a confidence, between us."

"I know better than to mix in family spats. Hate to see this one, though. You and your uncle are both fine chaps. But have no fear, I'll respect your wishes. Your secret will be safe."

During the days of delay, the temperature soared to nearly a hundred. Men snarled and pushed in the narrow companionways, and came close to exchanging blows over the most trivial disputes.

Shortly after Saturday's five o'clock inspection, Paul was sitting in a hot patch of deck shade amidships, reading a newspaper, when he was startled by a yell. "Watch out, that piece is loaded!"

He jumped up to see an infantryman swaying unsteadily in the shadow of the bridge. The man swung a revolver back and forth in a woozy arc. "He's drunk, where'd he get the stuff?" someone asked. Half a dozen men near the soldier began backing away. No one answered the question.

The soldier was young, towheaded, naked to the waist and covered with sweat. Behind Paul, Jimmy whispered, "Better get ready to dive for the deck."

One of the soldiers shifted position slightly, provoking a scream from the towhead: "*Stand still!* First one who moves, I shoot."

Suddenly, boots hammered the iron deck; Colonel Roosevelt strode by Jimmy and Paul. He pushed through the small group of onlookers caught within range of the revolver and stopped ten feet from the drunken man.

"What's going on here, soldier?"

"I can't stand it down below no more, it's so hot your brains fry. I'm going over the rail and I'll kill any son of a bitch who tries to stop me."

"Calm down, calm down. Tell me your name." Silence. "Soldier, that's an order."

The towhead almost stammered. "T—Tom Strawbridge. Second Regiment. What the hell's it matter?"

"It matters quite a lot, Tom. To you, to me, and to all these men. I want you to grasp that revolver by the barrel. I will then step forward and stretch out my arm. You lay the gun in my hand."

"Go fuck yourself, four-eyes."

Roosevelt stiffened, but that was the only hint of anger. He dabbed his chin with his bandanna. Plucked at the sweat-darkened front of his khaki blouse. "Tom, listen to me carefully. I am going to walk over to you and take that gun. You are not going to shoot me. You know what the consequences will be if you do. Prison for the rest of your life. You don't want that."

He started walking.

"Surrender the gun and there'll be no charges, you have my word on it. Everyone's upset by this heat, no one's going to blame you or punish you, so long as you give me the piece."

He moved forward slowly as he talked. He was within a yard of Tom Strawbridge. The soldier's hand trembled dangerously. Suddenly Strawbridge grimaced, clasped the butt with both hands and pointed the revolver at Roosevelt's head.

Men behind the colonel gasped and ducked, but Roosevelt stepped in fast, one long stride. He shoved the muzzle upward with his left hand, tore the weapon away from Strawbridge with his right.

The colonel and the private stared at each other. A man said, "Shoot the crazy bastard."

"No. I gave my word. Some of you fellows lead him to his bunk. Give him coffee, let him sober up. And keep this away from him." He slapped the revolver into the palm of the nearest soldier. Three others surrounded Strawbridge, who broke down suddenly and cried.

Those few moments of danger cleared away Paul's doubts about the colonel. He might be a zealous self-promoter, but he was a cool head, and a brave man.

On Sunday afternoon, Colonel Roosevelt arranged a demonstration for the Luxograph camera. He brought out a soldier Paul had previously seen around the ship, a man in his forties who was trying to look younger by putting blacking on his crinkly hair. The man was tall, stringy, plain-faced; but he had arresting green eyes. He dangled a lariat from his hand.

"Dutch, allow me to introduce Sergeant Hugh Johnson. We have one hundred and sixty certified cowboys on our roster, and he's one. The sergeant hails from Riverside, California. He's prepared to show you some fancy tricks with his lasso."

Johnson said little, but his exhibition for the camera was exceptional. He whirled the rope up and down from his head to his ankles, then jumped in and out of the spinning loop. Even Jimmy was impressed. Paul filmed two and a half minutes of Sergeant Johnson doing rope tricks. He was amused because Roosevelt edged forward to a position behind Johnson; he was prominently in the picture, waving his hat, clapping, and grinning.

"This will put the Rough Riders on at least forty screens in the Middle West, Colonel," Paul said when they were through.

"Then you've done yeoman service for the regiment. Here's a small token of appreciation." Roosevelt handed him a clean polka-dotted Rough Rider bandanna.

Paul broke into a big smile. "Colonel—sergeant—thanks very much, both of you."

"Put it on," Johnson said.

"No, no, I'll save it. It's a fine souvenir. Perhaps very valuable someday."

He folded the bandanna into a square, folded it a second time and tucked it in his shirt pocket. Colonel Roosevelt and Sergeant Johnson exchanged perplexed looks.

□ □ □ □

The band from the 2d Regulars played every night at twilight. The men who gathered to listen had one predictable request. Paul was heartily sick of it. But it followed him as he wandered away toward the stern on Sunday evening.

> "I went to the animal fair,
> The birds and the beasts were there.
> The big baboon by the light of the moon
> Was combing his auburn hair . . ."

They sang it boisterously, booming it over the water. Paul leaned on the rail, pondering Michael's words on the pier.

With your experience, I'm sure a place could be found.
I can assist you with contacts. Pop off a cable or two.
Why not? One place is as good as another . . .
Think about it!

If he let Michael help him, if he established a base in London and lived in rented quarters wherever the picture assignments took him, it would be an admission that the baker of Wuppertal had told the truth about America; that it wasn't the perfect place many imagined and hoped it would be, and Paul would discover this, and leave again. But it was more than a general disillusionment tempting him to listen to Michael. It was rejection by his family. The crushing loss of Julie . . .

Tampa Bay had a strange, almost sinister look this evening. Small silvery swells rolled in from the Gulf. To the northwest, a rampart of black cloud was rising swiftly. A crooked thread of lightning dropped from the clouds to the horizon, where the sky glowed an eerie dark green. The wind was stronger.

> "The monkey, he got drunk,
> And sat on the elephant's trunk."

He saw a tug making its way from ship to ship. A naval officer balancing himself on the tilting deck shouted through a megaphone. The tug was too far away for the officer to be heard.

> "The elephant sneezed and fell on his knees,
> And that was the end of the monk,
>   the monk . . .
> That was the end of the monk."

The tug headed for a transport anchored astern of *Yucatan.* The wind churned the bay, sending waves over the tug's bow. Thunder stuttered. The tug swung past the transport on the starboard side, then plowed toward *Yucatan.* The black clouds rolled above the anchored vessels.

Yucatan pitched in the whitecapped waves. Lightning flashed, followed by a crack of thunder seemingly right overhead. There was a brassy smell of burning in the air. Then the tropical rain began to pour.

The concert ended in a melange of sour notes. Men scrambled for cover. Paul could now read the name of the tug, *Lizzie C.* She rolled and pitched wildly; men on her deck used boat hooks to keep her from smashing against *Yucatan*'s iron hull.

The drenched officer with the megaphone was calling to the bridge. Soaked by the rain, Colonel Wood and Colonel Roosevelt were at the rail amidships, trying to hear. Wood cupped his hands around his mouth. "What's that? What did you say?"

"There are new orders," blared the voice from the tug. "You are to make ready to sail."

Early on the morning of June 14, Tuesday, pillars of black smoke rose from the stacks of all the transports. After a week of delay, they were almost ready. Fine weather had returned; sparkling sunshine, indigo water, a fresh breeze.

Paul scanned the shore with borrowed binoculars. The piers were almost deserted. Some ragged black youngsters were playing tag while waiting for the ships to leave. Among huge middens of paper and broken glass, one last saloon keeper and two of his whores were loading canvas into their wagon. Yards of red, white, and blue crepe paper floated in the water, bleeding out colors.

Paul and Jimmy set up the camera in *Yucatan*'s bow. Jimmy cranked to film a panorama of the harbor as signal lights blinked, sailors with red and white semaphore flags sent messages between ships, torpedo boats and cutters sped about boarding last-minute complements of men and provisions.

The armada sailed that day. It consisted of more than eight hundred officers and more than fifteen thousand men. There were four hundred stevedores, teamsters, and clerks aboard. Nine hundred and fifty horses and thirteen hundred mules; ammunition, foodstuffs, and dismantled wagons; artillery that included seven-inch howitzers, five-inch guns, field mortars, and the four Gatlings. The largest military expedition ever sent outside the United States was under way beneath fair skies. Its goal was clear.

So was his, perhaps.

Think about it . . .

There was a sense of a burden lifting. Couldn't he just imagine Uncle Joe's reaction when he heard about his nephew going to London? Paul relished the imaginary scene. *Germans are great grudge-holders, you know.*

He was at the bow rail again, alone, the warm breeze blowing against his face, tossing his unruly hair. He'd gone to his grip, dug to the bottom, and found the badly bent stereopticon card. He remembered a significant moment before he left Berlin. A picture card showing the Kaiser and his family torn in half; left behind to cast away the old, as a gesture toward the new. In meeting the transformed Mikhail Rhukov, listening to his encouragements and offers of help, Paul thought he'd come to such a moment again.

He studied the two frames showing the harbor and the lady of Liberty with her torch raised high. How many hopes that picture represented. Hopes, and bitter defeats. Some of the bitterest of his life.

Joe Junior had once called him naive about America. Well, it was so. In the persons of Wex and Shadow, America had given him a wonderful new craft; a lifelong profession that could take him to all those places he'd wanted to see since he was little. But that could never compensate for the loss of his family, and the girl he loved.

Now another place beckoned him. Not a new home; he was through with that stupid child's dream, he hadn't any *home*. Rather, he'd have a roving commission, a base in Europe, to help him forget all he'd yearned for and lost. Forget at least occasionally. Never would he be completely rid of the pain.

Paul was holding the stereopticon card delicately, its edges against his palms. *Think about it!*

He tore the card in two and dropped the right half overside. An updraft caught it, whirled it high a few seconds, then flung it to the water. It was instantly gone in the foaming bow wake.

He slipped the other half of the card into his shirt pocket. No more symbolism; just another souvenir.

He turned his back to the wind and lit a cigar. While life was far from perfect, and the anguish of failure in America, the loss of Julie, would never leave, he could begin to look forward to the future again.

Assuming—Michael's words—*we all get out of the bloody Cuban jungles alive.*

Part Nine

WAR

1898

Our war for humanity has unmasked
itself as a war for coaling stations,
and we are going to keep our booty
to punish Spain for putting us to
the trouble of using violence in
robbing her.

1898
WILLIAM DEAN HOWELLS, author and critic

It has been a splendid little war; begun
with the highest motives, carried out
with magnificent intelligence and
spirit, favored by that fortune which
loves the brave.

1899
JOHN HAY, United States Ambassador to England

100

The General

THIRTY-TWO BLACK TRANSPORTS sailed for Cuba, steaming a thousand yards apart in three long lines. The voyage was expected to take three days; very soon it was clear that it would require five, or more, because the slowest vessels —transports towing a pair of multidecked barges and a schooner carrying large water tanks—set the pace for the rest.

As it turned out, Joe Crown traveled not on *Segurança*, the headquarters ship, but on a smaller one, *Allegheny*, the command ship for Wheeler's cavalry division.

It was irksome to be isolated from the high command aboard *Segurança*; Wheeler complained loudly and often that he and his officers knew nothing about their objective, though many bets were laid on Santiago, the fortified harbor on Cuba's southeast coast. A large part of the expeditionary force had remained behind in Georgia and Florida, to train during the summer. Presumably those units would make an assault on Havana later. But no one knew for certain.

On *Segurança* deal tables were set up for the clerks in the first-class saloon and a pair of typewriters clattered all day long, spewing out lists of materiel and the order of debarkation. On the fore and aft decks, troopers lounged in the tropical sun. On a web of laundry lines, khaki shirts waved and snapped in the ocean breeze, along with heavy half sections of shelter tents washed and hung out to dry.

Rations for officers and men consisted of army hardtack, bacon, canned tomatoes, beans, and that vile "canned fresh beef," which Wheeler, Joe Crown, and most of the others refused to eat. The only thing that tasted good was the strong morning coffee.

Just before sunset on Wednesday, a smudge of land appeared off the port side. Corporal Willie Terrill, Joe's orderly, identified it for him, using one of several maps bought in Tampa. "Cape Romano, sir. We should clear the Keys sometime tomorrow and be headed east above Cuba."

Next morning Joe awoke to find the sea ahead thick with new arrivals. Fourteen gray Navy warships out of Key West, sent to surround and guard the convoy. By now the transports were strung out for twelve or fifteen miles. All day long, in tranquil seas, cutters and torpedo boats raced back and forth with orders to the captains to close up.

Late in the afternoon *Allegheny*'s starboard rail filled up with excited men pointing to the south. Joe had his first look at a thin blur of land where sea and sky joined. That was Cuba. An involuntary shiver of dread prickled his spine.

Shortly before midnight Joe and Wheeler strolled the deck together. Occasional pinprick lights flashed on the Cuban coast. "Heliograph signals," Wheeler said.

"Not lighthouses?" Joe said.

"No. The government maintains lighthouses along that coast, all right. But my adjutant mapped the locations—they're all dark. Which means the enemy is getting ready for us."

"Do you think it'll be a long and costly war, sir?"

"Long, I don't know about. But any war is costly for its victims. You know it only takes one small bullet to send a man down for eternity. To that man, and his loved ones, a war is costly even if it lasts but five minutes." Wheeler yawned. "I think I'm ready for bed. The motion of the sea is lulling. Enjoy it while you can, Joe. There won't be much rest for us on shore, I reckon. Good night."

"Good night, General."

Wheeler loped away and disappeared down a lighted stair. Joe stayed on deck, watching the heliographs flash and thinking of his own mortality. Thinking, too, of many things Estella Rivera said during that long, strange night of confession and revelation in the Tampa Bay Hotel.

On Sunday morning, June 19, Joe attended the nondenominational church service on the afterdeck. As he sat with head bowed during the long prayer, his mind turned back to Wheeler's words about a single small bullet. What if such a bullet sent him down to the dark? Were his business affairs in order? Yes, reasonably so, although there was no one chosen, or trained, to run Crown's.

That concern was quickly swept aside in favor of the more important one, his family. He'd made a wretched botch of his relations with practically every one of them. And he'd even come perilously close to violating the marriage vows he'd respected since the day he spoke them. Not committing that sin was more a tribute to Estella Rivera's perceptions, and her strong morality, than to anything he'd done.

Joe Crown had always been a regular churchgoer. But in the privacy of his heart and intellect—and with a fair degree of guilt—he had long ago admitted that he couldn't accept portions of the Scriptures literally. He doubted that the various biblical personages had undergone supernatural experiences. Angels descending on beams of light. Bushes turning to fire . . . God Himself speaking from the flames. The miraculous life of Christ was such a difficult issue in this regard, Joe refused to think about it.

And yet, with Estella, he had gone through something akin to a religious experience. He'd had a kind of vision, revelation—a dazzling light-burst of truth that illuminated the wrong path he'd taken as he followed the god he'd worshiped for so many years. *Ordnung.*

Oh, he still believed in the worth of order as a productive force in human endeavor. But order, authority, control—those were merely desirable ends, not deities to whom a man had to offer human sacrifices from his own family. Estella had shown him that, and much more.

While the chaplain droned on, Joe prayed that he'd live through the coming war. He prayed for time and the opportunity to rectify his worst mistakes, as Estella said he must. At the end of the prayer, his "Amen" was soft but fervent.

The armada rounded Cape Maisí on the eastern tip of Cuba late that day. Speed was again reduced. At dusk, searchlights from the warships began to rake the coastline. A cutter bore General Wheeler over to *Segurança* and a meeting with Shafter. At half past ten he was back, reporting to his officers in the first-class saloon.

"General Calixto García came out from shore with an armed escort. He's a handsome old bird, forehead wound and all. Here's the upshot. Admiral Sampson wants a direct assault on Santiago, the harbor and the town. But it's a mighty flinty objective."

One of Wheeler's aides unrolled a map of the southeast coast.

"Take a look at the position of the town. Notice it is secluded inland, almost five miles from the harbor mouth. They say Santiago's one of three places Christopher Columbus may have landed when he thought he found the Indies. That landing would have been a Methodist picnic compared with what we're up against."

Wheeler tapped the map. "The harbor entrance is protected on both sides. Here, by a strong battery in the Morro fortress—here, by the Socapa heights battery. If that isn't enough, Cuban intelligence says the channel's thick with mines wired up to firing switches inside the Morro. General Shafter's dead set against a direct attack, he read in some book about a British campaign against this same place a hundred years ago. The British were slaughtered. Shafter doesn't want any part of an assault up cliffs two hundred feet high, and I can't say I blame him. He and Sampson will meet García on shore tomorrow to discuss it further."

Joe raised his hand. "Sir, do we have any say about these plans?"

"Not so far. I don't like it much, but I'm hamstrung. This is Shafter's game. Let's hope he knows how to play it right."

On Tuesday, June 21, the convoy was still steaming sluggishly westward off the south coast of Cuba. *Allegheny* passed the entrance to the Bay of Guantánamo, which six hundred and fifty men of the 1st Marines had stormed and secured ten days before. Somewhere back in the bay, Joe presumed the Stars and Stripes were flying.

Santiago was now about forty miles ahead. With a telescope, Joe scanned a shoreline that was both breathtaking and daunting. White waves rolled and crashed, driven by winds that grew steadily stronger through the morning. He'd been told that prevailing onshore winds created a rough surf every day.

Above the breaking waves rose sheer limestone cliffs, and behind them, heavily forested hills that reached still higher to become a striking mountain range, the Sierra Maestra. Misty gray clouds hung on the tops of the mountains. The dark green forest below looked thick and wet, with here and there a bit of a narrow trail showing. It was a beautiful, desolate scene. And a difficult place to land, and march, and fight.

And what of the Spaniards? Supposedly as many as twelve thousand were assigned to defend this southeast coast. Where were they hiding? They could be lying in wait within the range of his telescope, totally concealed by the dark, wet jungle. And it could be assumed that they knew much more about fighting in the tropics than did Arizona cowhands, Harvard sprinters, or colored men who'd been stationed on the treeless Great Plains. He couldn't rid his mind of Wheeler's remark.

It only takes one small bullet . . .

The convoy anchored well offshore as the sea grew steadily rougher. The warships were farther out, steaming in line and spreading themselves in preparation for a bombardment. During the afternoon, Wheeler took a hundred turns around the deck, and then a hundred more, impatient and angry because he'd found out that another strategy conference was going forward without him, this one at a little inland village called Palma.

Around four o'clock a lookout spotted signal pennons flying on the headquarters ship. Wheeler threw on his linen duster, dress sword, and old black hat. "We're ordered to *Segurança*, boys. This may be it."

A cutter bore Wheeler, Joe Crown, the other senior officers and their aides to the black-painted vessel. General Shafter convened his meeting in the main saloon, under electric lights that made the sweat on his face glisten. Shafter had taken off his blue frock coat. His shirt was tentlike, his suspenders stretched tight over his enormous belly. He seemed more elephantine than ever, and pale, and tired, as he sat waiting in his special oversize chair while his aides set up a map stand.

Joe took a seat in the last row, in a cloud of cigarette smoke generated by the German attaché. The man had grown tiresome with his Prussian hauteur and his boasts about a farseeing German war plan whose essentials were already formulated. He said the vaunted "Schlieffen Plan" was so carefully thought out and so meticulously reviewed and revised whenever European alliances shifted, not even the most formidable military powers—Russia, England, the hated French— would be able to stand against it in the event of war. Finding himself seated beside the attaché, Joe tried to set aside his irritation and be cordial. For his part, von Rike had the good manners to shift his cigarette to his other hand.

While they were waiting, Joe asked, "Did you go to the conference on shore?"

"*Jawohl.* By muleback!" Von Rike rolled his eyes. He kept his voice low. "The site was a thatched hut. There were a few Cuban troops standing about. They have rifles but no shoes. A mongrel lot—*Negerin* and mulattoes—I saw not one white face. When our group arrived, they laughed openly at the sight of the general in chief. You should have seen him trying to dismount. A ship's hoist would have helped." He threw his cigarette on the deck and twisted his boot heel on it. "One really wonders if he can survive the heat and the terrain."

General Shafter tore loose his metal collar button and dropped it on the small field desk beside his chair. He rolled to his feet with a wheeze of effort. "Gentlemen, tomorrow morning, as soon after daylight as practicable, we will invade the island of Cuba."

There was an excited ripple of approval. Joe sat up very straight, every nerve alert. Shafter lumbered to the map. He looked more like a disheveled tavern keeper than a soldier. He took a wooden pointer from his principal aide, Lieutenant Miley.

"This afternoon at Palma, speaking to Admiral Sampson and General García, I outlined what I consider the only acceptable strategy. We must take Santiago, but not by direct attack. The cliffs around the harbor argue most forcefully against that. We are a long, long way from the Civil War. Heavy casualties are not expected by the public and, in my view, won't be tolerated. Therefore I propose to position the Army *around* Santiago"—his pointer touched crosshatching on the northeastern shore of the bay—"strike hard to break through enemy lines, overcome the string of Spanish blockhouses which protect the town, then press quickly for a surrender. If I must put the strategy in one word, the word is 'rush.' *Rush!* American soldiers can no more fight a protracted campaign in this climate, at this season of the year, than they can put hands into a bonfire without burning themselves."

Like some angry buffalo, Shafter lowered his shaggy head and peered at his senior staff from under his thick eyebrows as he described alternative landing sites that had been considered. There were three, where natural breaks or notches occurred in the limestone cliff barrier at the shore. He pointed out the Aguadores Ravine, four miles east of Santiago. The hamlet of Siboney, eleven miles farther. And seven miles east of that, a site identified as Daiquirí.

"Tomorrow, gentlemen, we will commence our landing here—" He struck the map with the pointer, nearly toppling the stand. "Daiquirí. Lieutenant Miley has prepared notes on what we may expect to find. John?"

Young Miley covered it quickly, reading from a notebook. Daiquirí was a settlement named for a nearby river. It had been the headquarters for the Spanish-American Iron Company, but the war had suspended operations, and the American mining engineers were gone. "What we'll find there are some zinc huts, palm-leaf cottages, machine shops, and a roundhouse at the end of a rail spur which goes inland. If the line is still intact, we will be able to transport men and horses to Siboney."

"From there," Shafter said from his chair, "we'll strike northwest, over the trails, and invest and capture Santiago."

"John." The peremptory voice belonged to Brigadier S. S. Sumner, Joe's opposite number in command of the 1st Brigade.

"Sam?"

"Is there a good beach where we propose to land?"

Miley looked uncomfortable. "There is a beach, but it's small. We hope it will be adequate for an operation of this size. Luckily there's also a long pier, used to unload ore hoppers into lighters that tied up there. The pier stands high above the water—thirty feet or more." Joe heard some groans.

And Sam Sumner wasn't satisfied. "The winds are pretty damn strong on this coast. And the later in the day it is, the rougher the surf. Happens without fail."

"We must take our chances, General. Orders will be typed and distributed within two hours. The order of landing is as follows. First to go in will be General Lawton with the 2d Division, and the four Gatling guns. General Bates next with his independent brigade, and then General Wheeler's cavalry." Fighting Joe made no attempt to hide his displeasure at being last.

"Shortly after daylight, Admiral Sampson's fleet will begin diversionary bombardments along a twenty-mile sector of the coast. Each soldier is to carry his blanket roll, canteen, field rations for three days, and a hundred rounds of ammunition. After we land all the men, we will land the mules and horses."

Colonel Leonard Wood of the 1st Volunteer Cavalry stood. He was about Roosevelt's age; a Harvard medical school graduate who'd joined up years ago as a contract surgeon and found he liked Army life. He had close-cropped blond hair, blue eyes, burly shoulders, hands that were large and callused. Joe found him an unlikely combat soldier, like so many in this expedition. Including himself.

Wood asked, "Is there a hoist of any kind on the pier?"

"No, Colonel, there is not."

"Then how do the animals land?"

"You will swing them off the ship in slings and let them swim."

Wood turned pale. Again Joe heard murmurs of discontent. The landing was beginning to seem improvised; dangerously so.

Joe Wheeler bounced to his feet, plucking at his white beard. "Sir!" Shafter recognized him courteously. "When we land, do we know what to expect in the way of resistance?"

Shafter hooked his thumbs in his suspenders. His eyes darted nervously. "General García's scouts have provided us with good information on fortifications in the area. There are earthworks, breastworks, trenches, and rifle pits. There is a Spanish blockhouse on the heights."

"But how many soldiers waiting for us?"

Gloomily, Shafter said, "We don't know."

Wednesday, June 22. Reveille sounded at half past three in the morning. Joe had packed his kit after supper, handed it to Corporal Willie Terrill, strolled a few minutes on deck, then crawled into his bunk, where he spent most of the night tossing and worrying.

Allegheny's deck was packed with men before daybreak about five o'clock. Heavy mist lay on the mountains. The village of Daiquirí—what could be seen of it—looked dead as a graveyard. Through his telescope Joe watched a verminous yellow mutt running on the narrow beach. A string of empty ore cars stood on the high pier. A thread of smoke rose in front of a thatched cottage; someone had built a cook fire, then gone away.

Already the wind was blowing hard onto the shore. Already little crests of white water showed. A hundred and fifty boats would be used to ferry the troops. There were steam launches, each with a chain of longboats tied behind it; the launches began to position themselves around the transports as the sky brightened and the mist on the mountains grew luminous. Joe had donned his frock coat and dress sword. He could remember few times when he'd been so hot and sticky.

Distantly, toward Santiago, a series of rolling explosions brought a cheer from the crowded decks of the transports. Sampson's squadron had begun its diver-

sionary shelling. The warships assigned to the landing maneuvered into line—
Wasp and *Hornet, Scorpion* and *Vixen* and *New Orleans.* Shortly after nine-thirty,
the first gun turret boomed and spewed white smoke. High on a hillside behind
Daiquirí, a great geyser of earth and debris erupted. The second salvo blew up a
cottage close to the beach. More cheering . . .

The bombardment continued for half an hour. Wheeler paced up and down
near Joe, muttering uncharacteristic profanities. He didn't like the high swells
breaking with a roar on the narrow strip of beach and crashing against the iron
pilings of the pier. You had only to glance overside and watch a longboat rise on
the crest of a wave, then crash like an elevator car with its cable cut, to know it
was a dangerous sea.

Excited cries whipped Joe's attention toward the shore. A bare-chested man
with black hair ran to the end of the pier waving a pole with a square of white
cloth tied on. Some straw-hatted horsemen came galloping through the village,
brandishing a Cuban flag and hallooing to the ships. Wheeler said, "By damn.
The Spaniards must've pulled out during the night. Those boys are on our side."

The shelling stopped. Palm huts burned throughout the village, sending black
smoke upward. A large circular structure—the roundhouse?—was also burning.
The rising smoke mingled with the mountain mist.

Gangway doors were opened in the hulls of the transports, near the waterline.
Rope ladders were let down. At half past ten the first men climbed down the
ladders toward the longboats. Tensely, Joe watched a man miss a heaving boat
and crash into the water. Burdened by his rifle and cartridge belt and blanket
roll, he sank. He bobbed up again, yelling, and was dragged into the boat.

One launch after another pulled its crowded longboats alongside the pier.
When an incoming wave lifted one or more boats high enough, the men jumped
for it. Around noon, two black troopers from the 10th Cavalry made the jump,
missed the pier, and landed in the water. From the deck of *Allegheny* Joe could
hear their terrified cries. A Rough Rider officer on the pier threw his hat aside
and dove in, to no purpose. The troopers were trapped as the waves hurled their
boat against the pier, then flung it away. On the piling Joe saw patches of blood.
In the water, a campaign hat floated.

The two black soldiers were the first fatalities. Those who rode the longboats
near the beach, then jumped out and waded ashore, had an easier time of it.

By afternoon, the waters off Daiquirí resounded with the neighs and brays of
horses and mules dropped over the side from slings on davits. Most swam to the
beach, but some were too frightened or not strong enough. Finally heading
ashore in a longboat, Joe counted nine dead animals floating. Roosevelt was on
the pier, screaming and gesturing with his hat. Had he lost a mount?

The surf foaming onto the beach swarmed with men, some of them civilians.
One, a man in a wide-brimmed straw hat, was wading ashore with a moving
picture camera and tripod on his shoulder. A second man wearing a derby
slogged behind him carrying a large canvas bag. At long distance, Joe couldn't
identify either man, but he supposed one was the camera operator he'd met,
Bitzer.

In the buffeting wind, Joe's longboat convoy neared the pier. General
Wheeler, very agile, had no trouble leaping from the boat to grasp the hands of

two enlisted men. "You're next, General," Corporal Willie Terrill said as the longboat dropped again. Joe stepped up on the thwart.

The longboat rose swiftly. When the orderly shouted, *"Now, sir,"* Joe leaped. His right foot hit the pier firmly, yet somehow he slipped. He windmilled his arms, toppling backward toward the boat still high on the wave crest. He heard Corporal Willie Trees shout. Willie's big hard hands hit the small of his back and threw him forward. He landed on his chest, scraping his jaw. His legs dangled over the water. He dragged himself forward, pushed up on hands and knees, his heart pounding.

He stood up and dusted off, acutely embarrassed to have arrived on enemy soil in such an undignified and unmilitary way.

Six thousand men landed at Daiquirí by the day's end. Since Wheeler and his staff had to wait for their horses to be brought up, they went on a walking tour of the shelled village. Wheeler had already announced his intention to ride inland for a personal reconnaissance before dark.

Daiquirí was mud streets, smoldering huts, and damaged buildings. The officers hurried toward the roundhouse. Greasy smoke billowed from its shot-out windows, making the eyes smart and racking Joe with a fit of coughing. Half the roundhouse roof had caved in. A crowd of about fifty Cuban soldiers—black, tan, and many shades between—came running toward the officers, screaming *"Viva los americanos!"* A couple of the Americans brandished their swords and returned cries of *"Viva Cuba libre!"* Joe didn't join in; he wasn't impressed by the shoeless, shirtless rebels, several of whom fell in step and held out their hands, pleading for money. One man plucked at Joe's shoulder strap as if he wanted it for a souvenir. Joe knocked the hand away. The man spat a curse in Spanish and ran off.

General Wheeler had already loped off to the other side of the building. Joe and the rest hurried after him and found the single railroad track running into the jungle. It was a sight he'd seen many times on the march through Georgia and Carolina. Cross ties broken; rails pried up and bent after being heated. In the war, rails twisted like that were "Sherman's Hairpins."

Wheeler slapped his old black hat against his leg. "We'll transport no men on this line. Joe, find out where they've got to with those damn horses. I want to go inland before Shafter tells me I can't."

"Sir," Joe said with a fast salute. He and his aide, Tyree Bates, walked swiftly through the village. They located their mounts on the beach and Joe yelled at the wranglers to get them moving. Following the horses on foot, he was pulled up short by a sight that confused him. Two weary men were unloading a camera and tripod from a longboat. Tied behind it was a second longboat holding three large wooden crates and riding much lower in the water.

Lieutenant Bates stopped. "Something wrong, General?"

Joe heard an insect whining at his ear. He slapped it, then wiped the mosquito's bloody remains from his fingers. "I just want to ask a question of those men. I'll catch up."

Bates hurried away. Joe waded into the surf as the men hoisted their camera to bring it ashore; it was twice as large as the one he'd seen earlier. The young man giving orders wore a houndstooth cap and a natty but water-soaked jacket. Joe knew him.

"Hello, Bitzer. I thought I saw you come in some time ago."

"Not us," Bitzer said, unhappily. "Shafter wouldn't allow any civilians off the headquarters ship till now. Davis is ready to crucify him. Maybe you saw one of the other crews, Paley's, or the one traveling on *Yucatan*."

"Where are they from?"

"Bill Paley's out of New York, on assignment from Edison. The other two work for American Luxograph in Chicago. One of 'em I don't like, but the chief operator's a good egg."

"What's his name?"

Bitzer's eyes had a curious, evasive look. His assistant walked up at that moment and noticed his partner hesitating, as if he couldn't remember. The assistant said, "Crown. I think his first name's Paul, but everybody calls him Dutch."

101

Rose

ON THE AFTERNOON before the Daiquirí landing, in a pawnshop on Fourteenth Street, Rose French pointed into a display case.

"Let me see that one."

The pawnbroker, a genial Irishman with thinning red hair and dainty freckled hands, unlocked the back of the case and reached in for a small silver-plated hideout pistol. It had over-and-under barrels, a stub trigger, fancy crosshatched walnut grips. He laid the weapon in his left palm and presented it with a flourish.

"Very fine piece, my girl. Is it for yourself?"

"Oh, yes," she said. Even after so many days, her left eye remained swollen. Purple and yellow bruises marked the places Elstree had savaged her. The pawnbroker was studying the damage in a speculative way. "Recently I was assaulted in broad daylight. Assaulted and robbed," she added quickly.

"I can see." The Irishman gave a cluck of sympathy.

Rose tested the weight of the piece. Light. "Is this well made?"

"Remington is one of our finest marks."

"Is it powerful?"

The man leaned over the case and pointed down to an even smaller derringer. "The Vest Pocket .22 caliber is the weapon usually preferred by ladies. But I'd not call it powerful compared with the one you're considering. The piece in your hand is a two-shot .41 caliber. At fifty feet, it's dangerous. At ten to twenty, it will drop any assailant, even a brute who preys on women. Put it in his face at three to five feet, his sainted mother won't recognize him."

"Well," Rose said with a musing smile. Her tongue crept over her puffed and discolored lower lip. One of Elstree's blows had driven it against her teeth, tearing it open on the inside. Her mouth had bled for days. She handed the weapon to the pawnbroker.

"It sounds ideal. I'll take it."

102

Dutch

AT FIVE O'CLOCK in the afternoon, General Wheeler ordered men to the abandoned blockhouse on the knobby hill above Daiquirí. One carried a folded flag.

Paul looked for Jimmy. He was nowhere to be found—the second time he'd absented himself since they came ashore. Annoyed, Paul dropped his grip, lowered the camera from his shoulder and checked the meter. Fifty feet left. That was lucky; along with his own small suitcase, Jimmy was carrying the canvas bag with the fresh and exposed magazines.

Paul knelt in the mud to shorten one tripod leg. Then he took off his straw hat and fanned himself. Sadly, he saw that spatters of mud had stained the fancy blue hatband.

High above, men appeared on the blockhouse rampart. Paul checked the lens. It had steamed over. From his shirt pocket he took the folded polka-dot bandanna from the Rough Riders and gently wiped the curved optical glass. Just in time, too. The Stars and Stripes ran up the blockhouse pole. Paul started cranking. It would be a grand finish to his footage of the longboats, the men wading in, the smoking ruins of Daiquirí.

A thundering yell from hundreds of throats greeted the flag. Offshore, a ship's whistle bellowed, then another, then a chorus of them. Paul was pensive a moment; how he'd hoped, once, that it would be his flag. Perhaps that was just another of the naive dreams his cousin Joe had scorned.

All at once Jimmy sauntered out of the drifting smoke, suitcase and canvas bag clutched in his left hand. In his right he had one of the long, wicked bush knives called machetes.

"Where did you get that knife?" Paul asked.

"Took it. Never mind where."

Paul held his temper. "We need to find a campsite. Let's look for Colonel Wood's regiment. I saw them moving inland." He hoisted camera and tripod to his shoulder and picked up his grip with his other hand. The backs of his calves and thighs ached from the day's labor. "When we're settled, I have to search for a friend. I want to be sure he wasn't one of the two men who drowned."

Jimmy fanned himself with his derby. "Those were niggers."

"Black men. Yes." Jimmy looked mystified. "Also, I need to load a new magazine."

"Sure, but I bet it's a waste of time. Film's probably rotting in this heat."

The same thought had occurred to Paul. He didn't like to dwell on it.

Behind Daiquirí, a large grassy flat stretched away to a lush green wall of jungle. In the open area, the 1st Volunteer Cavalry was encamping for the night.

To the right as they approached was a lagoon crusted with yellow scum. On the left, well away from the lagoon, they found space to put down their gear. They had one rubber ground cloth packed in the canvas bag. Paul knew Jimmy would want it. He didn't propose to argue. It would be a long, soggy night.

At the headquarters tent he found Lieutenant Colonel Roosevelt, whom he asked about the 10th Cavalry. Roosevelt said the 10th had begun a late afternoon advance toward the village of Siboney, seven miles away.

"I'm going that way to hunt for my friend," Paul told Jimmy. "See if the regiment can spare some beans and hardtack. Also, we need water. I heard there's fresh water in the mining company tanks. You can fill the canteen while I'm gone." Jimmy stared at him, idly swinging the machete. Paul said, "I will be back."

"Yeah, be sure to hurry, I wouldn't know how to get along without all your advice and orders."

When is it all going to explode? Paul thought as he left. He was afraid the answer was, soon.

The road to Siboney was misnamed. It wasn't a decent wagon road, but a hilly trail snaking overland between the limestone cliffs along the coast and the rail line the Spaniards had torn up during their retreat. The trail had been hacked from a tropical forest of cactus, Spanish bayonet plants, thornbushes, and coconut palms. It was narrow, barely able to accommodate a six-hitch freight wagon, and murkily dark. Thousands of trailing vines made the surrounding tropical forest all but impenetrable.

The advance of men and animals on the road had slowed to a walk. By the time Paul found black soldiers, it was stopped. The troopers of the 10th had fallen out to smoke and rest on their muddy blanket rolls. Paul approached a white first lieutenant with a day's growth of beard and a shirt sweated through front and back.

"Person?" the lieutenant snarled. "Of course he's alive for Christ's sake, why wouldn't he be? He's up the line somewhere."

Paul rushed ahead, avoiding outstretched legs for another half mile, and suddenly spied Ott Person's homely face. "Ott. You're all right!" he cried as he ran up. The black soldier scrambled to his feet.

"Hey, Heine, what you doing here?"

"I heard that two men from your regiment were drowned at the pier. I was afraid—"

"That it might be old Ott? I'm too mean and ornery to go like that. You was worried about me, huh?"

"I always worry about friends."

"I'm pleased to know I fit in that company. You're my friend too. Here, squat down, rest yourself. You ever feel such heat before? I don't need to go to hell when I die, I already know what it feels like." From the pocket of his sweated khaki shirt he took a tobacco sack and packet of papers. "Fix yourself a smoke."

"Thanks, I have a cigar." It was his last from Tampa. He cut the end with his clasp knife and bent forward to the match in Ott's hand. Farther up the trail, a black trooper with a harmonica began to play "The Stars and Stripes Forever" in a slow, almost melancholy way. It was appropriate music for the end of an exhausting day.

"I mean to tell you, I don't like this here place," Ott said as they smoked. "I want to get out an' go back to the States. What d'you figure to do when this war's over?"

"Take my pictures back to Chicago, if I get any good ones. After that, I think I am going to look for a job in England."

"Hoo-eee. That's clean across the ocean, ain't it? What's wrong, you don't like the U.S. of A.?"

"Some things about America are good. But not all. I think I expected too much from your country. Others have told me that. When I landed at Ellis Island, I had every hope that America would be my home forever. But I don't belong there. I think it's time to try another place."

"Heine, don't do that. You're a good man. Our country needs folks like you. Don't run off and leave everything to the mean ones, that fat-faced sarge in Tampa and bastards like him. We got 'nough of them already. Ain't there nothin' would make you stay?"

"There was a girl. If I could have had a home with her. But it's impossible, she's gone."

"They's lots of nice handsome white girls in America. I bet plenty of 'em could make you happy."

"No, Ott. But thank you for your kind words. I'd better go now, it's a long way back to my partner and the equipment. Please take care of yourself."

"Sure enough will, Heine, you do the same. And don't you leave too soon, I got to pay my debt."

The harmonica sang its strangely sad tune as Paul waved and took the trail to Daiquirí.

A sickle moon shed a wan light on the camp. Paul gave the rubber ground cloth to Jimmy, then rolled on his side in the damp grass, put the straw hat over his cheek and his eye and vowed he'd sleep in spite of everything conspiring to prevent it.

There was a lot. A rusty light pulsed in the sky above Daiquirí; the mine company's machine shops were still afire. Offshore, the warships played their searchlights over the shelled village, the jungle, the mountains rising steeply four or five miles inland. In the distance, the rebel troops of a general named Demetrio Castillo sang Spanish songs. Nearer, sentries called out regularly. Insects droned. In Paul's very gut there was noise; he was famished. Jimmy had brought back a canteen of fresh water and one skimpy ration of tinned beans and hardtack, which they'd divided.

In spite of the light and the noise, the heat and the damp, Paul drifted off. He woke violently, to Jimmy's screaming:

"Jesus, what is it? Mother of Christ, get it off me!"

Paul bolted up. The hat fell from his face. By moonlight he saw Jimmy lying on his back, batting at something on his chest. Something large, round like a saucer, with flailing appendages.

Something crawled on Paul's leg. He looked down and yelped. The same kind of creature was marching up his pant leg toward his belly where his shirt had come loose, exposing his skin. In the grass all around, he heard rustling and clicking.

Paul struck the crab off his leg. It was a hideous thing, with two long, waving pincers, two round eyes on stalks. It had a mouth of sorts; the lips were like horny beaks. As he watched them open and close, open and close, a paralyzing terror took hold of him. It was the terror of a child's nightmare, when you were helpless in the dark, the demon was all-powerful, and there was no one to aid you.

He was trembling now; unable to move. Another crab crawled onto his thigh. Around his boots, half a dozen more waved and clicked their pincers. Jimmy was still yelling and hopping from foot to foot, though he'd flung off the crab that woke him. Similar disturbances had broken out among the shelter tents of the regiment.

Jimmy jumped over near Paul and began to stamp on the crabs. Their shells cracked loudly. They emitted faint sounds oddly like a piteous crying. A sergeant ran up as Paul tottered to his feet. He recognized the lanky Rough Rider from California, Johnson. "Land crabs," he exclaimed. "A whole damn army of 'em."

Jimmy gasped, "I woke up with one crawling on my *face*, for Christ's sake!"

"Colonel Wood said the crabs aren't really dangerous 'less a man's wounded. What they want is bloody meat. He said they'll come for that by the hundreds." Johnson tromped on another crab and ran off to alert someone else.

Still shaking, Paul said, "Help me pick up the gear. We're moving."

"What good'll that do? They're all over this fucking field. One of those crabs gets me, or some greaser's bullet, it's all over. I should have left before now. Shouldn't have come at all. Maybe I'll give you notice right here."

"Jim, we're going on. We have a job. You aren't going to quit on me. That would be the act of a coward."

"You son of a bitch. You call me a coward—you so much as think it—I'll chop your fucking head off." He grabbed the machete, whirled and slashed at some tall grass. The stalks fell soundlessly on the broken shells of the crabs. Out in the dark, hundreds more were rustling and clicking . . .

"Jim, calm down. I didn't call you a name, I just said that *if* you left now—"

"Shut up, I heard you."

They stood glaring at one another in the moonlight. Suddenly exhaustion took the starch out of both of them. Paul said, "All right. Truce. Let's move." Jimmy snatched the rubber sheet from the ground, and they shifted their gear to a new location on the flat. But every time they settled down, the sounds of the land crabs intruded, and they both jumped up and thrashed about in the grass, Paul with his hat, Jimmy with his bush knife, to drive the creatures away. There was constant noise and shouting in the shelter tents of the Rough Riders too; the tents afforded little protection from the invaders. For everyone camped on the flat that night, sleep was elusive.

In the morning, bleary and miserable, they ate hardtack and drank tin cups of lukewarm coffee. Then they set out for Siboney, speaking only when necessary. Ahead lay seven miles of a rank green purgatory.

The trail was choked with heavily burdened soldiers, teamsters fighting their wagons up and down the grades, strings of mules laden with provision sacks, water casks, wooden ammunition boxes, pieces of dismantled Hotchkiss guns. Hanging vines repeatedly knocked Paul's hat off or snagged the camera on his shoulder. Twice, the dirt of the trail crumbled or sank from under his boots and he fell. Each time, he twisted onto his back to cushion the camera. Even with their difficulties, they made better progress than did most of the soldiers.

They came upon a large wagon piled with crates, all with the same black stenciling. PROPERTY AMERICAN BIOGRAPH CO. NEW YORK USA. The wagon was mired in mud. Paul recognized the houndstooth cap of the driver. "Billy!"

"Hallo, gents. Hell of a mess here."

The near front wheel was sunk halfway to its hub. Sleeves rolled up, Billy Bitzer was quirting his two mules while his assistant Len dragged on their head-stalls. "You're welcome to ride along if we can get out of here," Bitzer said.

Paul and Jimmy fell to, straining to turn and lift the sunken wheel. Bitzer applied the quirt and Len pulled from the front. Sweating heavily, Paul yelled, "It's coming, a little more, we've almost—" Suddenly the wheel rose and the wagon lurched forward, on solid ground again.

"Damn fine work," Bitzer said, hugely pleased. "Stow your camera and gear and let's go."

Paul laid the Luxograph on top of the considerably larger Biograph camera, in a space between Bitzer's crates of storage batteries. He climbed up beside the cameraman. Jimmy chose to walk in front with Len. The going was slow, but Paul was glad to ride for a while.

"Say," Bitzer said abruptly. "You won't like this much, but I'd better tell you. Your uncle, the general—he knows you're here."

"How?"

"I met him on the beach. He recognized me from Tampa. He asked about the other picture crews. I kept my mouth shut but—" He nodded to his assistant out in front. "Len spilled it. Your name. He didn't know he was doing wrong."

With a grim look Paul said, "He wasn't. But now I'll have to face my uncle sometime, it's inevitable. I can't hide and do my job too."

After traveling half a mile, they discovered another foundered wagon. Both of its near wheels were completely off the trail. The wagon was tilted at an angle of about thirty degrees. Wildly waving his arms, the portly driver called, "Lads! Hello! Help me here, won't you?"

"My God, it's Paley." Bitzer reined the mules; he and Paul jumped down.

Paley of the Eden Musée looked dreadful. His fine striped trousers were torn and smeared with dirt. His white linen shirt was ripped at the shoulder and stuck to his body like a wet rag. He lurched up to them. "Fellows, I'm sick. I have a raging fever. And now the rear axle's cracked. Help me, won't you? We're all in the same profession, aren't we?"

"*Today* we're all in the same profession," Bitzer muttered to Paul. To Paley he said, "Out of the way, I'll have a look."

Bitzer knelt behind the wagon and reached under to grasp the axle. Paley was swaying erratically and mopping his face with a monogrammed handkerchief. "Can it be fixed?"

"Well, it's pretty badly damaged. Let me look again."

Bitzer's hand disappeared under the wagon. There was a sudden crack; the back wheels tilted inward and the rear of the wagon bed dropped. Bitzer pulled his hand away just in time.

"It isn't cracked, it's broken clean through the middle. Tough luck."

"For God's sake, boys—I must get to the front! Is there room in your wagon?"

"Afraid not."

"Then find someone to assist me, won't you?"

Bitzer fanned himself with his cap, pious as a funeral mourner. "I'm sorry, Paley, I don't have much influence, I'm just a nobody, remember? Dutch Crown here, he's just a nobody too. But if we run into General Shafter or General Wheeler, we'll see if they can spare a squad to come back and help you out. So long."

They left William Paley clutching the side of his wagon; he appeared to be crying. Paul didn't want to laugh at Paley's misfortune, but something in him took a keen delight in the repayment of snobbery. When they were safely away, he said, "Billy, you are a wicked fellow. You broke the axle."

"What d'ya mean? All I did was touch it. Do unto others the same way they did to you! Let the arrogant bastard sit there and bawl. He's the competition. This is war."

Shortly after noon, the wagon rolled down a hill near the village of Siboney. At the foot of the trail they came upon two land crabs devouring the remains of a rat. Their bodies were an orchid color, with splotchy markings of black, orange, and light yellow. They waved their pincers and turned their little stalked eyes toward the noisy wagon. The mules didn't like them, and brayed.

Paul had never encountered anything, anywhere, that filled him with such a complete and consuming fear. The wagon creaked on but he shuddered for minutes afterward.

Bitzer let them off at the edge of Siboney. Paul sensed that professional rivalry was taking over; the Biograph team wanted to proceed on their own. That was fine; so did he. He thanked Bitzer, shook his hand, and waved as the Biograph men drove away.

Although Siboney was slightly larger than Daiquirí, it was just as poor and shabby. Huts and flimsy houses straggled down the sides of a gulch running from the foothills to the shore. At the far end of a curving beach, drab fishing boats were tied at a dilapidated pier. Transports anchored offshore were disgorging men into chains of longboats; there were at least six thousand more troops to be brought in.

All along the beach, naked soldiers swam and splashed in the surf. The sight produced a rare smile from Jimmy. "Let's set up the camera. Wouldn't the girls in Chicago love all those dicks in the wind?"

"Somehow I don't think Iz Pflaum would love it." Tired, Paul put down his gear and sat on an abandoned sack of coconuts. He held out his hand. "Borrow that?" Jimmy surrendered the machete with a show of reluctance. Paul nicked a coconut and sucked out the milk. It was sweetish; he didn't care for it. Still, it surpassed the foul water they'd been drinking.

Paul and Jimmy found a campsite among the hundreds of men who'd put up shelter tents or simply squatted in the open. The site was exposed to the wind, and made rough by broken shells in the sand, but Paul hoped the absence of long grass would mean fewer land crabs.

He wandered the beach until he found an officer who knew something about the creatures. The officer said the crabs were scavengers and lived in fields, swamps, and mangrove thickets for a distance of eight or nine kilometers inland. Although more numerous at night, daylight didn't frighten them. Remembering the rat on the trail, Paul said, "That I know."

As he returned to the campsite, he began to limp. His feet were blistered. His legs ached from ankle to hip; his back hurt from carrying the camera. The tripod had worn raw welts on both shoulders under his shirt; the one on his left shoulder was oozing blood. He peeled off his shirt, clenched his teeth, and washed the welt in salt water from the surf.

Jimmy had disappeared on another of his mysterious excursions. *Let him rob half the population, I don't care,* Paul thought wearily. He found an Army private reading a magazine and sunning himself and gave him fifty cents to watch their gear. Then he set out for the center of the village.

Siboney was crowded with armed Americans ready to fight. Every minute or so Paul had to jump out of the way of a mounted courier riding at the gallop. He spoke to several noncoms and officers, but none of them knew when the advance would begin. Turning away from the last of these futile encounters, he was looking directly into the sun. He threw his hand in front of his eyes and stepped into the shadow of a shanty. When he lowered his hand, there was Michael Radcliffe. As if by magic.

Michael was swinging the heavy knob-headed walking stick he'd carried in Ybor City. He looked cool and dry and clean in a straw boater, fashionable suit of lightweight white flannel, pointed shoes of black leather offset by vamps of white canvas. His single concession to the heat was an open shirt without cravat.

"Greetings, my friend. You look totally at sea."

"Like everyone else, Michael. Do you know how or when the campaign will go forward?"

"Absolutely not. It really doesn't matter to me, I've set up my base and shall report all the action from a table in a convenient cantina, just there." He pointed with the stick.

Paul was ready with a jibe, but a clatter of horses distracted him. A party of officers was trotting out of the village in the direction of Santiago. He recognized

General Wheeler's white beard. He stiffened when he saw the rider immediately behind Wheeler. Observing the reaction, Michael said, "Which one is your uncle?"

"The second one."

"I've seen him before. Strikes me as a tough bird."

"Definitely."

"But you don't want him to discover you, isn't that so? You don't want to speak to him."

A part of him wanted exactly that; yearned to approach his uncle. But he said, "No, why the devil should I?"

Michael pondered a moment. "Considering all you told me about your banishment from his house, I reckon that's a reasonable question. You'll hear no more about it from me. Care to join me in the cantina for a smoke and a drink?"

As they walked, Paul said, "Have you met Captain von Rike, the attaché from the German Army?" Michael said he had. "Don't you remember him?"

"Should I?"

"He was in the rail yard in Berlin seven years ago, the first time you popped out of nowhere and sneered at my art. He was with the group of officers timing the unloading of the Buffalo Bill train. He was a lieutenant then."

"And only a captain now? Well, advancement is never rapid in a peacetime army. People swear that they detest war but secretly they adore it. So many benefits. Field promotions. Fat supply contracts. The chance to bed some lovely creature on short acquaintance because she's mad to show her devotion to the brave lads in uniform . . . von Rike, eh."

"Yes. I didn't like him then, I don't like him now."

"Better get used to him. He and his army colleagues are the new Germany, along with the German Navy, and the Kaiser. An unholy trinity if ever God made one."

The cantina was small and relatively clean. The portly proprietor sold Paul a half dozen short cigars for a few pesos. The beer served couldn't rival Crown's, but it was cool, and he was thirsty. Michael said his gin was "barely palatable." Paul lit one of the little cigars. It was strong, but he enjoyed the taste.

Michael asked the proprietor whether women were available in Siboney. The proprietor said most certainly, he would be happy to make arrangements. "Later," Michael said, waving him off. He started to drink. "Why the devil are you looking at me that way?"

"Just curious. Do you worry about your wife when you're away from home? I mean do you worry that she might behave the way you do?"

Michael wasn't offended; amused, rather. "Cecily? Never. She's an honorable woman. She also has a regular companion for the theater and social affairs."

"A man?"

"Indeed. Anthony Albert Parsons. Actor. Positively the handsomest, most rugged chap you ever saw. If I had his looks, they'd be queued up for a quarter of a mile at the footboard of my bed. Anthony happens to prefer his own gender. In the vernacular, he's a poof. Probably knock you silly if you said it to his face. Damn shameful waste, if you ask me. But he doesn't. Cecily adores Tony. I like him awfully myself." Michael sighed as he laid his stick on the table. "Selling out must make a chap soft. There was a time when I loathed every living creature."

"I think I remember," Paul said. They both laughed.

After a silence, Paul drew a deep breath.

"Michael."

"Sir?"

"I would like to take you up on your offer of help in England."

"Capital! I'll write a cable to my father-in-law instanter. Pop it onto one of the dispatch charters to Key West, it will be sent from there. They're laying cable from the States to Cuba, but I understand it's to be restricted to military chatter. The yellow king, Mr. Hearst, must have had inside information. He sent his own yacht and a small fleet of dispatch boats to carry copy."

He leaned back in his chair; stroked his chin. "I am absolutely delighted you've abandoned your starry visions of America. You have passed through the gates of wisdom. Congratulations," he said as he offered his hand.

A moment later a shadow fell between the squeaking half-doors of the cantina. Crane sauntered in, a flat leather dispatch pouch hanging over one shoulder. A notebook bulged the pocket of his tan hunting suit, which was stained with the dirt of the trails and camps. His smile was amiable, but Paul had the same impression as before: his eyes held too much sadness for a man not yet thirty.

"Stephen, sit down," Michael said. "You always know more than any of us, though God knows how, since I only encounter you in places like this."

Crane took a seat and called for a Kentucky bourbon. "*Cubano whisky único, señor,*" the fat proprietor advised him. "*No americano, yo sentiro.*"

"Then the local stuff will have to do." The proprietor waddled away. Crane unsnapped the dispatch case and threw some yellowing sheets on the table. "Newspapers, boys? There's half a *Tampa Times,* a two-page weekly rag from Key West, and a *New York World* ten days old. I gathered them up on the beach."

Michael picked up the New York paper and started. "Ugh. What's this filthy stain, blood?"

Crane was amused. "A topkick had a can of tomato soup in his kit. There was some sort of squabble for possession. I lifted the paper while the pugilists were going at it."

Disdainful, Michael dropped the *World* on the table. "Tell us what you know, Stephen. I'll pay for the drinks."

"You may be getting a bad deal, but I accept." The proprietor delivered the whiskey. Crane licked his lips and rubbed his fingertips together as he looked at it. "Here's all the information I have at the moment. Up in the hills, the Spaniards are holding a strategic road junction. Some of General Castillo's infantry probed up that way, got into a heavy skirmish, and came hightailing back. We'll have to force the junction to reach Santiago. Beyond the junction on a flat plain, there's a little burg called Sevilla. Castillo's scouts claim its the best campsite, if not the only one, between here and the objective. I understand Wheeler's gone up the road to reconnoiter the Spanish position."

Paul said, "We saw him leave."

"I'm not surprised he wants to see for himself, he's a fire horse. Been moaning and cussing all day because Shafter's kept the cavalry in the rear, behind Lawton's regulars and Bates's volunteers. But I think something's dawned on old Joe. The elephantine one is still rolling around out there on the ocean. Until he lands, General Wheeler is senior commander ashore. If he moves fast enough, he may call the tune. He may get what he wants."

Michael leaned over the table. "You mean a bit of a go?"

"Exactly." Crane sipped his whiskey. "Holy heaven. This is swill." He took a healthy swallow anyway. "Getting anything good with your camera, Dutch?"

"Yesterday I filmed parts of the landing. I also have footage from my transport. There is a lot showing Colonel Roosevelt."

"Always ready to pose, Teddy. You don't know it, but you may already be part of the election campaign of the next governor of New York."

"What I want most are scenes of combat."

"Then take my advice. Follow Joe Wheeler. Except for those two colored gentlemen who met their maker yesterday, this war has been God damn sanitary. From here on I think we'll see blood."

Crane was right about Wheeler's moving fast to take advantage of temporary seniority. After dark, with ship searchlights raking the beach and hundreds of men bathing nude in the glare—one of the most unlikely sights Paul had ever witnessed, and one he photographed with no hope of Shadow's distributing it— there came word of an early-morning march. The objective was the Spanish defense line guarding the main Santiago road where it joined a lesser one at an abandoned village, Las Guásimas, named for a species of tree growing there. The Spanish were entrenched on hilltops above the road. General Wheeler, General S. B. M. Young, and General J. E. Crown were to advance along the main road with eight troops of regulars: four from the 1st Infantry, four from the dismounted 10th Cavalry. Taking a roughly parallel route on a foot trail which wound through the hills closer to the coast, Wood's Weary Walkers would march toward the same objective—the junction at Las Guásimas.

Because Uncle Joe's command would advance on the Santiago road, Paul decided to accompany the Rough Riders on the coastal trail, assuming they'd allow it. He still wanted to avoid his uncle. He wasn't sure how he'd react, what he'd say, if they met. His impulse to hurt Uncle Joe with an announcement about London had passed; making the decision and informing Michael had purged it somehow. But he'd have to tell his relatives. If not in person in Cuba, then by letter when they returned to America. He owed them that much consideration, especially Aunt Ilsa. The whole matter induced a weighty fear that Uncle Joe wouldn't care.

He washed his dirty clothes in the surf, and himself as well. All along the beach, huge bonfires were blazing. Naked men knelt at the water's edge, doing their laundry. Other men, naked, danced goatishly around the fires, bobbing, shouting, singing. You might have thought them pagan priests of old until you identified the songs. "The Animal Fair." "A Hot Time in the Old Town Tonight."

Periodically, raffish bands of Cuban irregulars galloped their starved ponies along the beach. They fired volleys at the sky, surely heard by the Spaniards in their works not three miles up the main road. Some jumped their ponies over the lounging Americans, hooting at the joke. The searchlights swept back and forth, lighting the way for crowded longboats hurtling shoreward on the whitecapped rollers. Before the boats could beach properly, many a soldier jumped fully clad into the shallows, splashing a comrade or dumping hatfuls of water on his own head. Altogether, it was hard to imagine a more bizarre spectacle. Paul thought of it as a military *Walpurgisnacht.*

He laid the washed clothes near the flickering fire they'd coaxed from some soft wood. He hoped everything would dry by morning, so that he could store the clothes in his grip, which he intended to leave at the cantina. He had one dry shirt and pair of pants left in the bag; they smelled moldy when he pulled them out.

Jimmy sat close to the fire. The camera and canvas bag were just behind him, protected by a large piece of oilcloth. Jimmy's beard was a grimy stubble reaching halfway up his sallow cheeks. At his open collar, the heavy chain of his holy medal showed. He drew the edge of his machete lightly back and forth over his thumb, occasionally wetting the thumb with his tongue.

"So tomorrow's when we get shot, huh?"

"Tomorrow is the day we film some fighting, if we are lucky. I am going to ask permission to go with the Rough Riders."

"I wouldn't cry if they told you to go to hell."

Paul walked to the Rough Riders bivouac; the regiment had come over the trail from Siboney in the late afternoon. The first person he recognized was Hugh Johnson, the leathery Californian with the cold green eyes. "What're you up to, Dutch?"

"I want to go with your unit if Wood and Roosevelt will allow it."

"Talk to Wood, Teddy's spitting nails. Has been ever since they drowned his horse Rain-in-the-Face at Daiquirí. Good luck."

Paul went on to Wood's tent, glancing up as a few fat warm raindrops splashed him. While he stood outside the tent, waiting, it began to rain in earnest, raising steam clouds from the ground. When his turn came, he was shocked by Wood's appearance. The sturdy and vigorous colonel of the 1st looked pale and spent. He sat with his elbows on a packing crate desk, slowly rubbing his fingers up and down his temples while Paul stated his request. At the end, Wood frowned; Paul feared he'd say no. The man was a calculating professional; the soldiers called him Icebox.

"Davis is coming with us, and Mr. Marshall of the *New York Journal.* I suppose we can't very well deny equal treatment to you and Bitzer. Paley is in the hospital. God only knows how Mr. Bitzer will keep up, hauling all those storage batteries. Do you have a lot of gear?"

"Some, sir. My partner and I can carry it easily."

"All right, permission granted. But you must stay at the rear. You must clear the trail instantly if someone orders it. If you don't, we'll run over your equipment, and we'll run over you."

"Understood," Paul said.

"I'll tell you what I told Davis and Marshall. Tomorrow won't be a Sunday stroll in the park. You'll smell powder before the day's done. It's likely some men will die. You could be one of them."

"Even so, sir, I want to go."

"Then be ready to move at 3 A.M. We'll start as soon as we can thereafter. Pass that along to Bitzer if you see him."

Paul thanked Wood and left quickly. He searched for Bitzer for half an hour but couldn't find him, so he gave up. It wouldn't be hard to be ready at three. With the warm rain falling steadily, there'd be no sleeping on the beach at Siboney.

Friday, June 24; half past five in the morning. Wood's command was assembling at the foot of the trail.

Only a few men had horses: Davis and Marshall, the correspondents; two of Wheeler's aides; Colonel Wood; Major Alex Brodie, a tough little Army veteran who led the 2d Squadron; and Lieutenant Colonel Roosevelt, commanding the 1st Squadron. Roosevelt rode Little Texas, the second of two mounts he'd brought.

Most of the soldiers were in good spirits, even though they'd camped in the rain and now stood shivering in wet clothes. Richard Harding Davis looked typically dry and neat in his familiar dark blue coat, high collar, cravat, and a flat-crowned felt hat with puggaree trailing behind. He introduced Paul and Jimmy to the other journalist, Marshall, whose long white duster was spotless. How the reporters stayed so clean, Paul couldn't imagine. He and Jimmy were a pair of muddy scarecrows.

They waited with camera and canvas bag at the rear of the column. There they fell into conversation with a bowlegged private who introduced himself as Jerry Pruitt. He had a slow, drawly way of speaking; said he hailed from Texas, where he worked as a cowhand on a huge ranch called Main Chance.

Among the Rough Riders Paul heard a good deal of discussion about the guns they lacked. They were supposed to march with a dynamite gun and two rapid-fire Colt's machine guns, but all three pieces were lost in the confusion of ordnance wagons at Daiquirí or Siboney. It seemed to create apprehension, as did speculation about the weapons of the Spaniards—Mauser rifles, with smokeless powder. "I hear them Mauser bullets can go nine, ten inches deeper into a block of yellow pine than these Krag rounds we got," Jerry Pruitt said dolefully.

At five forty-five the column began its advance, four abreast. Paul shouldered the camera, Jimmy the canvas bag. Jimmy had left his jacket and suitcase with Paul's valise at the cantina; he was down to his shirt sleeves, rolled above the elbows. The machete rode in his belt.

Just as the march started, Bitzer and his partner Len arrived with their bulky camera and several storage batteries packed into a mule cart. There was no room for the Biograph men in the cart; one walked on either side of the mule. Paul dropped back to say good morning.

"So you got the word. I'm glad. I searched for you last night with no success."

"Thanks." It sounded hollow. Bitzer eyed the trail. "With this load we'll be lucky to keep up. Anyway—stay safe."

"You too, Billy."

The first part of the advance was arduous, up the steep trail that snaked across the hills behind Siboney. Very quickly, the trail narrowed, squeezing the four-abreast formation to single file. There was no cadence; the Rough Riders moved as fast as the terrain would allow, each man watching his footing, jumping rain-carved ruts or thick creepers. Every step left an imprint in the earth. Despite the thick umbrella of trees, Paul knew the sun was up; he felt the heat.

The heavy jungle made it impossible to send out flankers. That increased the sense of danger; vulnerability. Bitzer's mule cart fell behind. Every few minutes Paul looked back to check on it; the fourth time, it had disappeared behind one of the humps in the trail. He felt bad for the Biograph men. On the other hand, competition was competition; he wasn't unhappy to be in the lead.

In about an hour the column crossed the last ridge and headed down into more open country. For a while the trail was relatively steep. Then it leveled, meandering between small round hills; walking was easier.

The sky was brilliant blue and cloudless. The march was already producing casualties. Paul counted more than a dozen men sprawling or sitting in the grass, overcome by the heat. Those who had fallen out avoided the eyes of those passing. Jimmy said the stragglers were the smart ones.

To their left lay rolling fields of tall yellow grass, separated from the trail by five-strand barb wire. Quite a few cuts had been made in the wire; by the Spaniards moving through, Paul presumed. On the right the ground sloped gently down toward the unseen main road, where Uncle Joe and the other senior officers would be advancing with their commands. Paul's column was too far away for a clear view of the Spanish works, although it was possible to glimpse one small blockhouse on the hilltops above the road junction.

Between the trail and the road, the terrain consisted of tall grass, dense stands of chaparral, and scattered clumps of coconut palms whose trunks slanted up at angles of forty-five degrees. Some of the low trees and shrubs forming the chaparral showed blossoms bright as a flame. Here and there a scummy lagoon glinted. Two buzzards with hooked beaks and leathery wings circled above, waiting.

By half past seven the men were sweating hard and grousing about the heat. Colonel Wood halted the column and an order was passed back. *"Fill your magazines and stop your talking."* The men readied their Krag-Jorgensen rifles. Unlike the rest of the Army, the Rough Riders had smokeless powder. Wood and Roosevelt and Brodie had demanded it.

Jimmy sat down on someone's discarded blanket roll for a smoke. Paul lit one of his small cigars. He noticed that wear and dampness had cracked the tips of his boots.

He shielded his eyes and again scanned the ground between the trail and the enemy fortifications. He'd studied a picture of Spanish uniforms; peaked straw hats were standard issue in the tropics. He saw none. He heard no firing. He commented about it to Private Pruitt, who shrugged.

"Mebbe they pulled back a'ready." Somehow Paul doubted it.

The heavy air was alive with the hum of insects. The ominous calm made him nervous. He kept scanning the hills. There wasn't a sign of the enemy.

Jerry Pruitt offered his canteen to Paul and Jimmy. Jimmy snatched it; drank long and greedily. Finally he passed it to Paul, who shook it. Very little was left.

Jimmy had held water in his mouth. He spat it onto a handkerchief to wipe his neck and cheeks.

The march resumed at a slow pace set by those in the lead. Presumably General Wheeler's men were moving forward in similar fashion on the inland road. At 8:15 a sudden boom startled everyone. "Hotchkiss gun," said an officer. "Got to be one of Wheeler's."

Over toward the road, a cloud of white smoke arose. Paul set the tripod in the grass but before he could turn the crank, the smoke dissipated. Then came a crashing volley of rifles; not from the road, but directly ahead—the front of the column, where Cuban scouts and men of L Troop had taken the point. Krag-Jorgensens began to return fire. Paul's heart pounded. "Here we go."

"Jesus and Mary," Jimmy said in a tremulous voice. He crossed himself. He was pale as the belly of a fish.

Firing quickly became continuous. It crackled on the distant road as well as on the trail. Mingled with rifle volleys was a stuttering Paul took to be machine guns.

He ran part way up a low hill on his right. From there he saw Roosevelt's squadron breaking toward the road, in what must be an attempt to link up with Wheeler. Roosevelt's men plunged off the trail with machetes and sabers swinging, clearing the heaviest brush in front of them. Major Brodie's squadron continued the forward advance; presumably Brodie would flank the enemy at the Las Guásimas junction.

Paul ran down the hill and hoisted the tripod to his shoulder. The weight tortured the raw place under his shirt. Early this morning the broken skin had been oozing pus.

"Jimmy, let's go forward."

Jimmy was squatting on the ground. From under the brim of his derby, he eyed his partner.

"Jim, what's wrong?"

"Not a damn thing. This is where I stop. I ain't catching any spic bullets this morning."

"I can't carry the camera and that bag too."

"You don't need the bag, you got enough film. I'll be here when you get back."

Hot, tired, and not a little frightened by the sounds of battle, Paul lost patience again. "I'm sure Honoria Fail will be proud of your heroism." Jimmy grabbed the machete lying in the grass; started to scramble up. Paul shouted at him. "Sit down, shut up, you and I are finished as partners."

"We were finished a long time ago, you snotty kraut bastard. Go on, get your ass shot to pieces."

Red-faced, Paul spun around and rushed forward with the camera. Firing was steady as he followed the red and white guidons of the 2d Squadron through the low hills to the edge of a level area. At the other side stood a number of sand-colored buildings with red tile roofs and several large, irregular holes in the walls. What was it, an abandoned ranch? From the way the front ranks were pumping rounds into the buildings, it was clear that Spanish troops were laid up there, raking the level area with their fire. But there were no puffs of black powder smoke to reveal their positions.

The Americans advanced across the level area with dogged steadiness. One section of the line would rise up, run eight or ten feet, drop down, and shoot. Then another section would run up past them, establishing a new forward line. Men cried out, pitched over with terrifying suddenness. Still the line advanced, Wood and Brodie in front, leading. To the credit of the volunteers, you couldn't tell them from those few who were regulars.

On the right flank, similar lines from Roosevelt's squadron were moving through stands of palm and coconut, toward the unseen road. Paul glimpsed Roosevelt on horseback, brandishing his saber. Beyond him, the Spanish works were at last clearly visible: bastions of flat stones piled up on the ridges above the road, and at least three small blockhouses. Poking above the stone breastworks were a few pointed crowns of straw hats.

Paul carried the camera close to the rear of the American line. He jammed the tripod in the grass, preparing to crank. He heard a noise near his ear; instinctively ducked. The air was full of that sound, something between a bee's buzz and the hum of a twanged wire. Mauser bullets . . .

He happened to glance forward and to the left, where he saw Pruitt. As if his attention had willed a tragedy, Pruitt's hands suddenly flew into the air. His rifle fell at his feet. His body seemed to fold to the ground like a discarded rag. Hunched down, Paul ran across the level area to reach the private from Texas.

Jerry Pruitt was sitting up, kneading the front of his khaki shirt with both hands. The shirt was soaked with blood that leaked through Pruitt's fingers and over his wrists. Pruitt's eyes were glazed but somehow he recognized Paul. He tried to speak through clenched teeth. Paul shook his head to show he didn't understand.

Pruitt closed his eyes. A peaceful expression relaxed his face. Very slowly, he fell backward, away from Paul. He settled gently in the grass. Sunlight played on his smooth-shaven left cheek, where a huge blue fly landed and walked around.

Paul stood up. The firing remained loud, yet he heard a new sound, quite distinct in the taller grass behind Pruitt. A rustling; a clicking . . .

"Medical corpsman?" he yelled at the top of his voice. "Where's the surgeon?" But neither a corpsman nor Lieutenant Church, the regimental surgeon, was within earshot.

The first of the plate-sized crabs sidled into view. More flies were crawling on the dead soldier's face, a black wriggling mat of them. It was a strange, timeless moment, standing there on the level ground with a dead man at his feet and bullets flying and spending themselves in the dirt. He was shaken by knowledge of his own mortality.

He pulled off his straw hat and wiped his dripping forehead with his sleeve. The sun was fully up, blinding him. In that moment he changed; entered some new state wholly unfamiliar. He felt a monstrous burden come down. He hated its weight and somehow knew he could never remove it. The transformation was final. The boy Pauli Kroner was gone forever.

He turned away from the searing light of the sun. The moment of epiphany passed, and time began to run again.

□ □ □ □

He rushed the camera to a new position and managed to shoot a few feet of Mr. Marshall, the correspondent, writing with his notebook on his knee while the Rough Riders pressed on across the level area, pouring fire into the buildings. Someone cried, "Brodie's hit, he's down!"

Roosevelt came spurring back from the direction of the road, his polka-dot bandanna flapping at the back of his neck. He'd pinned it to his hat brim to improvise a havelock. He flung himself from the saddle and ran up to men clustering around the fallen squadron commander. Following Roosevelt, Marshall suddenly lurched sideways and dropped to his knees. He fell on top of his notebook, a huge bloodstain showing on the back of his white duster.

Paul carried the camera forward again. He wondered how long his legs would hold out. He came to a sprawl of four bodies; recognized two. Sergeant Ham Fish and Captain Capron, commander of L Troop. He grieved for all four; brave men who had taken the point, and fallen.

The Rough Riders were still charging and firing as they closed on the bullet-pocked buildings. Paul stared at the bodies. Professional instinct told him he should crank off some footage while he had a chance.

Are you stupid? Shadow will hate it. Pflaum won't show it. Do you seriously think that Illinois storekeepers and Ohio widows will pay so much as one cent to see bloody corpses with flies swarming on them? The evidence of the capacity of civilized men for killing?

In his head, a second voice began to argue:

Maybe nobody wants to see it. But it's the truth.

Roosevelt waved his hat and shouted encouragement at the front of the line, where he'd taken Brodie's place. Another Mauser bullet passed close to Paul, its low buzz seeming to mock him, saying it had spared him but the next might not. Wex Rooney loomed gigantically in his mind:

Tell the truth. Nothing else matters.

He tilted the camera and turned the crank, filming the dead point men of L Troop.

Soldiers were spilling from the rear of the red-tiled buildings; men in conical straw hats and uniforms of blue-striped seersucker. Paul cranked furiously as one Spaniard after another burst into the open, threw down his rifle, and fled. A flag bearer dropped the red and yellow banner of Spain. He didn't run back to pick it up; other men were already trampling it. While the khaki line flowed forward in pursuit, passing its wounded, passing its dead, rifles and pistols shattering the morning, Paul kept cranking.

The Rough Riders had swarmed into all the buildings. There were a few shots, loud but hollow-sounding. An officer with white bone jutting from a gashed arm came dragging past from the right flank, going toward the rear. Paul stopped cranking. "Sir? What's happened?"

The lieutenant grimaced; he was young to have so many teeth replaced with gold. "The Spaniards are holding on to their positions on the road. Wheeler's dispatched a courier. He wants Lawton to send up an infantry regiment." He staggered on, toward the trail to the rear. The image of his ghastly smile, all the gold teeth, lingered with Paul. It took him a moment to collect himself.

As he reached for the crank, he checked the meter. He swore. Five feet left. He'd have to go back, find Jimmy, or the canvas bag if Jimmy had abandoned it. He left the camera and more than two hundred feet of exposed film of the battle, the ghastly corpses, the long grass all beaten down and wet with blood that would look black on a screen.

He walked a quarter of a mile. He passed a Rough Rider trying to tie his own tourniquet, a stick and a pocket handkerchief, around his left arm. He stopped long enough to help the soldier finish.

He passed a dead Cuban scout, his ragged white blouse pierced by at least five hits, his face already ravaged and ripped by half a dozen land crabs. Like so many of the insurgents, the scout was a boy; fourteen, fifteen at the most. Paul picked up a stone and hurled it with great force, breaking the orchid and yellow shell of one crab and scattering the rest. As soon as he moved on, they returned.

He made the mistake of glancing back. He saw a crab use its claw to tear out the boy's left eyeball and crush it like a pale olive. Paul gagged and bent over and threw up what little food was left in his stomach.

He heard Jimmy before he saw him. Heard him grunting in a strange way, as though expending effort. Paul ran through a gap in the barbed wire beside the trail. Jimmy was there in the long grass, shirtless, kneeling on a soldier's body. Beside him lay the canvas bag. The machete in his right hand was bloody.

Jimmy's head whipped around. Paul recognized the lieutenant who'd come in from the right flank. The man was dead. Half his gold teeth were missing. They lay winking and sparkling in the grass by the lieutenant's ear.

Jimmy saw Paul's expression and gave him a queer, shamed smile, as though hoping Paul could be mollified that way. Links of his neck chain winked in the sun.

"Just makin' a little profit before I go."

"You killed him, he only had an arm wound."

"Hey, look, why should you care about—"

Paul flung himself forward on top of Jimmy with a cry of rage.

103

Julie

RAIN FELL ON BELLE MER. It washed the marble terrace and speckled the reflecting pools in the garden. It was a summer rain, late in the afternoon; warm, torpid, melancholy.

It fit Julie's mood. Despite her resistance, the darkness was tiptoeing into the corners of her mind. The familiar darkness that brought apathy, and sorrow, and drove her to bed.

In the music room, she searched through a dozen cylinders for the Victor Gramophone, all purchased by her husband. "Sidewalks of New York." "Anvil Chorus." "Home Sweet Home" as a cornet solo. "Alabama Coon," a Negro novelty with a clog-dance effect. She chose Strauss's waltz *"An der schönen, blauen Donau,"* played by the Germania Philharmonie. It reminded her of Paul. He was on her mind almost constantly of late.

Gazing out through the tall streaming windows, she thought it strange that she should be so sad, crushed by a sense of failure, now that she'd taken her first tottering steps to freedom.

All winter long in Chicago, she'd brooded about her situation. She had to free herself from Bill; free herself, and then search for Paul. Even if it took years to find him. Even if she devoted her whole life to it, and never succeeded.

She had laid her plans with great care, and a maximum of secrecy. She told no one, not even her Uncle Ike on Fifth Avenue. She expected that Bill would attend the August race meeting in Saratoga as he usually did, and when he confirmed it two weeks ago, she went into New York City alone. She invented an elaborate lie about needing to consult a medical specialist about a female complaint. Propriety forbade probing questions about such things, even from husbands.

In the city, with a marked classified column in her trembling hand, she paid for a six-month lease on a furnished flat half a block from Madison Square. Paid in cash. Bill provided her with money of her own, for which she needn't account. She told the landlord her name was Mrs. Jesse Vernon, recently widowed, and that she would move in as soon as she sold her cottage on rural Long Island.

Afterward, exhilarated by her daring—the revelation of a bit of the courage Paul and Aunt Willis always said she had—she had sat in Madison Square, rather brazenly, by herself. While her brow cooled, she planned the next step.

She would leave Southampton when Bill was away. She wouldn't say goodbye to him, she'd simply disappear from his life and make no contact with anyone who knew her. She decided she mustn't see her mother for at least a year, first because it might put Bill on her track, and second because she did not want to give Nell an opportunity to weep and collapse and predict her own imminent demise unless Julie returned to her husband, thereby hushing what would surely be a thunderstorm of scandal.

Perhaps her scheme wasn't clever, but it was all she could think of, all she could manage, given the challenge of dragging a little courage from her tortured heart . . .

She glanced up with a feeling that she was no longer alone. Someone was walking across the terrace; a woman. She was wearing gloves, a nondescript cape, and a sunbonnet that hid her face. At first Julie thought she might be a servant from another house, on an errand. But servants had no reason to enter the mansion from the Sound side.

The woman peered through a tall French door, moved to the next one and there spied Julie, who had risen and was standing beside her chair. The woman tapped the wet glass.

Someone lost and wanting directions, Julie decided. She went to the door, unfastened the latch, turned the handle.

"Yes, may I help you?"

The woman thrust forward abruptly, showering Julie with raindrops. Julie was startled but not alarmed. The woman tore at the ribbon tied under her chin and snatched the bonnet off. Julie's hand flew to her mouth. The woman's face was a mottled mess of purple and yellow bruises, lacerations, and scar tissue forming under one eye. There was an odor of staleness on her clothes.

The woman was young, dark-haired; perhaps she'd been attractive in a coarse way before someone beat her. Little alarms resounded in Julie's head. She remembered the bell pull, on the wall behind her.

The waltz came to an end. All that issued from the amplifying horn was a rhythmic scratch, repeated endlessly. Before Julie could demand the intruder's name, she said, "I'm Rose. You're Bill's wife?"

The familiarity worsened her anxiety. "Mrs. Elstree, yes. I really don't understand your forcing your way in here. Be so good as to tell me—"

Rose interrupted. "I want to see him."

"For what purpose? Who are you?"

"Who am I? I'm Bill's friend. He kept me for a while. In New York. Then when he was through with me, he dumped me over. I had a stage career, do you think I can have one now? Some of these marks are scars, they'll never go away. Do you think he gave a God damn? Not him, he's the one who did this."

Julie stepped back, the angry words landing like blows. She'd grown used to Bill's philandering, but actually confronting one of his lovers was bizarre and frightening. She didn't like the wild look in Rose's eye.

"I guess you could say I'm his discarded trash, Mrs. Elstree. I'll tell you one thing I am for certain. I'm the mother of his baby."

Julie felt as though a huge knot had been yanked tight in her breast. She couldn't breathe. Around and around went the Gramophone cylinder, filling the dark room with its amplified scratch.

"You're—accusing my husband of getting you with child and then beating you?"

"Nothing less, Mrs. Elstree. When Bill found out about my condition, he said he was walking out. When I said I wouldn't have it, he put me down with his fists. It's lucky he didn't kill the baby." She took a firmer grip on a small reticule she was carrying. "Now that's enough talk, where is he?"

What does she want? Julie thought. *Money?* The young woman's disturbed expression, her violent speech, said it was more than that; something physical, threatening. How easy, then, to surrender Bill. If the woman was even half truthful, he deserved whatever he got. How easy to say, "He's upstairs, changing for supper," and then tug the bell pull to ask a servant to fetch him . . .

Julie loathed Elstree as she'd never loathed anyone. But she couldn't do it. She said, "He isn't home."

"Liar," Rose said. "I saw the carriage come in ten minutes ago. I was hiding in the lane. I paid my last dollar for the ticket from Manhattan, I won't be turned away. Sit down, we'll wait for him. He'll join you for supper, won't he?"

"No, he has other plans, a bridge game at his club." She spoke too fast; the lie was evident.

"Oh yes? Well, we'll wait anyway." Rose opened the reticule and pulled out a derringer pistol with over-and-under barrels. "Shut off that damn talking machine, it gets on my nerves. Walk slowly."

Julie obeyed. In a moment the Gramophone was silent.

"Come back and sit down."

They sat on brocaded chairs, on opposite sides of an Oriental carpet. Sun was trying to break through; it cast a moving pattern of rain between them. Rose held her gun out of sight beneath the reticule in her lap.

Julie felt cold perspiration on her hands. Despite everything Bill had done to her, the way he'd hurt her on their wedding night, threatened her when she asked for a divorce—despite all of his unfaithfulness, abuse—she couldn't let a man she'd taken as a lawful husband walk into the music room and take a bullet. If she did that, her conscience would flay her until her last breath.

"Fine place you got here," Rose said. "He's told me about it but I never thought I'd see it. My first look will be my last, too."

"Rose, be sensible. We can talk. Put the gun away."

"Not a chance." She leaned forward suddenly. "Not a fucking chance, you bitch."

"Please, there's brandy in the next room. A glass will calm you down, help you think twice about—"

"Shut up, someone's coming."

Julie heard the footsteps. She prayed it was a servant. But she knew Bill's tread too well. The music room door handle turned and he stepped in.

"Julie?"

"Bill, she has a gun!" Julie screamed.

"Rose," he said, not intimidated. "What the hell are you doing in my house? You've made a grave mistake."

He strode to his left, reaching for the fringed bell pull. Julie leaped from the brocaded chair, intending to throw herself on her husband, shield him, in the wild hope that the woman wouldn't shoot her, only wanting to shoot him. But her slipper caught the edge of another area rug, and she staggered. That misstep put him in the open, by the bell pull. He yanked it. Rose shot him.

Elstree stared down at the stiff bosom of his shirt. He'd dressed formally for the evening, his custom when he and Julie dined at home. Between the second and third diamond stud a red flower grew. He looked infuriated. He yanked the bell pull three, four, five times, until the tapestry sheath tore off the wire, and plaster dust showered down from above. His hair whitened in a moment.

Rose ran toward him; she stopped a yard in front of him and whipped up the derringer, steadying it with both hands. Julie screamed, "*No!*" and threw a small ornamental vase, but it missed. Rose fired the second round. It tore through Elstree's neck and out the other side, painting the wall with blood.

"Ah, my God," Elstree said wearily. He sat down awkwardly against the baseboard. His eyes closed, his head lolled over on his shoulder, then his torso sagged and he fell forward on another Oriental carpet.

Powder reeked in the damp air. Rose threw the empty derringer to the floor. Julie heard servants coming; she ran to the door. Rose dropped to her knees beside Bill. Incredibly, she was crying. "Bill, Bill, oh darling, Bill." She fondled

Elstree's hair; kissed his powdered cheek again and again; got his blood all over her sleeves and gloves.

Julie tore the door open. "In here, hurry." Rose staggered to her feet and ran out the nearest French door, disappearing along the terrace. Servants crowded into the room, snapped on the electric chandelier, exclaimed and sobbed over the sight of the master bleeding on the carpet.

"I tried to save him," Julie said. She was crying too, a huge, remorseful burst of tears, beyond rational control. "I tried, I tried, you've got to believe me."

The town constable apprehended Rose French as she was fleeing the village of Southampton on foot. That night, in the small jail, the turnkey rushed to the cell in answer to Rose's cry and found her lying in blood. The fetus was lost.

William Vann Elstree III had already been removed to a local mortuary for preparation.

104

Dutch

PAUL LANDED HARD on Jimmy, his knees in Jimmy's ribs. Jimmy heaved upward, throwing him off. Both were stunned.

They got up about the same time, standing six feet apart in the trampled grass. Paul held out his hand. "Give me that thing."

With both hands on the machete's hilt, Jimmy said, "Here," and took a ferocious swipe at Paul's head.

Paul jumped away. He heard and felt the end of the blade pass near his cheek. While Jimmy's momentum was still carrying him through the swing, Paul lunged forward and drove his knee into Jimmy's groin. Jimmy let out a grunt of pain and dropped the machete.

Both of them crouched to retrieve the fallen weapon. Paul was faster. He seized the sweat-slippery haft, whirled the machete above his head once and sailed it away into the long grass.

Throwing the machete left him with his back to Jimmy. Jimmy's fist slammed the back of his head. Paul staggered; Jimmy grabbed his shoulders from behind and threw him sideways. Off balance, Paul went down.

His jaw slammed the ground near the bloodstained gold teeth. Jimmy kicked him in the ribs. Paul flopped onto his back, writhing. Jimmy dropped on Paul's belly with both knees, seized the canvas bag, and jammed it over Paul's face. Paul clawed at it, suffocating. Jimmy held on. Paul knew he'd die unless he freed himself. He flailed with his fists, hoping to hit Jimmy's head. He missed repeatedly. Then his left hand made contact; he grabbed Jimmy's hair and yanked.

Jimmy tumbled away; the weight of the canvas bag lifted. The tropic sun blinded Paul. He flung an arm over his eyes, sucked air into his lungs. Pain raged in his body where Jimmy had struck and kicked him.

While he lay gasping, trying to gather strength, Jimmy scooped up the gold teeth and stuffed them in his pockets. He snatched the canvas bag and jumped through the break in the barb wire. Paul rolled on his side and watched him cross the trail and plunge into the brush. Jimmy was stupidly fleeing inland, toward the road where the regulars were still exchanging fire with the enemy. Perhaps the fight had disoriented him.

Why in hell had he taken the film magazines? Paul wondered as he staggered up. They weren't worth anything. No, that was wrong, Jimmy would get satisfaction from stealing and destroying what Paul needed. He ran through the break in the barb wire, giving chase.

On the other side of the trail the grass sloped away toward coconut palms scattered through the chaparral. Paul ran hard, his arms pumping. Twice he heard the buzz of Mauser bullets close by. Clouds of powder smoke hung above the Santiago road, but there were no similar clouds above the fortifications on the ridge, nor anything to reveal the location of a single Spanish sharpshooter.

The nearer Paul came to the road, the louder grew the gunfire. Weaving between trees, he lost sight of Jimmy. Then he heard a cry, and a crashing in the underbrush. *He's fallen!*

Paul ran harder. He burst from the chaparral onto the sloping bank of one of the lagoons seen before. Jimmy had slipped in the mud; Paul came on him as he was struggling to his feet, his hands and shirt covered with black muck.

Jimmy saw Paul and threw the canvas bag at him. Paul ducked; the bag sailed into the tall grass. Jimmy ran to the right, along the bank. Again his feet went out from under him. Yelling, he landed on his rump in the shallows.

Jimmy's hair straggled over his forehead. His eyes glared in a dull, bestial way. How did the world create someone so willful, venal, cruel? For a moment, Paul wanted to run down the bank and finish him—rid the earth of him. But he only stood there, his fists trembling a little. A smile flickered on Jimmy's filthy face. "Come on, come on—what's stopping you? Yellow? Sure. Yellow." Jimmy laughed at him.

With a *chug*, a Mauser bullet hit a palm tree behind Paul; splinters stung his neck. Scruples had undone him and Jimmy knew it.

On the ridge line beyond the Santiago road, one conical sombrero poked up, then immediately vanished again. Paul walked unsteadily to the canvas bag, pulled it out of the high grass and dropped to his knees. He had the magazines, there was no more reason to fight. He fumbled at the knot in the drawstring.

Jimmy came bounding up the bank with wrists crossed and both hands on the chain of the holy medal. Before Paul could defend himself, Jimmy dropped the chain over his head. "Now," he said, pulling hard as sweat rivered off his face, "now I got you. Guess my old man was smarter'n yours. He was a gent, but he taught me how to fight. Didn't he? *Didn't he, you son of a bitch?*"

Caught on his knees, Paul couldn't stand up. He tore at the constricting chain. The big links cut into his neck. Blood began to seep between them. Jimmy grunted as he pulled the chain tighter. His hate-twisted face swam above Paul; he had the advantage, there was no way to defeat him with cleverness. If he could

be defeated at all. Paul's strength was sapped. Everything seemed to be darkening.

Jimmy grunted like a man sunk in sexual pleasure—*"Uhhh, uhhh"*—each grunt
a savage two-handed yank on the chain. Blood ran from under the chain in half a
dozen places, streaking Paul's throat, staining his shirt collar. Jimmy was going to
kill him.

He refused to let it happen. Not here, not this way. He seized Jimmy's belt
with both hands and pulled hard. Jimmy fell against Paul and they rolled down
the slope into the shallows. Jimmy's left hand let go of the chain.

Paul pounded his fist into Jimmy's gut, knocking him sideways, flailing and
splashing. Tiny insects darted away over the surface. Paul hit again. Jimmy's right
hand tore away from the chain.

Dizzy to the point of sickness, Paul somehow got to his feet. He moved backward up the bank, one step, two, lifting the bloody chain over his head. He threw
it on the ground and stamped on it repeatedly, churning the mud until the chain
was buried. Jimmy watched him from the shallows like some animal wounded
and maddened by tormentors. He managed to lurch out of the water and stretch
out his hands, as if to choke Paul again. Paul turned his body sideways, waiting.
When Jimmy came a step closer, he kicked Jimmy's crotch again.

Jimmy's eyes glazed. Paul put all his remaining strength into a right-hand
punch that lifted Jimmy and hurled him back into the lagoon with a great splash.

Jimmy showed no sign of wanting to rise from the shallows, where he was
bracing himself on his hands. He looked whipped, but Paul took no pleasure from
it. *Look for the bag. See if the magazines are all right.* He turned away from the
lagoon, walked a few steps along the bank. He heard the buzz of the Mauser
bullet just before he felt it strike his back.

When he came to his senses, his nose was resting in the mud. He'd been hit
about halfway down his back, the right side, behind his ribs. It hurt like the very
devil; agony.

He watched Jimmy slog up from the shallows, a grin breaking over his filthy
face. "Well, I guess I win the pot in this game, huh? Anything you want me to tell
Shadow and the folks in Chicago? No? All right, then I'm going. You have a good
time, you and your friends." He grabbed Paul's hair, lifting his head. "I hope they
take hours to kill you, you fucking kraut know-it-all. I hope they take forever."

He pushed Paul's face into the mud, then threw his head back and laughed. He
disappeared in the direction of the trail. He was so happy, he forgot the canvas
bag, if he'd ever really wanted it.

Above the noise of gunfire, men shouting orders beneath the blanket of smoke
on the road, Jimmy's merry laugh drifted out behind him. As it faded, Paul heard
another sound. His eyes grew huge.

He tried to get up; couldn't. He lay bleeding and staring into the long grass
that grew around the bank. The long grass full of rustlings and clickings . . .

The first land crab sidled out of the grass, pincers waving, little round stalk
eyes quivering in the air. Its horny maw opened and shut, opened and shut.
Another one followed, and another, and more after that.

The largest crab, the one nearest Paul, stopped a moment, and Paul fancied he could see in those stalked eyes some vicious and hungry demon relishing the meal to come. He dug his fingers into the mud. Pushed up, then fell back, too weak.

Working its mandibles, waving its pincers, the crab sidled next to his cheek. Climbed onto his face.

Clicking, rustling, the other crabs converged. Two of them nipped at Paul's head. He felt others on his bare arms; on his legs; in his groin. He shut his eyes and bit on his lower lip. *They'll kill me, tear me to pieces.* He had no more courage, it was all drained by the fight, the bullet wound, now this . . .

A claw nipped his cheek half an inch below his left eye. He screamed.

The crabs seemed to sense his weakness; his helplessness. They began to pluck and tear at his face, his hands lying beside his bleeding body. The pain really wasn't so bad. No more than a sharp peck, like a bird's beak. But what it represented broke him. He cried.

He wasn't ashamed of his terror because he was no longer even aware of it. Blood trickling from beneath his eye mingled with spittle trickling out of his mouth. Gradually his sobbing stopped and he droned, "Finish it, finish it, finish, *finish.*"

He heard a thrashing and crashing in the long grass. *Mein Gott,* what next? . . .

"Lord, Roy, looka them damn things."

"Kick 'em off, don't stand there, they's 'bout to eat his eyes."

A rifle butt flicked a crab from Paul's face. The pincer tore his nose as the crab let go. The rifle butt swept back and forth, broomlike. In the glaring sky Paul saw a black balloon floating.

A round black face, bright with sweat.

He saw a hat, a blue shirt, a scarlet bandanna. Where had they come from? Up the trail from the rear, to relieve Wood's command? The first black soldier shouted, "Some of you niggers get up here an' help me, this boy's 'bout to bleed to death. He may be gone a'ready."

A second dark face appeared in the sky, and then a third, impossibly ugly.

"Let me lift him up, I'll carry him to the rear."

"Ott, you can't, you half sick with the fever."

"Get out of my way, I said I'll carry him and I mean to do it."

Paul's eyes lost focus, the sun darkened, and that was the end.

105

The General

HEADQUARTERS 2D CAVALRY BRIGADE, U.S.A.
Camp Near Santiago de Cuba, June 25, 1898

ADJUTANT-GENERAL CAVALRY DIVISION:

SIR: By direction of the major general commanding the Cavalry Division, I have the honor to submit the following report of the engagement of a part of this brigade with the enemy at Guásimas, Cuba, on the 24th inst., accompanied by detailed reports from the regimental and other commanders engaged, and a list of the killed and wounded . . .

Leading from Siboney there are two roads, or, more properly, trails, one to the eastward, the other to the westward of the little town . . .

After having carefully examined the enemy's position, I prepared to develop his strength. Canteens were ordered filled; the Hotchkiss Battery was placed in position in concealment at about 900 yards, and Bell's squadron was deployed, with Norvell's in support . . .

The Spanish forces occupied a range of high hills in the form of obtuse angles, with the salient toward Siboney. On discovering the enemy, I sent a Cuban guide to warn Col. Wood. Knowing that his column had a more difficult route, and would require a longer time to reach the position, I delayed the attack some time in order that the development of both flanks should begin simultaneously. During this delay Gen. Wheeler arrived, and was informed of my dispositions, plan of attack, and intentions. After examination of the position by him, and his approval of my action, I ordered the attack. It was executed by officers and men in a manner which won the admiration of the Division Commander, and all present who witnessed it . . .

It was impossible for the troops to keep in touch along the front, and they could only judge the enemy's position from the sound and direction of his fire. The fighting on the left flank was quite remarkable and, I believe, unprecedented, in volunteer troops so quickly raised, armed, and equipped. Both Col. Wood and Lt. Col. Roosevelt disdained to take advantage of shelter or cover from the enemy's fire while any of their men remained exposed to it —an error of judgment, but happily on the heroic side . . .

The chief results following from this action with the Spaniards are: A test of the valor of the opposing forces; the spirit of superiority I believe it has fixed in our own; the opening of the way to Santiago de Cuba; and the gaining of a beautiful camping-ground for our Army on the heights overlooking that city, which can now easily be taken at our leisure.

Very respectfully,

Jos. Crown,

Brigadier General, U.S. Vols.

106

Willis

ON SATURDAY, June 25, the day that Joe Crown wrote his report, the chartered Red Cross ship SS *State of Texas* was anchored in Guantánamo Bay. She was carrying rations, blankets, medicines, and bandages for the rebels in the interior. Clara Barton and the volunteers with her were expecting to accompany the supplies overland.

After the ship dropped anchor, they were informed this was impossible because the head of the bay was still in Spanish hands; the Red Cross could do nothing at Guantánamo for the time being.

About midday, there came telegraphed news of the Las Guásimas fight. The previous day, General Joe Wheeler's command had overcome a Spanish force and sent it into retreat toward Santiago. Like all such victories, it was not without cost. Sixteen Americans killed, and fifty-two wounded.

Miss Barton held a hasty meeting with her volunteers, and spoke to the ship's captain. She told him there were wounded men only forty miles to the west. Steam was up by two o'clock in the afternoon. The *State of Texas* sailed for Siboney.

At twilight the relief ship anchored in the midst of warships, transports, steam cutters, lighters scattered in a huge half-moon around Siboney.

On the trip from Guantánamo, Willis had been told Siboney had no proper harbor, nor any pier large enough to handle oceangoing vessels. Now she saw it for herself, standing at the rail smoking her tenth hand-rolled cigarette of the day. The Cuban tobacco from Tampa was strong and probably bad for her, like a thousand other things in her life, from pastries oozing cream filling to liaisons with younger men who always left for perfectly logical reasons, or were snatched away by fate. So far she had survived it all. And she would continue. But as she grew older, it grew harder.

A short distance from Willis, Clara Barton was watching a longboat struggle to put out from a temporary pier built by Army engineers. By mutual consent, Clara and Willis separated when Willis wanted to smoke. They were dear friends, but Clara abhorred tobacco in any form.

Clara was just five feet tall, but her powerful presence made her seem larger.

She was incredibly energetic for a woman of seventy-seven. She could work eighteen or twenty hours without a complaint, a yawn, or any more nourishment than a cup of strong tea. Her features were hawkish, her eyes brown, missing nothing. Her hair, worn in a grandmotherly bun, showed no gray. She traveled with a wardrobe of nearly identical calico dresses and gingham aprons. She said it saved time otherwise wasted on deciding what to wear.

At last the longboat got under way in heavy swells. No fool about the attitudes of men, Clara had declined to be the first ashore, sending instead her chief physician, Dr. Anton Lesser, to deal with the Army medical officers. Dr. Lesser had gone to offer the assistance of the entire volunteer staff of the Red Cross ship —physicians, five trained nurses, and two skilled helpers, Willis and a widow named Mrs. Olive Shay.

Fighting an onshore wind, the longboat took thirty minutes to reach the ship. Short of breath and looking overheated in his tan duster and souvenir planter's hat from Tampa, Dr. Lesser joined Clara Barton on the deck, forward of the wheelhouse. Willis threw her cigarette over the rail and quickly moved toward them.

"Do you see those two houses, just there on the beach?" Lesser pointed them out. The houses, both dilapidated, were separated by about fifty feet of sand.

Clara nodded. "Which house belongs to the Americans?"

"The one nearer the pier. The other's full of Cuban boys. Both houses are absolute pigstys—no one's cleaned them. There are no blankets, no pillows, the wounded just scattered about on the floor higgledy-piggledy. I stepped on roaches, swatted flies—and they're supposed to be hospitals!"

"We'll clean them, Anton," Willis said.

"Did you tell them that?" Clara asked the doctor. "Did you tell them we have buckets and brooms? Brushes, disinfectants—and more than a hundred folding cots?" Mrs. Shay joined the group, together with one of the trained nurses. Dr. Lesser looked distraught.

"I told them. I spoke personally with the Army surgeon in charge of American casualties on the beach, a Dr. Francis Winter. He and I didn't hit it off at all. I recognized his type. Reads the Army rule book once and likes it so much he memorizes it. Dear ladies—he said our help wasn't wanted and wouldn't be accepted."

Clara rocked on her heels. "Are you joking?"

"I regret to say I am not."

Mrs. Shay, a petite redhead, was outraged. "He refused the help of the Red Cross?"

"He did. Emphatically."

Willis said, "Why the hell would he be so stupid?"

"He cited Army policy. Women don't belong in a war zone. They're not as qualified as male doctors and orderlies. They should stay safely at home. Those are a few samples of his claptrap."

"And it comes from the topmost office in Washington," Clara said. "Surgeon General Sternberg himself. I know, because my home is only seven miles from the capitol, and I hear things. Sternberg insists female nurses can't be trusted in the field. He uses words like 'skittish' and 'flighty.' It's the same ridiculous song the Army medical department sang in the Civil War. Great heavens—thirty years, and we're still fighting for acceptance."

Lesser nodded gloomily. "You're right, Winter's only reflecting the policy of his superiors. But he has authority on the beach."

Willis smacked the rail. "Let me go in and talk to the bastard, I'll straighten him out."

"Oh, no, Miss Fishburne," Lesser exclaimed, "I don't think that's a good idea. You are refreshingly forthright, but Winter's exceedingly pompous. I fear candor would only worsen matters."

"Well," said Clara Barton, "if the American doctors won't accept our help, perhaps the Cubans will."

"Certainly a possibility," Lesser agreed.

"Then we shall land as soon as it's light in the morning, and offer our services. At the same time, Anton, you and I will go over the head of this Dr. Winter, to the chief Army surgeon. I can't imagine that all the medical officers in General Shafter's command are idiots."

Willis wouldn't have wasted five cents on that wager. But she didn't say it.

107

Dutch

HE AWOKE in some kind of house, within sound of the surf. The room was filthy and dimly lit.

He lay on a hard floor. He had never hurt so much. He felt as if his whole body had been punished with flails, but especially his back, midway between shoulder and hip on the right side. With every breath, a fierce pain stabbed him there.

To his left, illuminated by kerosene lights, two men in bloody smocks worked over a soldier lying on a table. One of the men was suturing the patient's thigh. Paul was mesmerized by the glitter of the big half-moon needle. The doctor swooped the needle into the patient's leg and pulled it out again, trailing bloody catgut. The patient screamed.

"More ether," the doctor shouted. He was sweating brutally.

From the next room someone called, "That was the last. They can't unload any more until the wind calms down and the surf drops. In the morning, maybe."

"Of all the God damned half-baked excuses for a hospital—"

The other doctor reached out to steady him: "We've got to finish, ether or no ether."

Paul watched the shiny needle rise. The soldier screamed again.

Paul's head was clearing a little; drawing up memories. Jimmy. The chain around his neck. The bullet. And the land crabs. He could feel them. He shuddered, making a little noise. The doctors looked at him.

He remembered dark faces seeming to float in the sky. One belonged to Ott Person . . .

His mind drifted again. Sometime later, another doctor appeared. This one wore a cleaner smock. He was an older man, portly and losing his hair. He had a round face pink as a cutlet, and a self-important air. He carried a medical chart.

"I am Dr. Winter, the surgeon in charge. How are you feeling, my lad?"

The false bonhomie angered Paul. "Terrible. I have never suffered pain like this."

"Even so, you're a very lucky fellow. The bullet pierced cleanly, and passed through. No organ damage. Two broken ribs, that's the worst. But we're puzzled by the abrasions around your throat. Was something wrapped there to choke you?"

Paul propped himself on his elbows; excruciating. "My partner attacked me. Then he ran off. I don't know what happened to him."

"Well, I certainly can't tell you."

"What day is this?"

"Saturday morning." The doctor tucked the chart under his arm and brought out a gold watch. He tilted the dial toward the kerosene lights. "Just a little after 3 A.M. Lie down, please. Your wound is dressed, we've taped your ribs, but you'll have to recuperate for at least a week."

"Impossible! I have to work," Paul said, struggling up again. "I'm here to take moving pictures of the war."

"So we were told by the man who brought you in." He poised a pencil over the chart. "There's been a great deal of confusion. We never got your name. What is it?"

"Paul Crown. American Luxograph Company."

"Just your name," the doctor snapped. He wrote it down.

"Where is this house, Doctor?"

"Siboney."

"When I was hit, I was up in the hills."

"Yes, the soldier I referred to carried you all the way here on his back. Big buck nigger. I don't know who he was, I can't tell one of them from another. I insist you lie down and rest."

Dr. Winter walked away, once again allowing Paul to see the silvery flash of the needle, followed inevitably by the scream.

Saturday morning a civilian with a familiar face came in. He peered around, spied Paul, and pulled up a stool. His natty jacket and houndstooth cap were unspeakably dirty. Paul smiled sleepily.

"Billy."

"Hello, sport," Bitzer said. "I heard you were laid up here. How're you doing?"

"I am going to make it."

"Well, I guess you'd better! Got a couple of important things to tell you. First, your camera's okay. Some soldiers found it abandoned by that ranch house at Las Guásimas. They turned it over to me. I stored it with the V Corps provosts."

Panicky, Paul remembered the canvas bag left in the chaparral. Would it still be there? Would the heat and rain ruin the magazines? He struggled up. "I have to get out of here—"

"Nah, no hurry," Bitzer said, shaking a cigarette from a pack. He offered one to Paul. Paul shook his head. Bitzer struck a match. "Everything's holding until they can move enough men and supplies to forward positions. That'll take six or seven days, maybe more."

"Are you sure my camera's all right?"

"Absolutely, I checked it over. The lens is fine, so's the crank mechanism. I don't think a drop of rain fell on it, either. You were pretty damn lucky. I still wish I had that camera, it's a honey."

"Decent of you to look after it," Paul said. "We're competitors."

Billy Bitzer's grin managed to be tough and warm at the same time. "Yeah, but your name isn't Paley. That's the other news. Paley went home. He got too sick to work. Never shot a single frame of the action. He left for Key West yesterday. Nobody's holding a wake."

He put on his cap and squeezed Paul's shoulder. "Get well, friend."

"Thank you, Billy. For everything."

"Forget it. See you in the trenches."

Later that day Paul was dozing when someone shook him. He said, "No," rolling his head from side to side without opening his eyes. He wanted to sleep.

The hand jostled him again. "Come on, Heine, wake up. I only got a little while." Groggily, Paul looked at the ugly face of Corporal Ott Person.

Ott hunkered down and cast an eye over the room, now crowded with seven men lying on pallets. Flies buzzed. Roaches crawled on the walls.

"This place ain't fit for pigs. Can't they get you cots in here?"

"I guess not." Paul struggled to prop up on his elbows. Under a thick pad of dressings, an invisible razor cut a long slice in his side. "They're short on supplies, doctors—everything. They say you brought me back here, Ott."

"Down the trail. Owed it to you."

"How did you happen to find me?"

"Wasn't looking for you, that's for certain. Didn't even know you was up that way. They sent for two troops of the 10th to relieve Wood's command. We double-timed up the trail an' spread out to find Joe Wheeler. My squad happened to be the one that passed by the place where you was layin', that's all there is to it."

"I'll think of some way to repay you when I'm out of here."

"Heine, stow that. Tol' you before, I'm the one had the debt to square. You really want to do something for me, you stick around after this war's over. Be an American."

Paul drew a deep, slow breath; even taking it carefully that way, the pain was ungodly. "Ott, I can't do that. I have an opportunity in England and I'm going to take it. All my life I've wanted a home. Wanted to belong somewhere. You know what my home is? A furnished room. A hotel. A suitcase."

Ott tugged up his red bandanna and swabbed his cheeks. He seemed to be perspiring heavily. "Could be worse. My first one, it was a two-room shanty with a leaky roof an' a red clay floor. I know how you feel 'cause of that gal you lost.

But there ain't no place on God's earth won't disappoint you sometimes, Heine. 'Merica may be a wagon with one bad wheel, but it carries a lot of folks farther than they ever thought they could go. Did that for me in the Army. Did it for you, too—learned you how to use that camera. So don't turn your back. Please don't."

Paul shook his head. Ott had to understand. It was over. The half of the stereopticon card stored in his valise in the cantina was just what he'd called it on the ship leaving Tampa. Another souvenir.

Ott stood up, powerfully tall, casting a long shadow on the wall. They looked at each other.

"Well, I spoke my piece. I'll go now." He untied the knot of his red bandanna and wiped the back of his neck, his face, and his throat. "Lord, it's a reg'lar furnace in here." Paul was puzzled. A stiff breeze was blowing from the sea, cooling the house and driving out the stale air. Yet Ott was covered with sweat.

"Whew, mebbe I need a few minutes on that beach 'fore I go back to camp." Ott stuck his bandanna in the back pocket of his pants, set his campaign hat on his head, snapped the strap under his chin. "So long, Heine. You look me up soon as you're out of here. We'll talk some more about you stayin'. I don't give up easy."

Next morning, Sunday, Dr. Winter brought a young officer to see Paul. "This is First Lieutenant Criswell. He wants to ask some questions."

"Frank Criswell," the officer said, leaning down to shake hands.

Paul used his elbows to prop up again, this time with a little less pain. Winter snapped his fingers and an orderly rushed a stool for Criswell, who sat as the doctor left.

"Mr. Crown, I'm an aide to Major Groesbeck, acting judge advocate of the Fifth Army Corps. You are the chief camera operator with the film company known as American Luxograph?"

Apprehensive, Paul said yes.

"You had a partner, one James Daws?" Paul nodded. "Will you describe him? As to character, I mean. What sort of fellow was he?"

Had? Was? What did that signify?

"Sometimes Jimmy's all right. He can be very agreeable if he feels like it. But he has—how should I say it? He has another side. He grew up poor and wants badly to be rich. I think he will often take the easy way over the right way. I try to work smoothly with him but I confess I've never liked him. Not the way you like a true friend."

"Did the two of you have trouble on the day of the fight at Las Guásimas?"

Startled, Paul said, "Yes, we did."

"Please describe what happened."

Paul said he and Jimmy had followed Colonel Wood's command that morning. "Up near the ranch house, I found Jimmy trying to pry gold teeth from the mouth of a dead soldier. He may have killed the soldier, I saw the soldier earlier and his only wound seemed to be a broken bone. When I tried to stop Jimmy's mutilation of the body, he turned on me. He tried to—*ersticken*—suffocate me, is that the right word?"

"It is if that's what he did. Continue."

"I prevented it and he ran off. I chased and caught him and we fought. He tried to choke me with the chain of a religious medal." Paul touched the scabby wounds on his throat. "I got the best of him but then a Spanish bullet hit me. He left me to the land crabs and the vultures and that's all I know. Why are you asking?"

Criswell reached into the pocket of his clean blue blouse for a small notebook; turned pages. "Daws showed up in Siboney that same afternoon. Approximately at dusk, he stepped onto one of the fishing boats docked at the village pier. A motorized vessel." Paul recalled Jimmy's studying the boats when they arrived.

"Daws attempted to hire the boat to run him to Key West. He offered a good sum, so the captain was agreeable. We keep a sentry posted at the pier. The man on duty that night was a Corporal Bray. He overheard Daws hiring the captain and advised him that the fishing boats were temporarily under the control of Admiral Sampson and General Shafter, for military use only. Daws stepped on the boat and insisted he was going to Key West. Private Bray ordered him off the boat under penalty of arrest. Daws pulled a knife, stabbed Bray in the stomach, and threw him in the water. By now it was almost dark, no one saw the incident except the captain, or realized there was trouble until the sentry cried out."

"What happened then?"

"Bray's cries were heard by soldiers on the beach, who pulled him from under the pier where he'd hooked an arm on a piling to save himself from drowning. Amid all the confusion, Daws must have terrorized the captain because the fishing vessel put out for Key West. Corporal Bray related his story to the surgeons, but he expired before he could depose under oath. Therefore we have no legally admissible statement to use against Daws."

"And Jim escaped?"

At last, Lieutenant Criswell smiled. "To the contrary. Shortly after he stabbed Bray and commandeered the boat, we alerted the Key West station. When the fishing boat docked on Saturday and Daws stepped ashore, he was arrested. Little attention was paid to the captain. He pulled away from the pier at full throttle and escaped to sea. He can't be found. So I am here to ask for a deposition from you, Mr. Crown. If you'll make a formal statement under oath, and sign charges of attempted murder against James Daws, we can put him in prison where he belongs. You're our only hope of justice for Private Bray and his family."

"Of course I'll sign charges. Jim was a bad actor—isn't that the American expression?"

Criswell nodded and stood up. "Pay us a visit as soon as you're able. Anyone can direct you. And thank you."

"Certainly, Lieutenant. Goodbye."

Paul lay down again, strengthened by the knowledge that his testimony would put Jimmy Daws in prison. Sometimes there was a measure of justice in the world after all.

On Sunday afternoon Dr. Winter escorted another visitor through the maze of wounded on the floor. Sourly, the physician said, "You're a popular fellow, Crown. There he is, Mr. Radcliffe."

Michael snatched a stained white handkerchief from his breast pocket and waved it under his nose. "The smell in this place! Is it the reek of wounds, or medical ignorance?"

He said it loudly, so the retreating Winter would hear. Winter slammed the connecting door normally kept open.

"Indeed there you are," Michael said, leaning on his walking stick. His face, normally porridge-pale, was red and peeling. A folded and yellowing newspaper stuck out of a side pocket. "Taken me forever to find you. I never thought to look here, I had an ominous feeling you'd been killed in that dirty little scrap on Friday. The doctor gave me a rough account of what happened to you. You're a nervy chap, Paul, but you take too many risks. I wrote a perfectly satisfactory dispatch about Las Guásimas without leaving the cantina."

Michael looked considerably grubbier and tattier than he had last Thursday; a bit like the Rhukov of old. His white flannel suit bore streaks and smudges of dirt, and two sinister dark brown stains. The white canvas vamps of his fine black shoes were water-stained. Even his gold-wire spectacles hadn't been spared; one earpiece was badly bent.

And his beautiful straw boater was missing. Paul questioned him about it. Michael said, "Whores follow wars. The former can be as violent as the latter. Please don't ask me to be more explicit." Paul laughed.

"Have you been forward at all, Michael?"

"A mile or two up the main road, yesterday. Pretty damn dull it was. Here's something more exciting. As promised, I sent off my message to London. Built you up splendidly. His Inkiness replied that he is indeed keen to organize a picture company. So, when you come to London, dear Papa Otto wants to interview you personally. Until then, stay away from aggressive men, white or brown, equipped with bullets."

Michael left soon after, saying the smells were intolerable reminders of his former life. Halfway to the door, he stopped. "Oh, here. Want this?" He waved the newspaper from his side pocket. "Mr. Hearst's yellow rag from New York. Two weeks old."

"Is there anything in it besides this war?"

"Just the usual collection of the sad, the sensational, and the nauseating. Two innocent children burned to death in a tenement because the fire escape was in disrepair. Another truculent pronouncement from Kaiser Bill. Some society bloke sent to his reward by the bit of fluff he was keeping on the side. Bedding sale at the R. H. Macy store—"

"It's hard to sit up, I don't think I want to do it to read old news."

"Fine, I'll chuck it. Cheerio."

Paul was elated by Otto Hartstein's message. Despite the heat and the continual harrowing outcries of the wounded, he felt a good deal better, his own pain notwithstanding. First Criswell and then Michael—two stunning surprises since he awoke in the hospital house. Certainly there couldn't be more.

It wasn't the first time he was wrong.

108

Julie

THAT SAME SUNDAY AFTERNOON, on the terrace at Belle Mer, Julie confronted her mother across the green iron table.

"You scandalized everyone when you refused to attend the funeral, Juliette."

"The scandal began before that, Mama. We couldn't hush up what happened. That Bill was shot by a woman of low repute whom he kept in the city. Bill was my husband in name only. He abused me—hurt me physically—beginning with our wedding night."

"You never told me this. Not a word."

"Would you have listened? Would you have believed me?"

Nell sipped tea from a Spode cup. She looked embittered. And suddenly, fixing her eye on her daughter, she looked hostile.

She had arrived from Chicago on a sparkling cool afternoon; temperate for late June. She was, as always, elegantly and correctly dressed in a conservative gown with heavy braid embroidery, a satin underbodice and satin belt. In the entrance hall she had taken off a smart felt hat draped with ostrich plumes, handing it to the maid along with her umbrella. Everything was black; gown, braid, plumes, umbrella—everything. Julie wore a stiff white linen yachting skirt and a shirtwaist of white foulard with navy polka dots; very summery and gay. Nell found it another subject for disapproval:

"Let me also say I find your attire outrageous. Couldn't you at least wear a black armband?"

Looking quite composed, Julie gazed at her mother. *Don't let her see how it feels inside* . . . "Mama, why should I? I don't mourn Bill, he was a bad man."

"Surely you loved him a little—"

"Not an iota. I love Paul. Mr. Crown's nephew—the boy Papa drove off. I've never loved anyone but him."

Nell struck her cup down hard on the saucer. Julie heard the crack. Never mind, there was money for another. There was money for ten thousand saucers and cups. In his masculine smugness, his confidence in his own power and dominance, Elstree had never adjusted his will to take into account his wife's growing and unconcealed antipathy. He might have done so if she'd borne him an heir, but it hadn't happened. As a consequence, she inherited everything.

Nell raised her voice. "I do not approve of your behavior."

"Well, I'm sorry, Mama. I'm afraid you no longer have anything to say about it."

Nell sat all the way back in her iron chair, gripping the arms. Anxious, Julie watched her mother closely, waiting for the next assault.

Unexpectedly, it took the form of tender entreaty. Nell rose and rounded the table. She was extremely frail; more than a little tottery. Her palm fell gently to Julie's high-piled hair. Julie tilted her head away from the contact. Nell's cheeks showed spots of pink suddenly. She touched Julie again, pitching her voice low.

"What have you done to your beautiful hair? It's so dull. You've not cared for it properly."

"There are more important things—"

"Than womanly beauty? Oh, how wrong. How wrong." The stroking hand moved up and down, seductively. "Come home. Home to Chicago. I'll make it shine again."

Terrified birds beat their wings in the cage of Julie's breast. *Be strong, be strong.* Aunt Willis had again tried to encourage her when she paid a visit to Chicago last March. The moment Elstree met Willis he detested her, just as Papa had. Speaking privately to her aunt, Julie had confessed that her marriage was sham, and the only person she loved, or ever would, was Paul. She didn't tell her aunt about her plan to leave Bill because at that time it was amorphous, nothing about it certain except her need to escape. By her mere presence Aunt Willis strengthened her. She drew on that strength now.

"Juliette. Julie, my sweet baby—I insist you come home. You know I'm not well. I'm feeling short of breath this very moment—"

"Mama." Julie took her mother's wrist in a gentle but firm grasp. She lifted Nell's hand away from her hair. "I almost destroyed my own life by giving in to you. I think I have done enough for your health. More than any daughter should. It's time I looked after my own."

"*Juliette.*"

Nell's mouth worked like that of a hooked fish, silently. Her ringed hand groped behind her for the table's edge. She staggered, but she found the iron chair with uncanny accuracy. *What a consummate actress.* Julie had never thought of her mother that way before. *She will have to find a new role, this play is over.*

She tried to remain solicitous; soft-spoken. "I'm sorry you're ill, Mama. We have an excellent doctor in the village, Dr. Lohman. I'll go in and telephone him at once."

She started for the French doors. Nell reeled into her chair, the horror of betrayal in her eyes. "I don't want a doctor. I want an obedient daughter."

Julie stopped and turned around. She shook her head.

"I am going to telephone the doctor. You sit there, Mama. Rest."

The physician arrived in his shay within the hour. By then Nell had called for her carriage, and her luggage, and left, with one parting thrust.

"You have grown into a wicked woman. I don't know how it happened. I gave you everything. All of my experience, all of my love. I suffered the filthy, unbearable pain of bringing a child into this world and this is how the child repays me. You must have fallen under the spell of sluts like my sister. I disown you. My door is closed to you forever. You will never see me again."

109

Dutch

MONDAY. TWILIGHT. Paul awoke with a sense of someone standing near. Opened his eyes to a gleam of a golden star on a shoulder strap.

The face surmounted by silver hair combed straight back was exactly as he remembered it from the moment he stumbled through the front door on Michigan Avenue, although tropic sun had reddened the skin. The mustache and imperial were typically neat. But the brown eyes held an uncharacteristic nervousness.

"Paul. *Mein lieber Neffe!*" My dear nephew.

"Uncle Joe—"

"Will you allow me a short visit?"

"Of course—certainly," Paul said, not sure it was a wise reply. Savage feelings were already stirring. This was the moment he'd yearned for and, at the same time, dreaded.

"Is this too great a surprise, my presence here?"

"No, sir. I've known for some time that you're attached to General Wheeler's staff. I saw you from afar in Tampa."

"But chose not to make yourself known."

"Uncle Joe—please—sit. You'll find a stool over there by the wall."

Eight other casualties were being treated in the room, all of them, like Paul, lying on the floor. Two of the men were awake, openly staring and listening. Uncle Joe noticed the attention. "Are you able to walk?" he said to Paul.

"If I go slowly. I was up this morning for half an hour, sitting in the window watching the sea."

"Could we go outside and talk? I noticed a bench. Come, take my hand."

Paul grasped the strong fingers with his right hand, pushed with his left, and got up smoothly, though not without pain. "Lean on me. Put your arm across my shoulder." Paul almost smiled; there was the old, unconscious tone of command. But he obeyed without objection. It made things easier.

"It's pleasant out here this evening," Uncle Joe said as they left the malodorous house. "Quite warm—this way." In a moment Paul was seated on the bench with his bare feet in the sand. The setting sun flamed on the sea and shore. Through the open windows of a second house a short way down the beach, women in gingham dresses could be seen moving back and forth with brooms, basins, trays. Another woman, middle-aged and thin, was outside, hanging wet sheets on a clothesline. He'd been told the women were American Red Cross volunteers, led by Miss Clara Barton, who was quite famous in the states. Dr. Winter and the other American surgeons refused to explain why the volunteer help was restricted to the Cubans.

Lifting his sheathed saber out of the way, General Joe Crown seated himself next to his nephew. Paul asked, "How did you find me?"

"Things have been hectic, as you might suspect. Only this afternoon did I have a few moments to look over the roster of our military and civilian wounded. I was astonished to find the name Paul Crown. This is the first moment I could get away from my duties to see if it really was you. On the roster you also have a middle name, in parentheses. Dutch."

"That's mostly what I'm called anymore."

"You're one of these moving pictures fellows, I was told. Like Mr. Bitzer from New York."

"Yes. I work for a company in Chicago."

"I want to hear all about it. I want to know everything that's happened. But first, Paul, I must say this to you. I made a dreadful mistake. I wronged you by turning you out. I learned that in a very private and telling way. I'll try to explain, if you wish, but before I do—"

He broke off, sitting stiffly, shoulders squared. He was the perfect military man, save for the uncontrollable tears.

"—I must ask your forgiveness. I won't be surprised if you refuse me."

Paul looked at his hands. "It's true I had terrible angry feelings for a long time after I left"—*and I still have some*—"but I never stopped being your blood relative, or forgot the many kindnesses you showed me. I have made mistakes too. We ought to forgive each other, I think."

Uncle Joe put his hand over Paul's, holding tightly. Paul was near to crying himself. "Thank you," his uncle whispered. *"Thank you."*

A salt breeze was coming off the water, refreshing after the rank smells of the hospital house. Uncle Joe composed himself. "This picture business. I remember you spoke of it before. Please tell me about it."

"It's a profession I've come to love. Also, I seem to have a talent for it. I could never say that about anything else. I always wanted to draw, be an artist, you know. This fulfills that wish. With one difference. Now people can recognize the subject of my pictures." His uncle laughed.

As briefly as he could, Paul described Wex Rooney, and the instruction Rooney gave him in the art and craft of still photography. Next came Colonel R. Sidney Shadow III:

"A profane man. Fraudulent in many ways. But I like him. From the colonel, who isn't a colonel at all, I learned how to do what I'm doing now. It's what I propose to do for the rest of my life."

"You learned this in the Levee district? How did you survive in that sink of iniquity?"

"Very well, actually. I grew up in the streets of Berlin, remember."

The general stroked his beard. "I have heard of these living pictures, naturally. But I've never seen one."

"Very understandable, respectable folk don't go to them. I'm convinced that will change. The living pictures can do much more than entertain. They can educate. Bring the whole world to people who otherwise would never see it. Pictures can show great events like this war. Friday, before I was wounded, I filmed scenes near Las Guásimas. I'm not sure my film will survive the heat and damp, but if it does, the pictures will be shown at Pflaum's Music Hall in Chicago." He looked at his uncle. "I would like you to come see them. Perhaps you'll change your mind about their worth."

"I will come." Uncle Joe gripped his hand again. "I promise."

They continued to talk as the twilight shaded into dark, with thousands of stars alight over the Cuban coast. Paul asked many questions.

"How are Fritzi and Carl?"

"Fritzi is more insistent than ever about a stage career. Carl attends his private school in New York. He has learned to play the game of football. It isn't a gentleman's game in my opinion, not like baseball. But he is very good at it. He is not very good at his studies."

"And Cousin Joe? Do you know where he is?"

"Alas, we don't. He's never come home, nor written. We've engaged Pinkerton's National Detective Agency several times, but they can't locate him. At intervals your aunt receives curious souvenirs in the mail, sent anonymously. Stalks of wheat. Little candies shaped like California oranges. She feels Joe Junior mailed them to her to say he's all right. But the last one arrived months and months ago, with none since. She's fearful something has happened." Heavily, he added, "She has never gotten over the loss of Joe Junior. She never will. I bear the responsibility."

Carefully, Paul said, "You know, Uncle, Cousin Joe didn't rebel against you to hurt you. He only wanted to be like you. Independent. Strong. His own person."

Steel came into the general's voice. "He was not like me, Paul. He was a radical."

"But he truly loved you and Aunt Ilsa. He just got mixed up with some bad people, and bad ideas." After a hesitation, he said the rest. "Did you never have an idea that was wrong? Not one? If you didn't, you must be a saint."

"Oh yes, I've had many. Many! I finally confronted that fact in Tampa. You astonish me, Paul. You were a boy when you came to us in that terrible storm. Now you speak like a man."

Paul smiled. "I was twenty-one on the fifteenth of this month. I have lived like a man for a long time now."

Another silence. The surf purled. Horsemen galloped through Siboney, shouting.

Paul said, "You spoke of an experience in Tampa—"

"Yes. I learned many things, from a person you'll never meet. A woman. On very short acquaintance, she saw me more clearly than I had ever seen myself. I told her about you, and Joe Junior, and she said I must have caused the trouble by attempting to play God, when there is only One who can do that. I believe"—the confession came hard, but when it came, it was firm—"I have been too insistent on authority. Control. Everything in place, perfectly correct. Correct as I saw it! This woman you'll never meet—and your aunt will never know about, although nothing improper occurred—she helped me to see that I had been tearing myself apart, that I had torn our family apart, by continually seeking something that is unobtainable within a household or the world at large. I think I began my misguided pursuit because of what I saw in the Civil War. The horrible disorder. Death and cruel injury meted out solely by chance. I denied that part of human existence by trying to purge it from my own life. But reasons are not excuses. In my pursuit of some kind of rational order I went too far. I can't escape guilt by saying it's a common failing of Germans, passion for order, although it is. I must accept full blame for my mistakes and their consequences. I have. I do."

There was a long pause. Paul sat very still. Uncle Joe cleared his throat.

"You will return to Chicago when the war is over, Paul?"

"I will."

"Your aunt will be overjoyed. Your cousins, too. We will welcome you back to the family eagerly, if you'll allow that. I will use my contacts to help you with this new career. I know a great many important and influential—"

Paul interrupted. "I won't be staying in Chicago, Uncle." In a few sentences, he explained about Michael, and Lord Yorke, and London.

"London? You intend to take a job there?"

"If it's offered."

"You'll leave America?"

"My profession lets me live anywhere."

"But America is your home now! You made it so."

And circumstances unmade it.

Sensing Paul's resurgent anger, Joe Crown said, "If this is because of me, I beg you once more to forgive me. I'll do anything in my power to make amends."

"What happened between us isn't the reason I'm leaving. I lost the one thing in America I wanted most. The one person."

"The Vanderhoff girl."

"Yes. I wanted to make a home with her but she married that rich man. It's time I explore some other place. Some other country."

"What can I possibly do to change your mind?"

"Nothing." There was just the slightest edge in Paul's next words. "The control of the matter is mine."

The general was stricken silent. Paul was tired; his wound was hurting badly. "I believe I should go in, Uncle."

"Yes, certainly, I've kept you too long."

Uncle Joe helped him to the stoop of the house. "I'm going to leave this place soon," Paul said. "I must film more of the fighting."

"You have a few days yet, we're still struggling to move men and materiel to forward positions. I'll visit again, but if my duties prevent it, I'll look for you in the field."

"I will do the same, Uncle."

"Excellent. Till then—"

The general put his hands on Paul's shoulders.

"Please take care of yourself."

He gave his nephew a clumsy but fervent embrace and walked away quickly, striding up the beach with fine German precision. Paul watched until he disappeared in the dark.

110

Willis

A YAWL took them ashore in choppy sea Sunday morning. The harried doctor in charge of the Cuban house welcomed them warmly. In fact he almost wept when, through an interpreter, Clara described the supplies available from the ship, and said that she and the other women were willing to work without stint until the hospital house was clean and sanitary.

It desperately needed their attention. Little piles of sand and debris clogged the corners of the dingy rooms. Mosquitoes hovered. The smells were vile. Pus, blood, urine, feces. Two dozen Cuban soldiers were scattered throughout the house. A few were fortunate enough to rest on scraps of blanket or on grimy pillows that had lost most of their down filling. The others had the bare wood floor. Willis identified three who were almost surely dying. All of them had torn white trousers that were uniformly filthy, but fewer than half of them had shirts. Their bandages were dirty rags. They were inmates of a little hell of suffering, and Willis was unbelievably glad to be in the midst of it. At last, the Red Cross unit was fulfilling its mission. Willis hadn't seen a newspaper since they sailed, except for one old *New York World* with pages missing. She didn't care, there was work to do. She got down on her knees with a soapy bucket and began to scrub floors, she and the other volunteer, Olive Shay.

Miss Barton marched through the house like a field general, trailed by the grateful physician and the interpreter. "We have kerosene for lamps, we must use them to light these rooms. We have screen wire coming ashore, we'll cover the windows so we don't have all these flies and insects."

Two orderlies, ragged boys, were preparing to roll one of the wounded onto a blanket stretcher. The soldier was raving. His skin had the saffron tint of jaundice.

"That man's deathly ill, why are you moving him?"

In a hushed voice the Cuban physician said, *"Fiebre amarilla."* He rattled out several more sentences in Spanish. Scrubbing in the next room, Willis listened. She heard one phrase clearly. *Vómito negro.* She'd heard it before. The interpreter translated for Miss Barton. "Yellow fever. In the night he threw up blood. It's a certain sign. He must go to the quarantine camp in the hills, he can't stay here."

Clara Barton quickly inspected the young man. She shook her head in a sad way. "And he'll go nowhere else." She waved the orderlies on.

Willis felt a cold wind of mortality brushing her. From the place where she was scrubbing, near a window, she could see the young boys carrying their burden through the deep sand to the camp, wherever it was. The death camp.

She blew a straggly lock of graying hair out of her eyes and plunged the brush in the bucket. Soap smelling of disinfectant cascaded from the bristles. She locked both hands on the wooden back and scrubbed as if devils from hell were sitting on her bent back.

Willis slept four hours on Sunday night. The women were organized to sleep in shifts, occupying three cots crowded into what had once been a pantry or storeroom. When Willis awoke, she washed walls. She changed bandages sodden with yellow pus and brown blood. She brought bottles or pans to the wounded and helped them while they relieved themselves; stood at the tiny iron stove in purgatorial heat, frying mush she served with a special concoction of stewed dried apples and prunes, a dish they called Red Cross Cider. She assisted with the amputation of a soldier's mangled foot and only felt like throwing up once, and then just for a few seconds. Clara did no less than any of them. She led them by example.

Despite the heat, and the insects, and the stenches, and the heartbreaking cries of the young Cubans, there was an exhilaration in being here; a sense of purpose and meaning Willis found missing from her life at other times. Even men couldn't provide satisfaction to match it. To be happiest, she thought ruefully, she should have been born into some alternate universe of constant irrevocable disaster and suffering.

Shortly after noon on Monday, Dr. Lesser brought a visitor, a slim man in a bedraggled uniform. On the collar tabs of his sweated blue shirt he wore small metal crosses; medical corps emblems already tarnished and pitted by the climate.

"This is another of our volunteers, Miss Willis Fishburne," Lesser said as he made the rounds between the cots. "Willis, this is Major Lagarde, chief surgeon in Siboney."

Lagarde shook her hand primly. "Miss Fishburne. My pleasure. It's amazing what you and the other ladies have done here in a very short time."

Willis took a tobacco sack and a paper from her apron. "Damn shame your doctors think we're unfit to offer the same help to American boys."

Dr. Lesser rolled his eyes behind the major, who was apologetic. "Yes—well—possibly—steps will be taken to correct that error."

Yes, and we'll have a snowfall by noon, too, she thought as she went out to smoke. She was astonished when Clara came dashing in about five o'clock that afternoon, highly excited.

"Ladies, attention. Tomorrow we begin cleaning and tending the American house. Major Lagarde just issued the order. Dr. Winter is preparing a written apology."

Early on Tuesday, June 28, Clara Barton and her women invaded the American house. The routine was much the same. Sweep, tack up screens, wash down walls, scrub floors, set up cots, burn filthy blankets, cook, pass drinking water. They were able to devote more time to the tasks than they had in the Cuban house because there were several Army surgeons handling the medical chores, assisted by orderlies. Willis noticed that the men guarded their responsibilities jealously, leaving only the dirtiest jobs to the nurses and volunteer helpers. It irked her no end, but Clara said nothing, so she didn't either.

Dr. Winter, a large jowly man, tended to snarl when he asked any of the women to do something. He'd been strongly reprimanded, and he resented it as he resented the presence of women in his little domain. But he didn't try to impede their work in any way. He was merely a cross, curt, self-important son of a bitch at all times.

Throughout the day they heard occasional news from officers and noncoms coming and going. The campaign against Santiago had bogged down while men and supplies were moved forward over a single rutted road which had once borne the proud name Camino Real. There was an almost lighthearted air in Siboney; a great deal of bragging and boasting about the Las Guásimas victory, as though that were the whole war.

By Tuesday evening, three days of unremitting work began to tell on Willis. She had spells of double vision and severe aches in her finger joints, knees, and back. Even so, she decided she should familiarize herself with the names of the patients. Until now they had been merely faces.

"That one is a civilian?" Willis said, studying a roster blotted and stained in many places.

Hester Huff, one of the trained nurses, said, "Yes, he's listed as a camera operator. There are several with the Army, I understand."

"What in the world is a camera operator?"

"He photographs those motion pictures they show at variety halls. Have you ever seen any?"

"Once, at Hammerstein's in New York. Pretty trivial stuff. It's a novelty. Won't last." Hester agreed. "What happened to the young man?"

"A Mauser bullet hit him in the back. Dr. Winter said he was lucky, it passed through, only breaking two ribs. He's already protesting that he has to leave."

At the moment he wasn't protesting but sleeping, on his side, one bare shoulder showing above the sheet. The boy had a muscular build and a lot of unkempt brown hair, long and shaggy at the back. Willis said, "I've noticed he has quite a few visitors, including that brigadier with the beard." She tilted the roster in the direction of a flickering kerosene lamp. "What's his name? I can't read it."

"Paul Crown. He's General Joe Crown's nephew."

In the small hours of Wednesday morning, he awoke. He called for a drink. Willis had been waiting for the moment all night, her stomach hurting from nervous excitement.

She'd been in and out of the house many times, rolling and smoking too many cigarettes, pacing up and down the beach, unable to relax, or even contemplate sleep. Surely it was the same one. Surely it wasn't merely a coincidence of names. Another physician, Dr. Burmeister, had confirmed that Brigadier Crown came from Chicago.

"Here you are, young man." Willis handed the tin cup to the sleepy patient. Then she put down the stool she'd carried to his cot. Across the aisle, a wounded

Rough Rider sobbed in his sleep. The kerosene light on a crate by the door was trimmed low; the room was quite dark.

The young man made a small sound of discomfort as he hitched onto his hip and braced on his elbow to drink. Over the cup's rim his friendly blue eyes traveled from her face to the stool, curious. Willis said nothing.

He drained the cup and returned it. It was easier now that she was seated. "Thank you very much." A German accent. Oh, God, there could hardly be any doubt . . .

She pulled her stool closer. "Young man, my name is Miss Fishburne. I understand yours is Paul Crown?"

"That's right." They both spoke softly.

"Where are you from, Paul?"

"The company I work for is located in Chicago. I have lived there since I emigrated from Berlin."

Willis ran her tongue over her lips, which were unexpectedly dry. "Are you by any chance related to a Chicago brewer named Joseph Crown?"

A wariness sprang into his eyes. "Yes, he's here, with the Army. General Crown. I am his nephew. Do you know him?"

"Not personally. But I know you. You're the one. You are the one."

"What do you mean?" Paul strained up, as if by sitting, bringing himself closer to her, he might understand. "I'm sure we've never met before."

"That's true. Lie back, rest—I have things to say to you." Gently, she pushed him down again.

"There's a girl named Julie Vanderhoff, you know her, don't you?"

"I do. I mean I did."

"So do I. She's my niece. My first name is Willis."

He gasped. "She talked about you, often. Very fond of—*agh!*" He'd pushed up again; the exertion wrenched something. He fell back, breathing hard. Willis ran her hand over his forehead. Cold and damp.

"Listen to me," she said softly. "You know Julie's married. Elstree, the department store heir. Her mother, my dear considerate sister, forced her into it. Julie detests her husband, and rightly so. I visited her in March, in Chicago. I was introduced to Elstree for the first time, and within five minutes I wanted to kidnap her from his clutches. He's a wastrel, and arrogant. What's more, he's a notorious philanderer. I know this for a fact because I had him investigated by a detective agency when I got back to New York. Mr. Elstree spends time with prostitutes and kept women nearly as often as you and I brush our teeth. Julie could find enough evidence to divorce him and fourteen others, why the devil she hasn't, I don't know."

He was too stunned to speak. Willis was able to take a deep breath.

"This is the long and short of it, Paul. Julie's miserable. It's you she loves, no one else. She told me so in Chicago. I'm positive she'd leave Elstree in a moment if you asked her. As soon as you set foot in the States again, you go to her. Steal her away from that immoral bastard, damn the divorce laws. Go to her the minute you're back. If you don't, both of you will regret it the rest of your lives."

Reflecting the kerosene light, his blue eyes had a feverish gleam. "Where can I find her, Miss Willis?"

"She spends summers on Long Island. Southampton. Elstree has a mansion on the ocean. Belle Mer is its name . . ."

111

Dutch

ON THE FIFTH DAY after the Las Guásimas fight—Wednesday, June 29, 1898 —Paul walked out of the American hospital house shortly after sunrise.

On the freshly swept stoop, Miss Fishburne hugged him to her flat bosom, kissed his cheek, and once more charged him to find Julie as soon as possible. He promised.

Dr. Winter appeared in the doorway and once again warned him that he wasn't recovered, and was ignoring the best medical advice, at his peril. Sick of the man and his pomposity, Paul said, "Yes, Doctor, if I die I'll remember that. Thank you for your good care."

Winter glowered. Paul hobbled away in the ankle-deep sand, his taped bandages itching under his shirt, his back wound still hellishly painful. His head was awhirl with all that had happened while he lay on his cot. Julie . . . did he dare believe there was a chance?

Not yet. He'd tell no one. Not Uncle Joe, and certainly not Michael. He would heed Miss Fishburne's charge and investigate, swiftly, the moment he was back. But he wouldn't—daren't—expect a happy outcome, much as he longed for it. He mustn't even try to imagine what it would be like.

One more heartbreak would be too much.

He visited the cantina. Yes, his grip was safe. He paid the proprietor another dollar to continue to guard it, fortified himself with a *cerveza*, and set out for the lagoon where he'd fought with Jimmy. Reaching it would require a hike of two or three hours, very hard in his weakened state. He never for an instant entertained a thought of not going.

The Santiago road was choked with six-mule wagons hauling supplies to the forward positions around Sevilla, or returning empty to Siboney for new cargo. The daily downpours had flooded several creek crossings and turned the Camino Real to mire. A stalled driver told Paul the supply convoys had been moving up and down the road since Saturday. He began to tally the evidence, counting wagons abandoned because of broken axles or other mishaps. He got tired of counting when he reached twenty-five. Finally he was able to veer off the road and into the tall grass, where he'd chased Jimmy.

The sight of the lagoon, the memory of what nearly happened to him there, sent awful shivers up and down his back.

He began to search the surrounding grass. He found the canvas bag almost at once. It lay where it had fallen.

Mold covered the bag, and beetles had crawled inside. Very likely the exposed magazines were ruined, but at least he could take them back to Shadow as proof that he'd tried. He slung the bag over his shoulder and went in search of the bivouac of the 10th Cavalry.

The first sergeant of Ott Person's troop turned him away brusquely:

"Ott ain't here. He's bad sick. Night before last they took him to the yellow fever camp."

A spur of the old railway to Santiago ran up into the foothills of the Sierra Maestra. The fever camp had been established at the end of the spur, because of the convenience of shipping patients there on open flatcars pulled by a small switch engine. On Wednesday evening, exhausted though he was from all his walking, Paul rode the train to the camp.

He sat on a flatcar with his legs dangling down. He was the only passenger, traveling with eight pine coffins held in place with chains.

In the jungle on either side of the track, tropical birds whistled and cawed. It was almost dark, the air heavy with humidity. He constantly slapped insects. His bandages had started to smell. Miss Fishburne would change the dressing tomorrow.

He had talked with her about yellow fever late that afternoon. There was no defense against the disease, she said. You either caught it or you didn't. She described the symptoms. A furry tongue, constipation, sometimes nausea and vomiting, and, always, a sudden high fever. Paul remembered Ott's rubbing his sweaty face when he visited on the coolest evening.

Severe prostration, headache, and muscle pain were followed by the final symptoms of jaundice, poisoned urine, and what Miss Fishburne called hematemesis. "In soldier's terms, the black vomit. Blood coming up. A few recover at that stage, but most don't. The doctors have no idea of the cause of yellow fever."

He wondered whether he was risking himself with this excursion. Well, it didn't matter, he had to see about Ott's condition.

The little train slowed. A low-hanging palm frond brushed his cheek, like the tickling hand of death. Ahead he saw lanterns, blurred splotches in the night. The switch engine's drivers gave a long squeal as the train reached a rusty turntable at the end of the spur. Paul jumped down and walked toward the lanterns. One hung over the door of a guard booth, the others above a new gate of unpainted lumber. Beyond the gate, lamplit tents were scattered on the hillsides. Here and there a solitary figure moved among them.

When he reached the gate he was able to read the sign over the entrance. The legend was painted in large red letters.

WARNING
—QUARANTINE CAMP—
U.S. Army Medical Corps
No Admittance Except by Authorization

Not far inside the gate stood a wagon piled with white sacks. Their size and shape registered belatedly; each held a body.

He walked to the wooden guard booth. The sentry stepped out with his hand on the butt of his revolver. Paul tugged off his straw hat so the lantern shone on his face. Before he could speak, the guard said, "No civilians allowed here. You'll have to go right back."

"I came to ask about a friend. Corporal Person, 10th Negro Cavalry."

The sentry reached inside the booth for a stack of loose sheets held together by a spring clip. He leafed to the second page and tilted it under the lamp. "Othello Person. You're a tad late. He died this morning. He's in one of those bags on the wagon. I can't let you any closer. You have to go back. Sorry."

Paul turned around and stumbled toward the switch engine. Ott's eyes seared his memory. Ott's face; and his entreaties.

Ain't no place on God's earth won't disappoint you sometimes, Heine.

I don't know of a better country, and I've read on the subject.

Our country needs folks like you. Don't run off and leave everything to the mean ones, that fat-faced sarge and bastards like him.

Don't turn your back. Please don't . . .

In sorrow and confusion, Paul let the tears come.

That night he made his bed in the sand, against the wall of the Cuban hospital house, covered by a blanket Miss Fishburne brought to him. When he awoke in the morning, he was surprised at how deeply he'd slept. Perhaps it was to escape thoughts of Ott.

It was Thursday, the last day of June. Siboney was a ghost camp. Since Saturday, nearly fifteen thousand men had been moved forward beyond Las Guásimas. In the tent where he waited for Lieutenant Frank Criswell, a garrulous sergeant said the supply wagons had gotten so bogged down, cavalrymen had been leading trains of pack mules back and forth from Siboney. General Shafter still insisted he had to resupply the troops by any available means, even though it cost precious time. Time the Spaniards could use to prepare their rifle pits and trenches, barb wire and breastworks and blockhouses around Santiago.

"Grapevine says there's a Spanish relief column," the sergeant told him. "Near on to four thousand men, marching from Manzanillo. And ever' day we waste means one more day for rain, and the fevers. Mighty nasty things are bein' said about Pecos Bill 'cause of the delay. Some are callin' him plain incompetent. So now he's in a big damn hurry to attack." Lieutenant Criswell walked into the tent, inducing a sudden reticence in the sergeant.

With Criswell's help, Paul wrote his deposition, and signed it. "We had another signal from Key West," Criswell said then. "The provost court convened yesterday. Daws will be sent back to Illinois for trial." Criswell held up the limp foolscap sheets. "This should guarantee he'll go to prison."

A chapter closed. Paul was grateful.

He stood up too quickly. Criswell's face swam out of focus. He grabbed a tent pole and held tight. The dizziness passed.

"Lieutenant, if that's all—"

"Yes, we're finished. Where are you going now?"

"To load my camera with my last magazine, then walk up to the front."

"Better hurry. Word's out that the attack will be made tomorrow morning. After all the delay, Shafter wants to go against everything at once—the San Juan Heights and the fortifications at the village of El Caney, farther inland."

"Where is General Shafter's field headquarters?"

Criswell unrolled a map and pointed out a spot immediately north of the main road, between the village of Sevilla and a hill marked El Poso. "They carried the general up there in a huge chair like a throne, God knows where they found it. They fixed poles to it, and eight men hoisted it on their shoulders. Shafter looked like a rajah. I saw it and I'll never forget it. Thanks for helping me do my job, Dutch. Good luck with those pictures."

Travel to the forward area was hard; everything was moving that way—infantry, cavalry, artillery caissons drawn by sweating horses. In the distance, above the trees, floated a large football-shaped object, bright yellow; below it hung a basket gondola with many ropes dangling from it. It was the Signal Corps observation balloon, positioned somewhere over the Santiago road. Paul had heard about it but not seen it before.

He had one last magazine, four hundred feet, carefully loaded into the Luxograph with a prayer that the climate hadn't fogged it. If there was to be fighting, he must have pictures. He had to concentrate, forget Ott's death if he could, and Julie, and Uncle Joe. This was the moment when he was called to do his job.

He reached the headquarters about one in the afternoon. Tables and chairs were set out beneath trees festooned with Spanish moss. There was constant commotion; couriers leaving and arriving on foot, horseback, muleback. Officers arguing over maps. Paul assumed the largest white tent belonged to Shafter, who was nowhere in sight.

He unfolded his tripod about twenty feet from the conference tables. He got some stares, but no one interfered. At least not for five minutes. Then a balding officer with thick spectacles and pale pinkish skin stomped toward him. The officer had doffed his blouse in favor of a limp white shirt with sleeve garters.

"I'm Major Gilyard, what the devil is that contraption?"

"A moving picture camera." Paul's dislike of the man was instantaneous. "You haven't seen one before?"

"Back home I go to church, mister, I don't hang out in the tenderloin. What's your purpose here?"

"I understand General Shafter will be holding a council of war this afternoon. I want to photograph some of it for audiences in—"

Gilyard's saber flew from its sheath and slashed sideways, whacking a chip from the tripod, toppling the camera. Paul yelled, *"Was tun Sie, Dummkopf?"* What are you doing, stupid? As he leaned down to pick up the camera, Gilyard put the point of his sword against Paul's neck.

"Listen, you. I don't know what you said but pay attention to this. The general is suffering heat prostration, or something close to it. He won't permit himself to be photographed, he'll have you bayoneted first. If he doesn't, I will."

"Major."

Paul recognized Uncle Joe's voice before he turned and saw him. Uncle Joe was in shirt-sleeves and suspenders, his red cheeks gleaming in the heat.

"Put up that saber. We don't bully civilians, especially reporters."

"But he—"

"Put your sword up, Gilyard. Or go on report."

Gilyard's face turned redder than Uncle Joe's. He rammed the saber into the sheath and walked off muttering something about the damned volunteers.

Joe Crown shielded Paul from the others and spoke quietly. "Gilyard was right, Shafter's unbelievably touchy. Much criticism is falling on him. Roosevelt has spoken against him openly. Called him criminally negligent. I advise you not to risk more trouble by staying here. Photograph somewhere else."

"All right, Uncle Joe." Paul's eyes darted to the nearby officers, most of whom, excluding Gilyard, were paying no attention. "I heard the attack will begin tomorrow, is that right?"

"Yes, in the morning. Very early. It's no secret. We're going forward against the San Juan Heights and El Caney at the same time. I must go now." He gripped Paul's arm. "Take care of yourself."

"I will, Uncle. Thank you."

Uncle Joe gave him an affectionate smile and strode back toward the conference tables.

Troops continued to move forward all that night. At half past three, a thunder and lightning storm drenched the advance for half an hour. Paul took shelter under the bed of a foundered wagon and stripped off his shirt to wrap the camera. Soon he was chilled, his teeth chattering. No matter; he must have pictures.

Before dawn, Friday, July 1, white mist formed in the low places below the fortified heights protecting Santiago. The Americans confronted the heights from the far left, south of the main road, to the village of El Caney four miles north. The village was defended by a stone fort, El Viso. Smaller blockhouses and, presumably, trenches were waiting on the San Juan Heights.

At first light, General Lawton's division opened its attack against El Caney. Lawton's small battery of old three-inch field guns began to whack away at the Spanish entrenchments. By nine o'clock an advance was under way. The Spaniards defending the area enjoyed both superior visibility and artillery supremacy, and they had an additional advantage—the telltale smoke from every round of black powder fired by Lawton's men.

As Lawton was advancing, the left pressed forward along the Santiago road. A critical place in the advance was a low ford on the Aguadores River, a stream the Americans marked on their maps as the San Juan. The bright yellow observation balloon was hovering above the ford. Spanish guns quickly found the range and pierced the balloon. It deflated, sank, struck the trees by the ford, and draped over them limply. It provided a highly visible target for the enemy artillery, precisely locating the river crossing. By midmorning the ford of the Aguadores earned the name Bloody Ford.

Paul pushed toward the ford with the camera, among black cavalrymen advancing on foot, and a few men already wounded and stumbling to the rear. The roar of artillery and the crackle of rifle fire was constant. The smoke was heavy, tending to choke the lungs and make the eyes sting.

Nearing the ford, Paul came upon a lanky, hawk-faced civilian seated on a white horse at the roadside, seemingly oblivious to the shell bursts. The man, slightly pop-eyed, wore a black overcoat and a white sombrero. His blue eyes danced about, taking in every aspect of the scene. He looked hard at Paul's camera, then gave him an icy little smile. There was something almost unnatural about the man's calm. As if none of the danger or suffering affected him, only the martial spectacle.

Paul caught up with a white officer; the one who'd come to his room in Tampa. "Who was that civilian on horseback, Lieutenant?"

"Why, merely one of the gentlemen who promoted this war," Pershing said. "His yacht's anchored at Siboney. That's Hearst."

A thunderous burst overhead scattered shrapnel on the road. "Down!" Pershing shouted, a moment late. Two of his black soldiers fell, badly hit. The throat of one opened and spurted blood. Paul crouched, listening to the shrapnel slashing the foliage. Something struck the tripod. He found a sharp triangle of metal embedded in one leg. "Can't someone get that God damn balloon out of the trees?" a man yelled.

"Keep quiet, keep moving," Pershing said in a firm voice. All around him, Paul saw terrified faces; eyes huge with a realization that death was close. Close as the artillery firing from the San Juan Heights; close as the shell bursts that rained metal on the column struggling forward.

He followed Pershing and his men down to Bloody Ford.

The water at the ford was brown and swirling with darker streaks. Immediately to the right, toward El Caney, a pennon with a red cross identified a dressing station set up on the bank. In the center of the river, six officers sat on their horses, waving and calling encouragement to the men. "Hurry up." "Come on, lads." "Get across, you'll be safer." Frail Joe Wheeler was one of the six; Uncle Joe was another. All seemed astonishingly calm, though surely, inside, they must be churning with fear like everyone else.

Lieutenant Pershing jumped into the shallows at the ford. As each of his black soldiers reached the water, Pershing gave him a little nudge, a little pat, a supportive word. "Go on, Bob. That's it, Linc, straight across. Hurry up, now, don't stop."

Paul was standing just short of the water. The whistle of a shell made him look up. The first of Pershing's men were at midstream. There a stout black corporal lost his footing; he dropped his Springfield in the river, the unforgivable sin. Uncle Joe booted his horse forward and leaned far out of the saddle, extending his left arm so the soldier could grasp it.

He grabbed Uncle Joe's arm with both hands. The shell burst. Shrapnel ripped the water all around the men. A piece of it went into the corporal's head like a knife cleaving melon. As he sank, still holding Uncle Joe's arm and dragging him from the saddle, Paul saw a bright red blotch erupt on his uncle's left thigh. Uncle Joe's horse went down, but got up after it made a huge splash. Uncle Joe had managed to free his boots from the stirrups. "Get him out of there, save him," Paul shouted, quickly laying his camera at the roadside and jumping into the water.

Three other soldiers had gone down between Paul and his uncle. They blocked his way, and so did Lieutenant Pershing, who was angrily trying to stop two men fleeing to the rear.

Somehow Uncle Joe managed to keep a stiff arm on the shallow bottom, and his head above water, until a corpsman from the dressing station reached him and lifted him over his shoulder; Paul was still struggling to get around Pershing and the runaways, but he saw Uncle Joe's head bounce against the corpsman's back. His eyes were closed. Water streamed off his hair.

The corpsman staggered upstream toward the dressing station. Uncle Joe's leg trailed in the water, blood like a black dye pouring from it. Paul picked up his camera and wove through the underbrush toward the open-sided tent with the red pennon.

The corpsman laid the general on a litter seconds before Paul arrived. Uncle Joe's face was pale as milk. At the far side of the tent, a surgeon was sawing the leg of a black soldier biting down on a hickory baton while an orderly dribbled whiskey into the corner of his mouth. A white soldier without a shirt was on the nearest table. A haggard surgeon probed a large and exceedingly gory wound in the soldier's chest. The surgeon shouted at Paul. "Stay the hell out of here unless you're bleeding."

"This officer is my uncle. I want to know how badly he's hurt."

"For Christ's sake, I'm working on this one. Shoulder straps don't get you special attention here. You'll have to wait."

Paul watched Pershing's black soldiers pouring across the ford. The artillery and small-arms fire crashed without letup. "I can't wait. I will be back."

He shouldered the tripod and waded into the bloody river.

Beyond the Aguadores, the land opened out to another grassy plain broken here and there by barb wire fences. The plain ran upward to the San Juan Heights, and to a lower eminence on the right, Kettle Hill. Here Colonel Roosevelt led a fierce attack shortly after twelve o'clock.

All the commands had gotten horribly tangled. The cavalry's right was mixed into the infantry's left. Guidons and bellowing sergeants tried to reassemble their units, without much luck. Paul found himself in the middle of men from the 6th Infantry protecting themselves as best they could behind clumps of palmetto. There was a great deal of blood on the grass, and corpses were strewn about. On the heights, nothing could be seen of the Spaniards except for an occasional conical hat poking up near some large, well-kept farm buildings. The fire from up there was steady and decimating. It left no trace of smoke.

At 1:15, a furious *brrrr* from the left made Paul jump. Parker's Gatling Gun detachment, across the ford at last. The Americans now had mechanized fire to counter the artillery on the heights.

Officers shouted orders for an advance. Men stood up, raised their rifles, began moving forward. Across a broad front, the infantry and cavalry charged San Juan Hill at a rapid walk.

The Spaniards poured down their fire. Sheets of flame seemed to spring from the heights. Men in front staggered or swayed, then fell, sometimes with a strange and beautiful grace. Somewhere to the left, hidden by smoke and the terrain, the Gatlings drummed steadily.

Doubled over to make a small target, one of the military attachés ran up beside Paul. He scanned the forward line with field glasses. Paul knew him; Major de Grandpré, from France. The attaché shrugged in the direction of the advance. "Very foolish. But very gallant."

Paul set up the tripod. He reached for the crank.

There was a sudden burst of fire; a keening cry. Panting, Paul looked back; saw a scattering of dead and wounded. With his head spinning from heat, exertion, the strain on his wound, he hoisted the camera and ran a few steps more, into the lung-burning smoke.

The Gatlings roared. The Spanish fire cut down the Americans climbing the hill, infantry and cavalry, black and white, tangled together without organization but advancing steadily, without pause. Paul saw Roosevelt going up among black men from the 10th, brandishing a revolver, hallooing and waving them on.

He wanted pictures up there. Once more he slung the tripod over his shoulder and ran uphill through the smoke, toward the spurting flames that marked the crest.

The Spanish soldiers were tough fighters; they didn't give up easily. They poured heavy small-arms fire at the first Americans reaching the heights. Roosevelt was among them. He and some black cavalry and some of his Rough Riders were forced to shelter where they could, firing as the Spaniards readied a counter-charge. Paul lay prone just to the rear of the group. He lay embracing his tripod and practically kissing the camera, his right hand crushing his straw hat to his head, as if that would somehow stop a bullet.

He heard intimidating screams; watched the Spaniards rise from their trenches to attempt to overwhelm the attackers. Roosevelt kept shouting encouragement, risking himself by leaping up to fire his revolver. More and more soldiers were coming up the hill, and superior numbers made the difference, along with the devastating fire of the Gatling detachment. The countercharge quickly fell apart. The Spanish began retreating to the hills and vales lying between the heights and Santiago.

About half past four the shooting stopped. Paul was finishing his last frames, running out the magazine with the camera tilted to look into Spanish rifle pits. The stench in the pits was vile, and the contents gruesome. Dozens of dead soldiers in bloody seersucker uniforms lay where they had fought and fallen. One, a man with a bullet hole in his forehead, held his hat in a way that sug-gested doffing it to a lady.

Audiences at Pflaum's would probably loathe Paul's pictures of the dead bod-ies, and the rest of what he'd filmed, if it came out: the final slow climb to the summit by the blue and khaki line; the dash to surround a blockhouse and the farm buildings. The Spanish flag being torn down. He'd even cranked while an infantry major came upon a wounded Spaniard and killed him with three shots. The smoke-spurts from the officer's pistol showed clearly.

Before the Spaniard was hit by the first bullet, he shrieked for mercy. Americans would hate the scene because it disgraced one of their own. Paul hated it for a different reason. It was despicably inhuman. Then he thought of Wex and said to himself, *Yes, but the pictures are the truth, and people should see.*

It was possible to look out toward the southwest and clearly see the red-tiled adobes of Santiago a mile and a half away. Surely the Spaniards there saw the American flag floating over the Gatling-riddled blockhouse; surely they knew the end was coming.

Still, it was by no means a certainty yet. Down in the gentle vales between the heights and the town, hundreds of Spanish soldiers were reestablishing their lines. Dirt flew as they wielded their trenching tools.

A man in a boater and white raincoat came walking along the exposed hilltop, past a Spanish two-pounder canted crazily, one wheel shot to pieces. It was Crane.

Paul was too tired to do more than nod hello. In the drifting smoke he cranked the camera with an arm he wished he could break off, so badly did it hurt. He was still filming the rifle pit. Crane walked around him, out of camera range, and gazed down.

A shot rang out. Another. Crane took off his boater, calmly turned and peered at the shallow valleys, the source of the shots. Some of the Spanish soldiers were beginning a harrying fire.

An infantry officer wagged a pistol at them as he jogged by. "You civilians get off this hill, you're not impressing anyone." Crane and Paul paid no attention. Several more shots resounded. Paul heard the familiar buzz of Mauser bullets.

He checked the counter and saw he'd run out of film. He sank down on his haunches beside the tripod. Suddenly he remembered Uncle Joe. He must find out how he was. But not this moment. Not for a bit. He was spent.

"Incredible, eh, Dutch? In the *Red Badge* I only imagined it. This is ten times worse."

Paul nodded dumbly.

"I wonder how Dick Davis is feeling. I wonder if he still thinks we're a race of gentlemen. Well, I'd better go on. See as much as I can. Watch out for yourself, now."

"And you, Stephen."

Jotting in a notebook, Crane walked away. Paul saw him look into another rifle pit and shake his head in solemn wonder.

112

The General

SIX PILLARS OF SMOKE rose from Santiago harbor next day, visible for miles. Steam was being raised by the ships of the blockaded Spanish squadron—two destroyers and four large cruisers, including *Infanta María Teresa,* flagship of Admiral Cervera. To the American troops, and the American ships waiting offshore, the smoke meant one thing. Cervera would attempt to break out.

Sunday morning, July 3, the first Spanish vessel steamed from the harbor at half past eight. The other ships followed at ten-minute intervals. Soon, big naval guns were thundering, and a smoke pall hid the sea.

Cervera's ships attempted to escape to the west. The American vessels gave chase, maneuvering to fire salvos whenever possible. Commodore Winfield Scott Schley directed the battle from aboard *Brooklyn,* but it was *Iowa* that scored the first fatal hit on *María Teresa.* Pipes ruptured; Spanish sailors died screaming in scalding steam. *Iowa* made a second direct hit, and a third. With his flagship in flames, and every man aboard destined to perish if she stayed on course, Cervera ordered the helm turned toward shore, where the burning vessel grounded. Those still alive leaped overboard to safety.

One by one, the other Spanish ships were grounded or sunk. The battle was over at a few minutes past one o'clock. Almost five hundred Spanish seamen had died, but only one American. The Navy began to pick up prisoners from the sea and the beach; seventeen hundred and fifty in all. One was Admiral Cervera. He was treated with all the dignity and courtesy his rank and the rules of war demanded. His bravery and humane concern for his crew were much admired by the Americans.

Full of opium pills for pain, Joe Crown listened to the noisy sea battle and watched the smoke rise as he lay on a cot in a field hospital tent. He was going to recover, though the surgeons said the shrapnel wound in his left thigh would have killed him had not the doctor at the temporary station by the river stopped the bleeding in time. News of the great victory reached the field hospital late in the afternoon. Weak as he was, Joe joined in the cheering.

On that same Sunday, he learned later, General Shafter sent a letter into Santiago under a flag of truce. He warned the Spanish high command that at 10 A.M. Monday he would begin shelling the town. He requested that all women, children, and foreign nationals leave before firing commenced. The exodus began before sunset. By the time the American bombardment opened precisely at ten the following morning, several thousand civilians were in makeshift refugee camps around the settlement of El Caney. The American Army lacked the rations to feed them. Hunger and illness came quickly.

During the next few days, the Spaniards defending Santiago counterattacked several times, with little success. The Americans had built bombproofs and dug trenches into which they lowered the Gatlings, minus their wheels. Protected by their deadly fire, American soldiers gained ground a little at a time. There were bloody engagements, and casualties on both sides. But the end of the campaign was no longer in doubt.

Contemplating the increasingly hopeless situation, the military commander at Santiago, General Arsenio Linares, instructed General José Toral to commence negotiations for a surrender with honor.

The first meeting between American and Spanish officers was held July 13. Discussions went smoothly and rapidly. With terms agreed upon, all that remained was the transfer of power. It was scheduled for noon on Sunday, July 17. General Shafter would enter the city then.

While this was going on, Joe Crown lay in the field hospital; Paul visited him every day or so. Paul had no more film and was exceedingly anxious to get out of Cuba. Joe was fascinated by his nephew's passion for his work, although he still considered it a raffish trade and could see no real worth in it, nor any future. Nevertheless, he would honor his promise to attend the first showing of Paul's pictures in Chicago, if there was one.

By the end of the week Joe was on his feet again. The wound still hurt unmercifully, but he could hobble about with the aid of a stick with an L-shaped handle. His orderly, Corporal Willie Terrill, had cut and shaped the stick from a single piece of tough cieba wood. When the victory procession assembled on Sunday morning, Joe was present in full uniform.

He surrendered the crutch stick to Corporal Terrill and, with considerable pain, put his left boot in the stirrup. Corporal Terrill understood the difficulty. He put his hands on the general's buttocks and boosted. Joe was white around the lips. But he sat his saddle with correct posture.

General Shafter led the advance into Santiago, astride a huge powerful cavalry horse which nevertheless looked swaybacked, and occasionally whinnied pitifully to protest its mountainous burden. Joe rode beside Fighting Joe Wheeler. The long column of American officers was trailed by a band of reporters walking or riding horses and mules. Paul was back there, on foot, carrying a soiled valise. Joe had seen him earlier in the morning; he was disheveled, as usual. He was also thin from too little food. He wore a polka-dot bandanna tied around his head, pirate fashion. At least it hid his uncombed hair. His camera and film were being looked after by someone reliable, he said.

The ride wasn't a particularly happy one. Talk was minimal, voices subdued; many men held handkerchiefs over their mouths. The Spanish dead had been thrown in shallow mass graves, covered with just a few inches of dirt. Carrion birds had clawed their way to the corpses, ravaged them, and left the remains to rot in the sun. Dead Spanish horses, still saddled and covered with maggots, were decomposing all along the road.

In Santiago, to their great surprise, the Americans found whole companies of bedraggled Spanish soldiers crowding the stoops, alley entrances, balconies, for a view of their conquerors. Faces showed curiosity; even, occasionally, friendliness. Joe saw little overt hostility.

There were tiny children on the cobbled streets, too. Children with bloated stomachs pushing out the fronts of coarse smocks or dresses made from old sugar sacks. Santiago was starving. It confirmed what Joe had learned in the Ohio 5th Volunteer Cavalry, long ago. There might be certain accomplishments in war, certain brief celebrations. But there was no real joy. None.

In the broad and handsome plaza, an enormous crowd waited, pressing against the buildings on all sides. There was no cheering, no shouting, virtually no talking as the conquerors rode in. The hoofs of Shafter's laboring horse rang sharply on the cobbles.

The American officers dismounted, save for General Shafter, who had previously advised the Spanish high command that he would not dismount at any of the treaty ceremonies, since, without his special set of stairs, it would be impossible for him to remount.

The bell in the tower of the old cathedral clanged twelve times. A Spanish color guard marched to the flagstaff and hauled down the red and yellow banner of Spain. An American color guard smartly raised the red, white, and blue. Joe Crown felt no thrill of pride, merely watched, expressionless, until the flag reached the top of the pole, where it hung limp; there was no wind.

Behind him, a regimental band struck up "The Stars and Stripes Forever." Joe stood with perfect military correctness. But he wept inside.

Ilsa, I'm tired of war. I want to come home to you. I want to bring Paul back to us, heal our family, find our son if it's humanly possible.

Ilsa, I love you. I have made so many mistakes. I am so very tired.

113

Dutch

BETWEEN THE BATTLE on July 1 and the cavalcade to Santiago sixteen days later, Paul enjoyed visiting Uncle Joe in the field hospital behind the lines. His uncle was mending well; impatient to be up and doing.

"About once a day he tells us how we should conduct our business," a surgeon confided outside the tent. "Then he catches himself and withdraws the comment. Or he calls it a suggestion, merely a *suggestion.*"

Paul's wound hurt less every day. The Army doctors insisted on changing the bandages for him when he visited Uncle Joe. Someone had passed the word. "General Crown's nephew." He was amused.

He put his camera in the care of an accommodating quartermaster captain who had seen flicker pictures in New York City, and liked them. He hitched a ride on a freight wagon over the rough trail to Siboney, collected his valise from the cantina, and went searching for Miss Fishburne.

She was gone. The SS *State of Texas* had put to sea and was standing off

Santiago, awaiting permission to dock with bedding, clothing, and food for the civilian refugees from the town. But Miss Fishburne wasn't aboard the ship. In the days immediately after the fighting at the San Juan Heights, General Shafter had begged Miss Barton to move some of her staff to the front lines. They had set up an aid station in the jungle but according to reports were no longer there. Left behind in Siboney were two nurses and the other civilian volunteer, Mrs. Olive Shay, who related all this to Paul.

From the tiny office used by the correspondents to file their stories, he sent a collect cable to Shadow.

RETURNING SOON AS POSSIBLE WITH MANY EXCITING WAR
SCENES IF FILM SURVIVES INTENSE HEAT AND DAMP.
REGARDS DUTCH.

He found some discarded Army documents and a pencil and took them to the cantina to which he'd gone with Michael. A glass of warm beer at his elbow, he used the backs of the sheets to write a three-page letter to Wex Rooney at the Nu-Age Photograph Salon in Charleston, West Virginia.

He told Wex he'd been wounded, and had found his uncle serving as an Army brigadier, a great surprise. They had effected a reconciliation of sorts. He believed his uncle still disapproved of his chosen craft.

He described some of his adventures on the battlefield. He said that in determining what to film, he had tried to fulfill Wex's charge that pictures should tell the truth. He hoped Wex would be able to see his films someday, and closed with a wish that his mentor was still enjoying the company of the boardinghouse proprietress, whose name he couldn't remember. He folded the sheets carefully and tucked them in his valise. He'd buy an envelope and stamp and mail the letter in the States.

Doing all these things, he still had trouble keeping his mind off Julie. He knew he shouldn't build up false hopes, but how could he prevent it? The war was virtually over, everyone said so. He'd be going home within a month, to see whether his film survived, then to search for her.

No, put that in reverse order. He'd search first. The film would keep a little longer.

He ran into Billy Bitzer and talked it over with him. Yes, Bitzer thought the Biograph laboratory in New York might process Paul's negatives as a courtesy, provided Bitzer set it up first. He promised to telegraph the company from Florida. Everyone assumed they'd be returning to Key West or Tampa, and Paul intended to be on the first transport carrying civilians. In Florida he'd exchange his return ticket to Chicago for a ticket to New York. London was there in case everything Miss Fishburne said proved wrong. London was his escape hole.

On the night of the surrender ceremony in Santiago, when he was thoroughly tired of bloodshed, and delay, and hungry for a little ease, some good companions, he ran into Michael. Michael's suit was miraculously white again. He was still hatless, and sunburned.

Grinning, he said he'd discovered a cantina whose proprietor was ignoring God's ordinance about Sundays and keeping his doors open while there were

Yankee dollars to be made. He took Paul there just at dark. The cantina was on a crooked street, and packed with men drinking at tables in smoky lamplight.

Five minutes after Michael and Paul sat down, Crane walked in. Unfortunately, five minutes after that, so did Sylvanus Peterman. All four sat at a round table with two chairs vacant.

After they'd ordered, boots came thumping across the grimy floor. "Oh God," Crane groaned under his breath. The German military attaché clicked his heels and bowed.

"*Liebe Herren.* May I join you? My usual drinking companion, Commander Lieutenant Paschwitz, attaché of our Imperial Navy, is indisposed."

Michael became absorbed with the ceiling. Paul studied knife marks on the table. Crane wasn't happy about the visitor, but decency forced him to wave him to an empty chair. "*Vielen Dank.*" Von Rike pulled the chair out, then bent to brush off the table before placing his cap on it. He bowed a second time. Snapped his fingers. "*Bier, bitte! Cerveza! Schnell!*"

With the surrender consummated, there was a convivial air in the cantina; a great deal of shouting, singing, joking. Paul and the others at the table proceeded to drink rapidly, and in quantity. It seemed a happy, relaxing thing to do.

Before long, they were all drunk. Michael, Peterman, Crane, Paul, the attaché.

They were drunk on Cuban whiskey ("There is either cayenne or cat piss in this," Crane said while drinking it as fast as possible), or local beer—really not half bad, Paul thought, if you drank enough, and forgave the Cubans for calling it *Cervezo tipo Pilsen,* lager, when it was the color of molasses. To supplement the drinks they had Cuban cigars, dirt cheap at the bar and magnificent to smoke. Like slightly warm melted silver in the mouth.

"We're going to acquire new territory, we deserve it," Sylvanus Peterman said vehemently. He reached for his brown beer bottle. Over a dozen empties littered the table. "The world is ours now. Time, events—almighty God—have put on us the responsibility to reform, educate, civilize, backward societies. Heathen countries. It's a mighty burden, but we're up to it. You've heard Colonel Roosevelt—"

"Endlessly," Michael said.

"The new century that's coming belongs to America."

"I *beg* your pardon," von Rike said, turning away from Peterman and swilling beer like any commoner.

"Jingo, jingo, jingo," Crane sang tunelessly. He waved his empty glass to keep time. A brown hand took the glass to refill it.

"What do you think of this war, Radcliffe?" von Rike asked. "As an Englishman."

"Piss on Englishmen. I speak for myself. I think this war's venomous. Disgraceful. Nationalism is in the air, and never more so than in America at this moment. Still, you won't hear me condemning the Yanks to the exclusion of others. Given the slightest evil pretext, everyone's for patriotism—"

Von Rike was starting to look offended. Paul was drinking and smiling because Michael's pronunciation and diction were unbelievably British-Oxford-Cambridge-upper class; flawless.

"—and patriotism is a banner in which callous old men wrap strong young men so the strong young men will happily become cannon fodder in service of the slogans manufactured to hide corrupt motives. Don't believe me? Why are we here, my good lads? To cover a *patriotic* crusade!"

Peterman said, "I never saw you anywhere up front covering anything." Von Rike snickered.

"The crusade of the jingoes," Michael went on. "It's nonsense. But countries are all the same. Men are all the same. Never learn."

Crane toasted him with his whiskey. "I knew I liked you."

Von Rike said, "I beg to differ with your cynical and rather insulting remarks, Radcliffe. In my nation there is a new moral strength inspired by high goals which would undoubtedly earn a sneer from you."

"There is also a plan for Germany's next war, the Schlieffen Plan of 'ninety-five, do you deny it?"

"Of course I don't deny it, Count von Schlieffen is an astute and patriotic chief of our general staff, he wouldn't sit idly by watching traditional enemies conspire against us."

"Who does he mean?" Peterman asked Paul.

Paul said, "France and Russia," rather loudly.

"Exactly," von Rike said. "Traditional enemies of Germany sliding into an unholy embrace."

"Enemies you propose to defeat by attacking France first, through the Low Countries, subduing her, then rushing your armies across Germany by means of your fine railways to open a second front against Russia."

"You know a great deal about the Schlieffen Plan, Mr. Radcliffe."

"You Germans hardly keep it a secret, Captain von Rike."

"Railways?" Paul said, a little behind the conversation because of drinking.

"Not for nothing did they study Buffalo Bill's Wild West train," Michael said. Von Rike was startled, and puzzled.

"Look here," Crane said to the attaché, "do you deny Germany has global ambitions? You study Admiral Mahan, don't you?"

"Indeed yes. *The Influence of Sea Power Upon History* is a work that will reshape the world. The Kaiser admires it so much, he provided a copy for every officer of the Imperial Navy. Also selected Army officers, I am proud to say. To reach its goals the fatherland must have a two-ocean navy, the newest coal-fired battleships, and a global network of stations to refuel them."

Crane said, "To what goals do you refer, Captain?"

"*Lebensraum,*" Michael intoned in a mocking way. "*Weltmacht.*"

"What's he saying?" Peterman asked, jerking on Paul's arm.

"Living space," Paul said.

"Snatched from others," Crane said.

"World power," Paul said.

"Well," Peterman said, "Uncle Sammy may have a thing or two to say about that."

"Then there'll be a mighty collision," Michael said.

"Drinks here, God damn it," Crane shouted.

"I've seen the ships building," Michael said. "I've seen the rifled cannon." Paul remembered the Krupp gun. "Armageddon in our lifetime. *And the number of the army of the horsemen were two hundred thousand thousand. And the nations were angry. And there were lightnings, and thunderings, and an earthquake, and great hail. And the cities of the nations fell—"*

"What claptrap is that?" von Rike said.

"Revelation of St. John the Divine." Around the table several eyebrows rose. "You're surprised a villain like me knows his Bible? Some of the wisest words in all of human history. Pity they're religiously ignored. Tell me, *mein Kapitän.* Has the dear old fatherland really got the balls for what I just described?"

"Rubbish. St. John the Divine—pfaugh! We draw our character and strength from our leader—"

"Answer my question."

"—you know perhaps that his was a breech birth. After many hours of labor by his mother Princess Victoria, he was extracted by forceps, which permanently injured his left arm. Many people know that."

"It's the reason his left hand's always on his sword hilt in pictures," Paul said. "The left arm is shorter." He drank a third of a new bottle of beer.

"What many people don't know is this. The birth injury deprived the young crown prince of his sense of balance. He could never play games properly. Most important, he could not ride a horse, which his mother considered essential for a monarch. She instructed the boy's tutor as to what to do. His Majesty was put on a pony in the riding ring. Of course he fell off. He was put on again, he fell again. Over and over, he fell, they put him on. He wept from shame. Some called him the weeping prince. Days, weeks, months—they put him on the pony no matter how he wept, no matter what his pain. Out of that pain there came accomplishment. There came pride, and strength. His Majesty learned to ride. He also learned the power of the will." Von Rike showed them a clenched fist. "Anything is possible when the will sets the course."

"Shit yes," Crane said. "The Kaiser and his *will* got rid of the man who practically created your fucking empire single-handed."

"Bismarck," Paul said to Peterman.

"Do you think I'm some schoolboy? I know that," Peterman spat back.

Michael said, "Arguably the most important man on the world scene in this century, excepting perhaps the runty Corsican who lost his mind and most of his army when he attempted to conquer my motherland. I was born in Russia."

"Probably a yid, too," Peterman said.

"Peterman." Crane leaned forward. "You're a fucking little worm." He almost slid off his chair. "More whiskey here!"

"Bismarck had to be thrown out," von Rike said. "For years he deceived those he was supposed to serve. He pursued his own schemes and visions. When our traditional enemies were constructing or expanding significant colonial empires, Bismarck opposed a similar expansion of German sovereignty. When he was finally forced to reverse course, what colonies were left for us to acquire? South West Africa. East Africa. Togo. A collection of worthless shit-holes unfit for human habitation. Further, Bismarck continually spoke against a two-ocean navy even though our new Kaiser endorsed it. The damned old bastard played Europe like a chessboard, according to his personal design. A secret treaty here, a secret treaty there—even with the slimy treacherous Russians—"

Michael said, "I remind you I was born in Russia."

"—and those fornicating *Englisch*."

Michael said, "England is now my adopted country."

Von Rike leaped to his feet. "Then you're twice *ein dumm anmassender Schweinehund!*"

"Which translates as stupid sneering bastard," Michael said as he jumped up. He came around the table and hit von Rike in the jaw, slamming him down into his chair. Von Rike lurched up again and grabbed the nearest brown bottle. After two blows on the edge of the table, the bottle broke. Michael stepped away, backward, and fell over an empty chair at the next table. The privates and corporals around the table were goggling.

Michael struggled to his feet but he was clearly shaken. Silence rippled out to all corners of the cantina. "I do not suffer insults to my person," von Rike said. He drew little circles in the air with the jagged end of the bottle. "Not quite as fine as a saber, but it will serve. I hope your loved ones will recognize you again."

"Captain, stop!" Paul exclaimed, on his feet now, behind the attaché. Desperately, he looked for help. Crane was too drunk to intervene, Peterman too frightened. The American officers and men were still confused about the nature of the fight. The proprietor was moving from the bar with a shotgun, but not fast enough. Von Rike drew his arm back, preparing to lunge at Michael. Paul jumped him from behind and held him by the elbows.

"Take the bottle away from him, Michael."

Michael seized von Rike's arm with both hands and banged it over his knee. The bottle neck dropped and rolled.

Paul let go of von Rike. "Captain, I think it would be best for all if you left. We didn't come to this island to fight each other."

"Oh, I'm quite willing," Michael said, "now the odds are equalized. Want to step into the street, my fine Prussian knight?"

Von Rike had his temper under control. He straightened and brushed his tunic. He picked up his cap and wobbled toward the door. Michael righted his overturned chair.

"Gentlemen," he said, sitting down. "I fear we just looked into the face of the future. Not too pretty, is it?"

Peterman sank into his high collar with nothing to say. Crane looked like a mourner at a funeral. "Landlord," he called, "put that fucking shotgun away, we definitely need more drinks over here."

The noise level in the cantina returned to normal. Paul refused more beer. Burned into his mind were the fanatical blazing eyes of Captain von Rike, of the new Germany.

On Monday of the last week in July, General Nelson Miles led five thousand men into Porto Rico, a second bastion of Spanish resistance. Within days, Santiago heard that Miles was overrunning the enemy almost as fast as Shafter had in Cuba.

Meanwhile, the SS *State of Texas* had at last been permitted to dock. The civilian refugees had returned, some of them finding their homes looted by American soldiers, all of them discovering a lack of food. Miss Barton's shipboard crew quickly off-loaded large quantities of rations, and soon there were temporary kitchens serving gruel and soup and bread. The *State of Texas* steamed back to an offshore anchorage, observing self-imposed quarantine to protect those left aboard. It was the fever season.

Paul was walking near the waterfront when he suddenly spied Julie's aunt. She was working at a long trestle table set at one side of the street, under a canvas tarpaulin. Behind her, two other women were cooking over charcoal braziers.

Miss Fishburne finished serving soup to three ragged men, saw she had no more customers, and stepped back to wipe her forehead with her apron. Paul was shocked by her haggard and sickly appearance.

"Miss Fishburne!"

"Paul!" She leaned across the table and threw her arms around him. "You came through."

"All the way up San Juan Hill with the first charge. I shot some fine film, if it comes out."

"How is your wound?"

"Healing. It hurts some. But when I'm busy I forget it. I looked for you in Siboney and couldn't find you."

"We went to the front in two wagons commandeered from the Army and got to where we were needed, the First Division Hospital—three canvas pavilions with open sides and some of those field tents they call dog kennels. My God, what a sight. Eight hundred wounded already there, and more coming in. Men lying naked in the tall grass because the shelters were full. Clara was furious about it, and about the filth, the lack of supplies—and the number of casualties. She blamed them on officers sending men against rapid-fire guns."

"We had four of our own. Terrible weapons."

"Yes, I know. It does us no credit. We set up our tarps and braziers and unpacked our food cartons. At night the surgeons worked by moonlight for fear of snipers. Once or twice when they felt safe, they lit candles. Hundreds of candles, gleaming in the dark within sight of the sea—it was beautiful, but it was terrible, too. It made Clara very sad. She said it reminded her of the night after the battle of Antietam, the single bloodiest day in the Civil War. That night both sides used candles to search for their dead. She said—Paul, I'll never forget this. She took my hand and said, 'Willis, it's the same old story. What gain has there been in thirty years, for women or for human kind?' "

Miss Fishburne gave a kind of shiver, throwing off the memory. "I'm an old woman, I talk too much. Let's get to the important question. Are you going to go in search of my niece?"

"As soon as there's a ship, I'll be on my way."

"Bless you—oh, bless you!"

She saw a ragged family bearing down on the table. "I must go to work again. We have hundreds of these poor starving people to feed three times a day."

She blew him a kiss and drew her ladle from the kettle. When she spoke to the family in halting Spanish, she smiled; she had a wonderful smile, Paul thought. Immersed in her work, the years seemed to slough away and he glimpsed the handsome young woman she must have been long ago. He liked her very much.

He waved and went on.

□ □ □ □

By August 7, Sunday, negotiations were under way between the United States and Spain for a permanent peace protocol. Early that morning, Paul and his uncle walked down the Alameda, Santiago's waterfront promenade. Paul kept the pace slow, because Uncle Joe was still hobbling. He went everywhere with the L-handled crutch stick.

Paul and his uncle were discussing Bismarck. The former chancellor had passed away on July 30. Paul described some of von Rike's remarks before the fight. Uncle Joe responded sharply. "And after the French were defeated in 'seventy-one, who does he imagine kept the peace in Europe all these years? Bismarck was devious, but not in a catastrophic way. The Kaiser is devious, and a war monger to boot."

Ahead of them, at the dock, the chartered transport *Miami* swayed gently on her mooring lines. Paul could hardly contain his excitement, or believe his fantastic luck. *Miami*, the first vessel to carry American troops home from Cuba, would sail on the evening tide. She wasn't going to Florida but straight to the eastern tip of Long Island; a place called Montauk Point, where an emergency quarantine camp was being built for those among the returning troops who had been stricken with yellow fever.

When Paul heard of the ship's leaving, he had gone immediately to his uncle. Explained to him that it was important to rush his film magazines back to Chicago the fastest way. "I don't need a berth, I can sleep anywhere. I'm desperate to see whether there are pictures, or whether every frame is fogged. If I got anything at all, Pflaum's will want a showing soon, before it's all stale."

He wanted to tell Uncle Joe about Miss Fishburne, and what she'd said about Julie. He didn't because he didn't know how his uncle would feel about his attempting to steal another man's wife. If indeed she was there in Southampton, waiting to be stolen.

Uncle Joe had worked through Fighting Joe Wheeler, who intended to travel on *Miami* to carry his report, and others, to Washington. Day before yesterday, Paul had learned there'd be a place for him on the transport. Elated, he sent another cable.

MRS. W. ELSTREE
"BELLE MER"
SOUTHAMPTON,
LONG ISLAND
NEW YORK USA

URGENT I SEE YOU ON A MATTER OF OLD BUSINESS. WILL ARRIVE SOON. YOURS VERY SINCERELY. P. CROWN.

Paul and his uncle neared the ship. The Rough Riders were already queued up at two gangways. Most of them wore new khakis; old uniforms and bedding were being burned outside of town. The noxious smoke drifted everywhere.

There were wounded going aboard *Miami*. Some of the wounds were permanent. The Californian, Hugh Johnson, had taken a hit at El Caney, and the surgeons had amputated his right foot. Paul had seen Johnson in the field hospital where he'd visited Uncle Joe. Johnson was being fitted with a new foot made of cork.

"Could we go a little more slowly, Paul?"

"By all means. Take hold of my arm." Soon they were standing in the shadow of *Miami*'s great iron prow.

"Well, Nephew, best I leave you here so you can join one of those lines. Your gear's aboard?"

Paul nodded. "My camera and canvas bag. Last night."

Uncle Joe tucked his crutch stick under his arm to free both hands. "We'll meet again soon. I will manage to get a message to your aunt. She'll be overjoyed. I confess to the same feeling." They embraced. *"Wiedersehen, mein*—no, I can't call you a boy any longer, can I? *Auf Wiedersehen, lieber Paul."*

"Wiedersehen, Onkel."

"Chicago," Joe Crown said.

"Chicago."

Sowieso, für ein bisschen Zeit . . .

For a little while, anyway.

The next week or two—Long Island—would determine the rest of his life.

With a regimental band playing her out of port, *Miami* left Santiago in a glorious sunset. She rode low in the water, so overcrowded was she. Most of the officers, including Roosevelt, had created temporary hutches for themselves on deck. Paul didn't even have that much shelter. He curled up on the riveted iron plates with his camera beside him and his canvas bag for his pillow. *Rheinland* once again. Somehow it made him smile.

Miami docked in Fort Pond Bay on the south shore of Long Island on Monday morning, August 15. A quarantine officer held the vessel offshore overnight, for reasons never clear to the men aboard. Finally, about half past ten next morning, the engines rumbled again, and she proceeded to the pier. Paul could see a crowd, waving hats and small American flags on sticks. The band on board crashed out "Rally Round the Flag, Boys."

Hawsers were thrown to the dock and tied. Colonel Roosevelt and frail Joe Wheeler were on the bridge with the captain. Both waved to the crowd, but Roosevelt did it boisterously, grinning to show all those white teeth. A man on the dock cupped his hands and yelled, "Hurrah for Teddy Roosevelt, our next governor! How are you, Teddy?"

Roosevelt leaned over the rail. "I had a bully time and a bully fight. I feel as big and strong as a bull moose."

More cheering.

Paul was shoved and buffeted toward the gangway by impatient soldiers. Though it was a fine day, sunny, with a balmy Atlantic breeze, the land beyond the pier looked uninviting; sandy, scrubby. Paul asked a man on the dock if he knew a place to rent wagons and buggies. "Bennett's Livery. That road, 'bout a mile." With his tripod on his shoulder and his canvas bag and valise in his other hand, Paul set out at a rapid walk.

He rented an ancient piano-box buggy with a seat whose upholstery was torn, and paint that hadn't been touched up in years. The plodding old mare would go only so fast. It was late afternoon by the time Paul negotiated all the rutted roads, passed through tangled woods, and reached the village of Southampton.

Every store owner displayed flags or bunting, to celebrate the official Spanish surrender two days ago; those aboard *Miami* had heard about it during a brief stop at Jersey City.

He tied the buggy in front of Denny Brothers Hardware, having glimpsed a tall, middle-aged woman wielding a broom inside. He vaulted over the hitch rail and darted through the door.

"Ma'am, I am a visitor, can you give me directions to the Elstree house?"

"Belle Mer." The tall woman pointed. She had white hair center-parted and done in a single thick braid at the back. "First Neck Lane to the shore, left on Dune Road. It's the only house there." The woman was courteous to Paul despite his accent and raffish appearance.

"Thank you so much." He hurried out. Her voice caught him on the plank walk:

"No one there but the caretaker. All the servants were sent back to Chicago."

"I thought rich people stayed in summer homes until September."

"You aren't from around here, are you? Bill Elstree was shot and killed a few weeks back."

Terror . . .

"Who killed him?"

"Some woman he kept in the city."

Relief.

"And the widow? Where is she?"

His intensity, the strain in his voice, made the woman suspicious.

"I don't know as I should go telling just any stranger."

"Please, it's very important. I—" *Think. Quickly!* "I have a message to deliver. From someone in Germany who is quite close to her. I absolutely must find Mrs. Elstree. You can trust me."

"Maybe." The woman pointed to the buggy. "What's that queer thingamajig on legs?"

"My camera. I am a camera operator. Have you heard of living pictures?" She had. "I was sent to photograph Colonel Roosevelt and his Rough Riders." True enough, but it was in Tampa, and Cuba. "I have just come from the transport on which he arrived, now I must deliver my message."

"The living pictures. Fancy that." Obviously no one in these remote parts could invent something so outlandish. "I hope you made good pictures of Roosevelt because you're out of luck with the other part. Mrs. Elstree left a week ago."

"For Chicago?"

"Why, she didn't stop around to share that information with me."

"You say the caretaker's at the house?"

"Henry Prince. One of the Shinnecocks."

"I beg your pardon?"

"Shinnecock Indians. The tribe living along the shore. One more thing I can tell you," she said as he swung up in the buggy. "The place is already for sale. They say Mrs. Elstree's never coming back."

□ □ □ □

He raced the mare down the sandy lane as fast as she'd go, and had no trouble finding the mansion. A semicircular drive of white sand and oyster shell had been raked smooth; the buggy wheels disturbed it. Two large marble urns flanking wide stone stairs were tied with yards of black crepe, tattering in the weather. When the mare stopped, the click of hedge shears could be heard.

Paul followed the sound to the east face of the mansion. There he found a small, stocky, black-haired man at work. "Are you Henry Prince?"

"I am." The man lowered the shears, taking Paul's measure.

"My name is Paul Crown. From Chicago. I am an old friend of Mrs. Elstree. In the village I was told she's not here. Can you tell me where to find her?"

"I can't. I don't know. She showed me steamship folders a few days before she left. We talked about places. Paris, the Greek isles, Egypt—"

"She has relatives, maybe they know."

"They don't. Least, her uncle in the city, Mr. I. W. Vanderhoff, doesn't. He telephones every day or two, asking if I've heard from her. She has an aunt somewhere but the woman moves around." And Paul didn't have Willis Fishburne's address. Julie had given it to him in Chicago, but he'd thrown it away, considering it useless. Foolishly, he hadn't thought to ask for it in Cuba.

After another speculative look at Paul, the caretaker went on, "Guess there's no reason I shouldn't tell you my opinion. I think Mrs. Elstree disappeared because she wanted to disappear. Went away to heal herself. Don't know whether she'll be able to do that. She's one of the best people I ever met, but she was hurt bad. Mostly by him."

"Her husband?"

The caretaker nodded. Tapped the point of the shears against the wall. "Lot of sorrow in this house. Got into her like a sickness. And that mother of hers!"

"Also from Chicago—"

"She was here only one time. Mean, spiteful woman. You could spot it in a minute. Sorry I can't help more."

Paul thanked him and left. His sole hope now was Mrs. Vanderhoff, in Chicago.

In New York City he found a cheap hotel. Early next day he called at the American Biograph offices at 841 Broadway, sixth floor. He introduced himself as a friend of Billy Bitzer, who had not yet returned. Bitzer had, however, telegraphed, as promised. For a price, the owners would be happy to develop Paul's negatives and strike prints. Paul telegraphed Colonel Shadow for authorization of the expense and got it.

All the magazines were ruined, fogged, except the last. That four hundred feet was mottled and streaked. There were sudden white flares in the frame. But the images were spectacular. As he sat in the dark and watched the print projected, he decided it should be called "Conquest of the San Juan Hill." He thought Wex Rooney might admire it.

"Great stuff," said the projectionist when he emerged from his cubicle at the end. "Were you turning the crank?"

"Yes."

"Looks damn dangerous."

"Yes."

The projectionist shook his head enviously; he was about Paul's age.

A front-office man saw Paul to the door with his ruined negatives, the good one, and two prints. "Tommy says the footage you shot down there is sensational. Might be a spot for you with Biograph. Billy's telegraph was mighty high on you."

"Your offer is generous, I appreciate it. But I wouldn't be able to take a job in New York, I will either stay with Colonel Shadow or leave the country. Thank you for your kind assistance."

He rode an overnight train to Chicago. His camera was tagged and stored in the baggage car. He kept the canvas bag of film between his feet.

The car was second-class; smelly and uncomfortable. He stared at the passing night without seeing anything. He could pay for a Pullman, but that would be a waste. He knew he couldn't sleep.

The train chugged into the Dearborn Street depot at half past twelve in the afternoon. Paul hired a cab, and ordered the driver to go directly to the Vanderhoff mansion.

When they arrived on Prairie Avenue, the driver said, "Shall I wait, sir?" Paul stood frowning at the house. Every window on every floor was curtained.

"I think you'd better."

The cold and craggy servant who opened the front door refused to let him step in. Paul craned to see past the man. Sheets hid the furniture.

"I would like to speak with Mrs. Vanderhoff, please."

"She is in California for health reasons. The length of her stay is indefinite."

"Her daughter, then? Mrs. William Elstree—"

"Mrs. Elstree has not been here. We know nothing of her whereabouts. Mrs. Vanderhoff has no contact with her. Good day."

He slammed the door.

Wearily, Paul walked down to the curb. All right, it was settled. A dark part of him had guessed it would turn out this way. He would deliver the film to Shadow and, at the same time, give notice.

He climbed the familiar stairs, smelling savory kitchen odors. He knocked at the kitchen door and walked in. Mary was at the stove, the colonel at the table in his undershirt, noisily sucking cabbage soup from his spoon.

Mary reeled against the stove and nearly burned her hand. "Oh my God."

"Kid!" Shadow cried, jumping up, dropping his spoon, spilling soup, flinging his arms wide. "It's you! Put those things down. Have some soup. Mary! A bowl, a spoon—look at him, he's skinny as a hairpin. Food!"

"Right away, Sid."

Paul set the canvas bag on the table. "I'd like to show you the pictures first. The weather ruined all the magazines but one. But that one is pretty good."

"If it's half as good as what you sent, they'll go wild at Pflaum's. That stuff from Tampa—the orange groves, the cavalry drills, the alligator, and that coffee mill gun on the beach—Iz Pflaum was ready to kiss me when he saw the ticket lines. Come on, let's look."

In the darkened parlor Shadow projected the print. Silent images of destruction and death flickered on the screen, casting a changing silvery pattern on the stunned faces of the colonel and Mary. Shadow continually voiced wonderment, heavily laced with oaths. Sitting next to Paul, Mary ran her hand up and down the inside of his leg, moaning, "Oh, *no!*" frequently. When the film ran out, Shadow flicked on the lights.

"Kid—sensational. No other word for it."

"Thank you, Colonel."

"Were those men shooting real bullets?" Mary said.

"All the time."

"And you were that close? A bullet could have gotten you! Why didn't you hide?"

"If I hid, how would I get the pictures?" He poked at his brown hair which, as usual, seemed to be sticking up in several directions. "Could I wash now, and have a bowl of soup?"

"Anything you want," the colonel cried, beaming.

"Afterward I need to speak with you about something important."

Shadow took it hard. He begged Paul not to quit. He promised to raise his salary. Said he'd insist that Iz Pflaum use Paul's name in advertisements; promote him as "the star camera operator" of American National Luxograph.

"Kid, you're an ace. You came through in style. I worried a lot after I sent you down there. Guess I had good reason." Paul had told of his misadventures with Jimmy. "They hauled Jimmy back into town with cuffs on him. He's in Cook County right now, headed for Joliet."

"I signed charges against him."

"You may have to testify."

"If I have to, I will."

Shadow toyed with his coffee mug. "I'll be square with you. I was worried but also damn sore about all the expense money you were spending. Telegraphs! Cables! My God, you wrote novels, not messages!"

"Sid," Mary hissed.

"All right, all right, we'll forget it. It's forgotten! Those pictures are incredible. I mean *incredible*. You're a brave young man." For once he sounded sincere. "Now I want to hear everything, every detail. Mary! More soup. Beer, coffee— whatever he wants. *Anything!*" he said, slapping the table like a prideful father.

They talked for over three hours. At the end, Shadow dismissed the matter of Paul's notice by saying they'd discuss it after the premier showing of "Conquest of the San Juan Hill." All the issues could be resolved, money could take care of anything.

Paul sighed, said he really needed to visit his family tonight, and fled down the stairs.

In the great house at Michigan Avenue and Twentieth, all the family cried when he walked in with his valise.

Fritzi cried and flung herself on the floor of the front parlor, so overcome was she. Carl cried, a few manly sniffles suitable for a burly football player not quite sixteen. Aunt Ilsa cried to overflowing. Louise from the kitchen cried. Manfred Blenkers didn't cry, but he said, "Here, please, allow me," and took Paul's dirty, stained bag, then worked his hand like a pump handle.

"Do you know the good news?" Aunt Ilsa said. "Your uncle will be home in a few days. He is in Tampa at this moment. All the volunteers are coming home. He will have ten days of leave, then go to Washington to report and muster out— oh my heavens, this is too much." She fanned herself with her handkerchief.

"I knew you were coming but not the exact moment. You must sit. You must rest. Supper will be ready soon."

She plunged into the kitchen and personally warmed the sauerbraten and dumplings left from *Mittagessen;* brought these to the table with Louise's help and supplemented them with platters of wurst and cheese. Paul stuffed himself and drank two steins of Crown lager. Fritzi couldn't wait to hear his war experiences, and when he had related just a few of them, she pretended to swoon with excitement. Twice.

Later, Aunt Ilsa saw him to his old room and drew his bath. After he'd soaked and pulled on a flannel nightshirt and settled himself, she knocked and tiptoed in.

"May I sit a moment, dear?"

"Of course you may." He hitched to one side under the coverlet. One of those delicious August cool spells had swept into Chicago, refreshing the air with a hint of the chill of autumn.

"Oh, Paul. Dear Paul. *Willkommen.*" She threw her arms around him and hugged him fiercely against her formidable bosom. "You met my Joe in this strange war. Patched things up, he said so in his telegram. How extraordinary. I'm so glad. What now for you? A good rest, yes? Then back to work making your films?"

He drew a long breath. Shook his head. "I gave Colonel Shadow my notice this afternoon. I'm leaving for London as soon as possible. I'll take a job there."

Aunt Ilsa rocked back. "London? But why? Your home is here. If not in this house—that I can understand—then America. America's your home now, Paul."

"Nein, Tante Ilse. Mein zeitweiliges Heim nur." My temporary home only. "The home I wanted was a home with Julie and she's gone, no one knows where."

"A terrible tragedy, the death of her husband. Quite a scandal, too." A desperate breathiness came into his aunt's voice. "But please, don't be hasty. We could hire an investigation agency to search for her, as we did for Joey, several times."

"But they didn't find him."

She bowed her head. "No."

He took her hands in his. "You've been wondrously kind to me, Aunt Ilsa. We won't be out of touch, ever. But I must leave this country. It's time."

She searched his face for a long moment; saw he was determined. She rose, kissed his cheek, and gave a little motherly tug to the sheet, to make certain he was properly covered. She went out silently. Not until she was gone did he realize something was different.

She hadn't called him Pauli.

114

The General

LATE AUGUST. Munching on a pickled herring, he tap-tapped his way from the hot kitchen to the stifling front hall, leaning on the cieba wood stick. He had slipped back into civilian garb, civilian life, easily enough. But his thigh wound hurt most of the time. He listed slightly when he walked.

He checked the lock on the front door. He checked every door every night; Germanic habits of thoroughness didn't change easily.

He heard a footfall and discovered his daughter peeping out of the music room. Fritzi was in her flannel nightdress, barefoot. She was seventeen now, still flat-bosomed and lean as a scarecrow. But her air of hoydenish liveliness only increased as time passed. It seemed to rivet the eye of the most casual observer, he'd noticed. It even made her pretty, or at least enormously pleasing, in certain kinds of light.

"Papa, might I speak to you a moment?"

"*Fritzchen,* it's half past ten."

"I won't take long. Please?"

He followed her into the music room, where she faced him soberly and said, "Cousin Paul is going to leave the country, that's definite?"

"I believe so, yes."

"Everyone's moving on." She stood up straight, looking him in the eye. "Papa, you know I'm going to be an actress."

"Is that what you wanted? To tell me nothing's changed?"

"Yes, Papa, that's all. I don't want you to forget."

He sighed.

"I can't pretend I like this very much, Fritzi. But I suppose I must be resigned. I learned a few lessons while I was gone. I won't hinder you. I'll help you financially if you need that. I'll even—"

He cleared his throat.

"—give you my reluctant consent. If it matters."

"Oh, Papa, yes, it does! Thank you!" She jumped to his arms. They embraced warmly, then stepped apart.

"One more question, Papa. Do I have to call you General now?"

With a teasing smile, he said, "Everyone else does. I'll think about it, *Liebling.*" He patted her. "I'll think about it."

"Papa, are you teasing me?"

"Teasing? Would I do that? Your own father? The general?"

They looked at each other gravely for a few seconds. Then she saw the truth in his eyes, and burst out with laughter. Father and daughter walked up the long staircase in the dark and silent house, arms around each other's waist, voices murmuring.

A half hour later, he lay naked beside Ilsa in the familiar bed. His ardor had taken her by surprise. Now they were resting.

The room was black, all the windows open. No air stirred; no stars shone. The cieba wood stick was propped against the night table where he could reach it. The house was still, everyone in their beds. Paul had gone back to Shadow's. He'd stayed at the Crown house only two nights, moving his belongings to the Levee before Joe arrived home from Florida. Until the first showing of his film, Paul thought he should live where he worked. He'd come to supper several times, though. Relations were more or less normal again.

Around the country, the war was still the topic of the moment. A giddy spirit of victory prevailed. Bunting and flags fluttered on stores and office buildings and front porches. The jingoes in Congress and the editorial rooms of certain Chicago papers were saying America would wrest territory from the hands of the beaten enemy. The conquered island of Porto Rico, perhaps even the Philippines. Schoolchildren were writing essays on "Our New Empire of Democracy" or "America, A New World Power." What a glorious war it had been, to achieve all that! Or such was the opinion of fat-butted politicians and purblind editorialists who had never dirtied their hands and their trousers and their memories in a war. Joe had served in two. He never wanted to serve in another.

Because a powerful, youthful, prideful spirit was abroad in the country, Pflaum's Music Hall was spending a lot of money to promote the premiere of "Conquest of the San Juan Hill." There was prominent mention of Paul in the newspaper advertisements. Only this morning, Joe had clipped the one from the *Tribune*.

Exclusively at PFLAUM'S!
·
"CONQUEST OF THE SAN JUAN HILL"
·
Personally Photographed
by
AMERICAN NATIONAL LUXOGRAPH'S
Ace Camera Operator
PAUL "DUTCH" CROWN
·
"He Risked His Life for These
Thrilling and Authentic Scenes
of Our Brave Boys in Action!"
·
EVERY PATRIOTIC AMERICAN
MUST SEE THESE PICTURES!

After the premiere showing, Paul would leave America in a cheap cabin on a steamer bound for Southampton. He had his ticket, already booked with money provided by a friend in London. The same journalist who was luring him to work there. Joe had discussed it with his nephew more than once. Pleaded with him to give Chicago, and his adopted country, a second chance. Paul said no. He was polite but adamant. Joe laid a great part of the blame on himself.

Needing comfort, he rolled over and kissed the hollow of Ilsa's neck. Her skin was damp from their lovemaking. He continued to kiss and nuzzle her, then moved his hand down the front of her nightgown. She surprised him by giggling.

"Joe, I feel foolish. We're too old."

"Never too old to show you care for someone."

She tangled her fingers in his hair and rolled to face him. The warm breath from their mouths mingled. She kissed him and whispered, "No. Never too late for that."

A little later, cooling off again, he lay with his arm under his head, staring up into the dark.

"Ilsa."

Drowsily: "Yes?"

"I would like to make another search for Joe Junior. Hire the detective bureau once again."

"I think it's futile. The silence has lasted too long. Nothing mailed to us in many months."

"Still, I would like to do it. And regularly thereafter." He paused. "That is, if you'll consent."

"I consent. There are far worse ways to spend money. Far worse things to spend it on than hope."

"Even if you believe it's a vain hope?"

She ran her fingers lightly down his bearded face and once more kissed him, sweetly and tenderly.

"Yes, my dearest. Even then."

115

Dutch

SEPTEMBER. Torrential rain falling. Gutters overflowing. Cabs impossible to find. In spite of it, Pflaum's Music Hall was sold out for the first showing of "Conquest of the San Juan Hill." Shadow had badgered and wheedled Iz Pflaum into spending six or seven times his usual modest budget for display advertising. Solely from this advance publicity, the colonel had signed up four new locations in other states. Six more potential exhibitors of Luxograph films had come from out of town to attend the premiere, one all the way from Denver.

In front of Pflaum's, with gale force wind blowing sheets of rain past the streetlights, there was a raucous, ill-tempered jam of private carriage drivers and their vehicles, Nicky Speers among them. Each driver strove to outmaneuver the others and release his passengers under the jutting marquee. Rain had already shorted out six of its electric bulbs.

In the lobby, wearing patent leather shoes, tails, white tie, and a wing collar that was too small, Iz Pflaum greeted newspaper writers and other important people volubly, if fuzzily. Paul had arrived a half hour early, and at that time Shadow told him Pflaum had already consumed half a quart of bourbon. With every other remark or jocularity, Pflaum unconsciously hooked a finger in his collar and jerked. It didn't help; his face grew steadily redder.

Shadow himself was suavely elegant in a new amber-colored frock coat, starched shirt with black bandanna, tapered black trousers, black knee boots, and his big white sombrero. He was busy joking and wheedling and making deals with the out-of-towners in the main floor promenade, which had doors to the lobby on the outer side, doors to the auditorium on the inner. Mary was with him. She had squeezed her breasts into her tightest corset, then her most revealing bodice, and she presented this view of rosy flesh constrained and overflowing to each visitor. Mary also helped her man by passing out kisses and sly winks like cigars.

Iz Pflaum had scheduled the short film after the variety program due to begin at eight o'clock. Paul was extremely nervous. He stood alone, twisting a brand new checked cap bought for the occasion, together with his handsome new plaid suit, with Aunt Ilsa's attendance, advice, and money. She had overridden all his protests.

The doors to the lobby kept opening to admit patrons. He saw Nicky Speers with the Crown carriage under the marquee. Uncle Joe jumped out and helped Aunt Ilsa alight. Next came Fritzi and Carl.

Aunt Ilsa and Fritzi embraced Paul, and Carl shook his hand. Uncle Joe didn't want to prolong the meeting. "I believe we should find our seats, it's almost eight." As he stepped past Paul, he squeezed his arm. "I hope it will be a huge success."

Pflaum had put them in the third row on the left aisle, directly behind Shadow and Mary. Paul had the aisle seat, with his aunt to his right, then Uncle Joe, Fritzi, and Carl. At five past eight, as the last stragglers were rushing to their places, the electric chandelier dimmed and there was an eruption of nervous coughing and rustling of specially printed programs. Pflaum's band leader, Professor Ludwig Teasdale, stepped to the podium in the pit, pivoted flamboyantly—a deliberate play for a hand, which he got—and began the overture.

No one wanted to see the variety bill. The juggler was hooted so rudely, he missed a step and lost control of the spinning Indian clubs. One fell on his head, the others thumped and rolled all over the stage. From the gallery there were loud requests for the hook.

The other acts didn't fare much better. Finally, mercifully, the variety show ended. The lights came up while the screen was rolled into place behind the velvet curtain. The curtain parted again, to vigorous applause.

Iz Pflaum had programmed twenty minutes of the subjects Paul had photographed in Tampa. Blanket-tossing and cavalry drill. The alligator and the Gatling gun scything down the palm tree. All had been exhibited at the theater soon after Paul sent them from Florida.

More applause, and the curtains closed once more. A hush fell. The house lights came up, so Professor Teasdale could be seen raising his baton. The orchestra struck up "The Stars and Stripes Forever." The audience responded with clapping, whistling, stamping.

At the end of the piece, an arc light threw a hot white circle on the curtain. Into the spotlight lurched Iz Pflaum. He delivered a purple and occasionally garbled introduction of Colonel R. Sidney Shadow III.

The colonel bounded to the stage, flourishing his sombrero. He took the spotlight and began another time-wasting speech. He lauded the virtues and benefits of the living pictures, as well as his personally designed and constructed camera and projector. He expressed his strong opinion on the worth of "actualities"— films of real people, real events—as against fanciful story films. By now there was a good deal of grumbling, coughing, and foot-shuffling. Shadow ignored it and introduced his "ace camera operator."

By prior agreement, Paul merely stood at his seat while the arc light sought him and bleached and blinded him. He waved and sat down to applause and a few whistles.

"And now, ladies and gentlemen—my fellow citizens of this great city, and this great land—"

"Get it on, damn you," a man yelled from the rear. There was more hooting, clapping, whistling.

With unruffled aplomb, Shadow bowed and made a sweeping gesture with the sombrero. His voice boomed from the stage apron. "Prepare yourselves for the most remarkable, the most thrilling and—yes, honesty compels me to say it—the most harrowing and soul-stirring living pictures you have ever seen, or ever will—"

The curtain began to part to reveal the screen again.

"Conquest of the San Juan Hill!"

Fanfare and drumroll from the pit. Paul sank low in his seat, fairly twitching with nerves. The screen began to glow and flicker with scratchy, jerky images of the war he remembered too well.

During the last sequence, the stark views of the Spanish dead in the trenches, the bugler in the pit blew "Taps." Although the dead belonged to the enemy, they had belonged to the human race as well. There were no outcries against the Spaniards, only silence.

Paul glanced from the corner of his eye. Uncle Joe's profile was silver and black as the images changed. He sat motionless, gripping the arms of his seat. Paul heard Aunt Ilsa and Fritzi weeping, then the commotion of a woman fainting somewhere in the rows behind.

On the screen there was an abrupt cut, to a great billowing American flag with forty-five stars whipping in the wind. Paul had photographed it on the roof at Shadow's request, and patched it to the end of the war footage. It rescued the audience from grim scenes of death, and brought them to their feet in a thundering ovation. Uncle Joe was among the first to stand.

During the pictures Shadow had sneaked into the seat beside Mary. Now he jumped up and leaned over to hug Paul and slap his back. "They loved it. Even that grisly stuff—" He kept pounding. "God damn it, kid—Dutch—you brought home the goods, you're a God damn genius." He was incoherent. He was crying. The base, crude, dishonest R. Sidney Shadow III was *crying*.

The aisles filled with spectators equally overcome, Uncle Joe among them. The family milled, everyone trying to talk at once.

Aunt Ilsa: "Paul, you were in such danger, I didn't realize."

Carl: "Swell stuff. Exciting as the devil."

Fritzi: "I thought I'd expire with fright. Oh, we're so proud of you!"

And Uncle Joe, holding onto his arm, ignoring the buffeting of those trying to get past. There was a strange look on Uncle Joe's face. He was ashen; shaken. "It was so real. I have never seen anything so real, except the battlefield itself. I was transported, I felt I was there again. Climbing the hill with Roosevelt's men. Smelling the smoke. Hearing the guns, the cries of the wounded. Walking among all those dead. It moved me very much."

He turned away, took a starched white handkerchief from his pocket and blew his nose.

"Come, Ilsa. Children."

He stayed beside Paul as they slowly ascended the crowded aisle. "This isn't the low trash I thought it to be, it's honest, important work," he said. "History lives in those pictures. Before you leave us, you must tell me how the process works. The mechanics—every detail."

"I will, Uncle, certainly." He was euphoric over the vindication. Astonishingly, then, came a wave of remorse about parting from the Crowns.

But his ticket was purchased. Lord Yorke was waiting to meet him in London. The whole world was opening. The world he'd never thought he'd see.

The sluggishly moving crowd brought Ilsa, Fritzi, and Carl to the doorway. Fritzi dropped her program. Everyone stopped while she bent to find it. Outside, Iz Pflaum was waving his hands like semaphore flags. "Dutch, hurry, we have journalists waiting to speak to you. Mr. LeGrand of the *Tribune*, Mr. Wickwire of the *Daily News*, Mr.—"

Paul couldn't hear clearly in the hubbub. Just to his left, the last row of the center section was empty save for one person still seated. A woman in a coat with a black fur collar, gloves, a large hat with a gossamer gray veil. While he was taking notice of her, she stood up. She lifted the veil.

"Paul."

Julie held out her arms to him.

"I made a vow to find you."

She had a large suite at the Palmer House. Paul spent the night. They made love hungrily, and talked.

Every drape was drawn against the hammering rain. A single dim table lamp in the sitting room had been left on. Its light fell through the elegant archway and enabled them to see and feast on each other. While they talked, they sprawled, or sat with arms around drawn-up legs, naked and innocent as children.

She explained that she had left the Long Island mansion for a flat already rented in New York. There she had done exactly what Paul's uncle and aunt had done, but with greater success. Hired detectives. The firm's Chicago bureau made inquiries in the Crown neighborhood. No one had seen or heard of Paul in some time. The chief of the bureau was ready to approach Ilsa Crown when he noticed one of the many advertisements for Pflaum's special showing. There was the name Paul Crown.

"I rented the Manhattan flat to have a place to hide after I left Bill. I found the courage to do that because you and Aunt Willis always said I had it, if only I could call it up. It didn't work out quite as I planned. Bill was shot to death right in front of me. Then I quarreled with my mother because I wouldn't do what she asked. There was terrible guilt. The old trouble started to recur. The sadness—wanting to hide forever. But I fought it. I had something to help me this time. You. Knowing you were alive somewhere. Knowing I could find you if I tried hard enough, took enough time, spent enough money—heaven knows there's plenty to spend. Elstree was one of the richest men in America."

"And you've inherited all of it. I will never make a tenth as much in my entire life."

"It won't be a problem, I won't let it." She kissed his mouth; caressed his cheek and let her eyes rove his face. "I couldn't let the sickness defeat me—keep me from you. I promised myself that if I did find you, and you had someone else, I'd go away. But not without telling you once more that I love you, I'll never love anyone else."

He took her in his arms. The rain beat on the curtained windows. He bore her down gently and joyfully to the bed.

Shortly after dawn, he awoke to feel her leaving their warm nest of blankets. Her flanks shone in the dim light from the sitting room.

In a dark corner of the bedroom, a drawer slid in and out. She returned with something in her hand. She was between Paul and the lamp; he couldn't see the object.

He was puzzled when she clambered onto the mussed bed and knelt next to him. Her black hair cascaded to her waist. The lamplight falling on it made it shine.

"Paul dearest, I swore that if we were ever reunited, I'd ask you to do something. I hope you won't think it too strange. It's very important to me."

"Of course I'll do it, you know I will."

"And not ask why?"

"You're making me curious. I may ask someday."

"Fair enough." Her hand rose. Metal flashed. He saw what she'd brought from the drawer.

She leaned down to his face, pale dark-tipped breasts touching the flat of his chest. She kissed him gently, yet with ardor. Then she laid the silver scissors in his hand.

"Cut my hair."

Late in the morning, at the telegraph desk downstairs, he wrote a cable to Michael Radcliffe at the *London Light* in Fleet Street.

REGRET WILL NOT BE COMING TO LONDON. SITUATION
COMPLETELY CHANGED. PLAN TO STAY WITH PRESENT
EMPLOYER. AM MARRYING YOUNG WOMAN I SPOKE ABOUT.
WILL SEND NEW ADDRESS SOON. ALSO TICKET REFUND. FULL
DETAILS WHEN WORK BRINGS ME TO EUROPE. THANK YOU
FOR YOUR KINDNESS AND GENEROSITY. YOUR FRIEND ALWAYS.
DUTCH.

Part Ten

HOMECOMING

1900–1901

I am the family face;
Flesh perishes, I live on,
Projecting trait and trace
Through time to times anon,
And leaping from place to place
Over oblivion.

1917
THOMAS HARDY, *Moments of Vision*

116

Dutch

MONDAY, December 31, 1900; the eve of the new year. Germans called it *Sylvesterabend.*

It was the cusp of the new century as well. As the newspapers repeatedly and ponderously pointed out, years ending in zero concluded a series from one to ten. Thus 1900 was the last of a series that started with 1891. The twentieth century would begin in the first minute of the first day of January 1901—tomorrow. Among people Paul knew, there were varying reactions. Uncle Joe with his passion for numbers of course had it correctly, and scoffed at those who didn't. Colonel Shadow was irked to be told he'd lived with a misconception for years. Mary said she'd tried to explain it last New Year's eve but the colonel had been too far gone into champagne.

In addition to this mathematical news, for weeks every paper and periodical of substance had been delivering visions of the future from pundits of large and small reputation. There were predictions of high-speed trains operating on a single magnetized rail; hemlines rising indecently; underground moving sidewalks to keep pedestrians out of the weather; more deaths from violent collegiate sports; more business degrees for "new" women; an armored, bullet-shaped, steam-driven "touring carriage" for sight-seeing on the African veldt; German "commercial expansionism" in the Orient; crowded mountain slopes as the masses discovered the new winter sport of "skeeing"; completion of a trans-Panama canal, an engineering project under discussion for years; further assassination attempts on kings and presidents; cities patrolled from above by policemen riding in the gondola baskets of gas-filled airships; mounting danger to white civilization from "the Yellow Peril" or, alternatively, "disappearing barbarism" thanks to America's benign civilizing influence; Earth decimated and all human life destroyed by meteor showers from space.

These clashing forecasts of the twentieth century vied with the ongoing trivialities of daily life reflected in neatly boxed and illustrated advertisements for washing powders, hand soaps, fashions, memory-training courses, antiseptic hat liners ("Kill That Smell!"), machines that harnessed canines to a treadmill to drive a cream separator ("Double Dog Power!"), electric health belts with built-in battery pouches ("Quickly cures all nervous and organic disorders, whether arising from natural weaknesses, excesses, or indiscretions!").

But on the last day of the old century, the world was pausing not only to reflect but to rest. The latest edition of the *Tribune* carried little more than minor news on its front page. A sleeping car quarantined in Colorado with a case of smallpox aboard. A custody fight over a child in Kenosha, Wisconsin. A weather forecast of a severe cold wave, with fair skies but temperatures plunging below ten degrees tomorrow morning. There were large display advertisements relating to the holiday. Elstree's was featuring an End-of-the-Century China, Glassware, and Crockery Sale.

On that Monday afternoon, Paul and his family and friends went to court.

Paul had bought a new three-button cutaway sack suit for the occasion. He was damnably uncomfortable in it, because he also had to wear a tall celluloid collar and cuffs, and a bow tie Julie tied for him before they left home. The tie was already canted at forty-five degrees, and threatening to come undone.

She'd taken a comb to his hair, too, to little avail. Paul knew he was disheveled but it didn't matter, his wife looked smashing in her tailored dove gray suit with silk-faced lapels, a winter cape of matching gray, and a simple gray felt hat with a bow of royal blue velvet.

He loved her with an undiminished passion. He loved her gentility, and her innate kindness to others. She was intelligent and good-humored. Her health was improved. She walked at least two miles every day.

Though still subject to spells of gloom, she was slowly freeing herself of them, and, in an unassuming way, developing an independence her mother would have hated. Yet Julie was entirely feminine. And she wore fine clothes well.

The same could never be said of him. Everyone except his wife and his family called him Dutch, and he was far more comfortable in Dutch's wardrobe. He even thought of himself as Dutch now.

He was twenty-three, and with a young man's confident egotism he considered himself worldly. And not without reason. Today, however, he was visibly nervous waiting in the courtroom with the cold slanting light of late December spearing through grimy windows. The hearing was scheduled for two o'clock. The large, noisily ticking wall clock showed ten after. God, how he craved a cigar.

A whole troop of well-wishers had come along with Paul and Julie. General Joe Crown sat on the first row of the spectators' section, behind the railing. Beside him were Aunt Ilsa, Fritzi, and Carl.

Paul's uncle had become the Republican Incarnate. He was still enjoying a certain elation because McKinley and his running mate, Roosevelt, had swept aside Mr. Bryan as well as the radical Socialist Gene Debs in the November election. Uncle Joe had poured a great deal of personal time into the state campaign for the Republican ticket, and he'd donated large sums to the national war chest. He was anticipating invitations to the President's dinner table as a result of his generosity, and he was pleased that Paul was acquainted with Vice President Elect Roosevelt from the war.

Paul's aunt was no longer campaigning against spirits, wines, and beers. The change had come when she discovered her husband had quietly rehired his three sales agents, and added a fourth. There was an angry confrontation, so Fritzi told Paul. This time it was Uncle Joe who gave in, permanently relocating Dolph Hix and the other three men, making them managers of agencies in Madison, Austin,

Memphis, and Pierre, South Dakota. The man with the least seniority got Pierre, South Dakota.

With that issue resolved for the present, Aunt Ilsa had taken up a new cause. She had headed a campaign for money to send a Hull House observer to the first World Peace Conference at the Hague in May of 1899. Aunt Ilsa needed her causes; she was lonely in the mansion with her children gone. Paul took Julie there to dine at least once a week when he wasn't on a trip. At other times, Julie went alone.

Carl was home from Princeton for the holidays. Aunt Ilsa had overcome her husband's continuing suspicions of people and institutions in the East, persuading him that no finer education could be had for their son. Carl was eighteen, with enormous shoulders that suited someone who played the murderous, sometimes lethal game of football. A generous donation from Joe had somehow persuaded university admissions officers to look tolerantly on Carl's less then brilliant academic record.

Fritzi, who five days from now would be twenty, had taken a short leave from her company and rushed from Albany, Georgia. She was on tour with Mortmain's Royal Shakespeare Combination. The troupe's founder-manager was an aging actor calling himself Ian Mortmain; he had been born Ezra Cooler in Montgomery, Alabama. Fritzi said this was merely her "apprenticeship," and she'd soon move on to better companies and theaters.

Fritzi was supernumerary, assistant wardrobe mistress, part-time cook, and occasional performer. She played one of the witches in "the Scottish play" (she refused to say its title aloud, as many superstitious actors did), but her most important personation was a trouser role, Viola in *Twelfth Night*. Uncle Joe and Aunt Ilsa had traveled all the way to Owensboro, Kentucky, to see her perform. Uncle Joe still disapproved of the profession, but proudly said his daughter was outstanding, and garnered the most applause at the curtain.

Fritzi said she was "insanely jealous" of Paul because he'd been to the theater in London's West End while awaiting War Office clearance to go to South Africa in the fall of 1899. At the Prince of Wales's Theater, he'd seen not one but three idols of the English stage, Mr. Forbes Robertson, Mr. Gerald du Maurier, and Mrs. Patrick Campbell, in a new comedy.

And now here they were, all together in the courtroom even though their lives had diverged and changed markedly in the last two years. There was only one void. Cousin Joe. Paul wished he were there too, but he'd disappeared entirely, and little was said of him. It was too sad a subject, especially for Aunt Ilsa.

Spotted about in other seats were Paul's friends and mentors. Colonel Shadow was present, smelling magnificently of bay rum and high-priced cigars. Mary Beezer had put on her best and gaudiest dress. Still unmarried, she and the colonel had left the Levee and moved into quarters more suitable for a new prince of the living picture medium. They had a six-room suite on the top floor of Allerton's Hotel on fashionable North Michigan, above the river.

Shadow was in a transitional period. Becoming less interested in building and furnishing projectors, with operators, for a lease fee of eighty dollars a week, and more interested in producing and leasing the pictures themselves, for a price of seventeen cents a foot. But he hadn't given up tinkering. Before Paul went overseas to film the war between England and the rebellious Boer farmers of South Africa, Shadow supplied him with a new-model Luxograph. The camera featured a mount for interchangeable lenses and a geared platform with a lever to allow smooth panoramic movement from side to side. Nicer effects were possible with the new model, but there was a price. The camera weighed thirty-two pounds more than the one Paul carried to the San Juan Heights.

Fidgeting next to Shadow and Mary was Ollie Hultgren, the assistant who had replaced Jim Daws and gone with Paul on his picture trips ever since the summer of 'ninety-nine. Ollie was Swedish, twenty years old, a slim-hipped, long-faced boy with curly blond hair and eyes of a blue that shaded toward violet. He was a gentle person, a loyal friend and a smart helper who could be a chief operator in his own right one day. Paul had already urged that on Shadow.

The most flamboyant woman in the cold and drafty room was Julie's aunt. Over her flared skirt Miss Fishburne wore a short, snug coat of bright red—a Parisian automobile coat, she called it—set off by a plumed black hat and rolled black umbrella. She'd thrown her expensive coat of black Baltic seal fur over the next chair.

Perhaps the most special visitor, at least for Paul, was Wexford Rooney. Wex had sat up on a train all night, in company with his stout, blunt-jawed wife Lucille. This was the former widow Suggsworth of Charleston, West Virginia. She'd sold her boardinghouse in order to finance her husband in a new Temple of Photography in Lexington, Kentucky. Wex said his studio was highly successful, though how this could be in a place where horseflesh abounded and sporting gentlemen wagered on everything from the speed of two-year-olds to the accuracy of their watches, Paul couldn't imagine. Nor had Wex enlightened him.

Wex did look prosperous. His green suit was finely cut and sewn. He was shiny of cheek, merry of eye, grinning like an elf alongside Lucille, who was a full head taller and considerably wider. So far Uncle Joe had said very little to Wex or Shadow or their consorts.

Paul stood up. He opened the gate in the railing; stepped through to the judge's side and looked at the empty dais, then the clock. He reopened the gate and sat down again. Julie put her gloved hand on top of his. "He'll be here, don't worry."

He gave her arm a gentle pat, to thank her. She was the absolute joy of his life. The only trouble was, because of his work he didn't see enough of her. She had adjusted.

They were living on the sunny first floor of a two-story apartment building on tree-lined Paulina Street, in the pleasant neighborhood of Ravenswood. The house was just two blocks from the Ravenswood depot of the Chicago and North-western Railway, which ran frequent trains to and from the central city. It was an ideal location for a young family whose breadwinner worked in town.

Julie had sold Belle Mer at a large profit, and Elstree's Chicago townhouse as well. She'd kept a small cottage in a summer colony on the eastern shore of Lake Michigan, but Paul, traveling so much, had never been there.

He was proud of her because she was slowly and thoughtfully giving away the

Elstree millions. It would take years, perhaps decades, since huge profits from the department stores annually spilled back into the estate.

In philanthropy Julie was a novice. So she'd worked up her nerve, written, and then, by invitation, called on an American eminently qualified to guide her giving, Andrew Carnegie. While Paul was in Texas this past autumn, she'd traveled by steamship across the Atlantic, then out of London by train, to the one home of several he owned that Carnegie loved best. This was Skibo Castle, on Dornoch Firth in the wild and beautiful north of Scotland.

The monumentally wealthy "laird of Skibo" spent two days advising Julie. "He told me he feels strongly that any rich man who dies with all his money is a sinner. A bad citizen of this world. He devotes himself to many causes, but the two most important are the movement for world peace and building libraries. When he was a bobbin boy in Scotland, he and the other factory boys were allowed to use the private library of a nobleman. It was there he began a passion for self-education, and books. He and his family immigrated to America almost fifty years ago. And look what he made of himself. When I left, he escorted me to the carriage personally, kissed my hand, and called me a wiselike girl. 'What is that?' I asked. 'Why,' he said, 'in Scots it's a girl who is sensible, proud—and self-reliant.' Perhaps I really, really have come out of the dark at last, and become a person." Paul assured her it was true.

Julie never saw her mother, nor heard from her. Nell Vanderhoff had come back from her California "nerve cure" more than a year ago. Shortly after, a letter from the Vanderhoff family attorneys informed Julie that a new will had been drawn, eliminating her.

Wex had moved over to conduct an animated discussion of photography with Shadow. A door at the side of the dais opened. Paul jumped up as a pudgy man with a pink turnip nose came in, carrying a paper folder, a Bible, and a ledger. He wore an ill-fitting suit, not judicial robes. Just a courthouse hack. Deflated, Paul sat down again.

The man reached up to place the folder on the judge's dais, then sat at a table in front of it. He opened his ledger and inked his pen. Finally he deigned to notice those on the other side of the railing.

"Folks, Judge Müller will be here any moment. He's in the building. He encountered terrible traffic after dining out at noon. Mr. Crown, where are you at?"

"Here," Paul said, standing.

The clerk gestured commandingly. "Step in here, if you please. We need to handle this right quick—"

"After forcing us to wait twenty minutes," the general grumbled to Ilsa.

"—the court closes at four, for the holiday." The clerk sat back, fingering his lapels and enjoying his authority.

Paul was in this courtroom on this bitter afternoon because of Julie. She was in her third month of carrying their child.

They'd been trying to conceive a child since the very night of their marriage in a civil ceremony in October, two years ago. Paul's frequent, often abrupt departures, and his long absences, didn't improve their chances. Also, Julie had a history of trouble with pregnancy. She'd lost the only child conceived with her first husband. Finally they were successful.

On a snowy night early in December, they had been sitting in front of a fire in their parlor while snow drifted down outside a great bay window overlooking Paulina Street. They held hands and talked softly of the marvelous prospect of parenthood. The parlor was quite large, but it had a snug feel because, in the proper Victorian way, Julie had crowded it with furniture.

One of the important pieces was a rosewood étagère whose shelves displayed the growing collection of souvenirs from Paul's travels. And the globe, which now bore many more dots of dark red enamel. Tampa, Cuba, Egypt, the Suez Canal, South Africa, Texas, Paris, London—it was beginning to look as though the world had a case of measles.

One special souvenir hung on an otherwise uncluttered section of the wall, between the hearth and the display shelves, where the eye was drawn to it naturally. The left half of the stereopticon card, which Julie had framed and presented to Paul for his twenty-third birthday in June.

The flames danced, consuming the fragrant apple wood. Paul had drunk two bottles of Crown lager and was feeling warm and mellow. Behind them, the Victor Gramophone brought from Belle Mer softly played one of Julie's favorite pieces, the gentle and compelling Negro spiritual theme from Dvorak's Fifth Symphony.

"Paul."

"Mmm?"

"I don't like to ask for things. I don't do it often."

"No, the last time, as I recall, it was a simple request involving a pair of scissors."

"This would require a little more of you. Once again, it's important to me."

"Name it."

"Wait till you hear." She took a breath. "I know your feelings. I know the offer from that British peer tempts you. But if we're to stay here, I'd like our son or daughter to have American parents. Two of them."

While the impact settled on him, he looked at the framed picture of the ship's bow and the Statue of Liberty Enlightening the World . . .

Now here he was in the courtroom.

The clerk filed his nails.

The noisy Regulator clock ticktocked.

Carl folded his arms and let his eye wander, whistling the piano piece called "Ragtime Rose" that was a hit all over the country.

"Please don't, I'm reading," Fritzi said without looking up from her copy of *When Knighthood Was in Flower.*

Uncle Joe complained loudly about people who weren't punctual. "And he's German. It's true! He lives on *die Nordseite.*"

Aunt Ilsa murmured soothing monosyllables.

The courtroom grew steadily colder.

At 2:35 the private door opened and the Honorable Jacob Müller of the circuit court roared in, damning Chicago's vehicular traffic in a voice that could have been heard at the Stock Yards.

The judge flounced into his high-backed chair between the American flag and the flags of the state and municipality. He took a full half minute to adjust his robes. He didn't look at Paul, who stood in front of the dais, curiously tight with anxiety, suddenly unsure that this was the right step.

From Müllerstrasse in Berlin to Judge Müller's chambers in Chicago. From Pauli to Dutch. What a long journey . . .

Marriage to Julie, settling down in their flat, hadn't quite ended the journey, as he'd expected and hoped. He still needed a sign; the sign of which old Frau Flüsser in Berlin had spoken. He didn't know where it would come from, or how he'd recognize it. But he needed it, to banish the deep and haunting questions of childhood; put a clear mark at this journey's end, even though he surely had many others ahead in a lifetime of his chosen work.

He didn't dare say any of this to his wife; didn't dare tell her he was safely anchored in the happiest of marriages and yet still adrift on a wild sea, rudderless, with no chart, no light, no compass—

No sign to show him where he truly belonged.

The Honorable Judge Jacob Müller put on pince-nez, opened the folder, and examined Paul's application. He looked down from the high place.

"You are Mr. Crown?"

"Yes, your honor."

"I'm ready to take your declaration. The clerk will attend, please."

The courthouse hack stumbled from his desk with the smaller book. The judge said, "Left hand on the Bible, right hand raised, if you please, sir."

Paul obeyed. He swallowed several times but the lump in his throat wouldn't go away.

"Paul Crown, do you declare under oath before this court that it is your bona fide intention to become a citizen of the United States of America?"

"I do."

"A little louder, please."

"I do. I do!"

"Do you further declare that you renounce forever all allegiance to any foreign prince, potentate, or sovereignty, and particularly, in this instance, allegiance to His Majesty Kaiser Wilhelm the Second, of the country of Germany, you being at this moment a citizen or subject of said country?"

"I do, yes."

Judge Müller's pen scratched.

"So sworn, so noted, so entered."

The judge laid his pen aside, removed his eyeglasses, shot up from his chair, and leaned over to shake Paul's hand.

"Congratulations, Mr. Crown. Come back in two years, we'll make it binding."

Since 1898, Paul's road to this courtroom in the last hours of the last day of the old century had been colorful, convoluted, and, at times, highly dangerous. Shadow's appetite for "actualities" had only been whetted by the Spanish war films. He had also realized that money spent traveling a camera crew to a remote location, however wasteful it seemed at the time, could yield a bonanza. No longer did Paul have to argue to justify every penny.

Whenever Paul reflected on the variety of experiences he'd had by age twenty-three, he was awestruck. The Spanish war had merely been the start. When Admiral Dewey returned in triumph in September of 1899, Paul and Ollie Hultgren photographed his cruiser *Olympia* from a tossing tugboat in New York Harbor. That same day, when the Admiral received a ceremonial sword at City Hall, Paul passed out dollar bills to cut a path to the front of the enormous crowd, where he and Ollie could record the ceremony on film. The admiral glared at him several times; Dewey hated all photographers.

In competition with Albert Smith of the Vitagraph of New York, Paul and Ollie sailed for Britain when the war broke out in the fall of 'ninety-nine. Great Britain and the South African Republic had been wrangling for years about control of internal affairs. But the principal motivation for the war lay in the rich veins of gold in and around Johannesburg. The mines of the Rand deposits were largely owned and controlled from London.

What precipitated the war was an ultimatum from President Paul Kruger of the Republic. All British troops had to be withdrawn by the eleventh of October 1899. Britain responded with an immediate buildup of troops on the borders. The deadline passed. On October 12, the first shots were fired.

It was in London, on his way to South Africa, that Paul at last met Michael's father-in-law. Michael was already in South Africa for the *London Light.* A nasty trick of fate put him in Mafeking, an insignificant town about eight miles inside the west border of the Transvaal, where he interviewed Colonel Robert S. S. Baden-Powell, commander of the Bechuanaland Protectorate Regiment hastily moved to Mafeking after Kruger's ultimatum. When fighting started, five thousand Boers swept down on the town and threw a siege cordon around it, catching Baden-Powell, and Michael, by surprise.

Paul learned this from Lord Yorke, in the proprietor's immense office on the top floor of the *Light* building on Fleet Street. Lord Yorke explained that Mafeking had suddenly assumed strategic importance because it was a junction on the rail line to Bulawayo, Rhodesia, in the north. During the troop buildup, large quantities of military supplies had been shipped to the junction and stored. Thus a tiny town of fifteen hundred whites and about five thousand African blacks became a vital target for the Boers. Michael had the misfortune to be standing bang on that target at the wrong moment. Lord Yorke related all this sourly; he seemed to disapprove of his country's involvement in the war.

He changed the subject. Paul's reputation had preceded him, he said. After a half hour of questions, Lord Yorke offered Paul a high salary if he'd come to London and organize a picture unit. Lord Yorke looked like a frog and spoke like an angel, in a sonorous voice quite at odds with his jowls and pop eyes and oiled black hair. Paul could barely withstand his blandishments, in the office, then at Lord Yorke's regular luncheon table at the Reform Club in Pall Mall, and finally at supper at Café Royal.

"You must come over," Lord Yorke kept insisting.

"My wife is in America. That's where I belong, sir."

He said it, but deep within, doubt remained. When he got home, he didn't mention the offer to Shadow. When he told Julie, she said, "Do you want to go?"

"Part of me does. You are more important. You, and our child."

"Your happiness is important to me, Paul."

He smiled but didn't reply. To this minute, even though he'd acceded to her request at the fireside and said yes, he'd make his declaration of intent, he was damnably unsure.

After receiving clearance to enter the South African war zone, Paul and Ollie had bought passage on a small Greek freighter outbound from Tilbury on the Thames. They debarked at Durban, South Africa, on December 12, 1899. The very next day, who should Paul see coming toward him on a dung-littered street, wearing polished boots and cavalry trousers, double-breasted blue jacket and cravat, tall white tropical helmet and puggaree, but Dick Davis. Davis hurrahed, and hugged Paul, and treated the two cameramen to supper. Ollie was overawed—doubly so when Davis pointed out a bewhiskered civilian dining with two Army officers.

"Dr. Conan Doyle. Mr. Sherlock Holmes himself. He's here to set up relief hospitals and at the same time write some dispatches. I've seen a bit of his copy. He should stick to fiction and medicine."

Movement in the war zone was tightly controlled by the military, who also controlled and censored all copy sent out of the country by journalists. Every dispatch had to reflect favorably on the Crown and its military arm. With the appropriate permissions in hand, Davis, Paul, and Ollie hired a Cape cart drawn by two horses in tandem, and took on a pair of dark Kaffir boys—one to cook and one to tend the animals.

They reached Pietermaritzburg, the supply base of General Buller, and from there traveled northwest toward Colenso on a munitions train. Paul carried a Mauser pistol in a belt holster, bought in Durban; Davis's suggestion.

Two hours up the line, a dozen Boer riflemen on horseback charged down from the crest of some low hills and attacked the train. Davis was forward in the only passenger coach, which carried officers. Paul and Ollie were playing cards on a trunk in the baggage car. At the first shot, Ollie rolled back the door and held the tripod rigid on the bouncing, swaying floor while Paul cranked. A young Boer controlling his horse with his legs rode so close to the train, Paul could see the gray irises of his eyes. The young Boer fired his rifle directly at the camera. Luckily the train was bouncing. The bullet buzzed over Paul's head by a matter of inches. He snatched out his pistol. The Boer saw it and galloped away. Officers returning small-arms fire from the coach ultimately drove off the attackers, at a cost of two lives.

Separating from Davis, Paul and Ollie traveled on horseback with their Cape cart and their Kaffir boys. They filmed some of the fight at Spion Kop, tallest of a chain of kopjes—hills—when Buller tried to force the Tulega River and was repulsed. There was much confusion during the action, and Paul and Ollie slipped away before it was over. Paul didn't want their equipment confiscated because they'd filmed scenes of a British defeat in progress.

Once again they met Davis. He was coming up to the front. He told them where to find a Boer encampment by striking west. The Boers were friendly to neutral journalists; they wanted their side told. He'd visited with them and begun to change his original, unfavorable opinion.

"They seem dedicated idealists. Hard, maybe, but no harder than their enemy. They live simply and they say they want only one thing. To avoid the yoke of the Empire. The censors don't like what I've written about the Boers lately. The hell with them."

Paul and Ollie and the Kaffirs easily found the encampment, about a hundred men with half again that number of horses and a couple of small fieldpieces. It was one of many similar small bands of Boers who operated independently, moving and striking at will. Riding on the commando, they called it.

The leader, Captain Christiaan Botha, was a rangy man with sun-browned skin, a long beard, and a broad-brimmed hat with a feather in the band. His uniform was like no other Paul had seen, consisting of sand-colored boots and shirt and trousers of muted dark green, the color of leaves in a forest without rain. A huge sheath knife dangled from the captain's belt. A Mauser rifle and two leather bandoliers, full, lay on his cot.

Captain Botha shared his best food with the visitors and talked easily, if rather smugly, afterward:

"By spring we expect Her Majesty will have nearly five hundred thousand of her best in this little country. We have perhaps eighty thousand males in total, and no more than forty in the field at any one time. How is it that a small number of farmers dare to challenge the world's mightiest empire? I will tell you. One, we are fighting for our homeland. Two, we are born and brought up on horse-back. Able to move like flowing water over this terrain, which we know well. All that the queen's regulars can do is march in textbook formation and execute tactics memorized at their war college. We have beaten them all winter, every-where. We shall continue—rather like the American chaps who turned back a redcoat army stupid enough to march in formation up Bunker Hill, against the muskets of rebels afire with their cause. Now, a proposal. How would you like to visit a Zulu kraal?"

Captain Christiaan Botha led them, on horseback, with only one subaltern accompanying. Paul and Ollie were more than a little terrified by their first sight of the tall, muscular Zulu warriors coming to meet them with spears and shields.

Botha took the two of them to the chief's hut. It was four o'clock, and in the hut, which did not have a pleasant smell, the elderly chief proudly gestured to a sparkling silver tea service on a polished tea cart. "Holy God in heaven," Ollie whispered to Paul. "Am I mad?"

The chief of course didn't understand. Christiaan Botha assured Ollie he was completely sane. In an attempt to civilize the Zulu tribe, the British had arranged for sons of certain chiefs to receive schooling at Oxford. Many had returned to Africa with English wardrobes, English books, and possessions bought in English stores, although the civilizing process as such failed. The chief's son was one of those who had been a college man for a time.

The visitors sat cross-legged on the ground, drinking their tea. The chief wore a silk top hat suitable for an opera house, and proved an agreeable fellow. On request, he ordered some of his young warriors to dance for the camera, beating their shields. Paul cranked. If it came out, the footage would be wonderful.

The siege of Mafeking was lifted by relief forces early in May of 1900. Michael was already infamous throughout the British high command and War Office for hostile dispatches he'd managed to sneak out of the besieged town. The moment the siege was lifted, he was expelled from the country. He went to Paris because his father-in-law advised that he might be jailed if he returned to London too soon. While Ollie sailed for America with the now-battered camera and gear, Paul took a different ship, bound for Marseilles, to visit his friend.

Europe was in turmoil. It was a year of violent strikes. Steelworkers in Vienna. Glassworkers in Belgium. Field labor in Bohemia. German and Belgian coal miners. Paul had the eerie feeling that a hundred ghosts of Benno Strauss were haunting the continent, fomenting class warfare.

In Paris he watched three separate showings of *Cinderella,* the newest story film by Georges Méliès, a former conjurer and associate of the great illusionist Robert Houdin. Now Méliès was creating illusions for the screen. His newest picture was four hundred feet; six thousand four hundred frames. Probably the longest story film so far.

Paul and Michael were once again reunited at a great fair, the Paris Exhibition, for which the city had been beautified and the Metro underground constructed. Two of the largest and most popular exhibits were those of armament companies. Schneider-Creusot showed long-range cannon, Vicker-Maxim an array of rapid-fire machine guns.

Once again the two friends visited a magnificent Russian Pavilion, and there rode in a finely detailed replica of a Trans-Siberian Railway carriage. Outside, paintings depicting sunlit grain fields and pretty peasant huts unrolled on a continuous canvas.

Michael, as usual, held forth. When an attendant put his head in to snarl that they must make room for others waiting, Michael simply waved and spoke curtly in Russian—"Press. Shut the damn door."—and kept on talking about Mafeking.

Mafeking sums it all up (Michael said)—the failure of men, and the failure of organizations and governments. Mafeking's a bloody hole. Tin roofs, dirt streets, damnable heat, dogs and chickens running amok. We were imprisoned in that place two hundred and seventeen days, can you imagine? When the shelling slacked off after a few weeks, the Boer cordon shrank from five thousand to about fifteen hundred. The noble commandant, however, kept inflating the number in his reports. It was something like fifteen, sixteen thousand by the time we got out. Do you wonder Baden-Powell's the darling hero of the Empire?

Early on, he called the journalists together for a lecture on procedures and expectations. He personally would review and censor all copy. Nothing critical of the conduct of the siege, or his officers, would be transmitted, or tolerated. During the siege the telegraph was never cut, I can't explain why except that the Boers are fairly civilized.

It was a strange kind of imprisonment. The Boer artillery wasn't that plentiful, or that good. One large siege gun, Big Ben, plus some old brass cannon sufficient to poop in a few rounds at intervals, to remind us we were pinned down.

All the while, Baden-Powell sent out the cheeriest of reports. "Everything fine. Four hours of bombardment. One dog killed." He was determined to be a stalwart, and keep morale high. Whilst the siege was going on, we enjoyed cricket matches on Sunday—blasphemous to the Boers, they're religious people. Baden-Powell also organized billiards tournaments, concerts at the Masonic Hall, amateur theatricals. Acted in several of those himself. Oh, he kept up with his strategical duties, too. Bleeding Jesus, didn't he! He took a megaphone and paraded about the town perimeter shouting false orders about false attacks by nonexistent forces. The Boers at Mafeking could have run us over at any time, and I don't know why they didn't.

The word "siege" conjures up privation, but actually the officers ate well in their messes. We civilians ate well. There were all those foodstuffs piled up at the rail junction, a mountain of them. However, the poor wretched niggers had nothing. Were *given* nothing. They starved.

Baden-Powell put in a system of rationing for 'em. Sold 'em horsemeat soup for three pence per bowl. They scavenged in army garbage. Well before Mafeking was relieved, five or six hundred perished from hunger.

I've painted a queer picture, but it wasn't entirely bloodless. Now and then some of the Tommies did have a real skirmish with the enemy. A bit of slaughter to pep things up. I personally watched a group of our plucky lads dash out and overcome a sector of the Boer trenches. With victory in hand, our lads used their bayonets and swords to stab and decapitate every last Boer, dead or alive. I threw up.

To the end, Baden-Powell approved, or disapproved, every word we sent out. Suggested little improvements. You were smiled upon if you filled your dispatches with references to "our indomitable soldiers" and "the sterling qualities that created the Empire" and "fighting for glory or the grave." Absolute shit! And the journalists went along. Never dared suggest the real reason for the fighting—the defense of the interests of British mine owners, speculator combines, London investment banks heavily into mine finance. The usual secret oligarchy of old boys who send young boys to die. No one wrote about that. My profession disgraced itself utterly.

Out of profound revulsion spiced with boredom, in late February I began to alter my method of work. Each time I took up my pen I wrote two dispatches, one for Baden-Powell and another to be sneaked out by a Kaffir boy I could trust. I asked my father-in-law to print only the second set. He bravely did so because he opposed the war, he and my Cecily were members of the Stop-the-War Committee, along with Lloyd George and a mixed lot of others. I sneaked out a total of four unfavorable dispatches. Because they were published, I was promptly shown the border when Mafeking was relieved.

Unnecessary, really. No one believed the bad stuff because the government propaganda was too massive, too effective. Music hall picture programs included films of a Red Cross tent being ripped apart by Boer fire while valiant nurses, doctors, and orderlies were treating wounded. Actors. It was all a sham, the pictures were made on Hampstead Heath. You've told me they commit the same fraud in America.

In this life I have developed a vast Dickensian distrust of every sort of bureaucratic structure—armies, corporations, governments. I have a constant and unshakable faith in the essential venality and cupidity of those who own or control such bodies. The South African war validated all my beliefs again.

Ah, Paul—why do we go on? Why do we deceive ourselves, proclaim that we're uplifting our brothers and our sisters with the scientific marvels of the new age? Uplift is a fiction we created to hide the truth. We love the slime. The human animal is a cowardly and vicious beast. And think how much worse it will be when he has his hands on quantities of rapid-fire guns, cannon that can hurl a shell twenty miles, airships capable of dropping explosives on civilian populations . . .

A dark time, the next century. The beast is already prowling. He smells blood coming down the wind. Armageddon.

Nothing to do, I suppose, but have a drink, have a woman, try to survive for one more day.

Paul returned to America to find Bryan and Debs running for President in November, and his friend Crane dead at age twenty-eight. Crane had died of tuberculosis in June, at the *Kurpark* in Badenweiler, Germany. Paul knew the spa by reputation; it was famous for treating respiratory disorders. But not successfully in this case.

Shadow was jubilant about the South African pictures. "The yellow dogs at Edison hired two hundred derelicts and did the Spion Kop battle at West Orange, New Jersey. A cannon fired too early and a couple of the fake soldiers got hurt. Serves them fucking right for trying to deceive the American public."

Shadow gave him a bonus, and considered new assignments.

The Philippines were a possibility. An exotic locale. Jungle fighting. General Arthur MacArthur, United States military governor of the islands, was trying to subdue insurgents dedicated to ridding the country of foreign rule—first Spain, now the United States, which had been given the Philippines as part of the peace settlement of 'ninety-eight. But Shadow hadn't yet found men to train for a second camera crew, and he was reluctant to have Paul and Ollie out of the country for another extended period.

On Saturday, September 8, the elements provided an epic subject in the state of Texas. Galveston Island, southeast of Houston, was nearly destroyed by the winds and storm tides of a monster hurricane. Thousands of lives were lost, more than half the island destroyed. Paul and Ollie connived to get aboard a special relief train sponsored by the *Chicago American* of W. R. Hearst.

The train arrived in Texas City on Thursday, September 13. The storm had broken the bridges to Galveston like matchwood. Paul and Ollie stared in horror as their crowded scow bore them to a pier still standing at Twelfth Street.

They filmed on ghostly streets where an upright section of brick wall or a smashed piece of furniture was all that remained of human habitation. They saw Miss Barton and other Red Cross women cooking in a soup tent.

On the beach, black banners of smoke marked sites where bodies were being burned in kerosene-soaked pyres of alternating layers of lumber and flesh. At first bodies had been taken into the Gulf on scows and dumped, but hundreds of them floated back to the shore.

The smell of the fires was appalling, and so was the smell of the silt that lay two and three inches deep everywhere. In two days, they accumulated scenes that stunned audiences to silence.

And so it went, the hours and days rolling into weeks and months, sweeping Paul from one side of the globe to the other, one remarkable sight or experience to the next, exactly as he'd dreamed in the little windowless room in Berlin. Unbelievably, the dream had come true.

But his home life was always close to a shambles because of it. Tomorrow, New Year's Day, he and Ollie had railway tickets to New York. A new Ellis Island had opened on December 17, rebuilt after a disastrous fire in 1897 destroyed the original wooden buildings. Millions of immigrants were pouring into the country, including a great many Jews from Eastern Europe. Ellis Island was a topic of the moment. Shadow wanted an "actuality."

The train would leave at half past ten in the morning. Tonight, however, was all his, and Julie's. Tonight there was Uncle Joe's party, to celebrate the new century, and Paul's intent to become a citizen.

The party was held at the city's newest German restaurant, *Zum Rothen Stern*, the Red Star Inn, on North Clark Street at Germania Place. The owner had created a near-perfect replica of a Bavarian public house, using dark wood paneling, leaded glass windows inset with Teutonic crests, wrought iron lanterns, tables and chairs of white ash, stuffed moose and elk and boar heads, elaborately painted beer steins, a long menu of German specialties, and a staff of good-humored but mercilessly efficient waiters in short black jackets and long white aprons. Most of the waiters were middle-aged, and fat.

The owner, a forty-year-old immigrant from Cologne, greeted them at the door. "*Guten Abend, Herr General,*" he said, bowing.

"Good evening, Herr Gallauer." Uncle Joe looked around. "Happy to see such a large crowd. Your restaurant has enjoyed great success in a short time." Gallauer stroked his little Vandyke, pleased. "Is the private room ready?"

"But of course. The Cottage Room. Follow me."

Every table in the main dining room was full, and the noise level was high. Their private room opened onto the main section at the rear, and Uncle Joe, who seemed in a festive mood, suggested they leave the double doors rolled back. This pleased everyone, making them feel a part of the spirit of celebration pervading the restaurant.

The banquet Uncle Joe had arranged was huge, and altogether German. To begin, steaming china tureens of soup, a choice of oxtail or creamy asparagus-based *Rahmsuppe*. Next the waiters brought bowls of a house specialty, *Leber-klösse;* eating a Red Star liver dumpling or two was supposed to settle the stomach in preparation for the main courses—tonight, platters of roast pork, roast veal, mutton, rabbit, venison, and potted ox joints. Sauerbraten was served, with vegetables and fresh hot loaves of light and dark bread. Desserts would be a selection of traditional puddings and stewed fruits. All of this was liberally supplemented with spirits. Not only Crown lager and Heimat, but Mumm's champagne and Frankish wine in stubby oval bottles of green glass. *"Trocken!* Your driest and best," Uncle Joe demanded.

The table was U-shaped, with places assigned by little cards Aunt Ilsa had lettered. In the main section of the restaurant, the strolling accordionist was playing "The Stars and Stripes Forever" while people clapped and stamped to the beat. The march was a favorite of Paul's, and he heard it everywhere— parlors, concert halls, saloons, street corners—as if Sousa's melody summed up America's mood of strength, optimism, growing importance in global affairs.

The accordionist came into the private room and asked what they wished to hear. A familiar German folk song, perhaps? Carl said, "Play 'Ragtime Rose.'" Mary Beezer and Willis applauded. Though not fond of that sort of music, Uncle Joe was soon tapping his foot. At the end, he tipped the accordionist lavishly.

"Two dollars?" Aunt Ilsa gasped, palms against her cheeks.

"Once in a century, why not?" Uncle Joe leaned over to kiss her cheek. Paul thought that an excellent idea. He kissed Julie on the cheek. She pressed the back of his neck with her hand and whispered an endearment.

Paul lit a cigar. He called for the pitcher of Crown lager, which Carl passed. He poured his third tall glass. In the public section of the restaurant, people were laughing, singing, even shouting. It was still only half past nine.

The party grew louder and more convivial. The guests left their seats between courses. Julie spoke earnestly to Aunt Ilsa, telling her she really should meet Mr. Carnegie someday, because he shared Ilsa's passion for world peace.

Shadow dashed out into the smoky main room to fetch back the accordionist. "I want a cakewalk," he said, tipsily rearranging chairs to create space. The cakewalk was the most popular dance in America, and Shadow insisted on demonstrating his familiarity. "I didn't wear that fu—uh, that rotten minstrel blackface for nothing. Here we go, Mary."

Colonel Shadow and Mary did a cakewalk, receiving enthusiastic applause.

Wex cornered Paul and quizzed him about his travels. Paul in turn wanted reassurance that Wex was doing well; wasn't squandering his profits on Kentucky horse racing.

"Are you serious, my boy? Look at my dear wife over there. She has a fine head for figures. She keeps the books, controls our funds, and gives me a small betting allowance every month. When it's gone, there isn't any more. I tried to filch a little extra one month right after we moved to Lexington. Lucille caught me and threw me on the floor. Then she sat on me and lectured. She's as sweet as they make 'em, but she has an iron will, and the constitution of a wrestler. It doesn't pay to argue with Lucille, God bless her. She's what I've needed for years. She tamed my worst demons. No, there's a better way to put it. She ordered them to move out."

A bit later, Paul overheard Miss Fishburne talking spiritedly with his aunt. Miss Fishburne had imbibed heavily of champagne and was looking better for it, he thought. She'd been rather glum and tired when she arrived the night before. Julie had discovered the reason; her aunt was recovering from a failed romance with a handsome young Portuguese named Fernando, captain of a charter yacht berthed in Monte Carlo.

"I can't decide what to do next, my dear Ilsa. I'm mad to study plein air painting in Provence. Or sail to the Hebrides. I've always wanted to visit Japan to see Kabuki theater—all those chesty men playing fragile geishas, it's too much! Of course I could settle down at a spa and read Count Tolstoy's *War and Peace* to the end. I've started it nine times. Right now I'm having hellish difficulty with a book called *The Interpretation of Dreams*. It's very controversial. Written by some Viennese alienist no one has heard of . . ."

Aunt Ilsa was enraptured. Or, possibly, overwhelmed.

Paul next observed Miss Fishburne speaking to the formidable Mrs. Rooney, waving her champagne glass for emphasis.

"Take some unsolicited advice, Lucille. Be very nice to your husband or someone may snatch him away. I find him utterly charming. Rather like a leprechaun with brains."

Shortly thereafter, Miss Fishburne joined Julie while the waiters brought in hot coffee and glasses of schnapps. Julie and her aunt discussed Nell. Julie's aunt was twirling yet another full glass of champagne.

"Better you don't have a mother any more, that's my opinion. My dear sick sister was never remotely fitted for the role." Julie barely had time to agree before Fritzi pulled her chair next to theirs. Fritzi had been trailing Julie's aunt since they met, because Miss Fishburne had seen every noted actor and actress in America and Europe. Henry Irving, Salvini, Ada Rehan, Sarah Bernhardt. William Gillette, famous for his spellbinding personation of Sherlock Holmes. Tyrone Power and Beerbohm Tree and Joe Jefferson and Ellen Terry and Maude Adams and Richard Mansfield and Mrs. Fiske and Mrs. Leslie Carter and a young beauty named Ethel Barrymore, related to Mrs. John Drew. And Ethel's brothers, Lionel and John.

Fritzi was agog. "Mrs. John Drew is the only famous one I've met."

"Don't worry, you'll meet them all," Miss Fishburne assured her.

Julie said, "You'll be one of them, Fritzi. People will be wanting to meet you."

"Fritzi," Paul said from down the table. "I have a surprise. I saved it until tonight."

"A surprise for me? What is it?"

"Day before yesterday, the post brought a letter from Michael. He mentions a friend named Stanislavski, who's operating an extraordinary new art theater in Moscow with a partner, a well-regarded playwright and acting teacher. The two hope to start their own school; so Michael wrote to them, about you, some time ago. His letter yesterday says that when they're ready to accept their first class of apprentices, they'd be pleased to give your application every consideration—assuming you'd have the wherewithal to travel to Moscow."

"Oh—oh." Scarlet with excitement, Fritzi pressed her palms to her face; Paul thought she might swoon. "That's so exciting, Paul. What do they mean by wherewithal?"

"Money," Uncle Joe said dryly. "Steamer and rail fare. Little incidentals like food and clothing and shelter."

"I'll get it, and I'll go. It may surprise you, Papa, but I've heard of this new Moscow company. The most advanced in the world, everyone says."

"Everyone *you* know," Carl said loudly. "I never heard of it."

"Well, I suppose we could help finance a trip at the appropriate time," Uncle Joe mused, reaching for his schnapps. Fritzi ran over to kiss him, and then Paul.

Paul lit a third cigar. Uncle Joe hadn't said much to Shadow so far, probably deeming him too raffish. Now Paul watched Shadow weave around the table with a tall glass of Crown's. The colonel stopped to toast Uncle Joe.

"To you, sir. This is the best fu—uh, most delectable lager beer I've ever tasted. I'm converted. A Crown man forever."

"Is that a fact? Excellent, Colonel. You must tell me about this picture business you're in. Please, sit down." Uncle Joe indicated a chair, which was all the invitation Shadow needed. Seated, he flung an arm over Uncle Joe's back, startling him.

"Well, General, I'm in what you'd call a transitional phase. I want to shift out of exhibition into production. Widen my distribution of Luxograph pictures. Organize more camera teams. I'll never find another operator as good as Dutch, but maybe I'll turn up some close seconds."

"Why this change, may I ask?"

"In production the numbers work out better."

"Numbers. Ah. Can you give me an example?"

Shadow snatched a pencil from an inner pocket and scribbled on a menu at furious speed. Soon Uncle Joe was leaning down next to him. Their heads were practically touching. Paul laughed.

A few minutes later, Paul excused himself to visit the gentlemen's. On his way back through the main dining room, he was startled to see Uncle Joe standing in an aisle, red-faced, in some kind of confrontation with Hexhammer, the newspaper editor.

117

The General

HEXHAMMER intercepted Joe when he was on his way to the gentlemen's. The younger man was neatly dressed, as always. This evening there was an addition: a wide red-and-black ribbon around his neck, with a bronze-finished medallion hanging from it. The medallion bore an embossed double eagle, the symbol of Prussia.

Hexhammer bowed. "Herr General Crown. I understand that honorific has been yours ever since the Spanish war."

Ignoring the mild sarcasm, Joe said, "That is true."

"Celebrating with your family, as I am with mine?"

"Yes. Is that a decoration, Oskar?"

"Indeed so. The Order of the Red Eagle, Fourth Class. Bestowed by the Kaiser himself, for special services to the Pan-German League. We are very active, here and in the fatherland. In Berlin, the league is undertaking an elaborate study to establish, scientifically and unequivocally, that the pure-blooded German male or female is distinct from all other racial types, mentally and physically."

"Distinct, and superior?"

"I'm confident the evidence will show that, yes. These are exciting times. At the urging of Admiral von Tirpitz, and with the wholehearted endorsement of His Majesty, the Reichstag has authorized a twenty-year construction program to equip Germany with an additional—"

"Thirty-eight battleships. I do read the papers." *Though not yours.*

"Loyal German-Americans in Chicago are drafting a letter of commendation, to carry as many signatures as we can secure. The letter will go to League headquarters in Berlin. In the letter we applaud the stronger navy, which in turn will guarantee stability of German colonial—"

"Oskar, excuse me, I am in need of the facilities."

"Just a moment more. I assume you wouldn't care to add your signature to such a letter?"

"You assume correctly."

A little smile played on the editor's mouth. "I wanted to be very sure, you see. Your positions will not be forgotten, Herr General. Nor your hostility. There will come a time when you'll regret your stand."

"Oskar—" Joe reined his anger with difficulty. "Meeting you is always unproductive. You strain my patience and upset my stomach. Stand out of my way, please, before I do what I threatened to do one time in my office. Knock you down."

Before Hexhammer could react, Joe said, "Happy New Year to you and yours, Oskar. That's American speech, in case you don't recognize it."

He marched away to the lavatory.

At a few minutes before midnight the accordionist began a familiar *Neujahrslied* in the main room. Almost at once, people were on their feet, swaying, bellowing the sentimental farewell to the old year.

> *"Das alte Jahr vergangen ist,*
> *Das neue Jahr beginnt.*
> *Wir danken Gott zu dieser Frist,*
> *Wohl uns, dass wir noch sind!"*

Thanking God for the year past, and for allowing them to celebrate the new . . .

Then Herr Gallauer and his waiters called for quiet. Herr Gallauer had obtained a ship's bell, which he rang with a mallet while eyeing his large gold pocket watch. Stroke by stroke, the last seconds of the year were counted down. On the twelfth stroke, people threw streamers, and pounded the tables, and shouted, *"Glückliches neues Jahr!* Happy New Year!" Everyone, including the Crowns and their guests, kissed and embraced and uttered sentimental good wishes.

Mary Beezer burst into tears. Willis hailed a waiter for another glass of champagne. Wex Rooney thought that a good idea and held up two fingers. His wife pulled his hand down.

Joe gave a strong hug to each of his children, then Paul, Paul's wife, and finally Ilsa. Over her shoulder, he observed his nephew. Paul was standing with his head canted forward so that his forehead touched Julie's. His hands rested on her shoulders. He was murmuring to her, and she responded with an adoring look. Joe had never seen his nephew so happy.

Outwardly, he too was happy; exuberantly so. He sang and cheered with the rest. But some of that was pretense. With his remark about a time of confrontation, Oskar Hexhammer had cast a shadow on the evening. Joe Crown really didn't take the remark, the threat, personally, even though it was meant that way. He put it in a larger framework. A global framework. The fever of nationalism was high, and both his old homeland and his new one were traveling strange and unfamiliar courses. In the year of Joe's birth, 1842, Germany had existed only as a clutch of quarreling city-states and districts, and America was a rural land with much of its wealth undiscovered, much of its industrial potential unrealized. Now both nations were mighty, and prideful, and eager to demonstrate their strength and importance to the world. Joe prayed their courses would never collide.

118

Ilsa

IT WAS HAPPENSTANCE, Ilsa's answering when the front bell rang on New Year's morning.

Joe had left about seven, after a hasty *Frühstück* of coffee, salami, and a hard roll with unsalted butter. He complained of a headache from all the celebration last night, but he went to the brewery anyway, because it would be quiet and he could weed through the thickets of paper forever sprouting from his desk. He'd promised to be home by two for their annual dinner celebrating the feast of St. Sylvester.

Fritzi and Carl were still in their rooms. Ilsa hoped Carl was now too old to shoot off firecrackers in the garden. Any excessive noise in the house got on her nerves. Another sign of age.

Julie would come for the afternoon meal, but at this hour she would be at the depot, saying goodbye to Paul and his helper. Ilsa wished her nephew hadn't left so soon. She loved having the whole family together at the table on holidays, but it was becoming impossible. That was the way of the world when children grew up.

Customarily, Manfred would have answered the ring at the front door but he was away for a week, visiting Helga's family in St. Louis. They were Manfred's family now; his only family. Helga Blenkers had passed away during the summer, after exposure to a chilly rain brought on pneumonia.

The house smelled of fish. Louise, who was really getting too old and feeble to prepare large meals, insisted on serving a traditional carp with the other dishes this afternoon. The young people probably wouldn't eat it. They would already be stuffed with Louise's *Glücksschwein*, the little good-luck pigs of marzipan, and the miniature chimney sweep figures baked from dough.

There was a second ring of the bell. "Wait, please, I'm coming," Ilsa called.

She opened the door and saw a tramp standing there, supporting himself with a crutch under his right arm. She couldn't see him clearly because of the dazzling winter sun. She wished for youthful eyesight again.

Even so, a few details registered. The man was slightly built, with the start of a small paunch, which struck her as wrong because he seemed young. Curly hair fell over his collar; a heavy beard concealed his chin and neck. He wore a patched mackinaw of red-and-black plaid, pin-striped pants that must have belonged to a discarded suit, and a cloth cap that cast a shadow slantwise below his nose. His right trouser leg was pinned or sewn up just above the ankle; his right foot was missing.

It flashed through Ilsa's mind that Germans said the first person you encountered outside your house on New Year's Day had special significance. Seeing an old woman meant bad luck for the coming year, a young man the opposite. What did a tramp signify? She had no idea.

She raised a hand in front of her forehead to shield the sun. "I'm very sorry," she began; she'd recited the same litany often. "We don't feed anyone at the front door."

"Mama."

"If you will go to the back—"

"Don't you know me? Mama, it's Joe."

119

The General

ABOUT HALF PAST TEN, *Brauerei Crown* was quiet as a church. Working in shirt-sleeves, Joe was swiftly clearing his desk of some of the unwanted or unnecessary paper. Stefan Zwick had come in as well, on his own, and Joe could hear the satisfying sound of his clerk slowly and diligently typing in the outer office.

Hard work was an excellent antidote for the gloom generated by Oskar Hexhammer's predictions last night.

The telephone rang. Stefan answered, then put his head in.

"Mrs. Crown is calling."

Annoyed by the interruption, Joe abandoned a column of cost figures and reached for the instrument. "Yes, Ilsa?"

"Joe, I have some news."

Her low voice was a signal that something had happened. He forgot everything, rocked with fear of a tragedy.

"Tell me."

For long seconds, there was silence on the faintly humming connection. The news was so terrible she was unable to repeat it. A dozen gory alternatives flashed in his head, but of course not the right one.

"Joe Junior. He is here."

"Here?"

"Here, in the house, yes, I answered the door an hour ago, there he was."

"I'll drive home immediately. I must talk to him."

"Joe, don't come home. Not for a while. This time I will talk to him."

Angered, vaguely hurt, he exclaimed, "It's my duty, I'm his father."

"I will talk to him this time. Remember what Carl Schurz said. There is such a thing as being too German. I will do it, then you can see him. I don't know why our son came home but now that he has, I want him to stay if he will. I want to heal the old wounds, I don't want them opened again."

"But—"

"Joe." She was so quiet. Yet there was a definite declaration; a warning. *"I will do it."* He'd never heard such metal in her voice.

Now he was the one who was silent. She'd changed. The world had changed. His whole family had changed. But so had he, he realized with a mingling of amazement, bewilderment, and not a little sadness.

"All right, Ilsa. I'll come home later."

"Not too soon. A few hours. Thank you, my dear one."

He put the earpiece on the hook, missing it once before he hung it properly.

"Stefan," he called in a voice grown weak.

"Sir?"

"Close the door if you will, please."

Not accustomed to requests so politely stated, Stefan Zwick poked his head in again. He was concerned about the look of strain on his employer's face. He retreated at once. The door closed with the gentlest of clicks.

In Larrabee Street Joe could hear some boys whooping and playing in the cold morning air. He sat staring at the black upright telephone standing in a bar of slanted sunshine. It was a new century, in a world that was so changed he sometimes recognized nothing but a few outer trappings. Sometimes he was convinced he was a total stranger in this new world, as he was in America when he first stepped onto its soil, a young greenhorn, in the year 1857.

Well, never mind, never mind. Shattering changes had come, and gone, and the Crowns survived. He would survive. Absolutely he would. The strength of the family was his strength. And now he had a reason more compelling than any he had known for a long time. His boy was home. With the aid of lessons painfully learned, Joe would keep him home.

120

Dutch

ON THURSDAY MORNING, the third of January, Paul left Ollie at the hotel and walked down Sixth Avenue. There were seventy-six million people in the United States, and half of them seemed to reside in New York. Half of those seemed to be abroad this morning, despite the bitter weather. A new subway like the one he'd ridden in Paris was being dug underground, to siphon off some of the pedestrian traffic. Paul doubted it would help much.

Overhead, the Sixth Avenue Elevated rumbled and roared and blew cinders down on the unwary. In the street there was a gigantic crush of horsecars and private vehicles, a crush made all the worse by the alarming presence and honking bulb horn of a steam-driven horseless carriage. Common as they were becoming, steam- and gasoline-powered cars never failed to amaze Paul, and frighten anything with four legs.

He missed Julie terribly, as he always did when they were apart. But he didn't miss the three-piece suit, celluloid collar and cuffs he'd worn to court, and to the party. He was at work again, able to dress in the comfortable outfit he liked because it set him apart. His shirt was khaki, matching his cavalry riding pants. For Christmas Julie had given him the newest fashion sensation, riding pants flared at the sides, a style said to originate in Jodhpur, India; he hadn't had the nerve to put those on yet.

With the khaki he wore black boots and a long black leather coat with a heavy red flannel lining. An expensive black-and-brown-checked golf cap, a present from Aunt Ilsa, and the polka-dot bandanna of the Rough Riders around his neck completed the outfit of the chief operator.

At the corner of Sixth and Seventeenth, he turned into the large and handsome two-story mercantile emporium of the F. W. Woolworth Company. Somewhere in his rounds yesterday, arranging for filming at government sites on Friday and Saturday, he'd lost his winter gloves.

As he stepped into the store, he heard piano music. It came from a high circular platform near the front doors. The platform was completely surrounded by racks of sheet music. A red-haired song plugger finished a march, nodded to acknowledge polite applause from his audience of eight shoppers. The plugger laced his fingers together, cracked his knuckles, adjusted his stool, and played several arpeggios to introduce "The Blue and the Gray," the most recent hit of the famous Paul Dresser. The plugger sang the ballad in a high, clear tenor.

"A mother's gift to her country's cause
Is a story yet untold—
She had three sons, three only ones,
Each worth his weight in gold."

Paul walked by, whistling the tune softly. He found the glove section and began sorting through bins holding various styles and sizes.

"She gave them up for the sake of war,
While her heart was filled with pain.
As each went away, she was heard to say,
He will never return again . . ."

He found exactly the right pair. Gauntlets of black-dyed leather with warm fleece linings. The salesgirl took his money with unusual friendliness and a glance of invitation. Paul just smiled. She put his money and the sales slip into a metal basket, hooked the basket on an overhead wire, and yanked a bell cord hanging from the ceiling. A pulley system whizzed the basket along the wire to a cashier on the mezzanine. A few moments later the basket came sailing down the wire with change and the bill stamped PAID.

"Would you like these wrapped, sir?"

"No thanks, I'll wear them."

She handed them across with a little pout of her well-rouged Cupid's bow lips.

Paul headed for the street while the plugger plaintively sang the second verse. The mother who had lost three sons found them waiting for her at the gates of Heaven. In full uniform. The applause for the sentimental song was enthusiastic. While performing it, the pianist had gathered a larger crowd, including a man whose appearance, from the back, plucked some faint chord in Paul's memory. The man's brushy black hair stuck out in many directions.

Paul stepped to one side for a partial view of the man's profile. The man was young; about his own age. He wore a proper and expensive Prince Albert suit of medium gray and a gray silk cravat, maroon with thin gray diagonal stripes. Over his arm he carried a gray overcoat. Lively eyes, vivid blue, darted over the racks of sheet music. Paul recognized him.

The plugger again laced his hands together, cracked his knuckles, and shook his fingers in the air while smiling to keep his audience. He hit the keys and swung into another hit of the moment, "Ragtime Rose." Half a dozen of the racks were filled with copies of the piano piece. The name of the composer, Harry Poland, was printed large in scrolled type.

The young man with black hair bounced up and down on his toes, accenting the complicated rhythms with little shakes of his head and flicks of his elbows. He was beaming, immersed in the music. Slowly, Paul walked on around the platform. Absolutely no mistake . . .

Across the carpeted platform, the young man noticed him. He and Paul were opposite each other. Paul waited, smiling in a tentative way. The young man frowned, obviously turning inward to search his memory.

His mouth fell open.

Paul grinned, snatched off his golf cap, and walked swiftly back to the other man.

"Herschel?"

"*Pauli?*"

"Herschel Wolinski."

"It's I, yes, Herschel, your friend!" His accent was surprisingly light. With a whoop, he tossed his overcoat on the platform and threw his arms around Paul, slapping his back and shouting, "Pauli, Pauli!" Annoyed listeners shushed them. The pianist was the most annoyed. Herschel said to him, "Stop the dirty looks, keep on playing, it's my music."

He leaned back, gripping Paul's shoulders. "It's really you?"

"It is, Pauli, or Paul, whatever you want—I have a lot of names in America. What do I call you? Herschel, or Harry?"

"Harry. Now and forever."

"How long have you been here?"

"It will be four years in March. My mother passed away and my sisters chose to remain behind. I told you I'd make it, didn't I? I never doubted. I have a new name, as you noticed. It's very American, don't you think?"

"Yes, I like it, it's catchy." Still amazed, Paul picked up a copy of "Ragtime Rose." He opened it; gazed at the incomprehensible black notes.

"You wrote this."

"I did. Actually I wrote it some time ago, to be played slowly. That was not—ah—practicable. I chanced to be in a saloon one evening listening to a black entertainer from St. Louis. He played piano pieces in this tricky time. He showed me how. The Negroes call it raggedy time, or sometimes just rag. I threw out the old version of my music and produced this one, in raggedy time."

"And it's a hit, I hear it everywhere."

"I must say modestly—that's so. Sales to date are two hundred thousand and climbing. It's published, as you see, by Howley, Haviland, the firm in which the great Paul Dresser is a partner. I started there as a song plugger, like that fellow playing, but they soon promoted me to staff composer. I do all right composing marches but I am not good with ballads yet. This piece is my favorite. Mr. Dresser hates it. He regards it as a threat to the sweet style in which he writes. But he recognizes music that will make money. Mr. Dresser likes money."

"Herschel, I cannot believe this."

"Nor I, really." He remembered something. Made a pistol of his hand; cocked his thumb. "Bang, bang!"

Paul laughed, shouted, "Bang, bang," and fired back. Three spectators moved away. A floorwalker strode toward them. The plugger, no longer the center of interest, hit sour notes to show his pique.

Herschel didn't care. He snatched Paul's hand and waltzed him around as if they were at a ball. Herschel's head bobbed in perfect three-quarter time.

The prim floorwalker confronted them. "See here, we can't allow—"

But they were already gone, arm in arm, into Sixth Avenue. Herschel had stuck a copy of the song in Paul's coat pocket, calling over his shoulder, "I'm the composer, I get free copies."

□ □ □ □

RAGTIME ROSE

They drank beer through the afternoon, adjourned to Charles Rector's splendid restaurant at dusk, and there dined on venison steaks, with many glasses of red Bordeaux to wash it down. They could hardly stop talking.

Paul finished his seventh or eighth glass and brushed his fingers over the sheet music on the tablecloth, now stained with wine. "You deserve success. This is a very pretty piece."

"Well, maybe not pretty. But catchy. And American, one hundred percent."

"You've done so well here. It's wonderful."

"You know I was determined to reach America. When I succeeded, I was determined not to fail. New York is so costly, but I've been lucky. I have other jobs besides my regular one at the publishing house. I work a lot as a rehearsal pianist for stage shows. When my schedule permits, I am the onstage accompanist for Miss Flavia Farrel."

"The Irish Songbird. Surely."

Herschel's cheeks pinked. "Miss Farrel is a demanding woman. But she is a joy to serve. I am slowly learning to do her musical arrangements, and I also provide certain physical comforts which she requires with great regularity. I'm only too happy to oblige. She's twenty years older than I, but a handsome and generous woman. She has taught me many things." He blushed. "Please don't ask me to be more specific."

He filled Paul's glass, then poured the last of the wine for himself. "Of course what I want most is to compose all the time. Not for hire, for myself. I know very little about formal musical theory. I am taking a night course."

"Let's leave," Paul said suddenly. "I'm thirsty for some good beer."

"So am I. Old friend."

Their whereabouts soon blurred in Paul's mind. At one place on the Bowery they exchanged addresses, and Herschel clasped Paul's hand and promised to visit Chicago, to meet Julie. They were picked up at half past two in the morning, reeling along lower Fifth Avenue in the freezing air, happily intoxicated. They spent the night in a jail cell, singing the melody of "Ragtime Rose" over and over, without words, while the inmates of the other cells cursed and threatened.

At seven in the morning, his head bursting and his eyeballs on fire, Paul telephoned Ollie at the hotel.

"Bring money for bail. I'll explain everything. Did you hire the launch? Good. Pack the equipment. We're filming at Ellis Island before noon."

Herschel heard none of this. He was still in the cell, curled up in his fine Prince Albert suit, snoring.

"Everything all right?" Paul said.

"Set," Ollie said.

"Here they come."

The Luxograph was set up on the esplanade at the Ellis Island immigrant depot, a much more substantial building than the one Pauli Kroner and old Valter had passed through. The new structure was solid red brick, accented with sand-colored stone. The docking area along the esplanade had become one side of a U-shaped ferry slip; on the other side, west, landfill from the subway excavation had extended the island for a new hospital standing half completed in the chilly sunlight. Paul had had the strangest feeling as they arrived in their launch; he'd never imagined he would see Ellis Island a second time.

A squat ferry named *Weehawken* was churning toward the open end of the slip, her decks thronged with newcomers from steerage. Today's arrivals were off the *Karlsruhe* of the North German Lloyd line, Bremen. Winter crossings were rough, and Paul understood this had been one of the worst in recent memory. He could imagine the emotions of the immigrants as they faced their ordeal.

The ferry chugged into the slip and warped toward the esplanade with engines at low speed. Ollie crouched over the camera with his cap reversed. The Lux-ograph lens pointed at the anxious faces behind the rail.

"I'm grinding, Dutch."

"Get as much as you can, it's good stuff."

The ferry's port side bumped the esplanade. Crewmen leaped off with mooring lines. In the forefront of the crowd waiting for the gangway to be lowered Paul saw an old gentleman with a fine guardsman's mustache. All of his possessions were in one large bundle. He looked bewildered; frightened. So did many others.

When the ferry tied up, the gangway was swung out. An officious crewman lowered the rope and jumped back. The old man threw himself forward with great energy, obviously fearful of being trampled by younger or stronger people behind him. A uniformed official pointed to the main doors of the baggage hall. "That way, hurry it up."

Men and women surged off the ferry, pushing, exclaiming, snarling at each other. Someone bumped the old man; he staggered. Paul grabbed his arm to prevent a fall. He pulled the old man out of the crowd, supported him with one hand while he reached down to rescue his bundle.

The old fellow was trembling; didn't even notice the camera. "Here, sit down. Catch your breath." Paul helped the old man sit on his bundle. His old wrinkled cheeks were red from exertion.

Ollie kept grinding as the immigrants streamed up the walk to the doors. The old man fanned himself with his fisherman's cap. "*Vielen Dank. Es ist so schwer. Die Reise war so lang und stürmisch.*" Many thanks. It's so heavy. The trip was so long and stormy. Paul nodded to show he understood.

In a few moments, recovering, the old man stood up and shook Paul's hand. He spoke rapidly, still in German. "What a pleasure to meet you. My first American."

"I'm not really—" Something stopped him. In German he said, "Yes, wel-come."

The old man cast an anxious glance at the doors. The immigrants seemed to be vanishing into a black cave. "I must go in there?"

"Yes, but you mustn't be scared of the officials. Some of them get tired and yell a lot. But most of them are decent men."

"Your German is excellent. You are a countryman?"

"Berlin. Some time ago. A long time ago."

"I'm Swabian." Paul had recognized the accent. "A little town I'm sure you never heard of. Schwäbisch-Gmünd."

"I know it well. My family's from Aalen, just up the road."

"Imagine that. A neighbor, clear on the other side of the ocean." The old man glanced at the doors again; all the other arrivals were inside the lower hall, where immigration officers were shouting at them. The ferry was preparing to cast off and back out of the slip. Farther out, a barge waited to come in with another load of people and baggage.

"I'd better hurry and find my place—"

"There's plenty of time. I'll help you rejoin your group." Paul took the old man's paper tag from the breast pocket of his corduroy jacket. "Four-two. Follow me." Ollie ran out the magazine and was surprised to see his partner moving away with the old man holding fast to his arm, like a child.

"I didn't know whether I should attempt the journey. I'm sixty-eight years old. My trade is the loom. Weaving fine fabrics."

"You'll find work, good workers are always wanted. It's the lazy ones who don't last long."

"That's a good German attitude. But I don't mind telling you, I've heard awful stories about this island. How they turn back most everyone."

"No, no, it isn't true. If you're healthy and act confident, there's no problem. You look fine to me. Is someone meeting you?"

"My brother Reinhardt."

"Good, that makes things easier."

The old man gasped when he saw the chaotic hall packed with tired, fretful newcomers. Shafts of winter sunshine splashed the staircase in the center. Strident voices roused memories in Paul. "Manifest two with me. *Zwei, hier!*" "Keep moving, keep moving." "Manifest four this way. Step lively!"

"Manifest four, that's you. Let the gentleman through, please, he took a bad fall back there." They fought their way forward to the proper spot. Paul patted the old man's shoulder. "Stay with your group. Good luck."

"Thanks again, so much. I'm sorry I took you for an American."

Paul looked at him. There it was at last. The sign.

"But I am."

He waved the old man on.

Saturday morning was warmer, with low clouds moving across the harbor, blown inland from the Atlantic. Now and then the sun brightened the clouds and flashed on the water. A nice effect for the camera.

The launch tied up at the pier and they unloaded their gear. The occasional glimmers of sun subtly changed the color of the copper-green robe of Liberty Enlightening the World. On the way inside, Ollie said, "Where are we putting the camera, up on that balcony at the base of the statue?"

"Higher. We're going all the way up to the torch. There's a catwalk, holds fourteen people."

Ollie stopped, stricken. "That must be two hundred and fifty feet, Dutch."

"Something over three hundred, straight up through her arm."

"Are there steps?"

"I was told there's an iron ladder, like the ladder for a hayloft."

"We can't carry this heavy camera up a ladder!"

"Yes we can, the climb is only forty-two feet. You'll go first, and pull, I'll hold on below. That way, if there's a slip, you can still hang on."

"While you try to catch the camera?" Ollie looked green.

"Come on, it won't happen, this is a lark. You'll remember it always."

"Sure, if I live through it."

Paul showed his letter of authorization to one of the guards at the entrance. The guard gave them a choice of an iron stair winding upward, or a cable-driven elevator. They didn't take long to decide.

As the cage rose slowly toward a stair landing, Ollie was bug-eyed at the superstructure dropping past them. Paul tried to appear blasé but he found the interior of the statue equally awe-inspiring, and not a little eerie. There was a whole webwork of pig-iron braces, the armature, supporting the skin of the statue. Each brace was specially curved for its particular place, its particular task.

It was cool in the elevator, but Ollie was sweating. In hopes that he'd relax, Paul pointed out the sway bars Alexandre Gustave Eiffel had designed into all four corners of the statue, to allow it to move a few inches in any direction in a high wind. Ollie didn't listen. Paul remarked on the thin, armadillo-like copper plates forming the skin, each mounted so that its top would tilt in slightly when the wind blew. "What they say is, the statue moves and breathes. Otherwise it couldn't withstand a gale."

Ollie still wasn't listening, he was muttering to himself. Praying? Paul wondered.

The cage stopped at a second landing, where another guard inspected their papers, then stepped back to show the narrow iron ladder on the other side of a curved brace.

"All yours, boys. Door up above is small, you'll have to stoop some. It's windy up there, so don't get careless."

"Oh God," Ollie said. He looked at the guard, looked at Paul, tipped his head back and looked up the ladder, which seemed to grow smaller, more insubstantial, the higher it went in the statue's arm.

Ollie crawled under the brace. Paul lifted the camera over it, then crawled under himself. Ollie wiped his hands on his pants, took a breath, held it, and stepped up on the first rung. From the second rung, he reached down to take the camera with his left hand while Paul supported the tripod.

Up they went, a perilous step at a time. Paul leaned the camera against the ladder, gripping it with one hand, holding a rung with the other, while Ollie used two hands to move up, then pulled the camera after him. Soon Paul was sweating as hard as his partner. He looked down and wished he hadn't. The guard on the second landing was already small as a doll. He heard the wind moaning around the outside of the arm.

"You all right?" Paul said when they were three quarters of the way up. Ollie was hauling the camera to the next rung. Suddenly Paul felt the weight shift; Ollie had let the camera slip.

Paul teetered for a moment, the rung cutting into his left palm, the tripod braced against his chest as the camera threatened to tilt back over his head; fall . . . *All over*, he thought.

With a lunge, and a curse, Ollie snagged the camera with one hand, leaning outward from the ladder at an angle of almost forty-five degrees.

They stopped a couple of minutes in the half-dark, to let their heartbeats slow, and to gather strength. They made it the rest of the way without incident. Near the top there was dim light coming through a series of round windows at the base of the torch.

The door to the outer catwalk was less than five feet high, and narrow. Ollie had to force the door open with his back; when he did, more light spilled in, making things a bit easier. Bending, twisting, pushing, struggling, Paul got the camera through the door, safely into Ollie's hands, and climbed out on the catwalk after him.

They were three hundred and five feet above the ground.

Paul clutched his cap; up this high, the wind seemed formidable. Grasping the rail and looking down, he found the perspective of the statue strange and dizzying. It occurred to him that if he chanced to fall, he might impale himself on one of the spikes of her crown.

With Ollie's help he moved the camera around the catwalk to a point overlooking the ship channel. Paul unfolded the tripod. Ollie said, "Damned if we didn't make it."

"You'll tell your grandchildren about this day."

"What ship is it again?"

Paul said, "*Statendam.* Holland America line, from Amsterdam."

"Immigrants, right?"

"Plenty. I contacted the local office to make sure."

"When's she due?"

He snapped open his pocket watch. "Now."

But she was not yet in sight, so Paul stepped to the rail again, gazing around him. New York and the harbor traffic and the sea channel were patterned with sun and shadow. Mist clouds flashing with yellow sun flew by the torch. He gulped when he felt the copper lady sway. He held the rail with both hands until the swaying stopped. He remembered old Valter when *Rheinland* steamed in past the statue. How excited he was, reading from his little guide book . . . but no less excited than the boy Pauli.

What did it all mean, this journey of his, this search, this passage through time and distance and hundreds of experiences, thousands of people, different identities—Pauli, Paul, Heine, Dutch? He thought he could answer the question because the answer flowed back to the very beginning, when he was adrift in Berlin, asking himself where he belonged—if there was any place at all. Asking where home was—if he really had one.

Yesterday he had seen the sign. His place was with Julie, here in America. Here he was loved, and here also men were free. Free to do good, and free to do evil, but free. Freer, perhaps, than in the repressive and decaying autocracies of the Old World. Hundreds of thousands were still coming from the Old World, lured by the promise of freedom symbolized by the torch whose frozen copper flame rose up behind him.

Michael Radcliffe, who dwelt in clouds of pessimism, said there was a new world threat, a new outbreak of an old sickness of nationalism, and millions would die of it before many more years passed. The increasingly willful Kaiser and his military clique were prime carriers. So were certain Americans such as Colonel Roosevelt, now the Vice President. Paul himself was infected with it to a degree. This statue, the vista before him, and what was in his heart because of them, gave proof.

The land he'd chosen wasn't perfect, but neither was he. There was something more important. America had given him his love, his family, and his purpose. And the freedom to search for all three. The old doubts, the old questions, the old warnings of the baker of Wuppertal were laid to rest.

A great whistle blasted in the ship channel. Out of the mist came the prow of the Dutch ship. "You're right," Ollie said, "I can see them all over the deck down there."

A tug small as a toy sped toward the steamship, tossing up a wake. Another followed. *Statendam*'s whistle blew again, so resoundingly, Paul thought he felt the statue vibrate once more.

Out of the glowing mist came the ship. Paul crouched behind the camera on the catwalk high above the harbor. He swiftly turned the bill of his cap to the rear.

"I'm cranking."

He was home.

Afterword

For I believe enthusiasm no bad spirit in which to realize history to yourself and to others.

Admiral MAHAN

ONE DAY in the spring of 1991, in the midst of work on this book, I had lunch with a friend from the history department of the University of South Carolina. We talked about the art and craft of presenting history in a class or a book, and of scholars who write to promote a personal theory or viewpoint, arranging details and slanting the text to validate a certain interpretation of a life, a major event, an epoch. Marxist, perhaps; or Freudian. My friend shook his head over that. He said, "Our first responsibility is to tell what happened."

So it is with this novel, and the cycle of novels to follow. *Homeland* begins at the point where *The Kent Family Chronicles* concluded, 1891. Its purpose is to introduce a new cast of characters—a new family taking its place alongside the Kents, the Mains, the Hazards, and the descendants of Mack and Nellie Chance —and through them, to relate in an entertaining way some of the history of the twentieth century. "To tell what happened." Given America's global role in the last hundred years, sometimes called "the American Century," that amounts to tackling world history.

The first step is *Homeland*. Its development and preparation were made possible by the unstinting help of various people and institutions I called on. Before I thank them, I should add a couple of footnotes to the story itself.

The state of women's health is not exaggerated. Ignorance and inattention were epidemic, treatments bizarre, inappropriate, or altogether absent. No one raised an eyebrow if a woman was repeatedly afflicted by the popular "neurasthenia"; it was almost expected. Men placed themselves in charge of women's bodies with little more than their egos to guide them. The so-called new women helped bring the issue into the light.

We have descriptions of cardboard ships "blown up" in tanks of water, for the camera, to simulate the sinking of the *Maine*. Shadow's little film is adapted from these contemporary accounts. Audiences of ninety-six years ago weren't really fooled by such fakery, but the medium was so new and novel, the pictures thrilled them anyway.

Pioneer filmmakers Albert E. Smith and Billy Bitzer carried cameras to Cuba in 1898, as did the reportedly obnoxious William Paley of the Eden Musée. Some of Paul's experiences are drawn from memoirs Smith and Bitzer published in later life. Film buffs will recognize Bitzer as the cameraman who shot *The Birth of a Nation* and many other D. W. Griffith pictures. He was Griffith's indispensable right hand for years.

General Joe Crown's report after the Las Guásimas fight is a free adaptation of reports written by General S. B. M. Young and Colonel Leonard Wood.

The shingle weavers in the Pacific Northwest succeeded in organizing their first union in 1901. But this did little to mitigate the perils of their strange trade.

The iron ladder leading up to the torch catwalk of the Statue of Liberty was closed to the public in 1916.

Here are the people and institutions so generous with their time and information. I deeply appreciate their help and their many kindnesses. But I have to say, as I always do, that they are in no way responsible for the content of this book; the manner in which the research material was put to use. Any guilt, creatively speaking, is mine.

I have always had a special affinity for libraries and librarians, for the most obvious reasons. I love books. (One of my first jobs was shelving books at a branch of the Chicago Public Library.) Libraries are a pillar of any society. I believe our lack of attention to funding and caring for them properly in the United States has a direct bearing on problems of literacy, productivity, and our inability to compete in today's world. Libraries are everyman's free university.

On a more personal level, libraries are the places to which I turn for basic research. So, starting close to home, I salute the small but dedicated staff of the Hilton Head Island library, especially Ruth Gaul, Librarian, and Mike Bennett and his predecessor, Sue Rainey, specialists in tracking down hard-to-find volumes.

Thanks also to Alan Amoine, Chief, Special Collections Division, United States Military Academy Library, West Point; Paul Eugen Camp of Special Collections at the Library of the University of South Florida, Tampa; Peter Harrington, Curator of the Anne S. K. Brown Military Collection at Brown University; my dear friend Mrs. Joyce Miles of the Dayton and Montgomery County, Ohio, Public Library; Barry Moreno, Librarian at the Statue of Liberty National Monument; Eric L. Mundell, Head of Reference Services at the Indiana State Historical Society, Indianapolis; my friend and fellow delegate to the 1991 White House Conference on Libraries and Information, Robert E. Schnare, who helped me first with *The North and South Trilogy* when he was head of Special Collections at West Point, and this time as Director of the Library at the Navy War College, Newport; Jeff Thomas, Archivist at the Library Division of the Ohio Historical Society, Columbus; Evelyn Walker, Rare Book Librarian at the Rush Rhees Library, University of Rochester; Ray Wemmlinger, Curator of the Hampden-Booth Theatre Library at The Players in New York—"that certain club" to which

I'm proud to belong; and the Westminster Reference Library in London, England.

I gratefully thank the *Landesarchiv Berlin* for providing many helpful maps and explanations of the city circa 1890. With their help, my walking tours of Berlin fell into proper perspective.

Most of the basic preparation for the book was done at the Thomas Cooper Library of the University of South Carolina, Columbia. I thank the professional staff, as well as the dean, Dr. Arthur Young, and Dr. George Terry, who directs the work of all USC libraries and collections.

The man who opened the door to a close association with the university is not here to receive proper thanks. In the fall of 1989, after I delivered a public lecture sponsored by the USC Department of History, the departmental chair, the late Dr. Tom Connelly, invited me to accept an appointment as a Research Fellow in the department. I leaped at the chance, because it opened to me not only a fellowship with working scholars, but faculty privileges at the various Carolina libraries—no small boon. Tom Connelly was a tall, lanky Tennessean with an acerbic wit that overlaid a generous nature. He was also a Civil War scholar of distinction; and he could write superbly. His study of the real person behind the legend of Robert E. Lee, *The Marble Man,* is a great book. Racked by disease, he was strong till the end. I knew him just a little more than a year, but I treasure that association, and his kindness.

Other USC historians who have been equally kind, and have helped in specific ways, are the current Chair of the History Department, Dr. Peter Becker, and two special friends, Dr. Lawrence Rowland of the USC at Beaufort, and Dr. Tom Terrill at Columbia. I must also thank Dr. Carol McGinnis Kay, Dean of the College of Humanities and Social Sciences, who has supported and encouraged my increasingly strong connection with the university.

Cutting across departmental lines, I owe a debt to Dr. Bert Dillon, Chair of the English Department, who offered help, and answers, when I urgently needed them.

Valuable research work was done at the Statue of Liberty and Ellis Island, our national monuments in New York Harbor. For facilitating this, I am indebted to Superintendent Ann M. Belkov and Assistant Superintendent Larry Steeler. Park Ranger-Interpreter George Tonkin was a helpful guide to Ellis Island. Supervisory Park Ranger Peter Stolz demonstrated an impressive knowledge of the Statue of Liberty, its design, construction, and history. I thank all these good people for their help and hospitality.

Others who aided in important ways are Dr. Sarah Blackstone of the School of Drama, University of Washington, Seattle, author of a valuable and entertaining dissertation on the vicissitudes of the Buffalo Bill Wild West Show on tour; Philip L. Condax, Senior Curator, Department of Technology, George Eastman House International Museum of Photography in Rochester, New York—in whose theater my wife and I received an incredible education in film, for fifty cents a showing, from 1960 to 1965; my brother-in-law, Dr. Luther Erickson of Grinnell College; Paul Fees, Curator of the Buffalo Bill Museum, Cody, Wyoming; Robert Fisch, Curator of Arms at the Museum of the Military Academy, West Point; Peg Hamilton of the faculty of Hilton Head Prep; my dear friends Carl and Denny

Hattler; my son, J. Michael Jakes Esq. of Washington, D.C.; Philip C. Katz at The Beer Institute in Washington; Robert Keene, President of the Southampton Historical Museum and town historian of Southampton, New York; Siegfried and Ilsa Kessler of Hilton Head Island and Aalen, Germany, who reunited me with my long-lost family and thereby planted the seed for this story; composer and native South Carolinian, my friend Mel Marvin; Charles Miller of the Cartographic Division of the National Geographic Society; my son-in-law, Michael H. Montgomery Esq.; Jay Mundhenk, who generously shares his Civil War expertise whenever I ask; Kate Parkin, my wonderful U.K. editor whom I will sorely miss at HarperCollins, London; Rosalind Ramsay of Andrew Nurnberg Associates, London, my overseas agents; my cousin, Thomas Rätz of Aalen, and his dear wife Elfriede; our friends Richard and Barbara Spark; Linda Wilson of the office of Senator Strom Thurmond in Washington, who cut through miles of bureaucratic red tape to answer questions about citizenship requirements a hundred years ago; and Dr. Lewis N. Wynne, Executive Director of the Florida Historical Society.

When I had special questions or problems, expert detective work was done by David Follmer, who really knows his native city of Chicago (his only flaw seems to be an unfortunate preference for the White Sox over the Cubs), and by the ever-reliable wizard of libraries and data bases, Dan Starer of New York City.

And lastly, but very importantly, there is Kenan Heise, who supplied a basic library of city history from his Chicago Historical Bookworks, Evanston. Kenan also gave me valuable guidance at several key points.

At Bantam Doubleday Dell, I've received unstinting support and encouragement from Jack Hoeft, now CEO of the organization; Steve Rubin, who heads Doubleday; Linda Grey, in charge of Bantam when I signed on; and Lynn Fenwick, associate editor and keeper of order in the domain of my editor—of whom more momentarily.

My attorney, Frank R. Curtis Esq., kept my spirits up at a particularly dark time before this project began. His counsel and good humor have continually sustained me.

Of course I always owe an unpayable debt of love to my wife, Rachel, who endures book after book, the dark and the light, with courage, forbearance, and affection. Friends, too, have been supportive, and uncritical, when forced to listen to my all too frequent kvetching. I refer particularly to Carl and Denny Hattler and Bud and Doris Shay of Hilton Head.

Now for the most unique acknowledgment in any of my novels—perhaps in historical novels generally. The wonderful ragtime piano piece appearing on page 773 was of course not written by the fictitious Harry Poland, but was done at my request—enthusiastically—by a musician who studies and loves ragtime, and the whole period in which it flowered. He is an internationally recognized star in the firmament of composers for musical theater. One of his greatest scores was written for the musical *Rags*, a double-edged title which referred to immigrants in the period of the show (which was the period of this novel) and also to the music they found in America; music lovingly re-created in new and captivating songs. Broadway critics sent the show to an early—too early—grave, largely because of an unwieldy script. But the show has become something of a legend, and is still being performed. Some call it "the musical that won't die." The composer of *Rags*, and of "Ragtime Rose," is my friend Charles Strouse. Charles, my deepest thanks.

Finally, what to say about the strongest helper of all, my editor and longtime friend, Herman Gollob? Words really are inadequate, but I can try to find a few.

In pursuit of a good book, Herman rigorously applied—to borrow the phrase of another great editor of mine, Howard Browne—"patience, cajolery, and the knout." Very much like a skillful psychiatrist, Herman drew out of me a book I didn't know was there.

That is what makes a great editor great.

In 1901, William Dean Howells wrote the following warning. "Paradoxically, our life is too large for our art to be broad. In despair at the immense scope and variety of the material offered it by American civilization, American fiction must specialize, and, turning distracted from the superabundance of character, it must burrow far down in a soul or two."

In other words, we must be satisfied with American miniatures because we can't paint American murals.

Well, we can try.

While I was at that task, one of the political polls in the spring of 1992 put forth this depressing statement. "Over 60 percent of those polled think America is a nation in decline." Similar polls continue to tell us Americans believe that never again will their children and grandchildren live better lives than did the generations preceding them.

It gives me pause. Perhaps it's folly to write a novel about hope in a time of profound national confusion, even despair. But I try to mirror the realities of the past that I explore. "To tell what happened." At the time of this story, people were swept along on a flood tide of hope. America symbolized virtually limitless opportunity. Here, no problem was unconquerable. Here, children and grandchildren would prosper, and rise, to heights beyond the most extravagant dreams of their forebears who struggled to make the journey to these shores.

Hope brought my grandfather to America. My grandfather and millions of others. Surely that hope was in some ways uninformed; naive, sentimental. Given so much freedom, an American could be as cruel, devious, venal, unprincipled as the next. If not more so.

Some went home, disillusioned. But more stayed; many more. Hope was in the air.

I hope Americans will be able to say that again someday.

—John Jakes

Hilton Head Island, South Carolina
Greenwich, Connecticut
May 1990–October 1992